APR 2 4 2001

Taylor, Janelle.
Three complete novels
                28.00

Three Complete Novels

JANELLE
TAYLOR

Three Complete Novels

JANELLE TAYLOR

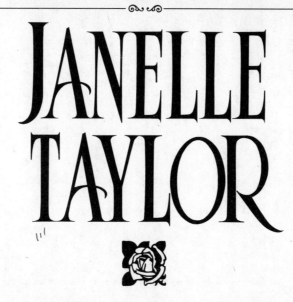

PROMISE ME FOREVER

FOLLOW THE WIND

KISS OF THE NIGHT WIND

WINGS BOOKS
New York • Avenel, New Jersey

This edition contains the complete and unabridged texts of the original editions.
They have been completely reset for this volume.

This 1993 edition is published by Wings Books,
distributed by Outlet Book Company, Inc., a Random House Company,
40 Engelhard Avenue, Avenel, New Jersey 07001,
by arrangement with Zebra Books, an imprint of Kensington Publishing Corp.

Random House
New York • Toronto • London • Sydney •Auckland

Printed and bound in the United States of America

Library of Congress Cataloging-in-Publication Data
Taylor, Janelle.
[Novels.   Selections]
Three complete novels / Janelle Taylor.
p.   cm.
Contents: Promise me forever—Follow the wind—Kiss of the night wind.
ISBN 0-517-10011-8
1. Man-woman relationships—Southern States—Fiction.
2. Historical fiction, American. 3. Love stories, American.
I. Title.
PS3570.A934A6 1993
813' .54—dc20 93-19516 CIP

8 7 6 5 4 3 2 1

Contents

PROMISE ME FOREVER

1

FOLLOW THE WIND

301

KISS OF THE NIGHT WIND

603

Promise Me Forever

DEDICATIONS AND
ACKNOWLEDGMENTS

To Carin Cohen Ritter, the best editor and adviser an author can have.

To Michael Taylor, the best husband and research assistant an author can have.

To Randall Floyd, who gave me the idea for this "Black Widow" plot from one of his "Southern Mysteries" articles in an Augusta newspaper.

To Sonia V. Migliore de Helfer, professor at Augusta College, for her translations into Spanish.

To Linda Pritchard, who furnished me with many maps of historical Augusta, including an 1875 one with all the names of the original streets, businesses, sites, and residents of that time period.

To the wonderful ladies in the Athens Welcome Center and Athens/Clarke Historical Foundation, who provided me with 1875 data and period maps on Athens, my hometown.

To the ever-patient and helpful staffs of the Augusta–Richmond County Library and Evans/Gibbs Library for research assistance on all settings and topics used. My adopted towns of residence.

To the nice ladies in the Savannah Welcome Center, the staffs of historical sites, and friendly residents of the lovely and gracious Savannah—one of my favorite Old South towns.

To my Readers, with hopes you won't think mistakes are made when I use the original names and locations of streets, sites, monuments, etc.. All of these are accurate for 1875 in Athens, Augusta, and Savannah. I would also like to remind a few worried readers that characters' unfavorable opinions of certain people and places do not reflect those of this author.

Chapter

1

"You sure it's legal to buries Mr. Phillip in secret, Miss Rachel? Mercy, this be the third husband you done laid to rest in less than three years. All that nasty tawk about you is bound to start all over again."

"It can't be helped, Lula Mae," Rachel informed the housekeeper. "I don't want trouble with the law or for more gossip to start and delay me before I can get away to take care of important business. This happened so fast. I need time to think and plan. You and Burke will have to keep silent until I figure out how to report this."

"You going to sells them gun and bullets cumpnies, soaz you'll have money to leaves here afore the law comes chasing you again? What abouts that shipping cumpny here?"

"I'm not going to get rid of any of them right now; I can't, but I need to check over the two out-of-town companies immediately. I'll tell Phillip's three partners he's away on business. I doubt they'll become suspicious for a while. Later, I want to sell everything and leave Savannah. I can't breathe anymore without creating gossip and dangerous suspicions."

"How you gonna hide this under the covers that long?"

"If my claim he's out of town doesn't work, I don't know yet. But I'll find a way; I must!"

Lula Mae clucked her tongue like a mother hen. "I kin jest hears them mean tongues wagging 'bout the Black Widder and her new prey. My bones are aquivering in fear. This time, Miss Rachel, they'll arrest you for sure, even if they don't find nary proof you be guilty."

"I'll check the house from bottom to top to make sure there isn't any proof I caused Phillip's death. The law didn't find any evidence against me the other times, and they won't find any this time. But before I get tangled up in another investigation, I need answers to some big questions. I have to go to Augusta and Athens to see George and Harry."

"What questions you need be answered, Miss Rachel?"

"Nothing for you to worry about, my dear friend. When I get things settled, I'm gone from Savannah, probably from Georgia. Of course you'll come with me, Lula Mae; I couldn't do without you." Rachel released a long, heavy sigh. She was so weary and scared. "The law has tried its damnedest to get me for three murders; I know how this fourth death will look to them and to the townfolk. This time they'll be determined to slam a prison door behind me. I can't make any mistakes, Lula Mae, so I'm going to handle this slowly and carefully."

Lula Mae patted the young woman's shoulder. "You was too smarts for 'em those other times."

"That isn't how I would describe it, but clever wits help when you're under attack. For certain, the minute this news is out, Earl Starger will be slithering around like the snake he is. That man could really harm me. He's the one who needs killing. If he doesn't leave me alone, I might oblige him," Rachel murmured, too exhausted and dazed to be aware of how what she was saying might sound to another person. She needed to get away from here so she could think clearly and make plans. She prayed for her husband's troubled soul and for herself. "Good-bye, Phillip. If you'd been more careful, this wouldn't have happened. It was too soon for you to die."

"Spring's the most awfullest time to go adying."

"No time is any better or worse than another, Lula Mae," she responded, though the spring of 1875 looked as if it was going to be the hardest time of her life, if she survived it. "I'll get back to the house. Burke will finish up here. He sent Jim and Henry on errands so they wouldn't be involved in this. I don't want them getting scared and making a slip to someone. Burke will make certain this grave isn't noticeable."

"Come along, Miss Rachel; I always takes good care of you after these things happen. You jest git weak as a kitten fresh from its ma when it's over. Let's git you in the house to rest up a spell whilst I tend my chores."

Rachel Anne Fleming Barlow Newman McCandless followed the trusted housekeeper to the lovely Georgian house. At twenty-one, Rachel was alone again. She envisioned what loomed ahead. The Savannah authorities would be all over her and their home as soon as she released this shocking news. She would tell the truth, but would she be believed, when even *she* suspected there was more to Phillip's sudden and painful death than the cholera she was blaming? She recalled his last words, the strange and frightening mutterings only she had heard. The smartest and safest thing for her to do was investigate what Phillip had told her before she went to the law.

At the front steps of the slate-blue wooden house with its rust-red trim, Rachel halted and instructed: "When Burke finishes with the burial, Lula Mae, bring him to me."

*

None of the three people saw the man who watched their actions and listened to their words. The tall, black-haired figure remained concealed behind a large live oak. His blue eyes, as dark and stormy as a violent ocean, exposed the mixture of anguish and fury he was experiencing. What Dan had learned about this sinister woman since docking last night and what he had just witnessed raced through his mind as he formed a grim opinion of his brother's wife. No, he corrected in bitterness, his brother's widow.

When he and his first mate had visited a local tavern late last night, Dan hadn't revealed who he was to the chatty bartender, a man who delighted in talking about the notorious and beautiful woman Phillip McCandless had married. He and his best friend had pretended they were sailors who were seeking work on Phillip's ships and wanted to know everything about him before signing on with his Savannah firm. They had acted intrigued and appreciative.

Dan squeezed some facts from all the enlightening rumors: At eighteen, Rachel Fleming had come to town and wed a rich older man; a month later Barlow's son died from a suspicious fall; two months later, her first husband was dead under curious circumstances. The police had investigated her as the cause of both deaths, but couldn't prove the men had been murdered. Gossip had begun, and the townspeople started calling her the Black Widow. She had waited only two months before preying on a rich but young man, then buried him in four months, a result of another dubious fall. That incident had evoked a second investigation—a longer and more persistent one—and had induced more gossip. Still, the authorities failed to find enough evidence to even arrest her.

Following her second husband's death, a local newspaper had carried a front-page article headlined "Beautiful Black Widow: She Mates and She Kills!" To protect itself from a lawsuit, it hadn't used names or dates and had called the story a "fiction"; but everyone had known it referred to Rachel, and had believed it, including the bartender. The insidious vixen had then been cautious enough to sit in her golden web for a year before stalking her next victim. She had entangled his brother, who was dead now after spending eight months in her silky arms. Her motive for burying Phillip secretly escaped him, for she couldn't claim her inheritance until she reported his death. All of her victims had been wealthy, and she was the only heir each time. Or so she believed. No one—including a desperate Phillip—knew for certain that Dan was still alive.

Dan wanted to storm the house to drag the treacherous female to the law. Yet something halted him from taking swift and rash action. This clever female had gotten away with killing two previous husbands and, if he didn't handle this matter with cunning, she might get away with Phillip's death. He couldn't permit that outrage.

The hazy contents of Phillip's last letter haunted him; it had been an urgent cry for help that had reached Dan too late. But he would see that justice was done. The information Rachel sought in Augusta and Athens must hold clues to her motives. Before he exposed this vixen's foul deed, he wanted those answers, too, as evidence. He would return to town, take care of his cargo, seek more information about her, then come back later to meet his sister-in-law to study her for himself. This time, that little predator would pay, with or without the law's help. . . .

*

"You sure we should burn all the eveedence, Miss Rachel?" the housekeeper asked. "How you gonna prove your story then?"

Rachel glanced at Lula Mae and Burke. All three people were dressed in old clothes and gloves to prevent contact with the items they must handle. If they were contaminated with cholera as Phillip's symptoms suggested, the disease could be spread by touch. "It has to be done for our protection, Lula Mae. I want everything Phillip touched last night and this morning burned or sterilized."

"I opened every winder, but it won't be doing much good until we git rid of this mess." Lula Mae looked at the rumpled bed with its stained and smelly covers.

"Mr. Phillip shore wuz pow'ful sick las' night," Burke remarked. "Ah'll see too it dese covers are burned good. We don't wants no mo sickness here."

Rachel met the black plantation manager's woeful gaze and replied, "Yes he was, Burke. Maybe a doctor could have saved him. I feel guilty about how he suffered and the attention he needed and never received."

"No, ma'am, he wuz too far gown down the heaven road, Miz Rachel. A man cain't be called back onest he's awalkin' it with angels. Folk 'round here gonna be pow'ful scared whenst they hears 'bout dis sickness."

"That's why I want it handled quickly and quietly, Burke. We don't want to create a panic. If only I'd known Phillip was ill last night, I would have done something for him."

"No, ma'am, Miz Rachel. If'n you been in here whilst the fever wuz on him, you'd be ailin' or be dead this mawnin' yerself. Twernt nuttin' you could do."

She knew Burke Wells was right, but it hurt nonetheless. When she had come to him early this morning, Phillip had appeared still drunk. The room had smelled horrible. She had opened the curtains, lifted a window for light and fresh air, then gone to check him. Phillip had rubbed an aching belly as he mumbled wild and crazy things in a desperate rush to warn her about some imminent peril. Then he had seemed to lapse into unconsciousness. She had felt his brow to find him cold, not burning with the fever she'd expected, and his skin had looked withered in the faint dawn light. She had lit the lamp nearby to examine him closer. His drawn face had been a strange color and his pulse had been so weak she could barely find it. Before Rachel could summon Lula Mae to fetch a doctor, Phillip had roused for a short time, mumbled more dire warnings, then died while she stood there helpless and in shock.

Rachel eyed the bedside table where several whiskey bottles lay on their sides. "From the number of bottles he emptied, he was terribly thirsty," she remarked. "Even drunk and ashamed, he should have called to me. He wanted to be left alone, so I obeyed. I shouldn't have, because it was so unlike him to have behaved that way. I don't know why he did this to himself. We have to burn these garments and gloves and scrub our bodies. We can't risk spreading this disease or catching it."

"Yessum, Miz Rachel, Ah un'erstan," Burke agreed.

"I'll starts water boiling and warsh them dishes. You wants me to throw out the food left over? It might be gone to the bad."

"I don't think tainted food was Phillip's problem, Lula Mae, as you and I haven't become ill after eating the same things, but, yes, do it just to be safe."

"When me 'n' Mr. Phillip went fishin' day afore yesterday, I seed him drinkin' dirty water from dat river 'hind us. I tol' him black water wuz bad."

Rachel knew cholera was said to come from eating contaminated food or from drinking contaminated water, but she didn't think the contents of the Ogeechee River, which ran along the western boundary of the property, was the cause of Phillip's death. "Many people drink and fish from the river, Burke. If there was a problem with its water, we would have heard about it. But it wouldn't hurt to mention that to the law."

"It's gonna be most awful when they comes."

"I know, but I'll have to report it soon. Phillip's gone, so it won't matter if I wait a while before putting myself through another investigation. He insisted the business is urgent, so I'll take care of that first. It's certain the law won't allow me to leave afterward."

"Dat law shouldn't be so bad to you, Miz Rachel."

"We know I didn't do anything wrong, Burke, but they won't see it that way. You can bet your life they'll give me trouble."

"You have witnesses dis time, Miz Rachel. Dey cain't hurt you."

"They'll only think you two are lying to protect me."

Burke Wells looked offended that anyone would dare question his word and honor. His dark eyes sparkled with anger and his fingers stroked his black mustache. "Deys bedder not go amessin' with me 'n' mah friends."

"Thank you, Burke, but I don't want you or Lula Mae getting into any trouble because of me. Just tell the truth, then it's up to them to believe us or not." She smiled as the strapping man mumbled under his breath about setting the law straight if they fooled with him and his loved ones.

Rachel and Burke stripped the linens from the bed, removed the feather mattress and pillows, and carried them outside to a clearing. They hauled several wash tubs there, then filled them from the well near the house so they would be prepared to battle any blaze that might sneak its way from the safe area. The black man tossed lantern oil on the pile and lit it. The empty whiskey bottles were broken and tossed into the roaring flames; later they would be buried after the fire killed any disease on them.

While the linens and bedding were being consumed and dark smoke rose skyward, Rachel asked, "Burke, did Phillip give you anything to hide for him in the last month or so?"

"No, ma'am, Miz Rachel, why'd you akst me dat?"

She trusted and liked the manager and housekeeper, but she didn't want to draw either of them into this mystery. She offered a logical explanation, "Sometimes Phillip didn't want to worry me about business problems, but if there are any and he's hidden papers about them, I need to know, and now!"

"No, ma'am, Mr. Phillip didn't gimme nuttin' to hide for him."

Rachel sighed in disappointment, which Burke mistook as exhaustion.

"Why don' you git in the house and res', Miz Rachel? Ah kin tend dis fire. Ah'll holler if'n Ah needs help. You looks pow'ful tired."

The blaze was under control, so the new widow thanked him and went to the house.

Lula Mae had opened all windows in the guest room and kept the door closed to prevent the stench from wafting through the rest of the two-story house. When Rachel joined her upstairs to help with the repulsive but necessary task, Lula Mae had finished her kitchen chores and had begun to mop up splatters. Any area Phillip might have touched where a smidgen of the dreaded disease might have been left behind had to be cleansed.

Rachel looked at the woman who was working so hard. "I'm sorry you have to help with this mess," she said. "I can do it, if you mind."

"I reckon I cleaned up worse messes in my life. When Mr. William or his son was sick, they ruint many a cover and floor. When I'm done, I'll toss these rags on the burnin' heap and bury this bad water. Won't be no sickness left in this house when I'm finished. The air's better a'ready."

As Rachel went to work with hot soapy water on the bed's woodwork, she murmured, "Why did this have to happen to me, Lula Mae? I'm not a bad person."

"A body hasta takes what the Lord keeps on his or her head. Don't let on it don't hurt bad. A good cry never did a body no harm."

Rachel halted to look at the woman whose stern-looking features made many think she was mean and cold. Today, concern and affection for Rachel seemed to soften them. Rachel knew Lula Mae to be one of the kindest people alive. The woman's words and her own thoughts stirred up memories.

As Rachel scoured the bedside table for smeared fingerprints and drops of whiskey that had escaped the fallen bottles, she murmured, "I wish I could keep his death a secret forever and not go through all that again, but I can't sell any of Phillip's holdings without exposing his death. How can I just walk away and leave everything that is rightfully mine? How can I start over somewhere else without funds?" And if she tried to flee, what all would happen to her if those faceless and nameless "enemies" tracked her down?

"I hate to see more trouble coming up the road," the woman said, "but do what needs doing. I'll stand by you."

She smiled. "You always have, Lula Mae, and I'm grateful."

Rachel slipped into deep thought as they continued their work. For some inexplicable reason, her kind and gentle husband had gotten heavily inebriated following a visit from Harrison Clements, his business partner in Athens. She didn't know what had transpired between the two men, but it had sent Phillip McCandless over the edge of a dark precipice. She wondered what Phillip's strange mumblings meant. In slurred speech, he had talked about her life and all she owned being in danger, about enemies who could get to her anywhere and any time and who would stop at nothing to get what they wanted, and about her selling everything to repay a debt she didn't know existed as it was the only way for her to stay alive and safe. What was the mysterious deal that she must honor, and where was the money she must return to its owner? And why was it hidden? She knew it had to do with guns and ammunition, with strange phrases like "you can't go to the law," and "you'll be blamed."

She didn't want to be blamed for whatever was involved. She remembered the terrible incidents—"all those warnings came"—over the last weeks to which he must have been referring. She had assumed they were unrelated crimes: the ship that was burned and sank, the warehouse that was vandalized, the two seamen who were beaten, and the dockworker who was slain. "Don't double cross Harry and. . . ." Scary words from him.

What if Harry did something wicked to Phillip last night? Rachel wondered in fear. *If it shows, I'll be blamed, not him. The law would never believe me over him.*

Whatever was going on, it was real and dangerous, as one worker was already dead. She couldn't go to the authorities with a wild mystery and become entangled in it. If she didn't solve it herself, she could be in even worse trouble than from a third investigation of husband killing and "Black Widow" gossip.

"That's all, Miss Rachel," Lula Mae announced. "I'll takes these rags and burn 'em. You git washed up and rest a spell. Supper'll be ready on time."

Rachel started to ask Lula Mae if the clues meant anything to her, but changed her mind. Some things were too personal or dangerous to confide in friends or employees.

Rachel didn't know any other woman who had lost three husbands, not even as a result of the war with the North. Yes, she reasoned, cholera did run its lethal course in a matter of hours to a few days, and death resulted from massive and swift loss of body fluids. But arsenic had the same effect as the symptoms Phillip had displayed. She knew about diseases and poisons, because she had lived on a plantation nearly all of her life where accidents and illness were commonplace and where items with deadly ingredients were used—both facts the law and townfolk knew, and had tried to use against her when William died.

Rachel glanced around the spotless room. Phillip was gone, forever. She couldn't believe it, even though she had helped wrap his body in clean sheets and hauled it to the site where Burke had dug a secret grave. She felt guilty over not washing and dressing him for a proper interment, but none of them had wanted to touch anything that might be infected by the cholera. Phillip didn't even lie in a coffin; his grave wasn't marked and he hadn't been given a service. None of that could be helped, she told herself, then closed the door to keep from looking into the room again.

Rachel's mind was in turmoil as she bathed and dressed. She had not wept over her husband's death because she was so angry with him. She was afraid of what loomed before her because of both his loss and the mystery he had mentioned for the first time on his deathbed. Phillip had been the one man she felt she could trust, the man who had taken away her wariness of all men; now, her faith in him was shaken. He had deceived her, endangered her, and deserted her. Yes, she fretted, she had a right to be angry and bitter.

As Rachel brushed her dark-brown hair, her thoughts returned to the path that had brought her to this point in her life. She had not had good luck with men. From the day the lecherous Earl Starger had entered her life, most had proven themselves untrustworthy and selfish.

Rachel dismissed Earl from mind. Maybe, she speculated, the war had brought forth the animal instinct in men: survival at any cost and take anything you desire to prove you're the strongest. She wasn't certain what had happened to men, but she knew her father and brothers and male friends had not been this way years ago. Some day in the far future when all of this was years behind her, hopefully she would find—

Rachel's thoughts were interrupted by a knock at her door. She opened it. Lula Mae stood there, looking hesitant. "Is something wrong?" Rachel asked.

"You have cumpny. It's a man, a stranger, who wants to see Mr. Phillip. You wants me to send him away?"

Rachel released an annoyed sigh. She didn't want to be disturbed tonight, or have to begin her false tale on this horrible day before her mind cleared. "A stranger?" She repeated Lula Mae's words.

"Yes. He says he has important business with Mr. Phillip."

"Business?" She came to alert and her heart drummed in trepidation.

"Yes, Miss Rachel. What must I do?"

She witnessed the housekeeper's worried look. "Tell him I'll be down shortly. We don't want anyone getting suspicious. I'll speak with him."

"Should I serve coffee or spirits?"

Southern hospitality was expected, so she said, "Coffee will be fine."

The older woman nodded and left.

Rachel checked her appearance in the mirror. She summoned her wits and courage, then went to face her first challenge since Phillip's death. As she walked along the lengthy hallway toward the stranger, she saw that Lula Mae had left him standing in the entry hall, no doubt with hopes of her mistress sending him on his way fast. Rachel noticed how his size and presence seemed to fill the doorway and how they pulled one's full attention to him.

She halted her approach with a few steps left between them to prevent having to strain her neck to look into his face. Her gaze met his as she said, "I'm Rachel McCandless, Phillip's wife. How may I help you, sir?"

Dan had met beautiful women before, but this one possessed even more allure than he had noticed from a distance this morning. He wondered why she had chosen Phillip as her third victim. Surely there were plenty of men in town with more wealth. To begin his own ruse, he extended his hand and said, "My name is Captain Daniel Slade, Mrs. McCandless. I'm here to see Phillip. Will he be down shortly?"

Rachel accepted his strong hand and shook it, noticing how he stared at her. She forced a polite smile to her lips and replied in a serene tone, "I'm sorry, Captain Slade, but my husband is out of town. I don't expect his return for many weeks. May I be of service? I take care of business matters whenever he's away."

Dan feigned surprise and displeasure. "I don't understand. Phillip was expecting me. Is he in Athens or Augusta? May I join him there?"

Rachel tensed, but kept control of her expression and voice. "I'm afraid not. He's in Baltimore to check on several new investments. I don't anticipate his return until the end of April or middle of May."

To dupe her, Dan gave a heavy sigh and frowned. "That's too long to wait. Where can I reach him? My business is pressing."

Her anxiety mounted in fear of this handsome stranger causing trouble for her before she could leave home. Yet she retained her poise, a skill she had learned over the years when people were cruel to her. "I'm afraid I can't help you there, either. Phillip said he'd be moving around and he'd contact me, but he hasn't done so yet. What is the problem? Perhaps I can handle it, or tell you who can help solve the matter."

Dan watched and listened for clues to her personality and character. She seemed at ease, as if she were telling the truth. Nothing in her mood, expression, speech, or manner exposed her as a new widow—his brother's widow and Phillip's murderess. He put aside his grief to carry out his task. "The business is between me and Phillip. He offered an old friend a good deal on an arms and ammunition contract. I wrote him of my acceptance and arrival date. I don't understand why he left, knowing of my imminent arrival. My ship docked tonight, and I came straight here with the money."

Rachel glanced at a large carpetbag on the floor. "Money? For a weapons and ammunition deal?" Suspicion filled her.

Dan perceived a curious reaction to his false claim, but it seemed a logical fabrication. He thought fear and panic had registered in those odd-colored eyes before she hurriedly composed herself. Her response was strange and unexpected. He nodded as his reply.

"Why don't we sit while we talk?" she invited, motioning toward the formal parlor. She needed time to think and to recover her wits. As they entered the spacious room, she indicated for him to be seated on a floral sofa and she took the matching chair across from it. The positions allowed her to study him while conversing. "Special orders usually go through Harry in Athens, not through Phillip here. What was it for, a custom-made weapon and special-size ammunition?" she questioned, even though she had caught that the mentioned items were plural.

To make the alleged deal sound important, Dan corrected, "No, for three thousand rifles and enough ammunition for each one to last for months of fighting. There's a conflict raging in the Mediterranean area, and I agreed to buy and deliver needed arms."

Rachel decided she must lead him on to learn all she could about him and his curious business. "Isn't such a deal illegal?" she asked.

Dan looked surprised, then grinned. "Stars, no. The Americans are assisting the battle against Turkey, though not publicly, of course. Guns and ammunition are needed badly there. I'm a private shipper who will deliver them for a tidy profit. Phillip said he could arrange the order for me. Why would you think your husband would become involved in something illegal?"

Rachel eyed him intently as Phillip's warnings about "war, freedom, and need guns badly" echoed through her mind. But there were contradictions: the money "must return" and "hidden" did not match with the captain bringing along his payment, and "Cuba" was a long way from Turkey. Contradictions, yes, if Daniel Slade was telling the truth. "I didn't say I thought Phillip would do anything illegal," she said, "But it isn't past evil and greedy men to lie and cheat or kill to get what they want. Are you sure the shipment will go into the hands of the right side?"

Dan was cognizant of her quick intelligence. "Since I'll be delivering them into American hands, I presume so, unless our country is wrong to interfere. I don't get involved in politics, local or foreign. But I do try to sail on the right side of the law." He grinned again. "Of course, some things are never what they appear. I'll head to Augusta and Athens. Maybe his partners know about our arrangement and have my order ready for transportation to Savannah. Harrison Clements' company is in Athens, isn't it?"

Rachel smiled and thanked Lula Mae as the housekeeper served the coffee. Both added sugar to their cups, but neither took milk. She waited until Lula Mae returned to the kitchen before continuing the conversation.

The use of Harry's name instead of George's or that of both men seized her interest. A daring plan came to mind. "Yes, it is. If you can wait until Monday morning, Captain Slade, I'll be leaving by train for both companies. Phillip asked me to take care of business there during his absence. Please feel free to come along with me. I want to learn if Harry knows about this curious deal of yours that Phillip didn't mention to me, and I also want to make certain it isn't detrimental to our firm. I wouldn't want Phillip misused by an 'old and trusted friend.'"

"Don't worry, Mrs. McCandless; I would never do anything to harm Phillip or his businesses. And I wouldn't do anything, even for a lot of money, to get myself thrown into a boiling sea of trouble. I'd be delighted to ride along with you. I appreciate the assistance, and the lovely company. Phillip is a lucky man to have a wife with such beauty, charm, and wits."

"Did you know my husband well?" she asked, unaware she used the past tense, as Captain Daniel Slade was distracting and disarming. She sipped the sweetened black coffee as she observed her guest.

Dan caught Rachel's slip, but didn't point it out. As he summoned the best response, he sipped his coffee to conceal the slowness of an answer. Her appeal was potentially dangerous. Her unblemished skin was an olive gold, her features small and perfect. She looked delicate and angelic, though he knew she wasn't. Her brows and lashes were the deepest shade of brown before it became black, as were the silky cascading waves of her hair that flowed over her shoulders. Her eyes were a fusion of pale yellowy brown with just a hint of grayish green, encased by a dark-brown band. She was clad in a simple day dress in a hue of grayish green that almost enticed her hypnotic eyes to reflect the color of it, but fell short of victory. Her gaze possessed strange power and magic. He was astounded and vexed she could sit there so serene and poised after what she had done today. She seemed the perfect reflection of a genteel lady! He placed an empty cup on the table and replied, "A long time ago, Phillip and I knew each other well and were very close. I'm looking forward to seeing him again. We'll have plenty to talk about."

"You were close friends?" she probed after witnessing a curious look of affection and fond remembrance in his seawater-blue gaze.

Dan assumed she would be less doubtful of him if she believed they were close friends, not just business acquaintances. "Yes, years ago in Charleston. That's where we're both from. You knew that, didn't you?" he inquired to test her knowledge of Phillip's past.

"I knew Phillip was from Charleston, but he didn't talk much about his life there.

With his family dead, it seemed to pain him too much to speak of the past. But I'm surprised he never mentioned such a close friend."

Dan again caught her use of the past tense. "I left Charleston in '71," he said truthfully, "and haven't seen him since. He contacted me through the mail. He seemed eager to make our deal. It must have been something urgent and unexpected to call him away like this."

Both were silent as Rachel rose to refill Dan's cup. She added two spoons of sugar as she'd seen him do earlier, then she replaced the silver pot on the matching tray, took her seat, and straightened her skirt. She retrieved her cup and sipped her coffee, as if waiting for him to go on.

As she served him, Dan concluded she didn't know anything about him, which was logical since Phillip had been told he was long dead. Fortunately, she couldn't cull anything from their appearances, as Phillip had favored their father and he favored their mother. His parents . . . But that was his tormented past. Right now, he had to deal with a painful present. He had to use every skill he possessed to weave a web of his own around this lethal beauty. She would never get away with murdering his brother.

Rachel observed Dan as he drank his coffee and seemed to slip into the past. She noted the conflicting array of emotions that flickered in his stormy blue eyes. She perceived an aura of mystery, a hint of tragedy, and troubling secrets in his personal life. It was easy to recognize those feelings which matched hers. She was baffled by how such a strong male could feel, and suffer, so deeply. It drew her to him, despite her previous warning to stay wary of this potent stranger, this possible enemy. Perhaps she was too tired and distressed to think clearly.

She reflected on Phillip's dying words: "He'll come soon and help me." Dan could be an old and trusted friend. If not, he might offer clues to the perilous mystery. In hopes of making light of the strained moment and contradictory emotions tugging at her, Rachel remarked in a skeptical tone, "I don't recall any correspondence to or from you, Captain Slade. If you and Phillip were so close and he was looking forward to your visit and to renewing your old friendship, why didn't he mention you to me?"

"Call me Dan, please. We'll be traveling together soon, and I hope we will also become good friends. As for Phillip's . . . secrecy, if that's what it was, I can't explain it. Knowing him, he probably wanted us to meet before he related past tales of our. . . ." He paused intentionally, chuckled, then finished, "Our devilish misadventures. We grew up together, so we have a long and colorful past."

Rachel wished she could relax her stiff guard and strained nerves. Her emotions advised her not to suspect this charming man of evil and treachery. Since Phillip *was* in the arms business, it was natural to have more than one deal in the works. Daniel Slade's arrival and contract must be coincidental. Yet her survival instincts warned her to stay alert and wary in case she was misjudging him and being duped. It wouldn't be the first time a man had fooled her.

"Something I said annoy you, Mrs. McCandless?" he asked when she frowned, then looked angry.

Rachel calmed herself again and smiled. "No, my mind just drifted for a moment. To an unpleasant topic, I fear. Pardon my lapse in manners. It's been a diffi—" She halted and flushed. *Don't relax, Rachel.* "It's always strange if Phillip's away and business problems arise. I'm nervous about making a wrong and costly mistake."

Dan saw how her eyes and smile could cause a man to forget all else if he weren't careful. But there was an aura of wariness around her that kept him on guard. "I can't imagine a smart woman like you ever making a mistake. If you weren't married to an old and dear friend, I'd be tempted to . . ." He let his words trail off suggestively, then put on an expression of near embarrassment. "I'm sorry, Rachel . . ." He switched to use of her first name in a husky tone meant to ensnare her interest. Women had told him he was handsome and charming. He had never used his appeal as weapons before today, but he must do and use any ploy necessary to entrap his brother's killer. Rachel Fleming had an abundance of similar traits and she had used them in sinister ways. "Pardon my lapse in manners, too. It's not that I've been at sea too long or don't have self-control where friends' possessions are concerned, but you're the most beautiful woman I've met and I . . . behaved badly for a moment. It won't happen again, so please don't be nervous around me."

As he smiled, Rachel saw bright white teeth amid a darkly tanned face with handsome features. His wide smile seemed to make his face glow and his dark-blue eyes sparkle with boyish mischief. There was a power, a magic, an energy that permeated the air around him. His movements were fluid and effortless. He had manners, excellent breeding, and education. He was masculine and self-assured, but not arrogant—not that she had detected so far, at least.

She had buried her third husband this morning, so how could a stranger have such a stirring effect on her this soon? Because Phillip's death seemed unreal, her mind answered, and because this sea captain stole nearly all her sense of reality. *Be wary of him, Rachel.* "You're forgiven, Captain Slade, and thank you for the compliment. I can tell you're a southern gentleman, so I'm not worried about spending time with you." After he encouraged her to call him Dan again, she asked, "When did you arrive? And where are you staying?"

It took Dan a few moments to respond, as he was lost in the swirling depths of her eyes. They seemed to possess the power to penetrate his very flesh. If only she were genuine . . . But she wasn't. It riled him to realize how looking into that exquisite face made him feel warm and tingly. If he didn't know better, he couldn't imagine this vital creature as a cold-blooded murderess.

Dan lazed against the back of the sofa and lied. "I just docked and came straight here." He motioned to the carpetbag. "I brought along my things because Phillip invited me to stay with him. Since he's gone, I'll return to my cabin on the ship and wait there until we leave."

Rachel needed privacy to search for clues and that hidden money. Since he had docked tonight and was a stranger, hopefully he wouldn't hear the malicious rumors this weekend and form a false opinion of her. "I'm sure Phillip would expect me to extend our hospitality to his old friend, but I don't think it's proper for you to stay here with him gone. Gossip can be a vicious and destructive thing. We can meet after breakfast on Monday at the Central depot on Broad Street, about eight-thirty. Buy a ticket to Augusta. After we finish there, we can continue on to Athens."

"That's perfect. Thank you, Rachel, for your help. I'll leave my first mate in charge of my ship and crew. I'll see you at the train station. I don't think we should mention our trip together to anyone," Dan suggested as he stood to leave. "As you said, we don't want to inspire naughty gossip. Phillip would never forgive even a good friend for sullying his wife's name. We'll talk again on the train."

Rachel liked that precaution. She smiled. "Thank you, Dan. I appreciate your kindness and understanding. I'll see you to the door."

Dan lifted his bag and followed her. He felt her eyes on him as he mounted a rented horse and rode into the encompassing darkness. He turned to see her close the door, then he halted. *He* would never fall prey to her powerful charms, but it was easy to understand how she had woven her webs and lured her victims into them before they realized what was happening.

Don't worry, Phillip; she won't get away with killing you, Dan vowed silently. *Damn you, Black Fate, for not getting me here in time to save my brother's life! I needed to see you, big brother; it was too long. Now you and Father are both gone before the past could be settled. He died hating me and mistrusting me, but you, Phillip, desperately sent for me in your hour of need. I failed you again, and I'm sorry.*

He dismounted, deep in thought. *I never wanted to be involved with lies and tricks again; they're too damn expensive. But I'll carry off my ruse, even if I have to lure that little enchantress into marriage myself to expose her. No matter how long it takes, I'll complete this task before I return to the sea. I swear that on your grave, Phillip, and you know I always keep my word.*

Dan glanced toward the area of large live oaks where his brother lay without a coffin and denied a headstone and burial service. The patches of visible soil were a dull grayish brown. Spanish moss hung from the massive trees and appeared a ghostly gray in the light of a full moon. Shadows danced on the ground as a breeze stirred the "old man's beards" and silent spring leaves. The croaking of frogs reminded him there was a river, the Ogeechee, not far away where murky water flowed between banks where tree roots were exposed and swampy vegetation and moss-laden cypress grew. He heard crickets singing and caught the lonely calls of an unknown bird in search of something in the night.

The heavy-hearted man looked toward the direction of the river, westward from the house. That was how he had sneaked up on the secret burial this morning. He had rented a horse from a town livery, ridden to his brother's property, then dismounted before reaching the house. He had secured the animal's reins to a bush, then walked near the river as he moved closer to the lovely setting. He had wanted to slip up to the house without notice, to surprise Phillip, to be able to see the first expression on his brother's face at close range. Instead, he had spotted a husky black man, a plain older white woman, and a breathtaking young creature hauling a sheet-wrapped body toward an area of dense trees, then lowering it into the earth beside a freshly dug mound of sandy dirt. He had frozen in midstep, concealed himself, and spied on them.

He hadn't noticed anyone but those three around, and his heart had begun to pound. He had slipped from large tree to large tree without being discovered. But he had heard them, heard enough to pain his heart and infuriate his mind and demand vengeance.

When he docked in Charleston a few days earlier, he learned his father was dead, and his brother had moved to Savannah and was in deep trouble. "I may be killed if I don't do what they want," he had written to Dan.

They? Why didn't you put more facts in your hazy letter, Phillip? If I don't keep your death a secret for now, I'll never learn the truth. I have to know why and how you died. Hear me, big brother, I'll do it or die trying.

A chill crept over Dan's flesh at that intimidating thought. He stared at the lovely house and shook his head. *No, my little beauty, you won't murder me, too. I'll be camped nearby and watching every move you make until we leave. Take one false step tonight or tomorrow, and I'll get you for sure.*

Chapter

❦

2

"That's all for tonight, Lula Mae," Rachel said. "Thank you for everything you've done today. Get to bed and rest. I'm sure you're as exhausted as I am."

"I knows you be bad off, Miss Rachel, but you forget your troubles and sleeps tight now. I left you a biscuit with fried ham in the server. You didn't eat enough for a biddy. If you needs anything, you holler for me."

"I will, but don't worry about me. I'll be fine."

"What did that stranger wants with Mr. Phillip?"

Rachel refused to draw the loyal woman into her troubles. "Just business. I handled it and sent him away. It's all right."

The older woman looked as if she wanted to press for more information, but she merely bid her mistress good night and left the room.

Rachel followed her to the back door. She watched the housekeeper move across the raised walkway to another matching structure that held the kitchen in the front and Lula Mae's quarters to the rear. On either side was a set of steps. To the left, a cobblestone path headed to the privy; at one point, it took a turn to the smokehouse, and at another veered off around the smaller building to the back gate. To the right, another walkway led to the well beneath a conical roof and separated to continue to a garden gate in one direction and to the wash shed in the other. Beyond the wooden fence to the rear of the home were a carriage house, stable, and corral. All structures were painted in slate blue with rust-red trim to form a picturesque sight.

Rachel closed the door and leaned against it. The Georgian house was lovely and comfortable. The hall where she stood traveled the width of the house, but a striking archway separated the span into two entry areas. All the interior doors, windows, moldings, panels, and fireplaces were painted a slate blue. The plaster walls were tinted off-white, and the floors were shiny brown wood with small rugs in strategic spots. The entire decor of the house was meant to evoke feelings of happiness, security, and beauty. But Rachel felt none of those things tonight.

She doused the lamps, returned to the back entry, and climbed the steps. As she went down the hallway toward the front of the house, she didn't even glance at the other rooms before she entered the bedroom she had shared with Phillip. She shut the door, needing to seal herself in a private and protective setting. So far from town and on a large plantation, she had never worried about peeping eyes and unwelcome intrusions during the night, so she didn't draw the drapes. She removed her garments and slipped on a nightgown.

As she brushed her long tresses, she looked into the mirror above her dressing table. The gown had been a gift from Phillip on her twenty-first birthday last February. She had laughed and told him the bloodred provocatively cut garment in Chinese silk was shameful and risqué, but it was the most comfortable one she owned. It clung to her body as if made to her measurements, and the material felt sensuous—almost delightfully wicked—against her olive-toned flesh. Phillip had loved it, and had paid a hefty price to get it. Maybe that was why she wanted to wear it tonight, to make her think of happier times and tender moments. She didn't want to remember him in the same light in which she recalled Craig Newman, but his betrayal caused those feelings to assail her nonetheless. Phillip had made her feel loved, trusted, and safe; so why had he deceived her in the end?

The bedroom suddenly felt stuffy, almost suffocating; she needed fresh air. Rachel entered the hallway and walked onto the wide porch which ran the full length of the house and matched the one below it. She leaned against a sturdy corner post.

Rachel stared at the full moon and wished it were bright and warm sunlight shining on her chilled body. The evening was not cold, or even very cool, but strange goosebumps covered her bare arms and raced along her body. She had the eerie sensation of being watched, but sighted no one in the shadows beyond the fence-enclosed yard. She told herself she was being foolish, that it was the events of today that had her on edge. Still, unable to shake the uncomfortable feeling, she returned to her room.

Phillip's belongings were everywhere to remind her of his past existence. Soon she must pack up or give them away, perhaps to Burke Wells and the other two workers. They only had four employees, as they didn't farm the land themselves; they used the sharecropper system.

Rachel had loved this plantation and house, and it had been a good home for her and Phillip. But it didn't feel the same after today; it was . . . distant and cold. She felt a stranger in her bedroom, an unwelcome guest. When matters were settled, she must sell Moss Haven and leave. She had no one in Savannah to entice her to remain, as Lula Mae could go with her. She could never return home to White Cloud—the Fleming cotton plantation between Savannah and Augusta. But, she worried, where could she move to and what would she do when this was over? She didn't have answers yet.

Get to bed, she instructed herself silently. *You have a lot to do before you leave town. And you aren't guilty, so don't be forced to live like you are.*

*

Dan stood in the shadows beyond the house, still staring at the upper porch. He couldn't believe what he had seen—the scantily attired creature in that fiery red, seductive nightgown. He knew he hadn't been seen, but the apprehensive woman had been nervous about something; perhaps she had sensed his powerful gaze as he gawked at her. Yes, *gawked,* he admitted with displeasure. Stars above, she was ravishing in that seductive outfit with near-black hair tumbling around her shoulders! The moonlight had played over her olive skin like a lover's caress. At around five four and probably one hundred ten pounds or so, she was quite slender, but possessed a shapely body that made a man's hands itch to stroke it. Her lips—the full lower one and the heart-shaped upper one—enticed a man to cover them with kisses, and her silky hair urged masculine fingers to bury themselves within its luster. He understood how the other three men had fallen victim to this enchantress.

He had lingered near the house to see if anyone came to call tonight. Did she have a partner in this foul deed as "they" in Phillip's letter had suggested? The only surprise he had received was sighting Rachel McCandless on that porch like a sultry goddess bathed in moonlight. He wiped perspiration from above his lip, smooth after a shave earlier. He licked his dry lips, then took several deep breaths to calm himself. His reaction to her was perilous; he could not for a single minute forget who and what she was! If so, he was as big a fool as her past victims. *Sorry, Phillip.*

*

An hour later, Rachel left the bed where she had tossed and turned. Her roaming mind would not let her sleep. If something vital was hidden in the house, she wanted to know *now*. She lit an oil lamp, as a candle would not provide enough light for her task. With Lula Mae sleeping in her quarters and the workers' houses at a far distance, she felt she wouldn't be discovered. She decided to start her exploration downstairs.

She took Phillip's keys from the dresser bowl where he kept them and left the room to enter the combination private sitting room and office to the right of the back hallway. She set down the lamp and unlocked her husband's desk. She searched each drawer and compartment, finding nothing out of the ordinary. After she relocked the desk, she focused on the cozy room, probing the short sofa and two chairs, but her fingers detecting nothing hidden inside them. She looked behind the pictures, but found no concealed holes.

Rachel crossed the hall to check the serving area, a small room adjoining the dining room where dishes, glasses, and utensils were washed and kept. To prevent a fire hazard, the kitchen was in a separate structure. She knew Phillip would not hide something valuable in Lula Mae's domain, so there was no need to check there. Cabinets were above and below the L-shaped counter and the square table in the middle of the floor with its two chairs. Rachel looked inside each one, but as expected, discovered no clues.

She entered the dining room. It was spacious and uncluttered, with a long table, eight chairs, a serving buffet that stood on one carved leg and was mounted to the wall, a linen chest for tablecloths and napkins, a hutch for china and silver, and a few decorative vases and pictures. She looked under and inside each piece and behind all the pictures and the mantel mirror. She examined the edge of the fireplace to conclude the bolection molding had not been tampered with. She examined the plaster walls, wood dado, and chair rail. As far as she could tell, no area looked disturbed since her and Phillip's arrival last August.

Rachel knew she must not skip anything and she entered the formal parlor, noting its beauty and charm as always, and searched the room. She paid close attention to the fireplace where a slate-blue mantel with carved sides and top encased the brickwork. The large painting over the mantel was heavy, but she worked until she could inspect behind it. She sighed in frustration: not one clue found!

Rachel returned to the combination office/sitting room to search the desk once more. Nothing! She closed and locked it, then slammed her palm against the wood, which repaid her blow of frustration with a stinging hand. She winced and rubbed it until the discomfort ceased.

"Where did you hide that money?" she questioned her dead husband in frustration. "You said if I didn't find it, I would be as dead as you are. If the money and that arms deal are so important and dangerous, why didn't you give me better clues to this damn mystery? Why didn't you confide in me about your trouble? Tomorrow I'll search everywhere else. If I don't find anything, I'll search your office Sunday while Milton is in church. If I don't find anything there, either, I hope to heaven I learn something from George or Harry about what's going on. Someone must hold the key to this mystery! Oh, Phillip, why did you leave me in such a terrible mess?"

Rachel took the lamp and went to her room upstairs. She doused the flame and climbed into bed. She was restless and tense, but soon, her exhausted body and troubled mind let her sleep.

*

Dan saw the light go out in her room. She had gone to bed, a second time. He knew for sure that there was more to this situation than what he'd witnessed. Now he understood her reaction to his mentions of money and an arms deal.

Unable to sleep himself, he had watched the house after Rachel had left the upstairs porch. She had not remained in bed more than an hour before starting a search of the downstairs. The house had several windows in each room to provide plenty of light and fresh air, so he had gone from one to another as he observed her curious behavior. At last, thanks to the two-inch opening of the bottom sash, her angered words had told him what she was searching for and why she was so upset.

Dan tried to reason out the clues to this painful riddle, but he didn't have enough of them to form a clear picture. He grasped why her trip out of town was so urgent. But why had Phillip warned her about danger before his death?

*

"Why don't you rests today whilst I gits the warshing done?"

"That sounds good to me, Lula Mae," Rachel replied, as it offered her the seclusion she needed to continue her search. She watched the housekeeper lift the clothes basket and go to the shed near the well. The arrangement was perfect for doing the laundry, even during the winter, because coastal Georgia had such short and mild ones. Although there was a water closet upstairs, bathing was also easier to do in the shed.

Rachel went upstairs. She looked through everything in the bedroom, including a thorough examination of the fireplace. She searched the guest room where Phillip had spent his last night alive. The water closet and sewing room were next, but still the truth eluded her grasp.

Rachel sat down in a rocker in the room where she and Lula Mae did their sewing. It was supposed to be a nursery, when and if that time had come, which it hadn't. She didn't know if she had failed to become pregnant with Phillip's child because they hadn't made love but a few times or if it was the result of her difficult pregnancy with Craig's child and the subsequent miscarriage. The doctor who attended her had said she might either have trouble getting pregnant or might never be able to again. Phillip had known that possibility; it had dismayed him, but he had accepted it. Rachel did not think she could ever accept never having a baby. One day she wanted to have safety, happiness, true love, a real marriage, and that would include children.

She decided to go to the attic, before Lula Mae finished outside, but that use of time and energy were as fruitless as the rest of her search.

*

Lula Mae came inside to tell her mistress she would be in the kitchen working, as she needed the wood stove to heat the irons. Two were needed, one would get hot while the other was cooling during use, and they were exchanged as necessary. Her first loads had dried quickly in the fresh air and sunshine, and she wanted to finish the laundry today.

"I'm going for a walk to clear my head and to loosen my body," Rachel said. "I'll return soon and help you put everything away." She left by the back door, went down the steps to the left, and followed the cobblestone walkway toward the carriage house.

At the back gate, she glanced toward the vegetable garden where Burke and his two helpers were working. They should be busy for hours, so she wouldn't be disturbed during her task.

Rachel entered the structure that was painted and trimmed to match the house. A comfortable carriage, built by a local craftsman in town, sat cleaned and polished and ready for use, as Burke always took pride in and care with his chores. She glanced at the harnesses on the wall pegs, an extra wheel leaning against one side, and the repair tools on a workbench under which a stool rested. She looked through the chest where blankets were kept to cover legs during chilly or cold weather. Nothing!

Rachel strolled to the barn. Earlier, Burke had turned the horses and milk cow into the pasture to graze, drink, and exercise. She checked the stable and hayloft. Another futile search. After careful study, she decided nothing could be concealed in the small privy or wash shed and smokehouse where she and Lula Mae visited frequently. That left nothing else to examine, except the shipping office in town tomorrow.

*

Rachel was a skilled horsewoman, so she didn't use the carriage or have Burke drive her into Savannah Sunday morning. Whatever happened to her, she didn't want Burke or Lula Mae involved, and she told the housekeeper and manager of the plantation she was going for a long ride for relaxation. Moss Haven was about fifteen miles southwest of town, but the route was an easy one to travel. For protection she carried a derringer in her drawstring purse. Being in the weapons business, Phillip had given it to her and taught her how to use it.

Savannah . . . Rachel entered the edge of town and thought how much she enjoyed the loveliness of this city. As she walked her mount up Broad Street toward the waterfront, she looked at her surroundings. She smiled as she recalled how Savannah was often compared to an exquisite woman—one conceived, born, and reared in beauty and charm. Thanks to Sherman's kind heart, her face and body remained unscarred by the vicious war years ago, unlike many other Georgia towns that had not fared as well beneath his crushing boots.

Savannah was desired by South and North, and long ago by British and Colonists. She was graceful, elegant. Built upon a forty-foot bluff and surrounded by marshland, she was situated fifteen miles from the Atlantic Ocean. The waters at her feet carried her name and provided a natural harbor for ships. She was a prosperous and generous creature who shared herself with planters, merchants, factors, bankers, shippers, and numerous other businessmen. She provided them with such goods as tobacco, rice, cotton, lumber, and indigo. Her limbs were adorned with spacious and pretty squares. Around those grids marked out by Oglethorpe in 1733 were beautiful homes whose various architectures—Georgian, Colonial, Greek Revival, Gothic, Regency, Federal, and Italianate—nestled up to one another and were trimmed with lacy ironwork as if a blend of expensive cosmetics adorned her appearance. The sizes and styles of the homes displayed the varying tastes and wealth of their owners. Around them were walled gardens, massive live oaks with lacy drapes of moss, and abundant spring flowers in all colors. Rachel could hardly wait for gardenias, her favorites, to show their lovely white faces this summer.

She preferred the plainer route she was taking over a more picturesque one which would take her past the homes she had shared for such short times with William

Barlow and Craig Newman on two of the twenty-four town squares. She passed Central Station where she would catch the train the next morning and guided her horse to Congress Street, past the eighty-foot water tower and the town market near Franklin Square to reach Ellis Square. She rode up Barnard to Bay Street and turned left. She heard the striking of her mount's hooves against the ballast stones used to pave most of Savannah's streets, stones that were brought over on ships to give them weight until they were dumped in port to take on cargo.

Rachel dismounted and secured her reins to a hitching post. She sighted very few people, and none she knew. She glanced down the two blocks separating McCandless & Baldwin Shipping Firm from the custom house that cleared their imports and exports. She looked across the wide street at Factor's Row. She had been there many times with her three husbands. On the river's level, numerous adjoining buildings rose above Yamacraw Bluff. They were connected to the higher ground by iron bridges from the upper floors and by cobbled alleys or circular stairsteps. A retainer wall to hold the sandy bluff intact was made of those same ballast stones, as were the stairways and winding alleys.

Factor's Row was the heart of the cotton industry in this area and to those nearby. The lowest floors of the buildings held cargo to be shipped elsewhere, mainly cotton and other valuable southern crops and items. The upper floors provided offices for cotton brokers and other businessmen. One of the tall buildings on the far end, between Drayton and Abercorn streets, belonged to her husband's company. Since her husband was dead, it was partly hers now. It was used as a warehouse to store incoming and outgoing cargoes on ships owned by McCandless & Baldwin and by other firms. The warehouse that had been vandalized was on this end of Factor's Row.

Rachel glanced down Bay Street. She noticed the telegraph poles and gas lamps that lined it. Many people who lived in town now had gas lamps in their homes. Huge live oaks with their ever-present moss trim were abundant and she heard birds singing, as spring was in bloom and they loved this time of year. In three days, it would be April.

"Stop looking at the sights, Rachel, and get on with what you came to do," she said aloud, warning herself against further dillydallying.

Upon her return from her trip, she must go to see their lawyer, banker, and insurance broker to settle Phillip's will and holdings. But first she would have to visit the location down the street where Police Chief Robert Anderson worked . . .

Despite the warmth of the late March day, shivers raced over her body and chilled her heart. She wouldn't think about that problem now.

Rachel used Phillip's keys to unlock the office door. She was glad church was in progress and that most Savannahians attended, whether it did them any good or not. Rachel scolded herself for that wicked thought, as not everyone in town disliked and ostracized her. Yet the ones who didn't seem to feel that way did not give her support when trouble befell her. But everyone had their own little worlds to tend and protect, she supposed. They couldn't be expected to defend another's, a stranger's.

Rachel's gaze traveled the papers in Phillip's desk, the books atop it, and the letters in a drawer: all shipping business, nothing about an arms deal with either the Athens or Augusta companies. There was no mention of "Cuba," and she didn't know anyone there. She wondered why Phillip had mumbled, "Go see him. . . . He'll help. . . . He'll stop them. . . . Only hope. . . ." She pondered the "he" in bewilderment. She, too, was sorry Phillip "got you into this mess."

Nor did Rachel find any notations about Captain Daniel Slade, which concerned her. She checked Milton Baldwin's desk, but all his drawers were locked with his own keys. She rummaged through the small corner desk she had used, but it was empty, as her position had not been filled since she quit work to marry her boss.

Rachel still suspected that Phillip had created the position just for her and had paid her salary out of his own pocket. The work she did—running errands, filling out reports, doing correspondence neatly, keeping the office clean, making appointments when the owners were gone, and notifying captains of their schedules—Phillip and Milton could have handled themselves. In fact, Phillip had never liked to send her on errands, especially to the warehouses or to clients, where someone might be rude or pushy. He had always been protective, and perhaps a little possessive, of her.

Rachel pulled the combination to the safe from its hiding place and went to kneel before the four-foot-high black box. Her nervous fingers twirled the dial, going from one number and direction to the next. She opened the heavy door, relieved the combination had not been changed. She sat down on the floor and reached inside to grasp a stack of papers to examine them. Beneath them was a packet of money, bound with a red ribbon.

Rachel lifted it in quivering hands, stared at the bills, then counted them. Some people, she concluded in disappointment, might consider five thousand dollars a lot of money, but she knew this wasn't the large amount Phillip had mumbled about during his dazed state.

A knock at the door interrupted her thoughts and startled her. She barely suppressed a scream as her head jerked in that direction and she dropped everything. *Discovered! Exposed! More trouble and accusations!*

Her heart raced, her mouth went dry, and her breathing altered to fast and shallow gasps. Milton wouldn't knock at his own office door. It could be a dangerous enemy spying on her. What if Chief Anderson or one of his many officers had seen her enter and concluded she was up to no good? What if the law insisted on speaking with Phillip about her curious behavior?

Rachel turned to the gaping box to hurriedly conceal her action and herself, but it was too late. She heard the door open and then after someone came inside the room, heard it shut. She knew she would be sighted immediately and froze in panic, knowing how this would appear to Milton Baldwin or the authorities. Even if it were an enemy or thief, her purse with the derringer was out of reach. She gave a heavy sigh, put aside the money and papers, and stood to defend herself, if she could.

Rachel's eyes widened, then closed a moment as she sighed again, this time with relief. "Captain Slade, what are you doing here? You startled me. How did you get inside? I thought I locked that door."

She had, but the handy Captain Daniel Slade McCandless alleged, "Obviously you didn't, and that was careless of you, Rachel. Being here alone could be dangerous, especially with the safe open and money inside." He nodded in the direction of it, as she had walked forward to meet him. No doubt she hoped he hadn't noticed that fact, as she looked as if she had been caught committing a crime and was relieved *he* had found her here instead of someone else. There was no denying she was afraid of something and someone. "If you're finished working, I'll escort you home. I brought a light meal we can share here or have a picnic along the way."

Rachel glanced at the basket he was holding before her wary gaze settled on his merry one. He looked as tempting as his unexpected offer, but she wanted to get out of there fast. She came up with what she considered a good excuse, "Neither would be wise, Captain Slade. We might be seen together and inspire wicked rumors. Besides, I have packing to do for my trip. I came to fetch some papers I'll need to carry out Phillip's business requests. I just finished and was about to tidy up and leave."

Dan sent her a broad smile and a coaxing expression. "A beautiful woman shouldn't be on the road alone, Rachel. We can meet outside town and I can escort you home."

"There's no need. I'll be fine. We don't have many criminals around Savannah, and I have a derringer in my purse for protection if I should run into one. But thank you for your concern and offer. I don't know how long my business will require, so I plan to pack for a few weeks away. If that's a problem for you, Dan, you can return any time you wish."

Dan shrugged his shoulders. "It's not a problem. I can't sail until my order is ready for shipment. One doesn't find many wives so involved in their husbands' businesses. Phillip must have great faith in your capabilities."

"Before we married, I worked here for Phillip," she reminded him, "so I am acquainted with all of his dealings and holdings. That's why I'm baffled by not knowing about your contract and friendship with him, and furthermore I found no mention of you or your order in his files."

Dan grinned and murmured, "So, that's how you two met. I'm surprised to hear about a genteel lady working; that's most uncommon."

Rachel couldn't tell him they had met through her second husband, as Phillip had been Craig's main shipper. Nor could she tell Dan that Phillip had befriended Craig, whom he didn't like or trust, just to be near her as often as possible. Yet, she used part of the truth, which he might already know, "I needed to support myself, and Phillip offered me a job here. I accepted immediately because many men are hard to work for."

"No doubt because of jealous wives and sweethearts."

"Perhaps a few, but that wasn't my meaning."

"What was?" he probed, looking quizzical.

"Candidly, many men take advantage of a woman alone."

"I'm sure that would be a problem for a beauty like you."

Rachel felt uncomfortable about the topic she shouldn't have broached. "Looks have little to do with some men's wicked behavior. Some think you owe them more than a well-done job to earn a decent salary."

"Sounds as if you've had a rough time with men."

She noticed that his playful smile had been replaced by a serious look. "Not with all of them, thank goodness. But often it's hard to tell the bad ones from the good ones until you get to know them."

Her response sounded to Dan as if she didn't bear hatred and mistrust for the entire male sex, as a killer of them surely must; but he assumed she was only bantering skillfully with him. "You don't have to tell me Phillip was different, one of the good ones. I know he would never misuse an innocent young woman. As to finding no mentions of me and my cargo here, that doesn't seem odd to me. This is a shipping firm, and I have no need of one. I have my own clipper, remember? I would imagine my order would be listed in the books of his other companies, as my business is with them." Dan quickly protected himself against what she would, or rather wouldn't, find in those books. "Unless this was a private deal between old friends. Maybe Phillip didn't record our contract; he was having the order sent to him to keep me from paying a higher profit mark-up if I went through his partners. It isn't uncommon for a friend to do another friend a big favor. Phillip was like that, a good man bone deep."

Rachel didn't refute the fact that even if it were legal, that would be cheating partners out of their rightful share of profits. In light of her husband's mumblings, didn't know anymore if her deceased mate would do something illegal or unscrupulous. "How did you meet Phillip?" she asked suddenly, wanting to test him to see if story would be consistent.

Dan noticed her skeptical look. "Living in close proximity in Charleston and being almost the same age, we went to school together, shared mutual friends and interests, and we were both in the shipping business. Phillip and I were not alike, but we became good friends."

"That would make you around twenty-nine?"

"Twenty-eight this past January, ten months younger than Phillip if I recall correctly. He did have a birthday the first of this month?"

Rachel didn't want to remember the young age at which Phillip had died. She nodded. "Did he tell you in his letters that he had married last August?"

"Yes, he did, and he sounded very happy about it."

"So why did you seem surprised to meet me? You stared at me when I introduced myself as Mrs. McCandless."

Dan sent her a wry grin and drawled, "Guilty as charged, ma'am, but I have a good defense. Phillip wrote you were beautiful and charming and well bred, but I assumed he was biased in your favor. He wasn't, and it caught me by surprise. Frankly, I expected pretty, not ravishing."

She stepped away from this magnetic man before his force overpowered her. "Thank you. I'm pleased to hear my husband bragged about me to his friends. What else did he say about me?"

"Nothing, except that you were a very special lady, his joy and pride. I think he wanted me to meet you and form my own opinion."

"I hope it's a good one. You didn't say how you knew I was here in the office."

Dan was ready with an answer to that expected question. "I'm staying at the hotel across the side street. I thought a change of scenery and diet would be nice for a while. I was about to take a walk around town when I saw you enter. I gave you time to do whatever work you'd come to do, purchased this basket, then came to join you. It *is* mealtime, so I hoped you might be hungry. Are you sure you won't sneak off for a picnic along the road home? We can get better acquainted. Since Phillip isn't here to fill me in on the last four years, you can do it for him. I doubt I'll still be in port when he returns from his trip." He was certain she was attracted to him, a feeling that clearly made her nervous. Excellent, he praised himself. If he had to romance the truth out of her, so be it, but he didn't want to appear a wife-stealer or a man who viewed women lightly. No doubt she would simply think he was enamored of her.

Rachel didn't know how to take his behavior, as merely friendly or flirtatious? "We can do that on the train and during our journey. It's unwise to be seen dallying with such a . . . an attractive man during my husband's absence."

"Thank you for the compliment, and I understand." Dan cautioned himself not to press and panic the skittish creature. "See you tomorrow."

Rachel walked to the safe, replaced the items, then locked it. She straightened anything she had disturbed to conceal her visit. "You leave first, then I'll follow shortly."

"You forgot your papers," Dan reminded.

"I don't need them. I have the information inside my head. Until morning, Captain Slade. The train leaves at nine sharp. Don't be late."

Dan chuckled and gave a playful admonishment.

"*Dan*, remember?"

"Good-bye, Dan."

"Good-bye, Rachel. Nine sharp," he repeated, then grinned.

Rachel watched the tall and handsome man depart with his basket swinging on a strong arm. He had to be at least six two, and was well built. He appeared all lean and hard muscle. He was certainly tempting, and no doubt many women had fallen prey to his charms. She couldn't and mustn't; she had to stay on guard to protect her mission and supposed marital status. She hung the drawstring purse on her wrist, took one last look around, then left. This time she made certain the office door was locked behind her. She mounted and walked her horse down Bay Street to Broad, then headed for home.

*

Rachel was only a few miles from where Moss Haven property began when a shot rang out and rent the silence of the lovely afternoon. A bullet whizzed past her, close enough to be heard and almost powerful enough to be felt. She urged her horse off the dirt road, dismounted with agility and speed, then jumped behind the protection of a large tree.

She leaned against it as she tried to slow her rapid heartbeat and clear her head. She jerked the fabric bag from her wrist, relieved she hadn't hung it over the pommel as she was inclined to do while riding. She yanked on the string to open it and fumbled inside for her derringer with trembling fingers. Clutching the little weapon in her grasp, she waited and listened for an enemy's approach. She knew the small gun had a short range, whereas the rifle in her foe's hand had a long one.

Rachel's breathing came in shallow, rapid gasps that dried her lips and mouth. Panic surged through her. She struggled to regain her wits, to be ready to defend her life. Someone had fired at her! Was this a scare tactic or a real threat that had missed her by inches?

Time passed without another shot. Her frightened horse had calmed down and was grazing contentedly nearby. Hugging the tree, she peeked around it with caution. Her gaze searched the other side of the road and tried to pierce the concealing woods beyond it. She strained her ears to detect any footsteps. Nothing.

She wondered if it was only a stray shot from a careless hunter, but doubted it was an accident. She wondered if it could have been a warning by whomever was responsible for the destructive episodes Phillip had mentioned on his deathbed, done by someone who didn't know he wouldn't be affected by another threat. But if that was true, how would she know?

Rachel wondered if Daniel Slade was who and what he claimed and if he had had enough time to get a horse, trail her, and . . . But why would he want to terrorize her or harm her? He had seemed so nice and polite, and so sincere. Maybe she was wrong about him. She recalled the eerie sensation of being watched last night after Dan's visit, and had dismissed her feeling as raw nerves and fatigue. But . . .

Earlier, Dan had suggested escorting her home *safely*. If that had been a hint to her needing his protection, she had missed it. During their journey together, she needed to study him carefully. She could not afford to misjudge him or to relax to the point of exposing herself.

Maybe she had misunderstood one of Phillip's ramblings. When he had said, "Killing me," perhaps he hadn't been referring to his illness.

Tomorrow she would be on greater alert when she met Dan!

Chapter

3

"You been gone a long time, Miss Rachel. I had a good notion to send Burke looking for you. I thawt something bad had happened to you." Rachel had taken time to recover her poise before reaching home. She had decided not to reveal the alarming incident to keep from worrying her servants. "I'm fine, Lula Mae; you worry about me too much. I've been riding and thinking. I have a lot on my mind."

"You bound to, Miss Rachel, but you'll be safe again soon."

"Right now I have to pack for my trip tomorrow. When Burke comes by, tell him I'll need him and the carriage at seven-thirty in the morning."

"Why cain't you jest sell everything and leaves, like he was still alive?"

"His partners wouldn't buy me out without contacting Phillip. I can't lose everything that rightfully belongs to me. Phillip doesn't have any other family, so I'm his only heir. Besides, if I tried to move away and sacrificed all his holdings, his partners would get suspicious of not hearing from him or seeing him and they'd begin an investigation. If the authorities had to hunt me down, which they would if I left mysteriously, I'd appear even more suspicious to them."

"I don't like you being hurt like this, Miss Rachel. It ain't fair."

"I know, Lula Mae, but I'll have to reveal the truth soon. If the authorities don't believe me, they can dig up his grave and examine his body."

The woman was horrified. "They won't dares to touch cholera dead."

"I hope not; I don't want his resting place disturbed. Once the news is out, I'll get a headstone to mark it. Now I'd better get packed. I don't have to leave any orders; you and Burke know what needs to be done while I'm gone. If anyone comes to visit, tell them Phillip and I are away on a trip. That should stall matters until I get back."

Rachel went upstairs and Lula Mae entered her bedroom to assist her mistress with folding and packing garments for her trip, even though the young woman had told her it was unnecessary. "I hate to see you leaves. Be careful out there alone. I worries about you when I ain't around to takes care of you."

The new widow looked at Lula Mae, smiled, and said, "Ever since I married William and moved into his house, you've looked after me. I couldn't have gotten through his loss and everything that happened to me afterward if you hadn't helped me, my dear and loyal friend."

"I shoulda been there when Mr. William died: I didn't knowed when I visited him that day, it was his last one; he seemed fit as a spring chicken."

"The doctor said it could have been his heart, but the law still isn't convinced. My opinion is that he never recovered from the loss of his son."

"That was a mitey strange fall that boy took when he broke his neck."

Rachel halted her packing. "That's why the law questioned me about it again after William died only two months later, leaving me as his heir. Most people still think I had something to do with both deaths."

Lula Mae patted her cheek. "I know you didn't, you sweet angel."

"I wasn't sure you'd believe me, either, Lula Mae," Rachel said. "You didn't like me when I married William. I was afraid you'd had your eye on him and felt I'd taken him away from you."

The thirty-eight-year-old spinster stopped working to laugh in amusement. "I was only worried 'cause you was so young. Mr. William and his son was like my brother and nephew. I 'bout raised that boy after his ma died when he was ten and I was hired to takes care of him and the house. But I saw how fonds you was of Mr. William, and I saw how he treated you like a daughter."

Rachel grasped her meaning, and stopped herself from blushing with embarrassment.

"Mr. William took good care of you, like I does. If I hadna been gone for three months at my sister's, you wouldna married that Craig Newman."

"It wasn't your fault, Lula Mae. I was young and scared. The law was harassing me, and people were saying such awful things about me. You know why I married William and why I left home." Rachel's gloom deepened. "So much happened after Sherman blazed across Georgia. If those carpetbaggers and Yankees hadn't put such high taxes and harsh rules on us, we could have saved the plantation. It wasn't fair or right, Lula Mae."

"Don't you be worrying over things that cain't be changed," the housekeeper soothed.

"That sounds easy, but it isn't. I tried to change things plenty of times, but nothing worked right for me. Craig appeared to be the only one who believed in me and tried to defend me. But I was certainly fooled by him."

"I'm sorry I wasn't there to help you, Miss Rachel."

"I was hurt when I thought you were ignoring my messages. I was alone and scared. When you finally returned to work for me I was so happy."

"Me, too. Mr. Newman was bad. He didn't want me working for you."

"I'm sorry Craig fired you, Lula Mae, but I couldn't stop him. He was so angry after Governor Smith canceled those state bonds and he lost so much of my inheritance from William. He did it to punish me."

"We was both hopping mad when he gots rid of me," Lula Mae said with bitterness. "He had no call to do that; I done a good job in his house. He didn't even hires nobody to take my place. It wasn't right or proper for a lady to do her own cleaning, cooking, and warshing. Mercy be on my head, but I was glad when you was free of him. Bad men don't deserve to live and hurt people."

"Craig was a bad man, Lula Mae, but I didn't wish death on him," Rachel refuted. "You know how he was when he got angry or upset. You visited me the day he died and you saw what a terrible mood he was in."

"His brother weren't no better. Taking all your money and leaving you pore. The law shoulda been chasing them 'stead of you!" The overwrought woman slammed down the items in her hands so hard that she toppled a stack of neatly folded clothes on the bed. She scowled and went to work straightening up the mess she'd made.

"Sorry, Miss Rachel, but it gits me worked up. You knows I was working for them Terrells. Mercy, they was hard folk to please! That was the worst year of my life. I couldn't work for you, 'cause you was near penniless, pore thing. I needed food and a bed."

"But you gave me a little money—as much as you could spare," Rachel pointed out. "And you came by to tend me every time you could when I was recovering from my miscarriage. I don't know what would have happened to me if it hadn't been for your kindness and loyalty."

"It weren't right for peoples to be mean to you when you never done nothing wrong. They forget their Christian duties not to judge or be cruel to others. It was most awful how wicked men tried to bed you on the sly and how women wouldn't have nothing to do with you and talked about you something fierce, right to your face! Just mean and jealous witches."

"I wanted to stand on my own two feet," Rachel admitted, "and I could have if people had allowed me to do so. But what can one expect from people who welcomed that destructive Sherman into their homes and handed him their beloved city on a silver tray? Perhaps it was done, as they claimed, only to spare Savannah from the same fate as Atlanta and the other towns that evil Yankee razed, looted, and burned."

"Things seemed good for us after you married Mr. Phillip," Lula Mae reminisced, "but here comes that bad trouble again. It seems you cain't get away from it, Miss Rachel. It follows you around likes a black shadder on a sunny day."

"I know, Lula Mae, and I can't seem to shake it. Phillip seemed like good luck for a change. I hoped my past would be forgotten or ignored in time, when everyone saw how happy we were and how safe he was. Now he's dead after getting drunk like Craig did that last day. It's a scary pattern that frightens me so."

Lula Mae halted her chore and looked at the young woman. "You and Mr. Phillip acted more like good friends than husband and wife. Were you truly happy and in loves down in your deepest of hearts, Miss Rachel?"

Rachel wondered if the housekeeper knew her so well or was merely unusually perceptive. "Happy? To be honest, Lula Mae, I'm not sure I even know what real happiness is. Not since my family and home were taken from me because of the war. We didn't believe in or practice slavery, yet, my father and brother are dead because of it, and my family and home were lost." That reality had ruined her life. "I don't hate all Yankees," Rachel murmured. "Many came south to be genuine reformers; but some won't allow us to forget our old way of life or grant us time to accept the new one." But today Rachel didn't want to think about the South's lingering dilemma. She had worries closer to home and heart to resolve.

"What am I going to do if the law comes and arrests me?" she plaintively asked Lula Mae.

"I won't let them or anyone harms one hair on your pretty head."

"Thank you, Lula Mae," she said, but knew there was nothing the kind woman could do to save her from whatever her fate would be.

Both worked in silence as the packing neared its end.

Rachel noticed that the bitterness she had seen in the housekeeper's expression and heard in her voice had vanished. She prayed hers would drain away, too, as she needed all of her energy to work on her problems. Somebody had shot at her today, but she would be out of that culprit's reach tomorrow. All she could do was wait to see if a message came to tell her who and what was behind this afternoon's threat. If it came to Phillip, she would be the one to receive and read it. If Phillip had been murdered and her life was in danger, she would take no risks that would allow an enemy to succeed again. She couldn't report the shooting to the police; that might entice them out to Moss Haven to ask questions. She would advise Lula Mae and Burke to be alert and careful during her absence, but not expose why. And soon, she would have the opportunity to study Daniel Slade closer.

*

As Burke and Rachel rode away in the carriage the next morning, Lula Mae observed their departure. She shook her head and frowned. "You be up to something, Miss Rachel, and you shoulda tolds me what it is," she muttered to herself. "I know you better than you know yourself. You always pluck the wrong man to marry. You're truly like me and don't need no man messing up your life and doings. Most men ain't worth nothing nohow. Most jest uses us and throws us away when they don't wants us no more. You should never let no man hurts you like that Newman beast did; I seed your bruises and such. No man deserved dying more than him!"

*

In town, Captain Daniel Slade McCandless was having his last talk for a while with Luke Conner. "Learn all you can," he said to his first mate, "but don't draw attention to yourself or to me. I don't know how long I'll be gone. Stay at the hotel; I'll send telegrams there to keep you informed." Dan thought Luke almost always looked as if he were about to grin over a joke; he had a playful air, a boyishly roguish charm, and a pleasant manner that Dan thoroughly enjoyed. They made perfect companions and had been best friends for four years.

"You be careful, Dan," Luke cautioned. "If all we've heard about your sister-in-law is true, she's a dangerous woman."

Dan saw how concerned his friend was. "I know; her own words at Phillip's grave incriminated her. That story I told her made her plenty nervous, Luke, and I can tell she doesn't trust Phillip's partners. And from what I sense, she doesn't know whether or not to believe me."

"What if she knows who you are?" the brown-haired man ventured. "You did give her part of your real name. What if she recognized it?"

"She didn't react as if she'd heard it before."

"If she's a good actress, she wouldn't; and no woman would be a better one than a successful murderess."

Dan reflected on that. "I don't think Phillip ever spoke about me or even knew I stopped using my last name after I left home. She said Phillip told her his family was dead and that he didn't want to talk about them."

"Then, why did she invite you, a stranger, to travel with her?"

"Obviously to study me to see if I'm embroiled in her mystery. Somehow Phillip was forced into a trap. I told you what his letter said about needing help fast and about not telling Rachel anything or he would be in more trouble and danger than he already was. That makes me even more suspicious of her. Maybe she got him into a raw deal and something happened to the money. She was searching hard for it yesterday, so I know she doesn't have it, and that scares her. Phillip must have hidden it as insurance, but died without revealing its location. Then he must have warned her she would be responsible for returning it. I wonder why he would do that, Luke."

"If Phillip didn't tell her about the deal and money until he was dying," Luke speculated, "it could be his revenge against her for killing him—put her into an enemy's peril. She has to find it and return it or her own scheme could be exposed. If she does know or suspect who you are, my friend, maybe she thinks you know where the money is hidden, so she's turning her charms on you to extract that information. Why else would a one-day widow who loved her husband be sailing toward you so fast?"

"I don't think that's her motive for inviting me along. Phillip had to love and trust her to marry her, especially with her bad reputation, but I doubt she loved my brother or any of her husbands. Besides, Rachel hasn't listed that far in my direction, Luke, though I admit I have caught her eye."

"Not yet and not here. She has to protect herself against more gossip and suspicions. Wait until she gets you away and see how she behaves then."

Dan didn't want to think about that possibility. "This would never have happened if she'd known Phillip had a brother who would come after her. It's because of that damned ship we were supposed to sail on in '71! If we hadn't changed to another clipper at the last minute because of the problems aboard, we'd be at the bottom of the sea with those unlucky sailors. We were in too much of a rush to have our names removed from the seaman's role in port. I didn't even remember that mistake until I was given Phillip's letter last week. I never knew they thought I was dead. Phillip was desperate, so he prayed it wasn't true. He wanted me to get him out of trouble again. It all comes back to the arms deal and missing money. Rachel's true motive is in that mystery; she's not just after an inheritance."

"She probably wants the hefty profit from it, but you'll foil her," Luke said with confidence in his friend. "If anybody can romance the truth from her lips, it's Captain Slade. You've never let a pretty face and shapely body sway your judgment before."

"Not even when I bedded the woman my father loved and wanted to marry?" Dan scoffed. "Damn that scheming bitch!"

"That was different, Dan, a mistake, and we both know it."

Agonizing memories flooded Dan's head. "I let that flaming-haired vixen get her claws into me. My father never forgave me, Luke, and I don't blame him. From the time I was born, he had a grudge against me. I couldn't help looking like my mother, and it wasn't my fault Mother died giving birth to me. If anyone's to blame, it was he. He shouldn't have gotten her pregnant again a month after Phillip was born. That was too soon and she was too weak. I told him so one day when we quarreled; I think he hated me even more because I forced him to face the ugly truth; it was cruel of me."

"That's over, Dan, and you can't change the past. I thought you'd resolved all that bitterness and anguish, but Phillip's loss has apparently brought it back to the surface. Don't let it eat away at you, Dan. Bury it now."

"That's easier said than done, Luke. If only I could have seen Father and Phillip one last time to make peace with both of them, it would be over, one way or another. At least my conscience would be cleared by my overtures. Now, it's still hanging over my head like a sharp cutlass."

Luke clasped Dan's shoulder with a firm pressure and sent him an expression that revealed his love and support.

Dan nodded in gratitude. He dropped the matter and returned to their original conversation. "Rachel wouldn't be concealing my brother's death if she's after his money. His partners would never let her drain the companies of enough money to make murder worthwhile anyhow. If Phillip died of natural causes, that would be simple to prove."

"Maybe it isn't," Luke speculated, "or doesn't look that way to her. If she's innocent this time, she could be afraid she'll be arrested and convicted unjustly. That would be ironic."

"If my ravishing sister-in-law isn't guilty, my friend, the law wouldn't be so interested in her. They don't believe her, and neither do I."

"If she *is* scared and was looking for escape money, why didn't she take that packet you saw in the safe? As you said, she was searching for something particular, something important."

Dan picked up his bag to leave. "But if not that money, what could it be?"

"Damaging evidence that needs destroying? Or clues to this deal?" Luke surmised.

"Could be either one, Luke. I aim to find out everything soon."

"If she sets her eye on you, Dan, protect yourself. I'll see what I can learn about her family and servants. And about that Earl Starger she mentioned."

"I have a few tricks of my own to use on our pretty prey . . ."

*

Rachel purchased a ticket at Central Station while Burke placed her luggage on the loading platform for a porter to put it aboard the train.

"Don't you worry none while you're gone. Me 'n Lula Mae'll takes care of ever'thin'. You can depen' on us."

"I know. Burke, and thank you."

"Mr. Phillip'd be proud of you, Miz Rachel. You be handlin' dis real good. And don't you be scared. Ole Burke won' let no harm come to you."

Rachel smiled and embraced him. She didn't care what anyone in the South said about a white woman showing affection for a black friend.

"Bye, Miz Rachel," he said. "You takes care now."

"You, too," she said.

She hadn't seen Dan outside, and she didn't see him inside the car she was assigned to use. She sat down and waited.

"Good-morning, Mrs. McCandless," the familiar voice said over her shoulder. "May I join you since we're the only people occupying this car?"

The wary widow smiled as she put her ruse in motion by teasing the grinning man. "Since our mischief can't be observed, please join me."

Rachel moved her skirt out of Dan's leg room. She was wearing a simple outfit—a promenade polonaise and a demitrained skirt that lightly swept the floor in the rear. The material was a brownish green that enhanced the color of her eyes, a dye Phillip had mixed just for her.

"You look lovely this morning," he remarked as he settled himself in the aisle seat next to her, getting his own deceit underway.

"You look nice yourself, Cap—Dan."

"That's mighty kind of you, Rachel," he drawled.

Yes, she had noticed his appearance. He was clad in an obviously expensive suit that was tailor-made for his manly physique—a deep-blue waistcoat with striped trousers in blue and brown and a neat cravat with a tiepin at his throat. Beneath was a brown vest over a tan shirt. He looked comfortable in his dress garments. He cut a dashing figure this morning, and seemed in high spirits, yet she wished he would stop smiling at her as he did and wished the sparkle would leave those seawater eyes. This man was too irresistible for his own good, for *her* own good. It was hard to concentrate on deluding him when he stole her wits and breath with ease and swiftness.

A whistle blew—loud beneath the covered platform—to indicate their impending departure. They heard hissing steam and felt the tug against the tracks as the train began to move. It did not increase its speed until they cleared the town, then headed northwest at a steady, rocking pace with its wheels sending forth clickity-clack repetitions as they struck the iron rails.

As she gazed out the window, Rachel opened a safe conversation. "I hear they're having a terrible railroad strike up North," she said. "The papers say working conditions are so awful and dangerous that men have walked off their jobs and refuse to return until changes are made. They've reported all sorts of crimes they say are the work of a group called Molly Maguires. I hope it doesn't spread to here. Most of the interior crops and goods are sent by rail to Savannah for shipment to other ports, and things they need are sent inland by rail. Of course, if goods can reach Augusta by wagon, they can be sent downriver by steam or keel boat."

"You seem to pay close attention to anything that might affect your affairs. That's smart, Rachel."

"Phillip taught me well. The '73 Panic and Depression warned people to watch for danger signs and to ward off trouble before it struck. My father was smart like Phillip, too."

"Does that mean he's dead? Of course he is, or you wouldn't have been working to support yourself. I'm sorry, Rachel."

"He and my older brother were killed in the war. We owned a beautiful plantation between here and Augusta: White Cloud where we raised cotton. That's how it got its name. When the fields were ready and you gazed out over them, it looked like a giant snowy cloud covering the earth."

This was what he needed, more information about her. "Did your family lose it during the war? Was it burned and looted?"

"No, we were lucky there," she revealed in a bitter tone. "But postwar taxes and expenses were destructive."

"What happened to your home? Where is the rest of your family?"

"Another brother drowned shortly after the war. The others . . . If you don't mind, I don't want to talk about this anymore. We won't be passing near the plantation; it's farther east than our route."

Dan realized these were all clues to her dark past, ones he needed to probe later if Luke didn't have the answers when he returned. He saw how the conversation had dulled her eyes with remembrances of bad times. Her voice and expression exposed the strain she was experiencing, which told Dan she wasn't totally unfeeling. Despite his suspicions and caution, her soulful mood tugged at his heart. While he regained his control, he pretended to gaze out the window beyond her, when actually he watched the baffling array of conflicting emotions that flickered on her face and in her golden-brown eyes.

For a time they both looked out the window at the stretch of pines and cedars with intermingled hardwoods that seemed to go on forever. At some points, they passed plantations and farms and saw workers in the fields. One pasture was dotted with cattle and a few horses. They came to an area where several boys and girls were waving and yelling at people on the train. He observed how she smiled dreamily as she watched them.

The bartender had told him she had been married three times but had no children, just large inheritances from each. Dan tried to imagine his brother and this beauty as a wedded couple, but he couldn't. "You and Phillip don't have a child; that's a shame. Your expression says you're fond of them."

"We've only been married eight months, remember?"

"Then you two want children someday?"

"Yes, if it's possible. Some couples . . . Look, isn't that lovely?" she asked, changing the subject. "Everything is so green and alive. I love this time of year. I suppose you miss many seasons while at sea."

Relax her, old boy. Let her think she's learning all about you. "A world of blue can be peaceful and enjoyable, Rachel. I love the sea. I was born to be a sailor. The *Merry Wind* is my home and family. She's never failed me. She's sleek, fast, and beautiful. A clipper with three masts, miles of rigging, and sails enough to fill a big house. She's the most beautiful sailing vessel ever made—long and lean with sharp bows and raked masts. You've never seen a more thrilling sight than a clipper knifing through a wind-swept sea with a white curl at her bow as she tosses aside an occasional spray. She doesn't have that bone-jarring lift and plunge into the water like other ships. She just skims across the surface like a strong hand over a calm pond. Her flapping sails are like musical heartbeats to me. Yep, she's my home, family, and love."

"I take it you're not married?"

"Only to the sea. She makes a challenging, unpredictable, and bewitching wife. She'll steal your very heart and soul if you let her. But she'll take your life if you don't master her."

Rachel didn't mean to relax in his company for a single moment, but she couldn't help herself. "I've never been on a clipper before, only a large steamship once. You make it sound so exciting."

His gaze met hers. "It is. It makes the blood sing through your veins. Maybe I can take you on a voyage one day."

"That would be won—" Rachel halted and composed herself, dashing aside the contagious emotions he had evoked within her. "I'm sure Phillip and I would enjoy a trip on your . . . lovely wife." She laughed.

The train made a few stops at small towns with tiny depots. The whistle would blow on approach and departure. Steam would hiss like an angry snake and send clouds of misty white breath billowing away from its sides. It would move onward with its steady sounds and lulling motion.

Despite the numerous stops, no other passenger entered the car they were sharing. They remained secluded in the quiet and intimate setting, sitting side by side with shoulders touching and occasionally one's knees rubbing the other's as the engine took them around bends.

"Somehow I can't picture Phillip McCandless as a plantation master," Dan commented.

Let him think he's getting to know you, Rachel. "He isn't. We use the sharecropper system at Moss Haven. Our plantation is divided into large parcels where other families live and work. They pay us by giving us half of their crops, mostly cotton and indigo. We own the land, houses, work animals, and tools. We supply the seeds and other necessities. Phillip sells the crops to brokers in town, and the profits are split down the middle. We only have four people who work for us: Lula Mae, our housekeeper, Burke Wells, our manager, and two helpers. Burke takes care of our private property and sees to the needs of the sharecroppers. We only keep a few stock and raise a family garden. This method saves us a lot of time, work, and aggravation. If their crops fail one year, we have other holdings to see us through. So far, that hasn't happened."

"Your staff is mighty loyal. That housekeeper looked annoyed with me for bothering you the other day. She's mighty protective, isn't she." He chuckled.

"She's always been that way. She calls me *Miss* Rachel and has trouble forgetting I'm a grown woman. But I don't mind. She's been good to me."

The train halted for a time at Tennille. The passengers were allowed to get off to stretch their legs and to buy a snack if they wished. Dan went to purchase them something to eat. He returned with a napkin of cold fried chicken, still-warm biscuits, hunks of cheese, and an open bottle of wine.

He spread another napkin across her lap, then one across his thighs. He held up the food for her to make her choices. Rachel took some of each and thanked him. Dan pulled two glasses from his pockets and poured wine into one. He passed it to her, then filled his own.

"I'm sure you paid a pretty sum for this lovely feast."

"We're worth being pampered today, aren't we?" he jested.

"Yes, and its fun." How curious that he should make her feel so relaxed and happy while simultaneously making her tense and worried.

"Do you like Savannah, Rachel? Are you and Phillip planning on living there permanently?" He listened as he ate a chicken thigh.

"It's a beautiful town. Phillip never mentioned moving again. He seemed happy with his change from Charleston. Why do you ask?"

"I just never thought about him moving away. He loved it there. But Savannah does put him closer to his other businesses. Why did he merge the McCandless shipping firm with Milton Baldwin's?"

She chewed, swallowed, then answered, "Savannah already had several shipping firms, and both of theirs were smaller. To be competition for trade, they needed to be large and powerful. I also think Phillip wanted someone helping to run the firm when he was in Athens or Augusta."

"How did he get into those businesses? They're both odd choices for a gentle man like Phillip who was never a hunter or a fighter."

"I don't know. I assumed he always owned partnerships in them. He didn't inherit them from his family when they died?" she asked Dan. *Listen close, Rachel.*

"No, the McCandlesses were never involved with arms and ammunition."

"I can't answer. I never thought to ask him that question."

"Did he spend much time with them?"

"A few days every five to six weeks. He seemed content to let George Leathers and Harrison Clements run those two companies. That's why I found it strange that he worked out a personal deal with you."

"Probably because we're old friends." Dan was confused. Since Rachel was a clever actress and cunning murderess, she shouldn't make the mistake of using the past tense so often when she talked about Phillip. Why did she?

They finished their meal as the conductor yelled, "Awl-la-board!"

Dan put away the leftovers and napkins, but refilled their glasses with pale-red wine. "To an interesting and successful journey together," he toasted, then tapped his glass against hers.

"I hope it will be," she concurred, and smiled at him. She relaxed in the comfortable seat, sipped the wine, and viewed the landscape.

The Coastal Plain of the lower part of Georgia was flat in most areas. As they journeyed toward Augusta, the terrain began to alter. Hills with gentle rolls and fertile valleys appeared and increased in frequency. The soils changed colors where the hard brown or red clays of the northern section met with the sandy yellow and gray ones of the southern section. They crossed tree- and vine-shrouded streams and rushing rivers that wound through the land like wriggling snakes. Wildflowers and bushes bloomed and displayed new cloaks of verdant leaves. Forests of pine—some tall and slender, others short and thick, both laden with brown cones—and hardwoods of oak, maple, poplar, hickory, and scattered dogwood ran for miles along the tracks and for miles backward from the front rows. Recently planted fields of cotton, tobacco, corn, and vegetables showed green sprouts in their fertile brown beds. The train moved past houses, farms, barns, pastures, stock, workers, and dirt roads. Soon they would arrive at their first destination.

Augusta . . . Where Savannah was comparable to a genteel lady, Augusta was like a child—busy, impatient, eager, growing constantly, ever-altering, but always retaining some of its original appearance and traits.

Phillip had told her it was the primary manufacturing city in Georgia, was the first inland trade center, and one of the state's largest cities. Named for Princess Augusta, mother of King George III, it was nestled against the Savannah River. Because the winters there were short and mild, it was a resort for northerners and rich inland planters. Augusta was a rail center, large cotton market, and a textile giant with her numerous mills, factories, and foundries.

As the train slowed at the edge of town, they went over rolling hills and through verdant flatlands. They moved past open spaces of rusty-red dirt and areas crowded with pines. They saw mills on both sides—some as high as five stories, their chimneys making them appear even higher. Twice the tracks crossed the city canal system that furnished the companies with power.

They reached Union Station on schedule, a huge complex of buildings that covered many blocks. The train halted inside a large depot with wooden platforms and wide windows.

Rachel wondered if Dan noticed her trembling, both from his touch as he helped her descend the train and from the task that loomed before her.

"I'll get a porter to bring our luggage out front. Wait for me there."

"I'll hail a carriage and be ready to leave when you join me."

Rachel walked outside and glanced around. Plenty of public carriages were nearby, as well as private ones and wagons waiting for freight. She caught one driver's eye and motioned him to her. He reined his team and jumped down beside her. "My companion is claiming our luggage," she informed him. "We're staying at the Planter's Hotel on Broad."

Dan and the porter joined them and the men loaded the baggage. Dan tipped the man, thanked him, then assisted Rachel into the carriage and climbed in behind her. When they were settled, the driver clicked his tongue and flicked the reins to urge the horses into motion.

The carriage headed up Campbell Street. When they reached Greene, Rachel pointed to a structure in the middle of the intersection of the next block. "Look at that, Dan." The driver halted a minute for them to get a good view.

"George lives nearby. He said it's called Big Steve. They ring it for fires and other emergencies. The tower is five stories high and the bell in the cupola weighs six thousand pounds. I wonder what it would feel like to climb all those winding steps and look out over the city."

"About as scary for you as it would be exciting," he responded. Dan had scaled riggings much higher than the bell tower, a few times even while swaying in bad weather. It always gave him a surge of power and burst of heady stimulation to see his sleek ship and the rolling sea far below him.

"While we're here, we must see the sights."

"That sounds nice," he agreed, but was miffed by her cheery mood when she was a recent widow.

The carriage moved on toward the hotel. The streets were wide; some were paved with cobblestone and Belgian blocks. In the middle of many of them were lovely parks or landscaped areas. Azaleas and other flowers were in full bloom. Trees—redbuds, pines, magnolias, dogwoods, and assorted hardwoods—also lined the sidewalks. They saw lovely homes in Victorian, Classic Revival, Greek, and Georgian architecture. Occasionally upper porches were shaded and decorated by entwining wisteria.

The carriage reached Broad and the driver halted until he could cross the street which was congested with wagons, carriages, riders, and walkers. It was aptly named, as twenty wagons could sit side by side in its great width. Brick-and-wood buildings two and three stories high stood shoulder to shoulder in both directions; some displayed balconies where owners lived above their businesses. Telegraph poles stretched out along one side on Broad, and lampposts lined both sides. Two blocks down and six blocks up in the middle of the street were two city markets, one with a large cupola that held a giant clock that revealed the time as ten minutes past five.

When it was clear, the driver urged his team across the tracks of the horse-drawn city trolley and turned left. They rode half a block to the corner of Macarton Street where the Planter's Hotel was located.

Dan's alert senses detected the nearness of the Savannah River, two blocks away.

"I hope this hotel will suit you, Dan."

"It looks impressive," he said, noticing that it filled the width of the block.

Rachel looked at the large structure. A street-level veranda stretched across the front and down one side. Above it, a porch offered guests a tranquil area for relaxing, with one side covered to provide shade in hot weather or cover during a shower. "We should take third-floor rooms if possible. That way, our rest won't be disturbed by talkative late strollers."

Dan paid the driver after he returned from carrying their baggage inside. The man flashed him a toothy grin for the large tip and left.

"You mustn't keep paying for everything, Dan. I have my own money."

"It wasn't much; it won't ruin me," he jested, then grasped her elbow and guided her to the registration desk. "Two of your best rooms, preferably on the top floor and side by side, please."

While the clerk studied his book, Rachel glanced around. The lobby was all done in polished oak with matching pillars for ceiling support; clustered around them were sitting areas for socializing with friends, with business associates, or with strangers who needed to be welcomed in the proper southern style.

"Three-eleven and three-twelve are available, sir. Ten dollars a day, including breakfast. We have the finest dining room in town with reasonable prices and delicious meals. How long will you be staying with us?"

Dan looked at Rachel for the answer.

"One week, please. We'll leave on Monday, the fifth of April." She watched the clerk record the dates, but didn't look at her companion.

Dan was surprised by her response, as it was a long stay just to carry out simple business. He'd know her motive soon, because he didn't plan to let her out of his sight except to sleep and dress, or not at all if she decided he would make an excellent victim number four. Under the grim circumstances, that wouldn't be a betrayal of his brother. Yet he assumed she would not pursue him or another man until she found a safe way to expose her husband's death—unless, of course, she was so confident and bold that she would do as she pleased. She seemed taken with him, but that could be another pretense.

"The bellman will see you to your rooms and deliver your baggage. I hope you have a pleasant stay with us. If you need anything, let me know."

In her most polite tone, she said, "Thank you, sir, I'm sure we'll have a lovely time in your city. Come along, Cousin Dan, let's get settled in and have dinner. I'm ravenous."

As she joined the bellman nearby, Dan followed behind her swishing skirt and swaying hips. He noticed how dark her hair looked against the ripe-olive-colored garment. This woman utterly amazed and perturbed him. She behaved as if she truly were on a holiday, as if she didn't have a care in the world!

They reached their rooms and waited for the bellman to separate their baggage. When that task was done, Rachel and Dan tipped the sunny-haired young man, who nodded his gratitude and left.

Standing in their doors, Rachel smiled and said, "I'll be ready in one hour, Captain Slade, as soon as I unpack and freshen up."

"I'll knock on your door at six-thirty sharp." Dan noted that her cheeks were lightly flushed and wondered if sharing that bottle of wine on the train was the reason for their rosiness and her merry mood.

Rachel locked her door and walked to the bed, beside which her trunks had been placed. She unfastened the buckles and unpacked them.

As she looked into the oval mirror, Rachel observed how pink her cheeks were. As far as Daniel Slade was aware, she was a happy woman, wed to one of his oldest and best friends. She had to be very careful how she behaved around him or he could become suspicious of her morals.

Dear Phillip . . . She spoke silently to her dead husband. *I tried to love you as a wife and to desire you as a man, but I couldn't. I believed you understood and accepted that reality. Perhaps you didn't and you're punishing me with this dangerous mystery. Somehow I must find the key to unlock this prison you've placed me in. If you truly loved me, guide me to the clues I need for release and freedom.*

Rachel donned a simple but lovely cornflower-blue dress that was trimmed in ivory lace and small ribbons. She pinned up her long dark hair in a stylish manner, then secured a matching blue silk flower just above her ear. As she finished putting on her hose and slippers there was a knock at her door. She glanced at the clock on the dressing table and smiled.

"I see you're punctual, Cousin Dan," she greeted the captain at the door. "I'm ready."

"Why *Cousin* Dan?" he asked.

"That's how I'll introduce you along our journey so no one will think anything wicked of our traveling together."

As they strolled down the lengthy hallway toward the stairs, Dan asked, "How many times have you been to Augusta with Phillip?"

"Only once. We came around the Christmas holidays. We spent two days with George's family, and another two with Harry's in Athens. Phillip considered his business partners the closest people to his family. As you know, his real family are all deceased. The men spent time with business and socializing with their friends. I was left in their homes with their wives. I didn't get to see much of either town, so I'm looking forward to this holiday. I'd also like to get to know his partners better. With Phillip not around I can do that better."

"You sound as if you don't trust them," Dan hinted as they descended the steps.

"Why would you think that? I hardly know them."

Dan couldn't say that when she was relaxed her eyes looked like a pale yellowy brown of melting honey and when she was tense or guileful, they looked more greenish brown, the hue they were now. She also seemed to hold them open wider when she was nervous. So he merely commented: "The way your voice sounded, and the fact that you're staying around more than a day or two."

"Will that interfere with your schedule?"

"No. In fact, I can use a holiday myself. I've been at sea a long time and I'll be heading there again soon. I can use a little fun. Right now, a delicious meal will be perfect." He gestured down the hall. "There's the way to the dining room."

They were met at the door and seated at a table near a window. The eating area was busy tonight. After their orders were given to the waiter, they looked at each other across a white-linen-covered table with glowing candles and fragrant flowers in a shallow cut-glass bowl. Soft music from a violin filled their ears helping to calm their tensions.

Rachel realized this evening was not going to be easy while staring into that handsome face with its enticing blue eyes and smile as bright as a thousand candles. She had to lighten the heavy romantic aura and distract them both. "Tell me about your travels around the world. I imagine you've been to many exciting places and had countless adventures. Entertain me with colorful tales."

Dan recognized her ruse and concurred it was a good and needed one. She was far too ravishing and enchanting tonight to be ignored. As their turtle soup came he began to relate tales of some of his voyages. He was well into his third story when their dinner arrived: baked ham, stewed tomatoes, green beans, and biscuits with honey. The meal was served with coffee and a heady red wine. Between bites, Dan continued his stories, and she listened or asked questions or made comments.

The candles between them were burning low when the waiter set down their dessert plates, which were heaped with fruit dumplings covered with a hard butter sauce.

Rachel glanced at the enticing sweet and laughed. "I'm stuffed. I don't think I can hold another spoonful."

Dan swallowed his second bite, licked his lips, and tempted, "It's worth the pain, Rachel; it's a wonderful dish—sweet and spicy at the same time, so very crispy, and with a sauce that slides down your throat with ease. Surely you can't deny yourself such a treat just to prevent a little discomfort later. Some things are worth doing, then paying the price for later."

For a moment, Rachel had the wicked thought that he wasn't talking about the dessert. His blue eyes seemed to leap with flames that could consume her. She had the thought of leaning over and licking the sweet sauce off his full lips. Or slipping into his arms and covering his mouth with hers, right here in front of everyone. Rachel used her lagging strength to free her gaze from his. She took a bite of the dessert, then said, "Very good."

The waiter asked if they'd like more coffee. Dan looked at Rachel, who shook her head and said she was too full to finish the tempting dessert and was ready to leave. Dan instructed the man to add the meal to his hotel bill.

"If I can't tempt you with finishing your treat, let's leave. Would you care for a stroll down the street? It's well lighted and looks safe."

"No, thank you, Dan, not tonight. I'm tired from a long and busy day. I'll meet you in the lobby at eight for breakfast. Afterward, we'll go visit George Leathers. Perhaps he knows about your contract."

"Ah, yes, business first and play later. Wise choice, Mrs. McCandless. Shall we go?" When Rachel put down her napkin, Dan assisted her with her chair, then put his hand at the back of her waist and guided her toward the lobby stairs.

At her door, Dan smiled and bid her good night.

"Good night, Dan. I'll see you in the morning."

Dan watched the door close and heard it lock, just as he heard it squeak when it was clear she remained there leaning against it. He wondered what she was thinking and feeling, and plotting. Whatever her plan, it would get under sail tomorrow. He went to his adjoining room.

Rachel heard his departure and wondered why he had lingered. Who and what was Captain Daniel Slade? What role did he have in her destiny? Whatever it was, it had begun the moment he arrived at Moss Haven last Friday. Was Dan a villain or a hero? she wondered. *Worry about this tomorrow—whatever it brings,* she instructed herself.

Breakfast passed in light conversation between Rachel and Dan. Their waiter returned, cleared away their dishes, and refilled their coffee cups.

When the tables nearby were empty of hotel guests and they had privacy, Rachel moved their talk to a serious vein. "When we visit George this morning, don't forget you'll be introduced as my cousin from Charleston. I plan to tour the company and pretend we're on a holiday. If George offers to entertain us, I'll accept. As far as he's concerned, we're here on vacation. After I soften him up in a few days, I'll ask to see the company books. Hopefully by then he won't object."

"I'm confused, Rachel. If you're here on business, why not say so?"

"Because my task is a secret for now."

"You don't trust me? How can I help out if I'm in the dark about what you're trying to accomplish?"

Rachel pretended to ponder his words. Phillip hadn't mentioned Daniel Slade to her, but neither had Phillip told her much about his past, so maybe that wasn't too strange. She had come up with a plan that would seem to include him, yet not enlighten him to her motive. "All right, Dan, I'm going to trust you because you're Phillip's good friend. He's thinking of selling his shares of the companies, but he doesn't want his partners to get worried about him pulling out or checking up on them. I did his books at the shipping firm, so I understand records. He wants my opinion about their values by studying the assets and liabilities."

"Doesn't he get business reports from his partners?"

"Yes, but he wants to make certain they're accurate."

"I see, you hope to catch them off guard to get an honest figure."

"Neither man should suspect me or what I'm doing. The two companies are separate, but they do joint deals. I want to see if either or both partners act suspicious or nervous as if they have something to hide."

Dan noticed that her eyes had that greenish cast again and were held wider than normal; it told him she was lying through those beautiful white teeth and soft lips as easily as she was breathing through them. "Do you know enough about guns and ammunition to be a fair judge?"

"Yes. I've read all of their reports, and Phillip's taught me all he knows about them. For comparison, we've gotten prices, models, sizes, and lists of materials from other companies. I've studied the diagrams of weapons and types of cartridges. I know enough to spot when something's wrong. I know how gunpowder and shells are made. I know how different guns work, and who owns their patents. Phillip wanted to make certain that if anything happened to him, I could take his place if I wanted to. Besides, I find it all fascinating." She had refreshed herself with those manuals and papers Sunday night to make sure she had the facts clear in her head.

"Guns and bullets are fascinating?" he teased the woman whose eyes were now that amber shade that might indicate honesty. But for all he knew, it could be only an effect of lighting.

"Yes, how they're made and how they work. Isn't it the same with your ship? You want to know how every inch of her works."

Dan smiled. "That's right, Rachel, and I do."

"I'm certain that's so. You seem like a man who needs to know everything that's going on around him, especially if it involves you."

"Do you and Phillip think he's being cheated? Is that why he wanted to handle my contract himself?" He complimented himself for being astute and alert enough to throw in his last question to supplement his cover.

Rachel hoped her ruse with Dan would make her questions and curiosity about George and Harry sound logical. "Perhaps. Both businesses were earning nice profits until mid '73, at which time Phillip was told things had slacked off. They said orders were lower, and material prices and salaries for skilled workers were higher. After the war ended and things settled down, surplus arms and ammunition were sold off. With the fighting over, not as many weapons were needed. Big companies like Remington and Winchester gobbled up the foreign markets. But Phillip figured that most southerners would replace weapons confiscated from them after the war—for protection and hunting." She sipped at her coffee before continuing. "I'll be able to tell if more supplies are being purchased than make the amounts of the sales listed that he's paid for. I plan to check items ordered against items made against items sent out or in inventory against recorded sales and profits. Any discrepancy should stand out. For example, if large amounts of supplies are ordered to make cartridges, but only a few sales are recorded and the inventory is low, that would point out an inconsistency— that unrecorded goods were going out. Phillip doesn't believe that sales have dropped off or as much as they're telling him. He thinks secret deals are being made. That would be easy for his partners to accomplish since he isn't around much to see what's going on."

If he didn't know better, her fabrication would sound convincing. "Phillip certainly did himself a good turn when he captured you. I see why he didn't hesitate to leave you in charge or to send you here on this clever mission. Do his partners know how enlightened you are?"

"No, not yet." She liked the way Dan seemed impressed by her wits and skills. True, she did know all those things, and would continue to pretend that was her task. "And I won't behave as if I am. I want them relaxed enough to make slips. One last caution, Dan. If your deal with Phillip isn't recorded in those books, don't mention to either George or Harry that it was a previous arrangement. Perhaps his secrecy is a kind of test. We'll tell them we came to place your order, then see if they already know about it. If they don't, since you need your arms in a hurry and Phillip isn't here to tell us how to handle it, we'll put it through the books. Is that all right?"

"I'll go along with you. Problems with either or both companies could affect my order. I came a long way to carry out my business, so I don't want it to be a waste of time and energy or a loss of a nice profit."

"Profit is what concerns Phillip, too. If the companies aren't making hefty ones, he wants to rid himself of those drains on his finances. He's checking out replacement investments now, so he's serious about this."

Dan set down his cup and asked, "What kind of investments?"

"I don't know. He said it will be a surprise." She didn't care for the foul taste of this deception, but it couldn't be helped. She liked Dan and wished she could solicit his assistance, but she couldn't risk trusting him.

Dan didn't point out the hole in her fake tale, but she must have caught that oversight, because she came up with a valid explanation.

"Phillip didn't want to arrive and demand to study the books himself because he was afraid, if things were accurate, that it would create ill will. That would tell his partners he had suspicions of them. It probably wasn't wise, but he's always accepted their word and reports without question or intrusion. Since they're out of town and he lets them run the firms, he stayed out of the accounting end. Phillip was actually a silent partner or more like a shareholder. I've been trying to get him more involved; that's why he wants me to get the facts for him. If I'm smart and lucky, I'll find a clue in the records to help him make his decisions."

Dan thought he should reason with her. "If they're taking orders on the sly or not recording the full profits, that wouldn't show in the books, would it?" he asked. "Surely they would conceal such devious actions. Why would they act nervous or suspicious if they know nothing can be found or traced?"

"Isn't it human nature for a man who has something to hide to worry he's made an error someplace that someone might catch?" she asked. "Something overlooked, like a freight wagon rented when no order is listed to be hauled to the wharf or depot that day? No matter how clever a criminal is, doesn't he usually make at least one tiny slip that eventually gets him exposed and caught?" She observed him closely.

"In most cases that's true." Dan decided not to press her further and make her skittish. He worried about how easily and thoroughly she lied and how fast she caught and covered her mistakes—except for that recurring use of referring to Phillip in the past tense. He needed for her to make slips, big ones! Dan cautioned himself to keep a keen eye and clear head. *Move slow and careful, but let her think you're bewitched by her. Maybe she'll try to use you to save her, then you can snare her.*

"Are you ready?" Rachel asked when his cup was empty.

"Let's go entrap our first villain."

Rachel witnessed his roguish grin and the devilish glint in his dark blue eyes. "You like confronting challenges and dangers, don't you?"

His smile broadened and made deep creases near his mouth and eyes. "Yep, I do. They keep one alive and alert. Entertained, too."

She observed his expression and listened carefully to his tone. "You're not like Phillip in that area. He likes things calm and safe and simple, as I do. He doesn't want his life to be complicated or to change drastically. Nor do I."

"He's still reserved and mellow? Still prefers smooth sailing? I thought moving, new ventures, and marriage would have changed him."

For a while, Rachel needed to have pleasant thoughts about the man who had rescued her from a terrible situation and who had shared eight peaceful and safe months with her. "He hasn't changed since I've known him. He's sensitive, caring, and even-tempered. He enjoys life and having a good time, but he's soft-spoken and quiet. He's a kind and special man."

Dan watched her gaze into empty space as if calling Phillip's image to mind and remembering the good times with him. He was unprepared for her remarks. If one didn't know about her, one would think that was real affection and respect in her now limpid gaze and softened voice. She was clearly so talented in deceit that he couldn't detect bitterness, resentment, or hatred for his brother in spite of what she had done and why she was here. He was angry, but made certain his feelings were cloaked. "Phillip was always that way. Fair and honest, but restrained. He never liked trouble or problems, and he was almost generous to a fault. Growing up, he was shy, a mite withdrawn and self-protective. But I rid him of some of that and got him into a few mischievous deeds."

In view of her perilous dilemma and how little she knew about Phillip's life before she entered it, she realized how secretive he had been. He had never discussed his past, claiming he liked to live in the present. She thought she had known him and his work; it was obvious now she hadn't. There was another side, another personality, to him that he had guarded and hidden. She had witnessed only the good and tender side of her husband, but there was also a dark and unknown one that had made an illegal deal with dangerous men. "I wonder why Phillip was like that," she murmured, partly for her own curiosity and partly to coax needed revelations about him.

Dan figured that if he kept talking about Phillip, she would, too; and he'd learn more about his brother since their separation. Dan wanted to discover how and why Phillip had changed over the years, as his brother would never have done what Rachel hinted at that night when she searched their home. Yet Phillip must have gotten himself into a bad situation: his letter, her remarks, and this trip were leading to a perilous road Dan knew he must travel if he wanted truth and justice. No doubt she was testing him to see if he knew enough about Phillip to be who he claimed.

"His father. Stephen McCandless," Dan replied, "was a tough man in business and at home. You could say I was a mite reckless and spirited when I was growing up, so McCandless thought I was a bad influence on his son. He raked me over several times for taking Phillip off the straight and narrow, but I didn't want Phillip to be like his old man. I'll admit I went too far sometimes to give him spunk, but it was because I loved him. At times he was too gentle and tender-hearted for his own good. Phillip toughened up some after he went to work for his father and started dealing with other men. Gave him mettle and a new perspective." Dan saw how attentive and interested she was. "I don't mean to imply he was a weakling; he just didn't care for ill feelings and disruptions or embarrassments. He wanted everyone to get along and be happy. He would have made a good diplomat; he preferred peace and love. He never liked to see anyone or anything harmed. He took up for me plenty of times when I was mischievous or stubborn."

"He's still tender-hearted and protective," Rachel remarked. "His gentleness and understanding were two of the things that drew me to him. He would go to almost any length to keep from hurting someone he loves."

"That's Phillip McCandless all right."

"Was his father cold and mean?"

Dan quelled the bitter memories that question evoked. "Not to Phillip or to his wife. Phillip was born with the old man's image, was his pride and joy. Fortunately, he didn't inherit his father's worst traits."

"You obviously didn't like Mr. McCandless."

Dan was ready to get off this painful subject. "I never got to know him that well. We didn't get along or see eye to eye. He was afraid I'd corrupt or mislead his . . . son, maybe pull him off to sea with me." Dan caught himself before using the accurate word *favorite* son. *Watch it, old boy.*

That last comment astonished Rachel. "Was Phillip ever tempted to become a sailor or ship captain?"

"No. He didn't like water or ships. He got seasick." Dan didn't tell her his brother had been scared of the deep ocean and of drowning ever since a near-fatal mishap when they were young boys.

"Maybe he was afraid of them," Rachel surmised. "There was a storm when we took our short trip to New Orleans, and he almost panicked. He checked the weather several times before our return home and was nervous during the entire trip. But he didn't like to expose his fears to anyone. If he was afraid of anyone or anything, he always tried to conceal it. I suppose he thought it would make him appear weak to admit them."

After that childhood mishap and Dan's alleged loss at sea, he could understand Phillip's fears and hatred of the ocean. "No man wants to expose his flaws to others, Rachel. We all have some, but we like to hide them, keep them under control, not allow them to rule our lives."

Both wondered why Phillip had changed and how he had gotten into his dangerous predicament, but neither could broach that subject.

The dining room had quieted down with the departure of most customers. Their waiter arrived and asked if they wanted more coffee. Rachel and Dan told him they were finished and leaving, but both hated to end the informative conversation.

They hired one of the drivers of the three phaetons that were lined up outside the Planter's Hotel to take Augusta visitors to their destinations. Dan assisted her into the carriage and sat beside her. Rachel gave the driver the address, then settled herself into the comfortable seat.

"Did I tell you how lovely and refreshing you look this morning?" Dan asked. "If not, it was an oversight."

Rachel smiled and thanked him. The dark-haired beauty opened her parasol and held it over her head to protect her eyes from the sun's glare. She was attired in a ladylike ivy promenade outfit that nonetheless flattered her figure. Her hat of tightly woven straw with its sprigs of flowers and an ivy ribbon band had a curved brim that Phillip had said called attention to her face. A fabric drawstring purse rested in her lap. Her husband had helped her select this outfit down to the last detail, and she loved it.

The phaeton headed up Broad with the click-click of hooves striking the pavement and with a dipping bounce as the wheels made contact where the stones were put together. The street was busy with freight wagons, carriages, mounted riders, and a horse-drawn trolley that was making its way along the tracks on the other side of the street. They passed various businesses, a few warehouses that ran the depth of the block, and the west-end town market. Behind it was Citizen's Fire Company #8, with men working on equipment in preparation for an emergency. To assist the firemen, there were water pumps and fireplugs at intervals in the long street.

At McKinne, they turned left. Houses mingled with businesses. Dogs chased each other and barked. Birds sang in trees that were in or near blooming: dainty dogwoods dressed in ivory gowns, radiant peaches adorned in pink, majestic magnolias eager to open their large shell-shaped flowers, and lovely redbuds with tiny clusters of crimson petals. Some yards were aglow with color: sunny daffodils, flaming red, pale-pink, and snowy-white azaleas, rose-hued quince blossoms, and sprawling yellowbell bushes. Grass was as green and supple as spring leaves; so were countless wild onions and pesky weeds. It was a glorious day and tranquil setting.

Rachel studied Dan while he looked the other way. His dark-gray jacket hugged his broad shoulders and a single button fastening at the tapered waist exposed his narrow torso. His striped trousers did not fail to hint at the long and lean legs beneath them. He didn't look discomforted at all by the standing collar of his shirt or the cravat tied neatly at his neck. He was a man who took pride in his appearance.

To her relief, he had seemed to accept her devious explanation this morning. Unless she was wrong, he had looked and sounded as if he had known Phillip too well and had too deep an affection for him to have been lying about their mutual past. Surely Dan would despise and mistrust her when he learned she had beguiled him. But it couldn't be helped, she excused herself. Too much was at stake—her life and freedom. She tried to calm her apprehensions, but it was hard with her next challenge looming ahead.

Dan sensed her attention to him. Phillip's widow had looked at the sights, smiled, and chatted as if relaxed; but she wasn't, and he knew why.

They halted at the corner of Mill and Ellis streets. The Augusta Canal was in sight, as were tall buildings with towering chimneys atop them.

"Is this it?" the driver asked when neither person moved nor spoke.

Rachel glanced at the structure with a large sign reading AUGUSTA AMMUNI-TION COMPANY and said, "Yes, thank you."

Dan got out and extended his hand to Rachel, who lowered her parasol and grasped it. He felt her tremors as she exited the carriage, and he was glad she was nervous, as it made her vulnerable to his plans.

After the phaeton left, Rachel's gaze met his with anticipation.

Dan looked over the building with a two-story center section, a small one-story connection on the left, and a large wing to the right. Constructed of wood painted gray with blue trim, it had many tall windows and one chimney. On the two front doors were signs with red lettering that read: ABSOLUTELY NO SMOKING IN-SIDE. "Let's begin our work," he suggested.

Rachel knocked on the office door. No one responded. She tried the door; it was unlocked. "Let's go inside," she said.

George's office was neat and clean and uncluttered. In the front right corner stood a tall rack with a hat and double-breasted jacket. In the left corner was a easel holding a board with a display of the company's cartridges.

Rachel walked to George's large oak desk. On its surface were yesterday's newspaper, a lamp, a box of cigars and a clipper, an inkwell with pen on a carved base—a gift from Phillip last Christmas—and two letters. Rachel lifted the mail and read the names, but did not recognize them. The trash can beside it was empty. No company books or papers were in sight for her to sneak a peek. It was a good thing, as the part-owner opened a side door to the adjoining building and entered his office.

George Leathers' eyes widened in surprise. "Rachel McCandless, how nice to see you." He came forward, held out his hand, and smiled.

Rachel accepted the polite and friendly gesture and replied, "Nice to see you again, George. This is my cousin and dear friend, Captain Daniel Slade from Charleston." As she introduced Dan, she noticed no unusual reaction in Phillip's partner, who was clad in a brown vest and pants and a white shirt with sleeves rolled up a few turns.

George Leathers stepped closer to his second guest, extended his hand, smiled again, and said, "Pleasure to meet you, Captain Slade."

"Dan, please, and it's good to meet you, sir. Cousin Rachel has spoken highly of you."

As they talked, Rachel observed the older man. His hair was almost all gray and the matching mustache almost concealed a thin upper lip from view, but it was neat and made George look distinguished. He had heavy brows over long and narrow brown eyes, but not the kind that gave one a feeling of deceit. His nose was large, but suited the squarish face whose angles were broken only by drooping pockets of age-weakened flesh on either side of his chin, as George was of medium height and weight, though not stocky.

George glanced around and inquired, "Where is that partner of mine? Did I miss seeing him? I was in the laboratory on the other side."

"No, Phillip isn't with us," Rachel told the fifty-two year old man with a pleasant expression and genial manner. "He's in Baltimore for several weeks on business." She didn't detect any suspicious reaction to that news. "Dan came to visit me and has business here and in Athens, so we're making a holiday of it while Phillip's away. Dan's been at sea on a long voyage, so he needs time off to enjoy himself. He's never been to either town and I didn't see much when I was here last time, so we're staying until Monday morning."

"That's nice, Rachel. I'll be delighted to show you two around while you're here. I can use a little relaxation and entertainment myself."

Rachel put on her prettiest smile. "That's wonderful, George, and very kind of you, if it doesn't interfere with work."

"Have a seat while we chat." George took his chair and motioned to two others for his visitors. "Unless you have plans, I can fill your schedule except for Friday. I have appointments that day, but in the evening there is a big party at a friend's home. I'm sure he won't mind if I bring you two along. It will give you a chance to meet some important and nice people."

"Sounds marvelous, too tempting to resist. Don't you agree, Dan?"

"Sounds like what we both need, Cousin Rachel. Thank you, sir."

"We accept your hospitality and kindness, George."

He leaned back in his chair and smiled. "Excellent. Of course you'll join me and Molly Sue for supper at our home tonight, won't you?"

"We'd be delighted to come. I look forward to seeing Mrs. Leathers again. The last visit, she gave me some wonderful recipes. Naturally our housekeeper, Lula Mae, doesn't cook them as good as your wife, but we have enjoyed them nonetheless. Perhaps she'll share more special ones with me."

Pride and love glowed in George's brown eyes. "I'm sure she will. Molly Sue is the best cook I've ever known. It's too bad Phillip couldn't come with you. He's working too hard. He looked tired the last time I saw him. I hope he gets a little rest while he's away. How long will he be up North?"

Rachel feigned a look of dismay. "Six to seven weeks, he said. I miss him already, and he's only been gone a few days. Thank goodness I have Dan to keep me company and this trip for diversion."

George's fingers toyed with the gold chain to his vest-pocket watch. He glanced at a calendar on one wall and looked concerned. "That's a long trip."

"Yes, I know. Is there any pressing business?"

George stroked his mustache. "Not before his return. I did want to chat with him about some changes I have in mind, but they can wait."

"I suppose you're busy working on that large and important order Phillip mentioned," Rachel remarked in a casual tone.

George curled his fingers around the arms of his chair. "Yes . . . Did Phillip send me any special instructions? Or send anything else?"

He had hesitated, as if unsure of what to say, or perhaps wondering what or how much she knew about it. She thought it wise to put the nervous man at ease. "No. Is there a problem? Did he forget something in his rush to leave? His urgent trip did come up unexpectedly."

"Not really, but he said he was sending word soon on a new project. I'm sure he'll handle it when he returns. Nothing to worry about."

"He didn't mention anything to me, but you men never tell us wives very much about business. I hope it won't slow you down to entertain us."

"Certainly not. We have good men working for us. They don't require much supervision. You're a ship captain, Dan? Do you work for Phillip?"

Rachel and Dan both noticed how George changed the subject.

"I have my own clipper, work for myself, and live on my ship, the *Merry Wind*. I have friends and acquaintances who hire me to deliver cargoes for them around the world. When I'm not doing that, I usually pick up my next job and shipment wherever I'm docked. My base is Charleston; that's where I receive my mail and most job offers."

"It sounds as if you stay busy and on the move."

"Most of the time. I had to bring a load of ironwork to Savannah last week, so I took time off to visit with Cousin Rachel and her husband. It made better ballast than stones, and there was a good profit in that heavy load. If you ever have need of a private shipper, George, I'm for hire at reasonable prices."

"Sorry, Dan, but I either use the railroads or Phillip's firm. I always try to refer any business I can to him. He's been a good friend and partner for years. Since you're both from Charleston and in shipping, I suppose you knew Phillip before he moved to Georgia and married your cousin."

Dan wanted to ask how many years and how the two had met and gotten into this business together, but it was better for that to wait until later. Too many questions could make the man even more nervous than he was. "No, I'm from Alexandria, Virginia. I started using Charleston as my home port after Phillip left. Most of my regular customers shipped out of there, so it seemed a good idea to change locations. It didn't matter much to me, since I'm not around often. Before we leave town, I do have an order I'd like to place with you."

George assumed it was a small and personal one, so he didn't press it at that time. "That sounds good to me; I can use the business. We'll discuss it during the week and make out a contract. Have you ever been in an ammunition factory before?" After Dan shook his head in the negative, George asked if they would like a tour of the company.

"We'd enjoy that very much, if you aren't too busy," Rachel answered enthusiastically.

"Certainly not, Rachel. Besides, your visit is long overdue." He stood and said, "Follow me, but stay close and don't touch anything."

As they trailed behind George to the door to the adjoining structure, Rachel looked at Dan and smiled. She was delighted by how he had handled himself and by how quickly he came up with appropriate answers.

Dan grinned and winked at her, also pleased with his performance.

Rachel enjoyed Daniel Slade's company and attention. She hoped he was trustworthy. She had never met anyone like this fascinating man who exuded virility and confidence. She was certain there would never be a dull moment with him.

Sometimes it was awful to be a woman whose life was controlled by men and their whims. Perhaps Lula Mae was lucky in not needing a man to protect and support her, but most women did and wanted it that way. It was the natural way of life for a father to have that role while a girl was growing up, then for a husband to take over when she was older. Women were born to be obedient daughters and helpful sisters, then dutiful wives and good mothers. But where did the single woman fit in the scheme of life? If she were moral and genteel, only with a man, in wedlock. If she lost one mate, she was expected to find another. That was what southern society taught and demanded of her. But what happened if cruel fate kept defeating her life's purpose? Rachel knew that answer too well. A southern woman could not afford a stain upon her honor. If she earned one, it was as damaging as a witch's mark burned into her forehead for the whole world to see as a warning to avoid her. Somehow, some way, she had to destroy the unjust brand on her, the brand of Black Widow that alleged her to be a destructive predator of men.

They had climbed the stairs to the top floor of the middle structure. She pushed aside her crazy thoughts and listened to George Leathers.

"This is where it begins," he said with pride, waving one hand over the large area. He picked up blocks with indentations of different sizes and explained bullets molds and ball-making. He motioned to a hot cupola in use and informed them that they melt the lead there, "one of the few locations we allow a fire, but away from anything explosive."

He guided them to another area of the floor. "These men are making shell casings. The rims are marked to indicate rim or center fire," he said, then related the differences and how each worked. George looked at his guests to make certain he was talking in terms they understood before he urged them onward to the front of the second floor.

Far from the fire in the vertical furnace and separated by a thick wall was the shell-loading area. "Powder is measured or weighed, poured into a shell, and the ball seated atop with the right amount of pressure."

"Fascinating," Rachel murmured. "So many steps to make one."

"That isn't all," George said, but didn't know she knew that.

They went down the steps to the first floor. "This is where boxes are made and labeled with sizes. Over there is where the finished cartridges are stored until they're packed." George continued strolling as he talked and pointed to different tasks in progress. "In here, we store our chemicals and materials." He moved to the next room. "Boxes and cases are shelved and orders are filled from here. We box by fifty cartridges with twenty boxes per case to make one thousand cartridges, unless it's a special order for less. Supplies come by river or rail, and are sent out the same ways."

"There's so much to this business. How do you keep it all straight?"

He beamed with pride. "Been in it a long time, Rachel, so it's second nature to me. One last stop, the most dangerous and delicate one. Make sure you don't touch anything in here or lean against any counter."

They entered a large and well-ventilated laboratory. It was cluttered with work and storage stations, laboratory equipment and instruments, chemicals, and packing containers. Three men were busy, but only one halted his task a moment to glance at the guests with his boss.

Rachel and Dan both noticed that nowhere along their tour had George interrupted his workers to introduce either the men or them.

"This is the dangerous and delicate area of powder-making. We treat cotton or wood pulp with nitric and sulfuric acids to make nitrocellulose. Nitrocel is unstable and volatile. It decomposes rapidly to explode. The power of the explosion relies on how much it's nitrated and the sizes and shapes of the granules. You don't want any flames or accidental impacts in here. We have mild winters, so little heat is needed to keep these workers warm. If the weather gets too cold, we close down this area." George was serious as he said, "I don't like to take any risk, no matter how small, of blowing up this place. We get our power from the canal system that runs through this part of town. The white chemical is potassium nitrate. That yellow crystal-like is sulfur. The dark one is charcoal. They're mixed in a seventy-five to ten-to-fifteen ratio, then all you need is nitrocel and it's finished. Any spark or impact will ignite that blend, and it has to be keep dry until it's weighed or measured and put inside shell casings."

Rachel looked at the large stores of chemicals and final mixtures. "Doesn't this create a terrible danger of accidental explosions? This is a wooden structure; a fire would burn it to the ground in no time. I hope you and Phillip have plenty of insurance and a safety plan to evacuate men."

George and the nearby worker, the one who had glanced at them earlier, looked as if her question was strange. "Insurance is expensive, which is understandable for this business, but we're well covered and have safety drills often. My employees are skilled and experienced, and we don't allow smoking near the building. We sit alone on this site, so there's no threat from other burning structures reaching us."

"That's a relief, but it still seems so dangerous. Wouldn't a brick building be better? Have you and Phillip thought about that change?"

"Wood burns faster and easier, but brick would explode, too. We've never had an accident, and I don't expect any in the future."

"I hope not," Rachel murmured, and wondered why the man with the wire-rimmed glasses kept sneaking peeks at her over them.

George removed his watch from his vest pocket and looked at the time. "Oh, my, it's almost one o'clock. I wish I could spend more time with you this afternoon, but I have errands to run. I'll tell Molly Sue to expect you for supper at six. You remember where the house is located?"

"Yes, I think so."

"Are you staying at the Planter's Hotel again?" George asked Rachel.

"Yes, it's so lovely."

George gave them directions to his home and suggested they use the trolley. "That should be fun for you, and the weather's nice. I have my carriage outside. I can take you back to the hotel."

"That's kind of you, George. We'll have time to rest and freshen up before we come to your home. And we thoroughly enjoyed the tour."

"Yes, sir, we did," Dan concurred.

*

At the hotel, Dan and Rachel enjoyed a light snack in a cozy corner, as it was too long to wait between breakfast and the evening meal.

"George sounded as if he was expecting an important message or delivery from Phillip," Dan remarked, "then passed over it lightly when you questioned him about it. Wonder what that was about?"

"I don't know. Phillip didn't mention anything pressing before he . . . left home. George certainly has a lot of men employed and they seemed very busy for a company whose business has slacked off. He didn't even seem that enthusiastic about your order, as if he has more trade than he needs."

"He probably thought it was small and personal, and I didn't want to distract him with its size. Maybe they're working on that big special order."

Rachel's thoughts had drifted when Dan made his remark and caught her off guard. "What big and special order?" She tensed, fearing he had made a slip that proved he was involved after all.

"The one you mentioned to George earlier."

"I guess my mind is elsewhere, such as on dinner tonight at his home. I hope we can learn more than we did this morning, which wasn't anything other than George acting a little tense and that man staring at me."

A waiter came and offered more coffee. Dan let him fill his cup, but Rachel said she was finished. The man took away their dishes and left.

"I noticed that, too," Dan commented. "The one in the laboratory. Maybe he was just taken with your beauty and charm, Mrs. McCandless."

"Thanks, but he gave me an eerie feeling." Rising, she said, "I'm going to my room to rest before I freshen up for tonight's adventure. I'll meet you at my door at five-fifteen. Does a trolley ride sound fun to you?"

"It surely does. I'll finish my coffee and see you later. Rest well."

*

Rachel was glad one of the water closets on this floor was only a short distance from her room. She had washed off in a basin last night and this morning, so she wanted a long and soothing bath before tonight's adventure.

When she finished and returned to her room, she began to gather what she needed to dress for the upcoming episode. Within moments, she halted and frowned, then checked the room with thoroughness. Alarm consumed her. As she had certain ways of folding and placing items, it was obvious someone had searched through her things but tried not to make it evident. Yet nothing was missing! A thief would have stolen her jewels, so she ruled out that possibility. Surely, she surmised, a maid wouldn't risk being caught or reported for nosy mischief that could get her fired.

A daring sneak had explored her room. George or Harry or the unknown client? Maybe the culprit was seeking that missing money or written clues to her involvement. Someone, she reasoned in dismay, was trailing her and had known she was absent. It could be the same villain who had spied on her at home and shot at her!

What about Daniel Slade? Rachel didn't want to think of him, but she had no choice, as she must consider any potential foe. In each instance, he had the opportunity to be responsible. If Dan was guilty, his only motive could be some entanglement in the mysterious deal. At times she believed and trusted him; at others, she didn't. Mostly he appeared open and honest, saying and doing the right things for an old friend. Yet sometimes she sensed he was holding something back. Maybe that was normal behavior for a man who was trying to resist a friend's wife, or maybe it was something else . . .

Rachel cautioned herself to be more leery of him and everyone. She didn't like being watched and intimidated, especially when she didn't know why and by whom. She wondered if she should mention to Dan that she had noticed the search, but she decided it was best to keep the matter a secret for now. She prayed it wasn't him behind the evil deed.

*

The trolley stopped to pick up passengers. Dan assisted Rachel and another lady aboard. Everyone took their seats and the driver urged the horses onward past the railroad tracks on Washington Street.

It halted near a fountain for several people who lived nearby to get off and for one to get on. While they waited, Rachel and Dan glanced down tree-lined Monument

Street to their right to see the fifty-foot signer's obelisk in the center of Greene Street, standing tall and proud of its meaning before City Hall with its cupola of the temple of justice.

"Phillip told me the last time we visited that it's made of granite blocks from Stone Mountain," Rachel said. "He said two of the three Georgia signers of the Declaration of Independence are buried beneath the obelisk. Isn't that fascinating? Important men resting there forever."

"It certainly makes an unusual headstone. When I die, I want a small and simple one above me, just large enough to let people know someone is buried there so they won't trample my grave in ignorance," he remarked as if teasing, but it was actually to prick her about the lack of a marker on his brother's grave.

"That isn't funny, Dan," she scolded.

Dan witnessed anguish in her multicolored eyes, an unexpected emotion that caused them to shine with moisture. He wondered why she employed this ruse. "I'm sorry, Rachel," he said. "Death never is a laughing matter."

The trolley was moving along the city tracks again. They passed the east-end town market with Fire Engine Company #4 behind it. They went right onto Lincoln, down three blocks in silence, and halted at Telfair.

Rachel got off while Dan was paying the driver. When he joined her, she began walking toward Elbert Street where George lived in the corner house.

Dan captured her arm to halt her movement. Something was amiss, and he couldn't allow his clever groundwork to be destroyed. "Wait a minute, woman. All of a sudden you're giving me an icy shoulder. Did I hurt your feelings back there? If so, I said I was sorry."

His expression and tone seemed so genuine that for a moment she forgot her doubts of him. "I'm the one who's sorry, Dan, for being so rude. It wasn't intentional. You see, my father lies buried somewhere in an unmarked grave. With so much fighting going on, all the soldiers could do was dig a hole, drop a body in, then cover it and leave a man resting where he'd fallen. His entire unit was slain before any of them could report where the ones to die first were buried. Sometimes there are good reasons why a man doesn't have a headstone on his grave. It's sad, and shouldn't be that way. When you made your joke, I thought of people walking and laughing and children playing on the earth covering my father without even knowing he was there."

Dan gazed into her misty eyes of dark honey and reluctantly concluded she was telling the truth. "I understand, Rachel. That must have been hard to accept."

"I don't think I ever will. That war should never have happened."

"I agree. Things should have been settled other ways. I was fourteen when it started and eighteen when it ended. I didn't do much fighting, but I sneaked through enemy lines many times carrying messages."

She gaped at him. "You were a Confederate spy at that age? How could your parents allow you to do something so dangerous?"

For a brief time, Dan lost his wits as their gazes fused. "My mother had died and my father couldn't have stopped me, even if he had wanted to or tried. I like to think of it as being a blockade runner on land. I witnessed some pretty awful things, enough to keep me away from fighting as much as possible. I guess I'm as peace-loving as Phillip."

Rachel caught how quickly Dan rushed past his first sentence, as if he regretted making that painful confession. This man had suffered during his lifetime, as she had. That similarity and their intimately secret work together on this trip drew her closer to him, even though she failed to grasp that steady weakening. An exchange of smiles caused her to unwillingly lower her guard. "I'm sure Phillip's father was glad you didn't take his son along during those adventures. We'd better move on; it's almost six. This is one adventure and challenge we'll share, Captain Slade."

"The first of many, I hope. Let's make sure to stay on extra alert tonight."

Chapter

5

Dinner was delicious, and passed in polite conversation between the four people. George told them about Augusta, which Rachel and Dan found interesting.

While Molly Sue was clearing away the cups after the final coffee service, Rachel asked, "How did Phillip get into the ammunition business with you? With him in Charleston and you here, how did you two meet? I've never thought to ask him before, but realized this afternoon I didn't know."

"Harrison Clements introduced us in January of '73," the mild-mannered man replied. "Harry and I both needed an investor to add capital to our businesses. Phillip wanted to get into other interests, so he joined both our companies. He was a good choice, particularly since he was moving to Savannah the next month and could handle our shipping needs. That saves me and Harry money because Phillip gives us a low rate."

"How did Phillip meet Harry?" Rachel inquired in a casual tone.

"I don't know. I've known Harry since the war ended, but we aren't close. We've done joint contracts many times over the years. Phillip joined my company and Harry's in February of '73, and it's been good for all of us."

Rachel watched George as she said, "I'll have to ask Harry when we reach Athens next week. Dan wants to place an order with him, too."

"It's good to keep the earnings in family businesses," George replied.

Rachel concluded the man didn't appear tense or suspicious about her visit to Harry. She was glad, because she liked George and Molly Sue. Perhaps, she reasoned, George was only supplying ammunition without knowledge of it being illegal. She hoped so. "It's late, so we should be going," she said. "It was a marvelous dinner and evening."

"Yes, it was," Dan concurred. In fact, he had enjoyed himself too much! This skilled woman had a hazardous way, regardless of how hard he fought it, of making him relax and respond to her. This weakness was a threat to what he must do. He couldn't allow himself to forget who and what she was for a single moment. He didn't comprehend why it was so difficult to remember that at all times. Perhaps because this creature seemed to have an awesome power to beguile him. He must toughen his resolve and chill his heart to ensure she became his victim, not he, hers.

"I'll bring the carriage around front and take you to the hotel. The trolley has stopped running, and it's too late to catch a phaeton or walk back in the dark. This area is safe, but no need to take chances."

While he was fetching the carriage, Molly Sue said, "George has wonderful plans for you this week," and related them. "I hope it's all right with you that he's filled up your time here. He so enjoys doing things like this."

"It sounds wonderful. You will join us as much as possible, I hope?"

"Of course. It's like a holiday without leaving town. I'm so glad you came to visit, Rachel, and brought this nice cousin of yours."

"You and George are most kind and hospitable. Thank you."

"I've never had a better meal, Mrs. Leathers," Dan complimented. "I hope that when I find a wife, she can cook only half as well as you."

Molly Sue blushed with pride. "A real southern gentleman. We don't see enough of them anymore. Stay this way, Captain Slade. Some lucky woman will thank heaven for a good man like you."

"You're most kind and generous," Dan replied with a broad smile.

Everyone said good night, then Rachel and Dan departed.

*

"It was fun, wasn't it?" Rachel said at her door.

He lazed against the frame and murmured, "Yes, it was. I could get used to living on land if it were like this all the time."

"Divorce your wife and leave the sea?" she jested.

"That would depend on my finding a better one to replace her."

Rachel studied Dan. "You haven't searched very hard. I'm sure plenty of women would leap at the chance to become Mrs. Daniel Slade. I'll bet you have females in every port around the world pining over you."

Dan kept his gaze on hers. "Pining over me isn't the problem. I have to find one I pine over."

"That does make all the difference, doesn't it?"

"Absolutely. Trouble is, every time I see one that might suit me, she's taken. I don't think it would be wise or safe to snatch another man's love. It's a shame you aren't available, Rachel. You and I seem much alike and we get along well. That's rare for a man and woman."

Rachel felt a warm flush cover her body and rose her cheeks. "Thank you for the compliment, Dan, but you don't know me that well yet. I could be a terrible person masquerading as a proper lady."

Dan sent forth a chuckle, but was intrigued by her reaction. "I've met plenty of women around the world, Rachel, and I know a real lady when I see one. You're just too modest and nice to agree with me."

She looked at the muscular man leaning against the doorway with his arms crossed over a broad chest. He was so alluring and special, if he was genuine. "I do try to be a lady, Dan," she joked, "but it's hard sometimes."

Dan laughed and straightened himself. Stars above, she was tempting and dangerous! *Cool your loins and clear your head, old boy. She's only your target, not an ordinary woman to dally with or pursue.* "Probably as hard as it is to be a gentleman at all times."

Beneath his smoldering blue gaze, Rachel became apprehensive. His husky voice was trailing over her flesh like a gentle caress. His masculine smell was attacking her senses. His nearness was tantalizingly perilous. "It's late," she said in a strained tone. "We'd better say good night. I'll meet you for breakfast at eight before our first tour."

"Good night, Rachel. Thanks for including this lonesome old seadog in your lively existence for a while."

She was confused and touched by his last remark. "You don't seem to be a man who would ever have reason to be lonesome."

"That's because I'm masquerading as a carefree bachelor."

"One day that will change. Don't rush into any relationship until you're certain it's the right one for you though," she advised in a serious tone.

"How does one know when and if it's the right one, Rachel?"

She lowered her gaze, lost her smile, and replied, "I don't know the answer to that, Dan. I just know that misjudgments can be painful and costly. When you choose, make certain you aren't wrong."

"That sounds like the voice of experience talking. Why?"

Rachel forced a smile to her lips, met his probing gaze, and said, "I was referring to my mother. She made a terrible choice for a second husband. After Papa died and things were so bad, she was frightened and alone, so she rushed into marriage with an awful man. It was wrong for her and her family. It's caused us a lot of anguish, and we're all paying for it."

Dan perceived that she was being only half honest, that part of her words included her own experiences. But which ones?

She berated herself for that disclosure. "That's enough reminiscing tonight. It solves nothing and keeps pain from healing. I'll see—"

Dan caught her cold hands in his warm ones. He realized with annoyance that his heart was racing and that he didn't want to leave her. "I understand. I had a hard time growing up myself. We can't change the past, but we have to find a way to keep it from hurting us the rest of our lives."

She made the mistake of gazing into his blue eyes and was engulfed by their flames. "What way did you find, Dan?"

"I haven't yet, but I'm still looking and trying," he admitted.

"Maybe we'll both succeed this year."

"I hope so, Rachel, for both our sakes. It's never too late to try."

Is it too late for me this time to keep from being destroyed unjustly? Rachel wondered. *Too late to find a man like this who would*—"Good night, Dan. Thank you."

Dan released her hands and moved a few steps away. "Sleep well, Rachel McCandless. I'll be waiting for you in the morning."

Rachel entered her room. She walked to her bed and sat on its edge. *If only you would truly be waiting for me in the morning,* she thought, then let her tears flow. She wept for the loved ones she had lost, for the unhappy changes in her life, for what might have been, for Phillip, and for what she knew could never be with Daniel Slade —the first man to reach her "deepest heart," in Lula Mae's words, and the first to enflame her passions. She knew she couldn't pursue him. Even if he were for real, he was married to his ship and the sea. Even if he were attracted to her, she couldn't win him, not with her black past and with the lies she'd told him. Except for the loyal Lula Mae, she was alone again, with more malicious gossip and another vile investigation looming before her. She yearned for her lost parents and siblings. She craved peace of mind, safety, and happiness. She hoped she had not misjudged Phillip, as she had Craig. She hungered soul deep for Captain Daniel Slade.

Dan stood at the secret entrance to her room and listened. The desk clerk had told him about the hidden doorway between the two rooms, concealed by the movable chests. He had unlatched his and pushed it aside to see if she said anything enlightening, as she had that night in her home, but so far she hadn't. He was relieved the freshly oiled hinges didn't squeak. He was baffled by her loss of restraint. An evil and dangerous woman should be colder and have more self-control. . . .

Dan heard the bed squeak as she stood to undress. With caution, he pushed the chest in place and relatched the hinges. The truth eluded him, taunted him, and tormented him.

*

Rachel was satisfied with what she saw in the mirror. She felt better after purging her pent-up emotions last night and was relieved her eyes were not red and puffy from it, thanks to a restful sleep. She had slipped a note under Dan's door, changing their breakfast from eight to nine to give them less time together before their appointment with George at ten-thirty. Until her troubles were solved, she had decided to keep their relationship in check, limit it to friendship and proper behavior. All she should concentrate on was carrying out her reason for this trip. She must not flirt with Dan again, or allow him to flirt with her, as they had done last night at her doorway. It was too dangerous, too soon . . .

Rachel joined him in the lobby. Dan rose from the chair where he was sitting with a newspaper in one hand and a cup of coffee in the other. She smiled and said, "I hope you aren't starving. I needed more time this morning to make myself presentable after our late night."

"You always look more than presentable, Rachel. Are you ready to eat?"

"Ravenous," she said, then gave a merry laugh.

Dan offered his arm and guided her toward the dining room. The yellow dress flattered her olive skin and dark-brown hair. She seemed calm and cheerful, which surprised him after what he'd heard last night. She was so unpredictable and as enigmatic as the mystery that brought them here. "We've a busy day ahead, so it's good you got plenty of rest."

"I feel much better this glorious morning. No more depressing talk like we had last night. We're supposed to be having fun while we work."

"Reprimand noted, Mrs. McCandless, and I fully agree. Being drawn into the dark past is no fun at all. We'll make sure it doesn't happen again."

"Good," she remarked as they were seated at a window table. She glanced outside. "Isn't it a lovely day? Not a cloud in the sky."

Dan's eyes scanned the horizon. "Looks like smooth sailing to me."

*

"There's our guide approaching in his carriage," Rachel said.

They joined George and rode west on Broad Street with Rachel in the front seat, a yellow parasol held over her head, and Dan in the back one. Their host pointed out sites and talked about them as they journeyed toward their first destination miles away.

George halted the carriage. "There's a major part of our heritage—the old Confederate powderworks," he related. "During the war, it was the largest gunpowder factory of the South, actually one of the largest in the world." As he told them about it and pointed out various structures, Rachel and Dan gazed at the enormous span of buildings whose architecture reminded both of a Norman fortress.

"Since Sherman didn't raze Augusta and we had the canal and plenty of mills, we were able to recover quickly from the war. I suppose he didn't think he needed to destroy us after he sliced the Confederacy in half and cut us off from our supply center. Most of our employees worked here during the war. That's why they are so skilled and experienced."

"That's good news," Rachel said. "After you told me how explosive and sensitive gunpowder is, you know, I was concerned about fires and safety."

"No need to be worried. Augusta has fifteen fire stations, underground water pipes, and pumps around town. Let's head on; there's a lot to see."

Rachel saw Dan out of the corner of her eye when she faced George to talk. She quelled the desire to turn and look at him. It was good they were not sitting together, so she could *almost* keep her mind off him, off the question of whether or not he was a physical, as well as emotional, threat to her.

At the toll house for the planked Summerville Road, George halted and paid the charge. They went right and rode into a verdant hill section which slowed the team and carriage. "Many of these houses were built in the late 1700's and early 1800's by rich folks as retreats from the summer heat, floods, and insects downtown," George informed them. "Some of them belong to inland planters or rich northerners who spend their winters here. If you look behind us, you can see a grand view of our beloved city."

Rachel and Dan simultaneously twisted in their seats. Although three miles away, Augusta was in full and splendid view on the flatland. As Dan turned frontward before Rachel did, their gazes met, locked for a moment, then were broken as she, too hurriedly, he noticed, faced forward once more.

George halted the carriage at a long road to their left and said, "This is the Augusta arsenal. Most of it was shut down after the war. You could say it ended for us on May third of '65 when the arsenal surrendered." He reveled in telling them all the details.

George guided his team up that roadway toward the structure with architecture similar to that of the Confederate powderworks. The parade ground still showed traces of past use. Trees were planted along both sides and ever so often there were pyramids of old cannon balls.

"There were four major arsenals in the South, and three of them were in Georgia. We had the supplies, power, rails, river, and ocean to make our state crucial to the Confederacy. Even when the Yankees blockaded our coastline, our ships still got in and out of Savannah. That's why it was so important to Sherman. After he destroyed our rail center in Atlanta and took control of Savannah, the back of our nation was broken. I don't know why he left those vital cities intact: Augusta with her powderworks and arsenal, and Athens with her manufacturing of arms, but I'm sure glad of it."

"Didn't Harry say that private arms were made here at one time?" Rachel asked.

"Yes, by Leech & Rigdon, then Rigdon-Ansley. Ah, there it is, your surprise for today," George announced with a cheerful grin.

Rachel glanced down the drive, lined with mounted cannons and stacks of their black balls, to a large and lovely cottage. She didn't have time to question her host further about how Harry got into the arms business or if he was a native Athenian or if he was involved in the war's arms manufacturing.

"Bellevue Cottage, home of Octavia Walton Levert. Her grandfather was one of the signers of the Declaration of Independence; he and Lyman Hall are buried beneath the signer's obelisk downtown. She lives here with her aunt, Mrs. Anna Robinson. We're to have lunch with these fine ladies. You'll enjoy them immensely. It's one o'clock, so we're right on time." He tucked away his pocket watch, then told them about Octavia.

Rachel's nerves became as tight as a French corset two sizes too small. Whatever, she fretted, would she talk about with such an intelligent, widely traveled, educated, and polished woman? A woman so well known around the world would surely find her dull and simple. If she had known about this important lunch, she would have dressed differently, better. She trembled as the carriage stopped before the residence.

Dan noticed her apprehension. He smiled and whispered, "Don't worry; they'll adore you, as everyone does. Just be yourself, Rachel."

That's easy for you to say, she scoffed silently, *you handsome and charming rake! They'll love you at first sight, like all women must do.*

*

Hours later, Dan assisted a smiling Rachel back into the carriage. A few pleasantries followed, then the visitors rode away with the two ladies waving and Rachel and Dan responding in like manner.

"That was wonderful, George. I don't know when I've had a better time. They were wonderful, special ladies. Thank you for bringing us to meet them. Octavia is lovely, so well bred and well mannered."

"They keep our Old South ways alive and fresh, don't they?"

"Yes, George, they certainly do," Dan agreed.

"You had a good time chatting about foreign places and people with her, didn't you?" Rachel asked, her body half turned in the seat as she spoke to Dan.

He rested his arms along the back seat and carriage side. His blue eyes trailed over her serene face as he answered. "It was quite enlivening and refreshing. I also enjoyed reading that poem to her from Edgar Allen Poe. It was much lighter than his usual style."

"You like to read?" Rachel queried.

"Sea captains have plenty of time for books during voyages. Jules Verne, Mark Twain, and Thomas Hardy are three of my favorite authors."

"Ah, the adventurous tales for a man with a wild heart and restless spirit," she jested, and watched him grin in amusement.

"You'd be surprised how much their works teach you about people."

"I've read many things by all of them. I love to read, too. Perhaps I should become an author and write down my adventures for sale." Rachel wanted to bite off her loosened tongue after it made that foolish mistake.

When she appeared dismayed over her slip, Dan subtly rescued her. "I'm certain you would earn a fortune on them. Wait until we complete our trip and you'll have many more, like today's, to add to them."

"I saw the photograph of Dr. Levert on the piano. He was a fine-looking gentleman. I'm sure she must miss him something terrible."

Dan grinned at how the cunning creature changed the subject from her past. "We should locate a photographer's studio and have a picture taken of us on our holiday as a souvenir remembrance."

"I know a good one downtown," George interjected.

Dan leapt on that assistance from the man who didn't guess they weren't related. "Give me his name and we'll see him Friday afternoon. We can do our sitting dressed in party clothes to look our best for posterity."

Rachel laughed. "You're such a joker, Cousin Dan."

"I'm serious. It would be fun, and will give us a nice keepsake."

"He's right, Rachel. You should capture pleasant times in pictures."

"If you two insist, it's fine with me."

"I insist," Dan murmured.

"Friday it is," she responded, then faced forward because his sensual grin was weakening her resolve not to be more heavily attracted to him.

The entertaining tour continued as they made their way back to the hotel where they parted company for the day.

*

"Either George is a nice and sincere man," Rachel speculated at dinner, "or he's cleverer than I can ascertain and he's keeping us occupied and away from the company. What's your opinion of him?"

"If he's a dishonest and treacherous man, it certainly doesn't show in his personality and behavior. I like George; he impresses me as kind and generous. I think the reason he acted strange at the company when you spoke with him is because he didn't want to discuss business with his partner's wife or with a woman. Other than changing the subject to distract you from an uncomfortable topic, he seemed open and trustworthy."

"That's good, because it matches my opinion of him and his conduct. I would hate to think of George being guilty of my suspicions."

Dan knew which suspicions she really had in mind. "We are having a wonderful time, and you're getting good information for Phillip."

"Yes, I am. I'm enjoying your company and assistance. Thank you for coming along and for being such a gentleman."

Dan grasped her implications and sly warnings. "Me, too, Rachel, and you're welcome. Have you contacted Phillip yet?"

Rachel lowered her fork from her lips. "What?" she asked.

"Have you sent Phillip a telegram to let him know how things are going?" he explained, to see how she would react.

"No. I told you at home, I don't know how to reach him. He knows where I am and what I'm doing. If he wants news, he'll contact me. I'm sure he realizes it's too soon for me to have any facts for him."

Dan swallowed his piece of ham. "You're right. Maybe he'll cable you in Athens. Then we can let him know I've arrived and that I'm with you. That should keep him from worrying about you being alone on this journey."

Rachel calmed herself. "I'm sure he'll be delighted to learn his best friend is protecting me for him. If a telegram is delivered to my room along the way, I'll tell you immediately, so you can respond with me."

When a bellman came to their table and told Dan he had a message at the front desk, he said, "I'll check on it while we're waiting for dessert."

Rachel observed his retreat with intrigue, as it was odd for their dinner to be interrupted unless it was an emergency.

When Dan returned after ten minutes, he seemed winded to her, as if he'd rushed to do something. "A problem?" she asked.

"No, but I'll tell you about it later," he hinted with a sly grin.

They finished eating and walked to her door. Rachel unlocked it and turned to say good night, to find him grinning. "What is so amusing, Dan?"

"Your surprise," he murmured in a husky voice and pointed inside to a vase of flowers. "You said this was your favorite season, so I thought a little bit of spring would brighten your room and give you pleasure."

She looked concerned as she asked, "How did you get them in here?"

"They arrived while we were dining. The bellman came up with me to unlock the door so we could put them in place. You don't mind, do you?"

"Of course not. It was kind and gracious. Thank you. Good night."

"Good night, Rachel. See you in the morning." He assumed she made her hasty escape because she was worried he had seen her perfidious mischief on the bed.

Rachel walked to the table and roved her gaze over the lovely and colorful arrangement. She couldn't decide if his gesture was friendly or romantic. The card with them did not help answer her query: "Rachel, they can't compare with your beauty, but I hope you enjoy them. Dan."

She withdrew a daffodil and smelled it, smiling with delight at the heady fragrance. She went to the bed to place it on her pillow to give pleasure during the night, as she often did with gardenias during their season.

Something was lying there—a folded note and a small vial of white powder. She tensed as she put aside the daffodil to grasp the two items. A sick feeling caused her heart to drum. She read the note on hotel stationery. Dread and panic made her heart race faster and her hands shake.

She read it again: "I want you and I'll get you, whatever it takes, in life or in death. Leave your husband or you'll soon be a widow once more. Divorce him or desert him or use this on him; I don't care, but get free and be mine this time or else you'll be sorry. I need you and must have you."

Rachel gaped at the vial of poison in her trembling hand. She had to get rid of it fast before it was found in her possession! Whoever had written the note didn't know Phillip was dead, but was following her and scaring her. Anyone who saw it would think she had penned it, as the script matched hers! She didn't know if the contents were the insidious truth or a cruel joke. Who, she fretted, had done this horrible deed, and how?

Dan didn't have an alibi this time, either, but he couldn't forge her handwriting without a long sample and lengthy practice. The brief message she had slipped beneath his door this morning was not sufficient. She had no tangible reason at all to distrust or suspect him.

As quietly as possible, she left her room and went downstairs. She located the bellman who had summoned and accompanied Dan earlier. She questioned him about anyone else being let into her room for any reason during her stay. He told her no one could enter a guest's room without permission from the desk clerk. Rachel checked with the other man, to learn that only one person had done so—Daniel Slade, and tonight.

"Did you notice anything lying on my bed?" she asked the bellman.

"A note and a small bottle of medicine. I put them on your pillow. I didn't read it or bother anything, ma'am. Ask Captain Slade; he saw me."

"Did he read the note and see the . . . medicine?"

"He saw them when I moved them, but he didn't touch either one. Is something wrong, Mrs. McCandless?" the desk clerk inquired.

She smiled and lied. "No. It's only that the note was very private; so, when I found it moved, I wanted to make sure no one had read it."

"I swear we didn't, ma'am. Delivering the flowers only took a minute."

"Thank you, and don't worry about it again." The bellman left and she said to the clerk in a pleasant tone, "I have important personal papers in my room, sir, so please don't let anyone inside for any reason. Have future messages and gifts left with you, then contact me to come for them."

"Yes, ma'am; your request will be obeyed," he replied politely.

"Thank you, and good night." As she returned to her room, she prayed Dan had mistaken the vial for medicine, too. She hoped he wouldn't remember her having it when he heard the horrible rumors about her soon. If he did, she knew what he would think!

*

Rachel took her same precaution of a breakfast that allowed only enough time to eat. Last night it had been difficult to share a leisurely dinner in the cozy dining room. She didn't want every meal to be a chore where she had to stay on strenuous alert against reaching out to Dan or risk making slips when she became too disarmed.

She pushed aside her fears and worries over the recent threats. She needed a clear head to concentrate on George and Dan. She reminded herself that the original incidents in Savannah had begun before Daniel Slade's arrival, so it was doubtful he was behind them; that made her think he couldn't be blamed for the ones dogging her on the road. Still, she would keep an alert eye on the enticing sea captain and on her surroundings.

George picked them up at nine-thirty and gave them a detailed tour of the inner city. When they reached the waterfront, he halted the carriage and they got out near the city wharves. Steamboats and keelboats plied their trades at the location, which was loud and busy with workers. Homes, businesses, and enormous warehouses were lined shoulder to shoulder along Bay Street. Two covered railroad bridges crossed the river less than a block apart. Nearby was another bridge for use by the general public.

Rachel saw the sparkle that entered Captain Daniel Slade's dark-blue eyes as he gazed at the wide and swift Savannah River and the boats. He appeared filled with energy and excitement to be near water again. When George asked Dan a question, she listened closely to his response.

"Ever been tempted to give up the sea, Dan?"

The captain didn't take his softened gaze from the rapid currents. "Not yet, George. Haven't found anything worth replacing it and my ship."

"I understand that feeling. This river is a powerful and unpredictable one. She serves us well until heavy rains cause her to flood into the city."

"Flood the city?"

"That's right, Rachel. She usually overflows a little once or twice a year, but Augusta has suffered four terrible floods. What we need is a levy to control her over-abundance. We sit close to her banks and we're low. When she's too high and dumps water into the canal at a heavy rate, it spills over into the town and residential areas. Where Molly Sue and I live, it's been pretty safe over the years from much damage."

"What about at the company?" Rachel questioned. "Since it's beside the canal, is there much danger of things getting ruined when it floods? You said the powder and chemicals had to be kept dry. A flood there could create a terrible financial loss for you and Phillip."

"No problem so far. Let's continue on," George suggested.

At their next stop, without leaving the carriage, George said, "This is Cotton Row, one of our most important locations, our life-blood. We still do well with to-bacco, but that white stuff is the ruler. King Cotton—what a history and tragedy that's been for the South," he murmured before going on. "We're second only to Memphis in the cotton trade, and second only to Savannah in shipments of it to northern and foreign markets. Our buying and selling spans the world. You've never witnessed such a commotion and such excitement as the height of the season in September."

George stared off into space with a dreamy gaze. In a few minutes he shook his graying head, and said, "If you two are hungry by now, I know a special little cafe not far from here. Wonderful food and clean as my home."

"That sounds good to me, George. After we finish, I'd like to go to your office to get my business with you settled, so I can forget about it."

"Suits me," George agreed with a genial smile.

*

At the Augusta Ammunition Company, Rachel and Dan were in for several surprises and new clues to her mystery.

"How do you keep track of different orders, George? Can you show me the books so I can see and understand how it's done? I'd like to learn more about Phillip's business so I can talk with him intelligently about it. I'm sure he would be surprised and pleased by my interest and knowledge."

George looked anxious about her unexpected request. "I wish I could help you, Rachel, but it's impossible on this trip. The books aren't here; they're with our accountant, and he's out of town this week. He's working on financial reports for us, hopefully to show us where we can cut costs to save money. They'll be finished by the time Phillip returns. I'm sure he'd be delighted to teach you all you want to know."

Rachel sensed that George was deceiving her, but not because of the mystery engulfing her, but rather because he didn't want to show the reports to her without her husband's approval or to expose his private earnings. "That's fine, George," she said to relax the nervous man.

Dan spoke quickly to lessen the tension and to distract George from Rachel's intimidating request. "I did my figuring, and I'll need eighteen hundred cases. I'll pay cash in advance before I leave town so I won't have to worry about hiring someone to deliver the payment to you later." Dan knew he would have no problem selling that size order somewhere during his future travels, so he wasn't risking the investment in his cover story.

George's brown gaze widened in astonishment as he scribbled notes. "That's 1,800,000 cartridges! It's . . . $30,006! I didn't realize you meant an order this big. I would have discussed it and taken it sooner. I can use the cash. Do you mind if I ask why you need so many cartridges?"

"Certainly not. We have a small force in the Mediterranean area, and they're expecting trouble by the end of summer with Turkey and her surroundings. I was in port when they mentioned sending an order for arms and ammunition. I requested the assignment and received it. When Rachel planned this holiday, I decided to mix business with pleasure. I want Phillip's two companies to fill my orders. I'll try to stay in port until it's ready. When can you have the cases in Savannah ready to be shipped out?"

Rachel leapt at the chance to gain information. "Will that be a problem or take long, George? I know you're already working on that other big contract Phillip mentioned before he left home."

"I had it started before Phillip canceled it, but Harry stopped by last Friday and told me Phillip had changed his mind again and to get back on it fast. I have my men working as quickly as possible to make our deadline. It'll be in Savannah by May fourteenth as promised."

His words reminded her of Phillip's frantic mumblings. May fourteenth was six weeks away. "I forgot who Phillip said it was for."

"I don't know, just Phillip's name is on the contract. He's handling the order, delivering it, and collecting the payment."

"Harry didn't mention the customer's name, either?"

"No, Phillip's handling the arms deal the same way."

Rachel did not point out how preposterous that sounded. "It's big and important. How many cases are involved?"

"Thirty thousand."

Rachel's eyes widened this time. "That's . . ."

"Thirty million cartridges." George supplied the amount for her. "We're charging $16.67 per case, so the contract is for five hundred thousand dollars. We give a discount on large orders like that; normally we charge eighteen dollars a case. I'll give you the same lower rate, Dan, because your order is large."

Dan didn't get to thank him, because Rachel murmured, "Five hundred thousand dollars for your end of the deal? With Harry's share added to it, that's a huge amount of money. How are the companies supposed to be paid? When? If anything happened to stop the order after it's made, we'd have a terrible loss."

The gray-haired man nodded agreement. "The balance is to be paid on delivery by Phillip's ship, to Phillip himself. He assures us nothing can go wrong. I hope he's right. I'm working on borrowed money to fill this size order. You're right, we could be ruined if the deal fell through. Who else would take such a load off our hands?"

"You said *balance,* George. What does that mean?"

"Phillip already has an advance of half the money owed to both companies. He's to collect the other half on delivery."

Rachel speculated that with Phillip dead, George and Harry stood to earn a great deal of money. They could pretend the deal didn't exist or fell through, then keep and divide the large payment. But if George was telling the truth about not knowing who the buyer was, how could she discover his identity? Unless Harry lied about knowing. What if Harry had received the advance already, perhaps when he visited Phillip last week, but her delirious husband didn't recall that fact? Worse, what if something had happened to it while in Phillip's keeping? Whoever it belonged to would demand it or the merchandise. Unless George and Harry were paid, it was doubtful they would honor "Phillip's" deal. That would leave her responsible for what had to be a . . . million-dollar-at-least trap! "You say it's to be delivered to Phillip in Savannah on May fourteenth?"

"That's right; then he's supposed to come straight here to settle the account. He did promise to send half of the money for working capital by now; that's what I was concerned about the other day. With him gone until the deadline, I'll have to borrow more money to work with until his return."

"What about my payment and order, George? Won't that help out?"

"It will help some, Dan, but supplies and salaries are expensive. What caliber do you want?"

Dan gave the size for the rifles he planned to order in Athens.

"Rim or center fire? We can make them either way."

"Centerfire gives less trouble on the battlefield."

"I have some in storage that size. I can have the others ready and send them on the same day I rail down Phillip's contract. Is that all right?"

"That's perfect timing, George," Dan said. "Thanks."

*

Before they retired to their rooms to dress for the theater and dinner with George and Molly Sue Leathers, Dan remarked to Rachel, "That's a big contract Phillip worked out with somebody. Seems he's bringing more orders and profits into the companies than his partners are. He'd probably earn more if he was in business by himself.'"

Rachel recalled her fabricated tale to Dan and felt she must defend it to prevent suspicions at this vital point. She could only come up with one idea, a rather strong one. "This doesn't make sense, Dan. If the companies are on the verge of such large profits that Phillip knows about and can't be cheated out of, why would he be thinking of selling them? Why would he be concerned about secret deals by his partners when he's made two himself? I'm utterly baffled."

Dan perceived her ruse. "You'll have to let him explain when he either contacts you or you both return home. That deal is large enough to supply an army somewhere. If a soldier fired fifty bullets a day every day, it would keep ten thousand men in shells for months of fighting. He surely became lucky; it's even better than my deal. That's a big shipment of questionable cargo to clear customs. I wonder how he plans to get it past them. I have a letter of clearance for my arms," he alleged, knowing he could get one from a friend before he left Savannah. "It seems strange he would take off like this when both his partners are waiting for partial payments from him and he was expecting my arrival and business. That doesn't sound like the Phillip McCandless I know; he's always dependable. It will be interesting to see what Harry has to say about all of this when we reach Athens."

Rachel hadn't thought about clearing the shipment through customs, but Dan's mention aided her ruse. "Yes, it certainly will. Perhaps that's where Phillip's really gone, to work out a problem with customs—and he didn't want to worry his partners. He might have sent me here just to distract them during his absence. I'm afraid I'm confused and annoyed, so I'll excuse myself before I say something I shouldn't. I'll be ready to answer your summons at my door at six-thirty."

As she turned to enter her room, she halted and faced him again. "Dan, if you have so much money with you, please be careful. Don't let anyone overhear you talk about it; that could provoke a robbery."

Dan had mentioned the money with hopes this rumored seductress would think him rich and would come closer to him as choice for her next victim. Yet she appeared genuinely worried about his safety. That was odd . . . "Don't fret, Rachel. I've taken care of myself since I was a boy."

"I've taken care of myself since I was a girl, but sometimes things come up one can't control or handle alone. Just be careful, will you?"

"I promise, and I'll take care of you, too. Get dressed, so we can have a great time and forget our troubles," he urged, his hands nudging into her room before he rashly yanked her into his arms and kissed her.

"I'll be prompt and shipshape on time, Captain sir." She gave him a mock salute and closed her door.

She had obtained a few clues, and they frightened her. With Phillip's protection gone and perils confronting her from two directions, the temptation to entice Daniel Slade became overwhelming. She asked herself if she should resist it or surrender to it. Perhaps tonight would provide an answer . . . First, she had to bathe and dress.

*

Dan surmised Rachel hadn't shown him the clever note she had written to herself because she realized he would recognize her handwriting. Too, the reckless contents would reveal her Black Widow past, which she surely hoped was unknown to him.

She almost always caught her slips before they could damage her! Perhaps she had wanted to use it to make him jealous, to entice him to pursue her faster. Perhaps she had hoped to use it later as an alleged threat against Phillip to make her appear innocent of his murder.

Dan wondered how she would react when she received a real note in a few minutes. He had taken the precaution of having Luke Conner pen it for him before leaving Savannah. He had sent a message with the flowers so she could compare his script to that of his deceitful note; the difference should dupe her into not suspecting him. He wanted to make her nervous and afraid so she would make mistakes or would turn to him for protector and confidant. He slid the note under the water-closet door while she was bathing and left in a hurry before he was sighted by anyone.

Rachel heard a noise and glanced in that direction. Her eyes widened as a paper was shoved under the door. She froze for a moment, then leapt from the tub. She wrapped a bath sheet around her, crept to the door, then unlocked and opened it. She peeked into the hall, but it was empty, so she rebolted the door. The wary woman lifted and unfolded this second note. It was not on hotel stationery and was not a forgery of her script.

> *"Weave me an enchanted web, my beautiful love. Capture me with your magical strands. I will gladly risk my life to spend only one blissful night in your silken arms. I must have you or perish. I will give you any amount of money and all the jewels you desire to become my mistress or my wife. I am a rich and handsome man, and a skilled lover who will pleasure you as you have never known before. I will never harm you and I will never allow others to hurt you. I will take you anywhere you wish to go, far away from your past troubles and sufferings. I will make you happy. If your answer is yes, wear silk flowers in your hair tomorrow as a sign. If it is no, I will keep craving you from afar until you change your mind and need me."*

Rachel trembled. The words were meant to sound romantic, but they were intimidating. Was it from the same person? If so, what did the sneaky man really want from her? She dreaded to imagine. She had torn up the first note, then discarded it and the poison in the chamber pot. This one she would keep, to see if she could discover whose handwriting it was. It did not look familiar. And its tone was not menacing like the first note . . .

Rachel finished her bath and returned to her room. She compared the script to Dan's card. As hoped, they had bold differences. Yet she couldn't show it to him and reveal her predicament; it would expose her past at a delicate time. At least this proved that the threats weren't coming from Daniel Slade. Didn't it?

She couldn't contemplate the matter further, as she had to hurry to prepare for dinner and the theater with the Leathers and Dan. But the next day she would do her best to unmask her wicked spy.

Rachel had told Dan she would skip breakfast this morning, sleep late to rest up for the night's activities, and meet him for lunch and a long stroll.

The meeting in George's office yesterday kept racing through her mind and troubling it deeper. When Phillip had mumbled about money, never had she imagined it was at least a million dollars! That was more than enough to provoke an evil man to recover it at any cost or to seek lethal revenge. When Phillip didn't deliver the shipment on schedule, the client would be forced to come and check on it. She dreaded to imagine what would happen in six weeks when he arrived and challenged her.

Rachel thought she must contact Milton when she returned home to see if Phillip reserved a ship. To solve this mystery before the deadline, she needed a destination and client's name. If the deal was legal, maybe something could be worked out to everyone's satisfaction. But then she realized she was fooling herself; no one—especially that client—was going to believe she didn't have the money or know what was going on. If only she could ask Dan to help her solve this mystery, but she couldn't because he might learn the truth about her. He'd never understand or accept what she'd done, not after she reported Phillip's death. *But at least after that's handled, you can . . .* she thought.

Rachel frowned, and spoke aloud to the empty room. "You can what, you stupid fool? Let him deceive you like Craig and Phillip did? You can't trust him. Phillip rants all those crazy things on his deathbed, then his supposedly old friend shows up the same day. You sense you're being spied on, then someone shoots at you. Your room is searched, then you receive two intimidating notes. No doubt someone thought you'd be fool enough to keep that vial of poison and get caught with it when you returned home. That would certainly get you blamed for Phillip's death, just like all the others. He's so clever and evil that he forged your handwriting so you couldn't show his first note to anybody. Every time, Daniel Slade had the opportunity to be behind those sinister deeds. I'll wear the flowers in my hair today and see who responds to that message. If only you are who and what you claim, Daniel Slade . . ."

As Dan sat on the floor and listened through the secret entryway between the two rooms, these were not the words he had expected to overhear. He asked himself if he could be wrong about Rachel, if she could be innocent of all four deaths. He wondered if cruel fate could be to blame or if a jealous rival could be framing her. If she was innocent, he couldn't harm his brother's widow, his sister-in-law. Maybe his curious doubts were nothing more than the results of having not seen Phillip in so long, or seen him dead, or known her in the past. What he had been confronted with was a beautiful woman who was charming, tantalizing, and genteel appearing.

He had observed Rachel's proper, but cheerful and relaxed, behavior during the last few days at Octavia Levert's home and at the theater last night. With her cloudy past, and this hazardous mystery hanging over her, how she could be so poised and so lighthearted? Once in a while, he glimpsed moments of panic, sadness, and confusion in her face. If only he knew the real Rachel, knew the whole truth. But he didn't. How would he feel and behave if she weren't guilty of those crimes? Being attracted to him didn't make her a bad person. Nor did marriage to Phillip mean she had loved his brother. For certain, there was more to the puzzling situation than Rachel McCandless being a Black Widow. There were the curious arms deal, an enormous amount of missing money, and Phillip's involvement with them. If only she weren't so skilled with her pretenses!

He was responsible for the spying, room search, and the second note, but not the other incidents. But if Rachel wasn't, then who was? Dan recalled that he hadn't seen the first note and vial when he examined her room on Tuesday, a search she hadn't mentioned to him. Either someone had put the items there during dinner or she had them with her in the water closet.

Don't be tricked, old boy, Dan warned himself. *She's putting on a superb performance for you in there. She knows about the secret passageway and she hopes you're listening so she can be certain you're duped and duped good. I doubt she knows you're Phillip's brother, but thinks you're an enemy. You'll just have to convince her you aren't. Get your sly romance sailing faster, old boy.*

*

"I set up an appointment for us with the photographer George suggested," Dan told her as they ate lunch. "We're to be in his studio at six, dressed in our finest. He says we'll be finished in thirty to forty-five minutes, and can make our seven o'clock party on time. He isn't far away."

"You've been out this morning?" she inquired. *Doing what else?*

Miffed I didn't overhear your little ruse? he mentally scoffed, but smiled and jested, "Of course, sleepyhead. I'm unaccustomed to lying abed late. I walked down to the riverfront and enjoyed the fresh air and exercise. I ate breakfast, too, but I was ready to eat again."

"I shouldn't have skipped it; I'm starved. This is delicious," she remarked of the chicken and dumplings.

"For certain Buelly isn't this talented. Do you cook, Rachel?"

"I can, but don't do much of it; Lula Mae gets her feathers ruffled if I try. You don't know Lula Mae Morris. The kitchen and housework are her domains, her prides and joys. She doesn't believe in a lady, the mistress of the house, doing menial chores. She doesn't accept the death of the Old South. I'm supposed to be a pampered and spoiled southern belle who doesn't lift a finger."

"I can tell by the laughter in your eyes that you're teasing me."

Rachel grinned and nodded. "You're learning me too well, Dan."

"I hope so; I'm trying," he admitted. "You're a fascinating woman."

"The truth is, I help her with some of the chores, but cooking and ironing are two things she prefers to do alone. I plan the menus, set the table, and help with the dishes. She likes for me to spend my time reading, sewing, and taking care of my appearance. It makes her happy to wait on me, so I try to let her do so as long as possible. But when

I get bored or annoyed, I put my foot down and dig into work. When I'm in that kind of mood, she ignores me and lets me have my way."

Dan reflected on the heavyset nanny and housekeeper who had raised him and Phillip. Maw-maw had been a kind, intelligent, and gentle black woman. She had been like a protective aunt—no, a mother—to him, one of the few people who could and would stand up to Stephen McCandless about his ill treatment of his youngest son. She had come with his mother from their cotton plantation when his mother married Stephen McCandless, a woman freed as soon as she was purchased, a woman who had loved them and been loved and deeply respected by them. Her death couldn't have hurt him more than if she *had* been his mother. She had died shortly before his last quarrel with his father. That loss had pained him deeply. Perhaps suffering from it was why he had bedded Helen and—

Rachel witnessed the unknown memories that evoked a pleasant, then tormented, look on Dan's face. She wondered what he was thinking about. "Tell me more about you and Phillip in Charleston," she encouraged, then realized she had broken into his thoughts when his eyes rushed to her as if he'd been caught doing something he shouldn't have.

Dan could not tell her about Maw-maw in case Phillip had mentioned the woman who had raised him. "Curious about those devilish things we did?" he teased as he obtained control of himself.

"Yes. I haven't learned much about Phillip's past, so it's about time I do, don't you think?" What she wanted to learn more about was Dan.

"We men are protective and defensive about our mischievous years and deeds, but I'll tell you, if you promise not to tell Phillip I exposed us." He waited for her to nod. "We got into the regular boyish pranks and troubles. You had brothers, so you know how they are, always into something they shouldn't be." When he saw the reaction his last statement inspired, he hurried on to get her mind off her own tormented past. "One of our favorite pastimes was playing hide-and-seek in the McCandless warehouse near the wharf. We especially liked the fall when it was filled to capacity with cotton bales. We'd jump from one to another all around the building until we were covered in dust and had white fuzz in our hair and stuck to our clothes. It'd take an hour to get cleaned up to go home so the evidence wouldn't expose us. We weren't allowed to play games like that because they were dangerous; a fall that far could break a neck or limb."

Reared on a plantation, Rachel had similar memories of picking and playing in cotton—but piles of unginned, unbaled, and dusty clouds of white. She didn't want to distract Dan by mentioning that fact. "You love dangers and challenges, don't you?"

"Guilty as charged, Mrs. McCandless," he confessed with a broad grin. "I remember one time when we sneaked aboard this ship and vowed we were going to stow away to conquer the world together. We even had food and water with us. But Phillip turned coward at the last minute and sneaked off the vessel. I wound up in Alexandria, and in big trouble. Was my father angry with me! But Phillip came to my rescue; he took the blame, said we were only playing hide-and-seek and the ship took sail."

"Did you still get punished?"

"In a way," he answered, but didn't explain.

"What happened to your family and shipping business?"

"My family all died, and I lost control of the firm. After I left Charleston in '71, I worked as a sailor for three years until I earned enough money to buy my own clipper to work for myself. Fortunately I've been very successful and prosperous."

The waiter arrived to refill their coffee cups, clear away the dishes, and serve their dessert. As the man did so, they remained quiet.

Dan recalled the day he left home after the fight with his father over his mistake with his father's intended. He loved his brother, but there were times when he had resented Phillip for being his father's favorite—no, *only*—son. Growing up with Stephen McCandless had created hard times during childhood and teenage years. Poor Phillip had been caught in the middle—wanting to please their father and wanting to be friends with his brother. Sometimes Phillip had enjoyed and taken advantage of being the favorite, but that was normal for a young boy. Other times Phillip had hated being trapped between their father and his younger brother. When he himself started sailing on McCandless ships, it had kept him away from home much of the time, which suited him and his father. During those years, he only saw Phillip when he was in port for short periods. After he had left home and stayed gone so long and became successful, he had mellowed and matured. He had wanted to return home to set things right with both Stephen and Phillip. Now . . .

After the waiter left, Dan discarded his past and continued the conversation. "I've been on my own for years and have managed fine. What about you, Rachel? How did you reach this point in your life?"

Rachel decided to tell Dan a few things about her, as he could discover them if he checked on her. If he had done so already, it would make her seem honest and open. If he hadn't, it might evoke empathy and understanding when she needed them later. Besides, Phillip's wife and best friend would share this type of get-acquainted conversation.

Rachel selected her words with care and spoke them slowly. "I was born and reared on the plantation. Mama married Papa when she was sixteen. Within nine years they had five children: three boys and two girls. They were so in love, and we were all close and happy. Then the war came. My father and Robert were killed in battles. Things got bad at home. Mama did her best to shoulder the responsibilities, but she was scared and lonely and didn't know how to run a big plantation. When taxes and expenses worsened, we almost lost everything, and that terrified her. I was twelve when she panicked and married a Yankee carpetbagger who promised to take care of her. Earl was four years younger than Mama, but she was so beautiful that it didn't make any difference. Our friends and neighbors were angry with her for surrendering to the enemy while wounds from the war were still too fresh. He pretended he was rich and in love, but all he wanted was to get his hands on White Cloud. It would have been better to lose it than to let that snake take control."

"What about the rest of your family?" Dan coaxed.

"Randall drowned the next year while he was fishing with Earl. He was a good swimmer, but his shirt got caught on an underwater limb and Earl said he couldn't rescue him before it was too late. The twins, Richard and Rosemary, ran away from home in '69 and '70 and no one knows where they are, not even if they're alive. Lordy, how I miss them! None of us got along with that Yankee. I think he was mean and hard on us on purpose to drive us away from home. He didn't want a houseful of children who weren't his. He succeeded, but Mama refused to believe it was her husband driving away her children. She still thinks we all betrayed and deserted her. I left home in '72 when I was eighteen because I couldn't get along with him, either. I wish Earl Starger had never entered our lives. I hate him for what he did to us."

Dan remembered her cold words about Starger over Phillip's grave. "What happened after you left home?"

"I moved to Savannah. I met Lula Mae when I arrived and we became friends. She's been a big help to me over the years. I went to work for Phillip in January of '74, and I married him in early August of last year."

Dan noticed the gap of time in her story, but she *had* spoken the truth without revealing too much. That surprised him. "George said Phillip moved to Savannah in February of '73. Did you meet soon after his arrival?"

"We met in April of that year through a mutual friend who's dead now." They had met through Craig Newman, but she dared not mention her second husband. "Speaking of George and Phillip, did Phillip mention this big contract to you in his letters?"

Dan knew she changed the subject to get attention off herself. "No, but he had no reason to. If he'd been home when I arrived, I'm sure he would have boasted about it. *I* would have. It should make a nice profit for all three partners. At least one third of the contract has to be profit, and divided three ways would make a hundred thousand dollars each. That's an excellent return on an investment. If he's thinking of selling two of his partnerships, what about the third one—the shipping firm?"

For a while she didn't know what to say. "I don't think so," she finally managed.

"Maybe he's planning to sell all three and become a full-time planter."

"He hasn't mentioned anything like that to me. Would he do that?"

"It wouldn't surprise me, Rachel. He never liked ships or water. He would make the perfect country gentleman. I'd bet he loves plantation life. It could be why he bought Moss Haven and not a house in the city."

Phillip had told her that he bought the plantation with winning her in mind, to get her out of Savannah, but to still be near it for business. "Dan, may I ask you a personal and serious question?" she asked suddenly.

He put down his fork and leaned forward. "Of course."

Rachel decided how to phrase her queries to simultaneously cover her ruse but also to obtain information. "You said this mysterious order is large enough to supply a big army. What if it isn't legal? What if Phillip can't get it cleared through customs? If it falls through, the Augusta and Athens companies could be ruined. Would Phillip do something like that to destroy his partners? To punish them for cheating him? Even if the two companies were no longer profitable, he would lose his original investments in them, whatever those amounts were. But if he's being cheated and deceived, he might not care about that money. Does that make sense?"

"Phillip never courted problems, but he was always honest and kindhearted. Your reasoning makes sense for some men, but it doesn't sound like the Phillip I knew."

She was happy with his answer. "Who could make such a large and expensive order?" She asked.

Dan played along with her probe. "Don't worry, Rachel. It isn't for another rise of the South; the contract isn't that large. And Phillip would never supply arms to men trying to overthrow a government somewhere, and it's too big for an outlaw gang. Maybe it's a secret military contract; there are plenty of problem areas around the world, some even in our own West with Indians. Phillip has a good head for business, and he never liked trouble. The contract must be legal or he wouldn't go along with it."

Cuba, her mind hinted, but she didn't have time to speculate on that possible clue from Phillip's dying words. "Didn't you hear George? He said Phillip canceled it last month, then he and Harry talked last week and reinstated it. That means Phillip had doubts about it. Maybe he feared he was being duped. I don't like this secrecy. Something is terribly wrong."

Dan agreed. "Has Phillip kept important secrets from you before?"

"I don't know," she admitted. "I didn't think he kept anything from me until this came up. Then there's you . . ."

"What about me?"

"Why did Phillip keep you, his past, and your deal secret?"

"Am I the reason you're doubting him, because you didn't know about me? If so, Rachel, that's not valid; men often don't mention such things."

"Not even to their wives?"

"I can't answer that one; I've never had a wife."

"If you love someone and marry them, it seems to me you tell them everything. There isn't anything about me from the time I was born until last Friday that Phillip didn't know."

"Everything, Rachel?"

"Yes, Dan, *everything*. That's how it should be. If a marriage is good and going to last, it must be based on love and trust, on sharing and caring, the good and the bad."

"You're a wise woman, Rachel McCandless."

"I learn from observation and experience. I've witnessed good and bad marriages and I know what makes the difference." How she wished she had learned that truth long ago, but she knew it now. She wouldn't make another mistake with another man and another marriage, even if she had to remain unmarried the rest of her life, even if she lost her inheritance from Phillip and was dirt-groveling poor, and even if she were defenseless and terrified.

Dan forced himself not to ask about her marriage to Phillip or about her first two marriages. Her gaze was a mixture of emotions. She seemed upset, uncertain, and vulnerable—yet resolved and strong. "We could speculate on this for weeks, Rachel. Let's keep searching for clues together. If we don't get answers from Harry in Athens, we'll have to wait until we see Phillip and he explains. Don't let this mystery ruin our holiday; worrying over it won't help. Let's go for our stroll, relax, and enjoy ourselves. Let's forget about work this afternoon."

"You're right, Captain Slade. Why don't you take command and steer us to a happy port?"

"That's the most tempting offer I've ever had. Let's ship out, mate. I'm going to help you forget all your troubles today."

"I'll hold you to that promise, sir. I'm ready."

They left the hotel and headed eastward. When they came to the town fountain in the center of the street, they walked over to it and sat down on the wide ledge around the rectangular pool. The day was sunny and clear, a beautiful early April afternoon.

Rachel trailed her fingers through the water and listened as it trickled over the compote-shaped levels of various sizes. "Do you miss the sea, Dan? Does all water remind you of it, like the river did the other day?"

"You're very perceptive, Rachel. I suppose it's true, because it's the only thing I've known and had for years. It's a vital part of me."

She watched him gaze in the direction of the Savannah River only two blocks away as if the currents in it had a powerful pull on him. The city wharves were straight beyond their location, and they could hear the sounds of steamboats and workers. She wished she could have that same potent effect on this unique man. How wonderful it would be to have his eyes sparkle or glaze over dreamily because of her as they did over ships and water, to be the only important thing in his life. She wondered if Dan would believe the terrible gossip about her, and if he would be interested in her once he learned she was not married. It was foolish to be thinking such reckless things until she was certain he wasn't involved in her perils. "Do you ever think of leaving the sea and giving up your ship and voyages?" she asked.

"If a good enough reason came along, I suppose I would."

"What kind of good enough reason would it have to be?"

"Something that fills my life, heart, and soul more than they do."

"That's the perfect, best, and only answer."

"That's the only reason anyone ever does anything, isn't it, Rachel?"

"People search for better choices, but they don't always make them. Or they don't turn out to be the best after one's made them."

"Mistakes give us experience, knowledge, and growth. Mine have accomplished all those things. Have yours, Rachel?"

"Some have and some haven't. It all depends on whether the action affects only me or includes others. If something involves other people, you're not always in control." Rachel stood. "You aren't keeping your promise, Captain," she teased. "You're letting your first mate get gloomy on you."

Dan grasped her hand and tugged on it. "Come along, woman. I'll keep trying until I succeed."

They reached the busy east-end market with its tall pillars and high tower displaying a cupola and large clock. They turned right onto Centre Street, strolled to Greene, and turned right again. They slowed to look at the Confederate cenotaph, obelisk, city hall, and "Big Steve" bell tower. They didn't break their meditative silence or stop holding hands. They absorbed the lovely sites, balmy weather, and each other's company. They took another right onto Campbell.

At Broad, Rachel glanced at the market clock and said, "It's four, Captain; better steer us into port for repairs for tonight's activities."

"At your command, Mrs. McCandless. Come with me, please."

Both noticed that no one followed or approached them during their stroll. Dan had seen her play with the silk flowers in her hair, but he made sure he did not mention them. Rachel wished her signal had worked, but presumed Dan's presence had foiled a meeting. If anyone was trailing and spying, she couldn't see or sense it.

*

Dan gaped at Rachel when she opened her door after he knocked.

"Is something wrong? Isn't this appropriate?" she questioned, looking down at her dress.

"You're absolutely ravishing. Stars above, woman, are you trying to enchant every man who'll be present tonight?"

"You are far too kind and generous. Come inside while I finish pinning the flowers in my hair. It will only take a moment."

Dan didn't tell her it was improper to enter the room where she dressed and slept. He came inside and closed her door, but stayed near it, almost afraid to get any closer to the alluring beauty.

Rachel was dressed in a satin gown of dark rose with rich pink trim. The square neckline was edged with pink ruffles and lace and creamy pearls. The puffy short sleeves ended with ribbon bands and ruffles. The bodice drifted down into a fitted waistline where a wide silk ribbon banded it, then was bowed in the back. Its tails were joined by two others to make staggered drops of three different lengths near each hipbone. The front of her skirt was in three layers, the first ending at her knees, the last at the floor, and the third between those two. Each layer was bordered in delicate embroidery of pink flowers with pearl centers. The longest was cut apart in the back, pulled up and over to each side, secured near the bow, and allowed to settle into soft folds as the decorated hem drifted lazily to the floor. The exposed section from waist to floor was frilled in many vibrant pink lacy tiers that flowed into a sweeping train.

He had seen her slippers and stockings when she lifted her hem to walk to the dressing mirror. Both were dark rose to match her gown, as was the fashion. Her silk slippers revealed the same pattern of embroidery as on her evening dress. Her only jewelry were pearls on her ears and a gold wedding band on her finger, but she needed nothing more to enhance her breathtaking image. He watched her finish securing several sprigs of silk flowers in her hair, which was pulled away from her face, pinned in the back near her crown, and cascaded into curls and ringlets to the top of her neckline. She lifted an ivory silk shawl with a swingy fringe border, tossed it over one arm, and collected her satin bag.

"You look splendid, Captain Slade," she said, approaching him. "Evening clothes suit you. Turn around and let me admire you for a moment."

Dan did as he was asked. She liked the low-cut waistcoat with its wide lapels, narrow velvet collar, velvet cuffs, and lengthy tails. The straight-cut trousers and vest matched its dark-blue color. The vest was tailored low, and the jacket was to be worn unbuttoned, so his fancy white shirt with a pleated frill completed his perfect look.

"With you on my arm, I'll be the envy of every woman present. Shall we go and capture our moment of perfection forever?" she teased.

"The sooner, the better," he murmured.

*

In the photographer's studio down the street, the man had them posed for their first picture. Rachel sat on a velvet stool while Dan stood slightly behind and to her right. The man positioned them, moved back a few steps, and checked them from head to foot.

"Perfect, ye look elegant an' bonny," the photographer said in his Scottish brogue. "Dinna move a muscle." He walked behind his camera on a tripod, checked the shot through the lens, looked back at them, and said, "Smile as tha happy couple ye are." As they obeyed his instruction, he took the first picture. "I'll be wan'nin' two ta be sure ta get a guid one. Stay still."

Dan didn't move as Rachel's heady perfume teased his senses. Her curls grazed the skin on her back, near where his fingers made contact with that enticing bare flesh. His genial expression did not change as worries stormed his mind. If Phillip had had the cash, it was more than enough for someone to kill him for. If she was determined to keep it, all she had to do was claim she didn't have it or know about it, and no one could do anything to prove otherwise. After inheriting Phillip's estate, she wouldn't have to touch it for years and risk exposing her deceit and theft. Maybe that was what she had in mind with this trip, to initiate her defense. Maybe he was along to aid it, to be used as a witness, to be set up as her next protector and victim. If only she didn't look so . . .

The photographer told them to switch their positions. Rachel's hand rested atop Dan's broad shoulders, an action which aroused both.

As they awaited the shots for the second sitting, Rachel inhaled Dan's manly aroma that blended with his Bay Rum cologne. Her body was touching his, but she yearned to be even closer. She wanted to run her trembling fingers through his head of glossy, midnight hair. She longed to snuggle into his strong arms, to seal her mouth to his. He was appealing and magnetic, powerfully and dangerously so. He was a man she could respond to with passion, a man who could steal her heart. But he could break it just as easily if she weren't careful.

The photographer changed their positions a last time, placing them side by side on a longer velvet seat. As they moved, they exchanged quick smiles. Their bodies touched and warmed, their scents mingled and enticed, their spirits tempted and taunted and tormented.

When the session was over, Dan paid the photographer and ordered the best copy of each pose for both of them.

"I'll hae them at yer hotel by Sunday. Check with tha desk clerk. If there be a problem, dinna hesitate ta contact me."

"I'm certain they'll be perfect," Dan assured him.

"Thank you," Rachel added before they departed.

*

As Dan paid the carriage driver, Rachel stared at the enormous Palladian Georgian home, awed by its size and beauty.

A servant answered Dan's knock at the door. The immaculately clad man with excellent manners bowed, welcomed them, and ushered them inside a lengthy hallway. He took Rachel's shawl, then escorted them to go, into an oversize drawing room.

Dan and Rachel paused beneath an archway sided by fluted pilasters. As with the outside, rococo detailing was used inside on the woodwork. The drawing room extended the length of the house, but was skillfully separated into three areas by a series of columns to match those at the entrance and archways. There was no mistaking the craftsmanship and designs of Chippendale furnishings, again in the rococo style. The decor was obviously done by someone with superb taste and plenty of money.

"It's breathtaking," Rachel murmured to her companion, who agreed emphatically.

The sitting areas were filled with guests. George had told them there would be forty tonight. A talented female played a piano in the center section, sending forth soft music into the well-lighted setting.

George and Molly Sue Leathers came forward with the Powers to greet them. "May I introduce your host and hostess, James and Jane Powers? This is Rachel McCandless, Mrs. Phillip McCandless, wife of my business partner. This fine gentleman is her cousin, Captain Daniel Slade from Charleston, who owns his own ship and business."

Pleasantries were exchanged, then Rachel complimented, "Your home is the loveliest I have ever seen. Thank you for having us here tonight. It was most kind of you to accept George's request to include us."

"Please make yourselves comfortable. Ask for whatever you desire. Meet everyone and enjoy yourselves. Dinner will be served at eight."

"There are plenty of people for you to meet," George said. "Come, and let me introduce you to some of them before dinner is announced."

*

Rachel took her place and looked around the table to see who was sitting with her and Dan—all twelve appeared important and wealthy people, all were nice and charming. She was relieved.

A bevy of servers and butlers bustled around three tables. Red and white wines, coffee, tea, and water were poured into an assortment of crystal glasses at each plate.

The menu was thorough and delicious. To avoid having to pass along and possibly spill something, the servants brought around each choice for the guests' selection. Tiny silver bells sat before each plate to ring for another helping or assistance.

Dan observed Rachel's conduct and found her charming, well bred, and an excellent conversationalist: a southern belle to the finest degree of training. She knew how to behave in this opulent setting, and looked the perfect image of a lady.

Dan continued to watch her from the corner of his eye as she dined and chatted with those nearby. She seemed to be having a marvelous time. Her olive complexion had a glow of health, merriment, and self-confidence. He wished she didn't look so ravishing and radiant, as it made her too distracting and appealing. The more he was around her and the more he learned about her, the more he was confused. He had met devious, scheming, and heartless types before. How could Rachel conceal those traits so expertly and without dropping clues to expose her true nature? As she had said earlier, no matter how clever an evil person was, one couldn't hide a true self from everyone and all the time . . . It was frustrating to entice her physically closer while trying to stay distanced emotionally. He couldn't allow himself to forget his behavior was only an entrapping fantasy. He just wished his chore weren't becoming so difficult.

While after-dinner liqueurs were being served in the drawing room, the men enjoyed their pipes and cigars, and people gathered in groups to converse, Rachel excused herself to visit the powder room.

Before she could rejoin Dan near the piano, she was halted by Jane Powers and a stranger near the archway.

"This gentleman wants to meet you, Rachel. His name is Harold Seymour; he's here with his aunt. He's taken with your beauty and charm, my dear, but I've warned this smitten bachelor that you're married."

"You do me an injustice, Jane," the neatly dressed man drawled in a thick Southern accent. "I told you, this lady looks familiar to me, and I haven't had the opportunity to make her acquaintance yet."

Jane laughed and sent him an incredulous look. "Harold, this is Rachel McCandless, *Mrs.* Phillip McCandless, from Savannah. Her husband is the partner of George Leathers."

"Ah, yes, the lovely Mrs. McCandless from Savannah. Now I know why your face is familiar. You've had quite an interesting life, Rachel. As a newspaper reporter, I've read many articles about you and your adventures. Would you do me the honor of granting me an interview?"

Rachel was caught off guard. How dare he mention something so private and embarrassing—and revealing—in such a luxurious, social setting! How dare he use her first name in that intimate and suggestive tone!

"Rachel is famous?" Jane Powers inquired, showing great interest.

Rachel sent her a fake smile and said, "I'm afraid not, Jane. My husband is the important one in our family. I was simply mentioned in stories about him." Before she could try to extricate herself further from the alarming situation, one of the guests summoned Jane to answer a question.

Rachel focused on the newspaper man to bring his damaging idea to an instant stop. "An interview with me, Mr. Seymour, would be dull and useless to you. Besides," she continued sternly when he tried to interrupt and persist, "I do not grant them to anyone. I'm afraid I haven't met many reporters who write the truth as the person involved relates it. Most have been rude, aggressive, and insensitive. I try to stay clear of such men, as my life is private, not a tasty treat for public consumption."

Harold had his eyes glued to hers. "Ah, yes, protection of privacy would be important to a beautiful and famous lady like yourself, but—"

"It is, Mr. Seymour, and thank you for the compliment. If you'll excuse me, I must be leaving. It's late, and I have an early train to catch in the morning. I must thank my host and hostess and bid them farewell."

"Are you sure you can't spend a few moments with me tonight or in the morning before you depart?" he wheedled. "I won't be rude or callous. I find your story utterly fascinating and the gossip surrounding you misinformed. Isn't it past time you tell your side and call a halt to nasty rumors?"

Rachel did not smile as she responded, "No, Mr. Seymour. I neither have the time nor the inclination to do so. Good night and good-bye."

Rachel walked to Jane and James Powers. She waited until they finished their talk, then said, "It's time for me to leave. The evening was delightful. Thank you for including me and my cousin. If you visit Savannah, please allow me to repay your hospitality and kindness."

They chatted for a moment, then parted. Rachel's eager gaze located Dan. He appeared to be enjoying himself and having no problem in this formal setting. She presumed he had come from a wealthy and refined family and had training and plenty of practice in the social graces. She went to Dan and told him she was ready to leave.

Dan knew she was upset and in a hurry to escape from what had appeared to be an unpleasant and apprehensive chat with a man across the room. He had asked the gentleman with him for the intruder's identity. The moment he learned it was a newspaper reporter, Dan assumed the man had recognized the "Beautiful Black Widow" from Savannah and was harassing her. It was obvious she had handled the man with expertise, but he didn't want to give Seymour another chance to expose her. "I'm ready. I need fresh air, exercise, and sleep," he said.

*

Dan paced his room as he made plans. He had to put his romantic ploy in motion tomorrow, convince her he was falling in love with her.

Chapter

❧

7

As Rachel dressed for her breakfast with Dan, she prayed she wouldn't run into Harold Seymour. She hoped he wouldn't check with the hotel clerk to make certain she'd told the truth about leaving. Being caught in a lie would make the aggressive reporter more curious and bold, as he already aroused her suspicions. He could have seen her arrive, recognized her, and, hungry for a juicy story, searched her room and left those two notes to make her susceptible to his interview request. If he didn't pester her again, she would ascribe last night's meeting to coincidence, which would mean she hadn't unmasked her tormentor.

For a while she had suspected her stepfather of spying on her and perpetrating all the insidious deeds. White Cloud wasn't too far from Savannah and Augusta for him to make quick trips to harass her as always. She had discarded that angle, though, as Earl Starger had been very direct with his wicked desires in the past. So, she mused, who did that leave?

The more she was with Daniel Slade, the more she was tempted and persuaded to trust him. She told herself she mustn't confuse his emotional threat with a physical one. Perhaps she would learn enough about him if she become more—but carefully—responsive to him.

If that inquisitive reporter came around and asked revealing questions, how would she explain her dark past and lies to Dan? Yet it would be too suspicious to everyone, including Dan, if she made a sudden change in departure plans.

She met Dan in the lobby. "Did you rise early again this morning?" She asked.

"Always, Rachel; it's in my blood. Did you sleep well?"

"Yes I did, and I needed it. Wasn't the dinner party marvelous?"

"I had a splendid time. But I always have a good time with you. I'm going to miss you, Rachel, when I ship out again. I'm afraid I'll be hard pressed to find such perfect company and good friendship elsewhere."

"Hard-to-please man, are you?" she teased, warmed by his words.

"One of those flaws you haven't noticed yet."

"Being discriminating isn't a flaw, Dan. What's more precious than one's time, pleasures, and friendships?"

"You're right, woman. It's a strength, not a weakness."

"I wouldn't imagine you have many, if any, weaknesses."

"You'd be surprised to learn I probably have plenty of them."

Rachel laughed. "That's a sneaky way of not admitting to having any."

"I should have left out *probably,* because I do have some."

"Such as?" she probed, unwisely sealing her gaze to his.

Dan imprisoned it. "No way will I expose them to you, woman."

"Why not? How else can I get to know you better?"

"With you as such a good influence, maybe they'll vanish, so there's no need to tell you about them to hold against me later."

"I would never hold anything against you, Dan. People change over time, and hopefully for the better."

"You don't, Rachel."

She was confused. "What do you mean?"

"How could perfection be improved?"

"Perfection? Me? Surely you jest. Or you don't know me well."

"I hope to by the time we return to Savannah. If not, it won't be my fault or from a lack of trying."

"I wonder if you like me as much if you really knew me?"

"What a crazy question," he said.

"I'm on my best behavior, of course. When I'm not . . ." She grinned and left her brazen implication dangling in midair.

"So that's it, you're a skilled actress who's pretending to like me."

"Certainly not. Of course I like you, Daniel Slade. Who wouldn't?"

"Because I'm Phillip's friend and you're a well-bred young lady?"

"Certainly not. I like you because you're nice and fun to be with, because you're a real gentleman and I can trust you."

"I'm a gentleman only because it's necessary with a friend's wife. If you weren't married to Phillip McCandless . . ." He left his suggestion hanging.

"You wouldn't be a gentleman around me?" she quipped.

"That isn't exactly what I meant," he replied, looking embarrassed.

"If I weren't married, Daniel Slade, I wouldn't be a lady around you."

The waiter intruded at that moment and silenced their provocative words.

*

George and Molly came to fetch them and they traveled for a few miles on the road toward Washington, Georgia, chatting about the party and the guests. When they arrived at their destination, George drove slowly so the couple could get a good view of the impressive driveway that was lined with majestic magnolias, some in bloom with their eight-inch shell-shaped flowers. At the far end of the drive stood a square, two-story house with white pillars around all sides, a gallery that encircled the second floor, and a cupola atop the roof.

When the carriage halted, the Berckmans came to greet them. They were shown into the house with its thick cement walls that held in winter heat and kept out summer blazes. They chatted for a while with the Belgian family, then left with Prosper on a tour of world-famous Fruitland Nurseries.

They enjoyed walking among the flowering trees and colorful bushes. Bees darted here and there, collecting nectar. Graceful butterflies fluttered around the countless blossoms and cheerful strollers. Birds sang and flitted about. Brown thrashers searched among dead leaves for bugs and worms, rapidly tossing debris in all directions during their task. The day was clear and sunny, and Rachel and Dan were at ease for a while.

They returned to the house to share tea and small cakes with the family. When it was time to leave for their next activity, she and Dan thanked their host and departed with the Leathers.

A mile down the road, George asked Rachel if she wanted to stop to purchase honey from a beekeeper, some of the best in the state.

"That's sounds wonderful, George," she said. "Thank you."

George halted the carriage on the edge of the dirt road. Rachel and Dan walked to the wooden stand to make their purchases from an elderly gentleman. Rachel bought a case of six jars, while Dan bought two cases to take to his ship. He paid for all three.

"You must like honey," she commented.

"I love it. When you're happy and relaxed, it's the same color as your eyes," he remarked as he accepted his change and waited for their order to be placed in crates. "I've never seen that shade before, sort of a pale golden brown with a very dark ring encasing them."

"I get this color from my father's side of the family, the Flemings. I take after them. I don't favor Mama or her side. She has blond hair and green eyes. Even at forty-five she's beautiful and slender and looks my age."

The packaging was finished. Dan lifted the small crates with ease.

"Yours are the color of the deepest sea," she said.

"Do honey and water mix?" he asked with a roguish grin.

She couldn't answer, because they reached the carriage and because she couldn't think of a clever response to the romantic query. He noticed so much about everything, including her. That both pleased and panicked Rachel.

Dan placed the cases on the floor between them and the carriage left.

"You two get along well," George remarked. "It's nice to see families and kin who are so close."

Rachel and Dan exchanged guilty looks, then conspiratorial smiles.

"Yes, sir," Dan murmured. "We do get along better than most people. Cousin Rachel and I are best friends. We have a long history together."

"I hope you get back this way again soon, Dan. We've enjoyed your company," Molly Sue told him.

*

They headed to the city parade grounds, which were composed of ten acres with a group of trees near the center. Wagons and carriages were parked along the four streets and people milled around, chatting and laughing.

"Winter is our season to play baseball, because harvest is over and it's still mild here. The team gathers one Saturday a month to practice during the spring and summer. Men and older boys from town make up the opposing team. It's fun and relaxing to come over and watch. We usually have a picnic afterward. It draws the community closer together."

Molly Sue handed the two men quilts for them to sit on to observe the practice and to join the merriment. As they strolled across the grassy lot toward the gathering of people and players, George made a shocking but unintentional revelation to Rachel and Dan.

"Phillip loves baseball and horse racing season. We have our races in the winter, too, at the Lafayette Course south of town. Gamblers of all ages and sexes visit during that time. I'm not a gambling man, but Phillip surely loves to place bets. He even likes to wager on the cockfights and billiard tables. We have a few gambling establishments, but I don't frequent them. I've always let Phillip go alone or with others. Hard-earned money is too valuable to toss away on games and horses. I've seen Phillip almost lose his shirt some days," he chuckled.

"I didn't realize Phillip liked to gamble," Rachel murmured.

"Oh, my, have I talked out of the wrong side of my mouth?"

"Don't worry, George, I won't tell him you mentioned it. There are certain pleasures we women shouldn't interfere with, right, Molly Sue?"

"You're a smart woman, Rachel," she complimented, then frowned at her husband in a way that told him to keep silent on the matter.

Gambling? A regular bet maker? Phillip McCandless? Enough to be an expensive and hazardous weakness? Enough to lose . . . Rachel didn't want to ponder those possibilities any further at the moment.

"Here we are. Just spread your quilt, have a seat, and enjoy yourself," George said.

Rachel glanced around the crowd and searched for Harold Seymour. She didn't see him and sighed in relief, though he could still come later, she knew.

Dan witnessed her tension and noticed her scan the crowd. He knew why. As he pretended to watch the teams practice, he drifted into deep thought. His brother had never been a gambler, but it sounded as if Phillip had gained a love of that expensive and risky sport. Dan prayed it hadn't become a weakness, a dangerous threat. If a man owed someone a lot of money, he would be tempted to do anything to settle that debt. Or if a man gambled with someone else's money and lost all or part of it . . . Dan didn't want to think his brother could be so foolish. If—

"Did you see that, Dan? It's going for a mile before it lands!"

"He's a hard and straight hitter, George."

"Some of these boys amaze me. We have a good team this year."

The practice continued for another hour before the picnic began. Molly Sue and George fetched the food basket from the wagon and spread out a feast on a tablecloth on the grass. They chatted as they feasted on cold fried chicken, pickles, biscuits, and strawberries.

Dan watched Rachel lick her greasy fingers and use her tongue to collect the crisp pieces of chicken that clung to her lips. "Don't let anything get the best of you, Cousin Rachel," he jested.

She leaned forward and pushed a ripe strawberry into his mouth. "Aren't they the finest you've eaten?" she asked, then licked her fingers.

"Sinfully so. I should also buy two cases of them for my ship."

"They would be ruined by the time you set sail."

He stopped nibbling on the chicken to reply, "I keep forgetting my holiday is so lengthy; I'm unaccustomed to being in port so long."

"Do your men stay aboard the ship when it's docked?"

"Some do at all times. They rotate taking shore leave. It isn't wise to leave a ship unguarded in port even if your cargo's been unloaded."

"I know what you mean. One of Phillip's ships was robbed, burned, and sunk last month. It was loaded to sail, but fortunately no crew was aboard to be attacked. Phillip's firm had to cover the client's loss, and it was a very big one."

Dan scowled at that news. "Did they catch the culprits?"

"No. We also had a warehouse vandalized last month, then a dockworker was murdered. It seems trouble comes in bunches. The police are too busy chasing people for minor offenses to spend the time needed to catch real criminals."

"That happens everywhere, and it's a shame. I'm sure those incidents upset a peace-loving man like Phillip. If Phillip hasn't taken the precaution to hire men to guard his possessions, he should. Sounds to me as if that bunch is rotten and needs attention."

"That's a good idea; I'll tell him." Rachel concluded Dan hadn't known about those threatening episodes, and congratulated herself for her cleverness in mentioning them.

"If you two don't mind," George said, "Molly Sue and I are going over yonder to speak with some friends. We'll return shortly."

"So, you were the baby of your family," Dan remarked when he and Rachel were left alone. "What was it like to live at White Cloud? If you don't mind talking about it," he added.

"Until the war, wonderful. It was one of the most beautiful and prosperous plantations in Georgia; I suppose it still is; I don't know, because I haven't been there in years. Mama and Papa knew how to throw such grand parties and everybody loved them—my parents and the splendid events. People came from miles away to attend. Sometimes I would sneak out of bed, peek through the railing, and watch the dancing for hours. Until I was caught," she added with a laugh.

Her tone and expression became somber as she went on. "After my father died and Earl came, it was awful, like living in a prison. Nobody was happy anymore; nobody smiled and joked. The air in the house always seemed cold and hostile. We'd get up, eat, do chores, eat, study lessons, eat, and escape to our rooms until bedtime; then repeat that depressing schedule the next day, and the next, and the next. After the twins left, things didn't get any better. Earl kept me and Mama on the plantation like captives, as if he was ashamed of us. I was educated at home by private tutors and taught the social graces every southern girl should know. But Earl rarely gave me a chance to practice them on others, unless he gave a big party to show off to everyone. Then he'd flaunt us like expensive possessions. Some old friends and neighbors wouldn't attend White Cloud functions or even speak to us anymore. I can't blame them for viewing Mama as a traitor and weakling. She changed so after Papa died. By the time I was eighteen, I was suffocating; I couldn't wait to get away from there. I still don't understand why Mama can't see how terrible he is," Rachel murmured with sad eyes, then went silent as the Leathers returned to join them.

*

As they entered the hotel, Dan tried to imagine a proper young lady of eighteen being thrust into the world alone to support and defend herself. Did that harsh experience and her losses explain why her first choice was a man old enough to be her father? Yet he suspected there was more to her reason for leaving home than she had confessed. Why wouldn't a killer of men get rid of the one she despised and resented the most?

As they strolled through the lobby, a waiter approached them offering them two mint juleps, as the drink was a hotel treat on Saturday nights.

Dan looked at Rachel in askance, then grinned before she could reply and said, "Yes, that should relax us nicely for a good night's sleep."

The waiter lowered his tray and handed each a tall glass filled with ice, which was covered with a golden-brown blend of sugar, bourbon, and mint leaves. It was a potent mixture, a symbol of Southern tradition and hospitality.

Rachel and Dan took their drinks and strolled onto the second-floor veranda to sip the juleps and chat before parting for the night. Others were there for the same purpose, so the couple sought a quiet and private area. They sat in comfortable rocking chairs with a small table between them. For a while, they only enjoyed the pleasant evening and heady refreshment. Their moods mellowed, their spirits soared, and their bodies warmed with the intoxicating drink and the close proximity of the other.

"Tell me about Turkey and why arms are needed there," Rachel coaxed, needing a distraction from Dan's overwhelming pull.

Dan lowered his glass from his lips, licked them, and replied, "If you're not familiar with that area, you'll need some background on it first."

"I'm not, so a history lesson is required."

"At one time, Turkey pretty much ruled that part of the world under the Ottoman Empire. Years ago, people of certain areas started demanding better treatment and independence. The Tanzimat Reforms were issued to appease them." Dan related the problems for and between the Christians and Muslims of the region, then halted to sip his drink to wet his throat. To keep from staring at her, he rested his head against the chair back and gazed toward the building across the street.

It was night, but the waning moon and gas lamps cast soft glows on the cozy setting and highlighted their features. Most of the other people had left the porch for late dinners, strolls, visits, or to retire to their rooms. It was becoming more intimate and romantic in the shadows.

Rachel was partially turned in her rocker to watch Dan as he spoke. He had the most compelling smile and arresting blue eyes she had ever seen. His complexion was darkly tanned from hours on his ship's deck beneath the sun. His features were bold and rugged. His hair was as dark and shiny as a crow's wing in the moonlight. He caused her heart to flutter and her slumbering desires to awaken.

Dan lowered his glass. "Some reforms worked, despite opposition. But the sultan was left with too much power and control. The rebelling peasants asked for help from other European and American powers. The sultan has run up a big foreign debt, and one he is unable to repay since the '73 worldwide financial crisis and Depression."

Rachel remembered that panic, an event that had helped push her into Craig Newman's arms and life, into his wicked power.

"No nation will loan him more money, so he isn't about to give up any of his profitable possessions. When war breaks out, other nations will get involved, mainly Russia; the United States can't allow her to steal control of such a large and important region." Dan hoped his truthful explanation would satisfy her curiosity.

"It sounds awful, but crucial. Everyone wants freedom," Rachel said and thanked Dan for the interesting information. "It's late now and we have church early in the morning. If you've finished your drink, we'd better go to our rooms and retire. My glass is empty, and I feel it working on me from head to toe." She laughed and rubbed her tingly nose. She hadn't intended to consume the whole drink, but had, she was so distracted by him.

Dan held her elbow as they walked up the steps to the third floor. In her weakened condition, it was the perfect moment for his next move, as he could always blame his own light head for his loss of self-control.

The hallway was empty and quiet. Dim lights cast seductive glows and shadows. He guided Rachel to her door. Dan asked for her key to unlock it. After doing so, he led her inside. "I'd better help you, woman," he said as excuse, chuckling all the while. "You don't seem too steady afoot right now."

Rachel gave a soft laugh. "I'm not," she responded. "I shouldn't have drank all of that mint julep. I'm not used to strong spirits. My head feels like a bird in dizzy flight."

"I know what you mean; I'm not a drinker, either, and that mixture was potent. You need any help with unreachable buttons?" he offered.

"I don't think so, but thank you." She looked up into his eyes, and their gazes locked. "You're the kindest man I've ever known."

"And you're the most bewitching woman I've ever known. It takes a strong will not to caress this satiny skin, this silky hair, and these soft lips." As he mentioned those forbidden areas, his defiant fingers trailed over each one with sensuous caresses. His thumb rubbed over her parted lips as he fused his eyes with hers. He felt her tremors of arousal, and he witnessed kindled desire in her gaze. He noticed how her breathing became fast and shallow and how her cheeks flushed even brighter.

Dan's eyes never left hers as he slowly lowered his head and sealed their lips, bringing fiery flesh into contact. His arms circled her back and drew her against him. He closed his eyes as his lips feasted on hers. His deft tongue explored her mouth and danced wildly with hers as they savored the taste of each other and the lingering one of the drinks. Dan groaned in need, tightened his embrace, and deepened his kiss. She was responding to him. Was it her unleashed passions or the debilitating bourbon controlling this blissful but wanton behavior?

Rachel allowed the rapturous feelings to continue for a while. Flames of desire leapt throughout her body. Her heart raced and she felt weak and shaky. She had never experienced anything like this with any man. She yearned to give free rein to the emotions, to let them sweep her away. She couldn't, though, not yet, not until the mystery of Phillip was clarified between them. She didn't want to give Dan the worst— a wicked—impression of her. She decided the best path of escape was to go limp in his embrace as if she'd passed out.

Dan caught her sinking body and carried her to the bed. He sensed it was a defensive ploy, but he had learned what he needed to know. Tonight wasn't the time to further explore her weakness for him. They still had work to do before their return to Savannah, work that could be halted by a guilty conscience or fear of a repetition of their behavior. He removed her shoes, covered her, and gazed down at her. Assuming she was awake, he murmured, "Stars above, Rachel McCandless, you're too much of a temptation to resist. I wish you weren't married, at least not to a good friend of mine. I can't steal Phillip's wife or compromise her. You're much too special for that. It's best to ignore this accident; it wouldn't have happened if we hadn't taken those drinks. If you recall this weakness tomorrow, I hope you forgive it and don't mention it. For us to discuss it would expose things better left hidden. Sleep well, my fetching siren." He kissed her forehead and left the room. He locked the door and shoved the key under it into her room.

Rachel rose quietly, removed her clothes, and returned to bed without donning a nightgown. The cool sheets rubbed against her flaming flesh. She curled to her side and nestled her face against the pillow. She had made a thrilling discovery; Dan did want her, and, if not for his friendship with Phillip, he would pursue her. She had to trust Dan, and couldn't think of a tangible reason not to do so. For a while she would pretend their indiscretion hadn't happened. What she had to worry about was Dan's reaction to her deceptions. She must pray, and pray hard, it wouldn't destroy any chance she might have with him in the future, because she wanted him. Forever.

Fears attacked her. If no man who married her could survive long, could she endanger Dan's life? Wouldn't it be wiser and safer, she reasoned, to try to become his lover, not his wife? It couldn't injure her reputation, as that was already ruined. Besides, Dan loved the sea, his ship, and his adventurous existence. With her as his mistress and waiting in port for his visits, that arrangement should suit the carefree bachelor fine. Besides, there was a strong possibility she couldn't have children, and Dan would surely want them.

"Please don't hate me and spurn me when you learn the truth about me," she murmured to herself. "I swear, I'll promise you forever as your mistress."

Rachel heard a squeak, leaned up, and glanced toward the armoire. She listened, but heard nothing more. She surmised that Dan was putting away his clothes in the next room. She would enjoy doing all Dan's chores for him, but probably would never get the chance. Besides, it might only be a physical attraction to her he felt. He might never want to marry a three-time widow, one husband having been his old friend. Then again, she could be mistaken, and prayed she was. She cuddled into the soft mattress, closed her eyes, and went to sleep to dream of Captain Daniel Slade.

*

As the singing of hymnals finished and the crowd took their seats in the large church, the pastor rose to stand behind his podium. He passed his gentle gaze over his flock, smiled, and opened his Bible.

He began with shocking words: "In Exodus twenty, verse thirteen, the Good Book says, 'Thou shalt not kill.' Most people believe that only means not to take another's life. I tell you, brethren and sisters, it means far more. There are many other ways to kill. You can murder someone's reputation with cruel lies or by spreading destructive gossip. You can murder someone's spirit by crushing it until it dies. You can murder someone's hopes and dreams by preventing them from coming true. You can murder someone's will by forcing him or her to be weak and useless so you can be stronger. I say to you, obey the Fifth Commandment in all ways."

Rachel hadn't attended church in a while, but had been reared to do so and taught to honor the Bible's words. She had tried to obey the Ten Commandments she had learned as a child. Even if she had surrendered to Dan, she wouldn't have committed adultery. "Until death do you part," the Book commanded, and it had, from all three husbands. Yet, she couldn't vow she hadn't broken the last one. She had coveted, hungered, and envied what others had: good names, friends, respect, honor, and happiness. Sometimes she was jealous of others for having what she wanted, and experienced bitterness and resentment for being denied. She wished every person who had been cruel to and judgmental of her could hear this message and obey it.

Dan observed Rachel from the corner of his eye as the minister talked, but didn't see a smidgen of guilt exposed on her face. They had eaten their early meal in a hurry, and neither had mentioned the heady incident last night. Both had put on cheerful moods and sunny smiles and chatted like good friends. He had seen Rachel relax the moment her gaze finished scanning the church and found no reporter. After the service, they were to have Sunday dinner with the Leathers, say their farewells, then return to the hotel to pack.

*

At the hotel, Dan collected the photographer's envelope from the desk clerk. He went to Rachel's room and knocked at her door.

She opened it and smiled, but looked tense. "Are you all finished this quickly?"

"I haven't even started yet. I went downstairs to get the pictures. They were just delivered as promised. They're excellent, beautiful. I'm well pleased." He withdrew and handed her three photographs. "Those are yours. These are mine," he said, shaking the envelope and grinning. "Real treasures."

Rachel looked at all three. She smiled and concurred, "Yes, they are wonderful. He did a splendid job. Thank you, Dan. I would invite you in to chat, but that wouldn't be proper."

He nodded agreement. "Besides, I have to pack, and you have to finish your chore. I'll meet you downstairs at seven for a light meal."

"I'll have something sent up, so I won't have to stop work. This takes a long time. And after I finish, I need to rest. We have to rise, dress, and eat early to get checked out and to the station by eight-thirty. The train leaves at nine, and we first have to buy the tickets we ordered."

Dan reasoned her plans were meant to protect them from another untimely temptation. "That's fine with me. Tomorrow will be a long and busy day. I'll see you in the morning at seven. Good night, Rachel."

She almost sighed aloud in relief for his understanding. "Good night, Dan, and thank you again for these lovely pictures."

After she closed her door, Rachel recalled what George had said today about telling Phillip to send that advance to him as soon as possible.

Rachel knew George was worried, but she believed—hoped—he had told her everything he knew about the mysterious order. She still wanted a look at the company books, but that wasn't possible, not on this trip, at least.

*

They boarded the Georgia Railroad train at Union Station. Everything had gone as planned this morning. They settled back in their seats and waited for departure. It wasn't long in coming. The engineer gave several blasts of the whistle, then put the train into motion. At first it traveled slowly and carefully through the southwestern side of town, but when Augusta was left behind, it increased its speed. Soon the wheels were rolling with their clickity-clack sounds, steam was rolling over the top of the line of cars, and passengers relaxed to enjoy the day-long trip.

This time, their car was filled with people, and Rachel and Dan were sitting across from each other. The noise made conversation difficult, so they soon ceased trying to communicate with curious listeners nearby. For a while, they gazed out the windows as they passed forests of pine and hardwoods. Grass was long and green in the fields, wildflowers were abundant and colorful, and stock grazed in contentment. Fields were plowed and planted with a variety of crops, many in cotton or wheat or oats, but sometimes in seemingly endless rows of tobacco and corn.

Both held books they had purchased to while away the hours, but mainly used them to keep from staring at each other. Their knees often touched as the train veered around a bend or they altered their positions, as the seats faced each other. They would glance up then, smile, gaze a moment, then focus their eyes on pages which hadn't turned in a long time.

The sea captain watched his bewildering sister-in-law from beneath lowered lashes. He wondered if Rachel could suffer from a strange mental derangement that compelled her to mate and kill. What if she couldn't help herself and didn't even remember doing those vile deeds once they were over? How could he find out for sure? Marry her and let her attempt to murder him seemed the only answer.

He speculated about a pattern to the mysterious deaths. Nothing about the three men or her mating schedule seemed to match. If the devastating war had done something to her mind, and her motive was determination never to be poor or vulnerable again, but she had the missing money hidden and would soon have Phillip's inheritance, she could spend a year in disarming mourning as she had before marrying Phillip. That lengthy timing would put a snag in his ruse to romance, wed, and then expose her.

It was easier to blame a madness that she wasn't even aware of for her insidious actions than to believe this woman could be capable of plotting and carrying out four cold-blooded murders. That would explain why she didn't act guilty and how she kept from dropping any incriminating clues.

If he doubted her guilt in the least, he couldn't do anything necessary to destroy her. But if she were only clever, dangerous, and daring, and if she had defeated the law many times and gone free, he had no choice but to use any ploy to entrap her. Soon he would know which course to sail with her.

There were routine stops in numerous towns along the route to let passengers on and off and to unload or load freight. They had their longest one at Union Point, where the tracks forked to head either right with a branch to Athens or left along the mainline to Atlanta. They ate lunch at a small cafe near the depot. Afterward, they took a muscle-loosening stroll. They didn't stray far from the small station as they walked along the tracks on a dirt road and looked at the landscape. Verdant leaves mingled with white or pink flowers on plum, peach, and pear trees. Sunny daffodils and purple rabbit's ears blossomed in a profusion of beauty nearby.

"I love spring," Rachel murmured as she watched bees and butterflies at work amidst the blooms. She saw birds searching for worms, bugs, and insects. She noticed tall green pines reaching for a sky that was cloudless and a rich blue. A mild breeze stirred the flora and leaves. "Everything is so alive and vivid, as if all things are filled with magical energy and eagerness. Everything's reborn, given a new chance to be better than before. It's inspirational, isn't it?"

"I've never thought of it that way, but it's true. You're a very sensitive woman, Rachel McCandless. You constantly amaze me and—"

The whistle blew its warning to reboard, to which the conductor added his shout. "We'd better get back to the train. We don't want to get stranded here until the next one comes along tomorrow."

*

The engine and line of cars halted on Carr's Hill, across from the one-hundred-fifty-foot-wide Oconee River and east of Athens. No trestle had been constructed for it to continue on into town, and wouldn't be until 1881. Warehouses, a depot, and several freight, stage, and carriage companies were located at the terminus of the Georgia Railroad and lined both sides of the tracks with structures of various sizes. Hack drivers, drayers, and freight haulers met the train to compete for business. After the baggage was unloaded, separated, and claimed by passengers, returning residents and visitors were taken across the bridge and into town.

Rachel and Dan's carriage climbed a steep slope which was lined with homes, a canebrake, woods, and cornfields. Their driver, a student at the local college, filled their heads with facts. Athens, located below the stirrings of the Blue Ridge Mountains, was nestled among the rolling hills of North Georgia, which were covered with pines, hardwoods, and red clay. Named after Athens, Greece—another city of beauty, prosperity, and culture situated atop scenic hills—it was a town of wealth and refinement, of education and industry, of enormous homes, and a mixture of both hurried and relaxed lifestyles. If they wished to tour the city later, he asked that they please hire him as their guide, as he needed the money for tuition. Rachel told him of course they would if their schedules matched.

The driver halted at their hotel. Across the street was the University of Georgia campus, established ninety years ago. Dan paid the student, who eagerly rushed away for another pickup.

The Newton House Hotel was a three-story, redbrick structure with white decorative work over its numerous windows. On the second floor, a free-hanging covered porch ran half the length of the Broad Street side and half the width of the College Avenue side. Double doors with glass sidelights and oblong fanlights led into a well-furnished lobby. Two polite bellmen lifted their baggage from the stone sidewalk and carried it into the hotel. It was lovely, the couple remarked, as grand as the Planter's Hotel in Augusta.

They registered and were shown to their rooms, which were across the hall from each other. It was six o'clock and they were hungry, so they decided to eat before unpacking and resting. They locked their doors and went to locate the dining room, to find it another cozy setting.

"Tomorrow morning we'll visit Harrison Clements and see what he has to tell us. I wonder what it will be . . ." she murmured.

Chapter

8

On Tuesday, the sixth of April, Rachel and Dan hired a carriage that took them down Broad Street to the Oconee River to the Athens Arms Company owned by Harrison Clements and Phillip McCandless.

Before they knocked on the office door, Rachel reminded Dan: "Don't forget what I told you at breakfast; Harry is smart and tough, so we have to move slower and easier with him than we did with George."

Dan eyed her. "You don't like him very much, do you?"

"I don't know him well, but he hasn't made a good impression on me. He seems smart in business, but there's something about him that makes me wary. I'm sure you'll see what I mean. It's his eyes. He has a disconcerting and sneaky way of squinting them or lifting one brow. I never feel comfortable around him. See if he strikes you the same way. Phillip claims I'm being foolish."

Dan shook his head. "I've never seen you be foolish, Rachel. I'll watch him closely. I'm sure you're right. Something has to be lurking below his surface or you wouldn't have doubts about him."

"Thanks for your confidence in me. Let's go face the lion in his den," she jested with a smile.

Dan heard men talking, so he didn't knock. He simply opened the door to catch the part-owner off guard. He pushed the door aside and stepped back to allow Rachel to enter first.

The man who had been sitting lazed back in a chair, his legs propped on his desk, got to his feet with speed and agility. The two men with him merely turned in their seats to see what had caused their friend's curious reaction.

"Rachel McCandless! What are you doing here?" Harrison Clements asked, sounding as if she were an annoying intrusion.

"Harry, how nice to see you again," Rachel murmured in a sweet and soft southern drawl. She smiled as she slowly walked toward his desk. "I do hope I'm not interrupting anything, gentlemen."

"Not really," the man with thick and wiry flaxen hair replied. His light-blue eyes narrowed, then one brow lifted quizzically. "What are you doing here?" he repeated as he came around the desk to meet her.

Phillip's warning, "Don't double cross Harry and the . . ." raced through her mind. She cautioned herself to be careful around Harry, who possibly was her enemy. With feigned vivacity, she related the same false tale she had told George about Phillip's sudden business trip up North and her holiday with her "cousin," whom she introduced. If Harry recognized Dan's name, it didn't show, and Rachel was relieved. "I thought a visit with you and a company tour would be nice today if it's no bother. If you're busy. . . ."

"Let me finish with these gentlemen, and I'll be with you two."

Rachel watched Harry guide the two men to the door, step outside to speak a few words in a lowered tone, then return to her. While he was doing so, she studied the man's boxy face, chiseled features, and deep-clefted chin. He looked as if he spent a great deal of time outdoors, as his skin was dark and his hair appeared sun-streaked. Harry held himself stiffly, as if he were annoyed and on alert; and she was certain it was her unexpected arrival that caused his reaction. She noticed there had been no introductions of her and Dan, which seemed rude.

Harry joined the couple inside his office, next to the arms company along the Oconee River. His ice-blue gaze roamed her face as he asked, "Now, what's this about Phillip taking off to places unknown?"

Putting on an innocent expression, she shrugged. "He left on business right after your visit," she said casually. "He said he'd be gone for six to seven weeks. Baltimore was his first stop, but he could be anywhere by now. That naughty husband of mine hasn't even contacted me yet."

Harry glued his eyes to Rachel's face. "Why did he go? What kind of business?" he asked in an almost demanding tone.

Rachel grasped the man's surprise and suspicion. "I haven't the faintest idea, Harry. Phillip said it was urgent and unexpected. He said he had to handle it promptly and it would require that long."

"That should put him back home the first or second week of May."

After he frowned and narrowed his gaze once more, Rachel asked, "Is there a problem? Phillip didn't mention one before he left home suddenly."

"No, I just wanted to see him before the fourteenth of next month."

Harry sat down, but didn't ask Rachel or Dan to take seats. He looked worried, and she surmised that it was because he would be out of a big profit if Phillip spoiled their secret deal. He probably wished he himself had handled the negotiations and collected the advance. He had to be angry with Phillip for concealing the money and perhaps refusing to pass it along to the company, or to him. "May we sit?" she asked.

"Of course. I'm sorry, but I have things on my mind today."

He didn't appear sincere, but Rachel pretended not to notice. "We just left Augusta and a wonderful visit with George and Molly Sue. They showed us around town and kept us busy for six days. They're so nice and hospitable, but of course you know that about them. George mentioned a large arms and ammunition deal the two companies are doing together. Is that what you're concerned about, Harry? I know Phillip's a partner and he's away now, but he doesn't normally handle much of the two companies' affairs. He leaves most of that to you and George."

Harrison Clements stared at her a moment, his probing gaze digging into hers to uncover clues. "We don't have any problems with any of our contracts, Rachel," he answered, "I only wanted to discuss an expansion during the early summer with him. I was just wondering why Phillip didn't mention this trip to me when we talked on the twenty-fifth."

He's probably asking himself if I know anything, Rachel mused. *Did Phillip send me here on a fact-gathering mission? What did Phillip's secret trip mean?* Rachel pushed aside such speculation. "I don't know. Unless," she created with a bright smile, "it was because he didn't know about it when you were there. A telegram arrived early Friday morning and he left soon after your departure by train. A little sooner, and you two might have run into each other in town."

Harry leaned forward. "A telegram? From whom? From where?"

Rachel felt a surge of power and excitement at tricking this unlikable man. "He didn't say. He only said he had to sail to Baltimore for six to seven weeks about a new investment, something urgent and sudden. You sure there isn't a problem? You seem disturbed by this news."

Harry straightened. "No problems, Rachel. I just need an agreement about the expansion before May fourteenth so I can sign the contract and hire a builder. This time of year, they get busy and filled up fast. When you hear from Phillip, tell him to contact me immediately. Maybe that urgent business was why he was in such a bad mood during my last visit."

Rachel noticed he didn't say to ask him, but demanded to tell him. She also caught the sarcasm in his voice during his last statement. As sweetly as she could manage, she replied, "I didn't notice a foul mood before or after your visit with us. He did seem preoccupied, but not upset. You know Phillip; he always keeps his worries to himself. He was excited over a new prospect when he left; he said he would surprise me with good news when he returns. I can hardly wait to see what he's getting involved with this time. He needs so many different interests to keep him interested."

"Just tell him to cable me as soon as possible."

"I will." She changed the subject. "May we tour the company? Dan and I would love to see how guns are made."

Harry glanced at the stranger with her. "It has to be quick and quiet; the men are busy and I don't like to distract them. Errors in products cost money, and even lives sometimes. Follow me," he instructed.

As they did, Dan winked at her and nodded his approval of her conduct.

Rachel sent him a warm smile of gratitude. He had kept silent but watchful during her talk with Harry and she appreciated his assistance.

Harry showed them into the factory where many men were laboring to make parts or to assemble them. They stopped only a few minutes at each work station, and no introductions were made. Harry pointed out the construction methods and gave them the names of parts. He showed them how breech action worked on a rolling block rifle and moved on to where a lever-action rifle was being put together and explained its functions.

As if she was ignorant of gun-making, Rachel observed and merely asked a simple occasional question. Yet she paid close attention to the diagrams the men used, and made an astonishing discovery. She stared at the weapon design, an old Henry model that had been improved later by Winchester. When Harry exhibited the next model, she recognized it as a Spencer, a lever-action repeater with a spring mechanism that held the cartridges in the butt . . . She knew those facts from the manuals Phillip had given her to study.

"We also make and sell slings, swivels, and sights. We have a testing range outside town; I do most of that job. Laying a rifle gives me a thrill. Pardon me, Rachel, that means to adjust the sight to compensate for any left, right, or downward drift of a cartridge after it's fired."

Expert with a rifle, like the villain who shot at me? "How fascinating. You must be an excellent shot."

"I am," he admitted without modesty.

Rachel wondered how Harry and Phillip had gotten their hands on registered designs. Had they purchased the rights to use them, or had they stolen them and used them illegally? She thought it best not to ask any questions in that area, since they would reveal her knowledge on the subject. If stolen, exposure could ruin the company and could lose her the truth. She could not understand why Phillip, if he had known, could be involved in criminal activities. Had she misjudged him, as she had Craig? Whatever the truth, she must wait until later to deal with it.

On the way out of the factory, Harry remarked, "We used to make arms for Winchester and Remington when they were too busy to fill all their orders. After the weapons were constructed, we'd ship them to their companies to have their trademarks placed on our superb workmanship. When they expanded, they didn't need our help anymore. I hated to lose those valuable contracts, but that's how things go in business."

Rachel remembered being told how surplus arms had gone on sale after the war. It would have been simple for a skilled gunmaker to get his hands on certain models, take them apart, study their workings, then draw his own patterns. No matter that it was stealing the inventors' ideas, works protected by law. Phillip had never mentioned buying licenses to use those patents; since he had taught her so much, he wouldn't have overlooked that important fact. Yet, how could Harry do that foul deed without Phillip's knowledge and consent?

"You two will have dinner with me Friday night," Harry said. "I'll send word where to meet me. You are staying at the Newton House again?"

Rachel faked a smile. "Yes, we are, and thank you for the invitation."

"Well, now if you don't mind, I do have work to do this afternoon."

Not so polite a dismissal, she mentally scoffed. "Thank you for taking the time to show us around. We'll see you Friday night."

"You said you're planning on sightseeing?" Harry hinted.

"Yes, we're going to do just that," Dan said.

"Nice to meet you, Harry, and thanks for the tour," Dan said. "I've never been inside a gun company before. Quite interesting."

"I'm certain you'll have a good time with your cousin this week. If you need anything, send word to me."

"You're most kind and thoughtful, Harry."

*

Rachel and Dan halted at the top of the hill to catch their breath at the five-points section, three blocks from the hotel.

"He didn't even offer to act as our guide or even to entertain us at night after he finishes work. He probably wants to avoid me as much as possible. I'm sure you noticed how fast and reluctantly given our tour of the factory was. At least George offered us one and did it with leisure. I thought it rude neither man introduced even me to the workers; I *am* a partner's wife. And that stupid excuse about expansion! He was lying, covering himself for needing to get in touch with Phillip soon. He's probably worried about Phillip checking on him and his deals through me."

"Why didn't you tell me Phillip had just sailed when I arrived?"

Rachel was stunned by his query. She expected comments on her observation of Harry. "You didn't ask when he departed. Does that matter?"

"No, I was just wondering if there was a reason."

"Phillip left home the morning you arrived in town. You just missed seeing him." She got off that unsettling subject fast. "Harry rushed us through the tour so swiftly, I didn't have time to learn or see much. They're certainly busy for a company making so little profit."

"It's probably work for that big contract all of you mentioned."

"That's what I assumed, too. I'm glad you decided to wait a few days to place your order. It will give us the opportunity for another visit, as I'm sure Harry won't extend another invitation. That man can be so rude."

"I noticed," he concurred. "Your opinion of him seems accurate to me. I can understand Phillip liking and working with George Leathers, but Harrison Clements isn't his kind. That friendship baffles me."

As they walked to the hotel, Dan said, "You go inside and rest until supper. I'm going over to the telegraph office to send word to Luke Conner, my first mate. I want to let him know we've reached Athens in case he needs me for anything. I'll also locate that young student about acting as our tour guide for the next few days."

Rachel looked puzzled and Dan gave her his explanation.

"Because Harrison Clements struck me as a careful man. It wouldn't surprise me if he has us watched and followed. If we don't play the holiday game, he'll get suspicious of us. We'll give him a few days to be duped and disarmed, then work on him again Friday night. That suit you?"

She was pleased and impressed. "You're clever, Daniel Slade, very clever. I'm glad you're here to prevent me from making mistakes. You and Phillip are so different for best friends."

"We didn't used to be. I guess we've both changed a great deal."

"I suppose so."

*

Rachel and Dan enjoyed a late breakfast as they waited for their guide to finish early morning classes and fetch them. When Ted Jacobs arrived a little after eleven, he was bubbling with energy and excitement. The fair-skinned, auburn-haired youth was slim with hazel eyes. He announced they would begin their tour across the street at the University of Georgia campus, as he was between classes and had two free hours. The couple followed the jaunty youth across the dirt street to the sidewalk.

"This cast-iron arch is patterned after the Georgia state seal," he explained. "Only seniors and graduates can walk through it. Other students and visitors have to use these stone stiles. Follow me, please."

Rachel and Dan obediently used the stepway over a cast-iron picket fence. They began at the library and Ivy Building, where Ted related their histories and functions. They continued on to Demosthenian Hall, behind which stood Moore College for the agricultural and mechanical arts—two skills of importance to this agricultural and industrial location.

Ted halted them to say that the Demosthenian Society was established in 1803. "It's a debating society," he explained, "to improve the mind and to give practice with speaking. I'm a member. With a little more practice, maybe I can become a famous politician. Our biggest rivals and competitors are the Phi Kappas. That's their hall across the way." He pointed across the quadrangle to the left side of the campus. "Phi Kappa was created to give Demoses something to think about and practice on. They have secret signs and meetings; their favorite prank is to steal our notes before a big debate."

The college chapel was next, a Greek Revival structure with six tall columns and windows that almost stretched from roof to floor. They came to New College as the chapel bell signaled the changing of class. Students—male and female—hurried to and fro: some silent and thoughtful; others laughing and chatting. They waited there until the activity ceased and all was quiet again.

Ted guided them past Old College, the campus's oldest building. "Students used to meet under trees for classes," he said. "Some families, especially wealthy planters and businessmen, moved to Athens for their sons to attend this college. Most liked the town and stayed. My father owns a large cotton farm near Danielsville, too far to travel every day, so I room and board here. We had a fire in our barn last year that destroyed nearly all of our cotton before we could haul it to market. I take jobs like this to see me through until this year's picking and selling. You were kind to hire me."

Rachel perceived that the young man was a little embarrassed about his confession and predicament. She smiled and said, "Everybody has hard spells, Ted, and needs help. We were lucky you needed this job or we might have stumbled around on our own and missed your informative lessons. This is more enlightening and enjoyable."

"She's right, Ted." Dan concurred. "Besides, you'll appreciate your education more by helping to pay for it, and you'll probably study and learn more this way. If you're interested in politics, it's good to meet a lot of different people."

Ted beamed with delight. "That's very true, sir, ma'am."

After Philosophical Hall, they strolled toward the campus entrance. Ted told them about two colorful town characters: Joe Keno and Deputy Marshal William Shirley. "You'll see both plenty of times during your visit."

At the arch, they halted to chat a while longer, then the bell in the chapel rang loudly to signal the changing of periods again.

"I have to go to class now, but I have all day tomorrow free," Ted said, "Would you like to continue our tours around town?"

"That will be nice, Ted. What time shall we look for you?"

"Let's start at nine; that will give us plenty of time to see many things. Bring a picnic with you for noontime. We'll take all day, if that suits you."

"It sounds perfect. We'll see you at nine in the hotel lobby. Hurry to class before you're late," Rachel coaxed with a smile as she noticed students rushing from building to building with books burdening their arms.

"You want to take in those sights he mentioned during our stroll?" Dan ventured after Ted left them. "He told us all about them. And," he added with a grin on his face, "we need to stay busy having fun, because, as I suspected, we're being watched and followed. Don't look around," Dan cautioned as she started to do so. "I have my eye on him, so don't worry. We'll play the holiday guests as alleged. Come along, partner."

The couple crossed the street and strolled up College Avenue. There was a gentle rise to the terrain that did not urge them to strain as they walked along the tree-shaded street. At the intersection of College and Market, they looked at the confederate monument in the center of it. The Athens Baptist Church, with its tall white belfry atop, was on one corner.

Businesses and homes intermingled and complemented each other with their lovely architectures and neat facades. They turned down Market Street and walked toward Town Hall in the center of the street one and a half blocks away. Rows of chinaberry trees grew to its rear. Ted had told them the first floor was used as the city market and jail; the second, for town meetings, entertainment, school events, community suppers, trials of men incarcerated downstairs, and debates for local and state politicians. Until the new courthouse was completed, it served in that capacity, too, as the county seat had been moved to Athens from Watkinsville three years ago.

"Do we still have our shadow?" Rachel inquired, acting casually.

"Yep, about a block behind, but keeping step. Make sure you pretend not to notice him. He doesn't come close enough to make a threat. If he does, let me handle him. I'm in a protective mood today."

"Aren't you always?" she teased, sending him a radiant smile.

They stopped at a cafe for lunch. That day's specialty, which both ordered, was fried ham, red-eye gravy, biscuits, and buttered grits—a true southern meal that could be eaten and savored at any time of day or year. The busy cafe was popular with the local citizens and the tables were close, so Rachel and Dan only talked about the sights.

When they finished, they strolled to the Stevens Estate at the corner of Hancock. They stopped to admire the enormous Greek Revival mansion with its two formal boxwood gardens, numerous outbuildings, several wells, a fruit orchard, and vegetable garden.

"Ted didn't exaggerate; it's wonderful," Rachel murmured.

"That it is, and a large place to keep up," Dan remarked.

"Do you ever miss having a home?" she inquired.

"I do have one—my ship," he corrected with a lopsided grin.

"I meant one on land."

"Not since I left my family home in Charleston. I suppose I'll want one some day when I get too old and feeble to sail the world."

"You're teasing me, Daniel Slade."

"I know, but your question isn't one I can think about at this time."

Rachel thought it wise not to probe him on the matter.

The couple strolled toward the hotel and passed it. The block beyond contained Long Drug Store, owned by Dr. Crawford Long, a noted surgeon who discovered ether anesthesia. Standing outside the store was a wooden statue of a man grinding medicine in a large metal vase with a wood stick shaped like a baseball bat. According to Ted, the town citizens affectionately had named the statue "Tom Long." Rachel and Dan didn't halt until they returned to Jackson Street and entered a gallery of art. With leisure and enjoyment, they examined the paintings on display and for sale.

Dan paused before one of a three-masted ship, its hull tossing whitecapped waves beneath a stormy sky, her sails billowing in an invisible wind. "That's a beautiful clipper. Reminds me of the *Merry Wind*."

Rachel eyed his wistful expression and the powerful painting, and decided she must have it. It didn't seem to surprise Dan when she purchased it, and she wondered if he thought she had done so to remind her of him after they parted.

Dan carried the wrapped painting to the hotel. Rachel halted abruptly as they entered the room, then he heard her gasp. His astonished gaze took in the same sight over her shoulder.

"Look at this mess!" She scanned the ransacked room, then began to check her belongings. "Nothing's missing," she finally said, "so it wasn't a common thief. It's probably Harry's doing! He must not have believed that tale we told him." She noticed something white at the edge of the rumpled bed and she retrieved it. "What's this?" she murmured, examining the clean handkerchief to find the initials D. S. on them.

Dan watched her make that stunning discovery. "It's one of mine, Rachel, but I didn't drop it here. How could it fall out of my pocket? Besides, I still have mine," he said, drawing a matching one from his back pocket.

"You don't have to worry about convincing me of your innocence. You've been with me every minute since I left my room. I was wondering who and why someone would try to frame *you* for this."

"I don't know, but I certainly don't like it. It seems inconceivable that Harry would go to such trouble to leave this here when he thinks we're cousins." Dan peered out the window. "Rest before dinner," he suggested. "I'll meet you downstairs at seven. If I hurry, maybe I can trail our shadow to his boss. That could give us answers about who's doing all this to you."

Dan left in such a rush that Rachel didn't have time to ask questions or to give cautions. She went to her window and looked down on the street. Her gaze located the man who had followed and watched them all day, who had lingered a while to make sure they didn't leave again. He headed down Broad toward the river in the direction of Athens Arms Company. She watched Dan sneak along behind him at a safe distance. She prayed the captain wouldn't be seen and caught and that he wouldn't attempt to get too close to eavesdrop on the imminent meeting of spy and boss. Clues were one thing, but his safety came first.

Don't you dare get hurt or killed helping me, Daniel Slade, Rachel silently instructed. *Harry Clements is dangerous; I should have told you that. You don't know what you're getting yourself into with me. I would die if anything terrible happened to you. Please don't take any risks, and hurry back.*

Worried, Rachel stared out the window for a long time, until the sun set and dusk appeared. She saw the lamplighter going from lamppost to lamppost lighting them one at a time, a stick in one hand, a lantern in the other, and a three-legged dog tagging along behind him with a running-hopping motion.

At least she knew Daniel wasn't behind this new incident. Maybe he wasn't responsible for any of them. Until today, she hadn't seen or sensed anyone following her. For all she knew, Dan hadn't written that card which had come with the flowers, and the script on the second note could be his! But how could he have forged hers on the first one? It was a vicious cycle of guilty or innocent.

She glanced at a clock on the mantel. Seven-fifteen. She poured water from a floral ewer into a matching basin and refreshed her face and washed her hands. After brushing her long hair, she checked her garments. She hadn't straightened her plundered room and she was a little mussed, but there wasn't time to now.

Rachel glanced around the lobby, but Dan wasn't there. They had scheduled to meet at seven for dinner. *Where are you?* she fretted.

Chapter

9

Someone tapped her shoulder, and Rachel turned to respond. "Dan!" Forgetting all else, she hugged him in joy and relief. "Where have you been? I was worried sick over you."

Dan embraced her for a moment and found himself wishing he could hold her longer, but too many people were in the lobby to risk exposure of their kinship ruse. His hands grasped her upper arms gently and he leaned her away from his enflamed body. He chuckled to release his sudden tension. "Why? You're the one who's late," he jested.

"I watched you leave from my window and stayed there until dark. I didn't see you return. I've been so frightened," she admitted.

Dan knew she hadn't created the plundering incident, so she might have told the truth about the other ones he had overheard her mention in Augusta. If so, she had a persistent enemy and a reason to be afraid. Still, nothing had proved her innocent of Black Widow allegations. "I returned by the side entrance. I've been on the porch reading the newspaper. When I didn't find you here, I checked in the dining room, then went upstairs to see if you were delayed."

"We must have just missed each other. What happened?"

"About what?" He forgot his earlier task, as she was so tempting and distracting, so touchingly moved by fear and concern for him.

"With our spy," she whispered, her gaze staying locked with his. He was safe. He was with her.

"Oh, the spy." He released his hold on her arms. "He went into Harrison Clement's office and stayed about ten minutes," Dan answered in a low tone. "I couldn't get close enough to overhear anything. I didn't want to chance being discovered."

"So Harry is having us watched and followed. I wonder why."

"Probably doesn't trust Phillip any more than Phillip trusts him, and he must not have believed our ruse about why we're here."

"Did I act suspicious when we saw him?" She fretted aloud.

"Not that I could tell; a skilled actress couldn't have done better." But, Dan recalled, she had noticed something during their tour, some clue she hadn't shared with him—not yet. It had to do with the weapons the men were constructing, and she had told him she knew all about arms-making. Her expression and reaction had given away that fact to him, but probably not to Harry who didn't know how smart and informed she was.

"I was about to send for the marshal to report you missing. If it hadn't been dark and I was familiar with this town, I would have come looking for you myself. Next time you check in with me when you return," she chided.

"Yes, ma'am," he said playfully as she dropped the touchy subject.

"It isn't funny, Dan. I was worried and scared."

"There wasn't any reason to be, Rachel; I'm always careful. I never challenge uneven odds."

"Such as the powerful ocean?" she quipped.

"Ah, but I'm acquainted with all her phases, so there are never any surprises."

"She's never beaten you, Dan, never defeated you?"

"Not yet, thank the lucky stars."

"But that luck might give out."

Dan grinned, as if failing to perceive her seriousness. "Rachel McCandless, are you asking me or warning me to give up the sea?"

"We've become good friends, Daniel Slade. I wouldn't want anything to happen to you. Every day at sea is challenging danger, isn't it?"

"Ocean violence is rare, Rachel. And there's no more peril than on dry land. Probably less."

"Are you sure?"

"As positive as I can be, Rachel, so stop worrying. Let's eat. I'm ravenous." He was confused by the curious change of topic.

*

As they dined, Rachel coaxed, "Tell me about this Luke Conner."

"Luke's thirty," Dan related, between bites and sips. "He has brown hair and lively blue eyes, the kind filled with boyish mischief. He looks as if he has a permanent grin on his face and in his eyes. He's so good-natured, it breaks free a lot."

Dan thought a minute about Luke. "He's cheerful, smart, dependable, and level-headed. The men trust and respect him; so do I. He stands by me in any situation, good and bad. He loves the sea and sailing. We're both adventurers at heart. Luke's easygoing, but he can be tough and strong when the situation demands." Dan sipped his tea, which was spiced with fresh mint. "We've been tight friends and constant companions for four years. Where one goes, the other goes. We met on the ship I took when I left Charleston in '71. We forged a tight bond during that voyage, and we've been together ever since. After I purchased my ship, I signed Luke on as first mate, and I've never been sorry for a moment. The *Merry Wind* has been my home for years, and he's been my family. Luke's like a brother to me, and he feels the same way about me."

Rachel was warmed by those revealing words and the strong feelings behind them, was even a little envious of that relationship. Hearing about the kind of special relationship that she had been denied through no fault of her own made her a little melancholy and bitter. "That's wonderful. I haven't had a best friend since I was a child. I played with the plantation workers' children until Mama married Earl. He said it wasn't proper and stopped it. Earl didn't like for visitors to come around much, so I didn't meet many girls my age who were acceptable to him.

"Of course," she conceded, "we didn't have many close neighbors with daughters my age because the plantations were so large and far apart. After I moved to Savannah, I wasn't given the opportunities and time to make friends with other young women. Oh, I had acquaintances, just not close and best friends like you described. I've missed that." She sighed heavily, then forced a smile. "Lula Mae is my friend, and so is Burke, the manager. But they're older, and I'm their mistress. Sometimes I think Lula Mae still views me as a child. She tries to protect me and teach me and discipline me as if I were her daughter. I suppose that's why I don't get any closer to her; it could cause a problem if I had to overrule a decision of hers or reprimand her. I owe her a great deal, so I let her get away with things I might correct others for doing or saying. If it doesn't seem that important, I allow it to pass unchallenged."

"Everybody needs a good friend, someone to confide in, someone who stands by you no matter what comes along, somebody you trust and respect."

"But how do you find such a person, Dan? How can you be sure they'll stand by you in dark times or not betray you?"

Dan sensed she was serious, perhaps even testing his feelings, his reaction to even bigger revelations. "You found *me*, Rachel. I promise you can speak freely to me. I would never betray you, to anybody. I could make a good best friend even if I'm not a female."

We'll soon see if you mean what you say . . ."This topic is gloomy. However did we sink into it? Order me a tempting dessert and put me in better spirits." She laughed softly with her voice and expression, but not with her gaze.

Dan noticed, and it curiously pained his heart. He believed those admissions were true, tormenting, and difficult. The fact she could reveal such private and poignant feelings told him how close she was getting to him and how much she trusted him in certain areas. If only he could trust and believe her, and didn't have to betray her.

*

On Thursday morning, they met with Ted Jacobs in the lobby. The hotel cook had prepared a sumptuous picnic basket, even loaned them glasses to go with the wine, along with a tablecloth and utensils. They got into a rented carriage and headed off to tour Athens.

Rachel and Dan were both amused by the redhead's enthusiasm, but they suppressed their laughter at the way he often leapt from topic to topic like a jumping frog. It was only when he turned his back to drive, that they exchanged grins and soft laughter. They realized how much fun they had together. They were relaxed and content, even though their shadow was tailing them again.

As they turned onto Milledge Avenue, Ted pointed out how much larger the lots were in an area which had many trees and meadows and a few branches. The streets and roads were dirt, but the hard-packed Georgia clay gave up little dust at their slow pace and that of the carriages they encountered. He pointed out many homes of famous residents along the picturesque route—mostly in Federal, Greek Revival, and Victorian styles.

Their next stop—a long one—was at a female institute. Ted reveled in telling about it being "one of the highest honors to be known as and be called a 'Lucy Cobb Girl.' Now, families from the North send their daughters South to get refinement and culture and social graces. That's ironic."

The sun was high, so Rachel held her parasol over her head and leaned closer to Dan to shade his eyes, too. Their shoulders and legs touched. The heady contact affected both of them, and they had a difficult time paying attention to their guide's words and the sights.

They reached Lumpkin Street and turned left, back toward town. Ted soon pulled to the side of the street. "Let's stop here for our picnic."

The serene, woodsy, flower-filled meadow bordered the estate of an ex-governor and the college campus. It was a perfect selection. Tall oaks and thick magnolias presented a lovely setting and welcome shade. They spread out the tablecloth and sat down on the grass around it. As they feasted on the delicious fare and sipped tepid wine, they chatted about what they had seen and would see.

When Ted asked questions about them, they related the same tale they had told Harry and George. It was doubtful, but George could have warned Harry of their impending visit and Harry could have hired this innocent-faced boy to meet them and to stay with them during their visit. The couple had discussed that possibility, then dismissed it because of their shadow. Still, it paid to be careful and alert. Dan and Rachel watched everything they said and did in his presence, which took extra effort, but it didn't prevent a good time.

Their tour continued along Lumpkin past the university to the cotton-factoring location. There, the student, a fountain of information and overflowing with energy, said, "Athens is one of the largest cotton markets in the South and probably in the world. Outside of town in every direction are farms and plantations of immense sizes. After cotton is picked, hauled in, ginned, and baled, you see stacks of them every-where, I mean *everywhere* along the streets nearby. It's a big and profitable business."

They traveled up Thomas Street toward the area called Lickskillet, the original location of the rich gentry, which now belonged to Prince and Milledge avenues. Ted pointed to a large Victorian home on the corner and said, "I suppose you know that's where Harrison Clements lives."

"Yes, I was there for a short visit before last Christmas," Rachel revealed. She waited to see if Ted would make further comments, but he didn't. Neither did she.

At the hotel entrance, Ted informed them that he had tests the next day and was visiting his family Saturday. "But I can show you around Sunday afternoon," he said. "You must see the old botanical gardens before they go to ruin."

Rachel smiled genially at the slim youth. "That sounds like a delightful way to spend Sunday afternoon, doesn't it, Dan?"

"It certainly does. We'll be waiting for you after church." Dan paid the agreed hourly fee and added some more money to it.

The youth beamed as he saw the large tip. "You're most kind, sir."

"You are most informative and interesting, Ted," Rachel said. "You've shown us a wonderful time. Thank you. Until Sunday afternoon."

As they watched the student head down the street to return the rented carriage, Rachel asked, "Is he still there?"

"Yep, our spy has stuck to us all day. I bet he's starving if he didn't bring along a picnic, too. Just for meanness, we should stroll until dark and exhaust him, but we won't. Let's just get washed up and have dinner."

*

Friday they walked up and down and in and out of blocks of town. They halted here and there to shop, having fun together and relishing the merry chase they were leading their shadow on. She purchased several sweets, including fresh baked cookies and candy called "bucket mix" from a confectionary store. She waited outside the hotel while Dan carried those items to his room, and she pretended not to see the spy who had to guess they were leaving again soon or she would have gone inside.

Dan returned and their adventure continued. They stopped to have lunch at a restaurant, but hurried to prevent their spy from having time to eat or risk losing sight of them. It was amusing to punish and outwit the hired man, who couldn't even stop for a drink to wet his dry throat or to be excused. Afterward, Rachel bought gifts for Lula Mae, Burke, his wife, and the other two workers at the plantation.

As they strolled along, Dan carried her packages, but didn't make any purchases himself. He had a pleasant time just being with and watching Rachel play the perfect holiday traveler.

The more they were together, the closer they became and the higher their desires increased. They cared about what happened to each other; as they worked in intimate secrecy as a team and they shared—without knowing it—common goals, dreams, hopes, and interests.

When Rachel and Dan were too weary to continue with their mischievous ruse, they returned to the hotel to relax before bathing and dressing for dinner with Harrison Clements. His message, more like a summons, had awaited them at the front desk telling them where to meet him.

*

At eight o'clock, the couple entered Fabeer's, a restaurant known for fine and leisurely dining. They were shown to Harry's table, to find him alone and sipping Irish whiskey without water or ice or a mixer. As they were being seated, Rachel asked where his wife was tonight.

"She's visiting kinfolks out of town. I must have forgotten to tell you. It will just be the three of us for dinner. I hope you don't mind."

Rachel didn't believe him. She guessed that his wife was at home or he had sent her away. No doubt it was to provide an excuse not to socialize with her and Dan and to prevent the woman from making a slip. "That's a shame, Harry; I was looking forward to seeing her during my visit. Please tell her I inquired about her and shall see her during my next one."

"When will that be?" Harry asked, then sipped his drink.

"I have no idea. I suppose whenever Phillip asks me to come along with him, perhaps during the summer or fall."

The waiter arrived and asked if the couple wanted a drink before ordering dinner. Rachel and Dan didn't glance at each other as they shook their heads, but Harry insisted. "Bring them champagne—your finest, William. This is a celebration. We're here to enjoy ourselves."

Later, as they dined, Harry questioned, "Are you and Phillip doing all right? Are your problems over in Savannah?"

Rachel grasped his meaning and panicked. "Everything is fine, but thank you for your concern." She quickly changed the subject. "When we were visiting with George, he mentioned something I'd never thought about: How did you and Phillip meet, and how did he become your partner?" *Focus the attention on him, Rachel, and off you.*

Harry couldn't hide his surprise at her unexpected queries. "Phillip's never told you?" he asked, stalling.

Rachel laughed and replied, "If he had, I wouldn't be asking you. George said you introduced him to Phillip and helped them become partners. Suddenly I realized I didn't know how you two had met or how my husband had gotten into the arms business, or even when he had done so. Surely there's no reason why I can't be enlightened, is there?"

"Why would there be?" he asked as his answer. "Phillip and I met when I was visiting Charleston in late '72. A mutual friend introduced us, and we liked each other from the start. During a conversation one day, we both discovered we wanted business partners and came to an agreement he would join my firm. After his father and brother died, Phillip wanted to leave Charleston and start fresh in another place. He wanted to get away from all those bad memories and gossip. I suggested Savannah as his new port and introduced him to Milton Baldwin. Milton's shipped for me for years, and he needed a partner just as George and I did. Arms and ammunition go together, and it made a nice circle to have Phillip involved in all three companies. The idea appealed to Phillip, so he joined all of us in early '73. So far everything's worked out well for everybody involved."

Two things stuck in her mind: Philip's brother and Harry's prior relationship with Phillip's shipping partner. Harrison Clements was like a ringleader who had created that little "circle" he used. Once more she realized how little she had known about the man she had married and buried. She echoed, "Brother? I didn't know Phillip had one."

It was Dan's turn to panic. He hadn't thought about either partner knowing about him or knowing people in Charleston. Since Phillip's wife hadn't known about his existence and alleged demise at sea, he had assumed his brother hadn't told anyone about him. Of course this cunning man could have investigated Phillip's history before or after taking him on as his partner. If Harry knew the whole story, he himself was in deep trouble! He waited and listened to see if he would be exposed to her. Since Harry didn't know Phillip was dead, wouldn't he think such revelations might create problems between him and his partner? He recalled that Harry had visited his brother the night before Phillip died and that Harry had a strong reason to be angry with Phillip.

"I can understand why Phillip wouldn't mention his lost brother," Harry said. "It's still much too painful for him, even after all these years."

"But Phillip told you about him," she said in an accusatory tone.

Harry shrugged broad shoulders and responded, "Only once and just a few words, because he knew I knew about him. He was drowned at sea in '72 when his ship went down in a violent gale. Another vessel witnessed the sinking, but couldn't help. The captain and crew didn't get the sails down in time; the waves flipped her on her side, and the weight of the sails and masts dragged her under too fast for rescues. The entire crew was lost."

"They were certain his brother was aboard?"

"No doubt about it at all. The crew registers in port with the ship's company before sailing. His name was on the role and he's never returned."

Rachel observed a look of unconcern and a lack of sympathy about the matter. "How awful for Phillip and his father," she murmured.

Without sensitivity or caution, Harry related, "The worst part was the nasty scandal his brother left behind before he sailed to his doom."

Why, she wondered, was Harry telling her such private and painful things? Was he angry with Phillip and trying to punish him by causing trouble between husband and wife? "What scandal, Harry?" she asked.

The man did not hesitate to answer, "I don't know the details, but it was a nasty triangle between Phillip's father, brother, and a woman they both wanted. The Mc-Candlesses tried to keep it quiet and concealed."

"But Phillip told you about it?" she probed.

"No, James Drake, that mutual friend who introduced us, told me. You're from Charleston, Dan. Did you ever meet James, Phillip, or Mac?"

"Mac?" she echoed.

"Phillip's brother—Mac," Harry clarified. "That's all the name I know."

Dan did not expose his relief. "No, the McCandlesses were gone when I moved there from Alexandria, and I haven't made Drake's acquaintance yet. I'm not in port very much or for very long periods."

"Is that how you met Phillip, when he married your cousin in Savannah?"

Dan put a genial smile on his face as he used his ruse. "That's right, but I've only seen him a few times, and not in a very long while. I docked the afternoon of the day he sailed in the morning. Rachel and I decided that while we were catching up on family and old times, we'd take this trip and have fun. A few more days of relaxation and entertainment, and I'll have my land legs back." Dan was aware that Harry had not asked them if they were having a good time in town or what they had been doing for the last few days. He knew why, because Harry was having them followed. Yet, as clever as Harry seemed, in Dan's eyes that was a reckless oversight. Perhaps the man's second one, since he had searched her room too casually and made no attempt to have it appear a robbery.

Everyone ate in silence for a few minutes as they studied each other.

Rachel worried that if Dan had grown up with Phillip and they had been best friends as he told her, he should have known about this brother and the scandal. Doubts about him returned. He could be one of her enemies after all, and Captain Daniel Slade might not be his real name. Maybe he had come along to investigate the mysterious arms deal for himself or his partners. She would question him later about these inconsistencies. If she didn't ask natural questions, he would be suspicious. No doubt Dan would come up with a cunning way to explain his deceits and she would be compelled to let him do so and pretend to believe him. Again . . .

"So," Harry spoke first, "you two are enjoying yourselves here. That's good. Athens is a nice town and has plenty to offer visitors."

"Yes, it does." Rachel concurred with an amiable smile. "We hired that university student I mentioned to you. He's made a splendid guide. He knows so much about Athens, so our visit has been fascinating."

"I know something you'll enjoy even more than sightseeing; I'm attending a party tomorrow night at the Fabeer's, the people who own this restaurant. I mentioned you were in town, so you two have been invited. It's at eight o'clock; no dinner, but plenty of treats and drinks, and there'll be dancing. Would you like to attend?"

"That sounds marvelous, Harry. Thank you," Rachel accepted for both her and Dan.

"I'll give you the address before we part tonight and see you there. Make certain you save several dances for me, Rachel. With your husband absent, a beautiful woman like you will be popular with the men."

"You're too kind, Harry. Thank you for the compliment."

"I speak the truth," he said, then, changing the subject, added, "The evening will be formal. Did you come prepared for special events?"

"Dan and I are prepared for anything," she said with a false smile.

"Excellent. More champagne?"

Rachel sent forth faked merry laughter. "I fear I've had too much already. If I don't stop now, I'll become all giggly and sleepy."

"What about you, Dan? It's a superb bottle."

"As with Cousin Rachel, I've had my limit, but thank you."

The meal and polite talk went on for a while, then they all departed.

*

Dan asked, at Rachel's door, "What did Harry mean when he asked if you and Phillip were all right and if your problems were over?"

Rachel tensed. "It's a personal matter, if you don't mind."

"Of course. Sorry I intruded. You looked upset, so I was concerned."

"Only because of the curious way Harry mentioned it. He isn't involved in that matter, so he should keep his nose out of it."

"I hope it isn't trouble with Phillip in your marriage."

"Certainly not. We're . . . fine in that area."

"Then I won't mention it again."

"Speaking of not mentioning things, why didn't you tell me about Phillip's brother and that scandal Harry revealed tonight?"

Dan was ready with the response to sate her normal curiosity and to quell her new doubts with part of the truth. "Phillip didn't like to talk or even think about them. When I realized you didn't know either story, I decided it wasn't my place or right to expose them and create problems between you two. Harry shouldn't have betrayed Phillip's confidence. If he was a close and true friend, he wouldn't have."

"Did you know Mac, too?" She witnessed a look of anguish and sadness on his handsome face that appeared sincere and honest.

In a strained voice, he admitted, "Yes, and we were very close. I didn't learn about that ship sinking until after Phillip left Charleston."

"But you said you left in '71 and haven't seen him since then," she pointed out. "So how do you know how he felt about those two matters?"

His gaze fused with hers. "From his letters, Rachel. James Drake was not a friend of ours and he's not a nice fellow. I don't know how or why Phillip got involved with that despicable character after I left town. James and Harry shouldn't gossip about Phillip behind his back, especially to you."

So Phillip had been tormented by wicked gossip, just as she was. That could have been the reason why he was drawn to her and wanted to protect her—kindred spirits of a sort. "I've been wondering why he did."

"It sounded spiteful to me. I think there's a problem between them."

Rachel thought that perhaps the deaths of his father and brother had changed Phillip from the man her companion had known, *if* he had changed. She still couldn't trust him and decided to do some more probing. "Was Phillip ever secretive with you and his other friends? As he was about this new deal, according to his partners?"

"Not exactly. Why?"

"This long trip he's on and this secrecy about his past," she partially invented. "It wasn't like him not to confide in me. He has a surprise in store, but it has me worried. Harry, too, from his behavior and expressions." *Something strange is going on, and it makes me nervous.* "Phillip should have told me everything before he . . . left home."

"I'm sure he'll explain all matters when he returns, so don't fret."

"And if he doesn't?"

"Then it's nothing to worry about, Rachel. Phillip never did anything illegal when I knew him and hasn't mentioned anything like that in his letters to me. He was always too afraid of getting caught and being humiliated to be careless or to break the law."

Phillip a coward? "Explain," she coaxed without a hint of a smile.

"Just teasing. Relax, woman. Everything will be fine soon."

"I hope so. One last question, what was the scandal about?"

Dan exhaled loudly. He frowned. "I don't know if I should—"

"Yes, you're the perfect one to tell me the truth," she interrupted, "and it's past time I knew what made Phillip like he . . . is. His brother drowning at sea explains why Phillip is so terrified of ships and the water. It explains why he suddenly moved to Savannah. We've learned how, why, and when he got into the arms and ammunition business. If you tell me about the scandal in his family, it might clarify other things about Phillip. Please, I need to know. Phillip won't object; I won't tell him."

Dan tried to stall, as he didn't want to delve into Mac's—his—past tonight, particularly that agonizing mistake with his father. He hadn't thought of or been called that nickname in years. He was positive Harry didn't know Captain Daniel Slade was Mac McCandless and he hoped the offensive man didn't do any checking on him anytime soon. "This isn't the place to keep discussing private matters, not in the hall where we can be overheard. I'll relate the story tomorrow as we stroll."

"No, tonight. Come into my room to talk. It shouldn't take long."

"What if somebody sees this improper behavior?" he reasoned.

"We're cousins, family, kin, remember? We'll behave; I swear it."

The chilliness in her gaze and tone warned Dan that her doubts had returned, her confidence and trust in him were shaken, and she was afraid of him. Yet her need to know the truth outweighed the fear of being alone with a possible threat. Her courage impressed him, and matters needed repairing fast. "All right, Rachel. On your terms," he added.

Chapter

10

They sat down in two chairs placed before a window and with a round table between them to form a small sitting area.

Dan tried to relax, but couldn't. His heart raced in dread. He prayed Rachel wouldn't realize he was talking about himself, as he had no choice except to reveal the cruel situation to win back her trust. "This is difficult, Rachel; I was very close to Mac."

Rachel sensed deep anguish that couldn't be an act, and tried to help him begin. "Who was he like, you or Phillip?"

"Me." he murmured, gazing off into space across the room.

"So you two were closer than you and Phillip?" she prompted.

"Much closer."

"What happened?" she coaxed. "Harry hinted at a romantic triangle."

Dan leaned forward, rested his forearms across his thighs, and interlocked his fingers. "Not exactly. In fact, not at all, but that's how it seemed to McCandless. It was a tragic misunderstanding, and it tore that family apart. Stephen—Mr. McCandless—and Mac died before they made peace. It started years ago with a greedy and treacherous woman Mac saw on occasion. Nothing serious, mostly social and physical—if you know what I mean—but she wanted to capture Mac as her husband."

"I understand your meaning. He saw her to satisfy himself physically, but she wanted to snare him as her husband."

"That's the truth, Rachel. All three were wrong, if you ask me."

"Everybody makes mistakes when they're young, Dan. Men do those kinds of things without stopping to think of the consequences. Often a woman agrees to a liaison because she loves a man and thinks he loves her and will eventually marry her when he doesn't have the same feelings or intentions. Sometimes the woman is trying to entrap the man; and sometimes he's only using her and misleading her to get what he wants. Those are cruel and reckless tricks with high prices. So, how did it involve the father and create a scandal? How did it all affect Phillip?"

"I suppose it actually began long before that. You see, Mac and his father never got along; there was always trouble and bad blood between them. Sometimes Phillip was caught in the middle of their disputes. Mac never could please old man McCandless, so he eventually stopped trying. Mac was a sailor for his father's firm, while Phillip did the office work. During one long voyage, that sorry vixen decided that if she couldn't win young McCandless, she would ensnare his father, getting her into their wealthy and well respected family one way or another. While Mac was gone, she became involved with Stephen. But Stephen fell in love with her, wanted to marry her, and didn't know about her relationship with his son. When Mac returned, she gave it one last chance to see if she could win him. Mac wasn't interested, but he'd had a terrible quarrel with his father, so he used her to help him settle down. As you said, that can lead to costly mistakes. Stephen found them in bed together and believed his son was being vindictive by stealing his intended. With their troubled history I can understand how Stephen would feel betrayed, embittered, and spiteful. They had a vicious fight that almost came to blows. Mac returned to sea, but not on one of his father's ships. He signed on with the one that sank, leaving no survivors. Stephen and Phillip got word about the tragedy. I was gone, so I didn't hear the news for a long time. I still can't believe what happened."

"Somehow people found out and gossiped about them?"

"Probably overheard their last quarrel. Stephen broke his betrothal to that selfish witch. I heard she left town and disappeared. I can assure you, Rachel, she was a heartless and conniving female who would do anything to get what she wanted. In Mac's defense, I have to say she had him fooled, too. He honestly believed she wanted the same things from their relationship that he did: a fine time in bed, nothing serious or permanent. And I promise you that isn't a biased opinion."

"So the father and son never made up before they died."

"No, but I'm certain Mac would have settled the matter in time."

"You liked him and trusted him, didn't you?"

"Nobody has ever been closer to me."

"I'm sorry, Dan, but that explains a few things to me."

"About what?" he asked, meeting her comforting gaze.

"About you and Phillip. I can understand why neither of you would want to discuss that painful affair. A lot of people were hurt, and it's terrible that so many have died without making peace. Did it cause trouble between Phillip and his brother when their father made those mistaken accusations against Mac?"

"Yes. At first Phillip was angry and hurt; he didn't know which one to believe. He loved and needed both of them. I tried to tell him Mac's side, but he wouldn't listen; the matter was too fresh. You see, if he sided with Mac, he would lose his father and his inheritance. If he sided with Stephen, he would lose his brother. Phillip never got a chance to make that choice, since Mac got on that ill-fated ship. I don't know what Phillip would have done if Mac had returned from that voyage. I like to think he would have believed Mac and helped him convince Stephen of the truth. Perhaps Phillip feels guilty over both their losses. It's too late for him to ever settle the matter now."

Naturally Rachel thought Dan meant because Stephen and Mac were dead. The unknown truth was that a father and two sons were dead with a bitter tragedy buried with them.

"This news made you mistrust me, didn't it?"

"Yes," she admitted. "What if Harry checks on you and learns we lied to him? That can cause more problems."

"That's the risk I'm willing to take to learn the truth. Even if he discovers I was close to Phillip for years and we aren't cousins, it won't matter soon. Your problem with him won't take much longer to solve." Dan moved before her on his knees. He captured her hands. "I'm your friend, Rachel; you can trust me. Haven't you realized that by now?"

She looked at the ceiling to avoid locking gazes with him, as that always disarmed her. "I want to trust you, Dan."

He wiggled her hands to force her gaze to meet his. "Then why can't you?" he asked. "What have I said or done to make you doubt me? I only kept a secret I didn't think I should reveal, and you suggested the deceits in my cover story. I merely embellished it to prevent doubts in Harry. If I had exposed the truth of us growing up together, Harry would have gotten nervous about our closeness and suspected Phillip sent his old and trusted friend here to investigate him." *And surely would have checked me out!*

"You're right, Dan, but trust is hard for me sometimes. Phillip was the one person I felt I could trust completely, but now I find he deceived me several times."

"Keeping a painful episode in his life from you isn't exactly deceit. I'm sure you'll be told the truth one day."

She freed her hands, and the captain stood. "But there's more, Dan. This trip, this secret deal . . ." She stood, but looked at the floor.

"I'm sure Phillip has good explanations for them," he said, but knew what her real meanings were. Dan grasped her chin, lifted her head, and locked their gazes once more. "Being ignorant of something important has a tendency to make one nervous, even afraid. But I'm here with you."

Rachel needed and wanted him so much, she was tempted to throw herself into his arms, confess all, and surrender to him. "I suppose I'm just tired and being foolish."

"Then get into bed and get some sleep. We'll talk again tomorrow." He bent forward and placed a light kiss upon her lips. "I won't let anything unjust happen to you, Rachel McCandless."

Would you feel that way if you knew the truth? she wanted to shout. Instead, she said, "Thank you, Dan. I don't know what I would do without your help. I'll see you in the morning."

He kissed her again on the forehead as a father would a weary child about to retire. "If you need anything, Rachel, I'm across the hall."

She needed him to hold her, to kiss her, to take her away from this perilous nightmare. The black truth would kill that golden dream. She walked him to the door. Before he opened it, she said his name and he turned. She placed her hands on either side of his bronzed face, pulled his head downward, and gave him a quick and light kiss on the mouth. She gazed into his eyes a moment. "Thank you, Dan. Good night."

"Good night, Rachel." He left, and heard the door lock. He knew he had repaired some of his broken rigging, but not all of it. She was weakening toward him and he could have pressed his advantage with her, but something deep within him hadn't permitted it. It would be wrong and cruel to seduce her tonight. Years ago, he had taken Helen whenever he needed his lust satisfied, but it was different with Rachel. Helen had been eager, willing, persistent, and experienced. With Rachel, there were strong feelings involved, contradictory feelings he didn't quite understand, powerful feelings he couldn't deny or ignore. Despite his fierce battle, she had gotten to him. She had woven her magical spell around him. She had spun her silky strands over his heart and body. She seemed willing to give him a night in her arms, perhaps a few months in her golden web. But could she promise him, or any man, forever? That was a tormenting mystery he had to solve soon, as he couldn't allow his traitorous heart and loins to cloud and overrule his head.

* * *

During the next morning and afternoon, Rachel washed her hair and stayed in her room while it dried. She rested and tried to read, and constantly thought about Daniel Slade, her stormy past, her shadowy present, and her cloudy future.

*

At seven forty-five, Dan knocked on her door to escort her to the Fabeers' party. Rachel put on a sunny smile and cheerful disposition and answered it.

"You look exquisite, Mrs. McCandless," he murmured.

Dan was wearing the same suit he had worn in Augusta, as it was the only formal outfit he had brought on the trip. Rachel was clad in an off-the-shoulder gown in sapphire satin that was edged with black lace and blue silk flowers, as were the short puffy sleeves. A row of black ruched trim journeyed from the neckline, over each breast, and down to the bottom of the first of three layers of her skirt. Her fabric bag matched the gown, as did her silk slippers. Around her neck and on her ears were black pearls, gifts from Phillip. Her dark hair was secured into leafy curls, and received no accessory tonight. A black lace shawl was over one arm.

"Ready on time, Captain Slade."

"How do you do it, woman?"

"Do what?"

"Get more beautiful every day."

Rachel smiled and quipped, "The same way you get more handsome every day, kind sir. Shall we go? We don't want to be late."

*

They reached the Fabeer home, a majestic and enormous Greek Revival mansion with ten Doric columns and a long wing attached on each side near the rear. Fancy gas lamps provided light for guests.

A well-dressed butler escorted them inside the foyer, led them down a hall, and halted them at a columned archway. "Madame, sir, this area is for quiet conversing," he instructed. "Through the arch there is the ballroom for dancing. A small sitting parlor is near the front door. Refreshments are provided in all rooms. The privies are located to the right of the drawing room. If you do not find what you require, tell one of the servants. Your hosts are in the ballroom if you care to greet them first. I will see to your wrap, madame. Have a pleasant evening." He took her shawl, bowed, and left them standing in a large and formal drawing room decorated in the French style.

Women were begowned and bejeweled in their finest, and men were attired formally for the elegant event. "My goodness. This is—"

"Intimidating and impressive," Dan filled in for her with a grin.

She laughed and agreed. "Quite accurate."

Harry came forward. "The first dance is mine, Rachel," he said. "I'm sure your cousin can find a partner. The rooms are filled with ladies eager to be noticed and whirled around the ballroom floor."

Rachel didn't have time to accept or refuse as the man seized her hand and pulled her into the brightly lit room where musicians were playing in one corner. She went into Harrison Clements' coaxing arms and away they danced, her fabric bag swinging from a ribbon tie around one wrist.

Harry looked her over from head to waist. "You look ravishing tonight, Rachel. No woman should be as tempting as you."

She smelled the alcohol on his breath, but knew he was not drunk. "Such flattery from a man can swell a woman's head, Harry. You must be careful with your extravagant compliments, kind sir."

Harry removed some of the distance between them. "It's the truth, my lovely vixen. It seems our mates had a simultaneous need of privacy and diversion. We shall have to keep each other company tonight. Will it be a burden to such a coveted prize as you'll be this evening?"

Rachel played the coquettish southern belle to the height as she laughed once more and murmured, "How could it be?"

"Splendid. I wonder if Phillip McCandless knows how lucky he is."

"I beg your pardon?" she hinted as if confused by his meaning.

"To have such a treasure for a wife," he clarified with a sly grin.

She sent him another false smile, then lowered her voice to a silky whisper as she replied, "I hope he does; but I'm lucky, too, to have him. Phillip is a wonderful and special man, the perfect husband."

"Ah, too bad," he said, then chuckled as if teasing.

Rachel did not appreciate the way Harry was behaving tonight. She did not like Harrison Clements at all. She didn't trust him, and she didn't enjoy the amorous game he was playing. If he was testing a lack of morals, her fidelity to Phillip, the rumors about her, or a possible attraction to him, he would be disappointed in all areas. No matter how much she wanted clues from him, she would never behave the wanton to obtain them. As they danced in silence for a time, she wished she were in Dan's arms. She saw him dancing with a lovely young lady attired in a gown with a soft bustle. The two were laughing and chatting and seemed to be enjoying each other's company. A surge of jealousy and envy shot through her.

"Is there a problem, Rachel?" Harry inquired. "You've tensed."

She met his ice-blue gaze, smiled, and apologized with cleverness and skill, "I'm sorry, Harry. I was thinking about Phillip. Your words reminded me of him, up North and alone, while I'm having such fun."

"Don't worry about Phillip; he always takes care of himself."

"Whatever do you mean?" she asked, feigning an innocent look.

"If there are gambling parlors around, he's being entertained."

There it was again, she fumed, a mention of a weakness for gambling. She laughed merrily. "Phillip McCandless a serious gambler? You jest."

Harry was vexed as he scoffed, "No, I don't. You mean you haven't witnessed how much he loves and how often he engages in that costly sport? But, of course," he added with that sly grin and narrowed gaze, "he wouldn't tell his beloved wife about such a weakness, now would he?"

"Are you serious, Harry? Phillip has a weakness for such things?"

"To the point I worry about it, Rachel."

"Oh, my, I didn't know. That's dreadful, Harry. I must speak to him about it when he returns. It could get out of control if he isn't careful."

"I just hope it hasn't done so already," he murmured as the music halted. "I shall fetch a drink to quench my thirst. I'll see you again soon."

Rachel moved to the side of the dance floor and watched Harry's departure. He held himself rigid, as if angry. It was true she didn't know Phillip loved to gamble, not until George mentioned it earlier. And she fretted over why the important money was missing. Surely Phillip wouldn't . . .

Dan came to join her. "What did he have to say tonight?"

Rachel did not hesitate to expose Harry's curious and bold conduct.

"He's up to no good, Rachel. Be wary of him," Dan warned.

"I know, but why, and why tonight? He's never done this before."

It didn't escape Dan that Harry's wife was called away suddenly and that Harry was making an amorous move toward Rachel. He recalled his wild speculations about a jealous lover or envious male who desired Rachel enough to kill to win her. "When did you meet Harry?" he inquired.

"After Phillip and I were married. Why?"

"I just wonder if he tried to romance you while Phillip was doing the same. That might be what he's up to, trying to romance clues out of you."

"Well, he's wasting his time and energy. It won't work."

"Or maybe he's trying to provoke you into making slips."

"That won't work, either. I don't like that man."

"It doesn't show when you're with him; that takes skill and practice, woman. Why don't we dance before others claim us?"

"I think we should find our host and hostess, meet them, and thank them for our invitation," she suggested.

The Fabeers were nice but showy people, they both decided after the brief encounter, and they were glad when the two were summoned away by friends.

As they danced, Dan said, "He's watching every move you make."

"Who?" she asked, too distracted by being in Dan's arms, one hand on his powerful shoulder and the other clasped within his.

"Harry. He hasn't taken his eyes off of you. I can't blame him. You are the most exquisite creature here."

"Phillip never used such affectionate terms. On whom have you used them, Captain Slade?"

He chuckled. "I haven't used them, but I've heard plenty."

"I see," she murmured with a skeptical tone.

"You don't believe me. You think me a cunning seducer of women?"

"Are you?"

Before he could answer, Harry intruded for another dance, which passed too slowly for Rachel's liking. Afterward, several men requested the "honor" of dancing with her. Five dances went by before Rachel could rest and return to Dan's side. A pretty girl of about eighteen was flirting openly with the dashing sea captain.

"Cousin Dan, I'm exhausted. I have great need of refreshment. Would you two care to join me while I fetch something to quench my thirst?"

Dan introduced the two women, who smiled and spoke politely to each other. "May I bring you something, or would you prefer to come along and select it?"

The girl looked miffed by Rachel's interruption. "Later perhaps."

As they entered the adjoining room where beverages were being served, Rachel whispered, "She didn't like me."

"Who?"

"Your little conquest. She was about to pounce upon you, Dan."

"I would much prefer for . . . What would you like to drink, ma'am?"

"Champagne. Let's have another toast. The other one is old."

Dan ordered two glasses of pale gold liquid. "It's your turn."

"Mmm, let's see . . . How about, to best friends forever?"

"Perfect, if you mean it."

"I do."

He tapped his glass against hers, and they both took sips from their own. "You're having fun tonight?"

"Yes, except the times I have to put up with Harry."

"Speaking of the demon, here he comes again to steal you from me." "I shall save you," he whispered, taking her glass and quickly setting it down to whirl her away before Harry reached them. "See, I told you I would protect you from all evil."

The remainder of the evening passed in delightful moments with Dan, pleasant ones with other notable guests, and distasteful ones with Harry.

At eleven, Dan whispered, "Our hosts are at the door. Why don't we say our thanks and farewells, then sneak out while Harry is fetching another drink? Our carriage is waiting outside."

"That's a grand idea. Lead on, sir. I'm in your care."

They followed his suggestions and returned to the hotel. At Rachel's door, they said good night until morning.

*

The champagne had made Rachel thirsty, but her ewer was empty. She took it to the water closet down the hall to refill it, leaving her door unlocked a short time. When she reentered the room she headed for the other side where the table was located. She had taken only a few steps when a hand clamped over her mouth. Startled, she dropped the pitcher; it shattered and splashed its contents onto her dress.

A chilling voice whispered in her ear, "Do not scream or fight, *Señora* McCandless or this knife will slide into your heart."

Rachel felt the blade tip pressed against her back. She froze in panic.

"This is only a warning for your husband. Tell him not to double cross me or his beautiful wife is dead. He has taken my money, so he must honor our deal. Do you *understand?* Nod your head."

Rachel obeyed, trembling, as her alarm mounted.

"I am going to blindfold you so as you cannot see me when I release you and leave. If you do, *señora*, you must die. *Comprende?*"

Rachel nodded again. She held silent and still as he tied the dark band across her eyes. She was shoved to the floor and ordered not to move for five minutes. She heard the door open and started to yank off the cloth.

"No, no, *señora*, not yet," the icy voice scolded.

Time passed and she detected no noise or presence, but she was afraid to disobey her tormentor in case he was still lurking nearby.

"Rachel, why is your door—" Dan didn't get out *ajar* before he saw the astonishing sight. He rushed to where she lay on the floor, face down, with broken glass and water around her. He helped the shaking woman to a sitting position as he asked her what happened.

He removed her blindfold as she related the terrifying episode. Her frightened gaze locked with his concerned one. "What is this all about, Dan?"

"I don't know, Rachel, but it won't happen again. From now on I'll come inside and search your room every time we return to the hotel. When you're alone, keep that extra bolt pushed into place . . . Are you hurt?"

She looked at her hands and arms. "I don't think so. He must have been hiding beside that chest," she surmised as she motioned to the tall piece of furniture near the door. "When he put that knife to my back, I didn't know what he was going to do as a warning to Phillip."

"Let me see if you're cut back there." As she leaned over, his keen gaze found a prick in the satin between her shoulder blades, but no injury. "Sit in the chair while I pick up this glass."

Rachel watched him gather the broken pieces of the ewer. The rug was soaked, but she would ignore that tonight. It was time to enlighten Dan to a few things, as the incidents were becoming perilous and frequent. "This isn't the first warning I've been given."

He glanced at her. "You're referring to your room being ransacked?"

"No, but that was one of them. That Sunday after I left Milton's office when you visited for the picnic, somebody shot at me on my way home. He followed me to Augusta and my room was searched there, too. His first one wasn't messy like the second one, so he must have been in a rush."

Dan placed the collected shards in the basin until morning. "Why didn't you tell me about these threats?"

Rachel intentionally didn't respond. "He, or somebody else, sent me two notes while we were in Augusta. I don't know if they're connected to this trouble, because they were . . . romantic."

"Romantic? What do you mean?"

Leaving out all hints to her past and reference to the vial of poison, Rachel told him what the messages had said. "I took them as jokes or flirtations."

"Why didn't you give the flower signal to draw out the culprit?"

"I did, but no one responded."

"That was risky to attempt alone. You should have included me."

"I realize that now. I won't take any more chances of getting hurt. I don't think the two matters are related. I believe the two notes were mischievous pranks of somebody in Augusta; I haven't received any here. The other incidents, however, are clearly results of Phillip's mysterious deal. I think it's illegal and that he's gotten involved with unsavory characters."

"You're probably right. The best thing we can do is keep probing Harry for clues, then discuss it with Phillip when we all get home. It sounds to me as if he should return the advance and cancel this contract. No amount of profit is worth these risks. But don't worry, I won't let any harm come to you. I'll deliver you safely back into Phillip's arms."

Rachel shuddered at that horrible thought.

Dan grasped her reaction, but said in a gentle tone, "You're still shaken. Why don't I leave so you can retire? Lock the door after me."

As he headed for it, she halted him. "Dan?"

He halted and faced her. "Yes?"

"How did you find me tonight?"

"I went for a walk and saw your door cracked when I returned." He had done so to release his tension and frustrations, to keep his pleading loins and treacherous heart from ignoring the cautions inside his head.

"Thank you for checking on me and for cleaning up the glass."

He thought of something he had overlooked in his concern. "Did you notice any clues to your attacker's identity? Voice, size, accent, or such?"

"He was about your height and spoke in a whisper, with a Spanish accent, I think; and he used a few Spanish words. We haven't seen or met anyone he reminds me of; if we do, I'll tell you. Thanks again, and good night."

"Good night, Rachel. If you need me for anything . . ."

She smiled. "I know, you're nearby."

*

They attended Sunday services at Athens Baptist Church. After dining at the hotel, Ted Jacobs arrived for their next tour. It was a pleasant day under a clear, sunny sky for their downhill walk on West Broad to Finley Street. Rachel held a parasol and Dan's hand to steady her balance on the steep decline. They soon learned that Ted had not exaggerated. The botanical gardens were still lovely, despite years of little care. The landscaping was magnificent. One of the willows was grown from a cutting from Napoleon's tomb. Other trees, shrubs, plants, and flowers—thousands of varieties and species—had come from all over the world. There was a serene lake and countless walking trails, and all were laid out with skill and beauty. As they strolled through still passable and pretty sections, Ted talked about past and present Athens.

As the vivacious student got a little beyond them on one path, Dan whispered, "Our shadow didn't follow us here. I haven't caught a glimpse of him since the entrance. He's probably hiding there because he knows we'll return by the same route." That was why he hadn't released Rachel's hand and denied himself that pleasure. She must be enjoying their contact, too, because she made no attempt to break his grasp. She appeared to have settled down from her scary experience last night, one that still had him worried and angered.

Ted chatted about his home, the techniques of growing cotton, past days of Old South glory, and the war. He brought Rachel to full alert when he said, "The Yankees confiscated all arms and ammunition; people couldn't even hunt game for food. That's why Mr. Clements's and your husband's firm grew so prosperous and important: Folks had to replace their weapons to hunt and for protection against foraging Yanks."

"In peacetime people don't require many arms or much ammunition. That's wonderful for the South, but less profitable for our company," Rachel commented.

"It's still busy, Mrs. McCandless. I tried to get a job there after classes hauling arms to the train depot, but Mr. Clements already has wagons and drivers he uses. When I pick up passengers, I see their wagons moving all the time to their warehouse at the terminus. They must rail out regularly, because that warehouse can't hold that many long crates."

"I'll put in a good recommendation for you with him, if you'd like," Rachel offered, and Ted thanked her enthusiastically.

Before they reached the last bend in the path and would come into view of their spy, Dan released his hold on her hand. Rachel knew why. They returned to the hotel and after Dan paid and tipped the student and said they'd let him know if he was needed again, bid farewell to Ted.

Rachel and Dan freshened up before eating downstairs, then retired to their rooms, after watching their shadow go off duty for tonight.

*

The next day they had lunch at a cafe, then stopped at the Clements & McCandless Gun Company on Lumpkin Street. They entered the store, which was partly Rachel's now, and were greeted by a friendly clerk.

"What may I show you nice folks today?"

"I'm Rachel McCandless, Phillip's wife, and this is my cousin, Captain Daniel Slade. We are in town on holiday and thought we'd look around in here to see what our store carries."

"Help yourselves, folks. If you need anything, call me for service."

"Thank you, sir," she said to the man who suddenly looked nervous.

As Rachel checked over the weapons, ammunition, and items offered for sale, Dan observed the clerk as he went into a stockroom and spoke with a young boy who left in a hurry by the back door. He joined Rachel and told her the man was no doubt warning Harry about their presence.

In less than twenty minutes, Harry arrived at the store. He looked surprised to see them. "Rachel, Dan, how nice to see you today. I missed your farewells at the dance the other night."

Rachel put on her most ladylike expression. "When we were ready to leave, we didn't see you anywhere to say good night and to thank you for obtaining us that invitation. The evening was splendid."

"What plans do you have for today?"

"Not much. We've stayed so busy that we're taking it easy today. We were strolling and noticed the store so we came in to buy gifts for friends. My manager will love one of those carved and engraved knives. You carry more varied items than I realized. As you know, I didn't see the store when we visited before Christmas. I'm very impressed and pleased."

"Select what you want, then have it placed on Phillip's account."

"How delightful, purchases without payments," she jested.

"I was going to contact you two earlier about joining me for the opera tonight. I've been so busy that I allowed too much time to slip by. I hope it isn't too late. Do you have other plans for this evening?"

"Only for dinner at the hotel. We'd love to join you at the opera. Is that all right, Dan?" she asked her companion.

"Sounds entertaining to me, Cousin Rachel."

"Excellent. I'll pick you up in my carriage at seven-fifteen. The performance begins at eight. That should allow plenty of traveling and seating time. See you later." He spoke to the clerk, then left.

Rachel made several purchases to cover her tale to Harry. Dan did the same with one of the superb knives for Luke Conner.

*

During the evening at the Duepree Opera House very little conversing could take place while listening to one traveling Italian group. That relieved Rachel and Dan, who put on faces of enjoyment.

As Harry dropped them off at the hotel, Dan said, "I want to place an arms order with Phillip's company before I leave. What time is convenient for me to speak with you tomorrow and to sign a contract?"

"One o'clock?"

"Fine, see you then." After Harry rode off, Dan pointed out that Harry didn't seem surprised about his news or ask any questions about the number of rifles he intended to purchase. "That's strange," he observed. "I wonder if George sent word to him about my intention or if he pressed George for information about us."

"How else could he have known you'd do business with him after our arrival? That disappoints me. I was hoping and believing George could be trusted. Ted, too. I pray I'm right about those two."

"I think it's best if we don't trust anybody completely, Rachel. We know it was curious that the clerk summoned Harry as there shouldn't be anything odd about Phillip's wife visiting his store. We must stay alert. We only have a few more days here."

*

Rachel and Dan sat down before Harry's desk, and the part owner of the company relaxed in his chair. She listened and observed as the men talked.

Dan explained his cover story about the imminent conflict in and around Turkey and why he was purchasing the arms. He related his order for ammunition from George Leathers in Augusta, with a delivery date to Savannah of May fourteenth.

"How close to buying three thousand weapons can I come with a hundred thousand dollars? I have the full payment with me, so you'll get the money in advance. How soon can they be ready?" Dan told Harry he wanted the lever-action repeater with the tube loader through the butt, and gave the cartridge size of a center-fire shell he had ordered.

Harry was surprised and pleased. "That's a big purchase, Dan. I received a telegram from George on Saturday about your order from him and impending one from me, but he didn't reveal it was this large. Since you hadn't mentioned it to me yet, I thought you'd changed your mind about using us. Can you get it cleared through customs in Savannah?"

"I already have a letter of permission," Dan lied, "so no problem there. I also want gunsights and slings on them."

As Harry did figuring on paper at his desk, Rachel concluded George had not alerted Harry of their arrival, so Harry's astonishment had been real. Perhaps after spending time on Tuesday and Friday with her and Dan, Harry had telegraphed George for information about their Augusta visit. George must not have told Harry anything intimidating, considering his amorous behavior Saturday night. As they had played their holiday ruse well, Harry should be fooled about her motives for coming to see him.

Harry looked at Dan. "I can let you have 2,860 rifles with attachments for that amount. They can be in Savannah by May twenty-fourth. How does that suit you and your schedule?"

"Perfect. I was impressed by that rifle you showed us the other day. I'm certain the soldiers will be more than satisfied with that model. I'll keep one for myself and give a few to my men."

"It's a good choice, Dan, and a dependable weapon."

"Won't that interfere with our deadline for that big order Phillip obtained?" Rachel inquired. "How can you make that many in such a short time?"

"Ten thousand rifles doesn't take forever to construct, Rachel. I already have the dynamite ordered. It should arrive soon. The entire order will reach the port there on time as promised, as will Dan's."

Rachel struggled to hide her astonishment at those revelations. "Dynamite? From you? Why not through George?"

"We hope George doesn't find out about that part of our joint deal," Harry continued. "Phillip wanted me to order it elsewhere, because it was cheaper than their Augusta company could make, and our Athens company profit will be higher. Of course, everything depends on Phillip getting the money to me soon, at least the advance for half of it. A five-hundred-thousand-dollar order that goes wrong could ruin us. That's a lot of weapons to lie around long."

"Five hundred thousand dollars? That certainly is a large deal, especially when added to the matching one with George. My goodness, a million-dollar purchase!"

Harry's frosty blue gaze narrowed. "Phillip didn't tell you? I assumed you knew after what you said earlier." He frowned when she shook her head. "He didn't give you the details, but I guess it doesn't matter if I do. We're getting three hundred thousand for arms and two hundred thousand for dynamite, gunsights, and slings. By the time Phillip collects his share of our profits here and his share from George's order, he'll make a tidy earning on one deal. Before long, you'll have a lot of money to spend. I'm delighted he obtained that contract, but I can't do much more about it until I get the advance. Partner or not, I can't take risks like that. He should have let you and Dan bring the money to me, or brought it himself before he left town for so long. It puts me and our company in a financial bind. I don't like doing business this way, but Phillip assured me nothing can go wrong at this point."

"Why didn't you collect the money when you visited him?"

"He had a silly excuse about wanting to deliver the advances to me and George on that following Monday," Harry scoffed. "I hope nothing's happened and that isn't where he's really gone, to repair the damage. I must say, George is worried, too. We both have our necks out on this deal."

"Because Phillip backed out of it once before, you're afraid he'll do so again?" she ventured.

"Yes, and that was foolish. You can't sign a contract, take five-hundred-thousand dollars in advance, then cancel the deal. That's bad business. When he balked in late February, I was worried. But after a serious talk with him during my visit he told me and George to get on with the orders."

Rachel realized the two partners had restarted the orders the day Phillip had died and that both could be ruined if that deal didn't take place, a deal her husband had wanted terminated.

"I can't deliver arms and George can't deliver ammunition on May fourteenth if we don't get the advance first. The client could take possession, then not pay the balance. I don't even want to think about that."

Rachel tried to appear calm. "I'm sure that won't happen, Harry; Phillip wouldn't allow it to fail. Who is this rich and important client?"

"I don't know, and that worries me. Phillip said it was confidential and that he would assume full responsibility for all facets of the deal. He took the order, he's to deliver it on one of his ships, and he's collecting the money. Are you sure you don't know where I can reach him?"

Rachel didn't believe Harry was that uninformed about business so vital. "I'm sorry, Harry, but he's out of touch. I'm sure nothing will go wrong. If Phillip doesn't return by the fourteenth of next month, surely the client will come to the house to check on his late order. If that happens, I'll contact you and we'll handle the final details. We certainly don't want to jeopardize a deal of this size, or risk damaging the companies. If Phillip doesn't return on schedule, I'll help out any way I can."

"Why wouldn't he return on time?" Harry asked.

Rachel shrugged her shoulders. "Storms at sea, sudden illness, or a problem on the ship could slow him," she speculated. "I doubt any of that will happen, but I'll keep alert for a problem and for our client's arrival."

"That still doesn't account for the unpaid advances, Rachel—a half a million dollars," Harry retorted. "As soon as Phillip contacts you, ask him where it is, then hire a guard to deliver it to me and George."

"Perhaps Milton can give us the client's name and location. Since Phillip is using one of their ships, it's probably recorded in their books."

"It isn't, because I've already telegraphed Milton for assistance and he says he doesn't know anything about it. I don't like the way matters are going and I don't like being kept in the dark. Phillip shouldn't have left at this time or withheld those advances. I hope nothing's happened to them, because I don't know how he could repay that much out of his pocket. We'd appreciate any help you can give us, Rachel, to carry out this deal. You can begin by locating that money and getting it to us fast. If we fail, everybody is out of a big profit and we can all lose our shares of the companies."

Rachel knew those warnings were true; and it sounded as if Harry was directing them straight at her, not as messages to relay to Phillip. She'd examined the Savannah firm's books to find no shipping schedule for the order or for that date, as Milton had claimed. She possessed no client's name, no destination, and no advance, yet, a million dollar order and the companies' survivals were at stake, and maybe hers, too . . .

"Do you mind if I see the company books while I'm here?" she asked. "I can give Phillip a report about how much that advance is needed."

"He's already received a financial report, Rachel, so he knows the condition of the company. Besides, I couldn't allow anyone to study them without a letter of approval from Phillip, not even his wife."

She faked a smile. "I understand. It is not a problem. I would like to see the warehouse at the depot; it's the only part of the company I haven't visited."

Harry shook his head of flaxen hair. "That would be a waste of time, Rachel. It's just a big, empty, and dusty storage building."

"You're right; I wouldn't want to get filthy seeing nothing. We'll be returning home early Thursday morning, so I doubt we'll see you again during this visit. I want to thank you for those lovely evenings."

"You're welcome. Just tell Phillip I need word from him immediately."

"I will, Harry, but don't worry; I'm sure this delay isn't serious."

"It had better not be," Harry said with barely suppressed anger.

*

"So, what do you think, Rachel?" Dan asked.

"I don't know, Dan. That mysterious deal has everyone crazy."

"Phillip will settle them down after he returns."

"Harry and George are right to worry; I'm worried, too. Something about this deal, the money, and Phillip's sudden . . . departure is strange."

Dan pretended not to notice her near slip. "You aren't suggesting Phillip stole the advance and ran off with it?"

"Of course not. He would never leave me behind."

To get closer to her, Dan sounded skeptical as he remarked, "I hope not, Rachel, because as Phillip's wife and heir, you'd have plenty of enemies after you for their payments or goods. You don't suppose Phillip's been paid the entire million dollars, do you?"

She hoped and prayed not. "I honestly don't know, Dan. The more I hear and see, the more I'm baffled."

"Stars above, Rachel, there's no telling what they would do for that amount if someone took it from them. Money can make murderers of some men. Don't forget, you've already been threatened several times."

"If Phillip didn't return, do you think I'd be in greater peril?"

If she were terrified, she might turn more to him, so he said, "Damn right I do. It's a good thing I'll be around to protect you until this mystery is solved. I have to stay in Savannah until after the twenty-fourth when my guns arrive. By then we'll know if there's trouble in the wind for you. I won't sail until I know for certain you're safe."

"Thank you, Dan. You're the best friend I have." She hesitated, then entreated, "May I ask you one other thing?" He nodded. "Was Phillip a big gambler like George and Harry implied? Do you think he could bet with another man's money? Gamble enough to possibly lose that advance?"

Dan gave serious consideration to her question. "Not the Phillip I knew. But we've been separated for years, Rachel, so I can't answer for certain. You've never picked up any clues about him having such a weakness?"

"No, never." She closed her eyes and murmured, "I pray it isn't true."

Dan sent up that same prayer, but he replied with half-truths and clever guile. "Maybe there's a good explanation for Phillip's actions. Maybe he hasn't given them the advances because he doesn't trust them fully. Maybe his trip is his way of avoiding them so he can hold on to the money until the last minute. If they drew him into their companies in '73 with lies about their conditions, then claimed slacked-off trade to cover those deceptions, Phillip may just want to handle this deal himself, protect and take his profit, then sell out like he told you."

"Do you think, when Phillip backed out in February, it angered Harry or George —or both—or the client so much that one or all of them were behind the incidents I mentioned to you, sort of as warnings to get it started again?" When he looked confused, she clarified. "You remember, the ship that was destroyed, the warehouse that was vandalized, the two seamen who were beaten, and the dockworker who was killed?" He nodded again, and she continued. "The shipping firm had to compensate those clients and families, so it cost Phillip and Milton a lot of money, and Milton wasn't happy about it. You don't suppose Phillip felt responsible or felt his client was guilty so he used the advance to cover those payments, do you?"

Dan was impressed by her intelligence and her reasoning powers. "I don't know what to think at this point, Rachel. Let's wait until we return home and ask Phillip for answers before we jump into the wrong ocean looking for them ourselves." Dan stretched and yawned. "It's late and we're tired, so I'll see you in the morning. Get some rest and sleep."

Dan needed to check out a suspicion fast. The more he learned, the more confused he became. He was having strong feelings that this mysterious deal could have something to do with his brother's death and that Rachel McCandless might be innocent.

*

By the next evening, their last one in Athens, Rachel and Dan hadn't seen much of each other. He had gone to the telegraph office across the street to send cables to Burke and to Luke telling of their arrival schedule for pickups at the railroad station in Savannah on Friday.

Rachel had a lot of packing to do and stayed in her room most of the afternoon, sorting and folding items. At seven, after a light meal taken in the room, someone knocked on her door. Rachel hoped it wasn't Harry and was tempted not to respond. Besides, she couldn't see him or anyone, as she was wearing only her red silk nightgown. "Who is it?"

"It's Dan, Rachel; I need to speak privately with you. Now."

She hesitated as she looked down at her scanty attire. It was reckless, but she called back, "Just a moment, Dan; I'm not dressed." She pulled a concealing housecoat over the gown, secured the belt snugly, and answered the door. To keep out of sight of a guest who might be passing by, she stood behind the door as she allowed him to enter. She closed and bolted the lock. "What is it? A problem?"

Dan stared at her with mouth agape and blue eyes wide. He had seen edges of red silk near her ankles and knew what she was wearing beneath that shorter robe, and remembered all too well how it looked on her.

Rachel flushed and murmured, "I told you I wasn't dressed properly, but your voice sounded as if it was important?"

"I sneaked to the depot warehouse last night. That storage building was filled with crates, oblong, rifle-size. Harry lied to us."

"Why did you take such a risk? Harry is dangerous."

"Because I knew that if he had lied, he would rush to move them in case you sneaked a peek inside as we were leaving in the morning. I went back just now, and he does have men moving them to another building. If something deceitful isn't going on, he wouldn't take that action."

"What shall we do about it?"

Dan used the best words he could think of to give her an opportunity to confess everything to him. "Nothing this trip. We'll report it to Phillip when he returns. Let him investigate and discover what's going on. Don't get more involved, Rachel; you've had tastes of how dangerous this matter is. Phillip shouldn't have sent you here to nose around, and I think that was a devious story he told you. I think he was hoping, with your wits, you'd stumble across something he wants to learn. Frankly, I'm disappointed and annoyed with him for placing you in peril."

"I'm sure it wasn't intentional, Dan. Surely Phillip wouldn't endanger me. I'll go home and try to solve the matter from there."

Rachel was convinced Dan wasn't a threat to her. He was too caring, helpful, and protective to be wicked. He had become a good and close friend. They worked well together. She was heading home to face her other problem, one that could destroy her budding relationship with Daniel Slade. She could lose him before she could win him.

Dan could not resist her allure. He pulled her into his arms and lowered his mouth to hers. She did not resist him, but responded with mutual desire and eagerness. His mouth feasted on hers, then left to trek over her face, to press his lips against each feature.

Fires leapt within Rachel's body, powerful and unfamiliar ones. Her heart raced. Her breathing changed to short and shallow gasps between heady kisses and a fierce hunger chewed at her core and urged her to feed it.

A matching hunger gnawed at him. Dan's body felt hot and shaky all over as it reacted to her intense response.

What will he think of me if I surrender to him while he believes Phillip is alive? Rachel suddenly wondered. *After he hears the awful rumors about me, will he think I yielded to ensnare him as my next "victim"?* She told herself she should wait until after he knew the truth. If he wasn't genuine and he spurned her, it would be better for her if she never learned what it was like to have him only to lose him. In a near breathless whisper as his teeth nibbled at one ear, she said, "We mustn't, Dan, not yet, not tonight."

He felt her stiffen and heard her words. He looked into her flushed face and tormented eyes and he took a deep breath to steady himself. "I'm sorry, Rachel, but I just can't seem to resist you. I've never met a woman like you. Stars above, I wish you weren't taken!"

In a ragged voice, she confessed, "I've never met a man like you, Daniel Slade. I've never felt this way before, and it scares me."

"Not even with Phillip?"

She lowered her lashes as if ashamed to admit the truth. "No, and that troubles me. We must fight this attraction for each other, at least for the present."

"We've been trying hard to do that, Rachel, but it's there. We both felt this pull between us the first time we met and it gets stronger each day."

"I know, I shouldn't have brought you on this trip with me."

His hand lifted her chin to lock their revealing gazes. "That wouldn't have changed our feelings. You needed me here. You wanted me here."

"Yes, but it isn't right. Not now, not yet. Soon, when things are different, we can test these feelings and decide what to do about them."

"This might be the only time we have together, Rachel, but I would never force myself on you or beguile you into surrender."

She craved him so much that she panicked. "It's too late for us, Dan." He wouldn't believe her or trust her again after her impending exposures.

"It's too hard to resist you, woman, and impossible to reject you."

"Give us more time, until everything's settled after our return."

"What if it isn't settled like we want it to be? We have a serious decision to make. I want you, if only once before we're forced to part."

Her heart fluttered in suspense and she wondered, *What decision?*

"I know it's wrong and cruel to pursue another man's wife, especially when that man is so close to me. But our relationship is real and it's right. No two people are more suited to each other than we are. Phillip will have to understand and accept that reality, accept your loss. We didn't set out for this to happen, but it has. You feel the same way about me, don't you?"

To Rachel, it sounded as if he was referring to more than a casual relationship, to more than enjoying stolen moments for a short time. There was only one reason why Phillip would have to accept her loss, and that was so he could win her. With courage and boldness, she replied, "Yes, Dan, I need you. But I don't want to make a mistake and get hurt again. After everything is revealed, you might not want me anymore."

He did not probe her hint on purpose, not tonight. "I will never betray you or desert you, Rachel, no matter what. I'll accept as much or as little of you as I can have, for as long as I can. Is that being selfish?"

Lost in the swirling depths of his ocean-blue gaze, she murmured, "No, Dan, it isn't; and I feel the same way."

As Dan's mouth covered Rachel's, each knew it was too late to prevent what must and would happen between them tonight.

D an doused all lamps except one, which he lowered to a soft glow. He flung aside
the covers of the bed, removed his boots, then his shirt. He looked at Rachel, who
hadn't moved or spoken during his actions. He studied the luminous eyes demurely
glued to his bare chest. She appeared unsure of herself, as if she weren't familiar with
an intimate situation. She had been married three times, so she couldn't be a nervous
virgin. She looked so delicate, so graceful, so enchanting. He was mesmerized by her
potent allure.

He admitted that Rachel McCandless had stolen his mind, his heart. She moved
him in strange and powerful ways. He neither totally distrusted or believed her. He
knew he should resist her, but wanted to surrender to her. He yearned to comfort and
protect her, but feared he must punish her. He longed for her to be innocent, but
wasn't convinced she was. The contradiction of emotions and thoughts was eating at
him. He felt in control of his ruse, but out of control of himself. If circumstances were
different, he would be wooing her. He had never met a woman who intrigued and
bewitched him like she did.

Rachel watched Dan's movements with panic. Love and desire—what did she
really know about such emotions? No man had ever made her feel warm and tingly and
helpless inside. She had never lost herself in the smoldering depths of any manly eyes or
experienced the overwhelming urge to boldly fondle a virile chest or to surrender
wantonly to any man. Surely love and passion were unique and all-consuming, and she
did love and desire Daniel Slade beyond reason or will to resist.

Dan wondered how she had the power to make him ignore all else except his
yearning for her. "Come to me, love," he murmured. He did not have to ask twice or
rush to her side to guilefully seduce her.

Rachel obeyed his husky enticement. He gently grasped her chin and pulled it
toward his to seal their lips in a heady kiss. He was too near and too compelling to
refuse. There could be so little time left to explore their feelings and to strengthen their
bond. Her heart rebelled against the possible loss of him. His embrace was strong and
comforting. His mouth left hers to nuzzle his chin against her hair. His lips claimed
hers with hunger and possessiveness; they burned those sweet and forbidden messages
across her unsteady senses and hazy brain.

A dizzying sense of power and unruly desire coursed through Dan's body and
mind. His passions soared at her touch. She was warm, willing, and bewitching. Her

allure was too powerful to resist. His mouth sought hers in an exploratory kiss. He was trapped in a world of fiery need and didn't want to seek freedom, not now, not ever.

Yet Dan perceived a tension and uncertainty in her. He leaned back and gazed into her beckoning eyes of melting honey. He observed the ever-changing emotions which flickered in them. A tug of tenderness suffused his taut body. He saw that she was afraid and doubtful.

Rachel's gaze traveled each line of Dan's handsome face. He was the most striking man she had ever seen. She had never imagined any male could be so devastatingly magnificent, so overpoweringly attractive. His kisses were so insistent, so demanding, so persuasive, so wit-stealing. It alarmed her to be like soft clay in his hands, ready and willing to be molded into any shape he wanted.

Dan pushed a lock of darkest brown from her face. His eyes roamed the olive surface of satiny smoothness. He worried when she lowered her head and gaze. Something told him she was a rare gem ready to be cut into a valuable and precious stone by the right craftsman. He savored the heady task before him. "Don't be afraid of me, Rachel, I would never hurt you. Look at me, love."

All of Rachel but her eyes responded to his tender and coaxing voice. She fretted that she wouldn't know how to respond correctly, how to pleasure him, how not to disappoint him. What if the act wasn't like the blissful preludes? What if she froze up as with Phillip? What if it hurt or became rough as with Craig?

When she married Craig Newman, she hadn't even considered the conjugal bed. Lordy, how naive and innocent she had been! He had taken her without gentleness or romantic inducements. When he discovered she was a virgin, he had joked about William Barlow denying himself of her treats. After that horrible first night, he had taken her only three more times during their four months of wedlock. Each had been swift and rough, as if he was trying to hurt her.

With Phillip, it had been different. He had shown her sex didn't have to hurt or humiliate, and had been furious with Craig for ravishing her so uncaringly. Even so, she hadn't been able to relax and enjoy the act as Phillip urged her. Because he knew she didn't care for the physical intimacy, he had initiated it only a few times during their eight months of marriage, while hoping it would change one day.

Now she was facing a new challenge. The difference this time was that she wanted this man. She met his gaze.

Dan read her anxiety, and dreaded a last-minute withdrawal. "Relax, love," he coaxed, "This isn't an unpleasant chore to be done quickly and gotten over with. Yield completely to the waves of ecstasy," he entreated hoarsely. He knew he must use all his talents to rekindle the heated response she had felt earlier. His head lowered once more and his tongue deftly plundered her mouth. His masterful lips seemed to brand her mouth, cheeks, and throat—every inch of her face and neck. All restraint left her as he guided her toward total submission. Flames of passion leapt and burned rampantly within her. She wanted and needed this to happen, and tonight.

Dan trailed his tongue over her parted lips, nibbled at them with his teeth, then tasted the sweetness of her mouth again. His hands untied the sash at her waist. He eased the robe from her shoulders and let it fall to the floor. His lips trekked over the flesh he had bared. His fingers quivered as they moved under the straps of her red gown and slipped it off her shoulders. The material flowed down her shapely body to expose skin that was even silkier than the garment. With leisure and delight, his hands caressed and fondled and stroked the areas he had exposed to them. He set out to tantalize, stimulate, and pleasure her.

His mellow tone whispered soft and stirring words into her ears. She trembled within his grasp. His embrace was blissful, and his romantic onslaught was captivating. A curious mingling of languor and tension surged through her. Her mind was rapturously dazed by a fierce longing for him and she never wanted those breathtaking sensations to halt.

Dan lifted her naked body and placed her on the bed. Quickly he discarded the remainder of his garments, as he didn't want any of those flames he had lit and fanned to go out or burn low. He joined her and pulled her into his arms. His mouth covered hers.

Rachel cast her inhibitions and doubts aside. She stroked the virile body touching hers. Its strength and beauty titillated her senses. His hands, calloused from hard and steady labor, did not hurt her. They were strong and skilled hands, gentle ones. From his sable hair to his firm middle to his warm feet, Daniel Slade was appealing. His actions were slow and deliberate, as if he were memorizing every inch of her body and attempting to enflame every part of it. Never had her breasts been sensitive to a man's touch, pleading to be caressed and kissed. Her body and mind throbbed with need.

Dan groaned as his own desires burned wildly with the urge to consume her. She was like a drug, powerful and addictive.

As Dan's head drifted down her throat and his lips worked at her breasts, Rachel watched him in the glow of the lamplight. Her tension was heavily laced with anticipation, but she wasn't sure of what. She was eager to explore the mysteries of love and sensuality with him. Her hands played in his midnight hair and stroked his bronzed body. She enjoyed the way his muscles moved beneath her fingers. When Dan's face returned to hers, she murmured, "I don't know what to do, so you'll have to tell me or show me."

That confession—honest from her golden brown gaze—surprised and confused him. "Are you sure you want to do this, love?"

Her voice was constricted by desire as she replied, "Yes."

His fingers caressed her flushed cheek. "All you have to do tonight is relax and enjoy yourself," he told her. "Do whatever seems natural or pleasing. There's plenty of time to teach you anything you don't know."

Without shame or reservation, Rachel beseeched, "Teach me all, Dan, tonight; I want to experience every sensation and emotion with you."

That plea captivated and thrilled him. Confident in his prowess, he vowed, "You will, Rachel, tonight and forever. There's no need to rush. We belong together." Dan was perceptive to her desires and insecurities. As his mouth roved hers, his fingers drifted into her dark hair and played in its silky fullness.

Their tongues touched, teased, and savored. Their hands caressed, stimulated, and enticed. Their bodies demanded closer and more intimate contact. Tonight, there was no turning back. They would delve into the magic that enchanted and united them. They would be anchored together in heart and flesh.

Rachel was nervous about her lack of skill, but Dan was being patient and gentle and stirring. His broad shoulders were followed by a flat waist and narrow hips that extended into long and supple legs to form a splendid physique and she responded to and devoured every kiss and caress, every unspoken promise of what was yet to come. Her hands roamed his neck and shoulders. Her fingers played in the black curls on his muscled chest, then traveled his hard back of rippling hills and satiny planes. The bud of her womanhood came alive and tingled with previously unknown pleasure as he stroked it. Her pulse raced and her breathing labored. Every spot he touched was responsive. She knew why she had never felt this way before. Love made the difference; she loved and desired Captain Daniel Slade!

Dan had difficulty breathing, thinking, and mastering his cravings. He felt as heavy as a rock, but as light as a feather. The range of emotions he experienced astonished him. When his lips and hands aroused her to writhing and coaxings, he parted her thighs and entered her as he murmured, "Ride with me, my love. Capture me and hold me tightly. Be mine, now and forever." As she did as he entreated, her exotic scent called out to him even more than that of seaspray. She intoxicated him more than strong whiskey could, a thousand barrels of it.

Rachel tensed, inhaled, and panicked for a moment when his manhood slipped within her, but she instinctively arched to meet him. As he entered and withdrew many times, she was astounded by how wonderful it felt. The hair on his chest stimulated the peaks on her breasts. His mouth held hers captive. A curious tension built within her, slowly at first, then rapidly. She clung to him and responded in the ways he whispered into her ear. She was being fed a delicious meal yet her hunger increased and her tension mounted, and she didn't know why.

Dan moved with caution and gentleness, but he didn't know how much longer he could keep control. He had delivered women into the throes of passion before, but none had ever responded this way or ever affected him like this. His rhythmic strokes were sending her along an upward spiral, but he was climbing just as fast as she was. He took her with an intensity and hunger that were new and stirring, with tantalizing leisure that erupted into a turbulent fervor. He scaled heights he had never reached before. He couldn't understand why she knew so little about the act of love, yet he sensed that was true. She caught his pattern and tried to match it, but it was an instinctive reaction.

Rachel was swept away in a flood of ecstasy. She inhaled sharply several times and stiffened and clung to him. She moaned as her first climax seized her and carried her away. "O-o-o-h, my, what's . . . ha-pen-ning? O-o-o-oh . . . O-o-o-oh . . . Oh, Dan . . . This is wonderful. I never . . . knew—" Her breath caught in her throat as the powerful sensations assailed her body and stole it.

Control deserted Dan as she moaned, writhed, and clung to him; and the truth of the thrilling matter reached his mind. Wave after wave crashed over his fiery body. He allowed the raging storm to carry him away with her. As overwhelming spasms conquered the woman beneath him, his molten juices mingled with hers. His release spilled forth joyously. He plundered her mouth and womanhood until every ounce of need was sated. The release was powerful and stunning; he trembled from the force of it. Unknown satisfaction and unfamiliar contentment engulfed him.

A golden aftermath seemed to glow in the room and within them. She lay in his arms, as breathless and tranquil as he.

As Dan trailed kisses and strokes over her flushed face and body, Rachel was calmed by the tenderness and gentleness of them. Surely he wanted her as much as she did him. Surely everything would be all right when he discovered the truth. Surely nothing this powerful and special could be destroyed. "I've never felt anything like that before."

"I know, love, and I'm glad you found it first with me."

"Is that how it's always supposed to be?"

"Yes, but it only happens between certain people."

"People who . . . desire each other as much as we do?"

"Yes, Rachel." He sensed a vulnerability in her. He cuddled her. Maybe he had found the missing piece to the puzzle of Rachel McCandless: no man had ever captured her heart or won her surrender. She had not given herself to any of the three men she had wed, and buried. That meant she must feel differently about him. If that was so, she surely wouldn't try to murder him after he tricked her into marriage. If he had won her heart and changed her, though, he might never learn the truth . . . If she did suffer from a form of mental disease and she couldn't help herself. . . .

"I never expected anyone like you to come into my life, Captain Daniel Slade. I hope you don't sail out of it for a very long time."

He knew why she was worried and afraid, and he was, too. He didn't know if his reply was the truth. "I won't, Rachel," he said. "I swear."

She closed her eyes and prayed it was true. Monday would tell her if it was or wasn't. Even if it was, it might not make a difference when . . .

*

Rachel and Dan left Athens on the Georgia Railroad train. They did not peek into the company warehouse so the man watching them would have good news to report to Harrison Clements. They surmised the crates would be replaced as soon as they departed.

They sat side by side, but played their kinship roles with perfection to fool a possible spy Harry had put on the train. It was wonderful being together, even if they couldn't touch and had to battle with their eyes to keep their gazes off each other. After the passionate and blissful night they had shared, each felt more confident about the other's feelings. Each knew what was facing them soon, but they ignored that problem for now.

The train halted at Union Point for a lengthy stop, and they had lunch there again and another peaceful stroll. It continued on to Augusta, following those same numerous stops in small towns and at water tanks.

They dined and spent the night at the Planter's Hotel, but did so in separate rooms in case anyone was spying on them and because people there knew them as cousins. If Harry and George were in cahoots, George could be having them watched at this point. Or one of the travelers who had gotten off the train and registered here could be Harry's hireling. It was best not to let either partner discover how close they were, not yet.

Dan had wanted to request the same rooms they had occupied before, but he couldn't without revealing knowledge of the secret passage between them. It wouldn't be wise to spark doubts in her, not when their relationship was so new and fragile. He, like Rachel, had to be content to gaze at the three photographs taken during their visit here and yearn for their second union.

After an early and quick breakfast, they went to the station and this time boarded the Central Georgia Railroad. During the last leg of their adventurous trek, they whispered and made plans.

"If Phillip has returned home, send me a message," the cunning Dan advised. "I'll come out to speak with him about our business. I won't cause you any problem if you decide you want to stay with him instead of me."

Rachel's heart pounded in dread before he could finish. When he did, she was relieved and ecstatic, which showed in her honey-colored eyes.

He said what he knew she needed to hear, "If you choose him out of some sense of loyalty and conscience, I'd be tempted to battle for you, but that would be destructive to all of us. Please, Rachel, don't take him over me for those reasons. I'll make you happy, and you'll never be sorry."

Her reply was curious. "I can't see you this weekend, Dan, even if Phillip isn't home. We must be careful until our problem is resolved. I have to come into town Monday morning to handle pressing business, so I'll meet with you afterward. Then we'll have our serious talk, I promise. After you hear what I have to say, you can tell me if it changes your feelings."

Dan comprehended what she had to do—see the authorities about his brother's death and secret burial, then confess everything to him. After she did those two things, he would know at last what to do about her. If she deceived him again or failed to make a full confession, he would know he couldn't trust her and he must proceed with his original plan of exposing and punishing her. "I'll check on my ship and crew while I'm waiting to see you. You're mine now, Rachel McCandless. Don't forget that for a minute."

"I hope so, Dan. I can hardly wait until we're alone again Monday. It seems like the end of time, but it's only a couple of days. No matter what happens after our return, I do want you, I swear it."

They reached Central Station in Savannah at four o'clock. Burke Wells and Lula Mae Morris were waiting in a carriage for Rachel, and Luke Conner was standing on the boarding platform waiting for Dan. "We'll get off separately and not speak here," Dan instructed. "We don't want your servants or any observers to know we've been traveling together. Until Monday, my love."

"Until Monday, Dan." She gazed at him as if dreading to part, as if she feared it would be their last time together.

Dan understood and sent her a smile of encouragement and support. "Don't worry, Rachel, everything will be all right. We'll be together soon."

"I hope so, Daniel Slade," she whispered, then left her seat and the train to join Lula Mae and Burke. As she did so, she glanced at Luke Conner, Dan's first mate and close friend. They exchanged smiles, and she wondered how much he knew about her, about them. *What if he's heard the false gossip about me and he tells Dan?* she fretted. Yet she detected no repulsion or anger in his sparkly blue gaze. *Please, God,* she prayed, *don't let them hear the ugly rumors until I can explain them to Dan.*

Rachel smiled at the black manager as he met her. "I'm afraid I have more baggage than I left with, Burke, but some are gifts for all of you. The porter will help you with my trunks and packages."

"You be too kind, Miz Rachel. I'll fetch 'em fur you."

The housekeeper smiled and greeted her warmly, but didn't ask questions.

*

At home, Lula Mae said, "We been missing you more 'an a starving man misses a good meal. You rest them weary bones a spell. I'm fixin' your most favorite supper. And thank you for my presents. You've always been a kind girl with sweet thinking and a good heart. How dids the trip pass?"

"Phillip's partners were nice to me, but neither will be pleased by the telegrams I send them Monday after I visit Chief Anderson. I didn't tell them Phillip was dead; I just weaseled information out of them."

"They bounds to be hopping mad when they hears Mr. Phillip be gone to heaven. They'll be all over you like insects in August to buys out them cumpnies. Men don't wants no woman partner. You oughta sells them fast. After you tawks to the law Monday, it's bound to be bad off for a spell."

"I know, Lula Mae, and I dread it but I can't wait any longer. I can't do anything with the three companies until I report Phillip's death."

"When it's done and over with, why don't you go visit you ma for a spell and git away from this sad house and mean town? Folks gonna be at your neck again, trying to strangle the life from you."

"No, I can't. Earl's there. I never want to see him again."

Lula Mae came to Rachel and placed a hand on her shoulder. "When times are most awful, a girl needs her ma. This trouble's been eating at you since you left home. Makes peace with her, Miss Rachel."

"I told you why I can't go home, Lula Mae. He's terrible and wicked."

"Why don't you write your ma and aks when he's gonna be gone away on business?" the housekeeper suggested.

"Earl might find out I'm there and return before I leave. I hate him."

"I'll goes with you and protect you. I won't let him or no man hurt you again. I know you don't like him, but you need your ma and I'm a betting she needs you. It jest ain't right to be living like this."

"You're right, Lula Mae, but that isn't my fault. Mama chose him, and that choice drove her children away. She's the one who has to make peace with us. She won't do that if it means losing that vile husband of hers."

"I'm real sorry about this, Miss Rachel. It's a good thing you got me to tend you, since your ma won't."

*

As Rachel snuggled into her bed, a mixture of joy and sorrow and fear plagued her. She wondered if it were plausible to be cursed to walk the earth alone, to be fatal to any man who wed her, to be doomed to bear no children. Dare she test that incredible theory by risking Dan's life? What if she was allowed to love and be loved, but not to have any man as a mate? Maybe she was jinxed through no fault her own. Who could answer such frightening questions with knowledge and not think her mad? A man of God, a physician of the mind, or a scientist? She certainly couldn't visit a fortune teller, as she'd been taught they were the servants of the devil.

If there was no such thing as a curse, what or who had killed her mates? Surely, as the law and public kept telling her, and she had even suspected, it was unnatural to lose three husbands in less than three years.

How she loved Dan, and wanted him, but she feared he was out of reach. Merely thinking of him warmed her heart and stirred her body. She recalled what he had said in Athens and on the train, but would an evil curse spoil the first happiness and real love she'd known since before the war devastated her life?

*

At the hotel, Dan was talking with his best friend and first mate. He related what he had learned and done during his near three-week absence. He hadn't risked sending his news to Luke Conner by telegram, so the developments astonished the brown-haired man.

"If you have serious doubts about your sister-in-law's guilt, you must have good reasons. You've become a good judge of character and situations, my friend. I know you to be a fair and just man, so you won't harm her if she's innocent."

Dan scowled. "That's the hard part, Luke, determining if she is or isn't guilty. I don't like being duped, and she's done that to me plenty of times; but I can understand her motives. I want the truth, no matter what it is. I don't know what to think or believe anymore."

"Maybe that's because you've gotten too close to her to see clearly."

Dan frowned again as he admitted, "You could be right, but it seemed the only way to get information out of her. If Rachel has a partner, I haven't found any clues to him; nor have you, obviously. When Phillip said 'they' in his letter, I assumed it meant Rachel had selected victim number four and they had killed him."

"You don't believe that now?"

"Not from what I've seen and heard."

"You mean because she's listed so far in your direction?"

"Yes and no. Just because she's attracted to me doesn't prove she killed Phillip or she doesn't have another lover somewhere. I keep telling myself it's possible she hasn't acted guilty because she hasn't committed any crimes. Some of her conduct could have to do with concealing resentment toward Phillip for getting her embroiled in danger. I've tried not to let gossip, those past investigations, her inappropriately gay conduct, and Phillip's last words mislead me. If she didn't love my brother, and with her struggle for survival weighing her down, she could be hiding her true feelings. Stars above, I did as good of an acting job as she did! I finally won her trust and affection. With the right motivation, anybody could dupe another person. I have to admit, under the circumstances, she had no choice but to delude me."

Luke was concerned for his captain. "Even if those deaths are only strange quirks of nature, she seems to be a hazard to the survival of the next man she chooses."

"Or she's being framed," Dan said. "If the deaths weren't her fault, somebody close to her might be behind them. They could be the work of a female rival, someone who hates her and wants to destroy her. Or a rejected lover who keeps making her available so she can pick him the next time she's free."

"That isn't impossible, Dan," Luke concurred, "nor any wilder than your sister-in-law being a Black Widow."

Dan jumped up to pace off his rising tension. "I know; that's why I'm so baffled and frustrated. What if it is insanity, Luke?"

"I don't know about such things, my friend; that calls for an expert. But I did learn her opinion of Earl Starger doesn't match anyone else's. From what I've been told, he's well liked, well respected, and good-natured. He's never been in trouble and doesn't seem to have an enemy in the world. He's smart, hardworking, and devoted to his wife. Nobody even hinted at trouble between Rachel and her stepfather. From all appearances, he's done his best to help her after every problem. If he's mean and cruel, only she knows those traits."

"That doesn't prove Starger doesn't have them," Dan reasoned in her defense. "There has to be a reason why she hates him so much."

"Maybe she resents him for taking her father's place. Yankees did kill her father and brother. And you told me another brother was with Earl when he drowned. She could hold him responsible for all three losses . . . I used a pretense when I visited White Cloud. It's a beautiful and prosperous plantation, now, but from what I discovered, Earl brought it back from the brink of ruin. Rachel's mother is quite beautiful herself, and appeared happy. She was ill and on medication, so I only spoke with her a few minutes."

"What day did you visit there?"

"On the first. Why?"

"Was her stepfather at home?"

"Not in the house, but out in the fields. Why?"

"The night before was when note number one appeared in her room."

"I was camped nearby. I didn't see or hear him return during the night. That would have made a long ride home, but it's possible. Didn't you say the note was in her handwriting?"

"Yes, but Starger would have samples of it, living in the same home. And a rich man could find someone to make accurate forgeries. What else did you learn?" Dan asked, almost sounding desperate for another suspect.

"I couldn't find a single hint about a spurned suitor. The only female rival I could find is a woman named Camellia Jones. She had her hook out to catch both Newman and Phillip, but was defeated by Rachel. She's from a wealthy and prestigious family, a bit spoiled and hot-tempered, but no scandals. If she's a vengeful murderess, it didn't appear that way. I think you stand a better chance of romancing information out of her than I would."

"I'll work on that angle later. What about her servants?"

"The housekeeper's been with her for years, loves her and defends her. She was working for Barlow when Rachel married him. Nobody seems to know much about her. Wells was on the place when Phillip bought it and I didn't hear anything bad about him. I didn't get to search her home; somebody was always around when I checked, so it seemed too risky."

"Anything else?"

"Very few people I approached were reluctant to discuss their local legend. Those who refused didn't defend her or have good things to say about her. I noticed that most people relied on gossip for their knowledge; few actually knew Rachel herself. I found one big inconsistency: Craig Newman. Remember how the bartender and others said all her husbands were rich and she was the only heir?"

"Yes. What about it?"

"That isn't the case for husband number two. Craig had a brother named Paul . . ."

Luke went on to expose several shocking revelations and when he finished, Dan realized this pit got deeper and darker every day. Could Rachel McCandless ever climb out?

*

Saturday morning was a cloudy and gloomy day that promised rain by nightfall. At nine, Lula Mae rushed to Rachel's room and told her she had company, that same stranger who had "bothered" her before she left home.

Rachel glanced out the window and saw Dan in the front yard. Her eyes widened and she was confused about his reason for coming today. "It's all right, Lula Mae; I'll go outside and speak with him."

"I don't trust that man, Miss Rachel. Something about him . . ."

"Don't worry. Just go about your chores."

Rachel joined Dan in the yard, and they walked a short distance from the house for privacy, as Lula Mae was standing in the doorway and eyeing them. "What are you doing here, Dan? I thought we agreed—"

"I'm sorry, Rachel," he interrupted her chiding, "but I had to see you. I went to Phillip's office so I know he hasn't returned. Baldwin is miffed, but he accepted that message you left him about Phillip's trip."

"What's so urgent that it couldn't wait until Monday? If anyone sees you here this weekend, it could mean trouble for me, for us."

"You worried me, woman, with the way you talked yesterday. You implied that what you have to tell me Monday will change my feelings about you. It also sounded as if you doubted my pledge to you. The more I thought about what you said and the way you looked, the more concerned I got. What's troubling you, love, besides telling Phillip about us?"

Rachel took a deep breath, held it a moment, then exhaled. "I guess it doesn't matter whether I tell you today or Monday, or if you hear it before the authorities. It's something terrible, Dan, a secret. I was going to confess it to you after I saw Chief Anderson. Phillip died the morning you arrived in Savannah. I couldn't tell you that day because there were serious things I had to investigate first, in Augusta and Athens. Please, let me explain everything before you get angry and lose all trust in me. I—"

"Miz Rachel, the law's acomin' up the road!" Burke suddenly appeared to give the warning.

Rachel went pale and trembled. "They must know. Why else would they be coming now? This is going to complicate things. I buried him in secret, without reporting his death to anyone. With my past—"

"Stay calm, Rachel. It might be nothing," Dan advised, pleased she was about to reveal everything to him, but dreading what that might be.

"You don't understand," she fretted aloud in panic. "They'll try to hang me this time. I'm innocent of everything, I swear it."

"This time?" Dan echoed, as if ignorant of her dilemma.

"I can't explain now," she hurriedly said. "They're here. I'm sorry, Dan. What I'll say is the truth; I hope and pray you'll believe me, because *they* won't. I'll explain everything in detail later, everything, I swear."

Two men with badges on their jackets dismounted, secured their reins to the picket fence, and looked at the couple approaching them.

"Mrs. McCandless," one said, "we're here to ask a few questions for Chief Anderson. And who might you be?" he asked the handsome stranger.

"Captain Daniel Slade of the *Merry Wind*. I'm an old and close friend of Phillip's. I came to do business with him."

"That's difficult, isn't it, Captain, since Mr. McCandless is dead? Tell me, ma'am, why didn't you report your third husband's . . . death?"

Rachel didn't like the way this interrogation was beginning. She knew Dan was observing and listening as intently as the lawmen. She was relieved she had begun her revelation to him to prevent him from being totally shocked by the news. At the word *third*, he had glanced at her. There was nothing she could do except stand there helpless and hurting while he learned about her past in this vile manner. "I was coming into town Monday morning to see the authorities."

"Isn't that a long time to wait, ma'am? He died three weeks ago. Why bury him in secret and wait so long to report it? What happened out here on March twenty-sixth?"

Rachel realized he had some of the facts, and they looked bad. She hated for Dan to discover the truth about her like this, and wished belatedly she had told him everything sooner. "I didn't know there was a time limit involved, sir. I had pressing business to tend for Phillip in Augusta and Athens at his two companies there. Before he passed away, he asked me to handle it immediately. I didn't think it made any difference if I took care of it first. Does it?"

The man looked her up and down with a surly expression. "It seems mighty strange that business is more important than obeying the laws."

"It isn't, sir, but circumstances couldn't be changed. There are some serious problems with our two out-of-town companies. I promised Phillip I would go check on them. I assumed an investigation would ensue and cost me valuable time, so I made my trip first. As you can see, I'm here now. Have I broken a law by delaying my report?"

He didn't answer, but asked instead, "Why did you bury him in secret, ma'am? No doctor was called that I can locate, so he must not have taken ill. A quick death happened with Mr. Barlow, too, didn't it? Was it from another . . . accident, as with Mr. Newman or Mr. Barlow's son?"

Rachel didn't like the sarcastic and suggestive way he spoke. She worried over what Dan must be thinking, but she warned herself to try to remain in control and to stay polite; but that was near impossible with the hateful man. "He died from cholera, sir. He took ill late Thursday night and was dead by early the following morning. My people and I buried him and burned everything he'd touched. I didn't want to create a panic in town. You know how people are terrified of that contagious disease. I didn't run away, sir; I returned from my trip and I was coming to see you on Monday."

"How do we know that's the truth?"

Rachel wanted to shout, Because I said it was!

Dan answered for her. "It *is* the truth, sir. I was here when Phillip died. It was from cholera, as Mrs. McCandless said."

"How do you know it was cholera?" the offensive man asked Rachel, after eyeing Dan from head to foot as he'd done with her.

She tried to maintain her poise as she related the symptoms.

"Don't you think it's mighty strange you've lost a third husband in such a short time?" the lawman asked. "Less than three years, isn't it?"

There, she fumed, Dan had heard the worst about her. "Yes, sir, but none of them from crimes I've committed."

"Why would you use that word, ma'am?"

The man looked as if he had cleverly pounced on a slip she'd made. Outrage and torment flooded her. She narrowed her gaze and said, "Because after every one of them died—of natural causes or true accidents—you lawmen have come and interrogated me for hours and harassed me for weeks, made not-so-subtle accusations, and behaved as if I did away with them. We all know the rumors and gossip, sir." Vexed and angered, she challenged, "If you doubt me, come along and I'll show you where Phillip's buried. You can dig up his body and have a doctor examine it—as many doctors as you please. Just glove your hands and burn anything that touches it, because you can catch or spread that awful disease if you don't take those precautions." The two men looked as reluctant as she'd imagined they'd be about examining an infectious and decomposing body. The longer that threat worked, the better it would be for her, as the more his body would . . . "I have nothing to fear, because I'm not to blame, this time or the other two times."

"Three times," the daring man corrected. "You certainly have bad luck with husbands and marriages."

Rachel no longer tried to conceal her anger. "What are you implying, sir?" she demanded, gluing her fiery gaze to his cold one.

"Just what I said, ma'am. As for you, Captain, tell me more about why you're here and why you didn't convince Mrs. McCandless to report this matter."

Dan was furious about Rachel's treatment, guilty or not. He disliked these two despicable men. He grasped why she had dreaded and postponed this exposure. "Phillip and I are old friends. We grew up together in Charleston. We have a pending business deal. I docked Thursday night the twenty-fifth and came here early Friday morning. It was when I asked to see him, Mrs. McCandless went and found him ill. Phillip passed away too quickly to fetch a doctor."

"But you said he took ill late Thursday night, ma'am."

Rachel knew she had to explain with an honesty that she hoped would be apparent to even these disbelieving men. "I didn't know he was sick that night. Phillip did some heavy drinking after a talk with his Athens business partner about those serious problems I mentioned earlier. He had started vomiting and was feeling embarrassed, so he slept in the guest room. I found him very sick the next morning and realized it wasn't from drinking, as I'd thought the night before. It was too late to save him or to send for help." Rachel was baffled and intrigued by Dan's prior words, his bold lies, but she didn't have time to think about them. No matter what he had alleged, she stuck with the truth to avoid entrapment.

"Slept in another room, you say?"

Rachel glued her gaze to his to make him uneasy. "Yes, sir. Wouldn't you spare your wife of such foolishness? I regret I didn't learn he was so ill before it was too late to help him, but I can't be blamed for an innocent and natural mistake. There were several empty whiskey bottles on the bedside table to lead me to that erroneous conclusion."

Lula Mae told the investigators in a sharp tone, "It happened jest like she said. I he'ped clean up that awful mess. It was cholera."

Burke related his story about the fishing trip and Phillip drinking from the river. "Miz Rachel said it wasn't the wahter. Ah he'ped bury him an'burn stuff. Ah's seed dis afore. Miz Rachel didn't do nuthin' wrong."

In a blatant attempt to frighten the two employees, the investigator said, "You two will sign sworn statements it was cholera? You know you can go to prison for lying, for helping to conceal a crime if one was committed?"

Burke and Lula Mae looked offended and angered.

"Don' be threatenin' us. We done tol' the truth. Ah'll put mah hand on the Good Book an' swear it," the black man warned with boldness.

"I will, too," Lula Mae added, "You ain't gots no right to say such things to us or to Miss Rachel. A gooder body never lived and suffered such troubles."

"You have Mrs. McCandless's word and that of three witnesses, sir," Dan asserted, "so I don't see a reason to doubt what happened her weeks ago, yet, you seem to be implying you do. I'm confused about the way you're asking your questions and treating a fine lady. You appear to be interrogating her as if she were a dangerous criminal."

The chief's investigator scowled at the sea captain. "You'll sign a sworn statement, too, Captain Slade, before you leave?"

Dan sent him a scowl in return as he replied, "Of course."

"When will that be, Captain?"

"I can follow you to town this morning or come by any time you say."

"I meant, when are you sailing?"

Dan grasped the insinuation. "Not until May twenty-fourth."

"Why is that?" the man was forced to ask.

"My business. I have orders in with Phillip's partners that will be delivered here on May fourteenth and then the twenty-fourth. That's what I came for and what I'm waiting for, if you care to check, sir."

"How long have you known Mrs. McCandless?"

"I met her after I docked last month. Phillip wrote me he was married, but this was our first visit."

"Do you mind if we examine the house and grounds, ma'am?"

Rachel knew what they hoped to find—evidence against her, so she could be charged, arrested, and convicted of murder this time. She was positive they would look for poison in any form or container, but she knew none was present. Still, she asked their reason in an almost surly tone.

"To make our investigation thorough," was the answer. "I know you weren't expecting us today, but I'm sure your home is presentable."

"Go right ahead, sir. Lula Mae, show the *gentlemen* around the house. Burke, when they're finished inside, let them see any place on the grounds they desire. We have nothing to hide from such *upstanding* lawmen. Answer any questions they have. I'll wait here for you, if you don't need me along. You didn't say, sir, how you knew Phillip was dead and buried?"

"We received a message at the office. We don't know who sent it."

"Do you always act on anonymous notes?" Rachel asked in a cold tone. "Or did you make an exception this time because I was involved?"

The man scowled once more, then followed Lula Mae into the house.

Rachel and Dan watched the lawmen enter her home to search it. She thanked Burke, and the manager, who was still fuming, returned to his chores until he was summoned to guide them over the grounds.

"They're looking for evidence I killed Phillip, but they won't find any, because I didn't. They won't give up on this matter easily. They'll try their best to prove I murdered him."

"Try to relax, Rachel, until they're gone. One of the men is peeking out the window now, watching us. Let them leave before we talk."

Rachel sat in a swing, swaying back and forth as her mind filled with tormenting doubts. She couldn't understand why Dan had corroborated her shocking story when he couldn't know whether or not it was true. And how had the law discovered this deed? The only person who could have known and summoned them had to be responsible for Phillip's death . . .

Dan perceived what Rachel must be thinking and feeling. Even if she were guilty of his brother's murder, he had to keep her out of prison to get at the truth. He had to wait until that mystery was solved. He had assumed her servants would not expose his lies, either out of loyalty and love or out of complicity with the alleged crime. But some deep instinct told him she wasn't guilty. Or was that only his desire and love influencing him?

When the two lawmen returned later, one said, "We have no evidence to arrest you on, ma'am, but this investigation isn't over. This case will stay open until we're convinced your third husband died of natural causes. Chief Anderson might want a doctor to check the body, so don't go moving or hiding it. I'm sure we'll be seeing you again real soon. You do understand that some poisonings look like cholera, so we have to be certain."

That was too much to take without lashing out. "How dare you! Charge me and arrest me, or get off my land with your vile thoughts and wicked minds. I'm not a Black Widow, and there's no way you can prove I am. Unless you have undeniable evidence, don't you speak to me like that again. If you do, I'll be the one pressing charges against you."

"Don't go getting upset, ma'am. You can't fault us with only doing our duty. You have to admit these deaths are strange."

"Why shouldn't I get upset and angry? You've put me through this three times. I'm tired of the innuendoes and implications and hateful gossip. I am innocent of any wrongdoing."

"If that's true, ma'am, you have nothing to worry over."

"If that's true," she mocked scornfully. "How foolish and cruel you are. I suffer three tragic losses, and you want to imprison me for crimes!"

"You must admit, ma'am, four deaths in a short span are suspicious."

"Uncommon perhaps," Rachel corrected, "but not suspicious, not when there isn't any proof I did something wicked."

"I beg to disagree, ma'am, but four strange deaths have to create suspicions, especially when you inherited so much money afterward."

"I didn't inherit anything from Craig Newman," she argued, "His brother even took all I inherited from Mr. Barlow, and the law did nothing to stop him. That was an injustice, and I was left in near poverty."

"Until you married Mr. McCandless. He was rich. Now's he's dead."

She didn't let the other matter drop. "What motive did I have for killing Craig? I was left with nothing. I didn't marry Phillip for a year. I worked and supported myself, which I'm sure you know."

"You didn't know he excluded you from his will, isn't that right?"

"That's correct. What wife would assume such a wicked thing? Everyone in town knows what a mean and spiteful and adulterous man Craig was. But I didn't kill him because he was evil. I didn't kill him, period."

"With Mr. McCandless dead, you're a rich woman again. Correct?"

"No. I told you earlier; two of his companies are in financial trouble."

"But you still have the shipping firm and this plantation."

She ignored the comment. "Phillip was a good and kind man. I loved him," she said, but didn't add, as a brother. "If it were any woman besides me involved, would you feel the same?"

"I would certainly hope so, ma'am."

"I doubt you would," she scoffed. "If that's all . . . ?" she hinted.

"For today, ma'am. Good-bye. I'll be speaking with you again later, Captain Slade. You staying here?"

"No, I'm at the hotel on east Bay Street. Room eleven."

"You want to ride back to town with us?"

"No, I haven't finished my business discussion with Mrs. McCandless."

After the men rode off, Dan murmured, "It won't look good if they learn we took that trip together and told everyone we were cousins. They're going to wonder why you didn't tell George and Harry their partner is dead. What's really going on, Rachel? Why did you dupe me, too?"

She glared at him. "I want to ask that same question, Dan. What happens when they learn you lied about when you arrived and about being here when Phillip died? That could get us both into trouble."

"I didn't lie to them about my arrival time, Rachel. I knew your staff loved you and were loyal, so I assumed they wouldn't expose me for trying to help you. I didn't tell you I'd docked earlier because I didn't want to make you uneasy wondering if I'd heard the terrible gossip about you."

"You knew about me when you visited?"

Dan nodded.

Her gaze narrowed in mistrust and anger. "You lied so you can extract your own vengeance? Is that why you seduced me? You hoped to prove to Phillip I was an adulteress as well as a murderess to save him from my evil clutches?"

Dan seized her arms and shook her. "It wasn't like that, Rachel. It *isn't* like that. I didn't know Phillip was dead, and I didn't believe the gossip. With Phillip gone, I didn't want you to feel uncomfortable around me. I know the rumors can't be true, because Phillip wouldn't have fallen in love with you and married you. He was a good judge of character. I've gotten to know you and have come to those same conclusions. Damnit, woman, I love you and believe you! Why did you tell me so many lies?"

"You . . . love me?" Distraught and frightened and hoping to be persuaded his words were true, she asked, "Why should I believe you?"

"Because it's the truth, and deep inside, you know it is."

Still, she had to challenge, "You're only saying that to beguile and disarm me. You're only trying to dupe me into making a confession of guilt, but I can't, because I'm not guilty of any crime."

Dan read her feelings and knew what she needed to hear. "How could you make love to me and doubt me this much?"

"In my experience, men are liars and users. Phillip was the only one I could trust, or I thought I could. But he lied to me, too, and I don't know why."

In a gentle tone, Dan asked, "How did he lie to you, Rachel?"

"Don't you know?" she accused in anguish. "Aren't you in on that mysterious deal? That's why you're really here! That's why you lied to them—to keep me out of prison to honor the deal or to return your money! I don't have it. I don't know where he hid it. Without the advance, George and Harry will never supply your arms and ammunition. Beat me or threaten me or kill me, but I don't have your money."

"I don't know what you're talking about, Rachel. The only deals I have with Phillip's companies are the ones you know about. This big and secret deal all of you are dancing around each other about isn't mine. That missing money isn't mine. If it were, I would tell you."

"I don't believe you. I can't," she said, hoping to be convinced.

"If it were my deal and lost money, wouldn't I be calling you the liar now?" he reasoned. "Wouldn't I be demanding you carry out Phillip's bargain or return my advance, or threatening you if you didn't? Think, love, and feel. We've become close. Don't you know you can trust me?"

Rachel met his tender gaze. "I want to trust you, Dan; I need to trust you. But it's hard and scary. My life and freedom are at stake. I've lost control of everything, and I don't know how to get it back."

"Let me help, love, please," he urged. "I can't do that in ignorance. What is the truth, Rachel? Don't I deserve to be told? You were starting to tell me when the authorities arrived. Finish it now. Even if I were your culprit, what difference would it make if you told me the truth?"

Rachel knew she had to take a chance he was being honest and sincere. Even if he weren't, it might save her life. "I pray to God I can trust you. If I'm wrong, I'm either in deep trouble or I'll clear myself with Phillip's enemies. It's a long and painful story, so be patient while I tell it. Let's sit over here," she suggested and guided him to a grassy spot beneath the shady live oaks dripping their moss.

Chapter

12

Rachel settled herself and began. "This is not a short and simple tale. It's going to be difficult for me, and it isn't going to be easy or pleasant for you to hear. I hope you'll be kind and understanding, even if you can't forgive me. When a person is backed into a corner, as I was, one is afraid and desperate and wary of others; it's only natural to be secretive and defensive when one's life and freedom are in peril. I know how terrible this is going to sound, but please listen patiently and try not to judge me harshly."

Dan nodded and waited to hear what she had to say.

"I need to start where it all began long ago when the horrors of war and losing Papa changed Mama. When things became so bad afterward, she seemed to panic. Maybe Papa was the one who gave her strength and courage, and she lost them after those tragedies. My mother was raised as a pampered and genteel southern belle with privileges and without worries. I'm sure it was hard for her to shoulder the responsibilities of a plantation and family. As things got worse, she couldn't face poverty and humiliation. She thought she needed a man to take care of her, southern women are reared that way. She was only thirty-seven and quite beautiful when that Yankee opportunist Earl Starger convinced her he had the money and power to protect her and her children. It didn't take long before all her children were gone. But she blamed us, accused us of hurting and betraying her after all the sacrifices she had made for us 'ungrateful' and 'selfish' children."

Dan grasped the bitterness within her, but kept silent.

"It wasn't like that, but Mama can't face the truth. I've only seen her once since I left home, and that was by accident. She acts as if she truly believes I've brought a terrible scandal on the family name. One day she'll be unable to ignore the truth, and I feel sorry for her when that happens. The reason I left home was because Earl was mean and evil; he wouldn't keep his pawing hands off me. If I were going to murder any man, it would be him!" She halted to calm her anger.

"The older I became and the more I blossomed into a woman, the worse it got with Earl. Oh, he tried to hide his groping behind games, teasings, and affection, but I wasn't fooled. When I was brave and angry enough to scold him, he played innocent and told me I was the one with a wicked mind. After one incident, he even warned me no Union judge or marshal would listen to the wild rantings of a vindictive southern belle against her devoted and respected Yankee stepfather. He must have thought I was scared of him and that threat, because he became even bolder.

"William Barlow was a friend of the family and our cotton factor, too. He was a true southern gentleman, kind, and generous. When I was eighteen, he caught Earl trying to ravish me in one of the cotton storage sheds when he came to do business. William was furious; he already detested Earl Starger, so his hatred increased."

Rachel shuddered as she recalled that offensive day. "William had always been like an uncle to me and the others. When he witnessed Earl's lechery and my peril, he asked me to marry him to get me away from the dangerous situation. He didn't want me as his wife; he couldn't be a husband to any woman because of a physical problem. He said I could divorce him when I found someone I loved and wanted to marry. In November of '72, I became his wife, but it was really more like his daughter. Then, the next month, his only son had an accident. We lived in a large, three-story home in town. His bedroom was on the top floor with a balcony, and he fell from it. I heard a scream and found him. I summoned help, but it was too late; his neck was broken. The doctor said he was sick and possibly feverish and dizzy. He must have gone onto the balcony to cool off and fell over the railing."

"Was anyone else present in the house?" Dan had to ask.

"Not that I know of; William was at work and Lula Mae was shopping, so I was alone with him. When William died two months later, on my birthday, the authorities thought it was strange for a healthy and rich man to die suddenly after three months of marriage and leave his young wife wealthy. The doctor said it could have been a heart attack, but the law wasn't totally convinced. We didn't share a bedroom, so I didn't find him until the next morning after he'd died during the night." She related how Lula Mae was with her ailing sister from February to April, so she had been alone with her husband.

Rachel gazed into space as she envisioned that awful scene. "He had a look of terrible pain frozen on his face, but the doctor told the chief that he didn't detect any almond odor on William's mouth which would expose a poisoning. They were suspicious of me, but couldn't find any evidence to charge me with two murders. It didn't take long before those nasty rumors started about me being a Black Widow. Most people wouldn't have anything to do with me. I didn't know the cotton factoring business and I was tormented by vicious gossip. Lula Mae was still at her sister's taking care of the house and family until the woman got well. I hadn't seen her since she'd visited the day William died. That selfish woman was so determined to keep Lula Mae around as long as she needed her help that she destroyed all my letters to Lula Mae so she never realized my plight. Without my only friend for comfort and advice, I was completely alone. When the Panic and Depression of '73 struck, I was afraid I'd lose everything William had worked so hard to earn. Earl was hounding me to come home, but I knew couldn't ever return."

Rachel shifted her position. As she did so, she noticed Lula Mae observing them from a window. She knew the housekeeper was worried about her and was no doubt wondering what was taking place. She would explain to the woman later. "Craig Newman was a business acquaintance of William's. He was in textiles and milling. I'd met him plenty of times. He was twenty-four, polite, charming, and almost handsome. I was so vulnerable and frightened that I foolishly allowed Craig to convince me to marry him two months later. It didn't take long to realize he had married me for my money. Isn't that a twist, but who would believe it?"

Dan sealed his gaze to her eyes, and found them honey-colored. If he had gleaned that clue correctly, she was being honest so far.

"The trouble was, Governor Smith announced that many of the state bonds were fraudulent. He canceled almost eight million dollars in bad ones. People protested, but it didn't do any good. That's where William had many of his investments, so half of my inheritance from him was lost, and that made Craig mad. When he died from a fall down the stairs, his will left everything, including William's money, to his brother; and that was legal. We'd only been married four months, but I had discovered what a cunning and evil man he was; I had no respect or affection left for him at his death. Of course the law was delightfully intrigued and started another investigation of me. I was in the backyard working in the garden and came in to find him dead at the bottom of the steps, his neck broken, like William's son. They finally had to rule it an accident, because I had no motive and he was drunk. I didn't tell them I didn't know I had been excluded from the will."

"You were alone with him?" Dan had to ask again.

"For most of that time, yes. Lula Mae came back to work for me in May, but Craig fired her in July, out of meanness. I did all the chores at home. The law thought it was strange that no servants were employed and present, as if I'd planned his murder and didn't want any witnesses. They didn't seem to believe it was Craig's doing to be hateful. Lula Mae explained to the law that I was telling the truth, so they couldn't charge me."

Rachel didn't look at Dan as she disclosed, "Craig Newman was a bad man, but I didn't wish death on him. Lula Mae knew how he was when he got angry or upset. She visited me the day he died, and saw what a terrible mood he was in. He began drinking first thing that morning; that's why I was working in the garden, to stay out of his reach until he calmed down. When he was in one of those black fits, he became violent."

"I'm sure it didn't help matters you hated him by then," Dan probed.

"No, it didn't, and it was hard to conceal those feelings. I dared not tell the police how cruel he was and give them reason to doubt me." Rachel felt she should reveal an important fact. "I only slept with Craig a few times as his wife; he had a mistress, and everyone knew about it except me. I never made love to him, Dan. I didn't even like the act because it was so painful and violent those few times. I realized later that he was being that way on purpose, that it didn't have to hurt and shame."

She hurried on out of modesty. "I won't go into all the details, but things were worse than ever for me. The gossip was malicious; the jokes were cruel. Even one newspaper carried a so-called fictitious story about a Black Widow who mated and slew after she got what she wanted. Earl was harassing me again. The authorities were keeping a close eye on me." She revealed her pregnancy, miscarriage, and her vile treatment by Craig's brother. "When Paul found out I was carrying his brother's child, he provided support for a while, but after I lost the baby, he was as bad as Craig had ever been. Paul accused me of getting rid of the child and accused me of stalking him as my next prey. He told lies that had people hating me even more than before." She explained how she couldn't find a job, and how Lula Mae had helped her. She told him how alone, frightened, humiliated, ostracized, and almost penniless she was.

"Phillip was Craig's shipper, so that's how we met," she continued. "We became friends. Phillip perceived how terrible Craig was, so he only pretended to be Craig's friend to be near me; he told me that later. But he was out of town during my worst time after Craig's death, the investigation, and my miscarriage. When he returned and discovered what had happened to me, he was furious. He hired me to work for him, and he eventually proposed. I couldn't marry again so soon and make another mistake. I knew the rumors would chew at me and Phillip. He was too kind to be treated as I was. By then, I was wary of most men. I was resentful of all my troubles. But Phillip was so good and persuasive that I agreed to marry him a year after Craig died. I just wanted my life to be peaceful and safe and honorable again." She took a deep breath to soothe her raw nerves.

"I loved and respected Phillip, but I wasn't in love with him. In most ways he was like a brother to me. We did have a real marriage, but only a few times. He knew how I felt about sex and why, so he didn't press the matter. He hoped in time I would come to love him and be a real wife to him. I hoped the same thing, but it never happened. When he died so suddenly, I knew what would follow; the law would investigate me again, and more feverishly than ever. I knew his death would suggest poisoning, as William's had. If it was cholera, I needed to bury him fast and sterilize everything. If it wasn't, I didn't know who had murdered him. He even implied on his deathbed that I would be blamed."

Those words brought Dan to even greater alert and attention.

"All those deaths are strange," Rachel admitted, "but I'm not responsible. Every trap I got myself into, I fell into a worse one by trying to escape it in the wrong way. I never want to be incriminated again. When I get my life straightened out, I want to make a fresh start far away from here. I know William and Phillip loved me, but Craig only wanted to use me. Phillip gave me back my courage, strength, and pride; but I panicked when he left me so unexpectedly and mysteriously."

She looked at Dan. "Maybe I'm bad luck for men. Maybe I'm doomed to never have a mate or . . . I know I won't be in a hurry to risk another man's life to prove I'm not cursed by an evil force. That might sound crazy, but I have three reasons to convince me I really am jinxed. Earl Starger wants to spite me for humiliating him with William and for spurning his wicked advances. He wants me back home so he can punish me and fondle me again. And there's Camellia Jones; she had her eyes on Craig first, then on Phillip; she hated me for winning both, so she fans the gossip. I wish she *had* won Craig; he was evil beneath that boyish charm. But they aren't the only ones who've hurt me. People call me a Black Widow behind my back, and sometimes to my face, the same ones who were nice when my husbands were around."

When she halted, Dan asserted, "Even nice people can't help but be curious and talkative. You must admit, it's . . . unusual to lose three young and healthy husbands in such a short span, and under what appears mysterious circumstances. It's bound to create curiosity and suspicion when such a young and beautiful woman is involved, especially one who inherited a lot of money. Considering your past troubles, Rachel, it wasn't wise to bury Phillip in secret."

"I had to," she said. "Gossip and another investigation aren't the only reasons why I did it. Something terrible is going on; Phillip was in big trouble. Maybe he was hoping you could help him when you arrived; maybe that's what he was mumbling about when he said, 'He's coming soon; he'll help me.' That's why I had to rush to Athens to see Harry."

In view of his arms-contract story, he couldn't admit that Phillip hadn't known if he was alive and on the way, so he couldn't have been referring to him. "You just implied he was in trouble and danger. From whom? About what?"

"He refused to worry me about it. After Harry's visit, Phillip got drunk, really drunk, and talked crazy." She repeated the story she told the investigators. "When I checked on him, I thought he was still drunk; several empty bottles were lying on the table nearby. He started babbling in half-sentences; nothing made sense and he used no names, except Harry's. When he died I was numb, and I panicked. I had to see what I could learn about his warnings to me before I subjected myself to a lengthy investigation and possibly prison. I couldn't allow any needed facts to be destroyed while I was being questioned and harassed. When you appeared, I didn't know who or what you were—friend or foe. Until I was convinced it was friend, I couldn't tell you the truth. That story I told you about why I was taking the trip was a ruse to mislead you. I had to come up with a logical motive for what I was doing. It also seemed the only way to pull clues out of his partners. I can't solve anything until I discover what's going on. I never expected anything to happen between us; that took me completely by surprise. I wanted to trust you so much, but I knew it would complicate matters until I could be honest."

"It caught me by surprise, too," Dan murmured. "But go on."

"Phillip was scared, Dan, very scared and worried. He wasn't himself for the last few months." She related her husband's last mumblings. "He said I would be killed if I didn't honor some deal or return the money. I didn't know about the deal, and I don't know where the money is hidden. I've searched everywhere, but I can't find anything, money or facts. That's why I didn't extend my hospitality when you arrived; I had to search the house and grounds. That's what I was doing in his office in town, but I found nothing there. Where could he hide so much money? If he received that advance George and Harry mentioned, it would be around five hundred thousand dollars. Why wouldn't he tell me where it was, if not returning it to its owner could get me killed or blamed for theft? I know Harry is somehow involved."

Dan couldn't help but wonder how much the money meant to Rachel, as it offered her a means to get out of her trap and out of the state. Did she know about Phillip's letters and know his identity and wonder if Phillip had told him where the money was hidden? Rachel wasn't his only suspect anymore; still, he mustn't trust her too soon or too far, and he mustn't expose his identity and motive until later. "Repeat what Phillip said before he died. Maybe there is a clue hidden there."

Rachel complied, then asked, "Do they mean anything to you? Do you see why I was distrustful of a stranger who mentioned an arms deal?"

"I understand." Heaven help him if she was a superb actress and these were all lies to dupe him into helping her, but it didn't sound that way.

"With my past, I also searched the house to make sure nothing was there to incriminate me," Rachel confided. "I feared that if Harry or the unknown client did something to Phillip to cause his death, evidence might have been placed inside to frame me. With Phillip and me out of the way, that would leave Harry—and George— to earn a big profit from this curious deal. Maybe someone poisoned Phillip; cholera does have the same symptoms as poisoning. Maybe someone figured that with Phillip dead and me inheriting his share of the companies, a woman could be terrified into carrying out their bargain. You heard George and Harry say Phillip tried to back out of the contract, and he told me that on his deathbed. Maybe that's why somebody had to get rid of him. That's what my trip and all the bantering were about; we were all trying to see what and how much we all knew. It's such a hazardous mystery, Dan. I don't know what to think or whom to trust."

She sighed heavily. "I'm going to search the shipping office again tomorrow. I have Phillip's keys, and Milton never works on Sundays. With luck, which I've always been low on, I'll find a name and destination to enlighten me about this deal. Maybe I overlooked something last time. Don't you see, Dan; I had to find clues before I exposed his death?"

Dan nodded. "How do you think the law learned about it? Isn't it odd they pounced on you today, as if they knew your movements?"

"I surmised the same thing, and it scared me. I know my servants are loyal, so I trust them. Maybe Earl is having me watched, saw what I did, and he exposed me. Maybe Phillip's unhappy client is spying on me, killed Phillip, and alerted the law to have me blamed, or to get it into the open so I'd inherit the money and complete the deal. Or maybe Harry knew Phillip was dead, guessed what I'd done, and he sent that anonymous message to get me into trouble and out of his hair. I'm sorry, but I even suspected that maybe I had misjudged you and you did it."

That last statement didn't shock him. "I didn't know he was dead, so I couldn't put the authorities on to you," he alleged. "Believe that, Rachel. As for Harry, he seemed genuinely surprised to see you there and to hear Phillip was away on secret business. He was worried and angry."

"I know, but I don't know why. The more I learn the bigger this mystery gets."

Dan changed the subject for a moment. "One question, Rachel; you said you didn't love Phillip, correct?"

She hoped the reason for his concern in that area was his feelings for her. "That's true, not as a wife should. That's why I could . . . do what I did with you. It wasn't adultery, Dan; he was dead and I was a widow. I'm sorry you didn't know so you wouldn't chastise yourself about his betrayal."

Dan didn't know if he should be happy, disappointed, or suspicious that she hadn't loved his brother. He had to get to the bottom of the truth, no matter how deep and rotten the barrel that held it. He wanted to trust her, but he couldn't drop his guard, not yet. "Don't worry, Rachel," he comforted. "I won't let anyone harm you. Phillip was my friend; he'd expect me to help and protect his widow. I'm sorry I arrived too late to save his life, even if I intended to steal something precious from him. We'll solve this mystery together and punish whoever's to blame."

Rachel was captivated by Dan and his words. She yearned to have his help and love. "Are you sure? It could be dangerous and deadly. It might even tarnish both our images of Phillip if he was involved in something illegal. If he was, it could either have been by coercion or by choice. He warned me not to go to the law. I wouldn't have anyway, because they'd never believe me. You saw how they acted earlier, so you know they would think I was daft or covering myself if I told them I thought Phillip was murdered by an enemy. And, if I mentioned this mysterious, maybe illegal, deal and the hidden money, they'd think I was involved in that crime, or the money was my motive for doing away with another husband."

"I think you handled matters in the best and only feasible way."

"Thank you, Dan. I need to tell you more about those incidents during our trip."

Afterward, she said, "You can see why I couldn't tell you everything at those times. I still don't know if those two matters are the work of the same person. It scares me to know somebody can forge my script; it could be used for an incriminating note."

"Or for a false confession," Dan ventured. "You've been shot at and threatened. If you were killed and a note left behind in your handwriting, everyone would think it was suicide from a guilty conscience."

"Don't even hint at such a horrible event," Rachel said, then abruptly changed the subject. "Another thing: when we were at the arms company, I noticed something I'm sure is illegal, and I don't see how Phillip couldn't have been aware of it." She explained about the patents on the weapons she had seen the men making and why she'd said nothing about it. "That isn't all: the law seemed intrigued by your presence and corroboration. I don't want to endanger your life by helping me. The authorities might think you aided me in murdering Phillip so we could be together."

"We'll have to be careful how we behave toward each other. If we appear too intimate this soon after his death, it won't look good for either of us. You keep that derringer close and stay alert, woman. Lock your doors and windows, and watch out for strangers. If someone killed Phillip and there's that much money hidden around here, you could be in peril."

"But I searched every inch of the house and grounds nearby."

"It could be buried in the woods, Rachel, or near any one of these trees. It might never be found."

"But I'll be held responsible! No one will believe I don't have it."

"For now, love, all we can do is search the firm's office tomorrow, then wait for that mysterious client to lay claim to his order."

"But I couldn't find anything in Phillip's desk or the safe," she pointed out in dismay," and Milton's was locked."

"Don't worry, I can get into most locks." He might as well confess that talent today, as she'd surmise it later and perhaps doubt him again. "That's how I got into the office last time when you were there; I wanted to see you again, but I figured you wouldn't answer the door."

"So, I didn't forget to lock it?" She eyed him with confusion.

"Nope. I thought about you for two nights and all of Saturday and Sunday morning. When I saw you go into the office, I had to see you again."

"You come to town to do business with an old and dear friend; you hear horrible gossip about his wife; you find him mysteriously gone when he's supposed to be awaiting your arrival; I invite you along on a private trip—so you decided you needed to study me closely?"

"I told myself I only wanted to get acquainted with the wife of my old friend, a woman who exuded mystery. The truth is, I realized later I was fascinated by you. I never intended to have these feelings for you or to indulge in glorious lovemaking with you; blame yourself for being irresistible."

Rachel returned his provocative smile. "That was sneaky. You scared me silly when you walked in that day while I was searching the office and safe."

"I can understand why. Sorry, love."

His blue gaze was tender and enticing, her heart fluttered. "When I said what I had to confess could change your feelings for me, this is what I meant. Does it, Dan? Do you hate me and mistrust me now?"

"No, Rachel. When it comes to your fourth and last husband, you'll promise me forever, won't you?"

She gaped at him. He was . . . proposing! How could a carefree, adventurous bachelor and avowed seaman love her so much this fast? His old and dear friend was barely cold in his grave and she was being investigated for Phillip's supposed murder; but Dan was wooing her and proposing marriage to the deceitful, recent widow within a few yards of his friend's final resting place! Daniel Slade did not strike her as being an impulsive person. Perhaps it was only his way of telling her his feelings were serious, but he didn't expect an affirmative reply today or ever. Her heart could not help but hope and her body warm, but she fretted, "What if I'm bad luck, Dan? I couldn't bear for you to die. I couldn't say yes until I'm convinced I'm not cursed by fate."

"Give me time, woman, and I'll prove you aren't a murderess or a jinx," he said in a commanding tone. "I'll stake my life on it."

"With my past, that's exactly what you'd be doing. Don't rush this, Dan. There's so much to resolve, and we must protect ourselves from gossip."

"As long as I know you love me and want me and you'll eventually consider my proposal, I'll wait for you and I'll help you with this mystery."

Joy and relief flooded her. She prayed this wasn't too good to be true. "I do want you, Captain Daniel Slade. When it's safe, we'll become lovers until we're both convinced we want a long future together."

Dan got to his feet, having noticed she hadn't confessed love in her wary and uncertain state. "It's time for me to leave before I lose my head and seize you right here and now. Remember, love, spies can be watching you at any time. Don't do anything risky or foolish. I'll meet you at the door to Phillip's office at ten tomorrow."

"I wish you didn't have to go," she mellowed enough to admit, "but it's best for both of us. Good-bye, Dan, until morning."

"I love you, woman, so take care of yourself while we're apart." He walked to his horse, mounted, waved, and rode for town and Luke.

When Rachel went into the house, Lula Mae rushed to her side to make sure she was all right. "I was 'bout to bring you 'freshments, but I thought you didn't want to be bothered whilst you talked."

Rachel had seen the housekeeper gazing out one of the windows several times. She smiled and said, "I'm fine. There's nothing the law can do to me, because I'm not guilty. But I am thirsty and hungry. Lordy, I'm glad that's over with; I was dreading that chore Monday."

"Why did he stay so long, Miss Rachel?" Lula Mae asked. "Who is that man? Why did he lies for you?"

"He's an old friend of Phillip's; he came to do business with him. I took him to Augusta and Athens with me, so he could place orders with both companies. It looked so bad for me that he wanted to protect me as a last favor to Phillip. I didn't tell you he was going because I didn't want you to worry over me traveling with a handsome man at a perilous time like this."

The woman frowned and chided, "That ain't like you, Miss Rachel, to lies to Lula Mae."

"I didn't lie, my friend," Rachel corrected. "I only kept a secret."

Lula Mae's frown deepened and her tone was stern. "Secrets been gitting you into trouble for years. What if the law finds out he lied?"

"They won't, unless you or Burke tell them. I can trust him."

"You don't know the man! He could be tricking you to get you."

Rachel was dismayed by the woman's unusual behavior. "We're friends, Lula Mae; he's going to help me solve some business problems. I'll be careful how I behave around him; I promise."

"Is there a reason to be careful?"

For the first time, Rachel did not like the woman's tone and boldness. Yet she tried to remain calm and polite, as she thought Lula Mae was probably just upset and worried. "Of course; the law will probably spy on me for a while. I wouldn't want them misunderstanding our friendship or putting Dan into trouble. I need to ask you one question; did you see anyone hanging around here while I was gone? I can't figure out how the law learned about Phillip."

"I ain't seen nobody around here. You know it wasn't Lula Mae or Burke who tawked. Mighty strange goings on, if you aks me."

"I agree, but let's not worry too much about it. With Phillip's death in the open, I can get on with taking care of his affairs."

"You gonna stay here?"

"I haven't decided; there hasn't been time to think ahead that far. I'll let you know when I do; I promise." Rachel couldn't tell the housekeeper about her love for the sea captain or her hopes of marrying him one day. "Whatever happens, Lula Mae, I'll take care of you, as you've always taken care of me. You'll never be poor again. Even if they haul me off to prison, I'll see that you're provided for first."

"I love you, Miss Rachel, like you was my own child."

"I know, Lula Mae, and I'm grateful to have you."

"When I said I didn't see nobody whilst you was gawn, I didn't means nothing happened. I don't wants to scare you, but somebody searched the house whilst I was at church Sunday. Nothing was stolen, not even the money in the cashbox. Ain't that strange as can be?"

"Thank God the culprit didn't leave anything here to incriminate me today! We'll keep our eyes open wide for more mischief."

After the woman left for the kitchen, Rachel went to her room and unwrapped the painting she had purchased in Athens. She exchanged it with the one hanging over her bedroom mantel. She stepped back, admired it, and envisioned Dan in that scene. He was everything she wanted and needed in a man, in a husband. He wasn't stubborn; he bent when necessary. He was understanding and forgiving. He didn't dwell on injured masculine pride. He was caring, tender, and gentle; yet he was strong and confident. Love, she concluded, was glorious; and lovemaking with the right man was sheer rapture. Whatever it took, she would not permit Dan to be harmed in any way or by any one because of her, not even by the cruel fate that might have cursed her.

*

Rachel answered the knock at the front door, as Lula Mae had retired for the night. She discovered a knife was used to pinion a note to the jamb. She freed the paper and read it. She stared into the darkness, but saw and heard nothing to indicate the villain was lurking there. She locked the door, relieved only a threatening note had been awaiting her this time.

*

As soon as the door to the shipping firm's office was locked, Dan pulled Rachel into his arms and kissed her. At first it was slow and sweet; then, urgent and swift. His mouth claimed hers many times between treks over her face and nibbles at her lips.

Rachel returned the ardent kisses and clung to him. Once more those flames of desire danced within her body and tingles raced over her flesh. Her hunger for him was so intense that she was tempted to brazenly sink to the floor and make wild and wonderful love to him.

Dan had to struggle against that same temptation and to master the emotions she unleashed within him. He groaned against her mouth. "Stars above, I want you so much, Rachel McCandless. You've woven a spell over me."

She hugged him tightly and replied, "I want you, too, Dan. I ache all over to have you again. I never knew what I was missing until you taught me what lovemaking is. Now, I think or dream about you almost all the time. Will it always be this special way between us?"

"Yes, I know it will. I wish I could take you here and now, but that's too dangerous, even with Luke standing guard to sound a warning to me."

Rachel looked up into his smoldering gaze. "He is?"

"I asked him to see if anybody followed either or both of us. If anyone approaches, he'll whistle a message. We can't be found locked in each other's arms if a visitor showed up unexpectedly. They'd never believe our story. It's hard, woman, but we have to resist those urges today. Soon, we can have each other any time we want."

"Lordy, that sounds wonderful. I crave you so much, Daniel Slade."

"As much as I crave you, my delicious siren?" he teased.

"My heart is so full of yearning, I fear it will burst any moment. I feel like a wild animal who wants to claw off your garments and devour you. I can't be blamed for this new wantoness; you're responsible."

"You don't know how happy and proud that makes me to be the first man to awaken your passions."

"Does it bother you there were two others before you, one your best friend?" she had to ask.

"I wish I were the first and only man; but, in a true sense, I am. No man has received your passionate response except me."

"You are the first and will be the only man I surrender to that way."

"Does that mean you'll make that special promise to me?"

She playfully nibbled his chin to conceal her reaction to the implied proposal this time, as she had expected him to drop that stirring idea for a while. As if she misunderstood, she murmured, "Yes, I shall sail away to paradise in your arms whenever you desire me. But don't ask me to honor my word to become your lover until this mystery is over."

"What if you can't solve this puzzle or things get too perilous and you have to give up everything here to steal away with a lowly sea captain? I have money, love, but not the wealth you're accustomed to. I don't have a home, except for my ship. Frankly, I don't have much to offer you but myself."

She embraced him and, knowing he needed reassurance, vowed that was all she wanted and needed. "The only time I worried about money," she said, "was when I was near poverty and people wouldn't allow me to earn my living. If I found that hidden money, I would return it to its owner and be done with this mystery. He could work out his deal with Harry and George and not involve me. But I was Phillip's wife and only heir. Is it right to throw away everything he worked for and owned when I'm not guilty of anything?"

"If you had to lose it all to have me, Rachel, would you?"

"Are you asking me to forget everything and flee with you? Even if it makes me appear guilty of murder and theft? Even if it causes something to surface that will blacken Phillip's name without me here to protect it? Just let George, Milton, and that wicked Harry take control of Phillip's shares? Is that what I must do to prove my desire for you is real? To prove wealth means nothing to me by tossing it all away? In fact, I intend to divide the plantation between Lula Mae and Burke for their loyalty and friendship."

He surmised she was testing him about marrying her for her wealth as Craig Newman had done. "Have you already promised it to them?"

"For helping me to conceal a crime? Is that what you mean?"

"How could you even ask me such a thing?"

"The same way you asked me such curious questions. At times we seem to know each other so well; at others, not at all."

"What I meant was, if this deal is dangerous and illegal and unsolvable, and you get drawn into trouble with the law over it or over Phillip's death, would you escape with me to avoid prison and separation? Even if you'd lose everything by not staying to fight a battle you might win?"

"If it ever looks that bad and threatening, yes, I will. But you have to understand that for years I've lived under a cloud of doubt and suspicions and gossip. I want my name cleared, my honor and pride restored. I want people to learn they were wrong, cruel, and unjust. I don't care if I can never return here; it's only been pain for me anyway. I just don't want people saying they were right about me all along. I don't care what they say about Craig Newman, but I don't want them joking about William and Phillip being fools in marrying a deadly criminal like me. They were good men, Dan; I don't want their memories stained because of me."

He smiled and hugged her. "You're quite a marvelous woman. You're much stronger and braver than you realize. You'll get through this with me at your side. It's past time the truth about you came to light; I promise to help you prove it to everyone. I guess I got crazy for a minute. Every time I think about something taking you away from me, I panic."

"You?"

"Why not? I've never been in this situation before. I'm learning from scratch, just like you are. Now that I've found the woman I've waited for, I won't take any risk of losing her."

She caressed his clean-shaven jawline. "You've already won my heart, body, and soul. What more do you want?"

"You beside me every waking and sleeping moment."

"Won't you tire of me if I'm like a chain around your neck?"

"Never, my love. I'll hang a pretty ornament on you, right here," he said, lifting her left hand to motion to her third finger. His gaze settled on the golden wedding band his brother had given her; the realities of Phillip's loss and his motive for beginning this romance surfaced to haunt him.

Rachel noticed how her love's smile faded. "Should I take it off, or wait a while? I am a widow, and it's probably known publicly by now."

Dan stared at the ring as he envisioned his brother placing it there with love and trust for this woman consuming him. Was Phillip dead because he tried, any way necessary, to earn more wealth to lavish on this beauty? Phillip had never been adventurous, never overly brave. His brother had always feared the consequences of mistakes and the humiliation of their exposure. Breaking the law and stealing from clients wasn't like Phillip. What had changed him? Or was it, *who* had changed him? Rachel?

"Dan? What's wrong?" she asked in concern and alarm.

"Sorry, Rachel, but I was thinking about Phillip. Everything's happened so fast and I've only been thinking about you, about us. It just struck me that he's dead, gone forever."

If Rachel had any lingering doubts about Dan and his claims, they vanished as she witnessed the grief and sadness in his troubled blue gaze. "You're right, Dan, but I believe we've intentionally ignored his loss to keep from suffering over it. We can't bring him back. We haven't betrayed his love and trust by surrendering to our feelings for each other. All we can do for our friend Phillip is to make sure his name isn't blackened. If there is a crime and a reckless mistake involved, I hope we can resolve it without a scandal to stain his memory. I did love him and care about him."

Dan fused his gaze with hers. "I know you did, Rachel. I suppose it didn't seem real because we've been separated for so long and I didn't see him die. Maybe I kept thinking your ruse about his trip was real and he would return home any day now. Seeing that ring brought him to life."

Rachel understood his meaning. She remained silent while he dealt with his anguish and loss and quelled his guilt over her.

Soon Dan smiled wryly and suggested, "Let's get busy before church is over and Milton decides to make a visit here. If he's in on something strange with Harry, he could be on alert."

"Before we get started, I need to show you the warning I received last night." Rachel took the note from her bag and read it to him. "It says, 'Do not double cross me, Señor McCandless, or your wife is dead. If you think you can protect her from us, ask her how many times we have threatened her and been close enough to keep our word. There is no place you can hide her we cannot find her and slay her. Do as you agreed and she is safe.' It was pinned to my door with this." She held out the knife to him.

Dan examined the weapon. "It's the kind anyone can buy almost anywhere, so no clue there. You didn't see or hear anyone?"

"No, thank goodness. But this tells us one important fact: the client doesn't know Phillip is dead, so he couldn't have murdered him."

"Don't be misled, Rachel. The message could be for you and was only meant to appear it's to Phillip so you won't think he harmed him. The timing is suspicious, as if Phillip's heir needed to be warned before the news of his demise was announced . . . Let's talk about it later; we have to finish here before church is over and Baldwin's on the streets."

Dan jimmied the lock on the man's desk without damaging it. Rachel pulled out a record book, opened it, and scanned the pages.

"Look at this, Dan!" she shrieked in excitement. "A notation about a cargo ship reserved on May fourteenth to sail to Haiti. Isn't that close to Cuba?"

"About forty-eight miles away, within sight from a mountain or crow's nest on a ship. You mentioned Cuba yesterday. Who do you know there?"

"No one. At least, I don't think I know anyone. These two sets of initials mean nothing to me. C.T. and J.C.," she murmured. "This is Milton's handwriting, so he isn't totally in the dark."

She reasoned aloud to stimulate Dan's astute thoughts. "Harry said Milton denied knowing who the client is, but that could have come from loyalty to Phillip by honoring Phillip's request to hold silent. I wonder if Milton's been told Phillip is dead. The authorities said they looked for a doctor who might have been summoned to tend Phillip, so they questioned others before confronting me. They must know I told Milton that Phillip was up North on business. They might even know I deluded his other partners, and even know where I was. Maybe they didn't tell me because they hoped to entrap me. I'll bet I shocked them when I told the truth. They can't prove you lied to help me, so they're bogged down with three witnesses in my favor. I wish I knew which of his partners is lying. Since only initials are listed, maybe Phillip was the only one who knew the details of this deal. I wonder if Milton would reveal anything if I questioned him. With Phillip dead, I am his partner, so why withhold facts? If Milton's involved in this wild scheme and it's trouble, probably not."

Dan was intrigued. "Tell me again what Phillip said about Cuba."

"I don't know what it all refers to."

"Then repeat every word you heard, Rachel."

She obeyed his request as best she could: "Your life, everything in danger. . . . Enemies, get to you anywhere. . . . Stop at nothing . . . to get what they want. . . . Guns and ammunition. . . . Must return the money. . . . Sell anything to repay them. . . . Only way to stay alive and safe. . . . Need guns badly. . . . War. . . . Freedom. . . . He'll come soon and help me. . . . Don't double cross Harry and the—Must honor the deal. . . . All those warnings came. . . . Tried to stop deal. . . . Killing me. . . . got the money hidden. . . . You'll be blamed. . . . Can't go to the law. . . . Go see him in Cuba. . . . He'll help. . . . He'll stop them. . . . Only hope. . . . Sorry got you into this mess. . . ."

Dan scowled as he studied the words for clues and facts. Perhaps Phillip *had been* referring to him as the first helper! It was fortunate his brother hadn't called out his name during delirium. Or had he? No, he didn't believe she knew his true relationship to Phillip.

"I can see why those words frightened you, Rachel, for they hold definite warnings. In your place, I would have taken the same course of action. It surely sounds as if Phillip took their advance and hid it. That would match the hints those two partners gave us. I wish I knew who he was talking about in Cuba; I don't recall any friends or business associates there. If a treacherous or greedy friend got him into this deal, he wouldn't have suspected anything was wrong; but something happened to change his mind. Until we get a real clue about the final destination, it wouldn't do any good to sail there; it's a big island with too many people. We couldn't go around asking who ordered arms and ammunition for a rebellion."

"What do you mean?"

"Cuban Rebels have been fighting for their independence from Spain since '68," Dan related. "A purchase of that size and price could only be to fight a war for freedom: that's what Phillip's clues imply. The American position is one of sympathy but noninterference. Of course, we almost got drawn into the conflict two years ago when Spain captured the *Virginius* and executed fifty-three sailors. She was a gunrunning ship, Cuban owned, but some of the crew members were Americans and she flew the American flag. Trouble was averted when King Alfonso XII wisely compensated the families involved—if you can pay for lives you've taken! From what I've heard, horrible atrocities are going on there, so Spain isn't endearing herself to us. We already have trouble with her in other locations: Puerto Rico, Guam, and the Philippines. Those are major shipping routes that have to be protected. The rebel leaders are Antonio Maceo and Carlos Manuel de Céspedes; so you can see, those initials don't match these in the book."

Rachel was alarmed. "If one gun-running ship was captured and sailors slain, that means it is dangerous and deadly to supply arms. It also means our government is trying to remain neutral. If we interfere by providing arms, or they had, it means trouble with the authorities—trouble I don't need. Selling weapons to rebels is risky, and must be illegal."

"And profitable, very profitable, Rachel. Did Phillip need money?"

"Not that I knew of, unless it had to do with a gambling debt. The news that he was a gambler came as a shock to me, if it's true. Both men may be lying for a reason."

Dan liked the way Rachel always seemed to give his brother the benefit of doubt and to protect Phillip's image when possible. "I hope they're wrong."

"Now that my husband's death is exposed, I can check his will, bank account, and all records. I'll start on that tomorrow. And I'll speak with Milton, too. I bet he hates the reality of us being partners, or just being in business with a female; so will Harry and maybe George. Tell me, Dan, how do you know so much about Cuba?"

He chuckled and scolded in a playful tone, "Suspicions about me returning already, woman. Shame on you. I'm a sea captain who delivers cargoes around the world. If I don't keep up with the trouble spots, I could get myself and my crew killed and my ship sunk or confiscated."

"I understand, and shame on you for thinking I didn't," she chided. "I told you about those incidents Phillip considered warnings; from Harry's words about the backdown; the timing matches for that to be true. Those were violent crimes I want solved. Do you think Phillip meant they were killing him, or his guilt or illness was killing him?"

"Either or both, or neither. Maybe it was the fever talking."

"Not with cholera."

"I haven't seen it up close; what does it do?"

She hated to relate how his friend had died. "Vomiting, diarrhea, cramps, fast and heavy drying up of the body, cold and withered skin, drawn face, faint pulse, and enormous thirst. It's infectious, painful, and swift. It usually is spread through contaminated water or food. That's why Burke thought Phillip caught it from drinking that filthy-black river water. I'm certain it wasn't that, or others would have contracted it."

"How does that imitate a poisoning?"

"Arsenic has the same symptoms."

"What was that about almonds that you mentioned concerning William's death?"

"Strychnine can look like a heart attack if the right amount is used. The victim sometimes grabs his chest and has a grimace of agony on his face that freezes there if death is rapid."

Dan pushed aside how his brother had spent his last day on earth, in agony and alone. His heart pumped turbulently with dread at Rachel's revelations, her vast knowledge of such matters. Slips? *Surely not.* "That's gory, but fascinating. How did you come by such learning, woman?"

13

Rachel wondered if Dan was trying to sound casual but was really tense. It was best to be honest. "Some from the plantation, from poisons used to kill rodent and weeds. Some from Craig, about chemicals used in the textile and milling processes. And some from doctors during the investigations of me. Does it make you nervous to discover I know so much about those things?"

"Don't be foolish," Dan scolded. "You said Phillip might have been poisoned; I wanted to know how you came to that speculation. It's evident Craig didn't think you were capable of murder or he wouldn't have told you such things. Did you have other suitors between your husbands?"

That took her by surprise. "That's a strange question."

"From a jealous lover?" he teased. "There isn't anyone around who's going to battle me over you now that you're free again, is there?"

"No. The only men who approached me were making lewd advances. They wanted to bed me but not risk becoming one of my victims. Most of them shied away in terror of me putting an evil spell on them."

"Ah, fear of the Sea Witch stealing their souls," he jested.

"Can you be so sure of me this soon, Dan? You've heard the rumors and you've witnessed what the law thinks of me. You know I buried Phillip in secret, and you only have my word for why I did it. I could be lying about everything. How can you trust me?"

"The same way you can trust me, Rachel—on blind faith and feelings."

Should she confess that her heart coaxed her to accept him swiftly and totally, but her wary mind cautioned her to go slowly and to hold back from committing herself fully? She wanted to follow her heart, but her bad experiences with men warned her to listen to her keen mind. "I suppose I'm just anxious about how rapidly and unexpectedly we got so close. I worry about making another mistake with a man. I have to be certain it's you I need, not just a man to protect me when I'm so vulnerable and afraid."

"After what you've suffered, I can't blame you for having doubts and worries about all men. Complete faith and love will come, Rachel, if you don't fight it out of fear I'm like all the others who've hurt and used you."

"You aren't like any man I've ever known. Maybe that scares me more. Your power frightens me sometimes. You, Daniel Slade, can hurt me more than anyone has if you aren't being honest and sincere."

"The same is true of you, my enchanting siren. No woman has been this close and special to me. I want you so much that, even if I learned you were guilty of being a Black Widow, I would still love you and want you; I would believe the power of our love is strong enough to break that curse on you. I never thought a woman would get to me as you have. You're right; it *is* scary. It will take adjusting on both our sides. We won't rush it, love. Let me finish checking this book and locking Baldwin's desk, then we must leave."

As Dan read and turned pages, Rachel observed him. She told herself she shouldn't be so skittish and leery. They cared about each other and about what happened to each other. They were being helpmates to each other. They shared most of the same goals, dreams, and hopes. Even when mistrustful, neither of them was childish, petty, vengeful, or reckless. Weren't those qualities and traits of true love?

"We're all finished. Let's leave while it's still safe."

"What now?" Rachel queried.

"You handle your normal business with the banker and lawyer. See what response you get from Harry and George from your telegrams to them tomorrow. See how everyone reacts to this news. Then all we can do is wait for May fourteenth to see who comes and what's in store."

"What about us, Dan? We can't risk seeing each other at home or in town, not with an investigation of me in progress."

"We're friends and business acquaintances, so that will cover the visits."

"That isn't what I meant," she murmured, her cheeks flushing.

Dan pulled her into his embrace and kissed her. "Don't fret, love; we'll be together soon; I promise. But for now, we must get out of here; it's late. We'll meet for lunch tomorrow, in public to prevent suspicions, in the cafe down the street at one. You can tell me all you've learned."

They kissed a final time, checked the office for slips, and departed.

*

Again, Rachel was shot at on her way home. Before she could dash for cover, she decided to see if it was only a scare tactic. She halted and glared in that direction. As suspected and hoped, no second bullet or enemy approached her position. Assured somebody wanted her terrified but not dead, courage and daring filled her. "Stop threatening me or the deal is off!" she shouted. "Be nice and everything will be fine!" Those words provoked no response, so she rode for Moss Haven.

*

Early Monday morning, the two police investigators arrived at Rachel's home. They told her they had come to take down affidavits about Phillip's death and secret burial. Rachel, Lula Mae, and Burke were placed in different rooms with closed doors. Rachel guessed it was to prevent them from overhearing each other and was done without warning in hopes of ensnaring them in a lie. She knew the aggressive men would compare their words with hopes of discovering inconsistencies.

One man took down her explanation in detail, while another did the same with Lula Mae and Burke. She presumed they would take down Dan's statement, too. She prayed that after telling him everything he wouldn't make a mistake and get all of them into trouble.

"Why did you lie to Mr. Baldwin, Mrs. McCandless?" the surly man asked Rachel. "That point confuses me."

"It was to gain time to carry out important business details. If I had told them Phillip was dead, they would have panicked and we couldn't have completed our business. As long as they believed I was acting on Phillip's behalf, they cooperated. I'm sure you realize that men do not like doing business with a female, not even a wife. I deceived Milton Baldwin until I could finish in Athens and Augusta, then meet with him in person to take Phillip's place in their firm. It wasn't wise or kind to leave him a note or drop that shocking news in his lap, then take off for several weeks. I didn't want to leave him worrying over how his partner's death would affect him and their firm. I needed to be present with plenty of time for discussion. Besides, I didn't think I should tell them such news before I told the law."

"What business could be that important?"

"This is a confidential report and paper, is it not?"

"Of course, ma'am."

This time she had to lie. "That's good, because Phillip's motive could create problems and ill will if his partners learned why I truly went to see them. Phillip told me there was a big problem with a very large deal he had worked out with a client, a deal that is crucial to the survival of those two companies. He suspected that his partners were stalling orders, perhaps even making secret deals and not paying him his total share of the profits. As you recall, I worked for Phillip before I married him; I understand books, orders, inventories, and such. Phillip wanted me to get the facts about the companies' actions. The trip was planned early Thursday. Before he died on Friday morning, he begged me to rush there to do my snooping before they learned he was dead. He said that if they panicked, they might lie and cover the truth. The crux of the matter is, he thought he was being cheated. He wanted me to catch them by surprise with an unexpected visit before they could destroy evidence of their guilt, so I pretended Phillip was away on unrelated business and I was on holiday."

"Did you obtain the facts you needed?"

"Not really. Neither man would let me study the company's books without Phillip being present or sending a letter of authorization. I'm afraid neither my husband nor I thought of that angle. I plan to telegraph them today about his demise. Now they won't have any excuse to keep me from the books; after all, I am their partner. Will there be a problem with me taking another short business trip soon? I assure you I shall return home."

"After I examine your statement and the affidavits of the three witnesses, I'll inform you if you can leave town," he replied.

"Tell me, sir, how and when did your office get this tip?"

"A letter was slipped under our door last Thursday morning."

Rachel realized that was when she and Dan were leaving Athens. Who had known her schedule? Dan, her servants, Luke Conner, the men in the Athens and Savannah telegraph offices, and possibly an unknown spy. "What did it say? Surely I have a right to be told why an anonymous note influenced you."

"There's no reason not to tell you, ma'am. It said: 'Phillip McCandless has been dead since March 26. His wife killed him. She buried him in secret. She went to Augusta and Athens on March 29 to steal his companies. She will return late April 16. Get that murdering Black Widow this time.' We figured it was simple to learn if Mr. McCandless was alive and the letter was a joke. But with you gone and him claimed gone, we couldn't. We did what little investigating we could during your absence."

"I want to view this letter, sir, to see if I recognize the handwriting."

"That might be helpful, if it were possible. But it vanished Friday night."

Rachel gaped at him. "You mean it was stolen from a police station!"

"I'm afraid so, ma'am." The man appeared embarrassed and annoyed.

"Doesn't that strike you as odd, sir? Who would provide a tip, then steal it? For what reason?"

"To get an investigation underway and to keep from being involved."

"But breaking in and stealing are crimes," she reasoned. "Only a fool would do such things in a police station. Doesn't it make you wonder how this informer got his information and why he altered it into lies?"

"I figured somebody slipped up on you, saw what you were doing, got suspicious, left without being seen, then reported it to us."

"So why accuse me of murder, if all this person saw was a burial? And why follow me to see what I was doing and where I was going?"

"I hate to say it, ma'am, but probably because of your past."

"As there wasn't a crime, sir, it seems to me that someone was trying to get me into trouble for revenge or spite. Did the script look feminine?"

He was intrigued. "Why would you ask that?"

"Perhaps it was a woman who loved and lost one of my husbands."

"That's farfetched, ma'am."

"No more than me being accused as a Black Widow, a murderess."

He scratched his head and flicked nonexistent dust flecks from his jacket.

"You have to admit, ma'am, there were good reasons for our doubts and questions every time. It was printed neatly, but I can't say if a man or woman wrote it. I will tell you that this case isn't closed yet. If we find discrepancies in the statements, we'll need to question all of you again. If any other clues come up, we'll check them out. Chief Anderson hasn't decided about having a doctor examine the body; that's still a possibility."

"Whatever you need to do to clear me, do it swiftly, please."

"I'll try my best to have this case solved very soon. If you have nothing else to say, read this carefully. If it's correct, sign it."

After he left the room, Rachel mused on what she'd learned. Lula Mae and Burke couldn't speak correct English, much less write such a letter; and they'd never betray her. Too, others had known her schedule: Harry and George. The tip proved someone knew when Phillip died and how he was buried. It was strange why the culprit didn't report her deed that day, or on the Saturday or Sunday afterward; the waiting period bewildered her. Why say she was trying to steal his companies? By inheritance, they were hers. Perhaps that part of the note was meant to mislead her and the law.

Rachel didn't want to speculate on Daniel Slade, but . . . Having heard the rumors about her on Thursday, had Dan arrived here Friday and witnessed her behavior, assumed she had slain his old and dear friend, then set out to entrap her? She reflected on their many days and one passionate night together. Had knowing Phillip was dead been the reason why he could seduce his old friend's wife—no fear of betrayal? No, she concluded, if Dan believed she murdered Phillip, he would handle the revenge himself, after he was certain she was guilty.

*

Later, in Savannah, Rachel entered the telegraph office and sent messages to Harry and George: "Sad news. Phillip died. Gave no client name. Cannot find money. Will await client arrival May fourteen. Need facts on deal before honor. Rachel McCandless." *One task out of the way today.*

She went to McCandless & Baldwin Shipping Firm to handle the second. She did not knock, and entered to find Milton at work at his desk.

The green-eyed man glanced up, looked at her a moment, and stood. He smiled and said, "Hello, Rachel. This is a pleasant surprise. Come in and sit down. You won't believe what happened while you were away. The police came to see me Thursday with a foolish story that Phillip is dead."

Rachel watched the man with his black hair and even features as she responded, "I'm afraid it's true, Milton; Phillip is dead. He came down with cholera and died on the twenty-sixth of last month."

"My God, it's true! Why didn't you tell me sooner?"

To Rachel, he appeared shocked, but seemed to recover quickly. "I'll explain that in a moment. First, what did the officers ask you?"

Milton's quizzical green gaze settled on her face. "They came by and wanted to know where Phillip was. I told them he was away tending to other business; that's what I believed. They asked if he'd acted strange before he left; I said he hadn't. They told me about an anonymous letter claiming Phillip was dead, that you'd killed him and buried him secretly. I said that was mad, that you and Phillip love each other and are very happy. They wanted to know who he used as a doctor. I told them, and they left."

"Did you send that news to Harry or George on Thursday? Or later?"

"Certainly not! I thought it was nothing but a cruel joke."

"Did the police speak with you again Saturday after they saw me?"

"No, they couldn't: I was off fishing with friends. I haven't received any messages or visits since Thursday. What's going on, Rachel?"

She hurried on with questions she needed to learn the answers to. "What do you know about this big arms and ammunition deal with the other two companies, the one you're shipping out on May fourteenth?"

He hesitated a minute. "Nothing much, except the date and two men's initials. For some curious reason, Phillip wouldn't discuss it with me. I assumed it was a private deal. What's going on, Rachel?" he asked again.

Once more she ignored his query to continue her line of questions. "You have no idea about the names that go with those initials?"

"No. Why? And why does Harry want to know about the deal, too? He and Phillip are—*were*—partners. Why wouldn't he be informed? He telegraphed me to ask the destination of the delivery ship. All Phillip told me was to write down Haiti. Is there, *was* there a problem between them?"

She tried to be clever to delude him, to use clues to extract other ones. "I'm not sure yet. That's why I had to rush off to Augusta and Athens. Before Phillip died, he mentioned a mystery and asked me to check it out immediately. After he died I rushed off to carry out his last wish before this news was exposed. I'm sorry I had to deceive you for a short time, Milton, but I didn't want you dropping a hint to his other partners; and I wanted to wait until we could sit down and talk in person. Do you understand?" She put on her most innocent look.

The thirty-two-year old man murmured, "I suppose so . . . . What do you want to do about your share of the firm?"

She noticed he changed the subject to a selfish topic. "I'd like to go over the books with you first, then decide."

"Certainly, Partner. We can do that right now, if you have time."

"The sooner, the better. Thank you, Milton." She observed him as he pulled Phillip's chair over to his desk, unlocked a drawer, and withdrew a ledger. He opened it and located the section he wanted. He didn't seem too grieved over her husband's death, and that troubled Rachel. Neither did he appear distressed to have her as his new partner, if he'd given that much thought yet. He looked up and smiled at her.

"If you'll have a seat next to me, we'll begin. It won't take long."

Milton was right, it didn't. "As you can see, we're in deep debt," he remarked as he finished his explanation. "Current shipments are just barely keeping us afloat by covering current expenses; not much left over to pay rear bills. Those attacks recently cost us plenty to settle them. Phillip, you now, and I are fortunate we both have other investments for support."

Rachel eyed the ledger. It didn't look altered, as it would if he'd been warned to do so before she viewed it. But how did she know there wasn't another book for other ships and cargoes? Should she believe this was the whole stormy picture? Did she have any reason to distrust Milton Baldwin?

"I'm looking forward to the large payment for delivering that cargo on the fourteenth," he said. "I assume it will proceed. We—you and I—surely need it. There's just too much competition these days to make this business profitable anymore. I've been seeking new clients and trying to recover old ones we've lost to cheaper prices; so far, it doesn't look promising. We sold off two ships last month to cut expenses; keeping so many idle in port was draining us of needed money. If something good doesn't happen soon, selling everything won't even get us in the clear or leave us with much—if any—profit. If Phillip hasn't already told you how terrible matters have gotten, I'm sorry you're having to hear it from me today."

"So am I, Milton, and I was in the dark. It doesn't look good."

He shook his head. "No, I'm afraid it doesn't. If I locate a buyer, are you interested in selling out before we sink?"

"I suppose so. But we'll discuss that possibility later. I do have to leave; I have several other appointments today. Thank you again, Milton."

"If you need any help or advice, Rachel; you know where to find me."

She feigned a smile. "That's very kind of you. Good-bye."

As she walked to the cafe where she was scheduled to meet Dan, Rachel fumed. *Why offer friendship now when you and your wife haven't socialized with me in the past unless it was necessary! Your partner and supposed friend is dead, and you didn't seem to care much. Why?*

Dan was waiting for her. She put on a cheerful smile and joined him.

"Good morning, love," he whispered. "How are things going?"

"Not good at all today. The—" She halted when the waiter arrived to take their orders, then left. "The law showed up very early to take our statements. Have they seen you yet?"

"Early this morning, but a nicer officer this time. I made certain my story will match yours. Lula Mae and Burke knew to say I was present?"

"Yes, I explained things to them after your departure Saturday. That's the only lie they had to tell. Have you noticed any shadow following you?"

"No, and you aren't being followed, either. Luke's across the street near a tree. He just gave me the clear signal. You look upset."

Rachel related her meeting with Milton Baldwin. "It seems all three of Phillip's companies are in almost desperate need of money. That gives more and more of a reason why he would accept a mysterious deal like this."

"Are you in financial trouble, love?"

"Certainly not. I'm seeing the banker, insurance broker, and lawyer after we eat. The companies need money, but I don't think they're broke. I have the plantation and earnings from sharecropping. I'll be fine."

"If you need anything, please tell me."

She tried not to stare at his handsome face. "Stop worrying."

"I will worry until we can risk another meeting on Thursday and you tell me all is fine. I wish you didn't have to do this alone."

"I can manage it, honestly." She told Dan about her home being searched during their absence and about being shot at again. "Whoever it is isn't trying to kill me, just terrify me. Frankly, it's making me more angry and defiant than afraid. We'll finish this later; here comes our food."

*

Rachel received astonishing news at the bank: their account was almost empty, barely enough there to pay one month's expenses! And that was if she managed it carefully. She had only a little cash at home in her household money box. She stared at the large withdrawals almost every month and wondered where that money had gone. She fretted it had been lost due to Phillip's gambling. Almost penniless . . . That fact evoked horrible reminders of her days near poverty after Craig's death. She left the bank in a state of dismay and confusion, and nibblings of anger.

Her visit with the insurance broker was worse. Phillip had canceled his insurance in February! The man said it was because he couldn't afford to continue it. He said it was a shame it was dropped so close to when it was needed, but Rachel did not detect a wicked implication in his words or manner. The man was polite and sympathetic.

As she walked toward the lawyer's office with a heavy heart, Rachel imagined what people and the law would think if they learned about the cancellation of the insurance: that Phillip had feared for his life and had done it so his murderess couldn't inherit his wealth after she did away with him. She dreaded the new gossip which was sure to come soon and felt her resentment and anger increase.

The lawyer did give her a little good news: she was Phillip's sole heir to his shares of three businesses and the plantation. Yet, the man revealed that her husband had seen him on the street on March twenty-fourth and he had asked for an appointment on the twenty-ninth "to discuss a serious legal problem," but, of course, hadn't kept it. Rachel told him that she didn't know what the meeting would have covered, but she suspected it was to obtain advice about the illegal deal. She was glad he didn't hint at her husband's intention to change his will to exclude a woman he feared.

The lawyer informed her that Phillip had mentioned he might want to sell his two out-of-town partnerships, as they weren't profitable anymore. Nor did he like having businesses so far away. He told her Phillip had hinted at putting the sale money into the shipping firm to get it back on solid ground. The man studied the file to make sure he had covered everything.

In view of the big deal, she mused, how could Phillip think or say the two companies weren't making money? Unless he intended to break that mysterious contract . . . Or to take his profit first, then sell? Had Harry or George—or both men—known of Phillip's plans to break up their partnerships? Would they do *anything* to prevent losing a needed investor? Or perhaps Phillip had planned to sell out only because he needed cash. It was odd her husband hadn't mentioned such things to her.

Rachel thanked the lawyer for his assistance and left. She stood outside his office for a time, thinking and planning her next step. She had no insurance, and virtually no money in the bank. She wouldn't receive support from sharecropper earnings until fall, five months away, if no disaster occurred to destroy the crops. With the three companies in trouble, so was she. Milton had exposed that about the firm; and George and Harry had implied it about the arms and ammunition companies. If that mysterious deal fell through, all those holdings could collapse.

These revelations had to explain why Phillip was so desperate to make money any way necessary. Phillip would never want to lose his masculine pride and be humiliated by financial devastation. He could have used that advance to gamble with, hoping to earn enough winnings to rescue himself, then back out of the hazardous deal with a polite refusal, rich from using their money as a stake. If he had been so foolish and couldn't face ruin, humiliation, and perils, would he take his life to avoid them? Rachel couldn't answer that distressing question and didn't want to think about it.

She asked herself if the other partners could be just as desperate to save their reputations. It was possible that Harry had exploited Phillip's weakness and plight to coerce him into restarting that order. Both had warned that without the advance, the deal couldn't go through, even if it were legal. Rachel trembled in dread. Even if she sold Moss Haven and all three partnerships, she could not collect enough to replace five hundred thousand dollars if she were forced to be responsible for its loss. If she knew the deal was legal, she would have asked the lawyer about that angle. But she was in enough trouble without taking more risks. She had inherited Phillip's section of the assets but probably his shares of the companies' debts, too. She wondered if Dan's orders and payments would make any difference with the companies' finances. She hoped so.

Rachel knew she had to learn where she stood. She returned to the telegraph office and sent Harry and George a second message: "Am your partner now. Please send financial report fast. Will check company books soon. Advise when ready and convenient. Rachel McCandless."

As Rachel waited for Burke Wells to pick her up in the carriage at the agreed time and location, she was lost in thought over her troubles. She had been married three times to wealthy men, but had virtually no inheritance. She had been a fairly good wife and done nothing wrong, but she was believed to have murdered all her husbands and the son of one of them. Surely she was cursed by wicked fate! She yearned for Dan's strong arms to give her courage and comfort.

She was tempted to go to his hotel and to fall into his arms, to entice him to take her away from all these troubles. But she couldn't. That would make both of them appear guilty of murdering Phillip to be together. They would never make it out of port on his ship before the law tossed them into jail. Besides, she had to stay here and fight these cruelties against her, to put an end to the evil spell on her, to be free to marry Dan without risking his survival.

Burke arrived and she got into the carriage. They rode home in near silence as the manager comprehended she had worries on her mind.

"Burke, I need to speak with you and Lula Mae about something important," she told him as she stepped down from the carriage. "Please come into the house after you put away the horses."

When the three gathered in the kitchen, Rachel said, "I want to thank both of you for doing so well with the authorities. I hated to ask you to tell that one little lie, but without Captain Slade's help, I doubt those hateful men would have believed us. They probably would have carted me off to jail, even with no evidence I'd done something wrong."

"We done just like you said, Miz Rachel. Gawd won't go ablamin' us for he'pin' you. Ain't no call fur dem poleece to be botherin' you. Dey'll be pow'ful sorry dey messed wif us if dey do. De worst is over."

She took a deep breath, then murmured, "I wish it was, Burke, but I received bad news in town today." She lightly skimmed the story of her financial condition. It wasn't necessary for her servants to know the private details, only that rough times on the plantation were ahead. "For a while, until I get matters settled, we'll need to be careful with spending."

"You cain't be saying you're bound to lose all your stuff, Miss Rachel?"

She looked at the shocked housekeeper. "No, Lula Mae, but probably some of it. That business I hurried out of town to tend is crucial for keeping those companies alive. There's a problem with a big order; if it fails, we'll all be hurt. But everybody is working hard to make sure it succeeds. Mr. Baldwin is looking for a buyer for the shipping firm here. I've agreed to sell out if he does. But I don't think either of us will have much money left after the firm's bills are paid. We just have to wait until the crops come in and pray nothing happens to them."

"Ah inspect dem ever' week, Miz Rachel. Dey's doin' fine. It looks to be a big year. Don' you go aworryin'. Gawd looks after His children. Ah'll keeps dem share-croppers workin' hard."

Rachel's heart warmed. "Thank you, Burke."

"No needs to worry 'bout eating, Miss Rachel," said Lula Mae. "The smoke-house and pantry holds a gracious plenty. It won't be a long spell afore the garden comes in. Unless the cow goes dry, she gives a bounty of milk and butter. I'll tends the garden every morning to make her give us all she can. Nothing'll go to waste; I'll can all we don't eat whilst it's fresh. I won't buy nothing at the market we don't has to have."

Rachel sent her an affectionate smile. The woman always came through for her during the worst of times. "Thank you, Lula Mae. I knew I could depend on you two for help and understanding. Nobody has more loyal workers than I do. I love you both."

"I bet yo're plum worn out, you pore girl. You need a hot supper, a long bath, a sip of whiskey, and a good night's rest. I'll tend it for you."

"You're right, Lula Mae; thank you. I plan to go back into town Wednesday, Burke. I'm going to try to borrow money from the bank against the crops. If they'll let me have a loan, it will solve our troubles for a while."

"Ah'll be ready when you wants to go attendin' to dat bisness."

"Lula Mae, would you like to ride along with us and do any shopping? It will give you a chance for a nice diversion."

"I mite could go, Miss Rachel; that sounds most wonderful to me."

"Then, you'll come along. We'll leave around ten o'clock Wednesday."

*

Tuesday, Phillip McCandless's obituary appeared in local newspapers. Rachel read it quickly, then, again, slowly. Nothing was mentioned about cause of death. Nor was there a hint about the investigation she was enduring, but she was certain anyone seeing it would assume one was in progress, also as usual. She prayed no aggressive and rude reporter, like that Harold Seymour in Augusta, would come to plead for an interview. She told Lula Mae if that happened, not to let him inside the house and to say she wasn't available.

Lula Mae Morris and Burke Wells had on protective airs today, and she was grateful for their love and concern.

Rachel realized with sadness that she could not purchase a headstone for Phillip's grave until her finances improved. Burke said he would make one she could letter herself until she could afford a proper one. He left the house to tend that chore promptly. He also told her he would make a mound over the grave and pretty up the area since the site no longer had to remain a secret. That pleased and relieved her.

During the day, Lula Mae helped Rachel remove Phillip's clothes from their bedroom. They hauled them to the washshed for Burke to go through first for his selections, then the two workers. If anything was left, Burke was to give them to less fortunate and hardworking sharecroppers on her land. Items of value, such as his watch and a diamond stickpin, she placed in her household money box and would decide later what to do with them.

As Rachel slipped off her gold wedding band to put it away, she pondered a curious point: there was nothing—in their bedroom, the attic, the rest of the house, and the outbuildings—of Phillip's personal effects to enlighten her about his past. She found no picture, letter, memento, or anything from the days between his birth and his arrival in Savannah. It was almost as if he hadn't existed before coming here to live! Or had he, in a moment of anguish and turmoil, destroyed all reminders?

If not, perhaps he had them stored in a trunk somewhere, such as in the office storeroom or the warehouse downtown. She must ask Milton. It would be nice, and perhaps enlightening, to see some keepsakes of his past.

*

It was near one o'clock in the morning when Rachel was awakened by loud noises. She jerked up in bed and listened. It sounded like rocks slamming against the house! The commotion ceased before she could reach the front window and look outside. Her gaze searched the yard and nearby area for movement, but she saw nothing. Her heart pounded, but she couldn't cower there in terror. She retrieved her derringer and crept downstairs. She knew the windows and doors were locked on the first floor as Dan had cautioned her. She sneaked to a window and scanned the area once more, but everything appeared normal. She slipped to the front door, leaned her ear against it, and listened. She heard nothing but crickets and frogs.

Rachel took in a deep breath, then released it. Her lagging courage resummoned, she placed her hand on the knob and eased the door open as silently as the oiled hinges would allow. She peeked into the yard. The waxing moon would be full in three nights and light was plentiful. Her gaze lowered to the porch, which was littered with rocks. The odor of fresh paint filled her nostrils and her alarmed gaze saw the reason for it: ugly names and hateful messages were scrawled in black paint on the porch floor and on the house front and door.

"Damn you, you coward!" she yelled into the shadows at a distance, in case the culprit or culprits were still lurking there.

Lula Mae came running around the house, shouting her mistress's name to avoid getting shot by accident. She was carrying a shotgun and a lantern. "Miss Ra—" The woman fell silent as she gaped at the awful sight and her pale-faced mistress. She propped the weapon against a post, rushed to Rachel, and embraced the trembling and tearful female. "Lord have no mercy on them bastards! Kill them all for doing this most awfullest thing! You all right, Miss Rachel? They didn't hurt you, did they? Speak to Lula Mae! You hurt some place?"

Rachel gathered her wits and control. "I'm unharmed, Lula Mae. They were gone when I came downstairs, or they're hiding out there in the darkness to witness the effect of their cruel mischief. The rocks awoke me. Look what they painted on my home!" she cried in distress.

In a mixture of moon- and lanternlight, both gazes read the words scrawled in black paint: KILLER, BLACK WIDOW, WHORE, and GET OUT.

"It's starting all over again, Lula Mae," she murmured. "How can they be so cruel? How can they judge me guilty and evil without proof? Will I never receive the benefit of doubt? Will this damned curse never end?"

Lula Mae patted her shoulder and coaxed, "Comes insides, Miss Rachel. I'll fix you some warm milk to calm yore jitters. Those bastards won't come sneaking back to do more hurt tonight. We'll pick up them rocks and paints over that mess tomorrow. Don't go aworrying 'bout it tonight. Burke's home's too far away, so he cain't hear what happened. We might aks him to sleeps in the barn or carriage house for a spell."

"I'll be fine, Lula Mae. And don't go to any trouble with firing the stove and preparing hot milk this late. I'll take a sip of brandy. From now on, we'll keep our guns loaded and ready to use if those villains try this again."

"If they do, Miss Rachel, we'll shoot ever blamed one of them! It's bound to be bad awful for a spell. I'll have Burke hangs lanterns on the porch so we can see their wicked faces when we shoot them. The law won't do nothing to stop them, but we will."

"You're right; it's useless to report this incident to them. They don't care what happens to me. You get back to bed, and so will I. There's nothing we can do to-night."

"You want me to stays in the house with you?"

"That isn't necessary. I'll lock the doors and keep my gun nearby." Rachel didn't want to set a pattern for the housekeeper being underfoot at night, especially if Dan . . . Her love, she wanted and needed him. She wished he were here. It would be a while before that was safe; and without a doubt, things would get much worse before that glorious day.

*

Wednesday morning, Rachel and Burke left for town. Lula Mae insisted on staying at Moss Haven to guard the house against another attack. As the two departed, the housekeeper went to work on the damage.

*

Rachel sat waiting for Burke to return from his errands, as the meeting at the bank had not taken as long as expected. The man's rejection of her loan came fast and easy for him, or so it appeared to her. He claimed that with the companies in such bad shape and with the uncertainty of the crops, she didn't have adequate collateral for a loan. The last reason was because she refused to put up Moss Haven to back a loan. She couldn't allow anything to take her home away from her, as failure of repayment would do. She wouldn't take that risk until it became absolutely necessary. One hope remained: she had jewelry she could sell, gifts from Phillip.

Excluding her servants and her secret lover she was on her own now. Things appeared grim, hopeless, and perilous, but she was resolved not to be defeated. In three weeks and two days, she would discover if that big contract was legal and if the client would be understanding about the lost advance. If those two things came true and the investigation halted, all of her troubles would be over and she could have a future with Dan.

A terrible reality struck home: no, she wouldn't have an answer on May four-teenth! Phillip was supposed to sail with the cargo that day. It would take a while for the client to realize it was overdue, then more time for him to come and investigate why.

She couldn't understand why she hadn't heard from Harry and George by now;

that made her anxious. If something good didn't happen soon, she would be at the end of her money by the last day of May. Would Dan think she had known of her troubles all along and had set out to entrap him for her survival? Would he—

Rachel's heart suddenly thudded and her gaze widened in disbelief and alarm. To avoid being noticed by passing people who might gape at her, she was sitting sideways on the end of a bench that faced the river and was located in a garden area between Bay Street and Factor's Row; she was almost concealed behind a cluster of large and flowering azaleas. As she glanced toward the street to check for Burke's approach, she saw Captain Daniel Slade strolling down the other side of the street with Miss Camellia Jones on his arm!

Rachel leaned out of sight, but peered through the bush limbs to watch them. They were laughing and chatting as if old and close friends! Fury and suspicions flooded her mind. She wondered if that wealthy witch had hired Dan to ensnare and destroy her for revenge. Phillip's past relationship with the flaming redhead would explain how Dan had known about her husband, and the cunning male could have fabricated the rest of his tale.

Anguish knifed Rachel's heart, and anger ruled her mind. She could imagine Camellia's laughter and taunts when the hateful witch exposed their ruse: for once, the "Black Widow" had fallen under a predator's spell.

Rachel was relieved when they rounded the corner at Abercorn and were gone from her sight. Desperate to get home, her gaze searched the street for Burke's return. She saw him coming, and rushed to meet him. She scrambled into the carriage and urged him to leave fast.

As he flicked the reins, Burke asked, "Mo trouble, Miz Rachel?"

"The banker said no to my request for a loan, but don't worry. I have another plan in mind. We aren't whipped yet, Burke, and we won't be."

"Dat's de spirit, Miz Rachel," he complimented with a grin.

"Stop at the police office," she suddenly ordered as they neared it.

"What you be wantin' in there?"

"I'll only be a moment," she said, hopped down, and went inside. She had to learn if Dan had betrayed her in his affidavit. She could use a request to leave town on business as the motive for her visit.

The meeting didn't take long, as the investigator told her everything was fine so far with the case, which wouldn't be closed for a while longer. It was all right if she needed to take another business trip, he said. This time she smiled and thanked him before they parted company. She didn't mention the vandalism at her home last night, and she wouldn't do so unless it became threatening to their safety.

"Home now," Rachel instructed Burke when she was again seated in the carriage.

"Ah seen Mr. Bal'win like you said, Miz Rachel. He said nary a trunk of Mr. Phillip's was 'round that he knowed about."

She was disappointed, but said, "That's good, Burke. I appreciate you tending that chore for me."

Rachel still thought it was odd for Phillip's personal effects to be missing, but there wasn't anything further she could do about that riddle.

When they reached the plantation, Lula Mae had discarded the rocks and covered the horrible black words with slate-blue paint. Rachel gave the weary housekeeper and manager the news, both bad and good. She thanked them and told Burke it wasn't necessary for him to sleep near the house as a guard. Exhausted in mind and body, she went upstairs.

*

Rachel entered the water closet to freshen up for dinner, though her appetite was missing and eating was only to appease her housekeeper. She barely suppressed a scream as her alarmed gaze watched a venomous spider struggle futilely to escape the slick-sided basin. She lifted a note from beside the spider's prison: *"Marry me this time, my beautiful Black Widow. If you keep seeing that sea captain, I'll fill his bed with hundreds of these poisonous beauties. No man will ever have you except me."*

Marry who? She thought, her anger rising. *You never reveal yourself. You didn't respond to the flower signal. Why not?* She realized this note was cold and threatening and was written in her script, as the first one. It was as if the same person hadn't written the second and romantic note! If not, who and why? Dan . . .

Rachel realized she mustn't tell Lula Mae and frighten the woman. Her friend, who had done her work today with a shotgun nearby, would be distressed to learn a culprit had sneaked in the back door to terrorize her mistress in her own home.

*

Thursday morning, a response was delivered to Rachel from George Leathers. Her Augusta partner began by saying he had sent a letter rather than a telegram to keep what he had to say private. He was shocked by Phillip's death and conveyed his sympathies. Rachel knew he would be dismayed and angered by her recent ruse after he learned the actual date Phillip had died. She would handle that explanation when she saw him tomorrow, as she intended to take the train to see both partners in person. George related that the Augusta company was near bankruptcy. With that advance lost, he didn't know if he should ship the order and risk the client canceling it or demanding part of it for the payment taken. He advised that as soon as the contracts were filled, the company should be either closed down or sold, according to which action could be best. After their debts were settled, he anticipated a loss.

George wrote that he planned to retire and live off other investments. He apologized that she would get little or nothing from the sale. Without the profit from that big deal, the outlook was bleak. He enclosed a report to verify what he had said and he added that he had deceived her about the books being gone because he didn't think Phillip would have wanted her to know how terrible things were with the company, as his partner was well informed about the conditions.

The news upset Rachel, but it wasn't unexpected. It was nearing time to handle another nasty facet in her life, and she dreaded it.

Rachel put on her most flattering dress and groomed her dark-brown hair. She must look her best when Dan called this afternoon as scheduled. She wanted the treacherous beguiler to see what he was losing, to yearn to make love to her again. She wouldn't let on she knew about his relationship with Camellia Jones, as that would expose a deceit. She would drop him as a hot iron. She would not allow him to see how much and how deeply he had hurt her. From this day forward, she must never trust another man! Lula Mae was right; most of them only wanted to use a woman!

Just then the housekeeper knocked on her bedroom door. "Cumpny, Miss Rachel," she said nervously. "He's in the parler. I'll be in the kitchen if you need me. I got food on the stove needs watching."

"That's fine, Lula Mae. Tell him I'll be down shortly. Don't serve any refreshments. He won't be staying long." After the housekeeper left, Rachel checked her image in the mirror. Pleased with her appearance but broken-hearted, she went with lagging courage to face her traitorous lover to reject him.

As she entered the formal parlor, Rachel gaped at the man lazing on the sofa. Her body went cold and rigid. He smiled and rose to greet her. This was not the confrontation she had expected. "How dare you come here! Get out of my home, Earl Starger!"

Chapter

14

"Calm down, girl. I read about Phillip McCandless's death in the newspaper. I had to come see if you were all right. Do you need anything?"

Rachel gaped at the forty-one-year-old man who was attired in immaculate and fashionable clothes. "What do you care!"

"Don't you think it's past time to forget our little misunderstanding?"

Her wide gaze enlarged even more in outrage. "Misunderstanding! You beast, you attacked me."

"If I got too friendly trying to earn your affection and acceptance, I'm sorry. If you hadn't jerked away from my fatherly hug, your shirt wouldn't have gotten ripped. I was only trying to calm you down and silence you before others heard the commotion and misunderstood, as William did. I didn't mean to scare you or hurt you, Rachel. I would never do that."

She glared at the hazel-eyed man whose unruly brown hair usually looked as if it were wind-tousled, but today was combed neatly. His long and thin features had an aristocratic appearance, but the man actually had no genteel blood or feelings. "You're a liar! I hate you, Earl Starger."

The visitor sank to the sofa as if weary. "I'm sorry you feel that way, girl, because you're wrong. Your mother has cried every week since you left home and got into so much trouble. How can you be so cruel to her? Come visit her, Rachel. I swear, I won't hug you or peck your check, or even touch your arm while passing in the hall. You have my word of honor."

Rachel remained standing near the entrance to the room, her body rigid and her cheeks flushed with strong emotion. "You have no honor! You tricked Mama into marriage with pretty lies and devious charms. You weren't rich. You only had enough money to pay off our taxes and debts."

"I never claimed to be rich, girl. If you hate me because I wasn't, that isn't my fault. I did save the plantation for you and your family."

"Saved it for us? That's a joke!" She stared at the reason she had been driven from her home and why her last thirty-one months had been like a sojourn in Hades. No matter how much Earl tried to mask the aura of evil, danger, and lechery around him, she saw and felt it. He could be charming and could fool others easily, but not her. His faded hazel eyes were cloaked in concealment now, but she had seen that gaze filled with a wild and intimidating glint. "I'm supposed to believe you randomly chose a beautiful widow with a prosperous plantation in trouble to invest your life savings in,"

Rachel fumed, "but fell in love with her immediately and married her two months later. You came to our home with a plot to bewitch and entrap Mama, and you'll never convince me any differently. You're a greedy and deceitful carpetbagger! You came to get rich off White Cloud and to take advantage of our troubles. You practically imprisoned me and Mama on the plantation while you played the wealthy and respected planter in town with your Yankee friends. You're the reason my brother Randall is dead, and the cause for Richard and Rosemary leaving home. If Papa and Robert were alive, they'd kill you for what you've done to us."

Earl exhaled loudly as if frustrated. "The war is over, girl; there isn't any North and South anymore, only the Union, the United States. Throw away your hated and bitterness or it will destroy you. Your mother loves me, and I love her."

"Love? You don't know what love is."

Without raising his voice, Earl countered, "And you do? Did you love William Barlow or Craig Newman or Phillip McCandless when you married them? Or even by the time you buried them? No, you only wanted riches and a means of escape. You can't find happiness that way, girl. Come home for a visit, get your head cleared, and let me prove you're mistaken about me. You can leave any time you want and return home."

"You can't dupe me, you evil snake. One day Mama will see the ugly truth about you. Then your hold on her will be broken. And that day can't come soon enough to please me."

Earl stood and came toward her. He halted his approach when she took a few steps backward as if to flee the room. "She isn't my captive, girl. If she didn't love me and trust me, she could end our marriage."

Rachel sent forth cold laughter. "Mama would never create such a scandal, and you know it. She'd endure her predicament to the end before humiliating herself and staining the family name by allowing anyone to learn what a fool she'd made of herself by marrying you."

"The only scandals our families have known and suffered are because of *your* mistakes, Rachel. Don't make any more. Get your life changed and your mind unclouded."

The only black cloud I see is in your eyes! Rachel thought. "With your help?" she sneered sarcastically.

"I'll do whatever I can to repair the damage you've done to yourself. Maybe you can't be blamed for being confused back then, not after what the war did to your family and home. You've had plenty of time and numerous opportunities to experience life to know my actions were innocent, only affectionate."

"Are you mad? What I've done to myself! I'm not guilty of any of those accusations. If I were, I'd be in prison or hanged. Or if I were capable of murdering someone, you would be my first and only victim."

"How can you despise me so much, Rachel? It's eating you alive. Your hatred keeps forcing you to make bad decisions. Can you get out of trouble a third—no, a fourth—time? You can't keep on like this and survive, girl."

She attempted to trick him into making a slip. "Why, because you'll kill me next time instead of murdering my husband to force me back home into your evil clutches? Or you'll make certain there is convincing evidence left behind to insinuate I'm to blame, so I'll be jailed?"

"Rachel Anne Fleming!" Earl cried, "Do you hear what you're ranting? Have you lost your mind for certain, girl? There are good doctors up North who can help you with your illness. Let me hire one of them to—"

"You bastard! I'm not insane, or evil, or cursed, or duped, Earl Starger! You're the one who needs his head doctored and cured. They have ugly names for men with your vile weakness and wicked behavior."

Earl shook his head. "If I didn't know how ill-minded and scared you are, I would be angry; and I wouldn't offer to help you. But I know you're sick and need help; so does your mother."

"I don't want or need any help from you. I would rather die than to lower myself that much."

"If you don't get your life changed, the authorities will take care of that ridiculous threat for you."

"Another veiled threat, my despicable stepfather?"

"I haven't threatened you today, or any other day, girl. You take every word I say and twist it. You're determined to paint me black with evil. What can I say or do to prove it isn't true?"

You act as if you're playing to an ignorant audience, not to someone who knows you and can't be fooled by your evil talents! Rachel fumed silently. "You've harassed me for years, ever since we met."

"How can love and concern be harassments?"

"Don't try to confuse me with your words, you beast," she scolded in a frosty tone. "We have nothing to say to each other, and we never will. Get out of my home and off of my property. Don't ever come back."

"What shall I tell your mother?"

"She knows where I live, if she cares about me and wants to see me."

"She can't travel, Rachel. She's been ill, very ill. I think she's heartsick over you and the other children deserting her and ignoring her."

Worry and alarm flooded Rachel. "Has she seen a doctor?" she asked. "How bad is it? Or is this another clever and cruel trick to fool me? To entice me home?"

"I took Catherine to see a doctor in Waynesboro on the twenty-sixth of last month and again last Thursday. He examined her and gave her two tonics. If she's not better by the sixth of May, I'm to take her to him again. I think seeing you would improve her health. That's why I risked your wrath and hatred today. If you refuse to come visit her, at least write her a letter."

"So you can steal it, read it, and hopefully learn all my secrets?"

"Rachel, Rachel, don't be so heartless and foolish. Even if what you claim was true, how could I endanger you with your mother and servants present? Bring along your own servants for the protection you think you need from me. Hellfire, carry a gun in your pocket if it makes you feel safer! I'm only concerned with your mother's health."

Rachel didn't believe him or trust him, but she sensed something serious was afoot. "I'll think about both of your requests. Now, leave," she ordered him. She had to write, had to learn if Earl was away with her mother on those two dates. If it was the truth, Earl was out of the picture as a villain. If not . . .

"All right, girl, if that's the way you want it."

"It is, for now. Good-bye, Earl," she stated in a stern tone.

"Good-bye, Rachel; I hope you come to your senses soon."

As he reached the door, Rachel said, "Oh, yes, and you can stop sending me those crazy notes, stop following me, stop searching my room wherever I go, and stop shooting at me. Your threats and attacks don't frighten me."

Earl stared at her as if bewildered, then exhaled and shook his head in pity and frustration. "If anyone is harassing you, Rachel, it isn't me. Hire a detective to watch me so you can get that wild idea out of your head. They're only delusions, girl, imaginings of an ill mind. Get help before it's too late. But if they did happen, you best hire someone fast to protect you."

She had hoped to catch Earl by surprise and evoke a slip, but it hadn't worked. In fact, he looked sympathetic, as if he really thought she was mad.

*

Lula Mae knocked at Rachel's bedroom door once again. "More cumpny, Miss Rachel," the housekeeper announced to her agitated mistress. "That sea captain."

The young widow's chilly gaze met Lula Mae's worried one. She surprised the woman by ordering in a whisper that couldn't be overheard downstairs, "Don't serve any refreshments this time, either, Lula Mae, because he won't be staying long. I'll get rid of him as fast as possible, this time for good, I hope. I wish he didn't have to remain in port so long until his orders arrive from Athens and Augusta. He's becoming *too* friendly, and I don't like it. I'm tired of men trying to charm me and use me. I won't be sweet and polite today, so maybe he'll stop calling on me."

"Yessum, Miss Rachel; I'll do that for you."

She checked her appearance again in the mirror. Her cheeks were still a mite flushed from her quarrel with her stepfather, but her lingering anger should help her through this necessary episode.

The unsuspecting man stood and smiled, but Rachel frowned. His gaze altered to one of confusion. "I wanted to send you a message, Captain Slade, but things have been too hectic today," she said in a formal manner. "I wanted to suggest you don't come to visit this afternoon, or ever again. I've given our relationship a great deal of study and concluded it won't work. It isn't wise for us to see each other again."

Dan was shocked and baffled. She looked and sounded so cold, not frightened or angry. He probed for a reason. "Our relationship has gotten too close and deep for mistrust. Is this withdrawal from me because you're scared of your deep emotions for me?" he surmised.

"I like you as a friend, Dan, and I enjoyed making love with you, but you've become too serious and demanding too fast to suit me. I've recently buried my husband, so I'm not ready for love and marriage again."

"What?" he murmured in disbelief.

Rachel had practiced this difficult scene many times inside her head, so she seemed to play it now by rote. "I appreciate what you did for me with the authorities, but that's all settled now. I must continue with my life and settle pressing business matters. I can't be distracted by a futile relationship with you. Please don't be angry and spiteful by going to the police and telling them you lied. That would get you into deep trouble with the law and place me in a terrible position. I would be forced to claim you tried to seduce me and, when that didn't work, you became vindictive and want to get me into trouble now by changing your story. You did sign a sworn statement," she reminded in a sweet voice. "Let's part as friends, all right?"

Dan shook his head as if to awaken himself from a bad dream. "What in stars are you talking about, woman?"

Rachel faked her most innocent look and tone. "I'm trying to reject you with kindness. I don't love you or want you, Captain Slade. I'm sorry if I gave you that false impression while I was under such pressure. I'll admit I was wrong to surrender to you and wrong to let you believe we had a future together. It happened because I was too distraught and grieved to think clearly. We had fun together. We liked each other. We spent a passionate night together. But that's all. And just to clear your conscience, I didn't kill Phillip or any of my other husbands, so I wasn't using you as a needed witness. However, you did provide me with one when things looked bleak that day, so I'm grateful. As you'll recall, I did not ask you to lie or to help me. That was your idea."

"What's happened, Rachel? This is crazy, wrong, a damn lie!"

"No, Captain Slade, it isn't; and I'm sorry if I hurt you. All I can say in my defense is that you caught me at a weak moment and I behaved foolishly. Please don't call on me again. It was brief and fiery, but it's over."

Tormented and bewildered, Dan accused, "Why, so you can find a richer and more respected man as victim number four?"

Although he was a cruel traitor, it cut her heart to chide, "Don't behave like a boy who's lost his first love. I don't intend to have a number four. As I told you, my luck with husbands isn't good."

"You don't need another rich husband because you found that advance?"

Rachel frowned and exhaled loudly to expose her annoyance. "No, Dan, I haven't. In fact, I won't inherit very much from Phillip at all. That isn't the point. Men are trouble for me. I don't plan to have another one in my life, except for maybe a brief night of passion."

Dan stared into her muted gaze, but today he lacked the power to penetrate it. "This isn't my Rachel McCandless talking."

"I warned you several times that you didn't know the real me."

"If this is a taste of the real you, then you're right."

"Please, Dan," she urged in a guileful tone, "don't make me hurt you. End this with dignity and pride. You had what no other man has had from me; can't you be satisfied with that knowledge and gift?"

"No, Rachel, I can't. I love you and I want you. Damn it," he pleaded, "you love me and want me, too! Why are you doing this to us?"

Rachel presumed he was only cajoling to preserve his cruel ruse. "What I'm doing is trying to keep you from falling any deeper into this futile pit you've dug for yourself. I like you and enjoyed you, but that's all; I swear it. Please let me help you out of it with kindness."

Dan knew something terrible was wrong, but he couldn't surmise what it was. It wouldn't do to press her today; she looked firmly resolved to end their love affair. Yet he perceived love, anguish, and deceit in her. He had to find out whatever had inspired those emotions before he pressed her for more answers, for the whole truth. "All right, Rachel, I'll back off for now. But I'm warning you, I won't give up on us until you prove I'm wrong. When you come to your senses and get rid of these doubts and fears, you know where to find me until May twenty-fourth. If you haven't cleared your head and gotten courage by then, I'll be gone, and so will your first chance at real love and happiness. If you need me for anything, I'll be available."

Rachel could not conceal her astonishment at his words and behavior. It was a struggle to regain her poise and wits. "Thank you, Dan."

"Thank you, Dan?" he echoed, his tone and gaze sad. "That's all you have to say after what's happened between us?"

"You won't believe this, but I truly wish it could be different."

For the first time, Dan felt she was being honest with him. For the first time since she'd entered the room, her eyes were like liquid honey, not like a frozen grayish olive green. "So do I, Rachel, so do I." Without another word or a farewell, he left the room, mounted, and galloped away.

Rachel watched his hasty departure from the parlor window. Her heart ached. Her body was exhausted. Her love for him raged at her spiteful conduct, but her mind congratulated her for her convincing act.

I love you, Daniel Slade. Why couldn't you have been different from the others? If you weren't a fraud, I would have given myself fully and forever to you.

"Is he gawn?" the housekeeper asked from behind her.

Rachel sighed heavily, "Yes, Lula Mae, and for good."

"Why be so sad, Miss Rachel?"

"It was harder than I imagined, my friend. He is in love with me."

"Does that makes you weak and sorry?"

"Sorry for him, yes; but weaken toward him, no. I did what I know is best for me. That's what I have to think about these days—me and my two best friends, you and Burke. You are my family. I don't need others."

"Do you want something special to make you feels better?"

"A long and hot bath, a glass of sherry, and a delicious supper," she responded with gaiety she didn't feel. She needed to clear her head before writing to her mother tonight.

"That's my Miss Rachel, stronger than any man."

God help me if I made a terrible mistake today, Rachel fretted after the housekeeper left to take care of her requests.

*

"She did what?" Luke Conner asked. "Did I hear right?"

"You did, my friend. Now, what we have to find out is why."

"You honestly believe she loves you?"

"Without a doubt, Luke, without a doubt."

"Then why did she do this?"

"That's what I intend to learn."

"You know I'll help any way I can. But what if you've been wrong about her all along? What if she is a Black Widow? What if she was only using you as a witness? And what if she has located the money?"

Dan was confident as he said, "There's no way she was pretending in those areas, Luke. What we have to do is trace her steps for the last few days since I saw her. Somewhere along that path is the clue to why she changed and what's troubling her."

"You don't think she found something that revealed your identity and she assumes you're betraying her?"

"I don't think that's the problem. Phillip packed up all his memories and left them in that trunk in Charleston with our family lawyer. I have it stored on the ship. I doubt my brother brought anything along on his move. Phillip remembered how many scrapes I got him out of years ago. He always believed I was the stronger, smarter, and braver of us two. He hoped I was still alive somewhere, would get his cry for help, and would show up by some miracle to get him out of his bind. That's why he left that letter with our family lawyer; that's why he hired a private detective to search for me. It must have cost him plenty, but he didn't give up. I can't give up, either. I have to save Rachel; that's what he really wanted from me. He knew he was too far gone for rescue, but he loved her enough to want me to save her from harm. Somehow he got entangled in gambling and saw this illegal deal as his way out, but he panicked when he realized what it could cost him. By then it was too late; he'd probably lost the advance staking himself to one last big score."

"You don't think he killed himself?" Luke asked in dread.

"No, I think somebody else did it for him, somebody who either needed or wanted him out of the way, or out of Rachel's life."

"That Jones vixen?"

"I don't think so. When I saw her the other day, she did all she could to blacken Rachel's name, but I doubt she's a murderess. Camellia is too smart to risk losing everything on revenge. I was going to tell Rachel about my ruse with that little minx, but I never got the chance."

Luke grinned and his light-blue eyes sparkled. "So, we track her moves for the last three days and discover what frightened her."

"That's the plan, my friend. I've gone over everything from every angle, Luke, and I've faced the truth: I love her, I want her, and I need her. I don't believe Rachel McCandless is capable of murder. I believe her only involvement in this arms mystery is the mess Phillip left her in. Something in the last few days has shaken her faith in me, but I'll win it back. Either that or she's running scared of risking my life on her jinx theory. I could be blinded by love and desire, but I won't accept that until I'm given positive proof she's a criminal. She's mine, Luke. I've never loved or wanted a woman like this before. I won't lose her to fate, to an enemy, or to her mistaken fears."

"After you free her from the past, then what?"

The captain grinned. "I'm going to marry her and sail away with her."

"If I know you, there'll be no stopping you until you succeed. I'm checking on your other suspicions. We'll get answers soon."

＊

At Moss Haven, Rachel was too distraught and angry to care if it was dark and dangerous outside or if a stealthy culprit was observing her action. Besides, with the loaded derringer in her pocket, she wished the despicable snake would approach her for retribution. She replaced Phillip's marker that had been yanked from its location and thrown onto the front porch. She used her bare foot to pack dirt around the wooden stake that was lettered with his name, then the distressed widow gazed at her third husband's resting place and wanted to weep to release her tension, but she mustn't weaken. She returned to the house and went to bed; she needed rest for the events that loomed before her during the next few days.

＊

When Rachel arrived in Augusta on Friday afternoon, she hurried to the ammunition company to see George Leathers before he left his office. She told the carriage driver to deliver her baggage to the Planter's Hotel and to inform them she would be there soon to register for the night. She paid him for his assistance, and he drove away.

Rachel entered the office to find the gray-haired man sitting behind his desk and reading the local newspaper. He stood quickly when she arrived, but looked hesitant and apprehensive.

"After what's happened," George began, "I shouldn't be surprised to see you here today, but I am. Your local paper sent Phillip's obituary to mine, so I saw the date listed. It was a shock, Rachel. What were you doing here having a good time when Phillip was already dead? Why didn't you tell me? You deceived me. I don't understand."

Rachel knew she looked tense. "Please sit down, George," she said, "and listen to my explanation. It was hard to pretend I was on a holiday and to dupe you, but I had a good reason. Before Phillip died, he told me he had qualms about the big deal; and that's why he backed out of it. Incidents occurred to intimidate him into restating it." She revealed the ones that had happened in February. "Phillip never received a verbal threat that I know of, but he was certain either the client or Harry—or both—was behind them."

His brown eyes widened. "Harry? What are you saying?"

She put her new plan into motion. "You must hold everything I tell you in confidence. Can you do that for me and Phillip?"

George nodded.

She took a deep breath and divulged, "Harry was pressuring Phillip about this deal. Both companies need money badly, so Phillip was going to honor the bargain. Something happened, I don't know what, to convince my husband it might not have been legal. It might have something to do with supplying arms and ammunition for a Cuban rebellion." She halted again to relate what Dan had told her about that possibility. "He didn't have time to expose everything before he died from cholera. He warned me this client and Harry could be dangerous, not to trust them. But he also advised me to honor his part of the deal. He knew he was dying and told me to check out both company's books before I told anyone he was dead. He didn't have time to explain why that was important. I thought I could learn something from you and Harry if I withheld the truth. This might sound ridiculous, but I think Phillip might have been murdered."

George appeared baffled. "But you said he died of cholera."

"That's what the symptoms implied and what I told the authorities. I didn't think it was wise or safe to mention my suspicion of murder or an illegal deal that could get us all into trouble. Besides, I had no facts to go on at that time, and only have a few gathered now, but no real evidence."

George stroked his mustache as he questioned, "Phillip actually suspected Harry of being deceitful and dangerous?"

"Yes, he warned me not to double cross Harry, whatever that means." She repeated a few of Phillip's mumblings and related some of the threats against her to give George a small but clear picture of her dilemma. "Do you see why I was so alarmed and frightened, why I had to fake a holiday and dupe you? I'm sorry, George, because I don't think you're involved in this mystery. I have to confide in you, but I can't do the same with Harry, not yet. I'm going to visit him tomorrow and see what I can learn. I can't reveal to him all I've told you, so I'll tell you what to say to him if he contacts you. Will you help me? If this deal is legal and it was nothing more than feverish rantings, we're all fine. But if it's true, we'll have to decide how to handle it. We don't want our reputations and lives placed in jeopardy."

"We certainly can't honor the contract if it's illegal," George said. "I wish Phillip had told me the truth before we stuck our necks out this far financially."

"Phillip needed money badly, George," Rachel thought she should disclose that fact, "and knew both of you do, too. He kept the contract a secret because of his suspicions. He was taking total responsibility for it."

"You mean, he was going to go through with it anyway?"

"Yes. But if anything went wrong, he was going to take full blame. He was the one who made the mistake, so he was hoping to finish the deal and forget about it. He was sorry he got all of us into this mess. He wanted me to carry it out, but he left me with too few clues and facts to do that. To be honest, George, Phillip left me in terrible financial condition. All three companies are hurting for money. I hope we can honor this contract."

"I'm sorry to hear that. Of course I'll help you, Rachel. It sounds like quite a challenge; it'll get the old blood to flowing swiftly."

"There is one big favor I'll need. Please send the order, so I can use it as bait to discover if we can sell it as planned or if we have to back down. If I don't have something to use, I can't get answers from the client when he arrives to check on late delivery. I'll be responsible for the merchandise. If anything happens to it, you can have my share of the company as payment. I'll put that in writing, so you won't worry about me reneging."

"That's generous and gracious of you, Rachel, but your share isn't worth what I have invested in the order. But I'll trust you and do as you request."

She sighed in relief and smiled. "Thank you, George; it will be a big help. Let's both pray the deal can proceed as planned. Didn't Captain Slade's large order help out our finances any?"

"I'm afraid not. I used the money to pay back salaries and to buy supplies to complete that big deal. I still had to borrow money from the bank. But your cousin doesn't have to worry about not getting his purchase."

"That's another thing, George; Daniel Slade isn't my cousin. He's an old and close friend of Phillip's. They grew up together in Charleston. He arrived the morning Phillip died. But it is true he came to do business with Phillip, and his two orders are legitimate. He agreed to pretend to be my cousin and to be on holiday while I took care of private business. But that's something else I don't want Harry told yet. We also thought it would look better if I were traveling with kin, instead of an unattached male."

George shook his head in pity. "You've had a lot to endure and to handle alone, Rachel. I'm sorry. Phillip was a fine man, a good partner. I'll miss him. Was there trouble when you reported his death?"

"The usual investigation, which isn't closed yet." She related what had taken place. "Now do you see why I'm apprehensive and suspicious? And that isn't all. When we were in Athens, Harry had us followed every day and night. Dan trailed our shadow back to Harry's office for his report. I caught Harry in lies several times, but I didn't let on I had. That makes me distrust him even more. To be fair, there may be logical reasons for his strange behavior, but I can't risk exposing what I know."

"I hate to say it, Rachel, but I agree," George said. "Harry's always been a strange man. It may be unfair of me, but I think he's capable of doing such evil things. When he came to see me after his last visit with Phillip, he was abrupt and cold, outright angry. He came close to threatening Phillip if anything went wrong. But it seems stupid on his part to kill Phillip before the deal was finalized. He says he's in the dark about the client's identity and location."

"But that will be simple to discover when the client comes for his order. Maybe Harry assumed I'd be easier to control than Phillip. Have either of them ever mentioned buying licenses to construct patented arms?"

That change of topic confused him. "No, why?"

Rachel disclosed her suspicion in that area, and saw George's eyes widen in astonishment. "If Phillip knew, he didn't say anything or halt it. But I prefer to think Harry is the only one involved in that crime. With the arms being shipped so far away, he knows the chance of being exposed is slim. That also gives Harry an excellent reason to go through with the deal; he can't sell patented weapons in the United States. He's already trying to force my hand by saying he won't supply the arms without the advance, but can't get rid of that many weapons anywhere else, and the company will be ruined. I'm still searching for the money; Phillip hid it well."

"What a mystery," George murmured.

"Yes, it is, and we're stuck in the middle of it. I'll keep you informed of everything, by letters sent here for privacy. We won't know much more until the end of May or beginning of June; it'll take that long for the client to realize there's a problem and to come to Savannah to check on it."

"You shouldn't face him alone, Rachel, if he's dangerous."

"Dan will be there," she lied to calm him. "He has to stay until his arms are ready and delivered. He says he'll help me before he sails."

"That's good. I liked him."

"He's a nice and kind man," it pained her to allege, "as you are, George. Please forgive me for duping you, but I had to get to know you better before I was assured I could trust you completely."

"After all you've told me, I quite understand. You're a clever woman, a strong and brave one."

She sent him a warm and honest smile. "Thank you, George. Now, when Harry questions you, as I'm sure he will, I want you to tell him that I duped you, but that I've apologized. I was only trying to discover the condition of the business before I told you of Phillip's death, as if I feared you'd cheat me out of profits. Tell him you don't think I trust you completely and that you're angry with me for lying. I was also very interested in the big deal, but don't know much about it. I told you I don't have the money, but you aren't certain. Say I told you Phillip became ill fast, lost consciousness, and didn't tell me anything before dying. Tell him I've agreed to go through with the deal, but I want to sell my share of both companies as soon as the deal is completed. Say it all depends on whether or not a new arrangement can be made with the client, since I don't have his advance."

"That will get him furious at you, and suspicious of you."

"That's what I want if I'm going to get any clues out of him. I hope he does threaten me and try to force me to continue the deal; that will tell me how involved and desperate and dangerous he is."

"I'll worry about you, Rachel."

"Thank you, but I'll worry about you, too. Guard yourself well, George. I wouldn't put it past Harry to try to get rid of both of us so he can collect the entire price. I don't believe he's as ignorant about all of this as he claims. Harry's too devious and greedy to trust Phillip this much. Only an honest, trustworthy, and loyal friend and partner like you would let Phillip handle this deal the way he has. I promise you that Harry won't cheat us out of our shares of the profit, if there is one."

"I still hope there is, Rachel, to save us. As I told you I am going to sell out and retire when all my business is finished. What about you?"

"Me, too, George. You can begin work on a sale any time. I'll agree with whatever price and terms you say are fair."

"I'm happy you decided you could trust me and confide in me, because you can, Rachel. I would never betray you, and I'll do all I can to help you."

"I'll be traveling on to Athens in the morning to confront Harry. I should be home by Monday or Tuesday night. After Harry questions you, let me know how he reacted and what he said during your meeting."

"You're certain he'll come to see me?"

"Positive. He'll want to make certain both of us are fooled."

"If Harry is responsible for those incidents and for murdering Phillip, I hope you get the evidence to have him arrested and punished."

"So do I, George." She realized she was still duping George a little, but that couldn't be helped. She couldn't expose every detail to him, not yet. But she did feel as if he were being honest and sincere, and that relieved her. After warning him to be on guard for threats, she bid him farewell.

*

When Rachel arrived in Athens on Saturday afternoon, her luck wasn't as good as it had been in Augusta. Harrison Clements was away for the weekend, and not expected back until late Sunday night. His wife was with him, or so the housekeeper told her. She left a message she would be at his office first thing Monday morning for a business conference. She assumed Harry had seen Phillip's obituary, too, and was nervous over her deception.

*

Rachel scowled in annoyance as she found another note on her pillow after having dinner downstairs. She had almost requested for her evening meal to be sent to her room, and wished she had. The daring suitor was on her trail again! She hated being pursued this way and was sorely puzzled by how the man got in and out of her room without her noticing his presence. Didn't that have to mean she didn't know the culprit? Once more her script was used and there were threats against Dan's life if she saw him again. Soon, considering how closely she was spied on, the pursuer would know Daniel Slade was out of her life. She concluded that this matter had nothing to do with the arms deal, so she would ignore it. Until he revealed himself to her, she couldn't spurn him or discover why he used a forgery of her handwriting for his messages.

*

At six on Sunday afternoon, there was a knock on Rachel's door. She considered not answering it, dreading to initiate a quarrel with Harry in her room. But, she reconsidered, it might only be a bellman with a note saying Harry had returned home, gotten her message, and was ready to confront her in the morning.

Rachel opened the door. Her gaze widened and she inhaled sharply. "What are you doing here?" she gasped. "How did you know where to find me? What do you want, Daniel Slade?"

Dan nudged her backward and pushed the barrier aside. He entered her room, closed the door, and locked it. "We're going to have a serious talk, woman. It's time to clear the air once and for all."

Rachel retreated a few steps and gaped at him. An obstinate gleam filled his dark-blue eyes and his clean-shaven jaw was clenched in resolve. She wasn't prepared for this situation. Her heart hadn't chilled enough against him. Gazing at him seemed to weaken her need to spurn him. "About what? I said all I had to say at home. It's over, Dan; accept that."

"It's only beginning, Rachel McCandless; accept that," he corrected, as he placed a gentle but firm grasp on her upper arms.

She attempted to free her body and gaze, but could accomplish neither. "Don't be stubborn and childish, Dan," she urged. "Or spiteful."

"Those aren't my intentions. I only want to love you and help you. Those are the same things you need from me."

She stared at him. *Don't weaken or be tricked.* "You're wrong. I—"

"You're going to listen to me, woman! I risked my neck to keep you out of prison. I lied to your partners to help you obtain clues. Luke and I checked out your family and servants to see if one of them is framing you. We searched for a jilted or unrequited lover who would kill to free you for himself. We looked for a jealous and spiteful female rival who wants to punish and destroy you. We know you aren't responsible for those crimes. I even courted that repulsive vixen Camellia Jones this week to see if she's to blame for your past troubles. I do everything I can to assist you, but you turn your back on me and close your heart against me. Why? It isn't because you don't want me as much as I want you. What is it then? What happened to make you reject what we both know you want? Are you that wary of all men? Are you that afraid of a permanent love?"

Rachel was overcome with shock and bewilderment. When she retrieved her stolen wits and breath, she inquired, "You've been seeing Camellia to spy on her?"

Dan comprehended he had guessed right, thanks to his and Luke's excellent tracking skills. But all wariness had not left her muted gaze. "Yes, and it was hard, but I did it for you. She hates you and wishes you dead, but I don't think she would murder your husbands to obtain vengeance. She loves herself and all she has, too much to take such a risk. It's the same with the others we've been checking on; we haven't found a reason to incriminate any of them. Not yet, but Luke is still working on those angles in case we've missed a clue." Dan saw he had her full attention. "There isn't a spurned sweetheart or lover in your past, not that we could locate," he continued. "You married every man you became involved with. I couldn't find any woman, except that arrogant Camellia, who would want to be spiteful. We couldn't locate any family members who would want or *could* extract revenge, not even your stepfather. True, Craig's brother hated and distrusted you, but he's been living up North a long time. The only way he could be responsible for Phillip's death would be through hiring someone to kill him, and he'd have no motive for the deaths of William and his son. If it's a plot against you, and I firmly believe it is, it began with your first marriage. For a while, I even suspected that Lula Mae had her eye on William, but from what I hear, she doesn't care for any man. Besides, she wasn't around when the first three people died. I was inclined to believe your stepfather was the culprit, but he has alibis for the two days in question." He suddenly changed the subject. "Did you know your mother is ill?" He explained his last question, though she already knew the facts.

Rachel comprehended how much Dan had done for her. "Yes, but how did *you* learn all of this?"

Dan grinned, as he knew she believed him. "Luke and I have our ways. We can be most cunning when a situation demands it. This one does, Rachel. If I don't solve both mysteries, I'll lose you. I warn you, you skittish vixen, I won't give up without a fight."

She tried to suppress a smile of amusement. "How did you find me?"

"Burke likes me and trusts me. He knows how you're suffering and he knows I love you and want to help you."

She looked alarmed. "He gave away my whereabouts?"

"Only to me, Rachel, and for good reason. You can trust him completely." Dan wished he could tell her everything, but he couldn't take that risk now. If she learned he and Phillip were brothers and he had set out to entrap her, it would do more damage or undo the repairs he was making.

He cupped her face between his hands and entreated, "Can't we test these feelings for each other? I won't press you for more than you're willing to give or more than you can share. But give me, give *us,* a real chance. We're so well suited. Can't we at least make a commitment to give our wonderful feelings for each other a try? If you say no, I'll have to get out of your life completely. I can't risk being hurt."

Convince me, Dan. "I told you; I'm probably cursed and jinxed."

He shook his head. "I don't believe that. You have an enemy, have had one for years. We'll find out who it is and why; then this evil will be over."

Persuade me, Dan. "I might not want to marry again."

"I don't want to, but I will settle for you as my lover, if you insist."

Reassure me, Dan. "I might not be able to have children. My pregnancy and miscarriage were hard on my body; vengeful gifts from Craig. The doctor's words weren't promising. You'll want an heir someday."

That took Dan by surprise. Share no children with this special woman? Never have a child of his own? No son to carry on the family name? But, she had said "might." What was more important: having his love and no children, or having children with a woman he didn't love?

Rachel's heart pounded as she watched him contemplate that sad news. *Induce me, Dan.* "You could say it doesn't matter, and it may not at this time in your life, but later it will. You'll make a wonderful father, Dan; you deserve that gift. If we became lovers, it would be painful for both of us to part eventually so you could marry and have a family. The longer and closer we're together, the more difficult it will be for us to end our liaison. If you want me for a while, that shouldn't be too perilous to our emotions. We'd have to be careful and secretive, but I would agree."

"Is that why you discarded me? To spare my feelings?"

Tell him the truth, Rachel. "No. I mean, not totally. I have worried over those things, but I was trying to shut them out of my mind."

"Then what happened between Monday and Thursday?"

"Camellia Jones. I saw you with her on Wednesday."

Dan feigned surprise, then enlightenment. "So that's it. That's all?"

He chuckled and hugged her. He leaned back, gazed into her eyes, and declared happily, "What a relief! You thought I was bedding her?"

Get it all into the open. "That, and more."

"What, love? Tell me, so we can clear up this misunderstanding."

Don't let him think you're silly; explain. Rachel related the doubts and fears that had assailed her when she saw them together.

Dan cuddled her in his arms. "I can understand why you would think such things," he said soothingly, "but it isn't true; I swear it, Rachel, on my name and honor. I love you and want you. I didn't know Camellia until I arranged to meet her to test her."

Trust him! "I hope I'm not being foolish and reckless, but I believe you." She explained her behavior on Thursday and apologized.

Dan said the right thing, "If I were in your predicament, I would have jumped to the same conclusions and behaved the same way. I should have forced you to listen to me, but I was too stunned. I've missed you, woman, and been worried about you. I didn't like you leaving like this all alone."

"It was probably good I did; I learned a few things and put another ruse into motion." She told him about her meeting with George. "You don't think I was wrong to trust him and to entice his help?"

"No. I think it was a good idea, a clever plan."

She explained what she had in mind for Harry Monday morning. "Think it will work?" she asked.

"Sounds splendid to me." His gaze locked with hers.

"There's more, Dan; your life is in danger."

"You aren't cursed, love," he refuted before she clarified.

"I don't mean that." She told him about the notes she had received Wednesday and yesterday that threatened his life. "I can't even use them as evidence because the culprit forged my script. He probably knows you're here now."

Dan caressed her cheek. "Don't worry, love; I'll protect both of us. One day all of this will be over and we can be together as man and wife."

"Why not be together tonight?" she suggested bravely.

"Nothing would please me more, Rachel. Nothing."

Love me, Dan, and never leave me, her bold heart urged. Then her cautious mind only allowed her mouth to say, "Love me, Dan. Now, please."

Just as Dan pulled her into his arms, another knock sounded on her door. "Don't answer it, love, and whoever it is will go away soon."

Rachel glanced at the clock on the mantel and frowned. "I can't. I placed an order for my dinner to be delivered at seven. I'm sure that's who it is," she surmised as the knock became more persistent and a voice called out her name. "Hide under the bed while I take the tray."

Dan complied and Rachel opened the door to a bellman holding a tray. "Just place it on the table," she instructed, eager to have him gone. Flames of desire licked urgently at her body, and she needed to douse them.

Rachel thanked the young man and tipped him. She closed and locked the door following his exit. Dan scrambled from his hiding place and looked at the meal that was sending forth fragrant smells.

Rachel went into his arms, fused her greedy gaze to his, and murmured, "The only thing I'm hungry for at this moment is you, Daniel Slade. Feed me before I perish of starvation."

"You dinner will get cold. Are you sure?"

"Need you even ask?" she replied, and kissed him ravenously. "Well?" she coaxed as she pulled her lips from his with difficulty.

Chapter

15

That was all the permission and encouragement Daniel Slade McCandless required. He was more than ready to take a second sensuous voyage with her, to find again rapture in her arms and body, and to quench his thirst for her. He knew that fulfillment would last only a short time, but he would bond her to him so tightly tonight that she would be available forever when he wanted and needed her.

Dan unfastened the two clasps on her paletot top. He slipped it off her shoulders and tossed it onto a chair. She turned for him to undo the laces of her pompadour basque. His fingers trailed down her arms as he removed the fancy blouse. He undid the button of her walking skirt, bent, and waited for her to step out of it. He tossed that garment onto the pile he was making on the chair. His hands grasped the tail of her yoked chemise and lifted it over her head. Her full breasts greeted his gaze as she turned to face him. It feasted there a moment before his trembling fingers tried unsuccessfully to unfasten the button on her lace-trimmed knee-length drawers.

Rachel smiled and assisted him. She flung the undergarment away. As Dan squatted to remove her slippers and hose, she didn't feel modest or apprehensive as she stood there naked before the man she loved and desired. In fact, she found it arousing to have him undress her.

When his last task was completed, Dan stood. His eyes roamed her olive skin with admiration and pleasure. "You're exquisite, Rachel. Every inch of you is perfection. Not a flaw on your body."

Rachel hadn't been pregnant long enough for streaks to mark her breasts, stomach, thighs, or buttocks. In a way, she was glad, as this way there were no reminders to Dan that she had carried another man's child within her body. Not that she was happy about not bearing Craig's child, as it would have been *her* child, perhaps her *only* child. But she wouldn't think about that torment tonight. If the doctor was mistaken and she did become pregnant, she would marry Daniel Slade in a moment.

"My turn," she murmured, her gaze like two golden-brown embers that were ready to be ignited by a view of his naked body.

Rachel grinned as Dan held his arms out and enticed, "I'm all yours, woman. Do with me as you wish."

Rachel slid his jacket over his broad shoulders and flung it aside as she tried to control merry giggles. With seductive leisure, she unbuttoned his shirt, then peeled the snug-fitting item away to expose a hard chest with its fuzzy black covering. She placed her fingers on either side of his neck at the collarbone; with a snailish and stimulating pace, she drifted them down his chest, wandering them over his flat nipples, teasing them across the ridges of his rib cage, and halting them at his trim waistline. She squatted to take off his boots, then stood to unfasten his pants, bent again to remove them, with Dan assisting her by lifting one leg at a time. When all of his garments were discarded, her brazen gaze could not resist journeying him from raven-black head to bare feet. She wished there were more light, as no lamp had been lit in her room yet. She had only the lingerings of daylight coming through the two windows to aid her scrutiny. She had never done a study before of the male body, but she relished it with this man she loved. As her palms flattened against his muscled chest and her gaze locked with his, she murmured, "This is perfection, Daniel Slade. You're magnificent. You make me feel so brave and bold. You cast off all my doubts, fears, and restraints. You have made a wanton and greedy woman of me. I have no shame or inhibition with you."

"Isn't that how it should be between true lovers, Rachel?" he asked in a voice made husky from his unleashed emotions.

"I didn't know that fact until I met you, but now I know it's true."

Their unclad bodies pressed together as they kissed. The contact of their flesh enflamed their passions to even higher levels. His teeth nibbled at her neck, her shoulder, her ear. She sighed in contentment. Their fingers traced over naked flesh, noting the textures and contrasts of each. They were eager to unite their bodies and to sate their hungers, but they proceeded with deliberate leisure.

As Dan's fingers caressed her upper body front and back, hers roamed his chest and shoulders. She wriggled when his hand moved along her spine in a tickling manner, then caught her breath as both grasped her buttocks and drew her close against him. Her fingers roved his back and savored the feel of rippling muscles as his body moved to tantalize her. She stroked his arms and enjoyed the sensation of his hair against her palms. She wanted to touch and explore every inch of him.

Dan lifted her and laid her on the bed, not even tossing aside the covers. He wished darkness hadn't stolen the outside light, as his eyes wanted to feed on her tasty skin. He had only the filtered glow of a full moon to view her by. His hands, nose, lips, and ears must be his eyes tonight. His mouth covered hers with a demand that stole his breath.

Rachel inhaled the manly scent of his body, which mingled with an enticing cologne from the islands southeast of America. His mouth tasted minty, delicious, and provocative. His tongue danced with hers in an erotic manner to a silent, seductive beat.

Dan's lips traveled down her slender neck to compelling mounds of sweet flesh. His tongue played with the taut and succulent buds it found there. It circled them over and over, hardening them even more. One hand caressed its way along the path to her triangular forest of dark-brown. The hair in that location was downy soft, and the mist of her arousal dampened it. His fingers caressed her silky valleys as he teethed her nipples lightly.

Pleasure, sweet and tormenting, ensnared Rachel. It began deep within her womanhood, mounted and teased, then sent charges over her entire frame as if tiny lightning bolts striking her flesh from head to foot. She writhed and moaned, her need for him great and urgent. Every inch of her was sensitive and responsive to him. She was so alive and happy with him. She couldn't imagine losing him. Her pleasures increased, but so did her yearning for more; this time, she knew for what.

Dan was thrilled and encouraged by her fiery need and responses. He obtained added pleasure from the delight he was giving her. He eased atop her, parted her thighs, and obeyed her mute summons to possess her fully. The contact was again staggering to his control and impassioned senses.

Dan was enchanted as Rachel's legs curled over his thighs and she matched her movements to his. Her mouth clung to his, as her flesh glued itself to his. She urged him onward with her actions and words. If any lingering doubt that this was the woman for him had existed someplace in Dan's mind or body, it was vanquished forever. He had experienced rapturous lovemaking with other women, but it was different with Rachel, a special feeling that totally consumed his heart, his soul, his whole being.

She felt the same way. If any doubts had lurked within her, they were gone, conquered by the emotions and sensations she was sharing with Daniel Slade. It was a union of more than hungry bodies; it was a fusion of spirits, a forging of their cores. Her senses reeled freely and wildly, compelling her to total abandonment. He was all she needed.

Rachel's unbridled responses and bold actions heightened Dan's desires and coaxed his full possession of her. Her ardor and need inspired him to hold nothing back. Passion's flames engulfed him in a fiery and blazing glow that only she could extinguish. His lips and hands roved her luscious figure and mouth, bringing her to uncontrollable tremors of desire. She uttered feverish moans as she became breathless with need for him. She arched to meet every thrust. Her words and movements provoked him to a swifter pace. Loving him like this was sweet torment. Though she wanted the stimulation to continue, she craved release. "I love you, Dan," she confessed without awareness she had spoken.

The sea captain heard those whispered words and his heart drummed with joy. Yet he knew she wasn't conscious of uttering them. She was ensnared in the throes of love, passion, and overpowering release. He cast his control aside and joined her in an explosion of sultry elation.

Both were damp with perspiration from their exertions. The salty taste of passion touched their tongues as they kissed each other's faces and necks. They relaxed in the languid afterglow of their potent experience, snuggling together to bask in its warmth.

"I told you I would fight for you, woman," Dan chuckled "but I never realized a battle could be so pleasurable and victorious."

"If this is how you fight, my dashing sea pirate, I'll gladly challenge you every day and night."

"Rachel McCandless, how brazen you've become."

She joined in on his laughter. "You cannot blame me, Sir Pirate. The fault lies with my instructor. He is determined to teach me the skills he knows. Alas, I fear I am most eager and receptive to his tutoring."

"You best take advantage of this class, my lovely and greedy student; there is no guessing when another one can be taken."

Rachel kissed him, then murmured against his mouth, "I am all ears, eyes, hands, and senses tonight, my talented teacher."

"Give me a moment to rest, then I'll make you starve, make you anticipate, then sate you fully."

"So far, you've always kept your word to me. I shan't allow you to break it tonight. Shall I feed you my chilled supper to give you needed strength? I fear I am not properly attired to go downstairs for a hot one."

After a time of kissing and cuddling, Dan got out of bed. To guard their privacy, he drew the drapes before he lighted a lamp. He encircled his manly region with his shirt, then secured the half-covering with a knot near one hip. He checked the dinner tray for anything appetizing.

Rachel donned a loose night robe, secured it with a sash, then joined him. "Let's see," she murmured as she eyed the meal. "Bread, fruit, spring salad, dessert, and cheese appear our best choices. The meat and vegetables are cold and greasy by now. The coffee's cold, too, but we have a glass of water to share. I'll use the spoon and you take the fork."

"I could dress and fetch us a hot meal from downstairs."

"Half of this is fine with me. But if you want something else or need more food than this for nourishment, I will get you another tray."

"This is plenty for me, too. I don't want to exercise later on a full belly."

Her adoring gaze roamed his tousled black hair and twinkling blue eyes. "Daniel Slade, how brazen *you've* become since ensnaring me."

They shared laughter and exchanged smiles.

As they dined off the same dishes and shared the same drinking glass, Dan announced, "It's past time you got to know Luke Conner and my crew, and visit my ship to see how I live. That will help you get to know me better. We'll take care of that matter when we return to Savannah. Unless you're afraid I'll take to sea the moment you're aboard and steal you."

She laughed, but retorted, "You wouldn't do that because you don't want me to appear as if I'm fleeing crimes because I'm guilty and scared. You don't want the authorities chasing me down."

When Dan finished chewing and swallowing a piece of bread and cheese, he refuted, "But you aren't guilty of any crimes, my love."

"The authorities aren't convinced yet; and Harry would make another charge against me—theft of that missing money. He'd think I was escaping with it." She ate a few spoons of canned fruit.

"How could he report lost money from an illegal deal?" Dan queried.

"It isn't illegal," Rachel disclosed, "or so he claims. George told me Phillip got clearance from customs. Harry has the papers in his office. If customs approved the shipment, it might be legal." She took a bite of salad.

"That's a surprise. It puts a hole in our conclusions."

Rachel shrugged. "Maybe, but maybe not. We don't know what Phillip said or did to get those papers. They could even be forged, like my notes."

"You're right. But you can still visit me on the *Merry Wind.*"

"That wouldn't be smart, Dan. We can't risk exposure."

"Bring Lula Mae along."

"That wouldn't help much; she's my loyal servant and friend."

"Bring Milton Baldwin along then. Tell him you want to visit me and see my clipper, but you don't want to inspire any nasty gossip."

Rachel lowered her salad-filled spoon. "That might work, and I'd love to see your world and meet your friends. Perhaps Milton would like to see such a fine and beautiful ship, too. I'll let you know when I make a decision."

"Has anything else happened since I saw you?"

Rachel gave Dan the important news. She told him about her stepfather's visit and about her mother's illness, which Dan had already known. "I wrote Mama a letter before I left home," she revealed. "Her answer will determine my next action."

"No wonder you had the anger and strength to try to break from me."

"I'm truly sorry about that, Dan. I was mistaken and rash. After all that happened last week, I'm surprised I've retained my sanity."

Dan stopped eating to question her words. "What is it, Rachel? Did your meetings go badly?"

She didn't want to reveal her financial condition to him, but Burke might have already told him things were terrible, and she didn't want Dan to think she was keeping secrets from him. Yet she wouldn't paint the entire black picture tonight. "Yes, I'm afraid they did. Phillip recently canceled his insurance, and the news from the bank was depressing. That, atop what I'm learning about the finances of the three companies doesn't look good financially."

Phillip left her near penniless? What had happened to his wealth? Gambling, a costly search for him his brother, and bad investments? "Do you need money?" Dan asked. "I can give you or loan you what you need until your problems are resolved."

A self-employed sea captain didn't have the amount she required to extricate herself from her dilemmas, and she wouldn't accept it even if he did. "No, thank you. I'll be fine. I have some money at home, and I have future earnings from the share-croppers. I've told all three partners I will agree to sales when they can work out deals, but only after this problem is solved."

Sell his family's business, even if it was tied up with Baldwin's? "Why not keep the shipping firm for support, in case the crops fail?" he asked.

She ate two spoonsful of salad. "That isn't wise or safe. All of them are in sorry condition. When I inherited Phillip's assets, I also inherited his shares of their debts. I'd rather be free of any future risks of financial ruin."

To make his question sound casual and his mood appear calm, Dan worked on the dessert as he asked, "How will you support yourself?"

She didn't mention the jewelry she planned to sell to tide her over until better luck arrived. She couldn't help wondering why he didn't propose again to get her out of her predicament. Had he decided a mistress would suit his adventurous lifestyle better? "I have land not in use by sharecroppers. I can either farm it or raise cotton or indigo. I do have years of experience and knowledge in that area."

"Will it earn you enough to support yourself?"

"If not, I'll think of something else later. There's no need to waste wits and energy at this time worrying about a problem that's not definite. I have other troubles to concentrate on."

"Such as explaining this sudden trip to the authorities?"

"No, there won't be a problem there. I stopped by to ask permission before I left town; they said it was all right to come. My case file is still open, but they aren't getting anywhere with their investigation against me. They won't either, unless there is faked evidence to frame me."

"I don't like these pranks and threats. Are you locking your windows and doors, and keeping a gun handy?"

"Following orders as you gave them, Captain Sir."

"This isn't a funny situation, woman," he chided with tenderness.

"I know, but I have to keep a sense of humor or cry. Too many times I've allowed a group of hateful and cruel people to push me into bad circumstances; I won't allow that to happen again. I have to believe there are plenty of good and kind people. I merely have to make certain those wicked ones don't provoke trouble for me."

Dan was pleased. "You've had numerous bad experiences, Rachel, but look at the strength, pride, and courage they've given you. I doubt you'll fall into another trap trying to find peace and happiness and respect."

As they finished eating, they made plans for the next day, then returned to bed to once more find bliss in each other.

*

Rachel lifted her hand and knocked on the door of Harrison Clements' office. She wished Dan were with her, but they had agreed it was best for her to confront Harry alone. She wasn't afraid; she felt strong and determined. Part of that had to do with Dan's love and his faith in her. Part of it was the result of wanting to defeat the flaxen-haired man who opened the door and glared at her.

Harry's ice-blue eyes were like frozen chips. A scowl lined his rugged face and his square jaw was clenched. His body was rigid, as if poised for a physical attack. None of that dissuaded Rachel from her task and she knew she appeared calm and poised.

"Get inside and sit down," he ordered, "so you and I can have a serious talk! What the hell is going on!" he shouted at her as she followed his command.

Rachel took a seat, arranged her skirt, then met his furious gaze—all without changing her pleasant expression and losing her air of self-control.

Harry rounded his desk and dropped into his chair. "Phillip was already dead when you came up here and pranced around town as if everything was normal!" he accused, "I saw his obituary in the *Southern Banner*. What was that sneaky pretense about?"

Rachel focused on his face as she coaxed, "Calm down, Harry, or we won't be able to clear up this matter without ill will."

"Calm down?" he exploded. "What is this scheme of yours?"

"If you'll relax and listen, I'll explain everything. Phillip knew he was dying and instructed me to check the company books before I reported his death; but you refused to let me study them. You have no excuse to deny me access now, *partner*. Why didn't you respond to my telegrams?"

He glared at her. "Because they were stupid, and a bunch of lies!"

"You don't have to get belligerent and hateful, Harry. I was only carrying out Phillip's last request. We didn't know each other well, and I believed it better if you didn't know at the time I was your new partner. But you were too busy to give me much time and attention. George was nicer and more cooperative than you were. However, he is a little annoyed with me at present for duping him, too. I saw him yesterday and tried to smooth things over, but it'll take time."

"You expect us to believe Phillip used his dying breaths to tell you to check on us, but didn't have the time or sense to tell you where he hid the advance? I'm no fool, Rachel, so don't treat me like one! You can't keep that money; it belongs to his two companies. We've both borrowed from banks to invest in this deal of his, so it must be turned over to us or we're all ruined, including you. Is that what you want? Is that what *he* wanted?"

She removed a fabric bag from her wrist and placed it in her lap as she replied, "Of course not. But I don't have the money. That '*stupid*' telegram from me told you that."

"If the two companies bankrupt because of your greed, you'll be hurt, too. As our partner now, our debts are half yours. Turn it over, and I'll forget and forgive you for this little weakness."

"That's kind and generous of you, Harry, but impossible. Phillip was delirious; he didn't reveal its hiding place. But he did mumble about something being illegal and about trying to stop it." She saw him tense in dread of the reference to what Phillip had confessed to her. "Was he referring to this big deal that nobody seems to know about?"

"Don't be absurd! It is legal. One thing I do have is that clearance paper from Savannah customs. It came in the mail, so Phillip did handle that angle, as I insisted before proceeding further, before he died on us."

She faked a look of surprise. "It is legal? Customs will clear it through port? You have a signed paper in your possession?"

"Why does that shock you?"

"It's all been so secretive and mysterious that I assumed . . ." She left those words hanging for effect. "That's why I said I'd have to meet with the client first, to make sure before we honored the bargain and got into trouble. If Phillip wasn't referring to his deal, then to what?"

"How should I know? You were at his side and didn't even understand him. Now that you know it is legal, you can stop refusing us that payment. We both need it badly, and today, Rachel. No—weeks ago."

Rachel pretended to trust Harry and to be honest with him. She had to convince him she wanted this deal, that she was just as frustrated and baffled as he was. "I don't have it, Harry, believe that or not. I would turn it over to you and George if I could find it. As you pointed out, my neck is on that chopping block with you two. I searched the house, grounds, and Phillip's office at the shipping firm, including the safe. I've been to the bank, to our lawyer and our insurance broker. I've questioned Milton. Nothing. I don't know where else it could be hidden. It doesn't make sense. Because of Phillip's mumblings I feared my life was in jeopardy and that the client is dangerous, and I've been getting threats since the day after he died. I was hoping to get answers from you last time, but you claimed you were in the dark. Maybe it was only his illness talking nonsense."

"If that client loses his money and doesn't get his orders, he might well become a threat to you. How would you feel and react if someone stole all that money?"

"Phillip didn't steal it! He hid it for safety. He just died before he could pass it along to his partners or reveal its location to me."

"He had no reason to withhold it."

"Why did he, Harry? Didn't you two trust each other?"

He scowled at her. "I trusted him; that's why I allowed him to keep me in the dark. Obviously he didn't trust me, or he was using the money to stake his gambling weakness."

Rachel put on a look of horror. "Don't even say or think that, Harry. If it doesn't show up soon, we're all in terrible trouble."

"Just you, Rachel," he refuted. "You're responsible for the missing money. It was in your husband's possession, and you've taken his place."

"How am I to blame? Is there a law to say a wife automatically is responsible? I don't know where else to look, Harry. I'm open to any suggestions you make. If Phillip asked someone to hold it for him, the chance of that person—who is now rich! —coming forward to hand it over to us is nill." She feigned a look of alarm and pretended she wanted to be helpful. "Phillip told me to honor the bargain, but he didn't explain how. I was hoping to get clues from you and George during my last visits, but you both claim ignorance. I didn't even know how much the contract was for until you two told me, and it shocked me to learn it was so large. We must find a way to save it."

"How can we do that, Rachel?"

"Since you don't know the client, you can't tell me if he'll be understanding about our dilemma and be willing to renegotiate. Milton has Haiti recorded as the destination of the cargo, a May fourteenth shipping date, and two sets of initials: C.T. and J.C. But he says he doesn't know more than that about this mystery. That isn't much, if any, help to us. We don't know where to anchor at Haiti or whom to meet there. We have one path still open: the client will come to see me when his order doesn't arrive, and we can go from there. Or there is another possible angle: the men who go with those initials could arrive on or before May fourteenth to escort the cargo to its owner. If so, we'll have contacts to work through to get started on saving this deal." She saw how Harry eyed her differently, as if pondering her honesty and deciding if her speculations had any value.

"Did you tell all of this to George?"

She forced a look of embarrassment. "No, you said last time he doesn't know anything, even about the dynamite. I didn't want him getting angered and refusing to keep his end of the bargain. We need ammunition to go with our rifles." She lightly glossed over the fabricated story she had asked George to tell Harry. "Was I right to handle him that way?" She saw how he mellowed a smidgen, and that gave her a heady sense of power.

"It was smart and for the best, if we hope to save ourselves."

To check his reaction to another suspicion, Rachel asked, "If this deal fails, Harry, maybe we can find another buyer for those arms. What about the Indian troubles out west? The Army might need ammunition and rifles. We could offer them a deal by taking less profit ourselves. That's better than suffering a loss and risking ruin. Or maybe we can find a foreign market where there's trouble and need. I could ask Dan for suggestions. He's still in port awaiting his two orders. He sails around the world and keeps up with trouble spots to safeguard his ship and crew."

Harry leaned back in his chair. "Those are great ideas, Rachel, but I've already thought of them and checked out every potential customer and location, just in case the worst happened. Companies bigger and more important than ours own and control all of them."

"All of them?" she echoed and looked distressed.

Harry nodded.

"Oh, my, that's terrible. If we can't find the advance or another customer, the only thing left to do is make sure we save any part of this deal we can."

"How can we take a five-hundred-thousand-dollar loss?"

"Surely a third of that would have been profit," she pointed out.

"But that leaves $333,333 to cover. I can't do that."

"Neither can I, Harry." She set out to prove she was desperate and sincere by exposing some of her predicament, which he might already know about from Phillip or his spy. "I'm almost penniless, so I need this deal to succeed. Phillip didn't leave me any insurance; he canceled it two months ago. All three companies, even if I sold my partnerships, can't earn me much. Phillip's bank account is almost empty, my household cash box is very low. The sharecroppers don't pay off until September, and that's if nothing drastic happens to their crops. All I have to cover an emergency is jewelry I can sell. I can't get rid of Moss Haven and have no home. You must help me save this deal, Harry. Please. You need the profit, too, to save the business."

"The only reason I haven't shut down or sold out is because I was waiting to complete this last deal before doing so. Arms don't make money anymore, Rachel.

Phillip was going to get out, too, when this was over. He was damned lucky to find this rich and needy client. I'm already into another business, but I can't take money from it to save a dying company. It's in Atlanta, where I'll be moving when everything here is settled. That's where I was this past weekend, finalizing the terms."

Rachel urged a pitiful look to her face and sound to her voice as she murmured, "What am I going to do?"

"I don't know, Rachel, but I can't be of any help to you. I'm sorry."

Presuming he cared little or nothing for her husband, she fumed, "Damn Phillip for getting us into this bind! I'll bet it's because of his gambling! How could he be so foolish and weak? I never knew he had such a problem or I would have put an end to it. That's the only thing that could have gotten him into this financial disaster he dropped in my lap. I've told Milton and George to sell out, to make the best deals they can. I'll tell you the same. But will you give me time to save ourselves before you do it?"

Harry observed her for a moment, then said, "I might as well. The order is almost done. It might be crazy, but I'll complete it with hopes you can use your beauty, wits, and charms to save us."

Rachel interpreted his wanting to continue the preparations as a clue. Perhaps he even concluded she would bring forth the money later if she had no other choice. "Thank you for the flattery and confidence," she said. "I swear I'll do my best. Whatever it requires to solve this mystery and my problems, I'll do it." She knew he didn't comprehend her real meaning, but that was fine.

"Don't go marrying our rich client to win his aid," he joked.

"He may already have a wife," she quipped, as if she'd thought of it.

"If he doesn't, I'm sure he'll be enchanted and tempted by you. He'll try his damnedest to ensnare a rare gem like you as part of his new deal."

"Thank you again . . . may I ask you a question that baffles me? Why did you allow Phillip to handle such a crucial deal in this illogical way?" she rushed on before he could object to her question.

"Because he was a friend and partner, one I trusted. When he said he had to honor somebody's confidence, I believed him. I didn't have any reason at that point not to do so. I don't know if you're aware of it, but Phillip took heavy losses during the '73 Panic and Depression. Maybe that's when he started gambling and ran up heavy debts. Or perhaps it was following those family deaths and scandal. He found this mysterious deal and client, as you called them, and I agreed to help him try to recover his many losses. I suppose I also got greedy and excited about making a big profit, so I allowed myself to get pulled in deeper and deeper."

Rachel didn't believe that claim for an instant. "Why didn't I ever suspect Phillip had money problems?"

"Men don't usually tell women those things. I also felt partly to blame for his problems getting worse. When he invested in my company, it was doing fine. We had contracts to make weapons for Winchester, Remington, and a few others. But they expanded their businesses and canceled the contracts, just dumped us out in the cold after years of helping them out with expert craftmanship and always honoring our deadlines. They gobbled up all the other available markets, American and foreign. With their names and reputations, it was easy to steal all the customers. A company of this size and with two partners to support can't survive on small or personal contracts. Business keeps slacking off every month."

Rachel heard and witnessed bitterness over those crippling losses, and assumed that was why Harry—and perhaps Phillip—were illegally using those makers' patents for the rebels' arms. Still, she held silent about that suspicion to prevent tipping her hand about her knowledge.

"This could be a dangerous situation, Rachel, not to honor a contract with a rich and probably powerful man, to tell him your husband lost his money either by hiding it or gambling it away. When he arrives, do you think he'll believe you and I know nothing about the money? I doubt it. He's going to be furious. Duped men do crazy things when crossed. You have to find that money or replace it."

She skillfully clenched her hands and licked her lips as if scared and tense. "I've already explained, Harry. I can't. I'm on the brink of poverty. Are you sure he paid Phillip?"

"Phillip told me and George he had."

"Then who would he trust to hold that large amount for him? And why?"

"I have no idea, Rachel. But you can study the company's books to prove I didn't receive it. As my new partner, they're open to you."

"There is one last point I'd like to mention, if it's true." She noticed how that tone seized his full attention. "The firm's record lists Haiti as the destination for the cargo, but Phillip mumbled something about Cuba, about war and freedom, about needing guns badly. I had forgotten about it until I saw Haiti listed. Dan told me rebels are battling there for independence from Spanish rule. He said a gun-running ship with an American flag and partial crew was attacked and men hanged. Spain had to compensate the families to avoid a conflict with us. Publicly, our country is staying neutral, but perhaps not privately. If the shipment is for Cuban rebels, that could explain why Phillip had to keep it a secret."

"You could be right; it sounds logical."

She felt that Harry knew all she was telling him, but revealing she knew a few things could evoke a slip from him. With cunning, she speculated, "If it is a confidential military operation or assistance, that could be how Phillip got that custom's clearance. He's been in shipping all of his life, and he owns partnerships in arms and ammunition companies, so someone he knew or who discovered those things about him must have approached him as the best choice to fill his needs. Maybe he didn't tell Phillip where the order was going and why. Or if he did, Phillip was willing to aid their cause, or make a big profit on it. All you've told me about Phillip explains why he agreed; he was desperate. But it sounds as if something happened to give him doubts; that's why he changed his mind and halted the deal. So, why didn't he return the money? You said he told you he still had it the day before he died. By then he had changed his mind a second time and restarted the contract. The only reason I can guess why is because of several horrible incidents that occurred in February."

After she related them to him, she surmised, "Phillip must have taken them as warnings not to back out; he even mumbled something to that effect during his delirium. I can understand how urgently the rebels need their orders from us . . . but enough to do such evil things to get them? And what will they do to all of us if we don't comply with them or return their money? Damn Phillip for dying before he could tell me everything! Those aren't many clues for us to work with, Harry. What do you make of them?"

"What did he say on his deathbed? Did he call out any names?"

Rachel knew why he was worried. With her most innocent voice and expression, she repeated only the rantings she had used so far to dupe him.

"Will you go through with the deal if it is for rebels?"

"Yes, if there's no trouble. Phillip cleared it through customs, so it must be legal.

One thing I will demand from this client is proof of a signed contract between him and Phillip and proof the money was paid to my husband. Evidence first, negotiations second."

"If the deal's confidential, maybe there is no contract or receipt."

Rachel frowned, but concurred, "You could be right, but I will question him on those points. When Milton gave you the destination, did you have any suspicions the shipment was for Cuba?"

"I have to admit that I did, but dismissed it as foolish. I didn't have your knowledge to tell me I was wrong. I don't want any trouble from this matter, Rachel. I wish I weren't involved in it, but I am; *we* are. You'll have to find a way we can honor this deal or find us a safe way out of it. We have to protect our lives, families, friends, and holdings against potential revenge. Let's get it over and done with as soon as possible, so we can both make fresh starts."

"What if we discover our client was behind those deadly incidents? What if Phillip did return the money, but they refuse to admit it and try to force us to hand over their purchases?"

"He still had it the day before he died, or he told me he did. He promised to bring it to me the following Monday. When you came here and claimed he was gone for weeks, I was furious and baffled. You don't think he killed himself because he lost it, do you?"

She permitted her expression to show doubt and sadness. "I honestly don't know what to think, Harry. I hope he didn't. No matter, he left us in a tight and perilous bind."

"If those incidents were warnings, that kind of man doesn't play games. If we trick him, he'll have us killed. Nobody twisted Phillip's arm to make this deal, but they'll do more than twist ours to make us stick to the bargain he made. That worries me."

"Me, too. We'll either have our answer in two and a half weeks or a few weeks afterward. Let's pray it's a good one." She sighed heavily. "This discussion has worn me out emotionally and physically. Do you mind if I rest this afternoon and go over the books with you tomorrow?" That would give him time to telegraph George to check out her story and be duped further.

"That's fine with me. How about dinner tonight? My wife is still in Atlanta looking at homes and making new friends. We hope to be moved and settled in by the end of the summer. I apologize for being angry and crude earlier, but I didn't understand the situation."

"That's all right, Harry; it was my fault for deceiving you, but I was so confused and desperate. I'm glad you forgive me. Dinner sounds marvelous, but Dan is with me, so I should bring him along. He's at the hotel or out playing around town. It would be hard to claim it's a private business dinner when we've spent hours on it today." She perceived his annoyance.

"I didn't realize he'd come along again."

Rachel laughed. "He tracked me down last night at the hotel. He was miffed at me for taking off alone. He doesn't realize I don't need a man's protection for such a simple journey. He and his family are old-fashioned; they believe a lady must have an escort wherever she goes."

"That isn't a bad idea with a woman as ravishing and tempting as you, especially in light of those threats you said you've been getting."

She observed that lustful gleam in his eyes again, but she smiled. "Thank you once more, partner. One favor, I don't want to discuss business in front of him tonight, if you don't mind. These matters are personal, just between us, not for my relatives' ears. What are our dinner plans?''

Harry set a time and place, and Rachel agreed. They spoke a few minutes, with him telling her what time to be in his office tomorrow on Tuesday, April twenty-seventh. Then she departed, with the man almost painfully drilling his powerful gaze into her retreating back.

*

On Friday, Rachel dressed to go into Savannah to meet with a jeweler to see what he would offer her on several of her expensive pieces. As she did her grooming, she reflected on the past few days. The dinner Monday night with Harry and Dan had passed without problems, as had her meeting with Harry the following day. As far as she could detect, the books had not been altered and Harry had been truthful about the company's condition. According to a cable from George yesterday, Harry had gone to see him on Wednesday, and George had carried out Rachel's request to delude him.

She and Dan had spent a passionate, stolen night together in Augusta Wednesday while en route home. Upon her return yesterday, a letter had awaited her from her mother. To Rachel's delight and relief, Catherine Fleming Starger was feeling better and wanted to visit her daughter next weekend. Rachel had sent her mother a prompt plea to do so after Earl had informed her of the older woman's illness. The only part of the letter she found disappointing was her mother's confirmation of her doctor's visits, with Earl as her escort, on the two days in question. That told Rachel her stepfather couldn't be in two distant places at the same time, and Earl Starger would never hire anyone to do his dirty work!

*

By one o'clock, Rachel was relieved again when Adam Meigs offered and paid her a fair price for the jewelry she sold him. She was to go to Milton's office to entice him to visit Dan's clipper with her this afternoon, but a stunning and malicious episode occurred to prevent those plans.

Chapter

16

"My, oh, my, what do we have here?" a sultry voice with a heavy Southern accent taunted from the doorway. "The merry murderess buying herself new trinkets with her deceased husband's money? Or mayhap trading in gifts for prettier gems with which to ensnare her next victim? If Phillip McCandless had married me instead of recklessly choosing a Black Widow as his mate, he would still be alive and well. Who are you adorning yourself for this time? Who is the fourth victim, Rachel?"

The dark-haired widow turned to confront the tormenting redhead whose striking tresses tumbled down in untamed perfection. Camellia's cattish yellow-green eyes exposed her shallow character, and the woman's sharp claws were unsheathed again today. Before Rachel could leave to prevent an embarrassing scene, the twenty-five-year-old viper created one.

"Only a heartless bitch like you could dump a fine man like Phillip McCandless in an unmarked grave and not give him a decent burial or allow his many friends to say a proper farewell."

Rachel's sherry-colored gaze altered to one with of grayish green as anger consumed her. She glared at the aristocratic beauty with her full, pouty lips and unmarred oval fair-complected face. To her, Camellia's long and slender neck reminded her of a snake's with head held high to strike. Again, the auburn-haired vixen spoke before she herself could, while Rachel eyed the two grinning friends with Camellia who laughed encouragement and nudged each other in amusement.

"Oh, yes," she drawled in a breathy purr, "I know all about your wicked deeds. I have many friends in the police department, more than you have in this entire area. You've entrapped yourself this time. I'm surprised you're still strolling around free, but it won't be for much longer."

Rachel concealed her alarm at those intimidating words and wondered if there was any truth to them. Even if something had come up which she hadn't been questioned about yet, she bluffed with poise, "Well, you're misinformed, and most rude, Miss Jones. Didn't your family and tutors teach you proper manners and good breeding?"

Camellia looked as if she was astounded that Rachel gave any response, as if she'd expected her to burst into tears and run away. "How would you know about good breeding, as you don't possess any? You're a vicious criminal, and you'll get caught and punished this time. Your file is still open, wide open."

Rachel realized her calm and strength vexed the other woman. In a sweet tone she replied, "I won't quarrel with you, *Miss* Jones. You know nothing about me or the real situation, despite tales from your gossipy and mistaken spies. You're the one who's vicious and hungry, eager to devour me out of spite for stealing Craig and Phillip from your grasping clutches."

Camellia's eyes widened and her mouth gaped. "If either or both could speak from their graves or be allowed to choose again, there would be no contest or comparison between us!"

Rachel knew she had touched a raw nerve, and couldn't help but pick at it to silence her foe. "You're absolutely correct; you would suffer two defeats again. A hateful, spoiled, and selfish witch like you could never land a smart fish, no matter how pretty and expensive your baited line was."

Camellia clenched and unclenched her fingers, as if preparing them to attack her despised rival. "How dare you insult me!"

Adam Meigs shifted nervously behind his counter. He wanted to halt the episode, but Camellia Jones was too valuable a customer to offend. He hated being placed in this distressing position.

"The same way you dare to insult and harass me," Rachel retorted. "I've offered you peace and friendship many times, but you persist in being my enemy and tormentor. You create lies about me and fan the flames of unjust rumors. You try to humiliate and hurt me at every turn. Grow up, malicious little girl, and clear your head of such destructive traits; that's the only way any man is going to lean in your direction."

Camellia gasped in outrage. "You arrogant and stupid bitch! I'll—"

Rachel riled her more when she interrupted to chide, "That's what I mean, Camellia. Your quick temper and foolish hatred defeat you every time. I'm not the reason you're still unmarried; *they* are. I didn't steal Craig and Phillip from you, because you didn't own either one. You have beauty, money, and social rank, but some men don't consider those as important enough reasons to marry a childish woman like you. Even if I were guilty, which I am not, you have no reason or right to behave like a—"

"Shut up! Don't you dare call me names or I'll claw your eyes out!"

Rachel noticed the silky hands with long nails that lifted for a moment, flexed a warning, then lowered and tightened into fists. She saw the fiery glint in the woman's gaze. "I see, you can call me whatever nasty names and vile words you wish, but I'm supposed to cower and hold silent in return? I've done that in the past, but no more. I was afraid if I got angry and fought back with people like you, I would do damage to myself even more powerful than those stupid investigations and cruel gossip. I realized I was mistaken. I'm not guilty, so I don't have to behave as if I have something to be ashamed of or to fear. My case file can stay open forever and the authorities won't find any incriminating evidence against me, because there is none, because I didn't harm any of those four people."

"Three dead husbands and a son in three years?" Camellia sneered.

"Strange and unfortunate, but of natural or accidental causes." Rachel roved her gaze over the three people as she vowed, intending to shame the women, "One day, all of you doubters and persecuters will discover I'm blameless. I hope you and others will be adult enough to apologize then."

"Apologize to you? When it snows in July!"

"Stranger things have happened, Camellia; I know from experience."

As if just noticing the pieces of jewelry lying on a cloth on the counter, Camellia snatched up one she recognized, having seen Rachel wear it to a party. Enlightenment flooded her, and she grinned cattily. "I've heard Phillip's companies aren't doing well.

I guess this proves it. Having to sell off jewels to eat, my unlucky spider? I'll take them all, Mr. Meigs, every one. You *have* purchased them?" she asked, and Adam nodded.

Rachel fumed at knowing this vixen would have those precious items she'd been forced to part with for survival. She hated the thought of Camellia wearing anything chosen for her by Phillip. She knew the redhead would gloat every time she wore them, as if displaying trophies of victory. "Good-bye. I hope we don't meet again soon, if ever. Mr. Meigs, I—"

Camellia grabbed Rachel's arm to prevent her departure, astonishing everyone in the store. "I haven't finished my say, you—"

Rachel exposed her anger on purpose. "Oh yes you have! You—"

"No I haven't! You forget Captain Daniel Slade as victim number four. I'll see you hanged before he's dead and buried like the others."

Rachel feigned bewilderment. "Whatever are you babbling about?"

Camellia put her flushed face close to Rachel's lovely one. "We both know the answer to the question. Toss this one back into the pond, Rachel. You hook him and harm him and I'll kill you myself, or have it done for me!"

Again, everyone present was shocked by the redhead's icy threat, even though they all assumed she didn't mean it.

"Not that it's any of your business, Miss Jones, but we're good friends; and it will remain that way, no matter how it looks to you and to others like you. It wouldn't shock me to find your pretty nose stuck in my current troubles. If it is, be prepared to have it cut off."

Camellia gaped at Rachel in disbelief. "You're threatening me?"

"You made the threats; mine was a warning. Despite your wealth and prestige, the authorities won't glance the other way if you commit such a crime or pay for it to be done. I'll be certain to mention our meeting today, in detail, to those fine investigators when we speak again. Of course, if you speak with them first, please be sure to explain your meanings clearly to them."

"You'll be sorry if you try to blacken my name, you trollop."

"How so, dear Camellia? Please tell me more about your motives."

One of the woman's friends tugged on her arm and cautioned her to self-control. Camellia scowled, but heeded her advice. "Another time, my cunning Black Widow," she vowed. "Rest assured my eyes and ears will be on you. Make one slip and . . ." She slapped her hands together loudly. "You'll be squashed like a pesky mosquito."

Rachel locked her gaze with Camellia's. "Guilty or innocent, my blood on your hands would give you a thrill, wouldn't it?"

Before she could stop it, the reckless admission leapt from her pouty lips. "You have no idea how much."

Rachel grinned at that slip. "Oh, but I do," she purred. "Take heed, for my ears and eyes are on you, too. Who better than a twice-spurned lover, a jealous and vindictive rival, to frame the object of her despair? Did your 'friends' in Chief Anderson's office disclose that unexpected angle of their case? I doubt it. If I were you, I would watch my words and guard my steps well for a while or you'll be answering as many questions as I am."

Rachel turned to the uneasy jeweler, smiled, and said, "I'm sorry you had to witness such unladylike behavior from both of us, Mr. Meigs. Thank you for your kindness and assistance. Good afternoon."

Rachel's head was held high and her shoulders straight as she left the others gaping after her in stunned silence. She hadn't wanted to conduct herself that way in public, but had been given no choice except to defend herself and to hush Camellia. The bitter confrontation had drained her. Camellia's attention was on her today, so she shouldn't visit Dan on his ship, with or without Milton Baldwin's escort. Nor was she in a mood to see her partner in the shipping firm. Despite how much she yearned to see her love, Rachel had Burke head the carriage homeward where she could relax and think.

*

"What's going on, Miss Rachel?" Lula Mae asked.

Rachel caught the stern tone and serious expression on the woman's face. She was baffled. "I told you, Lula Mae, I had a terrible quarrel with Camellia Jones in Mr. Meigs's store. That's why I'm so upset."

"I don't means that. I mean with you and *that man*."

Rachel studied the nosy and bold woman and grasped which two words she stressed. "What do you really mean, Lula Mae?"

"He comes here out of nowhere to sees Mr. Phillip. You sneaks off with him. He lies to the law to keeps you outta trouble. You treats him cold and mean and takes off again. You comes home and you's friends again."

"I explained those reasons to you before. We *are* friends, Lula Mae. I was wrong about him, and wrong to be cruel to him."

" 'Cause he loves you and is helping you? I hope you ain't letting him fools you like Mr. Newman did."

Rachel told herself the woman was controlled by worry and affection for her, but she was nevertheless vexed with Lula. "Dan is nothing like Craig Newman, nothing."

The housekeeper frowned. "No more 'Captain Slade,' is it?"

Rachel hoped the woman would realize soon how much she was provoking her mistress and how difficult it was to master her annoyance and to withhold a stern rebuke. "Is there something wrong with us being friends?"

"I don't trust him."

Calmly, but strongly, Rachel replied, "I do."

"Too much, too soon, I'm afeared. It'll stir up more trouble."

"What reason do you have to dislike and mistrust Dan?"

"In here," the woman said, pointing to her stomach to indicate an instinct. "It tells me, and it ain't never been wrong."

It is this time, Rachel's mind argued. "Don't worry, Lula Mae," her gentle tone advised, "I'm walking slowly and carefully and with my eyes open wide. I won't be hurt or tricked again."

"I got reasons to worry and not believe you, Miss Rachel. I seed them pitchers in your room. I seed hows you two was with each other."

"What pitchers?" she queried, failing to understand the woman's pronunciation of *pictures*.

"Them of you and him on that sneaky trip, them pitchers in your drawer."

Comprehension filled Rachel and angered her. What she'd endured today atop her current troubles and perils caused her to lose control. "You've been looking through my things to check out your crazy suspicion? It's none of your business, Lula Mae!"

The woman took that scolding as an affront. Her shoulders jerked back and her body stiffened as her cheeks flushed. "I was putting away your warsh and seed them. You got so much on you these days, I was trying to do more chores to help you. This ain't no way to thank me or be kind."

Despite that explanation and the woman's hurt feelings, Rachel was miffed. "Why didn't you leave it on my bed as usual?"

"I told you," the simple woman said, "I thawt it would help you. When I seed them pitchers, I was scared. I thawt you was gitting yourself into a fix with him. I don't want you hurt more."

"You mustn't fret." She explained about the party in Augusta and alleged the pictures were George Leathers' idea, since at that time he believed they were cousins and they would make nice keepsakes. "There's no harm in having them made and in keeping them."

"Could be, if the wrong eyes sees them. Best to git rid of them."

Rachel envisioned burning those heart-stirring souvenirs and shuddered. She tried to soothe the woman's fears with deceit. "I've done nothing wrong with him, so why should I? They're lovely, and I looked my best that night. Besides, worrier, Dan is an old and dear friend of Phillip's, so why would anyone find our behavior offensive or wicked?"

"You forgitting the past," Lula Mae pointed out, "them investigations, the dangers you're in, those loose tongues awagging. It be crazy to look close to a man at this time. You know what mean folks will say; that you done chose number four and were acourting him afore Mr. Phillip was cold and stiff."

She and Dan were being careful to conceal their relationship so it shouldn't create more problems for her. "I'll have to take that risk, Lula Mae; I can't give up all my male friends and acquaintances to prevent more rumors. Gossip will plague me anyway."

"It's them kind of men that's harmed you worst, Miss Rachel. Keep 'em away till this trouble be over," she urged.

"I don't know how long that will be, Lula Mae. I doubt my file has been closed once since it was started years ago. No matter what I say or do, someone will find fault with it. I must live as normally as possible."

"Even if such foolishness gits you hurt?"

"I'll have to be the judge of what's best for me—not you or anyone else. I'm sorry if that sounds mean, but I have to rule my life from now on."

"You ain't never shut the door in my face afore. It's him, ain't it? He's the cause of you acting like this."

Rachel thought the woman sounded jealous and possessive; her resentment and intrusion were blatantly obvious. To keep peace, she said, "I'm under a heavy strain, Lula Mae. Dan is a big help and comfort. I need that support and strength right now. He isn't pushing himself on me."

"He wants you, Miss Rachel. He's achasing you. Cain't you see that?"

"Even if that were true—"

"He's gonna git you. I jest know it. I can feel it. It scares me."

Rachel was distressed by the woman's uncharacteristic behavior. She asked herself if the housekeeper was addle brained today. Or perhaps Lula Mae was only worried about her mistress losing everything and sending both out on their own again. Maybe the woman was scared she would run off with Dan and leave her to fend for herself.

"All I can say is calm down," Rachel appeased, "and thank you for such love and concern. I'll be fine, Lula Mae; we all will. This should be over soon, and things will be back to normal at Moss Haven."

As she shook her head, strands of Lula Mae's drab brown hair broke free of its confining bun. Her dark-brown eyes dulled with sadness.

"No ma'am, Miss Rachel, not this time, not ever again. I jest knows it. You gonna be hurt real bad this time. Lord have mercy on me; I cain't stops you from doing wrong. What's gonna happen to all of us?"

"Give me love and trust, and a lot of patience and understanding, Lula Mae, and I promise to make things better for us soon. I can't concentrate on solving our problems if we're quarreling. Please help me."

"You wouldn't break your word to me?"

"No, dear friend, never. As long as we've been together and as much as we've shared and endured, you shouldn't even have to ask that."

"You're right, Miss Rachel. I'm ashamed of myself. I'll help you."

"Thank you, Lula Mae. I'll take a long and cool bath in the wash shed. After my trip today, I'm hot and tense and dusty."

"That's jest what you need. I'll git everything fixed. When I'm done, I'll cook you the best supper you've ever had."

Rachel didn't argue with her over preparing the bath. "That's kind of you, dear friend. I'll go get my things and meet you in the wash shed. Remember where I told you I hid the cashbox if you need any for shopping. I don't want anything happening to the last of our money."

"Lord, have mercy on us, it best not."

*

At seven, Daniel Slade arrived to call on Rachel. He noticed how the protective housekeeper frowned at him when she opened the door. With few words, she guided him into the parlor and went upstairs.

Within minutes, a smiling Rachel entered the room and greeted him. Both were aware of the older woman's presence in the server where she was clearing away dinner dishes and leftover food. Rachel offered Dan refreshments, but he refused. They carried on a casual, genial, and innocent conversation until Lula Mae finished her work and left the house.

"Why didn't you come to visit me today?" Dan asked. "I waited and worried all afternoon. You did say Friday, didn't you?"

Rachel related her confrontation with Camellia Jones in the jewelry shop. "After that, I decided my mood would be better on Monday. I'm sorry you worried. I should have sent you a message, but I assumed you'd realize something had happened to prevent my coming, such as Milton being unavailable."

"That hateful witch," Dan muttered. He wondered what, if Rachel was low on money, she was doing in a jewelry shop? "Why were you there?" he blurted out.

Rachel decided to be honest with him. Dan appeared shocked and dismayed that things were that bad for her.

"Don't worry about the money, Rachel; I'll give you what you need. How much will it take to clear up your problems?"

"None now, but thank you. If things get bad, I'll tell you."

"You shouldn't have to sell your jewelry to support yourself. Are you too proud to accept a gift or a loan from me?"

"Yes," she admitted. "I don't want to depend on you or anyone right now. I must stand strong and tall to take care of myself." While she spoke, Rachel observed Lula Mae lurking near a side window. She was furious, but she didn't let on she had sighted the housekeeper. She tapped her lips with her forefinger to indicate silence to Dan. "Lula Mae at window," she mouthed, then winked at him and grinned as she set out to dupe the woman. "You were a good friend to Phillip, and you've been a good one to me. I appreciate all you've done and are doing to help me through this difficult period. If I need a loan to carry me to better days, I'll come see you. I have to be in town on Monday for business; perhaps we can have lunch and chat longer. I'm afraid I'm very tired tonight, if you don't mind."

Dan caught the clues for a meeting in a few days. He was vexed with Lula Mae for spoiling their visit and intrigued by the woman's stealthy conduct. He kept his voice and expression amiable as he said, "I understand, Rachel. Things like that are exhausting. Lunch Monday sounds enjoyable. Please don't hesitate to send Burke for me if you need anything or there's more trouble here. Why don't you see me out so you can rest?"

"Thank you, Dan," she said as they headed into the hallway. "That's very kind and generous of you."

The moment the walls on either side concealed them from view, they embraced and kissed. Their mouths feasted wildly and swiftly. Both knew the daring woman might come inside if they lingered too long.

"I'll see you Monday on your ship," she whispered.

"I love you, Rachel," he whispered. "You'll love me, too, one day."

"Could any woman resist you very long?" She grinned. "Who could possibly compete with or compare to you, Daniel Slade?"

"No one, I hope."

"Get along with you. I'll explain everything in detail Monday."

He kissed her and hugged her once more. "Good night, love."

She traced her fingers over his enticing mouth. "Good night, Dan."

Rachel opened the door and walked onto the porch with him. After exchanging waves she stood there while he mounted and departed. She went inside, locked the doors, the windows, then doused the lamps and went upstairs. She peered out the water closet window that overlooked the other structure and saw light glowing on the ground outside Lula Mae's quarters behind the kitchen. Rachel decided the woman had hurried to her room while Dan was galloping away toward town.

The widow was curious about why her longtime and loyal housekeeper would spy on her, on them. Was it from loving concern? Or something else? Dan's past speculations about another person being responsible for her misfortunes haunted her mind. If he was right, it had to be someone who had begun their evil work after she wed her first husband.

She asked herself again, as she had years ago, if Lula Mae had loved and wanted William Barlow. If so, had the unmarried woman felt betrayed when he chose a young and beautiful wife over an older and plain one? Lula Mae had visited them that fateful last day. Lula Mae had detested Craig Newman, and also had visited them on his ill-fated last day. Lula Mae had tried to persuade her not to marry Phillip, had warned her it would end in trouble. During the month before Phillip's death, Lula Mae had acted strangely around him, as if angry with him.

While Rachel was away with Dan, the older woman had their schedule and would have had the opportunity to contact the law. Maybe Lula Mae was smarter than she let on; maybe she could write a legible note like the one quoted to her by the investigator. Maybe the older woman hated all men; she certainly made enough statements to imply that feeling.

William Barlow and his son . . . Craig Newman . . . Phillip McCandless . . . Could an embittered spinster and alleged friend . . .

Don't think such wicked and crazy thoughts! Rachel cautioned herself. *Lula Mae Morris is strange at times, but she couldn't be capable of four murders!*

After receiving that letter from her mother, Rachel knew that Earl Starger had alibis on two crucial occasions. And he would never hire someone to do such crimes for him in the first place. He would do them himself with sadistic delight! It couldn't be her lecherous stepfather.

Camellia Jones? She was mean, but a doubtful suspect.

Craig's brother Paul? Hateful and spiteful, but also a doubtful suspect.

Rachel couldn't think of anyone else with a motive to kill her husbands or a satanic desire to destroy her. That eliminated everyone she knew! It compelled her to return to her wild theory about a jinx or a curse!

Suddenly, a terrible thought entered her mind. The doctor working on Craig's accident for the authorities had asked her if she ever suffered from blackouts or fainting spells. He had mentioned people doing things and not remembering them, and not being responsible legally for their actions during those times. She had believed then it was a trick to make her confess to escape arrest. Later, Phillip had explained such a mental condition—illness—truly existed.

The past flooded her distraught brain. When William's son died, she had been napping; it had been his scream—hadn't it?—that awakened her. When William died, she had been asleep in another room. When Craig took his fall, she hadn't heard any scream he might have let out because she had fainted while working in the garden beneath a hot sun and assailed by anxieties, and possibly from the strain of being pregnant, which she hadn't known at that time. When Phillip had died, she had been asleep in another room.

Could a person, she fretted in panic, do such horrible things and not realize them? Could one have an evil side that stayed concealed from even the person in question? Could there be a wicked force, another Rachel, living secretly and working insidiously within her? Had Earl's lechery and her hatred of him have birthed another being inside her?

God help me, surely not. That's crazy, impossible. Isn't it? she thought in confusion.

Rachel asked herself how she could make certain, and she couldn't think of an answer. She dared not go to a doctor, which might mean exposure! If her theory was true and she was dangerous and if a Black Widow curse ruled her other nature, her beloved Dan could be . . .

"Stop it, Rachel. There's no way, no way," she murmured, and panicked when she couldn't convince herself with absolute confidence of her sanity and innocence.

*

On Saturday, Rachel visited the sharecroppers with Burke Wells to assure herself and them that everything was fine. She wore a sedate black dress with long sleeves that became hot and itchy as the sun's heat increased during the first day of May.

After she returned home, she took a long and soothing bath with cool water from the well, then washed her dark-brown hair. She had not slept well the night before, so she was weary and edgy today. As she sat outside to dry her locks while the sun was setting, her mind drifted.

Ever since Rachel had caught Lula Mae spying on her and Dan, the housekeeper had been quieter than usual and very watchful of her mistress. Rachel wondered if she suspected the same awful thing she herself had thought of last night and was trying to protect her by keeping her away from all men, from any likely victim, and from the consequences of being caught. She dared not broach such a subject with Lula Mae, or with anyone.

She hadn't heard from Harrison Clements, George Leathers, or Milton Baldwin again; it was as if everyone was content to let her be a silent partner. Or perhaps they were all only awaiting what might take place in thirteen days, on the dreaded day of May fourteenth. At least nothing threatening had happened again at home or at the firm, so surely that was a good sign.

Her mother was coming for a visit next weekend, and perhaps at long last they could make peace, without Earl around to cause problems.

Dan . . . How she loved, craved, and missed him. She longed to be in his arms, to savor his kisses, to enjoy his caresses. He treated her with such respect and dignity in private as well as in public. They could talk freely and honestly now. But when either needed privacy or silence, the other didn't feel shut out. Their bond was strengthening and growing, but soon he would expect a commitment of marriage and a confession of love. Dare she give them before she was certain she wasn't a danger to him? Her worst fear, she told herself, could not possibly be true. But she knew the only reason she doubted her sanity and innocence was because she couldn't locate another suspect or explain her run of "bad luck."

*

On Sunday morning, as she'd done with Phillip until his death, Rachel and Lula Mae dressed and attended a small church west of town. She noticed that half of the people were nice, though not overly friendly or receptive. The other half stared at her and frowned as if she had no right to be in God's house because she was an unpunished criminal. The minister welcomed her return and gave his condolences about Phillip's death; he seemed sincerely kind and sympathetic, and she was grateful and relieved.

On the ride home, with Rachel in control of the team pulling the carriage, Lula Mae declared in an angry tone, "We cain't go there no more, Miss Rachel, not with them bunch of hypocrites being mean to you!"

"We can't hurt or deny ourselves to punish them, my friend. And I can't hide at home as if I have something to be ashamed of or to fear."

The woman hadn't argued or responded, and they had reached home in silence. Rachel sensed a change in the housekeeper and in their relationship, one that worried her.

After eating, Rachel worked in the yard on her flowers and bushes. She teased fingers over her gardenias and hoped they would bloom soon so she could place some in her bedroom at night and enjoy their dreamy fragrance. But that heady smell increased as they wilted and died, as if Mother Nature demanded such a sacrifice for their gift to people.

Rachel strolled to where her third husband was buried. She gazed at the home-made marker at one end of the oblong mound of earth. "If someone harmed you, dear Phillip, I will find them and have them punished," she murmured. "I'll solve this mystery. But you really made a mess of things for yourself and me! Wouldn't it be ironic if you're resting near where you buried that infernal money that might bury me if I never find it."

She stared at the grave for a while and mourned the loss of a good friend and rescuer when she had desperately needed one. "Where is it?" she pleaded. "I can't dig up the whole plantation searching for it."

"Searching for what, Miss Rachel?" Lula Mae asked, having heard her last two sentences during her quiet approach.

Rachel jumped and gasped. "You startled me; I didn't hear you." She lied out of necessity. "Phillip took our money out of the bank shortly before he died and hid it somewhere. I don't even know if it was on Moss Haven. I wish I could find it. Then we'd all be fine again."

"Why would he do that?"

"I don't know, my friend. He wasn't himself for a few months before his death. He must have had a good reason. If he hadn't been delirious before he died, he would have told me."

"He acted strange nigh unto the end. He stared at air as if he could see it. He sneaked whiskey. He wasted his food. He spoke mean to me. He even sneaked money from the cashbox. I was plenty worried."

Rachel didn't ask why Lula Mae hadn't told her sooner. "He had business problems on his mind. I'm sure he didn't mean to talk unkindly. But a man can't sneak his own whiskey or steal his own money in his own home."

"I didn't says he stole it. He jest acted on the sly the way he took it."

For gambling? she fretted. "I assumed he'd given it to Burke for supplies or seeds until he could get to the bank to replenish his wallet. I thought he'd forgotten to replace it, and didn't feel I should question him about his own money," she said.

"We wouldn't be bad off if it was still where it should be."

"We're fine now after I sold those jewels."

"Weren't right you had to go and do that!"

Rachel didn't want to argue again today, as such a talk might get out of hand while she was annoyed with the older woman. "Maybe not, but it's past, so let's forget it. Besides, I don't have much need for fancy jewels."

"I came to aks what you wants me to do with that pitcher you took down in your bedroom to hangs Captain Slade's?"

Rachel was almost provoked to break the promise she'd just made herself not to quarrel with Lula Mae today. "It isn't Dan's; it's mine. *I* saw it; *I* liked it, and *I* bought it," she replied, feeling testy. "You know I never liked those drab flowers in the other picture. It was hanging there when I moved in and I hadn't gotten around to selecting and buying a replacement."

"Why a ship?"

"I do half-own many ships and a shipping firm, Lula Mae, and we live in a port city where we see them when in town. It's lovely, very dramatic and inspiring. Phillip would have loved it, too. If he'd seen it first, it would be hanging downstairs over the parlor mantel. Don't you like it?"

"No ma'am, but I don't care much for pitchers of the ocean. You wants me to git rid of the flowers?"

"Just wrap it and store it in the attic for now. Let Burke help you. I don't want you falling and getting hurt." She ordered the servant to tend the chore because Lula Mae would rebel against her mistress doing that task, and she wanted this conversation and meeting over fast.

"I will, Miss Rachel. You be out here much longer?"

"No, why?"

"Ain't good for you to be fretting and suffering like this. Mr. Phillip shouldna left you so bad off."

Keep control, Rachel. "I'm sure he didn't mean to, Lula Mae."

"Did, all the same. I don't like how you been mistreated for years."

Rachel realized a problem was brewing that must have attention or it would become worse. She dreaded to do what she knew she must. "Lula Mae," she said after taking a deep breath, "I love you and appreciate all you've done for me over the years. I hate to scold or correct you, but lately you've been forgetting I'm your mistress. You've been sharp-tongued and nosing into my private affairs too much for even a close friend. You must stop or it will cause trouble between us." She observed, as with her last reprimand, how the older woman looked shocked and offended.

"Miss Rachel, how can you speaks so to me? Nobody loves you or tends you better than me. Why you wanta hurt me?"

"I don't, Lula Mae. But you've been treating me and correcting me as if I were a child, a misbehaving child. You question me about everything I say and do, and often challenge my actions and decisions. I have to choose my own friends and do what I think is best for all of us. And please don't speak so harshly about Phillip; he was a good man, just a troubled one at the end. I have so many burdens on me right now. Don't make things worse by forcing me to be bossy or mean to you. It hurts me when we don't get along."

"I'm sorry, Miss Rachel; I didn't know I was being so bad."

The woman sounded and looked contrite, so Rachel softened. "Not bad, my friend," she said, "just too protective. I am a grown woman. I can handle people and affairs myself. Right or wrong, they have to be my decisions. All right?"

"Yes, Miss Rachel; I'll behave myself."

Rachel smiled and added, "So will I, Lula Mae. Let's go have our pie and milk now. We won't mention this again."

They walked into the house and server together. Rachel poured the milk into glasses and turned to find Lula Mae staring at her while she toyed with the knife in her grasp.

"Is something wrong?" Rachel asked, then looked down to see blood dripping onto the pie crust and making tiny puddles. "You've cut yourself!" she gasped.

Lula Mae glanced at the injured hand as if she hadn't felt the pain. She frowned and snapped, "Look what I've done! I've ruined the pie!"

"Don't worry about the dessert." She tossed the woman a rag and said, "Wrap it tight to staunch the bleeding while I fetch bandages and medicine." She rushed to the cabinet in the water closet upstairs, gathered what she needed, and returned to tend the injury.

Afterward, Lula Mae stared at her bandaged hand and said, "Thank you. I'll toss out this pie and make another one."

"Don't do that right now. Go lie down and rest. You've worked too hard lately and you're tired. I'll cook supper for us tonight. No arguing."

*

Rachel needed to see Dan, but his pictures would have to sate that fierce yearning. She opened the drawer only to find all three gone and a note lying in their place. Again, it warned, in her script, to spurn the sea captain or else he would die . . . Rachel gaped at the last few words, "by your hand as with all the others. If you want him to live, give him up. I'll be the only one safe with you, as you could never murder me."

Someone had done this mischief while they were at church, as the pictures had been there this morning when she dressed. Lula Mae couldn't be responsible for their theft, as Rachel had received the other notes while out of town. Surely she herself hadn't . . .

* * *

Rachel dressed with great care Monday to look her best for Dan when she saw him this afternoon. First, she planned to visit Milton Baldwin to check on the firm's business. With good luck, maybe things had improved since their last talk. Maybe he could even make a profit payment to her. Surely he was paying himself a salary, so, as part owner, he should pay her, too. She hoped their conversation was pleasant and productive, as she wanted him to escort her to Dan's clipper to prevent gossip. But even if he didn't, she would go anyway, and let tongues wag if they wanted!

Milton greeted her cordially. He smiled and said, "I was planning to visit you this afternoon, so your timing is perfect. We have an important matter to discuss and settle."

Excitement surged through her. "You've found a buyer for the firm?"

Milton frowned and shook his head. "No, I'm afraid that isn't it. I didn't want to inform you of this problem earlier while you were still grieving. Now that you've had time to get Phillip's insurance and bank account, it *must* be handled." He withdrew a paper from his desk and handed it to her. "Read that agreement. Can you pay off this loan? I need the money, Rachel. Phillip promised he would pay it back by April sixteenth. If he couldn't, as you'll see by the terms, I get his share of the firm. I allowed you a two-week extension to deal with his loss and to get your affairs in order, but I can't hold off any longer. Do you want to buy back this loan paper or turn the firm over to me? It's sixty thousand dollars, and it's past due. Legally the firm is mine by default, but I wouldn't do that to you. Think about it a minute, then tell me your decision."

Chapter

❧

17

Rachel was crushed by the stunning news. Her mind shouted that this couldn't be happening. She wondered how much more defeat she could take. So much money was missing, both from the business and their personal resources. Where had it gone? Then a thought struck her. "How can this be true, Milton?" she accused. "I looked at the firm's books, remember? Nothing is—or was—recorded there about such a large loan, about *any* loan."

"It was a private matter between friends, Rachel. Phillip is the one who insisted on using his share of the firm to back it up. I agreed because I couldn't take a personal loss that big. I only loaned him the money because he was desperate and he had that important contract, so I knew he could repay it soon. I hate doing this to you, but I have no choice. Surely you can understand and accept my position. Do you want to repay it or default?"

"I can't repay it! Phillip didn't leave any insurance. Our bank account is wiped clean. Until that big deal is completed, neither Harry nor George could loan me that much, if anything. Those two companies are heavily invested in that mysterious contract, which only Phillip seemed to know about, until May fourteenth. If I sold Moss Haven to come up with the cash and something prevented that deal, I'd lose everything and be penniless. Besides, you told me and the books seem to indicate the firm is going to bankrupt soon, so why waste money I don't have on it?" Nor could she bring herself to ask Daniel Slade for a loan of that size. "I wish you had warned me about this earlier. It comes as a shock."

"I'm sorry, Rachel, but I thought you had enough problems on your mind; and I assumed, once Phillip's affairs were settled, this problem could be handled easily and quietly between us. I don't want to hurt you, but it's a lot of money, my money."

"Why would Phillip set the repayment date before he earned his profit on the deal? How was he planning to get money to get rid of this?" she asked, shaking the paper in her hand.

"I don't know. He chose April sixteenth. Maybe he was going to use part of that advance everyone says he accepted and hid."

"That wasn't his money to spend! This doesn't make sense," she murmured as she studied the signature on the agreement, which looked to be Phillip's. Everyone wanted the missing money, and everyone thought she had it. Were they using tricks on her to get their share? Was this paper authentic and the loan real? If Milton was lying, she couldn't prove it. She would lose one of her three holdings, and was receiving nothing in support from the other two. Instead of an imminent profit from the sale of one firm, it was being snatched away from her needy grasp!

"I'm very sorry to put you in such a vulnerable position, Rachel," Milton said with lowered eyes.

She locked her probing gaze with his unreadable one. "Do you honestly believe this is fair and right? Surely the company's assets—ships, two warehouses, this office, existing contracts, and whatever else—are worth more than sixty thousand dollars. Why couldn't an accountant figure up what I would have to relinquish to settle this amount? I could become a shareholder instead of a partner. I need financial support from this firm until I can sell off my other partnerships. That may take months, and they won't result in much—if any—monetary gain."

"That sounds logical and reasonable, Rachel, but it wouldn't work. The value of things on paper aren't the same as what one can actually get for them. When or if I found a buyer, I could never recover sixty thousand from a sale; we have too many debts to settle. I'd be lucky to make anything off such an action or to find a deal in my favor."

"Can you give me an extension, until the big contract pays off?" She ventured, to see how resolved or insensitive he was. "It's only a few more weeks. What difference would it make, since I can't repay the money now and, by defaulting, it wouldn't help you, either?"

"What if the deal falls through, as all of you seem to think it will?"

"Then I'll honor Phillip's loan agreement immediately."

"I'm sorry, Rachel, but I think that's a waste of time for me."

"You want the firm now, today, is that it?" she challenged.

"I want this distasteful matter settled promptly, yes."

"Why the sudden rush, Milton? What will a month matter?"

"If I have ownership and authority over everything, I can make some tough decisions and take desperate actions to save this firm and myself."

"Why can't you do that anyway?"

"Don't take this the wrong way, please, but I think I can work out my problems better if the name McCandless is taken off the firm. In view of your open investigation and your current partnership . . . I don't want to sound heartless, but your past and current trouble and reputation can damage the firm further. I've already had prospective clients imply you're the reason I can't obtain their business. A few old customers are balking on new shipments until you're exonerated; they don't want their payments to reward a . . . You know what I mean. I'm sorry."

Rachel observed him. From her past treatment by the townfolk, she couldn't call him a liar, but he was out to save himself, no matter how much she hurt. Oddly, she was angered—not saddened or frightened—by the probabilities of new or revived gossip and ostracism.

"Please do this the easy and friendly way, Rachel. I can have my lawyer Frank Henly draw up the proper papers to turn your share over to me, then have you come to his office to sign them before witnesses. If you resist, I'll have to let Frank handle it. I realize this agreement doesn't have witnesses and wasn't written up by a lawyer, but it *is* legal and binding. This *is* Phillip's signature. You don't want that publicity and exposure, and neither of us want to create ill will between us. Legally, we are no longer partners. Help me to make this transition simple."

Rachel wondered who had filled in the due date, and if it was the one agreed upon by Phillip. "I really have no choice, do I?"

"I'm afraid not. I'll have Frank prepare the papers for your signature, and I'll notify you when they're ready to sign. This is difficult for me, too, Rachel, so I'm happy you're settling it so peaceably."

She decided to test his motive and feelings one last time. "If I come up with the sixty thousand, I can buy back the agreement?" she asked.

Milton stared at her and hesitated, but said, "Of course. But it has to be on or before Friday," he amended.

"A week before I'm to be paid for that deal? That isn't fair."

"That's a shipping date, Rachel, not a closing and final payment date. There's no telling how long a voyage and delivery and collection of balance could take. I can't hold off that long."

She pretended to concede. "I just wish you had refused to loan Phillip money, at least that much, when you knew he had a gambling problem."

"Why he desperately needed the money wasn't my business, Rachel. We were friends and partners, so I helped him out of a tight bind."

"And put me in a worse one."

"That wasn't my doing or intent."

"Do what you must, Milton. I'll leave now. Good day."

As she stood outside the firm, Rachel worried over Harry and George having similar agreements that might take away the other two companies. If she lost all partnerships and Moss Haven, she would be in that same state of poverty as after Craig died. What or who had set this evil pattern in motion? How could she stop it? She couldn't turn to Dan as if he were her only escape. She couldn't give herself to him completely until she was on level ground once more.

Rachel was glad she had told Burke Wells to wait for her. She returned to the carriage and she had him take her to Bay Street, where she tipped a sailor to carry a message to Captain Daniel Slade of the *Merry Wind* that was docked below the bluff. She said to tell him something had come up, but not to worry or visit, that she was only changing their appointment to dinner at her home on Wednesday. She lingered there until she saw the man approach Dan's clipper and head up the gangplank, as the vessel with secured sails was visible between two buildings beyond a stone alley.

*

At home, Rachel told Lula Mae that Dan was coming to dinner on Wednesday, that her mother was visiting this weekend, and that she had lost the shipping firm. She couldn't decide which or if all revelations astonished the wide-eyed woman, who didn't comment on any of them.

*

Tuesday morning, Rachel was miffed by an announcement in the newspaper that was delivered by the mail carrier: "McCandless & Baldwin Shipping Firm is now under the sole ownership of Milton Baldwin." It was clear that Phillip's Savannah partner had wasted no time in letting people know he had pushed her out of the firm, so they needn't worry about trading there. He must have turned in this notice before meeting with her in order to meet the newspaper's deadline for publication! "So much for giving me an extension and handling this matter quietly, you sorry . . ." she muttered in anger.

*

Later, Earl Starger paid her another visit.

"What do you want this time?" she asked in vexation. She didn't know which caught her eye first: the lack of lust and smugness in his hazel gaze, the freshly combed dirty-brown hair, or the deceptively genial smile on his lips that softened his angular features and made him look sincere.

"Calm down, girl. I'm only staying a minute, and I won't even come inside. I wanted to thank you for writing to Catherine. It seemed to make her feel better. I'll be sailing to Boston tomorrow for three weeks, so why don't you visit her? While I'm away, you won't have to fear seeing me."

Mama didn't tell him she's coming to visit! "Is she strong enough to be left alone for three weeks?"

"Yes, and she has plenty of servants around for help and protection. If I've done things in the past to offend you, Rachel, I'm sorry, and it won't ever happen again. If we can't make peace and become friends, let us have a truce, at least for Catherine's sake. We've conflicted too long and too harshly. Join me in putting the past behind us. You have three weeks of privacy, so please go spend time with her."

Rachel was astonished by his cunning pleas and deceitfully contrite behavior, but she didn't fall for his ruse. Yet she didn't want to endure another bitter quarrel today so she said, "I may go. It sounds like a good idea."

"Do it. You wouldn't want things to end this way between you two."

Her heart pounded as she questioned a subtle threat against her or her ailing mother. "What do you mean?"

"Your experiences since leaving home and Catherine's recent illness should tell you that unexpected deaths do occur. Don't wait too long. I promise I won't do anything to prevent a reunion you both need."

"I'll think seriously about it."

"I hope so. Good-bye, Rachel. Take care of yourself."

She watched his departure with intrigue, and suspicion.

*

Dan arrived at six-thirty Wednesday evening. Even though they couldn't converse on more than a genial level as Lula Mae served them and they ate, Rachel detected that something was troubling Dan. She noticed it in the way he seemed to force his smile, the unrelaxed way he sat in his chair, and the lack of a usual sparkle in his blue eyes. She didn't think he could be angry over her not visiting him Monday, as she had sent a message and an invitation to dinner tonight. She would question his strange mood after the housekeeper was dismissed and they were alone. And she would make certain the nosy woman did not spy on them again tonight.

Before Lula Mae could serve their dessert and coffee, there was a knock on the back door. Rachel heard the housekeeper talking with a man, so she went to see who had called at this hour and for what reason. It was one of their sharecroppers who said his wife was having a baby and he needed help fast. Rachel observed how reluctant the woman was to leave her alone with Dan, as it wasn't like Lula Mae to refuse to help in a matter in which she was skilled.

"I can finish the serving and cleaning up, Lula Mae. Go along with him; his wife needs you. There's no time to fetch the doctor in town. I'll be fine until your return."

"But you has cumpny, Miss Rachel."

"Don't worry about us. Dan won't be staying long after we finish. I'll even leave the clean-up chores for you, if that will make you feel better about going."

"Jest let me git my things," Lulu Mae conceded with a frown.

After the woman left, Rachel returned to the dining room and explained the emergency situation, then served their dessert and coffee.

Dan was angry Rachel had sold his family's shipping business. He had planned to buy it from Milton and move it back to Charleston, where he wanted to settle down eventually with Rachel. He couldn't do that until after this perilous mystery was solved and he could expose his identity. "I saw something in yesterday's newspaper that surprised me, Rachel," he said. "Why did you sell the firm? I told you I would lend or give you whatever money you need for support. Why didn't you tell me first?"

Rachel didn't know why that matter disturbed him, but it certainly seemed to. "I didn't sell." She related how she had lost it on Monday.

That news stunned Dan, but it pleased him that she was innocent of his mental charges. "You believed him?"

"Not really, but what could I do? The signature on the agreement was Phillip's. I can't repay the loan, so why cause more trouble for myself fighting a futile battle?"

"Stall signing those relinquishment papers."

She stared at him. "Why? How? For what reason?"

"This secret loan is suspicious. If it were for a few thousand dollars, I'd believe him, but I doubt Baldwin would loan a man with a gambling weakness so much money, even with Phillip's share of the firm as collateral and especially when Baldwin's trying to convince you the firm is near bankrupt. He would try to force you to repay the money before accepting the terms." Dan had decided to hire a detective to check out Baldwin and this curious matter, but he would keep that intention to himself for a while. "If he presses you to sign, tell him to take you to court to prove the agreement is authentic and binding. See how he reacts to that situation."

"He'll be furious, then vindictive."

"That doesn't matter, does it?" Dan reasoned. "I'll be able to help you battle him. We need to get our hands on that paper, even if I have to steal it; that's the only way to see if it's real. Besides, without it, he has only his word he loaned money to my . . . friend."

"But if it is authentic, Dan, that wouldn't be fair or right of me."

"If necessary, I'll give you the sixty thousand dollars to repay him."

"No! The firm is in bad trouble and you'll lose your money."

"I think he's lying and bluffing, Rachel. Give me time to prove it."

Hope and suspense filled her. "How?"

"I'll think of a way after I give it careful study." Something compelled him not to relate his plan to her. He would send for that Charleston detective tomorrow. He would travel by train and could be on this case soon. "Don't sign those papers until we're convinced he's telling you the truth," he advised, then suggested what she should tell Milton.

"Oh, mercy, he'll become an enemy, too. I don't need or want another one. But all right, I'll do as you say, even though it's going to be big trouble."

"Trouble isn't new to you or to me. If we sink, we'll do it fighting."

His plan was cunning. "I'll trust you, Dan, and follow your lead. When you startled me that day I was searching the office safe, I had a stack of papers in my hand, but I put them away without looking at them. The loan agreement could have been there or in Milton's locked desk."

"We searched everything later, remember?"

"You're right! So where was it?"

"Probably didn't exist then."

"I pray that's true, Dan, and we find a way to prove it fast."

"We will. Two good things: your stepfather sailed for Boston this morning, and so did Camellia Jones. I checked on their schedules. Neither is returning for three weeks. At least they'll be out of your hair for a while."

Rachel liked that news. It meant no Earl to intrude on her mother's visit, and no Camellia to run into while flaunting the jewelry she had been forced in to selling.

"I have to leave tomorrow on a short trip," he disclosed, "but I'll be back next Wednesday. My crew is restless, and I've been offered a sweet deal to take a rush cargo to New Orleans. I hate to leave you at this time, Rachel, but we might need the money to finance this deal."

He was leaving! "I can't let you use your earnings to get me out of trouble. It isn't your problem, and there's a possibility of a total loss."

"It *is* my problem, Rachel, because you're involved and in danger."

She warmed and smiled, but she still didn't want him to go. "I wouldn't be if I could find that missing money."

"Why don't we search for it again? Lula Mae will be gone for hours. The timing is perfect. I might think of a place you haven't. Since I'm a man and a man concealed it, I may have a better chance of finding one's hiding spot."

"That sounds good to me. Let's get busy and hurry."

While there was daylight, they searched the outbuildings and around the house's exterior. Dan even took a lantern and examined every area underneath any raised structure. He tried to recall if Phillip had had any favorite hiding spots as a child and he checked those that came to mind.

As the inside of the house was explored, Dan tried to imagine his brother in those locations—the dining room while eating and chatting with Rachel, the cozy combination office and sitting room where he had worked and relaxed, the parlor where he had sat and perhaps entertained, the guest room where he had spent his last hours alive and in terrible pain and alone, the sewing room that had not been given a chance to become a nursery for an heir, and the master bedroom where his brother had slept and had made love to the woman he himself now loved and craved.

As they entered the parlor and sat down to rest, Rachel murmured, "See, nothing. No money and no clues."

"It could be buried anywhere on this large property."

"One strange thing I noticed during my first search; I didn't find any personal effects from Phillip's past, not one. Isn't that odd? It's as if he either destroyed or concealed his past before moving to Savannah."

"He could have left them stored in Charleston to avoid painful memories. I'll check on it for you the next time I'm there."

Rachel walked to an oblong side table. She lifted a decorative box and opened its lid to send forth lovely music. "Phillip gave this to me. Whenever I was sad or scared, he would play it for me as a distraction. Sometimes we would even dance around this room, laughing and talking. Despite all we've learned or suspect, Dan, Phillip was good and kind and special. He was my closest friend. I have to believe he knew what he was doing with this mysterious deal and, if he were alive, he'd know how to straighten out the mess. I'm sorry he died in such physical and mental torment. He didn't deserve that."

Dan was touched and pleased, but it refreshed the sadness and bitterness of his brother's loss. He turned to her and suggested, "Why don't we distract ourselves with a twirl or two, ma'am?"

They danced in silence as they comforted themselves and each other. But when they locked gazes, the close contact and romantic aura became too arousing. They didn't know when Lula Mae might return.

"How about a game of chess?" Rachel asked. "Phillip taught me how to play."

"Sounds perfect, just what we need," he teased and grinned.

Rachel smiled, then closed the music box and put it back in its place. She pulled out the chess board and pieces. She placed them on a small table, and they sat down to test each other's skills.

Soon, their eye and knee contact became too stimulating.

"We're fighting a losing battle, woman," Dan chuckled.

Before she could respond, thunder boomed over the house and caused her to jump and squeal. They were so enthralled with each other, they hadn't heard the distant rumblings or noticed the flashes of lightning that had moved closer and closer over the last hour. A violent storm broke over the area and rapidly sent down a deluge of rain amid noisy roars and brilliant flickers.

"Afraid of storms?" Dan asked.

"No, it just startled me. I'd better close the windows upstairs. Will you check the ones down here?"

Dan shut and locked all windows and doors on the bottom floor. When Rachel returned from doing the same on the one above, he grinned and said, "I doubt Lula Mae can return any time soon, if at all tonight. It's bad outside, and looks to be a long and dangerous storm."

As if taking his words as an invitation to rush into his arms, Rachel replied, "We should wait a little while, in case they left before the storm broke. If she isn't here in twenty minutes . . . Why are you grinning like that? Isn't that what you had in mind?"

Dan stroked her hair, then her cheek as he said in a husky tone, "Only every hour since Augusta and every minute since my arrival today."

"Then we think alike." Her eyes gleamed with anticipation and desire.

"That we do, my bewitching enchantress."

"Why don't you douse all the lamps downstairs, all except those in here? I'll freshen up. Join me in ten minutes, if she isn't back."

"Do you have a slicker I can borrow? I need to put away my horse."

"In the closet by the back door. Lock it after you return."

As she left the parlor, Dan noticed she had gone from twenty to ten minutes before—*Stars above,* his mind fretted. Could he make love to his brother's widow in his brother's house in his brother's bed, the same one where Phillip had—*Yes,* his heart and body replied, and he relaxed.

Dan found the slicker and went to put his mount in the barn, where he unsaddled him and tossed him hay and sweet feed to calm the nervous animal. Inside the back door, he bolted it and removed his wet boots.

Upstairs, Dan found Rachel standing at the end of the hall with the porch door ajar and gazing outside. He came up behind her and slipped his arms around her waist. She signed dreamily and leaned against him. He nestled his cheek against her fragrant hair. Both watched the storm.

The day's heat lessened quickly as breezes grew stronger and cooler. Moss was whipped about as the wind grabbed and shook branches as if trying to viciously rip the limbs from their trunks. Failing to do so, it snatched at their leaves and sent them scurrying across the yard. Spring flowers were yanked around, colorful petals torn off and sent flying to join the severed leaves and broken twigs. Ear-splitting thunderclaps sounded overhead; they shook the house and rattled the windows.

Lightning flickered like glowing fingers slashing into dark clouds to release a torrential rain. More peals of thunder roared and boomed like charges of dynamite going off in rapid sequence. The ground was soaked and visibility was nonexistent. As gusting winds slanted rain and fired it onto the porch, moisture reached Rachel and Dan in the doorway.

"Let's go make a storm of our own," he enticed as he nibbled at her ear and caressed her bosom through her garment.

Rachel turned in his embrace and kissed him as her answer.

Dan lifted her, closed the door with the hand beneath her knees, and carried her into the bedroom. Only a few candles were burning there, and they cast an intimate and romantic glow in the lovely room. Neither thought of who had shared this room and bed in the recent past.

Garments were cast aside as their bodies were stormed by the urgency and power of desires that matched those of nature's deluge. His hands locked around her buttocks and held her tightly against his pleading groin as she sat atop him. Her legs straddled Dan's thighs and her toes dug into the softness of the bed as she removed any remaining space between their straining bodies. Her hands wandered over his sleek body and roved the furry mat covering his chest. She thirsted for this man and she leaned forward to seal their mouths.

They meshed over and over to create a white-hot heat within them. As his hands roamed her naked flesh, his mouth trailed down her throat to taste the sweetness of her skin and to savor her heated response to him. Dan rolled her to her back so his mouth could tease over her torso and drift into the inviting canyon between her breasts. She moaned as his hungry exploration conquered the brown peaks nearby. Her words and movements encouraged him to continue his loving assault and to make it bolder.

Rachel's fingers stroked Dan's back and shoulders, then moved into his silky jet-black hair. He was driving her wild with his stimulation. She tried to do the same with hers.

They made no attempt to delay this heady meal, as they were starved for each other. Desires were unleashed and allowed to race where they willed and at their chosen pace.

Their tongues danced in a frantic and erotic mating ritual. Their bodies were joined, and they strove for a mutual prize. Thunder vibrated the house; lovemaking shook the bed. Lightning danced on the windows, and passions glowed within them. Joy and feverish need charged through them as powerfully as the storm was attacking the landside. Their pulses throbbed and their hearts pounded as they took and gave of rapture's delight. They desperately needed this unrestrained fusion of bodies and spirits. All that mattered to them was this special moment and their love.

Dan captured Rachel's face between his hands and kissed her greedily. He had an uncontrollable urge to make this woman a part of him.

The heat of their bodies intensified as their exertions increased. They labored until ecstasy was ready to burst within them to carry them beyond reality. When sheer bliss rocked them to their cores, they clung together and drank every drop of their lusty nectar.

After the staggering explosions ceased and calmness came, they remained entwined as they struggled to breathe normally. It was so muggy that their perspiration refused to evaporate and it dampened the sheets. Neither minded, as it was imbued with the erotic scent of sated passions.

"That was wonderful, Rachel. How can it get better every time?" he murmured in amazement and pleasure.

She cuddled against him and smiled to herself. That told her she didn't disappoint him with her skills that she knew increased each time they made love. "I don't know, but I'm glad it does. You're a superb teacher."

They embraced and kissed tenderly, relaxed and happy.

Pressed to his hard body, Rachel wished this were their home and they never had to leave its safety again. She wished no peril confronted them, no danger threatened them, no dark past haunted them. She prayed all of those things could be defeated soon.

Dan wrapped his arms more possessively around her and rested his chin atop her head. A mixture of calm and excitement filled him. Surely it would always be this way between them: stimulating, spontaneous, satisfying, heart-stoppingly wonderful, and tender. What they had found together was more than physical enjoyment. He shifted to fuse their gazes. "You steal my wits and self-control, woman. What am I going to do about this powerful hold over me?"

"Let me keep it, please; and I'll let you keep yours over me. We'll enjoy each other one day at a time. We'll make no promises or demands until our lives are settled. All right?"

Dan cuddled her into his arms once more and didn't respond. He asked himself if he would miss his present lifestyle at sea. Yes, but that was normal. Would he be content to become a landlover with this woman? If he gave up his ship and travels, would that change him or bore him? He didn't think so, not with a fascinating and challenging woman like Rachel at his side day and night. All he had to do was convince her they were matched.

While a sated and serene Rachel slept in his arms, Dan napped in a twilight state and kept an ear on the storm, as he didn't want the too-watchful housekeeper to return and catch them in bed together.

At four on Thursday morning, the strong forces of nature ceased attacking the area. Dan awakened Rachel and told her he was leaving before daylight to avoid Lulu Mae and to set sail. They kissed and embraced, then she accompanied him to the door so she could bolt it after his departure. She saw the lantern go out in the barn and heard him gallop toward town. She smiled in tranquil fatigue. Before returning to bed, she made certain no clues were left behind to expose their passionate night together.

*

When Lula Mae peeked in on Rachel, she found her mistress sleeping and alone. She sighed in relief and closed the bedroom door, to do her chores quietly in case the storm had kept Rachel awake part of the night.

*

At dawn, Dan sailed for New Orleans, with a valuable cargo stored below deck. If he hadn't agreed on Monday to accept this job, he wouldn't go, not after learning about Rachel's dilemma with Milton Baldwin. Nothing physically threatening had occurred recently and she and Burke were on guard against trouble, so she should be safe. He needed to get his hands on as much money as possible. Repaying that lost advance might be the only way to protect his love from vengeance and gossip, as no one would believe she didn't have it. She wouldn't be safe until the matter was settled. Whatever it cost him, he wanted to get the perilous situation behind them. Rachel's mother was coming for a visit, and her feared stepfather was far away. Threats had quieted down or ceased, and he would return next Wednesday, two days before the contract deadline. Still, he was uneasy as he took his last glimpse of Savannah for a while.

*

That afternoon, Milton sent Rachel a message that said the lawyer had the relinquishment paper ready, so would she come to sign it tomorrow at one o'clock in Frank Henley's office?

The deliverer waited while she penned a response: "I have company until Monday so I do not want to spend hours away from them or get in a sad mood. I will come to town next week to handle our business. I saw Tuesday's newspaper so you shouldn't have any problems over my 'trouble and reputation' hurting the firm before our meeting. Work on your old and prospective clients while waiting to see me. Good luck."

The messenger left with her envelope in his grasp, and the first step had been taken as Dan advised. All she could do was pray hard her love was right, or she was in for needless suffering.

*

Friday at five in the afternoon, Catherine Fleming Starger arrived in a carriage with a servant handling the team and protecting her along the journey from White Cloud, located halfway between Savannah and Augusta.

Rachel hugged her mother, who responded in like manner. Their past troubles and sufferings slipped away during the joyful reunion, as their recent overtures had broken the icy obstacle between them.

"It's been too long, Mama." Rachel said, with dewy eyes. "I've missed you so much. It was foolish of us to stay apart like that. Let's not ever quarrel and ignore each other again. It's been awful without you."

The letter from her daughter had shown Catherine how unfair they were being to each other. She had been closer to Rachel than to any of her children, and she had suffered from the barrier placed between them years ago. "I'm sorry we've both behaved badly, and we won't let it happen again," she vowed, also with misty eyes that exposed her emotions. "Now that we've made an effort to end our separation, we won't allow another to intrude on our new relationship. I should have been more understanding and patient; you were becoming a woman, and that's difficult."

"The war hurt all of us; I suppose we were both fighting changes in our lives. Please forgive me for hurting you and for staying away."

"If you'll forgive me for being blind and selfish. All I saw was my side, Rachel; I didn't realize you children were so miserable at home. I know Earl can be difficult and bossy at times, but a bachelor has to learn how to become a husband and father. Taking on a widow with four children wasn't easy for him, but I shouldn't have taken his side every time. I'm truly sorry."

"We both made mistakes, Mama, but we won't do so again." Held at arm's length, she studied her mother, who was paler and thinner than when she'd last seen her. Yet, she was still beautiful, with blond hair and green eyes and exquisite features. Until the recent and draining illness, Catherine had appeared to be in her early thirties; now, she looked her age of forty-five, and that saddened the daughter.

"Come inside and rest, Mama; I know you must be exhausted."

As they headed to the porch, Catherine responded, "It was a long and tiring journey, Rachel, but I'm so happy to be here. After receiving your sweet letter, I had to come and make peace between us. My recovery and Earl's trip created perfect timing for it.''

"Yes, they did. I'm so glad you came. I've missed you, and I've been worried about you. How are you feeling?"

Catherine smiled. "Much better, almost completely recovered. Of course, I look a fright after being ill and lying abed so long."

"No, you look wonderful—as ravishing as ever . . . She's here, Lula Mae!" Rachel shouted as they entered the house.

The housekeeper hurried from the server. After exchanging pleasantries and telling the servant to put the visitor's baggage upstairs, the woman went to finish dinner preparations, a special meal she had spent hours getting ready. She had told the male servant where to put the horses and where to take quarters for a few days.

"Where's Phillip? Isn't he home from the office yet?"

Rachel stared at her mother. "What?" she murmured in confusion, fearing her mother's mind had been affected by her illness.

Catherine smiled again. "Is he away on business like Earl? I so wanted to see him, too. You are happy this time, aren't you, Rachel?"

"Didn't Earl tell you the news? Haven't you read the newspaper?"

"Tell me what news?"

"Phillip is dead, Mama." When she saw the woman's shock, Rachel related how and when her third husband had died, ostensibly of cholera. "I can't believe Earl didn't tell you; it's been six weeks, and it's been in the newspaper. Earl came to see me twice since that awful day, on April twenty-second and this past Tuesday before he sailed. He didn't know you were coming to visit me, so I didn't mention it. Why is that, Mama?"

Catherine was dismayed by the revelation of her third son-in-law's death. "This comes as such a shock, Rachel. Earl probably didn't want to upset me while I was so ill and then recovering. You two have never gotten along, so I didn't tell him I was coming. I will after my visit here when he returns home in three weeks. Why did he come here? Did you two quarrel as usual?"

Rachel was tempted to confess all, but it would only hurt her mother who would never leave Earl, even if Catherine believed her accusations. They were making peace, so she didn't want to risk another conflict. It was best and kindest, at least for now, to let her mother remain in her safe dreamworld. "He came to make peace, too. We argued the first time, but then we were polite."

"Can you become friends and settle your differences?"

"No, Mama, and I'm sorry. He thinks I'm both crazy and guilty of murdering four people."

"But you said Phillip died of cholera. I don't understand. Surely you aren't in trouble with the authorities again."

Rachel explained about the secret burial, her exposure, and the still-open investigation. Yet she didn't reveal any of her perilous secrets.

"What are they going to do to you?"

Rachel gazed into green eyes filled with love and worry. "Nothing, Mama. I'm innocent, and the case will be closed soon. They have no evidence to arrest me on, because I didn't do anything wrong."

"What's going on in your life, Rachel? A three-time widow at twenty-one . . . Why do these terrible things keep happening to you?"

"I don't know, Mama, but it's been so hard on me."

"Will you be all right, my precious baby?"

"Yes, Mama, fine. I'm stronger and smarter now. Let's not talk about sad things anymore. How are you doing? Earl said you've seen the doctor twice. When? Why?"

"On March twenty-sixth and on April fifteenth. I was tired and weak all the time, but I'm better now. He ordered me to bed rest and gave me a tonic. They cured me, along with your letter. I've missed you so, Rachel. I miss all of my children."

Rachel wondered if she should be so unhappy about her mother confirming Earl's alibis for two important dates: Phillip's death and the police tip. "Have you heard from Rosemary or Richard?"

"No, but I wish the twins would contact me, at least write to say they're safe and happy."

"So do I, Mama. They will one day."

"If I hurt you and deserted you, Rachel, I'm sorry. I don't want anything to ever create another breach between us."

"It won't, Mama; our troubles are over. We'll both promise to write and to visit regularly."

Lula Mae came to tell them dinner was ready to be served. Rachel and her mother went into the dining room to eat and to continue their talk.

*

To both women's delight, the weekend passed with long and nourishing conversations and relaxing strolls that strengthened and brought a glow to her mother's cheeks. By the time Catherine headed for home on Monday morning, both were at peace with themselves and with their past.

But Rachel had learned something important: her stepfather hadn't been away from home in weeks, except to take Catherine to the doctor twice and on the two days he had visited her at Moss Haven. Rachel knew her mother had told the truth, and it almost disappointed her to mark Earl Starger's name off her suspect list: if nothing more, at least for writing the intimidating love notes. Who was left? Harry, the client, and a yet-unknown prankster.

*

Tuesday night there was another house-rocking and paint-vandalizing incident. This time, Rachel was certain it wasn't the spiteful work of Earl Starger or Camellia Jones, who were both far away. She assumed it had to be the malicious mischief of someone in town, perhaps young boys. As long as no one tried to harm her and her servants, she would allow them to get such amusement out of their heads and prayed they soon tired of their cruel sport. Once more the black letters were covered with slate-blue paint.

*

Wednesday, if Dan returned to Savannah, he didn't come to visit her, but another violent storm paid a long call on the area. Rachel stood at the window and observed it as she recalled how she had spent the last one.

*

Thursday morning, Rachel received a scolding note from Milton for her lack of a visit this week "as promised." It included a strongly worded summons to finish the matter tomorrow at ten o'clock. She dismissed the deliverer, after telling him to report her response would come later in the day.

She sat down to pen her reply: "As commanded, I will be in town tomorrow, but not to sign a relinquishment paper at Mr. Henley's. I will meet you in our office for a serious talk, after I have seen Mr. Henley to check on my legal rights in this strange affair. Until I am convinced that is Phillip's signature and, if so, that the repayment date is correct, leave things as they are. With such terms and so much money involved, I am suspicious of an agreement that had no witnesses and was not handled by a lawyer. I want to learn if I am legally responsible for a personal and unsubstantiated loan before I repay it or default, whichever way I decide to respond later. You appear in a great rush to have me out of the firm before tomorrow's deadline of Phillip's big contract; that arouses my curiosity, just as your insensitive attitude and harsh correspondences arouse my anger to defiance and investigation. If you press me at this time, I will be forced to battle you in court. I am sure this can be resolved soon if we do not challenge each other again. I will see you tomorrow morning."

There, she thought, her refusal and bluff—step two—were done as Dan suggested. She was amazed that, so far, her love had guessed Milton's actions with accuracy. She hoped he was back in port by now to lend her the courage and strength she needed to carry out stunning step three tomorrow. She couldn't imagine how Milton would react to this shocking development when it reached his hands this afternoon. She was eager to learn if Dan also had surmised it correctly.

*

Later, Lula Mae and Burke went into town for supplies and to deliver her message to Milton. Rachel kept hoping Dan would arrive while the servants were gone so they could talk without concern of being overheard, which was her motive for sending the two servants on errands.

*

When she heard knocking at the front door, she rushed to respond with a bright smile on her face. She inhaled sharply when her gaze touched on two strangers with dark-brown hair and eyes—Cubans, she decided in panic, a day early for their confrontation and alone with her.

Chapter

18

The first man's gaze roved her from head to foot, but the glint in his dark eyes was appreciative not lecherous. He was tall and had a pleasant expression on his handsome face, but she was tense and scared. She remembered that the attacker with a knife had used a Spanish accent and words. She listened with increased alert and dread.

"Buenas tardes, señorita. I did not mean to startle you. We have come to see Señor McCandless," he said in fluent English, then smiled.

Rachel struggled to regain her stolen poise and wits. At least his voice did not match her past assailant's. "He isn't here," she responded as she glanced at the second man, who appeared to be sullen and menacing. She took an instant dislike to him, and waited anxiously to hear his voice.

"Where can we find him, señorita?" the first man asked, drawing her attention back to him. "Señor McCandless asked us to meet him here today. You have no reason to fear us. We are *amigos.* Friends," he clarified for her.

She realized her apprehensions were apparent. She tried to calm herself and clear her head to meet this challenge, as fear was not a weakness to expose to enemies who would pick at that raw spot.

"You hesitate and seem afraid, señorita. Why?"

"Phillip McCandless is dead. Didn't anyone in town tell you that when you asked for directions to his home?" She noted a mixture of shock and dismay at her disclosure. She couldn't help but release a sigh of relief that the client's cohorts hadn't known that fact, which meant they couldn't have committed that evil deed. At least that much of this situation was good.

"We did not need directions to his *plantación,* señorita. When did this happen? How? Who runs his . . . affairs?"

Rachel was alarmed again. "You've been here before? When?"

"Seven *semanas* . . . weeks ago. Who are you, señorita?"

She didn't know if she should believe him. "Phillip died seven weeks ago on Friday, March twenty-sixth. When did you see him?"

"We visited him on Tuesday of that week." As he repeated his earlier questions, his genial expression and tone vanished.

Rachel decided to play ignorant for a while to glean clues. "He died of cholera. I'm Mrs. McCandless, his widow. How can I help you? What did you want with my husband?"

"Our order, Señora McCandless."

She feigned confusion, but felt he had known from the start who she was. "I beg your pardon?" she said evocatively.

"Are you his *heredera*, his heir?"

She faked greater bewilderment. "Yes, of course. Why?"

"You own his three companies?"

"I inherited half of each one; Phillip had partners in all of them. Why are you asking me such private questions? Why should I answer you?"

"Do you handle Señor McCandless's shares?"

She stared at him, for effect. "Yes," she finally said. "But I shan't tell you more, sir, until you explain what this is about. Who are you?"

"Carlos Torres. This is *mi amigo*, Joaquín Chavous."

Rachel eyed the handsome man, then the churlish one to his right. "I don't recall your names in my husband's books or from his lips. I know nothing of your past visit to our home, which I find strange."

"Señora McCandless was in town that day. He would not speak of us or our visit; our business was *secreto.*"

"Is this a personal or business matter?"

"This is very serious!" the second man snapped at her. "We are no fools!"

Rachel jumped, her eyes wide. She stared at him, but realized his voice discarded him as that suspect with an itchy blade.

"Relax, *amigo*," Carlos advised his foul-tempered friend. "Forgive Joaquín's mood at your bad news, but our business is important."

"I don't like his rudeness, Mr. Torres, as I know of no reason for it. If you'll explain what kind of business you had with Phillip, perhaps I can help you; or perhaps I can send you to the right person. But if Mr. Chavous persists in behaving so badly, you must leave my home immediately." Rachel knew she couldn't play totally dumb, as too much money was involved for the matter to be dropped, especially by Joaquín Chavous. It was best to fake enlightenment when he clarified and to work on resolving the matter.

"We paid Señor McCandless a lot of money for rifles and bullets. He was to deliver them to us *mañana* for shipment. Can you help us?"

Rachel allowed her expression and response to reveal she might have known about that. "Was it a very large and confidential order? A secret one for ten thousand rifles, many cases of cartridges, and other goods?"

"*Sí*, Señora McCandless. You do know of our bargain?"

"A little, and it isn't good news, I'm afraid."

"What do you mean?" Carlos asked, narrowing his dark gaze.

"Since Phillip died, I've been trying to piece together this puzzle he left behind, but the clues have been confusing and scant. From what I've learned from his partners and from things my husband mumbled on his deathbed, after you gave Phillip the five-hundred-thousand-dollar advance on your contract, he hid it for safekeeping. At least his partners tell me they never received the money. You see, Phillip kept the deal a secret from all of us. I don't know if that was by your order, but it left us in ignorance. We don't even know who the client is, where the shipment is to go, or what your terms included." Rachel saw how the man was staring at her oddly, and she tensed in panic. Yet he didn't interrupt.

"While Phillip was dying, he mumbled something about money and guns, but he was too delirious to make sense. That's the first I knew about your secret deal, which wasn't much. I went to see his partners—here, in Augusta, and in Athens—but they claim they don't know more than that, either. All they know is how much ammunition and dynamite and how many guns you ordered, and that they were to be ready for shipment tomorrow, with the destination recorded as Haiti. Phillip wrote down two sets of initials in his shipping ledger: C. T. and J. C.; so that must be you two. His partners said he accepted the five-hundred-thousand-dollar advance, but he never gave it to them. I've searched everywhere, but I can't find where he hid the money. Is it true? Did you give him a big advance?"

"You lie!" Joaquín shouted at her, his features and tone harsh.

Rachel glared at the belligerent man. "I don't know whose idea it was to keep your bargain a secret, but Phillip died without exposing it to me or to his partners. I have no reason to suspect them of deceiving me. In fact, they're all very upset about this predicament and about losing such a big order. I've tried to unravel this mystery, but how could I with so few clues? I was waiting until the client realized his shipment was late and came to me to resolve matters. I didn't know you were coming to get it. We are talking about the same contract, aren't we?"

"It is the same. But a . . . *predicamento?*" Carlos echoed skeptically, after his hand grasping Joaquin's arm firmly stayed the man's hot retort.

Rachel looked at him as if he must not understand that English word. "Of course, for all of us. You want arms and we need profits. Our companies can't fill your order without payment, and the advance can't be found."

"Advance?" Carlos echoed. His gaze locked onto hers in a piercing manner.

"You did pay him an advance, didn't you? Phillip hinted at receiving and hiding one while he was delirious; and his partners told me he had accepted one, but he never turned the money over to them. I told you, I searched for it many times and I can't find it."

"No, Señora Raquel, we paid him no *avance.*" He paused when she gave a loud sigh and smile of relief. He destroyed that happy reaction when he corrected, "We paid him *todo,* everything, *un millón de dólares.*"

"Please tell me that doesn't mean one million dollars," she urged.

"One million American *dólares.* We demand our arms immediately."

Rachel paled and trembled. "One million . . . Phillip had a million dollars of your money, not five hundred thousand?" Dread washed over her.

"*Sí,* Señora Rachel. We paid, so you owe us our guns and bullets. It would be dangerous to keep our *dinero,* our money, and refuse to deliver our arms."

Rachel absorbed three points: he was using her first name now without having been told it and in the Spanish version, he was threatening her with a surly look and tone, and he never mentioned wanting the money returned. "I don't have your money, sir," she said, "and Phillip's partners won't comply without payment. I'm sorry my husband kept this deal a secret and hid your money, but that isn't my fault, nor that of his partners. Actually, I only have your explanation of the bargain, so I have no way of knowing if you're telling the truth. All of us were kept in the dark, so we're at a disadvantage. It's unfortunate that your payment is missing, but you can't expect us to hand over goods we don't have the resources to pay for. The orders are being made with hopes this deal can be saved with new terms. In fact, the ammunition should arrive soon. But the rifles won't be sent until Harrison Clements gets paid."

Carlos's voice and eyes were hostile as he said, "He has been paid."

"You mean, you gave the money to Phillip and him? But he told me—"

"We paid Señor McCandless; they are partners. Señor Clements is in our deal; he gave his word. It would be unwise for him to betray our trust. You must convince him to . . . comply.''

"I've attempted to work it out several times. I tried to get them to agree to lowering our profit if you would accept less arms and cartridges than you ordered. To save this deal, we all have to be understanding and we have to cooperate. So far, he refuses to yield even a little.''

"That is your *problema.*''

"Why is it mine? I didn't know about this deal until recently, and then only by chance. If Phillip had died sooner, I wouldn't know anything.''

"You are the trusted wife and heir of Señor McCandless. We know of the rumors about you, señora. Do not try to dupe us and steal our money. That would be foolish and deadly; your bite has less power than ours. The same is true for your partners. All of you are in this bargain. All of you are responsible, and must honor it. If you wish to live, Señora Raquel, to protect your family and holdings, do not betray us. Warn your partners of the recklessness of their decision. I will give you and them *una semana,* one week, until next Friday, to have our cargo loaded for shipment home. It better be good news I hear when next we meet, or all of you will suffer for your treachery, and so will those you love.''

Rachel was terrified of his warnings, but she asked, "Why are you threatening me? Is this what you did when my husband backed out of your deal in February? Harry told me Phillip was going to cancel the contract, but changed his mind the day before he became ill and died. Did you commit those vicious crimes to scare him into changing his mind again?'' Rachel listed the lethal and destructive incidents before she challenged, "Do you need arms so much you'd do such wicked things to get them? Is that why Phillip backed out, because he realized what kind of men you are?''

Carlos stared at her oddly, then said, "We did not know such things. When we came three times, it was to make our deal, to pay our advance, and to deliver the balance. We came, we did so, and we left. No one here was threatened or harmed by us.''

She had an instinct Carlos was telling the truth. "If you didn't try to frighten and coerce Phillip, then who did?'' *Harry?* she mused.

"I do not have answers for what I do not know.''

With boldness and courage she had to force out, she asked, "Can you prove to me you paid Phillip? Do you have a signed contract or a receipt?''

"You have my word. It is true; you must accept it.''

"I'm to accept your word, but you don't have to believe mine?''

"*Sí,* because you do not have much money at stake.''

"You, not someone else, brought the money and made the deal?''

"*Sí.* We made no contract for the Spanish spies to find. We trusted your husband. He dared not trick us. The same is true for you.''

Rachel tested his wickedness. "What if I go to the authorities and report this misunderstanding and your threats? What if you're arrested?''

Unaffected by her words, he said, "We have *mucho amigos,* Señora Raquel; that would be *estupido* and costly to you and the others. Even if we are murdered, others will take our places. They will not believe you, either.''

"But I'm telling the truth!''

"Are you, Señora Raquel? It is *mucho dinero* and the temptation to keep it is great. Resist, or you will not live to spend it.''

"That's what his partners think, too; that's why they're refusing to help me resolve your deal. I swear to you, as I've sworn to them, I don't have it and can't find it. If you wish, search for it yourselves."

"*No importa,* the bargain stands and must be honored, or—"

He didn't have to finish or translate for her to grasp his meaning. Still, she tried to bluff him. "What if I disappear so you can't harm me?"

"Will all you own and love disappear for protection from us? Will your family and friends, and companies be safe if you betray us? We know many things about you and the others; we learned before we made our deal with your husband. Your mother's name is Catherine Starger; your *casa* was White Cloud. You do not care if we slay your stepfather. Your servants are Lula Mae and Burke. Many others live and work your lands. Your husband had no family, but he was an *hombre* who cared for others. Many men work for your companies. We know about the other partners, too. If you escape with our money, we will not need to hunt you down to punish you; I promise that others will suffer for your treachery. Is this what you wish, for others to pay for your greed?"

"No, please don't harm any of them because of what you think about me. I don't have your money and I don't know how I can raise it to cover our expenses, but I'll try." She related all she knew and all the two partners claimed they knew about the mystery, but it seemed to have no favorable effect on the two Cubans. "To solve it, I have to know more. Maybe that will give us a clue to where the money is hidden; that's what's holding up the deal. Who is the buyer, the man who sent you to get arms? May I speak with him to try to reach a solution?"

"No. The deal stands as agreed, no changes or refusals."

"When was this deal made? And for what reason? How was it made? If you want me to solve this riddle, you have to fill in some pieces."

"As you wish, Señora Raquel. We met in January and made a bargain. The advance money was paid. The order was to be shipped *mañana*. In February, Señor McCandless insisted on the balance. We brought it to him seven weeks ago. The rebellion grows worse every month. We need those arms *pronto*. We are to escort the shipment to a . . . rendezvous point."

"Where? Why did Phillip record Haiti when Cuba is actually the destination?"

"You do not need that information. It does not change or affect your *problema*. What you do not know, you cannot reveal to spies if captured and questioned. We are at war. Freedom fighters protect their lives and cause and their *amigos*. Never trick or betray desperate *hombres*, Señora Raquel."

She did not refute his last statement, but registered it. "How did you choose Phillip? Maybe the man who got you together is holding the money for him. With his name, I can recover it and settle this quickly and safely."

"Ricardo does not have it; he is in Santiago de Cuba. Our *amigo* told us of weapons and ammunition companies here. We learned your husband owned both, and a shipping firm. He was the perfect choice. We talked and made a deal. We honored our part. Whatever it takes, you and the others will honor his. As a father is responsible for the actions of his child, you and the others are responsible for the actions of Señor McCandless."

It was futile to argue. "Can you give me a little more time to persuade his partners to agree, and time to get the arms here from the other two towns?" she asked. "I'm not trying to dupe you, but I can't work this problem out alone, or quickly. We have to figure out where to get the money to pay for supplies and shipping. We aren't rich people, Mr. Torres, and it's a lot of money."

Carlos studied her muted eyes for a moment, then spoke with his friend in Spanish, but the pugnacious Joaquín seemed to disagree strongly with him. Even so, he told her, *"Una semana,* one week, Señora Raquel. If you fail or if you go to the authorities, we will be forced to . . . persuade you and your *amigos* how unwise and dangerous that is. *Comprende?"*

"I understand. I'll try to do my best to—"

"Do not try, Señora Raquel, *do* it. Many lives depend upon you, here and in my country. We have been taught cruelty by our rulers; we will not hesitate to use it to win our freedom from oppression."

"I'm sorry about your country's sufferings, Mr. Torres, but I'm not to blame for them. I know what war is like, what it is to lose loved ones; I felt those sacrifices many years ago. I know about the battle you've been fighting since '68, and, believe it or not, I hope you win. I wish my country didn't have to remain neutral . . . May I ask one more question?"

"Sí," he replied, and smiled.

"Is this deal legal? If we find a way to honor our part, can we get into serious trouble with the authorities here for selling to you?"

"If that is what frightens and stalls you, there is no American law against it. Your husband had a letter of clearance to ship us the arms."

"His partner told me he has a letter of clearance for customs, but I have to be certain it isn't illegal. If it is, you can threaten me all you want and I won't try to help you get your arms. I have enough troubles of my own without adding another one."

"It is *legal.* But it must be done . . . privately. *Comprende?"*

"Yes. A friend explained your fight for independence to me. He also told me about the ship Spain sank and the American sailors murdered. Can you assure us that won't happen again? I don't want to endanger my crew."

"It will not; you have my word. Answer me a question, Señora Raquel: What other troubles do you have, and will they interfere with our business?"

She knew they might hear the gossip in town, so it was best to try to ward off potential damage. "You said you knew of the rumors about me."

Carlos nodded, and she continued. "They aren't true. But the local authorities are investigating and watching me again. They aren't convinced Phillip died of cholera; they suspect me of killing him. They can't prove it, because I didn't. But that's partly why I couldn't go around asking questions about Phillip's mysterious deal and a lot of missing money; something like that would give them a motive they don't have. *Comprende?"*

"Sí, señora, but guilty or not is *no importa* to us, only the arms."

"It matters to me. I didn't kill him, and I don't have your money. If he hadn't died close to bankrupt, I would pay back your money and let his partners finish this deal with you. Right now, I'm in two predicaments, and I want out of both. Phillip left me almost penniless, so I can't repay you; and I can't allow that condition to give a false suspicion that I have your money. His desperate need for money must have been why he made a bargain with you. I didn't know he was facing financial ruin until I tried to straighten out his affairs, and it came as quite a shock. By then, if you care to check out my story, I had already been to see his partners about this mystery and the missing money. I know you'll kill me and destroy what little I have left if I don't help you. I would be a fool or crazy to want your money badly enough to steal it. I'm neither insane nor an idiot."

"That is *bueno*, Señora Raquel, as I would hate to burn down such a lovely *casa* as this and to kill such a beautiful woman."

"You would do that even though I'm blameless in all of this?"

Carlos glued his intentionally frigid gaze to her pleading one. *"Sí*, but it would pain me." He smiled as he coaxed, "Do not make me suffer for your foolishness and greed."

Rachel glared at him with a clenched jaw as she scoffed, "You don't believe a word of explanation I've given you!"

"It is *no importa* if I do or do not. My order is to return with our arms. If I cannot, those who stop me must die. I will do my duty."

She had no doubt he would do as he vowed. "It isn't fair to hold us responsible for a million dollars we never received. We can't handle a loss that big. You're expecting us to pay for your arms out of our pockets when they're near empty and when we don't even have proof you paid Phillip. Why can't you help us resolve this matter so none of us will get hurt?"

"It is not our *problema*, Señora Raquel, but we will solve it."

In an insulting tone, she replied, "I'm sure you will. Where can I reach you when I have news?"

Carlos gave her a lopsided grin. "We will reach you next Friday. If you try to trap or kill us, the *amigos* who take our places will not be as kind and generous as Carlos Torres is being today. When I next lay eyes on this beautiful face, . . ." he began as he caressed her anger-flushed cheek.

Rachel halted his flattering words as she slapped away his disturbing hand and glared at him. She panted, "Don't you ever touch me!"

"Ah, a woman with fire, spirit, and courage. She would make a fine *compatriota*, would she not, Joaquín?" The bellicose man grunted and frowned. Carlos finished his interrupted statement, "When I next lay eyes on your beautiful face, Señora Raquel, have good news for me."

She glared at him more forcefully and icily. "I hope I have good news for both of us. I want this offensive matter settled fast and for good."

Carlos chuckled in amusement and admiration. "You are smart, so I do not doubt your success. *Adiós*, flame of my heart."

Rachel watched the two Cuban rebels gallop away as if born and reared in their saddles. She sank against the porch wall, closed her eyes, and exhaled loudly to release her tension. Afterward, she felt limp and shaky. She didn't know how she had gotten through the terrifying situation. She had no doubt those men were lethal. If only Dan were here . . .

Why isn't he? her troubled mind asked. He had left her vulnerable at a terrible moment and he hadn't returned yesterday as promised. That had forced her to confront two dangerous enemies alone.

Old fears and doubts about him resurfaced to torment her. His absence today was convenient for her to be terrorized by those rebels. Was he one of them? The unknown client? Had his romantic pursuit and assistance been clever ruses to evoke what he believed was the awful truth about her, only an attempt to scare her into handing over the money she claimed she didn't have? Could she be so wrong about her love?

No, Rachel, you've judged a man right this time, she reassured herself. *He loves you and wants you. Something, perhaps bad weather, delayed his return. He'll be back soon and explain. Don't make a crime out of a simple mistake. Trust him. He's the only one who can and will help you.*

But how could even a strong, smart, and brave man like Daniel Slade defeat two dangerous rebels or the many Cubans who could replace them? Trying to save her from them could get him killed, as Carlos threatened, as those recent notes had warned. Yet, she couldn't go to the law for help. They wouldn't understand, or believe her, or help her. They would only think they had more charges to level against her: theft, fraud, gun-running, and probably more. She had no choice but to find a way to complete this deal, to save many lives.

*

Friday at noon, Rachel was sitting in Milton's office, a tangible strain in the air. She hadn't told her loyal servants about the Cubans' visit and she hadn't seen Daniel Slade yet. But she was determined to handle her troubles as best she could without endangering those she loved.

"I don't understand you, Rachel. What have I done to cause such hatred and spitefulness in you? I'm not to blame for your grim situation, so why punish me as if I am? I thought we agreed to handle this as friends, but I was mistaken. Would you please explain?"

She noted the antagonism in his tone and in his green gaze, but for once she didn't fear it. "I don't hate you, Milton, and I'm not being vengeful or ridiculously stubborn. You told me that day, after you shocked me witless with your news, that you were sorry to take away my share of the firm but you had no choice. Well, I have no choice but to protect myself. You asked me to understand and accept your position; you owe me the same consideration. I have only your word that paper and loan are authentic. As you said, it's a lot of money—mine as well as yours. The whole thing doesn't make sense, especially the repayment date. Neither does your rush to shove me aside. You agreed to a week's extension, then announced your takeover the next day. How did you get that news to the paper so fast? The only way was early that morning before you even saw me. The whole time we were talking, you had no intention of honoring your word to me."

Milton scowled as he admitted, "You're right; I turned in the notice before our meeting. I had to submit it before their deadline. I thought it was impossible for our decision to go any other way, so why waste time? When it did, it was too late to stop release of my announcement."

"Why didn't you warn me about it? You thought I wouldn't see it? And why did you write me that hateful and demanding summons yesterday?"

"Because you broke your promise to come in and sign the paper. I was angry and worried."

"More accurately," Rachel refuted, "you were afraid I would get that contract payment today and not have to default before the deadline you gave me. Is there any way you can prove that loan agreement is genuine?"

"Any court will agree it's Phillip's signature and the terms are binding."

"Will it, Milton? Are you absolutely positive?" To her, he looked nervous when she countered his statement without blinking an eye in fear.

"Did Frank Henley tell you otherwise?"

"I haven't seen him yet. I wanted to speak with you first. Neither of us wants trouble and a scandal at this delicate time."

"That's accurate. What do you suggest is fair?"

She noticed but ignored his sarcastic tone and look. "I've already met with that mysterious client, but the balance won't be paid until delivery of goods," she lied.

"Harry's balking on his part. As soon as I convince him to cooperate, the cargo can sail and we'll be paid. After that, you'll be paid."

Wide-eyed he asked, "You still want to remain as my partner?"

"Don't look so horrified. Being a silent and secret partner to protect business and to entice clients suits me fine."

"It doesn't suit me fine, Rachel. It could destroy this firm."

"Are you forgetting who owned the biggest company before you two merged? Forgetting who obtained most of the firm's clients?"

"Phillip never worked any harder than I did! Probably even less!"

Rachel was vexed by his resentment of Phillip. "You've lost another client, Milton. You can cancel the ship for Haiti today. The deal is on delay. But when it's ready, my client wants Captain Daniel Slade of the *Merry Wind* to deliver it. He's offered them a cheaper price and a faster voyage."

Milton jumped to his feet in outrage. "You can't do that to me!" he shouted at her. "I need that contract. Phillip and I had a deal."

With a serene tone, she said, "Show me a signed contract with my client and I'll tell him he must honor it."

Milton sat down. "I don't have one, and you know it!"

"Do I? It seems there is a lot I wasn't told by you, Harry, George, and even Phillip. I'm weary of secrets that have damaged me emotionally and financially. From now on, I'm fighting back against anyone or anything who tries to hurt me. If you're so confident you can win our dispute, take me to court and prove it." She saw Milton go pale and shaky.

"My God, you're serious! You'd fight this, right or wrong!"

"You're damn right I will!" she replied crudely to prove she was determined. "Push me into another pit and I'll claw myself out fighting."

Milton gaped at her in disbelief and alarm. He jumped up and paced as he reasoned on the matter. Finally he turned to her and said, "To save my firm and to prevent a nasty scandal, if you'll agree to stay a silent and secret partner, I'll grant you another extension. But only until your mystery deal is settled, one way or another. That's as far as I'll go. Agreed?"

Now she gaped at him. He had backed down. Maybe Dan was right about a ruse. Maybe Milton was running scared after being challenged. "I accept," she said to stall for more time to unmask him, as surely Dan knew how. "If you put aside the relinquishment paper for a while, I won't bring the court or Mr. Henley into our dispute."

"This time should I get your promise in writing and witnessed?"

She didn't let him get away with his sarcasm. "If you like. It might be a good idea, so you won't renege on my extension again."

"I was only joking."

Rachel knew his laughter and smile were forced. "I hope so."

"Who is this mysterious client?"

She stood and straightened her skirt. "I can't tell you."

"Why not? One of those secrets you said you despise?"

"No, my client insists on confidentiality. Sorry."

"I see. It doesn't matter to me who he is. Settle this fast, Rachel."

"You can bet I will. Good-bye, Milton. I'll send you news soon."

"I hope so, Rachel, and I hope it's good . . . Oh, yes, a load arrived earlier this morning by train from George Leathers. It's stored in our south warehouse."

"Thank you. I'll tend to it soon. If I were you, Milton, I would put a guard on the order. You don't want anything happening to it while it's in your care, just in case the client decides to use your shipping firm. You do recall those break-ins we had a few months ago. My client wouldn't be happy if anything happened to his ammunition. He doesn't seem to be a man you'd want to cross or disappoint."

"I'll take care of it immediately."

"That's most wise. Besides, another vandalism wouldn't look good to our clients."

"I promise you, it will be safe."

"I'll hold you to your word of honor. Good afternoon, Milton."

Outside the door, she congratulated herself on her success, thanks to Dan's clever suggestions. First, she had to send telegrams to George and Harry to update them. Second, she wanted to ride to Factor's Row to see if Dan's ship could be sighted. She wished she had thought of that sooner, as she was eager for his return. But if he was in port and hadn't seen her yet, she would have to discover why not.

*

Rachel stared at the sleek clipper anchored at the end of the docking area, almost concealed from view by numerous other ships. She wondered if it was an intentional action. She was tempted to board the *Merry Wind* to confront Captain Daniel Slade about his curious behavior. She decided to return home to await his imminent visit and needed explanation, whenever it came and whatever it might be.

Chapter

19

Rachel halted to await the rider coming toward her from Moss Haven. As he reined in beside her, she noticed Dan's look of concern.

"Please tell me you didn't get a message and went to meet with that mysterious client alone," he entreated.

"No, I've been to see Milton. Where have you been? You're late."

"A storm held up our sailing and slowed us again during the voyage. I docked a short time ago and rented a horse to come see you. Don't you know how dangerous it is to travel alone? Why didn't you take Burke? For heaven's sake, Rachel, some culprit's been inside and around your house many times; you certainly aren't safe out here by yourself."

"Everybody wants me to carry off this deal, so I'm safe. Those threats are to scare, not injure, me. I was hoping you were in town by now and we could have privacy. Let's get out of sight before someone comes along."

As they led their horses into cover of the dense woods, Dan refuted, "Even from the writer of those love notes? Neither of us believes it's the same villain. For certain he's crazy and dangerous. Don't do anything like this again, woman, or I'll lock you in my cabin to protect you. Understand?"

Rachel grinned in pleasure, caressed his tense face, and coaxed, "I've done fine on my own, so stop worrying so much."

"That's all I've done since I left last week. It was a stupid oversight not to leave one or two of my men here to guard you. I will next time."

Rachel smiled and thanked him. "Your bluff worked with Milton," she told Dan. "He was furious, but he says he'll wait for repayment until after this deal is settled. But he insists on keeping McCandless off the firm's name." She related the shipping partner's motive and her agreement.

"That's all right for a while, but not permanently. It won't be necessary once you're cleared of all accusations and the truth is exposed to everyone." Dan was positive the detective he had hired would unmask Baldwin soon. If the loan agreement was forged, maybe the same deft hand had written those notes to Rachel, which would solve two pressing matters. "Anything else happen while I was gone? Lula Mae said you haven't had any visitors today, so the client isn't wise to trouble with his order yet."

Rachel saved that shocking news until last. She told him about the house being rocked again, about their pictures being stolen and the note left behind during church, and about her mother's visit. Before he could reprimand her again for being out alone after those new incidents, she hurried on to reveal her other news. "I don't know why Earl didn't tell her about Phillip's death, but he must have wanted me to handle that unpleasant task for him. He had no idea she was coming to visit me, but he thinks I might go home during his absence. Mama's doing much better, Dan. But she did tell me Earl hasn't been away from home on those days I've gotten threats. It was obvious she was telling the truth, so he can't be to blame."

"I almost wish he were, so we could resolve part of the trouble."

"I felt the same way," she admitted. "I sent George a telegram to thank him; the ammunition was delivered this morning. Milton's having it guarded in our warehouse. I told George I'm working on new terms with the client. I have to make sure he doesn't get hurt financially helping me."

"I'll have the cases stored aboard my ship for safekeeping. We can't afford for anything to happen to that part of the order."

"That's a splendid idea. Thanks. I telegraphed Harry, too, but I don't expect any help or understanding from him. I told him to send me that clearance letter for customs to see if it holds any clues, and I practically begged him to send along some rifles to appease our client for a while."

"I've already sent Harry the money I made on the New Orleans voyage to buy another hundred rifles and gear. Added to what I've already ordered, it'll come to almost three thousand. If we can find ways to get up to five thousand, that'll cover the half Phillip was paid for. If this deal is legal, we can complete the rest of it and collect the balance."

"I'm afraid not, Dan. Phillip accepted the full million dollars, and our client sent men to pick them up; two Cubans visited me yesterday. I have a one-week reprieve. Besides, it isn't fair for you to buy arms to get us out of this mess; Harry and George are just as involved as I am. I can't let you invest in a deal that has no return profit. If the two companies can't come up with the money or goods, then we have to face the consequences. Harry will let you spend every penny you have getting him out of peril, but I can't. And I doubt the client will settle for five thousand or less arms when he's paid for ten. Don't you see, a million dollars makes renegotiations and reneging impossible? We can't even come up with five hundred thousand worth!"

As Dan held silent and stared at her, Rachel related the scary meeting in detail. "They said they haven't threatened Phillip or me, yet. Dangerous as they seem, I believe them. I bet Harry's behind all the threats, he wants this deal to go through no matter what. He thinks if he scares me badly enough, I'll 'find' that money and turn it over to them."

"Stars above, woman, you could have been killed! I shouldn't have left you alone. I have to sail again Sunday, but two men will remain here to protect you and I'm leaving Luke behind to do some snooping around. It's a bigger offer than the last trip, and we need the money for more guns. Don't argue with me; I'm not doing this to help the companies or your partners. My only concern is for your safety and survival. Crossing rebels is dangerous. Three orders from me should give us enough to bargain with, and we have George's ammo. If you, Harry, and George will cut your profits or cancel them, we may get enough to satisfy . . ." He halted and frowned. "No, not with a million paid. If it was only the advance involved and we could get together half of the order, this trouble could have been settled next week."

Rachel held silent as Dan slipped into deep thought to study the new developments. He was so clever that he might come up with something.

"I still need to go to Charleston, love. I want to see if I can find someone who might be holding the money for Phillip and doesn't know he's dead. I'll check with his old family lawyer and friends."

"That's a clever idea. See if anyone knows where his personal effects are stored. We might find a clue in them."

"I'll check out everything that comes to mind. I'll return in a few days, storm or no storm! You stay inside with doors locked and a gun handy this time. Promise?" He pulled her into his arms and kissed her. He was eager for the day when she became Mrs. Daniel Slade McCandless. "Is it too soon to propose again, woman?"

Rachel was taken by surprise, but kept her wits clear. "Yes, I can't think about another marriage right now. Even if I didn't have all these problems looming over me, I've been a widow for less than two months. Can't you imagine how people would react if I wed again soon?"

"What do we care what they say or think?" Dan quipped.

"I shouldn't and, if I were guilty, I wouldn't; but I'm not and I do. Besides, think of how a swift romance and marriage will appear to the law."

"You're right; I hadn't considered that. I forget we're both still under investigation. Any word from the authorities about your case?"

"None. I don't know if that's good or bad."

"It's a good sign, love. If they had any clues to work on, they would. They just don't want to tell you this soon you've been cleared again." Dan pulled her into his embrace and stroked her silky hair. "I know it's been hard on you, love, but stay strong and brave."

"I will; I have you to make certain I do. Thanks for everything, Dan. You're doing so much to help me and protect me."

He chuckled. "Because I'm selfish. I'm only thinking of myself. I love you and want you. The only way I can have you is to get you free of this mess first. If that costs me money, so what? I can always earn more, but I can't find another Rachel McCandless if I let something happen to you."

The happy woman nestled her cheek to his chest and listened to the steady drumming of his heart. "You're the most wonderful man alive."

Dan grasped her chin and lifted it. He sealed their gazes, then their mouths. Rachel responded, as she needed his comfort and touch. Soon, both were aroused by desires that craved to be sated.

Rachel struggled to regain her self-control. She dragged her lips from his with reluctance. "I'm sorry, Dan, but I can't make love here. I've been shot at twice not far away. Too many forces could be spying on us this very minute. I couldn't relax and . . ."

Dan hugged her tightly and murmured, "I understand, love. I'll escort you home, then get back into town. I want to see if I can locate those Cubans. Maybe I can learn more than you did from them. I'll get my ship loaded tomorrow, then sail at dawn Sunday. I'll see you as soon as I return. Don't forget; I'll have two of my men camped nearby to guard you."

*

Saturday, Rachel received a response from her telegram to Harry. He said he would send Dan's two orders on schedule, but he still refused to send any arms without payment, regardless of threats to her. The angered woman wondered if he would feel and do the same if he were receiving those threats. If he kept refusing, the hostile rebels might comply!

* * *

By Thursday, Rachel was becoming apprehensive. Things had been quiet since last Friday, maybe too quiet, she worried. After all that had happened recently, it was a nice, but suspicious, reprieve. Perhaps no new incidents had taken place because of the two men Dan had left behind, who were camped in the woods near her home.

Late that afternoon, one of them came to the house to tell Rachel his captain was waiting for her at the place they last met. She saddled her horse and galloped to the location in the concealing woods; this time, she tried to make certain she wasn't followed by backtracking, hiding, and other ploys. She slid off the animal's back into Dan's inviting arms.

"Lordy, how I've missed you," she murmured.

"And I've missed you, woman."

They kissed, embraced, and caressed until they were breathless and aroused. Before exchanging news, they had to share passions. Garments were cast aside, and they sank to the leafy earth to make love.

*

As Dan buttoned his shirt, he said, "I placed a third order with Harry today for another hundred fifty rifles. It's strange, love, but Luke hasn't been able to find a single clue to those rebels. You'd think two Cubans would stand out like gale clouds on a clear day. It's as if they vanished into a fog. Or they're hiding for protection. Luke couldn't even find the ship they came in on. You're the only one who's seen them."

"They certainly weren't figments of my imagination. They're only lying low until tomorrow. What did you learn in Charleston?"

"Nothing, I'm afraid. If Phillip's contact was there, I couldn't find him. I didn't pick up any possessions from anybody while I was there."

"I was hoping and praying you'd return with that money. Where can it be, Dan? You can't hide a million dollars just anywhere."

"I don't know, love; I wish I did. Don't be upset or discouraged."

"I don't like you earning money just to—"

He silenced her with a finger to her lips. "No more talk about that. Besides, we need bait for our trap. I may not have to pass them along. If not, I can sell them elsewhere and recover my investment."

"Keep a few for evidence. If Harry . . . That's it, Dan! I'll blackmail the sorry bastard. If he doesn't hand over those arms, I'll expose him for stealing and using registered patents. He'll have to cooperate."

"Don't go threatening him alone, woman. Desperate men are—"

"I know. *Dangerous.* But I'll finally get that snake. I should have thought of this sooner. I'll telegraph him tomorrow before we meet with the Cubans. This should gain another reprieve for Harry to get the arms here—at least part of them." She hugged and kissed him in her ecstasy. "At last, a good-luck charm. You, Daniel Slade."

*

Rachel and Dan responded to the message she received about a meeting five miles from the plantation. They reached the location, dismounted, and joined the two men who eyed them with wariness.

Carlos remarked, "You came with protection Señora Raquel, but it is not needed. What news do you bring? When do we sail?"

"There's been—"

"No, señor, she is the only one to speak," Carlos interrupted Dan.

When the blue-eyed American started to argue, Rachel stayed his retort with a gentle grasp on his arm and a smile. "I'll handle everything. This is Captain Daniel Slade of the *Merry Wind*; he's the one who'll deliver your arms when they're finished. We expect part of the order on Monday and the rest a week later. We should be underway by the first of June."

Carlos frowned. "That is not our agreement, Señora Raquel."

"Your verbal contract was with Phillip, Mr. Torres; he's dead and your payment is missing, so I'm doing the best I can to honor his part of the bargain. Either wait while I do, or take whatever action you wish. If you kill me or cause me more trouble, you won't get your *armas* or your *dinero. Comprende?*" she asked in a terse tone.

Carlos's scowled deepened, and he had to calm a riled Joaquín before he responded. "You are the one who does not understand, Señora Raquel. You are not in a position to threaten or to betray us. Do not try to do so."

"I'm not; I was merely giving you good advice for all our sakes."

"Look, she's doing everything she can to comply. She's paid for all she's ordered out of her own pocket, and I've agreed to ship them free as a favor to an old friend. She isn't the problem; her partners are. They're the ones balking. You can't blame them, either; they never got paid."

"How do we know that is true, *capitán?* We do not have our *dinero* or our goods. We will not sail without one or the other."

"Then give me another ten days to comply," Rachel entreated. "What harm can it do? I've tried to come up with money to cover our expenses, but I'm almost broke. All three of Phillip's companies are near bankruptcy, so are worth nothing. The bank refused to grant me a loan. Even if I sell my home, it will take time. What more do you suggest?"

"As I told you before, Señora Raquel, that is not our *problema.*"

"It shouldn't be mine! So give me the extension I need."

"We will think on it and contact you as soon as possible. Do not fail us, or you and others will *sufrir.* Do not *considere* it, *capitán,*" Carlos warned Dan as his fingers curled around the butt of his pistol. "Joaquín is swift and accurate. We have need of your ship and skills, so do not make him slay you. Even so, we have reported to our *líder.* If our next *comunicación* is late or missing, others will come to slay and destroy, not talk as we have done. To kill us will not end the threat to her; it will make it *peor,* worse."

"Don't threaten or scare her again," Dan warned in a frigid tone.

"Ah, so that is the *situación,*" Carlos murmured as he eyed the couple with a knowing grin. "If you wish to save her for yourself, *capitán,* do as we say. You will hear from us soon. *Adiós, amigos.*"

Rachel and Dan watched the two *rebeldes cubanos* depart.

"Damn! I should have had a man watching so he could follow them before they disappear again. We have to find a way out of this trap, love. They'll do what they threatened without remorse or hesitation."

"I know, Dan; that's why I hate for you to be involved. Maybe that telegram to Harry will work in our favor. At least it'll give us enough arms to bargain with. I'd love to see the look on his face when he reads it."

*

Saturday passed without the anticipated response from Harrison Clements, and Rachel was bewildered. She couldn't believe her blackmail threat didn't panic him into doing as she asked; no, *demanded.* She decided either he must be in Atlanta with his new business and hadn't gotten her shocking message or he was on the way there to challenge her.

* * *

Sunday afternoon, Rachel and Dan were strolling outside when two men arrived, the same investigators who had interrogated her after Phillip's death. Rachel tensed as she feared it was about that unresolved matter and the culprit stalking her had found a cunning way to incriminate her after all.

She tried to appear calm. "What can I do for you gentlemen today?"

The officer focused on Rachel. "Chief Anderson asked us to come out and ask you a few questions as a favor to the police chief in Augusta, to save him a trip to Savannah. Do you mind speaking with us, ma'am?"

"Of course not, but I'm confused. What does the Augusta police chief want to know from me?"

"Who murdered George Leathers and why?"

Rachel paled and shuddered. Chillbumps raced over her body. Her heart began to race and she wanted to faint. "George . . . is dead? How? When?"

"Yesterday. Someone blew up the company you two own. He and a worker were killed. One of his men said you were asking suspicious questions recently about explosions and fires. Why was that, ma'am?"

Rachel panicked. "You think I had something to do with his death?"

"Just answer the question, please."

She was tempted to refuse. "Considering the business we're in, they were normal worries, sir. He was giving me and Dan a tour of the factory and mentioned the dangers. I merely asked if we had safety measures and insurance to cover any problems. As a new partner trying to learn the business, why would my concerns seem odd to anyone?"

"When there's never been . . . an accident before, then one happens shortly after your visit and curiosity, it does, ma'am."

"I haven't been there since last month, over three weeks ago. You know when I went; I asked your permission, remember?"

"Yes, I recall our talk. How long have you known Mr. Leathers?"

Don't volunteer more information than he asks for, Rachel; be honest, but brief and careful. "Since I married Phillip."

"How many times have you seen him?"

"Three, with Phillip last Christmas and twice since he died."

"Did you like him?"

"He was a fine gentleman and good partner."

"Do you know if he had any enemies who'd want him dead?"

"How could I? We live too far apart and see little of each other. Our only connection is business. As I told you, I've only seen him a few times. Who would want to kill such a good-natured, kind, and genial man? I can't imagine him having enemies. Are you certain it wasn't an accident? George said gunpowder was volatile, that any impact or spark could set it off."

"No accident, ma'am. Dynamite and gunpowder were used deliberately. If I recall, you were having trouble with your two partners, suspected them of cheating you, and that's why you rushed off to see them before taking time to report your husband's . . . untimely demise."

Rachel remembered the deceit she had used in that conversation. "As I told you that day, on the first visit, neither partner would allow me to check the books without Phillip's permission. When I called on them after they knew of his death, both men permitted me to see all records. I found nothing to arouse my suspicions about any misdealings, and both men accepted my motive for tricking them earlier. I don't know why Phillip mistrusted them, but his fears were groundless."

"Where were you during the last two days?"

"I visited the telegraph office in town Friday; you can confirm that with the operator. I was home yesterday, and have several witnesses to verify my presence. There is no way I could have gotten there and back."

"She was here all day," Dan concurred, having held silent to listen and observe, and to make his presence again less noticeable.

"You were a witness for her last time. Do you stay around much?"

"I've been on trips to Charleston and New Orleans for most of the last two weeks. I returned Tuesday. I saw Rachel on Friday, and two of my men have been camped nearby since last Sunday. You can verify my movements with the port authorities, and you can question my men about hers."

"Why are they staying here?"

"Because somebody has been trying to terrorize her by playing cruel pranks. She's had her home rocked twice, things stolen from inside, been shot at, and had ugly words painted on her front porch."

"Why didn't you report those incidents, ma'am?"

"What good would it do? Even if you believed me, you couldn't help. We never saw the culprit or culprits involved."

"Probably just perverse pranks. They'll stop when things settle down soon."

"They *have* stopped since Dan kindly left his men nearby for protection . . . What other suspects do you have for George's murder?"

"None. Nobody saw a thing. The place is a total loss. I'm afraid you've lost that part of your inheritance. No insurance, either."

"What?"

"No insurance, ma'am. Didn't you know that?"

"George told me it was expensive, but he never said there wasn't any."

"So you were expecting a payoff?"

"How could I, when I didn't know about the destruction until just now? What about Molly Sue, George's wife? How is she?"

"I don't know, but the Augusta chief said Mr. Leathers had private insurance, so she won't be hurt like you are."

"That's not as important as George's death. Is it all right if I go visit her?"

"Chief Anderson doesn't want you to leave town at present. He's having a few curious matters checked out."

Rachel tried not to show her anxiety. "What matters?"

"Police business, ma'am."

"You will notify me when I can travel?"

"Yes, ma'am. You two are spending a lot of time together, eh?"

"Is it against the law to see friends and business clients?" Dan asked.

"Ah, yes, I recall; you're waiting for orders. Seems you're out of the Augusta one. Too bad. When will the Athens order come?"

"Tomorrow, if all goes as scheduled."

"Then you'll be sailing? Or staying to replace your loss elsewhere?"

"It arrived Friday, as contracted, if you'd care to verify that, too."

"How convenient for you."

Dan's reply was sharp and frosty. "Yes, it was."

"We'll be seeing you again soon, ma'am."

"I hope not, except to tell me you've found George's murderer and you've closed my other file."

"Mr. Leathers' murder isn't our case, ma'am. But if you think of anything that might be helpful, contact me in town."

Rachel and Dan noticed the officer didn't comment on her case before departing with his friend, who hadn't spoken a single word.

"Do you think the Cubans did it?" she asked in trepidation.

"They know their ammo is safe here, so it could be to scare you and Harry. But it seems crazy for them to move against any of you at this point."

"Should I have revealed that predicament to the police?"

"No, at least not yet; they might not be connected. Even if they are, we don't have any evidence to provide to help them catch the killer; and we could get ourselves into big trouble unnecessarily. I promise you, if the rebels are to blame, they'll be punished."

"Poor Molly Sue. I'll send her a condolence cable tomorrow. I can't explain to her why I'm not coming to the funeral of my partner, so, unless they told her I'm a suspect, she'll be hurt and confused."

"I doubt it, and she would never believe you harmed him."

"Why do people keep dying around me? I'm such bad luck."

"Calm down, love; this isn't your fault."

"With George dead, will I be responsible for all the company debts?"

"I don't think so. We'll ask your lawyer tomorrow."

"That's all I need, more trouble and debts! Damn, Rachel!" she instantly scolded herself. "What's the matter with you? George is dead; Molly Sue is hurting; and you're worried about yourself!"

"This has been a shock, love, so it's normal not to think sensibly."

"Is it, Dan? Sometimes I think I'm. . . . Let's have a stiff drink to get rid of our tension."

*

Monday, Dan came to tell Rachel his two orders from Athens arrived by rail: 2,960 rifles with attachments. He had stowed them aboard the *Merry Wind* for safety, and placed guards on duty around the clock.

A telegram was delivered while they chatted. A furious Harrison Clements challenged Rachel to come to his office to examine the licenses he had purchased giving their company permission to use those patented designs on the weapons he was making. He offered to sell her his share of the arms company and vowed he would not stay in business with such an "underhanded and unstable woman." He told her the customs letter was being sent to her, but no weapons at his expense were forthcoming, or were *ever* coming. "Don't ever threaten me again," he ended the communication.

Rachel glanced at Dan and said, "I hope the local authorities don't get hold of this telegram; I can imagine how it could damage me if anything happened to Harry or how it will make him look guiltless if this deal gets nasty and exposed. He may have licenses, but how do we know they're genuine? I'm going to call his bluff like I did Milton's!"

"Be careful with him, love. He's dangerous and unpredictable. As for us, we'd better put a little distance between us for a while. We don't want the law or our enemies guessing the truth about us. I'll see you Friday night, unless something happens and you send for me. I'll leave my men here."

* * *

Thursday, a man arrived by train with several papers from Harry. He hadn't halted along the route to sleep, so he wanted to rush his task and leave for a local hotel to collapse.

Rachel eyed the clearance paper for customs and decided it was authentic. She looked over the licenses to use those patented designs for weapons, as the man was ordered to let her examine them and for him to return them to Harry. They, too, appeared legal and in order. To forge handwriting and papers would be a simple task for a trained hand, but making fake seals to use on the two documents would not. It seemed that nothing illegal was involved in the arms deal. She must have been mistaken. If the payment could be found and the deal finalized, she would earn a fat and needed profit and no risks would be taken, but that was a big *if.*

The messenger took the papers she handed to him and left for town.

Rachel opened the remaining letter. She was alarmed by what she read: there had been a fire at the company and one worker had been slain. The damage was minor and wouldn't shut down or slow down business. Harry had posted armed guards for protection, and he knew of George's murder. He begged her to find and deliver the Cubans' money so the contract could be fulfilled before they were murdered! He closed by informing her that Dan's third order would arrive Monday, along with thirty extra rifles from him.

*

Later, Earl Starger paid her a surprise visit, having returned from Boston. The relaxed and smiling man handed Rachel one of the jewels she had sold to Adam Meigs, which was then purchased by Camellia Jones. "She was on the ship with friends going on holiday. She boasted of how you'd had to sell many pieces for support. It angered me, Rachel, so I talked her into letting me buy this one. I said it was for my wife, but I want you to have it as a peace token, along with this . . ." He placed the brooch and an envelope in her hand before she could withdraw it. "It's only a thousand dollars, but it'll help out until you get your problems settled."

Rachel shook her head and held the items out to him. "I don't want anything from you. I can manage fine on my own."

Earl refused to take back the money and diamond pin. "Consider them gifts from your mother for Christmases missed. Don't be proud and stubborn, Rachel. Taking money from family is less embarrassing than facing financial ruin and public ridicule. If you insist, think of it as a loan and repay it when you can. Don't create another scandal or more hardship for yourself at this difficult time." He changed the subject. "Did you go see Catherine during my absence?"

"No, I invited her to Moss Haven, and she came for a few days. We had a wonderful time, and she's doing much better. Why didn't you tell her you visited me twice? And why didn't she know about Phillip's death?"

"I thought you should tell her the bad news when you saw her. There was no need, in her ill condition, to have her worried over you longer than necessary. I should have told you she didn't know, but I forgot during our last quarrel. Have there been any problems about Phillip's death while I was gone?"

"None, but the case isn't closed yet. When did you dock?"

"Tuesday evening. I had business in town yesterday. I'm heading home after I leave here. Have you seen today's newspaper or heard from your Athens partner?"

"Why?"

"There's an article about trouble there yesterday. I also heard what happened with the Augusta company last week. What's going on, Rachel? Do you need help and protection? Can I hire a guard to watch over you?"

"Why do you ask that?"

"Before I left weeks ago, you mentioned getting threats. I admit I wasn't sure they were genuine, but the attacks on your companies tell me they are. Something's amiss, girl. If you need help or more money, tell me. That's all I have with me today, but I can send more. It won't obligate you to me. I only want to keep you out of more trouble and danger, I don't think Catherine could stand losing another child."

She told herself not to be fooled by his seemingly sincere worry. To prevent a nasty scene, she said, "Thank you for your concern and offer, Earl, but I'm fine. Please keep this news from Mama, if you can. The police should have those crimes solved soon. Besides, I'm perfectly safe; an old friend of Phillip's—Captain Daniel Slade—is in town on business." She watched for a reaction to Dan's identity, but saw none. "He has two of his crewmen protecting me at all times. Whoever was threatening me or playing pranks can't get near me anymore. I wish they would, so they could be unmasked and punished. I reported those incidents to the police, but there isn't anything they can do."

"It's good to know you're safe. You be careful, and I'll tell Catherine you're fine. Good-bye, Rachel. Contact us if you need anything."

"Good-bye, Earl, and thank you."

As a relieved Rachel observed her stepfather's departure, Lula Mae said from behind her, "That's the first time you two ain't fussed lack bitter enemies. What did he want?"

She related the gist of their talk, then handed the housekeeper the money. "Put it in the cashbox. We'll need it next week for bills."

"You took money from him? I cain't believe it. You hate him."

Rachel gave a heavy sigh. "I had no choice. I'll repay it later, even if I have more of a right to White Cloud earnings than that Yankee does."

"You two made peace?"

"Heavens, no. But I wasn't in a mood to quarrel with him. He'll never change, but he didn't harass me as usual, so no harm in being nice and sweet."

*

The following day was filled with more surprises. Rachel answered the door to find a man who introduced himself as an insurance broker from Macon.

"I came to give you this, ma'am." He handed her a packet of money. "As per Mr. McCandless's orders, if anything happened to him, I was told to deliver this hundred thousand dollars to you in cash. I'm sorry this visit took so long, but I just learned of his demise. If you'll sign this release form, the insurance money is yours and I can get on my way home before the last train leaves."

"I don't understand. I didn't know Phillip had a policy with you."

"He took it out in February and paid the cost through June. Mr. George Leathers had a policy with us, too. When I saw his wife Tuesday, she told me Mr. McCandless had died in March. Your husband's instructions were, in the event of his death to bring your payment in cash."

"This is most unexpected, sir, and greatly needed. Thank you."

After she read and signed the form, the broker left. Rachel stared at the bills in her grasp, wishing it were the missing million dollars. She wanted to keep the money for expenses, but it was more important to buy guns, to save her life and those of others.

She hurriedly freshened up, took one of the seamen as a guard, and went to see Dan in town.

*

"You sure you want to spend this on more weapons?" he asked.

"As you said with your money, our lives are more important. I'll telegraph Harry that the money's on the way; he has guns made and waiting, so he can ship them immediately, before our next meeting with those rebels."

"I'll take it to him myself, so we'll be certain he gets it and obeys. If I don't stop off anywhere and nap on the train, I can be there tomorrow."

Dan sent Luke Conner to Central Station to check on the rail schedule. While his best friend was gone, Rachel told Dan about the letter earlier this week from Harry and about Earl Starger's—pleasant for a change—visit. They discussed how Dan was to handle Harry.

When the first mate returned, he told Dan he had two hours to pack and get aboard, then handed his friend the ticket he had purchased.

"Good, that's gives us time to visit your lawyer, Rachel, to check on your position in the Augusta company. I think, if the company folds, with the books destroyed and George dead, you aren't responsible for its debts. We'll see. I hope so; that will take one worry off your mind. If I were you, I would get rid of my share of that Athens company fast before it leads to trouble. I know that leaves you with only the plantation for support, but don't worry; I'll take care of you. And you might get the shipping firm back if all goes well with our investigation. We'll work on it after this matter is resolved. Luke, I want you to stay near Rachel while I'm gone in case those surly Cubans approach her again."

*

After Dan left on the train, Luke and Rachel headed for the plantation in her carriage. Along the way, he remarked, "I'm delighted to finally meet the woman who's going to change my life."

"What do you mean?" she asked the brown-haired man who, as Dan had said, always appeared about to burst into a broad grin.

Luke Conner chuckled and his azure gaze mellowed. "You've stolen my best friend's eye and he's determined to settle down with you."

She didn't know what to say, so she hinted, "Settle down with me?"

"He has proposed, hasn't he?"

"Yes, but I haven't accepted. It's too soon."

The first mate's eyes took in her exceptional beauty. "You will. Dan never takes no as an answer to something he wants. I'm going to become the captain of the *Merry Wind* while you two stay home and create a family."

"Family? Dan wants children?"

"What man doesn't? You two will have beautiful babies."

Rachel realized it was time to remind Dan that she might not be fertile. If he was being dreamy-eyed about children, she had to impress upon him the possible truth. If he were not serious about her, Dan wouldn't have mentioned her and a future together to his best friend.

"Did I say something wrong or upsetting, Rachel?"

She smiled at Luke and said, "Of course not. Your remarks just caught me off guard. When a stranger woos a woman, she doesn't always know how serious or honest he's being. I guess this talk means he's both."

"Daniel Slade is the most sincere and trustworthy man I know. I hope you feel the same way about him that he feels about you. I wouldn't want him to get hurt. He's my best friend, my captain, and like a brother to me. You do love him and want to marry him, don't you?"

Rachel glanced at the handsome and genial man. True, he was being bold and nosy, but only out of love and concern for his friend. "I shouldn't be thinking about such things, Luke. Phillip was Dan's good friend and my husband. He's only been dead for two months, the same amount of time I've known Dan. I don't want to rush this attraction between us, and I don't want to risk more gossip about my marrying before Phillip's body is cold. You should advise Dan to slow down and get to know me better before he makes such a serious decision about his future. You know I'm still under investigation; if Dan and I look as if we've gotten too close too fast, the law could suspect us of doing away with Phillip. That might sound crazy and impossible to you, but it isn't when I'm involved. I don't want him hurt in any way."

"I understand, Rachel, but Dan will take care of everything for you."

"You've helped him investigate me and you've met me. Do you think I'm capable of being a Black Widow? Do you think I'm guilty?"

Luke fused his azure gaze to hers. "No, Rachel, I don't."

"Not even in the beginning?"

"I had doubts, but was never totally convinced," he admitted.

"I appreciate your honesty, Luke."

"Relax and let us take care of things for a while. One problem's done; that lawyer is getting you out of trouble and debt in Augusta."

*

Carlos Torres and Joaquín Chavous were waiting in the barn when they arrived. "Another conquest to protect you, Señora Raquel?"

She glared at the brazen man. "This is Captain Slade's first mate and best *amigo,* Luke Conner. You didn't have to murder George Leathers and destroy our Augusta company to terrorize us. I told you George had already sent his part of the contract; the ammunition is stowed safely aboard Dan's ship. The hold-up is Harrison Clements in Athens, but if you try to harm him again like you did Wednesday, we can't fill your order. Three men are dead, murdered. One company is blown up. Harm another person or set another fire and I'll go to the police and have you arrested. Is that clear?"

"I do not know who is threatening you or why, Señora Raquel, but it is not us. It would be foolish to harm people and places we need to fill our order. Is this another trick to stall or an attempt to betray your word? Monday is the final day to complete our business. If not, *accidentes* will occur and we will be behind them this time."

"Dan is in Athens now picking up part of the order. I have 2,960 rifles aboard his ship. Another 3,040 are arriving Monday. That's six thousand, and the full amount of ammunition. I need more time to get the other four thousand. Or rather, I have to find $127,000 to pay for them being made."

"Six thousand is not enough, Señora Raquel. We paid for ten. Get the others *pronto.* I will give you until Tuesday, *no más,*" he vowed coldly.

*

Luke escorted Rachel into town on Monday to meet Dan at the depot. The train arrived on schedule and they greeted each other with smiles.

"How did things go during my absence?" Dan inquired as he perceived a genial aura between his love and first mate.

Rachel glanced at Luke and smiled. "Would you believe your best friend charmed the frown off Lula Mae's face. My spinster housekeeper is most taken with him. If he were older, she would no doubt pursue him."

"How did you manage that magic, my friend? She can't stand me."

Luke sent Dan a lopsided grin and roguish shrug. "I'm irresistible."

"It's because you're a threat to her, Dan," Rachel quipped. "She's afraid you'll steal off to sea with her mistress and put her out of a good job."

"That's my intention, woman, if you ever agree."

"Luke's an excellent chess player. We had a wonderful time getting to know each other. For seamen both of you are superb riders."

"The old change-the-subject ruse, Luke; did you catch how easily and quickly she does it?" Dan teased. "She's leading me on a merry chase."

"I've never been dishonest with you, Daniel Slade, not about that."

"Being dishonest and being direct are two different things, love."

"Can we discuss this at another time and place, sir?"

"See, Luke, I get to her, but she doesn't want to admit it."

"Listen, you two mischievous sailors," Rachel put a halt to the bantering. "We have serious business to tend. What happened? The suspense is chewing away at me," she said.

"I have 3,040 rifles with me. Harry sent thirty extra as promised."

"How generous of him," Rachel scoffed. "I didn't scare him at all."

Dan related his news. "I did my best to persuade him to send the other four thousand and the dynamite, but he wouldn't. I pointed out we had George's ammo and wouldn't have to pay for it; it didn't make a difference. I told him you would sacrifice your share of the profit, and we'd paid for the 5,970 rifles out of our pockets. I even told him what you said about giving up your share of the company if he'd send only half of the remaining weapons. He still said no. He claims he can't write off $127,000."

"But we've spent $207,500 saving our skins!"

"He knows that, love, but it doesn't change his mind. He said the rebels have to take the ammo and six thousand arms and be satisfied. He thinks we've done all we can to straighten out Phillip's mess."

"We?" she echoed with a sneer. "It hasn't cost him anything!"

"He says he hasn't made any profit, either. Even sacrificing his profits and yours, the expenses are $334,000 for the full contract. He did agree to give up any profit, but he won't pay for arms out of his personal account and says the company's account is bare."

"He's as responsible as I am. Maybe more so."

"He doesn't see it that way, because Phillip accepted the money and you're Phillip's wife."

"It's because he thinks I have the money and I'll soon weaken!"

"That," Dan concurred, "and the fact he's riled about the trouble last week. He's posted guards at the company and his home for protection. He's nervous, but not budging. He's put the company up for sale, said you had agreed. He has the rest of the weapons ready and waiting, if we'll send the remaining $127,000. Giving up his profit is as far as he'll go."

"Well, the Cubans will just have to share in the responsibility. I can't come up with any more money. I've done more than my share."

"Let's tell Torres and Chavous we have the order and we're ready to sail." Dan suggested.

"What happens when we anchor and they discover the shortage?" Rachel reasoned. "You planning to dump the cases and flee before it is? They would be so furious about being tricked, they'd send Torres and Chavous back for the rest or for our heads."

"They're only messengers and escorts, love. They don't have the power to make decisions or changes. We need to see their leader and reason with him. Once he learns the whole story, he'll have to work with us to solve the rest."

"You're right, Dan. Besides, we need to discover who Phillip was talking about as our 'only hope.' Somebody must be there who can help us."

Dan decided to let Rachel think she was going along, but it was too dangerous. He would leave her behind at the last minute, along with two of his men for protection. "Let's get these crates loaded on the ship. We'll talk more later. Luke, get things ready tomorrow for sailing Thursday at dawn. Rachel you get packed tomorrow. When we see those rebels in the morning, we'll put our plan into motion . . . I'm starved. Who's for a delicious dinner?"

"Here come the boys with wagons," the first mate said. "I'll take care of these crates, then stay on the ship tonight, if it's all right, Captain. I'll meet you at the hotel at breakfast."

"That's perfect, Luke. Thanks," he said with a grin and a wink. "Well, woman, do you want to join me for dinner, say, the Pirate's House?"

Rachel realized Luke Conner had given them the evening alone for more than sharing a meal and conversation. Dare she risk spending the night in Dan's hotel room? What if they were still being watched?

Chapter

20

As Dan slipped into bed with Rachel, he yearned to embrace and kiss her. Both knew what loomed before them in the next few weeks, especially during the next two days. Even death for one or both could loom on the cloudy horizon. Tonight they would love as if it was their last night on earth. Tonight they would soar toward rapture's heaven on the wings of passion. Later they would worry about the perils confronting them.

Dan lay beside Rachel to hold and caress her. The hotel room was secure, and one lamp cast a soft and dreamy glow on their bodies. For a while, Dan made love to her with his eyes. He stored up exquisite images to carry him through the days of separation ahead, as he would not allow her to sail to the hazardous meeting in the Cuban stronghold. It was possible he wouldn't come out of this alive, and he couldn't risk her life, too. Yet he must do all he could to free her from that threat. His gaze roamed her face and body with tantalizing leisure. He saw a flush of arousal spread over her.

Rachel experienced an odd mixture of tension and relaxation. His gaze was so potent, so enticing, so flattering. Tingles and warmth raced over her. She felt as if she were being teased and pleasured simultaneously. She did nothing to hurry or to slow his thrilling sport.

Dan came forward until his bare chest made contact with hers. His lips ever so lightly brushed over her waiting mouth. His fingers trailed over her face as if mapping it in detail. He pressed kisses to every feature, then rained more down her throat. His mouth halted to bring the brown peaks of her breasts to life with loving moisture and titillating flicks of his tongue.

Rachel groaned as he ignited and fanned her smoldering desires into a raging fire. She savored and craved the way his hands roved her pliant body. As one hand drifted over her stomach, it tightened with anticipation of its continued trek toward her womanhood. She was stirred and tempted and could not keep from pulling his mouth back to hers. She wanted to taste him, to feel him, to surrender totally. Her hands traveled his body as they stroked his tanned flesh and admired its appeal. She closed her eyes to let her unbridled senses absorb everything about Dan and the blissful journey they were beginning.

Dan's loins ached for an urgent fusion of their bodies, but he mastered the urge to move too swiftly. He nuzzled her neck and ear as his nose inhaled her heady fragrance. His fingertips grazed her skin and admired its firm suppleness. He felt as if he had gulped ten bottles of potent whiskey, as she utterly inebriated his senses.

Rachel's fingers wandered into Dan's sable hair, loving the feel of it against her skin. She relished trailing them over his hard chest and sleek torso. With bravery and boldness, her hand worked its way lower and lower, over his taut abdomen, past lean hips, and to his manly region. Her fingers curled around his rigid shaft and stroked the fiery member that instantly responded to her touch. Her mouth melded with his as their tongues danced in fiery abandon.

Dan's lips returned to the rosy-brown nubs on her breasts and blissfully tormented them to increase her hunger for him. He vowed this would be a night she would never forget. His hands kneaded the flesh of her breasts and he gently worked at the buds on them. He felt bathed in wondrous sensation. He was calm yet his body felt as tight as a rope. He felt in control yet was spinning in a whirlpool of unleashed emotions. He grasped her firm buttocks and fondled them before pressing her feminine core snugly against him.

Rachel was captivated and enchanted by Dan. He was aroused to the point of driving within her with swift urgency but was sensitive and caring to her needs and pleasures. She wanted to tell him to enter her to appease his hunger, but she let him decide when the time was perfect. Her thrusting peaks were responsive to his sweet torments. She writhed as his fingers trailed up and down her sides, across her back, along her spine, and finally into her fuzzy brown triangle. The straining bud pulsed and heated at his attention. Her anticipation and desires increased. Soon her head was thrashing on the pillow as his deft finger entered her and dashed aside any lingering control and reality.

Mindless with desire, Rachel's hands moved up and down Dan's back with speed and pressure. They teased over sinewy muscles that rippled with his stirring movements, wandered to his taut buttocks. He had stolen her wits and was driving her wild with a fierce craving for him. Her fingers toyed in the crisp black hair around the root of his manhood. She felt him trailing kisses down her stomach and shifting his position to continue along her thighs, taking him out of her reach. When he brushed kisses over the pulsing spot that only he had pleasured, she stiffened in confusion. She lifted her head and looked at him, questioning the unknown experience and intense sensations he was evoking.

Dan sent her an encouraging smile that told her to relax. His strong and gentle hands stroked the silky inner surface of her thighs, each time just barely making contact with the inflamed area. One finger lovingly massaged the delicate peak as another slipped within her secret haven to create a pattern that matched that of his manhood when it was thrusting within her. The moisture and heat of her paradise told him she was eager and ready to accept and enjoy any pleasure he wished to give her.

Rachel remembered how she had thought that the physical act was either ugly and painful or something to be endured or only for a man's satisfaction. With the right man, though, it was clearly beautiful, magical, enslaving, and inspiring. For her, Daniel Slade was that man, the only man, the one who could entice her total and willing surrender. He could make her starve for his contact, feed her ravenous body until she was thoroughly sated, then leave her craving her next meal of his sensual treats. He reclaimed her strayed attention as he continued his loving assault on her senses. His mouth, tongue, and fingers, gave her pleasures she had not known existed. She squirmed as tension mounted within her. She wanted to relax, but couldn't. She was taut with anticipation of what she instinctively knew would be marvelous. Passion's flames licked at her body and seared it with his brand of ownership.

Dan realized she had reached the point of fiery abandon. He moved atop her, covered her mouth with his, and entered her moistness with a gasp. As if insatiable, she matched his pattern and labored with him. His lips greedily drank from the nectar of her mouth and hardened nipples. She was moaning and clinging to him. Her tongue teased over his lips. Her mouth was insistent upon his, then ardently fastened to his. He noticed how she kept pace with his movements as they worked in unison toward the same goal. He was coaxed to increase his ardent endeavors to give her supreme satisfaction. As bliss exploded within her, she nibbled at his shoulder and clung tightly to his body.

Dan was charged with energy. He discarded his self-control and scaled the summit to capture passion's peak at her side. His release stole his breath and shook his body. He didn't halt his labors until he was breathless and appeased, as was she.

A golden aftermath of the heady lovemaking settled within them. Both felt limp and fulfilled. Their hearts surged with love and peace. Their spirits were united, as their bodies still were interlocked. They hugged, then parted, to lie close in the intimate setting.

Rachel gazed at Dan. Though his prowess in lovemaking was immeasurable, he was so gentle and giving. She wiped beads of perspiration from his face and smiled into his twinkling blue eyes. Her adoring gaze lingered a moment on the white teeth revealed by his smile. Her fingers traced his strong and handsome features, then wandered into his damp ebony hair. Her gaze locked with his.

Dan knew he was viewing love and trust and contentment in her whiskey-colored depths. He was proud and pleased. He shifted to kiss her and to cuddle her possessively. "You're mine, woman, tonight and forever," he murmured as his teeth nibbled at her ear.

Rachel squirmed and giggled at the tickling sensation. "You are the most magnificent and unique man alive, Daniel Slade. If we did this every night, I could never tire of you or having you like this."

"Good, because I'm a greedy and demanding lover."

"Every time you take me, you give me exquisite pleasure. You're so generous and thoughtful. One day, you'll teach me enough so I can torment you and sate you in these same ways."

"Does that mean you'll agree to keep me around?"

"Except when you're at sea, I want you at my side day and night. I, too, have become greedy and demanding. I'll make you the best mistress you could ever find or train." She waited for his response to those words.

Dan refused to pressure her. He was positive she loved him and wanted him. When everything was resolved, she would marry him, because he wouldn't let her say no. "That's an irresistible offer and a promise, love."

Rachel grasped what his hesitation meant and smiled. "Yes, it is."

"I hate to roust you from this warm and tempting bed, woman, but it will be easier to get you home unseen at this hour than in the morning."

"You're right. I hate to leave, but it's safest for us. I'll get dressed." As she did so, she said, "I'm glad we ate up here instead of in a restaurant."

"It was sneaky of me, slipping you and the food in here."

"It certainly was, my sly hero. Just think . . . in two days, we'll be sailing the tropical seas. I wish . . . Will I see you tomorrow?"

"No, we both have many tasks. I'll see you when you come into town on Wednesday. You'll spend the night here, then board my ship just before sailing time Thursday morning. I don't want you around tomorrow and Wednesday while we're loading supplies and those arms, in case we have problems with customs. If that paper isn't in order and legal, I don't want you getting into more trouble. I won't, because I got it from Phillip and Harry, so I have an excuse for not knowing it was faked."

As she brushed her hair, she watched him in the mirror as he donned his garments. "You will send word if there's a problem?"

"Yes, but don't worry. I think everything will go fine. You can take care of messages to Harry and Milton late Wednesday. Better still, leave them to be delivered Thursday after we sail. We don't want interference with our departure." *After I'm gone, you won't need to tell them.*

Rachel didn't remind him she wasn't supposed to leave town, but she wasn't going to the police station to ask Chief Anderson's permission! She wanted to be with Dan, to make certain he wasn't blamed and punished for the shortage, and to spend time learning about his lifestyle. That would tell her if he could give up his adventurous existence or she could fit into it.

*

Rachel talked with her housekeeper as she packed, "I have to take this trip, Lula Mae, to finish that important business hanging over my head. If all goes well, I'll be paid a lot of money and our troubles will be over. When I return, if the police don't shut my file on Phillip's death, I'll have the money to hire a lawyer to force it closed. I want everything settled, so our lives can return to normal. It should take about two weeks. If those investigators come calling again, tell them I had to take care of business and I'll contact them the moment I'm back."

"But they told you not to leave, Miss Rachel. You'll git in trouble."

"Maybe, but I have to take that risk. Settling this deal is the answer to all my problems. Besides, if I'm away, whoever is playing those tricks on me will be thwarted and I'll be safe. This is the only choice I can make at this time. You stay on guard so you won't get hurt while I'm gone."

"I'll be worried silly till you git back. Where you going?"

"I can't tell you; it's a secret, the client's order. This deal is big and important; we can't risk someone forcing the truth from you or anyone."

"I wouldn't tell nobody."

"Not on purpose. Please understand, and I'll explain everything later."

"Wills Captain Slade be guarding you?"

"Yes, and Luke Conner, too. I won't be alone with Dan, so don't worry."

"I won't stop worryin' till you're home again. Why cain't Mr. Clements go?"

"This was Phillip's deal and there are problems with it. I have to go straighten them out and save it. Harry refuses. He's still angry with me about tricking him after Phillip's death. We have the arms company up for sale, but there won't be any profit from it, just debts paid off. That leaves me with the plantation to replace lost earnings from the three companies. I plan to start farming the rest of the land as soon as possible, maybe grow cotton or indigo, to supplement our income from the sharecroppers. I'll have to depend on you and Burke to help out more. We'll probably have to hire more workers, too. That takes money. But we'll do fine. We'll make a real plantation out of Moss Haven. Won't that be—"

Rachel straightened from folding her garments and listened. "Someone is knocking on the door. See if it's the message I'm expecting."

When Lula Mae returned, she handed Rachel a paper that told her it was time to set their daring ruse into motion.

"I have to run an errand nearby. I won't be gone long."

"I'm supposed to go check on Mrs. Willis. I'll goes while you're gone. I'll help you finish packing when we both git back."

"That's perfect, Lula Mae. Burke and the boys are working outside so the house will be safe from more pranks."

Rachel watched the older woman ride off in one direction in the carriage as she galloped off on horseback in the other. She was surprised, and perhaps a bit intrigued, by how well Lula Mae had taken the news about her impending trip. Perhaps it was a result of her clever disclosures about how they would soon be living. It might be the truth, as she should wait a while before marrying Daniel Slade. It wouldn't be fair to Phillip or good for her stained reputation to disallow a proper mourning period. No matter her final decision, it kept the nosy housekeeper off her back for now.

*

Rachel reached the location and dismounted. She saw Carlos smile when he noticed she had come alone. She ignored the irascible Joaquín and focused on the raffish leader of the two rebels.

"You no longer fear me, Raquel; you come alone; that is *bueno.*"

"So is my news, Mr. Torres. The ship is being supplied and your crates are being loaded today and tomorrow. Dan wants you to board the *Merry Wind* at five o'clock tomorrow afternoon. We set sail at dawn the next morning. To prevent any trouble at the last minute, the ship will move to the end of the channel and anchor there until departure time. Agreed?"

"You have the arms, ammunitions and explosives?"

"Everything is ready to be delivered. Dan's crew has been on shore leave, so they're being located and called aboard for sailing."

Carlos smiled and complimented, "I knew you would not fail me."

"You have no idea how hard and stressful this has been for me. If that's all for now, I have to get home and finish packing for the voyage."

Carlos showed his surprise. "You are sailing with us?"

"Yes. I want to make certain the cargo I've paid for gets to the right client. If anything goes wrong again, I can't put another one together. This deal is my work and my money, and I'm going to protect it until it reaches your leader's hands. If that missing money is ever found, it's mine. Is that understood?"

"*Sí*, Raquel. You have done well. I hope you find the *dinero.*"

"So do I, because I'm penniless. Every cent I could get my hands on went toward paying for this order all of you held me responsible for. The only reason I complied was to live. You don't know how tempted I was to tell all of you to go to the devil. But I knew you would hurt my family and friends."

"It is over; no more threats or dangers. We are *amigos.*"

"I hope so. If the Spanish attack us along the way, Dan won't let them board or confiscate his ship. You will guarantee our safety in Cuba? Once the order is delivered, we're free to go unharmed? No tricks or betrayals?"

"No Cuban rebel will harm you, Raquel. You have my word of honor."

"And that of your leader?"

"*Sí, mi líder,* too. After our bargain is met, we part as *amigos.*"

"One last question, Mr. Torres: do you swear you're innocent of all the threats and attacks we've received?"

"We have harmed no one in your country, Raquel."

"Good, because I couldn't let you get away with murdering those men."

"You accept my word?" Carlos asked, looking surprised.

"Yes. I don't like your intimidating behavior, but I believe you."

"It takes a smart and brave woman to challenge her enemies."

"First, she has to unmask them. I'll do that when I return home. I'll see you Thursday at dawn. I'm staying at the hotel until sailing time. Don't forget, be at the *Merry Wind* gangplank at five tomorrow. And, Carlos . . . ?"

He grinned when she also used his first name. *"Sí,* Raquel?"

"Don't let anything happen to you and your sullen *amigo.* I don't know the rendezvous place or your *líder's* name. After all I've been through, I wouldn't want to be blamed and killed for your losses and a late shipment."

"We will be most alert and careful until *mañana. Adiós,* Raquel."

"Adiós, amigo Carlos," she replied, having decided to try to make friends with him before she faced his leader with the shortage. Knowing all she had done to save this deal, maybe he would speak in her favor.

*

Wednesday afternoon, Burke Wells dropped Rachel off at the hotel, then delivered her baggage to the clipper. Two seamen stored it in their captain's quarters, as he wasn't there to tell them what else to do with it.

Rachel had written out messages for Milton Baldwin and the police, explaining she was away on vital business and would contact them as soon as she returned in two weeks. She had made out a telegram for Harry, telling him the same, but adding a request to stay ready to fill the rest of the order. She had given them to Burke to deliver and send tomorrow after she sailed.

Luke Conner came by to relate there had been no problem with customs when they inspected and cleared the cargo.

"That's a relief," Rachel said, "because I'm not convinced that permission paper is real. No matter; we used it in good faith and they accepted it."

"Dan will come by for supper and a chat later. The crew is gathered, supplies are laid in, cargo's stowed, and she's ready to sail with the morning tide. I'm going to miss . . . Savannah. I've enjoyed my visit. It's been quite interesting getting to know you and investigate you," he jested, having covered his near slip about Dan's intention to leave her behind in safety.

"We'll have plenty of time on the ship for more talks and chess games. I'm looking forward to tasting Dan's lifestyle and meeting his friends."

"Have no fear; you'll fit in perfectly and easily."

"Thank you, Luke; I needed to hear that."

*

Rachel answered the knock at her door, eager to see her love, who was early. She gaped at her stepfather and wondered how he knew where to find her. "What do you want, Earl?" she asked, trying to sound polite.

He came inside and she watched him as he fingercombed his wiry hair. "I saw you check in, but I was too busy to speak. Why are you staying here? Is there more trouble at home?"

"I'm only here overnight," Rachel said in annoyance. "This isn't a convenient time to chat; I'm expecting a guest for dinner."

"Captain Daniel Slade?" He scowled when her expression said he was right. "How do I know?" he asked for her. "The gossip is already making its ugly rounds, Rachel. How can you do something so foolish? It's too soon for you to be courted again. Don't you care about another scandal? My Lord, girl, you're still under suspicion for killing Phillip and George Leathers! Don't you realize how this quick romance will look to the police?"

Rachel closed the door to prevent them from being overheard by a guest. "What's wrong with having a male friend?"

"Friend? That isn't what he is, and nobody is fooled, girl."

"It's really none of your or their business. Please leave."

Earl was leaning against the door. He put his hands behind his back and locked it. "We aren't finished yet."

Rachel heard the click and glared at him. "Don't start this again," she warned in a frigid tone. "Get out or I'll scream."

Earl grinned and challenged, "Create more gossip and scandal? Your devoted and worried stepfather comes to offer his protection, comfort, and aid, but you attack him? Who would believe you?"

"Come near me and I'll kill you; or Dan will. He'll be here soon."

"I think not. He's already sailed with the evening tide."

"He's gone?" she murmured, then recalled Luke's near slip.

"That's right. It's just you and me. No servants. No weapons. No refusal. I'm sure that lowly sailor has had you many times, so now it's my turn. You owe me, girl. You teased and tempted me for years. Then you took off with that old man and humiliated me. Your mother doesn't have your fire and spirit; she gave it all to you. Yield to me just this once, Rachel, and I'll leave you alone forever. I'll give you whatever money and help you need."

"You're mad! I wouldn't surrender to you if my life depended on it."

"It does. You're penniless and no man will risk marrying you. All of your assets will be lost soon, then you'll be thrown into the street. I'm not asking or demanding you become my mistress; I just want to bed you one time to see what magic you possess to drive men crazy enough to risk their lives marrying a Black Widow. You don't even have to respond."

"My God, you *are* insane! Get out."

Earl pulled a jeweled knife from his pocket. "This little darling can mar your enchanting beauty, girl, or it can put a stop to your evil existence. If you die, no more victims will lose their lives."

Rachel panicked. "You can't murder me and get away with it."

"This pretty baby is a woman's weapon. Either you tried to stab me and fell on it, or you killed yourself in a moment of madness. Everybody knows you have to be either mad or evil to do what you did to innocent men. I would never risk my life marrying a bloodthirsty predator like you. Now, get your clothes off and get on that bed. I'm going to give you some fatherly love and discipline to correct your wicked ways. Do it, now!"

"No. I didn't kill any of them. I'm not insane. I won't bed you."

"You have no choice. Scream, and this knife will end your sadistic criminal life. Whether you realize it or not, girl, you're guilty. Why do you think your mother and I have been worried and afraid all these years? Why do you think she was scared to invite you back home? Because we've both witnessed your mad and dreamy behavior. Be glad we've never told the law about your lunacy. We thought it would stop when you met the right man and fell in love with him. But your hunger for money and your desire to give men pain won't let you. Show gratitude to me for not seeing you hanged."

She was trapped. "You're lying, you miserable and devious snake!"

"Am I? Think back, Rachel. Recall the times you've found things done without remembering doing them. Were you ever awake or sensible when any of your husbands died? You're sick in the head, but can't face it or admit it. Just like you refuse to admit you teased and tormented and encouraged me to fondle you and bed you. As soon as things got hot between us, you'd come around, panic, and accuse me of trying to rape you. Don't you see, girl? You couldn't stand for me to take your father's place so you tried to take me away from your mother. What little good you have inside always stopped you at the last minute. You blame men for the war that killed your father and brother and ruined your life, so you choose one to punish. Until you face the truth and get help, it won't ever stop."

"If I'm so sick in the mind, why are you trying to ravish me?"

"Because you owe me for all those years of painful games. After we finish here, I'll take you back to White Cloud. As soon as I find the best doctor to cure you, I'll send you to him and pay for everything. I won't ever touch you again. You have my word of honor. If you don't believe what I'm telling you, ask Catherine. She knows you're guilty. It's eaten at her for years and finally made *her* ill. The only reason she's getting better is because I've sworn to have you cured, with or without your consent. That's why she left her sickbed to visit you, to see if you could be helped."

"Mama would never believe such absurd lies about me. If she knew what you were really trying to do to me, she would kill you herself."

"After I'm done, tell her. I don't care; she won't believe it, not from her mad and wicked daughter. Enough talk. Strip and lie down."

Rachel was staggered by Earl's words and intention. She couldn't scream for help; either he would kill or disfigure her, or would create an ugly scandal and trouble, preventing her departure . . . Was Dan gone? Why else would Earl be so confident about not being interrupted?

"Get on with it, girl. This is ready for you," he murmured as he rubbed the hard bulge in his pants. "It's been ready for you for years."

"You wrote those notes to me, didn't you? You followed me to Augusta and left them in my room, and in my house. You had someone forge my handwriting so I couldn't show them to anybody. You put that poisonous spider in my basin and that vial of poison in my hotel room."

"No, Rachel. You must have done those things to convince yourself you're innocent. Have the police or a private detective investigate me; that's the only way you'll ever learn I'm not to blame. By damn, I'll even pay the cost to prove who's at fault! I'm tired of you calling me vile names and accusing me of filthy overtures. I'm tired of you treating me like a disease or a fool. The only reason you haven't told your mother about my so-called advances is because deep inside you know I'm not guilty and you'll be exposed for the wicked-minded creature you are."

"You'll never convince me I'm mad, so give it up."

"I don't have to convince you, we both know you are."

"I didn't shoot at myself, write those notes, or make those threats."

"If it wasn't you, check out your seaman when he returns. It could be his method of getting into your bloomers. Come on, girl; you understand my meaning. Scare you into falling into his arms for protection, then he's so overwhelmed by your beauty that he seduces you. And you're so damn grateful that you let him do as he pleases with you."

"That's a crude and spiteful lie, Earl Starger!"

"Rachel, Rachel," he chided. "How can you be so blind and rash?"

"Get out."

"After I get what I came after, what I've looked forward to for years, what you've offered, girl. Then you're going to a doctor up North for treatment. If I don't have you cured, we'll have to expose you to the police. We can't let you murder another man. If we keep quiet, we're as guilty as you are."

"How will it look for my father to sleep with me?" she scoffed.

"I'm not your father, so it won't be incest."

"It would be adultery; you're married to my mother."

"You came after me, girl, not the other way around. Everybody knows you have witch's powers. How can I be blamed for falling under your evil spell for one foolish moment?"

"I am not evil, cursed, jinxed, or guilty. Somebody else killed them."

"Who, Rachel? Only the insidious witch who lives inside you."

"Stop it. I won't listen to any more lies."

"Be thankful I'm saving Captain Slade from your lethal web. You like him, don't you? Just as you liked William and Craig and Phillip. If you snare him, girl, he's dead. Let him escape, and you get help."

"What about you, Earl? Why haven't I murdered you? I despise you."

"Because the evil one inside you knows I know who and what she is. She knows I'll expose her if she tries to murder me, too. She knows who started this game between us, and she wants me. Let her come out and take me. Go into your dreamy state so Rachel won't remember what happens between us tonight. She's the one telling you that you aren't sick so you won't allow a doctor to get rid of her."

Earl stepped closer and taunted her with the jewel-handled knife. Rachel backed away until she reached the wall. A table with a heavy vase was beside her. She waited until Earl stalked her and stood before her. As one of his hands covered her breast, she curled her fingers around the rim, lifted it, and struck him forcefully over the head.

The vase broke, and Earl staggered backward. His hand grabbed his bleeding head. He shook it to clear his dazed condition. He glared at the wide-eyed Rachel and saw the hatred and defiance written on her face. "Damn you, you little witch; you'll be sorry for that. I'll tell all I know about you."

As he came at her again with a blood-glint in his hazel eyes, Rachel used her riding boot to land a near-crippling blow to his groin. Earl collapsed in agony to the floor. Rachel grabbed his feet and used all the strength she could summon to work him out her door. She rolled the disabled man into the hall, relieved no guests were milling about. She closed and locked the door, and leaned against it to recover her breath.

Earl struggled to rise before someone came along and saw his injuries. He decided to slip into the closet across the hall until his strength returned. He was filled with hatred and a desire for revenge. His dark lust for Rachel changed into an evil hunger to see her crushed and punished for her deeds. He swore to himself she would never get away with what she had done.

Rachel jumped and gasped as someone knocked at the door she had swayed against. She feared it was Earl trying to get inside again.

"Rachel, are you there?"

She unlocked the door, yanked a startled Dan inside, bolted the lock, and flung herself into his arms. She was breathing hard and her heart was pounding. She held on to him for comfort and strength.

"What's wrong, love?" he questioned in alarm. He tried to put distance between them to look at her, but she clung to him. Dan waited a minute for her to relax her grip, but she didn't. "Rachel, what is it? What happened?" He saw the broken vase and grasped her distress.

"Earl . . ." She finally managed to get out one word.

"He's been here?" She nodded, but didn't look at him. "What did he do to you? If he harmed you, I'll hunt down the bastard and kill him."

Rachel was terrified and confused. If there was only a grain of truth in what Earl had said, how could she tell Dan? How could she plant such seeds in his mind? She mustn't, not until she returned to Savannah, went home, and questioned her mother. "We had a vicious quarrel. I don't want to talk about it tonight. He scares me. I'll be so glad to be away from here tomorrow. I'll deal with him after my return, once and for all. I wish we were sailing tonight. I'm afraid he'll come back. Can I stay on the ship with you tonight?"

Luke had told him about the near-slip he had made earlier. Dan wondered if she had guessed he was planning to leave her behind and this was a ruse to prevent that action. He had been downstairs for a while, delayed by Camellia Jones, and he hadn't seen her stepfather come or go. "That wouldn't be wise, love; somebody might see you. We have to wait until the wee hours of the morning to sneak you aboard."

"Then stay with me here tonight. We'll leave together when it's safe."

"Are you sure you should take this trip? Those Cuban rebels are going to be riled and dangerous when we deliver those arms and ammunition and they realize we've shorted them by thousands. If my ship is stopped and searched, we could get into trouble for gun-running."

"I don't care. I just want to be with you. I want to get away from here. I know the law will come after me about Phillip and George while you're gone. I may be hanged or in prison when you return."

"They don't have any evidence against you, love. Besides, they told you not to leave town until both investigations are over."

"They'll invent some, or that culprit stalking me will."

"You're only upset and not thinking clearly. When I return, you'll marry me. In a few years, when I'm safe and alive, the gossip will cease."

"That isn't funny."

"It wasn't meant to be. It's another proposal. If you don't want to stay in Savannah, you can sail away with me after this problem is solved. I can promise you a life of real adventure."

"Why would you marry me? I said I'd be your mistress. I've been married three times, and all three men are dead under suspicious circumstances. Either I'm bad luck or I have a deadly enemy. I don't want you killed."

"I'm willing to stake my life that you're harmless, woman."

"If you love me and want me, take me with you tonight."

Earl listened to the revealing conversation and knew he had been given his tool to exact revenge. Everything was quiet now, so they must be kissing or heading for the bed. In a rage, he left to fetch the police.

Luke saw the man eavesdrop, then leave hurriedly. He followed Earl Starger until he realized, after hearing him mumble about having the means to "get that evil bitch this time", where the man was headed. Luke rushed back to the hotel and alerted Dan to impending trouble.

"They'll send men to guard the wharf to make certain we don't escape while others come here to arrest us. Everything is ready to sail. Damn!"

"Let Luke hurry to the ship and sail her to Ossabaw Island. You and I can go to

Moss Haven, take a boat downriver, and meet him there. We'll tell the desk clerk we're going to dinner and that we're expecting a message, to hold it until we return. That should stall and fool them. If they question anyone at the wharf, no one will have seen us board your ship."

"She's right, Dan. We have to move and move fast. It'll take them a while to hear Starger out, then gather enough men to come after you. Even if everything's in order and legal, it'll take time to sort out this mess. Don't forget, we have two Cuban rebels and arms on board to be found."

Dan knew he couldn't leave her behind in danger. "Let's go."

*

Rachel and Dan padded down the Ogeechee River beneath a waning full moon. For the majority of their journey, they moved swiftly on the brackish water. At most places, the black river was wide; at a few, it was narrow. Several times they had to slow their pace to duck their heads to avoid low branches or bowed trees. The twisting route was bounded by impenetrable woods and swamp. Moss-draped cypress and oaks hung over the banks, often with their gnarled roots exposed. Rachel didn't want to think about the dangers that lurked in the water or on the shrouded banks.

"It's so spooky at night," she murmured, shuddering.

To distract her, Dan related his delaying run-in with Camellia, who had flirted and warned him about her predatory rival.

"I wouldn't be surprised if Earl convinced her to stall you while we quarreled. They both hate me, and they're friends."

"She wants me, and he wants you. Is that right?"

"Yes, but neither will win their goals. Is *that* right?"

"Absolutely correct, love."

"I'm relieved we got away without being seen and stopped. The law is probably still waiting for us to return from dinner. I'm glad Burke and Lula Mae didn't see us take this canoe. I hate for them to have to lie for me again. We're twenty miles or more from town, so we should be safe."

Dan noticed her nervous chatter. "This was a clever idea, woman; I'm happy you thought of it in your state. Starger really upset you this time."

Rachel stiffened a moment. "Yes, he did. I'll tell you about it another day. I don't even want to think about him, much less talk about him."

At least Dan knew she had told the truth, and he chided himself for having brief doubts about her again. But he knew they weren't out of danger yet. As soon as the authorities realized they had escaped—believing by Earl's report that they had done something wrong—somebody would be sent after them. He prayed they could get undersail before that happened. And he prayed what they were doing wasn't illegal, or they would both be . . .

When they reached the place the Ogeechee dumped into the Atlantic Ocean, they halted at Ossabaw Island to await Luke and the *Merry Wind*. They climbed out of the canoe and sat on the sandy beach beneath the moon.

"I hope Luke got the ship out of the channel and is sailing along the coast toward us. At least we have the evening tide in our favor. He'll have to go slowly this close to shore, and they have about twenty miles farther to travel than we did. He'll send men after us in a boat. We'll leave this canoe here. Try to relax and sleep until I sight them. Lay your head in my lap."

Rachel did as he suggested. She was exhausted from the chores and episodes of the last few days and the trip downriver. The setting was serene and romantic. The air was warm and smelled of salt. A breeze off the water was gentle and steady. The ocean lapped at the shoreline, giving off lulling sounds. Farther out, waves tumbled over each other and created white crests. Moonglow bathed Dan's face. She watched him as he gazed out to sea and witnessed its strong pull on him. Could he give it up for anything or anyone? Once they were away from her troubles and perils, would she want to return to them? To ever leave his side again?

"Are you scared about what we're heading into?"

"Yes and no," she replied with honesty. Was he safe with her? God help them both if Earl Starger hadn't lied to her . . .

Dan toyed with a dark-brown curl and worried. He wondered what Earl Starger held over her head like a silencing weapon. Something terrifying had happened between them, and he wanted to know what it was. *I thought we were past dangerous secrets, my love. What are you hiding from me now? You're mine, Rachel, and I won't let anything or anyone come between us. If I have to kill that bastard to protect you, I will.*

Chapter

21

Rachel stood on the starboard side of the main deck and observed a setting sun that painted an orange-gold shade across the horizon. Nothing was in view except the seemingly endless blue ocean and sky that appeared to touch far beyond them. Savannah and the troubles there were left far behind. The long and lazy days were underway.

She realized Dan had been accurate when he described the *Merry Wind*. She was one hundred ninety feet long, thirty-six feet wide, and five decks deep. Her stern was squared and her stem was gracefully curved. With a keel of solid rock elm, planks of teak, and copper sheathing to prevent barnacles, she was stout and splendid. She could haul eleven hundred tons of cargo, and was faster than a steamer. The sleek three-masted clipper skimmed the water's surface with ease and beauty, riding the waves as a soaring hawk rode air currents. She sliced through swells smoothly, creating no lift and plunge as most other ships did. She did toss an occasional spray, but mostly made a gentle white curl at her bow.

A breeze played through Rachel's long hair and teased mischievously at her skirt-tail. She closed her eyes and inhaled the fresh sea air. She felt serene yet restless, happy yet somber. Getting underway, settling in for the voyage, and doing routine tasks had taken up the day for Captain Daniel Slade, his first mate, and friendly crew. To keep out of their way as they scurried about and to avoid being an intriguing distraction, she had spent most of it in Dan's cabin, admiring its masculine decor and gazing out the numerous mullioned windows across the stern.

She wanted to tell him about her confrontation with Earl Starger, but she didn't want to use him like a vessel into which she poured her troubles and frustrations. It wasn't fair to overburden him when he was so busy with his ship and crew and was concentrating on the threats before them. She wanted to share everything with him, but hadn't he already taken on more than enough of her problems?

As the wind calmed, so did the flapping and fluttering of the many rows of sail that were wider and loftier than those of past designs. She listened as Dan gave orders; she saw how quickly, genially, and efficiently they were carried out by a crew that clearly respected and admired him. She watched men lower and secure sails for the night; she heard the anchor being released, signaling the end of their first day at sea on June third.

Crew members went in several directions, some to eat, some to relax, some to play games, and some to guard duty. Any who passed near her smiled and spoke, and she did the same in return. She hadn't seen the *cubanos* since boarding at Ossabaw Island following their escape. She knew they were using the only spare cabin, which had compelled her to bunk with Dan in his large and comfortable quarters. Dan had grinned when he told her she could use the bed and he would take a swinging hammock, but both knew that sleeping arrangement wouldn't last long. The crew and Luke Conner probably knew the same thing, but she didn't let it worry her.

As dusk closed in, the water took on a pearly gray-blue cast, as did the heaven above it. She hoped Dan would be finished with his captain's duties soon and would join her. She turned to see him striding across the deck toward her. His midnight hair was wind tousled and he was attired in a billowy white shirt, snug black pants, and shiny ebony knee boots. As he sent her a broad smile, she thought of a roguish pirate of days past when they roved the seas and took whatever captured their roaming eye. He was so handsome that he stole her breath and enflamed her body.

"How did you fare today, my love?" he asked in a husky voice that revealed he was just as aroused by the sight of her as she was of him.

"I think I'll make a good sailor."

"I had no doubts about it," he replied with a lazy grin.

"You weren't exaggerating, Dan, she's beautiful and swift."

"Haven't you realized by now that I never choose anything that isn't?"

Rachel smiled. "Thank you for the flattery," she said.

"I never flatter, woman; I speak the truth. I'm glad you stayed below for most of the day so I could concentrate on my work. Watching you here for the last hour has been a terrible strain on me. Several times I was tempted to seize you and carry you to my cabin."

"What would your crew think of a captain with such a weakness?"

"After getting a view of you, my enchantress, they wouldn't blame me. In fact, they probably can't understand how I quelled such an urge."

"What did you tell them about me? About my staying with you?"

"They know it's the only place I could put you, under my personal guard. I told them the truth, that you're to become my wife when we return."

"Dan! You know that's too soon for a recent widow to remarry. But let's discuss that matter at a later date."

"Always putting off the most important decision of our lives," he teased. "How can you keep tormenting me, woman?"

"I'm not. You know what choice I'll eventually make."

"*Eventually*, that's a naughty word."

"You are very demanding and persistent, Captain Slade."

"Sometimes that's the only way to get what you want."

"Is that how I have to behave to get fed tonight? I'm starving. The sea air creates a big appetite."

"For me or food?" he jested with a sly grin.

Knowing voices carried afar, she leaned closer to whisper, "Both."

"Come along, wench," he murmured, grasping her hand and drawing her toward the stern hatchway that led to his cabin.

Dan seated her at a table that was bolted to the floor. He took the chair opposite hers. "Be glad this is a short voyage and we'll have plenty of fresh food. On long ones, meals can get boring and unappetizing. Buelly cooked up his specialty to impress you: beef and vegetable stew, hot biscuits, fruit cobbler, and a bottle of my best wine."

"What do your men eat?"

"The same thing their captain gets. A well-fed and well-treated crew makes a happy and obedient crew."

"A Slade-made proverb?" she teased as she served her plate.

"It's worked so far. No captain or ship has a better crew than me." Dan knew he was fortunate that all his men, except Luke Conner, only knew him as Daniel Slade, not McCandless, so he didn't have to worry about someone making a slip to Rachel before he could explain that ruse. He told himself he shouldn't be upset with her for keeping a secret with good reason when he was doing the same thing. Soon it wouldn't be necessary. Yet he dreaded making that confession, and discovering her reaction.

As they dined, they chatted about ships, his crew, and foreign places he had visited. They were mellow and happy in their private surroundings. Through portholes and the ceiling they heard footsteps or voices above them as men on duty strolled the deck to watch for other ships risking night travel or for unexpected bad weather. They noticed the gentle rocking of the clipper and heard waves lapping at the copper-sheathed hull.

"How long will our trip take?"

"About five to five and a half days. With good winds, she travels fifteen to twenty knots an hour. Most days we'll continue moving for ten hours. If the wind holds and no problems arise, we should make Cuba by Monday night or early Tuesday. We'll stop at Andros Island to take on fresh water. I know of a sheltered pool where we can share a bath."

"That sounds most tempting. Have you used it before?"

"By myself or with male friends, you jealous wench."

"Good. I would hate to use my claws on a female rival," she said playfully.

*

When they finished, Dan loaded the dishes and leftovers onto a tray and put it outside his door so they wouldn't be disturbed later by the cook fetching them. He slid a bolt into place and turned to look at Rachel who was standing before the mullioned windows. He watched how slanted shafts of a three-quarter moon played over her dark hair. He doused the two lamps, allowing only a silvery glow in the room. It provided just enough light to make out the interior of his quarters and to silhouette the entrancing woman with her back to him. Dan walked to Rachel and locked his arms around her waist. He rested his cheek against her silky head.

She sighed dreamily and leaned against him, placing her hands over his. "After only one day, I see why you love this life so much. It's so tranquil but exciting. You have plenty to keep you busy, but not too much to prevent relaxation. It must be wonderful and stimulating to sail around the world seeing magnificent sites and having heady adventures. I could catch your contagious love for the sea and sailing."

"I hope you do, woman. It will be more fun with you along." He turned his head to brush a kiss to her temple and tenderly squeezed her.

Rachel's heart was filled with love and joy. His world wasn't scary after all, no grim threat to her and their relationship. She wanted to learn everything about him. She was ready and eager to take a risk on love. For the first time since childhood, she felt blissfully happy and safe. She twisted in his embrace, and her hands grasped his face. Rising on her tiptoes, she sealed her mouth to his. A fierce and urgent craving for him overwhelmed her.

Dan's arms tightened around her. His mouth meshed with hers. One kiss fused into another and another. His lips left hers to tease over her face.

Rachel leaned her head back to allow him to continue a stirring trek down her throat. Her fingers grasped the billowy shirt and worked it free of his pants and belt. She slipped her hands beneath it and caressed his hard chest. They moved over curly hair and honed muscles. They journeyed around his sides and up his back. She flattened her palms on the sleek surface and pressed him closer to her. Hungry to taste his flesh, her mouth trailed kisses over his neck. She heard him groan in arousal, and felt the proof of it between her hips.

When she parted them to discard her blouse and chemise, he quickly yanked off his shirt. They embraced, bringing their bare flesh into contact.

Dan used movements of his furry chest to stimulate her already taut nipples as he kissed her with unleashed passion. As their tongues played a heady mating game, Dan shifted his position to cup one breast and tantalize its peak. Rachel's hand roamed to the hardness in his trousers; through the material, she ran her fingers up and down its length. She heard him groan again, and thrilled to how much he wanted her.

Her bold fingers worked with his belt buckle. When it was conquered, she undid the fasteners of his pants and wriggled the garment below his firm buttocks. She captured and stroked his throbbing manhood. Her loving hand did not calm him; instead it made him more anxious to be within her. She released the sleekness of him only long enough to unbutton and drop her skirt, which she kicked aside. Without removing her pantalets, she spread the slit in the crotch with one hand and guided him toward her moistness with the other.

Dan grasped her seductive intention. He lifted her body, entered her, and held her in place by her buttocks as she rode him in a near frenzy to reach her destination. He was almost dazed by her unrestrained action and feared he couldn't hold back his pleading release for long. He spread kisses over her hair and face as she rocked upon his fiery manhood.

Rachel's legs were locked around Dan's hips. She tightened and relaxed them as she controlled this lovemaking session. The position rubbed and stimulated the bud of her womanhood. Even when she was breathless and fatiguing, she couldn't halt her movements. She was overpowered by the need to have him fast and now. It seemed like forever since she had feasted on his body, even though it had been only a few days. She rode him swift and hard until she was rewarded by an explosive release to her steamy journey. She writhed against his flesh, moaning in ecstasy and kissing him any place she could reach. "I love you, Dan, I love you," she murmured in the throes of passionate bliss, followed by noises of feverish abandonment and pleasure.

Dan began to spill his victory into her body, sheer rapture making him feel weak and shaky. As he finished, he walked her to the bed without breaking their tight hold on each other. He thrust a few more times to finish dousing the flaming torch. He was breathing rapidly, but his muscles were no longer tense. He felt limp, sated beyond belief. He withdrew from her and rolled to his side, carrying her along with him. He hugged her tightly. "Stars above, woman, that was wonderful. Absolutely amazing," he said as he exhaled between slightly parted lips. "I love you, Rachel McCandless. You drive me wild."

"I love you, too, Daniel Slade."

When she repeated what she had confessed earlier in mindless passion, Dan shifted to let his gaze pierce the shadows to view her face. It was too dim to see much, and he wished he had left one lantern or a candle burning. He wanted to see her expression as she admitted the truth at last, when he could hear it and she was conscious of what she was saying.

Rachel grasped what he was doing. She rolled to the bedside table. Using the safety matches there, she lit a candle, then returned to lie beside Dan. She locked her gaze to his and said, "I love you. Did you need to see my eyes to know I'm telling the truth?" she teased him and bit him gently.

"I've known it was true a long time, but I wanted to be looking at you when you finally admitted it. This means you'll marry me, right?"

She lightly bit him again. "Weren't you listening when I told you I might not be able to have children? Luke says you want them, and probably soon."

"*Might* is the magic word, love."

Rachel frowned and rolled to her back. "No, magic is hot fantasy; I'm talking about cold reality. Maybe no children, no heir, ever."

Dan half covered her naked body with his. He stressed, "*Maybe*, Rachel; it isn't a fact. You could be carrying my child this very moment," he ventured and caressed her lower abdomen.

Rachel captured his hand and halted its movement. "And I could never carry your child. Be realistic and honest, Dan. You know it's important to you. Don't fool yourself with wishful hopes. This could be another burden I'll have to bear. I can't let it weigh you down, too."

"Children or no children, I want you to be my wife."

She looked at the ceiling. "Now, but what about later?"

"I'd rather have you without heirs than to have heirs without you."

Her soulful gaze returned to his entreating one. "I'll make you a deal: I'll marry you as soon as I become pregnant. I must prove my fertility before we wed."

Dan tensed in worry. "But what if you're right?"

"If I am, we'll see if that changes our feelings and relationship. Better to test them before we commit than afterward. Right?"

"I don't like making bargains with my future, with my love."

"Think of how much fun you'll have trying to win me," she murmured as she nibbled at his lips and stroked his reviving manhood. "There's only one way to get me pregnant, remember?"

Dan spread kisses over her face and vowed, "If that's the only way to win you, woman, I'll work day and night on my task."

"I'll do all I can to help you succeed," she said, grinning.

*

Friday afternoon, Rachel stood on the forecastle deck of the clipper and chatted with the handsome *cubano*. She had told Dan of her assumption it was better to make a friend and ally of Carlos Torres than to treat him as an enemy. With reluctance, her lover had agreed. She knew Dan was observing them from the stern near the steering wheel. She tried to act poised and friendly, but she was apprehensive. "Tell me about your country and rebellion," she coaxed with a smile.

Carlos gazed across the ocean. He was unusually amiable as he explained. "She lives in glorious splendor, as you do, Raquel. Part of her is mountainous, but most of her is . . . plains and basins. She is one big island with *muchos niños*, babies. She provides a third of the world's sugar; but also fruit, *café*, and timber. The Central Valley where I am from is important; it is where much of our sugarcane, *café*, cattle, and timber is raised. When we anchor in Bahía de Nipe and go ashore, you will see for yourself how lovely she is."

Rachel leaned forward and propped her forearms on the railing to steady her balance. Although the brilliant sun was at their backs, she squinted from the glare off the water as the *Merry Wind* knifed through the windswept sea. "What about your people? What are they like?"

"Our people are farmers and fishermen, peasants and landowners. Most are *Criollos* whites born there. The rest are *Mestizos,* of Indian and Spanish mix, *Mulatos*—of Negro and Spanish mix, and *Amarillos*—Chinese. Slavery has not been abolished, but trade in flesh was terminated many years ago. *Mejicano* Indians and *Chinos* were . . . indentured to fill that loss. Most are *Católicos;* others—*Africanos*—are Santeria. We arrive before *huracán* season next month, but you get wet *muchos* times; it is our rainy season."

Rachel realized the closer they came to Cuba, the more Carlos Torres drifted toward his native language; yet, she grasped the gist of it.

"You will meet our leader and band of *rebeldes,* rebels. Our war cry is *'No hay nada más importante que la libertad,'* which means, 'Nothing is more important than freedom.' *Pronto,* you will see why we would kill for guns to free our land and people."

"Tell me now so I'll understand when we get there," she urged.

"You thirst to know *muchos* things, Raquel."

"If you were heading to a country where you didn't know the people, language, and customs, wouldn't you be the same way?"

"Sí. Ricardo was *mi maestro,* my teacher."

"If he knows so much about us, why wasn't he sent on this mission?"

"El es la mano derecha de Ramón," he said, shaking his right hand to make his point.

Right-hand man, she mentally translated. "Ramón is your leader?"

Carlos did not answer that question. "Your country is our biggest trade partner. She is our ally, but she fears to challenge the Madre Tierra and its ruler, King Alfonso XII; he is the son of Isabella and has ruled for ten years. The war began long before he came to power; we have battled for independence for eight years. We will continue to fight until we are free *hombres.* They tax us and control us as dogs or burros on ropes. They are *corruptores* and they let us say nothing in the *cortes* and *audiencias."*

When he paused, she asked, "What do those words mean?"

"Parliament and High Courts. They order their *soldados* to be brutal to control and cower us. We asked for *americana* help, but it has not come. El Presidente Grant and war leader *Señor* Belknap resist our pleas for help. Your government does not stop us from getting arms and supplies, but it has not offered or provided them. *Uno día* she will," he said with confidence.

Rachel straightened and faced him. "How did this rebellion start?"

"The eastern provinces banded together under Carlos Manuel de Céspedes, a wealthy planter. When the Orient Province declared independence in October of 1868, the battles began. *El Grito de Yara* was heard across the land: 'The cry of Yara.' Landowners want . . . economic and political freedoms; the farmers and workers want slavery abolished and political freedom for *todo el mundo.* De Céspedes freed every slave who would join the fighting. The Nationalist *líder* is a Black commander named Antonio Maceo. Our band follows his instruction. The soldiers of the government we battle are savage, but you will be safe in our *campo."*

"I hope so, Carlos, and I hope you win your independence."

"You are kind, Raquel, *una mujer valiente y lista."*

At the man's adoring expression, she did not ask him to translate his last few words. He had used the Spanish form of her name many times with a husky tone that worried her. She hoped he didn't think she was flirting with him. Surely Carlos knew she was the captain's woman. As she thought of herself surrounded soon by rugged and earthy rebels in a sultry jungle, she had to struggle not to panic or shudder in dread.

"You worry about something, Raquel."

"It's just the heat. I've been under the hot sun too long. If you'll excuse me, I'll go to my cabin and rest. It's been nice talking with you like this. We'll do it again before we reach your island."

"*Con mucho gusto,*" he responded, grinning at the flush on her cheeks that he did not believe was the result of the tropical sun.

"Good-bye," she said, and left the appealing *cubano* staring after her.

"*Hasta luego, llama de mi corazón,*" he murmured to himself, as the enchanting female truly did ignite a flame in his heart that called for her possession.

*

A little over three hours after setting sail Saturday morning, Luke Conner came to Dan's cabin. "The Grand Bahama Island is off the port side. It's miles away, but you can see it on the horizon. Care to take a peek?"

"Are those Cubans on deck?"

"Yes. Why? Are you having problems with them?"

Rachel frowned and sighed heavily. "Not exactly, but I think Torres is enamored of me. It might be best to avoid him today. You don't think there'll be trouble in their camp, do you?"

"Yes, but I'm hoping it can be settled quickly with their leader."

"Why don't we just drop the crates and those two and leave?"

"As soon as they opened them and discovered the shortage, with no explanation from us, they'd be after us before sunset. Other lives are at stake."

Rachel recalled the Cuban's threat toward her family and friends, and those toward her partners; so more than her own life was in jeopardy. If she didn't believe that, she wouldn't take this risk. "You're right, Luke. I just don't want Dan, the crew, and this ship endangered because of me."

"You love him deeply, don't you?" he asked in a serious tone.

She noticed that for once he didn't have his perpetual grin teasing across his handsome face. "Yes."

"So why are you afraid to marry him?"

She and Luke had become close friends during the days he had guarded her at Moss Haven and during the last week together. She liked and trusted Dan's first mate. Luke had a sincere air about him. She desperately needed to talk to someone who could understand her predicament and give good advice.

"Why don't we sit down and chat?" he encouraged. "I'm off duty."

Rachel's weary soul and restless heart responded to his kindness and warmth. She took a chair, and Luke pulled the other one around to sit near her. "It's all so confusing and frightening. I'm scared, Luke, scared of something happening to Dan if I marry him. I'm scared I can't have children, and he wants them. He's endangered himself so many times to help and protect me. I could get him killed here or back home. I would die if that happened. I love him and need him so much it panics me."

"Why, Rachel? Don't you realize love is a precious and rare gift?"

"I don't know how much Dan's told you about me or how much you learned while investigating me . . . ." she began, giving him a wry smile. "But there's much more involved. I don't know where to begin."

"Tell me the whole story; we have plenty of time. Maybe I can help. Maybe you and Dan are too close to the situation to be objective."

"I don't think anyone can help." Slowly and with anguish, she related her history to him. She paused only a moment before she revealed her deepest fears and Earl Starger's last visit at the hotel. "What if he wasn't lying, Luke? What if I am guilty of all those horrible deeds? What if I . . ."

The brown-haired man grasped her hands in his. With confidence in his azure gaze, he said, "You aren't crazy or guilty, Rachel."

There was anguish in her tone and expression as she refuted, "But—"

"No buts," he gently interrupted, tapping her lips with a forefinger. He wiped away a tear that had escaped her luminous eyes. "No madness and no guilt, woman. Trust me; I know you by now. He was wrong or lying."

"If he wasn't, Dan's life will be in danger."

"You could never harm Dan, just as he could never harm you. Love him and marry him, Rachel; you won't be sorry."

"Are you going to tell him about this talk? He'll wonder what's been keeping you down here so long."

"It isn't my place. You will, when the time is right."

They both stood and Rachel hugged him. "Thank you, Luke. You're a good friend to both of us."

"Any time you need a shoulder to lean on, mine's available."

*

Hours later, as the sun was setting in glorious splendor, they anchored near Andros Island—the largest of the Bahama chain—to take on fresh water. They would remain there until the morning tide. As Dan had promised, he took her ashore to the concealed pool for a quick bath and stroll.

The island was forested with Caribbean pine and hardwoods called "coppices," and woody vegetation of shrubs and vines. Earlier they had sighted a few fishing and farming villages a few miles upshore, but this area was unpopulated. The climate was perfect.

Rachel and Dan walked across a sandy beach holding hands. He led her into cool greenness that quickly encompassed them. She smelled heady fragrances. The only life they saw was frogs, lizards, birds, and small rodents.

When they reached the sunken pool, Rachel smiled. The turquoise water was shallow; it came from somewhere in the impenetrable forest.

"There's another one not far away; that's where the men will go to get fresh water for the remainder of our voyage and catch a fast cleaning."

"It's lovely, Dan, so *romántico*." She glanced at him suggestively.

He caught her sensual hint, shook his head with a grin, and said, "We best hurry; it'll be very dark in here soon. We can't linger."

As evening shadows closed in, they hurriedly bathed and left the cozy location. In his cabin, Rachel revealed her talk with Luke Connor this morning. Dan understood her fears, and told her the same thing Luke had. As if to prove how much he trusted her, he made passionate love to her.

*

Sunday, Rachel had another talk with Torres. She hoped and prayed it would help save their lives. "There's something I should tell you, Carlos. I don't have the entire order with me."

His dark eyes looked quizzical. "You have tricked me?"

"Not exactly, and please don't be angry. Let me explain. Your payment hasn't been found yet, so I had to come up with the cash to buy these arms and ammunition. Harrison Clements wouldn't let me have any without payment first, but the others are ready. George trusted me to pay him later for the ammunition, and he sent the entire order; it's aboard."

"What good are bullets without rifles, Señora Rachel?"

"I have six thousand. That's all the money I could come up with; I swear it, Carlos." Rachel explained in detail the financial misfortune that had befallen her. "Dan's helped all he could," she finished, "he's shipping the order free, and he paid for most of the arms. I thought this much of the order was better than nothing. The only things that saved me were Dan's generosity and not having to pay George for the ammunition. The company books were destroyed, so there's no record of my debt. I promise to keep searching for your payment. I swear, if I find it, I'll send the rest of your order. More than you ordered, to help your cause and to repay your kindness and patience. That's all I can do."

"It will not please *el lider*. He will not believe you."

"It's the truth. If you weren't threatening my family and friends, I would throw the crates ashore and disappear. No, I would have dumped this problem in yours and Harry's laps. I only came here to reason with your leader. I realized you didn't have the power to change the deal."

"*El lider* will not change it. We need those arms, Señora Rachel."

"We're no longer *amigos*? It's back to 'Señora Rachel.' If this will get you into trouble, Carlos, I'm sorry. You did your duty and trusted me."

"You must do your duty, or others will suffer. I will not be the one sent to . . . persuade you and your partner to give us what we bought."

"Please help me explain to your leader," she beseeched. "I've done all I can. Doesn't that count for anything?"

"Only victory matters, and lives in my country and in yours."

Tears welled in her honey-colored eyes and she struggled hard not to cry. She chewed on her upper lip to make the pain distract her from that "feminine weakness." She searched her brain for an escape route. In an emotion-constricted voice, she asked, "Will your leader give me time to sell my home to raise the rest of the money for your arms? That's the only thing I have left worth anything. It'll take time to find a buyer. If I rush a sale, the buyer will know I'm desperate and will offer little. I need a hundred twenty thousand dollars to get the other four thousand rifles and dynamite."

"Why does Señor Clements not help you?"

"Because he thinks I have the money and thinks that when I'm terrified enough, I'll turn it over to him. He says he didn't have anything to do with Phillip's deal, so he isn't using his money to pay for it. He's also furious about the company being set afire and a worker killed. He hired guards for the company and his home to protect them against another attack from you and Joaquín. He claims he isn't afraid of your threats."

"*Aja!* We did not do those things, Raquel. Señor Leathers could not; he was dead. If you did not, he has lied to you. He must honor the deal; he said this in the *documento* I took to *mi lider*, as did Señor Leathers. All three gave their word; they agreed to let Señor McCandless take the dollars and deliver the order. If you have paid for all we carry, Señor Clements is the only *hombre* to make *dinero* on this."

Rachel was vexed. "Why didn't you tell me this before?"

"I did not know you did not know. Señor Clements met with Ricardo on the isle of Bimini the week before your *esposo* died."

So that was why Harry had such a golden tan so early in the year! "I thought Phillip was the only one who knew about the deal."

Carlos shook his dark head. "He said he wished to increase the order and would sell us the next one at a . . . cheaper price. Ramón said we would do so when we get more *dinero americano.*"

"Has Harry been to Cuba? Has he met your leader?"

"No. He contacted Ricardo through de Céspedes. Ramón sent him to the meeting; Joaquín and I were in your country with your *esposo.*"

"So," she reasoned aloud, "Harry learned from Ricardo that Phillip had the entire million dollars. He came to force it out of Phillip, but Phillip must have been angry with him for going to Ramón behind his back. Phillip was already suspicious of Harry cheating him on other orders." To sway him in her favor, she quickly used the ruse she had fabricated at the beginning of this mystery to solve it. "That's why Phillip hid the money and wouldn't give it to Harry and George. He was holding on to it to make certain nothing happened to it. But where did he hide it? I've searched everywhere. My heavens! What if Harry saw where Phillip concealed it when he came to visit the day before Phillip died? What if Harry's had it all along? What if he murdered Phillip? How deeply was George Leathers involved?"

Carlos paid close attention. "He agreed to make and sell us the bullets. He signed the *documento,* but it had no names. If your *esposo* did not tell him about us, he did not know who we are or where the order is going."

"That's good, because I liked and trusted him. I'll bet Harry killed George to keep him silent and to keep from having to pay him. All this time Harry's been behind the threats and attacks to scare me into paying for this order. He's probably planning to kill me when I return so there'll be no witnesses to his involvement." She told Carlos about the notes she'd received in her handwriting. "He's hired someone to forge my script; he'll probably use it to write a suicide note so everyone will think I killed Phillip, took the money, was behind all those other crimes, and then killed myself out of madness and guilt. If his evil plot worked, he would be rich and safe from the law and from your people. But he won't succeed!"

When Carlos remained silent and watchful, Rachel ventured, "If his name is on the contract, he's responsible for supplying arms, too. Force him to give you the rest of them. I've done my part. Besides, you told me there wasn't a written contract. If I had known all of this earlier, I could have solved this perilous mystery sooner. Why did you lie to me, Carlos?"

"There is a paper, but it says *nada* you can use. Ramón buried it to keep it secret. It tells that our order was placed and for how much *dinero.* All *tres hombres* signed it. Your *esposo* signed again when he was given the *dinero.*"

"You must convince Ramón to give it to me. I can use it to prove Harry was involved with full knowledge of where the arms were going. Ricardo can give me a signed statement he met with Harry in Bimini."

"*No es posible.* Our deal must remain a secret. It is *urgente.*"

"Without evidence, Harry will get away with all he's done to us!"

"It is for Ramón to decide what is to be done. He will not be pleased at being tricked and betrayed."

"Then help me convince him Harry is the traitorous culprit."

Carlos glued his unreadable gaze to her pleading one. "I can only tell him what you have told me; that does not make it true."

"My name isn't on the agreement, so I'm not responsible."

Carlos pointed out, *"El nombre de su esposo* is, and he had the *dinero.* That is how Ramón will see it. *Qué lástima!"*

"If there's trouble in your camp, convince your leader to punish me, not the others. Let them leave unharmed. Agreed?"

"I can make no *promesas* for Ramón. It is his *decisión."*

*

It was nearing dusk on Monday when Bahía de Nipe, their anchoring sight, was approached. They had sailed within view of Cuba with her inlets, rugged cliffs, sandy beaches, and islets for hours. The hills and mountains of Sierra de Nipe and Sierra del Cristal loomed before them. The tropical air was balmy, and heady fragrances wafted on its currents. Along the irregular coastline, they had seen cultivated areas near the shore, light-green splotches surrounded by dark jade; the terrain had drifted into woods of valuable exotic timber, fruit trees, feathery palms, and mangrove thickets. It continued into fertile valleys and lush rain forests, Carlos told them.

Where the anchor was lowered at their rendezvous point, there were areas of short or no beachline between the ocean and verdant jungle. The water lapping at the hull was a purply blue, which became turquoise near the coast. The bay where they would land in a small boat was sided on the left and right with rocks, against which waves pounded and sent off white sprays.

"We will camp *aqui,"* Carlos pointed to the beach, "while Joaquín brings my people to get the arms. He will not return until *mañana.* You and Raquel will camp with me; no other *hombres* will leave the ship."

Dan tried to argue in an attempt to leave his love in safety and comfort, but Carlos refused to listen and agree. "She comes with us. *No argumento."*

As the boat was rowed to shore by Dan and Carlos, threatening gray clouds hovered above the mountainous region. They passed over coral reefs of various shapes, sizes, and colors. Rachel saw fish darting amidst the rugged and beautiful formations, and pointed them out to the others. Dan took a peek, but the two Cuban rebels did not.

The men dragged the boat ashore, and Dan helped Rachel get out. Their shoes sank into soft ecru sand. Carlos spoke with Joaquín in Spanish. The brutish rebel replied at certain points, nodded several times, and departed. He was swallowed almost immediately by the lush greenery.

Twilight closed in as they settled down for the evening. Rachel's gaze roamed the terrain that was a fusion of vivid colors and intoxicating smells. Bougainvillea climbed trees and hillsides to decorate them with red, purple, and white blossoms. Lacy frangipani in many shades added beauty to the setting. Other tropical plants, shrubs, vines, and trees were abundant in a wild array of enchantment. Rachel was eager for dawn's light to let her gaze feast on the alluring landscape, but dreaded what the day would bring.

*

A hand shook Rachel's shoulder as she slept on her stomach, dark hair concealing her face. She stirred, turned, and looked at its owner. Her gaze widened in disbelief as she discovered the identity of the "only hope" Phillip had mentioned. The American rebel gaped at her in the same manner, scowled in anger, then pressed a finger to his lips for secrecy.

Chapter

22

"You are Señora Phillip McCandless?" he asked loud enough to be heard by others on the beach.

Rachel stared at him as she replied, "His widow; Phillip is dead."

"I am Ricardo," the twenty-three-year-old man said. "I will translate for you. Ramón does not speak *inglés.*"

"You're American," Rachel said evocatively.

"*Sí,* but I have been many months with my *amigos. Venga,* come."

"May I . . . be excused first?"

The man with shoulder-grazing dark-brown hair and matching eyes turned and asked permission in fluent Spanish to grant her request for privacy. Ricardo faced her again and said, "It is fine, but hurry. Ramón is anxious to discuss the trouble between our sides."

Rachel stood and straightened her skirt. She looked at the roughly clad Cuban rebels, most with lengthy hair and short beards. Dan sat on the ground with his hands tied behind his back; he sent her a smile. Rachel's mind was too dazed to react. On shaky legs, she vanished into concealing trees to recover her wits and poise while she excused herself. She couldn't understand why Phillip had kept such a valuable secret. Anger and resentment toward her deceased husband resurfaced.

Rachel fingercombed her disheveled hair as she approached the large group of intimidating men who were studying her with keen interest. She wished she were more presentable and clear-headed for this vital meeting. She looked at Carlos, "Did you tell him everything I told you?" she asked him.

"*Sí,* Raquel, but he is *mucho* angry. The *rebelión* does not go well. Spanish soldiers attack and kill our *amigos.* We need the arms, and *pronto.*"

She looked at the man Carlos Torres nodded at. He appeared broody and truculent, his eyes as dark as his long and wavy black hair, and they were glacial and piercing. She trembled in dread.

With a deeply lined scowl and gruff voice, the rebel leader spoke to Ricardo, who nodded understanding and focused on Rachel.

"Ramón asks if you *comprende* how *importante* the arms are. He wants to know why you have tricked and betrayed him."

"I haven't, but it's a long story." As she explained the predicament from the beginning, Ricardo observed her and translated. She answered honestly the questions Ramón passed through his American friend and ally. She knew it was safest and wisest for her to be completely honest. When the talk ended, she watched Ramón pace and think. She tried to keep her hungry gaze from feasting on Daniel Slade—or on her brother!

Rachel was filled with a mixture of joy and sadness, of confusion and enlightenment. Richard had grown to over six feet; he was lean and hard and muscular. His olive complexion had been darkened by the tropical sun. He had become more handsome over the six years since she had last seen or heard from him. She wondered if he knew where his twin sister was, as Rosemary had ran away a year later. She yearned to hug him, to ask him countless questions, but he had warned her to secrecy of their kinship. To expose it could endanger her brother and further imperil her.

As if he didn't know the beautiful woman, Richard "Ricardo" Fleming ignored his sister. If he had known she was Phillip McCandless's wife, he wouldn't have gotten her enmeshed in this scheme gone sour, a scheme he himself had suggested. How could he get Rachel out of this mess and safely back to Georgia when Ramón wanted to kill her as a threat to the double-crossing Harrison?

The leader came to Richard and talked to him for a while. Rachel got the impression Ramón was asking his trusted friend's opinion of the matter and of her. She waited with rising anxiety until her brother turned to speak.

"Ramón says the *rebelión* is growing in strength and fierceness. He says he must have the rest of the arms so his *hombres* can battle for their lives and freedom. Without them, our cause can be lost. He says you must come to our camp until he decides what to do. You and the *capitán.*"

"Why can't we talk and decide here . . . ? Is he going to kill us?" Rachel asked in alarm. She didn't want to get far from the ship or be trapped in the jungle in unfamiliar surroundings and between opposing forces.

"If the ship is sighted, we cannot be near it. Our *hombres* will unload the crates and hide them nearby. We will return for them later."

"You didn't answer my question. Is he going to kill us?"

"I do not know. *He* does not know yet. Stay calm and quiet."

Rachel caught the subtle warning in his last sentence. She also noticed how her brother concealed his emotions with skill and perfection. She was amazed by how much he had changed. If it came to a choice between her life and his loyalty to the *cubanos,* which would he choose? Considering the odds against them, Richard didn't have a choice.

"You must understand we can not trust a stranger in wartime."

Rachel seized the clue "stranger" that said to continue their ruse. "Your friends were with me when I tried to save this deal. Killing us won't get you the rest of the arms. You'll only be helping Harry get rid of us. If anyone has your money, it's him. I would not lie to you," she vowed, her gaze fused with her brother's.

Without visible reaction, Ricardo told her words to Ramón Ortega.

Carlos chatted with his leader. It was obvious he was arguing on her behalf and just as obvious that he vexed Ramón. He looked at her and said, "I am sorry, Raquel, he will not listen to me. He says I am bewitched by you."

She thanked Carlos for trying. "What now?" she asked.

"Sit while we unload the crates," Richard ordered. "We must hurry before soldiers come and attack. Our lookouts say they are not in this area today, but they might approach undetected by sea."

Rachel joined Dan, but they didn't have time to talk, for her love was released just then to escort the Cubans to his ship to fetch the arms and ammunition.

Richard glanced at her to warn her not to try to escape. *"La junglas* is a dangerous place," he said, "and you will be shot. If you are hungry, eat while we work. That would be wise, as we have a long walk after when we finish."

"Do I have to sit here for hours in the sun or can I move around?"

"As long as you do not run away, do as you please."

"Thank you, Ricardo."

"De nada," he replied, a tiny gleam of a smile in his eyes.

"Vámonos, amigos! Dénse prisa!" Ramon shouted for some of the men to get moving and to hurry with their task.

Rachel walked to the shade of the swaying palms and leaned against one. She watched the small group get into Dan's boat and head for his ship. The others sat on the sand and chatted, occasionally glancing at her. She shielded her eyes against the blazing sun and observed their trip to the *Merry Wind*. She saw her love, her brother, and the rebels climb aboard. Rachel knew Dan had been warned to make no trouble or she would be slain.

*

Time seemed to move at a snail's pace as two boats went back and forth between the coast and the ship to unload the cargo. The men on the beach worked steadily as they carried the long rifle crates and small cartridge cases into the dense jungle for conceal-ment and later retrieval.

When the task was done, Luke and three seamen were ordered to take the boats to the ship to await Ramón's decision. The first mate looked at his captain with uncer-tainty and worry. Dan told his best friend to obey. With him and Rachel in the control of the rebels the crew couldn't risk a rescue battle or get enough men ashore in a group to fight one before taking heavy losses. The boats shoved off and returned to the *Merry Wind* to keep eyes alert for possible assistance with a daring escape.

Two Cubans were left behind to make certain Dan's crew didn't follow the others to attempt a foolish rescue. Before they settled down beneath shady palms, the beach and path were brushed clean of telltale tracks.

The trek to the rebel camp began. Cubans walked in front of and behind the captives, and several took positions beyond and to the rear of the group as lookouts. Ramón Ortega was close to the front of the column on the well-trodden dirt path; Richard journeyed at his side without glancing at his sister. Carlos was assigned to guard Rachel, and Joaquín was farther back with a bound Dan.

The trail ascended into hills and *sierras* of lush vegetation. The terrain was rug-gedly beautiful in its striking wildness. They crossed a savannah where cattle grazed on *paraná* grass. They saw coconut, payaba, banana, mango, cieba, palm, ebony, and mangrove, its roots above ground. Carlos told Rachel that most of their soil was fertile and could be cultivated year round. She noticed that bougainvilla and frangipani were abundant in many areas, sending forth a pleasurably intense fragrance.

They skirted *aldeas,* villages, in clearings where ground stolen from the ever-encroaching jungle was cluttered with *chozas*—shacks, huts, and mud-daubed wattles with thatched roofs of grass or palm branches. Carlos whispered the inhabitants were *guajiros,* peasants. The excitingly different landscape was verdant and dense. Vines climbed trees and hillsides, many varieties in splendid bloom. Ferns along the path teased at their legs and shoes. Rays of sunlight filtered through unfamiliar trees with thick foliage that was several shades of green and formed a canopy above them. They used a wooden footbridge at one river, to cross. At another point of the river's winding course, they forded at a shallow spot.

The leader halted them there for a rest and water break. Everyone sat on the ground, but kept silent in the vulnerable location.

Rachel couldn't see Dan because of the many men between them, but knew he hadn't caused his churlish guard any problem. She was glad she was in good physical condition, but the long walk in the tropical climate was tiring. She was also glad she had changed into pants, shirt, and boots to make the trek easier. She watched Ramón Ortega from beneath lowered lashes. His body and expression were taut with suspense and attention. The leader's eyes were in constant motion as they scanned for trouble. She had noticed how brittle and cold they were, and wondered what had made him into such a bellicose man. Perhaps years of fighting had changed him. Ramón couldn't possibly have been this way always, or her brother wouldn't be his friend and ally. Yet, what did she know about the kind of man Richard Fleming was today?

She observed how Richard stayed close to the leader, as if his bodyguard and adviser. She yearned to speak privately with her brother. She wondered at his reactions to their unexpected reunion and her peril, but Carlos halted her speculations, as he helped her to her feet, to continue the trek.

Butterflies and other insects darted among exotic blossoms. Birds were numerous and colorful and noisy, including tiny bee hummers and royal thrushes. Carlos pointed out several brilliantly shaded parrots. She noted the humidity had increased to rain-forest level, sultry, but not oppressive. She had seen small animals—lizards, frogs, spiders, and a rodent Carlos called a *hutía,* which he said was edible. She wondered when they would reach the encampment and how big it was. She knew, from the changing angles of the sun, that they didn't take a direct route to it, so she didn't know how far they were from the coast and the ship. Nor could she guess how to return to them if she and Dan escaped. She had tried to pay attention to their trail for later use, but it was too—

"We rest *aquí,*" Carlos interrupted her thoughts.

A waterfall seemingly burst forth in a rush of white liquid from the dark interior of the jungle and cascaded into a pool of bluish green. Trees, some with long brown pods or exposed roots, cloaked the shoulders of the lovely area. On three sides, tropical flowers and shrubs grew in abundance. Lacy ferns, moss, and lichen in greens and yellows covered banks and rocks of assorted sizes. Sunlight came through an opening in the leafy canopy above the pool, creating a goldish glow. The experienced fighters sat down and sipped from canteens, on alert with rifles across their laps.

"It's beautiful, Carlos. May I wash my face and hands?"

"*Sí,*" he said, and assisted her over rocks to a solid spot near the pool.

Rachel knelt at the edge, wetting the knees of her pants. She cupped her hands, scooped up water, and drank until her thirst was quenched. She used a handkerchief Carlos gave her to refresh her face. "That feels wonderful," she murmured. She wished she were alone with Daniel Slade in this romantic and intimate setting. It would be wonderful and arousing to swim naked and make love here. "How much farther to your camp?"

"One hour," he replied.

"Do you have more men there?"

"*Sí, muchos.*"

"Do you think Ramón is softening any toward us?"

"Do not ask questions I cannot answer, but do not be afraid."

She assumed he was under orders not to reveal anything to her. "*Gracias.* You've been very kind. May I take Dan a drink?" Carlos nodded. Rachel took the canteen he handed to her. She filled it with fresh water and walked to where Dan sat, with Carlos trailing her. She squatted before her love and smiled as she tipped the canteen to his mouth.

Dan's eyes never left her lovely and flushed face while he drank. When he nudged the container with his chin to indicate he was finished, she removed it. He watched her soak a handkerchief and wash perspiration from his face. It felt wonderful to his sweaty flesh. He smiled when she fingercombed his touseled ebony hair. "I'm a mess, eh?" he asked, happy to have her near to him.

"Not bad," she replied with a grin. "Do you have to keep his hands tied?" She asked Carlos. "With me in danger, he won't try to escape."

"It is an order from Ramón."

"Will you ask—"

"No, Raquel; it is not wise to anger him more."

"It's all right, Rachel; the rope isn't too uncomfortable."

"I don't like his being helpless in case we run into Spanish soldiers," she told Carlos. "There's a war going on here."

"Just keep a calm head on your shoulders; I'll be fine."

She looked at her love. "They have no right to treat us like this."

"Give Ramón time to cool off and think," Dan encouraged. "He has to realize the best thing to do is free us to get the other guns."

"He seems too cold and stubborn to make a truce. He won't trust us."

"What about Phillip's hints?" he reminded. "Will they help?"

Rachel chose her words with care. "I understand, but it won't work. Phillip kept too many secrets, more than we've discovered so far."

Dan perceived a clue in her words, but couldn't grasp its meaning. He wondered if it had to do with the American at Ramón's side. It didn't seem likely, as the two hadn't shown any recognition of each other.

"We must go," Carlos told the couple.

Rachel stood and Dan got to his feet. They exchanged one more smile before they took their places in the human column on the well-worn trail.

*

It was dusk when they reached the end of their journey, but enough daylight was left to reveal it was a large camp that spread out into several nature-made clearings. To the captive couple, it looked as if around a thousand men and at least fifty women made up the band. Food was cooking over low campfires whose smoke didn't seem sufficient to give away their location. The Cuban rebels were busy with evening chores and activities. The men cleaned weapons of various kinds, and most wore machetes and knives at their waists. Some chatted, some gambled, some smoked cigars, and others rested from scouting treks. There were a few lean-tos and tents, but most areas had only sleeping mats of banana or palm branches. Cloth sacks near those makeshift beds held the men's possessions. Despite the number of people and work in progress, the area wasn't noisy.

Rachel and Dan were placed at Ramón Ortega's campsite. The leader and "Ricardo" sat down to be served a meal by a lovely beauty with dark, flowing hair and expressive brown eyes. Her revealing looks and behavior toward the leader told Dan and Rachel that she was Ramón's woman.

Rosaria handed the couple metal plates with black beans, chicken, rice, and fried plantains. She passed them cups of strong *café cubano*.

The prisoners were ignored as everyone ate, and the two men talked in Spanish. Rosaria sat near Ramón, but didn't join the conversation. When they finished, she gathered the dishes and cups and left to wash them. One of the returning rebels came and spoke with *el lider*, who looked as if the news he received was infuriating. He sent Rachel a fierce scowl that made her tremble and conclude things weren't going well for his cause. Tomas kept pointing northward as he spoke swiftly with excitement.

Richard looked concerned and angered. "I'm going to talk with Ramón," he said to his sister. "Don't try anything foolish or you'll be killed. You're in greater danger from Spanish soldiers than from us, so stay put. This trouble has to be resolved fast and now."

Dan watched the tall and handsome man leave with the rebel leader, then disappear into the forest together. "Do you know who he is?"

Rachel looked at him and nodded. "My brother, Richard Fleming."

Dan gaped at her. "But you told me you didn't—"

Pressed for private response time, Rachel interrupted, "I didn't know he was here, and it came as a shock. He signaled me to silence when he woke me this morning. I don't know if he can get us out of this mess, but he'll try; I'm sure of it."

"Is that what you meant about Phillip keeping more secrets?"

"Yes. Carlos said Ricardo suggested the arms deal. They checked all three partners. Harry met with my brother on Bimini Island, remember? Phillip and Harry had to know I'm his sister, and maybe those Cubans did, too."

"Then why did they threaten you, and why are you a prisoner?"

Confused, she speculated, "Richard must not have been told I was Phillip's wife. He looked shocked to see me. Maybe, when the investigations were done, Carlos and Joaquín didn't make the connection or mention revealing names. Maybe they don't know Ricardo's real identity."

"You think that's what Richard is telling Ramón now?"

Rachel glanced in the direction they had gone. "I guess it depends on how close they are. Richard suggested the deal, and the alleged traitor turns out to be his sister! How will that look to Ramón and his band? Maybe exposing our relationship would be more damaging than helpful.

"Any time," she fretted, "he could be a prisoner like us. I don't want him killed just when I find him again. I haven't seen him since '69. There's so much I want to ask him and tell him. I wish we could talk for—"

Rosaria returned and Rachel fell silent, as she didn't know if the sultry woman could speak or understand English. Dan comprehended her caution. Rosaria tended her evening tasks, but occasionally smiled at the couple. Rachel returned her genial overtures, but felt since she was a captive she shouldn't offer to help with camp chores.

The hour grew late. Most of the men and women turned in for the night, but a few stood guard around the slumbering camp. The couple didn't know if an enlightening talk had taken place or if the men had gone on a mission. A sweet-smelling gentle breeze filled the air and cooled them. They heard frogs croaking, crickets chirping, and rebels snoring. Fires had burned to low and smokeless coals. The setting was deceptively peaceful. But somewhere in the dark and steamy jungle dangers abounded.

Rosaria placed a wide sleeping mat nearby and motioned for them to share it, having perceived their closeness to each other. The couple thanked her and lay down. Rachel cuddled close to Dan, drawing from his strength and courage. Soon, exhausted in mind and body, both went to sleep.

*

At dawn, they were awakened by Richard and brought food by Rosaria. When they finished, her brother and the rebel leader moved closer to talk.

"Can you get the rest of the arms if we free you?" Richard asked.

Rachel nodded. She didn't know how much or if anything her brother had told Ramón about them.

"How long will it take? Our position is fragile."

"A few weeks," Dan responded, "Three at the most. I'll pay for them."

Rachel glanced at her lover in confusion. "How?" she fretted.

"I'll find a way to get the money," he reassured her.

"We'll force Harry to hand them over without more money."

"Let's get this matter settled first, then work on him," Dan suggested.

Rachel looked at her brother and asked, "You'll release us?"

Richard smiled and said, "Today. You must leave before trouble comes. Do not let us down, Rachel; we need those arms and ammunition."

"You convinced Ramón to trust us?"

"Sí, I gave my word to a good friend."

"I won't fail you, Rich— Ricardo."

"Ramón wanted to keep you here as a hostage while Capitán Slade fetched the weapons," he disclosed. "He was going to murder you in a month if he didn't return with them. I persuaded him you spoke the truth and to let you leave. It isn't wise to keep such a beautiful woman in camp so long."

"I promise you the rest of the weapons will be in your hands soon, no matter what I have to do to get them and to protect her."

"We will trust you, Capitán Slade. But do not betray us again."

"Can we talk alone?" Rachel asked almost hesitantly.

Richard shook his head and whispered, "It is dangerous to share the truth with anyone except close friends."

Rachel grasped his meaning. "When do we leave?" she asked.

"Soon. The longer you stay, the greater the danger of your ship being confiscated and your crew captured. Our men are fetching the hidden weapons as we speak. They will arm many bands to battle our cause."

"I hope you win it. If there's any way possible, we'll send extra arms."

"*Gracias,* Rachel. Our cause is just, and we will win it; but it will require much time and bloodshed."

"Protect yourselves always. If—"

Tomas and Eduardo raced into the clearing and shouted warnings of an imminent attack by Spanish soldiers. Orders were given and passed along with swiftness and efficiency. The people hurried, but did not panic. The noise of preparations and excited voices were kept at a minimum. Well-trained and experienced rebels grabbed their weapons and possessions to scatter into the encompassing landscape. Only things too heavy or cumbersome to carry were abandoned along with the exposed campsite.

"Capitán Rafael de Cardova approaches. Take these," Richard said as he passed a pistol and machete to Dan. "Keep up and don't lose sight of me," he warned his sister, who appeared alarmed by the approaching peril.

Rachel and Dan followed Richard Fleming and a small band into the jungle. The couple ran as fast as they could, but felt vulnerable in the strange surrounding. Exotic vegetation slapped them in the face and nipped at their arms. Their breathing became labored and swift; their hearts pounded; their lips and throats dried. They didn't know if they would come out of this alive, especially if they became separated from the others.

"Come on!" Richard shouted when Rachel lagged behind with a stitch in her side and Dan slowed to grab her hand and pull her along.

It seemed as if they ran at top speed for two hours, with enemies blazing guns to their rear and with the cruel jungle trying to slow their pace with verdant and tangly obstacles. When shouts of *"Alto!"* were heard beyond and behind them, they left the dirt path to prevent being trapped between two forces of the government. Several skilled men took turns clearing a passable trail through dense vegetation with slashing machetes.

Rachel and Dan obediently followed her brother and Ramón. Their hearts throbbed in panic and from their exertions in the humid heat. They didn't notice their route or the lovely terrain as they mindlessly moved onward.

They skirted a sugar plantation with cane fields that stretched for miles. The thick blades could provide concealment there if necessary. Workers paid no attention to them, as they knew what was taking place with their liberators. They moved until darkness halted them and they stopped to hide and sleep for a few hours. Exhaustion and a lack of privacy prevented questions from being asked or answers given between brother and sister. But Ramón smiled and spoke to her in Spanish.

"He said not to be afraid," Richard translated. "He will protect you and get you out of here safely. He knows the jungle better than the soldiers."

"Gracias, Ramón," she said and smiled, seeing another side of the rebel leader, a kind and genial one she found pleasing. "After we leave here, we won't let you down; I promise."

Her brother told *el líder* her response. Ramón Ortega smiled and nodded. He handed Rachel his canteen, told her to drink, then sleep.

Dan was tense. He didn't know if his ship would be waiting when—or if—they reached the coast, as he had ordered Luke to sail if trouble arose.

*

At dawn, Richard awakened them. "The others are going to lead our enemies away from us so I can get you to the coast and the ship. Stay quiet, not a word; sounds carry far. *Comprende?"*

Rachel and Dan nodded. Ramón and his men headed to the right, cutting a slightly obvious path to entice pursuit and deception.

"We have to struggle through and try not to make our passing and direction noticeable." Richard instructed. He told Dan to take the lead, that he would cover their tracks. "No broken limbs or crushed ferns," he cautioned. "Wriggle around any obstacle without damaging it. Be ready to flee if I give the word. Get to the ship and sail. I'll hang behind to cover your retreat and lead them on a merry chase away from you."

"No," Rachel protested. "You'll be captured and killed."

"Do as I say, my sister, or we will all be killed for nothing."

"Why are you doing this? What are you doing here?"

"There's no time to explain, and the less you know the better for everyone involved. Tell Mama I'm fine and I'll be home in six to twelve months. I'll explain everything then. A friend of mine will contact you to help you with the rest of the arms. I told Ramón you're my sister and to trust you. Don't let me down, Rachel. I love you, my beautiful and brave sister. *Hasta luego.* Now, go, before it's too late to save any of us," he commanded in a stern tone.

With caution and skill, Dan urged her toward the coast, and Richard brought up the rear. Every time they stole a short breather, Rachel tried to question Richard in whispers, but her brother halted her, advising her to rest and save her energy and to wait for answers until later.

The desperate trek was arduous and frightening, but they succeeded.

When they reached the edge of the forest, Richard glanced at the ship beside Dan's but it didn't worry him. "Don't wait for a boat," he ordered. "Swim for the ship. I can hear the soldiers closing in." He rushed the couple across the beach where deep sand grabbed at their feet. "Go!" he demanded when his sister hesitated. "Take her now, Slade, or she's dead."

"Come with us, Richard," she urged in panic, reaching for his arm.

He eluded her grasp. "No, I'm safe here. Go!" he shouted again. He took a position on one knee a few feet away and began firing at his foes.

Rachel took in the danger. From one direction, Ramón's small group of rebels poured onto the beach to provide cover for the daring escape. From the other, a larger group of Spanish soldiers were in sight. She realized they were in the middle of what appeared to be a fierce battle in the making; the odds were against the rebel side.

"Get her out of here!" Richard demanded, looking worried.

As Dan yanked on Rachel's arm and dragged her into the aquamarine sea, she resisted and yelled, "I love you! Please come with us!"

"My place is here. Keep your promise. Damn it, Rachel, go!"

In that moment of distraction, Richard's vulnerable body was thrown backward as he was shot by government soldiers. Ramón and others reached him first. The rebel leader cradled the American in his arms like an injured child as the Cuban fired shot after shot at the advancing soldiers who dropped to their stomachs to make more difficult targets.

Dan pulled Rachel farther into the crashing waves, refusing to release her hand as she jerked to free it to return to her fallen brother's side. "No, love; we must leave. He risked his life to save yours. There's nothing we can do against such odds and unarmed." He had tossed his borrowed weapons back to Richard to have his hands free for swimming.

"Let me go," she pleaded, but Dan refused.

An excellent and strong swimmer, Dan headed for the boat rowing toward them. He kept his attention on Luke and on the three men with him who were covering the distance between them with speed and urgency. He heard shooting behind him and the pleas of the woman he was dragging by one arm, but he didn't halt in his intention. He saw another ship anchored near the *Merry Wind,* but didn't want to imagine who was aboard and why they were there, as neither was flying an American or other country's flag. His crew's behavior and a lack of response to the battle ashore told him it couldn't be a Spanish ship.

The boat met them and hauled them inside, then immediately headed back to the clipper. Rachel struggled to see the lethal action on the beach. Dan watched with her as Richard was thrown across Ramón's shoulder and taken away. Neither could guess if he was alive or dead, but he clearly wasn't being left behind to face the persistent Spanish attack. The rebels vanished into the jungle under heavy fire with the soldiers in swift pursuit.

Rachel collapsed into Dan's arms and wept in fear.

No one spoke after Dan shook his head to order them to silence. The boat reached the *Merry Wind* and they were taken aboard.

A man with white-blond hair and ice-blue eyes met the fatigued couple, along with armed American sailors. "I'm Peter Garrett," he introduced himself. "A United States special agent. I was ordered to come after you, Captain Slade and Mrs. McCandless."

"Are we under arrest?" Dan asked as he sized up the stranger.

Rachel prevented Peter's reply when she shouted, "You have to go ashore and rescue my brother. He was shot. We must get him home to a doctor. Please, Dan, you can't let them leave Richard here at the mercy of those Spanish soldiers."

"Your brother is fighting here?"

"Yes. Richard Fleming, an American. He helped us escape. We can't leave him; he's wounded and I doubt they have skilled doctors here to treat him."

"Let's talk in your cabin, Captain Slade; this is a serious matter."

"No, go rescue Richard!"

"We can't, Mrs. McCandless; that's Spanish soil and we're American officers. I'm sure his friends will take care of him. I was watching with my fieldglasses; he took a bullet in the shoulder and they got him away. Look for yourself; the soldiers are back on the beach, watching us. They're not in pursuit." He saw her hug the railing as her gaze studied the shore where only Spanish soldiers were watching them. "We have to sail before they alert their government to our presence; they'll send its ships to destroy ours. We can't be taken prisoner. I'll stay aboard to question you two." Peter Garrett ordered the armed sailors to return to his ship and to follow the *Merry Wind* close, with cannons aimed at her to halt a rash flight.

Dan knew he couldn't battle his country's forces. He put Luke in charge, then guided Rachel and the agent to his quarters. The two ships got undersail within minutes.

Rachel—dirty, sopping, her hair tangled—rushed to the mullioned windows and stared at the receding island where her only remaining brother lay wounded and in peril. She prayed for Richard's survival and safety as tears eased down her flushed and scratched cheeks. She didn't care if the salty liquid stung or how disheveled she looked. Her heart was filled with sadness, fearing his loss was final this time.

"If you have brandy or the like, Captain Slade, she can use some to calm her down," the blond-haired agent suggested. "So can you. I'm sure what you've experienced has been difficult."

Dan prepared two glasses. He walked to Rachel and pressed one into her hand. "Drink it, love, you need it."

Rachel tossed down the contents in almost one swallow to relieve her tension. As the fiery drink hit her throat, she coughed and struggled to breathe. Her soulful eyes watered even more and sent tears racing down her face.

Dan wiped them away with gentleness and soothed, "That'll make you feel better."

"How can I relax until I know Richard's alive and safe? Why couldn't we try to rescue him?"

"The forces against us were too large, love. I'm sure Ramón and the others will take good care of him."

Rachel faced the man with crystal-blue eyes and pleasant features. "You and your men could have helped! How could you leave an American in such danger? Don't you know or remember what the Spanish did to our sailors aboard the *Virginius* in '73?"

"Yes, but we couldn't interfere and create a nasty incident. America has taken a neutral stand for now. We're American authorities, so we can't risk provoking a war with Spain to save one man's life. Richard Fleming is there by choice, just as you two were. That's what we have to discuss. I was sent to capture you for gun-running and for possible connections to the murders of Phillip McCandless and George Leathers."

"That's a lie!" Rachel refuted. "We didn't kill anyone."

"If I'm going to help you two get out of this mess, you have to be totally honest with me. Tell me from the beginning, everything about you and what you're doing here. *Everything,*" he stressed.

Rachel looked at Dan in trepidation, but he advised, "Do as he says, love. We have no choice."

"But it might blacken Phillip's memory," she argued.

"We can't worry about that. Phillip got himself into this trouble with his eyes open wide. We have to clear ourselves."

"He's right, Mrs. McCandless. The charges and accusations are serious. To save yourselves, you have to be honest with me."

"We didn't kill George Leathers or my husband. You can't have any evidence to the contrary, unless it's forged or planted."

"What about gun-running?" Peter ventured. "Why are you two here?"

"We had a clearance from customs to ship arms."

"I know," Peter replied in a calm tone. "But to Haiti, not Cuba, where there's a rebellion in progress."

"How do you know we didn't drop off our cargo there before sailing here to visit my brother?" Rachel countered. "It's not far away."

Peter was impressed by her courage and wits. "Carlos Torres and Joaquín Chavous brought you straight here to deliver arms and ammunition to Ramón Ortega, and we all know that to be a fact. What I don't understand is why you're claiming to be Richard Fleming's sister."

"Because I am! I was Rachel Fleming before I married."

"No, you were Rachel Newman; that's what I was told."

"Richard and I were born on White Cloud, our family's cotton plantation in Georgia," Rachel said. "He ran away from home in '69 because of our cruel Yankee carpetbagger stepfather. Our father and older brother were killed during the war. I ran away from home in '72 when I married William Barlow. He died, so I wed Craig Newman. After *he* died, I married Phillip McCandless last August. I haven't seen or heard from Richard in six years. When I learned he was in Cuba, I visited with him. Is that a crime?"

"Your mother's name is?" Peter evoked.

"Catherine Fleming Starger."

"Do you have other brothers and sisters?"

"Rosemary is Richard's twin, but she ran away the year after he did. We have two deceased brothers, Randall and Robert; one died in the war and one drowned after our mother married Earl Starger."

After the genial agent nodded agreement to each fact related, Rachel asked how he knew so much about her and her family.

"I've been on this case since January, so I know everything about it," was his answer.

Baffled, Dan inquired, "If you knew, why didn't you stop it?"

"Because the arms deal was my idea." Peter observed the stunned reactions of both people. "America is publicly neutral and must appear to remain that way, so it gave us the means to supply arms to the rebels without involving the United States openly. I'm the one who found Phillip McCandless and gave the information to Richard; and he passed it on to Ramón Ortega as his idea. Since he was from Georgia, it was logical he knew such people and things." He saw their astonishment increase.

"Why would my brother and the rebels trust you?"

"Because Richard and I are friends and partners. Richard Fleming is a special agent for the American government; he has been for years. He couldn't tell you and risk destroying his cover; we need him in Cuba. She's a major supplier of sugar and other products, so we have to protect our interests. And we also believe in their fight for independence."

"You're telling me my brother is a secret agent for the United States?"

Peter smiled and admitted, "Yes. That's why I had to make certain you were his sister before I revealed anything to you."

Rachel was stunned. "How? When?"

"After Richard left home, he spent some time in Athens, Augusta, and Savannah. He decided to hire onto a ship to seek adventures around the world. During one voyage, he docked in Charleston. From there, he took a sugar ship. He liked that trade and Cuba, so he kept it up; that's how he learned to speak Spanish. We were in the same port one night when several bullies attacked me. Richard saved my life. We got to talking and became friends. I convinced him to become a fellow agent. We've done many missions together. Don't worry about him; he's smart and skilled. When things got hot in Cuba, since he knew the language and the island, he was assigned there fifteen months ago to spy and to protect American interests. He caused trouble with Spanish soldiers to catch the rebels' eye and trust. He joined up with Ramón Ortega's band and became close friends with him. Their biggest need was arms and ammunition. I found McCandless and passed word and money to him to make the deal. He sent Torres and Chavous to prevent him being recognized or connected to the deal. When problems arose and were reported to him, he alerted me to investigate."

"The million-dollar payment was from you, from our government?"

"Partly from our government, from private businessmen with interests there, and from Cuban landowners who want freedom. After I got the information to Richard, he sent Torres and Chavous to make the deal in January and to pass along the advance. In February, your husband sent a message to Richard that he wanted out of the deal unless the balance was paid. Richard sent the same two men to deliver it on March twenty-third, but he alerted me to trouble. I met with McCandless. When they went to escort the shipment home on May thirteenth, they were told of more problems. They telegraphed their contact in Charleston, who sent a message to Richard on a sugar ship. That's when Torres and Chavous took it upon themselves to do further checking on the partners and their families, to use the information as threats. They sent another message on May twenty-second. Richard received it on the twenty-seventh and alerted me again. I got the news on June second that McCandless was dead, the payments were missing, and his widow and partners were trying to renege on the deal. I reached Savannah on the third, after you'd sailed. The local authorities had sent for government help, because you'd fled the country out of their jurisdiction. Your stepfather reported you two were running guns to Cuban rebels, and the Chief told me you were a suspect in two recent murders and several past ones. He relished telling me your whole story. Naturally I couldn't say I was already involved, so I sailed here to handle things."

Dan probed for clarification, "You found Phillip for them?"

"That's right. When he got nervous in February, I met with him, explained the situation, and convinced him to stay in the deal to help his country. That's when he learned Richard Fleming was our contact, but he didn't tell me his wife was Richard's sister. From my study, I knew you as Rachel Newman. I doubt Torres and Chavous know Ricardo's American name, or mentioned the names of the widow or her mother in their reports. I knew the rendezvous point, so I came straight here. You were already ashore. All I could do was wait and hope for the best."

Rachel was angered and accused, "If Richard is your friend and partner, why didn't you rescue him?"

"I told you, we can't get publicly involved. Richard and I know the risks we take, and we accept them. He wouldn't want me to destroy this mission. Besides, we couldn't have gotten to him. We don't know where the new camp is located. Right now, the jungle's crawling with soldiers. The best way to protect Richard is to leave his survival to his friends there."

"What about that clearance letter for customs?" Dan asked.

"I was the one who supplied it."

Rachel realized that if the United States Government was at the heart of this matter and the money was lost on gambling, it would explain why Phillip had panicked after losing the advance; that would explain why he had demanded the balance to use to save himself and the deal. It also gave a reason for his moodiness toward the end. "How is Harrison Clements involved, and George Leathers? Did you approach them, too?"

"Only McCandless; he was in charge." Peter Garrett related the facts and his assumptions about every point and person, and they matched Rachel's and Dan's. "Tell me all you know and did," the agent coaxed.

Rachel and Dan complied, then she concluded, "Phillip must have been furious when Harry met with Richard behind his back. I'm sure Harry is responsible for those threats Phillip and I received. He might have the missing money."

"I have an idea how we can find out," Peter hinted, then explained.

"That's clever," Dan complimented the agent when he had finished. "What about us and the rest of the arms? We promised Richard we'd send them in a few weeks. If we fail, the rebels will either doubt him or they'll send Torres and Chavous to harm us."

"I'll take care of that, so forget about it. We have to protect you two and Richard's cover. By the time I finish with Harrison Clements, I hope to have enough to see him hanged for murder and other crimes."

"You probably can add one more," Rachel disclosed, then told him of her suspicions about the patented designs used. "If he forged those intimidating notes to me, he could have forged the licenses, and maybe Milton Baldwin's loan agreement to steal the shipping firm from me also."

Dan explained her meaning as Rachel sipped water to wet her throat, dry from hours of talking.

"We'll know the whole truth soon. Don't worry; I'll have you two exonerated of gun-running after we dock. I don't know what I can do about those other allegations, unless Clements exposes facts about them."

"You believe us?"

Peter smiled and said, "Yes, Rachel, I do. You're a very brave and smart woman. You've handled yourself well in this trying situation." He turned to Dan. "How did you get enmeshed in all of this, Captain?" he asked.

Dan had no choice except to use his original ruse, which he did. He would tell Peter Garrett the truth later and swear the agent to secrecy until he could tell Rachel everything in private and at the right time. He wanted to wait until all matters were resolved before he confessed his big secret. He didn't want to say or do anything to repulse or hurt his love at this delicate time and when she was so distraught over her brother's fate. He was amazed and pleased by the turn in events and relieved they'd done nothing illegal. Yet, Phillip's initial motives and the money were still missing . . .

As they completed their conversation, Dan realized that Peter obviously had not checked the details of Phillip's deceased family, as the agent hadn't seemed to know the name Daniel Slade. If he had, Peter surely would have queried the similarity.

*

By the time both ships anchored at Grand Bahama Island for fresh water on Sunday, June thirteenth, Rachel, Dan, and Peter had talked of their plans many times. Peter dismissed the other ship with orders to return to its home port while he stayed aboard the *Merry Wind* with two of his agents who would help entrap Harrison Clements in a few days.

At a lovely lagoon, Dan and Rachel were given their first real moments of privacy since anchoring at Cuba. She had used Luke's cabin while the three men shared Dan's larger quarters. At last, they were alone. The location was verdant and dense with tropical vegetation, trees, vines, and exotic flora. The setting was sultry and humid. Lacy ferns and feathery palms were stirred to life by a breeze that swept through the area in a rush. Wonderful smells clung almost intimately to the still air left behind. Unfamiliar flowers and blossoms on plants and vines decorated their romantic surroundings with color and beauty. The pool was an aquamarine shade, and most enticing. Their awakened senses took in nature's splendor, then each other.

As they embraced and kissed, she murmured against his lips, "It's been so long since we could touch like this. I've missed you."

"With Peter in on the case, we'll be free of all entanglements soon. Maybe he can help extricate you from those other troubles."

"I don't know how, Dan; they've been hanging over my head for years. If someone else is to blame, how could he find out and prove me innocent?"

He tenderly cuffed her chin. "After he's done with Harry, we'll turn over the notes and papers to him," he told her. "Maybe he has skilled men who can unravel the riddles in them."

Rachel didn't want to build up false hopes. "That would be wonderful. I want to be free and clear of all suspicions."

He gazed into her eyes. "When you are, will you marry me, woman?"

"I haven't proven myself yet," she reminded.

"Well, let's get busy taking care of that right now," he jested.

"Do with me as you will," she sighed seductively.

"How could any man resist an offer like that?"

Rachel's lips touched his, brushing them lightly with hers. Dan's arms banded her body and drew it close. It was nearing dusk, so they had little time to stay there. Both were aware of how long it had been since they'd made love with blissful abandon. Their hungers raged, and neither wanted to rush these precious moments, but they knew they must.

They parted to remove their clothes, too much in love and ensnared by passion to be modest. Dan bent forward to kiss the tip of each breast before traveling up her neck to tease her ear, then ravenously devour her parted lips. They kissed and caressed, stroking and stimulating each other. Their tongues moved with skill and eagerness. They were intoxicated and entranced by each other.

The palm of his hand moved over one breast in a circular motion to enflame and tauten it even more than it was, then went to the other to do the same. He used his mouth to sear fiery kisses and burning caresses over her quivering flesh. The sea captain voyaged over her bare shoulder, the hollow of her throat, and the pulse point that told him how aroused she was. His lips tasted and explored her sweet desire and heady surrender. He wanted to stir her to greater heights before he joined their bodies.

Rachel's arms were around him, and her hands drifted up and down his back. She enjoyed the hardness and suppleness of his muscles and skin. Her body tingled and smoldered from his touch. He was tantalizing and pleasuring her from head to toe. She was glad she didn't have to battle her need for him. She had longed for this staggering contact for days.

Dan's body was aflame with need, too, and scorching desire. Every place he touched with hands or lips was responsive. He yearned to bring every inch of her to awareness and blazing life. He was enchanted by the way she gave him free rein over her body and will with such deep love and trust. Her nearness was driving him wild. Her skin was as silky as a satin ribbon, its olive hue glowing healthily. Every part of her called out to him to touch it and adore it. Rapturous sensations assailed him as her hands wandered over his body. When his mouth fastened to hers, she slipped a hand into his hair to hold him there a while longer. He loved her and wanted her to be his forever.

Rachel felt enslaved to the man who had captivated and mastered her emotions, wits, and will. He was so giving, gentle, and caring. With every part of her, she wanted him completely, now and forever. She used her voice, newly acquired skills, and reactions to tell him so.

Dan's fingers roamed across her flat stomach to seek the brown forest and the vital peak that summoned his exploration and craved his attention. He wanted to warm himself in the steamy core. Soon, he had her writhing with unleashed passion, as was he.

Rachel's fingers roved his torso with delight, then trekked lower to stimulate his flaming need to a brighter and higher level. She teased down his sleek sides and captured the prize of love's war that could send her senses spinning beyond reality, beyond resistance or withdrawal. With gentleness, she stroked it and absorbed its warmth. She created more heat and strength. She thrilled to his prowess and response. Intense joy filled her when his body shuddered and she heard a groan of pleasure come from deep within his chest.

Unable to restrain themselves further, they fused their bodies. Dan tried to move with leisure and caution, but Rachel urged him to move swiftly and urgently, as she did. They rode the undulating waves of love's sea, reveling in its dips and crests.

Rachel sensed the strain he was experiencing to give her release first. She arched to meet every thrust, but allowed him to set their pace. She let him know when she reached the precipice. She labored with him as she fell over ecstasy's edge, then he quickly pursued her into the swirling depths.

Their mouths meshed when the triumphant moment arrived. They kissed and caressed until every sensation of the glorious moment was extracted. Afterward, they bathed and returned to his ship.

*

On Tuesday afternoon, they docked in Savannah. Rachel and Dan stayed aboard the *Merry Wind* while Peter Garrett went to see Police Chief Anderson. The couple waited anxiously until the agent returned.

When he did, Peter grinned and told them they had been cleared of gun-running charges: He had convinced the chief that Earl Starger had misunderstood what he overheard. The ecstatic couple listened as he related, "Anderson's investigator wasn't pleased you'd left town, Rachel, and made quite a fuss about it. I asked to view the evidence against you, and they don't have one piece or even a clue to incriminate you. I pointed out they couldn't arrest you or limit your movements without any to base it on. That investigator said they had intended to exhume McCandless's body to have it examined, but the doctor told them it was too late to accurately determine the cause of death. I made it clear the United States Government would be interested in a case they kept open and a citizen they harassed without a verifiable reason to do so. After our little chat, they understand suspicions and gossip don't count in the legal system."

"You mean they're dropping the charges against me?"

"You never *were* charged, just suspected and investigated. Since they haven't come up with any hard facts by now, they have to let the matter go."

"That's wonderful, Peter. But unless your ruse with Harry works and he's to blame, we might never know who killed Phillip and George."

"Most crimes have a way of being solved eventually," Peter told her.

Rachel was pleased for herself and Dan, but hated to see a killer go unpunished. "I hope so. What do we do now?"

"I'll leave first thing in the morning for Athens. I'll see you two the minute I return. Hope for good news."

"We will," Rachel and Dan replied at the same time, and smiled.

After Peter left for the hotel, Dan and Rachel retired to his cabin . . .

*

Peter and his two men left by train on Wednesday morning. Dan went to pick up a report left at the post office by the detective he had hired to check on Milton Baldwin. It told them something very interesting and helpful, so they went to Milton's office to confront him.

Milton asked what they were doing there. "The police are searching for you," he said, noting the odd way they looked at him. "It was in the newspaper two weeks ago, something about gun-running and murder."

"I've been cleared of all suspicions, Milton, all of them," Rachel disclosed. "I'm free. The newspaper will have to run an apology and retraction."

He appeared surprised and disappointed. "Did you deliver the cargo?"

"Yes."

"Then you have my money. That's why you're here?"

"No, but we have something else: proof that agreement is a fake."

Milton's expression altered. "What are you talking about?"

"Phillip didn't sign that loan agreement; his signature is traced. And the date is in your handwriting, not his. We have an expert witness who'll testify against you in court. You've broken the law, Milton."

"You're crazy, Rachel. I haven't broken the law."

"That isn't what the United States special agent thinks. Dan and I have spoken with him in detail. He believes you're in deep trouble. I'm not lying or bluffing, Milton; I'm taking you to court on this matter. And I'll win."

The man panicked. "Wait a minute, you two! That loan is for real. I'll admit that isn't the paper Phillip signed, but he owed me the money."

"Why don't you explain before we're forced to head to the police station?" Dan suggested. "Unless you prefer to tell your story to them."

"All right!" he shouted. "The loan was from Harry to Phillip, but I purchased it. Phillip borrowed sixty thousand dollars to cover a gambling debt, and he put up his share of the arms company as collateral. After he died, Harry came to me and suggested I buy it so I could use it to force Rachel out of the shipping firm. He thought if she was desperate for money to settle a debt or lose part of her inheritance, she would either have to honor the deal we all needed or she'd expose the fact she had the missing money when she took some from it to pay me. After those tricks she pulled on all of us, none of us trusted her or believed her. Harry had my name and company switched with his, Phillip's signature traced, and I filled in a date I knew you couldn't meet. When you called my bluff, I got scared and didn't want to press too hard and provoke you to examine the agreement too closely."

"That's fraud and forgery, criminal offenses," Dan asserted.

"What difference does it make which partner he owed or which company he would forfeit?" a frightened Milton reasoned. "The loan was real, and overdue. He couldn't pay it off and neither could she."

"That doesn't change what you two did to deceive and defraud her. We'll press charges and you'll go to prison. Unless . . ."

"Unless what?" Milton asked Dan.

The sea captain had already discussed the course of action with Rachel. "You agree to dissolve the partnership and divide the firm into the same shares as when you merged. That's how you can avoid prosecution."

"That isn't fair! I'll be out sixty thousand dollars!"

"And you'll be out of prison. We'll adjust the split to keep you from taking a total loss of the money, which Rachel doesn't have to do in light of how you tricked her. Is it a deal? Oh, yes, McCandless Shipping will be moving back to Charleston, if that influences your decision any."

"How would we work out the details?" Milton asked, cornered.

"I'll spend the next few days here working them out with you. Rachel has agreed to let me handle the matter for her because I know how shipping firms work. We should have everything settled within a week."

Milton thought a few minutes, then said, "We'll do it your way."

Rachel wanted the distressing situation ended, so she was polite. "Thank you, Milton. I want this handled swiftly and secretly. I don't want to hurt or embarrass your family because you made a foolish mistake. Over the years I've learned that gossip and scandals can be painful and humiliating. Don't you think this way will be best for everyone's reputation and business?"

Milton gaped at her in astonishment and gratitude. "I'm sorry, Rachel. Things were so bad, I got greedy and desperate. Harry's scheme sounded good at first. By the time I realized it was crazy and hazardous, I was in too deep to back out, and he wouldn't let me. I was also angry with Phillip for getting us into this trouble. If he'd kept his mind on business and kept away from gambling, this wouldn't have happened to any of us. If I was going to save myself, I had to get the notorious Black Widow out of my company. I know you can't understand how I could behave so recklessly, but I was under such pressure that I didn't think clearly. I'm glad it's finally in the open and can be cleared up. I never wanted to hurt you. I'm sorry."

"So am I, Milton. Sorry this happened. I'll be gone soon, and we can both be free of the past. I wish you good luck with your new company."

"That's more than kind and generous, Rachel; thank you."

"I'll head home, Dan, while you two begin your work and talk."

The sea captain walked her to the door and said, "I'll see you in a few days. Rest and get things packed for your move. Unless it's an emergency, stay out of town until everything is resolved."

"I'll wait to hear from you." Rachel left with two of Dan's men to protect her along the way and at the plantation until Dan and Peter arrived.

*

After Rachel explained matters to Lula Mae Morris and Burke Wells, everyone calmed down from the excitement of her return to Moss Haven. "I have half of Phillip's shipping firm back, so it should be earning money again soon. Captain Slade is handling it for me for a while. Isn't it wonderful? My files are closed; no more questions or investigations. Home," she murmured as she allowed her gaze to roam the lovely setting.

"Dat's good news, Miz Rachel. Ah told you to have faith," Burke said.

"I'll help you unpack. I bet you're bone-tired," was Lulu Mae's offer.

"Yes and no; I'm too elated to decide. As we speak, Harry is being investigated for Phillip's and George's murders. If he is found to be the culprit and there's proof, it will all be over at last."

*

Saturday evening, Peter Garrett arrived at the plantation. Rachel was disappointed that Dan wasn't with the agent, as she hadn't seen or heard from him in days. He had teased about letting her miss and crave him for a while to convince her how much she loved and needed him, but she hadn't taken him seriously. Yet she'd promised to stay home, and obeyed.

"Have you seen Dan?" she asked after they exchanged greetings.

"No, I assumed you'd both be here. Where is he?"

Rachel explained what had taken place with the shipping firm and what Dan was doing in town. "What did you learn from Harry?"

"Wait until you hear my news. My men and I pretended we were working for Ramón and we'd come to kill him over his refusal to send the arms and for stealing our money. We bound and terrified him until he was convinced his life was nearing its miserable end. I don't work that way often, Rachel, but I knew he was guilty and needed persuasion."

"I understand," she said, but wasn't sure she did.

"Harry tried to play the ignorant and innocent pawn in your game. If we hadn't gotten rough, he wouldn't have talked. I told him we have you and Dan captive in Cuba and we'd forced the truth from you two. He finally spilled all he knew before the night was over. He told us he doesn't have the money and how he'd tried to scare it out of you: He ransacked your room and had you spied on in Athens during your first visit there; he had a man threaten you with a knife and had your home searched. He shot at you, but only one time, and had your house rocked and painted. He sent that scary note about the deal, but not those weird love notes. It helped knowing all those things from you so I could question him about each one."

Peter took a breath and continued. "He even confessed to blowing up the ammunition company, but claims he didn't know George and that worker were inside. He knows we know he's lying about that part, and I'll get him to admit it soon. I have him under guard at the hotel in town. My ship's coming late Monday, and I'm taking him with me for more interrogation. I convinced him to tell me how he controlled Phillip. He altered the company books to make things look bad so Phillip would sell out to him. When Phillip came up with the arms deal, Phillip's desperate need of cash and the sorry state of his financial affairs gave Harry the means to keep Phillip from backing out. He has an interested buyer for the arms company, but you and his wife will split the profit after he's in prison."

Presently that wasn't her main concern. "What about Phillip's death?"

"We never could get Harry to admit he killed him or has the money. He was petrified, so I'm inclined to believe him. Evidently Phillip did hide the money from everyone, and either he did die of cholera or somebody else killed him."

"What about the guns for Richard and the Cubans?"

"Harry had them ready, so they're on the way there now. He had no choice except to turn them over to us. After he spilled his guts, I told him who we are, and he almost fainted. About those licenses, I have them in my possession, but he's already confessed they're forged. You'll be pleased to learn, that Phillip didn't know anything about that crime."

Rachel was relieved by that. "What you're saying is that my husband hadn't done anything illegal with the arms deal? His only mistake was creating gambling debts that made him desperate for money?"

"That's how it appears to me. He concealed the money to protect it, but that isn't a crime. If he used any of it for gambling, more than his share of the profit, that's a different story. Until or unless we locate it, we'll never know the truth."

"I almost wish I never find it, but we need it to pay bills and salaries for the arms, or to repay bank loans. With George's records burned, I don't know who the Augusta company owes. Of course, I'll try to pay any indisputable bill. Once we go over the Athens books, I'll make certain all honest debts are paid out of the sale price before Mrs. Clements and I split the profit. It isn't right for innocent people to suffer because George was murdered and Harry was crooked. If the missing money turns up, I'll let you know."

"You're a good woman, Rachel McCandless. Any message for Dan? I'll report my findings to him when I return to town."

She thought a moment, then replied, "Tell him I said hello and I miss him, but I won't disturb his hard work."

*

The following afternoon, Rachel visited with Dan's men in their camp nearby and brought them cookies and lemonade as a treat. They finished a card game as she approached. While they chatted, Rachel said, "I'm sure you're eager to set sail again soon. Is Turkey an interesting place?"

"Turkey, ma'am? Don't know, ain't never been there."

That took Rachel by surprise. "I must have misunderstood; I thought that was where you'd come from before you docked here."

"No, ma'am; we came from Scotland. Delivered a shipment of wool."

She assumed Dan's arms deal was a secret even from his crew. Or if the man knew about it, he must have been ordered not to mention it to anyone. If a secret, she wondered what excuse her love had given his crew for his trip here. "What made Dan decide to visit Savannah?"

"Don't know, ma'am. When we docked in Charleston in March, Capt'n Slade was in a rush to get here to visit somebody important. He don't talk about his private business."

"Where do you head after you leave Savannah?"

"Mr. Conner said we'd be sailing on Tuesday. Heading for Africa."

Again, she was surprised and intrigued. As the man sat cross-legged and chatted, Rachel viewed the paper lying on his thigh. "What's that?"

"My helper," he replied, then chuckled. "I can't ever remember from one time to the next which hand beats another in poker. Mr. Conner gave me this paper to use when I play. It's getting in bad shape."

"May I see it?"

"Sure, ma'am." He passed the fading page to her.

Rachel didn't care about the list of poker hands in winning order. What she wanted to study was the handwriting she was sure she recognized. "If I can borrow it for a short time, I'll make you a new copy."

"I don't want to trouble you, ma'am."

"No trouble. It's my way of thanking you for being a good protector. Enjoy the snack. I'll return this to you soon."

Rachel went to her room and retrieved a paper she had kept hidden. She lay the two on her bed and studied them. The list handwriting matched the flowing and neat script of the second love note she had received! Luke couldn't have delivered it; he was here. Dan was with her, so he must have. . . . But why would he send such a provocative message, then never admit it?

She paced the floor. No trip to or from Turkey. . . . No private arms deal . . . So why had he placed orders with Harry and George? To protect his cover lie about why he had come to visit Phillip? Again, why? Maybe he had witnessed the burial and suspected her of murdering Phillip. Or maybe he was an agent like Peter, assigned to keep Phillip in tow; when he died, Dan was ordered to stick close to her . . . Whatever the answer, she was thinking too wildly to confront Dan today. It was best to let him come to her and explain; surely that would be soon.

*

Monday morning, Lula Mae handed Rachel a letter from Harry, one postmarked the day she sailed for Cuba. "It's been opened and resealed," Rachel observed.

"The man who brung it didn't say nothing about that."

"Maybe Harry forgot something and he did it. Strange. Thank you, Lula Mae," she said, dismissing the housekeeper.

When she was alone, she ripped open the envelope and read the shocking letter. In dread, she read it once more:

Rachel

I had Daniel Slade checked out with friends in Charleston. He's lying to both of us, but you'll be the one to suffer. His real, or I should say full, name is Daniel Slade McCandless, known in the past to friends and family as Mac. By some miracle, he's Phillip's missing brother. I don't have to speculate on what his plans are for you, do I, my pretty spider who devoured his brother? He's trying to lure you into his web like you did his brother; then he'll turn on you and murder you before you can kill him, too. What a wicked trap you're in, my ravishing and foolish Rachel. You'd better get away from him while there's still time to escape. Oh, yes, the authorities came to visit me again today. They say they have new evidence against you and will be coming to arrest you soon. If I were you, I'd take that stolen money and get myself hidden.

She wasn't worried about the law, as no doubt that was concerning those charges Peter had destroyed. Dan was Phillip's brother? Harry wouldn't say something she could check out and disprove. She recalled their talk in Athens about "Mac." He had been telling her about himself! Perhaps Phillip had known Dan was alive and had sent for him, as he murmured on his deathbed. But Dan could be trying to entrap her! Maybe Peter had convinced Dan, as he had Phillip, to go along with the arms deal until it was completed, then work on his personal problem of revenge. If Harry wasn't responsible for those other threats, someone who had the motive and opportunities was. His claims of love and those proposals . . . What better way to expose a Black Widow than to marry her and ensnare her when she tries to kill you?

Cruel fate was making another attempt to hurt and destroy her. The first man she loved and wanted hated her and craved her punishment for something she hadn't done. If he had decided she was innocent and had fallen in love with her, he would have confessed the truth by now. Instead of being with her, he was in town trying to save *his* family's shipping firm, probably with plans to snatch it away from her. Would he actually go so far as to marry her to expose her? If he felt she had gotten away with past murders and might do the same with Phillip's, yes.

She had surrendered her all to him and told him everything about her. She had come to love him and trust him. But she should never have let down her guard with Daniel Slade *McCandless.* Lula Mae had mistrusted him and had warned her to do the same, but she hadn't listened. He had worked on the mystery only to clear his brother's name and to help their country. Should she confront him, or spurn him and leave? Could she let him see how he'd fooled her and hurt her? As with Craig and Paul, Dan would find a way to keep her from inheriting anything from his brother.

Phillip would hate you for what you're trying to do to me, she thought bitterly.

Edgy, confused, and tormented, Rachel left the house for a walk, her heart burdened by the recent revelations. She must think and plan.

*

In town, Dan made an elating and unexpected discovery. While going over records and bills, one entry stood out to him. It involved a favorite past hiding place of Phillip's, but one Rachel had said was impossible. It was obvious she hadn't known about the replacement or she'd have told him.

Peter Garrett arrived shortly after Dan found the clue. He explained his suspicion to the agent. "If I'm right, I know where the missing money is hidden. You have time to go with me before you sail?"

"I surely do," a smiling Peter replied.

*   *   *

Rachel heard voices as she neared the side of the house: Dan's and Peter's. She sneaked to the corner and peered toward the front porch. The bottom step had been demolished. After the facts she'd learned, she was compelled to observe and listen.

"Here's the missing money, Peter, just like I said," Dan remarked as he withdrew a large bag from its hiding place. He opened it and the two men eyed the contents, then exchanged grins of success.

Rachel was stunned. Had Dan known all along where it was hidden?

"There's a letter here to you from Phillip," Peter said. "And a picture of you two years ago."

So, Rachel fumed, it was true: Daniel Slade McCandless . . .

"I'll read it later; it's probably personal. I have one more thing to do here; visit my brother's grave, then go find Rachel. You've heard the gossip about her being a lethal predator. After I capture her in the web I've weaved, I'll expose the truth about her to everyone."

"What are you planning to do with her?"

"Just what I told you on the ship and in town."

Peter grasped his meaning, as Dan had related his love and marital intentions and his hopes of proving her innocence in past episodes.

"You want to walk to his grave with me before you leave?"

"Yes." Peter replied. "Maybe I can give you some suggestions about how to solve Phillip's murder and those of the other men."

Rachel waited until they were far from the house. She sneaked to the barn and saddled a horse. She walked him out the back door and across the pasture. She mounted and rode away, needing time to settle down before she faced Dan for an enlightening confrontation on both their sides.

The sinister culprit who had been stalking her for years watched her movements and followed. When he called out and she reined in to speak with him, he brutally punched her in the jaw and knocked her unconscious. With hatred and a hunger for revenge gleaming in his eyes, he held her limp body in place while he rode to a secluded shed on her property. He hauled her inside, bolted the door, and glared down at her. At last Rachel was at his mercy, and he would show none.

Chapter

24

Rachel awakened, her hands bound behind her with a belt and her jaw smarting from the blow she hadn't seen coming in time to elude it. She lifted her head and saw her sinister stepfather lazing against the only entrance, which was shut and bolted. He had her captive in an abandoned storage shed on her property, so he hadn't taken her far, which would be helpful if anyone realized she was missing and looked for her. The shed was large and cluttered with old tools and broken crates. Plenty of light came in through holes in the collapsing roof, but the structure was still sturdy. He was standing there gloating over his brazen deed, while she lay helpless near the rear of the shed. She didn't know how long she had been unconscious, but she doubted much time had passed, as he hadn't gotten antsy and tried to arouse her. She was frightened, but tried to look brave and controlled. In an insulting tone, she asked, "Are you mad? Don't you know this will get you into big trouble? A United States special agent is at my home right now with Daniel Slade. They'll come looking for me, and you'll be arrested for kidnapping and assault. Earl Starger, you untie me and let me go this instant!"

Unruffled by her anger and warnings, he laughed and replied, "I saw you sneak away, girl. I also saw them find that money all of you have been searching for. When you don't return from your walk and they can't find you near the house, they'll take it and go. That's all the agent wants. As for the sea captain, he'll assume you took off to avoid him, so he'll leave, too."

She glared at him. "How do you know about the money?"

He laughed again and said, "I know everything about you, girl; Lula Mae has kept me informed for years."

Rachel was shocked and dismayed. "Lula Mae?"

"That's right; she works for me."

It made sense, how he had always seemed to know her every move and condition! "What did you pay her to spy on me and betray me?"

Earl leaned against the door and crossed his arms over his chest. "Not much; she did it because she loves you and wants to protect you."

"How can that be true when she works for you?" Rachel refuted.

Earl stroked his elbow as he explained, "After Newman died, I hired a man to pose as a doctor. We convinced her that you're crazy, and aren't responsible for your actions. We told her if she watched over you and kept us informed of your condition and behavior, we wouldn't go to the police. We warned her how dangerous it would be to you and others if she revealed she knew the truth to you, so she kept silent all this time. We put on such a good act we had her believing an evil witch lives inside you and might jump out and attack anybody around if they learned she existed. We even told her that evil side would kill you to protect herself. Lula Mae believes in all that stuff about God and the devil; she thinks the devil and his helpers can work his evil on humans. She cried and wailed about her sick-minded baby and agreed to do anything to save you and protect you from his wicked clutches. She even believes you got rid of Newman's baby because of how he abused you during your marriage to him; of course, she hated him, too. That money she gave you for support so you wouldn't starve was from me. I couldn't give you too much or you would have become suspicious of where she got it. She believes I love you like a daughter and only want what's best for you. I made sure every talk she overheard between us went in my favor."

So, the woman *had* been spying and eavesdropping, but longer than she had realized, and for a much different reason from the one she had imagined. Yet the spinster's motive had been a good one. Poor misused Lula Mae, she fretted. "You tricked her and took advantage of her."

"That's right. She's a stupid, gullible, and superstitious woman. You made a mistake trusting her and confiding in her. When she learned you'd been asleep or had fainted when all those men died, it was easy to make her think you'd been under some evil spell you couldn't remember."

"She told you . . . everything about me?"

"Everything. I was supposed to pass it along to the . . . *doctor*. Of course, I already knew everything, and I mentioned those alleged fits you had at home. I told her how worried and afraid your mother was. Lula Mae believes I'm a kind and generous and tender-hearted man you've lied about. And that night at the hotel, I almost convinced you of your madness."

Rachel recalled how he had cast brief doubts in her own mind about her sanity and guilt, so a simple woman like Lula Mae might be easy to fool, especially by a "doctor." "You low-down snake," she sneered. "I hate you. You've never done one kind or good thing in your life."

Earl straightened and took a spread-legged stance with hands akimbo. "Come off it, Rachel. Be glad I got rid of those groping men for you."

Fear knotted her stomach and sent tingles of alarm over her body. "You . . . got rid of them? You mean . . . you killed them?"

"Of course. Don't look so surprised; surely you had suspicions."

"But Mama said you were home when Phillip died. Did you pay—"

"She knows only what I tell her she knows. She was too drugged on medicine to realize or remember my comings and goings. When I'd tell her what date it was, she believed me. She was too drunk on that stuff I got from the real doctor to even be aware of when I was or wasn't home. She doesn't know I was gone during those incidents that plagued you."

Rachel leapt on that clue to get answers while the insane man was in a boasting and cocky mood. "You're the one who was sending me those notes, following me, and threatening me!"

"Yes, and mighty clever of me if I do say so myself."

"Clever to kill four men in cold blood? How could you?"

Earl came over and squatted down beside her as he revealed, "William's boy was easy; he was sick and feverish; and you were napping. I knew it wouldn't be long before he'd be chasing you around the house and trying to sneak into your bloomers. I couldn't allow that to happen to my Rachel. I wasn't worried when you married Old Willy; everybody knew he couldn't hump a woman anymore. I figured, in time, you'd get an itch and I'd be around to scratch it for you. Don't you recall how contrite I was? I did everything I could to make peace with you."

"You didn't fool me; I saw through your little pretenses."

When she tried to sit up, Earl pushed her back down. "I know. That's why I had to put you in a hard spot. William's death was easy, too. Since you slept in separate rooms, I sneaked inside and forced him to drink that poison. I figured it would look like a heart attack, and he was so scared I thought he would have one. Then you'd be free and rich and come to me. When you kept being mean and distant, I helped Camellia fan the flames of gossip about you. I knew that if you were tormented enough by them, you'd run home eventually. But you fooled me; you married that Craig Newman. I should have left you in his trap longer so he could beat some sense into you. But I didn't like anybody doing my job for me or marring my property."

Rachel listened in horror as Earl Starger continued his confession. She didn't know how she was going to get out of this predicament, but she wouldn't let him ravish her without the fiercest struggle she could manage. If she escaped him, who would believe this incredible tale? She had to keep him talking in case Peter and Dan did come looking for her.

Earl's voice and expression were cold and cruel as he said, "I came to see you that morning. Newman was drunk and gave me a hard time. He ordered me to never come to his house again. I saw you faint so it gave me the opportunity to get rid of the bastard. I dragged him up the steps and threw him down, twice for good measure. I figured it would appear an accident. Even if it didn't, they couldn't prove you'd done it. I knew you'd be free again soon and be even richer. I should have killed Paul when he stole everything from you, but that might have been dangerous for both of us."

"Might?" Rachel scoffed. "It was dangerous for me, you beast. I'm lucky I wasn't imprisoned or hanged. How did you kill Phillip?"

"I sneaked inside like I did with William and poisoned him. He was so drunk, he didn't see me in the room. I poured the poison in the whiskey bottles and kept nudging him awake so he'd keep nursing on them. I gave him enough to kill him twice. I knew he'd be gone soon. I returned home, made sure Catherine knew I was there and what the date was, and waited for word to arrive of your new dilemma. When nothing happened, I came to check it out. Lula Mae told me how you'd buried Phillip in secret, even destroyed the whiskey bottles, and were leaving on a trip. She remembered how she'd begged you not to marry Phillip, on mine and the doctor's orders. She figured he was poisoned by you the night before and didn't want you being arrested. You saved us both from trouble when you hid his body for a time to rot away any evidence; that was cunning, girl."

His description repulsed her. "I didn't do it to protect you. I—"

"Oh, I know why you did it, that arms deal and the missing money. I bet I scared you silly when I shot at you that Sunday after Phillip died and sent you those notes. Clever of me to use your handwriting, wasn't it? I've practiced for years on letters and papers you left behind when you ran away. I had a feeling I might need that skill one day. When I left the vial in your hotel room in Augusta, your friend almost caught me. I was hiding under the bed when he and that bellman came to leave flowers. I saw that silly card he wrote. You made me furious, girl, when you started clinging to that sea captain. That's why I tipped off the police, to get you into trouble. Of course, that was a mistake; at the time, I didn't know about the other trouble you were in and that

Slade was only with you on business. But you spent too much time with him and started getting too close. I never overlook anything, girl; I even stole back my tip note to the police. And those whiskey bottles you burned and buried, they didn't have poison in them. Did you like the little spider I put in your basin?"

"It could have bitten me before I noticed it!"

"You would have deserved it for sleeping with that sailor. I saw those pictures of you two; I know sated looks when I see them. I enjoyed tearing them to pieces and burning them. He'll never have you again."

Rachel realized she was running out of time, as Earl was getting cold and hateful. And there wasn't much, if anything, more to brag about to her. At least she had discovered two important things: she wasn't to blame for any of the deaths and Dan was responsible for only one note to her, one written before their entwining trip and delivered early after their meeting when he doubted her, before he came to know and love her. Surely that was why he hadn't intimidated her further. "I should have guessed the truth when nothing happened while you were away. I thought it was because I had protection from Dan's men, and Mama told me you were home all those times I received threats. Why did you leave and let up on me?"

"I thought you needed a little simmering time. With those other men threatening you, I knew you'd be boiling soon and need my help."

"Is that why you alerted the police after our fight?"

"You provoked me, girl. It was your fault, but you got out of it."

"You tried to attack me!" she charged. "You tried to convince me I was crazy, a murderess. This time you'll be exposed and punished."

"That traitorous sea captain won't protect you. That interesting letter from your partner came while you were gone. I read it when I came to see Lula Mae. I told her to hide it until the right time came to give it to you. I warned her it might entice you to murder him out of revenge. I sneaked to the house this morning and told her to give it to you, to test your reaction. If you became angry and dangerous, we'd send for the doctor, I said."

"What are you planning to do with me?"

Earl trailed his fingers over her flushed cheek. "I'm going to enjoy you to the fullest, hurt you like you've hurt me many times, then kill you. I'll sneak your body away, bury it secretly, and forget you existed. No one will ever suspect me. They'll think you ran away after learning the truth about your lover, how he was betraying you. It's actually amusing you'll end up like Phillip did, in a secret grave. After things settle down, I plan to divorce Catherine and marry the rich and eager Miss Jones."

Rachel tensed. "She's in on this plot, too?"

Earl yanked her hair. "Don't be absurd. I wouldn't tell anybody my secrets. She and I have been just friends for years, but she took a different liking to me on the ship to and from Boston. That was a coincidence, but we've been lovers since our return, so I don't need you anymore. But I can't let you get away with what you did to me. I have to punish you. Once I've sated myself with you and you're dead, I won't think about you again."

Rachel tried a ruse. "Camellia is making a fool of you, Earl. She lost two men to me, so she's taking you away from my mother for spite."

Earl sent wild laughter into the shed. "That isn't true, girl. After I finish with you, you'll understand how enslaved to me she is. Maybe not, because I won't be gentle and generous with you like I was with her. Now let's get those clothes cut off and get busy. I have to get my alibi—"

The door was kicked in with a loud crash and Dan shouted, "Touch her and you're dead, Starger!"

Earl had instinctively dodged the splintered wood that was sent flying in all directions. He flung down the jewel-handled knife and drew his pistol. "I'll kill the witch first!" he yelled in frustration and madness.

A bullet from Peter Garrett's gun struck Earl in the shoulder, as the distance was too far and the danger too imminent for him or Dan to reach her deranged stepfather and disable him. The wild man staggered backwards a few steps, but raised his weapon to carry out his objective to murder Rachel. The second bullet made Starger's heart its accurate and lethal target.

Dan picked his way over the debris, lifted the bound Rachel, and carried her into the fresh air and sunlight. Peter followed to make certain she was all right, as Earl Starger was beyond assistance.

As Dan unfastened the belt to free her hands, he asked if she was hurt. "We hated to wait so long, love," he explained, "but Peter wanted his full confession to end this matter once and for all. We didn't know he had a pistol."

She was trembling and dazed. "How did you find me?"

"Burke saw him attack and abduct you. He came after us. We got on your trail fast. Thank God Peter's a swift and skilled tracker. We sneaked up outside just as Starger began confessing his crimes. Peter told me to hold off a rescue until he had his say. This clears you of all suspicions, love."

"I knew he was evil and mean," Rachel sighed, "but not to this extent. He probably made Mama ill just so he could keep her drugged to give him alibis. It's over; it's finally over—the mysterious deal, the suspicious deaths, my dark past."

"Now you can make a fresh start, Rachel."

"That sounds easier than it will actually be, Peter. Thank you for your help."

"Before I sail, I'll file a report with the police chief. Not only will your files be closed, I'll make sure they're destroyed. I'll also make certain the newspapers tell everyone the whole story. People around here will never gossip about you again. Plenty of them will owe you apologies."

"I don't care about that part. I just want everyone to know I'm not guilty. I want my name and reputation cleared."

"I'll see that they are, Rachel; you have my word."

"What about my brother? Will you find a way to check on Richard and let me know how he is?"

"Just as soon as possible, but I'm sure he's fine. He's a good agent."

"Peter," a nervous Dan asked, "will you take Starger's body back to the house? Rachel and I need to have a serious and private talk. There's something important I have to tell her, a long overdue confession."

Peter Garrett knew what Dan meant and his feelings were with the man for what was coming. "I'll head on into town and handle matters there. I'll postpone my sailing until tomorrow and return to the plantation later."

Dan helped the agent load Earl's body on his horse, then the man left. As Peter vanished from sight, the apprehensive sea captain returned to Rachel's side. "I don't know how to begin, woman."

Rachel looked at her lover and said, "You're right; we need to have a serious talk, Daniel Slade . . . McCandless. Mac! Don't you agree?"

Dan gaped at her in astonishment and dread. "You know?" When she nodded, he asked, "How? When?"

Rachel explained about Harry's letter, then told him about her other discovery. "You've lied and deceived me from the start. Why, Dan?"

"I'm sorry, Rachel, and I'm going to be totally honest with you," he vowed, and was. After he finished his story, he said, "You can believe me and forgive me and we can share a wonderful life together or you can doubt me and reject me, and we'll both be miserable. I love you, Rachel, with all my heart. And to hell with that 'deal' of yours. Even if you can't have children, I love you and I want to marry you. And not to prove you're a killer, either. We both know that isn't true. I've trusted you since before you tried to spurn me the last time. I kept putting off telling you the truth because something always came up to stop me—either perils or doubts you had about me or fear you'd turn against me when you needed me most. The timing always seemed wrong for exposing my secret. If you need time to think, I'll give it to you. Just don't make a hasty decision while you're hurt and angry. What else do I need to explain?"

"How did you know where the missing money was hidden? I saw you two recover it, and I heard what you said." She repeated the words to him.

"This morning I found a notation in the company books about Phillip ordering supplies to repair your front porch steps. When we searched the house and I mentioned that favorite hiding spot of his, you said no work had been done on them recently. But I found a bill indicating work *had* been done. I realized you hadn't known about it, so it was suspicious. I didn't know I was right until Peter and I checked."

"Phillip must have sent me to visit one of the sharecropper families or into town to shop," Rachel speculated, "because I didn't know about it."

"I believe you didn't know, and so does Peter."

"All this time it was right under my feet every time I walked them. If we had looked that night, we wouldn't have had to go through all this trouble."

"It's a blessing in disguise, love," Dan pointed out. "If we'd found and used the money, we wouldn't have learned the truth about everything. It was difficult and scary, but things worked out for the best."

"I guess you're right," she conceded. "But why did Phillip send for you? He believed you were long dead, didn't he?"

"Yes and no. He did for a long time, but he changed his mind. He hired a detective to track me; that's where part of his savings went. The man found news about a Captain Daniel Slade and sent word to Phillip. My brother hoped and prayed it was me, so he sent a letter to our family lawyer in Charleston. When I docked there, he gave it to me." Dan reminded her of the letter's hazy contents he had related earlier. He told her why he had returned home finally to make peace with his father and brother. He told her about the trunk he had picked up with all of Phillip's personal effects and said she was welcome to go through them. He revealed how the misunderstanding about his "death" had occurred.

"The ammunition company and shipping firm weren't doing well, but the arms company was in fine shape. Harry just convinced Phillip it wasn't, to serve his own wicked purposes. When we went to visit the first time, Harry didn't know Phillip was dead, so he was angry and bitter about him being away on that alleged trip and for holding on to the money. He used those early threats to scare Phillip and you. After he learned Phillip was gone, he was sure you had the money, so he became more threatening."

Dan paused, then went on. "Phillip used a lot of money to locate me, and he wasted a lot on gambling. He left a letter with the money to me. He said he was in terrible financial straits and accepted the arms contract to get back on his feet. He said he'd sworn off gambling, but he owed several bets. He did use two hundred thousand of the Cuban's money to try to win big, but he didn't. After he learned the United States Government was involved, he panicked. He didn't have any way to replace the cash he'd lost. He was afraid if he turned the shorted amount over to Harry, the bastard would kill him and keep it, and claim Phillip had lost it all gambling. He hoped I would get his other letter and come help you if anyone caused you trouble. He loved you and trusted you, Rachel. If he had been lucid the morning he died, he would have told you where the money was hidden."

"I'm sure he would have; he was a good and kind man. I'm sorry he got himself entangled in such problems. If he'd confided in me, maybe I could have helped him."

"Maybe some of it was my fault. If he'd known I was alive, maybe he wouldn't have punished himself with guilt and anguish."

"You can't blame yourself for Phillip's weaknesses."

"Just as you can't blame yourself for what Starger did to get you."

"If it hadn't been for his lust over me, they would all be alive."

"It isn't your fault he craved you. He was mad and evil, Rachel."

"But I kept giving him obstacles to remove."

"But you didn't know that."

"I know, but—"

He pressed a forefinger to her lips to halt her from punishing herself for something beyond her control. "No buts, woman. Just as Phillip chose his ill-fated course, so did Earl Starger. I'm sorry I didn't tell you the truth sooner. But there were times when you were reluctant or afraid to tell me things," he reminded. "We've gotten close over the last few months, love, so we can't let this come between us."

"How are things going at the shipping firm?"

That wasn't the response Dan expected or wanted, but he didn't press her. "Fine," he answered "We should have everything straightened out and divided in the next few days. I think Milton Baldwin is basically a decent and honest man. He just got caught up in a desperate ploy to end his troubles. He was aggravated with Phillip for creating problems for them with his gambling and moody behavior at work. When you, as his new partner, came under another dark cloud, things got worse. Harry offered him a way out, and he grabbed it without thinking. You'll have McCandless Shipping back this week. Do you remember enough from working for Phillip to run it?"

"You told Milton it was being moved back to Charleston."

"That was when I thought you'd marry me and move there to live."

"Do you think anyone here would trade with me, the Black Widow?"

"Why not? Everyone will know the truth soon."

"Even if they believe the report, they'd be too embarrassed to deal with me. Do as you promised Milton; move your family's company home."

Her words dismayed him, but her tone wasn't accusatory or bitter. "I don't want to take the company from you, love. I don't want to take away anything Phillip left you. He loved you; you're his widow and heir."

"That's because he thought you were dead. He would have left the firm to you if he had known you were alive. I think you should have it."

"Why, Rachel?"

"Because you'll need it to support a wife and hopefully a family."

Dan trembled with anticipation. "Does that mean. . . ."

"That I love you and want to marry you? Yes," she said with a smile.

"You understand and forgive me?"

"Yes, Captain McCandless, if your offer is still open to acceptance."

Dan swept her into his arms and hugged her tightly. "It is, love."

Their gazes met and they kissed, washing away the pain and doubts of their pasts. Their love was too strong and special to allow a mistake to destroy it. Their lips meshed many times until they were breathless.

"We have to stop this, sir. Peter will come looking for us soon."

"Only if you'll agree to marry me this week."

"How about Friday afternoon?" she suggested.

"Why so long?" he asked, putting on a painful but humorous look.

"We have matters to settle first: the firm, telling my mother about Earl, a talk with Lula Mae, and plans for a wedding. I don't care what people say or think, I want this last one to be done right and proper."

"A real wedding, eh?"

"Yes, for once, for a last time, forever."

*

Two days later, Richard Fleming arrived at Moss Haven. His shoulder was still bandaged and in a sling, but he was fine. He, Rachel, Dan, and Peter spent hours talking about their adventures. Her brother was delighted and relieved to learn Peter had shipped the rest of the arms last week, and they should have reached Ramón today. Richard was returning to Cuba after he was healed, but only for a short time. He had a big surprise for Rachel and their mother: he had located his twin sister.

"I've already sent Rosemary a telegram and told her to come here Thursday. With your good news, my request and arrival are perfect timing."

"Did Dan tell you the other good news?" Peter asked Rachel.

"About me keeping the arms money?" After the agent nodded, she said, "Yes, and that's wonderful. I can use it to settle the companies' debts in Athens and Augusta. I'll repay Dan his investment, then give any left over to Molly Sue Leathers. Harry's wife has the profit coming from the sale of the arms company and has other holdings for support, and Harry's family doesn't have a right to his share after what he did. Molly Sue lost everything except George's insurance, so she deserves his share: George was a good and honest man, and he did his part. Since my husband gambled away his share, it isn't fair for me to take any of what's left after the debts are paid."

"You used your insurance money on the deal and lost your share of the profit, so you're out a big sum of money. Phillip was my brother, so you don't need to repay me. The men who lost their jobs and earnings at the ammunition company need any remaining cash more than I do."

Rachel smiled at him. "That's very kind and generous, Dan. Molly Sue will take care of that part for us. I did receive a cable from that buyer in Athens; the sale for the company and store in town is being handled this week, as soon as those outstanding debts are cleared, which weren't as large as Harry claimed. At least the out-of-town matters will be resolved and I will make a little profit on that sale. Peter, what about problems with that illegal use of the arms' patents?"

"Those faked licenses have been destroyed, and the arms made by them are out of the country. We'll drop that issue. As soon as Harry's tried in court, he'll never get out of prison."

A special dinner was prepared and served by a relieved and happy Lula Mae Morris. The housekeeper, who was moving to Charleston to tend the couple's new home, hummed as she worked. Her frown lines had softened, as had her mood. With a heavy burden lifted off her shoulders, she was a changed woman, and a trustworthy one. She was ashamed of how she had been duped by Earl Starger, but everyone understood how it had happened and forgave her. Never again would she doubt or be disloyal to the mistress she loved as her own child.

*

Thursday, Catherine Fleming Starger arrived for the wedding of her youngest daughter. She was contrite over her mistakes, but she found it difficult to grieve over the deceitful and wicked man she had married. It would take time to get her life and emotions back under control, but she knew she could do it. As with Lula Mae, the still beautiful blonde was elated over not being blamed for her past mistakes.

That afternoon, Rosemary Fleming Sims and her husband reached the plantation from their small farm in Macon. She told her sister and mother how she had met her husband and where she had been living for five years in central Georgia. The couple had two children, both boys, who were staying with her husband's sister. She promised to bring them to get to know their grandmother, aunt, and two uncles soon at White Cloud and in Charleston. She said she hadn't contacted them since leaving because she didn't want the mean Earl Starger to know where to find her.

Rachel and her family had a wonderful and tearful reunion, together again in happiness for the first time since the war. They talked for hours, telling each other what had transpired for them over the years.

Later in private, Rosemary confided to Rachel, "I couldn't write or visit Mama because I wanted Earl out of my life forever. He was always pawing at me and I knew it would get worse if I didn't leave home. I was afraid to tell Mama about his wicked behavior because I feared he would hurt her. I saw him once and he threatened to hurt both of you if I ever saw or spoke to you again. I knew you had married and left, too, but I didn't know where to find you. He was vile and dangerous, Rachel; I think he killed Randall, but I don't want Mama to know; it would hurt her too deeply."

"You're right, Rosemary; we can't ever tell her. I suspected the same thing, and we all know now he was capable of murder. Thank God, he's out of our lives. I've missed you so much. I'm happy you're here."

"So am I, little sister. Tomorrow will be a glorious day for us."

*

That evening the Fleming family and Dan read the newspaper, and enjoyed the feature story by none other than Harold Seymour about Rachel's incredible experience as an alleged Black Widow. At last she was exonerated of all suspicions and allegations, and her name was cleared. They also noticed an article about a move north by Miss Camellia Jones. That was another secret Rachel wouldn't burden her mother with: Earl's affair and his intention to leave her for the flaming-haired vixen.

Rachel knew the police chief was sending a copy to Craig's brother so Paul would know who had murdered his brother. She was glad he would learn the truth, and hopefully it would make him feel guilty over his past mistreatment of her.

*

Friday at five o'clock on June twenty-fifth, friends and family gathered in the church outside of Savannah to watch Rachel Fleming Barlow Newman McCandless marry Daniel Slade McCandless, her former brother-in-law. Dan's ship hadn't sailed for Africa, so Luke Conner could be his best man and his faithful and genial crew could attend.

Nor had Peter Garrett sailed, so he, too, could be at the ceremony. Molly Sue

Leathers came from Augusta to share in the happy event. Milton Baldwin and his wife were also present. Burke Wells and his wife wouldn't have missed the joyful moment for anything and Lula Mae Morris, as with Catherine, wept tears of happiness. Also present to witness the occasion were lawyer Frank Henley and his wife, jeweler Adam Meigs and his wife, reporter Harold Seymour—who hadn't been invited, but who wanted to write one final story, the happy ending—and most of Rachel's sharecroppers.

The smiling couple stood before the preacher who was ready to begin the ceremony. Rosemary, her matron-of-honor, and the groom's best friend and first mate were positioned on either side of them. Richard had retaken his seat beside his mother after giving away the radiant bride.

"Rachel and Dan, friends and family," the pastor began, "we are gathered here today under the eyes of God and these witnesses to join this couple in holy matrimony." He read several Scriptures relating to marriage and their duties to each other, then asked them to repeat their vows.

In a soft voice, the bride in a lovely pale-blue dress responded, "I, Rachel, take you, Dan, to be my lawful husband, to love and to honor, in sickness and in health, in good times and in bad, for richer or poorer, and until death us do part."

After his instructions, the groom, handsome in a dark-blue suit, responded, "I, Dan, take you, Rachel, to be my lawful wife, to love and to cherish, to support and protect, in sickness and in health, in good times and in bad, for richer or poorer, and until death us do part."

After some words from the preacher, Dan slipped a gold band on her finger and said, "With this ring, I thee wed." He smiled and added, "Forever."

Rachel gazed into his adoring blue eyes and repeated, "Forever."

The pastor placed a hand above and below their clasped ones and said, "By the power given to me by God and this state, I pronounce you man and wife. What God hath joined together, let no man put asunder. I wish you much joy in your blessed union. You may kiss your wife, Captain McCandless."

Dan and Rachel faced each other. For a moment, they exchanged smiles and gazes, then kissed briefly. As they embraced, each whispered, "I love you" into the other's ear.

While they did so, the pastor announced that the guests would be dismissed to the grounds for a party where they could speak with the happy couple.

When they parted, certain people couldn't wait that long to give their congratulations and affections. Rachel was embraced by her older sister, and Dan was hugged by Luke Connor. Richard, Catherine, Lula Mae, and Burke joined them to do the same.

The newlyweds were guided outside to a location shaded by live oaks with lacy moss and set up with wooden tables and chairs. An assortment of food and sweets had been prepared by Catherine, Rosemary, and Lula Mae. Champagne had been furnished as a gift from Milton Baldwin.

Everyone, particularly the bride and groom, had a wonderful time chatting with friends, eating the delicious fare, and sipping champagne.

*

With a houseful of family and a ship loaded with crew, Rachel and Dan went to a hotel on the edge of town to be alone. A short time after arriving, the couple was undressed and in bed. They set out to weave golden webs of rapture and enchantment around each other.

"I love you, Rachel McCandless," he murmured and kissed her.

"I love you, Daniel McCandless," she responded before the next one.

Rachel gazed into her love's eyes. Her journey to find and win him had taken almost three years. At last the dark cloud over her had lifted, allowing glorious sunshine to replace it. She was wed to her fourth and last husband, to the only man she had ever loved or desired. The Black Widow gossip and accusations had been laid to rest. Dan had asked her to "promise me forever," and she had. For now, their bright future would be ignored while they concentrated on their present and each other.

Epilogue

"What are you doing, love?" Dan asked as he entered their bedroom.

Rachel glanced up at her handsome husband and smiled. "Catching up on correspondence. The only time it's quiet and calm enough to do so is when the children are napping or after they're put to bed at night. They're a handful of energy and curiosity. They keep me busy."

"You're the one who insisted on proving herself," he jested.

Rachel laughed and teased, "I'm not sure I meant three times in five years, my virile captain. You do want me to have time and stamina for you. I don't know how I would manage if it weren't for Lula Mae. I should tell you to order seaman Zed Tarply to stop courting her before we lose her."

"Did you ever imagine that grumpy spinster turning sweet and soft on men? She and Zed are behaving like youths experiencing their first loves."

"They are, and I'm happy for both of them."

"So am I. Everybody should be as lucky as we are."

As he removed his jacket and put it away, she asked, "Did your meeting go well? You're home early today."

Beaming with pride, he answered, "Yes, it did. I hauled in another big client and account. McCandless Shipping Firm is very successful and prosperous, woman. I'm glad we moved it back here. Milton's doing well, too. We've worked out a few nice deals together."

"I'm glad we settled our past misunderstanding. You were right; he is a decent man, and we all make mistakes. Is Luke coming for dinner tomorrow night? He docks this evening, doesn't he?"

"Yes. He's enjoying being the captain of the *Merry Wind* and has done a fine job of it these past years. He says she still handles as if new."

"Do you miss being at sea and roaming her decks?"

"I don't have time. Too much business to tend and too busy with my wonderful family. The few trips I make satisfy me . . . Who are you writing?"

She watched him approach with easy strides. Even after years of being with him, he still made her heart flutter wildly and her body flame with desire just by being near. "Mama and Rosemary," she answered, "living and working together at White Cloud is good for all of them. Mama's healthy and happy again. Even with Rosemary and

Tom selling their small farm and moving in with her, Mama's become strong and independent. Rosemary needs the help with her children; my heavens, six balls of energy to chase and keep out of trouble!" she murmured, referring to two sets of twins added to the two boys her sister had when Rachel and Dan married.

"Six children are a handful. I'm relieved ours came in ones."

"Me, too," Rachel concurred with a grin. "I bet those children love living on a big plantation and romping all over the place."

"Do you ever miss Moss Haven or Savannah?"

"No. I was wise to sell it to Burke Wells. He hasn't missed a yearly payment yet. He has his sharecroppers bringing in hefty earnings for him."

"That and farming the rest of his land. He's smart and hardworking. He was pleased to see me when I visited two weeks ago. He wants you and the children to come next time. Have you heard from Richard this week?"

"Today. I plan to write him tomorrow. I did tell you his last letter said Ramón and Rosaria got married?" Dan nodded. "Richard's being sent to South America this time. Something about trouble between Chile, Peru, and Bolivia. His skill with the Spanish language has been helpful for him again."

"Your brother did a superb job in Cuba. The truce won't last long, but at least it's quiet for now after years of fierce battle."

"He said they're calling the rebellion the Ten Years War. Sad, but it began long before '68 and it's still rumbling after '78. It isn't over."

"Richard and Peter expect a big and final war to settle things. Luke hopes it stays quiet, because he's been making runs to and from there."

"How is Peter?" she asked. "Have you heard from him lately?"

"Not in a few months. He's doing fine, still agenting," he teased.

"I doubt he or my brother will ever give it up; they love that exciting and challenging and adventurous life."

"When either or both find a woman like you, like I did, they will."

"Thank you, kind sir, but I'm the lucky one to have found you."

Dan leaned over and nibbled at her neck. Rachel giggled and squirmed. He held out his hand in seductive invitation. She met his gaze, read the enticement, and stood. Their mouths meshed in a heady kiss.

Nothing had changed their desire for each other over the years. They knew how fortunate they were to be so happy and prosperous. Their life and family were fulfilling.

They had moved Phillip's body to the McCandless family plot near Charleston, and all ghosts concerning him and the past had faded and vanished. Only good things seemed to happen to them now.

Following many kisses and caresses, they were breathless and burning with need. "I'll lock the door," Rachel said. "We don't have long, my love. Naptime only last two hours or less, and minutes are wasting."

Rachel turned after bolting the door for privacy. She gazed at the naked man awaiting her on the bed, as he had discarded his garments swiftly in his eagerness. His sable head was propped against the headboard with his back resting against pillows. His bare torso was exposed, but a light sheet concealed his lower half, a teasing ruse. She grinned.

Dan watched his wife walk to the bed and halt beside it to strip. She removed her shoes with mischievous leisure. She unbuttoned her dress and peeled it off her shoulders, then worked it over her hips, wriggling seductively as she did so. With playful tantalizing, she unlaced her chemise and slipped it over her head, exposing full breasts to his merry gaze. She worked her bloomers off and kicked them aside. Her body was still slim, sleek, and taut. Its olive covering was satiny to the touch, and he yearned to trace his fingers over it.

"You're tormenting me, woman," he said with pride and desire.

Rachel seized the sheet and whipped it aside, revealing his splendid form. "We promised we'd never have anything between us, remember?" She lay down beside him. Her dark-brown hair fanned out on the pillow and haloed her face. Her expressive eyes were like golden honey and filled with hunger for him. She raised herself to trail her fingers over his hairy chest, making tiny curls along her path. She felt his heart beating at a swift pace. Her fingers paused at his pulse point to feel it racing with need. She roamed his jawline, smoothly shaven and strong. She sent her fingers to journey over his lips and nose. She so enjoyed touching and arousing him.

Dan shifted to send his hands and lips to work on her exquisite body. He wanted to make her senses spin wildly, as she had his. He savored the sensation of her silky skin beneath his fingertips. He roved her in all directions as if mapping a route to paradise. His hands buried themselves in her lush mane and didn't seek freedom for a time as he kissed her deeply.

They embraced and clung together, relishing the intoxicating contact. They explored each other's body with equal and rising passion.

Dan's mouth left hers to travel slowly and purposefully down her neck, over her bare shoulders, and around her firm breasts. He brushed his lips ever so lightly at first over each taut peak to allow his hot breathing and warm moisture to tease and enflame the straining bud. He urged his tongue to lavish blissful attention there while he drank sweet nectar. He felt her quiver in anticipation and heard her groan with pleasure. He sent his hands on a sensuous mission to the steamy core of her womanhood. With skill and tenderness, he caressed her moist and satiny flesh there.

Rachel closed her eyes and absorbed the rapturous inducements. She dreamily stroked his muscular back, fondled his tight buttocks, and sought his throbbing hardness. She smiled when he sucked in a loud breath of air and stiffened for a moment as she caressed and stimulated his maleness.

Soon both were consumed by passion's flames. She didn't have to tell him she was ready and eager to have him thrust within her, and he didn't have to be told or urged. He moved atop her and slipped inside her. United, they worked as one to heighten their ravenous appetites and to appease them. They labored with skill and knowledge, as they knew from experience how to please each other and themselves.

"This is wonderful, Dan," she murmured against his mouth.

"Always, my love," he replied and sealed their lips.

They couldn't restrain themselves any longer. They ardently raced toward victory and captured it.

After, as they lay contented and aglow in each other's arms, both shifted their heads at the same time to gaze at the other. They exchanged smiles, then a tender kiss.

"I love you, Rachel, more and more every day."

"I always think I can't love you more or enjoy lovemaking more, but it happens every time. I think I've had the best experience of my life, but the next one is even better than all the others put together. I still feel weak and hot when you look at me or touch me. How I do love you, Dan."

He hugged her possessively as his heart surged with deep emotion. "Destiny, woman; we're matched, perfect for each other. I think I sensed that the first time I looked into this beautiful face and these unusual eyes. You bewitch me, wife, and don't ever break your spell over me."

"I won't, my love. Remember what you demanded and I promised?"

Dan smiled and murmured huskily, "Forever."

"Yes, Captain Daniel Slade McCandless, forever, and you'll get it."

Dedicated with love to:

my husband, Michael,
my two daughters, Melanie Taylor and Angela Taylor Reffett
and my son-in-law, Mark
And with
much love and pride for my first grandchild,
Mark Alexander Reffett

Acknowledgments and Thanks to:

the staffs of historical Forts Concho, Davis, and Stockton in Texas; the wonderful people in San Angelo and San Antonio; the staffs of the Texas tourists bureaus and chambers of commerces across the Lone Star State; and to the many friends we made as we researched and camped along my characters' trail. The staff at Fort Davis was particularly helpful with books and information. We arrived during a historical celebration that featured reenactments and demonstrations of fort life, 1890s clothing and weapons, riding formation-saber-pistol-cannon demonstrations, and much more. "Fort Davis is today one of the most complete surviving examples of the typical western military fort to be found" *(Fort Davis: Historical Handbook Number 38*, by Robert Utley). It was fun and educational to be present on such a special occasion. Thanks to all you Texans who made my research there so pleasant and unforgettable.

A special note of thanks to my in-laws, Joe and Betty Taylor, and to my friend, Terri Gibbs Daughtry, for teaching me so much about the courage and humor it takes to overcome disabilities. They were inspirations for Tom and Navarro.

Chapter

1

"A cold-blooded gunslinger is exactly what we need, Papa. A man who can strike as quickly and accurately as a rattlesnake, one without a conscience."

"Men like that can't be trusted, Jess. We'd never be able to control him. The way my luck is running these days, he'd rope up with Fletcher and betray us."

"Papa, you always said even a bad man has a crazy streak of loyalty toward the man who hires him or when he gives his word on something. If we pay him enough, he can be bought. If we don't get help soon, Wilbur Fletcher will own this land and we'll be buried on it. Or left to feed the coyotes and buzzards; that would be more like the evil bastard."

"Jess!" her father shouted in dismay. "Watch your tongue. Your ma and me never allowed you children to speak such words. This trouble is weighing heavy on all of us. It's got us to thinking, talking, and acting loco." Jedidiah Lane wiped the sweat and dust from his wrinkled face and took a deep breath.

"That's my meaning, Papa; we have to stop it soon or be destroyed. I know you don't want a dangerous gunslinger around and I know how you hate to seek help, but we must. The soldiers and Sheriff Cooper can't do the job, and we can't handle it alone. What else can we do?"

They had had this disturbing talk several times before, but Jed was still reluctant to admit he could not defend his land and family against the easterner who had itchy hands for his ranch and seemed ready and willing to do anything to get it. Jed ran his dirty fingers through graying auburn hair, then drew a bucket of water. As they did every day, he and Jess had halted at the well behind the house to wash up before going inside for their evening meal.

"Listen to me, Papa; the time for talking and praying is over. You know I would never suggest such a desperate plan if there was any other way to defeat Fletcher. What's so wrong with it? He has gunslingers on his payroll. We need a man who thinks like they do, a man who can outwit and outgun them. We can't fight and take care of the ranch at the same time. This is one of our busiest seasons. If we hire a gunslinger, he can handle Fletcher and his men for us while we tend to the branding and planting. At least he can teach us how to thwart him."

As Jed rolled his sleeves, he reasoned in a weary tone, "What can one man do, Jess? We have fifteen hands and it's made no difference. Fletcher still does as he pleases. If Sheriff Cooper or the Army gave us a little help, we could trap and stop that sorry bas—" He halted before saying the same crude word he had scolded Jessie for using.

"Over the years we've endured many hardships, but this trouble is different. We know Wilbur Fletcher is behind it. No month passes without another offer from him to buy our spread."

Jed splashed cold water on his face. His joints ached and he moved slower these days, reminding him that he wouldn't always be around to protect and provide for his loved ones. If only Alice were at his side. If he lost his mother, his children, and the ranch . . .

"Papa, you aren't listening," Jessie said, tugging at his arm and worrying over another of these recent withdrawals into dreamy distance. "The Army and the sheriff told us they can't do anything without proof. They won't even look for any until they have 'just reason.' I understand they can't camp here to observe; Fletcher would only lie low until they left. But they're the law; they should do something, anything. While they're waiting for him to make a mistake, he's getting stronger and bolder, and we're getting closer to that cliff he wants to push us over. Please let me ride into San Angelo and search for a gunslinger. I'll be gone less than two weeks. Then we can have this trouble settled before summer."

Jedidiah Lane looked at his daughter with indecision in his dark-blue eyes. Her reddish-brown hair hung to her waist in a thick braid that had loosened itself during her labors. Her face was flushed with excitement and anger. Jed shook his head when he saw that her sky-blue eyes that should be filled with peace and joy instead sparkled with determination and hatred. His gaze swept the petite body clad in men's clothing. She looked so fragile, but he knew she was strong. He was so used to having Jessie at his side and doing a man's share of work that he often forgot she was a girl. No, he corrected himself, at twenty-four, she was a young woman, a beautiful creature. He often worried that some man would steal her from him, and he didn't know how he would exist without her. "You can't go into a rowdy town like that, Jess. I'll send Matt or one of the hands."

That wasn't what Jessica Marie Lane wanted to hear. She needed distance to cool her anger and clear her head. She had to find a way to help her father. She also wanted time away from the trouble and her responsibilities. Though she loved the ranch and her family dearly, she needed time to relax and think. Jessie wasn't sure if her father realized just how dangerous Wilbur Fletcher was. It had been she and their foreman, Matt Cordell, who had convinced her father that Fletcher was behind their recent troubles. Her father had created the Box L and had made it succeed through many lean years. In a way, Jedidiah Lane didn't think anyone or anything could wrestle it from his grasp. It sounded as if she finally had persuaded him they needed outside assistance, and she wanted to select the best man for the job.

"I stand a better chance of finding and hiring the right man than any of them do, Papa. You know I can take care of myself. I'll take Big Ed with me and be on the alert every minute. You need Matt and the others to remain here to run the ranch and watch out for Fletcher."

"Maybe you can locate a retired Texas Ranger," Jed replied as a concession. "You know how skilled they are."

Her tone was respectful but firm as she said, "No, Papa. A Ranger has law running through his veins. He would try to handle this matter like an assignment, like a lawman. We need a man with a killer instinct, one who follows our orders, no matter what they are. We might have to do things a Ranger wouldn't allow. Fletcher doesn't respect or obey the law or any code of honor, and we can't either. Good men don't always win, Papa. Nor can we take a Christian attitude and turn the other cheek. This trouble isn't going to stop until one of us loses. To win, we have to fight like he does: mean, dirty, and clever."

Jed stiffened. "We aren't like that, Jess. We're good, honest, hardworking folk. If we start breaking the law, we're no better than Fletcher is. This thing has to be handled right."

"Good won't win over Evil this time, Papa, unless we fight Fletcher on his terms. You always say, 'When a man wallows in the mud, he gets up dirty.' The truth is, mud will wash off, Papa, but six feet of dirt can't be pushed away from the inside. We have to face bitter reality: it's kill or be killed."

Jed sighed wearily. "In the past, I've used my wits and courage to defeat strong forces, like those Apaches and Comanches and rustlers and even nature. Blood has rarely been shed on my land. I kept praying that Fletcher would give up his hunger for the Box L Ranch, might even return East or move to another area. Perhaps you're right in saying the man will never give up. If so, you must be right this time, too. I depend on you, Jess, and trust you completely. You're smart. You're proud and tough like me, but gentle and wise like your ma was. For twenty-six years, this has been my land, my heart, Jess. After I made claim on it with the government's approval, my Alice used her inheritance to buy our first stock and supplies. We worked side by side creating this spread. We faced droughts, rustlers, sickness, hunger, cattle disease, poverty in bad times, and my pa's death. Until we built this house with our bare hands, we lived in a tent, then a shack. We watched two sons die and we buried them out there. I watched my sweet wife suffer and leave me, and my hands were tied by God. Fate dealt me many crushing blows, Jess, but I overcame every one. Sometimes I'm too stubborn, and even reckless, but I won't give up to nothing and nobody. My sweet Alice and two sons are buried on this land; so is my pa. I'll be buried next to them one day."

Jed's voice grew hoarse with emotion. "Sometimes I got depressed and tired. But I haven't felt this helpless and angry since Alice and the boys died. Ma is getting old and weak, and Pa's been gone a long time. You've been like a son to me, Jess. I taught you to do anything a man can do, sometimes even better than most men, so you can take care of this spread when it's yours. If I have to die for my home and family, so be it. But I won't die without doing all I can to stay alive and to hold on." He drew another deep breath and wiggled his sore shoulders to loosen his muscles. "You best leave at first light before I change my mind. I'll go tell Matt and Big Ed our plan. Be real careful-like, Jess. If anything happened to you, I couldn't bear it. You're the rose of my heart and life, girl. When your ma was taken from me . . ."

"I know, Papa," she responded, hugging him in gratitude and to bring him solace. "I still miss her, too. I'll be fine. Before you can round up the calves for spring branding, I'll be home again, with help. You'll see, Papa, that rattlesnake won't bite us again without suffering several strikes in return."

Jessie watched her father head for the bunkhouse, his shoulders slumped and his expression somber. He hadn't reminisced this way before, and now she knew what had been on his troubled mind. Although they were closer than most fathers and daughters, Jed usually kept his worries and fears penned inside. Jedidiah Lane was a strong, tough, independent man and he had taught his heir to be the same way; but this frustrating situation was overwhelming him, and that saddened her.

It also made Jessie feel guilty about the many times she had resented being depended upon so much. She resented the fact that her older brother's death had caused this duty and burden to fall on her back, forcing her to make herself tough enough to bear them. She resented being a "son" instead of a daughter. She hated those feelings, but couldn't help them.

She wanted romance, love; marriage, her own home and children. But there was little chance of meeting and marrying anyone if her life didn't change. Even if she did meet a man, how could she *leave* with him? What would happen to her father, her grandmother, to her disabled brother, to this beloved ranch, to her immature sister until Mary Louise wed? If her father had an accident, who would take care of him and the Box L Ranch? Gran and Tom couldn't, and her self-centered sister wouldn't. She was trapped here by her responsibilities.

Besides, her blood, tears, and sweat were on this land, too. She loved it as much as Jed did. It would belong to her one day. She knew her father hadn't meant to cause her pain. He loved her even more than his other two children because she was so close and helpful to him. Jessie knew that her father had difficulty expressing love since her mother's death. She believed that he was afraid that whomever he loved deeply would be taken from him.

No doubt, she mused, her father yearned for a love to replace the wonderful one he had lost. Surely there had to be more to life than hard work for both of them. But how, when, and where could she find a true love?

By all accounts, Jessie fretted, she was a spinster! Was it, she asked herself, so terrible to experience nibbles of resentment once in a while? Was it so awful, so wicked, so selfish of her to sometimes think, *What about me?* To sometimes want to live her life for herself instead of always for others? Maybe someone special would ride into her life one day. *Stop dreaming, Jessie. You have work to do.*

*

"Father said you can do *what?*" Mary Louise shrieked.

Jessie glanced at her younger sister, whose dark blue eyes were wide with astonishment. "Ride to San Angelo to hire help against Wilbur Fletcher," she repeated.

"That is ridiculous! You and Father will get us all killed."

"It's the only path left open to us. I'm tired. We'll talk later," she said, hoping to end the conversation before an argument could begin. "We've been repairing cut fences and gathering strays since sunrise. I have to get packed. I'm leaving at dawn."

"I'm going with you," Mary Louise stated.

"You can't. We have to ride fast and hard. You know what that terrain is like. Besides, there isn't time for shopping or playing."

"I never get to go anywhere or do anything fun!" Mary Louise pouted. "I'm stuck in this godforsaken wilderness without friends or diversions!"

As she gathered clothes for her journey, Jessie reasoned, "One day, all this trouble will be over, and you'll have plenty of both. Be patient, Mary Louise."

"Never! It's too spread out and wild here. We're practically cut off from life by mountains and deserts. The only close neighbor we have is Mr. Fletcher, and you two think he's our enemy. None of you care if I grow old and die here. I hate it. Father should sell out and move us back to civilization."

Jessie knew it was futile to debate Mary Louise's last statement. Continuing to pack, she replied, "You're exaggerating. There are several towns and posts within a day or two of us. We go there for supplies and holidays. And there are other ranches within a few days' ride. We aren't that secluded, little sister."

"What good are they to me? I'm never allowed to visit them for more than a few hours or overnight. And there's no one proper to meet there. We have no entertainment, as you can't call barn dances much fun. I'm lonely and bored."

"There's plenty to do. For one thing, Gran needs help in the kitchen. You know she can't get around like she used to. She's seventy now and needs help. If you'd stop complaining all the time, you'd find plenty to keep yourself busy."

"With slave labor? I shouldn't have to feed chickens, milk cows, grub in the vegetable garden, clean house, and do washing. Father can hire servants to tend us. All my friends at school had them. We aren't poor, you know."

"We don't need to fritter away hard-earned money on servants when we can do our own chores. Besides, we don't have an extra room for a female helper, and she can't live in the bunkhouse with fifteen men."

"If Tom went off to school as I had to do, she could use his room like Rosa did before she ran off to marry that drifter."

"He wasn't a drifter. He was a seasonal wrangler, and she loved him. It was time for Tom to move out of Gran's room; they both need privacy. And you know why he can't go off to school. The boys would give him a hard time, and he'd be miserable. You're smart, little sister. If you help me with Tom's lessons each day, he'll learn far more than I can teach him alone. That would give you something important to do."

Mary Louise glared at Jessie, then flipped her sunny curls over her shoulder. "I'm no schoolmarm, and I won't be treated as one."

"Teaching your own brother isn't going to make you a schoolmarm. He needs help, Mary Louise. Between the two of us—"

"No. I do enough work around here as it is."

Jessie looked at her sister's perfect features, currently hardened by a pout. Mary Louise was two inches taller than her own five feet four inches. On occasion Jessie wished she had her sister's tame golden tresses instead of her own auburn hair that sometimes frizzed into small, loose curls or tufted on the ends to do as it pleased unless controlled by a snug braid. Her sister's eyes sparkled like precious jewels, expensive sapphires. The lucky blonde had an attention-stealing figure, whereas—even though she was four years older—Jessie was less filled out in the bust and hips. Men always noticed Mary Louise in a crowd. The bad thing was that Mary Louise was too aware of her exquisite beauty and the power it gave her. When it suited her, she used those charms and wiles without mercy. Jessie was glad she didn't have her sister's sorry attitude and personality, or Mary Louise's insensitive and selfish nature.

Annoyed by now, Jessie responded a little harshly, "You do very little, and you know it. Gran isn't a tattler, but I know she covers for your laziness many times. What have you done today? From the way you're dressed as if for a party, I doubt very little. It isn't fair to put your work on Gran's tired shoulders."

"It isn't fair to force me to live here and work like a servant."

Provoked, Jessie asked, "If you want to leave so badly, why don't you accept a position as schoolmarm in a large town or in a private school like *you* attended? It's a very respectable job. You're smart enough to do anything you wish."

"Smart enough to find a way out of here one day, but not by teaching brats!"

"I'm sure you will, little sister. Just make certain the trail you take from home is a good and safe one. Life isn't as easy as you think." Jessie realized that her sister was more bitter, spoiled, and resentful than she had imagined. That troubled her deeply, but she didn't want to deal with this constant irritation tonight. "You've been home from school for nearly two years, Mary Louise. It's past time to forget the East and stop making yourself so miserable."

"I am miserable. I hate it out here. There's nothing but heat, work, and solitude.

I'm beautiful and educated, but how can I meet a proper husband or friends in this wilderness? I will not wither and die as a spinster, Jessica!"

Ever since she'd come back from school, Mary Louise had been different. She called Papa "Father" and Jess "Jessica." The girl made everyone miserable!

The blonde continued. "This harsh land killed Mother. Look at pictures of her when she was young. She was beautiful and shapely. When she died, she looked old and worn. That isn't going to happen to me. She never recovered fully from Tom's horrible birth. It's too hard on a delicate woman out here, and I refuse to live and work and look like a man as you do, Jessica Lane."

"Tom's birth was difficult, but Mama died of a fever she caught from that drifter. You can't blame Tom," she scolded.

"If he'd never been born, she wouldn't have been so weak and gotten sick."

"Mary Louise Lane! That's a horrible thing to say."

"We're lucky we weren't born deformed, too. Mother had trouble bearing children; she lost two others, you know that. Father treated her as one of his brood mares. She was too frail after Tom to risk another child, but he didn't care."

"That isn't true," Jessie countered. "Davy died when he was two, and the other baby shortly after birth. Tom was seven years old, so Mama wasn't still ailing from his hard birth. That's a mean thing to say, little sister, and a terrible thing to think."

Undaunted, Mary Louise retorted, "If Davy hadn't died, you wouldn't be Father's son. You would be married and have children. If Mother were still alive, she'd have forced him to leave this ranch land by now."

"Mama loved it here. We all do, except you."

"If she were still alive, she'd hate it, too. She would realize what it was costing her to remain. It will steal our beauty and drain us dry, Jessica, if we don't get away soon. Talk to Father; he listens to you. We could have such a grand life near a big town."

"I love this ranch as much as Papa does. I'm sorry home and family don't mean the same to you any more. And I'm sorry you've been so unhappy since your return. We missed you those five years you were gone. You might be happier if you tried."

Chilliness filled the girl's eyes and tone. "If I were missed and loved so much, I wouldn't have been sent away and kept away for so many years. I can't be blamed for falling in love with civilization. I feel like a stranger, an intruder, here."

"That's your doing, little sister. But you were loved and missed. Mama wanted you to be educated as a lady in the way she was. Before she died, Papa promised her he'd make sure you were. If I hadn't been eighteen already, he would have sent me, too. The only reason I didn't go was because when I was the right age the war had just ended and there was still trouble back there. And we couldn't afford it after the war took its toll on everyone. Mama did her best to teach me here, just as I'm doing with Tom. Besides, Papa and I couldn't take care of you, Tom, and Gran properly while working the ranch. Gran was sick back then and had her hands full with Tom. Papa didn't send you away to be mean, Mary Louise. How can you resent the years back East? You so clearly love them as the best in your life."

"You wouldn't understand, Jessica. You've never seen the places I have or done the things I have. You've never had friends around all the time. I miss them. Letters aren't the same, and Father refuses to let me go visit them. If you knew what the outside world was like, you'd do anything to get away."

Jessie was aware she didn't have any close female friends, but she did have some nice acquaintances who she saw occasionally in town or on special occasions. There were plenty of men on the ranch and in town, but it was true that none of them courted her. Here, the hands sometimes treated her as a sister, but more often as "one of the boys" because she worked with them daily doing the same tasks. Only infrequently had a seasonal cowpuncher paid attention to her as a woman, but she had never been tempted to encourage one beyond a stolen kiss.

Sometimes, Jessie admitted, she did want to see other places, make real friends, do exciting things, and find love like she read about in books and old magazines. Maybe that was another reason why this trip to San Angelo was so important to her. But her place was here, and she had accepted that, not threatened to find a way to change it as Mary Louise did. Yet her sister was accustomed to another kind of life. Jessie was trying to understand her feelings, but Mary Louise was so greedy and rebellious. If that was what "civilization" did to a woman, Jessie concluded, she didn't want it.

"We're so different now, Mary Louise, but we *are* sisters. If only you would—"

"Sisters help each other, Jessica. If you truly love me and want what's best for me, you'll convince Father to send me back East, at least for a long visit. His stubborn selfishness is going to get us all killed."

Jessie knew if the girl left, she would never return, and perhaps that would be best for everyone. But she didn't want Mary Louise hurt or endangered in her desperation to escape the life she hated. The girl couldn't be reasoned with, so Jessie decided to drop the distressing matter for now. "I wish you didn't feel that way. I have to finish packing. Please go help Gran with supper."

"It's *dinner,* Jessica. How like a rough, unmannered man you've become over the years without Mother here to guide you."

Vexed, Jessie snapped, "What can you expect after being Papa's 'son' since birth and working every day like a man?" She instantly regretted her words and continued in a softer tone, "But you're wrong; I know I'm a woman. I want to find love and marriage one day, but first this trouble has to be settled. And it will be after I return with help."

Mary Louise grinned with satisfaction at Jessie's irritation. "How can you find a decent husband? All you see are crude cowboys, penniless drifters, and rough soldiers. If you married one, like moon-eyed Matt, you'd be stuck here forever, slaving on the land and pushing out babies. Not me, Jessica. I'm going to leave. I'm going to marry a rich and handsome man. I'm going to travel and be pampered as I deserve. Look at yourself in the mirror. You're as tanned as a cowboy. You wear your hair braided, and you hardly ever don a dress. The sun and work are sapping what little beauty you have. In a few years, even that will be gone. Perhaps even old Mathew Cordell won't desire you then."

Jessie gazed at Mary Louise, who was standing with hands on shapely hips and a devilish gleam in her deep-blue eyes. A challenging expression was on the blonde's face, but Jessie responded calmly. "Matt is our foreman and my friend, nothing more. He's never tried to catch my eye, not that he isn't ruggedly good-looking. I respect him. He's dependable, hardworking, and kind."

Mary Louise laughed mischievously. "And nearing forty. Of course, you are only ten to fifteen years younger! When Father dies, you'll need a man to help you. Matt's already well trained, and your choices are few. By all accounts, big sister, you're already a spinster at twenty-four."

The redhead frowned at those mean words. Jessie wondered what her sister had noticed about their foreman that she hadn't. Or was it a joke, an attempt to point out that the best choice of husbands was a man Mary Louise considered beneath them? Matt was a good man, but there was no magic between them, only friendship. "Why do you keep teasing me about him lately? Does he appeal to you too much for your liking, considering he's too poor and honest to be useful to you? I can't wait to see whom you choose to fulfill your dreams."

"It won't be a cowpuncher with dirty fingernails and dusty clothes. My choice won't stink of horses, sweat, and manure. He won't be uncouth and uneducated. He'll be wealthy, powerful, and educated. He'll adore me and spoil me."

Spoil you? You're already spoiled more rotten than old eggs in an abandoned nest! "I wish you luck, little sister. Until you find him, you have work to do. Papa will be angry if you don't get busy helping Gran with supper."

"Luck, Jessica, isn't what I need. I have wits, beauty, and determination. What I need is opportunity, and it will knock on my door one day very soon."

What you have are dreamy eyes, little sister, and enough greed to fill a thousand bottomless barrels. You're lazy, vain, and defiant. Who will want to tame a selfish critter like you? I wish Mama were here to straighten you out!

*

Jessica Marie Lane sat at the table with her father, sister, brother, and grandmother. Her emotions were in a turmoil after her talk with Mary Louise. To distract herself, she remarked, "The chicken and dumplings are wonderful, Gran. I wish I could cook like you. Every time I try, it never turns out like yours."

The older woman smiled. "I'm glad I cooked your favorite tonight. You be careful on this trip, Jessie. We'll miss you and pray for you."

Jed had told his mother about their plans before Jessie joined them at the dinner table. He glanced up from his plate and said, "She'll be fine, Ma."

Mary Louise scoffed, "I think it's an absurd idea, Father, and a dangerous one. When Mr. Fl—"

Her tone and words stung Jedidiah Lane. "It's not for you to correct me, girl. This is the only thing I can do to keep my land and family safe."

Jed's rebuke provoked Mary Louise to defiance. "You can sell out, Father. We could move to a more civili—"

"Hush such silly talk, girl. I claimed this land and made this ranch from blood and sweat and hard work. No man is going to drive me off it. You should be more like your sister," he added unwisely.

"I'm not Jessica, Father. You know how I feel about living in this wilderness. Let me visit Sa—"

"You've bellyached enough for everybody in Texas to know how unhappy you are. You've been stickier than a cactus since you came home from that fancy school. If I'd known it was going to ruin you, I would never have kept my promise to your ma to send you there. I'm tired of your grumbling and laziness and having to tell you ten times to do something or make you do it over to get it right. I told you a hundred times you aren't going back East to get worse, so don't ask again. I'm warning you, girl: Correct yourself and stop this whining or I'll straighten you out with a strap." Jed wasn't one to strike his children, but his younger daughter's disobedience and haughty manner had worn thin.

"But, Fa—"

"No buts or arguing, girl. I didn't raise you to be a weakling or a griper."

Mary Louise fell silent, but her eyes exposed the fury within her to everyone.

It was obvious to all present that Martha Lane tried to hurry past the awkward and fiery moment by questioning her son and oldest granddaughter about their plans to thwart Wilbur Fletcher. The talk went smoothly for a while.

Tom, the girls' thirteen-year-old brother, was excited and pleased about the decision to hire a gunslinger. "I can't wait to meet him, Jessie. How will you pick him?"

Jessie's sky-blue gaze met her brother's greenish one, and she smiled at him with deep affection. She saw him squint to see her clearly; the round glasses he had gotten from the doctor at Fort Davis were not strong enough to correct his bad vision. Jessie loved him dearly, and she wished his twisted foot and bad eyes had not made such a terrible mark on his young life. She knew that Mary Louise was embarrassed by their brother's disabilities, but she had not known how deeply the girl resented Tom. Jessie gazed at his freckled face and tousled dark-red hair. No one was more aware of Tom's problems than Tom himself, and that saddened her. Jessie's smile broadened and she said in a whispery, playful tone, "I'll play the fox, Tom, and sneak around watching them. Then I'll make my choice."

"I wish I could help," Tom murmured. "That Fletcher wouldn't give us trouble if I was big and strong and good with a gun. If I could ride and shoot, I'd take care of him for you and Pa."

"The best you can do for now, boy, is keep to your studies."

"I will, Pa," the boy replied in disappointment and with a hunger for approval.

Jessie looked at Tom's lowered head. "I'm sure you would be a big help, Tom, but you're a mite young to be taking on gunslingers and their evil boss."

Tom knew age wasn't his problem; his disabilities were. He smiled at his older sister who loved him and helped him more than anyone else. His forefinger pushed his straying glasses, for what little good they did him, back into place and he returned to his meal.

"You've been quiet, Gran. Are you tired, or just overly worried about me?"

Martha Lane looked at her eldest granddaughter. "Only a little, child. If there's one thing about you, Jessie, it's that you get done what you set your mind to doing. If it's a gunslinger you need, you'll come home with one. And I've no doubts he'll be the best man for the job."

"Thanks, Gran," Jessie responded gratefully.

After the meal and dishes were finished, Tom returned to his attic room to complete his studies. Jed went to his desk to work on the ranch books. Mary Louise, as usual, retired to the room she shared with her sister to write letters to old school friends and to daydream or plot an escape from the ranch. Jessie and Gran worked in the kitchen, preparing and packing supplies for her journey.

"You know this has to be done, Gran, don't you?"

"It's sad to admit, child, but it's true." A wrinkled and gnarled hand caressed Jessie's cheek with softness and love. "You have your pa's strength and your ma's gentleness, Jessie. You're a special girl. You've been a blessing to my son and this family. The Good Lord knew what He was doing when he gave you to Jed as a helpmate. Without you at his side, he might have given up during hard times. I know this secluded life is hard on a young woman, but times are changing. When Thomas and I came here with Jed and Alice, there was nothing but the land. Jed and Alice worked dawn to dark building this spread. Me and Pa helped as best we could. It's one of the finest in Texas, in the whole west. This home was built with love and care. Every board and stone was handled by a Lane. Every mile of this ranch has Lane tracks on it. To think of that evil man taking them away makes my heart burn with hatred and anger, and the Good Lord knows how I resist such feelings. Find us help, Jessie, but don't lose yourself in this bitter war."

"What do you mean, Gran?" Jessie asked.

"Fighting evil has a way of making a person grow hard and cold and ruthless. To battle a man like Wilbur Fletcher means you have to crawl into his dark pit to grasp him and wrestle with him. That takes a toll, Jessie. You get dirty. It changes you. Whatever happens, you can't allow it to change you in the wrong direction. Always remember who and what you are: a Lane."

Jessie eyed the proud woman who could be so tough when the occasion demanded it. She was lucky to have Martha as her grandmother, to be able to speak most of her mind to someone who cared and understood, who could be trusted. "I promise, Gran; the only thing that will change around here is Fletcher."

When they were done packing the supplies, Martha retired to her bedroom and Jessie went to sit on the floor beside Jed's chair in the large living area. The March night was cool, and a fire had been lit to chase away its slight chill. Jessie rested her head against her father's knee as she had done for years, though not lately. She felt as if he needed her closeness and affection tonight before her departure, and after his harsh words with his younger daughter.

As when she was a child, Jed stroked her loosened hair and murmured, "Come home safe, Jess."

"I will, Papa. Soon this trouble will be past. Be careful while I'm gone. Fletcher's daring and greed make me nervous. We have to work fast to win."

"I wish Mary Louise was more like you, Jess. What's wrong with that girl? She balks at every turn worse than a stubborn mule. She's been a splinter in my side ever since she came home. I wish I'd never sent her to that school. They ruined that girl. They filled her head with crazy ideas and dangerous dreams. She's so bitter and rebellious now. I don't know what to do with her. Every word I speak has to be mean and cold or she won't obey me. I think the girl hates me."

Jessie replied with care. "She's having trouble adjusting, Papa. Life here is so different from what she was used to in the East. It's remote and lonely without her friends and diversions. She had those things at school. She wore beautiful clothes, received lots of attention, and it changed her. She's not a Texan anymore. We can't blame her for being the way she is now. She was away from our love and influence too long. Be patient and gentle with her. Maybe that will help."

His voice cracked with emotion and fatigue as he said, "She won't let me, Jess. Every time I try, she takes advantage. It's next to impossible to get her to do her chores. I never have to ask you and Tom more than once to do something, and it gets done right the first time. Maybe she thinks I'll give up if she keeps battling me and making mistakes. She struts around like a spoiled lady. She's rude to the men and disrespectful to me and Ma. Sometimes I'm tempted to switch her good, but I'm afraid if I do, I'll be so angry that I'll really hurt her. If she keeps pushing me and testing me, I don't know how I'll behave, and that's bad."

"I understand, Papa. I pray that time is all she needs."

"That's what we need, too, Jess. Time to defeat Wilbur Fletcher."

"We will, Papa; I swear it." She yawned and stretched. "I need to go check Tom's schoolwork for today and give him assignments for when I'm gone."

Jessie halted before leaving the room and said, "Papa, if you can find something for Tom to do while I'm gone, it would help him. He feels so badly about being too young and unable to assist us."

"What can he do, Jess? It's too dangerous for him to ride herd with us or to help with the branding. He can't move out of danger fast enough. I can't even let him carry the pail after milking 'cause he trips too many times. I wish he had been born whole, Jess, but he wasn't, so we have to protect him."

"I know, but it's so hard on him . . . Good night, Papa."

"Good night, Jess."

Jessie walked through the kitchen and eating area and up the corner steps to Tom's attic room. She recalled with dejection how many times the railing had been loosened and repaired from Tom's pulling at it as he struggled upstairs with his club-foot. She wished he could run and play and ride like other children. Most tried every trick to get out of chores when Tom would give anything to be normal enough to do them. She tapped on the door, opened it, and entered the cozy room. Two lanterns gave brighter light than the average person required for reading, but Tom's bad vision made it necessary.

Jessie walked to the small table he used for a desk and fluffed his wiry hair. Tom removed his almost useless glasses to rub his tired eyes, then smiled at her through a narrow squint that created creases between his brows and around his eyes. She teased her fingers over her brother's freckled nose and cheeks. "Ready to get busy?"

After they went over the lessons Tom had done that day, Jessie told him to work on reading and on memorizing his times tables while she was gone. She instructed him to write down every word he had trouble saying or did not understand so she could explain them and give him the correct pronunciations later. She wished Mary Louise would work with him during her absence, but she knew the selfish girl would not. She dared not suggest that Tom ask for help and get his feelings hurt.

As she was about to leave, Tom asked in a pained voice, "Will I always be this useless, Jessie?"

Jessie's clear blue gaze met his anguished one. "You aren't useless or helpless, Tom. Please don't feel or think that way."

"I can't help it. I can't do much here. When we go someplace, I have to sit in the wagon and watch the others have fun. Look at what I have to wear," he said, pointing to the thick stocking over his clubfoot that Gran had made for him because he couldn't get a boot or shoe over the badly twisted foot. "People laugh at me, Jessie. They don't want to be near me, like they can catch it or something. I wish they could, so they'd know what it's like!"

"Sometimes people are cruel without meaning to be so, Tom. There are things they don't understand, so it frightens them. If life had turned out different, they could have been you. To hide their fears and relief, they joke about it."

The boy turned in his chair and stared down at his desk. "Please don't let anything happen to you, Jessie. If you and Gran left, I'd be here alone with Pa and Mary Louise. They don't like me. They're ashamed of me."

From behind, Jessie lapped her arms around Tom's chest and rested her cheek atop his head. "Papa loves you very much, Tom. He feels responsible for what happened to you, and it hurts him because there's nothing he can do to correct it. I know it's hard, but a person's behavior and attitude sometimes control other peoples'. If you act ashamed and defensive, they'll react the same way—or even worse than they normally would. Show how brave you are. Don't let this get you down or stop you from trying anything you want to do. It will be harder for you than for others, but your perseverance will reveal your strength and courage to everyone. Treat your problems with humor; that relaxes people. Sometimes you can hush mean people by saying, 'God gave me this busted foot. I haven't figured out why yet, but I know He must have a good reason.' Or say, 'I'm slow, but I'll get there eventually.' Always laugh, even if you're hurting inside. If you show you can overcome your problems or accept them, others will. Everybody has flaws and weaknesses, things they can't control, and it frightens them."

Tom loosened her affectionate grip and looked up at her with shiny eyes. With enthusiasm and confidence, he said, "Not you, Jessie; you can do anything."

Merry laughter came from the redhead. "I wish that were true, little brother. If so, I wouldn't be leaving in the morning. My weakness is in being a woman. If I were a man, I could battle Fletcher."

He looked puzzled and surprised. "You don't like being a girl?"

"I didn't mean that. I just don't feel like a whole woman. I've been a tomboy and cowhand too long. Now I don't fit into either sex. I had to be boyish to work the ranch with men, and I had to learn to do everything better to be accepted. One day I'll be their boss, so I need their respect and trust. I can do almost any man's chores, but I'm not man enough to challenge Fletcher and his hirelings alone. It feels kind of like that half-breed who worked here a few years back; you're in the middle with no real claim to either side." Jessie laughed and teased, "Why am I rattling on with silly female talk? I have to get some sleep. Work hard while I'm gone. This isn't playtime, young man. Always remember, Tom, a smart brain is better than a perfect body. What you can't do physically, learn to counteract mentally. A smart head can open some doors that strong bodies can't. Learn all you can, as fast as you can. One day, you'll be glad."

"I love you, Jessie. I'm so glad I have you for a sister."

"I love you, too, and I'm glad you're my brother."

"Even though I'm nearly blind and crippled?"

"But you aren't blind, and you can walk; those are blessings, Tom. Think of your troubles as challenges, never as ropes tying you to a post. Look what strength and courage they've already taught you; it can be more, if you let it. If I know my brother, one day he won't let this foot and these eyes bother him. Until then, young man, study hard and don't lose heart. Promise?"

"I promise. You always make me feel better. I just forget it when I'm around other people, especially when we leave the ranch." Tom hugged Jessie and kissed her cheek. "Be careful, Jessie. Come home safe, and soon."

"I will, Tom. I have more lessons to teach. Good night."

*

Jessie went to the room she shared with her sister, who was either asleep or pretending to be so. She donned a nightgown, put out the lamp, and got into bed. She was both excited and tense about her journey. She hoped nothing would happen tonight to prevent it. Fletcher had kept them busy for the past two days with his evil mischief, so hopefully he would be quiet for a time, at least long enough for her to get away unnoticed.

Chapter

2

Jessie saddled her horse, a well-trained paint that balked at anyone riding him except his beloved mistress, and secured saddlebags and a supply sack. A bedroll was attached behind the cantle, and two canteens hung over the horn. An 1873 fifteen-shot Winchester rifle was in its leather sheath. Belted around Jessie's waist was a Smith & Wesson .44 caliber pistol that loaded rapidly and easily and fired six times. She carried ammunition in one saddlebag and in her vest pocket. She knew, if a horse had to be dismounted quickly to take cover from peril, survival could depend on having a supply of bullets within reach.

Jessica Marie Lane was anxious to get on the trail before the hands returned from their nightshifts and reported any threat that would halt her departure. With the sun attempting to peek over the horizon, she had to hurry. Just as she was ready to leave, she heard men approaching her.

Jed employed fifteen regular hands, then hired seasonal help during the spring and fall roundups. Half of the men rode fence and did chores while the other half rested from theirs. The night/day schedule altered each week. As soon as the hands in the bunkhouse finished dressing and eating, they would replace the others to do the same before yielding to much-needed sleep.

The hands who gathered around to see her off and to wish her good luck were among Jessie's favorites and best friends. These seven men were unflinchingly loyal to the Lanes and had been with them for years. All were skilled at their tasks, and all were amiable men who loved practical jokes.

Rusty Jones was laughing as he joined her. The bearded redhead told them, "That biscuit shooter is airin' his lungs deep. I told him I was starving, but he ordered me out of the cookhouse till he sang out that vittles are ready. Come back fast, Jessie. I'll have a hot iron waitin' for you," teased the expert brander.

"We'll start bringing in the cavvy today," Jimmy Joe Slims said.

Jessie smiled, sorry she wouldn't be able to help gather the wild and half-broken horses to get them ready for the roundup.

Carlos Reeves, a skilled broncbuster, lit a cigarito, then rubbed his seat. "*Sí, amigo*, I haven't tasted dirt in a season. There's one stallion I'm eager to get my gut hooks into. I never could break him last time. I'm not over that defeat yet. That *diablo* is *demente*. Ride with eyes and ears to your rear, *chica*."

John Williams, a huge and strong black man who labored mostly as their blacksmith, said, "Miss Jessie, you be careful allee time. We'uns'll work hard tilst you git back. I gots yore hawse shoed good and ready to sling dirt if needs be."

"Thank you, Big John."

"Lasso us a real tough *hombre*, Jessie. Just tame him before you get him here," jested Miguel Ortega as he settled a sombrero on his broad back.

"*Jamas!*" shouted Carlos. "We don't want him tamed, Miguel. We want him eager to spit lead at anybody riding the Bar F brand."

"I'll be jumpy as a prairie dog with a rattler in his role until you get back," Jimmy Joe declared.

"Hold your reins, sonny," Rusty replied. "Ever'body knows those two abide each other 'cause the dog don't know that rattler is feeding on his pups."

"Biscuit!" Hank Epps shouted from the cookhouse, "Git yore grub whilst it's givin' the steam!" Yet the crusty and jolly old cook hurried to join them.

Jefferson Clark, another black man, said, "We was jus' tellin' Miss Jessie good-bye. She'll be gone nigh unto two weeks."

"Eh?" Biscuit Hank responded, cupping his ear as if his hearing was bad, but all the boys knew it was fine when Hank wanted to hear something.

"I'll be mounting up, Papa, so the boys can fill their bellies and get busy."

Jed embraced his daughter and urged, "Be real carefullike, Jess."

Mathew Cordell ordered Big Ed, "Take extra good care of her."

The burly man mounted his large sorrel. "I will, Boss."

Jessie smiled at Matt who was fingering his mustache. He had never been one for many words, but this morning he seemed more talkative than usual.

"You sure you don't want me or one of the boys to go with you two? That's a long and dangerous trail, Jessie. I'll be worried till I see your pretty face again."

What her sister had hinted at last night kept flickering in her mind. As she had told Mary Louise, Matt was good-looking. He was steadfast and loyal, but a mite serious and quiet when compared to the other hands. A breeze played in his hair and something curious glowed in his eyes of a matching dark-brown color. His gaze was deeper, longer, and stranger than she had noticed before. Or maybe she was looking too hard because of her sister's implication. "Don't be worried, Matt. I have to go," she told him.

"I figgered you would from the first time you mentioned seeking help," the soft-spoken foreman replied. "I've seen how your clever head works."

"A man don't stand a chance against Jess when she makes up her mind about something," Jed added. "Not even her pa."

"I knew she would win," Matt responded, grinning.

Jessie wondered if that was a soulful expression in his eyes when the foreman ordered, "Let's eat, boys. Jessie has to leave, and we got work awaiting."

Jimmy Joe nudged the half-Mexican and teased, "Yeah, Carlos is eager to git his britches warmed, his bones rattled, and his butt sore before dark."

"I'll take the spit and fire out of any horse you bring in, *amigo*."

"Why don't we start with that stallion who tamed you last time?"

"Hopping onto his saddle will be easier than getting into a bunk with tied-down covers. I was so tired last night, I didn't even loosen her reins before I jumped on her. Which of you *amigos* hobbled her so good and tight?"

The men laughed and glanced around, but no one laid claim to the joke.

Gran and Tom joined the merry group, but Jessie's lazy sister was still dressing. Mary Louise had been told to take over Jessie's morning chores during her absence but claimed she was "kind of behind" today. Jessie had awakened Mary Louise in ample time, yet her sister had not heeded her urgings to arise and get busy. Obviously Hank or a hand had done the milking and egg gathering. Jessie was glad she would be gone when their father learned of the girl's new disobedience which would surely provoke more anger and harsh words. The redhead didn't know what it was going to take to quash her sister's stubborn defiance.

Embraces and words were exchanged. Then Jessie mounted the piebald animal and bid them all farewell. Off she and Big Ed rode on their adventure.

For the first few hours, the riding was easy as they traveled over grasslands and hills that were scattered with short trees, scrubbrush, and yuccas. Here and there they encountered cactus: mostly prickly pear, ocotilla, and cholla. The area was lush and green, and Jessie always marveled at its beauty. Several buzzards circled high above in the clear March sky as they searched for food. Graceful antelopes darted about during their early browsing. They were plentiful—thankfully, more so than the many skunks and porcupines!

About twenty miles eastward was the old Comanche War Trail. The Indians had used that trail from North Texas for their raids into Mexico, particularly during the feared "Comanche Moon" in September. But Colonel Mackenzie had defeated the last big band in the Palo Duro Canyon in '74, two years ago. The survivors had been placed on a reservation in the Oklahoma Territory.

Jessie knew how lucky they were that her father had made a truce with them in the beginning, just as he miraculously had done with the hostile Apaches who sometimes rode to the west of their ranch. Both truces had proven to her that peace was possible when each side was honest and willing.

After a rest and water stop, they rode another two hours. The Davis Mountains were to their left and the Glass Mountains to their right. The Del Nortes near the Lane Ranch were left behind, as was the Bar F Ranch which they had skirted cautiously. In the distance, the mountains—that were mainly brown up close—looked purple. In every niche and cranny, wildflowers bloomed across the landscape, as spring was this area's most colorful season.

Jessie and Big Ed rested longer on their second stop and prepared a light meal. She was glad it was not summer, as this southwest section of Texas could blaze with life-sapping heat during that time. The terrain had begun to change; it was now semidesert. Many hillsides were dense with yuccas. Soon it would be desert with only occasional hills, mesas, and desolate scrubland. And soon they would be able to see for miles without obstructions on the flat and dry wasteland that would demand a slower pace as they weaved through wild vegetation.

From past trips to the town near Fort Stockton, Jessie knew that only one more stop in two hours or so was needed, then it would be another two hours' ride into town. If they encountered no problems, they should be there by five.

Jessie was right. Shortly after five, they made camp beyond town on the Comanche River. This area was known for Comanche Springs, a main stop in the parched Trans-Pecos region for the San Antonio-Chihuahua Trail, both upper and lower San Antonio-El Paso roads, the old Butterfield Overland stage, and the Great Comanche War Trail. Fort Stockton had been constructed in '58 to protect the vital route and its travelers against Indian hostilities, one of a chain of posts and camps built and manned for that task. During the war between the North and South, it had been occupied briefly by Confederate troops before the embittered Apaches almost destroyed it. In '67, it was rebuilt and heavily garrisoned, mostly by black "Buffalo Soldiers." Afterward, the small town of St. Gall nearby had flourished. With Pecos County officially organized last year and with St. Gall made the county seat, Jessie had no doubts the town name would soon be changed to Fort Stockton, as most already used that name.

Weary, but stimulated to be on the trail, Jessie ate little and slept little. By dawn, they were traveling again. They had avoided town, in case Wilbur Fletcher or any of his men were present. Jessie did not want her plan unmasked to the villain, who might follow them to discover the reason for such a journey.

The mesas and hills in all directions on the desert terrain would have slowed them if not for the rugged road. With luck, they would encounter little traffic this time of year: Butterfield had ceased its route in '61, any wagon trains from back East had not made it this far west yet, freighters usually passed earlier in the week and most used the lower road, and soldiers from Forts Stockton and Concho had little trouble with Indians to keep them on the move.

Because of the scarcity of water in this arid region, they could not head directly toward San Angelo. It was necessary to ride northeastward to Horsehead Crossing on the Pecos River, then along the upper road toward their destination. To avoid contact with possible trouble, as soon as they reached the middle Concho River, they would follow its bank into town rather than remain on the road.

They followed the same schedule of yesterday: ride two hours, rest, ride two hours, eat and rest longer in the heat of the day, ride another two hours, rest, then a last two hours before camping. That way, they would not overtire the horses or themselves.

Horsehead Crossing on the Pecos River was made easily in three hours. After watering their horses and refilling their canteens, they forded the shallow river and continued past mesas, hillocks, and an area where more yuccas and green amaranths—future tumbleweeds—grew in abundance.

The landscape rapidly drifted into a drier terrain that was sliced by intermittent arroyos that warned of flash floods to the unwary traveler who ventured into them at the wrong time. Except for the dirt road, this area was covered densely with mesquites, rocks of all sizes, and prickly pear cactus. In olden days, such obstacles would have made travel slow and difficult. The land was flat and the vegetation short, giving them a view of the harsh region surrounding them. At times, they could see in any direction for twenty miles or more. Winds gusted on occasion and stirred up dust that coated them and tickled their throats. What grass there was grew in bunches in the sand-colored earth. No clouds could be found in the azure sky, and the day was the hottest they had experienced so far.

Five hours later, they camped on the Concho River. In two days, by Sunday night, March twelfth, they would reach San Angelo. They were tired, and Big Ed wasn't much of a talker with women, so they ate and turned in for the night.

Up at dawn and after a hot meal, Jessie and Big Ed broke camp and mounted. They followed the winding bank for hours. Jessie was glad they were near the river where plenty of water was available for them and the horses. It was hot and dry beneath the sun, and perspiration formed quickly. It dried rapidly on their exposed flesh, but their garments were damp. She had not had a bath since leaving home, and was more than ready for one. She wished she could strip off her clothes and boots and take a swim, but knew that was unwise.

They made their last camp on Saturday night, thirty-six miles from their destination. Big Ed whistled and grinned while he tended the horses and Jessie cooked their meal. The redhead guessed how eager her partner was to reach town. She had given him five dollars for being such a good companion and guard; she knew where and how he would spend the money. She would pretend not to notice when he left her at the hotel to visit the local saloon and brothel to indulge in masculine pleasures. While he was doing so, she would finally take a long bath, enjoy a delicious meal, and get rested for her task on Monday.

The following morning, they rode through the area near the river. It was so dense with bushes, oaks, cottonwoods, and willows that they were forced to slip back into the rugged terrain nearby. The mesquite was thick, prickly pear cactus was more than abundant, and rocks of varying sizes and shapes were everywhere. At times, they lost sight, but not sound, of each other as they rode single file.

Big Ed was leading the way, and it was time for their first rest stop. Suddenly Jessie heard his sorrel whinny in terror. She heard hooves clashing against rocks. A loud thud reached her alerted ears, followed by a yell from her companion.

Jessie had been around broncbusting long enough to know when a man had been thrown. She called Big Ed's name, but received no answer. Evidently the wind had been knocked from his lungs and he couldn't respond yet—or he had been rendered unconscious. She urged her splotched mount forward as rapidly as possible. When her line of vision was clear, she saw the nervous sorrel backing away between mesquites from a cluster of rocks. The sound that caught her attention didn't need explaining: rattlesnake. Jessie drew her rifle and fired twice, striking the viper both times and nearly decapitating him. His body thrashed wildly as his life ended, but his muscles continued to work involuntarily.

Jessie sheathed her Winchester, then dismounted. She rushed to Big Ed's body. When she turned him, she saw the bloody wound on his temple. She couldn't awaken him. She bent forward to check for signs of life, finding none. The redhead settled on her haunches, resting them on her boot bottoms. She stared at the dead man. Although Ed had not been a close friend of hers, he was a good hand. She had chosen him because he was big and strong and dependable, and because she had known he wouldn't give her any problems on this job by trying to help her with the selection of a gunman. She had also wanted as much peace and quiet as possible for thinking, something none of her good friends would have allowed.

If only they had stuck to the road or she had come alone or they had taken a rest stop sooner, he would still be alive. What to do? she wondered. There was no point turning back, as she was too close to San Angelo and her crucial mission and Big Ed was beyond help. Should she carry him into town for burial? Would that bring too much attention to her, something she needed to avoid, especially now that she was a woman alone? She could not carry the body back to the ranch, a four-day ride that would attract buzzards and coyotes. Neither did she want to camp with a dead body each night. Big Ed had no family to notify. Wasn't burial here as good as in a strange town?

The sorrel's anxious prancing and erratic breathing seized Jessie's attention. The smell of blood and death made the beast nervous. Quickly she went to him to soothe his fears. When he was calmed, Jessie checked his legs for bites. She was relieved to find none. After tying his reins to a mesquite, she began the grim burial task.

Jessie took Big Ed's bedroll from his saddle. After removing his gunbelt, she rolled him inside the roll and bound it securely with Ed's rope. Locating an indentation in the earth, she struggled with the heavy burden until she had dragged the body there. For over an hour, the redhead gathered rocks and piled them atop the body until the mound was thick enough to keep animals away. Binding sticks together to form a cross, Jessie maneuvered it between rocks at one end of the stony grave, then placed Big Ed's hat upon the highest point. She said a brief prayer for him while trying not to feel blame for this fatal accident.

Jessie was exhausted and sweaty after her labors. She grasped the reins of the sorrel and her paint, then headed for the river. Locating a spot where they could make it to the water, she let the animals drink. Afterward, as the creatures grazed on grass nearby, Jessie knelt and splashed water on her face and arms, cleansing away the dirt and sweat and dried blood. She drank from the cool river, then filled her canteens.

She had seen men die before. One broncbuster had broken his neck during a fall. Another hand had been gored by an enraged longhorn. Her grandfather had died when she was young. She had been at her mother's side when Alice had left this world. Since then, she had worked hard to prove herself, to be the "son" her father needed. She knew Jed was leaving the ranch to her, as Tom couldn't handle it and Mary Louise hated it. She had to learn all she could, as her responsibilities were great. Now, a good man had been killed while helping her carry out her plan. She leaned against a tree and closed her eyes, feeling the need to have a good and cleansing cry for the first time since her mother's death.

*

By dusk, Jessie entered the town of San Angelo and saw a small hotel. First, she went to the livery stable to have the two horses tended. If the man was overly curious about her, he didn't show it. Taking her saddlebags, she walked a short distance to the hotel. This time, the clerk was very nosy about her reason for being there and for being alone. To silence him, she claimed she was visiting her brother, an Army officer at Fort Concho across the river.

The post had been built in '67, and Santa Angela had sprouted nearby, to be renamed San Angelo years ago. The area was lush and green because the three branches of the Concho River fused there. According to what the men on the ranch had told her, Concho Street was noted for rendering services and pleasure to off-duty soldiers. The men had also told her the town was famed for its near-lawlessness, making it the perfect place to locate a gunslinger, which surprised Jessie since it was so near a symbol of law and order. There were other reasons for the town's development, since it was on the route of the upper road and several forts were, or had been, nearby.

Jessie glanced around the room she had rented for a few days. It was furnished sparsely, but was clean. She had wanted to relax in a long bath in her room, but the clerk informed her she had to use the bathing closet at the end of the hall, one shared by the other guests on that floor. As the eating area had closed, he permitted the cook to warm leftovers and bring them to her room for an extra fifty cents.

As soon as she finished the meal, Jessie gathered her things and took a short, rushed bath. Fortunately, no one disturbed her. She brushed and rebraided her long hair, in her room, then, exhausted, the redhead went to bed, shutting out thoughts of Big Ed's death and the noise from down the street.

*

Jessie waited until late afternoon before venturing out to complete her goal. She had studied the town from her window. Some areas were rowdy, while others were less so. She didn't notice a church or a school nearby, and hoped that didn't mean these people were as bad as the boys had warned her.

She took several precautions. After banding her small bosom to her chest with a strip of snug cloth, Jessie attired herself in loose jeans, a roomy cotton shirt, and a brown vest that concealed her feminine figure. She used scissors to clip wisps of hair atop her head and alongside her face, hair that curled almost mischievously against her flesh. After positioning her hat, she fluffed the shorter strands around her face so it wouldn't be obvious that she was a girl with long locks stuffed out of sight. She unfolded the dirty bandanna and made smudges here and there on her face to detract attention from her clear, rosy complexion. Lastly, she strapped on her gunbelt, pushing it lower on her right hip.

Jessie eyed herself in the small mirror, and was pleased with her disguise. She inhaled and exhaled several times to slow her breathing and pounding heart. She didn't know if intimidation or panic or excitement ruled her senses.

Everything was ready. She closed her door and left the hotel.

Jessie slowly walked down the planked sidewalk, making certain she moved and carried herself like a male. She noted every wooden and adobe structure surrounding her. A few people passed her, mainly merchants and cowboys and soldiers. At the far end of the dusty street was a raucous saloon and brothel. Music and laughter wafted out the open door. Men entered and departed. A scantily clad female leaned over the second-floor railing to speak with a customer in the street. Gunshots rang out, then loud laughter.

Halfway down the street was another saloon, a quieter and cleaner-looking one. Jessie saw only three men enter it and none depart. Horses' reins were secured to hitching posts, most being at the end of the street. The nervous redhead didn't have to ask herself twice which saloon she would try first.

Jessie parted double doors—too high for someone five feet four to see over, and looked inside. Freshly washed lanterns—suspended from the ceiling—were aglow. A long wooden bar stretched nearly the length of one side, with an aproned bartender leaning negligently upon the shiny surface. Behind it were shelves containing numerous bottles of assorted liquors. Before it were tables and chairs, some occupied and many not. Two soldiers were drinking at the bar and chatting in low voices. Two girls swept down the steps, giggling and motioning to the uniformed officers, and joined them. Soon, the clinging couples vanished upstairs. At several round tables, men sat gambling, drinking, and talking. The smell of tobacco smoke filled the air, as did the odors of sweat, leather, the furniture oil that was used to replenish ever-thirsty wood in this arid region, and that particular smell that only western dust has.

The bartender glanced her way, then returned his gaze to the room. Jessie moved inside and sat at a table away from those occupied ones. She did not remove her hat, as cowboys rarely did so except in church or at home. Most just shoved them back on their heads, keeping them on as if the hats were part of their bodies. Even while sleeping in a bedroll, most covered their eyes with them.

Jessie tried not to appear nervous, but she felt herself quivering. She hoped no one would approach her as she only wanted to observe every man with a gun strapped to his waist. One man had to be a professional gambler, she decided, from his fancy white shirt, black silk vest, and black trousers. He fingered the cigar in his mouth as he studied his cards before placing his next bet.

An old man wearing a blue cotton shirt, baggy trousers, and red suspenders entered from a back room. He took a seat at the piano and began to send out playful tunes. The conversations became more difficult to hear over the music. Glass clinked against glass as more drinks were poured.

The bartender finally came to her table and asked what she wanted. "I'm waiting for someone," Jessie told him, "if that's all right."

He looked her over before asking if she wanted a drink. When she shook her head, he shrugged and returned to his former position.

A man arrived who must have just left the other saloon, as he walked none too steadily. He made his way around the room, speaking to almost everyone. From the customers' reluctant responses, Jessie assumed he wasn't well liked.

Time passed. The sated soldiers reappeared, had a final drink, and departed. The inebriated man was talking and laughing loudly in one corner with another cowboy. Snatches of boastful claims reached Jessie's ears. Or perhaps they weren't all boast, considering the cautious way he had been greeted earlier. The men present hadn't been rude to the obnoxious drunk, and an aura of tension had been in the air since his arrival. Yet, even if he were as good with his guns as he claimed, he wasn't the kind of man she was searching for. A man who loved drinking that much couldn't be trusted to remain sober at vital times.

Two men wore their gunbelts strapped snugly to their thighs, the usual sign of a gunslinger. One had a knife scar down his left cheek, telling her someone had bested him at one time and could probably do so again. The other appeared too nervous over the card hand he was holding, a good indication he couldn't bluff easily. The gambler with his sly grin and flashing dark eyes looked too deceitful to be trusted. There wasn't a good choice here. Perhaps she should visit the other saloon, Jessie reasoned uncomfortably.

The "soiled doves" returned and moved around the tables to obtain more business. They had approached the crude man first, but he had sent them scurrying away with insults and shoves. Jessie watched the females for a time, wondering what had driven them into such a degrading life, though a woman alone in the rugged west had little hopes of supporting herself respectably without a family.

A third woman came down the stairs. She halted at the bottom and studied the room of men, frowning in distaste as she noticed the intoxicated ruffian. Like the other girls, she was dressed in a satin-and-black-lace dress that reached halfway between her knees and ankles, but hers was a sapphire blue while the others wore fiery red. The woman in blue circulated through the area, stopping here and there to speak to customers she knew. She teased her fingers over the gambler's cheek, then bent forward to whisper something in his ear. The man looked up, patted her buttocks, and grinned broadly.

Jessie tensed when she headed her way. The woman smiled seductively as she took a seat facing the disguised redhead. Feathers in her blond hair fluttered as she leaned forward and propped her elbow on the table, then rested her chin on a balled fist. She licked ruby-red lips and spoke in a husky voice.

"My name's Nettie. What's yours, son?"

Jessie tried to lower her voice as she replied, "Jess, ma'am."

Nettie chuckled at the show of good manners and anxiety in the person she assumed to be a young man seeking his first experience with a woman of her skills. "This your first time in a saloon, Jess?"

"Yes, ma'am." Jessie shifted nervously in her chair and wanted to flee. This situation was crazy, but there were things she needed to learn and do here. She had to be brave and cunning and steadfast in her mission.

Nettie stroked the protruding flesh revealed by her indecently low bodice, a trick to lure men's eyes and heat their desires. "Calm down, son. Nettie can relax you real good upstairs. You ever had a real woman before?"

Jessie flushed a bright red at the unexpected mistake and lewd implication, a reaction she couldn't remember having to any situation. What to do? she wondered. If she didn't stick to her plan, this trip and Ed's death were for naught.

Nettie laughed again, a throaty and sultry sound. "You've come to the right woman, Jess. I've broken in more young pups than a dog has fleas. You want a drink to settle you down? There's no need to be shy or scared. I'm the best in town."

"I . . . I . . ." Jessie stuttered as she tried to decide how to extricate herself without being unkind or exposing her sex. If she revealed she was a female, this woman would be embarrassed and angered. Worse, her ruse would be exposed. That could lead to failure, and to trouble.

"You don't have to say or do anything, son. I know everything. You'll leave here smiling as bright as the sun and feel as loose as a busted feather pillow. Why don't we head upstairs and get acquainted in private?"

"I got money, ma'am, but what I need to buy is information, not . . ."

Curiosity filled the prostitute's eyes.

Jessie hurried on. "I'll pay you five dollars if you can tell me who's the best gunslinger in town. I don't mean a bragger, but a man proven to be an expert."

Nettie leaned over to peer under the table. "You're packing iron, son! You ain't looking to earn a reputation here, are you? You'll get yourself killed."

"No, ma'am. I want to hire him for a job. Rustlers are raiding my pa's ranch. We need a man good with a gun to defeat them."

"That's a job for the law, son. Why did your pa send you here?"

"The law can't stop 'em, ma'am. We know who it is, but we ain't got proof. A gunslinger could kill 'em or scare 'em. I rode a long way to hire help."

"You ain't from around these parts?"

"No, ma'am."

"Do I know these bad men?"

"No, ma'am. They live where we do, far away."

"Five dollars for a name?" Nettie glanced at the bartender to see if he was watching them.

Obviously the woman was tempted by the idea of cash for no work, especially money she could hide and keep. "I need a man we can trust, one who'll obey orders."

Nettie's voice was low as she leaned closer to whisper, "I know the man you need, but he ain't in town yet. He comes in with his three brothers every few days, but the other three ain't worth their salt. Josh is as good as a gunslinger comes and he's loyal to who hires him. His brothers are trash, but Josh would kill any man to protect them. Josh don't let 'em work with him, but all other times they're as tight as a noose at a necktie social. Their ma gave 'em all names starting with J: Josh, Jim, Jake, John. He's the man you want, son, fast as lightning and no heart against killing."

"I can wait around to meet him. What's his last name?"

"The money first. But don't let anybody see you give it to me. My boss won't take kindly to giving out such help."

Jessie pulled five dollars from her pocket and crushed it in her palm. She extended her balled fist across the table. Nettie's eager hands covered it, and the money was passed along without anyone's notice. The sly woman secreted the cash into her cleavage, then grinned.

Before Nettie could reveal the gunman's name, the half-drunk man came to their table and jostled it as he staggered. He seized Nettie's wrist and yanked on it. "Come on, Nettie. I dun paid fur you. I need release bad."

"What you need is a long piss, Jake. I'm busy. Get one of the other girls."

"I want you, woman. They ain't good like you is."

"I'm busy here, Jake. You'll have to wait a while."

Jake looked Jessie over with red-streaked eyes and a surly expression, then howled with laughter. He grabbed at Nettie again, but she scrambled out of reach and glared at him. "You turnin' down a real man for a snot-nose kid?"

"Behave yourself, Jake Adams."

Jake tottered to Jessie's chair and shoved on her shoulder. "Git outta here, boy. Git home to your ma and pa where you belong."

"Leave him be, Jake. We've already struck a deal, so you'll have to wait your turn."

"I ain't beddin' no whore after no boy just diddled her. Git, afore I'm riled."

Jessie saw trouble in the making. Several men had ceased their games to observe the action. The bartender was staring at them, but made no attempt to deal with the smoldering situation. The old man at the piano halted his fingers. Silence and tension filled the room. Everyone's expressions warned the redhead this was not a man to fool with. "You go with Jake, Nettie," Jessie said, "We'll talk when you finish. I'll wait here for you."

"Ain't no need to wait, boy. I dun rented this whore all night."

Jessie tried to appease the belligerent man. "What if I come back tomorrow, Nettie?" she asked the woman.

Nettie ruined Jessie's attempt by saying, "Don't be rude and stupid, Jake. This customer asked first, so he's next with me. Let's go upstairs, son."

"Ain't no way, woman, even if he only takes five minutes—if he's got that much strength. You git out of this saloon pronto, boy. Come back when you're dry behind the ears. Fact, you git out of town and don't come back. If you do, I'll whip yore arse all over this saloon."

Jessie had to cool the man's temper. She could see Nettie tomorrow. "No need to get upset, mister. I didn't mean no harm."

Jake punched her shoulder roughly. "Nettie belongs to me and my brothers when we're in town," he said. "Ask anybody, boy. Now git! Move faster, boy!"

Jessie stood, her right hand unthinkingly and unwisely settling on her gunbutt.

Jake backed off a few steps. With a threatening scowl, he shouted, "You challenging me for this whore, boy? I'll kill you where you stand!"

Jessie jerked her hand away from the pistol and half raised both hands, her palms facing the man. "No, mister. I don't want no trouble. I just wanted—"

"I don't care what you wanted!" Jake grabbed a handful of vest and shirt and yanked her toward the nearby doors. "Git movin' afore I use you to wipe dust and spit from the floor. Hell's fire, that's what you need, a good lickin'."

Jake balled his fist to strike Jessie, but Nettie seized his arm. "No, Jake! He's just a kid. Don't beat him! Somebody stop this crazy fool!" she shrieked, but no one came to Jessie's aid because the customers knew Jake Adams and his mean brothers too well to interfere.

With force and roughness, Jake threw Jessie against the slatted doors. Something kept them from opening and her from falling outside on her rear.

Jake mistook his thwarted effort as resistance from Jessie. "I warned you, boy. Now, yo're gonna git it. I'm takin' you outside to settle this. If yo're too yellar to draw against me, I'll whop you good. I'm gonna break yore fingers and yore laigs and make you crawl home. You won't never wanta come here and cross Jake Adams agin." He lifted his balled fist to begin his threatened task.

Before Jessie could react in self-defense, a man parted the doors and captured Jake's fleshy fist in midair. In the excitement, no one had noticed the stranger who'd been watching from outside.

"Leave the boy alone, mister. He'll leave peaceably."

Jake was enraged by the daring interruption. He jerked his hand free and glared at the man who stepped inside. "Yore nose don't belong in my business, stranger. Git movin' or you'll answer to me and my guns, too."

The challenger didn't back down. "Let the boy go," he ordered.

Jake backed off a short distance and planted his boots two feet apart. He placed his hands on his hips, near his guns. "Says who?"

"Me. No real man picks on a harmless kid. Don't shame yourself in public. Get back to your whiskey, cards, and woman. I don't like seeing boys pushed around or mistreated. He'll go home and there'll be no trouble."

Jessie couldn't take her blue gaze from her rescuer. His hazel eyes revealed no fear, only slow-burning anger and determination, a warning Jake ignored. Black hair peeked from beneath his light hat and lay against a darkly tanned face, one more handsome than Jessie had ever seen. This, she decided, was a real man. He was tall, brave, powerful, intimidating, and confident. With him assisting her, she was no longer afraid, but her wits were reeling.

"I'll give you one chance to git, mister," Jake said, bringing Jessie back to reality as she stood between them. "If'n you don't, we'll have to tangle."

"There's no need for us to fight. Let the boy go home, then I'll buy you a drink to make peace. We'll play cards and get acquainted."

Jake fumed. He shoved Jessie at the stranger to throw him off balance and get the upper hand, then grabbed for his gun. "No man—"

The stranger pushed her aside and she stumbled, then straightened herself. The black-haired man was holstering his gun before it seemed possible for anyone to draw and fire. Two shots had rung out: the stranger's accurate one and Jake's wild one as he fell backward, dead on impact with the floor.

Nettie smiled and said in a voice only Jessie and the stranger could hear, "Good riddance. You two best git fast. It was a fair fight, but his brothers won't see it that way. They're meaner than cornered rattlers. Nobody here will go against the Adams boys to help you. Hurry. They could be down at Luke's saloon. Sorry, Jess, but Josh wouldn't take your job after you got Jake killed."

"Thanks, Nettie, but I don't think I'll need him now," the redhead remarked, then sent a side glance at her champion to make her point to the woman.

Nettie smiled. "You're right, Jess. Get moving before his brothers come."

Obviously the stranger didn't want more trouble or attention, either, as he said, "I'm leaving, boy, and you should, too. No need to wait for trouble to strike if you know it's ahead and you can ride another trail just as easy."

Jessie watched him head down the street toward the stable at an easy stride. Nobody tried to stop him or to avenge Jake. She wasn't about to hang around and court danger, either! She ran to the hotel, stuffed her belongings into her saddlebags, and left by the back door. She rushed to overtake him before he left town. The stranger had paid for his horse's care and had mounted to leave.

"Wait!" Jessie yelled to him. Catching her breath, she added, "Let me ride out with you. I just have to fetch my horses."

The stranger glanced down the street and didn't see anyone coming after them but knew the boy might need help and protection for a while. "Hurry."

Jessie claimed her horses, paid the man, saddled her paint, and mounted. She joined her rescuer and off they rode with Big Ed's sorrel in tow. The redhead knew this was the man she wanted for her job. Somehow she must convince him to come to work for the Lanes. She never stopped to think of the peril in heading for the wilderness with a dangerous and mysterious man or imagine what he would and could do after discovering she was a woman. She was too excited and enchanted to think beyond, *I've found him*.

Chapter

3

They had galloped for twenty minutes before Jessie yelled to the man beside her, "Wait up! We're going in the wrong direction. I live the other way."

The stranger reined in his mount and looked at her. "This is the way I'm heading. You best skirt town and get home fast."

The redhead knew she had to talk fast. She saw surprise fill his hazel eyes when she blurted out, "You need a job, mister? My papa is looking for a man good with his gun. That's why I rode into town to search for the right one. Nettie was about to give me a name when that drunk interfered. We have big trouble with a man named Wilbur Fletcher who wants our land. With your skills, you can scare him off or teach us how to beat him. The law can't help us. He's tried to buy our ranch, but we won't sell. Now he's trying to scare us off or break us with losses. We need help before he kills us."

"I don't get involved in other people's troubles, boy. I saved you once, so git home while you're in one piece. I won't fight over you again."

"But you got involved back there even without my asking or paying."

"If Jake had tossed you out or only roughed you up a bit, I wouldn't have intruded. He was going to hurt you badly or kill you. I don't like to see young boys mistreated for no reason; it riles me into not thinking straight. Stopping Jake's hand was like giving him a challenge. I got you outta there in one piece. No reason for me to take more risks for a stranger. Jake caught me tired, thirsty, and mean. All I got back there was a bath and food. I didn't even get a glass of whiskey or rest. You got the wrong man. I take care of myself, nobody else."

Jessie had witnessed a slight reaction to her story, as if the gunslinger was moved by it and didn't want to be or show he was. "We can pay you good," she pressed. "You can pick any horse you want from our stock. We'll buy you the best saddle made. If you can't stay long, just teach us how to fight. A man like you has dealt with bad men before, so you know what to do. We don't. Please come home with me."

"Your ma and pa will whip you good for bringing home a man like me. You don't even know me, boy. I could be dangerous. I could rob you and leave you here dead. Everyone would think that drunk's brothers did it. Or I could ride home with you, do in you and your family, and blame it on that landgrabber."

Jessie shook her head and refuted, "You're a threat only to men like that bully and men like Wilbur Fletcher. If you wanted to harm me, we wouldn't have gotten this far from town, and you wouldn't have saved me back there if you're as bad as you think. If the law's after you, mister, we don't care. You'll be safe at our ranch. We need help real bad. You're the best gunslinger I've seen. You're fast and you're clever. A wicked man wouldn't stop to reason with an enemy before drawing his guns. He wouldn't waste time and trouble talking before he settled the matter with his pistols or fists. You left town easily and quickly so you must want to avoid trouble and attention. I'm sorry if saving me spoiled your plans for rest and a good time."

"You're wasting your breath, boy. The answer's no. My only concerns are my neck and freedom. I don't endanger them for anybody or anything. I keep to myself and stay on the move. All I got in the world is right here with me. It's time you learn nobody does anything for anybody without a selfish reason."

Jessie recalled her description of a gunslinger to her father, but her gut instinct said little of those harsh words were true about this man. Except, she thought, he did have keen wits, iron guts, and expert skills. She remembered what her grandmother had said about fighting evil—that it make a person hard, cold, and ruthless. A man like this must have done it plenty of times. He must be so alone, and couldn't be happy. That moved her deeply. She wondered what pain and hunger drove him onward in such a miserable existence. What was he searching and starving for? Himself? Importance? Some lost truth? Peace? Yet he didn't seem as hard, cold, and uncaring as he acted and believed. Maybe his fatigue had lowered his guard around her. Maybe he was trying to hide or control all good emotions so he couldn't be hurt. Whatever he had to prove, he could do it against Wilbur Fletcher!

"You do have a selfish reason to help us," Jessie persisted. "I can offer you a comfortable bed, hot food, rest, and money. All you have to do is protect our ranch and hands from that greedy bastard. Your horse looks ready to drop dead and that cheap saddle can't sit good. Stay long enough to earn new ones. When Fletcher sees we have help and won't be scared off, he'll have to give up."

As the man shook his head, she extended her hand and said, "I'm Jessie Lane. My father owns the Box L Ranch thirty miles east of Fort Davis, four days southwest of here. What's your name? If you have a famous reputa—"

"I don't, and I want to keep it that way," he interrupted, his eyes chilling. "Men with names don't get any peace or privacy. I'm not from around these parts, and I don't ride anywhere picking trouble. Name's Navarro, boy."

"That your first or last name?"

"Just Navarro." It didn't matter if he told the boy that much, as the law was seeking Carl Breed, Junior, and that wasn't his name. Even as he refused his offer, he realized a secluded ranch might be the ideal hideout for a while. He needed to replace the stolen horse and saddle, and to rest. He had escaped four months ago and put distance between him and that cruel northern Arizona prison he'd been in for two and a half years. He told himself to take what he needed and to ride on, but there was something about the boy's innocent face and pleading blue eyes that reached deep inside him and yanked at his feelings, emotions he thought he had destroyed or repressed long ago. This boy loved his family and was desperate to save them and his home, something Navarro didn't have. *Why not use them to help myself?* he asked. *It's his fault I didn't go unnoticed back there, so the little firehead owes me.*

"I won't mislead you; Fletcher has hired guns working for him. He's mean, evil, and dangerous. This job won't be quick or easy. But we'll stand a chance of winning with you on our side. Without you, we'll lose everything."

Navarro removed his tan hat with his left hand, mopped his brow with his other sleeve, and replaced it. Indecision filled him. This Fletcher sounded like a Carl Breed who needed and deserved punishment. What good had it been to rescue this boy if he allowed that bastard to terrorize and murder him? He knew what it was like to be used and mistreated by a cruel man, and bitter hostility surged through him. "What if Fletcher doesn't give up or I get killed by his men?"

"I'll kill him. I won't let him steal our ranch or harm my family. I would have taken care of him by now if it wouldn't get me into jail. My family depends on me. I can't help them from prison. We can't get any proof against him, but we know he's guilty. You can help us prove it or destroy the snake. You won't have to do all the work or take all the risks. I'll ride with you. Whatever happens, we won't let you take the blame and get into trouble; you have my word on it. Please, Navarro, take the job. I need you."

Navarro shook his head as those blue eyes pulled on him like a strong current and the sweet voice washed over him strangely. *You must be exhausted!* he reasoned to himself. "How would you kill him, boy? You can't even take care of yourself."

Jessie pointed to a broken branch at a distance. "See that busted limb?"

Navarro's narrow gaze located it and he nodded.

"Keep your eyes on it." Jessie pulled her pistol and fired. She pointed out five other targets and skillfully struck each one.

As she reloaded and holstered her weapon, Navarro remarked, "*Shu!* You didn't need my help back there. That gun's no stranger to your hand. There's something odd about you . . ." he murmured, staring intently at her.

From the Apache guests they'd had at the ranch, Jessie recognized the Indian expletive, but said nothing to the man. "I was trying to avoid trouble because I had to go unnoticed back there so no one would discover my mission or my sex." She removed her hat and allowed the long henna braid to escape confinement. "I'm Jessica Lane, but I'm called Jessie. Men like Wilbur Fletcher aren't afraid of a woman, no matter how good she shoots. And his men wouldn't hesitate to kill one if she got in their way. I'm good with a gun and horse, Navarro, but the odds are against me. With your help we can halt that bastard. Are you for hire? Name your price. My papa will agree and pay you."

Jessie knew it was daring and maybe crazy, but she casually loosened the plait and freed her hair into an auburn cascade that flowed down her back. Perhaps a woman would be more persuasive than a "boy," and she had to use all she possessed to ensnare him. After all, if he took the job, he would learn her sex soon. As she fluffed her locks, she heard Navarro murmur, "An *isdzan*. . . ."

Navarro's mouth hadn't closed yet. "Jess" was a *woman,* a beautiful woman. Her eyes were as light a blue as a spring sky. Her hair was the color of a chestnut mare under a brilliant sun that freed its fiery soul. The loosened flow of reddish-brown against her flesh softened her features. The startled man watched her use a bandanna to wipe dirty smudges from her silky skin. Her nose wasn't small and dainty, and looked as if it had been broken long ago, but it sat nicely on her smooth face. Her full mouth was appealing and inviting. He felt his breathing and heartbeat quicken as he gazed at her parted lips. Her eyes were large, too, but expressive and captivating, the kind that could draw a man into them like an enticing pool during summer heat. Her jawline almost traveled to a point at her chin but had been softly rounded at the last minute of creation. Her height must be about five three or four. Compared to his six two, she was a little bundle. Whyever, he worried, would a good father let her—

"What have you decided, Navarro? We need to get moving before we lose all light." Jessie felt strange under the scrutiny of those hazel eyes that were more brown than green. "Are you going to refuse your help and let Fletcher murder us or do you want to earn a nice payment for the use of your guns and wits for a while?"

Navarro let out a deep breath. He knew what hired guns would do with this beauty, and it angered him. He also knew what it was like to be totally helpless. She needed him, believed in him, and must even trust him to have discarded her disguise like this.

He couldn't do anything about his problems except try to outrun them, so going with her was as good as anything else he could do for a while. Luckily he came along while that drunk was attacking her. For all the help she was getting from the cowardly men present, Jake could have dragged her upstairs and . . . "Are you crazy, woman? Why would your father let you go into a rough saloon to hire a gunslinger? I should heat up your britches for pulling a stunt like this. Ride home before you get into more trouble. I can't fight beside a female. We'd both get killed." Yet he knew that female warriors could fight as well as men, sometimes better, as the Apaches were one of the few tribes who allowed skilled women to go on raids or into wars.

"Then I'll battle Fletcher alone. Hiring a gunslinger was my idea, but Papa finally agreed with it. I'm not reckless, Navarro; I wasn't traveling alone. I brought Big Ed— one of our ranch hands—with me, but he was killed in an accident yesterday. His horse was spooked by a rattler and he was thrown. I buried him under rocks about twenty-five miles west of town. This sorrel was his. I was too close to town to turn back, and what I have to do is important. You may not love or need anybody, but I do. I'll risk anything for my family and home. I'm sorry about whatever or whoever hurt you so badly that you lost all feelings of compassion. If you need another reason to help us, it's a high-paying job."

Jessie noted his defensive reaction to her perception of him. Quickly she went on. "Everybody knows San Angelo is a rough and ready town. That's where you find gunslingers, and it's closer to the ranch than El Paso or Waco. I was keeping to myself, watching and waiting for the best man to arrive. He did, when you appeared. If your answer is still no, then I'll head on to another town to continue my search. I can't go back to San Angelo and risk being recognized. But I'm not going home without help," she stated with determination.

His gaze darkened. "That's rash and dangerous, Jessie. The men you'll meet on the trail and in rough towns won't hesitate to use you any way they like. You're a beautiful woman, and all alone. It's crazy! You can't do it."

Jessie warmed at his compliment, unbidden concern, and smoldering gaze. "Then, help me. That way I won't get into any more trouble."

Navarro appeared surprised. "How do you know I'm any different, any safer to be around?" he reasoned, looking frustrated and uneasy.

"If you weren't, we wouldn't be sitting here talking like this. You strike me as a good man who's had a lot of bad luck. For some reason or reasons, you don't want anyone to get close to you. That's your business, Navarro, and I won't pry. But you can use this job, can't you? Is it so bad to help someone who needs you desperately while you earn a living?"

The desperado wasn't sure if he liked the way she made him feel. It was scary, and he hated being afraid of anything. If this woman knew the truth, or even *half* the truth about him, she would take off like a scared rabbit. "Don't you have any brothers? What about your father? Ranch hands?"

Jessie decided she had to be totally honest to win over this wary man. "Papa is getting old and stiff, and he's no gunman. My only brother has a crippled foot and doesn't see well. Tom can't run or ride or fight. The children at school teased him and picked on him, so I teach him at home now. We have fifteen men working on the ranch, but Fletcher has about twenty-five. Our hands are good men, but only two of them are highly skilled with guns: Miguel and Jimmy Joe. Papa's afraid if we do too much shooting back or if we attack them, it'll cause more trouble and danger."

Jessie's gaze remained locked with Navarro's attentive one. "We don't want to endanger our hands. They're more than our working men; they're friends. At first, Papa ignored their bouts of rustling and fence-cuttings, but it got worse. Sometimes they simply shot steers or horses and left them to rot as warnings. The men try to avoid Fletcher's hirelings in town, but it's hard to take humiliation for a long time, and those bastards keep provoking our hands. We've had men shot at while guarding the herd at night. We've had fires in the sheds, foxes locked in the chicken coop, herds stampeded —and more. Last week we found calves driven into mud and fighting for their lives. There were tracks all around the area. I don't know what he'll pull next. In fact, I don't think Papa realizes just how evil and dangerous Fletcher is. Papa's a strong and proud man, but he can't battle such odds, and that hurts him. I'm scared, Navarro, scared my family will be killed. I hate being afraid and feeling helpless. I'm not a coward or a weakling or a fragile female. I work as hard and long as any man on our ranch, but this is one trouble I can't handle for Papa. I know this is a desperate act, but it's the only way I know to solve it. When I thought Jake was going to kill me, I lost my wits and courage. The minute you walked in and took control, they returned. I need you as my partner in this."

Her confession and pleading expression caused him to admit, "Nobody has ever needed me, Jessie, just used me. I . . ." Navarro twisted in his saddle and looked to their rear. "Riders coming fast. Could be trouble. Let's get out of sight."

Jessie led the sorrel into the trees and scrubs. Navarro moved in behind her, but it was too late. Gunshots headed in their direction.

Jessie yanked her rifle free and dismounted quickly, dropping the horse's reins to the ground. Navarro did the same. They prepared to defend themselves.

"Probably Jake's three brothers," she surmised accurately.

Their pursuers dismounted and claimed the other side of the road not far away where better concealment and protection than their location was offered. Gunfire was exchanged.

"Your brother drew first!" Navarro shouted. "I tried to talk him out of it! Ask anybody in the saloon! He roughed up this girl, was about to beat her!"

To avoid a fight, Jessie added, "Jake attacked me! He was drinking and mean! He tried to kill us! We only defended ourselves! Ask Nettie and the others!"

"You killed my brother, and you'll die for it!" came the expected reply.

"We shouldn't have stopped so long to talk," Navarro murmured. "I had you on my mind and dropped my guard. That could have been anybody overtaking us."

"I'm sorry if I distracted you," Jessie replied, "but I had to get your help before you rode off. Now I've endangered you again. Look, they're splitting up."

Navarro noted movement in several directions. He had to clear his head of this tempting female. "They'll try to encircle us. Take the one moving to the left; I'll take the right. We can't let them cross the road and flank us."

The man in the middle opened rapid gunfire to give his brothers coverage, and Navarro had to respond. Bullets zinged and thudded on rocks and wood too close to ignore. Navarro returned what she concluded must be Josh Adams's fire. Jessie could imagine how good he was since Nettie had claimed Josh was the best. Was her partner, she worried, as skilled as their attacker?

The man to their right darted across the road. Jessie aimed her rifle and fired, catching him in the chest. He spun sideways and struck the dirt. Navarro did the same with the racing target to their left, causing each to fire in front of the other. As Jessie attempted to move out of Navarro's way, she placed herself in Josh's sights. The gunslinger lifted himself to get a clear shot. Navarro's instincts warned him and he shoved her to the ground as he jerked his pistol in that direction. It wasn't fast enough, and Josh fired first.

Navarro fell backward, his pistol falling aside. Jessie saw the bloody wound on his temple and was reminded immediately of how lethal Big Ed's had been. She prayed she hadn't gotten another man killed, especially this one.

Cursing filled her ears. She whirled back to see Josh heading her way, about to open fire on her again. She hit the ground, rolled several times to a clearing in the scrubs, and fired.

Josh gaped at the wound to his stomach. Every gunslinger dreaded a gut shot. He placed his hand over it, but blood gushed between his fingers. With hatred hardening his gaze, he headed toward Jessie once more.

"You're wounded!" she shouted. "Let it go! I won't shoot again if you leave!"

Josh knew the man with her was down, probably dead. Yet he had only one bullet left in his pistol and no time to reload in the open. He assumed she was too scared to fire again. "Hell no, bitch. You're dead!" He could see Jessie clearly by now, but her beauty and sex meant nothing to him. He had to kill her in revenge before he suffered a painful death.

Jessie's breathing was labored. Her eyes were wide. Her heart pounded. Her mouth was dry. The wounded gunslinger was dangerous and deadly. She didn't know how many bullets she had left, and there was no time to look or to fetch more. She couldn't risk wounding him again. Enraged, he would keep coming, even on a crawl. This time, she must take aim and—while looking into the man's face—pull the trigger and slay him. It was harder than returning fire or hitting a target she couldn't quite see. But if she didn't, Josh would kill her. The redhead did what she must. She squeezed the trigger and took Josh's life.

Jessie returned to Navarro's side and knelt. He wasn't slower than Josh Adams, but he couldn't kill two men at the same time. He had been struck while saving her life. If he hadn't pushed her aside. . . . She leaned forward with trepidation and listened for a heartbeat. Finding one, she nearly shouted in joy. Hurriedly she yanked her shirt free from her jeans and struggled to remove the binding around her breasts. She had tended enough injured men and animals not to be sickened by blood and wounds. Using a knife, she cut a length to bandage his head. The bullet had creased his temple deeply, but had not lodged there.

Navarro stirred and moaned, but didn't fully awaken. He roused just enough to help Jessie get him onto the saddle of the sorrel. To keep him from falling off, Jessie secured his hands and legs with cut strips of rope. She knew they had to get out of this area before someone came along and more trouble started.

The redhead unsaddled Navarro's horse and freed him. There was plenty of grass and water nearby, if someone didn't find him and keep him, but the mount was too old and tired to be of use to them during this emergency. Jessie quickly tied Navarro's belongings onto the sorrel and dragged his worn saddle into the concealing scrubs. She gathered and replaced their weapons, after reloading them. She swung onto her paint's back, grasped the sorrel's reins, and headed off to skirt town. With luck, no one would see them and she could find a safe place to camp on the Middle Concho River before nightfall.

An hour later, Jessie halted to check on Navarro. He was breathing fine, but still unconscious. There wasn't much light left, but she decided it was best to keep moving as long as possible, to get farther away from town and their deed.

Finally she was compelled to stop because it was too dangerous to push on in the dark. If it weren't for the short vegetation and seemingly endless horizon, she couldn't have traveled this far before night. Even if there had been a full moon overhead, she couldn't journey farther. With the mesquites, rocks, and cactus so abundant, another accident could occur. Too, dangerous creatures roamed at night in their search for food: deadly snakes, spiders, scorpions, and such. She wasn't afraid of coyotes; they were usually cowardly creatures.

She worked their way to the riverbank, feeling it was safer than the desert terrain nearby. Jessie knew that her piebald, Ben, was sure-footed, intelligent, and unskittish, but she didn't want to risk an injury to him or to the sorrel. She dropped the reins to both horses and dismounted. She cut Navarro's bonds, and the injured man's weight assisted her with dismounting him. He slid out of the saddle and landed atop her as she intentionally broke his fall with her body.

Jessie moved from beneath him and straightened his arms and legs. After unsaddling Ben and the sorrel, she let them drink and graze nearby. It wasn't necessary to hobble them or tie their reins to a bush, as Ben would never leave her side and the sorrel would remain close to the other horse. She placed Navarro's bedroll near him and worked him onto it, then positioned her own beside it so she could keep a vigil over him during the night. Head injuries were curious wounds that must be watched closely.

She dared not light a campfire, but longed for a cup of strong coffee. She looked in her supply sack and withdrew two cold biscuits. She searched Navarro's. Jessie grinned as she realized both had been prepared for a quick flight.

Hot and dusty from her exertions and ordeal, Jessie stripped and bathed quickly, knowing Navarro would probably sleep until morning. Besides being injured, he looked tired. No doubt he had ridden a long way before reaching San Angelo. She donned a clean shirt and jeans that fit better than the loose ones she had used during her disguise, but left off her boots. She knelt again beside Navarro, and carefully she removed the stained bandage, tended his wound, and rebound it.

Jessica Lane studied him in the dim light. His midnight hair was silky and nape-length, and looked freshly trimmed. It was cut to comb backward on the sides. A right part caused the top to sway to the left across his forehead in almost a playful manner. His thick brows were far apart, and they, she recalled, hooded deep-set hazel eyes. His straight nose flared slightly at the base. His tempting lips were full and wide, his cleftless chin below it strong. His cheek and jawbones were prominent, creating defined hollows between them that her fingers couldn't resist traveling.

Jessie's enchanted gaze slid over him. Navarro was tall and muscular. Her hands felt his arms to find them hard and well defined. He looked to be in his midtwenties. His skin was smooth and bronzed, and enticed her to caress his cheek where no stubble grew tonight. The white bandage made a striking contrast against that black hair and darkly tanned face. She wondered if he had Indian or Spanish blood, as his features hinted at one or the other. No matter, she didn't care.

He was dressed in a blue shirt, tan vest, and black pants. Without disturbing him, she removed his gunbelt. After laying it aside, she unbuttoned the top portion of his shirt. She could not resist slipping her fingers inside the cotton material to feel his flesh. His chest was hairless. It was smooth, yet hard. His skin was cool to her warm fingers. He was a magnificent specimen, like a wild stallion who roamed the wilderness alone, one who couldn't be captured and tamed unless he was willing. Asleep, his features were relaxed and softened. He was so handsome that her heart pounded and her body flamed with desire. He wanted to be so tough, yet something wouldn't allow life to harden him completely, and she was glad.

Jessie's gaze returned to Navarro's arresting face. He was her captive of sorts. She had him at her mercy. She was taking him home with her. She had saved his life, as he had done for her—twice.

She wondered if he would still refuse her job when he awakened. She wondered how he would feel about getting shot and then being saved by a woman. Some men would be embarrassed and riled and accuse the woman of being to blame. When a man was angry and ashamed, he often became defensive, even cruel, to hide his exposed weakness. She couldn't imagine how this gunslinger would react.

Jessie let her fingers trail over his bold features, and she enjoyed the contact with his flesh. If he knew, no doubt Navarro would think her wicked and brazen for touching a stranger in this intimate way. She had been around men all her life, but she had never experienced this overwhelming urge to examine one. The emotions surging through her mind and body were unfamiliar, but not unpleasant, though a little scary. As her fingers journeyed over his full lips, she imagined how it would feel to kiss him, to *really* kiss him. She lifted his hand and studied it. It was large and strong and bore marks of hard labor. She found that curious for a gunslinger, but her mind was thinking more of how it would feel to have those hands caressing her than for what purpose they had been used.

"Are you dangerous, Navarro?" she murmured dreamily. She removed a gun from its holster. It was a Colt .45, kept in top condition. "How many men have you shot and why? Who are you? Where do you come from?" She fluffed his dark hair and smiled. "What will you say in the morning? Will you help us? I hope so; I truly do." She replaced the pistol.

Jessie eyed him one last time before moving away. She wanted to learn about him. She wanted to be with him. That thought surprised her, considering he was close to a stranger. But there was something about this man, something that appealed strongly to her, something more than his exceptional looks. "Maybe you are dangerous, Mister Gunslinger. I've only known you a few hours, but no man has ever made me feel more of a woman than you have, and most of that time you thought I was a boy! The way you look at me makes my heart race like a wild mustang. I must be loco to carry you home."

Settle down, Jessie, she instructed herself. *It's probably because he saved your hide two times and you need his help . . . No, it's more than that, and you know it. But what? How should I know? How many men like him have you known? None. Get to sleep, girl, before he awakens and finds you fondling him. If he's going to work for you, he has to see you as a boss, like a man. What good in blazes would it do if he did see you as a woman? You can't lasso up with a gunslinger. Mercy, girl, why are you even riding down that silly trail?*

Jessie curled to her side on her bedroll. She snuggled under her cover and went to sleep. She knew Ben would warn her if danger approached.

* * *

Navarro awoke early the following morning. His head hurt, but not unbearably. He knew what it was to endure pain, so he suppressed it now with an iron will. His hand went to the injured area and made contact with the bandage. At first he was confused. He wasn't in a dark and musty cell. He smelled fresh air and saw pale blue sky above him. He remembered he was free. He turned his head to look at the beauty lying next to him. She was on her side toward him, cuddled under a blanket. Long, thick tresses of wavy auburn nestled around her neck and half obscured her face. He remembered getting shot, but not coming here. He knew the river was to the west of town and they had been riding eastward. She must have tended his wound and brought him here.

He lifted his head and glanced around. The paint and sorrel were standing nearby, unsaddled and grazing. His stolen mount was not in sight. He knew she must have released him. Dizziness forced Navarro to lie back again.

They were on bedrolls, side by side. He wondered how she had managed this feat. She must be stronger than her size and sex implied.

A morning breeze wafted over them. He couldn't resist cautiously moving aside her straying locks to gaze at her. Jessica. It was a lovely name for a beautiful woman. She was the kind of creature raiding Apache warriors would have captured and enslaved. The morning light adored her red hair and rosy-gold flesh. Her lips were parted, and he wanted to steal a kiss from them, but he controlled that wild urge. Jessie was most unusual. It was strange and stimulating being this close to a woman like her. Feeling aroused by their close proximity, he looked skyward and took a deep breath.

He had wanted to avoid trouble following his escape, but had landed right in the middle of hers. He told himself he should be hightailing it farther east, but he couldn't seem to force himself to leave his bedroll or her side. He was a long way from his trouble and peril, but he couldn't decide how determined the law would be to locate and recapture him. Yet he couldn't run every day and night. He needed time to rest and relax, to enjoy his costly freedom.

What, he admitted, he would like to enjoy most was the woman beside him. How sweet it would be to taste her lips, to stroke her skin, and to enter her body. He could rob her, rape her, kill or capture her as the Apaches had taught him, but somehow he couldn't do any of those things to Jessie. It wasn't because she had saved his life or he needed her job; it was something else, something odd. Besides, this lovely creature had enough pains without him giving her more, and he knew plenty about suffering. It had never bothered him to do what he must or wanted, but this situation was different.

Navarro was glad his wound was on his head instead of his torso. If she had removed his shirt to doctor him, she would have seen the lash marks on his back and shoulders, gifts from a brutal guard who loved inflicting torment and humiliation. He would have deserted Jessie rather than explain those scars.

Navarro's mind drifted to dark days in his past. He had been given a twenty-year sentence for a gold robbery committed by the Breed gang, his father's men. He had escaped prison once but had been too weak from hunger and the beatings he had endured there to get away. Things had been worse for him afterward: filthy clothes and cell, whippings for the slightest offense, starvation or inedible food, rats and bugs, forced labor under a desert sun without water to drink, the summer heat and winter cold of his cell, trips to the "black hole" for defiance, sickness without care, and no family or money for bribery of the guards. It had seemed hopeless, a death sentence.

The worst part was being closed in, locked in a tiny and dirty area. Sometimes he had looked forward to the hard labor just to get outside in the fresh air and sunshine. He would never go back to that hellhole. He would kill or die to stay free. If recaptured, this time he would hang for murder, as he had slain a guard to escape. His path was set now—stay ahead of the law and hangman's noose.

Bitterness gnawed at him. No one had ever loved him or wanted him his entire life, not even his mother and father. They had endured or mistreated him. Nobody had helped him during his troubles, not even when he broke free of his old life. If only he hadn't ridden with his father to punish him, to prove he was more of a man than Carl Breed was! It was bad enough to be either a half-breed or a bastard, but to be both was torment and shame. He had meant nothing to his own parents, so why should it be any different with strangers?

Yet Jessie had risked everything—her life, escape, her mission—to help him. She could have left him there to recover and flee on his own, but she hadn't. Why? Because he had saved her twice? Because she needed his aid at home? No, she had saved him from Josh Adams as repayment. She could have tended his wound, concealed him, then left him behind. She could have left the sorrel and saddle as payment of any debt she felt she owed him. Too, she could find a gunslinger who'd be happy to take her job for the price she was offering, one far better and more experienced than he.

Navarro was bewildered by her behavior. He didn't know much about caring, self-sacrifice, and friendship. He had been taught by his parents, the Apaches, and the whites he'd met that he was a worthless half-breed bastard. He had given up trying to prove them wrong. Yet Jessie wasn't a quitter, and she believed he was worth having around. Should he risk all to help her? What would await him at her ranch? He couldn't make friends there because he had trouble trusting people. He had to stay on guard every minute against recapture, and she would distract him. Even before prison he had to make excuses or tell lies about his past. He had been made to feel inferior, hostile, wary, and defensive. *Why chance being hurt and used again?* he asked himself. *If she knew the truth, she wouldn't want me.*

Sometimes he still had nightmares about horrible periods in his life. Sometimes his entire past was like a long bad dream. But he had learned that good dreams—you tried to seize them and make them come true—were like water that slipped through your fingers no matter how tightly you cupped them. No, a dream wasn't real and couldn't be captured, so it was foolish to try.

Since his second escape, he had survived by robbing a store for food, weapons, and clothes and by setting a false trail northward. He had lain low while they pursued him, then stolen a horse to make distance. Those actions made him a thief, as well as a murderer and a fugitive. He didn't know where to go or what to do—other than to keep moving, to stay on alert, and to keep to himself. So why get involved or halted by this desperate woman? He glanced at her again and saw she was awakening. Even so, he kept his troubled gaze on her.

Jessie rolled to her back. Accustomed to rising early even if exhausted, the redhead stretched and yawned. The moment her eyes opened and sky was viewed, she jerked upward and scanned her surroundings. Her wide-blue gaze settled on the man who was watching her. She took a deep breath, then smiled at him.

"I was startled for a moment. How do you feel?" she asked as she sat up and straightened her twisted shirt and fingercombed her tousled hair.

"Like I've been shot," he replied, the smile he returned feeling strange and tight on his face. "Thanks for saving my hide back there . . . Why *did* you?"

Relieved he wasn't angry and resentful, she smiled again. "I always pay my debts, Navarro. You saved me twice, so I still owe you. I released your horse; he was in bad shape. You can have Big Ed's sorrel and saddle. Papa won't mind, even if you refuse our offer of a job. I put your belongings over there," she said, pointing to his saddle-bags.

He noticed his gunbelt to his left. "That's generous of you, Jessie, but I owe you more than what little help I've given so far. You got a taste of what it's like to almost get killed. Still want to challenge this Fletcher and his boys?"

"We have to, or lose our lives and ranch. We won't be pushed out, Navarro. I doubt you know what it's like to be afraid. You can take care of yourself or move on. We can't. Sometimes I'm tempted to sneak into Fletcher's home and kill him. Yet, as bad as he is, that seems like murder to me. I want to get him in a fair fight or catch him red-handed for the law. After that trouble yesterday, I know I can kill him if I must."

"Then I guess I'll have to help. But you should know there have been times when I've been scared. Nobody wants to die. Only a fool is fearless all the time. The trick is to use fear to make you careful, but never to let it control you. You're real smart and cunning. Your trick in town would have worked if not for that Jake fellow."

"It worked out for the best. I got you instead of his brother Josh. That's who Nettie told me to hire. I had to kill Josh to save us. I left them lying there. I'm sure somebody will find the bodies and bury them. We're several hours west of town, so I think we're safe. You should rest today. Then we'll move out at first light tomorrow. That's a nasty wound you got. It scared me."

"I'll be fine," Navarro said as he tried to rise. "We can . . . Oh," he muttered as he touched his head and flattened out again at the wave of dizziness. "Whew, it's spinning like a dust devil. Pain don't matter, but I'm not steady yet."

"That's expected. Hard as it is for a man to lie around, that's what you need today. If anybody's searching for us, it's in the other direction. I'll make coffee and breakfast. You stay down a while."

Navarro was reluctant to obey her gentle order, but he did so nonetheless. He saw her disappear into the scrubs to gather firewood and to be "excused." Battling his condition, he did the same nearby during her absence. It felt good when he reclined once more. He hated feeling weak. His mother's people had taught him to ignore heat, cold, wounds, thirst, and hunger. No matter the suffering and hardship, an Apache warrior never complained. Morning Tears had told him that from birth, but his white outlaw father had never learned to do so. Navarro knew there was only one period in his life when he lost his strength. During his imprisonment, he had allowed the constant torment and cruelties to break him. Never again, he swore coldly, then suppressed memories of the brutalities he had endured there.

If anyone besides this woman was present, he realized he would force himself to his feet. Yet he was enjoying her tender care and genuine concern. It felt good to have someone make him feel so important.

Jessie returned with an armload of scrubwood. She built a fire near the river's edge. While it was burning down to cook level, she prepared the pot to perk coffee. Taking a knife, she sliced strips of salted meat and placed them in a frying pan. Pouring water from her canteen, she mixed a bowl of johnnycakes. While Navarro observed her, Jessie cooked their morning meal.

She moved his saddle to his bedroll so he could prop against it, which he did. She poured coffee into a metal cup and passed it to him. As he sipped the hot liquid, the redhead dished up their servings of meat and bread. Jessie settled down on her bedroll and devoured hers, as she was hungry.

"It's good," the black-haired man murmured between bites.

"Thanks. Now that we're friends and partners, how about a last name?"

"Navarro suits me fine. People get too close when they know you too well. I like to keep to myself. Hope you don't mind."

"No problem, Just Navarro," she teased. "I know how men like their privacy. That's about all I've been raised around, so I know how they are."

"You married?" he asked unexpectedly.

"No. You?"

"Nope."

"How old are you, Jessie?"

"Twenty-four. You?"

"Twenty-seven."

"Any family, Navarro?"

"None."

"Besides Papa and Tom, I have a sister and grandmother."

"How old?"

"Who?"

"Your brother and sister."

"He's thirteen. She's twenty. Unmarried, too."

Suddenly they both grinned at their sparse sentences. Jessie put aside her dishes and located a stick. She sketched a map in the dirt and said, "This is where I live. It's good grassland, and we have plenty of water. That's why Fletcher craves it so much. He's backed up to the mountains here," she revealed, pointing to the location. "He can't expand unless he gets our holdings. He also has to depend on windmills for water. They can go dry at anytime."

"That's in the middle of Apache and Comanche territory."

"You've been there?" she asked.

"Nope."

"The Comanches were defeated long ago, so we don't have trouble with them. Actually, we never did. Papa made a truce with them when he first arrived. He got the idea from John Meuseback in Fredericksburg. In '47, Mr. Meuseback made a truce with them and they never raided in his area. Papa earned their respect and friendship early on. Whenever they were in the area, he gave them tobacco, beads, cloth, blankets, and cattle, but never whiskey or guns. He always kept goods on hand as gifts for them. They trusted him and liked him. He wasn't a threat to them, so they were never a threat to us."

Navarro was intrigued. "What about the Apaches? I hear they still roam that area sometimes. They live by their own code: rob, but don't get robbed; kill, but don't get killed; capture, but don't get captured; trick, but don't get tricked. Most tribes prize cunning and deceit in a man more than raw courage or great prowess. A brave warrior is needed and followed only in times of danger; being a cunning and successful thief is more important to them."

"What about right and wrong? Honor? Don't they fear God's punishment?"

"None of that matters to them. They don't worship the one Great Spirit like most Indians. They believe in a Good Spirit and an Evil Spirit. They think the Evil Spirit rules the earth. They pray to him before heading into battle. That's why peace with them is so hard. They're too different from whites. I'm amazed you haven't been attacked."

Jessie wondered how he knew so much about the Apaches, but didn't ask him. He had volunteered more information than she'd expected, and to question him might silence him. She wanted to keep their talk light and easy, with the hope he would continue to open up to her. "The Apaches were harder to deal with . . ." she began, then halted to pour them more coffee.

"Papa came to that area on a military expedition with two engineer officers. They left San Antonio in February of '49 and headed for the Davis Mountains. Their mission was to plan out a road between San Antonio and El Paso. There were thirteen of them: the two officers, a guide, nine frontiersmen, and Papa. He was to record everything that happened for General Worth. Before they could pass through the area, they were surrounded by two hundred Apaches. The Indians escorted them to their village for a talk. There were five acting chiefs among them. When the officers convinced the Indians they were no threat, Papa's party was allowed to leave unharmed. While he was among them, he made friends with the five chiefs, and even with Gomez, a troublemaker who spoke against a truce. When he returned there in '50 to settle, the Indians remembered him. Of course, Papa tricked them a few times."

At Jessie's laughter and grin, Navarro asked, "How? They're masters of trickery. Gifts are fine, but once they're used up, they're forgotten. Just like a man is once he's served his usefulness to them. They live for robbing and killing; it's in their blood and upbringing. If they even suspect an enemy has a weakness, he's attacked. I've roamed enough to know you never let your guard down for a moment—like I stupidly did several times since I hooked up with you."

To stop him thinking about that brief weakness and to learn more, she asked, "What do you mean? They never tricked us or attacked us. Maybe because they believed Papa possessed magical powers."

"An Apache never attacks unless he's sure he'll win and without suffering losses. Each man is free to do as he pleases. They only choose a chief for a short time to lead a certain raid or battle, then he's a regular warrior again. If travelers or soldiers don't stay on alert and appear well armed—like your papa's group must have been—they're attacked without mercy. Once you enter Apache territory, you're spied on all the time. You never see them until it's too late. They watch everything and everyone. They're very patient and cunning. When they bite into a prize, they won't let go until death, like the badger. They learn how many men you have, what arms, what belongings, and your schedule. If you reveal strength and care, you're safe, even if they outnumber you. An Apache never takes a risk of defeat. If the plunder and odds are to his liking, you'll never survive his assault, even ten to one. Cheis, the one whites call Cochise, was a master of such strategy."

"Perhaps that's why they respected Papa so much," Jessie confessed. "He used deceit numerous times. Maybe they feared to harm him, for they are superstitious. He's told me stories many times about those days."

Jessie raised her knees and locked her arms around them. "He used a magnifying glass to show them how it could enlarge objects. He made fires by calling down the sun's power through a burning-glass. He also used safety matches, 'spirit sticks' they called them, to light fires. He pulled tricks with gunpowder inside gourds, and with magnets and a compass. He let them look through his fieldglasses, and that was big magic. It even frightened some of them."

Jessie grinned in amusement as she imagined such a scene. "One time he placed a white flower in his inkwell and let it turn black without dying. They couldn't believe a man could change nature's colors. He made them think his coat was powerful enough to defeat rain, but it was just an ordinary slicker. Papa always asked questions and listened, treated them with respect, and enticed them to show him their skills. He was good at sleight-of-hand; he made them think he could pull a coin or bullet from behind their ears. That amazed and frightened them. They believed he was a medicine man of great power and cunning. He gave the five leaders special gifts before he left, mostly the so-called magic items. He gave his metal hatchet and such to other important warriors. He knew he could replace them in El Paso, and he wanted these men on his side for the time he returned to settle there. He presented Gomez with a horse—they view horses like we do money. The leaders gave Papa a necklace with each one's mark on it. They said it would protect him from all Apaches. It did; not even renegades raided us. When the Indians rode in our area, they never harmed anyone or any animal with the Box L mark on it."

"That's amazing, Jessie. He must be a very clever man to outsmart them. He was wise to use his wits instead of strength to win their favor. They're taught to hate all races, especially the whites and Mexicans. They're raised from birth to see everyone not Apache as the enemy. It's easy to understand, since the Mexicans paid bounties for Apache scalps of any age and sex and the whites stole their favorite lands and made truce with the Mexicans. Farther west, grass and water are prized areas; those are the ones the whites stole from the Indian. Do you know that bad behavior in children is controlled by threatening them with the names of white men, like your bogeyman serves to frighten white children?"

"I've never heard that before. You've learned a lot during your travels, Navarro. I've never been many places or met many people. It must be exciting to see and do such things, to be totally free."

"A man can't always go where he pleases or do anything he wants."

Jessie noticed the bitterness in his tone. "Where are you from?" she asked.

"Here and there, everywhere and nowhere. I stay on the move."

"You don't have any place to call home?" she asked carefully.

"Nope. No home and no family. Just me and my itchy feet."

Without thought or hesitation, Jessie made an offer to the desolate man. "You can stay at the ranch as long as you like, Navarro. Our hands think of it as their home and us as their family. Most of them have been with us for years. It must be tiring and lonely not to have anyone or any place special."

"I've never noticed," he alleged, trying to sound harder than he felt at that moment with her gazing at him with those soft blue eyes and radiant face.

"Everybody searches for love, peace, and happiness in their own way, Navarro. Maybe that's what you've been doing all these years. Maybe you'll like the ranch and boys so much that you'll stay."

"Nope. I get nervous when I hang around the same place and people too long."

"Maybe you've been hanging around the wrong kinds too long," Jessie teased.

"I won't argue that truth, woman. But a man don't change easily."

"I'm sure of that. I live around fifteen to thirty men all the time. I know how stubborn you men are about changes of any kind or size. It's like a war."

"We have too few things in our lives that remain the same, Jessie, or too few things in our control. We like things that are familiar and easy. That way, we don't have to stay on edge or get into trouble so much."

"Little corners of peace in a room full of trouble and darkness?"

He mused a moment, then remarked, "That's a wise saying."

"Gran says it to us when we have problems. She says there are always bright places where we can find peace and safety in this large world of peril and sadness."

"Who is Gran?"

"My grandmother, Papa's mother. She's getting old, but she's a wonder. She's gentle and wise. After Papa, she rules our house."

Navarro studied the woman before him. *Tough but gentle,* he thought. Could she and the ranch be his little corners of peace during his time of trouble and darkness? He had known and enjoyed few bright places in his life. Maybe it was reckless to enter this one. He could be lulled into dropping his guard. Jessie had a power about her that was magical and intimidating. Maybe he would start wanting this woman and her peaceful surroundings too much, and he knew he couldn't have them.

"Navarro? Are you feeling all right? You look so strange. Maybe I should check your wound again." Jessie moved to her knees, closer to him.

Navarro held himself still and silent as she unwrapped the bandage and studied the bruised and torn area. He wanted this contact with her. Her touch was gentle. He closed his eyes and envisioned her as she worked on his pliant body. He heard her reach for her saddlebag. She smelled fresh and clean, and he knew she had changed her clothes during the night. He noticed her garments now fit snugger than before. He felt her fingers pressing the jagged edges into place for healing. Carefully she smeared medicine on the throbbing location, then rebound his head.

The redhead rested her buttocks on her bare heels and gazed at him. He almost appeared to be dozing. Her bold study of him last night surfaced in her mind to enflame her. For some ridiculous reason, she trembled. She felt as if she were near a roaring fire. Her knees were touching his hip, and the area was warm. She couldn't understand how *her* clothed flesh against *his* clothed flesh caused such tingles and excitement to race through her. She knew she should move away, but she didn't want to. Jessie told herself how crazy and dangerous such behavior was. "Is that better?" she finally asked.

Navarro opened those engulfing hazel eyes. "Yep."

As Jessie started to move away, the gunslinger captured her hands and lifted them in front of his face. Jessie watched him as he looked at her hands.

"Working hands. Gentle and kind ones," he murmured. "Thanks, Jessie," he added, then released them as swiftly as if they suddenly had burst into flames.

Jessie felt tense in this unfamiliar situation of being alone with an irresistible man. Their contact caused strange and powerful emotions to surge through her. Gran had always told her that it was dangerous to tempt a man with something he couldn't have. She knew little about this mysterious stranger's character and nothing about his background. Navarro could be dangerous. Yet the kind of peril she sensed had nothing to do with her physical well-being. It felt as if she were quivering from head to foot, as if her body were suspended over smoldering embers. She didn't know what to say or how to behave. From his expression, neither did Navarro. Yet they seemed to have matching needs, troubles, and hungers that drew them to each other.

Jessie could not blame the man for being aroused by the situation. They were adults. They were alone in what seemed more like a romantic setting than a desert wilderness. Though she knew she wasn't beautiful—even though he had said she was— she *was* pretty. No matter if she was dressed as a man, she was shaped like a woman. Gran had told her that sometimes it took very little to stimulate some men's passions to a hazardous peak. She wondered if Navarro found her desirable, then scolded herself for even thinking such a wicked thought.

Navarro broke into her mental dilemma. "Do I make you nervous, Jessie?" he asked. "Are you afraid of me? There's no need."

In a hoarse tone, she answered, "I'm not scared of you, Navarro. I'm just tired.

These last few days have been very difficult for me." Rising, she added, "I'd better get these chores done so . . . so we'll be ready to move out if trouble strikes." Jessie pulled on her boots. She began to gather and wash the dishes in the river.

Navarro watched her intently. Unless he was mistaken, she had lied to him for the first time. He *did* make her nervous, just as she made him nervous. Even if for the same reason, he shouldn't do anything about it. Jessica Lane was a special woman. He liked how she made him feel like a special person, too. Crazy and impulsive though it might be, he wanted to be around her longer, and knew he couldn't if he took advantage of her.

That thought surprised him because he had been raised by his outlaw father and his mother's Apache people to take what he wanted and when he wanted it. And he did want Jessica Lane. He wanted her more than any woman he had ever met, almost more than anything in his life. He didn't know about the white man's ways of courting, but he did know that any decent man wouldn't toss her on the bedroll and take her by force or try to persuade her to yield to him using deceit in order to win his help, which she so desperately needed.

Maybe he could trick her into surrendering to him, but it would be wrong. That word thundered through his keen mind. *Wrong?* He had been taught by both sides of his family that doing wrong was the best way for a man to behave. To be successful at it was the highest honor a man could achieve. Still, Navarro could not seem to accept or believe that. Maybe that was why he had never fit in on either side, though he had broken laws in both the red man's and white man's worlds, laws that made him an outcast and a wanted man. What did it matter to anyone, he fumed, that he had been forced to do so to survive?

Jessie completed her task and wondered what else to do to fill her time, thoughts, and energies. She wished they were on the trail homeward. Without a doubt, this was going to be a long and difficult afternoon in camp. She didn't even want to imagine the night ahead, alone under the crescent moon with him.

Chapter

4

Navarro pretended to nap with his head on his new saddle. He felt as if he had talked too freely with Jessie. He worried over the way she drew him out so easily, as deftly as a sharp knife working on a hide. But that was the center of it: she was easygoing and straightforward, and he hadn't been around many people like her. She had a way of making him tense at times, and totally relaxing him at others. The redhead was beautiful and desirable, but those weren't her main attractions; her inner beauty was that. He couldn't imagine what it would be like to be around her for a long time or how it would affect him. He knew he couldn't ever lower his guard completely, and she was smart enough to realize he was holding back emotionally and keeping secrets. When a person didn't know something, they always suspected the worst.

Navarro was annoyed with himself for revealing his knowledge of the Apaches, and wondered if she suspected the truth of his shameful birth. If other people could look at him and tell he was a half-breed, she could, too. So why didn't it matter to her? Most didn't want breeds around. *Shu.* Even his name branded him as the "entrails of the earth." Maybe he should change it, as his parents were never married; Carl Breed didn't think it was necessary to wed his Apache squaw, even after she bore him an unwanted son. The desperado knew he had to set some rules with Jessie; privacy was a must. Yet it was going to be hard to back off even a few steps. And for once, he didn't want to retreat.

Jessie sensed that Navarro was awake and deep in thought. As she filled the canteens, she reflected on what little she had learned about him. She tried to grasp hints from his past words and expressions. She couldn't forget what he had said just before their attack by the Adams brothers. What had created such bitterness, such an empty feeling of nobody loving or needing him? Something terrible had caused him to harden his heart, or to try to deaden it. Yet he seemed so forlorn and vulnerable, so hungry for affection, attention, and respect. He seemed so confused, so alone. Whether he knew it or not, Navarro needed to be needed. And she needed him.

Jessie wondered why he appeared poor, why he couldn't afford a new horse and saddle. His hands were calloused from hard labor, so why didn't he have money? His clothes were decent, his hair recently cut, and his weapons were new. Yet his pouches were so small to carry all his worldly possessions. She wished she had looked inside his saddlebags while he was unconscious, but snooping went against her upbringing.

Before it was time to begin their evening meal, she took a walk, being careful on the rocky terrain.

When she returned to their campsite, Navarro was gone. She listened, but heard nothing. She glanced around, but saw nothing. She knew he hadn't left, because the sorrel and his possessions were still there.

Jessie walked to the paint, who was grazing leisurely near the riverbank. She stroked the black-and-white stallion's neck, then hugged him. As he nuzzled his head against her shoulder, she whispered, "Can we trust him, Ben? A man like him can be unpredictable. Why in blazes does he make me feel so—"

Navarro came into sight not far away, and she fell silent. She watched him walk toward her, his gaze locked to her face. Those crazy tingles and hot flushes troubled her again. She focused her attention on her mottled horse.

Navarro joined her on the other side of the animal. "Does he bite?"

Jessie continued to stroke the loyal steed. "Not usually, but he isn't around strangers very much. He's very protective of me and won't let anyone ride him except me. Ben has a keen nose, so he'll warn us if danger approaches."

Navarro noticed the quavering in her voice. "He's good horseflesh. So is that sorrel. You sure your father won't beat you for giving him away?"

If Navarro's last sentence was meant as a joke, it didn't sound like it. "Certainly not. Papa lets me do what I think is best most of the time. He'll probably say the horse isn't reward enough for saving me twice. Papa never whips us, though I think he's tempted to do so these days with my younger sister. She can be unbearable at times. She's very beautiful and educated, but she's so spoiled and defiant." Jessie sighed in dismay as her rebellious sister came to mind. She wondered what Mary Louise would think of the handsome and mysterious Navarro, and what he would think of her beautiful sister. Jessie glanced down at her male attire, then envisioned her sister's lovely dresses and ladylike ways. How could she compete with such beauty for Navarro's eye? Her gaze locked with his watchful one again. She blushed at the line of her thoughts. "I'm sorry. I shouldn't have said that about her. It's just that she's been giving Papa such a hard time since she returned from school back East."

Vexed by the ridiculous jealousy and rivalry for this hired help, she pushed aside worries about Mary Louise. "Papa bred both horses. Carlos helped me break him. Of course Ben allowed me to tame him. He's one of those wild creatures who must be willing to change before he'll yield."

Jessie's blue gaze fused with Navarro's hazel one over Ben's splotched back. The closer they were to each other, the more the curious tension between them mounted. The gunman's hand slowly drifted over hers where it rested on Ben's withers, as if he hadn't noticed it there while stroking the animal. They stared at each other for a few minutes before both simultaneously looked away.

He wondered if her last sentence held a dual meaning, one about him. "A loyal horse is important. He can save your hide. A bad one can make you lose it."

As his gentle touch won over Ben, Jessie asked, "Are you angry I released your horse? I had no right to free him without permission. I was rushed and distracted."

"He was old and tired, Jessie. I only had him a short while, so we weren't old friends. My regular horse was stolen a while back, and he was the only one available at the time." He gazed off into the distance and inhaled deeply. It was crazy how lying to her made him feel bad. "I really couldn't afford a new one. I haven't worked in a while. Been moving around. That's why I decided to take your offer. The money, that sorrel and saddle, and creature comfort sound mighty appealing."

Jessie tried to hide her disappointment that his words hadn't mentioned compassion. "We didn't discuss your salary. Do gunslingers get paid a lot?"

Navarro watched the setting sun enhance the gold spirit in her red hair. Her blue gaze was guarded now. Her body appeared taut, as did her voice. "Don't know. I'm not one. Too dangerous. I like to stay alive."

His succinct and unexpected responses intrigued her. She stared at him for a moment, then reasoned, "But you're so fast and accurate. You're holstering your gun before most men clear leather."

Navarro shrugged. "Adams was drunk and slow."

"That doesn't change your abilities. I witnessed your reflexes back there. Don't men challenge you all the time?"

"I try to keep my skill a secret so they won't."

Befuddled, Jessie asked, "How do you survive, if not by your guns?"

"I bluff or keep to myself. I don't show off in towns. I keep my nose out of other people's lives. It usually works. If it doesn't, I move on."

"I meant, what work do you do for money?"

"Whatever strikes me when I need it."

"Anything illegal?" she hinted, boldly.

Navarro sent her a sly grin that softened his mouth and eyes. "I thought you said that didn't matter to you, that you wouldn't pry. You've already learned more about me than most people know. I've talked more to you in two days than I've talked to others in three years. I'm a loner."

Jessie flushed again; she'd blushed more since meeting Navarro than she had in years. "I'm sorry. I didn't mean to be nosy. I was just trying to get acquainted. For someone who doesn't like to talk much, you're very easy to talk to, Navarro."

He realized he had hurt her feelings. In a gentle tone, he replied, "Talk to me all you want, Jessie, but don't always expect answers. Too many questions make me nervous. Makes my feet itch to move on. Can't help it. That's the way I am. I feel relaxed enough around you to share a few words, but not more than that."

Jessie was relieved at his last words, but still she coaxed, "Please don't let my reckless mouth and forward manner drive you away, Navarro. I'm used to speaking my mind around men. About the only strangers I meet are some of the ones Papa hires as seasonal rovers to help with the spring and fall roundups. Some of them are the same men who return every season. We only keep fifteen regular hands year round. I'll try not to probe again. I'll make sure Papa and the hands don't bother you, either. But it will be hard. They'll make you nervous until they get used to you and you to them. They're a friendly group of men. They're always playing jokes on each other. If they do it to you, it means they like you and trust you and accept you as one of them, so don't get mad and quit." Jessie laughed and remarked, "I remember one joke they played on Big John. He's a black man who works mostly as our blacksmith. He used to be a slave, but Papa bought him and freed him. Big John is very superstitious. One of the hands dressed up in a white covering like a ghost, a 'haint' Big John calls them. The rest of the men pretended they couldn't see or hear the ghost as he moved around the bunkhouse. Jefferson—he's another black man who works for us—told Big John that only a man marked for death could see and hear Old Haint. They let him worry for hours before they revealed it was a joke."

Jessie laughed again before adding, "But Big John got them back. One night he yelled that Indians were attacking. While the men were running around outside checking out the danger, Big John filled their bunks with burrs. You should have heard the yells and curses when they crawled back into their prickly beds. Big John chuckled and told them Old Haint had done it."

"Don't the men ever get mad at each other for being tricked?"

"Of course not. They love practical jokes. It's a crazy way of showing affection and releasing tension from all the hard work. They never do anything mean or harmful or vindictive." Jessie inhaled deeply. It was getting late. "I'd best cook supper so we can turn in. If your head's all right, we'll leave early in the morning."

"It's a little sore, but I'm fine. The dizziness is gone."

"I should check it out and change your bandage."

"No need. It's best to leave it be tonight. I don't want the wound reopened." What Navarro didn't want was to get aroused by her touch again.

After a meal of beans, fried bread, and hot coffee, Jessie washed the dishes in the river and put them away. They had eaten in silence. In the last light of the day, she gathered scrubwood for the morning fire. While Navarro was out of camp, Jessie moved her bedroll away from his. Now that he was well, it was dangerous and improper to sleep so close to him.

Upon his return, the desperado noticed her attempt to put distance between them. He said nothing and took his place.

Jessie slept soundly all night, perhaps because she had slept little last night while holding a vigil over him.

Navarro observed her for a time. He knew he had to keep to himself at the ranch. He decided it was best to make up a story to tell her father and the men about his past to prevent suspicion. Maybe he should just kill this Fletcher, take the salary, and move on quickly. That way, neither he nor Jessie would be endangered by each other or that landgrabber or the law. No, he argued; he should help her outwit and defeat the villain to avoid attention from anyone. Maybe he should just ride in a different direction from her tomorrow. No, he argued again; if he did that, she had to ride home alone and face that bastard alone.

Besides, he liked Jessica Lane and enjoyed being around her. What was the harm in prolonging that rare pleasure for a while as long as he was careful?

*

Their third day together began with a quiet meal and some stolen glances. After they were packed and the horses were saddled, they headed westward along the Concho River. Jessie told him the direction she and Big Ed had taken and where they had stopped to camp. Navarro requested no changes in the route.

Jessie let Navarro take the lead, as men usually felt that was their job. The riding wasn't difficult, but they couldn't move along swiftly on the rugged terrain. The sun at their backs wasn't blazing down heat yet, and the spring morning was pleasant beneath a clear sky. She watched him whenever he was in sight, though mesquites often obscured her pleasing view. His shoulders were broad and his back was straight. He rode as a man born to the saddle.

While she was washing the dishes and packing her supplies, he had disappeared downriver to bathe and change clothes. He now wore a pale-blue shirt with his brown vest and jeans. His tan hat stood out against the midnight hair around his collar. Navarro's two holsters were strapped securely to well-muscled thighs. But not once had he glanced back at her so she could admire his face.

During the first break, he had barely talked. It was the same at midday and their afternoon stop. He was different on the trail than in camp, was on constant alert. Maybe he thought the law from San Angelo was searching for them, or some of the Adamses friends out for revenge. He frequently glanced around in all directions, but tried to keep his eyes off her. She knew that from the way his gaze darted away when she looked at him. Jessie feared he was withdrawing into himself again. Perhaps he had known few women, and didn't know how to react around them. She prayed that his feelings about people wouldn't change his mind about the job before they reached the ranch.

As dusk approached, Navarro chose a campsite. "This spot all right?"

"Looks fine to me. I'll get supper going while you tend the horses." Jessie looked at him and smiled apologetically. "Sorry. I'm used to giving orders to the hands, so don't mind my bossy manner if I forget myself with you."

"You *are* the boss, Miss Lane, and I'm the hired help. Don't fret over it."

Jessie smiled at his agreeable attitude. "The hands call me Jessie, not Miss Lane, so you needn't be formal when we get there." Hesitantly she added, "If you change your mind about the job before we get home, I'll understand. It's hard to take life-threatening risks for strangers. I'll still pay you for the safe escort home. The horse and saddle are yours, no matter what you decide."

"You changing your mind about me already?"

"Of course not. But I sort of pressed you into taking the job in a moment of weakness and gratitude. I was afraid after you thought it over carefully, you'd see how dangerous your task will be."

Navarro pushed his hat back from his face. "If I backed out now, you'd race off to another town the minute I was out of sight."

Jessie didn't break their locked gaze. "No, I wouldn't. Jake and his brothers taught me a good lesson. If you have to leave, I'll deal with Fletcher, me and the boys. We've endured his threats too long trying to prevent more trouble and bloodshed. It's payback time."

"How would you do that?"

"Do to him as he's doing to us. Take a lesson from him this time."

"That's what I was going to suggest when we made our plans against him. He'll get the message. Whatever he does, we do back, only twice as bad. We'll call his bluff, Jessie, then carry out our warning if he doesn't back down. We only have to make sure he can't prove it was us. You don't want the law winning his battle for him."

"We'll make certain we don't land in jail while that villain goes free!"

He saw anger and determination enlarge and brighten her blue eyes. "What if we do slip up and get caught? Jail ain't a place for a woman."

Jessie frowned at the possibility. "Don't even think such a horrible thing. We'll be clever and careful."

"It happens, Jessie. Prisons hold lots of innocent men, or men who were doing what they thought was right, or things they were forced into doing—or even tricked into doing. Why didn't you hire a lawman? Or someone with authority to battle him legally?"

Jessie explained to him what she had told her father about lawmen.

"You're even smarter than I realized. Sometimes the law can't be trusted."

"Does it bother you to think we might have to break the law?"

"Not if we don't get caught."

"Good. I don't like it, but it may be necessary," she admitted.

"You willing to do anything to defeat that landgrabber?"

"What do you mean by anything?"

"Anything, Jessie, anything to win."

He hadn't clarified, so the redhead wasn't sure of his real meaning. "It's like with

Josh and his brothers: kill or be killed. Yes, Navarro, I'll do anything to keep my family alive and our home safe."

"What if Fletcher wanted you in exchange for a truce?"

That question took her by surprise. Jessie was amazed that he was talking so freely once more after such a quiet and distant day. "Never," she replied. "I'd die first. I'd never let that bastard touch me."

Her last words stung the desperado, who viewed himself a half-breed bastard. "But you said *anything*. Your family could die, too, if that's the price he demands."

"My family wouldn't expect such a sacrifice from me. They wouldn't allow it. Papa and the boys would gun down that bastard before letting him take me. I meant anything but that. Besides, Fletcher hasn't shown any interest in me."

"That doesn't mean he doesn't have any. Is he married?"

"No, he isn't. He's in his mid-thirties, rich, and from a good background. Too bad it didn't have a better effect on him. He's been there two and a half years. But he's greedy. He wants to build a cattle empire in our area. He craves power. He has about a hundred thousand acres, and runs about thirty thousand cattle and horses. But he chose a bad spot to create his big dream. He can't expand without taking our ranch. He keeps about twenty-five regulars hired year round; that's a lot for a spread his size. It's clear he has so many men for a particular reason. To fight us."

"Seems crazy to box himself in like that. You sure there isn't another reason he wanted his land, or why he wants yours?"

"Not that I know of or can imagine. I hadn't thought about it that way. There is silver in the mountains southwest of us, but none near us that I know of. We do compete for beef and horse contracts at the army posts in our area. Sometimes that's a lot of money, but he's already rich."

"Is a man ever satisfied with how much cash or holdings he possesses?"

"No. But, most of them don't go around killing and stealing to get more, do they? I suppose I really don't know. I haven't left the ranch much."

"Would you marry a lawman for his help?"

Again, Jessie was stunned and intrigued by his line of queries. What was he seeking? Was he an undercover lawman? Was his style of life a ruse? Was that why he had helped her and hadn't harmed her? After hearing her story, was he going to the ranch to investigate her claims? If all that were true, which she doubted, what should she respond? Navarro made her feel safe, desirable, womanly. He often looked at her as if his gaze were a physical caress, as if he couldn't control his eyes and interest.

"Well, would you?" he pressed when she remained silent.

Jessie began unsaddling Ben as she replied, "Does anyone know what they would do to survive until the moment confronts them? I killed Josh for survival. I suppose it would depend on who he is and how desperately we needed his help." She placed the supply sack nearby. When Navarro didn't continue the conversation, she went to gather scrubwood for the fire to cook supper.

Navarro unsaddled the sorrel and let both horses drink and graze. He vanished into the treeline along the bank to excuse himself and to think while walking. When he joined Jessie at the campfire, their meal was almost ready.

As she handed him his cup and plate, their hands touched twice. "That means, you wouldn't marry a villain, but you *would* wed a lawman?" he asked.

Jessie glanced at him as he took up the conversation where it had left off earlier. She couldn't surmise his motive. She sat on the ground, crossed her legs Indian-style, and sipped her coffee. "I hope I wouldn't tie myself to a villain through desperation or ignorance," she answered. "Everyone has flaws and weaknesses, but that doesn't make a person bad, or all bad. As for a lawman, I can't imagine myself getting bound to one of them, either. Why do you ask?"

"Just testing your feelings about good and bad. I wanted to know how desperate, rather how determined, you are to win. I like to know a person's motives and restraints beforehand. I wouldn't want to risk my neck, then have you surrender to the enemy to make a truce to keep from being pushed off your lands. That kind of survival isn't worth the price you pay."

Jessie had the strange feeling his words applied to more than her predicament. "You mean like the Indians did when they went to reservations just to survive?" she said, taking a bite of the salted meat.

He shrugged. "I guess it's the same thing. Sometimes survival costs a person a lot. Makes you wonder if it's worth it at any price."

"It's a shame the way the Indians have been treated. I suppose peace is never easy."

"Nothing is ever easy, Jessie, nothing worth having."

"You're a very intelligent man, Navarro. We'll have no trouble defeating Fletcher with you on our side."

"You'll have plenty of trouble, woman. He won't be stopped easily. Don't have too much confidence in me. I'm only one man. How do you know a drifter like me won't take off if it gets too bad?"

"Sometimes all it takes is one good man to win a battle."

"How do you know I'm a good man?"

"Good or bad, all I need is a smart and brave man. You're both. I've seen it."

"You could be wrong."

"Am I?" she challenged.

"In all honesty, I don't know. Never had to take sides before. Always fell in the middle or outside of both. What if this Fletcher offers me more to work for him than you're paying me?"

"Papa said that was the danger in hiring a gunslinger who could betray us. But you said you aren't one. If you did move to Fletcher's side, I'd have to kill you if the time came and we battled face-to-face. Or rather, you'd kill me. I wouldn't stand a chance of defeating you. I could be wrong about you, but I don't think I am. I hope and pray I'm not. If you think there's any chance you'll cross over to the enemy, please don't ride any closer with me."

The desperado was moved by the unshed moisture that glistened in her eyes. Her voice was hoarsened by emotion. "Would it bother you to shoot me?"

"Yes, and it would bother me to see one of the hands do it. I know we're almost strangers, but it doesn't seem that way, except when you pull into yourself for hours. We've been together for three days, but it seems so much longer. We can be friends, Navarro, good friends. I'm sure of it. You might even like the ranch and boys and decide to stay a long time, even for keeps."

"I can promise you now, Jessie, I won't be around longer than it takes to do this job. Then I'm on my way. No matter if I did like it, I couldn't stay. I've never been able to hang around a place long. Don't say, give it a chance. It only causes me problems if I don't stay on the move. I don't make friends easily, so don't expect too much from me. I can promise you something else: Fletcher will never lure me away from you. I'll do your job any way I have to. Once it's done and you're safe, I'm gone. Don't beg me to stay. I can't."

Jessie was touched that the job now meant her safety to him. Still, he was warning her to keep her distance. Few men had made romantic gestures toward her, so why should Navarro? Yet, she wished he would. "How can you be so sure about what tomorrow will bring?"

"I'm twenty-seven, so I know myself and life by now. I can't ever shake the trail dust from my boots."

"Because you want it that way, or because something makes it that way?"

"Getting nosy again, woman," he scolded softly.

"Sorry again, Navarro. Let's finish eating and turn in. I'm tired and tomorrow's a long day."

"As you said, how do you know what tomorrow will bring?" he quipped.

"Some things in life are for certain."

He shrugged. "You're right, unless you die first."

"Dead or alive, tomorrow will still come."

Jessie did her chores when she finished eating. Afterward, she washed her face and arms and tired feet in the river. She brushed her hair, which had remained loose, and braided it. Navarro was lying on his bedroll with his hat over his eyes, so she claimed hers.

"Good night, Jessie," he said without moving or lifting his hat.

"Good night, Navarro," she responded, then shifted to her side so she wouldn't be facing him, wouldn't be tempted to stare at him. She mused in slight annoyance; for someone who didn't like talking and prying, he certainly did his share when it came to her. *Some things in life are for certain, unless you die first,* echoed through her mind. For certain, Navarro teased her heart with crazy feelings. For certain, she didn't want to halt those budding emotions. For certain, she didn't want to die before experiencing the passions he flamed within her.

*

They followed their same pattern on the trail: Navarro rode in the lead and was silent again today. He said his head was fine, and removed his bandage during their midday break. Since his dark hair concealed the wound, she took his word and didn't insist on checking it. He liked the sorrel, and from the way it nuzzled his hands during stops, the animal took to him. Navarro stayed on alert, and Jessie was glad he was so skilled and cautious.

But each time they halted, he seemed more and more restless. He walked around and tried to avoid her gaze. They reached the end of the river before sunset. Navarro suggested they follow one of the side creeks before camping, since anyone coming from the other direction would be eager to halt at the river nearest the road. It was still early, so Navarro took his rifle and went hunting for fresh meat.

"I'll be gone a while, Jessie, if you want to take advantage of the water."

Jessie hadn't had a thorough bath since Monday night while Navarro was unconscious, and today was Thursday. After she hurriedly collected firewood, she gathered her clothes and looked for a private spot. Navarro had been a gentleman so far, so she trusted him not to spy on her during such a private moment. She stripped off her garments and entered the shallow water. It was chilly, and she shivered. She bathed with speed, dried off, and dressed. She freed the braid and brushed her hair, allowing it to remain unbound. The shorter pieces—cut for her disguise—she fluffed around her face, and they curled fetchingly.

Awaiting Navarro's return, she mixed bread to fry and put coffee on to perk. When he did appear, he was carrying a skinned rabbit in his right hand and his rifle in his left. He came to a stop when she looked up at him from her chore. He stared, then shook his head. As if suddenly reluctant to approach her, he did so slowly. He held out the rabbit, and she took it.

"Thanks. It'll be nice not to have salted meat again tonight."

As the creature was exchanged, their fingers grazed each other's.

"I'll wash up while he's cooking," Navarro said. He moved as if anxious to get out of camp and away from her. He didn't return until the meal was ready.

Jessie handed him his plate of meat, bread, and beans. She noticed how he made certain their flesh didn't make contact. He sat down with his side toward her and began to eat. Was he trying to prevent himself from making advances? Or was he trying to show he wasn't interested in her as a woman? Or did he fear she wouldn't be receptive? Maybe she had duped herself into thinking he was just as attracted to her as she was to him. How embarrassing it would be to entice him if he wanted to be left alone!

The meal ended in strained silence. Jessie did her chores, then after checking Ben, she sat on her bedroll. "What's wrong, Navarro? You've been quiet all day." Usually he passed the ride in silence, but not all evening in camp.

His tone was gruff as he replied, "You relax me too much. I say too many things. I get too comfortable around you."

Jessie smiled, mostly to herself. "Is that bad?"

"A man like me can't stay alive that way."

"How will us becoming friends endanger you?"

"It lowers my guard. You're a beautiful and tempting woman, Jessica Lane, a damned distracting one. I've never known a lady before. I'm not sure how to behave around one. It isn't good for us to be out here alone."

Jessie's pulse raced. "I haven't been told that many times. Thank you, Navarro."

His surprised gaze shifted to her lovely face. He felt his heartbeat increase and his body tense. "You don't have a man at the ranch?"

"No. The hands are like my brothers, and there aren't many others around."

"Are those cowpokes blind or crazy?"

Jessie laughed to ease the tension within her and between them. "I've been raised around them and work every day with them, so they think of me as Papa's son or their little sister. I'll be their boss one day: Papa's leaving me the ranch. Tom can't run it, and Mary Louise would sell it to escape."

"I doubt many of them see you as a sister, Jessie," he refuted.

"If they don't, they keep it to themselves. Maybe they don't want to offend me since they'll be working for me one day. We ride herd and fence together, tend sick animals, help with foaling and calving, do roundups and branding side by side. Maybe I work them too hard for them to have time or strength to treat me as a woman. I don't mind; it gets the job done."

"How do they keep their eyes and thoughts off you long enough to work?"

Jessie glued her gaze to her half-empty plate. "When I'm filthy and dressed like them, they probably don't remember I'm not a boy. I fooled you and the others in town. I'm not very feminine."

"Where did you get that crazy idea?"

Jessie glanced up. He sounded angry. "The mirror and past experiences."

"Both lied to you. You only fooled everyone back there because you're clever and you wanted to trick them. If you wanted to play the woman, you could do it better than most. You stay Papa's son because you think it's expected of you. You have confidence in everything, except what you are and what you want. What *you* want, Jessie, not your family, not your duty."

"My sister is very beautiful and ladylike. Nobody ever forgets she and Gran are women. It's different with me."

"Only because you forget it, too."

"It's hard being a ranch hand and woman at the same time, Navarro."

"What's hard is being a son and a daughter at the same time."

"How would you know?" she snapped, irrational anger filling her.

"By listening to you. Everything has been for your family. You would sacrifice anything for them. What would you sacrifice for yourself?"

His last question haunted her, as she didn't know. "I have everything I need, a good home and a wonderful family. They would do the same for me."

"Even your sister? Would she die for you, Jessie? Would she do anything to protect your family and home? Would your brother? Your grandmother? Your father? Or would they surrender if the odds became overwhelming?"

Jessie knew he was serious. She asked herself what the others would do if defeat was imminent, if certain death would result if they didn't yield. "Mary Louise would surrender, but Papa, Gran, and Tom wouldn't. Neither would I."

"If your father loves you so much, why does he risk your life?"

"He doesn't; *I* do. You sound awfully cynical about home and family."

"I don't have either, so how would I know about them? I'm trying to learn what drives you and them before I get there."

"Love, honor, pride, and the hunger for peace, Navarro. Do you know about them?"

"Very little."

"Perhaps that's why you can't understand them."

"Perhaps."

She put aside her plate. "I'll teach you, if you're willing."

"Like that wild stallion, I have to be willing to be corraled and tamed?"

"That isn't necessary. You can still have those things and be free. Some of the men at the ranch have known hard lives before they came to us. Big John was a slave. Jimmy Joe's father beat him and worked him like one until he ran away. Miguel is probably still wanted by the law in Mexico; he was framed by a man who wanted his family's lands. His family was killed. Then Miguel was accused of murdering one of the landgrabber's men. If he hadn't escaped, he'd have been hanged. Others have bad pasts, too. We've never judged them. The ranch is their home. They're safe and happy there, and free to leave whenever they wish. Whatever made you so bitter, it will destroy you if you don't get rid of those feelings. Gran says that having to fight for yourself all the time makes a man cold, hard, and ruthless. Don't become like that. Find a place where peace lives, Navarro, before it's too late. If not at the ranch, then somewhere else, and soon." Her entreating gaze was locked with his tormented one.

"There is no place like that for me, Jessie."

"There could be, if you allowed it."

"I *can't* allow it."

"Why not?"

"Don't wait for me to answer, Jessie; I can't do that, either. Let's just turn in."

"All right, Navarro, we'll drop the talk. I don't want you losing your tongue again. More coffee?"

He extended his cup to her and she refilled it. "Thanks."

"You're welcome." Jessie carried out her chores and claimed her bedroll. "Good night, Navarro."

" 'Night, Jessie." He finished his coffee, rinsed the cup, and lay down.

*

The following day they journeyed for monotonous hours over a terrain that grew desolate. The road was dry and dusty, and the countryside was deserted. Winds frequently whipped around them and tugged at their hats and clothes. The mesquites and cactus were abundant. The landscape stretched out for miles around them, offering lengthy visibility. There were no clouds to shade them, but fortunately the day wasn't terribly hot. They passed buffalo gourds running along the rocky ground and prickly pear growing in clusters. Bunches of grass waved in the breeze. It was quiet, almost deathly quiet.

Yuccas appeared. Soon, mesas were seen in the distance with their flat tops. Hillocks broke the flatness of the landscape, as did occasional draws and arroyos. A whirlwind played to their right, then another danced to their left.

At noon, they ate the extra cold bread and meat that Jessie had prepared that morning in camp. They washed it down with tepid water, and didn't build a fire to perk coffee. They spoke a few words, but hadn't indulged in a real conversation since rising, even though they were riding side by side on the road.

Just before reaching Horsehead Crossing, Navarro halted and lifted himself in his saddle. His keen gaze stared at the area beyond them. "Lots of dust. Somebody's coming. Let's get out of sight. We don't want any trouble." He guided her into a ravine a good distance from the road and dismounted.

Jessie was surprised and pleased when he assisted her down, as she was a skilled rider. She watched him lead the horses into the deepest section and secure their reins to a scrub. He came back to where she awaited him and scrambled up the bank. He extended his left hand and pulled her up beside him. Their gazes touched for a moment as he steadied her, but they were pressed for time. They took their places where they could peer over short mesquites, crouching low near the edge until it was time to jump into the ravine to hide.

"It could be freight wagons, or soldiers, or a band of outlaws on the move," Navarro deduced. "Too much dust for one or two men. I'm not taking any chances with you."

"You think they saw us?"

"Nope. We were moving too slowly to create any signs at that distance."

"Is that why we've been traveling at this pace?"

"Yep. It isn't too hot for a faster one if we rested and watered the horses, but you can see a long way out here so it's best to be careful."

They watched the dust and movement get closer and closer. Men with extra horses rode steadily in their direction. Sounds of the travelers finally reached their alert ears. The mesquites were shorter in this area and they were a good distance from the road, but Navarro said, "Let's duck now."

He slipped over the rough edge, then helped her down beside him. They lay on their stomachs on the sloping bank. He kept her close, and his arm went over her back in a protective cover. "Don't talk or move when they reach us," he whispered. "Sound travels out here."

Jessie obeyed his gentle order. As the group neared, he gingerly slid farther down the bank and pulled her along with him. On his back, he pressed her head to his chest, and Jessie allowed the stimulating contact. Navarro remained motionless, and so did

Jessie. She felt the strength of his embrace and arms. She felt the warmth of his comforting body. She heard his heart beating at a steady pace. She inhaled his manly odor. She was safe in his arms. She relaxed with her cheek against him and her arm over his stomach. She closed her eyes. He was a splendid and wild dream, and she longed to capture it, to make it real.

A lengthy time passed, and the group was long gone. Jessie was so calm and relaxed in his arms that Navarro wondered if she had fallen asleep. She felt wonderful cuddled in his embrace, and he hated to end it. During his eight years with his mother's Apache people, he had seen how important women were to men, though he hadn't learned that by the way his white father had treated Morning Tears. Although few women were given names or mourned at death, life often centered around them. The most successful man had many wives, and proved his worth by being able to support them. When he failed in a raid, the wives ignored him and taunted him, and he hung his head in shame. He redeemed himself by bringing home many goods and gifts for them. He strutted under their affection and praise, as if the most important thing in life was pleasing them, though it was never said.

Apache women preferred a man who was a good thief over a brave warrior. They wanted to be the second, third, or fourth wife of such a successful bandit. To be a man's only wife meant he was poor and there was more work for her to do. Since Apache women could choose their own mates, it was usually a man who already had other wives. They were selfish, greedy creatures who wanted a husband who could give them many trinkets and supplies through deceit or robbery. His bravery was only valued if the white soldiers were attacking. Navarro had never cared for those women. He had supported his mother in the village, but never sought a wife. No doubt none would have tended the horses he staked before her parents' tepee, the sign she accepted a proposal, because he was only concerned about becoming a good warrior and surviving the white onslaught, not becoming a clever thief.

Jessica Lane wasn't like that. She was strong, brave, honest, and hardworking. She admired courage and honor and warrior skills. She would want to be the one wife and partner of a man, not share him with others to lessen her chores. She didn't seem to care about trinkets and false faces. She never shamed a man for revealing a moment of weakness, as when he was shot.

He recalled what she had said about love, pride, and honor. Pride was important to him, but he knew little about love and honor. He had lived a dangerous and destructive life, merely existing for twenty-seven years. He had been broken in prison, but Jessie made him feel strong and unconquerable again. Her attitude made him feel worthwhile. He hadn't realized he possessed hungers for peace and love or that he needed anybody until he met her. He wanted her, but not just sexually. She touched him, moved him, inspired him to crave a new and different life. Others had made fresh starts at her ranch after bad pasts. Could he? How long would it last before the law swooped down like a vulture and devoured him? How would Jessie feel if she learned the truth about him, his mixed blood and criminal life?

Sweat increased over his body, and it wasn't because of the sun on his front or the warm earth at his back. *Shu,* she was one irresistible woman!

Jessie felt the tension enter Navarro's body. She heard his heartbeat increase. She noticed the change in his breathing. She felt the moisture on his shirt.

"They're gone," he finally said, sensing the danger of lying there longer. *Run, Navarro! Get clear of this powerful temptation before you're trapped.*

Jessie lifted her head, and their gazes locked. He saw and felt her body react the same way his was doing, except her cheeks flushed and her eyes softened and glowed. The desperado wondered if she realized how she was looking at him, how she affected him. He wondered if he was reading her right. If he was mistaken and made a move toward her . . .

Chapter

5

Navarro wanted to kiss her, to hold her forever, to make her his; but such daring behavior could frighten her. He didn't want that; he wanted more time with Jessica Lane. To have it, he must earn it. If he tried to seduce her, she might think it was an unspoken price for the aid she so desperately needed. If she yielded to him, he didn't want it to be for that reason. He couldn't help but think that if she knew the truth about him, she wouldn't be looking at him with yearning in her blue gaze and she wouldn't be tempting him to steal the treasures she possessed. He could sate himself if she were another woman, a female for hire, but she wasn't. Jessie was a woman to love, not use.

Love? his flustered mind echoed. What did he know of that emotion? Very little. He couldn't start something, anything, with Jessica Lane because nothing could come of it, except anguish for both of them. Where could it lead? Nowhere. After spending days with her, he couldn't bring himself to hurt her. If not for his dark past, Navarro admitted with bitterness, he would go after her, wouldn't he? Yes. The strange answer flooded his mind. Here was a woman who knew how to love, to share, to hold on, to inspire self-worth. But his past did loom over him like dangerous storm clouds about to strike the land below with their cruel violence and undeserved destruction.

Jessie sensed the turmoil in Navarro. She read it in his worried gaze that he always seemed to try to keep impassive. Here was a troubled man, a man who didn't know his value and appeal, a man who bore resentment and scars from life's cruelty, a man in bitter conflict with himself and others. He was so confident and strong in some areas, and so weak and vulnerable in others. He must have known anguish and rejection many times in the past. Could he change? she wondered. Did he long to become different? Or was he so set in his ways that it was too late? Jessie wanted him, but it was too soon, if ever the time would be right with this tormented drifter.

If she enticed him, it could lead anywhere, nowhere. The time and place were wrong for seeking the truth of why they were drawn to each other, in both a physical and emotional way. If she did expose willingness, he could reject her, become angry at her wantonness, could run for cover far away. Also, he could think she wanted to surrender to him just to make certain he aided her cause. He already considered her self-sacrificing. She needed more time to get to know him, to get closer to him, to let him do the same with her.

"You think it's safe to leave now?" Jessie asked in a strained voice.

"Yep, the sooner the better."

Both stood and brushed off their dusty clothes. They went to the waiting horses and mounted. They wound their way through the dense mesquites and headed down the deserted road again.

They reached Horsehead Crossing. They crossed the wide and shallow Pecos River, journeyed to the Comanche River. Near it, the yuccas, mesquites, and cactus were joined by oaks and cottonwoods. Mesas lifted heavenward from the harsh terrain of rocks and light-colored sand. Fluffy clouds decorated the sky today. Ten miles above Fort Stockton, they followed a branch off the main river and found a safe and secluded campsite. They were stopping early this evening, but it was necessary. They didn't want to halt too near the post and town, and it would take too long to get miles beyond them. They dismounted and glanced around the lovely setting.

Navarro unsaddled the horses and tended them while Jessie collected scrubwood. After lighting a fire, the redhead went to the water to wash her face, hands, arms, and hot feet. It felt good to her to clean and cool her dusty parts. When she returned to the campfire, the handsome male had coffee perking and their meal in progress. Jessie was surprised and pleased by his participation in the chores tonight. He looked up as she approached. When she smiled and thanked him, he responded with a one-sided grin, as if he were only first learning to smile. Jessie took over the cooking, and soon they were eating a common trail meal of beans, fried meat, skillet bread, and coffee.

Little talk took place between them. When they finished, Navarro helped her wash the metal cups, plates, utensils, and cook pots. Supplies were put away for the night, and bedrolls were laid on areas swept clean with a brush limb. Each realized there were only two more hours of daylight. Each was aware of their strengthening attraction and of the night ahead.

As they both needed something to occupy their hands and minds, Jessie suggested, "How about a few hands of poker? I brought cards along for me and Big Ed, but we never got around to playing any games."

"You know how to play?"

"The boys taught me. It passes time when you're on the range guarding herds or while you're waiting for a mare to foal. We only play for fun—no gambling. I can use leaves for money, and you can use small stones. How about it?"

"Fine. A handful or certain number of stones and leaves?"

"Fifty each, so we can keep count."

"If you win, you want to know it, huh?"

Jessie laughed. "Don't you?" she teased.

"Yep."

They collected their "money" and sat down on Jessie's bedroll, facing each other. They heard the rippling and rushing of water as it passed rocks and twigs in the stream. The fire crackled and sent wisps of gray smoke heavenward. The odors of their meal left the area as an occasional breeze wafted through camp. The most noticeable smells were the dusty dryness of air belonging only to the desert and the smoke drifting upward from a dying blaze.

As Jessie shuffled the cards, Navarro pointed out the porcupine who had come to drink downstream from camp. The spiny, rotund creature took his fill and waddled off into the trees on the other bank, paying little attention to the couple. The paint and sorrel were at ease, whinnying softly ever so often, their hooves making noise as they shifted about as they grazed and drank. It was a pleasant evening and tranquil setting.

After Navarro cut the deck, Jessie passed out five cards each, facedown. They studied their hands and plotted strategies. Bets were made, and other cards replaced unwanted ones. Two rounds of raises ensued before Navarro called her. Jessie grinned as she pulled the winnings—leaves and pebbles—toward her with a hand of three jacks against his pair of kings.

"You are good. Never trust a woman smarter than you are, I've always heard."

"Then you have nothing to fear; it was pure luck of the draw. I was going for a pair, but that third jack leapt into my greedy grasp."

As Navarro shuffled the cards this time, he asked, "How big is your ranch?" He hoped that talking would distract him from his rising desires for her.

"Three hundred thousand acres. It's green land with rolling hills and lovely trees. There are some mountainy regions, but mostly beyond our boundaries. We have the Calamity River coming from the south, and the Alamito along our western side. Our grasslands are some of the best in Texas. It's beautiful, Navarro."

After dealing their cards, he continued with, "How much stock do you run?"

Jessie arranged her hand and decided which cards to replace. "One hundred thousand head of cattle and horses. We had more, but several periods of hard times thinned us out. We're rebuilding and strengthening the herds now. The panic in '73 devastated many ranchers. Papa was hurt by it, but not destroyed like many were." Jessie opened, Navarro matched, and she exchanged three cards.

"What happened?" The desperado asked. He had been in prison in '73 and hadn't heard about a panic. *Keep her talking and not tempting you, man.*

"The railroads were competing heavily for business from ranchers. The market was so good for beef the season before that some ranchers drove every head they could to Kansas stockyards: cows, heifers, yearlings, and immature steers. I don't know how much you know about ranching and breeding, but those are called stock cattle. The best cattle to market are four-year-old steers, males castrated as calves." Jessie raised Navarro's last wager. "Trying to get rich, some ranchers flooded the market, but the buyers didn't want stock cattle, just big and healthy steers, and few of them at that time. Most of the regular buyers didn't even come to town that season. Papa didn't have an advance contract from a packing house, army post, or Indian reservation, and we arrived late, the end of September, because of rustlers on the trail."

Navarro checked his hand and raised Jessie's last bet. "What happened?"

"All the ranchers could do was hold the cattle there, fatten them in stockyards, and hope to sell them the next season. Or they could return home, if they could afford to pay for another cattle drive. Supplies, wages, losses, and incidentals can add up to an unaffordable price. So can using stockyards for a long time. Most of the men had to borrow from banks to survive and to feed their herds. Their loans were due in October. When the Panic started back East, it moved here fast. The banks couldn't loan them more money or extend their notes."

Jessie matched Navarro's last bet, but didn't raise it. "What made it worse was the terrible corn crop that year. There wasn't enough to feed and fatten such large herds over a long period of time. What corn there was, was priced high. On top of that, the season had been rainy, so the grass on open range was bad. Some men shipped cattle ahead with hopes of making sales once their herds reached the East; it didn't work and they took awful losses. The Cattlemen's Association said the losses amounted to over two million dollars."

As Navarro planned his next move, Jessie related, "A lot of cattle had to be sold off just for tallow and hides. Many ranchers and bankers lost big. News came that the easterners didn't need or want more cattle. Papa divided and sold our herd to small buyers because we had good steers. Prices were low, but we had no choice. It was too hard on the cattle to drive them back home, and too expensive. Better to earn a little than to spend or lose more. The buyers knew it and took advantage of everyone. Usually a mature steer weighs around twelve hundred fifty pounds and sells for about three cents a pound. Papa got ten dollars a head instead of thirty-five to forty. He was trying to raise money that year to buy more shorthorns and blooded bulls for better breeding."

When she stopped talking and checked her hand, Navarro called her.

As she laid down the cards—two sixes and two aces—for him to view, Jessie said, "In a way, we were luckier than most ranchers; at least we still had our stock cattle at home, and horses for army sales."

Navarro grinned as he spread out a straight of two, three, four, five, and six.

Jessie eyed the cards and teased, "You had my six. I needed it for a full house. That would have beaten a straight."

"I'll only help you beat Fletcher and his gang, not defeat me, woman."

"One last hand to break our tie?" she hinted.

"Yep. You deal. Don't cheat, 'cause I'm watching you close." As she shuffled, Navarro remarked, "That was smart of your father not to drive his whole herd to market to get rich quick."

Jessie worked with the cards again. Hoping Navarro would open up more if she did, she kept chatting. "Papa's taught me a lot about breeding and marketing to prepare me for the time I take over the ranch one day. He's had a hard time over the years. He's faced hardships and failures many times, but they've never broken him. He lost two sons and my mama, and that hurt him deeply. Jedidiah Lane is proud and tough, but I think you'll like him. He's determined to succeed with the ranch and to hold on whatever it takes. Don't be upset if he's standoffish at first. He hates for others to fight his battles for him, but it can't be helped this time. He's been there twenty-six years." Jessie dealt five cards each. "Just as things look bright for him, dark clouds move in. He almost failed another time in '68 to Spanish Fever. Sometimes people call it Texas Fever. It was a hard time."

"How so?" Navarro inquired, watching her closely. She was so beautiful and tempting, and their conversation wasn't distracting him like he'd wanted.

"A lot of Texas longhorns were sold and shipped back East that season. Nearly every shorthorn they came into contact with died. The eastern ranchers, feeders, and butchers went loco; some lost everything, and blamed longhorns and Texans. They tried to pass quarantines and laws against shipping longhorns out of our state. Railroads began refusing to ship our cattle. When we tried to drive them to markets, we weren't allowed to travel over certain lands or use ponds for drinking. People became afraid longhorns would spread the disease everywhere."

After the opening round of bets, unwanted cards were put aside and others taken. A slow series of raises followed as they talked.

Jessie continued her explanation. "You see, Spanish Fever rarely troubles or kills Texas-bred cattle. But if you mix the herds or let eastern cattle graze the same land behind longhorns, the other herds die fast. For a while, people were afraid to buy or eat Texas beef. The easterners hated longhorns and Texans. We couldn't ship or sell our steers, because Papa mostly had longhorns. We only survived ruin because of beef and horse contracts with western posts and Indian reservations. That's when Papa got into crossbreeding."

"What kind of crossbreeding?" he asked.

"Papa bought two Durham bulls. Shorthorns gain faster on corn and certain grains, but longhorns grow faster on grass. Crossbreeding high-grade bulls with female longhorns improves the bloodline, quality of meat, and sales. There's a good change in their color, shape, and size. Some of the best and largest steers are crossbreeds. If you don't know a steer's been crossbred, you have to look close and be smart about it to realize the half-breed has Texas blood of the mother.''

The word "half-breed" stung Navarro. To conceal his reaction, he asked, "If your bulls are so important, do you keep them guarded from Fletcher?"

"We have two Durhams, one Booth, and one black, hornless Galloway. Papa keeps them near the house. Luckily the crossbreed looks like a shorthorn, but he's not endangered by Spanish Fever, like his Texas mother isn't. Matt makes certain the boys keep an eye on the bulls. We can't afford to lose them.''

"Who's Matt?" he probed, catching a new softness in her voice and expression.

"Our foreman, Mathew Cordell. He's a lot like you—quiet and serious," she explained at his surprised look. "You'll like him. Matt's easy to be around. He's been with us since I was a child. I call." She spread her hand: a flush of clubs.

Navarro exposed his cards one at a time: a full house of two fours and three queens. The last card revealed was the queen of hearts. As it touched the sleeping roll, his gaze locked with hers as if sending her a subtle message.

"You win again. That was fun, Navarro. We'll have to play again some time. It's almost dark so we'd better get some sleep. We have one more night and a day and a half on the trail.''

"You restless to get home?"

Jessie couldn't tell him that the responsibilities of home seemed far away and almost unreal at this moment. How strange, she mused, that only Navarro and this setting seemed real. It was as if they had been together for a long time. She wished she could spend more time alone with him, but duties and dangers called to her from far away.

Navarro was aware of the past six days between them, and of what little time remained before they reached the ranch. He wanted to hold her tonight, as he had in the ravine. He yearned to feel their lips and breaths mingle, to have her bare flesh against his, to have her murmuring his name, to unite their bodies in sheer pleasure. He warned himself he should run fast from this impossible situation, but he couldn't, not until she was safe from Fletcher and his gunmen.

The cards were put away. The horses were checked. The fire was down to embers, creating a soft glow. Night birds and insects sent forth their tunes and cries. A frog went "plip" as it jumped from a rock into the stream. Limbs and leaves moved in a gentle breeze, creating shadows and shapes on the ground. Stars twinkled overhead as if dancing in place against a darkening backdrop. Jessie and Navarro claimed their bedrolls and remained silent.

Jessie heard her own breathing. Her eyes adjusted to the darkness. She glanced at the shape that she knew was Navarro lying on his side away from her and the fire's last glow. A coyote howled in the distance, but she didn't fear it. She asked herself what she wanted and needed in life, from life. What would her father say if she chose this mysterious stranger to share it with, to share the ranch Jed had created from sweat, blood, hardships, and toils? What if she wanted Navarro, but couldn't win him? What if her father rebelled at their union? What if her father was willing, but something stood between them?

Jessie wanted him to be with her, to stay at the ranch. She wanted him as a friend, a helper, a lover, a husband. She had known many men who worked on the ranch and those she'd met in town or on cattle drives. But this man reached her, touched her, awakened her as a woman as no other man ever had. This was the man for Jessica Lane, she decided. He wasn't perfect, but who was? This was a man to whom she could give her all, a man whose children she wanted to bear, a man whom she could love and labor side by side with for the rest of her life, a man worth fighting for. She envisioned him laughing, talking, and being with her. She saw his smile, the glow in his hazel eyes, the tension gone from his body and mind. Those images filled her head as she drifted off to sleep.

Navarro propped on his elbow and watched Jessie. Her breathing told him she was asleep. He knew she had been restless since the sensual episode in the ravine. His troubled past seemed so distant tonight, as it had since meeting Jessie. But it was real, and he shouldn't allow himself to forget that for even a moment. The threat would never disappear; he had escaped prison, killed a man, and stolen from others. How long did he have with her before he must be on the run again? How should he handle that insufficient time? If only he could have her for a while—even once would make the coming dangers easier to accept. It would be unbearable to never have anything good or special in his life. Didn't he, didn't everyone who had been cheated by life, deserve a few of those bright corners she had mentioned? Trouble was, he could get entrapped there. Was helping and being with Jessica Lane for a short time worth the risk of his freedom and his life? He must decide soon.

*

Navarro and Jessie awakened; their gazes met across the space which separated them. A twig broke, capturing their attention. Both glanced that way and saw a pronghorn at the stream with her young. Jessie smiled at the sight of mother and child. She hoped Navarro wouldn't want to kill them.

The desperado wasn't even tempted. He recalled how the Apaches often captured birds and animals to give to their children to torture. The women in particular enjoyed watching their children learn that skill. Mercy was a rare thing for some tribes to feel or show, especially to their worst enemies, the Mexicans and whites. That was another way in which his Apache blood was not strong. Killing for survival was natural and necessary, but torturing for sheer pleasure was not.

Navarro shook such thoughts from his head. He stood and flexed. "Up, sleepyhead," he told Jessie, who hadn't moved from her supine position. She was far too tempting lying there with her unbound locks flaming around her lovely face.

Jessie stretched and yawned. "I feel lazy today. It's been a long journey. As soon as we get home tomorrow, we'll be put to hard work immediately. I dread it, but I want it over with. We'll plan our strategy at the ranch."

Navarro thought she appeared just as reluctant to get on the move as he was and to end their private time together. He gathered wood and lit a fire while Jessie splashed water on her face, then brushed and braided her hair. As he made coffee, she cooked meat and bread.

Within twenty minutes, they had finished eating and washing the dishes. Jessie tossed the blanket over Ben's back. The saddle was thrown over it, then cinched in place. She secured her saddlebags behind the cantle, and tied her bedroll atop them. Her rifle was sheathed and her rope was hung over the stock. She filled two canteens and looped them over the horn, then tied the supply sack in place. "Ready," she told Navarro, and mounted.

They bypassed the town near Fort Stockton, and the army post. They would camp once more tonight. Jessie didn't want to get home late and send the edgy Navarro into a bunkhouse of curious strangers. Nor did she want to disturb weary hands turned in for the night. This would be their last night alone.

*

As dusk approached, Jessie was disappointed by how quiet and reserved Navarro had been all day. During their rest stops and midday meal, he had kept to himself once more, and that troubled her. Each time they made progress with their friendship, he halted it and backed off again. It was as if he feared something would happen to spoil their budding relationship. Yet he had opened up more than she had expected. She would back off and let him relax.

As they skirted a rolling hill, Jessie halted him. "Look," she said, pointing at two men who were cutting fences beyond them. "Don't let them see us."

They retreated to cover. "If we go around the other way, we can slip up on them through those trees. Fletcher's men," she added.

They almost succeeded, but Jessie was sighted at the last minute as she sneaked up on foot while moving from tree to tree behind Navarro, who was leading their attack. The villains drew their weapons and opened fire. Navarro shoved Jessie to the grassy earth. The desperado and redhead exchanged gunfire with the two men. One was wounded in the arm and the other in his leg. Navarro surged forward and got the drop on them. Jessie joined him.

Navarro ordered them to strip. When they were down to their longjohns, he told them to mount. After he was obeyed, Navarro tied them to their saddles and slapped their horses on the rumps to send them racing homeward. "That should give their boss a message. We could have taken them to the law, but it wouldn't do much to stop your trouble. They wouldn't betray Fletcher. He would have them killed, even in jail. It's best if we handle that landgrabber."

"I agree. Once they get home, Fletcher will know about you."

"Doesn't matter. He would have known soon anyway. We can expect more trouble from this incident; men don't take humiliation well. Let's get this repaired."

"How? we don't have tools or barbwire."

"We'll use our ropes to close the gap. You can send men out tomorrow to mend it right. All we need to do is keep your cattle in until then."

Jessie noticed how Navarro always said "you" and "your," never acknowledging her father. Maybe he considered the problem with Fletcher hers alone, and that was why he was helping. That was good, because it meant he cared about protecting her.

When the gap was closed with strung ropes, Navarro replaced his knife and remarked, "This is good grassland, Jessie."

"It's some of the best. It cures up easily for superior winter feed. It fattens our stock quickly. It's kin to buffalo grass, and it's very sturdy . . . How do you like this area? Isn't it beautiful?" Her eyes were dreamy as she gazed around them.

He looked over the verdant terrain and agreed. "Yep, I can see why you love it so much. I'm sure you're anxious to get home."

She was, and she wasn't. Navarro was standing too close to be ignored. Her fingers reached up and lifted a section of his black hair. "How's the wound?" It was still discolored and not fully healed, but it seemed to be doing nicely.

He didn't step back or push away her hand. "No more pain."

"That's good. If I forgot to tell you, thanks for saving me that day. If you hadn't shoved me down and caught that bullet, I'd be dead."

"If you'd left me there, *I'd* be dead, so we're even."

It would be dark in an hour, as there would be only a half-moon tonight. "There's a line shack nearby. We'll camp there, then ride in tomorrow. All right?"

"Sounds good to me."

They retrieved their horses and headed that way. Within thirty minutes, they were dismounting at the secluded cabin used during the winter and during fall roundups. No one was around, and no smoke from campfires could be seen. Jessie knew the men should be gathering cows in the south pastures or be at the bunkhouse many miles away. They were alone one last time.

While Navarro unsaddled and tended the horses, she went inside with their supplies. She closed the shutters and barred them to prevent any lanternlight from escaping, just in case someone was in the area and might see it, especially Fletcher's hirelings. Later, she would bolt the door. As the evening was cool, the cabin wouldn't get too stuffy.

Jessie used the iron stove to prepare their meal. As the ravenous travelers devoured the food at the small table, she said, "Fletcher's been undercutting our prices so he can steal army contracts from us. He doesn't need money, so he can afford a cheap price. I don't know how long we can sell for less or refuse to sell. Papa's been keeping the books a secret since last winter. I know he made some large purchases for those last two bulls, and we didn't have many four-year-olds to market last season. Don't worry about your salary; I know Papa will cover whatever you ask for payment," she added, knowing how her words must have sounded.

Navarro halted eating to respond, "Don't worry about what I'll charge, Jessie. That sorrel, saddle, and food are about all I'll need for a while. When I get ready to move on, I'll need a little cash for supplies on the trail. For now, the same as you pay your hands is fine."

Jessie was surprised by those words. "But you could earn a lot of money with your skills, Navarro. We wouldn't cheat you out of a fair deal."

"About the only use I have for money is eating and ammo and feed for my horse. I don't stay in hotels; I like to camp in the open."

"What about saving up for something special, like a ranch of your own?"

"Not interested in settling down."

"How long can you stay on the move, Navarro?"

"As long as I need to or want to. I've got nothing to hold me down to one place. I took this job because it sounded exciting, and I needed to rest a while."

"Don't you ever get tired of moving around?"

"It has its bad points. Shame is, the good ones never outweigh them."

"What if they do one day?"

"I doubt they ever will."

"If they did?" she persisted, their gazes locking and searching.

"Like you said before, how can anybody say what tomorrow holds?"

They completed their meal and cleared the table. "Why don't you relax with your coffee while I wash off outside? There's a windmill and a tank for the cattle."

Jessie left him sitting there in deep thought while she bathed in the vanishing light. She put on the one skirt and shirt she had brought with her in case she needed to dress as a lady during her mission. She unbound her hair and brushed the dark-red locks. When she went inside, Navarro stared at her before leaving to do the same after saying he wanted to look his best for his new job tomorrow.

He returned as she was about to braid her hair before turning in. He bolted the door and dropped his saddlebags to the floor, then approached the table where she was sitting. On impulse, he entreated, "Don't capture it, Jessie; leave it free. It's like a red river and my hands want to jump into it." Ensnared by her beauty and the heady moment, he stroked her silken hair.

Jessie closed her eyes and savored his gentle and unexpected touch. When he halted and stepped away, she stood and faced him. "Navarro . . ." She hesitated and lowered her head. She knew he could ride out of her life at any time and be lost forever. This was their last time for privacy. If she didn't let him know how she felt tonight, there might never be another chance. Without his knowing the truth, he might not be tempted to stay with her. He needed to learn he was loved, he was wanted, he was needed for more than the job she offered. He needed to see that he was special, that he had a place with her if he dared to claim it. She had to give him something only she could give: her love, herself, her trust. She wasn't sure what to do, but her mother had told her that things like this always took care of themselves. Something deep within her seemed to say, *It's now or never, Jessie,* and she couldn't resist that urging.

Navarro told himself to back off, that he shouldn't have approached her, but he couldn't find the strength or will to do so. He lifted her chin and looked into her eyes. "What is it, Jessie?" he asked. She seemed confused and apprehensive. Was she afraid to be here with him alone tonight? Did she want to ask him to go outside to camp? Should he have done so and not placed her in this embarrassing and uncomfortable predicament? "Do you want me to leave? Is that it?"

Jessie misunderstood. "Of course not. I need you."

"I meant, do you want me to camp outside tonight?"

She had known almost from the first moment she had met Navarro that he was the man for her. But she had realized during her days with him that he would need convincing. Jessie decided in a split second that before they risked their lives fighting Wilbur Fletcher, she wanted to taste love, his love. He was the only man who had stirred her emotions in this powerful way. Her mother had been taken from her father. Her grandfather had been taken from Gran. Jake could have ended her life in San Angelo. Josh could have slain Navarro on the trail. Both could die soon from Fletcher's bullets. Life could be so short and cruel. Before death claimed her, she must experience the joys and secrets of love. Once they were bound in hearts and bodies, surely he would stay at her side. Her love would be what won him over and what held him in her life. She had to prove to him that she was a risk worth taking, a dream worth capturing, just as he was to her. "No, don't leave," Jessie admitted.

"It's dangerous for me to stay around you tonight," he warned.

"I know."

A merciless battle waged within the desperado. His mind shouted for him to run. But as he looked at her, his heart begged him to stay. "Do you, Jessie?" he asked. "I haven't known many women, and none like you. The problem is, we may not have much time together. It isn't fair to let you believe we do. If we're killed or captured or your father decides not to hire me tomorrow, this could be our only night together. That isn't much to offer a good woman like you." Navarro realized she didn't know how true those words were. Time was a prize he couldn't grasp and hold very long; yet, he couldn't tell her why. He didn't want her to learn what a terrible thing he had done.

Jessie admired his honesty, but rashly believed she could change his mind later. "Isn't one night better than none?" she replied bravely.

"For me, yes. For you, is it? Don't answer too fast. Once a deed is done, you can't ever change it."

Jessie's gaze roamed his features. Yes, she concluded, her last statement was true. "I want more than one night from you, Navarro. But if this is all you can give for now, so be it," she answered, her courage and resolve unfailing.

"Not just for now, Jessie, forever. Make sure you understand and accept that. I won't guide you down a false trail of pretty lies and broken promises like most men will to get what they want. You're too special for that."

"For as long and as much as you can share yourself with me, Navarro, I want you."

The desperado's heart pounded in desire and hesitation. If only he had met Jessie years ago when a life with her was possible. He had been cold and hard like a frozen landscape. She was a flaming sun that softened and melted his icy heart. If he let Jessie distract him and he stayed too long just to be near her, he could destroy himself. It would hurt them both when he had to leave, especially since he couldn't tell her why. Yet there was so little happiness in life, in his past and in his future, and none in his present if he didn't grasp this moment. Although he had little hope of surviving if he stopped running, wasn't this risk worth taking?

Jessie watched him battle with ghosts and worries that were trying to pull him away from her. A man like Navarro might never come along for her again. Having been raised as a son and heir, she was different from other women. It would take a special man, a strong one, to stand at her side. "This has nothing to do with you taking my job, Navarro. Whether you stay with me or leave for some reason, this is between us as a man and a woman."

Navarro made his choice, and hoped it wasn't the wrong one. "Even if you change your mind about surrendering to me tonight, I'll still work for you, Jessie. I've tried to hold back from you because that's best for us, but I can't any longer."

Jessie moved closer to him. "I've done the same during our journey. You're so different from other men I've known. None of them has made me feel this crazy way. If we die at Fletcher's hands, at least I'll have had you once."

Navarro pulled Jessie into his arms. No matter where his path led tomorrow, this was one night he would never forget. For a moment, he did nothing more than hold her, feel her against him, and tell himself this was meant to be. He lowered his head and kissed her. The contact was more potent than any whiskey he had consumed.

Jessie looped her arms around his neck and returned the ardent kiss. His embrace tightened and he moaned against her lips, revealing his great desire. She quivered at the force of their shared passions. Her body warmed swiftly and uncontrollably. Her pulse raced. She felt strange and wonderful all over. If she couldn't capture this dream, then she would enjoy it for one beautiful night.

Navarro was staggered by the stimulating way she was kissing and holding him. An intoxicating aura surrounded him, and his thoughts seemed to dance like grass in the wind. Her kisses and embraces were unlike those of the women he had paid to release him. His experiences with women were few and far between, but he felt that his sexual prowess would come alive with this unique beauty.

They shared many kisses that became deeper and more urgent. Navarro's lips trailed over the soft surface of Jessie's flushed face, then traveled down her throat and back again. He nestled his face against her hair and savored the feel of it on his cheek. His strong hands wandered up her back and drifted into those auburn locks, allowing her curls to tease over his fingers. He clasped her head to his chest and kissed the top of it. "Nothing in my life has ever felt as good as you in my arms."

Jessie heard his heart thumping, gaining speed with each minute he held her close. It was as if he wanted and needed her desperately but was trying to control himself and not rush their union. Her hands roamed his back and her fingers traced the strength dwelling there. His back, shoulders, and arms were taut and well muscled. Her fingers encountered defined ridges and ripples, like rolling hills and playful water. She was so happy and free that she feared her heart would burst with emotion.

Navarro meshed his mouth to hers as his quivering fingers unfastened the buttons on her shirt. He peeled it off her shoulders and arms, then dropped the blue garment to the floor. His fingers roamed her satiny flesh with slow and arousing movements. They slipped beneath the straps of her chemise and removed it with ease, as she had unlaced and unbuttoned it for him. His hands covered her breasts and reveled in their firm softness. Her nipples hardened into taut peaks as he caressed them while he kissed her with rising hunger.

Jessie was amazed and surprised by how stimulating his fingers felt at her breasts. She had expected his touch to feel good, but not this wonderful. She felt his hands releasing her skirt, and she clung to him to make certain he knew to continue. Assuming he didn't know how to loosen and remove her bloomers, Jessie released them and let them fall to her ankles. She was glad she hadn't put on her boots after her bath; she wouldn't have to part from him to discard them.

Navarro's hands ventured over the bare figure within his reach. She had a strong and agile body from years of hard work, but it was every inch a woman's body, an enticing woman's body. Her tanned skin had a rosy hue, and he felt no flaws on it. She was warm and stirring in his embrace. He wanted to feel her against his naked flesh. First, he had to put out the glowing lantern to conceal the secret on his back. He swept her into his arms and placed her on the bunk where her bedroll was spread. For a brief time, his gaze admired her beauty from head to foot. She made no attempt to cover her breasts or the reddish-brown hair between her thighs. She looked almost too beautiful to touch. He wanted to see her every minute they were making love, but what *she* saw could inspire dangerous questions. He doused the lantern, stripped, and joined her. Instantly her arms closed around him and her mouth fused with his, stealing all thoughts except those of her and this dream come true.

Jessie's fingers played in midnight hair as Navarro's lips adored her breasts. A curious tension gnawed at her, but the pleasures from his skilled mouth and hands were stronger. When he stroked her where no man had ever touched her before, Jessie moaned and squirmed in astonishment and delight. Having seen many animals breed before, she knew something of what to expect. There was no frightening mystery to be solved tonight. She knew what would soon take place, and she was eager for it to happen.

Navarro slipped atop Jessie. With gentleness, he checked to be sure she was ready for him. Then, with care and leisure, he guided his manhood to her welcoming portal. He rubbed against her several times to accustom her to his presence. When Jessie kissed him fiercely and arched toward him, Navarro worked himself within her. He noticed that she only stiffened slightly and inhaled sharply, then relaxed. She didn't cry or wince or retreat, and he was glad. When he was fully inside her, he waited a moment. He hoped he hadn't hurt her, as he had been told it could be rough for a woman on her first time. He knew Jessie hadn't been with a man before, and he was overwhelmed that she chose to give him a woman's most valuable gift.

It was hard for the half-breed to believe he could touch anyone—and especially a woman like Jessie—so deeply. People had always taken from him, never given to him or shared with him. Yet, all she wanted from him was *him*. She didn't care who or what he was. It stunned him that she wanted him so badly, that she liked him and trusted him, that she was honest and open and brave enough to claim what she desired.

The mild discomfort passed quickly for Jessie. Each time Navarro moved within her, it was sheer bliss. What a wonderful part of love this was, she decided dreamily. How beautiful and special to have their bodies joined as one, to have such powerful feelings racing through both of them, to discover such joy together. There was no way to fully share oneself with another except through lovemaking.

Their breaths mingled as their mouths worked as one. Their hearts pounded in unison. Their caresses teased and pleased at the same time. Their responses simultaneously thrilled and inspired. A bond was forged; she belonged to him and he belonged to her. Whatever happened in the future, nothing could take away the beauty and unity of this night.

Upward they climbed, seeking something Jessie could only wonder at. Skyward they urged themselves, growing breathless at the dizzying heights of their passion. And then together they reached a moment of ecstasy that made Jessie cry out with sheer pleasure. Navarro held her tightly, never wanting to let her go as they cuddled in sated tranquility.

"Jessie?" he finally murmured when his breathing was under control again.

"Yes?" she replied in the darkness.

"Are you . . . all right?"

Jessie smiled in joy. "More than all right, Navarro, the best." She heard him sigh in relief and felt him relax. She nestled into his beckoning embrace and rested her head on his shoulder. They were both damp from their exertions, but she didn't care. She liked the way his arms banded about her possessively and the way his fingers trailed over her moist flesh. She liked it even more when his hand grasped her chin and turned it to seal their lips. He seemed so happy and giving at this moment.

Jessie was right: Navarro had never felt better or freer than he did lying next to her and loving her. For tonight, he told himself, reality didn't exist, only this beautiful dream with Jessica Lane did. He closed his eyes.

As they drifted off to sleep, locked in each other's arms on the bunk, Jessie recalled the scars she had felt on his back during the heat of their passion. She had seen and felt Jimmy Joe's scars from beatings by his abusive father. She knew they were lash marks. She wondered who had dared to put them there. Someone had overpowered this strong and proud man, then whipped him brutally. Her mind was flooded with questions: Why? Where? When? Had Navarro killed him, or them? Did that cruel incident have anything to do with the obstacle between them? Did it have anything to do with his bitterness, wariness, and restlessness? Or were those feelings much older than the raised scars? They must have been the reason why he had undressed in the dark—not from modesty or a fear of alarming her with his nakedness. He hadn't wanted her to see them and question him. Jessie warned herself not to probe him about the scars or his past. That might drive him away. In time, hopefully he would trust her with the truth. If not . . .

Navarro awakened first and eased from Jessie's arms and the cozy bunk they had shared last night. The creak of the door only caused the redhead to sigh and roll to her side facing him. He slipped away to bathe and dress in privacy. When he finished, he sat in the open doorway to await her stirring. The troubled man leaned his dark head against the rough wood and worried about what Jessie would expect of him after their closeness.

She had said one night was enough for her, but would it be? Did he want her to feel that way? No. Would one night be enough to last him forever? How could it, when he craved her fiercely again this minute?

Navarro wanted so much more with her and from her, but that was impossible. What, he scoffed, did Navarro Breed have to offer Miss Jessica Lane? Nothing but a lot of heartache. On the run, he couldn't even offer himself, as if a half-breed bastard was anything for a woman like her to desire! He told himself that he should have kept his distance, done her job, taken his payment, and left. He shouldn't have allowed this complication to happen. He shouldn't have birthed false hopes in her or opened himself up for more torment. That's what deserting and losing her would be: utter torment.

Navarro glanced at the slumbering woman who had touched his heart and life as no other person ever had. *Shu,* she had his guts tied up in knots and his head dazed! He had never been one to think of the future. He had lived for the present, just surviving day to day, until Jessica Lane was thrown into his path.

The desperado told himself he was a fool, a silly dreamer on loco weed! Hadn't the Apaches who had partly reared him said never to go against overwhelming odds? Yes, his heart admitted, unless the prize was worth the dangers. Yet, he couldn't abduct her and flee to safety farther east. Even if Jessie was willing to give up her family and world to escape with him—which she surely wouldn't if she learned the grim truth about him —he couldn't allow her to do so. He wasn't the simple drifter she assumed him to be, and she would be endangered.

Jessie had him thinking and feeling and behaving crazy! Wife, home, family, love, and future—they hadn't entered his mind and tempted . . . no, *tormented* him before their paths crossed a week ago. Why, he demanded, did he crave those things now when it was too late? He would have to leave her soon, and in silence, but not until she was safe.

Through a fringe of thick lashes that were barely parted, Jessie observed the man in the doorway, as she had been doing since he sneaked from her side. She guessed he had crept from the bunk for the same reason he had made love in the dark: his scars. She had feigned sleep to give him time to dress and think, to accept this sudden change in his life. He looked so wracked by confusion and anguish, so vulnerable. Such feelings had to be new and hard for a man like him to accept.

Let him adjust on his own, Jess. No questions or pressures. Don't make him skittish or defensive. You don't want him to panic and run. Let him come to you when it's right for him.

Jessie stretched and made throaty noises to alert Navarro to her wakefulness. She sat up, holding a light blanket over her bare breasts. She smiled at him and said, "Good morning. I'm as sluggish as a desert tortoise today. You starving?"

Navarro stood and went to the potbelly stove. "Coffee will get you going, Boss Lady. I'll start our grub while you dress." He found her much too tantalizing there in the bunk and naked. Her soft flesh summoned him to caress it. Her lips beckoned him to kiss her. Her blue eyes called to him to rejoin her on the bunk. Her tumbling tresses of fire blazed their image inside his head. Her entire aura enticed him to claim what he had already won—her willingness for him to possess her. To take her again would give Jessie the wrong idea. No, his heart argued, the right one: that he had a weakness for her. He was relieved when she left to bathe and dress and ceased her pull on him.

When they sat down to eat the biscuits and gravy from the cabin's stores and to sip coffee, Jessie said, "In a few hours, no more dull trail food. Biscuit Hank is a good cook. The hands love his dishes. You'll have hot, delicious meals from now on. Sound good to you, Navarro?"

"Yep. What if your father's changed his mind about hiring help?"

Jessie assumed the man was trying to talk about anything except what had taken place between them last night. "He won't. We need you. I hope you'll like the ranch and everyone there."

"Feelings don't matter when you've got a nasty job to do."

"Friends matter, don't they?" she asked, the words slipping out of her mouth.

"Never had many. None I can think of these days."

"What about me? Aren't we friends?"

The look in her eyes compelled him to respond, "Yep. But it's strange, you being a woman and all."

A bright smile softened her limpid gaze and warmed her face. "You'll make friends with the hands, too. They're a good bunch. You'll see."

"I doubt they'll take to my kind, but don't worry about it."

"Don't sell yourself so cheap, Navarro."

"You count me too high, Jessie. I ain't worth much. Just a drifter."

"You're far more than that, Navarro. Maybe you'll change your mind about yourself while you're living and working with . . . us."

"Don't fool yourself, Jessie. Men like me don't change or settle down," he cautioned, and stole the smile from her face. He needed to prepare her for the inevitable and to prevent her from having hopes of anything permanent happening between them.

Jessie eyed him a moment, then shrugged as she reminded herself of her earlier decision. "Maybe, and maybe not. That has to be up to you."

"You're one stubborn, dreamy-eyed female. That can hurt you later."

Jessie laughed to ease her anxiety. "Papa and Matt would agree on the stubborn part. I prefer to think I'm steadfast. As for the other trait, I'm guilty. When a person wants something, they dream about it first. Then it takes hard work and persistence to make it come true. You can't give up until your fantasy is real. I dream of my family being safe, well, successful, and happy. I do all I can to make it happen. Wilbur Fletcher turned our beautiful life into a nightmare. I'm going to stop him. With your help and friendship."

"You have them, Jessie. But I don't want you getting hurt. You have to learn when to fight, when to compromise, and when to retreat."

Jessie knew his last statement had nothing to do with Fletcher, as Navarro would never back away from that villain. She let it pass unchallenged. "Getting hurt is a risk I have to take. If it gets bad, Navarro, *you* don't."

"Yes, I do. I've promised to help, and I will, no matter what."

"I thought you didn't make promises," she teased.

"Usually I don't, 'cause I don't hang around long enough to keep them."

Jessie forced herself to hold back asking why not. "That's fair and honest. Thanks. But I will understand if something entices you to leave our battleground." She stood and said, "We better get moving. I'm sure Papa is eager to see me home safe."

*

The house and other structures of the ranch came into view. Jessie saw Navarro tense and frown, then take a deep breath. "There she is, home," she announced.

Navarro saw a white house, a large barn, corrals, miles of fencing, an oblong bunkhouse, several smaller sheds, a chicken coop, and a large plowed area for a garden. He noticed cattle and men working a short distance from the neat settlement. Spring branding was clearly in progress. He counted nine hands.

As they approached the area, the sights, sounds, and smells of the task underway reached Jessie and Navarro. They rode to a corral near the barn and dismounted, then unsaddled their mounts and tossed the leather seats over the top rail. The sorrel and paint were placed in the corral for feeding and watering, as no currying down was needed after their leisurely ride this morning.

Jessie saw her wary companion check out his new surroundings, as if looking for signs of peril and a path of quick escape. When he asked what was in each direction, she told him, "Box L land for miles and hours, Fort Davis thirty miles northwest of us, Mexico several days southward, mountains and rugged hills to east and west—and Fletcher fifteen miles northeast. We don't get much company."

"What about the sheriffs and soldiers from Davis and Stockton?"

"We rarely see them unless we go into town for supplies. Let's find Papa and tell him I'm home. Follow me," she invited.

Jessie guided him through a gate and toward the men. The hands saw their boss's daughter coming and shouted greetings to her, all the while eyeing the man at her side. The stranger's walk, alert gaze, and strapped-down holsters told them who the new arrival was: Jessie's hired gunslinger. Tom almost hopped on his twisted foot, in such a rush to get to his sister.

The redhead hugged him and teased, "Did you miss your teacher much?"

His green eyes sparkled with joy as he revealed, "Pa's letting me help with the branding. I'm keeping the tallies," he added, referring to how the numbers and sexes of branded calves were recorded in a book.

"That's an important job for a thirteen-year-old boy. It's good that you're so smart in arithmetic and can handle it for Papa," she replied, fluffing his damp auburn hair. "You best get back to your post, Mister Thomas Lane, or you'll lose count and Papa will blame me. We'll talk during supper."

"Who's this?" the freckle-faced boy asked, squinting through dirty glasses to get a look at the man with Jessie.

"Navarro. He's the man I've hired to help us defeat Wilbur Fletcher. You can get to know him at supper. Back to work, young man; you're getting behind."

Tom obediently returned to his place, but kept glancing at the couple.

Jessie quickly introduced the ranch hands, each man nodding a welcome as his name was called: Rusty Jones with the irons, Big John Williams tending the fire, Miguel Ortega and Carlos Reeves as ropers, Jimmy Joe Slims and three others as two pairs of flankers, and Jefferson Clark as the marker. "Where's Matt and Papa?" she asked.

"Fletcher's been real nervy since you been gone, Jessie," Jimmy Joe replied before another could. "I hope Navarro is faster than a shootin' star with his guns."

As he labored, Rusty added, "We've done branded the new fillies and colts; weren't many of them. Best we can count, we got about fifteen thousand calves this year. The boss bred 'em real good last season. We got us four to six weeks' work to get it done. No wranglers came by to hire on, and Matt couldn't get any in town. It's Fletcher's doing. We think he's been buying off the seasonal help or scaring 'em off. Matt put nine of us on branding while the others ride fence and guard the herds. He and Jed are on the range now, but I don't know where. Lots of trouble while you been gone. Jed'll tell you at supper."

Anger flooded Jessie and danced within her blue eyes. "He'll pay," she vowed. "I'll tell Gran I'm home, then be back to help. Navarro, come with me," she said, thinking it best if he stuck with her for a while to avoid problems.

"Send Big Ed over after he's tended the horses. He's had his fun long enough. We saved some special work for him," Rusty teased.

The fire left Jessie's eyes. "Big Ed took a fall and broke his neck. I buried him outside San Angelo before I met up with Navarro. Rattler spooked his horse."

The men halted their tasks for a few moments of silence as that grim news settled in on them. "He was a good man. He'll be sorely missed," one said for all.

As they walked toward the house, Jessie told Navarro, "Our herd stays about the same size because spring calves replace the mature steers we sell off each fall. The heifers—those cows under three without calves—who come to age this summer, will be bred next season. Papa's working hard to improve our bloodlines. This time of year, the hands separate the cows with calves from the herds and bring them to the holding pens for branding. Once they get the Box L mark, they're turned loose to graze again. The best males are culled for breeding; the others are castrated to be raised as beeves. We have four graded bulls and about twenty good crossbreds."

"Sounds to me like ranching takes a lot of work and wits."

"It does. If we have about fifteen thousand calves, as Rusty said, it'll take them a month or more to finish the branding without help from seasonal wranglers. They can toss, brand, clip ear, and castrate a calf in about a minute. Working ten hours a day for six days, they can do about thirty-six hundred a week. But that's hard on the men. Papa usually gives them Sunday off, but without extra help, we have to work round the week because castration can't wait too long. You know the differences in cattle?" she asked, chatting to distract herself from her fury and from her worries about her father's safety out as he was with only four men.

"Nope. What are they?" Navarro aided her ruse.

"A calf is less than one year old, a yearling less than two, and a cow is a mature female. A heifer is under three years old and unbred, a steer is a castrated male being raised for beef, and a bull is used only for breeding. We raise and breed all except the steers; those we sell at four years, unless we need money badly at three. Fletcher's brand is the Bar F. You read brands top to bottom and left to right. A short, horizontal line is called a bar. It's placed over the F for his mark."

They passed Biscuit Hank on his way from the food-storage shed to the chuckhouse. She halted. "Got you another mouth to feed. I want him treated real good, Hank, 'cause I need him to hang around until Fletcher is whipped."

With Jessie, the crusty cook didn't pretend his hearing was impaired, as he did with the men. "I'll be jiggered! You *did* git yourself a hired gun." His merry eyes looked Navarro up and down. "Looks sharp as a knife to me, Jessie."

She was delighted by the compliment and reaction to her companion. "He is. He saved my skin three times before I could get him home."

"Sounds like you been havin' as much trouble as we'uns have. Yore pa's madder than a hornet with his nest under fire. That snake over yonder is strikin' ever few days. He knows we got our minds elsewhere, and he's cookin' up trouble."

"Like what, Hank?" she questioned in distress.

The thin-haired cook shifted the slab of salted meat to his other shoulder. He didn't want to reveal such dreadful things to Jessie so soon after her return. It was best to let his boss, her pa, tell her, especially about old Buck. "I'll let Jed tell you when he rides in. It's a long and sorry tale, girl. I got to git vittles goin' for the boys. After a hard day, they quit work, starvin' and jawin'."

Jessie understood his reluctance. "That's fine, Hank."

"Yore grandma's been he'pin' me with the cookin' and washin' 'cause I been doin' the boys' chores in the bunkhouse. They ain't hardly had time to suck air."

"As soon as I speak with Gran, I'll help them. They look like they need somebody to give them a rest stop. I hate to have them working on Sunday."

"Can't be he'ped, Jessie. Be seein' you later." He strode off in a rush.

Chickens clucked and scattered as the couple disturbed their scratchings on their way to the well-kept clapboard house. Eight posts lined the edge of the porch that traveled the length of it. Jessie and Navarro mounted the steps and entered a large sitting area with a fireplace on one wall.

As they walked through the homey room, Jessie pointed to their right and said, "Gran's room is on the front. Mary Louise and I share one on the back." Motioning to their left, she added, "Papa's room is there."

Straight ahead, they entered an oblong area where the kitchen and eating rooms were located. To the right was a bathing closet with a second door to the back porch. At the far end of the dining section, she told him those stairs led to Tom's attic room. Gran wasn't inside so Jessie led her companion toward the back door and outside onto the porch, where she heard noises.

Jessie sighted her grandmother and rushed to the well. She took the heavy bucket from the woman's stiff fingers and scolded in a soft tone, "You should let Mary Louise do this, Gran. You have enough trouble and pain with your hands without aggravating them. As soon as that part arrives, Papa can repair the pump and halt this chore."

With twinkling eyes and mirthful laughter, the woman returned Jessie's motherly concern. "I see you got back safe, child," she said. "I been worried plenty these past eleven days. So has your pa. And Matt, too." The older woman looked at the handsome stranger who, without a word, took the bucket from her granddaughter's hand and carried it inside. Martha's gnarled fingers grasped the railing as she pulled herself up the four steps to the porch.

Jessie knew this was one of the times when she didn't dare assist her aging grandmother, who was still proud and strong at seventy. "I'll tell Mary Louise to fill the kitchen barrel before I change to help the hands. Where is that lazy girl, Gran?"

"Gone," Martha replied, halting to catch her breath before explaining.

"Gone? Where? When? What happened this time?" Jessie asked in dismay.

"She was riling Jed about visiting her friends back East again. He wouldn't yield, but he didn't have time or spirit to be troubled, so he let her stay in town for a week. She'll be coming home next Sunday. She claimed she wanted to observe the schoolmarm to see if she wants to start teaching. Jed let her have her way this time. He dropped her off when he went for supplies Friday."

Jessie knew her father had complied to get his defiant daughter out of his hair during this hectic time, and she was angry that such action was necessary. She also knew that her sister had lied to get her way. "Mary Louise should be here helping you and the others, Gran, not playing in town. I don't know what we're going to do about her. Hank told me how hard all of you are working. You can get some rest now that I'm home. I'll tend the wash tomorrow. And I'll take care of the chickens, eggs, and milking. After I get you caught up with chores, me and Navarro are going to deal with Fletcher. We'll keep him and his men too busy to trouble Papa and the hands."

"This is Navarro?" Martha hinted, nodding at the dark-haired man who was leaning against the door jamb and holding a respectful silence.

"Where in blazes are my manners? Gran, this is Navarro; Navarro, my grandmother, Martha Lane, but everyone calls her Gran. You can, too." Jessie briefly explained about Big Ed and how she'd found Navarro. "You'll hear it all tonight, Gran."

"We owe you a big debt, son, for taking care of our Jessie. We couldn't do without her. She practically runs this place. Will, too, one day. I'll bake you a special pie for dessert tonight. You'll take supper with us?" she asked.

Jessie answered for him. "I thought so, Gran, so we can hear the news and make plans against Fletcher. Hank and the boys warned me it's bad news. With Big Ed gone, that leaves us with only twelve hands, Matt, and Hank. Blazes! How can we get branding and planting done without more help? Especially with Fletcher coming at us stronger and meaner than ever. Damn him!"

Martha inhaled sharply. "Jessica Lane! Watch your tongue, child. Your pa will be red in the face if he hears such words coming from you."

"I just get so mad, Gran, that they slip out. I'm sorry. I'll be careful."

"I know, child," Martha sympathized, patting Jessie's back.

"I'll get changed into some old clothes and boots, then fetch the water for you. I'll see you in a minute or two, Navarro. Wait here for me." Jessie left the room.

Martha Lane focused faded blue eyes on the quiet male whose height towered over her five-two frame. "Where are you from, son? What's your last name?"

Navarro straightened. "Colorado and Jones, ma'am," he lied.

"A man of few words like Matt," she teased.

"While Jessie changes, I'll fill that water barrel for you, ma'am," he said, then lifted two buckets and headed for the well with haste.

When Jessie returned to the kitchen, Gran remarked, "Your Navarro is short of talk, child, and a wary man, but I like him. Strikes me as a tough man who hides a gentle side. I can tell he's had a hard life; his eyes give it away."

Jessie glanced out the door at Navarro as he drew water from the well. "I'm sure he's had plenty of troubles, Gran, but he's a good man. He hasn't opened up much to me yet, but I hope he will. He seems so lonely, but doesn't seem to want anyone to know it. We'll talk about him later. He's coming, and I have to hurry." Jessie wanted to get away before her tone and gaze exposed her feelings and intimate behavior. She was glad her sister was gone for a while and relieved at not having to deal with the rebellious girl at this time.

"That's it, ma'am," Navarro said, placing the two buckets aside.

"Let's go," Jessie instructed, then led him outside. "Thanks for helping us. Do you mind hanging around me this afternoon while I work?"

"Nope. I'll help, too. Just tell me where I'm needed most."

"You don't have to, Navarro. This isn't what you were hired to do. I just thought you'd feel easier in strange surroundings around me."

Navarro's hazel gaze locked with her searching blue one. "I feel easier around you in any surroundings, Jessie. Just think of me as hired help and give the orders, Boss Lady." He grinned, then laughed.

Jessie liked the look and sound of both. She smiled. "Thanks. You're a mighty special man, Navarro. I hope Gran didn't intrude too much."

"Nope. She's a fine woman. I never knew either of my grandmothers, and only met one of my grandfathers. They're all dead now. I'm the only one of my family left." Navarro scowled and broke their gaze. He hadn't meant to reveal anything about himself, but Jessie had a curious way of culling out facts when he least expected it. "I told her I was from Colorado and that my last name's Jones. You might need that information with the boys later."

Jessie didn't think either claim was true, but she didn't challenge them. "Well, Navarro Jones of Colorado, let's get busy. It's going to be a long and hard afternoon. Know anything about branding?"

He was relieved by her acceptance of him and of what he was certain she knew were lies. "Nope, but I learn fast."

"Good, because we're shorthanded, as you heard."

*

Branding was a loud, dirty, dangerous, and fatiguing task. The odors of smoke, the sweat from men and horses, singed hair, manure, blood, and arid dust permeated the area. The air rang with the sounds of shouts, pounding hooves, bawling cattle, clanking irons, whirs of lariats, creaking of saddles and stirrups, and the hissing of hot iron to hide. Everyone sang herd songs and ballads to calm the cows and calves who were waiting impatiently to be separated for marking. Verses from "The Dying Ranger" and "Bonnie Black Bess" only partially settled down the cattle that were bunched tightly in the holding pens.

Miguel Ortega and Carlos Reeves, expert ropers, tossed their Mexican lariats around hind legs and dragged bellowing calves forward one at a time. Each man was skilled at cutting out calves and keeping up with the rapid schedule. Sombreros shaded their dark eyes, and chaps protected their legs from horn scrapes and chafing. During each day, they used several highly trained cutting horses, changing mounts when one tired. Carlos always said that geldings were best because they never had romancing the mares on their minds. Miguel teased him that he should know, since Carlos was the one who tamed and trained most of them.

Two sets of flankers were kept busy by the Mexican and half-Mexican vaqueros. One flanker from each pair seized the calf by its shoulder hide and flipped it to the ground, pinning it there by snug holds on its head and right foreleg. His partner, sitting on the ground, grasped the right hind leg with his hands, then pressed his boot against the lower one to prevent any movement. Today, Jimmy Joe Slims was paired up with three other men as flankers.

Big John Williams, their smithy, tended the fire. The black man kept the coals at the right heat and replaced the irons tossed aside after use. Rusty Jones, the ironman, made certain the tool was hot enough to leave its five-inch mark and a scab, but not hot enough to hurt the hide or blur the Box L mark. The bearded redhead applied light pressure and held the iron in place a moment.

While Rusty was doing his task on one end, Jefferson Clark worked as the marker on the other. The black man clipped the calf's ear to match that of all Lane cattle. He tossed the bloody piece into a pail to be counted and compared to the day's tally. The clip provided another means of identification in case a brand was altered or obliterated by rustlers and aided the ropers while cutting out unworked calves from the restless herd.

As soon as Rusty and Jefferson finished stamping and notching, the back flanker lifted the calf's upper leg—if it was a male—for castration. With skill and a razor-sharp knife, in about a minute, Jefferson split the sack, peeled out the testes, snipped the cord, tossed them into another pail, and stepped back to indicate he was finished. The area would drain, scab, and heal quickly. The calf was released to trot to its bawling mother.

Jessie relieved a flanker to rest and to get a drink or to be excused, then moved to the next weary and thirsty man. Navarro fetched water from the second well near the bunkhouse. He sharpened the knives that Jefferson tossed aside when dulled. He helped Miguel and Carlos by saddling and unsaddling their mounts while the two men took short breaks. He didn't know how to rope legs, or tend fires, or stamp, or clip ears. Within a short time, the men felt enough at ease to yell for his help whenever needed. Both Jessie and Navarro noticed how he was welcomed into the laboring group.

Navarro was too distracted by the flurry of activities and excitement to think about his past or to stay on his guard around strangers who were laughing and talking as they worked. Rusty even jested about them being kin because of the desperado's matching name, Jones. The fiery-haired ironman told them that Fletcher was in big trouble with two Joneses to battle. The desperado found himself relaxing and enjoying the work and genial company.

When Jessie and Navarro met at the water bucket to soothe their dry throats, he handed her the dipper and smiled through dusty features. Each used a bandanna to mop sweat and dirt from their faces. Their clothes and boots were a mess. They were weary but elated. His black hair was wet. Hers was braided and tucked beneath her hat to keep it as clean as possible. Her work clothes were faded and frayed, but his stolen ones were only a few months old.

"Supper and a hot bath are going to be wonderful," Jessie remarked. "But our bodies might refuse to move in the morning. You didn't realize what you were getting into, did you?"

"This wasn't the work I had in mind, but it isn't bad. You have a good place and hands, Jessie. I can see why you love it here."

"Then maybe we can entice you to stay around permanently." His smile faded, and she knew her words were a mistake. As if a joke, she added, "Surely you don't want us to do all this work alone. Trouble is, it never ceases. It's roundup and branding every spring, then roundup and cattle drive every fall. Not much adventure and excitement for a man with trail dust in his blood and on his boots."

"Sorry, Jessie, but that's true." He liked the way she seemed to catch her errors and correct them with genuine concern.

"Back to work for me. I'll take over Tom's place for a while." Jessie stepped around and over smelly piles of manure where flies buzzed. It was a familiar odor, so it didn't bother her too much. More flies buzzed around the discard pails of ear notches and testicles, attracted by the fragrance of blood. She shut out the noises of the area and concentrated on her tally after telling Tom to take a rest and praising him for doing a good job.

The freckle-faced redhead hobbled in Navarro's direction, dragging his twisted foot from fatigue. The boy was fascinated by the man he believed was a legendary gunslinger, paying no heed to the fact Jessie had denied it was so. While the stranger was talking with Miguel, Tom removed his glasses and cleaned them as best he could. "Need help, Mr. Jones?" he asked with eagerness when the Mexican returned to his roping.

"You can help me sharpen those knives for Jefferson."

"Are you gonna ride over to the Bar F and challenge Mr. Fletcher to a show-down?" the youth asked in a rush. "I'll bet you're real fast with those guns. I'll bet you gun him down with the first shot. He's real mean, Mr. Jones. I would handle it for Jessie and Pa if I was able," he murmured, frowning and slapping the thigh of his bad leg. He pushed his thick glasses back in place, as they had slipped down his greasy nose when he glanced at his filthy socked foot.

Navarro was moved by the boy. Though different from his own, Tom's problems clearly had a similar effect on his life and character. "Killing a bad man isn't always the best answer, Tom. Sometimes it's better to shame him and defeat him. Bloodshed usually leads to more bloodshed. A man has to prove he's stronger, wiser, and braver, or another troublemaker will take his place."

"How are you gonna defeat him?" Tom asked, intrigued.

"He's spooning out bad medicine to make us sick, so we'll do the same with him. When he's had enough, he'll back off."

"What if he don't?"

"We'll figure what to do when that time comes."

When Tom's glasses slipped again, the boy muttered as he shoved them back into place. Navarro bent over and retrieved something from the ground. He cut two lengths of rawhide from the long strip that had broken free from Miguel's saddle—thongs used for securing items to it. "Let me see your glasses for a minute." Tom handed them to the man, who tied a section of rawhide on each earpiece. He replaced the spectacles and knotted the rawhide ends behind the boy's head, then fluffed auburn hair over them. "There, that should keep them from falling again. Sweat and oil makes them slick on the nose. I knew a man once who did his like that to stop them from bothering him. Doesn't even show with hair over it."

Checking the snug fit with dirty fingers, Tom grinned and said, "Thanks, Mr. Jones. I never thought of it before. You're real smart."

"Like I said, Tom, there's always a way to solve a problem. Glad I could help."

"Some things can't be solved," Tom remarked with resentment. "I got this crazy foot that the doctors can't fix. I can't even hide it in a boot like you hid that strip with my hair so people won't stare and be mean about it. People laugh 'cause I'm clumsy. It ain't funny. They'd know if they had to live like this."

To be helpless and bitter were things Navarro understood. To be an outcast, to be stared at, to be mistreated, to be scorned and avoided—he knew about those, too. The desperado was surprised by the words that came from his own mouth and heart. "People are mean or curious when they don't understand something, Tom, or when they fear it. When you act ashamed, they think there's a just reason for it. I know it hurts to be different, to want something you can't have. Don't let it make you hard and bitter. Don't let it stop you from trying anything you want to do. It might be harder for you than others, but it's a challenge. Doesn't that make victory taste better?"

"You talk like Jessie. She's the only one before you to understand how I feel." Tom repeated what his older sister had told him before leaving to hire Navarro. "If Jessie says it and you say it, it must be true."

"You're lucky to have Jessie for a sister."

Tom brightened. "Yep, she's the best in the whole world. She loves me more than anyone. I don't know what I would do if anything happened to her. You won't let Mr. Fletcher hurt her, will you? He knows she's the one keeping Pa strong against him. I'm scared he'll try to get rid of her to make Pa sell. Don't tell them I told you. Pa would be mad."

"I won't tell anyone. Good friends have to trust each other."

"You'll be my good friend, too, like Jessie and Matt?"

"Yep, if you call me Navarro."

"Yes, sir, Navarro."

"Let's get busy, or the others will think we've quit for the day and start ribbing us." Navarro walked slowly to make sure the disabled Tom could keep up with his long strides. He saw Jessie send him a smile of gratitude, even though they had been out of earshot. It warmed him from head to foot.

Jessie knew something special was happening between Tom and her lover. Tom didn't take to many people, and she knew Navarro didn't, either. It was obvious Navarro had somehow won over her brother, and the other way around, too. She was overjoyed to see them striking up a friendship that hopefully would help both with their problems. What, she mused, a contradictory man he was! Her heart danced wildly and a hot flush raced over her body. If only things would work out for Navarro here, then perhaps he would stay with her.

"You missed two, Jessie," Jefferson whispered as he tugged at her arm.

The redhead blushed at her lapse of attention. "Sorry. It's been a long and tiring trip to San Angelo. I'll put Tom back on tally while I do a few chores before suppertime else I won't be able to get up or lift a fork. Tom! You take over here. I have to go. Navarro, I'll need your help."

Navarro followed her to the barn.

"The boys will be quitting in about thirty minutes. I thought you might want to get your bath and get changed into clean clothes while you still have privacy at the water shed. Some people don't like stripping in front of a bunch of strangers. So if you're shy, Navarro, you can be done and dressed before they finish. I have a few chores to do, then I've got to get scrubbed for supper. When you're done, come to the house. You can visit with me and Gran until Papa returns."

Jessie pointed the way to the overhang beside the chuckhouse where several wooden tubs were located. "You can fill one with the pipe from the well. Biscuit Hank already has water heating so you won't freeze. See the fire and kettle?"

"Yep, but don't you need me to do chores?"

"I can finish alone. If you want privacy, you'd better get to it," she said with a laugh. "You can claim any bunk that doesn't have possessions by it. See you soon."

She left to place their saddles in the barn in case of rain, to toss hay to the horses corralled nearby, to pen up the chickens for the night, to do the evening milking, and to get her own grooming done.

Navarro wondered if Jessie had felt his scars and knew he was trying to hide them. Such a secret couldn't be kept long, so he would think about handling it soon . . .

Navarro bathed in a hurry, then dried his muscled body. He dressed in a rust-colored shirt, dark pants, and a leather vest. His feelings were in turmoil. He couldn't believe that he had been talking and joking and working with strangers since noon. No one had mistreated him. He had been accepted as if he were a seasonal hand returning for new work. Their reaction to him and his to them baffled him. Never had he been so at ease in a group. The ranch was beautiful, like Jessica Lane. Life here seemed wonderful for everyone concerned, despite their troubles. He saw why Jessie loved it and would die to protect it. He admitted he wanted to stay there to help these people and to enjoy life. He hated the thought of returning to a barren and lonely existence. Yet his tension was returning. One fence remained to be approached and jumped; Jedidiah Lane . . .

Chapter

7

Navarro sat in the dining area that adjoined the kitchen, where Martha and Jessie were completing the meal. He sipped coffee as he listened and observed, answered a question here and there, and just enjoyed the novelty of being included in this cozy moment in a real home with a good family. When Jessie came to set the table, Navarro asked if she needed any help.

Jessie smiled and shook her head. "But thanks."

"What work do you do, son?" Gran asked.

"A little of everything and anything. Haven't tried ranching before. This is new to me. Hard work."

"Have you handled many problems like ours?" the older woman inquired.

"None, ma'am."

"But he'll do fine, Gran," Jessie vowed. "He's fast, smart, and good."

"He must be, or you wouldn't be here to speak up for him."

"That's true," Jessie murmured, smiling at Navarro.

"Ma, I'm home," Jedidiah Lane shouted from the front door.

"In here, son," Martha replied, "with Jessie and her friend."

Jed entered the room, embraced the girl who ran into his open arms, and said, "Sure glad you're home safe, Jess."

"Papa, this is Navarro Jones. He's the man I've chosen to help us."

Jed walked forward to shake hands with the tall man. "Good to meet you, Navarro. The boys told me how you pitched in and helped today. I'm much obliged. They told me how you took care of my daughter, too. Can't tell you what that means to me. This girl is my heart and soul."

Navarro noticed how the man looked at his daughter, eyes filled with love and beaming with pride. A surge of envy shot through him. "Like I told your mother, I don't know much about ranching and cowpunching, but I'm willing to lend a hand where needed. Until I take on Fletcher."

Jed glanced at Navarro. He wasn't what he'd expected in a gunslinger. Navarro seemed too kind and polite to be a hired killer. "I need to wash this dust off before supper. Then we'll talk. Matt's coming, Jessie, so set him a plate. I have plenty of news for you."

"I can't wait to hear it, Papa. The boys wouldn't give me a clue."

"That's good. No need to work it over twice. I'll be back shortly."

Jessie added a sixth place setting to the table. She smiled at Tom as he came down the stairs. "You look handsome tonight, Master Tom."

"You look beautiful, Jessie," he replied. "Don't she, Navarro?"

The desperado shifted from one foot to the other, then nodded. Jessie was wearing a blue cotton dress, and her hair was hanging free down her back. The wavy locks nearly reached her waist. The shorter curls framed her face and softened her bold features. The skirt swayed with her movements and captured his attention. There was no doubt tonight that Jed's "son" was a lovely woman.

"You act as if you've never seen me in a dress, Thomas Lane."

"Not much. I like your hair down. Ain't it pretty, Navarro?"

To her frustration, Jessie blushed again. "I always dress when we have company, young man. You stop putting Navarro in the fire with your questions. Besides, it's, 'isn't it pretty,' not 'ain't it pretty.' Your lessons are sorely lacking. I'll have you back to work at those books tomorrow."

"But I have to keep the tally. I'm doing a good job."

"Yes, you are, but studies are more important."

Navarro intruded before he thought about it. "He's needed out there, Jessie, with you being shorthanded. You and I have work to do. Who'll take his place?"

"Navarro's right, Jessie," Tom added, grinning at the man.

"Are you two plotting against me?" she teased.

Tom and Navarro exchanged feigned innocent looks and shook their heads. Tom laughed. Navarro shrugged and grinned.

"I see, two against one. You win this time, but you'll have to study twice as hard later. Agreed?"

"I promise."

"You promise what?" Jed asked as he returned.

Tom explained, then told how Navarro had fixed his glasses. Jed praised the gunslinger's ingenuity, then succumbed to Jessie's coaxing look. "The boys said you did work hard today, son. You're hired on until branding is over."

"Thanks, Pa. I'll do it good and right. You'll see."

Their other guest arrived. Jed introduced the two men. "Navarro Jones, Mathew Cordell. Matt was with me before the war. Then he came back when it was over. He's been foreman for ten years, but he's more like one of our family. I couldn't do without him, so follow his orders as if they were mine."

As they shook hands, Navarro studied the foreman. Matt was a few inches shorter than he was, and appeared to be in his mid-thirties. He was what women would call good-looking, with his brown hair and eyes and a neat mustache lining his upper lip. He realized how important this man was; he had heard his name many times from Jessie and the others.

"The boys broke you in hard before you could breathe."

"They worked me good today," Navarro responded.

Matt left the two men to walk to Jessie. He looked her over and smiled. "I can relax now; you're safe."

"I'll bet it's been quiet without me around to stir up things," she teased, and noticed how Matt's glowing eyes lingered on her. His gaze was soft and warm like melting chocolate, and she found his spellbound reaction to her flattering.

"Too quiet, Jessie, except where Fletcher's concerned."

"What's been going on?"

"Let's get seated first," Jed suggested.

Tom took his regular seat beside his sister. Jed and Martha did the same at the ends of the table. Matt and Navarro sat next to each other opposite Jessie and Tom.

The dishes were passed around and each person filled his plate. No one talked for a time as they prepared to devour the delicious meal of meat, home-canned vegetables, hot biscuits, and coffee.

"The boys told me about Big Ed. Sorry to get that news, Jess. What happened? And how did you meet Navarro?"

Jessie went over the highlights of those incidents. When she finished, with Jed's and Matt's eyes wide with fear, she added the news of the cut fence.

Jed's face flushed with anger. "We'll get it repaired tomorrow. He did the same on the east fence. We took care of it today. 'Course they rustled some cattle while the fence was down. We saw their tracks. That isn't the worst part, Jess."

"What is, Papa?" she asked reluctantly.

"We found Buck dead near the cut fence. That old dog must have sniffed trouble and tried to attack them."

Sadness and fury filled Jessie. "How cold and cruel can the man be, Papa?"

"While we were out during roundup, somebody sneaked over and killed some of the chickens. They were tied up along the corral posts. You see what we're up against, Navarro?"

"Seen any faces or horses you recognized?" he inquired.

"Nope. They're real careful-like. They're good about luring us away to do their mischief. I took your sister into town. She claimed it was to work with the schoolmarm, but I think she was getting scared after that chicken episode so near to home. It riles me to see them so cocky that they'll come so close to the house."

"Fletcher sounds like a determined man to me," Navarro commented.

"No more than I am, son." Jed flowed into the rippling story of how he settled this land and how he would never sell out to anyone.

"I can see why, sir. You have something special here."

"What kind of work have you done before?" Matt asked. Jealousy chewed on him, because he caught an alarming undercurrent between the handsome stranger and his Jessie. He prayed he hadn't waited too long to let her know his feelings.

"Whatever job is available. No family or a place to call home, so I stay on the move. Nothing to hold me in one area very long. I like seeing new places. Came from Colorado, but spent most of my days north of there. Jessie told me you're into crossbreeding." He changed the subject from himself and his past.

"You said you don't know much about ranching?" Jed hinted.

"Nope, but it sounded interesting."

"If I can get Fletcher thwarted, I'll get back to it. Longhorns can take heat, thirst, and hunger; but they're leaner and tougher and stringier than purebreds. I've been mating mine with Durhams, Booths, and Galloways for a few years. As soon as I get more money, I aim to purchase me some Angus and Herefords to blend in. It costs a lot to buy them and have them shipped here."

"I'll see what we can do to stop Fletcher from interfering—."

"First," Jessie injected, "we have to catch up on chores. I'll help Gran with the washing, chickens, and milking tomorrow. That north fence needs restringing. It only has our ropes keeping the stock in."

"I'll help with it, Jessie, if Matt will show me what to do."

She smiled at him. "Thanks, Navarro. Then we'll go to work on Fletcher while the boys handle the branding."

"What if Tom shows me where Fletcher's place is on Tuesday? I'll keep him a safe distance away. That'll leave all the hands to keep to their chores, and you can help your grandmother. I need to study his layout, men, and schedule before we make any moves. Is that all right with you, sir?"

"Please, Pa, I can do it. I'll do everything Navarro says. I promise."

Jed mused for a time. "Tom doesn't do much riding. If you'll take care of him, he can go. That'll keep Jess and the boys busy here."

As Tom began to rush Navarro with questions about their impending adventure, Jessie told him, "Later, Tom. Let Navarro breathe and eat." Her brother obeyed, though she saw it was hard for him to do so.

As the meal continued, talk drifted into areas unfamiliar to Navarro. He was as careful as Jessie about concealing their true relationship. If Jed learned what had happened between them on the trail . . . Then there was Matt. The desperado noticed how the foreman subtly watched Jessie; he looked like a starving man picking up every crumb of talk that she dropped, feeding on each smile and gaze, drinking in every movement. He saw how easily Jessie smiled, laughed, and spoke with Mathew Cordell. They had known each other a long time. Matt would be here after he was forced to leave. Jealousy nipped at him like an angry dog on a stranger's heels. He listened to every word and observed each person. The longer he sat hearing about people, places, things, and times he didn't know about, the more restless and nervous he became and the more slowly the evening passed. He was feeling closed in, as he had in prison. He needed fresh air, movement.

Jessie glanced at Navarro every so often, but tried not to stare or to expose her warring emotions. It was hard being this close to him without touching him. If her father even suspected the truth of her behavior, he would order Navarro off his property. She had to give Jed time to get to know her love, time to accept him. And the same was true of Navarro and her family. Yet she sensed the anxiety building within the man across the table from her. She saw how straight and stiff he was in his chair. She saw how he toyed with his fork and how his gaze darted about from person to person. He was panicking.

Impulsively Jessie wriggled off her slipper and slid her bare foot across the floor. When it reached her love's booted foot, she stroked his leg with her toes. She pretended not to notice when Navarro reacted to her bold action. She brought her foot upward until it rested on his knee. His hand drifted into his lap and his fingers closed over it. Slowly and sensuously Navarro's thumb caressed the side. When her grandmother suggested they serve the dessert, Jessie hated to cease the action that seemed to relax both of them. She pulled her foot away and eased it into her slipper. "Gran made a special dessert for Navarro."

The dried-apple pie was warm and tasty. Its odor filled the room. Navarro thanked the older woman, and devoured two pieces.

"More?" Jessie offered.

"Too full. Best meal I've had all my life, ma'am."

"She's trying to teach me all her secrets, but I'm not a good student."

"You're good at everything," Matt replied with a grin. She looked so beautiful and feminine with her auburn locks flowing freely and her trim body clad in a dress. Her blue eyes laughed each time her lips did, and he hungered to make her kisses his dessert.

"You're just saying that because you practically raised me, Matthew Cordell."

"Did a fine job, too."

Jessie loved Matt as a brother. Tonight he looked extra nice and was most charming. She wondered how different his lovemaking and kisses would be from . . . She rushed a response. "Thank you, kind sir. Tom, it's bedtime. You've a busy day tomorrow."

"But I want to talk to Navarro."

"There's plenty of time for that, young man. He'll be here a long time."

"I hope he gets our trouble settled fast," Matt said, looking at Navarro.

"I'll try. I'll know more after Tom and me do our spying."

Jed stood, and so did Matt. Navarro followed their lead. As Jessie and Gran cleared the table, Tom mounted the steps.

"Let's head for the bunkhouse," Matt suggested to Navarro. "Good night, Jessie."

"Good night, Matt. See you tomorrow, Navarro," Jed said. "If you need anything, just tell Matt. We couldn't run things without him; he's like my adopted son."

"You sure it's all right if I use that sorrel, Mr. Lane?" Navarro asked.

"It's yours, son. Jessie gave him to you. It's hardly enough for saving my girl's life. We'll talk money tomorrow, if that suits you."

"Don't worry. I know you'll be a fair man. A drifter don't need much."

The two men left the house, and Jed went to his room. Jessie tried to get her grandmother to turn in while she did the dishes, but Gran wouldn't allow it.

From the corner of her eye, Martha watched her granddaughter as she remarked, "Your Navarro is mighty mysterious and restless, Jessie. I hardly learned a thing about him. Real closed-mouthed."

"He's a loner, Gran; they're like that. He spends most of his time on the trail by himself. He doesn't get much chance to talk or sit in one place long. Don't poke at him too hard before he gets used to us. It might scare him off."

"You wouldn't like that, would you?"

"Like *what?*" Jessie asked distractedly, her mind having drifted to the bunkhouse as she wondered how Navarro was mingling with the hands.

"Don't you think you've gotten too attached to a stranger too quickly?"

"What do you mean, Gran?" she asked as she stalled for time to think.

"Since when does Jess Lane blush? Or put on a pretty dress? Or wear her hair down? Or fly away on dreamy wings?"

"Stop teasing me, Gran. I do it every time we have company."

"Navarro isn't company. He's a hired gunslinger, a paid worker."

"He's more than . . . that," she finished hesitantly. "He saved my life, Gran. He's going to help us defeat our enemy, save our home and lives."

"What else is he going to do here, child? Steal the boss's daughter?"

"No."

"You sound sad about that."

"Maybe I am. I know it's impossible."

"Nothing is impossible for you, Jessica Lane, not when you want it."

"*He* is, Gran. The minute his task is done, he'll leave. I'm sure of it. Just as I'm certain there is nothing I can say or do to keep him here."

"You hardly know him, child. Is that what you really want?"

"For the first time in my life, Gran, I feel like a real woman. He tugs on me in a new way, and I like it. He makes me think about having my own home and family. Is that so terrible even though I haven't known him long?"

"No, but I don't think you should share this news with anyone, Jessie, not your pa, your sister, Tom, or even with Navarro himself. It's too soon."

Jessie had always been able to confide in and trust her grandmother. Yet there were things about Navarro that she couldn't reveal or discuss. Not yet anyway. "I know, Gran. Why tell them about something that will never happen? Don't worry about me. I'm a grown woman. I'll be fine. At least it's gotten me to thinking like I should at my age," she teased.

"The right man will come along for you one day, like my Thomas did for me."

"You're right, Gran. When he does, I'll know it." *I do know it, Gran, and it's Navarro, whoever and whatever he is.*

*

Jessie was up early to gather eggs and to release the hens from their nocturnal protective coop so they could scatter and scratch in freedom until dusk, except of course for those sitting on eggs. She tossed hay to the horses corralled nearby, including her cherished Ben who had been named after her grandfather Thomas Benjamin, as had her brother. She milked three cows that stayed in the pasture close to the barn. Usually she did those chores in the morning and her sister did them in the evening, when Jessi did ranch tasks while Mary Louise did household ones with Gran. The redhead carried two pails of milk to Gran and one to the chuckhouse cook, along with a basket of eggs for the men's breakfast.

She placed both items on a table. "Morning, Hank. Smells good. I'll bet the boys' noses are sniffing the air already."

As Hank shoved another pan of biscuits into the oven, he responded, "Mornin', Jessie. The boys will be crawlin' outta their fleatraps anytime now. I'm 'bout to clank the ring. Don't let 'em trample you gettin' to it."

Jessie laughed. "I've learned to move fast at mealtime, Hank. I'll be helping Gran with the wash today. Tell the boys to leave their stuff on the bunkhouse porch and we'll do their laundry. I'm sure they're too busy to think about clean clothes, and we need them to stick to the branding. Everybody's chores will be twisted around for a while. If you need extra help, sing out. See you later. Want me to signal the hands as I leave?"

Biscuit Hank finished setting the tables. "Much obliged if you do. I'll get the milk and the coffee poured, and get these eggs to movin' in a pan."

Jessie approached the metal triangle that was suspended from the porch beam. She lifted the rod and clanged it against the three sides rapidly. Men came from beside the chuckhouse where the bathing area was located, hair damp and shirts sprinkled from washed faces and hands. She heard boots clattering on the bunkhouse porch as others hurried after yanking on clothes. She didn't see Navarro or Matt, and decided Matt must still be inside his private room at one end of the bunkhouse. Or perhaps he and Navarro were preparing to leave for their chore. Jessie waved and spoke to the Box L hands who passed her as she headed across the yard toward her home to enjoy her first meal of the day.

"Jessie, wait up!" a familiar voice called out and halted her.

She turned and smiled at Navarro. "I hope you fared well last night."

The desperado took in her snug jeans and green shirt that revealed a shapely figure. Her locks were braided, and the waist-grazing plait swung as she moved. The sections of hair she had cut in San Angelo for her disguise curled and framed her face in an enchanting manner. The colors of her fiery hair and rosy-gold complexion made her pale-blue eyes glow. They were large and expressive, and they shone with warmth this morning. He enjoyed just looking at her and being around her, but he wished he could pull her into his arms and kiss her. He cleared his tight throat to speak. "No problems. Most of the boys were turned in when me and Matt got back from supper. He says we'll ride out to mend that fence after we eat. Will you be all right here today?"

"Fine. I have plenty to do for Gran and the boys. The hands all took to you yesterday. So did Gran and Tom. He told me how kindly you treated him. Thanks, Navarro. You can't know what that meant to him, and to me."

"Yep, I do, Jessie, but don't ask why. He's a good boy. He just needs . . ."

"Needs what, Navarro?" she pressed when he fell silent and looked moody.

"Needs to be treated like everybody else. Not different. Not like a cripple in any way. Every time he's not allowed to do something, or at least try it, he sees more and more he's not whole. A boy's spirit can be crushed only so many times, Jessie, before it's destroyed. Pretty soon he won't care about trying. I'm glad your father is letting him ride with me, but . . ."

"Why did you stop again? You can tell me anything, Navarro."

He glanced at the ground. "Ain't really my business."

"If it can help Tom, please go on. It's between us. I promise."

Navarro's haunted childhood provoked him to intrude. "I think your father's doing it for the wrong reasons. If Tom suspects, it'll be worse than letting him go."

"Explain," she coaxed.

"He didn't want you and me out alone together, and he can't spare any of his hands. He's letting your brother go because Tom's the one least needed with the chores."

"I'm sorry to say I agree. You're very perceptive about people. Thanks for being honest and for trying to help. Anything you can do about Tom will be appreciated. You know, you're like an armadillo: beneath your hard shell, you're soft inside," she murmured, stroking his chest. When he looked disturbed by her touch and her words, she said, "Gran and I are washing today. Toss your clothes on the porch and we'll get them done for you. Don't argue," she teased when he started to protest. "We're doing it for all the boys while they're so busy."

"Navarro, grub's about gone! Let's eat and ride," Matt shouted, wanting to separate Jess and the gunslinger. He'd spent a sleepless night thinking about Navarro's pull on her.

Jessie smiled and waved to the foreman, who did the same to her. "Good morning, Matt. He's coming," she replied. "Sure you want to help?"

"Yep. We'll get things done, then work on Fletcher, if he lets us."

*

The hands returned to their seasonal schedule of breakfast, brand, dinner, short rest, brand, supper, and bed. Matt and Navarro rode northward. Tom kept the tally again. The other men rode range with Jed. Gran and Jessie did chores.

When it was nearing eight o'clock, Jessie built a fire under a kettle outside. While water heated, she gathered the men's clothes and linens, then sorted them. The redhead was glad there was no wind today to give them trouble with smoke in their eyes. She chipped soap off a homemade bar into the hot water and stirred it until melted, then drew water from the well and filled the rinse tubs, the task requiring more time and work with the pump broken.

Gran joined her. They scrubbed the clothes and linens on ribbed metal boards. The rinsed items were draped over sturdy cords that were strung tightly between posts, lower to the ground than usual because of Gran's short stature. Each time the water became too dirty or cool to do its job, Jessie fetched and heated more.

The task took the Lane women until three o'clock to complete, seven hours of sweaty toiling over the laundry tubs. Their muscles ached all over, and their hair was mussed, their arms and hands nearly raw. They were both soaked in spots from splashes. But more tasks awaited them. While Martha began the evening meal, Jessie used the soapy water to scrub the house and porch floors, then rinsed them using water from the other tubs. They would dry before dusk in the arid air. The tubs and kettle were dumped and stored. The dying fire was doused. The soap was returned to its place.

Jessie entered the kitchen and sighed wearily, but didn't complain about the hard labor. "Gran, I'll fill the water barrel, then get cleaned up while those clothes finish drying. I don't want you do anything more today than supper. I'll tend to the chickens and milking, then collect the laundry later."

Jessie thought the lines of fatigue and age on Martha's face looked deeper today. Though her grandmother had combed and rewound her white hair into a neat bun at the nape and put on a fresh dress, she could not conceal her exhaustion. Jessie wanted to take over preparing supper, but she knew Martha would not allow it.

Martha kneaded the dough for biscuits with sore hands. "Put some salve on those chafed hands after your bath, child. Is Navarro coming to supper again?"

"It wasn't mentioned. I don't know what time he and Matt will get home."

"Might be best if he sups with the hands. We don't want the others feeling jealous of a stranger getting favor. If he does come, bring Matt, too. If we make it look like we got business to discuss, the men won't take any offense."

Jessie heard the chow bell sing out while she was bathing. The bath felt so wonderful that she wanted to linger in it, but she didn't have time. She donned a paisley print dress, then brushed her hair. As she did so, she decided to keep it trimmed shorter around her face because it made her look more feminine. When all was straightened in her room and the water closet, she told her grandmother she was going outside to complete her chores, as dusk was near.

"Best hurry. Your pa's late. When he rides in, he'll be ready to eat."

"I won't dally, Gran," Jessie responded, merry laughter trailing her words.

As Jessie pulled the first piece of dry laundry from the cord, Matt joined her and asked, "Need a pair of extra hands? I'm sure you're bone-tired."

She glanced at the soft-spoken foreman and replied, "If you don't mind, I can use the help. I'm late with everything today. Papa isn't back yet, so supper is waiting on the stove. You and Navarro want to join us?"

"Just finished eating. You did good closing that gap with ropes."

Jessie placed folded pants on his extended arms. "It was Navarro's idea. How did you two get along?"

"He don't talk much."

Jessie laughed and teased, "Then it must have been a mighty quiet day out there." He was wearing clean clothes and his brown hair was combed. Even his mustache had been trimmed since his return. She looked into his chocolate gaze, and found it warm and searching. "Anything wrong, Matt?"

"How much do you know about this gunslinger?"

Jessie hoped the foreman didn't notice her startled reaction to his question. "He isn't a gunslinger, Matt, but he's as skilled as the best. I don't know his life history, but he strikes me as a good man. Was there a problem with him?"

"No, but there's something about him has me worried."

Jessie stopped her task to meet his troubled gaze. "Like what?"

"He ain't the kind to hang around a ranch."

"He's here because I hired him to do a job. Like lone eagles, even drifters have to light somewhere sometime to rest. Is it something he said or did?"

"No. I can't grasp it yet."

"When you do, come to me first, not Papa. I'm the one who chose him and hired him. If there's a problem, I want to handle it. All right?"

"Sure, Jessie. Just watch him close, will you?"

"Don't worry, Matt; I will."

The boss's daughter and the foreman carried several loads to the bunkhouse for the men to sort and claim. The hands thanked her. Navarro wasn't there.

Jessie closed the gate to the chicken coop and latched it. Night would engulf the landscape soon. She scanned the horizon for her father's approach but didn't sight him. Concern gnawed at her. Jessie halted at the structure where supplies, meats, and home-canned goods were stored for the Lanes and their men.

As she sealed the door to leave, Navarro said, "You been working hard."

Jessie turned to face him. "I wanted you and Matt to take supper with us when Papa returns, but he said you've already eaten."

"Hired hands don't eat with the boss much, do they?"

Jessie realized it was more of a statement than a question. "Not usually."

"I found my wash on my bunk. Thanks, Jessie."

"You're welcome." To keep him with her longer, she chatted about little things. "I was penning up the chickens and getting flour and rice for Gran. We're letting some sit over there in a separate coop to restock those Fletcher's men killed. We don't normally let this many keep their eggs for hatching, just enough to replace those we eat or the ones that stop laying with age."

"Owning and running a ranch involves a lot of work."

Jessie surmised he wasn't used to small talk but was seeking it to stay with her longer. That pleased her. "How did you and Matt get along today?"

Navarro glanced around while deciding what to say. Several hands were sitting on the bunkhouse porch as they talked and laughed, and one made music on a fiddle while Biscuit Hank blew on a harmonica. He knew Miguel, Carlos, and two others were inside playing cards. Although Matt stood in shadows near the barn, Navarro sensed the foreman's watchful gaze. It was obvious that Matt didn't trust him yet; but only because of the Texan's feelings for Jedidiah Lane's daughter. He had observed Jessie and Matt since his arrival. He wished he knew what their relationship was, but he dared not ask.

"Navarro?" she prodded as worry filled her.

The handsome man inhaled and met her gaze. "Sorry, Jessie. My mind drifted. I love this time of day. What did you ask me?"

The redhead didn't think he had forgotten her question. "Nothing. Here comes Papa. I'd best get inside and help Gran get our meal on the table. I'm tired."

"Will I see you before I leave in the morning?"

"I'll be up early, like every day. Good night."

" 'Night, Jessie."

*

While Jessie was doing the milking, her father and the foreman got Navarro and Tom on their way. She didn't like not seeing them off, and hoped Jed and Matt hadn't planned to exclude her. When her other morning chores were done, Jessie churned butter, ignoring her hands that still ached from yesterday. Later, as she heated the iron and pressed garments, Gran labored in the garden.

*

A stroll after supper brought strange revelations for Jessica Lane. After waving to her, Miguel and Carlos left the bunkhouse and walked to the corral. At twenty-seven and thirty-one, both men were good-looking and virile. Hard work had made their bodies strong and lithe. Miguel propped one foot against a post as his deft fingers toyed with a pistol. Carlos rested his buttocks against a horizontal rail; his cigarito sent smoke spiraling upward as the half-Mexican drew on it, then exhaled. Their attire—pants, jackets, hand-tooled leather belts with silver buckles, ornately stitched boots, and Spanish spurs—revealed their roots.

An uneasy feeling washed over her as she saw them leave the others and halt in her path, decked in their finery. Usually the men washed after a dusty day and put on the clothes they would dress in the next day. Carlos and Miguel hadn't done that tonight. She had an odd feeling they were waiting for her arrival.

In the fading light before a three-quarter moon rose, Jessie smiled and joined them. "Don't you both look handsome tonight?" she remarked. "Are you expecting a wagon of fort laundresses to pass through?" she teased, referring to the women at army posts who saw to the soldiers' pleasures.

Carlos chuckled at her naughty innuendo. Miguel smiled, revealing the whitest and straightest teeth she had ever seen. Or maybe they only looked snowy in contrast to his black hair, dark eyes, and deep tan.

"You look pretty tonight, too, *amiga*. I like your hair cut that way."

"Thank you, Miguel." She related the story of why she had cut it.

"You are lucky he arrived to rescue you, *chica*. He seems a good *hombre*."

"He is, Carlos. You know the Lanes only pick the best men for jobs."

"*Gracias, chica*. He is a strange one. Indian blood always makes Mexicans nervous. Our peoples have warred for many years with Apaches and Comanches."

"He told you he's part Indian?"

"He did not have to, *amiga*," Miguel responded. "His looks speak of it."

"Does that bother you two?" Jessie inquired, holding her breath.

"*Jamas*, so release that air, *chica*."

She exhaled, and they all grinned. "What else do you know about him?"

Miguel repeated the same brief story that Navarro had told her family. Jessie didn't believe that tale, but she didn't challenge it. Nor did she tell the two men of her doubts. "Do you like him?"

"He has done well, *chica*. But he must relax for us to learn him," Carlos said.

"It will take time, *amiga*," Miguel added. "He is a man with a shadow over his past. Such men keep a distance. He has known much trouble and pain."

"How do you know that, Miguel?"

"The scars on his back. When we washed last night, we saw them. He said an *hombre* was cheating at cards and he exposed him, then in a shoot-out, the cheater was killed. His brothers tracked Navarro and whipped him for hours. They left him for dead. But as you know, he did not feed the buzzards."

"He is not a man to be lashed," Carlos added. "It is certain he tracked those *hombres* and tasted revenge. A man such as Navarro Jones is always near danger. It runs in his blood as surely as restless dust fills his boots."

"Are you two saying I can't trust him?"

"He is part Indian, a man who lives with troubled spirits, a man who will kill to survive, a man who must be free or die. He has been hurt many times; this I see because I was like him long ago."

"Is that a yes or no, Miguel?"

"He will honor his word, but nothing more. He will fight to the death to do his job. Stay alert, *amiga*. He is a man to steal a woman's eye. He will not stay."

Jessie felt her heartbeat increase. "You did, Miguel. You said you were like him once. You changed. You stayed. What's the difference?"

"I had my revenge, my justice. I buried my past. Navarro has not. He is still searching for something, and I do not think he will ever find it. He is from two worlds, yet he fits in neither. He is the kind of man who destroys himself, and hurts anyone who comes too close to him. He is not bad and does not mean to harm those few he loves. It cannot be helped. He is a breed unto himself, *amiga*. He would not know how to survive if he changes. Do not try."

*

Wednesday moved at a steady pace for Jessie with morning chores and afternoon branding. By quitting time, she was exhausted. She bathed and dressed for the evening meal. Just as they began eating, Tom and Navarro returned. Gran reminded the excited boy to hold his story until after he washed up and sat down. Jessie was annoyed when her father told Navarro to return and give his report as soon as he ate supper. Jed also told him to bring Matthew Cordell along.

"We'll have cake and coffee while we talk," Jessie added.

After Navarro left to get cleaned up and eat, Jessie looked at her father and said, "That wasn't polite, Papa. We're eating, and you know the hands have finished. Hank probably has put away everything. He should have stayed."

"That isn't a good idea, Jess. I don't want a man like that getting too close to my family. Tom's already following him around and hanging on his every word. Tom, remember he's a wild gunslinger, not a man to pattern after."

"But, Pa—"

"Hush, boy. I know what I'm saying. I've seen his kind before. If we didn't need his skills, I wouldn't let him be here."

The tone in Jed's voice and the look in his eyes warned Jessie and Tom not to argue back, but both were disappointed and angry about their father's attitude. Tom stared at his plate, his joy and appetite gone. Jessie forced herself to eat to conceal her conflicting emotions.

Afterward, the room was quiet as no one tried to make conversation. Gran and Jessie cleared the table and washed the dishes. Jed remained in his place and sipped coffee. Tom was sent to his room to get ready for bed while the adults talked. The boy wanted to be included; he wanted to relate his stirring adventure. Jessie whispered to him that she would sneak up later to hear about it, which appeased Tom.

When the two men arrived, Jessie showed them to the table.

"Matt, would you like cake and coffee?" she asked.

Sitting to Jed's left, he replied, "Sure, Jessie. Gran cooks the best."

"Navarro?" she hinted.

Near the far end of the table, he answered, "Yes, Miss Jessie, I sure would like some."

When she served them, Navarro thanked her politely, and so did Matt. Jessie realized that Navarro was making a strong effort to show manners and correct behavior around the man who had been almost rude to him earlier. She hoped and prayed her father would not drive her love away.

"Fletcher's men were branding calves like your hands, Mr. Lane," Navarro related. "I saw about twenty men doing chores close to where he's settled. They were all unarmed, so they don't expect any trouble from us. I got a good look at Fletcher; Tom pointed him out to me from our hiding place. Couldn't hear what he said, but he didn't seem to be planning anything."

"How do you know that?" Matt asked.

"None of the men strapped on guns and rode in this direction. Didn't see anybody packing up supplies, either, planning to be on the range a while. Nice spread, but not like yours, sir. Fancy house with a walled yard like a hacienda. Two big barns. Not many longhorns in his herds. But he's got plenty of good horseflesh. Nothing with Box L brand that I saw. When the men changed shifts, I counted about five or six new faces from those doing branding. I didn't want to do too much riding around and risk being seen by men on the move. I got the layout of his ranch set in my head, and pretty much know his schedule. I'd say, from what I've learned here, he has about two more weeks of branding. That don't mean he won't pull some men to attack before he's done. From all Jessie's told me, he's to blame. But we can't act until Fletcher does. That is, if you want this handled like I think you do."

"How is that?" Jed asked, his stern gaze locked on Navarro.

The desperado shifted in his seat. "With as little trouble and bloodshed as possible. You want him defeated and stopped, but not killed. Whatever he's done, you're still a good man who hates to take the law into his own hands."

The room was silent as Jessie's father and the man she loved stared at each other. Finally Jed spoke. "You're right. I'm no murderer. I don't want him gunned down. He's been smart. No witnesses or proof to back my charges. He's got the sheriff and Army fooled. He claims rustlers are using these tricks to cover their thefts. Claims he's been having mischief over at his place, too. Says somebody might be trying to drive us both out of the area. He's a liar. Nobody's tried to buy my spread except him. What do you have in mind?"

"Me and Jessie decided to do to him whatever he does to you. He'll learn fast that your loss will be his loss. You willing to do it that way?"

"I don't hold to making innocents pay for the guilty's actions. I can't order no dogs and chickens slaughtered. We can't rustle any cattle, either. If we got caught, I'd be held accountable."

"I agree, sir. Why don't we wait for him to move, then make plans?"

The talk ended almost immediately, as all were tired and it was late. Jessie walked the men to the door, where she asked, "Did Hank give you any supper, Navarro? You got in late."

Matt answered for the reluctant man. "He didn't eat, Jessie. Hank was in the bunkhouse. Navarro washed up and changed."

"Don't worry over me, Jessie. I've missed plenty of meals before."

"You won't have to miss any here. I thought this might happen, so I held a plate for you in the warming oven. Wait here while I fetch it."

While he obeyed, Matt stayed with him. "She's a fine woman, Navarro."

"Yep, I can see she is." He thanked Jessie for the food when she returned and handed him a heaping plate. He left before his emotions ran wild over this good woman who always thought of others.

Jessie turned to find her father watching her. "Giving him food isn't the same as letting him join us, is it, Papa? We do need him strong and healthy."

"Sometimes you have too much heart, daughter."

"How can a person be too kind or too polite?"

"Good night, Jess" was his response.

"I'll go tuck in Tom."

Jed halted his departure to his room. "He's too old for that."

"I know, but I still enjoy it. He was so excited about his adventure, but he didn't get to share it with us. I don't want him to feel left out tonight."

"I was foolish to let him ride with that man. He could have been hurt. I would never forgive myself if anything more happened to him."

"You can't protect him forever, Papa. Victories can't be won unless challenges are confronted. If you have no victories and joys, what good is living? He has to try things to make him feel as close to normal as possible. Even if he gets hurt, he'll be happy. Let him grow, Papa. Let him take risks. Let him find his place in life. Let him know you're proud of him."

"Do I have to let him get hurt worse or killed to prove I love him? To let him be happy? I can't, Jess. Tom is different, and nothing can change that."

Jessie watched her father disappear into his room. She went upstairs to find her brother asleep. To let him know she had kept her word, she wrote a message on his chalkboard: "Navarro said you were a big help. Thanks. I love you. Jessie."

*

Just as breakfast was completed in the Lane home and bunkhouse, one of the hands galloped to the barn. He leapt off his sweaty mount and raced to the warning bell. He rang it with all his might. When everyone rushed outside, he hinted between gasps for breath, "Trouble, Boss, nasty trouble."

Chapter

8

Jed, Matt, Jessie, and Navarro surveyed the horrid scene before them. Along the Calamity River in the southeast section of their ranch was a terrible sight. They rode in silence for a time, then dismounted. The ranch hand who had delivered the grim news had remained behind to rest and eat.

"Fletcher didn't prepare for this foul deed overnight. I thought you said you saw nothing unusual on his land!" Jed declared in an angry tone to Navarro.

As Jessie eyed the numerous dead coyotes that were strewn along both sides of the bank and tossed into the shallow water, she was shocked. "It looks as if they go for miles, Papa. It's an awful trick, but you know his motive. It's to terrify the stock and drive them away from water. His men must have hunted prairie wolves every night for days to get this many. He must have stored them somewhere in secret until he had enough to use for his vile mission. Navarro told you he didn't ride Fletcher's range. Even if he had, this task was done elsewhere. Then the bodies were hauled here. He couldn't have known about it to warn us."

"She's right, Jed," Matt added. "His hands must have been busy with branding, so Fletcher must have hired extra men to hunt them and bring them to his ranch."

"He could have hidden the bodies in the mountains, Papa."

"Some were trapped. Mangled legs." Navarro pointed out examples nearby.

Jessie looked at the wicked destruction of life. The coyote was smaller and built lighter than the wolf. The timid prairie wolf was misunderstood and slain by most men but was a creature that rarely preyed on stock or wild game. Although cunning and swift—the coyote fed on rodents, hares, and vegetable and meat carrion. What made Jessie even angrier were the pups and mix-breeds slain along with parents who mated for life. Coyotes readily bred with dogs, and offsprings were called coydogs. Pups, surely entire litters, of both had been killed without mercy. She knew that Fletcher's hirelings had done this cruel task at night, as the coyote was a nocturnal creature that lived in burrows during daylight.

Jessie glanced skyward in all directions. It appeared as if hundreds of vultures, the clue that had alerted their ranch hand to trouble, either were circling the lengthy area or landing to enjoy the enormous feast. Countless black dots were seen against the horizon, indicating more carrion-feeders were on the way, as if something had rung a supper bell near and wide to summon them here. "Papa, we have to get rid of these bodies fast so the buzzards will leave. Our stock won't come near this area with the stench of death and decay so heavy in the air. We don't have windmills in this area. The cattle and horses will scatter or sicken from lack of water before the air clears and they settle down."

Jed tried not to inhale the putrid odor surrounding him. A mixture of rage and depression overcame him. "I'll pull the men off branding and have them collect and bury these poor critters."

"Fletcher has only windmills for water supply," Navarro ventured. "Right?"

When Jessie nodded, he suggested, "Blow for blow. If we haul these coyotes over to his place and drop them around his windmills, his stock won't go near them. Fletcher did the killing; let him do the burying."

Jed looked at his daughter's hired man with new respect. He brightened as that tit-for-tat idea settled in and excited him. "You're clever, Navarro. We'll send him back his message."

Despite the distressing scene around her, Jessie smiled in pleasure.

Navarro went on. "Me, Matt, and two of the hands can wrap them in blankets or old canvas, then ride 'em over by packhorse after dark. Fletcher won't be expecting it so he shouldn't have any guards posted. When me and Tom were spying, he seemed too cocky and confident to be on alert."

"He'll be hopping mad tomorrow. He'll deny he's to blame for this outrage."

"The only way he can accuse us of returning them, Mr. Lane, is by revealing he knows where they came from. He'll keep silent."

"By Jove, you're right again! He can't say or do anything without exposing his guilt. We'll get revenge this time."

Jessie had held quiet while Navarro impressed her father with his keen wits. She spoke up to refute. "Justice, Papa, we'll get justice."

Jed's dark blue gaze fused with Jessie's light-blue one. Lines furrowed deeper on his face as he grinned. "This time, Jess," he said, "revenge and justice are in the same bucket. We'll make plans right now."

Jessie changed Navarro's suggestion. "Me, Matt, Navarro, Pete, and Smokey can gather the carcasses in piles while the other hands keep to the branding. We can use those old blankets in the shed that you used for Indian gifts long ago. Talbert, Roy, and Walt are flanking today with Jimmy Joe. Papa, that leaves you and Davy to check on the frightened herds. In case Fletcher's having us watched today, Matt, Pete, and Smokey can wrap and load the bodies after dark while me and Navarro haul them to Fletcher's windmills. The work will go fastest that way. We have to be finished by sunup tomorrow. You sure you don't mind helping with this nasty chore, Navarro?"

"I hired on to fight Fletcher and his tricks; this is one of them. But you don't need to help with a dirty job like this, Miss Jessie."

"I've done similar tasks before, when we had stock die of disease or were gorded during a stampede. You and I only need to deliver about ten to each windmill. The rest, all of us can haul to his south pasture and dump."

Jed, eager to repay and rile his foe, said, "Let's head back and get prepared."

At the house, Jessie dressed in well-worn clothes and located old gloves that could be discarded later. She grabbed a bottle of flowery cologne, then rushed back to the corral with the food Gran had packed for them. Water was taken along in canteens, since the river was befouled with rotting flesh. She noticed that Matt, Navarro, and two hands were ready to ride. Another hand was to bring the blankets and packhorses to them later as a precaution against Fletcher's possible spies. Jessie tossed Navarro some old pants and a shirt that she had taken from her father's work chest, aged garments saved to be used only once for tasks such as this one. "Use these so you won't ruin yours."

Navarro changed in the bunkhouse and returned. As Jed and Davy headed out to check on the stock and hands started branding near the corral, the four men with Jessie rode southeastward to the river.

The group approached the first bodies of coyotes, pups, and coydogs in various stages of decomposition. Jessie asked each man to pass her his bandanna before he folded and tied it over nose and mouth to shut out as much of the stench of death and decay as possible as they worked. She dotted the cologne on the triangular cloths and returned them before securing her own in place. The men thanked her. Even though Jessie rarely wore the cologne, Navarro and Matt were stirred by the womanly air that filled their nostrils.

"I'll put it in my saddlebag. Don't hesitate to use it," she told all of the men.

Each began to drag the animals into piles. Often, skittish vultures had to be scared off with loud shouts and waving arms. The persistent buzzards simply flew to another body farther away and ripped into it, as if devouring their first meal in weeks.

Jessie thought the vultures were ugly creatures, but they served a purpose as they rid the land of carcasses. Their weak feet were big, made for walking and grasping. Their strong beaks, skilled at tearing into hides and meat, made her cringe at the thought of lying weak and helpless while carrion-feeders circled overhead.

Jessie shuddered and cast that horrible vision from her head. She looked at the pitiful creatures she moved to the growing piles along the riverbank. Brush wolves hunted alone or in relays. Many times she had listened to their nightly serenades of mingled short yaps and mournful howls. Killing them was wrong, as they rarely harmed mankind and his possessions. Although their pelt colors varied, most were a grizzled buff with reddish legs and splashes. Their long fur was coarse, their bushy tails black-tipped. Their golden eyes were mostly closed in death.

As the group labored, the sun's heat and brilliance increased. The fetid odor worsened. Flies buzzed and gathered on the furry mounds and on uncollected bodies. They worked all day—sweat, blood, dust, loosened fur and flesh clinging to them and making their horrible task harder.

They halted and put a distance between them and the rank location to try to rest and to eat a light meal. Both were almost impossible. At dusk, the packhorses and blankets were delivered by Jed and Davy.

Jessie persuaded her weary father to return to the house to get some sleep for the tasks ahead tomorrow while she, their foreman, and two hands rested after their lengthy chore. It was getting cooler, but she resisted putting on her light wool jacket and ruining it. She glanced at the setting sun that was providing the last remains of daylight. Soon a full moon would rise from the east and give them enough light to work through the night.

"This was a vicious and evil deed; it shows how twisted Fletcher's mind is," Jessie remarked as reeking creatures were loaded on packhorses and tied down.

"Get the next load covered and ready," Navarro told Matt. "We'll return soon."

Jessie and Navarro rode for the nearest windmill on their enemy's land. They were cautious during their journey, but didn't sight any of Fletcher's men, not on that trip or any of the other ones. She decided that the confident man must have allowed all of his men to return to his bunkhouse that night.

The malodorous task continued far into the wee hours of the morning. The couple hauled and discarded coyote bodies around each windmill. Bar F stock nearby hurried away from the fearful odor of death. They hated to punish innocent creatures for their owner's wickedness, but it wouldn't be for long, just enough time for their foe to get the message that they wouldn't stand still for such repulsive acts. Wherever the task was done, Navarro let Jessie ride ahead while he lingered behind and used his Apache training to conceal their tracks. He had told them that using wagons was unwise, as wheel marks were harder to cover.

Many carcasses were hauled to the south pasture on Wilbur Fletcher's spread and piled there to be found in a few hours. While Matt and the others burned blankets and took the extra horses back to the corral, Jessie and Navarro made their last haul northward. The plan was to join them afterward at the ranch, which was closer to their last destination.

After covering their trail, Navarro joined Jessie at a group of trees near their boundary. He saw her leaning against the largest trunk, appearing so still as to be asleep on her feet. She didn't move as he approached. He dismounted and went to Jessie, whose eyes remained closed. His gaze scanned the woman who was also smelly, filthy, and exhausted.

Navarro tugged at her arm. "Let's go, Jessie," he said, "so you can get into bed. You worked hard; you need rest."

Jessie forced her eyes open, eyes that were red-streaked and puffy. She was barely able to move or stay awake. "Worked hard for a woman?" she teased.

Navarro smiled and countered, "For anybody."

Jessie yawned and stretched. "I should have told them we'd camp here. I dread that long ride home. Blazes, I'm sore and tired. I'm sure you are, too."

"If we don't get back, they'll worry and think we've been captured. I'll help you. You can ride double with me." Navarro held her arm with one hand and circled her waist with his other one. At his sorrel, he released his grasp. He gathered the reins of the packhorses and secured them to a rope, which he tied to his saddle. He rolled the stained blankets and their gloves into a bundle that was strapped to one horse, to be burned later. He mounted, then bent over to pull her up onto his lap. When she was settled in his arms, he led the horses away. Her Ben followed. "Take a siesta. I'll wake you when we near the house."

Jessie looked up at Navarro's handsome face. It felt wonderful to be in his arms. How she wished they were going home to bathe and sleep together. After this episode, surely her father thought more highly of Navarro. If not, soon Jedidiah Lane would be compelled to alter his low opinion.

Despite her sorry condition and fatigue, she savored being so close to her lover. She wished they were camping somewhere secluded and private, with no one waiting for their return. "Thanks for all you did today, Navarro. You've proven I was right about choosing you. Papa was most impressed. I'm glad, because he's too distracted to think clearly these days. He doesn't mean to be cold or rude; he just has so many worries."

"I know, Jessie. It's as bad as you told me, or worse. I'm worried, too. This Fletcher shows a crazy streak. Crazy plus mean is dangerous."

"Whatever he does, be careful. I don't want anything to happen to you."

"The same goes with you, woman."

Their gazes locked—searching, speaking, revealing, caressing. Each moved toward the other, fusing their mouths in an urgent and needed kiss. Navarro stopped the horses and held Jessie as close as he could. The kiss drifted into others, each deepening and lengthening. This was a time in their lives when they needed each other for strength, help, and survival . . . and love.

Finally, each seemed to realize that they could not repeat the sensual experience they had enjoyed in the cabin six days ago, not here and now. But their attraction had grown stronger since they'd arrived at the Box L, and each knew it would grow even more during the days ahead. They would find a place to be together. That seemed to help them through this difficult moment when a union was impossible. Jessie smiled when Navarro kissed the tip of her nose, and both passed understanding to the other. Their journey home continued. Jessie fell asleep in Navarro's embrace. As the fugitive watched her slumbering peacefully, the feeling of tranquility left him.

The desperado tried to keep his yearning gaze and thoughts off the woman in his arms. If not for his criminal past, this was the woman he could spend his life with. The people here could change him for the better. They could give him peace and happiness. He wished there was a way he could obtain a new face so he could stay with Jessie forever. He wished they could keep riding, travel far away to where his past couldn't reach them. If he dared ask, would Jessie go with him? If she refused, was it worth it to seek a new beginning alone? If she agreed, what if his past did catch up with them? What would become of his love then, after she had sacrificed her home and family in Texas to be with him? He was taking too many risks to be with her now; he couldn't take more with her life at stake. He wanted Jessica Lane more than he had ever wanted anything, but . . . No, he decided, it was too dangerous and selfish. Once she was safe, their relationship must end.

When they neared the corral, it was almost sunup. Hands were stirring. Matt and Jed hurried to meet them. Her father had slept fitfully, worried about his daughter. Pete and Smokey had eaten and gone to bed. Mathew Cordell had awaited Jessie and Navarro's return.

Navarro walked the horses at a slow pace to avoid rousing Jessie. He motioned to the two men to talk softly. In a near whisper, Navarro asked, "Can I take her to her room, sir? She's exhausted. The job's finished, and our tracks are covered." The fugitive noticed the look of jealousy that gleamed in Matt's eyes.

Reluctant but helpless, Jed nodded permission.

Navarro left the other horses with the two watchful men and rode to the house. He dismounted with Jessie in his arms, and carried her into the house. Gran smiled and led him to Jessie's room. The older woman tossed a blanket over the clean covers so her granddaughter's dirty clothes would not soil them. Navarro laid Jessie down and removed her boots without awakening her. He glanced at Gran as she handed him a second blanket to place over her.

Jessie sighed and curled to her side, but remained asleep. She did not see Navarro nod to Martha Lane and depart to report to Jed. Navarro then ate and turned in until noon. As for the redhead, she slept until one o'clock.

Upon awakening, Jessie was told by her grandmother that Jed and Matt were riding the east boundary to check for trouble from their enemy. The older woman added that she had seen Navarro working in the branding pen with the hands. Before the women could say more, Tom came to the house on a break.

"Jessie, you're up! Navarro said you'd tell me about the coyotes. He's too busy to talk. Me, too. I'm keeping tally again. Pa said I was good at it."

Jessie related the grim tale of yesterday's and last night's labors. "I can't imagine what that wicked man will try next. Tell me about your adventure with Navarro. We haven't had a chance to hear about it, have we, Gran?"

The older woman coaxed, "Yes, Tom, what happened?"

The boy's eyes brightened. He told how he guided Navarro to the area and how they spied on Fletcher's settlement and men. "It was fun, Jessie. He don't treat me like others do. I hate when people pity me and stare at me. You know what he said? He said everybody can do something special. He said I just have to learn where my path is and ride it. I like him, Jessie. I hope he stays with us after the trouble is over."

Jessie thought it was best not to display her matching feelings before the watchful Gran. "It would be nice, Tom, but I doubt it," she said lightly. "Drifters don't like to settle down in one place long. He's not a cowhand. Once this trouble is over, there'll be nothing to keep him here."

Tom frowned, then asked, "You think the trouble will last a long time?"

"I hope not," Gran answered. "We have work to do."

"Speaking of work, you and I better get busy, Tom. I'll help with the branding until Papa and Matt return. I'll quit in time to help with supper, Gran."

Jessie and her brother walked to the noisy and dusty area. Navarro turned the tally task back over to Tom. The redhead eyed the weary flankers. "Navarro, think you can do Walt's job while I take Jimmy Joe's?" she asked.

Jimmy Joe glanced at the redhead and grinned. "You been lazin' around long enough, huh?"

"I deserved a nap, Jimmy Joe, after working day and night straight through. Maybe you're as tough as me and don't need relieving," she teased in return.

"You know I can't show up the boss's daughter. Take my seat fast."

Jimmy Joe let the bawling calf loose and jumped to his feet. "I need a good stretchin'. My arms and legs are tighter'n strung barbwire. Thanks."

"Want to try it, Navarro?" she asked again.

"I've been watching a lot. I think I can do it. I'll willing to try."

Carlos Reeves dragged a calf over to them with a rope around its hindleg. He grinned as the dark-haired man grabbed it by the neck hide and struggled until it was flipped to its side on the ground. "Pin his head with a knee across his neck. Grab his foreleg and bend it back. He won't be able to move if you hold tight."

Navarro followed the instructions. He watched Jessie seize the right hindleg and stretch it backward, then grip it firmly. Her right boot propped against the knee joint of the calf's lower leg and held it motionless. Rusty stamped the creature with the Box L brand, while Jefferson Clark notched its ear.

"Girl!" Jessie shouted to the black marker and to the tally keeper.

The next time Navarro took a calf from Miguel, he had clearly mastered the task. Jessie shouted over the noise, "Boy!" When the "ironman" moved, Jessie leapt up, placed her left heel against the calf's bottom leg, straddled its body with her right leg, and lifted the animal's top limb. Jefferson deftly castrated the male. Jessie released her grip and stepped aside, then Navarro did the same. The calf trotted to its bellowing mother, who nuzzled his bloody ear.

"I can't believe how strong and skilled you are, Jessie."

"For a female, Navarro?" she jested.

"This time, yep, for a woman." He looked at the brander and asked, "Is there anything she can't do as good as the best man, Rusty?"

"Nope. She can even use hot irons as good as me."

Jefferson chuckled and added, "She kin do my job, but she ain't as fast."

"Your job is my least liked chore, Jefferson. I'm glad you're good at it and never sick. I don't like paining any critter. But you boys are wrong. I can't do everything. I can't take over for Carlos. The last time I tried to tame a half-broken horse, he almost busted my arm and leg. Did get my nose. I'll leave that dangerous chore to the best broncbuster in Texas. Right, Carlos?"

The half-Mexican grinned. *"Acaso, chica."*

"Perhaps, nothing," she retorted with a merry laugh.

Miguel dragged a calf to them as the other roper returned to the herd.

"Miguel there is the best roper in Texas. He can lasso any part of a critter, even a lowered tail. I can rope heads, but I'm not very good at legs."

"That is because you do not practice, *amiga*. No need when you have me."

"You see, Navarro, I have talented help. I only learn enough to take over in a bind. I have to know a little about everything. How else can I give the right orders? If a woman's gonna be owner and boss, she best know what she's saying."

"Jessie does," Rusty remarked. "She couldn't know or do better if she was Jed's son. You never catch her sleeping on her elbow when she rides herd."

"I don't dare, Rusty. You'd ride by, knock it loose, and send me falling. He always sneaks up on unseasoned wranglers and teaches them a lesson the first week. One's head snapped so hard that I thought his neck was broken."

"That's 'cause he was six feet under in sleep. A man that deep won't hear or see nothing. He never napped on my shift again."

When Jimmy Joe and Walt returned, Jessie said, "I have to get washed up and help Gran with supper. You boys need anything else before I go?"

Everyone shook their heads "no" so Jessie added, "Navarro, you didn't hire on for this kind of work so you can knock off whenever you're ready."

"You're shorthanded so I'll help them finish today. Tomorrow I want to ride out and see how Fletcher is taking our challenge."

"I'll go with you. I'm sure he's furious and plotting something new."

Jessie took care of her other chores, then bathed and changed into a skirt and blouse. She went to the kitchen and assisted her grandmother with the meal.

When Jed and Matt returned, she was told they hadn't seen or heard anything from Fletcher or his hirelings. That made Jessie suspicious and worried, but all she could do was wait.

*

On Saturday, the bad news arrived before Jessie and Navarro went riding: Fletcher's men had destroyed a windmill in the area most lacking in water supply.

Jed's face flushed with new anger. "Just like us, he hit at a windmill. I can't keep stock from drifting into that area without posting men there, and I hate to pull any hands off branding. With no water around, the stock will be too far from the river and other windmills before they're thirsty. They'll start stampeding in a search for it, or get too weak to make it to another source. We'll have to repair that windmill today and move the stock to water."

"Wait, Papa. We have to get those calves branded so we can turn them and their mothers loose to graze. Big John can work on the repairs while Navarro and I stand guard for him. You and four of the boys can round up the scattered stock and get them to water. You should check other windmills and for cut fences. Matt can team up with Roy as flankers with Jimmy Joe and Walt. Hank can tend the branding coals, and Gran can cook extra for the boys. It shouldn't take but a day or two, if the damage isn't bad. Big John already has part of the job done; that's the windmill we were going to replace soon," she reminded him. Jessie had seen how upset her father was, and had taken control of the situation to give him time to clear his head.

"I forgot. It's that old one in the southwest area. We'll get supplies loaded in a wagon, then you three can head out. Be real careful-like, Jess. I don't trust Fletcher. He might have men waiting around to prevent repairs."

"Navarro and I can handle them, Papa. Don't worry."

Nails, hammers, saws, sharpeners, wood, hole diggers, food and water supplies, bedrolls, weapons, and new windmill parts were loaded on a wagon. Big John Williams, who usually tended the windmills by checking and oiling and repairing them, climbed aboard and flicked the reins. Jessie and Navarro mounted their horses and rode one on each side of the wagon. They headed southwestward.

Several hours later, they arrived at the scene of Fletcher's latest attack. Big John examined the damage while Navarro scouted the nearby area. Jessie waited for the large black man to give his opinion.

"Deys chopped 'er laigs an' head good, Miss Jessie. 'Er gears ain't bad. Shaft an' pump looks to be all right. I kin replace dem broken blades an' tail. I'll be needin' yore he'p wif dem busted laigs."

"Let's get unloaded and get to it, Big John. Just tell me what to do."

When Navarro returned and reported sighting no threat nearby, he helped Jessie and Big John get prepared for the task ahead.

As they labored, Jessie told him, "These are made specially for areas like this one. Would you believe a New Englander invented them? I'll bet he'd never even seen this kind of rugged countryside. Thank goodness we have plenty of wind. Ever since they came about in '54, they've helped open up dry areas out here." She explained how the windmills worked: the gears at the top were run by windpower on the eighteen blades, causing the mechanism in a box to force the shaft up and down to pump water. The liquid poured into a pond or large trough. The tail controlled the direction of the wheel, keeping its face into the wind. During rainy spells or to avoid pumping too much water on brisk days, the tail was folded to halt its work, as a wise man never risked wasting his precious water supply.

While Navarro assisted Big John, Jessie stood guard with her Winchester in her hands. She glanced at the two men as they cleared the four holes of old posts and debris, then placed the lower section that John had constructed in them. A second section was added, then a third. The loud sound of hammers against nails rang out across the quiet landscape, accompanied by the noise of sawing wood. John positioned the small platform and secured it to the tower. A temporary post was hauled up the ladder to aid with lifting the multivaned wheel. Navarro joined John on the platform to help with that task.

Jessie observed with apprehension as the two labored on the small surface so high above the hard ground. Windmills were twenty to thirty feet tall and she sighed in relief when Navarro climbed down in safety. She saw her love use a rope to pull the remaining parts and tools up to John. Soon the new tail was attached. Gears were oiled. The shaft and pump were checked again. As the last rays of daylight vanished, John turned the crank at the base to put the tail to work. The broad piece moved with the breeze. The wheel faced windward, and turned. After a few creaking sounds, the speed increased. The shaft moved up and down, and water poured into the trough. Jessie, John, and Navarro cheered.

It was too late to return home. While the men loaded the wagon to leave at dawn and placed bedrolls on the ground, Jessie prepared them a meal of fried meat, scrambled eggs, red-eye gravy, and warmed biscuits from Gran. The campfire glowed and crackled. Smoke drifted skyward. The smell of aromatic coffee teased their nostrils as a full moon shone overhead.

As they ate, Jessie said, "It's so quiet tonight, too quiet. I doubt there's a coyote left in the area. Those he didn't have killed have fled in fear. The pronghorns took off, too. Haven't seen one all day. Papa should have the stock back in this area by mid-morning. What next, I wonder?"

"He's a bad 'un, Miss Jessie. I dun seed his kind afore."

Jessie knew he was referring to his days of slavery. "I know, Big John."

When they finished and all chores were completed, Jessie asked, "Navarro, would you like to take a walk? I need to relax before I turn in or I won't sleep any."

Big John went to his bedroll and lay down. "See ya in the mawnin'."

"Good night, Big John."

" 'Night, John."

" 'Night, Miss Jessie, Navarro."

Jessie and Navarro strolled for a time, the moon lighting their path. Mesquites, small oaks, and yuccas grew in the area. They didn't go far in case trouble arose for their slumbering companion in camp.

Navarro noticed how the moonlight played on Jessie's red hair and brought out its fiery soul. He saw the shadows it created on her features. He was tense. He knew he wanted this woman, but he wasn't sure what to say or do. He craved her closeness, but feared an overture would mislead her. It wasn't right to keep pulling her toward him when he must eventually leave. To make love with her implied she was important to him, which she was—but important enough to compel him to remain here, which was impossible.

"You're a good worker, Navarro," she commented to start a conversation. "You've done about everything but use your guns for hire."

"That'll come in due time, Jessie. Fletcher is riding a steady course. He's getting bolder and meaner all the time, just like you said. Trouble is, we still don't have proof he's behind all this. We have to catch him with dirty hands. I have a plan," he said, then went on to explain it . . .

"That's very clever, Navarro. We'll try it Monday night."

"I hope you'll stay at the house. There'll be shooting."

She halted and looked at him as he did the same. "Afraid I'll get hurt?"

"Don't want you to take that chance."

"I must. This is my home and family in danger. One day when you and Papa are gone, I might have to defend them again. Now's the time to learn self-defense from the best. Unless you've decided you love it here and want to stay."

Navarro put a little distance between them and turned away from her. He stood with his boots planted apart and his hands on his hips, staring into the shadows as he considered his answer. He heard Jessie approach him, felt her closeness. "It's a good place, Jessie, but not for a man like me."

"You still have to leave, Navarro?" she asked in a soft voice. "Why?"

"Because of me. I got my reasons. Don't ask me to explain."

"Can't I give you any good reasons to stay?"

"I wish you could, but my answer's the same. I can't."

"You understand what I'm offering, don't you?"

"I don't think you understand it's not possible."

"You can have me, a home here, whatever you want."

It was the hardest thing he had ever had to say, "Even if your father said yes, and he wouldn't, I can't."

Anguish knifed her heart. She had spoken too soon, been too bold. "I'm sorry I was so brazen. I didn't mean to corner you. I was just hoping you had come to feel the same way about me that I feel about you. I won't embarrass you again. Your friendship means a lot to me. Please don't get upset and leave. I'll behave myself, I promise."

Navarro turned to look at her. "This is hard for me, Jessie. I do want you and need you. I just can't give you what you need. You're the settling-down kind, and I'm not. If I let you think I can be persuaded to stay, that would be wrong. You'd get hurt when I left. You need a man raised like you, a rancher, somebody who can share a home and family with you. I won't lie just to have you for a while. I like you too much for that. I can't stay any more than you can jump on Ben and leave with me tonight. You can't become a drifter and I can't become a rancher. We're too different."

"If I would become a drifter, would you ask me to leave with you?"

Navarro's heart was pounding. "I shouldn't answer that, Jessie. It could hurt both of us."

"Hurt me because you wouldn't ask or wouldn't take me along?" she pressed.

"Wouldn't ask," he replied, then saw tears glimmer in her eyes. "Wouldn't ask because you might say yes, and that would be a big mistake for you."

"What about for *you*, Navarro?" She had to know.

"What kind of man would I be if I let you sacrifice everything for a wild life with me? If you rode off with the likes of me, your father would never let you return. I know what this ranch and your family mean to you. You're willing to die for them! I'm not a match for them, Jessie. Don't be blinded by desire for me."

"If I didn't have a home and family, would you take me with you?"

"Yes, Jessie. I would ask you to go, and I would try to make you agree."

Jessie was elated, but confused. "You want me enough to take me with you, but still you can't stay to have me?"

"It's not that I don't want you enough, woman."

"Then what is it?"

"It wouldn't work for me to stay or for you to go. You've always lived here and had loved ones. Your life has been happy, safe, settled. Mine hasn't. You're asking me to fit into your life. I have to be free and on the move to be happy, Jessie. If I was crazy enough to accept, it would destroy both of us one day."

"But won't losing each other do the same thing?"

"It will hurt us but not kill us. When I leave, forget me."

"Why don't you tell me to stop breathing, too? That's as easy."

Navarro turned and walked away again. "Damn," he swore softly. He couldn't tell everything. If she didn't despise him afterward, she would try to help him by endangering herself, and him. There was no road open for them. It was rash and cruel to think he could clear one.

Jessie stepped before him. It was obvious that something was eating at him. He wanted her, but something had him convinced it wouldn't work. She must persuade him it could. "All right, we have no future, but we do have a present. Can't we share it as long as possible?"

"It's too little to offer a woman like you, Jessie."

"It's more than I have, Navarro. Isn't it more than you have, too?"

"To have you for only one day is worth any risk I'm taking."

That confession, his choice of words, intrigued and touched her. Somehow she had to discover what or who stood between them. Until then . . . Jessie leaned against his hard body and put her arms around his neck. She drew his head downward as she raised on her tiptoes to taste his kiss.

Navarro groaned as his arms banded her pliant body. His lips savored her sweet ones as his fingers slipped into her silky hair. He felt as hot as one of those branding irons in the smoldering coals.

Jessie tried to cling to him when he released her. "Don't pull away, Navarro. I'm yours by choice."

He had to struggle to retain his strength and will. That inner battle made his voice husky with emotion. "Then do as I say, Jessie. Not here. Not now. John could awaken. Fletcher's men could attack. Your father could arrive."

Those reasons to halt this passionate moment were real. "When? Where? How?" she probed, yearning for him. "My time with you is so short."

"If your father guessed the truth about us, he would hate me, but he'd try to force me to marry you to save your honor. When I refused, and I would have to, Jessie, he'd kill me. You know what that violence would do to you and your family. Don't tempt me to hurt you or them. Help me be strong for now. We have to be careful. Soon, I promise. We'll have plenty of time together. Alone," he added.

"You're the boss," she conceded. Yet she wished she could have him one more time before her beautiful sister returned home tomorrow. She dreaded to think what would happen when Mary Louise discovered this handsome man within her greedy reach.

As Jessie and Navarro dismounted, Mary Louise met them at the barn. Jessie looked at her younger sister, who was wearing a new and very pretty dress. Her blond hair flowed down her back like a river of soft sunlight. Her sapphire eyes were examining Navarro from head to foot, and Jessica felt a surge of irritation.

"I assume this is Navarro Jones, our new hand?" Mary Louise asked coyly.

"That's right," Jessie responded. "Navarro, this is my baby sister, Mary Louise. Did you learn anything in town, little sister?"

"Enough to know I was right in not becoming a schoolmarm. They work dreadfully hard and long hours and hardly earn enough to survive. No, teaching is not for me. What did you two do last night?"

"The same as everyone—slept after a hard day of work. Are your chores done? From that fancy dress, I assume you've been lazing around as usual. Is Papa back yet?"

"No," Mary Louise answered, her gaze still on Navarro.

"Then I would get my chores done before he returns. You left at a terrible time. Everyone's been doubling up to cover for you."

"Don't be so bossy, Jessica. I had a long and tiring ride."

"So did we, but the work isn't done yet."

"Don't mind my older sister, Navarro; she's a slave driver. Don't let her work you too hard for what little she's paying you. Gran and Tom told me all about you. How long will you be with us?"

"Long enough to settle the trouble. Then I'll be on my way." Navarro sensed the tension between the sisters. "Jessie, I'll take the horses and tend them. We'll see what your father has to say when he returns."

Jessie was delighted that Navarro didn't seem enchanted by her exquisite sister. "I'll find you when I finish in the house," she told him, then smiled.

Navarro smiled back, then nodded at Mary Louise and left.

Mary Louise's gaze followed him. "If I had known we had a man like that working here, I would have returned home sooner."

"And let Papa discover you lied to stay in town to enjoy yourself while we worked our hands raw?" Jessie scoffed.

Mary Louise's dark-blue gaze settled on her sister's light one. "Don't be a prude in men's britches, Jessica Lane. You know I had to lie to get away. If I could have, I would have stayed longer. I can't believe Father let you stay out all night with a stallion like that."

"We weren't alone; Big John was with us. We were working hard."

"On the windmill or on each other?"

"Mary Louise Lane! Whatever did they teach you at that boarding school?"

"I learned what real men are for. Have *you*, big sister?"

"You are a lazy, conceited, spoiled, naughty girl."

"I'm a woman, Jessica. Are you?"

"You surely came home in a foul mood. What ails you now?"

"Being back, of course. I did enjoy myself in town. It was pleasant to get away from this smelly place and this silly war you and Father have started."

"It isn't silly. Didn't Gran and Tom tell you what happened while you were gone?"

"Oh, yes, your ridiculous charges about Mr. Fletcher. You're wrong about him, Jessica. He couldn't have done those awful things. He was in town. I saw him there several times. He's quite charming and handsome, as well as rich."

"Fletcher was in town this week?"

"That's correct. I first glimpsed him on Thursday. He was still there when I left this morning. I wonder how he managed to be in two places at the same time."

"He doesn't have to be at his ranch for his hirelings to carry out his bloody orders."

"Do hired hands normally make plans and carry them out without obtaining their boss's permission? After you dumped those dead beasts on his land, who made the decision to attack our windmill? Mr. Fletcher was in town that night. If he's as intelligent as you and Father think, why would he give someone else that authority? I believe you're mistaken."

"I believe you're loco. He's to blame; mark my words, sister."

"I believe you and Father are going to get into serious trouble over this error. What is the law going to do when Mr. Fletcher makes charges against you two?"

"For what?"

"After what you did, Jessica, there must be a hundred things, starting with trespassing!"

"He'll have to prove it first. He can't. Surely you wouldn't betray us just so we'll be jailed and you can escape your miserable existence here?" Jessie said sarcastically. "You *are* desperate to flee, aren't you?"

"That's a cold and cruel thing to say."

"That's what *you've* been lately—cold and cruel to everyone. If you hate it here so much, perhaps you would be happier somewhere else."

Astonishment claimed Mary Louise's expression. "You want me to leave home? Why? So you can work on that handsome drifter? Are you afraid I'll outshine you, big sister? If I want him, rest assured I can get him."

"The sun would cease to rise first. He's a loner."

"Does a loner normally hang around so many people for so long?"

"When he's getting paid well for a job, yes."

"What is he earning, Jessica? Since we don't have enough money to hire help for Gran or enough for me to take a trip back East, it can't be much. If not money, what is holding Mr. Jones here? How intriguing . . ."

Jessie watched her sister through narrowed eyes. She feared Mary Louise intended to practice her wiles on Navarro. Mary Louise would never become serious about a man like Navarro; he didn't have enough money, breeding, and power to suit the girl. Yet her sister was not above playing with him, flirting with him just to have fun.

"Oh, yes, I almost forgot; Captain Graham wants those horses he contracted delivered tomorrow. He said if we couldn't supply them, Mr. Fletcher can. You have until noon Tuesday to get them to the fort."

"A day-and-a-half notice? That isn't fair. How can we round them up and herd them to the fort in such a short time?"

"You always get a job done when you want to, Jessica."

The redhead stared at her sister. "How did you get home? Papa was sending someone after you tomorrow."

"Mr. Fletcher offered me a ride."

Shocked, Jessie demanded, *"What?"*

"Come now, Jessica, your hearing hasn't gone bad yet."

"What if he had kidnapped you and harmed you? He's an evil man. He's our enemy. He's trying to destroy us. Papa will be furious."

"Everyone, including Sheriff Cooper, saw us leave together so I was perfectly safe. Father should be proud of my courage. I tried to charm our neighbor to learn all I could from him."

"What did you learn? Nothing! He isn't fool enough to expose anything to Jedidiah Lane's daughter. He probably was amused by your silly attempts to trick him." Jessie realized her sister had contradicted what she'd said earlier about Fletcher being in town when she left. She listened and waited for the girl to entrap herself.

"If amusement was what he felt, my foolish sister, I know nothing about men. He seems much too intelligent and well bred to do the horrible deeds of which you and Father accuse him. Besides, he's considering a move to Dallas."

"Don't be a fool, Mary Louise! He's not going anywhere. If he were, he wouldn't be trying to buy our ranch or run us off it. Don't you go near him again. That's an order."

"You aren't my parent, Jessica."

"If you disobey, you'll wish I were. When Papa hears about what you did, I don't want to be within a mile of the house."

Mary Louise laughed. "Maybe he'll send me back East to get me away from that dangerous wolf," she jested.

"What in blazes is wrong with you! Don't play with a hot iron like him. You may think you know all about lassoing men, but you know nothing about one like Fletcher. Before you know what's happened, he'll have you tossed on your back with his filthy brand on you just to hurt Papa. If you're so smart, sister, you'll see through his attempt to use you."

"A woman can be duped and used only if she allows it to happen."

"You aren't that naive, Mary Louise. But I'm afraid you are that cocky. Don't get anyone hurt trying to protect you from that beast."

"You underestimate me, Jessica."

"No, Mary Louise, I don't. You get in the house, get changed, and do your chores. I have to see Matt about those horses."

The blonde whirled gracefully and headed for the house. Jessie doubted she would obey her orders. There was something about her sister today, something that alarmed her. But Jessie didn't have time to worry about it now.

*

Matt took all the men who weren't needed on branding, including Navarro, to round up the horses to fill the army contract. They couldn't afford to lose it or to allow their enemy to get his foot in that valuable door. Jessie remained at the ranch to help with branding and to do her other chores. Jed had suggested she stay, and she hoped she wasn't misreading his motive for doing so. It would take the men all afternoon to gather the small herd and they would camp on the range, but she had done that many times in the past.

Mary Louise penned up the chickens, milked the cows, and helped Gran with the preparation of their evening meal. The redhead suspected her cooperation had to do with her sister's confession, which would most likely come during or after supper. And it did. When their father discovered Mary Louise's presence on the ranch, the girl claimed a friend had brought her home and that she would explain everything to him later in private.

After they had eaten and the dishes were being cleared, Mary Louise asked to speak with her father in the parlor. The two left the dining area. As the dishes were washed and dried and put away, Jessie and Gran could hear the talk in the next room. They were stunned as Mary Louise revealed her shocking actions to her father, but vowed good intentions as her motive.

Jed exploded with anger. "What in tarnation! Are you crazy, girl?"

"I thought you would be pleased, Father," she scoffed, "if I could learn something useful from our enemy. He would never suspect a girl of spying on him. When men are relaxed or distracted, they drop hints about things. I'm clever enough to pick up on those slips. It was worth a try, wasn't it?"

Jed was so furious that his responding tone was sarcastic. "Did Fletcher make any mistakes? No, but he saw and heard my daughter acting like she has no wits under her fancy hat! How could a Lane be so foolish and shameful?"

Mary Louise frowned. "I can't do anything right in your eyes, can I, Father? Sometimes I think the only child you love is Jessica. You keep me here like a prisoner just to punish me. That's mean and unfair. If I had the money, I'd leave tomorrow and you'd be rid of me. I could have a wonderful life back East, meet the right man to marry, and be happy. I can't do those things here."

Jed worked hard to control his temper. "You're unhappy because you're defiant, lazy, and disrespectful."

"Only because I'm forced to be that way to stand up for myself. If Mother were still alive, she'd make you face the truth. Let me go, Father. Please."

"Not until you straighten yourself out, girl, if you can. I'm scared it's too late; I'm scared you're ruined for good. And that's a bloody shame, Mary Louise."

"You mean I'll be straightened out when I start looking, acting, and working like a man as Jessica does. Even if I did that to please you, you wouldn't let me leave any more then than you'll let Jessica leave now and have a life of her own. She isn't your son, Father. You've ruined her by treating her like one. What man would want a rough and ill-mannered tomboy for a wife?"

Before he could prevent it, Jed's hand lifted and slapped the hateful girl. The blow sounded loudly in the quiet room, causing the startled Jessie and Gran to jump in the kitchen. "Don't you ever talk about your sister like that again! I wish you were only half the woman she is! If you keep up this way, girl, everybody around here will see you get a strapping every day. I'm warning you, Mary Louise, you've tried my patience too long. I never thought to see the day when I struck one of my children in anger. See what you've done to me."

The blonde rubbed her stinging cheek and glared at her father. "One day you'll be sorry for what you've done to me." She stormed from the room and slammed the door.

Jessie and Gran exchanged worried looks.

The older woman embraced her elder granddaughter. "Pay no mind to her, child," she soothed. "She's just rattling on to get her way. She's going to be trouble around here, just like that drifter is."

"Navarro is nothing like Mary Louise, Gran. I'll see to Papa." Jessie found him sitting on the edge of a chair with his hands over his face. "Papa . . . ?" she began hesitantly.

His expression exposed anguish as he lifted his head to meet her sympathetic gaze. "I hit her, Jess; I struck one of my own children in rage. Worse, it felt good. That girl will be the death of me. If I let her run off like she is, she'll be in all kinds of trouble. I'm tempted to do it to teach her a lesson, but your ma would cry in her grave. It's a battle of wills now, and I have to win."

"I know, Papa, and I'm sorry." Jessie couldn't blame Mary Louise's cruel words on the heat of anger, because she believed her sister meant them.

*

Breakfast passed in strained silence at the Lane table. As soon as his food was consumed, Jed left to begin his chores and orders. Tom returned to his job as tally keeper. Jessie helped with the branding. Mary Louise didn't apologize to anyone this morning. Yet she must have taken her father's whipping threat seriously, for she did all of her chores without being prodded, did them right and without complaint, but in cold silence.

The men returned with the herd by noon. Matt and two hands left immediately to get them to Fort Davis before their Tuesday deadline.

"Some of us better ride fence, Papa," Jessie suggested. "Fletcher knows the hands will be spread out with chores so he'll think it's a good time to attack. I'll go with Navarro if that's all right with you. I've been flanking all morning so I can use a break. You want to come along?"

Jedidiah Lane was still stinging from Mary Louise's words and feelings last night and was distracted by the problems surrounding him. "I'll stay here and see how I can help the boys, Jess. You and Navarro be careful-like. Keep an eye on those bulls. We'd be out of luck without them. See you at supper."

While Jessie was speaking with her father and preparing to leave, Tom told Navarro what had happened in the house last night. Navarro promised not to break his confidence with anyone, including Jessie.

As they checked out several areas and clustered herds, neither Jessie nor Navarro mentioned the spiteful incident with Mary Louise. They talked little, as both seemed caught up in their own troubled thoughts. As dusk approached, they returned to the corral. While unsaddling their mounts, Matt and the two hands rode in, with one wounded. Davy was assisted down and carried to the bunkhouse for Hank to doctor him.

Matt explained how they were attacked, the horses rustled, and Davy shot. "They were waiting to ambush us, Jed. We were penned down for two hours while the others got a head start. No need to try and track them in the dark; they're long gone by now. Besides, we can't spare the hands to go after them."

"You boys are safe; that's all that matters tonight. There's no way we can gather more horses and get them to the fort on time. I'm sure Fletcher is on the road with replacements. That troop will be mounted and gone before we arrive."

"Davy took one in the wing, but he'll be fine in a few days. Bullet passed clean through and didn't do much damage, just a lot of bleeding."

"You sure we can't track and overtake them?" Navarro asked.

"They headed straight for the border. With the lead they had, they'd be in Mexico before we could catch up. Those were strong horses; they can run 'em fast."

Mary Louise joined them, and Jessie suspected it was only because she wanted to be around Navarro. The blonde spoke to the men and behaved politely for a change as she listened to the grim news. Her hair traveled down her back like shimmering gold. Her sapphire eyes matched the color of her fashionable dress and matching slippers. Jimmy Joe's and Miguel's gazes lingered on her.

"Did you tell Fletcher about the horses being sent to Fort Davis?" Jed asked.

"I didn't have to, Father. There were many people around the boarding house when Captain Graham gave me that message for you. Everyone heard it."

"It was Fletcher; I'm sure of it," Jed murmured.

"Why don't you send someone to the fort to see if he drove horses there?" Mary Louise suggested in a cultured voice. "If he did, that means he had to know yours would be stolen. Certainly that would be a clue to his guilt, Father. If he didn't take advantage of the rustling, he didn't know about it."

"But, Papa," Jessie injected. "He won't try to make a sale in our place. He's too clever to expose himself in such a simple way. That means we can use Navarro's plan tonight. Fletcher will expect us to guess he won't fill the contract. He'll expect us to gather more horses in the morning to drive over and explain our delay. That troop can't leave without new mounts. What he'll do is rustle the horses in the west pasture to stop us. If we set a trap for his men like Navarro suggested, we'll get them. Then we'll have our proof for the law."

"You're right, Jess. He'll think that we'll try again tomorrow, not tonight."

"We should get moving, Mr. Lane, before his men reach that area."

"You boys heard Navarro; let's grab some supplies and get riding."

*

Nothing happened all night. Their anxiety made it a long one, and a lack of campfires made it chilly. The hands took shifts sleeping and watching the group of excellent horses. At dawn, they headed for the corral with the stock.

By the time they arrived, Navarro suspected why Fletcher hadn't fallen into their trap. "He's more cunning than I realized, Mr. Lane. He guessed we set a trap for him. He probably laughed all night thinking about us sitting out there getting tired and aggravated. I think I know what he's up to now. He believes we'll expect him to make another strike on the trail today so we'll send nearly all our hands as guards. That will leave the cattle unprotected. That's where he wants to strike. He doesn't want a small herd of horses; he wants a large herd of steers. That loss will hurt you most. I say you send only a few men with the horses; we'll set another trap for him with the rest. What do you think, sir?"

"Tarnation! You've got a good head, Navarro; you think like he does. That's what the snake is up to, I'm sure of it. Matt, take two men and get these horses to Captain Graham. Tell Sheriff Cooper what happened on the trail and here last night. Tell him to expect some prisoners tomorrow."

"I wouldn't do that, sir," Navarro advised. "Not unless you trust this lawman completely. If he's being paid by Fletcher not to help you, he could warn him and ruin our plan."

The older man scratched his graying auburn head. "Toby Cooper seems an honest man, but you could be right again. We'll surprise him and Fletcher with our success. You seem to know what to do, so I'm putting you in charge here."

The desperado nodded. "We should get the steers gathered into one area—a place with plenty of trees and hills for good hiding places. We don't want any saddled horses or guards in sight to give us away so I hope all or most of you can ride bareback when the time comes to chase them. If he has anyone spy on the house today, he'll think the boys stopped branding to take those horses to the fort so that shouldn't look suspicious. Tom, Gran, and Hank should work in the garden or keep to their chores to show some life around the house. Jessie should ride with us; she's an expert shot. We don't know how many rustlers he'll send so we best use every one we can." Navarro knew he hadn't mentioned the blonde standing nearby, but she was Jed's problem.

"Everybody get your supplies and weapons ready," Navarro instructed the watchful hands. "We need to get moving and concealed before he strikes again. I don't expect him to come at us until dusk or tonight, so it'll be a long wait again. But that'll give us time to get ready for 'em."

"What do you want me to do to help, Father?"

Jed glanced at the blonde in surprise. "Your chores will be nice, Mary Louise."

"I'll tend Jessica's, too, while she's gone."

"Thank you," Jessie told her, wondering what the girl was trying to pull. She was up to something; of that, the redhead was certain.

*

The hidden men stayed on silent and motionless alert all day. At mealtimes, they munched on cold biscuits stuffed with ham and washed them down with water from canteens. Their horses grazed nearby, ready to be mounted for the pursuit. Navarro had arranged them in a semicircle, with the herd flanked by a lengthy pointed top hill. With Matt and two hands gone, Hank at the ranch, and Davy in the bunkhouse wounded, that left Jessie, Jed, Navarro, and nine hands to face Fletcher.

It was only an hour past dusk when the action began. Masked riders galloped toward the gathered steers, passing between the Box L watchers. Fifteen men entered the attack area, making the odds fairly even. At a signal from Navarro, the Box L hands opened fire on the rustlers. The startled bandits reined up mounts, some so fast that the animals nearly tripped.

Firing back, the villains rushed for cover or escape. It was obvious to the bandits that they had ridden into a clever trap, but there were gaps between the Box L hands and many of the rustlers fled without injury. A few were wounded, but kept riding homeward. Some were trapped as the Box L hands jumped on their horses and closed the holes in their defense line. Two rustlers were killed and two were captured.

Navarro took control of the prisoners while the hands hurried off to settle down the frightened stock. He glanced at Jed and Jessie and remarked, "Their horses don't carry a brand; that's smart. But we know who you boys work for: Wilbur Fletcher." As he yanked off their masks, he taunted, "Didn't he tell you that rustling is a hanging offense? I don't recognize any of them. Jed, Jessie, do you?"

None of the three did, which struck Navarro as odd since he had spied on Fletcher's ranch, and the Lanes had lived near Fletcher for years. The same was true when the hands returned; no one recognized these strangers.

"This your first job for Fletcher?" Navarro questioned. "He hire more men?"

"Who's this Fletcher?" one surly man scoffed. "We been ridin' fur days from Mexico. We only wanted to cut out one steer to carve an' eat. We're starvin'. No call to shoot my friends. I'll pay you, an' we can ride on, mister."

"The only place you're riding is to jail," Jed informed the two cutthroats. "You'll be sorry you hired on with Fletcher to ruin me."

"You're talkin' crazy, old man. We don't work fur nobody in these parts."

"We'll see who's crazy when you're swinging from a rope."

The villain's eyes grew colder and narrower. "No hungry man will hang fur goin' after a little meat when he offered to pay fur it."

"If you aren't cattle thieves, why the masks?"

"Keeps dust outta yore nose when yore ridin'."

"Yep, grass stirs up a lot of that," Navarro said wryly.

"Papa, we need to move fast. We'll get these men and bodies on the way to the sheriff before Fletcher's men report back to him. You'd better guard the house good tonight. He may attack to get our evidence."

"You going, Jess?"

"One of us needs to tell our side to Sheriff Cooper. I think you're needed her more than me to give orders. We should meet up with Matt and the boys on the trail. By now they're camped somewhere on their way back home. If we don't hook up tonight, we'll probably join them tomorrow. Don't worry, Papa. Navarro and I can take care of ourselves on the trail. We've had practice."

"I don't like you two riding alone. Fletcher's men might come after you."

"He'll expect us to take his boys back to the ranch tonight, then haul them to the sheriff tomorrow. If he attacks anywhere, it'll be at home. You need all the hands there with you. Navarro and I can manage two bound men and two bodies."

"I suppose you're right. But don't take any chances, Jess."

"We won't, Papa. We'll turn them in, make a report, then come home. If we meet up with Matt, I'll keep him with us and send the other hands home."

"What about supplies?" Jed fretted.

"We'll take what's left from here. We'll make do."

Navarro had held silent. His heart had been pounding in anticipation of being alone with Jessie on the way back, until she mentioned they'd probably have company. "I'll take care of her, sir. You have my word of honor."

As Jessie prepared to leave, Jed told him, "Remember your word, son, 'cause I won't forget it. That girl's my life, so guard her good."

Navarro was a little unnerved by the man's subtle threat. "I will, sir."

*

Jessie and Navarro reached the town of Fort Davis at dawn. Their journey had been slow and cautious over the hilly and mountainous terrain. They headed for Sheriff Cooper's office and awaited his arrival.

The tall and lanky lawman didn't join them till seven. His gaze swept over the two scowling prisoners sprawled on his porch and the two bodies tied over horses at the hitching post. "More trouble, Miss Lane?"

"Plenty, Sheriff Cooper. We caught these rustlers red-handed." She explained their successful trap, then remarked, "Wilbur Fletcher's men."

"How do you know that?"

"We know."

"I can charge them and hold them for the judge next week, but where's your proof they work for Mr. Fletcher and he's behind your trouble?"

"He's to blame, Sheriff. Take my word on it."

"I wish I could, Miss Lane, but the law says I need evidence to arrest a man."

"You mean you still won't investigate him?"

"I can ride over to his place and ask questions. But if he's guilty, he won't confess. You men got anything to say?" he asked the sullen culprits.

"We're innocent, Sheriff. We wuz just ridin' along an' they attacked us. Accused us of bein' rustlers an' brung us here."

"He's lying! They were masked and trying to steal our herd! I have twelve witnesses who'll back up my word this time."

"That's enough proof for me to hold them." He checked the dead men, then rejoined Jessie and the quiet stranger at her side. "Don't know any of them. No brands on those horses to tie them to Mr. Fletcher. Haven't seen you around, either," the lawman remarked to Navarro.

The deceptively calm fugitive extended his right hand and responded, "Navarro Jones, Sheriff. Hired on with the Lanes three weeks past. From Colorado."

"We lost Big Ed in an accident, and Davy was shot Monday." Jessie interrupted, eager to take the sheriff's attention away from Navarro. "None of the regular seasonal wranglers returned to sign on for spring roundup and branding, and no new ones came by, either. We're short of men, and we can't get our work done with them attacking us. We think Fletcher's behind it. Have you seen any of his men talking with wranglers in town?"

"Nope, but it's mighty curious none of them came around for jobs like usual. What about you?" he asked the desperado.

"I hired him in San Angelo," Jessie replied. "We were there on business. Did Matt report what happened Monday?"

"Yes, before he left last night. He was anxious to get back to the ranch so he didn't stay the night. Like he said, no need to spend time tracking those men and horses. You must have missed him and the boys on the trail in."

"We took a different way in case Fletcher's gang tried to overtake and ambush us to set these two free before they talked. Do you know if Matt reached the fort in time to save our sale?"

"Yes. Capt'n Graham and a troop are riding your way tomorrow. Matt convinced them to have a slow look around. I plan to ride along and do the same. I'd like to get this trouble settled as much as you would."

"You'll stand a better chance if Fletcher doesn't know you're coming and lays low." Jessie knew it was best not to mention the coyote incident.

"What if Mr. Fletcher isn't behind it, Miss Lane? None of his hands have been seen. Nothing suspicious points to him."

"Because he hires strangers like these two and uses unmarked horses."

"We'll see what we can learn. The Army doesn't like anyone messing with their deliveries. That troop couldn't pull out until they got fresh mounts. Start tampering with the Army's schedule and they get riled. With both of us on the lookout, maybe we'll get somewhere. I know you got a long list of charges against somebody, but to be honest, I ain't convinced it's Mr. Fletcher. Why don't you rest up today and travel with us tomorrow?"

"That sounds good. We're tired and hungry. We left straight from the range after a long day. We didn't want their gang to have time to report and cut us off on the trail. What time in the morning?"

"About seven."

"What about them?" she asked, motioning to the prisoners.

"My deputy will guard them. The others go to the undertaker."

* * *

After a hot meal and baths, Navarro joined Jessie in her room. She was wearing a half-buttoned shirt and a light blanket was wrapped around her hips and legs. "Did we miss Matt on purpose?" he asked.

Jessie glanced at him and replied, "Yes, so we could be alone on our way back. Now that we're staying here today, we don't have to worry about the sheriff and soldiers being with us on the way home."

"You think they'll find anything? If Fletcher makes a mistake with them around, this trouble can be over in a few days. Then I can be on my way."

"I was afraid you'd feel that way. You don't mind remaining here with me until tomorrow, do you? Is that being too forward?"

Navarro went to her. "No, Jessie, I'm glad we'll have today alone. You think anyone will come to visit you?"

"No. Sheriff Cooper knows we rode all night and plan to nap. Can we . . . be together?" she asked boldly.

Navarro's hands cupped her uplifted face. He gazed into her eyes. She could be lost to him sooner than he had imagined now that the authorities were getting involved. He prayed there wasn't a wanted poster out on him and, if there was, that Cooper didn't have one in his office. The lawman hadn't seemed overly interested in him. "Yes, Jessie. I want you," he said at last.

Their lips fused in a soulful kiss that revealed their longing. Jessie's arms encircled his body as Navarro trailed kisses over her cheeks, nose, eyes, and mouth. It was as if he wanted to taste every inch of her face. He nestled her head against his chest and untied her hair ribbon to loosen her braid. With leisurely gentleness, his fingers worked to separate the wavy strands and spread her tresses around her shoulders.

He looked down at her. The red mane enhanced her complexion and made her eyes glow. "I want you so much, Jessie."

Her hand lifted to caress his cheek, then trailed several fingers over his full mouth. "I want you, too," she murmured. She fluffed the midnight hair over his left forehead, then traced the prominent bone structure under his brows, on his cheeks, along his jawline, and over his chin. Her fingers wandered across the hollows of his cheeks. "You're so handsome, Navarro. I can't think clearly when I'm so close to you. I want to kiss you a million times and that wouldn't be enough. I want our bodies touching with nothing between us. I want to feel the same way I did that night in the line shack." Jessie unbuttoned his shirt, parted the material, and looked at his smooth and muscular chest. She spread kisses over the heated skin, then caressed the firm flesh with her cheek. As they kissed with rising urgency, she removed her own shirt and pressed her naked chest to his, causing both to groan in fierce desire.

Navarro's hands trembled as they stroked Jessie's enticing frame. She was so soft, yet so firm. He pulled away only long enough for her to peel off his shirt.

"I'll wait for you in bed," she murmured against his mouth. Then she flung aside the covers and lay down, her gaze beckoning him to hurry.

Navarro quickly removed his pants and boots and joined her, pulling her into his arms. "Jessie . . . Jessie . . . Jessie . . ." He whispered her name over and over as his lips and hands explored her tingling flesh.

Navarro's touch made Jessie writhe with desire, and she eagerly caressed his strong, lean body until he was as frenzied with passion as she was. At last they could restrain themselves no longer, and as their bodies united as one, they savored love's delights. Afterward, sated and sleepy, they cuddled together, and slept in each other's embrace.

* * *

It was past two in the afternoon when they awakened. Navarro had shifted to his right side, and Jessie was curled against him on hers. Her left arm lay over his waist, and her hand was held in his.

Jessie eyed the numerous scars on Navarro's broad back. She pulled her hand free of his light grasp and felt the ridges. He had endured terrible agony. She shuddered at the thought of her love receiving such a violent lashing. She kissed the ridged skin as if to remove any lingering pain and hugged him.

Navarro shifted to his other side to face her. She rolled to her back. Tears were in her eyes. As one escaped, his right forefinger captured it before the moisture slid into her tousled hair. He read such concern and confusion in her gaze, yet she never asked about the scars. She wanted to, but knew she shouldn't. "The man who did it is dead, Jessie. You know what I told the boys happened?" When she nodded, he continued. "I thought they'd mention it to you. Did they tell your father?"

"I don't know. Miguel and Carlos told me while you and Tom were spying at Fletcher's."

"But you already knew about my scars."

"Yes, I felt them that night in the line shack. I've seen Jimmy Joe's, so I knew what they were. I'm sorry someone made you suffer like that."

"I didn't want anyone to see them, but I knew I couldn't keep them a secret at the ranch. They're ugly, and they spark questions I don't like to answer."

"If you ever want to tell me the truth, Navarro, you can trust me. If not, I understand."

"That's one of the best things about you, Jessie; you know when to step back to let a man breathe easier. Thanks."

"It seems we're good for each other, Navarro. We sense what the other needs most. We strengthen each other's weaknesses. We fill the lonely holes and brighten the dark corners of the other's life. That's rare."

"Nobody has ever been this close to me before. It's scary, but it feels good."

"I've had plenty of people close to me, but none like you, Navarro. I hate to lose you and what you bring to me."

"I know, Jessie, but it has to be that way. If I could change it so I could stay, I would."

"I know that's true, Navarro, but it still hurts for something so special to end. If you ever change your mind, will you come back to me?"

"The things that hold us apart won't ever change, Jessie. There's no hope."

"Never?"

"Never," he mumbled, then inhaled deeply.

Jessie squeezed her eyes closed and took a deep breath, too. When she opened them, she said, "I'll let you go if I must, Navarro, but not until I've tried everything to keep you."

"Don't, Jessie," he urged. "There's nothing you can do. False hopes bring nothing but pain; I know from experience."

"Then love me while you can." She pulled his head down and kissed him.

*

By six-thirty the next morning, Jessie and Navarro were ready to leave town. They had made love, eaten supper, made love again, then slept all night in Jessie's room. At dawn, Navarro had sneaked away to take care of a chore and to rumple his unused bed. They had met downstairs for breakfast, then headed for the sheriff's office.

Toby Cooper looked up when they entered the jailhouse. He tossed papers aside and revealed, "I have bad news, Miss Lane."

Jessie's eyes filled with fear. "Is it my family? Did Fletcher attack there last night to get back his men? Was anyone hurt?"

10

"Settle down, Miss Lane," the lawman coaxed. "That isn't it. Those rustlers you brought in are gone. And so are those bodies from the undertaker's office."

"You let Fletcher have them back? Why? I have witnesses this time."

"I haven't seen Mr. Fletcher or any of his men. My deputy was hit over the head when he peeked outside to check out a noise. He didn't see who done it. I found him out on the floor this morning. He's at doc's getting patched up. I looked around . . . but nothing. I'm sorry, Miss Lane. I never expected anyone to attempt a jailbreak here. Mighty daring of them."

"I should have guarded them last night," Navarro said grimly. "I should have known their boss wouldn't risk having them talk. When you check Fletcher's ranch, look for unbranded horses and wounded men. We winged several more who got away."

"Don't blame yourself, Navarro," Jessie told him. "We were tired. We've been working hard for so long." She told the sheriff about the windmill incident and fence cuttings, as well as the slayings of their dog and hens. "Rustlers and thieves don't do things like that, Sheriff Cooper. Fletcher wants to buy us out or scare us off our land. We won't leave."

"Mr. Fletcher was just in town," the sheriff said. "Then, he sent word in on Monday. He filed a report saying those same things had happened at his place. He accused the Lanes of being responsible. I told him, like I told you and your pa, we need proof."

"That lying snake!" she scoffed. "He can't get proof because we're innocent. We can't get it because he's clever. What else did he tell you?"

"About lots of dead coyotes being dropped on his land and around his wind-mills."

"We'd never do such a brutal thing. Besides, we don't have time to plot against Fletcher. We're trying to get our branding done without extra help. If Fletcher will stop attacking us, we can. But he won't."

"We'll try to get this mess cleared up soon. I don't want no range war between you two. We need to get to the fort. Capt'n Graham will be ready to leave a little past seven. We'll get to the bottom of this."

*

They reached home around four o'clock. After Jessie related the bad news about the jailbreak, Sheriff Cooper and Captain Graham talked with Jed about the situation between the two ranches. The lawman and soldiers intended to ride over the Lane spread for a few days, then head for Fletcher's to do the same. Though Jed and Jessie told them it was a waste of time, that Fletcher's gang would only lay low until they left, the troop split into four units and rode off in different directions.

As she watched them leave, Jessie said, "Fletcher broke his men out of jail before they could betray him. Those two are long gone and those bodies are well hidden by now, Papa. The authorities wouldn't be here if Fletcher hadn't made those crazy charges against us. We're under more suspicion than he is! At least the sheriff and those soldiers will keep him quiet and on his land for a while. With them on our range, we can put everyone on branding until Sunday. We'd best take advantage of this break. That snake will be crawling again next week."

*

Thursday through Sunday passed in a flurry of noisy, smelly, dusty, exhausting work. The herd of cows and calves in the holding pens were dwindling down, but not fast enough to relax Jed and Jessie. The hands labored hard and long hours from dawn to dusk. At quitting time, they splashed off, ate, and fell into their bunks. Yet Navarro found the time to teach Tom how to throw and use a knife, despite Jed's mute disapproval when he learned of it.

Jessie observed her brother and Navarro as their friendship grew stronger, and came to love the mysterious drifter more and more. She watched him with the hands, and she was delighted to see him fitting in better every day. Dreamy-eyed hope filled her. Although it was difficult being around him and keeping their secret, she did, and so did he.

Nevertheless, Mary Louise was suspicious and envious and watchful of the couple who spent so much time together. Martha saw the glow and felt the change in her elder granddaughter, but said nothing to anyone. All noticed how Tom was budding like a flower in spring, and knew Navarro was responsible. But Jed worried over how Jessie and Tom would react when the drifter left them behind.

*

Jed insisted everyone take Sunday off after the necessary chores were done. There was no guessing when they would be able to rest again. As usual, most of the hands met at the front porch to hear Jed read from the Bible and to sing a few hymnals, as there was no church close enough to attend.

Navarro leaned his back against the end post and gazed toward the large barn across the clearing. He dared not look at Jessie. She looked beautiful today in a blue dress and with her unbound hair shining in the sun. Their day in town consumed his thoughts. He wished his life could be that way all the time . . .

As the ranch service ended, the sheriff and soldiers stopped by to say they were leaving the Lane spread—having found nothing—to visit Fletcher's.

"Join us for ring toss, *amigo*?" Miguel asked Navarro.

"Later. I have something to do first, a surprise for someone."

Tom was disappointed that he couldn't accompany Navarro, but Navarro said he would understand why not this afternoon.

With Big John Williams, Navarro headed for the smithy shed, a structure that sat away from the barn in case of sparks that might cause a fire.

Jessie worked with Tom on his neglected lessons, while Jed pored over his books and visited with the men. Gran rested, and Mary Louise wrote more letters.

Jessie and Tom left the house when Big John summoned them to the smithy. She watched Navarro help her curious brother sit on top of a wooden barrel.

Navarro removed Tom's right shoe and the soiled sock on his left foot. "Close your eyes and don't cheat," he told the boy. Navarro worked a knee-high Apache moccasin onto the right foot, overlapped the soft material near the ankle and calf, then laced the side ties. He worked the other one on to Tom's clubfoot, then secured it. He had made them in this style so the leather shoes would go on the boy's twisted foot, and made them alike so they would not draw attention. Navarro helped the boy to the ground. "You can look now." As Tom eyed the moccasins, he said, "They're strong enough to protect against rocks, cactus, and thornbushes. You can walk or ride anywhere and not get hurt. I padded the left one to make it more level with the other for easier walking."

Tom moved about with less effort and discomfort. He beamed with delight. "Thanks, Navarro! How did you make 'em?"

"I measured your feet not long ago, remember?" The boy nodded. "When we were getting those Indian blankets to wrap the coyotes in, I saw a tanned buffalo hide and leather shirt the Apaches had given your father. They gave me this idea. Jessie said I could have them, but she didn't know why. I cut them to size. Then John helped me make the holes with a saddle tool, and we both stitched them. Buffalo hide makes a stronger sole than rawhide. Holding the stuffing in while we closed the seam was the hardest part. We're making you a second pair for when these need washing or you get 'em wet from rain."

Tom walked again, grinning and laughing. "This is easier, Jessie. My calf don't strain like with the sock. It don't show as much, either. I got shoes on like everybody else!" The boy went to Navarro and hugged him around the waist. With misty eyes and a choked voice, he said, "People won't stare at me now, Navarro."

Jessie saw that Tom's reaction touched Navarro deeply. Yet, the gunslinger obviously didn't know how to respond. His hazel gaze darted about nervously until, at last, he patted the boy's back and said, "You're welcome, Tom. But I didn't do all the work. John helped a lot."

Tom smiled at the black man and said, "Thanks, Big John."

"You be mighty welcome, Tom."

"I wanna show Pa and Matt." The excited youth hurried to do so, his head and shoulders high with pride and joy. John tagged along to watch."

Jessie's eyes were filled with happiness. "You're one special man, Navarro, but I knew that from the beginning. Thanks."

"It wasn't much, Jessie—just moccasins. Soft leather can be put on easier than a hard shoe or boot. Now he won't feel so different."

"Like you do, Navarro?"

"I guess, but my flaws can't be covered up like his can."

"I don't believe you have as many as you think."

"But the ones I have are bad, real bad. Leave it, Jessie," he entreated. "Let's go before someone wonders what's keeping us here so long."

Within an hour, everyone heard Tom's good news and saw him strut around. Mary Louise and Gran came to check on the commotion.

"They're Apache," Jed remarked.

"Yes, sir. I met an old man on the trail who made and sold them at forts and reservations. I watched him for hours in camp, even helped a little. I remembered how he'd done it. Hope you don't mind."

"No, 'course not. You made Tom real happy. I've had lots of dealings with Apaches. They can be sly and mean if you don't trick 'em into a truce real fast."

"Deceit's about all they know and use, sir," Navarro replied, not wanting to give Jessie's father any clues about his past. He saw Martha watching him closely again, and wondered why.

Gran thanked Navarro and she enthused over the moccasins, his cunning, and his generosity.

"He's making me another pair, Gran," Tom revealed, "for when you wash these or rain wets 'em. You can't hardly tell I got a bad foot."

"You're very clever and helpful, Navarro," Mary Louise murmured. "I'm amazed by how many talents you possess. We're fortunate Jessica found you for us."

Jessie glanced at her sister. Mary Louise had been on her best behavior since her quarrel with their father last Sunday. The smartly dressed blonde was walking, talking, and acting like a well-bred and well-educated lady. Somehow Jessie didn't trust the girl; a person couldn't change so in only a week.

"Thank you, Miss Lane," Navarro replied. "I'll join the boys for a game now."

Jed, Matt, Mary Louise, and Gran watched as Navarro walked away, and Jessie watched all five with great interest. She suspected that none of them wanted to like or accept Navarro. She wondered at their reluctance.

*

With the law gone, Matt assigned several men to ride guard around the ranch that night. As the hands left, Matt joined the men, who were tossing metal rings around posts fifteen feet apart. Others played cards, made or listened to music on the bunkhouse porch, or did rope tricks to entertain their friends.

At ten, Roy returned to the bunkhouse to roust Biscuit Hank for doctoring. Roy was in terrible pain with four broken fingers. While Hank tried to straighten and bind Roy's injured hand with Matt's help, Navarro fetched Jed. Jessie heard the noise and went to investigate.

In the bunkhouse, Roy claimed, "I fell, Boss, and bent 'em back. They snapped like twigs. I won't be no good for a long time—if this hand ever heals right. I'm heading for my uncle's ranch in San Antonio at first light. Davy's fine, so I won't trouble you with caring for me. You got enough work on your hands."

Roy took more swallows from the whiskey bottle that Hank urged on him for dulling the agony. The man grimaced. "Sorry, Boss. It was a crazy accident."

Jessie and Jed exchanged glances. "You sure it was an accident?" Jed asked.

Roy looked scared and nervous as he vowed, "It was, Boss."

"You've been with me for years, Roy. I've never known you to be careless."

Roy drank again and groaned in pain as Matt helped Hank set the breaks as best they could.

"You need a real doc for this mess," Hank remarked.

"They got two in San Antonio. My aunt can tend me good. I cain't work like this. No need for me to hang around and be more trouble."

"It's three hundred miles. You need doctorin' afore that," Hank protested.

"I'll go to Stockton and hitch a ride. Be easier than horseback. Won't cost much." Roy spoke without convincing the others.

"Mighty anxious to leave," Matt said. "Speak the truth, man."

The strong liquor took effect and Roy snapped, "You would be, too, if—"

"Who did this?" Matt insisted, interrupting. "We been friends a long time. You owe us the truth. A fall don't tear a shirt like that."

"He'll find out and they'll kill me next time. I hafta leave."

"Who?" Jessie entreated. "We'll protect you, Roy. Tell us, please."

"I cain't, Miss Jessie."

"Yes you can," she urged in a soothing tone.

Roy shuddered in anguish and fear. "I don't know. I swear it. That gang just called him 'Boss.' They broke my fingers so I cain't work. They said if I wasn't gone tomorrow, they'd git me. They got a spy here. That's how they know to do ever'thing. He'll tell 'em I talked. They'll ambush me."

"Spy? Who?" the redhead asked.

"Don't know, Miss Jessie. One of our hands is working for him. Maybe they scared him into doing it. They're real mean. There's lots of 'em. We cain't stop 'em. We'll all get killed. Sell out, Jed, or yore family could be next. If you tell the boys what I said, that spy will talk and they'll be gunning for me. I hafta quit and ride out, Jed. I hafta."

"Let him go, Papa. But you have to promise to come back to work when this trouble is over. Deal, Roy?"

"I will. Just don't say what I tol' you."

"We won't," Jed said to calm the shaking man.

When Roy finished the whiskey and was put to bed, Matt asked, "You believe we have a spy here?"

"No, 'course not. They were just scaring Roy off. I can't let him stay like that. Fletcher could get to him again and use him against us. Once a man breaks, he can't be trusted again. We won't tell the boys what happened until he's gone. That leaves us with thirteen men, me, and Jess. Anybody else you think can be scared off, Matt?"

"No, sir. Roy was the weakest and had been with us the shortest time. If any strangers or old hands come by, we shouldn't hire them."

"Why?" Jed questioned.

"Maybe Fletcher's gotten to them. Too risky."

"I have another plan, Mr. Lane, if you want to strike blow for blow."

*

Monday night beneath a waning crescent moon, the group Navarro had selected met at the corral. "Carlos, did you pick the darkest and best-trained horses for our raid?"

"*Si, amigo,* the best."

Navarro eyed the men in dark clothes and hats that would help them blend into the night. "Any of you wearing anything that might make noise?" The men all replied they weren't, as ordered. "I know you boys can ride bareback. We don't want anything to make sound and we don't want to be seen. The moon's on our side tonight, but we have to be careful. We can't allow any of us to be captured and turned over to the sheriff or Army. Anybody who makes a mistake or gets surprised takes the blame for the whole thing."

They all concurred. "Carlos, you ride with Jimmy Joe. Matt, you go with Miguel. Jessie will be with me. That'll split up our best shots and best riders. Keep your partner in sight. If you have to leave him behind to protect the Lanes and the rest of our group, be brave and do it. Just like we planned, dynamite the tops. Big John said that'll hurt him the most. If it breaks those windmills' fingers, good. If not, we'll settle for taking off their heads. Fletcher'll have to put lots of hands on them for repairs. That'll repay him and give us time to work."

"Where did you get this dynamite?" Matt inquired.

"At the fort while me and Jessie were waiting on the troops to get ready to leave. I got to talking to one of the soldiers and he showed me around. When the guard turned his back in the magazine, I stuffed three sticks in my shirt. I wish we had more. You have the time down?" They all said yes. "We need them to blow together. That'll cause confusion. Cut fences on your way back—but hurry. No chances. Me and Jessie will fire his south shed as we leave. As soon as you're back, curry your horse and release him, then get in the bunkhouse. If Fletcher rushes over, we want it to look like a regular night. We'll be going now, sir," Navarro told Jed.

"You boys be real careful-like," Jed warned. "Navarro, you take care of Jess for me. I don't like her going on this job. It's dangerous."

"I'll be fine, Papa. Navarro needs the best shots and riders in case of trouble."

*

Jessie noted the time on her father's pocketwatch. They hadn't seen anything but stock since they reached their enemy's land. Navarro climbed the windmill and tied the dynamite to the gear box on the wheel. At two o'clock, she told him to light the long fuse. He struck a safety match and did so, then scampered down to leap on his horse. They galloped for distance from the impending blast. It shook the night like thunder and lightning during a bad storm.

Watchful for approaching men, they rode to a pasture shed and set it ablaze. Again, they galloped away toward safety, and for home this time. On Lane land, Jessie halted her mount and called out for Navarro to do the same.

"What's wrong? Did you hear or see something?"

"No, but I need a kiss," she replied, edging her horse closer to his.

"We have to hurry," he responded, but released the animal's mane to lean over and cup Jessie's face between his hands. He kissed her with tenderness that rapidly turned into raging desire. He groaned as he leaned away. "We have to ride."

"I know, but I needed you for a moment. We have so little time alone."

"I wish that weren't so, but it is, Jessie, and it'll be that way for good."

"Please stop reminding me that I'll lose you, Navarro," she beseeched him.

"If I don't, you'll ignore it. I've come to know you well, woman."

"Yes, you have, better than anyone. You sure you can get along without me after you leave?" she asked, trying to keep her tone teasing and light.

"It'll be hard, but I have to learn, don't I?"

Jessie knew he didn't expect or want an answer, so she responded, "Yep. Just as long as I know it'll be as difficult on you as it'll be on me. Let's get home, partner." She nudged her mount and galloped off to give him that breathing space he always needed when she got too close.

*

Tuesday morning, Wilbur Fletcher arrived to see Jedidiah Lane. Mary Louise entertained their neighbor until Jed and Jessie reached the house. Martha had gone to fetch them and warn them of their enemy's presence. They found the man sitting in their parlor and sipping coffee as if he were an invited guest!

"What do you want here?" Jessie asked. "You're not welcome on Lane land."

"How dare you enter my home!" Jed added in a cold tone. "Mary Louise, you know better than to invite this rattlesnake inside. If you have anything to say to me, Fletcher, come outside. I don't want you fouling my home with your evil stench. But since we have nothing to discuss, just ride off the same way you came."

"And don't come back," Jessie finished.

Fletcher, looking annoyingly unruffled, set down his cup and rose. "You're a hard man to deal with, Jed. There's no need to be impolite or hostile. We *are* neighbors."

Jed walked outside in a hurry as he tried to master his raging temper. At the porch, he turned on the man and said, "You've never been a good neighbor. You crave my land, but you won't ever get your dirty hands on it. Never."

"I made you a fair offer. You're getting too old to manage such a large spread. Your son can't take over for you, and surely you don't expect these young ladies to do so. What kind of father are you to work them so hard and to keep such beauties secluded way out here? With my offer, you could have a good life in town. You're making Miss Jessie as hard and stubborn as you are."

"Jess can manage this spread as well as I can. And she will when I'm gone."

"She's a woman, Jed, a beautiful woman. She shouldn't have to shoulder such a burden because of your pride and selfishness. She should be married with children of her own. You're making that choice impossible for her. As for Miss Mary Louise, she's much too educated and ravishing to be trapped in a wilderness. And that son of yours, he could receive treatments for his problems in a big city."

Jed was furious. His face flushed and his sturdy body stiffened with barely leashed emotion. "Don't go telling me how to run my family matters! You don't even have a wife and children, so what do you know about them? Nothing! I never understood why you settled here in what you call a wilderness. Why don't you give up and move on? You've got plenty of money to buy a good spread somewhere else, near those big cities you like. You can't grow here with me in your path so you're wasting your time waiting and talking."

"Expansion is precisely why I want to purchase the Box L. You have the best grazing land and water supply in the southwestern area. I'll even raise my offer. Name a fair price and we can settle our business today."

"We have no business with you, Fletcher," Jessie remarked.

"Give it up, 'cause I'll never sell out, especially to the likes of you."

The brown-eyed man responded in a calm voice. "If you keep attacking me, Jed, you'll lose. You'll find yourself in prison very soon. Then what will happen to your family and property? I know you dumped those coyotes on me. You're also to blame for dynamiting three of my windmills last night. I've sent word to the sheriff about your crazy doings. He should be returning to question you this week. You've gone mad, Jed, and I'm sorry to see that happen. You have this insane idea I'm your enemy, but I'm not. I freely admit I want your spread badly, but I wouldn't do the things you've accused me of doing to get it. I don't have to resort to such vile actions. You'll lose this ranch all by yourself through your criminal deeds. When you step too far, I'll be there to buy this spread, and you'll be the loser."

Jed looked as if the man's words alarmed him, but still he claimed, "I don't know anything about coyotes and windmills, Fletcher. If you aren't behind all this trouble I'm having, maybe that ghostly gang you mentioned is harassing both of us. I'm a God-fearing, hardworking man. I don't fight unless I'm forced to."

"Don't be sarcastic, Jed, and don't lie. You're boxing yourself in with these undeserved attacks on me. I want to get this land legally and fairly."

"When would I have time to attack you? We're busy with branding. We're short-handed, but you know all about that. If you send your hirelings over here again to kill my critters, or do damage, or scare off any more hands, you'll be sorry. Plenty sorry," Jessie's father added with renewed courage and coldness.

Without raising his voice, Fletcher said, "Don't threaten me. I'm getting as mad as *you* claim to be. I've been patient waiting for you to work this craziness out of your head or for the sheriff to capture the real culprits. Neither has happened. The only change in our situation is that it's getting worse. The next Box L hand I see on my place will be shot for trespassing."

"If you murder any of my men, you'll hang. Toby Cooper and Captain Graham know us, have for years; they'd know you shot an innocent man. We both know everything you've done to me. I've been lying back too long while you challenged me. It's fighting time. You'll get everything you deserve," Jed warned.

Fletcher reacted to that threat by narrowing his dark eyes for a moment, then forced himself to relax again. He brushed some flicks of dust off his well-made suit from Dallas. He glanced at his neatly trimmed nails. "I'm sorry you feel that way, Jed, and that you're being so stubborn and unreasonable. When you finally give up because you go broke or someone gets hurt, my offer won't be as good as it is now. I sincerely wish we could work this out without more hostility."

"Why do you really want this ranch?" Jessie inquired.

Fletcher's eyes roamed her head to foot. "I told you why, Miss Jessie."

Beneath his brown gaze, Jessie felt she must look a mess. Mary Louise was right; he was handsome, virile, and well mannered. He was a smooth and clever charmer! "I don't think so," she refuted. "There are too many other places you can go and settle. If you want our land this badly, there must be a better reason than greed for water and grass. If you keep pressing us, the truth will come out. I wonder how that will affect the law's reactions."

Fletcher smiled, and his aristocratic features softened. His dark hair was combed from his tanned face. His hairline receded slightly at his temples to form a brown widow's peak in the middle. His brows were thick, his nose straight, and his mouth full. She had never paid much attention to his looks before; now she realized how appealing they were. If she didn't know the truth, she would think she was crazy to suspect such a dashing and polite man of attacking them in such horrible ways!

"You're a surprising and refreshing woman, Miss Jessie. You'll make some lucky man a very strong, intelligent, and dependable wife."

Jed didn't like the way his enemy was eyeing his daughters. "I should have claimed all the land up to the mountains; then you couldn't have moved in and started trouble. I only needed three hundred thousand acres, and I never thought anyone would claim land without water and much grass. 'Course with your wealth, you can afford to build plenty of windmills. Tell me, Fletcher; why did you box yourself in like that? You don't belong in a place like this."

"I saw this area and fell in love with it, as you did. I planned to live here a while, then move back East. I decided it would be easy to sell later for a nice profit if I created a nice spread. But the longer I remained, the more attached I became to my ranch. I decided I wanted to make it the biggest and best in this area. This is where I want to spend my life, so I'm staying."

"You're a big-city man. Your being here don't make sense, like Jessie said."

Fletcher glanced from Jed to Jessie, eyed her once more, then looked back at her father. "I don't need to explain myself to you or to anybody. When I want something, I get it, because I have the money and wits to do so. Eventually all of this will be Bar F land. The sooner you face that reality, Jed, the better for all of us. I don't want to ruin you to win, so don't force me to break you. You know I can undercut every deal you try to make. I can hire every seasonal wrangler who comes to this area and let them sit on my bunkhouse porch. How will you get your cattle to market then? I can purchase the supply stores in both towns, then refuse to sell goods to you or price them so high you'll go broke or wanting. There are plenty of ways to change your mind without violence. I'm a rich and powerful man. I'm smart and I'm determined. I don't need to resort to the sort of vile tactics you're using and accusing *me* of using. I won't tolerate them any longer. Attack me again, and it will be war between us. I don't have a family to worry about protecting, and I do have more men working for me. Think twice before challenging me again."

"You're about as innocent as the devil is about tempting Eve!" Jed retorted. "Sheriff Cooper and Captain Graham are keeping an eye on this area. You'll make a slip soon and be unmasked. We'll see how much your money matters then."

"They can't unmask me if I'm innocent. If I were you, I'd look for whomever my real enemy is and go after him. Somebody wants you out of here worse than I do. I'd ask myself who and why. Good-bye, Miss Jessie. Good-bye, Miss Mary Louise," he said, smiling and tipping his hat to the blonde standing in the doorway observing them. "I do hope you fine ladies will enlighten your father as to the error of his ways before this matter is out of control."

Jessie watched their neighbor ride away in a sturdy buckboard. He was joined beyond the house by three men who took guard positions on both sides and behind their boss. Fletcher traveled at a leisurely pace, his departure creating little dust. Jessie saw him constantly look from right to left as he surveyed the land he craved. "It's working, Papa; we have him plenty worried. If he weren't nervous, he wouldn't have come here to threaten us."

"How can a man look and sound so innocent and be so dang guilty!" Jed stormed. "No wonder they all believe him. He's like Lucifer, Jess; he can fool you if you aren't sharp-eyed and careful."

After Jed walked away, Mary Louise joined her thoughtful sister. "He's a real man, Jessica. How can you and Father suspect him of such wickedness? I was horribly embarrassed when Father was so rude to him."

"If you had to clean up after his evil deeds like we have, little sister, he wouldn't look so good to you!" she snapped. "I guess you realize now he lied about moving to Dallas!"

"What's biting your backside?" Mary Louise asked with a frown.

"Secretive men," Jessie replied, then hurried back to her chores.

*

Jessie told Navarro about their talk with Fletcher. "The liar!" she concluded.

"What if he *is* telling the truth, Jessie? What if somebody is trying to force out both of you? We don't have any proof it's him. He's only our best suspect."

Jessie stared at him. "Don't you start that nonsense, too. Mary Louise is convinced it isn't him. That smooth talker even has Papa questioning himself."

"The next time he comes around, I want to meet him and size him up. A man gives away a lot in his voice and gaze. Sometimes there are clues in his words if you listen close."

"That hasn't worked for me where you're concerned. But it has with Fletcher. I'm positive he's guilty, Navarro. I would never go against him if I weren't."

"I'll take your word and keep working on him for you."

Miguel called for Navarro to come give him a hand. Jessie watched her love walk away. She didn't know how long she could hold him here. He certainly did not intend to become a ranch hand. Her emotions were in a maelstrom. If they left Fletcher alone or only responded blow for blow, Navarro would have little but hard ranch work to occupy him. If they attacked continuously and won, Navarro would leave. Either way, she couldn't keep him very long.

*   *   *

Wednesday, things got worse. Scout and fifty steers were shot. "Scout was a trained longhorn who led our cattle to market," Jessie explained to Navarro. "He kept the herd calm, moving, and under control. He'll be a big loss. We'll have to get the others skinned. Some will have to be cut up and buried. We can't save this much meat or get it into town to sell."

"It's a good trail, Mr. Lane," Navarro told Jed. "I'll follow it while it's fresh. They didn't even try to conceal it. That's strange."

"I'll go with you," Jessie said.

Navarro shook his head. "You have too much work to do. I'll go alone."

"There could be trouble," she argued. "It might be an ambush. I'm—"

"All the more reason not to go, Jess," Jed interrupted.

"We can't let Navarro take such a risk for us, Papa."

"I'll be careful, Jessie."

*

Navarro reported back at dusk. "The trail led to Fletcher's land, but he had men riding fence so I had to turn back. By now they've destroyed it."

"I can't go blow for blow this time. I don't murder innocent critters to get even. We can't rustle his herd, either. That's too dangerous. Let me think a while."

*

Sheriff Toby Cooper arrived Thursday to question them about the windmills and fire. The lanky lawman looked distressed to be suspecting the Lanes.

"Where would we get dynamite?" Jed scoffed. "That's crazy! And we wouldn't start a fire, either. It could spread to my land. Ever seen a prairie fire? You can't stop one. I think Fletcher did those things so he could point a finger at me and away from himself. That rich bastard can afford to replace them all a thousand times without feeling a pinch in his pocket. If I wanted to hurt him, I'd shoot the bastard!"

"Don't do that, Jed, or I'll have to arrest you. I'm riding over there. I'll see what he has to say."

"Ask him about Scout and my steers!"

*

Cooper returned Friday afternoon. "All of his men swear they're innocent, Jed. I checked that trail you mentioned, but it headed south about a mile on his land, then vanished. Did your men happen to notice those horses weren't shoed?"

"They were shoed with iron, Sheriff," Navarro corrected. "I followed them to the boundary, but his men were all around so I had to turn back."

"Not what I saw. I think we got renegades in the area again."

"Somebody changed them to fool you. It's not Indians."

Toby Cooper eyed the stranger whose looks said he was part Indian. "That would be hard. I used to track for the cavalry. If anybody rubbed out the old tracks and made new ones, it didn't show. That takes real talent."

Navarro shrugged. "All I know is what I saw and trailed: shoe prints."

"We all saw them, Sheriff. They were shod horses. Did you check his barns for unbranded mounts?" Jessie inquired.

"Yep. None there. No strangers or extra men around. No wounded ones, either."

"Because he's hiding them somewhere. He's real smart, Sheriff."

"I don't know, Jed. A lawman can't follow a trail that isn't there. I'll be coming around more. I don't want you two killing off each other. Mind if I stay the night? It's late for striking out."

"You can bunk with the boys, and take supper with us in the house. We have to get back to work. Make yourself at home. Look around all you like."

*

Saturday, three men dug fresh pits in the spring-softened ground. Then others helped move the Lanes' and their hand's outhouses to new locations. The dirt was used to fill the old holes, and another task was completed.

For days, Mary Louise had been doing her chores and helping Gran in the garden without complaints, to everyone's surprise and pleasure. Yet Jessie couldn't forget her sister's hateful words several weeks ago.

Nothing terrible happened until Tuesday, six days after the cattle killings. It was dusk when billowing smoke was sighted and checked on by one of the hands riding range. Pete hurried to the house and rang the bell. "Fire! Fire in the hay shed!" he shouted as the clanking alarm sounded louder than his voice.

The men responded quickly. Barrels were loaded on rapidly hitched wagons, then filled from the well. The storage shed, where stock gathered in the winter to be fed, was three miles from the house. Last year's hay was dry, and it burned with ease and speed. The main concern was to contain the blaze. Everyone went to battle the fire except Gran, Tom, Mary Louise, and Jessie. The redhead stayed behind and inside the locked house to stand guard over the family with her Winchester. All peered out windows.

Jessica saw clouds of thick smoke rising and expanding against a darkening blue horizon. She knew the fire was a large one, but rolling hills obscured any sight of red flames. She frowned as the words "blow by blow" came to mind. This was twice Fletcher had used their strategy against them. She assumed it was only to terrorize them, since more hay could be grown this summer or purchased in town for any winter needs.

Agonized bawls and frightened "moo-ooo's" caught her ear. Her gaze darted to the barn that was slightly right to the front of their home. She knew her sister had milked the three cows, who stayed near the barn at night. Jessie sensed something was wrong. "Get my pistol and lock the door behind me," She told Gran. "I have to check on them. Don't come out for any reason."

"Don't go out there, child. The men are gone."

"Maybe they were lured away for a reason, Gran."

"That's why you shouldn't go out there alone."

"They could be firing the barn and bunkhouse, Gran. Or killing the bulls."

"What if lots of men are out there, Jessie?"

"I'll fire shots and scare them off, then ring the bell if we have trouble back here. Don't worry; I'll be careful. I'll sneak out the back way and work around."

Gran locked the door behind her. Jessie peered around the corner of the house. It was almost dark, and the waxing moon would give little light. The animal's cries compelled her forward. She made it to the bunkhouse without a problem and, hearing nothing inside, continued on to the chuckhouse. She eased around it and saw movement in the enclosed, small pasture where the milk cows stayed at night.

Jessie knew the dark shadow was not a Box L hand. Her squinted eyes searched for more movement, but could detect none. The cows had ropes around their necks that were tied to posts, holding them captive. One stamped and shifted and bawled. Another wriggled and cried out.

Jessie fired over the cow's backs several times. When she heard running in the other direction, she raced around the barn and past the smithy to cut off and hopefully capture one of Fletcher's men for the sheriff. But the villain had a head start and less obstacles than she did, and got away. He leapt on his horse behind a shed and galloped away. Jessie fired more shots at him, but despite her skill, he moved too fast and was too far away to wound or kill.

"Jessie!" Gran called from the front door. "You all right?"

"Fine, Gran! He's gone! I'll check on the cows!" She assumed the large bulls were safe. No shot had been fired from the man who surely couldn't get close enough to the powerful beasts to harm them in silence. She reached the crazed cows and tried to calm them as she did during her morning milking chore. The animals looked wild-eyed and they stomped their hooves and bawled. She couldn't see much in the darkness and through the fence.

Jessie propped her rifle against a post and fetched a lantern from the chuckhouse. She wriggled through the fence, then moved with caution closer to the nervous creatures. She held the lantern high to examine them, singing and talking softly. She fell silent. Her free hand clamped over her mouth, and she feared she would lose her supper. Disbelief and fury assailed her. With tears in her eyes and a lump in her throat, she checked all three cows. She couldn't help but sigh in relief that she had saved one from torment.

Gran and Tom headed to join her where a lantern revealed her location. "What is it?" they both kept asking the stunned girl.

"Go back!" she suddenly shouted, as if coming out of a trance.

"What's wrong?" they persisted, halting their steps.

"I . . . have to shoot two of them. Fletcher's bastard sliced off their teats! Get in the house. You don't need to see this. Hurry!" she ordered the shocked people who hadn't moved. She didn't want the cows to linger in agony.

On the way to the house, Gran rang the alarm bell that carried sound for miles. She hoped the men could hear it over the commotion of the fire and would respond quickly. She hurried Tom inside and closed the door.

Jessie took careful aim and shot the first cow, then the second. They hit the ground with heavy thuds. It was one of the hardest things she had ever done; the cows had almost been like pets. She calmed the last one and led it into the barn, confining it there. She cleaned the mess as best she could. Later, she wouldn't recall wiping blood on her clothes.

The dazed redhead called Ben and he came running to his mistress. She leapt on his back and galloped to the gate to the adjoining pasture. She bent over, unlatched it, flung it wide, and rode inside. She rounded up the protesting bulls and herded them close to the barn and house. She turned Ben loose nearby, then trudged to the dead bodies and bright lantern.

Riders came in, dismounted, and, sighting the lantern, hurried to her. Jessie didn't realize tears were slipping down her flushed cheeks.

Matt rushed to the woman he loved, scrutinizing her. "Are you hurt?" he asked. "There's blood on you, Jessie. What happened?"

She gazed into his concerned eyes and uttered in torment, "He cut off their teats, Matt; the bastard mutilated our milk cows. The fire was a trick to lure you men away. I had to shoot them. I got the bulls near the barn. They're safe."

Matt pulled Jessie's head against his chest as she wept. His hand behind it kept it there, as did his arm around her shoulder. "Don't cry, Jessie. It's over."

Jessie cried in his consoling embrace.

"I'm sorry, Jessie. We should have left guards here. We'll never leave you and the house unprotected again," he vowed, stroking her unbraided locks.

"Por Dios," Carlos murmured as he held up the lantern and the men examined the grim scene. "What devil would do such a thing? The man is *demente!"*

"Where is the third one?" Miguel asked, glancing around the area.

Jessie lifted her head, wiped at her eyes and cheeks, and replied, "In the barn. I heard the commotion and came to investigate."

"That was dangerous, *amiga."*

"I know, but something was wrong. I spooked him before he got to her, thank God. He got away. I wish I had killed him!"

"Don't worry, *chica,* we'll make him pay."

"How, Carlos? He's too clever and mean."

"We'll get him, Jessie," Navarro vowed from nearby. He wanted to hold her and comfort her as the foreman was doing, but he held his jealousy in check. "We won't be fooled again. I promise."

"Thanks, Navarro. Where are Papa and the others?" she asked, afraid to look at or move toward her love. She needed his embrace, but couldn't have it.

"They stayed behind to make sure all sparks were doused. I think he needed time to settle down. We heard the bell on our way in. We got here as fast as we could, but not quick enough," Matt told her.

"This was over when Gran rang the alarm."

The others arrived and the horrid tale was repeated. Jed stared at the dead animals. Despair flooded him, knowing it could just as easily be his family lying there instead of cows. This brutality knifed at his heart. "Maybe I should sell Fletcher some land with water, that section from his place to the Calamity, to stop this trouble. Less land is better than none."

"No, Papa! Navarro and I will stop him. You'll see."

"The trouble's gotten worse since Navarro came and we started fighting back. Tarnation, Jess, that could be you and Ma lying there!"

"But it isn't. He's running scared, Papa. We can't give up now. Not ever!"

"I'm the one scared, Jess, not Fletcher. It's real bad now. No man likes being broken, but I have to think of my family."

"He won't break us, Papa. We can't let him win. We won't be pushed out of our home and off our land. *Our* land, Papa. He has no right to it. We stand and win, or we stand and die as fighters. We're Lanes, and Lanes don't back down."

"She's right, Jed," Matt agreed, placing his arm across the back of her waist.

Navarro spoke up. "Even if he breaks you, sir, he won't be satisfied. You've resisted and attacked him. He'll probably take back his offer or lower it. He'll be expecting us to retaliate, so he'll have guards posted. We need to wait a while, then attack again."

"Every time we do, he does worse," Jed argued.

"If you back down now, sir, he'll win. Jessie's right; he's worried and desperate. He can't keep attacking forever. He knows we'll be on guard, too."

"I'll do it your way for a while, Jess. But if it gets worse, I'm making a deal with him so I can protect my family."

"He won't deal, Papa. He wants it all. If you suggest a deal, he'll know you're weakening. Then it *will* get worse, far worse. Are you ready and willing to give up everything we've built here to a man like him? Can you grovel before that bastard and ask him to take away your heart and soul, your life, Papa? Can you leave Mama, your two sons, your papa here with that filthy vermin? Can you let all the blood, sweat, tears, and hard work end this way? Can you, Papa? If so, tell me now. But I'll stand against him alone if you say yes. I won't let him get away with all he's done and take our land, too. I won't."

Jessie's words and intense emotions had the desired effect on Jed Lane. He hung his head in shame and dismay. "You're right, Jess. I'm not thinking clearly. I've never been a coward, until now. I just can't stand to lose any more of my family. We have to keep guards posted around here from now on. You go on into the house. Me and the boys will take care of this mess."

Jessie embraced her father. "You've never been a quitter, Papa. I knew you were only upset. I didn't mean to speak so rudely, but I had to clear your head. It will be hard to fight Fletcher, but we'll win; I know we will," she said with heartfelt confidence. "Don't get discouraged. Good night, Papa, boys, Matt, Navarro. I'll see you all in the morning. We can make decisions tomorrow when we're all rested." Jessie left.

As the men worked, Navarro contemplated what he had learned tonight. Jed was not as hard or cold as he had believed. Navarro knew the agony of being broken, and he had had only himself to consider and defend. He now knew how love could control a man's actions. Jessie had made him believe in himself, in the future, and in love. She had become his world, his soul, his golden dream. But she had entered his life when it was too late to save him. If only he could share everything with her. She was the proof love existed, that life was worth living.

Dare he, the fugitive wondered, stay and put a claim on her, then see if Jed would accept their decision? No, the law would never forget about his crimes. He had been sentenced to twenty years for a gold robbery and he had killed a man to escape what they called "justice," then robbed others to survive. What did it matter if he were innocent of the original charge? He was guilty of many others. If Fletcher discovered the truth about him, he could be used as a weapon against these good people. He had to take that risk for a while longer, as he couldn't leave them defenseless. He was ensnared in a bottomless trap and there was no way out for him, ever. And no matter what it took, he couldn't pull Jessie in with him to perish.

*

"Gran told me what happened," Mary Louise said. "I'm sure Wilbur wouldn't do such a horrible thing."

Jessie was exhausted and tense. "What did you do, complain to *Wilbur* about your chores so he lessened them by destroying our milk cows? Instead of siding with him, why don't you use your charms and talents to get him to stop attacking us?"

"Jessica Lane, that's mean and untrue!"

"Maybe so. I'm tired and upset. I'm going to bed. Don't jump on me tonight, little sister, because I'm not in the mood to be nice."

*

On Wednesday, Navarro suggested that he and Jessie sneak over to Fletcher's ranch to inflict damage there. "Fletcher thinks we'll be on alert and scared to strike at him again. But if I have him figured right, he'll have his men on patrol just in case he's mistaken. That means his settlement will be vulnerable. We can strike at his critters without harming them." He revealed his daring plan.

Jessie grinned. "You're so clever. We can't sit around waiting for him to hit us again. We won't tell Papa or the others so they won't try to stop us or worry. We'll sneak out after dark and slip over there."

She explained how.

*

Jessie and Navarro rode to the boundary between Lane and Fletcher land. He cut the top strand of barbwire so their horses could jump over without risking injury. Afterward, he tied a strip of rawhide to the sharp end and secured the gap so it wouldn't be noticed by anyone riding fence tonight. They made their way to the area where Fletcher had built his many structures. It was fortunate for them that their enemy had spaced their targets away from his home and bunkhouse. Too, there were trees to aid their secrecy.

The redhead and the desperado left their mounts a safe distance from the bunkhouse. With care, they sneaked to the first object of their mission. The pigs were rousted from sleep and urged toward the open gate, but their grunts weren't loud enough to endanger the couple. As if enjoying their freedom, the rotund creatures trotted off in several directions. By morning they would be scattered far and wide. The chickens weren't as cooperative; many clucked in panic at the intrusion. Navarro hurried them along by tossing a lantern into the roosting shed. The dry wood caught fire.

"Let's make tracks, woman," he ordered.

The couple rushed to the cover of the first tree, then slipped to the next and next until they were back to their horses. Commotion filled the area left behind. They mounted and walked their horses to prevent noisy galloping that would give away their location. Soon they picked up their pace and rode for home.

They didn't even make it to the cut fence before they heard riders coming. They halted and concealed themselves behind a group of trees. The men rushed past them, responding to the alarm bell that was ringing near Fletcher's home. When the men were out of sight, Jessie and Navarro returned to Lane land. With the barbwire he had dropped nearby, he rapidly repaired the damaged section, having learned how from Matt weeks ago.

They rode for thirty minutes before deciding it was safe to stop and talk.

"That was fun," Jessie remarked amidst laughter. "I can see his men trying to capture those hens and pigs. He'll be steaming like hot coffee."

"If we're lucky he'll pull men in to guard his house and barns tomorrow night. We'll cut a few fences and scatter his herd. I'm glad his ranch isn't as big as yours or there'd be too much land for us to cover. Fletcher should figure that we'll strike near his settlement again. He should think we'll believe that he expects us to hit a new target—his land—but we'll go after the same one again."

"What if he reasons like you, Navarro, and guards his fences and herds?"

"From what you've told me about him, he's too vain to think we're as clever as him. He doesn't realize how smart we are yet, but he'll figure it out soon. Right now, by trying to outwit us, he'll outwit himself."

"You're clever, Navarro. If you weren't here, I'd do exactly what he'd reason we'd do: hit the house again, expecting him to be on the range."

"That's why you hired me, so I'm only doing my job, Miss Lane." His tone altered as he remarked, "You were real upset last night. Are you all right now?"

"What he did to those cows threw me like a wild mustang. Killing is one thing, but mutilating is an atrocity beyond words. I needed you to hold me so badly."

"Matt did a good job of comforting you," he said before thinking.

"Jealous?" she teased, then reached over to caress his cheek.

"Yep," he admitted to her surprise, "but I have no right to be."

"You're right. You have no reason to be. Matt is like an older brother to me. He half raised me. We've been good friends for years. He's one of the nicest, most honest, and sincere people I know. He would do anything for a friend."

"I don't think he sees you as a little sister or only a close friend. I've watched him watching you, Jessie. Don't you realize he's in love with you?"

Jessie's eyes widened with surprise. "Mary Louise hinted at it several times, but I didn't believe her. I hope he's not, Navarro. I wouldn't want him hurt. He's never tried to romance me."

"A man doesn't go after what he doesn't think he can win, Jessie."

"Does that mean you knew I was leaning in your direction, cowpoke?"

"We both felt the pull between us. It was too strong to fight. If I hadn't gotten your signals, I wouldn't have made a move toward you."

"That's why I sent them, so you would have the courage to come after me."

"But I shouldn't have. A person shouldn't offer what he can't give."

"You've given everything you offered. You made certain I understood your position before I surrendered. You haven't misled me, Navarro. You've been clear and honest from the beginning. I appreciate and respect that."

Clear, but not totally honest, my love, his mind refuted, and guilt plagued him. "Only because a woman like you deserves to know where I stand."

"A woman like me only finds a man like you once in her life, Navarro. I wasn't about to lose what little time I could have with you."

"I wish it could be more, Jessie, honestly I do."

His tone and gaze touched her deep inside. "I know."

He pulled his eyes from her lovely face and said abruptly, "We have to get back. Fletcher's men might be on the move. We don't want to be discovered out here alone by either side. If we can't sneak back, what will you tell Jed?"

"The truth, that we outfoxed our enemy tonight. Since you'll be leaving when this is over, I don't think it's wise to tell Papa—or anyone—about us."

"I hate to make you be deceitful for me."

"People do what they have to do, Navarro. Right now you're more important to me than being fully honest with my father and family. It's strange, but I don't feel very guilty about it. Does that change your high opinion of me?"

"Nothing could ever change my high opinion of you, Jessica Lane. You don't know what you've given me and brought into my life."

"I know what you've done for me. Do I get a kiss before we leave?"

Navarro lifted her from her horse and placed her across his legs. He caressed her face, then hugged her with longing. His mouth covered hers.

For several minutes they kissed, caressed, and embraced. Bittersweet feelings surged through them. Their bond was powerful; their future was impossible. He knew it, and she suspected it. Yet they couldn't resist each other for as long as fate allowed them to remain together.

Navarro replaced her on her horse, then smiled sadly at the woman who had stolen his heart, who offered a beautiful dream that he could never capture. "Let's go before we get into more trouble."

At the ranch, the fugitive felt Mathew Cordell's gaze on him from the foreman's private room at the end of the bunkhouse. None of the other men along the two rows of bunks moved or spoke, and the desperado knew he hadn't disturbed any of them with his comings and goings. He was glad Matt didn't come out and question his behavior, but he would tell him of this night's work tomorrow to prevent trouble and suspicion, just as Jessie would tell her father. No doubt, Jed would be upset.

*

At first, Jed was angry, then he calmed himself. He was proud of his daughter's courage and wits. Yet he didn't like the time she was spending alone with the gunslinging drifter. He recalled what Roy had said about a spy, but he reasoned it couldn't be Navarro Jones. Surely no hireling of Fletcher's would destroy his boss's property, even if the villain could easily replace it. Still, that was a good way to win their trust . . .

When Jed mentioned that fear to Jessie, she gaped at him in disbelief and disappointment. "Surely you don't think such a terrible thing, Papa. Look how he's helped us. Besides, I found him and hired him in San Angelo. We met by accident, and he didn't know who I was."

"What if he was trailing you and watching you all along, Jess? What if that's why he stepped in and rescued you. To win your confidence."

"You're wrong, Papa. Navarro is a good man—different, but good and kind. Please don't mention your doubts to him or the boys. If they started treating him strangely, he could leave before he helps us finish this job. We need him, Papa."

"Promise me you'll be very careful around him. He worries me, and Matt, too."

Jessie knew why both men were concerned about her friendship with the handsome stranger. She cautioned herself to keep their relationship a secret. It wouldn't do for either Matt or Jed to guess the truth. Her respectable father would insist they wed, and a bitter confrontation would ruin everything. Another woman might force the issue with hopes it would be resolved in her favor. But Jessie had been around men long enough to learn you never backed one into a corner. If Navarro stayed or returned, it had to be his decision. "I know what I'm doing, Papa. Don't worry. I'll be on guard."

*

That night, to dispel Jed and Matt's suspicions, Navarro took Carlos and Miguel along with Jessie and him. The four cut fences along Fletcher's southern boundary and stampeded cattle from the man's property. Navarro had guessed right: Fletcher had his settlement guarded heavily, and no one was on the range to halt their actions.

*

On Friday, Jessie, Tom, and two hands went to the town of Fort Davis to purchase more barbwire and search for another milk cow. One wasn't enough to supply the Box L with milk and butter.

The group was almost home on Saturday when they were attacked by two men. They were going slow up a steep grade when shots rang out from behind rocks. Jessie saw Smokey fall off the seat to the ground and lie still. Pete fell back into the wagon where she and Tom were sitting, a bullet wound to his shoulder. The laboring horses stopped when the reins went slack, as did the cow tied behind the wagon.

Jessie grabbed her rifle, but no more shots were heard. She knew the general area from which the others had come, and she watched it closely for signs of movement. Navarro and Matt prodded their horses past them and toward the gunmen's location. While they waited, Jessie checked on Pete and kept Tom down. The cunning Navarro had been prepared for this, as he and Matt had been trailing them the entire time. But the assault had come too quickly to prevent Smokey from being killed and Pete from being wounded.

Matt joined them and said, "I'll get you home. Navarro's gone after them."

"Alone?" Jessie asked, looking frightened. "I'll take your horse and—"

"No, Jessie. He can handle two men. You work on Pete in the wagon while I drive home. If more men are lying in wait ahead, I'll need your guns."

"You're right, Matt." While the foreman recovered Smokey's body and tied it to his horse, Jessie tore Pete's shirt and bound his wound as best she could to staunch the bleeding. But her mind was riding with her love on the vengeance trail.

At the ranch, Hank removed the bullet and bandaged Pete's shoulder. Smokey was buried in a short ceremony. That left them with twelve hands, and one of those wouldn't be able to work for weeks.

When Navarro returned later, he reported that he had slain the two men who had attacked them. "I cut Fletcher's north fence, sent the horses galloping home with their bodies tied to their saddles, and rode here. I figured, since the horses were unbranded, it wasn't much good to save them for the sheriff. He couldn't prove they were Fletcher's men, but your enemy will get our message."

"Fletcher and his boys would only say they didn't know them," Jessie said.

"No way to tie them to Fletcher, sir. I figured it would be better to let him know that if he attacks us, we'll attack them. If some of his boys start getting killed, maybe it'll worry the others. So far, they've been safe from harm. It's time they learn it's dangerous to work for Fletcher."

"I hate killing, Navarro, but you did right. Leastwise, we know they were guilty and deserved to die. We got Smokey buried, and Pete will be healed in a few weeks. I'm glad you and Matt trailed my daughter and son. If not for that, they could be dead now, too."

"I don't think Fletcher will hurt your family, sir. He's trying to scare off your hands. He expects that to change your mind."

"Jessie's convinced me we have to keep fighting and holding on. Actions like these only tell me she's right. I'm sure that snake would double cross me if I said I'd take his last offer. He can't be trusted."

"At least Fletcher's out four men, sir—the two we killed in that trap and these two today. We're lucky we've only lost one to death and one to fear. I'll try to make sure you don't lose any more, Mr. Lane."

"Thanks, Navarro. Roy said he'd send a letter when he reached San Antonio. I can't blame him for leaving; his hand might never heal right. It ain't his land to fight and die over. Maybe when he's safe, he'll send evidence back to the sheriff about what really happened that night."

"Don't count on it, Papa; he was scared." Jessie sighed. "Smokey has a sister in Brownwood; we should write to her about his death and send her his belongings."

"Will you do it for me, Jess?" Jed asked wearily.

"Sure, Papa, tonight," she replied gently. As everyone was parting, she sent Navarro a smile that said, I'm glad you're back safe.

*

The month of April ended with a party to celebrate the completion of spring branding and no trouble from Fletcher for two weeks. During their respite, the hands and family had worked hard and fast catching up with chores with everyone doing more than his or her share. The cows and calves were back to grazing on the range, the garden was growing, and a big crop was anticipated. Soon fresh vegetables would replace canned and dried ones.

The part for the well had arrived, and Big John had repaired the pump to the house. Pete's shoulder had almost healed, and he was back doing light chores. The level of anger and frustration on the Box L had subsided during this peaceful reprieve.

After quitting time each day, Navarro had worked with the hands to teach them tricks to use during fistfights, how to shoot better, and how to set ambushes. Tom had followed him around and devoured every word and action. But Jessie feared her love was preparing the men for his departure.

When the hands played a practical joke on Navarro, it revealed to her how they felt about him. From what Jessie could see, Navarro appeared happy and relaxed at the ranch. She had seen him laughing and joking with the men. He had spent six weeks on their land—seven including the time alone with her—and Jessie wondered how much longer he could be persuaded to stay.

As Jessie chatted with Navarro at the party, she said, "I'm relieved the boys' joke didn't upset you. It shows how much they accept you. I'm glad you've earned their respect and friendship. You deserve them, Navarro. You've worked hard for us and taken risks beyond what we're paying you for."

"It's a good thing you told me beforehand about their tricks. I would have thought they were making a fool of me and trying to get rid of me." He nodded a greeting to Miguel, then continued. "Whew, that was the hottest chili I've had! When they all kept eating, I didn't want to hurt Hank's feelings. It took a bucket of water to cool my mouth and throat. My belly burned for hours."

Miguel had approached the two in the middle of Navarro's accounting of the story, decked in Mexican finery again this evening. "We didn't expect it to take so long for you to catch on to us, *amigo*. I was about to warn you when I saw smoke coming out your nose and ears, and your eyes were watering. You'll get used to us. We're good *hombres.*"

"Yes, you are," Jessie agreed with a bright smile.

"Me and Carlos want to know if you will teach us to use the bow and knife as you have taught Jessie and Tom."

"Sure, Miguel. I thought we might need silent weapons when Fletcher goes on the warpath again. One job I had in Arizona called for silence, and I used them then," he remarked, then wished he hadn't made that slip. "Since you two are Mexican and have had trouble in the past with Apaches, I wasn't sure if you'd want to work with Indian weapons."

"We have no problem with using them, *amigo.*"

Mary Louise had joined them, too. "Would you like to dance, Navarro?" she asked. "The men are making merry music. There's no need to waste it."

Navarro looked uncomfortable at the invitation and the girl's sensual smile. "Sorry, Miss Lane, but I don't dance, never have."

The blonde grasped his muscled arm and tugged on it encouragingly. "I'll be delighted to teach you. It's very easy and lots of fun."

"He said no, Mary Louise," Jessie told her sister, "so don't pull at him. Miguel loves to kick up his heels, so ask *him.*"

Miguel placed his hand on his hip and cocked his elbow at the blonde as he said, "I would be honored to share a dance with you, my lovely señorita."

Jessie saw the girl's look which said, 'My superior manners prevent me from refusing before others.' She watched her sister rest her fingers on the Mexican's arm and walk away with him.

Gran took Miguel's and Mary Louise's place with them. "You two having fun?"

"It's wonderful, Gran. You cooked so much delicious food. The boys are really enjoying themselves." They were eating barbecued beef, dried peas, roasted corn canned from last year's crop, and a mixture of tomatoes with okra. Jed was even serving a little wine and whiskey.

"The men deserve a treat, Jessie. They've worked so hard. Why aren't you dancing?"

"Navarro doesn't dance, Gran."

"Then I'll keep him company while you toss up your skirts. I know how much you like to dance, child. Go on," the older woman urged.

Jessie felt she had to go dance or her grandmother would wonder why she didn't. She excused herself from Navarro, approached the others, and asked Jimmy Joe to be her partner. The sandy-haired twenty-year-old was delighted. Afterward, friend after friend—Matt twice—claimed her hand for the next dances.

As they observed the merriment, the white-haired woman remarked to Navarro, "She's a fine girl."

"Yes, ma'am, she is," he concurred as he watched her do the Texas two step.

"I don't know what we'd do without her if she ever left."

"Why should Jessie ever leave home, Mrs. Lane?" he asked, pretending not to understand what the older woman was hinting at.

"Jessie's twenty-four. Women her age often take off to build their own homes. My son depends on her so much; we all do. Jessie's our strength and pride."

"From what I've seen, she doesn't have a sweetheart, so I wouldn't worry."

"How much longer will you be with us, Navarro?"

"Until this trouble is settled. If it doesn't take too much longer, that is. I get restless when I corral my horse and body in the same place for more than a few weeks. I like to keep on the move. When I accepted Jessie's offer, I didn't think it would take so long to help her win."

"You think Fletcher has given up his fight? You've dealt him some hard blows, and he's been quiet for two weeks."

"He's just biding his time and waiting for us to relax and drop our guard, ma'am. He hasn't backed down for good. A man like him don't give up his dream."

"Very few people do, Navarro, until they realize it's futile."

They chatted about ranching, breeding, branding, and the hands for a while, as Navarro continued to keep an eye on Jessie.

Jessie noticed Navarro was looking tense. She went to him and grasped his hand. Laughing, she said, "It's time you learned to dance, Mr. Jones." She practically dragged him away from her grandmother to the dance area where Mary Louise was moving around the circle with Carlos, and hands were partnered up with each other. All were laughing and talking—having fun.

Before they reached the group, Jessie whispered, "Sorry, but it's the only way I could rescue you, and I need to touch you or scream. I'm much too bold for my own good at times, but you're too handsome to resist."

"I can't dance, Jessie. I'll look stupid and embarrass both of us."

"Just watch what I do. Stand beside me," she instructed, and placed him to her left. She laid her open hand on her right shoulder and said, "Take my right hand in yours," which he did. She extended her left before his waist and said, "Grab this one, too," which he also did. "Now we step with our right foot, then flick our left foot toward our right knee like this," she said, and demonstrated the movements. "Three times. Pause. Repeat. Move with the music. Now, step, step, and switch sides." She continued the lesson, moving to his left. "Step, step, and switch back. Then, go again. That's all there is to it. Over and over. By the time the dance ends, you'll have it down for the next time. That's right," she encouraged. "You learn fast, Mr. Jones."

Navarro was stiff and reluctant at first, but he obeyed because it felt so good to hold her hands and touch her body. Each time she passed before him, her fragrance— the same one she had dotted on his bandanna during the coyote incident—teased his senses. Her flaming tresses played against his chest and sometimes tickled his chin. Her laughter warmed his ears, and her smile enflamed his heart. Her hands were calloused from hard work like a man's, but she was as gentle and refined as any woman could be. She could help any man become the best that was in him to be, including him if she was given the chance. He always felt so good, so special, so worthwhile around her. Soon, he was thinking about Jessie so much that he was dancing without difficulty. He was even dipping and swaying at the right times. "I felt foolish at first, but it isn't so bad," he finally admitted.

Jessie glanced up at him with a radiant smile. "You should try new things every so often so you won't miss so much fun in life."

He murmured near her ear, "New things are only fun if I do them with you, Jessie. You make me feel brave and daring. And you don't make me feel silly."

"That's why you should stick around me for keeps. We'd have a wonderful life together. I know there's plenty you can teach me. It's more fun learning with someone you . . . Sorry," she murmured when he tensed and faltered. "It slipped out. I won't say any more."

The music halted and Jed announced, "I'm afraid that's all, boys. It's late."

Jessie was bubbling with happiness and energy with Navarro beside her. "We were just getting started, Papa. Just a few more. Please," she coaxed.

"We begin a new week tomorrow, Jess. We all need our rest."

"But we've worked so hard lately. This is our first party in ages."

In a gentle voice, he urged, "No more arguing for tonight, and we'll have a bigger party after we defeat Fletcher. Is that a bargain?"

Jessie decided her father was nervous about her being so close to Navarro and was halting the evening's festivities to end their contact. "All right, Papa," she said obediently and smiled at him.

As Mary Louise passed Navarro, she murmured, "I thought you didn't dance."

"Jessie's stubborn," Navarro answered. "She wouldn't let me say no about learning."

In a seductive tone, she replied, "Next time, I'll be as persistent as my older sister." With a swish of her full skirt, she pranced toward the house.

"Mary Louise!" Jed called. "Help Ma and Jess with the cleanup back here."

The blonde turned and smiled. "Sorry, Father. I'm coming."

As the girl and Jed carried things into the kitchen, Mary Louise remarked, "I'm surprised that drifter has stayed around so long, Father. He seems to forget his place at times. Men like that think they can latch on to a wealthy lady and raise their stations in life. I don't like him being so friendly with me and Jessica. After all, he isn't one of the regular ranch hands. I hope Jessica isn't becoming too fond of him. He seems so rough and secretive, don't you think?"

Jed gave her a hard look. "What do you mean, girl?"

"Oh, Father," she murmured. "You know how Jessica is. She's so kind-hearted. I fear she doesn't see the danger in such men. She always wants to help everyone improve. I hope such goodness and generosity don't get her into trouble with Navarro Jones. There's something so very strange and frightening about him. I know you all like him, but I fear I don't trust him. He makes me nervous the way he watches me and Jessica."

"Should I say something to him?"

"Oh, no, Father. He would deny he meant anything bad, and perhaps he doesn't. I don't want to cause more trouble. I've been so bad of late, and I'm really trying to change. It's just that my life here is so different from what I was accustomed to back East. I realize I've been petulant and selfish. I'm sorry for giving you a bad time. I'll try to do better; you'll see."

Martha Lane overheard them and wondered what her youngest granddaughter was up to with her pretty lies, but she kept the curious conversation to herself.

*

Wilbur Fletcher visited them again Sunday afternoon. This time, he stood on the porch chatting with Mary Louise while Gran fetched Jessie and Jed. When the two arrived, both frowning, he said, "I thought you would want to know that two dead men were left on my property recently. I turned the bodies over to the sheriff so he can try to discover who they are. Do you know anything about them, Jed? They were put through a cut in my north fence."

"We haven't seen any strangers around here since your man butchered my milk cows and set fire to my hay shed."

"Is that why you had your men release my chickens and hogs and fire my coop? This retaliation for things I haven't done is old, Jed, old and tiring. If we work together, we might solve this mystery and put an end to our troubles."

"How would we do that, Fletcher?" Jed asked in a sarcastic tone.

"Join our men into small groups and let them ride both ranges. That way, you and I will know for certain the other isn't behind anything that happens."

"Get my men separate and alone so you can kill them or try to scare them off like you did to Roy, Smokey, Davy, and Pete?" he scoffed.

"If you've lost four men, I'm sorry. It sounds as if you can use my help."

"You haven't lost any hands to accidents like I have?" Jed hinted for a slip.

"No, I still have all twenty-five, strong and healthy."

"Why do you need so many hands for such a small spread?" Jessie asked, aware Navarro was standing nearby sizing up the enemy.

"So I'll be well protected during times of trouble, Miss Jessie, and so I'll be covered if no seasonal help comes around—like this year."

"Yeah, that was strange, wasn't it?" Jed said in the same accusatory tone.

"If you'd bothered to check around as I did, Jed, you'd have learned all of the ranchers in our area had the same problem. Perhaps this section is too hard to reach for them to keep heading our way each spring and fall."

"Covering your tracks in every direction, aren't you?"

"You're a stubborn and foolish man, Jed. I didn't prevent any wranglers from coming here, and I haven't harmed any of your men or animals. When are you going to see the truth and accept it?"

"I already have, Fletcher. You won't win. I'll fight as long as you do."

Wilbur shook his brown head and scowled. "But I'm not fighting you, Jed, not yet."

"We've had enough of your lies," Jessie said angrily. "You'll make a slip soon and we'll catch it. You're going to pay for all the evil you've done to us. I swear it."

Fletcher eyed her intently, then frowned. "I hope you aren't the one putting these crazy ideas into your father's head, Miss Jessie. I wouldn't want you to be responsible for getting innocent people hurt or even killed."

"The only crazy person around here is you, Mr. Fletcher. Papa doesn't need me to point out the truth to him. But I would fight you even if he yielded, which he won't. This is Lane land, and it will remain Lane land until we all die."

"I beg you, Miss Jessie, don't encourage his misconceptions. I'm innocent. Someday I'll expect apologies from both of you. Good-bye."

Jessie watched their enemy climb into his buggy. Another man was waiting for him, a well-dressed gentleman who had a pad on his knees and was writing or sketching upon it. She wondered who the stranger was. She didn't like the way he kept glancing at Navarro as he worked.

After Fletcher left, Mary Louise remarked, "He certainly knows how to control his temper, doesn't he? I'm certain he was furious inside. What do you think he'll do?" she asked them.

"I can't imagine. Nothing seems too brutal and daring for him."

"Father, if you believe he's truly that dangerous, why are you resisting his offer? What if he kills us all to get what you think he wants?"

"That's a risk we have to take, girl. This is our home. We can't give up."

*

Monday morning, May first, Jed and Matt left for Fort Stockton for a few days to set up cattle and horse sales for the fall roundup. Jed left Jessie in charge of the ranch, but asked her to avoid as much trouble as possible until their return.

While they were away, Jessie couldn't seem to get a few minutes alone with Navarro because someone always interrupted them. She began to feel as if her father had left orders to keep them apart! Then she scolded herself for being so suspicious of everyone.

She returned to Tom's daily lessons, but it seemed difficult for him to concentrate. He wanted to finish quickly so he could join Navarro and the hands, as he was allowed to ride with them on many occasions. The clever moccasin that Navarro had made for Tom gave him confidence and a more level walk, and Navarro had fixed the boy's left stirrup so his bad foot wouldn't slip through it. Tom also tied his glasses in place every day as Navarro had shown him weeks ago. The youth had come to think of Jessie and Navarro as his best friends, and that pleased her. Yet she worried about how Tom would react when Navarro had to go.

On Wednesday, Jessie had a quarrel with her sister. Mary Louise accused her and Navarro of creating more trouble and danger than they prevented.

"If you two hadn't done all those terrible things to Mr. Fletcher, he wouldn't be so mad at us. You have no proof he's to blame, Jessica. Have you ever considered you and Father might be wrong? What if he is innocent?"

"He isn't."

"How do you know?" the blonde persisted.

"I know."

"How? Wanting to buy our ranch just isn't convincing enough."

"It is for us."

"Why?"

Jessie glared at her sister. "Darn it, Mary Louise! It's just a feeling. By now we've all learned to trust our instincts."

Mary Louise moved before her again when she turned away. "Feelings and instincts can be wrong. What if you're battling the wrong enemy?"

Jessie tossed aside the laundry she was folding. "We aren't."

"Prove it to me. Show me any shred of evidence, any clue," she challenged.

The redhead picked up a shirt again. "I can't. He's too clever."

"Or he's innocent."

*

Thursday, her father and the foreman returned with shocking news. Jessie was furious when she heard what had happened.

"Not one contract, Papa? He blocked all sales? How can he do that?"

"He undercut every price I made, Jess. Read the telegrams for yourself. I can't sell for the same or less than the deal he's offering them. That would be giving away my steers. We'll have to wait until fall, herd them to market and hope for the best."

"But he doesn't have that many mature steers, Papa. How can he fill those contracts?" she asked in confusion and dismay.

"It's my guess he's buying out some of the other ranchers. He's paying top dollar and keeping them from having to make the cattle drive. He can afford to do that, Jess, but we can't. What's worse is if he stops us from getting to market on time or floods it before we get there. I don't know what to do," he admitted.

"Go to the Cattleman's Association, Papa."

"I wired them, Jess. He's already taken that precaution. He's made charges against us that have to be investigated and cleared before I can join and get their help. They won't meet again until after fall roundup; that's too late to do us any good. We'll need money by fall, Jess, and I'm doubtful I can raise it."

"The bank will see us through, Papa. We have good collateral."

"I'm afraid not, Jess. I already tried them. Fletcher has big deposits in both banks. He's threatened to withdraw and get his friends to do the same if they loan us money. That snake has thought of everything!"

"He can't do that, Papa! Surely it can't be legal."

"He has done it, Jess. He has blocked every path."

"Then we'll find a new one."

"I hope so. We have plenty of everything but cash and credit. We can't make it without one or the other. Fletcher was in town, watching and gloating."

"He was there?"

"Yep, like he knew I would be. Maybe we do have a traitor here."

That remark surprised her. "I doubt it, but I'll ask Navarro if any of the men acted strange or vanished for a while."

"Don't ask him, Jessie; ask Miguel."

"Navarro can be trusted, Papa; I'd stake my life on it."

"We have, Jess, many times."

"And we haven't been wrong."

"He's been getting us to attack Fletcher, not just defend ourselves. What if Fletcher's trick to win is using our retaliation to get us into trouble with the law? Navarro could make sure we're trapped and exposed one night. When he was over here, Fletcher said we'd defeat ourselves. Maybe that was a slip."

"He could hurt us only if he works for Fletcher, Papa, and he doesn't!"

"You've become mighty defensive of him, Jess. You spend more time with him than with your old friends here. Are you letting that drifter charm you?"

"Papa! I'm not a foolish young girl."

"No, you're quite a beautiful woman, Jessica."

He so rarely called her by her full name, Jessie almost shot back, *So, you've finally noticed I'm not a son!* She calmed herself and said, "If you're worried about my friendship with Navarro, don't be. He's leaving when this is over."

"Are you sure?" he asked, sounding hopeful.

"Positive, Papa. He's been very clear about it from the start. He only agreed to work for us for a while. It's taking longer than he planned, but I convinced him to stay on until the conflict is resolved. The only reason he's remained is because everyone's been so nice to him. If you and Matt start throwing around doubts about him, I'm sure he'll pull out. You know how much help he's been. We need him. With the branding over, we can concentrate more on Fletcher."

From the corner of her eye, Jessie saw Mary Louise standing in the doorway to their bedroom. A curious chill passed over her. She shrugged and dismissed it, then returned to her talk with her father.

*

On Saturday, Mary Louise caught Navarro in the barn alone. "We have to talk," she told him. "Something terrible has happened. Father will be furious about what I'm planning to do. He talked to Jessica last night about you. I think it's big trouble. We can't talk here. Don't let anyone see you, but follow me after I leave." She took a horse and headed away from the corral.

Navarro was intrigued and worried. He couldn't march to the house and ask to see Jessie alone, not with Jed there. He slipped away. When he caught up with Mary Louise, he dismounted and joined her. "What's wrong with Jessie?"

"She's standing between us," came the shocking reply.

"What?" he asked, looking and feeling baffled.

"You don't notice me with her around. Ever since I came home and met you, my head's been spinning. I become hot and weak all over when I'm near you. I want you, Navarro. I know it's bold and wicked, but I do." She fondled his chest as she entreated, "Kiss me before I die of hunger."

Navarro grasped her hands and tried to push her away. "No, Miss Lane. I—"

"Yes, Navarro," she persisted as she rubbed herself against him.

When she tried to pull down his head to kiss him, he scolded, "Behave, girl, or your father will whip both of us. I thought you said—"

"Not if he doesn't know about us. I won't tell. If he finds out and intrudes, something could happen to him." She sent him a sultry smile. "If you get rid of Father, Jessica will have to sell out and split the money with me. It'll give us plenty to start a new life together somewhere. If Jessica refuses, you can take care of her, too. Please, Navarro, my love, let's run away together."

The desperado was stunned. All he wanted to do was put distance between himself and this greedy creature. "Get mounted, girl. This isn't a game."

"Far from it, my handsome drifter. This is your chance to win both me and plenty of money. I'm yours for the taking. All we need is money to make our dream come true. You can blame Mr. Fletcher for Father's death."

The fugitive gaped at the blonde. "Either you don't know what you're saying, or this is a trick or a cruel joke. I don't want to take you, Miss Lane, or hurt Jed. Forget this happened. Let's go."

Mary Louise grabbed his shirt and yanked on it, causing it to rip. "I'm more beautiful and desirable than my spinster sister! I'm offering you two treasures. I'm more of a woman than she'll ever be. We're rebels at heart, Navarro; we're perfectly suited to each other. We can escape together."

Navarro couldn't believe he hadn't seen this coming. Mary Louise must have been planning this for days. "No, we aren't matched at all, Miss Lane. You shouldn't behave this way."

"We *are* alike," she argued, pouting and glaring.

"No," he stated in a firm tone to discourage her.

As Mary Louise shrieked, "Yes, we are, damn you!," she scratched his cheek.

Navarro backed away and stared at the raging beauty with the flashing blue eyes. She was nothing like her older sister, nothing. He rubbed his stinging cheek and saw blood on his fingers. "Why did you do that?" he demanded.

Mary Louise settled down and frowned. "I lost my temper. I'm sorry," she murmured as she lowered her head. "It's just that I've been craving you so long and so much that it's driving me crazy. Are you sure you don't want me, Navarro?"

He tried to be kind and polite as Jessie had taught him. "I'm sorry, but no."

Mary Louise waited a moment, then said, "A woman can't force a man to desire her. I was certain you'd feel the same way I do. I was mistaken. Give me a minute to calm myself, then we'll head home. I won't trouble you again. About Father and Jessica, I was only testing your loyalty and honor. I don't want them hurt."

Navarro watched the girl retreat behind a row of bushes. He wiped his injured cheek, and wondered how to explain it to everyone. He couldn't tell Jessie or Jed or the others what the girl had offered; it was too cruel, too shocking. He straightened his shirt, noticing several buttons were missing. He wondered if he should escort Mary Louise home or just leave her there. As he paced and waited, he heard a curious sound, like another rip, then a harsh slap!

Mary Louise returned with mussed hair, ripped and dirty dress, and scratches on her neck. She muttered peevishly, "I'm so clumsy today. I fell and made a mess of myself. My dress is ruined." The blonde mounted her pinto, grabbed the sorrel's reins, and raced from the scene with both horses.

Navarro was taken off guard and she was already too distant to halt her. He was befuddled and vexed. *What in . . .* Dread filled the wide-eyed man and stiffened his tall frame. His heart pounded. He ran after the vindictive girl who had taken his mount. He suspected she would drop its reins soon, if he was right about what she intended to do. He was; he found the animal grazing over the next hill. Winded from his run, he leapt on his sorrel and raced after Mary Louise. He couldn't overtake her in time.

As she neared the barn, the blonde screamed for help. Men came running to her aid. She fell off the horse into Matt's arms, sobbing and looking terrified. "Don't let him near me!" she shrieked and clutched at Matt as Navarro approached. "He tried to attack me! Navarro ambushed me and tried to rape me," she accused, then snuggled her face against the foreman's protective shoulder.

Chapter

❧❧

12

Mathew Cordell's astonished gaze locked on Navarro's angry expression. The foreman saw his torn shirt and bleeding scratches. Matt looked at Mary Louise's disheveled injured condition. He was perplexed and disappointed, as were the other hands.

"You've been one of us for months, Navarro," Matt said. "I can't believe you would do something terrible like this."

"I didn't, Matt; *she* did. Miss Lane asked me to escort her riding. When we halted, she got too friendly. I tried to discourage her, but she went wild and attacked me. Then she messed herself up like that and hightailed for home to get me into trouble. She even ran my horse over a mile so I couldn't stop her. I never touched her."

Jed and Jessie arrived during Navarro's denial and shocking accusation. The hands —who had been around the "drifter" for only seven weeks, but around their boss's daughter for years—didn't know what to say or believe. They knew the girl was defiant and unhappy, but they couldn't imagine anyone lying about such a serious thing. Jessie was stunned speechless for a time, fearing the outcome of what she was certain was her sister's spiteful mischief.

"That's a lie, you heartless beast!" Mary Louise raged. "You trailed me and waylaid me. I would never entice a saddletramp like you! Surely you don't expect everyone to believe I injured myself. Look at us; we're both wearing the evidence of your guilt."

Navarro's gaze narrowed and hardened at the destructive and wicked girl. "You know I never tried to—"

"Hush, both of you!" Jed stormed. "Girl, tell me what happened."

Mary Louise dabbed at fake tears. She repeated her wild tale. "I'm sorry, Father. He caught up with me and wanted to talk. I didn't realize he could be this dangerous. I know I've been terrible lately, but I'm not to blame for this trouble. Honestly I'm not," she vowed, her blue gaze widening in an attempt to appear truthful. "You know I've never liked or trusted him, so why would I entice him?"

Jed glared at Mary Louise who looked so like his dead Alice at that moment, then at Navarro, who was a threat to his family. "What did you do to her?" he asked. "I never expected something like this from you."

"I swear I didn't harm her, sir."

"Then how do you explain all this?" Jed argued, pointing to the "evidence."

Navarro related his side of the story, except for the blonde's idea about killing Jed and Jessie. He knew they would never believe that evil part, and it would cause them to doubt his other words. He finished with, "When she took off like this, I guessed what she had in mind. I raced after her to reason with her—"

"He's lying, Father! He—"

Irate, Jed thundered, "Silence, girl! Let me handle this. This is crazy, Navarro. Why would Mary Louise hurt herself to frame you?"

"I don't know, sir, but I'm innocent." Those words echoed through the fugitive's mind from a day long past when he had used them after being accused and arrested for that gold robbery. No one had believed him then, and he had been brutally and unjustly punished; he could tell that was going to happen again today. If not for Jessie and the changes she had wrought in him, he would curse them and leave without another word! "I'm innocent," he repeated, but knew it was futile. Fury and bitterness flooded him as he watched and listened.

Jed waved everyone to silence as he considered this matter. He had seen his oldest and favorite daughter, his helpmate, responding more and more to this drifter every day. There was no way he could allow Jessie to get tangled up with a saddlebum like Navarro Jones. This was the perfect excuse to get rid of him before the gunslinger won Jessie's heart. Jed knew how much he loved and needed Jessie, how much his mother and son needed her. "I've heard enough of this sorry affair. I have to fire you, Navarro. You can't stay. In addition to this new trouble, for all I know, you could be on Fletcher's payroll. Roy said we have a spy in our midst; that could be you."

Navarro was incensed. "That isn't true, sir. I'm loyal to the Lanes."

"I don't know what really happened out there. You've been a big help to us, but I have to let you go to keep peace around here."

"What about Fletcher, Mr. Lane?"

"We'll take care of him."

"Can you do it alone, sir? What about your family? They're in danger. I wouldn't touch your daughter; I swear it. Tell them the truth, Miss Lane."

"I did," the blonde vowed.

Jed exhaled loudly. "Even if it was a misunderstanding or a rash mistake, it's best for you to leave, Navarro. I can't take your side against my own daughter. I have enough trouble without adding you and her to it. Get packed and ride out."

"No, Papa!" Jessie shouted. "I know Navarro and he wouldn't do anything like this. It's Mary Louise's fault; punish her, but not him. We need Navarro, Papa."

"Are you calling me—your own sister—a liar?" Mary Louise shrieked.

Jessie glared at the devious girl. "I'm saying you're wrong, that's all."

"If you—"

"Silence, girl," Jed ordered a second time to prevent a hateful reply before the others. "Leave, Navarro, before there's more trouble. Be glad I have doubts about what happened and gratitude for all you've done or I would have the boys tie you to the corral so I could whip you good to defend my daughter's honor. Get riding, son, before I change my mind," he warned.

At that familiar threat, rage filled the desperado's mind, and it stiffened his body. It glittered ominously in his brownish-green eyes and tightened his jawline. *Framed again!* He was tempted to reveal how much the girl hated Jed and Jessie, but those incredible words would cause a fight for certain, and he couldn't lick this many men at the same time. No man, he vowed, would ever lash him again! Besides, Mary Louise was to blame, not the others, so why hurt them? He was fired, he told himself, so he had no choice but to leave.

All his life he'd been used, betrayed, and then discarded. Yet, after all this time here, he had thought these people were different. Only his sweet and brave Jessie believed him and had stood up for him. Yet, he admitted, he couldn't expect the other hired hands to go against their boss and friend for someone who was almost a stranger. His only regrets were how this would hurt Jessie and Tom. He dared not look at his love. "I'm innocent; one day, you'll learn that the hard way, sir." He stalked to the bunkhouse to pack, telling himself he should be grateful for an excuse to desert Jessie without having to explain the truth. But somehow, he wasn't.

"You can't do this, Papa! It isn't fair or right. He's innocent."

"Don't become disrespectful like your sister, Jess. I have to do what I think is best for all of us. Mary Louise, go to the house and get cleaned up. And do your chores without any back talk."

"Yes, Father," she replied, and hurried to obey.

"Let him stay until morning, Papa," Jessie implored, "so you'll have time to calm down and think clearly. We need his help."

"I can handle Fletcher from now on. I've been dodging my duty or letting others do it for me too long. This is *my* ranch and family. *I'll* defend them. You boys get back to work. Sorry you had to witness such a disgrace."

The concerned foreman and men also obeyed their distraught boss.

Gran, who had positioned herself and Tom on the front porch, urged the youth to go inside until everything was settled.

Tom protested, as he wanted to go to his friend's defense. "It ain't fair, Gran. He's innocent. He wouldn't hurt nobody here."

"You can't help him, Tom; your pa has spoken. Don't argue with him."

"But Navarro's my friend, Gran. At least let me go tell him good-bye."

"Your pa won't like that. And you don't want to make leaving harder on Navarro. He knows how you feel. Come inside."

Mary Louise reached the porch. All exchanged glances. She frowned at the suspicions she read on their faces. "I can see you two believe him over me!"

"You're mean, Mary Louise, a liar!" Tom accused, hurt and angry.

"I'm glad he's leaving. That drifter is no good; he's trouble."

The youth's florid complexion became rosier. His weak eyes squinted. "He is not! I hope Pa beats you for lying! If I was big enough, *I* would."

Mary Louise pinched his arm, and he jerked and yelled. "You only like him because he's pampered you like a baby. He can't change you to normal, Tom. Nobody can. Forget that road trash and being something you aren't."

Ignoring her aches, Gran straightened herself to her full five foot two. "Mary Louise! Hush your mouth, girl, or I'll tell Jed to whip you."

"Does everybody hate me and doubt me? I can't wait to leave here! My friends back East never treated me this horrible way." She ran into the house.

At the corral, Jessie was still reasoning with her father. "What's wrong, Papa? This isn't like you. He was working hard and fitting in well here. You shamed him and hurt him."

"Better to hurt a stranger than us, Jess."

"Is it, Papa? Cruelty backlashes. I'm going to see him before he leaves."

"Don't, Jess!" he said in a sharp tone.

Her blue eyes glistened with defiance. "Sorry, Papa, this is one time I can't obey. I brought him here. I gave him hope for friendship and peace. If you're going to steal them away, I have to let him know I'm sorry and I don't agree with you."

Navarro stalked past them with his saddlebags slung over one shoulder, his bedroll under his arm, a sack of supplies from Hank in one hand, and his rifle in the other. His holsters were strapped to muscled thighs, and his hat was low on his forehead as if to conceal his bitter gaze. He didn't look at or speak to either Jed or Jessie. The desperado packed his possessions and mounted. Off he rode at a fast pace, fearing he had seen Jessica Lane for the last time.

Jessie ran to the horse Mary Louise had used and swung into the saddle. She ignored her father's shouts as she pursued her lover. When she neared him, she yelled, "Navarro! Wait up!"

Navarro reined in, but didn't look back. He sat stiff in his saddle. When Jessie reached him, edged close, and finally faced him, he kept his gaze ahead. "What is it, Miss Lane?" he asked, his tone intentionally icy and his manner forbidding. It was time to go. Coldness would make it easier for both of them to part.

Tears moistened Jessie's light blue eyes. "You didn't say good-bye."

"Was there any need to? I came here leaving, like I do every place," he responded.

"I'm sorry Papa humiliated you and hurt you, Navarro. It wasn't right, and I told him so. He felt he had no choice but to defend her, even though the little witch doesn't deserve it. Mary Louise is miserable; she hates this place and wants to leave, but Papa won't let her. I wish he would. No, I wish he had long ago; then this wouldn't have happened to us. When Papa calms down, he'll be sorry and be ashamed of himself for treating you so badly. I believe you're innocent, Navarro, because I know you."

"Do you, Jess?" he asked, finally meeting her misty gaze.

The redhead realized that the two men she loved most now called her Jess. She didn't ask Navarro why he had decided to call her that today. "I don't know much about you, Navarro, but I know what kind of man you are. She lied to cause trouble."

"Are you certain?" he challenged, causing her to grimace.

"Please don't try to hurt me to make this parting easier, Navarro. We have so little time left, and I have some things to say. Even if I didn't know you and my sister, evidence doesn't lie. You're left-handed; those scratches, the rips in her dress, and that slap mark were on the wrong side for you to have inflicted them. I was going to challenge her about her so-called evidence, but tempers were too hot for reasoning. Papa usually listens to me, but not today. He's a good man, Navarro, but all his troubles are changing him. Don't think too harshly of him. He has a large burden on his shoulders. He doesn't want any of us to see how scared he is. Papa's fifty-four and he's worked hard, but he has health problems. Sometimes I see him rubbing his aching hands like Gran does. Sometimes I've seen him so stiff in the legs and back after sitting a long time that he can hardly get up from a chair or get off his horse. I've noticed a lot of little things that he tries to hide. I love him, Navarro, but he's wrong this time. Please camp nearby while I reason with him and try to force the truth from Mary Louise. I'm sure Papa will apologize soon and rehire you. Please give us time and patience."

Navarro wanted to warn Jessie about her sister's evil, but he couldn't bring himself to hurt her more than she was hurting now. Nor could he tell the redhead that he suspected Jed had believed him and had used the incident to separate them. To expose Jed's motives would cause pain and trouble, and wouldn't make it possible for him to win the woman he loved. Jessie had taught him to think of someone other than himself and of something other than his troubles. "No, Jess, he won't change his mind or apologize. A proud and stubborn man never backs down once he takes a stand. His conscience might plague him a while, but that's all. I told you in the beginning I couldn't stay long. I let you convince me to change my mind. It's best if I move on now."

"It's not best for us, Navarro," she refuted.

"Branding and planting are over, Jess. The men can concentrate on fighting Fletcher. I've taught them plenty of tricks they can use. Also, the sheriff and Army are involved now. Promise me you'll hang back out of danger. You've been a good friend, and I don't want you hurt, ever."

"I didn't mean best for the ranch or my family," Jessie clarified. "I meant for us, you and me. We've been far more than friends, Navarro. I don't want to lose you, especially like this. I love you."

That confession staggered him. He had longed to earn and deserve her love. Those were the sweetest words he had ever heard. He wanted to yank her into his possessive embrace, kiss her, hug her, then ride away with her in his arms and keep her forever. There was a heaviness in his heart as he had to say, "Don't, Jess. I'm not worth your love. I'm no good for anybody, not even for myself. There's so much you don't know about me, and I can't tell you. Don't love me, or you'll get hurt."

That was not the response Jessie wanted. "I can't help it; I love you. I need you. Stay here and marry me." He was leaving; she had to be bold. She saw his shocked reaction to her proposal, and she hurried on. "Papa can't stop us. I'm twenty-four. He'll have to accept my wishes or risk losing me if we were forced to leave together. I'll even convince him to send Mary Louise back East so we can all have peace. I can make you happy; let me prove it. Stay, Navarro. Make your home and peace with me," she entreated.

Here it was at last: Navarro's dream was there for the taking. How, he wondered, could she give up everything for him? That meant she loved him more than anything in her life, as he loved her. That was incredible, overwhelming, strengthening. He had to be just as self-sacrificing for once in his miserable life. "I wish I could, Jess, but I can't marry you or take you with me. I can't stay, either. The longer we're together, the worse it will be for us to part. We're too different, and you don't even realize how much. It wouldn't work, *tsine*." For a moment, he slipped back into his Apache days and called her *love*.

"Do I mean nothing or so little to you that it isn't worth a try?"

Her expression and words seared his heart. Maybe he should tell her the whole black truth and turn her against him. Someday, he would. "That isn't it, Jess. There's too much in my past standing between us."

"What? Any problem can be resolved, Navarro. Let me help. What we have is real; it's special. Don't make us lose it."

"It's too late for me, Jess. Too late for us. I've told you that all along."

"It's never too late, my love. What haunts you so painfully?"

Navarro told himself she was only in love with the man she thought he was. She didn't know he was a murderer, a thief, a half-breed, a bastard, the son of a cold-blooded outlaw and hostile Apache, a wanted man fleeing prison and the hangman's noose, a man who could destroy her and her world. He couldn't risk letting her or anyone discover his many secrets. He couldn't risk involving her in such danger. If he confessed the love that filled his heart to overflowing, she would fight even harder to win him, and he couldn't allow that.

It would be better, he decided painfully, to let her hurt a little now than to hurt a lot when his dark past engulfed and destroyed them. He couldn't let her watch him be captured and hanged. He had to be strong and unyielding for both their sakes. "You're a special woman, Jessica Lane. What you're offering is a valuable gift, but not one I can accept. Mine isn't a life I can share. I have to move on; that's what I need. You've had all I can share. I have nothing more I can give. You must believe me and accept that truth. I swear it."

"Why, Navarro? At least give me an explanation."

"Not everyone has the same needs and dreams, Jess. I'm a loner, a drifter, an adventurer. I can't become a rancher, a husband, a father. Not now, not ever. If I could, you'd be the woman standing beside me. I swear it."

Jessie sensed a terrible struggle within him. She was positive he wanted her, wanted to stay, wanted the life she was offering. Something wouldn't, couldn't, let him surrender—not yet. She had to keep him with her until she could unmask and destroy his demons. "Couldn't you hang around for just a little while longer? I'm sure Fletcher is about to make his big and final move. When he does, our war will be over one way or another. Please, only a few more weeks. Afterward, if you haven't changed your mind, I won't beg you to stay; I promise."

"I'll think about it. If you don't hear from me soon, you'll know I'm gone, for good. Before I leave, I want you and Tom to know I didn't attack your sister."

"We know. This is all because of me. Mary Louise is a mixed-up girl, Navarro. She has been ever since she returned from the East. She wants to hurt me because she thinks Papa favors me over her and Tom. She doesn't know what a burden it is to be his 'son' and heir. She probably realized how I feel about you, so she struck at you to hurt me. She's angry because I won't persuade Papa to let her leave home. There have been so many harsh words and feelings between them lately. For a while today, I almost hated her for being so vindictive and deceitful. It's awful to feel that way about your own sister, and I do feel sorry for her and I try to understand her side, but she makes it so difficult. Moving back East isn't as simple as she thinks. Besides, she is too immature and reckless to be on her own. I've talked and talked, but nothing seems to help. I'm sorry you were the target of her revenge against me. Please, Navarro, stay nearby until I can work out this situation. If Wilbur Fletcher learns you're gone, he'll attack with a fury. You're the only thing that's stayed his hand."

"If I hung around, your father would think I was up to no good. It's best if I leave. If he's worrying about me, he can't keep his mind on Fletcher. And that's dangerous for all of you."

Time, not pressure, is what you need, my love. Time to see what I mean to you. "If you don't return, always remember me. And if you ever need anything, you know where to find me. Anything, Navarro, no matter what Papa says."

"What I need and want, neither the white nor Indian God can give me."

He sounded so hopeless, so sad. "Nothing's impossible, Navarro."

"Some things are, Jess, some things are. Go home, and watch your back. Enemies can strike from where you least expect them. Be alert for that spy Roy mentioned in case it wasn't a lie. I think and hope Fletcher is going after the ranch in a different way now, by ruining you financially, and I can't help there. He's smart enough to know he can't keep attacking or the law will get him."

"He won't give up. Greedy, evil men like him never do."

"I hope you're wrong. Good-bye, Jess. Thanks for being a bright corner in my life. I won't forget you. Tell Gran, Tom, and the boys good-bye for me. And tell 'em I'm sorry about this trouble. Be safe and happy."

"How can I if you leave? At least kiss me and hold me a last time."

"I can't; Matt's coming to safeguard you. Good-bye, Jess. Forget me!" he ordered, then galloped away before he lost the strength and will to do so.

Jessie watched her lover's departure until Matt joined her. She looked at the steadfast foreman she had known nearly all of her life. They had spent most of their lives together, except for the few years when he was off at war. When the Yankees attacked, he had felt compelled to protect and aid his family in Georgia. They were all gone now, except for one brother whom Matt rarely saw or heard from. She was glad he remained quiet while she collected herself. Matt always seemed to grasp her feelings and knew how to respond to them. Whenever she felt trapped by her life, he was the one person who could lift her spirits. It wasn't so much what the sedate foreman said; it was his cheerful smile, his comforting gaze, his gentle touch that made her feel better. She couldn't imagine living and working without faithful Matt nearby.

She sighed deeply and said, "If ever a man needed and deserved understanding and acceptance, it's Navarro. I don't know what happened in his past, Matt, but he's had a hard and lonely existence. There's so much good inside him, but he's afraid to let it run free and risk being hurt worse. I'm sorry Mary Louise caused more trouble and heartache for him; I think he's suffered more than his share." Jessie looked at the foreman. "She lied, Matt. I don't know why, but my sister lied."

Matt grasped her hand and squeezed it. "There's nothing you can do about either one, Jessie" came his gentle response.

"I know, but it makes me so angry. We need him. He knows how to deal with men like Fletcher. He's the one who made all the plans and taught us how to use caution. When Fletcher hears that he's gone . . ."

"We'll have to face him ourselves. I won't let anything happen to you, Jessie."

"You've been a good friend for a long time, Matt. I really trust you and depend on you. It'll be up to us to keep Papa strong and not let Fletcher win."

"I would do anything for you, Jessie. Whatever you need or want, just ask me." What she wanted and needed, only Navarro could give.

"What about Navarro's pay? That's why I rode out. Jed gave it to me."

"I'm surprised Papa thought about that. I guess he didn't want Navarro to have a reason to return. He told me once he didn't need very much. Maybe last month's pay will be enough to see him to his next job."

"Did he say where he was heading?"

"No."

"Do you think he'll come back?"

"I doubt it. Papa was pretty cruel. Let's get back to the house. I want to talk to that dishonest sister of mine."

*

In a feigned tone of concern, Jessie asked, "What happened out there, Mary Louise?"

"I don't want to go over it again. It was horrible."

"I'm sure you didn't give all the details in front of Papa and the hands. Tell me everything, little sister. I found him and hired him. I feel responsible."

"I'm still too upset to repeat it. Perhaps later, another day."

"I'm going to be more upset than you are if you don't explain," Jessie persisted. "Did you flirt with him and things got out of control?"

"Heavens, no! All right!" she snapped. "He followed me on his horse. While I was strolling, he joined me. He wanted to know what you and Father thought about him. I asked why. He said he wanted to court me if Father and I didn't mind. Of course I was shocked and alarmed. I told him I didn't get friendly with hired help. He became angry, as if I had insulted him. He said he was as good as any man and he would prove it. He said no woman had ever resisted him or denied him his wishes. He grabbed me and kissed me. When I jerked my head back, he seized me by the throat to pull it forward again. That's when I got these scratches." She touched the ones on her neck.

"I warned him Father would kill him for hurting me, but he laughed. It was such a cold and cruel sound, Jessica. He said Father was a weak fool who would never challenge an expert gunslinger like him. I panicked. When I tried to run, he grabbed me and tore my dress. He forced another kiss on me, and I feared I would retch. He touched me . . ." The blonde put her hand over her left breast as she explained. "He fondled it as if it belonged to him."

When Jessie remained silent, the girl continued. "I clawed him and cursed him. That's when he slapped me." She rubbed her left cheek. "He got off balance while we were tussling, and I grabbed his shirt and pushed him to the ground. I ran to my horse and escaped before he could get up and catch me. It was frightening. I'm glad he's gone."

"There's something I don't understand," Jessie murmured.

"What is that?"

"How does a left-handed man scratch, tear a dress, and slap a woman facing him on the left side?" As she asked her question, Jessie demonstrated her points with her left hand.

Mary Louise backed away and stared at the redhead.

"If I use my left hand, as Navarro would have, you're rubbing the wrong side, little sister. On the other hand, if a right-handed person did such damage to him or herself, it would be on the left, as yours is. How strange."

Mary Louise glared at her. "What is your point, Jessica?"

"You're far too smart for me to have to explain. Did you stop to think how dangerous a man like Navarro Jones can be when crossed? I think not. Nor did you stop to think how furious Papa will be when he learns the truth. Not to mention what the men will think about such a destructive little liar."

"How dare you accuse me of making up something like this!"

"I dare because I know you and I know Navarro. I dare because we needed him in this war against Fletcher. I dare because you were cruel and spiteful. If you don't tell Papa the truth, I will. It will be simple for you to claim you were mischievously naughty, then afraid to tell the truth."

"Are you mad? They would never believe such a wild tale!"

"I think they already do. The only reason the men held silent was because you're Jed's daughter. The only reason Papa did was because your looks remind him so of Mama and that clouds his brain. Once their minds clear, who do you think they'll believe? You or me? The longer you hold to this story, the harder it will be to correct it."

"They'll believe me because it's obvious Navarro has you blinded!"

"Perhaps to you, but not to them," Jessie refuted.

"So that's why he . . ."

Jessie laughed. "Refused you, little sister, and it stung?"

"What's between you two?"

"Something you would never understand: respect and friendship."

"Is that all?" the girl asked with a sneer.

"If it were, what you claimed might have been true weeks ago. I would keep the windows and doors locked and never be alone, little sister. Navarro Jones isn't a man to wrong." With that intimidating warning, Jessie left the room with her sister gaping at her back and wringing her hands.

*

On Sunday, Jessie refused to go onto the front porch for the Bible reading and hymnals. Her absence was noted by everyone.

When Jed scolded her later, his daughter replied, "You read about love, charity, and forgiveness, Papa, but you didn't practice them yesterday. Why do I need to listen to meaningless words? Either Mary Louise was wrong or she was lying, and you knew it, or suspected it. Else you would have beaten him like you threatened. Navarro's left-handed, and that sure doesn't fit with Mary Louise's supposed injuries. You didn't have to fire Navarro. We could have kept them apart. If not, you can send her back East so we can have peace here again."

"Jess! You'd choose that saddletramp over your blood kin?"

"That *saddletramp* has been more loyal and helpful in a few weeks than Mary Louise has since she returned. Besides, that wasn't my point. She's determined to leave home. I think she created this situation to force your hand. I, for one, am tired of fighting with her. If she wants to ruin her life by striking out on her own, let her do so. Perhaps bad luck will teach her more than any of our words and deeds can. I can't abide a liar!"

"Even if she did lie, Jess, she has to stay home with us because she needs our help and influence. Under that circumstance, he couldn't stay. And you know the boys would always wonder if he could be trusted. How could we fight if we didn't all pull together?"

"Why didn't you ask them how they felt?"

"Do you think they would have sided with a gunslinging drifter over their boss's daughter?" he reasoned.

Jessie ran the men through her mind. "No, I guess they wouldn't, especially with you leaning in her favor. They're too loyal to the Lanes."

"Forget him and this nasty episode, Jess."

"With Navarro gone, I may not have to, Papa, because we might all be dead soon. I don't want to discuss it anymore."

Jed watched Jessie stalked from the house, and was about to go after her.

Gran halted him. "Let her be, son. They were good friends. They went through a lot together. She liked him and trusted him. She can't believe he's guilty."

Jed saw Jessie cross the yard, saddle Ben, and ride away. "Do you think he did it, Ma?" he asked his mother.

The white-haired woman looked at the troubled man and replied, "No, son."

Jed frowned. "Don't matter much now, does it?"

"I hope not."

"You think she's going to go to him?"

"No, son; he's gone. But I think you're going to wish he weren't for two reasons: Jessie, and Wilbur Fletcher. You should be grateful to that boy."

"For all the help he's been to us on the ranch and with Fletcher?"

"For that, and for not asking Jessie to leave with him. If he had, I think she might have gone. Don't look surprised, son. Haven't you noticed how she's changed since meeting him? She may dress and work like a man, but she surely isn't one. I think Navarro's the first man to make her realize she's a woman."

"Then I'm glad he's gone. That would have meant big trouble."

"Jessie deserves a life of her own, Jed."

"Not with a saddletramp like that! She's too good for him."

"That's her decision, son. If he ever comes back, don't force Jessie to choose between him and us. It's better for him to stay than for her to go."

Jed looked worried. "You think he'll return and cause trouble?"

"No. Something terrible is driving that boy to keep moving. It's a shame. I've watched him for nearly two months. He has a lot of good in him, but a lot of pain to cut out. If things were different, he could have been perfect for our Jessie."

Jed fretted for a minute. "Mary Louise, get out here!" he stormed. When she hurried to him, he demanded, "I'll ask you one last time, is he guilty?"

Her sapphire-blue eyes took on their most innocent expression. "Yes, Father; I swear it on Mother's grave. Jessica is enchanted by him, so she can't see the awful truth. He's much too dangerous for me to frame. If you had allowed him to remain here, he would have been after both of us to get at your ranch. You did the right thing, Father, to protect me and Jessica."

"If you're lying, girl, God help you—and us."

*

Wilbur Fletcher visited them again on Monday. This time, he offered to buy all or only part of the Box L Ranch. Jed and Jessie refused the offer.

"You can't defeat us by blocking my sales and loans and association membership," Jed said. "Nothing you do will change our minds."

"I told you, I have not nor do I need to use violence to win our conflict. These were my first moves against you, all legal, but not my last. If you can't get sales or loans, how can you hold on, Jed? You can't."

"No Lane has given up in the past, and I won't be the first. Get off my land!"

"He just wants to get stronger and to make us weaker," Jessie told her father after his departure. "He wouldn't be satisfied with a parcel of our land and water. He'll try to freeze us out little by little."

*

On Tuesday, Fletcher apparently replied with cut fences and rustled steers in the southeast pasture. A gang of masked bandits ran off the two Lane hands riding herd and raced the stolen cattle toward their southern boundary.

"I told you so, Papa," Jessie told Jed. "He's at it again because he knows Navarro is gone. Mark my words: it'll get worse and worse. Come on, Matt. Let's see where they're headed."

When they reached the boundary, they found more fences had been cut to allow for the villains' escape. Jessie glared at the trampled ground, then searched the horizon. "They're long gone, Matt. They're running the cattle fast and hard. They don't care about injuries or weight losses. This wasn't about selling good stock over the border. We could track them, but we'd probably ride into an ambush. I'm sure they're smart enough to let guards hang back until they cross the river."

"Best I can figure, they took about a thousand head. Running them like that won't give 'em much profit. It's just harassment. I'll rope up this gap like you and Navarro did. I'll send boys back with wire to repair it properly."

Jessie dismounted and handed the foreman her rope. She watched him as he worked, his eyes squinting against the bright sunlight. He looked especially handsome today in his light-blue-and-faded-red checked shirt. That and a dark-blue bandanna enhanced his deep tan. Brown hair peeked from beneath his tan hat. He had a strong, appealing face. He was so different from Navarro. His expressions and manner were easygoing while Navarro's were usually intense. When Mathew Cordell smiled, he did it with his eyes and mouth and face, and smiling came easy for him. Something seemed different about him today, though, and Jessie suddenly realized what it was. "You shaved off your mustache!"

Matt glanced at her and grinned. He removed his hat to mop the sweat with his shirt-sleeve. His brown hair was mussed, giving it a wind-ruffled look. Sections fell across his forehead and teased at his wide brows. She noticed how white and straight his teeth were, and how the creases deepened around his mouth and eyes. "It looks wonderful. No need to hide a handsome face like yours."

The foreman chuckled. "You've been teasing me since your first pigtail."

"That was so long ago, Matt. The years have been good for all of us until now. I don't know what we would do without you and the boys."

"Don't worry, Jessie. I'll do all I can to take Navarro's place." The foreman knew she didn't realize the full extent of his words. He wanted this chance to prove himself to Jessie. He wanted to show her he was as brave and smart as that drifter who had so impressed and charmed her.

"No man is as unselfish or honest, or loyal as you are, Matt."

He looked surprised that she had praised him instead of Navarro. Jessie smiled at him. Matt was all those things and more. "You're my partner now."

"I would die defending you, Jessie. You and your family," he added.

The warmth of his smile and mood relaxed Jessie. "You're my best friend, Matt. I know that's strange coming from a girl, but it's true."

Matt secured the last rope in place, then looked at the beautiful redhead. "You're no longer a girl, Jessie; you're a woman, a mighty pretty one."

Jessie laughed and jested, "I didn't know any of you boys ever noticed."

"Pants, boots, guns, and a braid stuffed under your hat don't hide it anymore, Jessie. You've grown up into a really fine woman. I'm proud of you."

"Thanks, Matt. That means a lot coming from you."

The foreman mounted. "Let's head in before they worry about us."

*

Wednesday morning, Jessie, Matt, and the hands mounted up soon after dawn to ride fence. Tom was given permission to accompany them for a while. Before they broke into groups to check each direction and the scattered stock, a blast came from the eastern section. Everyone glanced that way, then looked around as more explosions sounded from the west and south.

"What was that?" Jed shouted.

All scanned the horizon and listened. The thundering and tramping of thousands of hooves soon reached their ears. Dust clouds rose in all three areas and soon merged into one enormous billowing of flying dirt and grass. It wasn't long before they felt the ground trembling and heard snorts and bawls. Dynamite had spooked the clustered herds around their property and was sending the charging and terrified animals straight toward the settlement. Soon the frantic creatures were in sight. Stock of many sizes, ages, and colors made straight toward them. Longhorns had their heads lowered, and piercing horns aimed at targets in their paths. They dashed at full speed and headlong toward the shocked people, racing wildly and powerfully over everything in their path: bushes, grass, and rocks.

Matt took command in a second. "Let's go head 'em off!"

The foreman, Jessie, Jed, and the men galloped to control the stampeding steers and horses. All knew they had to join the mad rush and ride along the outer edge of the stampede. It would take brave and skilled riding to prevent the stock from trampling anything and anybody in their path, and the herd could be injured or ruined if not checked swiftly. During such a panic, limbs could be broken, horns snapped off, animals gored, and weight lost. Sometimes stock would speed for miles before halting or being halted. The noise of the horde rapidly became deafening and ominous as it closed the distance between men, fence, and beasts.

The men reached the herd and dashed alongside, trying to capture the animals' attention, with familiar voices and songs. Yelling and singing at the top of their lungs, they separated into point, swing, and flank positions, and worked to string out the bunched animals. They were skilled at this task, as cattle often stampeded during drives to market. Sometimes a storm set them off—or thirst, or rustlers, or predators. Or steers with panic habits; those had to be killed or sold to prevent spreading the perilous trait.

In the excitement, Tom kneed his horse and rode to help the men protect his family and property. Gran yelled for him to stop and return but couldn't be heard over the thunderous commotion.

Mary Louise grabbed her arm and shouted, "Let's get into the house before they trample the fence and us, Gran!" She almost dragged the protesting woman from the scene. Both knew what damage the charging beasts could cause.

Jessie's eyes and cheeks stung from the dirt and debris being kicked into her face. Dust choked her, but she kept riding and singing and shouting. Animals nearby were being hooked by long and sharp horns or tripped by entangled hooves. There was no time to think of anything except her task and safety.

Matt spied Tom riding ahead. Suddenly the boy, unskilled at riding and stampedes, was thrown from his horse as it panicked and reared, tossing him to the ground in the path of the charging herd. Matt spurred his mount into a swift run toward the awkward youth who was getting up as quickly as he could. His horse had galloped away, leaving the disabled boy in great peril. Tom began to run clumsily toward the barn, but there was no way he could outdistance the thundering hooves and deadly horns coming at him. Matt reached him, bent over, extended his hand, and yanked the boy over his legs. The foreman guided his horse to the left of the horde just before it trampled the earth where Tom had fallen.

The riders turned the lead steers to the right and began to create a wide circle, turning them into the center of the herd. They kept the tactic up as they gradually tightened the circle. "Milling" was hazardous to the herd so they tried to calm them as rapidly as possible to avoid any more injuries and deaths. When all the animals were traveling in the circle, they gradually slowed their pace. The singing of a hymnal by all finally quieted them.

Matt helped Tom to a seat behind him, and the shaking lad wrapped his arms snugly around his rescuer's waist. Matt told the men, "Water and feed 'em here until they're well rested and calmed. We'll take 'em back to pasture later. Sing 'em a pretty ballad, boys, 'cause they're still nervous. I want guards posted today and tonight. I don't want anything like this happening again."

Jed looked at his son and asked, "What are you doing here, Tom?"

"He took a little spill so I let him ride with me," Matt answered for the boy. "He's a mighty brave one, Jed. Tom, why don't you help the boys sing to the herd? You got a good voice. You can keep Jimmy Joe company." He helped Tom to the wrangler's horse.

The auburn-haired youth smiled at the foreman in gratitude for saving his life and for trying to ward off his father's anger. "Thanks, Matt."

"Help the boys settle 'em good."

"I will. It's all right, ain't it, Pa?"

"Go along, but be careful—and don't get in their way."

As Matt, Jessie, and Jed rode toward the barn, Jed asked, "What happened?"

Matt explained, then said, "He's just eager to help and be like us, Jed. Don't be too hard on him. He has to learn and grow. He won't be a kid much longer."

"He could have gotten you or one of the boys killed trying to save him from his recklessness. I don't want him riding anymore."

"I don't think that's a good idea, Jed. Those moccasins and the stirrup Navarro made for him have given Tom courage and confidence. He needs plenty of both. Life is hard and mean sometimes. We won't always be around to help him or protect him. He's got to learn to take care of himself. With lessons and practice, he'll get better. I'll work with him if you don't mind."

Jessie was glad Matt had been around and was close enough to them to speak his mind. She knew he was right about Tom, and she hoped her father would agree.

Jed took a deep breath and released it with a hiss. "You're right, Matt. Lord knows I would take away that boy's infirmities if I could. I don't want him hurt more, but I suppose he needs to learn to stand on his own."

After her father left them, Jessie met Matt's gaze and said, "You and I have a job to do tonight, partner."

Chapter

13

Jessie and Matt skirted the southern boundary of Wilbur Fletcher's land, as most of it lay northeast of the Lane ranch. Wearing dark clothes and riding dark horses, they traveled for hours beneath the crescent moon. Their target—a herd of fine horses—was kept near the eastern side where Fletcher's best grazing land was located.

When they reached the point where the fence angled northward, they followed it at a safe distance. Jessie hoped Fletcher wouldn't think of placing guards in that area. They reached their destination and halted, slipping off their mounts to check their surroundings for sights or sounds of danger. Hearing none, they proceeded to the fence with Matt holding Jessie's hand and guiding their way. It was a strong and reassuring gesture that caused her to lock her fingers around his.

There, in near darkness, Matt grasped Jessie's arm and stopped her from going farther. "Let me check it out first," he whispered. "Wait here."

Jessie sensed that he needed to prove himself to both of them, so she obeyed his soft command. She watched him maneuver through the strands of barbwire that she spread with her gloved hands and boot. Soon, shadows engulfed him. The redhead strained to hear every sound, ready to go to his aid if necessary. Time passed, and she grew worried. Matt was such an important part of her life and she couldn't imagine losing him. If he got killed helping her, she would never forgive herself. She implored God to protect him.

Jessie knew they were taking a big risk, but Fletcher had to be punished. With Navarro gone, she had to take control of the campaign against Fletcher. They couldn't sit back and await their enemy's next strike or simply keep retaliating blow for blow. For now, she didn't know what else they could do.

Matt reached her and talked over the fence. "All clear. No guards around. The herd is still grazing over there. Let's hurry. Stand back while I cut a big gap. You know horses are scared of wire and will balk around it."

Jessie stepped away for Matt to cut several sections. When one end was released, each strand of wire whipped back toward the next imprisoning post. Jessie knew those razorsharp barbs could tear bad holes in flesh and clothes, so she gave them plenty of room to dance in their freedom. Afterward, she helped Matt gather and toss them aside. With pieces torn from her father's old Indian blankets, Jessie snagged them on a few of the prickly knots to conceal their guilt. She scattered about beads from a broken Apache necklace. "There . . . that should confuse them, especially with us riding unshod horses. Big John will shoe them first thing in the morning. Shouldn't be any trouble for the Indians. All the Apaches and Comanches are gone from this area, except for a few renegades to the west." Before they mounted, she said, "I'm glad you're safe."

"Weren't worried about an old hand like me, were you?"

"Yes, but you aren't old. You only have ten years on me."

"Eleven afore too long," he amended.

They prodded their mounts into the pasture and rode to the horses. They herded the animals to the gap without any problem. Using ropes and whistles and encouraging words, they moved along at a steady pace. Once they were clear of Fletcher's property, they ran the herd faster. They traveled for over an hour toward the east. When they were certain the noise couldn't be heard by their enemy, they fired shots into the air to spook the herd onward. They knew the animals would run for a long time, then locate the grass and water ahead.

"He'll be mighty angry when his men find them missing tomorrow." Matt said grimly. "My pa always told us boys never to make a dangerous man angry, but you have no choice in times like these. It'll take 'em a while, but they should be able to recover all or most of them. Let's get home before light shows our faces."

"Thanks, Matt."

"For what? Tweren't much."

"For saving Tom's life and for helping me tonight."

"Knowing you, Jessie, you would have come alone if I had refused."

"Yes, I would have. But I'm glad you agreed. I feel safer with you here."

"I'm not as good with my guns and wits as Navarro, but I'd give my last breath protecting you."

"I know you would; that's why you mean so much to me. Home it is."

*

Jessie and Matt reached home just as dawn was lighting the landscape and hinting at a beautiful day. They were exhausted yet elated by their easy success. The smithy joined them at the forge as they dismounted.

"Good morning, Big John. Shoe them as quick as you can. I don't want Fletcher finding unshod horses on Lane land. Thanks for the help."

The black man smiled broadly and revealed snowy teeth. "Yessum, Miss Jessie. I'll git a fire het up and have dem hawses ironed afore vittals."

"You can eat first," she encouraged.

"No'm, Miss Jessie. I wants 'em dun afore dat bad man rides over."

"Matt will tell Biscuit Hank to keep a special plate hot and ready for you."

The smithy started his task as he hummed a spiritual song.

"You get some sleep, Jessie. We can tend the chores today."

"You do the same, Matt, at least until noon."

"I don't want to be abed when Fletcher gallops over here."

"He won't, not today. Those clues will fool him for a while. He'll wait to see how that rustling Tuesday and the stampede yesterday affect us. If I've got him figured right, he'll give us a week to watch and worry. Besides, he probably thinks we've sent for the sheriff and soldiers again, so he'll be careful. No need to report to them; Cooper and Graham can't help us."

*

Jessie was right: Wilbur Fletcher didn't appear until the next Thursday. When he did, it was on horseback and accompanied by Sheriff Toby Cooper. It was five o'clock, and the hands were changing shifts or tending chores. Big John Williams was finishing in the smithy. Biscuit Hank had fed one group of men and nearly had the second serving ready. Miguel, Carlos, Jefferson Clark, and others were unsaddling their horses after riding fence and herd all day. Jimmy Joe, Rusty Jones, and a few others were riding out to take their places as night sentries. Mary Louise was milking the cows. Tom was in the house with Gran who was cooking the evening meal and Matt, Jed, and Jessie were talking near the barn.

Father and daughter walked to where the sheriff, Fletcher, and two men hitched their reins to the corral. Matt and the others gathered around, too.

The lanky lawman looked at the Lanes and their hands. "Jed, boys, I have to ask you a few questions. Mr. Fletcher has made some accusations against you."

"About what this time?" Jessie asked with a disgusted sneer.

"Robbery" came the reply Jed, Jessie, and Matt didn't expect.

"Robbery? Of what?" Jessie inquired in a sarcastic tone.

"His payroll and bank withdrawal. His men were killed and robbed yesterday on the way home from the bank."

Jessie eyed Fletcher, then the sheriff. "You think we did it?"

"The tracks led here, Miss Jessie."

"That's impossible. Fletcher probably hid his money and is trying to frame us for a crime that never happened. How are we supposed to know about his money and travels?"

"You took it because I kept you from getting those sales and loans," the other rancher accused. "You said you'd find another way to survive. It won't be on my money, Jed. Turn it over and I'll have Toby drop the charges."

"We don't have your payroll. We don't steal or murder. None of my men have been off this ranch for a long time. I'll swear that on the Holy Bible."

"You'd swear anything to get back at me and for fifty thousand dollars!"

"Fifty thousand dollars," Jessie murmured, wide-eyed. This was the first time she had seen Fletcher lose his temper. If the theft was for real, she could understand why. "Isn't that a bit much for a small ranch payroll? Something is funny here, Sheriff."

The man glared at the redhead. "I ordered a new bull and stud. They're arriving this week. The man wanted cash."

"Then I'd say he's the only one who knew you'd be withdrawing so much."

"She has a point, Mr. Fletcher."

"She's wrong. The seller wouldn't know when I'd withdraw the cash."

"Neither would we, especially since we didn't know about the purchases."

"If you'll check my account, Sheriff, you'll see I don't have his money."

"No man would be fool enough to deposit stolen money, Jed. You need cash."

"I got plenty until I make my fall sales."

"How?" Fletcher scoffed.

"There are plenty of markets west of here—forts, reservations, mining towns."

Jessie wished her father hadn't mentioned their prospects. Now Fletcher would try to block them, too. She saw the man's brow lift in interest.

"What about that drifter you hired to fight me?"

"He's been gone almost two weeks."

"Why did he leave?" Fletcher asked.

"We had a private disagreement. I fired him. If he was still around, we would have seen him while riding range. We haven't."

"I want my money, Jed."

Mary Louise had ceased her task and joined the group. "We don't have it, Wil—

' Mr. Fletcher. That drifter left weeks ago as Father said, and none of the other men have left the ranch. We had a terrible stampede here, and my little brother was almost killed. My grandmother and I were in the middle of it, too. The men have been staying close to protect us. I swear this is all true."

Fletcher smiled at the blonde. "I'm sorry to appear so upset, Miss Mary Louise, but it is a great deal of money to lose. I'm relieved none of you were injured during that stampede."

"It would suit you fine if we'd all been killed," Jessie retorted. To the sheriff, she said, "We didn't contact you, sir, because we didn't think you could do anything about it. Dynamite was set off in all directions, and the herds were sent charging toward here. We barely stopped them before they reached the barn."

"Dynamite, you say?"

"Yes, sir."

"Sounds like the same man, or men, who blasted Mr. Fletcher's windmills. I'll check around to see who's been purchasing it."

"I doubt you'll find anything. Fletcher here probably had his hirelings steal it."

"You've a bad tongue on you, Jedidiah Lane."

"Better a bad tongue than a black heart and mind."

"This quarreling won't help matters. It's time we leave. I'll come back when I learn something, Jed."

"*If* you learn something," Jessie corrected the sheriff. "Mr. Fletcher is very clever and determined; but so are we."

*

That night in her bed, Jessie wondered if Navarro had robbed Fletcher before traveling on. Surely if he was still around, he would have contacted her by now. Torment filled her—the anguish of not knowing where or who he was or the true reason he had deserted her. But she could not bring herself to regret loving him. Navarro had brought her a wild, passionate, and reckless love just when she needed it most. He had made her realize it was time to think of love, marriage, home, and children. If the past few months were all she would ever have of him, now she knew what her life was missing. He had taught her it was time to think of her desires, and the future. She had done her duties and responsibilities for others; it was time to do them for herself.

How, she didn't know yet. Navarro's loss was too fresh and painful. Too, someday he might return to her . . . or for her. Yet, she admitted, there was little hope for that. All he had needed to say was *Wait for me, I love you, I have to leave for a vital reason,* or anything like that. But he had held silent. Whatever had driven him away, he had kept secret. He had accepted her job, done it as long as permitted, and ridden off saying he couldn't ever come back.

Should she, Jessie wondered, allow herself to hope and dream? Could Navarro kill the ghosts that haunted him? Tears slipped from her eyes into her hair as she sensed that whatever stood between them was too strong to forget.

*

On Saturday night, the sounds of gunfire, breaking glass, and galloping horses shattered the slumber of all on the Lane ranch. Men rushed from the bunkhouse, yanking on clothes and carrying weapons. But it was over; the danger had passed.

Matt and the other hands hurried to the house to see if anyone was hurt. Jed opened the door and shouted they were fine. The men continued on to join him on the porch.

"Damn that bastard! I told him we didn't take his money!"

Gran, Tom, Jessie, and Mary Louise came outside to listen.

The shaking blonde shrieked, "You'll get us all killed, Father, if you don't sell out! Even if it is Mr. Fletcher, we can't win."

"Hush, girl, we aren't backing down now or ever."

"They weren't trying to kill us, little sister. All the bullets were aimed for the tops of the windows. None of us is that tall."

"They still fired at us!" the girl argued. "Go after the sheriff."

"That won't do any good."

"Then send our men after them."

"And let them lure us away like before for a worse reason? We can't trail them at night, and their tracks will be covered by morning."

"I'll post guards around the place," Matt said.

"That's about all we can do," Jed agreed. "Whoever goes on duty, be real careful-like. Jessie might be right about them trying to get us to race after them so they can double back and attack again. Light plenty of lanterns; let them know we're on alert. If he's got men out there watching, the others won't return tonight."

"Tomorrow we can patch the windows until we can get new panes next week," Matt suggested. "It hasn't rained in a long time, but a storm could break any day now."

Jed gazed skyward and remarked, "Weather's been odd this spring. Been too warm and dry for this time of year, and getting hotter every day. The mills and rivers are dropping low. Keep your eye alert, Matt. After that dynamite stunt, a violent thunderstorm could set off another stampede. After all this rustling and the last panic and the shootings, I've lost nigh onto ten thousand head. That's near a three-hundred-thousand-dollar loss at market time, and that bastard is fuming over a mere fifty thousand! We also need to keep the garden watered so we won't lose our crop. I surely hope it rains soon. If it don't we'll be in a bind as tight as Fletcher's."

*

Sunday night, under a lessening full moon, Jessie and Matt waited until the wee hours of the morning before retaliating. From rifle range and different sides of the house, they rapidly shot out windows in Fletcher's home. Matt rushed to join Jessie at the assigned place.

They mounted and galloped toward safety. Men rushed to pursue them. Before long, they noticed a fiery streak like a shooting star.

Jessie's heart pounded and her blue eyes widened. "It's a flaming arrow! The bastard is signaling somebody ahead of us! He must have taken the idea from that Indian ruse we pulled. We have to hurry before we're cut off."

"They're trying to trap us between forces. Let's head south and return from that way. If we get separated, keep riding southward until it's safe."

"If I slow you or get wounded, don't stop, Matt."

"I'd never leave you behind."

"You must. The law will go easier on a distraught and emotional woman than on you. Promise me you'll obey. It's an order from your boss!"

To settle her down, Matt promised, but he knew he would never obey. He guided them southward to skirt Fletcher's ambush. "They'll head for the ranch to see who's missing. We can't waste time."

As dawn approached, they rode hard and fast. The terrain was a blend of grasslands and rolling hills. The ranch was in the midst of a series of little valleys full of trees and hillocks that was set inside a large valley surrounded by ridges and mountains that were no trouble to cross. Southward and northward were tabletop mesas and more desertlike territory. The flatlands were often dotted by amaranth: roundish green scrubs that broke free of their roots in fall, dried to prickly balls, and tumbled across the landscape forever like restless ghosts. This area was usually tranquil and fragrant; the many wildflowers made it seem as though a special garden had bloomed amidst the harsh surroundings as a gift from heaven. But now the lack of rain had left its mark, mainly in the wilting grass.

As they neared the ranch, they saw Wilbur Fletcher and a band of men nearing the settled area. "Let's sneak in the back of the barn," Jessie whispered. "I have an idea."

It was light now, so they had to be cautious. At the last gate, they unsaddled their horses and let them go free, away from the corral their foe was certain to check for sweaty mounts. They tossed their gear over the fence and hoped they wouldn't be noticed at that distance, as bridles and saddles had been needed for a swift getaway pace. If checked, the damp undersides would expose their recent use.

As the family and hands hurried out to see what the neighbor wanted this early, they slipped to the barn and entered by the back door, then bolted it from the inside. They sneaked to the front door and listened to the talk outside. They peeked through cracks at the hirelings who checked the home and bunkhouse.

"How dare you!" Jed thundered. "Sheriff Cooper will hear of this outrage!"

"Don't fight me on this, Jed!" Fletcher shouted. "I don't want to get tough, but I have to know who's missing. I see all of your men except your foreman. And where is that fiery daughter of yours? Two people attacked me hours ago. They couldn't have beaten us here. I had guards posted along our boundaries. Seems you're caught red-handed this time. What's it worth for me not to have them charged and imprisoned? It's dealing time, Jed; you've lost our battle."

Jessie sensed what was coming and prepared them while Fletcher ranted at her father. She pressed a finger to her lips for silence, then smiled. Matt watched with intrigue as she loosened his shirt from his pants and mussed his brown hair. She unbraided her own, tousled it, and tossed pieces of hay on both their heads and clothes. They exchanged grins.

Jessie opened the barn door and looked outside. The creaking of it caused all eyes to rivet in that direction. Looking as if caught during wanton play, she glanced at her father and shrugged. As she pulled straw from her auburn tresses, she said, "We're in here, Papa. We were . . . talking and haying the cows. We started tussling like children. You know how Matt and I are at times."

As she pushed open the door, Matt was brushing off himself and trying to gain control of his wayward emotions. The intimate illusion she had created was arousing, and he wished it were more than a deception. He hurriedly tucked in his shirt as if he thought no one was noting his action. He jammed his hat over uncombed hair with its telltale gleams of hay. "What's wrong, Boss?" he asked, knowing Jed would grasp their ruse and not be angry. Matt assumed Jed's uneasy demeanor was part of their ploy to mislead Fletcher.

"Mighty early to be cleaning the barn," Jed remarked with a feigned scowl, playing along with their clever stunt. He liked the way they looked and worked together, and was annoyed he hadn't pushed a closer relationship sooner. He didn't know why he hadn't realized before that Matt was perfect for Jessie and the ranch, and the foreman would keep her mind off that drifter should he return.

Jessie saw a curious twinkle in her father's eyes. "Papa, we—"

"Later, Jess. We have other business to handle." Jed turned to his foe and charged, "I know you only came here to see how we took your shooting party Saturday night. You can't trick me by claiming we shot up your home last night. If anybody did, you can see it wasn't us. Get off my property and don't come back. No more offers, 'cause they're useless. And if you ever send your men over here to shoot at my house again, I'll kill you, you sorry bastard."

Fletcher looked confused before he could conceal his surprise. "If everyone's here, it must be that drifter again. You lied about him leaving."

Mary Louise, wearing a pretty dress as usual, vowed, "He's really gone, sir. He tried to ravish me, so Father fired him over two weeks ago."

"The beast," Fletcher murmured, then looked her over as if checking for damage. "Maybe he's the one who's attacking both of us."

"You said shots came from two directions," Carlos reminded him.

"Perhaps he's hired a partner for profit against me and revenge against you."

"That is farfetched, *hombre,*" Miguel scoffed.

"You can see we're all here," Jed told him, "and you can tell none have been gone. Unlike you, we have no unbranded horses or strangers around. As you said, it must be somebody after both of us. We better watch our backs."

"I don't know how, Jed, but I'm sure you're behind the robbery, rustling, and the shooting."

"A third charge now? All you gotta do is send for the sheriff and prove it."

Fletcher's scowl deepened. "I handle my own affairs."

"Is that why you came over with him the other day?" Jessie taunted. "And why you have twenty-five men on payroll for a small ranch? Do you pay them to watch you do your own dirty work? I doubt it, Fletcher."

"You've inherited your father's nature, Miss Jessie, but you won't inherit this ranch. Before long, it will be mine," he warned. "Let's go, men!"

After they rode away, Jessie whooped with delight and hugged Matt. She could not resist planting a kiss on his cheek. "We did it, Matt."

The others, all except Mary Louise, understood the interchange and grinned or chuckled. As the couple hugged and others praised them, she caught on to their ruse. "Congratulations, Jessica; you two fooled them."

"He's too cocky, so he thinks we aren't as smart as him," Jessie said. "And just wait until he tastes our next sour trick. Right, Matt?"

"What is that?" the blonde inquired.

"I don't know. Matt and I haven't made it up yet, but it will be a bitter one." Jessie looked at the nodding foreman, sent him a conspiratorial smile, and squeezed his hand. She felt him return the meaningful gesture with a firm grip.

*

Monday night, Jed invited Matt to have dinner with them. During the meal, the foreman mentioned that the two men he had sent after the new windowpanes would return tomorrow so the panes could be replaced on Wednesday. They discussed the unusually dry weather once more. Matt told them the irrigation troughs from the well behind the house to the garden would prevent any loss of that crop.

When Mary Louise asked what their next plans against Fletcher were, Jessie replied, "We don't know yet. We have to be careful and sly, because he's on watch now. We have to come up with ways to discourage him. If he sees it's going to be an impossible battle, maybe he'll leave this area. There are plenty of good locations nearer to Fort Davis or on the high plains west of us. I'd like to see him leave Texas altogether."

"If he's guilty, Jessica, he's going to become more and more dangerous. If you two push him too far, those bullets might strike lower next time. I'm scared."

Gran patted her hand and said, "We all are, girl, but we can't let him win."

"If any or all of us are hurt or killed, will your victory be worth it, Father?"

"No Lane has ever been a coward, girl."

"Isn't it better to be a live coward than a dead hero?"

"For some people, it might, little sister, but not for us."

After the meal, Jessie and Matt took a walk. "This may sound awful, Matt," the redhead told him, "but I don't want our plans talked about around Mary Louise. There's something about the way she's acting about Fletcher that makes me nervous. I know she can't be warning him, because there's no opportunity. But I don't like her attitude. It might just suit her fine for him to run us off our land."

Matt grasped Jessie's hand as they strolled. It felt wonderful to touch her, to be with her, and to feel her voice covering him like a warm blanket on a cold night. He halted and placed his hands on her shoulders. Moonlight reflected in her blue eyes as she returned his steady gaze. "I've been here long enough to speak my mind to you and Jed. Even if it hurts, you two expect me to be honest. We're good friends, Jessie, so I'll tell you what has me worried. Have you stopped to wonder what Fletcher and Mary Louise talk about whenever he comes over? She would have time to pass along a few hints if she had a mind to aid him. I've noticed he's been coming around a lot lately."

Jessie reflected on their neighbor's many recent visits. Her sister was alone with the man on most of those occasions. On the few that privacy had been prevented, Mary Louise had spoken openly to their enemy in front of all. The redhead recalled what her sister had said after the robbery and window shooting when Fletcher rushed over, and realized there could have been hidden messages in her words. "I know how devious she can be, Matt, but surely we're wrong to suspect her. If only she weren't so desperate and determined to leave home, I wouldn't have these doubts about her. I do know for certain that she framed Navarro to get rid of him. But did she do it to help Fletcher or to weaken us into giving up?"

"I don't know. I hope we're wrong, Jessie, but watch out for her."

As she had done many times in the past, the redhead wrapped her arms around Matt's waist and rested her head against his chest. Especially tonight, she needed the strength and comfort from her longtime friend. "I'm glad I have you to talk to, Matt. I can trust you with anything."

Matt's hands traveled to her back, then drifted into her hair. She smelled so enticing, and her mood was so mellow now. He enjoyed holding her and sharing anything with her. He wished she realized how much he loved and wanted her, and wished that she felt the same. He knew it was too soon to expose his feelings, that Navarro was still between them. His voice was strained with emotion as he replied, "You can, Jessie; I swear it on my life and honor."

She heard the affection in his tone and felt the arousing effect of their contact. It warmed but worried her. Despite her longtime relationship with Matt and Navarro's desertion, to enjoy Matt's embrace made her feel traitorous to her missing lover. She knew she must pull away. "We'll talk again tomorrow while we're riding range. Good night, Matt."

*

As the shifts were changing the next morning, gunfire from the northern pasture captured their attention. Matt assigned guards to the house while he and other hands rode to check out the peril. Anticipating more dead steers, Jed and Jessie went along. After a few miles, they saw and heard nothing.

Jessie yelled at them to halt. "It's a trick, Papa! Let's get back home!" She turned Ben and galloped for the house with the men strung out behind her.

Rapid shots told her she was right, and she prodded the paint to a faster pace. The guards at the house had been ordered not to be drawn away from their protective posts for any reason, and they had obeyed.

As Jessie and the others thundered into the yard, Davy shouted, "That way! Something's up!" He pointed toward the eastern pasture closest to the settlement.

The riders headed in that direction. When they reached the villain's targets, it was a horrid sight. The four prize bulls were lying dead on the ground. Jed hurriedly dismounted and approached the huge bodies. He dropped to his knees and stared at them. Tears slipped down his cheeks as his hand stroked the expensive Durham. He balled his fist and shook it in the air as he cursed Wilbur Fletcher.

Jessie took command. "Rusty, see to Papa. Matt, Carlos, Miguel, Jimmy Joe, ride with me. We're going to catch those bastards and kill them." The angle of the bullets revealed the direction from which the shots had come. The five took off southward.

They rode for hours on the fresh trail, but couldn't sight the culprits.

"We'll never catch them!" Matt finally yelled. "They'll keep running as long as we're chasing them!" After the group halted, he suggested, "We better head back before dark."

Jessie glanced southward once more. She knew the foreman was right; those men would continue on into Mexico if necessary to keep from exposing their boss. She lifted her face skyward, closed her eyes, and took a deep breath. As she exhaled, she lowered it and looked at Matt. "I've never been one to believe in violence, but we have no choice now. I don't know if Fletcher was robbed of his stock payment or if it was a lie to frame us, but he hinted about bulls, then murdered ours. If it's dead bulls he wants, then he'll get them."

"That is dangerous, *chica,*" Carlos told her. "He will be expecting you."

"I'm learning fast from him, Carlos. Some of you will lure his guards away while Matt and I return his foul deed."

"What will your *padre* say, *amiga?*"

"I don't know, Miguel, but it has to be done. We must meet every challenge Fletcher makes. If we don't he'll win."

"She's right, boys. We can't let this go unpunished."

"Thanks, Matt. We'll make plans back home. I'll come to the chuckhouse after supper," she said, and knew the foreman caught the reason for her caution.

*

"What do you mean he's gone to confront Fletcher?" Jessie asked Rusty.

"He took off right after you did. He ordered me to take care of the bulls. He has two of the boys with him. I've never seen Jed like that."

It was nearing dusk and they were tired, but Jessie said, "I'm going after him. Papa's in danger. Fletcher will kill him, then claim it was self-defense."

The group hadn't reached the boundary when they intercepted Jed, Walt, and Talbert. They all reined in to talk.

"Why didn't you wait for us, Papa? That was reckless. Fletcher's men could have cut you down and claimed you attacked them."

The weary, dispirited man responded in a strained voice, "I told the bastard I would poison my water, burn my lands, and kill all the stock before I would let him take my life away. I told him I'm hiring as many gunslingers as he has and lining my borders with armed men. We'll shoot any man or horse belonging to him that comes near my place."

Jessie saw that he was too exhausted and depressed to keep his fury at full level. She hated seeing her father like this. But she had enough energy and fury to make up for what Jed had lost today. "What did he say?"

"Didn't bother him at all, Jess. He claims he'll outwait us. Said I would never harm my land. Said I can't afford to keep that many men on payroll long."

"It was easy because he knows it's true, Papa. You could never cut the heart from this land, and we can't afford the high price of gunslingers." Jessie's mind raced to Navarro. She wished he were there to lead them. They needed his wits and skills. Her father was losing hope and courage. Yet, as she had for weeks, she pushed him from her thoughts.

"Let's go home, Papa. You need to rest."

They reached the ranch after dark, a three-quarter moon lighting their way. The others came to greet them and to hear the news. Matt repeated it as Carlos and Miguel took Jed and Jessie's horses to tend. The redhead led her father to the house and handed him a glass of whiskey to settle his nerves.

"What happened this time?" Mary Louise asked.

"I'm sure Wilbur will tell you the next time he sees you. Leave Papa alone tonight. It's been a hard day. I'll help Gran get supper on the table. You come, too," Jessie ordered her sister, not wanting to leave her father to the girl's lack of mercy while his spirits were low.

"Father looks terrible. Tell me what happened," she persisted.

Jessie grasped the blonde's arm and pulled her into the kitchen where she revealed the news, which didn't seem to disturb her at all. "We're lucky Fletcher didn't use their visit as an excuse to kill Papa."

"Don't you think that's odd since you claim he wants to be rid of all of us? It would have been a perfect solution . . . for a guilty man."

Jessie glared at her sister. "He had a reason. A man like him doesn't do anything without a selfish reason." As the words left her lips, similar ones from Navarro the day they met sounded inside her head. She closed her eyes and prayed, *Please come back to us, my love. Wherever you are, hear me and return.*

"Jessica, are you all right?" Mary Louise asked. "You look pale and shaky."

"I'm just tired and angry. Let's eat and get to bed." What she didn't say was that she had a terrible feeling something worse was about to happen.

*

Big John put in the new panes on Wednesday, and Mary Louise washed them afterward. The hands did their chores in silence, as if some gloom hung over them and the ranch. The day was hot and oppressive, so most blamed the weather for their crazy moods.

While Jessie and Matt were checking on stock, a disheartened Jed rode to the family graveyard—located a little over a mile from the house on a lovely spot near a chapparel—to visit his wife. Alice, their two sons, and his father were buried there. The aging rancher was frightened for the survival of his remaining family. He didn't know if he should risk their lives by holding on here. If he could get Fletcher alone without his many guards, he knew he would kill the man and end this madness. But other matters troubled him, too: Mary Louise's hatred and defiance, Tom's disabilities and his sullenness since Navarro's departure, and the longing for the gunslinger's return that

Jessie was trying to hide. He felt guilty over separating her from Navarro. He sank to his knees beside his wife's grave, buried his hands in his face, and prayed for the answers to his problems.

*

Late in the day, as Jessie was walking toward the house, Matt caught up with her and grasped her hand. Jessie halted and looked at him. Something in his expression told her there was trouble. "What is it, Matt?"

"I'll go with you. I want . . . to see Jed."

Jessie knew the men had told Matt to tag along for a reason, and she realized the hands had acted odd upon their return. Her heart pounded, as she knew something was wrong. She jerked her hand free and ran into the house. Jessie rushed to the kitchen, then glanced into the dining room. She paled and trembled. Her hand covered her mouth and moisture sprang to her eyes. "No," she murmured in anguish, and the tears escaped rapidly down her cheeks.

Matt's arm banded her shoulder. "I'm sorry, Jessie. The boys told me he was . . . dead. I didn't want you to come in here and face this alone."

Jessie left his embrace to walk to the long table where her father's body lay. Her grandmother was lovingly bathing her son to prepare him for burial. Dazed, the white-haired woman sang a hymnal as she worked, as if oblivious to her granddaughter's presence. Jessie's eyes touched the wound in his chest. She knew from experience it was from a knife blade. "What happened?"

Martha Lane continued her chore as if she hadn't heard the girl's words. Jessie looked at her and knew it was best not to press her for answers at this time. "Tom! Mary Louise!" she shouted.

Both came to the kitchen from their rooms. Tom gaped at the sight and buried his face against Jessie's chest and sobbed. Jessie clutched him to her and comforted him.

Mary Louise glanced at her father and remarked, "He killed himself."

Jessie's tears and soothing words halted, and she stared at her sister. Anger flooded her. "How dare you say such a thing, you wicked girl!"

Mary Louise backed away a few steps, looking as if she expected her sister to attack her. "I'm the one who found him, Jessica. I rode to the graveyard to speak with Father about my leaving here. I'm frightened, Jessica. He was lying across Mother's grave. There was a knife in his heart, and he was holding the handle."

"Only because he was trying to pull it out when he died, fool! He was murdered! Fletcher did it. I'll kill him. I swear, I'll kill him!"

"I didn't see anyone there, Jessica. Father's face was still wet with tears. He couldn't have been dead long. If anyone else did it, I would have seen him."

"If you did, you wouldn't tattle! You'd do anything to get away!"

"I know you're upset, Jessica, but don't attack me like this. Even though we didn't get along, he was my father, too."

"I can see how your heart is bleeding over his loss," Jessie scoffed, as the girl didn't appear the least bothered by their parent's death . . . his murder.

"We'll get him buried quickly, then contact Mr. Fletcher about accepting his offer. The sooner we leave here, the better for all of us."

Jessie's light blue eyes enlarged with astonishment. Anger such as she had never felt before consumed her. "You're crazy! I would never sell to that bastard."

"You have no choice. Father is dead. We can't stay here. Be reasonable. I've already started packing. We should move into town tomorrow after the funeral. From there, we can decide where to settle. If you don't want to try it back East, Dallas or San Antonio would be nice."

Jessie stiffened, and she clenched her jaw over and over. "This ranch is mine now, little sister. Go if you wish, but get out of my sight before I punish you as Papa should have!"

"You don't inherit everything, Jessica! Tom and I get something. I want my part so I can leave this awful place. When can you give it to me?"

Matt grabbed the girl's arm and almost shoved her into the parlor. He closed the door to the kitchen and said, "Leave them be! Let them mourn in peace."

"You aren't a member of this family!" she snapped. "Get out of our home!"

Matt had never been tempted to slap a woman until tonight. He had to struggle to control his temper. "I won't let you torment them with your selfishness, girl. If you love your family, settle down."

"So you can walk in and take over Father's place?" Mary Louise sneered.

"I'm responsible for them. I won't let you hurt them more than they're hurting already. How can you be so cruel at a time like this?"

"This is Father's fault. He knew he was going to lose, so he took his life."

"Jed Lane didn't kill himself."

"It looks that way to me. If we don't clear out, we'll be killed, too."

"You just said he killed himself." He pointed out her contradiction.

"He did, but he let this trouble push him to it. Jessica can't run this ranch."

"Yes she can."

"With your help, Mathew Cordell? I know you want her—and the ranch. I won't allow you or anyone to steal what belongs to me."

"Nothing belongs to you, Mary Louise. Jed left it to Jessie."

"She's not an only child, Matt. I have rights, too."

"Do you?" he challenged.

"I'm sure a lawyer will see it my way," she threatened.

"I doubt it. Jed made certain his will was legal. I was with him. He knew you would try to cause trouble when he died so he fixed it so you can't. If I were you, Miss Lane, I would behave myself before Jessie kicks you out with nothing. According to the law, she can do just that."

"You would be delighted to help her do it, wouldn't you?"

"Yep, I would. You've been nothing but heartache to your family since you returned home. You lied about Navarro Jones, and we all know it."

"I should think you would be glad I got rid of him. It opened the door for you to pursue my sister. With him around, you wouldn't stand a chance of winning her."

"Winning a woman through deceit and pain wouldn't be worth much to a real man. If I were you, I'd be scared. Navarro Jones isn't a man to double cross. You better hope he doesn't return now that Jed is gone. Jessie would never make him leave again. A cold and hard gunslinger can find ways of punishing a person without killing him . . . or her. You *did* lie about him, didn't you?"

Mary Louise looked frightened for a time. "Think what you will. I'm packing, because we'll be leaving soon. You'll see," she murmured, then went to her room.

Matt returned to the dining room, where Jessie was helping her grandmother prepare Jed's body. He went to the grieving women and asked how he could help.

"We're almost through here, Matt," Jessie said softly. "Ask Big John to prepare a coffin. We'll bury Papa tomorrow. After this, Fletcher should lay off a while. He'll expect me to panic and sell, so he'll bide his time for a week or so. Can you take care of the ranch for the next few days? I'll have a lot to do."

"Anything you need, Jessie, just ask me or the boys. Jed was a good friend and a good boss. We'll all miss him."

Jessie tried not to cry again, but her heart was aching. She told herself she had to be strong for her brother and grandmother. Death was no stranger to her; she had lost her mother in '70 and her grandfather years before that agonizing day. It was difficult for those left behind to go on without their loved ones. She still missed them, and always would. She knew that time and love and hard work were balms for the heart, but even they didn't help much during the first months. "I put Tom to bed. He's so upset. He and Papa loved each other, but there was always a distance between them. I hope you can spend time with him over the coming weeks. You're his best friend, and it will help him adjust."

"I will, Jessie. What else do you need tonight?"

"You did the most important thing by getting my sister out of here. How can anyone be so cold?"

"I don't know, Jessie. She has problems. If she troubles you again, just call me. I'll take her into town to get her away from here if need be."

"Thanks, Matt. I don't know what we would do without you."

The men had worked hard since receiving the grim news. The coffin was completed and brought to the house. Matt and Rusty helped place the body inside the box in the parlor. They closed but did not nail the coffin.

Tom had finally fallen asleep. Gran was mourning in her room. Mary Louise was plotting in hers. Matt held Jessie in his arms at the front door and comforted her. The men were quiet as the death of Jedidiah Lane settled in on them.

Jessie climbed into her parents' bed, as she could not sleep in the same room with her unfeeling sister. She wept over her father's loss, and the guilt she felt over it. The road before her would be hard; she prayed she had the courage and wits to travel it. She swore revenge on Wilbur Fletcher. She ached for her love's return and comfort.

Where are you, Navarro? I need you. I love you. Please, God, send him back to me.

Yet she remembered his parting words. He had claimed it was too late for them, but wouldn't explain why. He had said that if she didn't hear from him soon, that meant he was gone "for good." He had ridden off shouting, "Forget me!" But how could she stop loving, wanting, and remembering him? It was as if cruel Fate had stolen the two men she loved and needed most.

*

Jessie rested her head against Matt's strong shoulder. Now she allowed the tears she had kept pent up during the brief ceremony for her family's sake to flow. Long funerals were hard on loved ones, so Jessie had made her father's short.

Gran had taken Tom back to the house in the wagon. Mary Louise had come and gone with them, and had kept her wicked mouth shut today. The men had replaced the earth around the grave and returned to their tasks. Jessie had remained at the gravesite to mourn in privacy, and the foreman had stayed with her.

Matt stroked her unbound hair. He let her grieve in silence. There was little anyone could say or do to bring real comfort during a time like this.

When Jessie mastered her tears and wiped her eyes, she murmured, "It's all my fault, Matt. I should have seen this coming. I knew Fletcher was evil, but I didn't believe he would go this far."

"You're not to blame, Jessie."

She looked up into his gentle eyes and refuted, "Yes, I am. I was the one who kept spurring Papa on. It was my idea to hire Navarro and to attack Fletcher. If I hadn't challenged him, maybe he wouldn't have responded this way."

"What Jed did and said after his bulls were killed is what set Fletcher off."

"But I kept pushing Papa to hold out and to fight back. If I hadn't he might have given in; then he'd still be alive. It wasn't worth his life, Matt."

"Jed needed your courage and wits to keep him strong, Jessie. He depended on you. If he had yielded to Fletcher, he would never have been the same again. What is a man without his pride and honor? Jed was too proud and honest to give up his existence. What's left if we throw away our dreams when the going gets hard or dangerous?"

"But I can't let anyone else get hurt."

"You can't back down now, Jessie," Matt argued. "If good men give in to bad ones, they get stronger and bolder with everyone. Soon, they rule everything. If you surrender, Jessie, the fighting and Jed's death were for nothing. Jed would want you to hold out."

"But what if it's Gran or Tom next—or both? How can I stop him, Matt? Nothing we've done has slowed him. I'm the head of the family now. I must think of their safety and happiness, like I prevented Papa from doing."

"You're thinking through grief, Jessie. You'd be sorry and angry you sold out. It would be too late to expose Fletcher and punish him. At least wait a while before you make any decision. The boys and I will protect you and the others. From now on, we stay armed and on guard every minute."

Jessie glanced at her father's final resting place. She reflected on all he had endured to create this beautiful and prosperous spread. She looked at her surroundings and thought of all her years on the range. This was her home. This was Lane land. She loved it. No one had the right to take it from them. With Mathew Cordell and the hands behind her, she could continue her battle to save it. Matt was right; that is what Jedidiah Lane would want.

Her gaze went to the fresh mound once more. "I didn't get to tell him good-bye or tell him how much I love him. It isn't fair, Matt."

"He knew. He knows, Jessie."

Fury filled her. "I want to know whose knife that was in his heart. It wasn't Papa's. I've never seen one like it. He didn't take his own life."

"It wasn't marked so I don't know how we can discover its owner. We didn't find any tracks, either. Somebody clever concealed them. This is why Fletcher didn't attack Jed on his land; he wanted his body found here and looking like he killed himself."

"Let's get back so I can check on Tom and Gran."

Matt mounted and pulled Jessie up before him, as she was wearing a dress and couldn't ride behind. She laid her head against his chest once more and wrapped her arms around his waist. Matt was so comforting, and she needed his warmth and tenderness. She never stopped to think how contact with her affected him.

Matt glanced down at the woman in his arms. He wished she could stay there forever. He loved her and wanted her with every ounce of strength and emotion he possessed. When her anguish subsided, he would confess his love with the hope she could come to return it one day.

*

On Monday, Jessie wrote a letter to the Cattlemen's Association and asked for membership as the new owner of the Box L Ranch. She explained their troubles and accused

Wilbur Fletcher of being responsible. She told them if they were men of honor and conscience, they would not allow Fletcher to prevent her inclusion in the association or be influenced by his money and status.

She and the hands were kept busy getting stock to water, as several windmills were running low and so was the Calamity River. They had never seen this area so hot and dry this time of year, and they were concerned.

Since Jed's loss, everyone had been quiet and sad. The men hadn't played any practical jokes on each other since that grim day last week. When music was played at the bunkhouse, it was soulful tunes that reflected the men's moods. Yet none of them doubted Jessica Lane's ability to run the ranch, and none quit.

That night, Matt, Carlos, Miguel, and Jimmy Joe sneaked to the adjoining ranch and slit the throats of Fletcher's prized bulls and studs. The ranch hands were accustomed to deft and swift slaughter of beast and fowl; they did their task with merciful quickness and skill that didn't cause the animals to suffer. It was a difficult course to take, but they all agreed with Navarro's blow-for-blow strategy to discourage their enemy. Matt didn't tell Jessie about their action until it was over, as he didn't want her to endanger herself by riding with them.

As she talked with him Tuesday morning, she was astonished to learn of their deed, and knew it had been done with compassionate speed. "That was a brave and generous thing to do, Matt. Thanks. No doubt Fletcher will be rushing over today with hot accusations. I'm ready for him."

But Fletcher didn't appear, and Jessie wondered why not. She also wondered why her sister was doing more than her share of chores without protest. Gran and Tom seemed to be adjusting slowly to the tragedy, but all of them were quiet and tense. Jessie blamed part of it on the inexplicable heat that blazed down on heads and land, greedily sucking the life from water and grass.

As she lay in her father's bed, having moved into his room, Jessie thought, *Wouldn't it be crazy if nature beat us both, Mr. Fletcher? If a drought is in the making, neither of us will have anything of value to sell.*

Dread and alarm attacked Jessie. *Please, God, we've had more than our share of danger and torment. Don't send more burdens to us. Let us find peace and happiness again. We miss Papa so much. Expose his killer. Punish Fletcher for his evil. You're a good and just God, so how can you allow this to happen to us? I want Navarro; I need him. Please guide him back to me. If you can't, then protect him and give him freedom from his torment. I've tried to understand and accept these troubles and losses, but it's so hard to face them alone. I've tried not to become bitter and hard. Please answer our prayers before I do. Protect Matt and the boys. Help Gran and Tom not to suffer so much. As for Mary Louise, Lord, I don't know what to say about her. I know she's the one who found Papa, but she couldn't hate him enough to kill him. I suppose it's wicked of me to have such awful suspicions, but I can't help but mistrust her. Help me in the days to come to do my best for everyone here.*

*

Wednesday, Fletcher arrived in the company of two men and Sheriff Toby Cooper. His gaze was narrow and hard. His aura was cold and threatening.

Jessie met them and glared at the man responsible for her father's death. "What do you want? Haven't you done enough to us? Get off my land!"

Fletcher scowled at her and the men who gathered around the redhead. "I came to see Jed. My bulls and studs were slaughtered Monday night. I know who did it. Toby is here to investigate. You'll all hang for this outrage."

"Investigate all you like, Sheriff, but not with him here! My father is dead. He was murdered last Wednesday. This ranch is mine now. I'm warning you before witnesses, Fletcher—if you or any of your hirelings ever step foot on Lane land again, I'll take it as a challenge and attack. And I'll kill you, you murdering bastard! You have no reason or right to be here. This ranch isn't for sale; it will never be for sale. Get out and don't come back or you're a dead man!"

Chapter

14

The sheriff had left yesterday without searching the Box L Ranch or questioning the hands further. As if in grudging acknowledgment of the Lanes' grief, so had Wilbur Fletcher.

Miguel returned from his shift of riding range. He approached Jessie and Matt at the corral. He pushed his sombrero to his back, then rested his hands on his pistols. "Bad news, *amiga:* I saw your sister giving a letter to one of Fletcher's *hombres* riding fence. I hung back. They did not see me."

Jessie looked stunned, then angry. "At least she can't warn him about our plans—because she doesn't know 'em! Let's keep her ignorant. Tell the boys to watch her and report anything suspicious to me or Matt. She's been near perfect lately. She knows better than to give me open trouble before she can get her greedy hands on escape money. I know what she's waiting and watching for—me to fail. She thinks I'll give up soon, sell out, and move. She's wrong."

"She probably wrote Fletcher telling him to be patient while she works on you," the foreman suggested. "He won't. We have to guard the house and barns, and that'll spread us thin on the range. He's done so many things, I can't guess what'll come next. What we need are more men for chores and guards."

"Matt's right, Miguel," she told the Mexican vaquero. "I'll send you or Carlos into town next week to see if any honest ones are for hire. Perhaps we can use my sister's treachery to our advantage with a trap for her new friend."

Jessie scanned the sky and frowned. "This heat is getting terrible. Matt, we should cut the grass in the east pasture before it wilts and dies. We need to have hay on hand if this works into a drought. Tell Big John to check the reaper. It hasn't been used in a long time. Once we get it cut, it'll be safe while it dries. Maybe we can hire more men before we need to gather and bind it."

"If Miguel finds help, they can work on a new storage shed while it's curing on the ground. We'll need to hay again later with our stores burned. If winter's as crazy as spring, no feed could ruin you."

"Let's not take any chances with this. I'll have to prove to everyone that I can run this spread. As soon as I get settled with Fletcher, we'll need to locate new bulls for breeding season. It's going to be a rough year without Papa. I'll need help until I can do it all."

"You don't have to do it all yourself, Jessie. That's what me and the boys are for. Just 'cause you can't do or know a few things doesn't mean you can't run this spread as good or better than your father did. Are you forgetting you gave half and sometimes most of the orders? You were right there with us day and night. You're smart and brave and quick. You were Jed's right hand. Have faith in yourself, boss lady; you can do it."

She had needed those kind words. "Thanks, Matt. I hope so."

Matt gently stroked her cheek. "I know so, Jessie."

"So do I, *amiga*. You will not fail."

She sent them a radiant smile of affection and gratitude. "I'm lucky to have you boys. I don't know how I would survive without any of you."

*

"What you did yesterday, Jessica, was like a slap to Mr. Fletcher's face. I wrote him a letter of apology and delivered it to one of his men today."

As if that were news to her, Jessie shrieked, "You apologized to the man who murdered our father and is trying to destroy us!"

"If he is guilty, don't you think it's wise to be nice to him?"

"I'd rather cozy up with a rattlesnake!"

"That would be safer, if he's guilty. A snakebite can be treated; death can't. Don't you care about what happens to us—Gran, Tom, and me?"

"Of course I do! But if you say, *if he's guilty* one more time, I'll smack you!"

"Listen to me, big sister: if he's behind all this as you believe, one of us needs to think clearly to deal with him. At least my letter might get us extra time before our enemy strikes again. You need that time to clear your head, Jessica. You can't go around provoking dangerous men. We'll all be killed. Wasn't Father's death enough tragedy for this family? Give up this fight before it's too late for all of us. Please, I urge you to reconsider his fair offer. If you keep attacking him, he might withdraw it, or you might get into trouble with the law. If you go to jail, what then?"

"I haven't been attacking him lately. We didn't steal his payroll or rustle his horses or slaughter his animals. We *did* shoot out his windows, but he did it to us first. Either he lied about those other things or somebody else is after him."

"Who would that be?" Mary Louise asked, and looked worried.

"How should I know? An evil man like Fletcher must have lots of enemies. You can't go around hurting and destroying people without making plenty."

"You think it's that Navarro?"

Jessie glanced at her sister's pale face and wide sapphire eyes. "Worried about him returning to get you for framing him, hmm? It would serve you right for lying."

"I didn't lie! If he hurts me, it will be your fault, Jessica. You brought him here. I'm not to blame for him misinterpreting my good manners."

"If you hadn't been out riding alone, it wouldn't have happened. It was stupid to leave the ranch with all this trouble we're having. One would think you don't consider yourself in any peril from your *friend* Wilbur."

"I don't, because I don't believe any of us are in jeopardy from him. But I *do* believe somebody is after us. A woman can't run this big ranch, Jessica."

The redhead realized her sister was contradicting herself. If Mary Louise didn't believe it was Fletcher, then, she would have been in peril from "somebody" during her ride—unless she had invited along an unsuspecting escort. She didn't point out those slips in anticipation of more. "Have you forgotten you're talking to Jed's 'son'? I've helped run this ranch for years. I know as much as Papa did."

"Do you, Jessica? You haven't had as many years to learn as Father did. And do you think cattlemen will work with a female, especially a young one?"

"They surely will," Martha Lane said from the doorway.

Both women looked at their grandmother. Her lined face and blue eyes appeared calmer today, as did her voice when she said, "Jessie won't have no trouble with any men. They like her and trust her. They'll do business with Jess Lane." Her white hair was in a neat bun at the back of her head and her cotton dress was clean and crisply ironed. Gran dried her gnarled fingers on her apron and joined them. "The good Lord put us all on this earth for a purpose. Jessie's is to take over her pa's place. She's more than capable of running it and prospering because she loves this land like my son did. She has her pa's pride and strength. It's time for you to settle down, Mary Louise. You've been too hard on everyone since you came back, especially on your pa and Jessie. I don't know what spoiled you back East, but you have to cleanse that stain from your soul. Jessie has a lot on her shoulders these days, and we have to pull together."

"What we need to do is leave, Gran," the blonde argued. "It's dangerous for us here with Father gone."

"It was dangerous afore he died, girl, but he didn't give up. Jessie can't either. A Lane was the first man on this land, and a Lane must be the last."

"When Jessica marries, Gran, it won't be Lane anymore. *If* she marries. Because if she keeps up like this, she'll never find a husband. She'll die a spinster, dressing as a man and working as one. I don't want that for me."

"I'll make a deal with you, little sister: behave yourself until this matter is settled, and I'll give you money from our next stock sale and let you go where you please. It'll be enough to support you until you can find a job—or a husband. I can't afford more than that because I have to replace the shed and the bulls, and I have other repairs to make. The more Fletcher costs me, the less I'll have to give you for your escape. If you have any influence over him, get him to back off until you're away safely."

"You'll let me move back East?"

"If that's what you want so badly, yes. You've been ripping at the guts of this family too long. If letting you strike out on your own is the answer to finding peace here again, then go and be happy somewhere else. You certainly haven't been here."

Mary Louise licked her heart-shaped lips. "How much money?"

Jessie controlled her mixture of vexation and joy. "I don't know yet. It depends on how many markets I can find and how much stock I can get to them. Mostly, it depends on Fletcher not preventing my sales and drives."

Eagerness was in her voice as the blonde asked, "When?"

"As soon as possible. I'll work on it next week."

"You promise?"

Jessie made a large X over her heart. "I swear it on my life and honor."

"Then I accept your bargain, big sister."

The two women stared at each other as different and matching emotions filled them.

*

Captain Graham and a troop of soldiers stopped by near dusk. "We were chasing renegades west of here, so I thought we'd stop by to see how you're doing. Toby told me about Jed's death. I'm real sorry, Miss Jessie. He was a good man. You had any more trouble since then?"

"None yet, but Fletcher will be at us again soon. He won't give up. Why don't you camp here for the night? It might give us another day of reprieve. Some of your men can find bunks with the boys, and the others can use the barn. I'll tell Hank to prepare you a good supper."

"That's real kind of you, Miss Jessie. If there's any—"

"Fire!" Davy shouted as he galloped toward them. "South pasture's ablaze!"

Panic shot through Jessie. "We have to get it out fast. The wind's blowing in this direction. As dry as the grass and mesquites are, it'll spread fast. You know what to do, boys. Let's go."

"We'll help," Captain Graham said. "Tell us what to do."

"Leave some of your men here as guards. Fletcher's skilled at luring us away with trouble so he can attack here. Get everything ready, boys. There isn't much water down that way with this dry spell."

They saw the billowing smoke and leaps of red dancers long before they reached the scene. Range fires were hazardous, as they engulfed anything and everything in their path: stock, structures, fences, and people. They could travel swifter than a speedy landslide and sometimes prevent riders or stock from escaping. The blaze was greedy as it feasted on the nourishing landscape. Where the mesquites were dense, fire created a wall of flames. It licked at wilted vegetation and consumed it, then jumped to its next meal. They knew, if it got worse, it would be impossible to control.

Matt and Jessie shouted orders to the soldiers who joined her hands to battle the roaring blaze. Where it had passed, smoldering wood and blackened land was left behind. Hot air blasted across their faces and bodies. Smoke hindered vision and breathing. This could turn her land into ashes, and Jessie wondered why Fletcher would damage the property he craved.

Horses with plows were used to furrow breaks to prevent the fire's spread. Men labored to groove the endangered area as quickly as possible, and worked to calm the horses that were balking in fear. Between the rows, others set control blazes to battle fire with fire.

Jessie and Matt rode around the waving ocean of flames to see how large and fast it was. Men tossed shovels of smothering dirt or buckets of water from barrels on wagons onto the fiercest sections. Trees and bushes had to be allowed to burn because it was too hot to get close enough to chop them down. Two men drove back and forth between the blaze and the nearest windmill. It took a long time to fill the barrels, as the water table was low.

Jessie was frantic as she watched and listened to the ravaging monster at work. The men couldn't seem to gain control of the surging blaze. Before a break could be finished in one area, the freedom-seeking flames were leaping in another direction as if trying to outsmart and outrun them. The main tasks were stopping the spread northward toward the settlement and westward toward the clustering, terrified stock. The Calamity River—which would protect Fletcher's land from his mischief despite its lowered level—was southeast. Yet they all knew that the farther south one traveled, the hotter and drier the terrain. If the fire got into that area, there was no telling how fast and far it would journey.

Jessie heard the crackling and popping of dry bush and limbs as they fell prey to this vicious predator. She and Matt dismounted and grabbed shovels. They worked with the others to slow its progress. She coughed and sneezed as smoke wafted into her nose and mouth. She yanked off her bandanna and tied it over them, but it didn't make breathing any easier in the searing heat. Her eyes stung and teared; she constantly blinked to clear and soothe them. She knew Ben, her faithful paint, would not panic and leave her in danger in case she had to escape the surging flames. She was grateful the soldiers had arrived in time to help.

Dusk closed in around them, but they didn't need light to see their task. Flames brightened the darkening sky like a million lanterns. Men shouted over the noise of the job at hand, and horses whinnied and pawed the ground in fright. Suddenly a loud crash was heard.

Jessie halted and looked up. It came again, louder and longer. It sounded like tin being shaken violently or the roaring of a cannon in the distance. The heavens bellowed again, then sent lightning zigzagging across it. "A storm!" she shouted, "Hurry, God, with the rain; we need it desperately."

Matt checked the ominous sky. "It's moving in fast, Jessie, without warning. I just hope bolts don't strike and set off more blazes."

"Don't even say that, Matt," she murmured in horror.

The crashing of thunder increased. The wind picked up. More jagged flashes of light flickered across the sky. The noise bammed and echoed across the land. The air seemed to vibrate from it. The volume grew louder and closer. Wisps of dark-auburn hair blew into Jessie's eyes, and she pushed them aside. One boom caused her to jump and gasp. As if sensing their peril, the flames raced to consume as much terrain as possible before nature called a halt.

The arid land seemed to pop and crackle from the heat of the weather and that of the fire. The tension in the air was palpable. The rumbling moved closer and louder. The lightning grew in frequency and length. The wind was brisk, but sultry. Drops of rain began to splatter on them and on the parched and blackened ground. Within minutes, the heavens opened and sent down a deluge of water. Flames sizzled and smoked in protest. Some areas hissed like venomous snakes or furious cats. Blazes died. Quickly soaked, the exhausted and filthy people halted their labors to let nature control itself.

"Pass the word along," Matt shouted. "Gather the equipment and animals. Let's head back. This storm is going to be a bad one. Careful with those tools; we don't want them drawing down lightning. Let's get to cover."

Rain came down in a furious rush. It created black mud that spattered their sooty boots and pants. They were drenched, but shouting joyously in relief. The drops came down so heavy and hard that they could hardly see, even though hats shielded their eyes from the streaming liquid. It didn't help that darkness—now that the fire was snuffed—surrounded them and no moon was in sight. They hurried to collect their tools and get back to shelter.

"Shouldn't be any more trouble tonight, not with this storm raging," Matt remarked as they mounted. "I'll get some of the boys to check on the stock. We don't want this storm setting off another stampede."

"Will you take care of our guests, Matt? Make sure they get cleaned up and fed good. All I want is hot coffee, a long bath, and a cozy bed."

*

"Everything's fine, Gran. The storm put it out. The Lord gave us plenty of help tonight with those soldiers and rain." As thunder and lightning ripped and roared over the house, Jessie took a deep breath. "It's a bad one."

"Usually is after being so hot and dry this long. You all right, Jessie?"

The redhead hugged her grandmother and smiled, then realized how filthy she was. "I got you dirty, Gran; sorry. I'm doing fine. This will perk up everything and refill our water supply. I was getting worried."

"I know, child, but the good Lord always steps in when we need Him most. We'll make it, Jessie; you'll see. You couldn't have a better man at your side than Matt. He'll help take care of us and the ranch."

Jessie smiled again. "We're lucky he came back after the war. He's the best foreman and friend we could have. You go on to bed. It's late, and I know you're tired. Hank said you helped him cook supper for all the men. Thanks."

"I saved you a plate. It's in the warming oven."

"Sounds good, but I need a bath first. I have to get this smoke and soot out of my hair before I turn in."

"I figured you would. There's water heating and a fire going in Jed's room so you can dry your hair before bed. A nip of whiskey to relax you wouldn't hurt, either."

Jessie laughed. "I had the same idea. I'll get cleaned up, then eat and dry my hair before I sneak a nip. Don't worry about this dirt I'm tracking in; I'll mop it up later."

Jessie kissed Gran's cheek and watched her enter the room across from Mary Louise's. The blonde hadn't come out to check on the fire and its results, and Jessie knew her sister was curled in her bed dreaming of her departure. Mary Louise was a sound sleeper, so the redhead didn't doubt she was slumbering peacefully. Yet, she wanted to check on her brother.

Jessie slipped up the stairs and peeked into his room. Tom had left a lantern low to chase away the darkness. "You asleep?" she whispered.

"Nope. Is it done?" he questioned as he sat up.

Jessie explained what had taken place. "You get to sleep and we'll talk more in the morning. I'm drop-dead tired. I'll hug you tomorrow; if I did now, I'd get you filthy, too. I can't wait to scrub all the dirt off. Good night, Tom."

"Jessie, you think Fletcher will try to kill you too? He knows that me, Gran, and Mary Louise couldn't hold out against him but that you could."

Jessie gazed at his freckled face of concern. His green eyes were squinted to see her better without his glasses. Having removed her soiled gloves, she ruffled his wine-colored hair and coaxed, "Don't worry about me, Tom. Matt and the other men will protect me. We're on guard better now."

The youth hugged her around the waist and nestled his cheek against her stomach. "I wish Navarro was here. He'd kill him for us."

Jessie returned the hug and kissed the top of his head. "So do I, Tom."

The boy looked up at her and asked, "Why did he have to leave?"

"Papa fired him and ordered him off the place, Tom. It was a mistake, but Papa thought he was doing what was best for all of us."

"It was wrong. Mary Louise is bad. She lied. Navarro was my friend."

"I know, Tom, but bad things happen sometimes. You must be brave and strong. Soon we'll defeat Fletcher, and everything will be good again."

"I miss him, Jessie."

She didn't know if he meant their father or Navarro or both. "Me, too, Tom. I'll let you in on a little secret," she whispered, then told him about her bargain with Mary Louise. "I hate for her to leave, but she isn't happy here."

"I'm not sorry. She makes everybody unhappy."

"One day you'll understand her better. She has problems, too, problems inside that we can't see. When she gets them straightened out, she'll be a good person again."

"I hope she don't come back until she's well."

"She won't; I'm sure of it. Now, get to sleep, young man. I love you."

"I love you, too, Jessie. I'll pray like Gran says for you to be safe."

"I can use all the prayers you can send up, Tom. We all can. Good night."

* * *

Jessie took a bath in the water closet off the kitchen and washed her hair. She dried herself off and donned a soft nightgown. She nibbled at the food Gran had left for her, then put it aside. She wasn't really hungry. She poured a small glass of her father's finest whiskey and took it to her new room, where she tossed a comforter on the floor before a glowing fire, glad the heat outside had lessened as the storm forced cooling windows shut. She brushed her wet tresses and sipped the fiery liquid. Tom's mention of Navarro had seared her heart as the flames had seared her land.

Jessie remembered she had left her drenched and smelly clothes on the floor in the water closet. She took a candle and went to toss them on the back porch. She unlocked and opened the outside door and dropped them there. Before she could close it, Navarro appeared before her. She did not cry out, but she did almost drop the candle in surprise. Light flickered over his dripping face and soaked garments. She blinked to check her vision.

They stared at each other until a bolt of lightning and clap of thunder startled them back to reality.

Jessie smiled and murmured, "You're home." She went into his arms and sealed her mouth to his. She didn't care that her gown was getting wet. Her heart raced in joy and her body flamed with desire. Another crack of thunder and flash of brilliant light parted them. "Come inside."

He shook his head. "Your father will be furious, Jess."

"He's dead. He was murdered last week." Her eyes filled with tears at the sympathy on his face, but she cut him off before he could speak. "I'm staying in his room now. Let's talk there. So much has happened." She grasped his hand, and they sneaked inside. Jessie locked the bedroom door and turned to let her senses absorb his presence.

She placed the candle on a stand and went into his arms again. "I've missed you so much. I was afraid you'd never come back. It's been weeks."

As he held her, he asked softly, "What happened to your father, Jess?"

She related everything that had taken place since his departure, and felt him tense with anger. By the time she finished, her emotions were running so high that she was crying softly in his embrace. "I needed you so much."

The desperado stroked her damp hair and cuddled her in his arms. "I'm here now, *tsine*. I won't let him hurt you again. I'll kill him this time."

Jessie looked up at him. "Where have you been? I didn't know where or how to reach you."

Navarro's hand pushed her wet hair off her face. "I've been spying on Fletcher's men. I watched them rustle those steers a few days after the trouble with your sister, then followed them to the border. There's a sort of way station across the river. Men were waiting there to take the cattle and drive them on into Mexico. I trailed the others back to Fletcher's ranch and saw him meeting with them. He's guilty all right. I can identify everyone involved, but I can't go to the sheriff. He wouldn't believe me without proof." He took a deep breath. "I got close enough to hear what they were saying. Fletcher was expecting a big payroll delivery the next day, so I ambushed his men and took it off their hands. I buried it just north of your ranch." He described the location in detail.

"If you ever need money, it'll be there. I can't get caught with it. After I robbed his men, I figured it was best to lay low about a week. I wanted to contact you, Jessie, but I knew your father would be furious if I showed my face again. When it was safe, I went back to Fletcher's for more spying. Nothing appeared to be going on, so I headed to town for supplies and ammo while it was quiet. I have to stay ready to pull out after I get him. I rested up at that line shack, then came here to tell you good-bye before I kill him and leave for good."

Jessie went over what had happened after the robbery in greater detail. She tried to ignore what he'd said about leaving. "You can stay as long as you like, Navarro. The ranch is mine now."

He didn't respond to her offer. "When I got here, I saw soldiers standing guard and knew something was wrong. I hung back until everybody rode in and got settled, then put my horse in the far corral where it wouldn't be noticed. My saddle's over the fence. I've been hiding under the back porch until things quieted down in here so I could tap on your window and get your attention. But when I was peeking in the kitchen window to see if anyone was still up, I saw you coming with the candle. I was afraid you'd see a shadow and scream."

"I'll give Mary Louise some of Fletcher's money so she can leave and you can stay," Jessie suggested. "She's afraid you'll return and get her for framing you. She'll be overjoyed to take the money and run."

"That isn't why I can't stay, Jess. I have to get rid of Fletcher and get on the road again. This battle is getting too hot and drawing too much attention."

Attention from whom? she wondered. "I want you to stay and marry me, Navarro. Not to help me with Fletcher, but because I love you and need you."

His face mirrored the agony that attacked him. "I wish I could, Jess, but you don't really know me. I'm a half-breed bastard, a real one. My name is Navarro Breed, if a bastard can use his father's last name. My father was a cold-blooded outlaw, a white man. My mother was Apache. They're both dead. His band was called the Breed gang. They terrorized the Arizona and New Mexico territories for years. My mother worked at a fort washing clothes and cooking for soldiers. When several of them tried to rape her, Carl rescued her and killed them. But he had a selfish motive; he wanted her, and she became his squaw. Morning Tears was beautiful, so he kept her a long time. I wish he hadn't," he said with bitterness.

"From the time I was born until I was six, we lived on the run between jobs they pulled. Or we hung around dirty and wild towns near forts while the men drank and gambled and fought until the money was gone. When I was seven, Carl needed to lay low for a while, so he bought a sutler store at Fort Craig. That was a pretty good time in my life. At least we had a house if not a home. I had food, clothes, safety. I got to attend school and escape into books, like Tom does. But the children were as cruel to a half-breed bastard as they are to someone like Tom, and so were the grownups. But I learned a lot about the white world, and I learned fast. I figured getting head-smart would help me escape my father someday. Years later, Carl was recognized and we had to go on the run again. It was worse than before. He was meaner that time because he had liked his easy life. He never cared about me, but Morning Tears wouldn't let him leave me behind. I would have been better off if they had."

Navarro walked to the hearth and squatted. He gazed into the dying fire. "I helped her tend the horses, cook, wash clothes, clean up after those bastards, and wait on them like a slave. They picked on me all the time—pinching, shoving, and smacking —and called me crude names. They loved calling me 'half-Breed' for the son of 'The Breed,' as the law called him. Carl thought it was funny, thought it would give me backbone and meanness. I never wanted to be like them. I hated them and I hated my father. Sometimes I even hated my mother for being so weak. She endured anything he did to her. When she worked herself into losing her beauty and shape, he started sharing her with his men and treating her worse. Sometimes I tried to defend her or get her to defend herself, but all it got me was a bad licking with a belt. Finally she got the courage to take me and escape to her people—or maybe she was just more afraid of staying. I was twelve. That's when I learned she was the daughter of a famous thief in her tribe. They welcomed her back, because she brought along the loot from Carl's last hold-up. The Apaches do whatever is in their best interest, and they needed money to buy supplies and weapons. Until I was twenty, I lived and trained as an Apache warrior.

"I was a skilled warrior, but they wanted a cunning thief more. My Apache name is Tl'ee K'us; it means Night Cloud. My mother chose it to help me fit in, but I never did. They believe in pure blood, and I didn't have it. I was a loner, an outcast. I supported my mother, but she was ashamed of me. When soldiers attacked the camp, most were killed or taken to a reservation. I escaped and drifted on my own for three years. I worked my way through Colorado, the Dakota Territory, Wyoming, and New Mexico area, but people were the same everywhere. Nobody wanted a half-breed drifter around. I saw deceit and hatred on both sides, more than I saw good on either. While I was resting at one of my father's old hideouts, he showed up."

His eyes hardened and chilled and his body grew taut. "I hated him. I wanted to prove I was a better man, that he couldn't match my new skills. Maybe deep inside I even wanted to have a showdown with him. I could have outdrawn him and his men. I practiced all the time to be the best. Nobody was ever going to use me or hurt me again. The men knew I was faster, so they left me alone. I rode with his gang for a while, until I realized how stupid I was being. Six months later, I was gone and he was dead. I can't say I was or ever will be sorry about that."

Navarro put his hands on Jessie's shoulders and looked into her eyes. "You showed me different, Jess. You showed me goodness, kindness, and honesty. You took away part of the bitterness and anguish I've kept inside for years. You taught me I wasn't worthless. You accepted me for what I am, or what you thought I was. You wanted to bring out the good you believed I had in me. You eased my loneliness and filled my emptiness. You never believed I could be bad. You trusted me. You made me laugh and feel happy. If I hadn't met you, I would be colder, harder, and meaner by now. I'd be that unfeeling gunslinger you mistook me for in San Angelo. You've done all of that for me, but it doesn't change who and what I am. I have devils inside me, so I have to keep moving or they'll eat me alive. I've lived in torment, Jess, and I can't let it do to you what it's done to me. If I stayed, it would. I couldn't stand to see you gobbled up by demons, too."

"I can help free you, Navarro," she promised, hugging him tightly.

"No, Jess, you can't; nobody can. I haven't told you all of it. Before I leave, I will. I owe you the truth and more, but answers are the best I can give."

"I don't care what you've been or done. I know the inside of you, Navarro. Whenever you free yourself, I'll be waiting for your return."

"Don't tie yourself to a burning post, Jess. Your father is gone. Make a new life for yourself. Don't wait for me to come back," he pleaded.

"I understand how you've suffered, Navarro. But miracles happen. Several happened tonight: the soldiers arrived, the rain came, and you returned. Don't give up hope. But I won't pull at you. Just be my friend, and partner . . . and lover until you must go."

"How can you want me after all I just told you?"

"You had no control over your birth or the things that happened to you as a child. The things you did later were because you were hurting and bitter. Whatever you haven't told me yet—I know that's why you can't allow yourself to break free. Most of all, I love you."

Jessie unbuttoned Navarro's wet shirt, freed it from his pants, and peeled it off his broad shoulders. She unfastened his gunbelt and laid it aside. She stood, pulled her gown over her head, and dropped it. Extending a hand to him, she beckoned, "Come to bed, my love. We have so little time left together."

The fugitive took her hand and obeyed. He could not resist the magic and power of her very essence. He let her guide him to the bed, where she lay down. Navarro removed his boots and struggled out of his wet pants, then joined her. He watched the candlelight flicker over her face and body. Her auburn tresses were spread over the pillow. Her skin was soft and rosy bronze. Her gaze seemed a darker blue in the shadows, and it enticed him to do more than stare at her.

"You're so beautiful, Jess." He lowered his head to kiss the tip of her nose, then trailed his lips across her face and down her throat. His quivering fingers traveled over her receptive terrain, and he explored it as never before. He wanted to visit every inch of her ravishing landscape. He wanted to let her know which path he was taking, the way he couldn't in this life. His mouth and hands journeyed over firm mounds and silky valleys and sweet ridges until she trembled with urgency for him to seek his way home.

Jessie's hands wandered over his smooth chest and strong shoulders. They roved his scarred back and taut buttocks. She sent her fingers to play in his damp midnight hair. She pressed his head to her neck and shivered with delight as his lips lavished kisses there. She felt the hard muscles bunched in his arms and across his back. He was a treasure worth fighting for. She grasped his head and guided his searching mouth to hers. She took and gave and shared numerous kisses until she was breathless.

Navarro entered her to brand her as his own, if only for this night. He looked into her lovely face.

Jessie's fingers traced the lines of his brows as she savored the love and desire she saw mirrored in his hazel eyes. She knew with all her being that he loved her and wanted her. Her fingers began a circular trek, memorizing his features: across his left cheek, along his jawline, past his chin, up the other cheek, along his brow, down his nose, and to his full mouth where they teased his lips. His movements were tantalizing and bittersweet. She was torn between wanting to claim the sweet ecstasy that awaited them at the end of this long-awaited journey and wanting their passionate ride to continue forever.

Soon there was no choice in the matter. Their desires ran wild and free. Their kisses and caresses were urgent, demanding, thrilling. Their bodies worked as one; their hearts beat in unison; their spirits soared to heaven together. Ripple after ripple of wondrous sensation washed over them. They didn't even notice the storm outside for love's storm that raged within them, and they savored every moment—every sight, sound, taste, and touch—of each other before resting in each other's arms.

"I love you, Navarro Breed, and I want to share a future with you. Can't you see now that nothing in your past matters to me. Nothing you can ever say will change how much I love you and need you."

"It will, Jess; believe me, it will. Soon, I'll tell you the rest and you'll understand how impossible our situation is."

*

When Jessie awakened the next morning, Navarro was gone. She knew he had intended to sneak out before dawn so he wouldn't be caught in her room. Yet it would have been so wonderful waking up in his protective and loving arms. She was eager to hear what else he had to tell her; yet she dreaded the truth. She didn't want to think about why he felt he had to go. In all honesty, it didn't matter to her. Whatever he had done or whoever he had been in the past was over. Navarro had changed. He had wanted and needed to do so and he had, but still he vowed it was too late. Something deep within her said it was the truth.

Jessie left the bed and put on her clothes. She donned a lovely dress and left her hair unbound the way Navarro liked it. She glanced out the window and wondered where he was. The rain had stopped, and the day promised to be beautiful. She made her bed, straightened her room, and went to the kitchen.

No one was up in the house yet. She knew they were all tired. As quietly as possible, she slipped out the door. Jessie saw Navarro standing at the corral with Matt, Carlos, and Miguel. She went to join the men. They looked at her as she approached. Matt's gaze lingered the longest on her glowing face.

"Navarro, you're back," she said to him. "It's good to see you. Have the boys told you what's been happening here?"

"Yes, and I told them where I've been." He repeated his tale as if it were the first she had heard of it.

"Thank you, Navarro. We can use your help. Things have been so bad here."

"I'm sorry about your father, Jess. He was a good man."

"Yes, he was. Papa would want me to go on, and I will."

Captain Graham approached and talked for a while. After the officer promised more help if needed, Jessie watched him depart for the fort with his troops.

She noticed how the men easily accepted Navarro's return and were delighted by his success during his absence. She realized none of them believed Mary Louise's accusations, and she was glad. Still, she saw that worried look back in Matt's eyes. Qualms about her wanton secrets nipped at her.

"We're riding back to the fire site to check on the damage," the foreman said. "Navarro's going with us. You want to come along?"

To ease Matt's concern, Jessie smiled and said, "I'll stay here. I have a lot to do. I'm sure Fletcher will stand back to see how that fire scare affects me. If he had men spying on us while we were battling that blaze, he knows soldiers are here. He shouldn't try anything with them around. Hopefully he doesn't know they're gone. Make sure he doesn't get within sighting range of the house. How is the stock faring?"

"No trouble. Some of the boys stayed with them until the storm was over. We'll graze them in other areas until that section grows back."

Jessie made certain she didn't send Navarro too many glances or treat him too special before the foreman and ranch hands. After the men rode off, she returned to the house and joined Gran, Tom, and her sullen sister for breakfast.

Mary Louise finished in a rush, then said she would leave to get her chores done.

Jessie observed her hasty retreat and asked, "Think she's about to slide backward again, Gran? She was awfully chilly this morning."

"She's been strange since she woke up. I think you're right about letting her leave soon. It will be good for all of us to have some peace."

"Me, too," Tom concurred.

"I have a surprise for you, little brother: Navarro is back. He's out with the boys on the range. You can see him later today." She told them what Navarro had been up to. "I didn't want to start a quarrel with Mary Louise until I could tell you two first."

It was only minutes after that news that the blonde rushed into the eating area and shouted, "Why didn't you tell me that gunslinger is back? "You know he hates me! He'll try to hurt me! He can't stay!" Mary Louise shrieked, her sapphire eyes filled with panic as she wrung her hands.

"Why don't you apologize and beg his forgiveness?" Jessie suggested.

The girl scowled in anger. "He wouldn't believe me!"

"Make up a good story to explain your wickedness. You're skilled at that."

"This isn't amusing, Jessica! He's dangerous. Why did he return? How could you hire him again?"

Jessie began her plan. "Navarro's been working secretly for us, little sister."

"Doing what, pray tell?" she scoffed.

"You don't need to worry your pretty head with dangerous business. Just keep to the bargain we made and you'll be gone soon."

"Not soon enough to please me!"

"Navarro won't harm you. He's a good man."

"I don't trust him!"

"Well, I do, and that's what counts around here."

*

On Saturday, Jessie and most of the hands rode fence and guarded herds. Navarro stayed with Miguel and Carlos, and Matt stuck close to Jessie. Even the bubbly Tom was allowed to ride that morning and he didn't leave Navarro's side. Mary Louise remained out of sight as much as possible. Gran observed everyone with keen eyes.

Tom had just returned to the settlement when trouble struck. Masked riders galloped into the yard and fired in all directions to force everyone to take cover while they did their evil tasks. The irrigation troughs from the well to the garden were roped and torn apart. The wooden V's were dragged and broken, then discarded. Other raiders raced their horses through the garden, trampling and unearthing the tender shoots and vines. They whooped and laughed as they worked to destroy the ranch's food supply.

Gran grabbed a rifle and shot at the villains, wounding one. The men returned the old woman's gunfire, and Gran was forced to take cover. But Tom didn't. He grabbed another rifle and sneaked to the front porch to shoot around the corner. The wounded attacker sent bullets flying in the boy's direction, and one caught Tom in the shoulder. As the merry band galloped away, Gran hurried to check on her grandson, but Mary Louise stayed hidden in her room.

When Jessie and the others returned home, they found Gran and Hank working on a pale and bleeding Tom. The bullet had been removed, and they were bandaging the boy. They explained what happened. Matt and the hands went to check on the damage.

Jessie hovered over her brother and told him how brave he was. Navarro offered encouraging words to both. The redhead saw how nervous her grandmother was, and she finally told her hysterical sister to get out of the room.

"Me and one of the boys should track them pronto," Navarro said.

Matt entered as he was making that suggestion and said, "I'll go with you."

"I'm done here," Hank told them. "I'll get some supplies ready."

Jessie looked at the two special men in her life. "I'm sending Gran, Tom, and Mary Louise into town where they'll be safe until we can settle this for good. Fletcher is getting bolder. He thinks that he can win now that Papa's gone."

Navarro and Matt vowed to stop him, then left together.

* * *

Early Sunday morning, the wagon was ready for the trip into town. Tom and Gran were made as comfortable as possible in the rear, with the boy's head in his grandmother's lap and a pillow at her back. Mary Louise sat up front with Davy, while Miguel and Jimmy Joe—excellent shots—rode along as guards.

Jessie kissed Tom and Gran and begged them not to worry. She told her sullen sister good-bye, then waved as the party left. She turned to the remaining men and said, "Let's see what we can do about repairing those troughs and saving the garden. I don't know when Matt and Navarro will return. Rusty and Carlos, you two stand guard. Everybody keep your rifles and pistols handy."

The ground wasn't as muddy as they expected, since the dry earth had sucked up most of the rain. Big John and Jefferson Clark repaired or replaced the troughs. Hank and Jessie worked in the damp soil to replant any seedlings that weren't damaged too badly; they filled in with seeds where plants were beyond recovery. They all knew how important the crop was for fresh vegetables in the summer and fall, then canned or dried ones during the winter and spring. A shortage would be costly or ruinous.

The remaining three men—Talbert, Walt, and Pete—rode range to watch the herd. Jessie had ordered them to return home if more trouble struck. She didn't want them taking chances against greater odds. Stock could be replaced, but men's lives could not. She prayed Fletcher had done enough damage for one week.

*

Miguel, Jimmy Joe, and Davy returned on Monday. Jessie's family was safe in town. The sheriff had come along, but there was nothing he could do without proof. But Toby Cooper pitched in and helped them that afternoon, then spent the night.

The lawman hadn't left before Navarro and Matt returned on Tuesday. The two men had trailed the raiders farther and farther south until they guessed the band was heading across the Mexican border to lay low for a while. They decided it was best for them to return before another band made the next attack.

Jessie was relieved to see both Navarro and Matt back safely and told them they had made a wise choice. Guards were positioned around the ranch, and the work continued as everyone waited tensely for their foe's next move.

Wednesday evening at dusk, Toby Cooper returned with a letter from Jessie's grandmother. She read it, then looked at Navarro and Matt. "Mary Louise married the bastard," she cried with growing fury. "My sister married Wilbur Fletcher! She's coming home tomorrow to get her things and move over there. It's time for our plan. Sheriff Cooper, if you'll agree, our war can end this week. Listen to what we say; then help us get the evidence you need."

Chapter

15

Jessie watched her sister as she packed her belongings. "How could you do this, Mary Louise? You know what kind of man he is."

"Yes, I do. He's rich, educated, handsome, and powerful. And he's most virile," she added with a sly smile. "I told you I was leaving soon. When Wilbur proposed, I jumped at his offer. He'll give me the wonderful life I deserve."

"What will you do when he kills all your family to get this ranch through you?"

"Don't be ridiculous, Jessica. Wilbur is tired of all this bickering and troubles. As soon as he finds a buyer for his ranch, we're moving back East. He has family there and several businesses. I'll have the life I've always wanted."

"He told you he's leaving?"

"Yes, and that's why I married him, among other things."

"You should only marry for love, little sister."

"Oh, I did."

"Love for the wrong things, Mary Louise. You've betrayed us, and maybe gotten us killed. Fletcher is only using you, you little fool."

The blonde's eyes revealed her hateful emotions. "What would you know about love? I have my dream now, so don't try to spoil it. Besides, you can't. If I were you, I'd start looking for a husband. But I hope you don't have eyes for that saddletramp. He won't be around very long. Remember that man who came here one day with Wilbur? He's an artist. He sketched Navarro Jones's face. Wilbur is having him checked out in every nearby state and territory. We know he's in trouble somewhere. As soon as someone recognizes him, he'll be gone or in prison. You can't share this ranch with a man like him!"

Jessie concealed her distress. "Why would you two think Navarro's in trouble with the law?"

"Wilbur can size up a man better than you two can. He had detectives searching for clues about that mysterious, no-good drifter, but he stopped them when I told him Navarro left. When he discovered the trash had returned, he put them back on the job. It won't be long before somebody shows great interest in your meddling gunslinger. I told Wilbur I had heard him mention Arizona, so he's sending one of his detectives there. I also told him how you two have been attacking him. You were right about me framing Navarro. I knew he was trouble and I was trying to get rid of him."

"You told him about us, and he's letting the matter drop? No way, little sister. How could you put nooses around our necks?"

"My loyalty is to my husband. I decided if I told him the truth, then let you know I had, you'd stop all this foolishness. Besides, Wilbur *isn't* behind it. I asked him not to make charges against you, and he's agreed to please me."

"It doesn't matter what you told him," Jessie insisted. "He can't prove anything against us. The law will think you're lying to help your husband. You wouldn't make a valuable witness against us. Who would believe a traitor and liar like you? No one. You're a bigger and greedier fool than I imagined."

The girl's dark-blue eyes sparkled with anger as she said coldly, "I told you, Jessica: he's letting it all drop and we're moving back East."

"Good, because he can't hurt us anymore. I'm hiring more men next week to ride fence and serve as guards. They'll have orders to shoot any man who trespasses on Lane property. While he was gone, Navarro contacted a man who'll loan me the money I need to repair all the damages your husband has done. He's a very rich gold-miner, and the man owed Navarro a big favor. I'm going into town tomorrow, then I'm meeting him on Saturday to pick up the loan. Navarro also worked out several deals with fort reservations to buy steers until my fall sale. I'm signing contracts in two weeks. Fletcher won't be a threat to me after Saturday. I'll have plenty of money to fight him with and to make this spread the best in the area. The miner is loaning me lots of cash against my fall roundup. I'll have enough money to buy out Fletcher so the next owner won't cause me trouble. We'll be back Saturday night. We're having a big party to celebrate. You'll understand why I can't invite you, *Mrs. Fletcher.*"

"It sounds as if we've both gotten lucky this time, sister dear. I wonder who you'll choose to share that wonderful life with," Mary Louise murmured in a taunting tone.

"Make sure you send me your address and I'll let you know."

*

Jessie, Navarro, and Matt rode into the town at Fort Davis on Friday. They took a different route and used great caution along the way. As soon as they arrived, they met with Toby Cooper to go over their daring plan. They were pleased to learn the sheriff was willing to assist them.

Since her love's return, Jessie had been unable to find more time alone with him. Tonight was no different, with Matthew Cordell in the room next to hers. She had been willing to chance exposure, but Navarro refused to risk tarnishing her name. What the desperado didn't tell the redhead was that he suspected the foreman was watching them especially closely because of Matt's love for Jessie and his determination to protect her from harm.

*

Saturday at noon, Jessie and her friends met with a stranger at the hotel, a man whom Toby Cooper had enlisted to aid their ruse. After a short time, she left with Navarro and Matt at her side, both carrying heavy saddlebags. The three mounted and headed for the trail back to the Box L Ranch. They rode in alert silence for half an hour before trouble struck.

At the sound of gunfire and pounding hooves behind them, Matt glanced over his shoulder, then shouted, "Get in front of us, Jessie! Ride hard and fast! We'll guard you! Go, woman!" he yelled when she hesitated. He wished she wasn't with them, but she had insisted on participating in this trap. Matt breathed a bit easier as she obeyed his last words with speed and skill.

Navarro and the worried foreman drew their weapons and, twisting in their saddles, exchanged shots with the gang pursuing them. Dodging and returning bullets, the three galloped toward the hidden posse of Sheriff Cooper, several deputized men, and a troop of soldiers under Captain Graham. The gang rapidly closed in on them from behind, and all realized they would not make it to help. They and the lawmen had guessed that Fletcher would make his move at least an hour from town. It was evident to Navarro and Matt that it was too perilous not to seek cover and take a defensive stand, as Jessie's life was at stake.

"Take cover, Jess!" Navarro shouted. "We can't outrun them!"

Over the commotion, the redhead heard her lover's command. She slowed and guided her paint into a dense, rocky area, then dismounted. Jessie grabbed her rifle and concealed herself. Soon, the two men joined her.

"Stay down," Matt instructed. "Hopefully the posse will get worried soon and come looking for us. Don't take any chances before help arrives."

The foreman and the gunslinger prepared to defend the woman they loved. Both knew they would sacrifice their lives if need be to save hers, a frightening fact Jessie was aware of too.

Jessie witnessed Matt and Navarro's love and concern for her. She knew she was fortunate to have two men who cared so deeply about her. She didn't want either to come to harm, so she disobeyed to help them fight. She prayed assistance would come quickly, as they were greatly outnumbered.

Navarro and Matt told her to stay down, but she replied, "We need all the fire-power we have. Don't worry about me, just think about them."

There wasn't time to argue with the determined female or to be distracted, so the men yielded to her resolve. All saw Wilbur Fletcher and his gang dismount and take cover a good distance from their location. In a loud voice they could hear, their enemy gave orders to his hirelings, who began to work their way closer to the pinned-down group. Men slipped around rocks in several directions.

"They're trying to encircle us and fence us in. They'll tighten our noose fast."

Jessie glanced at Matt, and he was eyeing her as if death was on their horizon. She sent him a smile full of confidence and undisguised affection. He returned it, then focused on the danger surrounding them.

"Take no risks, Jess." Navarro's voice broke into her troubled thoughts.

The redhead sent her love a radiant smile and nodded. "We'll be fine, you two. Surely the others will head our way soon."

"I hope so," Navarro murmured as he picked off another foe.

No one talked as the three faced different directions to protect each other. They heard Fletcher's voice increase in volume and agitation as his men were gunned down one by one. The desperate man worked his way closer to their place of concealment.

Jessie, Matt, and Navarro were unharmed so far, but it was looking bad to all three as more gunmen closed in on them from all sides. Fletcher and his men became more daring but used the protective terrain wisely. Jessie and her men knew there was no way to flee; they were trapped. If their ammunition gave out before the posse came to check on them and join the battle, they were all three dead, and the trio knew it.

"You shouldn't be here, Jessie."

"Yes, I should, Matt. He's after my ranch. He killed my father."

"Matt's right, Jess; we should have handled this danger."

"Don't lose hope, you two," she scolded in a softened tone.

Jessie was right; the large posse arrived with stealth and strength. A fierce gun battle erupted, one in their favor for a change. Their attackers panicked.

Determined not to be caught riding with his vicious hirelings, Wilbur Fletcher fought like a wild man. The gang knew they were exposed and outgunned; they struggled to escape. None made it. The bloody conflict—so long and costly to the Lanes—ended fast, with Wilbur Fletcher lying lifeless in the dirt, and those who survived surrendering their weapons.

As the lawmen and others gathered around the fallen bodies and captives, Jessie made a sweeping gesture and remarked, "There's your proof, Sheriff Cooper. I told you he was behind everything. I'm so glad you believed me and helped set this trap."

Toby Cooper looked at the ground and shifted uneasily. "I wanted it over with, Miss Lane," he admitted. "It was hard to believe Wilbur Fletcher could do such things. In all honesty, I expected to unmask somebody else here. You're lucky he decided to ride with them today. Strangers on unbranded horses would still have left questions about their boss's identity."

"There still is an unanswered question," Jessie murmured. "Why did he really want our land? I think it had to do with more than grass and water or expansion."

"I guess we'll never know," Matt commented, looking at their dead enemy.

Jessie nodded agreement. "Everyone all right?" she inquired.

"Only a few minor injuries on our side," Cooper replied. "We'll load these bodies, gather the prisoners, and head back to town. It's over, Miss Lane."

"It would have been over for us, too, if all of you hadn't agreed to help and arrived in the nick of time to save us. Thanks," she said, as she glanced around at the posse and smiled at them. "You can call on us for help anytime you need it."

They chatted as the men carried out the sheriff's orders. Then the lawmen and soldiers took the bodies and captives back to town and to close the lengthy case.

As soon as the posse departed, Jessie hugged and kissed the cheek of her foreman, then her lover. "Thanks, you two. You saved my life, my family, and my home. I couldn't have won this war without you. It's time to start learning how to move onward without Papa."

"You'll do fine, Jessie. You're smart and strong."

"Thanks, Matt, but I'll need you beside me every step of the way." She wanted him to know that Navarro would not push him out of her life and his home.

Navarro witnessed the easy rapport between Jessie Lane and Mathew Cordell; they appeared closer than upon his arrival in March. Envy surged through him as he thought about leaving his love behind with Matt. The foreman would probably stay with her forever.

"Anything wrong, Navarro?" Jessie asked, worried by his strained silence.

"Just tired and tense. We best ride for the ranch. We'll be lucky if we make it before nightfall. I'm happy this trap worked and you're safe. Looks as if my job's done around these parts."

Matt didn't want his rival's forlorn expression to work favorably on Jessie, so he said, "It's good you left Gran and Tom in town until everything is settled and Tom's stronger. Doc said he's healing fine, and doesn't have any permanent damage. That boy doesn't need more trouble in his life."

"Let's ride for home." Jessie said with a sigh. "We can finish talking there. I'm sure the boys are eager to see we made it out alive and well."

*

At the ranch, Jessie gave her hands the good news and the next day off, except for necessary chores that wouldn't take long. She asked Navarro and Matt to ride with her to Fletcher's home tomorrow to give the news about Fletcher to her sister. Navarro made a suggestion that surprised Jessie and pleased Matt: make the offer she had mentioned to Mary Louise on Thursday. He explained how to do it.

Jessie wished she could find time alone with her love, as she sensed the moment of parting had arrived. But the foreman must have sensed it, too, and stuck to the loner like a stubborn burr to a saddleblanket.

*

"I'm afraid I have bad news for you, Mary Louise. You were mistaken about your husband and, because of it, you're a widow now. I knew you would tell Fletcher about my loan, stock contracts, and new hands. I also knew he would try to stop them. He's already tried to kill our little brother and I knew he would come after me, too, so his wife could inherit the land he craved. He never intended to sell and move. He lied to you, or you lied to me." Jessie told Mary Louise all about the successful and fatal trap. "He's dead, and the trouble is over."

"You tricked me! You used me!" the shocked female shouted.

"That's right, little traitor. The sheriff and Army believed me, too; that's why they agreed to help expose him. He refused to surrender, so it's his fault he's dead. As for his widow, everyone knows what a treacherous girl you are. I also know now why you were so afraid of Navarro's return. You feared he would tell us how you tried to get him to kill Papa, and me, too, if necessary. How wicked you are! I can't imagine that Lane blood flows in your veins."

"It was only a trick to test his loyalty!" Mary Louise said huffily. "You know I would never hire anyone to kill my own family."

"You sided with Fletcher. How long have you been working with him?"

She glared at Jessie. "I haven't been. I'll admit I tried to pass clues to him, but that's all. I was terrified. I wanted the trouble over before we were hurt or dead. I can't help it if I fell under his spell and married him."

"I can see how grieved you are," Jessie scoffed. "Now, both Lane women are in the cattle business. Yet I fear you don't know enough to survive very long. Even with a good foreman, if you can find a man who'll work for a vile creature like you, you'll lose it all within a year. That's justice, Mary Louise."

"You're mean and cruel, Jessica. I can't stay here alone with these strangers. I don't know who I can trust among the hands. They could rape me and kill me and rob me after you leave. I have to go home with you until I can find a buyer and sell out, then move back East as planned."

"Would you like me to buy this place?" Jessie asked, "There are one hundred thousand acres, about thirty thousand head of stock, this house, and other structures. I'll offer you forty thousand dollars in cash; the balance will come in five-thousand-dollar payments every year until eighty thousand is paid, sooner if I can afford it."

"It's worth more. That isn't even a dollar an acre, and nothing for the cattle and buildings. I want more and I want the entire sale price now."

"But it'll save you the time and effort of searching for another buyer," Jessie countered. "There's no telling how long that will take. Not many men can afford a higher price or will want land dependent upon windmills for water and without room for expansion. The land isn't that good, Mary Louise; I only want it so another Fletcher can't move in and harass me. As for the stock, they'll replace those Fletcher rustled from us, so why should I buy them? Anyway, you don't have that many ready for market; most have years to mature. I'll have to pay men to tend them, feed them in winter and fattening pens at market, and hire drovers to drive them there. And you're forgetting you must be a rich widow now. What about those holdings Fletcher had back East? They must be worth a fortune, so why bleed your own family after all they've suffered from that man? I would imagine he also has a large account at the bank in town."

Jessie saw a glitter in the girl's sapphire eyes and could almost hear her avaricious mind racing in a lucrative direction. "You should be rich beyond your wildest dreams, Widow Fletcher. No matter—it's all I can afford. Forty thousand now and five thousand every year for eight years is a lot of money for support. If you invest it or buy a shop, it will earn you plenty to add to the rest. Are you forgetting I need to rebuild everything *your* husband destroyed? Breeding bulls don't come cheap; neither do sheds and windmills, or barbwire for all the fences he's cut. I'll have to hire seasonal wranglers for the fall roundup and pay for the cattle drive to Dodge. That's expensive and will take months. I know you're anxious to get back East and live in luxury. Maybe your widow's inheritance will sate your cravings for wealth, or you can find another rich husband to lasso back there. Take it or leave it. Let me know when you decide."

Mary Louise halted her sister's departure by yelling, "Wait! Let me think."

Jessie realized it was the hint about Wilbur's holdings back East that has swung the talk in her favor. "Well?" she prodded after the girl paced and mused a while.

"Where did you get so much cash? Is it from the robbery weeks ago?"

"I told you about the loan from Navarro's friend. Your husband and his gang were killed before they could steal it. I borrowed fifty thousand, but I have to keep ten to run the ranch with until fall roundup. It wasn't a gift, so I'll have to repay it." *Why shouldn't I use the bastard's money to buy his land?* Jessie mentally scoffed. *He owes me far more for all he did to us. With stock sales, I can come up with the other forty over eight years. The stock will be worth that much. It's perfect.*

"Are you sure you can come up with the payments? What if you don't succeed with the ranch? I'll be out forty thousand dollars."

"Even if I didn't, isn't forty thousand a lot to earn from such a brief marriage? Besides, you have the remainder of his wealth. Perhaps even a fancy mansion back there."

"I don't trust you, Jessica. You'll try to cheat me just to be mean."

"You know I wouldn't do that. I'll send for our lawyer tomorrow to draw up a legal contract. We can sign it Tuesday in his office. I can pay you; then, you can leave. There's a stage east on Thursday. You can be waiting for it. The sooner you lay claim to your husband's estate, the better. You don't want greedy relatives hearing about his death and rushing in to confiscate your treasures."

Mary Louise didn't think twice before seizing the golden opportunity. "That sounds fine. Let me gather a few things and we can go home."

"You *are* home, Mrs. Fletcher. But I'll leave Matt here to guard you. I want him to check over the remaining men and my new property. If you've forgotten, there are chores to be done here, too. I'll send a few men over tomorrow to stay here until the deal is closed. You'll be fine. You always are."

"What about Gran and Tom? I have to tell them good-bye."

"You did, when you deserted our family to marry our enemy. When Fletcher rode out with his gang, you could have sent word to the boys at the ranch to meet us on the trail to warn us, but you didn't. However, you can say what you like to them after our meeting. Gran and Tom are still in town. Surely you recall that our little brother was almost murdered a week ago. I'm going to fetch them Tuesday. We'll close our deal and go our separate paths. Besides, you need to stay here and pack for your long journey."

"You sure it's safe for me and Matt?"

"Yes, or I wouldn't let him remain behind. Fletcher's gang was different from his hired hands. Perhaps I'll keep some of them. I'll leave that up to my foreman. As soon as the deal's closed, we'll tear down the fence between us."

"You hate me, don't you?"

"No, Mary Louise. You're my sister, but I'm disappointed and angry with you. All you think or care about is yourself. One day you'll be sorry. You've caused us all a lot of pain, and I don't want you around us right now. Lord knows I wish it were different, but it isn't. You have what you wanted, so be happy."

The girl tossed her blonde hair over her shoulder. "I most assuredly will, Jessica. When I'm settled back East, I'll let you know where to send my payments."

"I'm certain you will."

"Tell Matt he can sleep in one of the other bedrooms."

"If you'll promise not to try to frame him like you did Navarro."

The girl frowned. "Whatever would I want with Mathew Cordell?"

"Since Fletcher's the kind of man who appeals to you, I can understand you wouldn't be interested in Matt. He's much too good for a cold and greedy woman like you."

"Don't provoke me into changing my mind, Jessica," she threatened.

"You won't, because it'll keep you here. But I'm warning you, little sister, if you don't sign those papers Tuesday, the deal is off *permanently*. Challenge me on this, and you'll pay heavily. I swear I'll let you flounder and fail to teach you the biggest lesson of your miserable life."

Jessie left the beautifully appointed room of the hacienda-style home. She walked through the walled yard and joined Navarro and Matt. "She took the offer. Are you sure you want me to have the money, Navarro?"

"Yes. You deserve it. Fletcher cost your family more. I'll go after it and see you two back at the ranch. My job's over, so I'll be leaving afterward."

Jessie rushed on to conceal her reaction to his words. "I told Mary Louise Matt would stay here tonight." She related the talk with her sister. "Do you mind, Matt? I don't want her coming home, but she *is* my sister. You think it's safe for you to stay here with their boss dead?"

"Navarro and I have looked the place and the men over good. It's all fine, Jessie."

"I'll have Davy and Rusty come over first thing in the morning. You tell the men what to do. Decide which ones you want to keep on, if any."

"I won't let you down, Jessie," the foreman vowed.

"I know, Matt. Thanks." Jessie turned to her lover who seemed to be pretending he wasn't watching her. She sensed how much he hated to leave her and end their relationship, yet she also sensed that he was anxious to depart as quickly as possible. She wished she knew why. "You sure you need to fetch the money tonight?"

Navarro glanced at the horizon and inhaled. "Yep," he replied. "I'll see both of you at the ranch tomorrow. I'll tell everybody good-bye, then ride out." Before Jessie could protest, the fugitive mounted and galloped away.

Matt was pleased that Navarro was still determined to leave, but he couldn't understand why the gunslinger would go. The foreman was certain the other man loved his life at the Box L, as well as Jessica Lane. He couldn't imagine why Navarro would rather return to lonely drifting and gunfighting instead of remaining with a woman who would no doubt marry him, bear his children, and make him a successful rancher and happy man. Something terrible had to be eating at Navarro and pushing him ever onward in search of peace.

To lessen her sadness, Matt coaxed, "Don't worry, Jessie; he'll be fine. Men like Navarro Jones know how to take care of themselves."

"I know, Matt, but he could have a good life here."

"Settling down isn't what he wants or needs, Jessie." He caressed her cheek as he urged, "Don't try to change his mind about leaving; it will hurt both of you. Part as friends; that's what he needs most from all of us right now. If he ever gets wandering out of his blood, he might return," he suggested, hoping Jessie would let the drifter go, and give him time to win her. He couldn't with Navarro present.

"You're right, as usual, Matt. I'll keep quiet. Thanks for the advice."

Matt smiled at Jessie and bid her farewell, glad Navarro would be gone soon.

*

It was nearing dawn when Navarro returned and placed the money in Jessie's hand. He had ridden all night to accomplish his mission. He looked tired and dejected. "I kept a little to see me to my next job somewhere far away. Your trouble's over, Jess. I have to leave now and I won't be coming back."

Jessie had slept little and her eyes were dark with worry. "Do you really have to go? I need you."

The desperado stared at the floor, then looked at her. "No, Jess, you don't. You're just tired and scared. Your father is gone and the ranch is yours now. In a couple of days, Fletcher's spread will be yours, too. You'll do fine. One day you'll meet a good man and marry him. Forget me, Jess; I'm nothing but trouble."

"How can I forget you? I love you. Please stay. I can make you happy. You can't keep drifting forever. I know you love me and want me, too. Don't be so stubborn and proud. Make your home and peace here with me, with *us* all. Please."

"Don't make it harder for us to part, Jess. I'll never forget what you've done for me. I took this job as a hiding and resting place, but I got too involved with you. I lost my head for a while. We can't settle down together. When your head clears after I'm gone, you'll know this is for the best."

"Will I, Navarro? You're the first man to make me want to be more than Jedidiah Lane's 'son.' You're a special man. How can anyone take your place in my heart and life?"

"Don't *you* be stubborn and spoil things for yourself, Jess. I hope I'm not the last man to make you glad you're a woman, a strong and beautiful and giving woman. Don't ruin the rest of your life because of me. I was wrong to let you believe this could last. I'm sorry I hurt you. If you remember anything about me, remember how well we worked together, what good friends we were."

"*Were*, Navarro?"

"It's past now, Jess, and the past can't be changed. I should know."

"I don't believe you. You said before you wouldn't say anything rather than lie. Now you're trying to pretend nothing important happened between us. That isn't true, and we both know it. I'll wait for you to change your mind. You can't run forever. When you realize that, I'll be here."

"Don't wait, Jess. I won't be back—ever. I can't. I'm a condemned man."

"What do you mean? You said you would explain everything before you left."

Navarro squeezed his eyes shut and inhaled deeply. "I dread this, Jess, but you have to know the dirty truth. I'm wanted for gold robbery, murder, and theft. I didn't commit the robbery, but I was arrested and imprisoned for it. The last time I was with my father, his gang stole a shipment of gold. I was at his hideout packing to leave when the law surrounded the place and attacked. Carl and his men were killed, but I was only wounded. I was tried and sentenced. I told them I wasn't guilty, but they didn't believe me. I spent two and a half years in a brutal prison in Arizona." He told her about the cruelties and deprivations he had endured, and how he had gotten the scars on his back. "I had seventeen and a half years to go. I couldn't take any more. I escaped into the desert one day, but was so weak that they recaptured me. Prison was even worse than the first time. I escaped again last November, but I had to kill the guard beating me. I set a false trail to Colorado, stole that horse and saddle and supplies, and rode this way. I was out four months when I met you. I figured the law was heading in the other direction and I needed rest, so I took your job. I only meant to stay for a little while."

Her hand grasped his. "But you're innocent. You had no choice."

He squeezed it and released it. "The law doesn't see it that way. You hang for murder, Jess. The longer I stay here, the tighter I feel that noose closing around my neck. I have to leave or all of you are in danger. If the law came here, you'd be charged with helping me. I can't do that to you or Tom or Gran. Fletcher sent out those sketches and detectives. Men could be on my trail this minute. If I'm caught, you'd have to watch me hang. You could lose everything you've fought for because of me. It isn't worth the risk, Jess. None of you would be safe with me around. Think about Tom and Gran, Jess, not about us. Besides, I was raised a wild Apache half-breed. I have trail dust in my boots and blood. I'm not the settling-down kind." He had to discourage her. He could never endanger her and the others just so he could enjoy his dream for a short while. He was angry and bitter. He didn't want to lose her and the life she was offering, but he had no choice. If only he hadn't killed that guard, he might have been able to give himself up, serve his time, and return to her a free man. Maybe he could have straightened out his mess then, but now it was too late. "It's ride or die, Jess. I have to move on."

"I could sell out and we could go with you," Jessie suggested. "Surely there's someplace where we'd all be safe and happy."

"No, Jess. This is your home; you can't give up now. I don't want you all living like I'm forced to live. You and your family and the boys are the only friends I've ever had. Don't ask me to endanger them. You've taught me how precious life is and how good it could be if I didn't have this black cloud over my head. You made me open up and feel things I never have before. They broke me in prison, Jessie, but you gave me back my confidence. You made me care about *how* I survived. I'll try to stay out of trouble and danger from now on. It's been good here, but I won't stay and I won't return. I mean it, Jess."

"Can you forget me, Navarro?"

"I won't even try. Don't want to. My only good memories are of the times with you. But a memory is all you can be to me, and me to you. Accept that, Jess, or you'll be as miserable and bitter as I was for years. I kept fooling myself about what was important and real in life. Don't make that same mistake."

"What's real and important is us, Navarro."

"Don't, Jess, please." For the first time in his life, Navarro wanted to cry. He couldn't reveal any weakness before her. She had to be protected.

"I can help clear you, Navarro. I can get the money to bribe those other guards to silence. I can tell the law what a fine man you are, what you've done for us."

"What good would that do, Jess? I'm guilty! I'm a wanted, hunted man—a killer, an outlaw. You don't know what prison is like. I can't risk having you sent there as my accomplice. I'd rather die than hurt you. If the law finds me, it's either more killing as a

means to escape or surrender to the hangman. And I can't risk involving the people I
. . . like most in this world."

"You'll be safe here, Navarro. Arizona is long way off. The boys like you. They're
loyal to me. They'd help me protect you."

"You're forgetting about Fletcher's sketches and his detectives. None of us would
be safe with a condemned man around." He tried another road to convince her. "I
have sand in my boots and the law on my back. It's riding time. Be strong and never
look back, Jess. Like the wind, I'll always feel you around me."

"You're too hard on yourself, Navarro. I don't care about your birth or blood."

He had to make her care, or think she did. "You don't care I'm part savage? You
don't care my white blood butchered my Indian blood and imprisoned the survivors
on a filthy reservation? You don't care I'm a bastard child? A killer?"

"I'm sorry about your mother's death and your father's cruelties."

"Don't be. They never loved me or wanted me."

"*I* love and want you, Navarro. You're good enough for me. You're good enough
for anyone. Don't be afraid to love, afraid to take risks to claim happiness."

"I've taken plenty in my life, Jess, and they all hurt me."

She stepped closer to him. "I won't."

He backed away, determined to keep a clear head. "But I *could* hurt you. I can't
chance that, Jess. I left my evil father three times: at twelve, twenty, and twenty-four.
But I was never free of him; his blood was always flowing in me, making me feel
worthless. I saw him gunned down, and I didn't even shed one tear."

"I don't blame you for feeling that way. But haven't you learned that not everyone can feel or show love, Navarro? My own sister is like that, and she didn't endure
the harsh things you have. She had a good life and a family who loved her, but they
weren't enough. Something happens to certain people to make them cold and hard
and selfish. Either your parents never learned about love and all that goes with it, or
things happened in their lives to kill that emotion. Maybe it was the way they were
raised, but you aren't like them. Sure, you've made mistakes, but you've suffered
enough for them. I don't care if the law is after you."

"I have to care for both our sakes, Jess. I'm not what Miss Jessica Lane needs.
Think of your family and friends and hands. Think of the people you do business with.
Think they want to deal with a half-breed bastard? Think we could keep me hidden on
the ranch forever? The truth would come out one day, Jess. It's useless. What about
children? You want to pass this evil Breed blood and peril on to them?"

"You aren't evil, Navarro. You gave up that kind of life, white and Indian."

"Blood don't leave your body unless you're dead, Jess. Your past can't be rubbed
out like a message scratched in the dirt. What could you tell folks when they asked
about me? Make up lies? Can you live like that for the rest of your life? Become hard
and cold, like me? No, Jess. It isn't fair."

"I'll do whatever I must to have you."

"I'm no good for you or anyone," he stressed.

"You're perfect for me, Navarro Breed."

"You're wrong, blinded, Jess. I used to think it wasn't my fault, but partly it is. I
could have run away as a boy. I could have left the Apaches anytime. I could have never
returned to my father. Inside, I'm just as bad, selfish, and heartless as my mother and
father were."

"Nothing in your past alters my opinion about the man you are today. You've
changed, Navarro. Can't you see that? You didn't stay for the money. You aren't giving

up what you want now for selfish reasons. Doesn't that tell you something about yourself? If you're selfish and heartless, how can you feel anything for me and the others? Why would our safety mean anything to an evil man? You have cause to be bitter and wary after what you've experienced. You have so much good and gentleness inside. No matter how hard you struggle to hide that, you can't. Don't try, my love. No matter how your parents raised you, you know the difference between right and wrong, between good and bad."

"My father and the Apaches taught me," he murmured, "when you see something you want, you take it and the risks be damned."

"Then why haven't you stolen me?"

"I have, Jess, in some ways."

"Are they enough for you?"

"They have to be. I've done lots of bad things in the past and made lots of enemies along my trail. If I stayed, it would only bring you even more heartache. How could I never step off this ranch or let anyone step onto it for fear of recognizing me? There could be—probably are—wanted posters out on me. You have seasonal hands in the spring and fall; you have cattle drives; you have contact with suppliers. I can't hide out, Jess. We can't seclude ourselves from the outside world. The more you expand, the more likely that someone who has seen my poster will arrive. You're listening, but you're not hearing me, Jess. It's too late for us. It's good-bye this time."

Jessie realized the truth in his tormenting words. She knew she couldn't stop him from leaving, but she would always go on hoping he would return. "No matter what you say, I'll wait for you. The law can't keep searching forever. Go somewhere safe and lay low. When enough time passes, come back to me. You can't change my mind about waiting. Can you love me one last time?"

"No, Jess; it would be too hard on us. Besides, the boys are stirring. There's no time left. You don't need a half-breed bastard outlaw fouling up your new life. You're chasing the wind. Let this wild and dangerous mustang go free to roam alone, or you'll get hurt trying to lasso and break him."

"You'll be back one day, Navarro. I believe that with all my heart. I want you to take something with you to remind you of me."

Navarro waited for her to fetch a locket with her picture inside. It was a tiny painting that she had commissioned for her grandmother's birthday. She opened it and showed it to him. "Would you like to have this?" she offered.

The fugitive took the necklace, stared at his love's image, snapped it shut, and pushed it into his pocket. He couldn't tell her he loved her; that wasn't fair with him deserting her. Anguish knifed his heart as he realized the wonderful life that was being stolen from him. He stroked her unbound hair and caressed her cheek, then dropped his hands to his sides. "I'm sorry, Jess. I'll miss you."

Tears glimmered in her eyes. "I'll miss you, too." She went into his arms and hugged him. "So much," she murmured. She lifted her head and rose on her tiptoes to kiss him. It was a bittersweet kiss that revealed love and torment, and he returned it urgently. She didn't try to cling to him when he pulled away, looked at her, then went and mounted his horse.

Jessie stood on the back porch, returned his last emotion-filled gaze, then watched his departure. She understood and shared his anguish and resentment. Something real and important had entered his life at last, but he couldn't grasp or keep it. This denial was the greatest cruelty of all, but she was helpless to save him. Not once had he said, *I love you,* though she knew it was so. If only she could be as convinced he would return one day. But somehow, a feeling of finality—like that of her father's death weeks ago— surrounded her. For the first time, hopelessness consumed Jessie. Tears escaped her eyes and flowed down her cheeks, and she hurried inside to let them flow freely, knowing her life was riding away from her this glorious day in June.

On Tuesday, Mary Louise came to the office where Jessie was awaiting her. The lawyer explained the papers and had both women sign them. There were three originals: one for each woman and one for the lawyer's files. Jessie gave her sister forty thousand dollars, and Mary Louise signed she had received it. Both agreed that the balance of payments were due in equal installments each June for eight years. He told them the deal was legal and final, then left them alone to talk.

Since they might never see each other again, Jessie said kindly, "It's done, Mary Louise. Why not part as friends? I love you, and I'm sorry life didn't work out for you here. I hope you'll be happy back East, and please be careful. You're a rich woman, and people might try to take advantage of you. Write us when you get settled."

"Don't be nice when it's too late, Jessica. If you're hoping I'll cancel your debt to me because I'm wealthy now, you're wrong. I'll never come home again. I hated it here. You and Father almost got us all killed."

Jessie was provoked by the girl's hostility. "Papa might still be alive if you hadn't framed Navarro and gotten him fired. If he hadn't been so troubled over his war with Fletcher and with you, he wouldn't have been there alone. You have your freedom and money, so I hope you enjoy them. They carried a big price."

"You fool. Father didn't fire him because of me. He knew I was lying. He did it to keep you and Navarro apart. You're all he's ever cared about and he couldn't risk losing you to another man. If you believed you could win a wild and dangerous man like that drifter, you're crazy. He's selfish and unfeeling. Tell me, what did you give him for this money?" she asked, tapping the bulging bag. "I know he stole it from Wilbur. I'm sure it had a big price, too."

"You're the one who's selfish and unfeeling, Mary Louise. I pity you. One day, money and looks won't be enough to protect you from life or make you happy."

"Says the miserable creature to the rich and respected widow. I'll bet you rolled in the grass with him many times. He's probably waiting for you in your room this very minute for a wild celebration."

"He's gone. His job is done. He left yesterday morning."

"Because you aren't woman enough to hold him. You're too much like Father."

"I'm sorry you resent me so much, little sister. I've suspected it for a long time, but I prayed it wasn't true. If Mama hadn't died when you were so young, maybe you would be different. Maybe you would possess a heart and a conscience. Maybe you would love home and family as the rest of us do."

"Mother's death isn't responsible for the way I am: Father is. He sent me away like unwanted baggage. I was alone and afraid. I made myself tough and smart. Then he forced me back to this savage land. He ignored me and was hateful to me. And to Tom. Only you pleased him and earned his love and respect."

"You're wrong, but I'm still not sure you know why. I'll tell you. Besides your sorry attitude and defiance, you're Mama's reflection. Haven't you noticed that in the mirror? You stare into it enough to have seen the truth. You were a constant reminder of what he lost. It was wrong, but he couldn't help himself. He loved her so much and he was so lonely without her. He loved you, too, but he didn't know how to show it, especially with you being so hateful and cold. The same is true of Tom. Papa blamed himself for Tom's problems. They made him feel helpless. It hurt him to watch Tom suffer. You've done your best to make everyone miserable. Go back East to the life you crave. I hope you find happiness there, and I hope you face the truth before it's too late."

"I will be more than happy; I'll be ecstatic. Wilbur's businesses and fortune are mine now. I'll live in grand style and leisure while you grub in the dirt and smelly manure to eke out a simple life. Be glad I accepted your meager offer until I could get my affairs settled. Be glad my marriage to him profited both of us."

"There's no need for us to continue this destructive talk. If you want to see Gran and Tom, do so; we'll be leaving in an hour. Good-bye, Mary Louise."

"Good-bye, Jessica. You've seen the last of me."

Jessie's intuition told her that last statement wasn't true, and she felt a surge of dread.

*

The following dawn, Jessie gathered the eggs and released the chickens from their coop so they could go scratching. She milked the cows and set them free in their confining pasture near the barn, then grabbed a pitchfork and tossed hay to the horses kept in the nearby corral. Several hands offered to assist her, but she declined their help. She needed hard work to occupy her mind. So many changes had occurred in her life lately, and she hadn't adjusted to them yet.

Matt witnessed the turmoil in Jessie and let her be without intruding. He went about his business, taking as much of the load as possible off her shoulders. Yet he found himself checking the horizon every so often to see if Navarro Jones was riding back to stake a claim on the woman they both loved.

When he sighted a lone rider that afternoon, he stiffened, but it was only Slim with the mail. He smiled as Slim handed him some letters without dismounting, tipped his hat, and left. He had forgotten this was one of the two days Slim was paid to deliver the mail each month.

Jessie ripped open the letter from the Cattlemen's Association and read it aloud to the foreman. "A little late, but good news," she remarked. "I wonder if I'm the first female rancher they've asked to join them."

"You going to?" he asked, noting the pleased and proud look in her gaze.

"Yep. I want as much power and influence as I can get before another Fletcher comes along. Besides, it's good business. I tried to get Papa to join, but he refused. After those Spanish Fever and Panic scares, I was surprised he didn't. I know it's only been in existence a few years, but banding together will make us all stronger. We'll attend their next meeting in Dodge after the cattle drive."

* * *

Thursday, Jessie, Matt, and some of her hands rode to the Bar F Ranch. The foreman selected which men he would keep on their payroll. Some were assigned to tend the pigs, chickens, stock, and garden. The chuckhouse cook was retained to feed them. Miguel and Carlos were asked to be assistant foremen over their new hands. Matt thought it wisest to mix the two sets of cowboys, and divided them between the two settlements as needed.

Jessie walked through the house with Matt. The first floor contained an enormous living area with a fireplace, couch, several chairs, tables with hand-painted oil lamps, costly paintings, fragile vases, a liquor bar with crystal glasses and a fine mirror, masculine desk, and billiard table. She envisioned a loving couple living there, then a happy family. Her mind easily pictured a husband stoking a cozy fire with children playing near its warmth on a wintry day. She imagined the couple snuggled together on the couch after their little ones were tucked in bed—kissing, talking, and sharing everything thing in their lives. Her mind's eye saw her filling the expensive vases with colorful flowers and filling the lovely lamps with oil.

The dreamy-eyed redhead cleared her tight throat and scolded her wandering thoughts as she realized the face of the man in her fantasy kept fading from Navarro's to Mathew Cordell's! She presumed it was because Matt was a homebody, a rancher, a familiar companion; while Navarro Breed was a camper and a drifter. It was difficult to imagine Navarro being comfortable in a house like this. Jessie cast aside such painful thoughts and comparisons.

She had never seen anything so grand. Matt followed her into a large dining room with Spanish furniture that matched the hacienda style of the house, then into a well-designed kitchen, and finally to a bathing closet on the back porch. They peeked inside and were amazed by the luxury they observed.

"He certainly enjoyed living high and fine, Matt. It's beautiful, all of it."

Matt liked the house and the emotions it stirred within him. He wondered why he wasn't uneasy in this opulent setting that should make a cowpoke feel as corraled as a Sunday suit and a choking necktie. He realized it was because Jessie was with him and because she liked the house, too, and fit perfectly into its surroundings. Nothing of Fletcher's wicked aura lingered there. It was a tranquil and inviting home, one he would enjoy living in with her.

They went upstairs wide-eyed and in silence. They saw a spacious area with a fireplace to warm the second floor. It opened into two charming guestrooms, an extra room, and finally the master suite. At one end of the large yet intimate suite were a closet and a bathing room, and each had a window facing the front yard. At the other was an inviting, private sitting area. The furniture was massive and dark, but artistically carved. To her surprise, the decor was lovely.

Both gazed at the large bed that looked comfortable and enticing. Both imagined sharing it with a mate and making passionate love there.

Those sensual thoughts stimulated Matt. He walked into the bathing closet and glanced out the front window. He needed to master the runaway emotions that the seductive setting had aroused. He mustn't close in on Jessie until she pulled free of Navarro, and there hadn't been enough time for that. But Matt's romantic fantasy was powerful and tempting, and he yearned to make it a reality.

Jessie observed Matt's broad back and pondered his curious behavior. His body had stiffened, his gaze seemed guilty, and his face looked slightly flushed. Perhaps the intimate setting disquieted him or gave him romantic daydreams similar to those she was experiencing. She noticed how his brown hair teased at his collar and how well his garments fit his muscular frame. He was handsome and appealing, more so than she had ever realized. He would make some lucky woman a fine husband, and he would be a marvelous father. Jessie felt envious of the female who would share such love and happiness, when she herself was so denied. She hoped the woman would be worthy of Mathew Cordell.

Jessie's gaze returned to the bed. She couldn't help but wonder how different it would be to share it with Matt rather than Navarro. Her foreman clearly had the traits of a loyal husband and good father. Would a wild and restless drifter like Navarro Breed feel tied down by such responsibilities? Could the fugitive change and settle down, if not for his peril? Her serene mood faded with such worries and doubts.

"Ready to go, Matt?" she asked, needing fresh air and a change of scene.

He turned and smiled. "Yep, but I sure do like it here. A fine home, Jessie."

"Yes, it is, Matt," she admitted. "For the right couple."

Outside, she glanced back at the facade of creamy red-trimmed stucco. Two arched windows were in the dining room and two in the living area. On the second floor, smaller versions were in the same places, in addition to one above the front door. A wall encircled the house, and colorful flowers and bushes were planted in spots along the matching stucco fence. She and Matt walked beneath the arched entrance, then smiled at each other, as if agreeing once more.

"I'll bet Mary Louise hated to leave this house," Jessie said. "Fletcher clearly put a lot of money and effort into it. Get Miguel and Carlos to lock it up for now. I'll decide what to do about it later. I'm sure some of the things inside are very valuable. Tell them to keep an eye on it." She took one last look at the place and left.

*

On Friday, Jessie wrote her letter of acceptance to the Cattlemen's Association and thanked them for inviting her to join. She related the news of Wilbur Fletcher's death and the circumstances behind it, proving her allegations.

Matt sent Big John Williams to oil the windmills around both properties, and Jefferson Clark went as his assistant. The foreman assigned several men to begin a new hayshed in the pasture and showed them where to construct it. Other hands were put to work on the garden, which was coming back nicely.

Tom was still either in bed or relaxing in a chair until his wound healed completely. Gran fussed over her two grandchildren every day.

As Jessie did the Saturday-afternoon milking, Matt returned from his tasks and joined her. She glanced up and said, "I still miss Sookie and Bess. I guess it's strange how milk cows become like pets. I miss Scout and Buck, too. I'd like to get another dog. You think any of the people in town have one?"

"Next time I go for supplies, I'll check around . . . You doing all right, Jessie?" he added hesitantly.

She caught his meaning. "Yes, but it's hard some days." Her hands halted their milking motions and she glanced at him over the cow's back. He was so kind and thoughtful, and she was grateful to have him. "It was terrible when Mama died, but it was worse with Papa. He and I were closer. His death was so violent, Matt. Do you think he suffered much?"

Matt rested his arms over the cow's back. "I pray not, Jessie. A wound like his usually kills fast. Try not to think about it."

She went back to work. "I can't help it, Matt. I keep wondering if his killer was punished. How do we know the murderer was one of the men with Fletcher that day? He could be free while my father's dead."

"You have to believe he was slain with the others, Jessie, or it'll drive you loco. If he wasn't, he'll get his due some day."

"I guess you're right." Jessie was pained by her recent losses, apprehensive about her enormous responsibilities, and soul-weary after the long struggle for survival and peace. There was so much to do. "Matt, you wouldn't ever . . ."

When she hesitated, the foreman coaxed, "Ever what, Jessie?"

"Leave again, would you? I don't know what I would do if you left me, too. I depend on you so much. You're my strength and courage, my right hand. I trust you for advice. You'd never let me fail or quit. Being with you and talking with you is so comfortable and easy. We've been good friends for a long time, Matt. I just want you to know how much I need you and appreciate you."

"Even if there's another war, I won't desert you, Jessie. I don't have any hankering to see other places. I'm happy here; this is my home and family."

"What about your brother? Do you hear from him much?"

"About once a year. I can't write him 'cause he's always on the move, like Navarro . . . You miss him, don't you?"

"Yes. He was a good friend. He risked a lot to help us. I wish he had stayed. He's a lonely and troubled man. We could have been good for him."

"He was in trouble, Jessie. I can't explain how or what, but he had a devil on his back. A man trying to buck one of those off is dangerous to be around."

"You're right again, but I'm sorry you are. Let's drop all this depressing talk. We need to decide what to do about Fletcher's brand. There's no way we can change a bar *F* to a boxed *L*. I guess, just keep them with Fletcher's brand; we have proof of purchase. You still think it's all right for us to leave tomorrow?"

"Yep. The men have their orders. I put Rusty in charge over here, Miguel and Carlos over there. They have plenty to keep them busy. If there's any minor trouble, we have enough hands to deal with it. We need to get to San Antonio and pick out those new bulls before breeding season. After we choose them, it'll take the boys weeks to drive them home across country."

"I'll be packed and ready to leave early tomorrow. The stage goes out of Fort Stockton at eight Monday morning. We'll be there in three days. That's a lot easier than horseback across country, and a much shorter trip. Maybe we'll have some fun there. Lord knows we need it and deserve it. You take your suit, and I'll take my prettiest dress. We just might kick up our heels, Mister Foreman."

*

As Jessie stretched out in her bed, assorted images and worries flooded her mind. It had been such a depressing day, and she didn't know why. The meeting with the new men at Fletcher's—no, *her*—ranch had passed without a hitch. Everything was going fine, except for Navarro's departure on Monday.

Yet, a terrible sensation of . . . She didn't know how to explain it, but an awful feeling of doom had attacked her two days ago and still lingered in her mind. She wished she could grasp its meaning, if it had one. Perhaps she was only exhausted and tense.

She must accept losing Navarro, as a life with him was impossible, would always be impossible. His parting words were wise and true. They had been rocks and havens for each other when each needed them desperately. Yet if they weren't meant to share a destiny, why was their love so strong and their separation so painful?

Chapter

17

Monday morning, June nineteenth, Jessica Lane and Mathew Cordell climbed into the stagecoach at Fort Stockton. Their horses would be boarded there and retrieved upon their return next week. They had eaten breakfast together, then headed out for San Antonio.

The stage traveled at a slow pace and halted every fifteen miles at swing stations to change teams. They headed eastward to the Pecos River, then southward to the crossing point, passing the ruins of Fort Lancaster on Live Oak Creek that had been evacuated in '61. Early afternoon, they stopped for a light meal, and finally around eight o'clock they pulled into a home station on the right bank of Devils River to spend the night. They could see the nearby ruins of Camp Hudson, deserted in '68. After a hearty meal cooked by the keeper's wife, the passengers went to their assigned places and turned in to sleep.

*

The bumpy journey continued southeastward after breakfast and followed the same schedule. They headed into the Hill Country where the stage often had to slow for rolling terrain. Hills and peaks were in all directions, and the coach seemed to roll as they did, but not as smoothly. The landscape was dotted with color from bluebonnets, Indian paintbrush, purplish verbena, daisies, firewheels, cactus, and greenery. Mesquites, junipers, live oaks, and occasional redbuds and willows covered the hills. Sometimes early in the morning or late in the evening, they saw bobcats, javelinas, coyotes, deer, skunks, and badgers. When the stage was slowed by terrain, they even glimpsed rattlers, mice, and spiders. On nearly every bush and rock, a variety of lizards sunned themselves, undisturbed by their passing. It seemed as if this area was alive with vegetation and life, even if it was hot and dusty inside the jarring coach.

On the right side of the Las Moras Creek they passed Fort Clark, established in '52 and still occupied. Heading eastward, they crossed the Nueces River. Nearing eight again, they halted for the night at Uvalde Station near the ruins of Fort Inge on the bank of the Leon River. It was close to the junction of the road to Eagle Pass at the Rio Grande border. Uvalde had been notoriously dangerous in the fifties and sixties, and the driver said it wasn't much better these days. He didn't need to advise the weary, bone-sore passengers to stay at the station and get a good night's sleep. They did.

*

It was nearing dusk when Matt said, "We'll be there soon, Jessie. Looks like we'll make it without any trouble."

"Good. I'm ready for a nice meal, a hot bath, and a soft bed."

They hadn't traveled as far that day; their progress had been slower because of the hilly countryside. Matt pointed to San Antonio in the distance.

As Jessie watched the town come closer, she remarked, "it's so large. I love it every time I come here. I hope Mr. Turly has some good bulls for sale."

"He always does, so don't worry."

They hadn't talked much during the journey because of the other passengers. They had watched the scenery, and dozed. Reading, as Jessie quickly learned, was impossible because of the bouncing ride. She ached all over, even more than she did after eighteen hours or more in the saddle.

The stagecoach pulled into the station at the edge of town. Matt helped Jessie down. He hired a buggy driver to carry them and their luggage to a hotel. After they registered, they were guided to their rooms. They made plans to bathe, change, and meet for dinner downstairs.

When Jessie came down to join Matt, he was waiting at the base of the steps. His hair was combed and waved from his face and his chocolate eyes were bright with pleasure and admiration. He smiled, revealing white teeth that stood out against his deeply tanned face. His garments—white shirt, black vest, coat, and pants—fit him like a glove, displaying his broad shoulders and trim waist. Mathew Cordell "cut a fine figure," as her Papa used to say.

Enchanted, Matt gazed at the female approaching him. Even though she was beautiful dirty and in work clothes and with a braid, she sure looked different all dressed up. Her auburn tresses were pinned up in lovely curls that bounced when she walked. Her gown was slightly off her shoulders. He found that golden expanse of flesh enticing. The neckline, lower than what she normally wore, made her neck seem longer and silkier. The puffy short sleeves revealed arms that were also golden and firm from hard work. The waist was snug and exposed her slenderness. The flowing skirt moved with her, and he realized how graceful and feminine she was. Never had she appeared more like a ravishing woman than she did tonight. He couldn't take his eyes off her.

Jessie walked around the foreman, eyeing him up and down. She smiled and jested, "We clean up good for ranch hands, Matt."

"You're beautiful, Jessie. I've never seen that dress before, or your hair like that. I'll have to fight the men off you tonight."

Jessie mellowed under his gaze and compliment. She smoothed her skirt as she replied, "Gran made it for me from a Butterick catalogue pattern. This is the first time I've worn it. I love it, but it feels so . . . sinful," she teased as she fingered her bare neck, then laughed. "The woman had her hair this way in the same picture. Does it look all right? I feel strange all trussed up."

"Like I said, beautiful. I've never seen a prettier woman."

She knew he was being sincere. "Thanks, Matt. I had to do something to get me out of the dark hole I've been in lately. I must say, you look handsome yourself. Don't grow a mustache again. You look so good without it."

"Then it's gone forever, Boss Lady. You ready to eat?"

"Starving. It's been a long time since that skimpy meal at two. I want the whole barrel: steak, potatoes, bread, pie, and wine. We deserve to treat ourselves tonight. It's been a long battle, Matt."

He stroked her cheek and urged, "Don't go sad, Jessie."

"You know me so well, Mathew Cordell. I'm trying, really I am. I just need a little more time to get used to all the changes this war with Fletcher brought."

"You will, Jessie, and I'll be there every step to help you."

"That's the only reason I haven't lost courage, Matt. Help me keep from making mistakes. Speak up anytime. You know I trust you and depend on you more than anyone."

"I feel the same way, Jessie. I'll always be right beside you."

Matt guided her into the eating area. Heads turned and eyes widened as they touched on the auburn-haired beauty in her flowing blue gown. Whispers started as people asked who she was. As they skirted one table, Jessie heard a man repeat what the clerk had told him: "She's Miss Jessica Lane from the Box L Ranch. She's the owner. She's knows as much as men, more than some. She's in the Cattlemen's Association. Here to buy bulls. Smart woman. Real tough."

"All that and beautiful, too." Jessie grinned at his friend's response.

The redhead had never thought of herself as beautiful, but from the way the men in the room were staring at her, it seemed to be true. It both surprised and pleased her. As they were seated, men continued to stare at her or glance at her. When she caught their flirtatious gazes, they nodded and smiled. Jessie felt a surge of joy and pride, and a splash of power, wash over her at their reactions. She quickly warned herself not to become vain like her sister, who used her looks as a weapon. She laughed softly. When Matt questioned her, she smiled and whispered, "If they could see me like I usually look, they wouldn't take a second glance."

"You're wrong, Jessie. You look beautiful all the time."

"Sure I do, Matt, even when I'm covered in dirt and sweat in men's clothes."

"Have I ever lied to you?"

"No, but you're prejudiced."

"Am I?" he countered, then grinned.

Jessie looked at his handsome face and gleaming eyes. "Yes, you are, but thanks. If you'll notice, Mr. Cordell, I'm not the only one getting bold looks. I might have to fight off some eager women for your attention tonight."

"No, Jessie, you'd never lose me to another woman."

He seemed so serious. She tried to pass it off lightly. "Good. Let's see if we can get some service. I'm ravenous."

Matt smiled again, then looked over the menu he had been handed.

Jessie fretted over her foreman's reaction to her tonight. She recalled what Mary Louise and Navarro had said about Matt's feelings for her, and that reflection frightened and dismayed her. The man had never made a romantic overture toward her, and she didn't know what she would do if he did. She told herself she was mistaken, that Matt only loved her as a friend, as a girl he had been around since he was eighteen and she was seven. He had worked for her father for four years before going off to the War Between the States for two years, then he'd returned. He had been twenty-four, and she an impressionable thirteen. For the last ten years, he had been the foreman of their ranch. Jessie remembered all the years they had spent together, all the days and nights they had shared. They had been and were still close. She always felt safe around Matt. Although she had had a girlish passion for him years ago, she hadn't thought of him in a romantic way since then. Still, Matt was a handsome and virile man. There were eleven years between them, but it seemed less of a difference as the years passed. He had been a quiet, soft-spoken, serious, and reserved man—until Navarro's arrival on the scene. Now, it was as if he had been jarred awake, as if he had felt threatened by

. . . Yes, a rival for her! No matter, her heart belonged to Navarro Breed, wherever he was.

As the pleasant and relaxing evening continued, Jessie found herself watching and listening to Mathew Cordell with great interest. It was strange how she had never seen or thought of him in this light before. Matt had always been there, always dependable, loyal, and hardworking, and always in the background. Lordy, she did not want to hurt him. She prayed that he didn't love her or want her, even though that would pinch her heart a mite. But it had only been ten days since Navarro had left, and she still couldn't believe she had lost him forever.

No, her heart cried, not forever. Yet Jessie realized the hopelessness of their situation. She remembered: "Don't wait, Jess. I won't be back, ever. I can't." She feared she had seen Navarro for the last time.

"Jessie? Is something wrong?" Matt asked for the second time.

The redhead looked at him and shook her head, causing her pinned curls to shimmer. "Just thinking about the past. I have to stop doing that. Sorry, Matt."

*

At Mr. Turly's breeding ranch, Jessie and Matt looked over the bulls he showed them. The bloodlines were excellent. They examined the animals' noses, ears, mouths, eyes, hooves, and bodies; they found all parts healthy. The man related his prices, then left the couple to speak privately and to take a final look at his superior stock.

When Turly rejoined them at the pens, Jessie said, "I'll take two of the Durhams and two of the Herefords." She pointed out which ones she wanted. "We've worked with Durhams, Booths, and Galloways before, but I hear others are having great luck with the Herefords. They're a fine-looking critter."

"Wise choices, Miss Lane. Some of the best breeding is being done between Herefords and longhorns. The meat is top grade and brings in a higher dollar."

Jessie eyed the white-faces, short horns, and red hide of the breed. "I believe you said the Durhams were two thousand each and the Herefords one each. That's six thousand dollars. Is it all right to send it with my men when they come for the bulls? I didn't want to travel on the stage with so much cash."

"The Herefords are younger; they'll need another year to fully mature for breeding. We have a deal. We'll sign the papers today. I trust you, Miss Lane. I've dealt with Jed many times. I'm sure sorry to hear he's gone. From the way he always bragged on his Jess, I'm sure you'll do fine."

"Thank you, Mr. Turly. Papa taught me a lot, and I have Matt to help me remember it all and do things right. I'll send the boys over as soon as I return home. They should arrive during the first week of the month."

*

Jessie and Matt spent two nights at the Uvalde and Devils River stations again. On the last day of their journey toward Fort Stockton, tired and sleepy, she dozed, her head falling against the foreman's shoulder.

Careful not to awaken her, Matt shifted toward the slumbering woman, slipped his right arm around her shoulder, and eased her head against his chest and neck. It felt good when Jessie snuggled closer to him and her temple nestled near his collarbone. Her left arm was between them and her hand lay on his right thigh. As she slept deeper, the redhead's right hand and arm moved across his lap and remained on his thigh. Her unbound tresses teased over Matt's hand and arm and against his chin. Jessie's familiar cologne wafted into his nose, and her body was warm next to his. As the stage jostled them, her left breast rubbed against his rib cage and he nearly jumped out of his skin.

Although the coach held six people and he was in the back left corner, Matt soon felt as if he and Jessie were alone somewhere, especially with his head leaning against the wood and with his eyes closed. His dreamy mind shut out all the surrounding sounds except her soft breathing. He felt the heat of her breath against his chest. He let his thirsting senses absorb the many sensations of Jessie. It was wonderful having her in his arms. He had longed for this moment for years, always loving her from a distance. But he had been afraid to approach her, unable to risk another tormenting rejection like the one that had driven him west at eighteen. He also hadn't wanted to back Jessie into a corner with an unwanted overture. Maybe it was time to take that risk. He yearned to kiss her. He could think of nothing more fulfilling than making love to her. He was in paradise, and he hoped the journey and her slumber would continue a long time.

The longer it lasted, the more Mathew Cordell was tantalized and enflamed. Sweat beaded on his face and dampened his entire body. He was as hot as a poker left in a roaring fire. His hands itched to stroke her silky hair and body, and it was a struggle to control those impulses. He wanted her so much, but feared how she would respond to his pursuit. Jessie was a unique woman: smart, honest, dependable, giving, and plenty of fun. When she smiled or laughed, tingles ran over him. It felt good just to be around her. He loved watching her do anything; she always enjoyed herself and did her best. He had seen her happy and sad, losing and winning, a playful tomboy and a ravishing woman, courageous and scared, gentle and tough.

As the yells from the jehu—driver—jingling harnesses, creaking coach, and pounding hooves stirred her foggy mind, Jessie found herself cuddled in Matt's arms. She was so drowsy and relaxed that she didn't care what the passengers thought of her behavior. It felt good to be held in strong, loving arms. That thought jarred her sluggish mind to reality. She straightened herself and squirmed to loosen her stiff body. She glanced at Matt, grinned, and said in close to a whisper, as others were sleeping, "You make a good pillow. Sorry if I squashed you. I didn't realize I was so exhausted. I'll be glad to get home. How much farther?"

Matt removed his arm from her shoulder and flexed as much as the coach space allowed. "About two hours. Our last stop is coming up soon. When we get home, you should take it easy for a while. You've been working too hard."

"There's so much to do, Matt."

"You have plenty of hands for chores and plenty of time until roundup."

"I hope everything is all right at home."

He smiled and coaxed, "Don't worry; I'm sure it is."

Jessie was eager to get there. She hoped Navarro had changed his mind and returned. If not, perhaps there was a letter from him. Of course, she wouldn't get it until the end of the month when the man brought their mail during his semimonthly delivery. She doubted if one would come this soon from her sister. Yet, she wondered how both were and *where* they were.

*

Jessie and Matt reached the Box L spread before dark on Monday. The ride by horseback across terrain that was partly desert had been long and tiring. When they dismounted, jovial hands came to greet them and question their mission. Gran and Tom hurried to join the merry group.

Jessie told them about the deal with Turly. "I want Jimmy Joe, Jefferson, and Walt to go after them. You two are skilled with stubborn beasts, and Jimmy Joe will make a good guard for the bulls and money. I'll send it with you boys. It's six thousand dollars, so be careful with it."

"Guard it with our hides and souls, Jessie," the grinning towhead replied.

"That's why I chose you," she teased in return. "Everything all right?"

"Couldn't much be better, Jessie. No problems. Those boys on the Bar F are doin' fine. We'll haveta get used to peace ag'in."

"I just wish Papa were here to enjoy it with us."

"We does, too, Miss Jessie. We gots dem mills oiled an' spinnin' good."

"Thanks, Big John. If you boys will excuse me, I'm falling in my tracks. Thanks, all of you. As soon as the fall sale is over, you'll all get a five-dollar raise."

*

In the house, Jessie hugged her Grandmother and scolded her brother in a soft tone. "You shouldn't be up and about yet, Tom. I want that shoulder healed perfect before you go to pulling at it."

"I ain't no baby, Jessie. It's about well. I can help out now."

"Not yet, young man. It's only been three weeks, and it was a bad wound."

"Aw, Jessie, let me outta the house. I ain't no chicken to be cooped up."

"No, you're a brave young man. I won't scold you for being rash, because what you did that day took courage and wits. You and Gran probably scared those men off before they could ruin the entire garden. I'm proud of you, Tom."

"You are, Jessie?"

"You know I am. You're going to be a big help to me. We'll have to work hard to make this spread one of the best. You're old enough to start doing other things, but you have some learning to do first. Matt's going to help you. Is that all right, Thomas Lane?"

"More than all right, Jessie. I can be like a regular hand, can't I?"

"If you don't lag on your studies."

He caught her hint. "Yes, ma'am. I'll do both good. I promise."

Jessie touseled his auburn hair. "You best start with cleaning those glasses so you can see, young man. They're covered with dust and greasy fingerprints. I'm taking you with me on my next trip to a large town. We'll see if we can't get a better pair. Matt also suggested we talk to a bootmaker to see if he can make boots like those moccasins Navarro made."

"Real shoes?" he said in excitement.

Jessie wished she hadn't mentioned her love's name. "If it's possible."

"You think Navarro's coming back, Jessie?"

As the three of them sat down to eat, Jessie replied, "No, Tom, not ever. I'll tell you a secret you can't share with anyone. Anyone, Tom," she stressed, and saw she had his full attention and her grandmother's, too, whom she trusted with her life. "Navarro did some bad things when he was younger and got into trouble. The law is after him. That's why he couldn't stay long and can't come back. He doesn't want to get us into trouble for hiding him and helping him."

"Navarro wouldn't do nothing bad, Jessie. The law's wrong."

"Yes, it is, Tom, but he can't prove it."

"We finally proved Fletcher was bad. Navarro can find a way to clear himself."

Before taking a bite, Jessie refuted, "It isn't that simple for him, Tom. He got tangled up with the wrong men. When the law came to arrest the guilty ones, Navarro was with them at their hideout. The others were killed in a shootout, and the evidence of the robbery was there. No one is alive who can clear Navarro of those charges. He was tried and sent to jail. It was awful there, he said. He was beaten and starved. He busted out and was on the run when we met in San Angelo. He needed a place to hide and rest for a while; that's why he accepted my job offer."

"It ain't true, Jessie. He liked us. He helped us," the boy argued.

"Yes, he did. He does care about us. That's why he stayed so long. He hated to leave, but he had no choice."

"We coulda hid him and helped him."

Jessie put down her fork and explained about Fletcher's sketch and the detectives. "Don't you see, Tom? He was in even more danger than before, and so were we if he stayed and they came after him. He didn't want a shoot-out here."

"It ain't fair! He's my friend. I miss him."

"Me, too, Tom, but life isn't always fair."

"I know that. Look at me," he scoffed, slapping the leg with its bad foot.

"Don't get down on yourself again. Navarro liked you. Life hasn't been fair to him, either, but he's doing the best he can to survive. He wouldn't want you to hurt over him. I only wanted you to know why it seemed like he deserted us."

"It ain't his fault, Jessie."

"No, he isn't to blame, except for making mistakes that entrapped him. Just remember the fine things about him and all the good times you shared. There's nothing else we can do, Tom. I'm sorry it has to be this way."

"We can tell 'em how good he is. We haveta do something."

"If they didn't believe us, then they'd know where to start looking for him. It could help them track him down. They might think we know where he went. We can't risk more trouble, Tom. We can't make things worse for him."

"You know where he is?"

"No, honestly I don't." Jessie returned to her meal and drink.

"When did he tell you all about himself, Jessie?" Gran asked.

"He talked to me before he left, Gran. He wanted me to know why he couldn't stay. It was very hard for him to confess the truth. When I hired him, I suspected something was wrong, but I didn't care. We needed him, and I felt I could trust him, and I wasn't wrong. Navarro isn't guilty of that gold robbery. They shouldn't have tortured him. In his place, I would have done anything to escape and to stay free."

"I figured he was in some kind of trouble, too. A real shame. I liked that boy. I'm sure he's had a rough life." Gran passed the biscuits and gravy to Tom. "Eat, you two, before supper gets cold."

Jessie nibbled on the fried chicken. She cut a piece of biscuit smothered in gravy and put it in her mouth. It was so strange not having her father and sister around . . . and her lover. As she chewed, she realized that henceforth everything was her responsibility and duty. It was scary. What if another disaster struck? Could she handle it alone? Life was back to hard work with no special love to hold her in strong, passionate arms. Navarro had made her into a woman, and she wanted to remain one. She wanted children, love, a husband; and she wanted them all with the handsome fugitive. But—

For the second time, Gran asked, "Jessie, did you hear me?"

After swallowing the milk in her mouth, the distracted redhead asked, "What?"

She repeated her request. "Tell me about your trip with Matt."

Jessie smiled and said, "It was fun, Gran. I needed the diversion. I wore my new dress." And she happily told them all about her journey.

* * *

The next morning, Jessie sent the three men and six thousand dollars to San Antonio. She stood at the corral with the foreman and watched them depart.

No mail had arrived from Mary Louise or Navarro Breed.

*

July Fourth dawned clear and hot. Many of the hands were given the day off to go into town for the celebration. It was to be a big one, as America was one hundred years old. Matt was going in the buckboard and taking Gran and Tom. They all balked when Jessie said she wasn't accompanying them.

"Please go on," Jessie told them. "It's getting late. You want to make town before dusk. I don't feel well enough to make the trip. Something I ate Sunday didn't agree with me. Don't worry; I'm just tired and run down. I just plan to lie around resting and reading. I might even do some sewing; I have a few things that need repairs."

"Come with us, Jessie. You can lie in the back until we reach town. I'll bet you'd be better by then. Don't miss the fun," her brother urged.

"I felt awful yesterday and last night, Tom. If it didn't pass by the time we reached town, I'd have a terrible day. I don't want to take such a long and hot ride to sit in a hotel room being sick. I'd rather suffer here."

"I'll stay with you," her grandmother offered.

"No, Gran. You go and look at the material that came in last week. Tom needs new shirts. He's growing faster than the yearlings. And we want to make those curtains for the kitchen. We also can use fresh vegetables. Our garden has a ways to go after what Fletcher's boys did to it. And we'll need more canning jars soon. Go and shop. Then Matt and Tom can help you with the packages. You need a diversion, too. Please."

"You're right, child. We do need some things. Take care of yourself today."

Jessie kissed her cheek and promised she would.

As the others climbed into the buckboard, Matt approached her and asked, "You sure you'll be all right here alone? What if somebody comes?"

Jessie grasped his worry about Navarro. "I'll be fine, Matt. Some of the boys are around. I'd really like to be alone for a while. I need to get some things clear and settled in my head. There have been a lot of changes in my life, too much too fast. I need to think and plan."

"I see. I'll take care of Gran and Tom, then. Get rested. I'll bring you a surprise."

*

Jessie wandered around the house. it was so quiet with her grandmother and brother gone. Her father had been dead for six weeks, and his loss had not become any easier to accept. Navarro had been gone for three weeks, and it seemed forever. She missed them both terribly. She even missed her sister and wondered if the girl was all right. She couldn't imagine how it would be if anything happened to Gran or to Tom.

She felt lonely and denied. Life could be cruel at times. She wished this house was filled with her own family's laughter. She wished a baby were nestled in her arms and her husband at her side. With all hope gone for winning Navarro, what was she supposed to do? His words haunted her: "I won't be coming back. I'm not the settling-down kind. Be strong and never look back. Don't ruin the rest of your life because of me." If he wasn't to be the man in her life, who was? When? How? Surely God wouldn't leave her alone, as her father had been after losing her mother. Now she truly knew how lonely and heartsick Jed had been.

But Navarro wasn't dead. How could she forget him and fall in love with someone else? How could she marry another man and make passionate love to him as she had to the fugitive who had stolen her heart? Yet, since she couldn't spend her life with him—a reality she had to accept—she must look elsewhere for a loving mate, as Jessica Lane *was* the settling-down kind. She was in her mid-twenties, and life's clock wouldn't halt while she healed a broken heart.

Jessie's stomach churned. She told herself to worry over this matter later.

*

Matt, Gran, Tom, and the hands returned the following day. Her brother was elated over the new dog in his arms.

"His name's Clem, Jessie. Mrs. Mobley was going to live with her sister in North Carolina. She couldn't take him with her." Tom laughed and dodged the countless licks that the mongrel tried to put on his freckled face.

Jessie patted the creature's head and grinned. "He's sure lively. Hello, Clem."

The new pet was quick; he lavished moisture on her hand before she could move it. Jessie laughed at the ticklish antics and rubbed the pup's head. "You'll like it here, Clem. Lots of room to run around and play with Tom."

"Can he sleep with me tonight, Jessie? He stayed inside with Mrs. Mobley."

Jessie studied the energetic brown-and-white dog. She saw how Tom's eyes gleamed with happiness and new life. "If you give him a good bath first. You don't want a bed of fleas."

Tom hurried off with Biscuit Hank to tend to that chore.

Matt helped them carry the packages into the house. While Gran was putting away her things, Jessie looked at the foreman. "Thanks, Matt," she said.

"You're welcome, Jessie. I bumped into Mrs. Mobley and mentioned we were looking for a dog. She begged me to take Clem and give him a good home. I didn't think you'd mind getting a grown dog instead of a puppy."

"Not at all. Tom loves him already. It'll be good for him to have a pet to tend. It'll take his mind off everything that's happened."

"How are you?" he inquired, concern evident in his voice.

"Fine today. I needed that time alone. Thanks."

"You don't have to thank me for everything I do for you."

Jessie hugged him and kissed his cheek. "Yes, I do. How else can you know I'm grateful? If I started taking you for granted, you'd look elsewhere for a job."

"Never." He playfully yanked on her long braid. "I know how you feel. You have eyes and a smile that do a lot of talking—do it better than most words can."

"That's 'cause you've been around me so long and know me so well. I'll have to remember I can't keep secrets from you," she jested.

"No need to, Jessie; you can trust me with anything."

She gazed into his serious eyes and said, "I know, Matt, and thanks." The moment the word left her lips, they both laughed.

Gran returned and asked, "What's so funny?"

"Nothing, Gran," she said, then winked at the grinning foreman. "How about taking supper with us, Matt? You can all tell me about the doings in town."

*

Two days later, the hands were assigned to check the stock for screwworms. Every summer, their navels, noses, and wounds were examined for the pest that could sicken them. Any found with the larva were treated.

Jessie rode with Matt almost every day for exercise and distraction. She wondered when and if this feeling of emptiness would leave her. She warned herself she must come to terms with the changes she could not control. She knew Matt was doing his best to draw her out of her low mood, and sometimes he did make her laugh and forget for a while. But when she was alone or a certain task or object reminded her of Navarro or her father, it was difficult not to sink into her dark and lonely pit again.

*

On July fourteenth, the bulls and hands arrived from San Antonio. Everyone gathered around to look the beasts over and to congratulate Jessie for excellent choices. For a time, she was filled with pleasure, pride, and excitement, and she laughed and joked with the men like she used to.

Later, a letter was delivered from Mary Louise Fletcher in Boston. It briefly related her trip, her new address, and how glorious her life was in "civilization" and luxury. The blonde told them that everything she had dreamed of was coming true for her. An unbidden twinge of envy pinched at Jessie's nerves.

"Well, at least she's out of our hair and happy," Jessie remarked to Gran.

"Or she claims she is. Mary Louise would never tell us if things weren't working out for her, not after the way that girl fought to get there. It's been so quiet and peaceful lately. Even with chores, it's almost lazy living."

"I guess that's why I've been feeling so sluggish for the past week. We worked hard and long to get rid of Fletcher. We're back to routine now. Matt's giving most of the orders and taking the burdens and fears off my back. He almost makes it seem as if the ranch is running itself. The men aren't having any problems or complaints, not even those Bar F boys we took on."

Gran laughed and teased, "You almost make peace sound boring, Jessie. You need to get some excitement and happiness back inside you, child."

"That's easy to say, Gran, but so hard to do. Sometimes I feel so lonely, and edgy and listless. Everything is work, or planning future work. I want to have some fun, like Mary Louise. Not the kind she's having, but . . ."

"Why don't you have a party? That'll liven up this place."

Jessie sank into a chair and exhaled as if exhausted. "It's too soon after Papa's death, Gran. It wouldn't be respectful. Besides, I want people to take me seriously. I have to prove I can run this ranch."

Martha walked to her side and stroked Jessie's hair with a wrinkled hand. "You're not Jed's son, child. You're a woman. You have the right to behave and feel like one. Don't try so hard to prove you're strong and tough. You *are*, Jessie, and it will show to others. Just be yourself."

"I don't know who or what I am any more, Gran. I was like Papa's son for years. Just as I was becoming a woman, I had to go back to that role."

"No, Jessie, you don't have to."

"Yes, Gran, I do. If I dress like a fancy woman and behave like Mary Louise does, I'll have trouble with the seasonal wranglers and with every businessman I deal with. They wouldn't respect a frilly woman."

"Most of them know you, child. They like you. They know you helped my son run this ranch. A dress and loose hair won't change their minds."

"If you'd been in San Antonio with me and Matt when I wore that new gown and did up my hair, you wouldn't say that. Those men didn't see a cattle rancher; they saw a creature to chase and capture. How can I discuss business with a man when he's eyeing my figure or face? How can I get him in the corral when he's only wanting to get into my bed? Everything I do right, somebody else gets the credit. It was Papa when he was alive; it'll be Matt now. I have to show everyone that *I'm* the Box L Ranch."

* * *

Jessie was still in her strange mood when the next week began and she helped her grandmother with the washing and other household chores. As with each Monday, Jessie's troubled mind marked how long it had been since the week when Navarro had left: five today. Watching the weeks move by made the redhead realize her life was miserably slipping away with daily routine: dawn's chores, eat breakfast, chores, eat dinner, chores, eat supper, and sleep.

For months, Navarro had awakened and tantalized her desires, worked by her side, helped her defeat a terrible enemy, and given her hope for love and marriage. Now all of those things were gone forever. She ached for his companionship and touch; she yearned for his smile; she wanted to feel alive again, to taste his lips, to join her pleading body with his to find pleasure and contentment. She craved to share every-thing with him, but she was fast draining of hope.

For months, she had stayed on alert for danger. She had lived on the edge under Fletcher's threats of violence and death. Her wits and courage had been tested daily. Now life was back to the routine existence of running a successful ranch. She was glad the perilous trouble was over, but it had cost her the two men she loved most. And with Mathew Cordell in control and with the hands loyal and skilled, she had little out of the ordinary to do.

*

Something different came up at the end of the next week. Miguel sent word that most of Fletcher's garden was ready to be picked and canned. Early Thursday, Matt helped the two women load their things, and he drove them there.

As Jessie had ordered, the house was opened so fresh air could battle the late July heat. Wood was ready for use, and plenty of water was available. Jessie and Gran set up their supplies in the kitchen, and both admired the display.

Soon, men were bringing them baskets of corn, beans, tomatoes, okra, potatoes, and other vegetables to wash, pick, and prepare for canning. Others were outside helping with shelling and shucking, as they needed extra hands during the busy and fatiguing chore. All licked their lips in anticipation of the vegetables and soups they would enjoy this winter.

Matt entered the kitchen as Jessie finished stirring the huge pot of vegetable soup and began rubbing the muscles of her lower back. "You made Gran take a nap and the boys take a rest," he said. "Why don't you stop for a while, too? You look tired, Jessie."

"I have to get this work done, Matt. I don't want Gran overdoing."

"You can't overdo, either, Jessie. If you keep pushing yourself like this, you'll collapse. You have plenty of help, and it doesn't all have to be finished today, or even tomorrow. Turn around and let me work your back." Matt's hands urged her around and he massaged the muscles near her waist. His fingers curled against her sides while his thumbs pressed and stroked the taut flesh beneath them. "You're tighter than strung barbwire, Jessie. Relax. Let me ease the pain."

As the deft foreman labored on her aching back, Jessie closed her eyes and surren-dered to his masterful touch. His pressure was firm and purposeful, yet gentle and persuasive. After a while, his hands moved to her neck.

"Lift your braid," he told her.

Jessie captured it, bent her head forward, and draped it over her face. His thumbs traveled up and down the stiff cords of her neck while his fingers rested on her collarbone. Jessie rolled her head to help loosen the sore area. Matt's hands drifted to her shoulders to give them attention and comfort. His knowing fingers eased the kinks in her upper torso. Soon, the redhead felt better.

"That's wonderful, Matt; thanks. Now I have to stir the soup before it sticks and burns." She went to tend that task, but hated to leave his soothing touch.

The foreman let her do her chore, then caught her right hand to pull her back to him. "I'm not done yet, Boss Lady." He guided her into a chair at the table, then sat down near her. "These hands need loosening, too."

Jessie watched Matt as he massaged the water-puckered skin and grumbling bones. His strong hands were rough from work. She didn't mind, as his touch was restorative and soothing. She gazed at his lowered head of dark-brown hair that fell in mussed waves toward a sun-bronzed face. Her gaze drifted down his neck to the hollow at its base. Dark hair was visible where the top buttons of his faded blue shirt had been undone in deference to the hot, dry day. The shirt fit snugly, emphasizing his broad shoulders. Where his sleeves were rolled to his elbows, she saw muscles honed from years of labor. She watched them move as his fingers worked on hers.

Jessie's eyes roamed upward to his face with its sunny smile and sparkling brown eyes. He was very gentle and soft-spoken for one so rugged in body and character. He was also quite handsome and virile. She wondered why Mathew Cordell had never wed. What had happened during his thirty-five years to keep him from choosing a wife and settling down on his own place? A woman couldn't find a better man than Matt to share her love and life, so why was he still unattached?

Matt glanced up to find the redhead's inquisitive gaze on him. "Is something wrong, Jessie?" he asked when she continued to stare at him.

Jessie liked the comforting sound of his voice. "No, just the opposite. I was thinking how lucky I am to have you around, Mathew Cordell." A broad grin came her way. His chocolate eyes softened and glowed. Yet, he looked suddenly shy and a little surprised by her words.

"Thanks, Jessie," he murmured, almost squirming in his seat.

Jessie warmed to his unfamiliar expression and mood. "No thanks are needed. It's the truth." He looked as if he wanted to say something, but felt he shouldn't. Jessie decided not to intrude on his private feelings. "That's what I needed," she remarked, pulling her hands from his and flexing them. "I best get back to work. The next time you overdo, I'll return the favor."

Matt smiled and replied, "I'll hold you to that promise, Boss Lady. Fact is, I might cheat just to get it," he teased.

"Mathew Cordell be dishonest? The seasons would end first."

In a serious tone, he said, "It would shock you what some men would do for you, Jessica Lane." He stood and replaced his chair. "I'll get busy, too."

Jessie watched him leave, then returned to the simmering soup. She pondered his curious words. She asked herself if she could be the reason Matt had stayed on the ranch and never wed. That seemed unlikely in view of the fact he had never tried to court her. Yet, if he did have romantic feelings for her, she had to be careful not to hurt him.

*

The two women and men remained on the Bar F to continue their task. Hank stayed home to prepare supper for the cowhands. Tom was with him to tend the chores he had taken over from Mary Louise. When the canning group halted that night, bodies were tired and hands were wrinkled from hours in water. The boys stayed in the bunkhouse. Gran spent the night in one of the guest rooms, Matt in another, and Jessie in the master suite.

She looked around before falling upon the inviting bed. She let her imagination wonder about the nights and days Wilbur Fletcher had spent in this room. Soon she should go through the clothes and possessions he had left behind. She would give Matt first choice, then pass the remainder to the other hands. She liked this lovely and comfortable Spanish-style house. It was a shame to leave it standing empty. Soon, she must also decide what to do about it.

As the redhead lay in the darkness, she wondered how Mary Louise had yielded to a man she hardly knew, a cruel and evil man. How many times had Fletcher and her defiant sister made love in this very room? What had it been like between them? Passionate and satisfying as with her and Navarro? Mary Louise was such a wild and reckless girl, such a greedy one. Would her sister miss her times with Wilbur as she missed hers with the desperado? Would Mary Louise seek to continue those carnal pleasures with another husband or a lover? Jessie couldn't imagine another man taking her lost love's place, but if she didn't allow one to do so, she would be alone for the rest of her life: lonely, empty, childless, and unfulfilled. Could she stand such a barren existence? She wished Navarro were there with her, holding her and kissing her and making love to her.

Jessie turned to her side. She couldn't get in a comfortable position. She was used to sleeping on her stomach, but her breasts were too sore to permit pressure on them. She realized she had missed her "woman's way" in early June and in July, too. She assumed all her troubles had affected her body. She felt puffy, and hoped her impending flow would ease the tension and discomfort she had been enduring recently. She wanted to be back to normal. She didn't like feeling queasy, exhausted and moody, like this. She had even halted her long rides with Matt because she was having to use the outhouse or chamber pot so frequently. It was bad enough to have her mind and heart not working right, but it was unbearably irritating to have her body fight her, too.

*

The canning was completed by Saturday afternoon. They left the filled jars in the kitchen, to be divided next week for use in both locations. They did have another round of canning to do soon when their own garden came in. They packed their things and were home before dark.

*

August arrived with a hot dryness that made the redhead even more miserable. She didn't want to worry Gran, but a strange illness was plaguing her. She prayed she hadn't caught a curious disease that would make her waste away. To hide it, Jessie rushed to the outhouse each time a wave of nausea came over her. She tried to conceal her fatigue and weakness. Sometimes she wanted to rest or sleep so much that she feared she would faint and expose her unnatural condition.

On Friday, a distraction came when Jimmy Joe asked if he could borrow a certain Mexican dress and mantilla to play a practical joke on Rusty Jones. When she saw Rusty arrive later, Jessie sneaked to the corner of the bunkhouse to catch the much-needed entertainment.

Jessie listened as the "woman" told the fiery-haired man with a beard that she was carrying his child as a result of the night he spent with her in the saloon two months ago. The confirmed bachelor didn't know what to say or do, except to ask her to repeat her astonishing story.

Jessie peeked inside for a quick look. The "girl's" back was to her uneasy victim.

The thick, dark mantilla concealed the towhead's identity, who spoke low and soft to prevent too early discovery of the practical joke. Jimmy Joe spoke good Spanish, and Miguel translated at certain points. The story—based on a real incident—worried Rusty.

Jessie knew enough Spanish to comprehend most of the humorous conversation, and Miguel's assistance closed any gaps she or the other men had. At first she was amused, and she had to cover her mouth to silence any giggles.

"I don't follow your story, señorita," Rusty said in desperation.

The "girl" explained in Spanish, "I carry your child, Señor Rusty. I am not a soiled dove as the others who work for Señor Bill. You were my first and only man. After you left my bed, I ran away from the saloon. I could not do such things again with strangers for money. Do you not remember I was a virgin?"

Rusty glanced at his friends, looking embarrassed and nervous. He motioned for their help, but they all shrugged and grinned. He scowled at them.

"Do you not remember, Señor Rusty?" The question was asked again.

The bearded man cleared his clogged throat and replied honestly, "Yep, I was first to . . . sleep with you, señorita."

"First and last" was the soft correction.

"I didn't force myself onto you, señorita, and you weren't no prisoner there. You said I didn't hurt you. Why'd you come to me with your bad luck?"

"My father and brothers learned of my shameful secret. They say I must marry the child's father. You must help me."

"Help you?" Rusty asked, panicking more each minute.

"Yes. We must marry. I must stay here with you. If we do not, we will be in much danger." The "girl" pretended to weep in sadness and fear.

"In danger?" Rusty echoed, shifting about as if his whole body itched.

"Yes. They will come here and kill you for dishonoring our family."

Rusty's gaze grew wide and alarmed. He licked his dry mouth. His quivering fingers played with his red beard. His legs trembled. "K-k-kill me?"

"*Sí*" came the dreaded response.

Rusty's face became a bright red. His gaze pleaded for help from the observant men, to no avail.

"You must do right by her, Señor Rusty," Carlos said.

The others agreed, nudging the man nearby and nodding their heads.

"And for your baby, Señor Rusty," one added. "Don't forget about him."

"Who says that seed's mine? I ain't never heard of having to wed no soiled dove after one night's fun. How do I know I was last? How do I know she ain't laying a trap for me? If I knew for sure she's telling the truth, I'd marry her to give my child his rightful name. But this is suspicious." Rusty swallowed hard. He tapped the "girl's" shoulder and asked, "How can you be sure I'm to blame? How do you know you got a baby inside?"

When the "girl" related her symptoms, Jessie paled and shook as she recognized them as her own. She had been around animals mating and giving birth all her life, but she hadn't seen morning sickness or been around a woman in the early stages of pregnancy since she was ten and her mother had Tom. The truth of her condition struck her hard. She felt weak and shaky and and scared.

Before she escaped to her room, she heard Jimmy Joe burst into chuckles and tease Rusty. The others joined in and howled with laughter. Jessie fled the enlightening scene and hurried to her bedroom for privacy.

She closed her door and paced the floor. How stupid and naive she was, she scolded herself. She had missed her monthly flow before, during illness or from other unknown reasons, but this time her breasts were sore and her body was puffy. She had passed her queasiness off to bad food and her sluggishness to hard work and tension. She had even ignored her crazy moods because of all she had endured recently.

Jessie reflected on her "woman's way" and her nights with Navarro. She had missed the first one in June, right after her love's return during the storm. She had skipped her July one, and it hadn't appeared earlier this month. That meant she had to be over two months' pregnant. What, she wondered in alarm, could she do?

Navarro had been gone since June twelfth, almost nine weeks. She hadn't received any word from him and had no idea where he was. She doubted he would ever return. Even if he sent a letter, he wouldn't tell her where to locate him. She was carrying his child, and he would never know!

Jessie waxed between happiness and fear. She caressed her stomach and thought of their child growing there. Apprehension flooded her as she realized it would be born a bastard. Her child would be forced to fight the same stigma and heartache that its father had suffered. No, she couldn't allow her child to be tormented. She had to think of something, she fretted, but what?

Visions of disgrace entered her turbulent mind. She would soil the Lane name. She would become the topic of horrible gossip. Having a child out of wedlock would tarnish her, her family, her home, not to mention her child. Everyone would discover her "sin" with the fugitive drifter. Her beautiful love would become something ugly and shameful, something destructive, if she didn't prevent it.

Jessie knew she had to make a decision fast. She would be unable to hide her condition in a couple of months. She figured up the timing and decided the baby was due in early March. Tears rolled down her cheeks as she realized that was the month she had met Navarro Breed. If only he would return . . .

Jessie's tears and panic increased as she told herself that was a hopeless dream. This was a problem—a stark reality—she had to work out alone.

Chapter

18

Saturday afternoon, Jessie let Tom go riding with Matt so she could speak with her grandmother alone. She could not put off telling her any longer. She had worried over it all night and had come up with an idea. Now she had to discuss it with Martha Lane. There was no use waiting and praying for Navarro to return in time to give their child a name before he had to leave her side again. She had stopped fantasizing he would ride up and pull her into his arms any day and make everything all right. But if he did, the redhead knew she would leave with him and take her family with them to begin a new life in a faraway place.

Jessie brushed her long hair to release part of her tension. She had been sick again upon arising, sicker than any morning thus far. But as the hours passed, so had her nausea. She put the brush aside, caressed her stomach, and whispered, "It's time, little one, to make plans to protect you from the hurt and shame your father endured."

Jessica walked into the kitchen. "Gran, I have something to discuss with you," she said. "I know you'll be hurt and disappointed in me, and I'm sorry. I'm in trouble, Gran, big trouble, and I don't know how to tell you about it."

Martha looked at the girl who stood there with lowered head and clenched hands. She went to her granddaughter and hugged her. "You're carrying Navarro's child," she said in a gentle tone to help Jessie begin.

Jessie's head jerked upward and she stared at the white-haired woman. Her blue eyes were wide and her mouth was open. "How . . . did you know? I only realized it yesterday."

Gran guided them to chairs in the eating area. She sat close and kept the redhead's cold, damp hands clasped in hers. Her voice and gaze were compassionate. "The Good Lord gave me three fine sons, but found it in His way to call them home to Him. A mother never thinks she'll outlive her children. I've borne and buried three children, Jessie, so I know the symptoms."

Jessie's eyes misted, her cheeks glowed, and her voice cracked with emotion. "Why didn't you say something? I must be stupid and naive, because I didn't make the connection until recently."

"How could you, child? You've been around men most of your life. I should have had a talk with you long ago, especially after I saw what was happening between you and Navarro." When Jessie looked surprised, the older woman continued. "I watched how you two reached out to each other. I've known you from birth, Jessie. I saw how he was changing you, and how you were changing him. But he's a drifter. I thought your feelings would pass after he left."

"If he hadn't had to leave, Gran, he would have married me. He loves me."

"I'm sure he does, Jessie, but that hopeless dream is over, gone with him. I knew you had troubles. I've seen you running for the outhouse many times, and I've seen how moody and weary you are. I was waiting for you to come to me."

"I would have come sooner, Gran, but I only learned what was wrong yesterday." Jessie explained how she had made her shocking discovery. "We love each other so much. We knew we didn't have much time together. At first I didn't know why. I didn't even believe Navarro when he kept swearing he couldn't stay long. When he came back that stormy night after Papa's death and the range fire, I needed him so much, and he needed me. I didn't understand how much until he told me he was leaving forever."

Jessie thought it was best for everyone if her grandmother were led to believe she had "sinned" only once, as Martha Lane was a firm believer in God and in right and wrong. It was hard enough for the older woman to learn about such a wanton weakness without having to be told it had happened several times. "I'm sorry, Gran."

"But you still love him and you're carrying his child," Martha reminded her.

"Yes, Gran, but I didn't want it to be like this. The best thing to do is move somewhere until the baby is born, or to live there permanently. I'll have to lie and say I'm a widow, so my child won't be treated as a bastard." Jessie related enough of Navarro Breed's history to let the woman know how he had suffered. "I'll wait another month to make certain Navarro won't change his mind and return. Then we'll leave before I start coming to season. We can decide afterward whether or not to return. I'm afraid people might guess the truth from the time of the baby's birth and its looks."

The older woman looked worried and distressed. "Sell the ranch, Jessie?"

"No, Gran. We worked too hard to keep it, and our family is buried out here. I plan to let Matt run it for us. In this fix, he'll do a better job than I could. Eventually I want to return and live here. This is our home. Maybe Navarro will find a way to end his trouble."

Martha squeezed her granddaughter's hands, then grimaced in pain from her arthritic condition. "Don't live in a dream world, Jessie. Face the truth, child; he can't ever return. He wouldn't, because he loves you and wants you safe. You'll be blooming soon, so you have to act quickly. A scandal can ruin the baby you're carrying and this ranch. You have a duty to them. Time is working against you, but there is another way. Do what you must, child."

"What is that, Gran?" she asked, near panic.

"Marry Mathew Cordell. He loves you, too. He'll understand and agree."

"Marry Matt?" she said, looking shocked. "Tell him about my trouble?"

"Soon words won't be necessary. Think about the baby, nameless and a bastard, even if you claim you're a widow. One day you'd have to lie to the child, too, or tell it the truth. Think of yourself, Jessie, shamed and ruined, alone and miserable, trying to raise a child without a father and away from your home. You don't know where Navarro is, and it's certain he won't return. Speak to Matt. He's a good man. He's loved you for years. He'll help; I'm sure of it."

"But it's wrong to use him, Gran. I'd be too ashamed to confess the truth. Matt thinks I'm a wonderful person. He'll be hurt and disappointed in me."

"Love is a strong and special gift, Jessie. It's forgiving and understanding. Let Matt give it to you and the baby," she urged.

"What if he doesn't want a soiled woman or to raise another man's bastard child? What if he was so angry he left us, Gran? Who would run the ranch for us then? I can't risk telling him and losing him."

"Don't down yourself, Jessie. You made a mistake during a hard time. Matt would never think badly of you, and he would never run out on you. Don't you realize he'll guess what's wrong when you desert the ranch? Isn't it better for the truth to come from you, child? He'll be hurt that you didn't trust him. You'd be surprised what some men will do to get the woman they love."

Matt had spoken similar words that day at the Bar F. Did he love and want her enough to take on such a burden? Should she give him a chance to help her out of a terrible predicament? Would he understand and marry her? Or would the truth destroy her in his eyes and heart? If he agreed, what would he expect in return? He would know she loved Navarro and had slept with him. How could he deal with such torments, if he truly loved her? Yet, her grandmother was right and wise. She had to act fast. Navarro was lost forever. She must think only of the baby, her family and home, and the Lane reputation. She had to take this risk, and pray she and Gran had not misjudged the foreman's feelings.

"All right, Gran; I'll talk to Matt tomorrow. If he refuses, but stays, we'll leave next week. If he leaves, I'll put Rusty in charge before we go."

*

Jessie and Matt rode to the scene of the range fire. Burned scrubs and trees had been cut and destroyed. Grass, wildflowers, and bushes were beginning to grow. Wind, rain, and cattle movements since that day in early June had scattered or trampled under the black surface. New greenery was taking hold. One had to look close to realize how much damage had been done.

Jessie glanced around and said, "The land is almost healed, Matt."

"Your heart will be healed soon, too, Jessie. Your father will always be with you, but the pain will soften more every week."

Jessie realized he misread her sadness. She dismounted and dropped Ben's reins to the ground. She walked to an unharmed tree and leaned her head against it. This task was harder than she had imagined, dreaded, it would be. She felt lonely and lost and and denied. She couldn't help feeling angry and bitter about all that had happened. A deep yearning for peace and safety chewed at her raw nerves and distraught mind. She needed someone to take away her pain. She wanted to be loved, held, kissed. She needed to feel special again. Could Matt fill those roles in her shattered life? Would he?

Matt joined her, sensing he had mistaken her problem. More than natural grief was tormenting his love. He longed to comfort her, to bring back his old Jessie. His hands grasped her trembling arms and turned her to face him. He saw tears rolling down her cheeks and moisture shining on her thick lashes. He pulled her into his arms and murmured, "Don't be sad, Jessie. You have me to take care of you and the ranch. What do you need so badly that hurts you this way?" Even as he asked his last question, he prayed her answer wouldn't be Navarro.

Jessie looked into his concerned gaze and more tears threatened to spill forth. She hated to hurt this unselfish man, but she was drawn to his tenderness and strength in her time of weakness. She was apprehensive about the challenges and responsibilities confronting her. She didn't want to face such burdens and fears alone. She had been a rock for others for years; now she wanted and needed a supportive pillar. She needed a powerful and dependable shoulder to lean on, someone to help her through the hard times ahead. She was in the arms of the best man for those tasks. She prayed that the awful truth would not turn him against her.

"I do need you so very much, Matt. You've always been nearby when I faltered. You've always been the one I could turn to for advice and loyalty and understanding. You know me better than anyone."

Aching to ease her anguish, Matt kissed her. His mouth was gentle, his kiss full of love and understanding, his arms protective and strong. The kiss was short, but filled with emotion.

Jessie pressed her face against his chest and cried softly. Her hands circled his waist and she clung to him for comfort and strength. When Matt embraced her and rested his cheek against her hair, his kindness flowed out to her.

He stroked her hair and coaxed, "Cry all you need, Jessie. Let all the suffering out. You've been strong for months for everyone else. I know how hard it's been for you. I'll do anything I can to lessen your pain and sadness."

Jessie looked up at him and said, "I wish you could, Matt. Nobody can help this time. I'm in bad trouble. I have to leave the ranch for a year or two. Will you take care of it while I'm gone? Gran and Tom are going with me." Jessie thought it was best if she exposed her problem, then let Matt decide how to deal with any part he wanted to take in solving it. She couldn't ask him to marry her; the suggestion had to be his. If he didn't make it, neither would she.

He was stunned by that news. "Leave? Why, Jessie?"

"I can't stay here, Matt. I'll be ruined."

He wiped at her tears. "No, you won't. I won't let you get hurt. The ranch is doing fine. *You're* doing fine. You're strong and brave and smart."

"Not as much as you think, Matt, and I have to get away soon."

"Give it time, Jessie. You can't run because you're scared. You aren't alone. I'm here. The boys are here. We won't let you fail."

"That isn't it, Matt."

He eyed her for a time, then asked, "Are you going to meet Navarro?"

Jessie lowered her head in guilt and apprehension. She was moving slowly, to prevent as much shock and anguish as possible. "No. He's gone; I don't know where, but he won't ever come back. But yes, it does have to do with him."

He was puzzled. "You can't stay because Navarro and your father are gone? Leaving is no answer. We'll handle whatever's wrong."

"That isn't it, either." Jessie turned away from his confused gaze. "It's me."

Matt was angry with himself for not realizing how much she had been suffering. He couldn't let her leave in this vulnerable state and have her meet someone else who might take Navarro's place. He had to be bold and persuasive to win her heart. First, he had to discover what was troubling his love. "What kind of bad trouble are you talking about, Jessie?"

Before she lost her courage, she confessed, "I'm . . . I'm pregnant, Matt."

"Pregnant?" he echoed in disbelief, that being the farthest idea from his mind.

Jessie faced him and rushed on. "Please don't think too badly of me. I had to tell you the truth because we're so close and I trust you like family. I have to go away to have the baby. We'll be ruined by disgrace if I stay and have it here. I don't know when I'll return. Will you look after the ranch until I do? Please. I can trust you and depend on you. I don't want to sell it."

He was silent for a time as Jessie awaited his reaction and response. It seemed an eternity. If Matt loved her, this predicament had to be just as difficult for him. The hurt look in his somber brown eyes ripped into her soul. She wished she hadn't done this terrible thing to him. How could he understand and accept such wanton wickedness in her? In shame and anguish, she murmured, "I'm sorry, Matt. I shouldn't have told you. Please don't hate me. I couldn't bear to lose you, too. I'll be gone soon, and you won't have to look at me."

"Navarro's?" he asked in a strained voice.

"Yes." She told him the same amended story she had told her grandmother. It was also best for Matt to think it had happened only once. "I'm sorry, Matt. You must be terribly disappointed in me. I can't undo this mess, so I should leave before it's discovered and the news spreads. It was wrong to burden you with such a terrible matter. I just felt so alone and confused." She turned away again.

Matt didn't ask if she loved the drifter, as he knew she must to have made love with him. His anger at himself increased. If only he'd been there to fill her needs, she wouldn't have fallen prey to Navarro's wiles! But he *was* here now when her need was so great. "Leaving isn't best for you, Jessie. Or the baby. Or the ranch."

When he pulled her around to face him, she reasoned, "I created this problem, so I have to solve it, Matt. What else can I do?"

"Marry me," he responded. "I'm the man you need. You can trust me."

Jessie had hoped and prayed he would say that but she had feared he wouldn't, out of torment and bitterness. Her surprise showed more than her relief and joy. "But . . ."

His voice and expression were firm as he said, "But nothing, Jessie. You don't have much choice. This is where you need to be. I know you love him, and I know he loved you. Don't look shocked. I've been reading the signs since he arrived. I prayed I was wrong, but knew I wasn't. I was glad when he left and mad when he returned, because I was afraid he'd hurt you—and he has."

"It wasn't all his fault, Matt. He didn't trick me or assault me."

"But he pulled you to him, knowing he wasn't going to stay here."

"It was a bad time in both our lives. We were weak and suffering. We needed something from each other. Was that so terrible, so wrong?"

The pleading look in her blue eyes knotted his guts. Sunshine highlighted her auburn hair. Despite her flushed cheeks, her lovely face was pale. She needed so much from him, more than she realized at this dire time, and he was eager to help her. He dodged her last, loaded question. "If I had been more aware, this wouldn't have happened. Are you sure he's gone for good this time? He returned before, and things between you two were . . . even stronger than I realized."

Her honesty was apparent as she replied, "I'm sure. He's in trouble with the law— a fugitive fleeing a noose is what he told me that last day. To survive, he had to go, Matt, and he can't risk coming back. He'll never know about the baby."

Matt finally understood, and he almost felt sorry for the desperado who had lost so much. Yet he was furious with Navarro for taking advantage of Jessie when the man knew their future was impossible. "I suspected something was wrong. I knew he didn't want to leave, but I could tell he had to go. The sooner we get married, the better it'll be. How about Tuesday?" Matt wanted his claim settled on Jessie before his rival could sneak a visit and change her mind about this solution or take her with him far away.

Guilt chewed at Jessie. "I can't do this to you, Matt. It isn't fair to marry you under these conditions. I can't strap you with another man's burden."

"What wouldn't be fair is for me to let you uproot yourself and your family when

I'm the answer to your problem. You wouldn't be strapping me down; I want to marry you. I love you, Jessica Lane; I have for years. I've waited too long to tell you. Become my wife, Jessie. I'll love you and take care of you forever."

The admission touched Jessie. Matt's clear gaze told her that every word was true. As he cupped her face with work-toughened hands and looked coaxingly into her misty eyes, his smile was reassuring and heartwarming. Yes, Mathew Cordell would make a lucky woman a perfect husband, and that woman could be her. She couldn't help but wonder what would have happened between them if Matt had revealed his love long ago. "Why haven't you said or done anything about your feelings for me?"

"Fear," he confessed, then sent her a wry grin.

She laughed and said, "I've never known you to be afraid of anything or anyone. Fear of what, Matt?"

"Rejection. Of causing a problem between us. When I came here at eighteen, I was running away from a busted love affair. I was going to marry a girl in Georgia, but she walked out the week of our wedding and married another man. I met Jed; we struck up a friendship, and I came to work for him. When I went back during the war, Sarah was there with her children. Her husband had been killed. She begged me to come back to her. I couldn't; it was over for me. My home was here. When I returned, you were thirteen and I was twenty-four. I watched you grow over the years. I've seen you in every mood and in every situation. I could tell you saw me only as an uncle or older brother. I was scared to approach you like this. If I had, maybe Navarro wouldn't have gotten to you. But things have a way of happening for the best. You've changed since knowing him, Jessie."

Matt's perceptions and gentleness evoked even deeper respect and affection from her. "I know," she concurred. "Before Navarro, I lived and worked as Jed's son. He made me realize I was a woman. Not many men have treated me that way, Matt, and it wasn't their fault. I was just one of the boys, not a female to be romanced."

Matt shook his head, causing shocks of brown hair to fall over one side of his forehead. His gaze seemed to sparkle with amusement at her mistake. For a time, the reason for their talk and his proposal vanished. Only the woman he loved and desired stood before him, toying with a loose button on his shirt. She was smiling at him with trust and affection in her eyes. "No female is more of a woman than you are, Jessie. You're beautiful. Don't ever doubt it again. Don't you remember that night in San Antonio? Men couldn't take their eyes off you, 'specially me. Every woman there was chewed up by envy."

"I must admit it turned my head a mite. I also recall how those women were eyeing my handsome escort. I was afraid one would steal you away."

"What would a fancy city lady want with an old cowpoke like me? I've lived in a saddle so long, I'm barely housebroken. Good thing you're a skilled rider. This wrangler needs training bad."

They laughed, and more tension left them.

Matt stroked her hair and waxed serious. "See, you can still smile and laugh. It sounds good to hear it again, Jessie."

His innocent remarks made her remember all that had saddened her, but she concealed her reaction. "You're so good for me, Matt, so good *to* me. I don't deserve such treatment, or a prize like you."

He grasped her hands and squeezed them. "That isn't true."

"Yes, it is. Look what a mess I've made of things."

"Trust me, Jessie; your pain will heal, just like this land healed. I should know. Lordy, Sarah hurt me bad, but I learned to live and love again. You can, too."

"I don't want to hurt you like she did, Matt. It's too soon to . . ."

"I know, but time passes every day. With Navarro gone and me here, I'll have the advantage. You won't be sorry, Jessie. I'll make you a good husband. I'll raise the baby as my own. I won't make any demands on you. If you come to love me and want me, I'll be here. But if we only stay close friends, I'll settle for that."

"You shouldn't have to settle for half a life, Matt. You're too special."

"But that life will be with the woman I love, Jessie. It's worth it to me. Besides, woman, you *do* love me. Not like I love you or hope you'll love me one day, but you love me nonetheless. Maybe that little seed will sprout and flourish."

Jessie gazed at his sparkling brown eyes. He was a dreamer, too. He wanted her as much as she wanted Navarro. If he had gotten over his anguish in the past, perhaps she would get over hers at some future time. What better man to share her life and love, to take Navarro's place? She could not help but return his appealing smile and catch his contagious mood. When his hand caressed her cheek and he entreated, "Marry me, Jessie," she relented. "All right, Mr. Foreman, I'll make you boss of the Box L Ranch and Lane family."

Matt whooped with joy. He lifted her around the waist and swung her around before kissing her. "I'll go hire the preacher tomorrow. We can marry Tuesday."

"What will the hands say?" she fretted, her fingers interlocked behind his neck. She enjoyed the way his adoring gaze engulfed her, the joy and relief he had given her, and the way he tempted her to stay in his embrace and to kiss him.

Matt savored the moment and the way Jessie was responding to him. Her behavior gave him hope about winning her love one day. "They'll think I'm the damned luckiest man alive. Have you forgotten we were caught in the barn together with straw in our hair?" he teased, that memory arousing him further.

"Everyone knows that was a trick," she refuted.

"What about all those nights we've been alone on the range? And what about our trip to San Antonio together? They'll think we finally yielded to romance."

"What about my protruding belly in a few months?" she retorted too quickly.

He saw her flush at the slip. He thought a minute, then said, "You're two and a half months along. That'll put our baby arriving first of March. We'll be on the cattle drive when you start showing, Jessie. By the time we get back months later, nobody should suspect anything. Babies do come early. But even if they guessed the truth, the boys wouldn't say anything; they'd think it's mine. It *will* be mine."

"You're such a rare and wonderful man. Are you sure this is what you want, Matt? Don't get drowned trying to save a sinking person."

Matt clasped her face between his hands again. "I love you, woman. This is all I want and need."

"What would I do without you?" she murmured.

"That's what I'm saying. I'll be good to you, Jessie."

"I know you will." She was about to hug and kiss him when he spoke again.

"I do have to ask one question, Jessie. What happens to us if Navarro returns?"

"He won't. But if he did, it wouldn't change anything. I swear it. The baby will be born and raised as yours with your name."

"What if you don't come to love me, and he wants you and the child back?"

"We'll be a family until death, Matt; I promise. Navarro couldn't stay here, and we couldn't go on the run with him. Our fates are cast. Until death do us part; you have my word of honor. I also promise to try to forget him and the past as quickly as possible, and to try to love you like you love me."

"I know you're scared and hurting, Jessie. But you're a Lane. Be strong and brave in the coming months. You can hide the pain until it's gone."

"With you there beside me, Matt, I'm sure I can. Thanks."

Matt grinned. "This time I'm thanking you, Jessie."

*

Matt rode in with the preacher late Tuesday afternoon. Jessie and Gran had been working hard on preparations, and all was perfect when they arrived. The boys and Tom had collected wildflowers that were placed around the parlor. Food was ready for the party afterward.

Jessie was nervous. Her morning sickness had passed earlier, and she was relieved. She was wearing a lovely white dress with lace and ruffles. It fit her snugly at the waist and flowed into a full skirt. Her hair was pinned up, then cascaded down her back in ringlets that Gran had helped her make with the metal iron. Despite the hot and dry August heat, her hands were cold and shaking. She fastened her grandmother's pearls around her neck and settled them over her pounding heart. She knew she was supposed to remain in her room until summoned.

As she spent the last remaining minutes as a single woman, she tried to keep Navarro Breed off her mind. Once she committed herself to Mathew Cordell, it would be for life. For the first time, Jessie prayed that her lost love would never return. When he left, he had said it was too late for him. If he returned, it would be too late for *her*, for *them*.

Good-bye, my love. I'm doing this for our child. We can't ever think of ourselves again. For the rest of my life, I'll owe Matt loyalty for this sacrifice. I love you, Navarro Breed. Wherever you are, be safe and happy.

Jessie heard the fiddle and harmonica begin the music the boys insisted on playing for the occasion. Her pulse raced with her increased heartbeat. Her mouth went dry. She trembled. It was time to seal her future. At the tapping signal on her door, Jessie opened it and entered the room filled with her family, friends, and future husband. She approached the minister and Matt.

Matt took her hand in his and squeezed it. Jessie looked at him and saw love and joy written on his face. He had changed into a suit, and looked very handsome. She smiled.

Matt felt as if his heart would burst from the elation rushing through it. Jessie looked stunning, though her icy, quivering hands revealed her anxiety and her face was a little pale, her cheeks a little rosy. But everyone would think it was merely wedding shakes. He held her hand firmly to give her strength and courage and felt her tighten her fingers around his. He focused his attention on the preacher standing before them.

Reverend Adams motioned the music to halt. He cleared his throat, glanced at the couple, and looked down at his worn Bible. "Dear friends, we're gathered in this home to unite this man and woman in the bonds of holy marriage in the sight of God and these witnesses. I shall read from the book of Ruth, chapter one, verses sixteen and seventeen: 'And Ruth said, Intreat me not to leave thee or to return from following after thee; for whither thou goest, I will go; and where thou lodgest, I will lodge; thy people shall be my people, and thy God my God: Where thou diest, will I die, and there will I be buried: the Lord do so to me, and more also, if aught but death part thee and me.' From Ephesians five, verses twenty-two through thirty-three: 'Wives, submit yourselves unto your own husband, as unto the Lord. For the husband is the head of the wife . . ."

Jessie's thoughts drifted as those serious words sank into her mind. She heard him quote, "For this cause shall a man leave his father and mother, and shall be joined unto his wife, and they two shall be one flesh." Again, she could not stop her mind from questioning the right or wrong of this marriage. Soon she would be vowing to Matt, before witnesses, and unto God . . .

"Mathew Cordell, do you take this woman to be your lawful wife?" Reverend Adams asked. "Will you love her, cherish her, protect her, support her, and guide her in all manners of sickness, health, in riches and in poverty, and amongst any perils unto death parts you as the Holy Scriptures command?"

Matt did not hesitate. "I do, until death," he said.

The minister asked the redhead, "Jessica Lane, do you take this man to be your lawful husband, to love, honor, obey, and cleave only unto him in all manners of good and bad, through health and sickness, for as long as you shall live as so commanded by the Bible?"

Jessie swallowed hard as those vows shot through her head. The baby. That was all that mattered, giving her child a name and fair chance. "I do, until death."

"Is there a ring?" the preacher inquired.

Gran removed her own wedding ring and handed it to the foreman. They'd decided to borrow hers until Matt could purchase one for Jessie. The redhead looked at the woman and smiled.

"A ring is a circle with no end, as love and marriage should be. It is the symbol of your vows before God. May your love remain as shiny and precious as this gold. Place the ring on her finger and say after me: With this ring, I thee wed."

Matt worked the gold band onto Jessie's finger and repeated the words.

"Hold his hand and say after me: I take this ring and thee I wed."

Jessie looked into Matt's eyes and repeated the words.

"By the authorities given to me by God above and by this state, I pronounce you husband and wife. As Matthew six commands: 'Wherefore they are no more twain, but one flesh. What therefore God hath joined together, let not man put asunder.' I congratulate you, Mr. and Mrs. Mathew Cordell. Let us pray."

All bowed their heads as the minister blessed the couple and their marriage. Afterward, the guests kissed the bride's cheek, shook the groom's hand, and gave them both merry advice. Tom hugged his sister and teased her, then talked with Matt. Gran and Jessie embraced for a lengthy time as the older woman whispered words of encouragement and comfort into the redhead's ear.

The festivities got underway with plenty of food and drink. Music and dancing started. Everyone was in a good mood.

Matt danced with his new bride. "That wasn't so bad, was it?" he murmured.

"It was a beautiful ceremony, Matt."

"You're what's beautiful today, Jessie. It'll work."

"We'll make it work." She snuggled close to him as she told herself this was the beginning of her new life. The preacher hadn't asked if anyone objected to the marriage, and no one had been there to do so. Navarro had left her over two months ago. If he had changed his mind, he would have returned by now. She had to face facts. That part of her life was over; Matt and the baby were her future. She was a wife and, in six and a half months, she would be a mother.

"You all right, Jessie?" Matt asked, looking down at her.

"Yes, my husband, I'm fine."

"You'll have to start taking it easier."

Jessie laughed. "It's not an illness, Matt, but I'll be careful."

Carlos, Miguel, Rusty, and Jimmy Joe claimed her hand for dances when the one with Matt ended. Guests ate and laughed and had a good time. When the hour grew late, the hands drifted out a few at a time. Finally, only the family and preacher were left inside, and he was to spend the night.

Gran and Jessie cleared away the food as the men and Tom chatted. Reverend Adams was shown to the room the two sisters had shared. Tom and Gran retired to theirs. Matt followed his lovely bride into Jed's old room.

"I was going to use Mary Louise's room, Jessie, but Preacher Adams has to stay over till morning. You sure you don't mind sharing with me tonight?"

"You have to stay with me every night, Matt, or people will wonder about us."

"I don't want you being uncomfortable. Who'll know if I use your old room?"

"Tom will be confused. I want him and everyone to believe our marriage is real and the baby is yours. We've known each other for years, and you are my husband. Hush now. We're both exhausted."

"I'll turn around while you change and get into bed."

"Always a gentleman," she teased, but was glad he was as she removed her dress and stood clad only in her chemise. "If I were always a lady, this wouldn't have happened."

Matt turned and scolded, "Don't ever say that again. Things like this happen, Jessie. Don't blame yourself."

The redhead didn't try to cover herself, but faced him boldly. "It required two of us, Matt, and we're both to blame. It was reckless and foolish."

Matt went to her, wrapped his arms around her, and urged, "Forget it, love."

"I'll try; honestly I will. I'm just so confused and shaky."

Matt's fingers stroked her bare shoulders. "You've been very busy. You need to rest. You aren't sorry you said yes to me, are you?"

"No, Matt, I'm not. Just give me time and your patience."

"You'll have them, Jessie,—as much as you need."

"I hate treating you this way. This isn't the wedding night you expected, I'm sure."

"What I never expected was to win you, Jessie," he refuted. "If it took Navarro to do that for me, I'm grateful to him. I only hope you'll want and need me one day as much as you did him. He came along when you were vulnerable. Now I'm doing the same thing. The difference is, I won you, and I'll never do anything to make you regret marrying me."

"I do love you, Matt."

"I know, Jessie. Get to bed." Matt released her, and turned his back again.

Jessie looked at her husband. She was glad she had him, and somehow she had to prove it. One day, she would, she vowed. She undressed and slipped on her night-gown. She crawled into bed and pulled the light cover to her neck. "Ready, Matt."

The foreman doused the lamps, undressed in the dark, and climbed in beside her. Their arms and legs touched as they settled in place, and Matt hungered to pull her into his embrace. But he must wait until she came to him.

Jessie closed her eyes and took a deep breath. She couldn't offer herself to her new husband to appease her conscience or to show her gratitude. The minister's words from the Bible returned to haunt her. It was her wifely duty to submit to him. But not now, not yet, her heart and mind commanded stronger than those vows.

Soon, despite Matt's desires and Jessie's tensions, both were asleep.

*

It was hours later when Jessie began to toss and turn. Visions of Navarro in prison flickered through her restless mind. She saw him being beaten, starved, and thrown in that black hole he had told her about. She saw bugs and rats crawling over his flesh. She saw him raging with fever, and no one came to his aid. She saw him laboring under the hot sun and pleading for water. She saw him broken, tormented, alone. She saw him praying for her not to forget him.

Jessie bolted upright in bed, her body drenched in sweat and her heart pounding. Flashes from the nightmare shot through her head and chilled her.

"What is it, Jessie?" Matt asked from the shadows.

"Just a bad dream. It's so hot."

"The windows are open, but no air is stirring. We need a good rain to cool things off. It's as hot and dry as it was before that last thunderstorm."

"I hope we aren't in for another one. I'm sorry I awoke you."

"Lie down and go back to sleep."

Jessie was shaking. She didn't know why, but she had the awful feeling something was wrong, just as she had two days after Navarro left. She worried that he had been captured again. If that were true, he was . . . dead, hanged for murder. Could that be why he hadn't returned or sent word? How could she learn the truth? She dared not write the authorities about him. If the worst were true, she couldn't change it. Wasn't it better not knowing his fate? Wasn't it better to think he was safe and happy someplace far away?

"Matt, will you hold me? I'm so frightened."

Matt gladly gathered her into his embrace. "About what, Jessie?"

"I don't know. I just have the feeling something terrible is about to happen."

"You're safe with me, love. Relax and close your eyes."

Matt stroked her hair until Jessie settled down and was asleep again. It felt wonderful to have her in his reach, touching him. She smelled so fresh and was so soft. He recalled the day in the stagecoach when she had slept in his embrace. She was his wife now, and that thought thrilled him. Some day, she would turn to him, and he would be waiting there to claim her. But first, Navarro's ghost had to be taken from between them. He didn't know how to do that yet. All he could do was be close when she needed him.

*

When Jessie awoke, Matt was gone. She was relieved she was alone, for she was ill this morning. She jumped from bed, pulled the chamber pot from beneath it, and heaved over the container until her sides and throat hurt. She felt awful: nauseated, tired, achy, and tense. The door opened and her grandmother—neat and smiling—entered the room.

"I heard you stirring and thought herbal tea might settle your tummy. My ma and grandma used this recipe for years; they passed it along to me. When I was ailing with my boys those first months, it worked on my morning troubles."

"Thanks, Gran. I feel terrible. How long does this misery last?" Jessie took the cup, sipped the soothing liquid, praying it would stay inside.

"Another couple of weeks. Your body's changing. It's nature's way of telling you to go slow and easy for a while."

"What would I do without you, Gran? You're always here when I need help the most. I've made so many mistakes, but you kept me from making another one."

"About leaving home?" the woman asked as she sat down beside the pale redhead and stroked her tangled hair.

Jessie was glad she hadn't said, "about running away." "I made the right choice, Gran, thanks to your wise advice. Matt's a wonderful man. I'll make this marriage work."

"What about Navarro, Jessie?"

"I have to forget him. I've settled my life. Navarro will have to do the same. We have to accept it's over for us."

"Is it over for you, child?"

"Don't look worried, Gran. It'll take time, but I have plenty of that. It hurts me and makes me angry that Navarro and I can't have each other, but I won't—I can't—dwell on the past. I can't become bitter. I have to give Matt the chance he deserves."

"That's a wise attitude, Jessie. You're a strong and courageous woman. You and Matt are good for each other. You're more alike than you and Navarro. Friendship and respect are important to a successful marriage. Matt and you have had those for a long time, so love will come if you let it."

"Gran, what if I never come to love Matt in that special way?"

Martha's gaze was gentle and encouraging. "Only take and give what your heart allows, Jessie. Don't be false with Matt. He wouldn't want you to pretend. Even if your love is never a blind, fiery one, you two will share a good life together. Sometimes a quiet and peaceful love is more rewarding than a dangerous and passionate one. Matt and Navarro are so different; that will help you not confuse them in your heart."

"I promise to give it my best, Gran; I owe Matt that much."

*

Jessie stayed in bed until her queasiness eased. She got up, bathed, and dressed. Gran prepared her a light meal so as not to upset her stomach again, which the redhead ate slowly. Afterward, she spent her time moving items to make room for her new husband's things.

When Matt returned after his chores, Jessie smiled and greeted him at the door. "If you'll get your possessions from the bunkhouse, I'll help you get moved in."

"You sure about this setup, Jessie?"

She laughed and said, "Of course, I am, Mr. Cordell. How can we get to know each other as we should if we live in different rooms?"

"I'm much obliged, Mrs. Cordell. I know this isn't easy on you."

Jessie looked into his eyes. "You make it easy for me, Matt. I promise to make you the best wife possible. There's only one difficult area, and we'll handle that after the baby's born. Is that all right?"

Matt looked at her rosy cheeks and bright blue eyes. He grasped her meaning. "I can wait for that day, Jessie. You just worry about staying safe and healthy."

Overcome with gratitude for his understanding, Jessie hugged him.

As Matt held her in his embrace, his spirits soared, knowing she was being honest and fair. "These next months will be busy ones, Jessie. I'm going to town next week to hire trained bronc peelers to get the cavvy broken in. If we're lucky, I'll find enough wranglers to hire on for the roundup and cattle drive."

"I'll let you tend to everything. I'm not in shape to help out these days."

"I'm not trying to take your or Jed's place, Jessie. I only want to do anything I can to take the work off you for as long as you need it."

"I know, Matt, and I'm grateful. I trust you completely; I always have. Besides, this ranch is ours now. You aren't the foreman any more; you're the boss."

"Rusty will be a good foreman. The boys like him and respect him. They won't have trouble taking orders from him."

"He was a good choice. Now let's get you settled before supper."

*

For the next few days, Jessica Lane Cordell continued to take things slowly. She remained at rest each morning until her misery passed, then helped her grandmother with housework or Tom with his book lessons. In a way, the redhead was enjoying her new womanly role. She could relax about her pregnancy with Matt to safeguard her and the child from scandal and heartache. Matt treated her with such tenderness and affection. She liked being made to feel special. She liked feeling feminine. The more she was with Matt, the more she adored him.

As he continued to court her with loving kisses and embraces, she had to admit she found his romantic attentions pleasurable. It was soothing to be held in his strong, cherishing arms. She had prayed that losing Navarro wouldn't embitter her to the point she couldn't feel passion and love for another man. She wanted her husband to stir the desires that Navarro had first awakened. She recalled how it felt to share herself with her lost love. She confessed that she wanted to experience those same passions and emotions again. Perhaps sex would be the final link in the chain to bind her and Matt together as they should be. Lovemaking had bonded her and Navarro, had proven and strengthened their trust. Yet, while she carried another man's child, she could not unite her body with Matt's. But she could work on giving herself to him emotionally until the time was right.

*

Late Friday, Jessie and Matt were standing on the porch watching a lovely sunset. He was behind her, his arms wrapped around her waist, hers clasped over them. She was leaning against his hard body with her head resting against the broad width of his chest.

"It's mighty hot and dry. Makes the men and stock restless," he said.

"But it's beautiful and peaceful," she remarked, gazing at the colorful horizon to the west. "Everything's settled down, Matt."

He bent his head downward to brush a kiss on her cheek. Jessie turned and nestled in his arms, her hands spread across his back. She listened to his heartbeat as her nearness increased its pace. His arms tightened, and he pressed his lips to her silky hair. She wondered which was better, to show her affection or to withhold it to keep from tantalizing him.

"Matt, does it make it harder on you when I get close? Should I stop?"

"I'm glad you can talk to me about anything, Jessie, and yep, it's hard being near you and not . . . You know what I mean. But it makes me happy to hold you, to have any part of you. Lean my way as much as you can," he coaxed.

Jessie pushed back enough to look into his brown eyes. "You're a very handsome man, Mathew Cordell. I'm lucky no girl lassoed you before I could. I do want you, but I have to wait until there isn't anyone between us."

"Navarro's ghost?" he asked.

"No, the baby. After it's born, I will become your wife in that way, too."

Matt's hands cupped her face, and he stared into her sincere gaze. He craved her so much, but her admission gave him the strength to wait for her. He understood and honored her feelings, her dilemma, her sense of duty to all of them. "I love you, Jessie.

Much as I need you, our future is all that's important to me." His mouth covered hers with a soul-searching tenderness and power that stole her breath.

At the corral, Miguel nudged Carlos and remarked, "We were wrong, *amigo*. She could not love Navarro and surrender so sweetly to Matt. It is good. They have been close for many years. *Sí*, it is a good match."

"Where is the law that says a beautiful señorita cannot love more than one *hombre*? I think she turned to him from loneliness and fear. But, *chica* is an honorable woman; she would never hurt or betray our boss. I wonder if Navarro will ever return. What will he do when he sees he has lost her?"

"What can he do, Carlos? It is done."

*

Jessie awoke before midnight. She was restless and edgy. She didn't know what was wrong, but something more oppressive than the heat weighed upon her.

"What's wrong, love?" Matt asked from the darkness.

"I don't know. I can't sleep. I think I'll sit and read a while."

"It's just the weather and your condition. How about warm milk and a rub?"

"That isn't it, Matt. I have that dark mood again."

"Why don't I sit up with you? We can—"

A rumble in the distance caught their attention through the open windows. Both pairs of eyes darted in that direction. The noise came again, closer, louder.

"A storm's brewing. Maybe that's it," he suggested.

Jessie got out of bed, walked to the window, and looked outside. She saw lightning not far away and heard the rolling sound once more—deep, heavy, continuous until muffled by its retreat. Matt's arms encircled her body. She remained tense and stiff, staring at the ominous horizon.

Matt's gaze followed hers. From the look of it, they ere in for a bad one. "I best go alert the boys. Don't want the stock spooked into a run."

The sky was dark and threatening. Thundercracks rent the hot air and roared off in all directions like angry beasts on the prowl. Lightning flashed, and branched into several limbs as it reached down from above to finger the land with its power. The house vibrated as the booming noises increased in volume and proximity. Shadows were dispelled for a time by flickers of brightness. Lightning attacked the terrain as rapidly as the peals of thunder shouted into the night. An eerie wind picked up and blew over the dry landscape, shaking anything in its aimless path.

"Don't go tonight, Matt. I want you with me. I'm . . . scared."

"You've never been afraid of storms, Jessie, but I'm here. Just let me get the boys to work, then I'll return." He hugged her, snatched on his clothes, and left.

Jessie kept her gaze on the sky. This was not a normal thunderstorm. Its strength was awesome; its warning was lethal. She trembled as lightning danced wildly in the sky, then sent forked tongues to lick at the earth. No Indian war drum could sound as intimidating as the claps of thunder over the house. She knew it was dangerous for any man or animal out tonight.

Jessie jumped and shrieked as she heard what sounded like an explosion nearby, bamming and echoing. The next siege began as soon as it was silent. The house seemed to sense danger and to shudder in panic. The windows rattled, their panes tinkling and their frames creaking in an odd way. Two loud bangs were discharged by a luminous thunderbolt that separated into several offshoots and struck the earth. Jessie jerked and screamed. She wished Matt would return. She was terrified, and she didn't know why.

The thunder and lightning were at full fury, foreshadowing a torrential rain. She wished moisture would pour down to cool the heat of the weather's rage. An ear-splitting blast charged through the house, causing it to tremble with alarm. Jessie knew it had been struck by lightning. She smelled smoke: fire!

Jessie rushed into the parlor, glanced about, and hurried toward the kitchen. Before she reached it, she saw the brilliance of flames from the back porch out the windows. Crackles said the hungry fire was spreading fast as it chewed at dry wood. In horror, she watched red devils jump from spot to spot to set them ablaze. The thirsting condition of the wood caused it to ignite and burn rapidly.

"Tom! Granj! Get out fast! The house is afire!"

Tom responded he was coming. Gran yelled she was yanking on clothes.

Jessie knew Matt was in the bunkhouse giving orders and didn't realize their peril, as the continuous claps and rolls were too noisy. She seized a bucket and pumped water as fast as she could, but it filled slowly from the lowered supply. She tossed the liquid at the blazing windows, then repeated her action. She realized it was futile, with the fire swift and the water sluggish. She saw ravenous flames licking or gnawing at the porch, bathing closet, and the roof. She knew it was already in the attic. "Tom! Can you hear me?" When he responded he was coming soon, she ordered, "Leave those things! Get down here! Now!"

Jessie reached the short hallway to her grandmother's bedroom. A surge of flames and blast of hot air swept from her old room and cut the redhead off from her target, forcing her backward a few steps. She held up her hands before her smarting face. Weakening beams overhead creaked and threatened to come crashing down before much longer. Tom moved slowly on his disabled let. The kitchen was under attack, and his escape would be cut off soon. Frantic, she shouted above the noise of the fire and storm, "Gran! Keep your door closed! Fire in the hall! Get out the front window! Fast, Gran! I have to get to Tom before he's trapped!" Jessie did not get a response. She glanced toward the burning kitchen where Tom soon wouldn't be able to pass, then at the obstructed hall to her grandmother's silent room. In a split second, horrible thoughts raced through her mind. If she rushed outside to break the glass to rescue Gran, she could never reach her brother in time. If she went after Tom, they might be trapped upstairs and Gran in her room. Her baby. . . . All of the Lanes could perish tonight inside this raging oven. . . . Where was Matt! *God, help us!* She had to act, now.

Chapter

19

M att rushed into the house calling for Jessie. He hurried to her side and ordered, "Get to the barn where it's safe. I'll go for Tom. The boys are getting Gran out the front window. They're hauling water, but it looks bad. Too high to fight. Move, woman!" he shouted to spur her into motion.

Jessie didn't obey. She saw her husband run toward the kitchen, but returned to her room to save some of their possessions. She threw clothes on the spread, tied the corners, and tossed the bundle out the window. She threw more belongings and the ranch books onto the sheet and did the same with it. She jerked open drawers, scooped up items, and crammed then into emptied pillowcases. Out the window they went. She heard shouts as men passed orders and buckets. She smelled smoke and saw it wafting into her room like thick mist stirred by a brisk wind. Crackles and pops entered her ears. A crash told her the back porch was collapsing.

Matt hurried into their bedroom with an axe he had fetched. "Can't get through the kitchen! I'll have to chop through the wall to get to the attic steps. Get out, Jessie, before the ceilings fall." Matt slammed the tool with all his strength against the wall into the dining area. Wood splintered and flew in several directions. He worked quickly and desperately, knowing time was against him.

Jessie was panicked. The only way to her brother's room was by the steps in the far corner of the eating area. The sole window overlooked the back of the house where the blaze was raging at its worst, making a rescue ladder impossible. She couldn't leave until she saw Tom's face and knew he was safe. She prayed as Matt swung the axe and broke into the partition. When the hole was large enough for him to slip through, he vanished into the smoky room of flames, holding a soaked blanket over his head.

Jessie heard his boots clattering on the wooden steps. She heard the dog barking in fear. She heard her brother's voice. Her heart pounded and she clenched her hands. Soon two coughing males appeared, and she cried in relief.

"Let's go!" Matt carried Tom to the front window and outside.

Clem's frantic barks caught her attention. Jessie rushed to the hole calling to him, and the dog ran to her. She helped him through the opening which was too high for him to leap over to safety, then carried him to the window and leaned over to place him on the porch. Clem took off toward the yard. As Jessie bent to crawl out, the window gave way and struck her head. Everything went black.

Gusts of wind whipped the flames into a wild frenzy. It swirled dry dirt and smoke into everyone's eyes. "No use, boys!" Matt shouted. "Pull back!" The men stopped fighting the determined fire and rushed to collect the family's possessions that had been tossed out the windows. Bundles were carried to safety in the barn.

"Where is Jessie?" Gran shouted.

Flames leapt into the dark sky over their home and brightened the wanton area. Smoke billowed. Walls and sections of roof gave way. Over the thunderclaps, voices, wind, barks, and pops of burning wood, Matt heard Gran and looked around for his wife. He saw Jessie's head in the bedroom window. He ran to the porch, jumped onto it, and shoved the sash upward. He held it in place with his knee while he pulled Jessie into his arms, then carried her down the steps. A loud crash followed them and sent fiery coals and ashes into the air. One burned through Matt's shirt and seared his flesh. He halted for Miguel to toss water on the area.

Matt entered the barn and placed Jessie on a blanket on the hay. By lanternlight, he checked her head. The wound wasn't bad, but it had rendered her unconscious. "She'll be fine in a while, Gran," he told the worried woman. "Watch her for me."

Matt left the barn. He watched helplessly as flames engulfed and destroyed it. He wished the rain would hurry. It was too late to save their home, but a downpour would protect other structures on the ranch from flying sparks. "Watch the other buildings. That wind is gusting embers all over."

"Sorry, Boss, but she's riding high and bucking stubborn," Rusty said.

The men stared at the consuming blaze. Lightning flashed in all directions. Peals of thunder followed each display of powerful light. More walls and sections of roof rumbled to the floor. Heat reached them even at their distance. Rain started, slow at first; soon, it was drenching them fast.

Jessie roused and sat up to find everyone observing the fire that was fighting for its life against ever-increasing rain. She saw bundles nearby. She stood, battled her dizziness, and walked to the doorway.

Matt steadied her with an arm around her waist. Jessie leaned her head against his shoulder. She watched the storm rage into full force. Her home was gone, like her father and Navarro. "Damn," she swore in distress. "I hate fires! This isn't fair. It's the third one we've had. That's more than our share. Why didn't He send the rain sooner to help us?"

"Don't get bitter, love. We still have more than most people do. We'll bed down here in the barn tonight, then figure what to do come morning."

The hands rushed to the bunkhouse to get out of the storm and to change into dry garments. Matt coaxed his wife and Tom and Gran from the grim scene and closed the barn doors. "Let's get dry and get some rest," he suggested.

Jessie looked at the four of them: filthy with soot, smelling of smoke, exhausted, and depressed. The soaked animal in Tom's arms gave off its own doggy smell. "Why, Matt? Haven't we been tested enough?"

"Don't, Jessie. Accidents happen. There was nothing we could do."

"He could have," she remarked with anger, glancing upward.

"We don't question the good Lord's ways, child," Martha told her. "Not everything, good or bad, is His doing and bad things aren't always His tests or punishments. Be thankful we're all alive and safe."

Jessie lowered her aching head and replied, "You're right, Gran. You, too, Matt. You saved my life and Tom's. It's just been such a long and hard fight to end this way."

"It isn't over, love. You have Fletcher's home. We can move there. Either we can stay there or we can rebuild here."

"That's a crazy twist of fate: Fletcher came after our home and land, but we wound up with his. We'll use his place until we decide what to do."

"*Our* place," Gran corrected, then sent her an encouraging smile.

Matt turned his back while the two women changed nightgowns. Then they did the same while he and Tom changed. He pulled bedrolls from the tackroom and spread them on piles of hay. "Let's turn in," he said.

Jessie took the roll beside her husband and pulled protective cover over her shaking body. She saw Clem snuggle next to Tom's warm body. Fatigued, she realized her grandmother and brother were soon asleep. Jessie curled closer to her husband's side, needing his strength and comfort. He turned toward her and wrapped his arms around her. His hair and skin still smelled of smoke and his face was smudged. She wriggled closer to whisper. "I'm glad you're here, Matt."

He looked over at her misty gaze and weary expression. "Me, too, Jessie." His mouth closed over hers and kissed her deeply, soothingly.

Jessie's hand caressed his dirty cheek, and she returned the more-than-pleasant kiss. As one drifted into another, she rolled to her back and her husband lay half atop her. His mouth worked a stimulating path across her face before returning to her lips. Jessie warmed to his touch. She did not once think of Navarro Breed. She closed her eyes and dreamily realized how skilled Matt was with kisses and caresses, and she enjoyed them for a time.

"I love you, Jessie," Matt murmured in her ear. "I'll always protect you."

She hugged him tightly and replied, "I love you, too, Matt."

As if knowing it was perilous to continue his amorous behavior, Matt halted it and cuddled her in his embrace. "Sleep, love."

Jessie was grateful for his caution. She knew now that she could respond to him when the right time came, but that was months away. Relaxed, despite the raging storm and devastating fire, she closed her eyes.

*

Jessica Cordell stared at the wet, blackened ruins of her home. The storm had ceased at dawn, but the ground was muddy from it. She walked around the fallen house twice, and saw nothing more could be saved than the few bundles they had tossed outside last night. The rock foundation and chimneys stood firm in place amidst dark debris. Broken glass lay here and there from heat-shattered windows. The stench of destruction hung heavy in the cooled air. She took a deep breath to settle her edgy nerves. Maybe a move would be a new and challenging beginning for her marriage to Matt, away from the room where her father had been washed and wrapped for burial and where she had slept with Navarro during the last violent storm. All that was gone; it was time to look to the future.

They had eaten earlier in the chuckhouse, and Gran was helping Biscuit Hank with the chores there. The other hands were out checking herds and fences to see how they had weathered the storm. Matt was hitching up a wagon to drive them to their new home a few hours away. When it was loaded, he joined her.

"Come away now, Jessie. Don't look any more."

Jessie turned to her husband and smiled to let him know she was all right. She was fortunate that morning sickness had not attacked her on this challenging day. She reached for his hand and curled her fingers around his. After what had happened between them last night, she felt a little shy with him. To cover it, she behaved more boldly than usual. "It's over here, Matt. Let's go home."

A broad smile made creases near his brown eyes and enticing mouth. He guided her to the wagon and helped her aboard. He fetched Gran and Tom. When all were ready, he flicked the reins and off they went.

*

Jessie put away their clothes in Wilbur Fletcher's old bedroom. Gran and Tom did the same in the two guestrooms across the hall. After warning his wife to take it slow and easy, Matt returned to the other ranch to give orders.

Hours passed as the two women took inventory of their new possessions. The windows were open wide to air the stuffy place. Jessie had men move the billiard table to the old foreman's dwelling, a large one-room structure on the other side of the bunkhouse, to the left of the hacienda-style home. Other furniture was moved by the men as the women rearranged the large parlor.

Jessie checked every area for fire safety. There were plenty of windows for quick escape. Yet she knew the stucco facade and the flat roof with *canales* for drainage wouldn't catch fire, so that eased her fears of another dangerous blaze. Jessie recalled the terror and helplessness that had overwhelmed her during the fire, and she never wanted to feel that way again. She would make certain everyone was careful with the lamps and candles—anything that could ignite.

*

After a bath and shampoo to remove the smell of last night's disaster and the sweat from her labors today, Jessie donned a simple cotton dress. As she brushed her hair, her gaze slid to her flat stomach. She tried to imagine it protruding with a child. "Ouch," she muttered as the brush was ensnared in her tresses.

As she worked with the auburn tangles, she walked to a small extra room beside hers that would be nice for the baby. She looked into the area and tried to envision a cradle and rocker there, and her child playing. She wondered what sex it would be and how it would look. Jessie admitted to herself that she was anxious about giving birth and about raising a child. She was glad she had Matt's help and love, as he would make a wonderful parent.

More so than the troubled Navarro, she admitted, as he had had poor experiences with his home life. She was glad she wasn't on the run in her condition, that she was safe and comfortable here. She knew that Navarro still had bitterness to resolve, something only he could do for himself, so it was probably best they had parted. The trouble that had drawn them together could have made them too dependent upon each other. Months ago, they had needed each other desperately. Now Matt could fill her needs. She and Matt were so similar, whereas she and Navarro had been so different. Yet Navarro had opened her heart and life so Matt could enter them. Yes, Matt would be a better father than—

"Anything the matter, Jessie?" Matt asked from the stairs.

She leaned against his strong body after he joined her in the doorway and kissed her cheek. "I was just thinking about what a good father you'll be."

The answer delighted Matt. He couldn't forget how she had felt in his arms last night, how she had responded to him. "You'll be a good mother, Jessie."

"I hope so. This new job is a scary one," she admitted.

"I agree. We'll work hard to do it right. Have you given any thought to whether you'd prefer to live here or try to rebuild on the other property before spring?"

Her husband followed her into their new bedroom. "Yes, I've been thinking about that all afternoon. We've got broncbusting, fall roundup, and the cattle drive soon. When you and the boys get back from Dodge, it'll be only a few months before the baby's due. That isn't the best time for construction or moving, or for spending a lot of money on materials and extra men. I don't think we should make any decisions until next spring, after roundup and branding. Let's see how we like it here this winter. It's a lovely, safe house, and large enough for our family. We have so much to do between now and March."

"Sounds good to me. I don't want you working so hard. You have to be careful of lifting heavy things."

"You worry about me too much," she teased with a grin, glad he did.

"That's a new job I'm loving, Jessie."

"Me, too," she concurred, knowing deep inside it was true.

*

On Monday, Jessie had some of the men begin work on a new smithy. She didn't like the location of the old site next to one of the two barns. It was a fire hazard that Fletcher had overlooked, one she didn't want. Her husband had agreed that the structure should be in a clearing by itself, as on the Lane property.

Matt left early that morning for town to buy supplies, things the women needed in their new home, and to hire seasonal workers for the impending tasks.

In bed alone that night, Jessie realized it felt strange not to have him at her side. She was already accustomed to his presence after only a week of marriage. The bed seemed larger with only her to occupy it. She missed his company and the sense of security it gave her. She was glad she had never shared this bed with Navarro. Nothing in this house could remind her of the missing desperado, except the child she carried. She told herself this was the last night, last time, she would think of him. She owed Matt her life, Tom's twice, her family name, her love, her earnest attempts to make him happy, and her fidelity of heart and mind and body.

You have to leave me in all ways, Navarro. I can't keep thinking about you. I must be true to Matt; he deserves that and more from me. Good-bye, my love.

*

When Matt returned late Tuesday, he found Jessie and Martha in the kitchen preparing supper. "I'm home, love," he called from the doorway.

Jessie dried her hands and hurried to greet him with a hug and kiss.

"I have several surprises for you," he hinted.

"What?" she asked. Excitement and anticipation brightened her pale face. She had been ill again both mornings during his absence, but was better by now.

"This is first." He pulled a gold band from his pocket and slipped it on her finger. "There, Mrs. Cordell. It's my brand," he teased.

Jessie eyed the wedding ring with delight. "It's beautiful, Matt. Thank you." She hugged him again. "What else?" she inquired, recalling he had mentioned several surprises.

"I hired wranglers for the roundup and drive. Had to offer 'em top dollar, forty a month. They'll be here a week from Sunday." Matt knew the long drive to market meant they would be separated for months, and he dreaded that time alone on the trail. Even more, he hated leaving Jessie in her condition to run the ranch and in new surroundings that might tempt her to do more work than she should. But mostly he was anxious over the possibility of Navarro's return during his absence. Yet Jessie had vowed she was his wife forever . . . To conceal his lingering worry, Matt continued with his news. "I got two broncbusters coming Sunday to break in the cavvy. I promised 'em five dollars a head. Between them, Jimmy Joe, Miguel, and Carlos, we'll have the horses ready in a week or less."

"That's wonderful, Matt. Papa would be proud of us. Things are finally getting back to normal. I'm glad."

"Me, too. Word spread about Fletcher's death, so drovers headed this way again. We have a big job before us, and I didn't want to lose 'em to other ranchers. I wired our old trail boss, and he accepted my offer. I promised him a bonus if he gets us there on time and without much trouble. You don't mind, do you?"

"Certainly not. He's worth every dollar. We need him." Jessie stroked Matt's stubbled chin and said, "This is *our* ranch now, Matt, so you don't have to check everything with me. Besides, you were the best foreman any ranch could have. Marriage hasn't made you lose that magic touch. We have plenty of stock ready for market, so we can afford the best hands. I want you, the boys, and our herd safe on the trail. And back home as soon as possible," she added.

Matt grinned in pleasure. "My last surprise is for you and Gran. With me taking both cooks, that'll leave you two tending the boys left behind for chores and protection. I don't want either of you working that hard so I hired extra help for the house and hands. She's waiting outside."

"She?" Jessie echoed.

"Margaret Anne James. She's all alone, Jessie, an orphan. Just eighteen. You know what jobs are around for women on their own. Annie is nice and kind. They were letting her go at the hotel. Most men will be gone for months this time of year, so they don't need two girls. I heard Annie pleading to stay on just for meals and board until business picked up again; she said there weren't any other jobs around and she didn't have money to travel to another town where there might not be any, either. I felt sorry for her, Jessie, and we can use her. I figured we could move the billiard table into one of the barns and let her have the old foreman's house. We need a strong back and extra hands to take the load off you and Gran. Annie can help with the housework and cooking, and whatever else has to be done. This way, you and your grandmother can get more rest—and especially you, love. You'll need it in the coming months. You've also got a lot of sewing and planning to do for the baby. Annie can help you tend him after he's born."

Jessie was moved by her husband's thoughtfulness. But a twinge of jealousy pricked her. She had never heard Matt talk so much about another woman . . . and so caringly. She admonished herself for her foolishness. Matt had a tender heart, and great concern for his wife. She didn't care to have another woman, a stranger, in the house, but the girl was needed. She hoped this Annie would work out for everyone, as she didn't want Matt disappointed. "Bring her in so we can meet her."

"Did I make a bad decision?" he asked, as she had hesitated a while. For a moment, he suspected he read jealousy in her gaze. Was that—

Jessie broke into his thoughts, "No, Matt, a good one. You're right, and you're the kindest man I've ever known. I'm a lucky woman to have you."

While Matt was fetching the girl, Jessie told her grandmother, "If we don't like her and she doesn't work out, Gran, wait until Matt's gone before we handle the matter. I don't want him hurt or embarassed."

"You're a good-hearted woman, Jessie."

Matt returned with Annie, who looked a little shy and worried. She had thick brown hair, grass-green eyes and dimples set in a lovely face. At five seven, she was taller than Jessie and had a fuller figure. The girl appeared to be older than eighteen, but Jessie assumed a hard life had aged and matured her beyond her years. Those unbidden twinges pricked her again as she eyed the young beauty at her smiling husband's side.

After Matt introduced them, the girl dipped at the knee, nodded her head, and said in a southern accent, "Pleased to make your acquaintance, ma'am. I want to thank you for this job, Mrs. Cordell. I need it badly. I promise I'll work hard. I don't drink strong spirits, use bad talk, steal, or sneak off to play."

Jessie warmed to the blushing female with trembly voice and earnest gaze. She smiled to relax her. Annie's green eyes were clear and honest. She spoke well and had good manners. She deserved a chance to prove herself. "Welcome to our home, Annie. I'm sure you'll do fine here. Matt will have the boys prepare your place for you. I'm sure you're tired after your long journey, so go along with him to get settled in. We'll go over your chores in the morning. Did you and Matt discuss wages?"

"Yes, ma'am. He offered the same as the hotel, twelve dollars a month. If that's too much, you can pay me less. I had to use my earnings for boarding and meals, so it's more than I was making in town."

"No, that's fine. I think you'll like it here, Annie. Just remember we have lots of men around who can be tempted by a pretty face. I wouldn't want to lose you and one of them about the time I get used to having good help."

The girl smiled at Jessie's teasing tone. "Yes, ma'am. You have a beautiful home. I've only seen a few as grand."

"Thank you. We've only been here a few days. Ours burned last Friday. We owned this one, too, so we moved here. Gran and I have some changes we want to make. You can help us with them later. Matt, see that Annie's settled in, then return for supper. I'll bring you a plate after we eat. If you need anything, you can tell me when I come over."

"You're all very kind. I'll do my best here."

"I'm sure you will, Annie."

The girl left with Matt. Jessie and her grandmother exchanged smiles of acceptance. They returned to their chore, chatting about Matt's actions. Tom joined them soon, and Jessie sent him to wash up for the evening meal. By the time the food was on the table, Matt walked in and took his place at one end.

"What do you think of her?" he asked the two women.

Tom replied first. "She's mighty pretty. I like her."

"We do, too, Matt," Jessie said reassuringly. "We're glad you brought her home with you. She'll be a big help, and you spared her from a terrible fate in the saloon."

"That should make her even more loyal and hardworking," Gran added.

"I'm sure it will, Gran." Jessie turned to Matt and asked, "What else did she tell you about herself? I didn't want to ply her with questions she'd already answered for you. She was a mite skittish, but I don't blame her. If I had refused her the job, she would have been in for a bad time."

Matt buttered his bread as he responded. "Her parents moved from South Carolina to El Paso when she was twelve. They died two years back when she was sixteen. Annie doesn't have any other family, and didn't know many people in town. Seems her father wasn't liked much and died in heavy debt. Men he owed took most of what she had to settle his accounts."

"That's awful, Matt. How did she live, alone and so young?"

"She helped a seamstress for over a year until the lady closed shop and left town; Annie had been living in her back room. The woman gave her enough money to survive on until she got another job. She worked in the El Paso Hotel until five months ago. The owner was mean and . . . demanding," he said, choosing the word carefully for Tom's adolescent ears. He knew the two women would understand his meaning. "She'd saved enough to take the stage as far as Davis. She was about out of money when she was hired at the hotel. Didn't last long with business going down."

"Why haven't I see her in town? How long was she there?"

"She worked at Morley's place at the far end of town. We never stayed there. Annie came about four months ago. She tried to get another job in El Paso first, but that spiteful man made certain nobody hired her."

"I'm sure he was trying to force her back into his employ." With her young brother sitting there with keen ears, Jessie didn't say what she felt about the wicked man and his doings. Yet it angered her to think of a young girl in such a helpless situation. She was glad Annie was a good girl and hadn't given in to the lustful beast. "Most women are vulnerable if they don't have a family."

"Unless they're strong and smart like my wife, who has her own ranch."

Jessie laughed and retorted, "Unless they have wonderful husbands who keep them from losing their . . . skins to men like that hotel owner and Fletcher."

"You could run this ranch without me, woman, and we both know it."

"Perhaps, but I wouldn't want to find out. I like being married to you, Mathew Cordell, and we shouldn't have waited so long to have so much fun."

Matt's eyes glinted with pleasure and desire. "We haven't had much of that since our marriage last Tuesday, but we will."

"Last Tuesday?" she repeated in amazement. "It seems so much longer."

Matt laughed heartily at her expression. "Because so much has happened. I guess I'm already like a comfortable old shoe. I've been around a long time."

Jessie was seated to her husband's right, with Tom across from her and with Gran at the other end. As Jessie turned toward Matt it was easy to forget the others were there as she lost herself in their teasing conversation. "Better that, Mr. Cordell, than a tight and painful new boot that doesn't fit and is paid for."

Matt grinned and grasped her left hand. He gazed at the gold band on her finger, his heart swelling with pride and love. Jessie had never seemed more relaxed and happy than she did tonight. It was apparent she had accepted him in her new life, and that she was trying her hardest to be a good wife. In time, their marriage could only get better. If Navarro didn't return and spoil it.

Jessie observed the tormented look that flashed in Matt's brown eyes like lightning before a storm. His grip on her hand tightened for a moment as something distracted and alarmed him. Her astute mind went over the clues—marriage, ring, claim on her—and realized what her husband feared could happen to his new life. Jessie squeezed his hand, capturing his attention, and gazed into his troubled eyes. "I love you, Matt," she said, "and I'm glad I said yes to your proposal."

"Oh, no, Gran, they're gonna get squishy on us. Wait till after supper."

Everyone looked at Tom's wrinkled nose and comical expression, and laughed.

"Sorry, little brother, but I am a new bride. We act crazy like this."

"He'll understand when the love chigger digs into his hide like it did mine."

"Oh no, they never will," the boy vowed with wide eyes enlarged by thick glasses.

"I'll remind you of that claim one day, young man, when you're chasing some lucky girl's skirt," Jessie warned in a playful tone.

Tom shook his auburn head. "I ain't gonna act loco over no girl."

"Love ain't loco, Tom; it's wonderful and magical. It's very special."

"Matt's right," Gran concurred, smiling at the man. "You'll see one day."

The boy didn't look convinced, but stayed quiet and returned to his meal. The others did, too. When the table was cleared and the dishes were done, Jessie headed for the one-room house where Annie was lodged.

The door was open, so Jessie called out and walked inside. "Here's your food, Annie. How is everything?"

"It's more than nice, ma'am. Thank you."

Jessie saw how misty her green eyes were. She realized what a difficult and frightening life Annie had had. But the girl was strong, brave, and smart enough to take care of herself for years and to seek a new start each time she had to. Jessie's tender heart went out to Margaret Anne James, as Matt's had in town. "I'm glad you like it. I hope you'll be with us a long time."

"Is there anything . . . you want to know about me?"

"Matt's told us what you related to him," Jessie admitted. "I'm sorry you've had such a bad time of it. That's over now, Annie. The boys here are good men; they won't give you any trouble. If anyone does, come to me. Most of them have worked for my family for years, but we do have a few new hands from the past owner of this ranch, so I don't know them well."

Annie caught her meaning. "I won't give them any reason to approach me, Mrs. Cordell. Sometimes manners and kindness are mistaken for overtures, so I'll be careful. I'll try not to make any mistakes here."

"Come to the house about seven in the morning. We'll start then."

As the redhead turned to leave, Annie said, "Thank you again, ma'am."

"You're welcome, Annie," Jessie replied. "See you tomorrow."

*

Wednesday morning, Jessie and Gran talked with Annie and showed her around the house. They discussed the daily schedule, went over the list of chores, and told the girl how they wanted them done.

The three women took to each other quickly. Over the midday meal, Jessie gave Annie a brief sketch of their family history. She told the girl she had only been married a short time, but didn't give a date. Of course, she might guess her secret one day, or someone could reveal the conflict in timing by accident. Jessie couldn't worry about what Annie or the hands would think about a seven-month baby. Surely everyone saw how happy and compatible she and Matt were, and they were aware how long the couple had known each other. She knew, with the men about to go away, the truth would be safe until spring. And as babies sometimes came early, perhaps others would be fooled when it arrived in early March instead of mid-May. But even if the hands suspected her secret, none of them would speak ill of her and Matt, and hopefully wouldn't suspect who the child's father was.

Annie and Gran finished talking about Wilbur Fletcher. "You're a strong and courageous woman, Mrs. Cordell," Annie said. "You're lucky your father was a good man. Mine wasn't. We had to leave Carolina because he was always into trouble over gambling debts. It wasn't any better in El Paso. If he and Mother hadn't eaten tainted food and died, I don't know what would have happened to us. Creditors came and took everything as soon as he was buried. It was awful. I know a lot about sewing, so I can help make clothes. A seamstress taught me."

Jessie didn't mention she would especially need that skill and assistance in two months when her figure started expanding. She also didn't comment on how Annie had changed the subject in a rush. "Please call me Jessie," She coaxed. "I'm only six years older than you. Mrs. Cordell sounds so matronly."

"And I'm Gran to everyone, child," Martha added.

"You're all so good and kind. I'm so happy Mr. Cordell was in town to rescue me. Some men can be so wicked, but I knew I could trust him. You're lucky, Mrs.—I mean, Jessie."

The redhead sensed the sad-eyed girl had secrets of her own, but she didn't pry into them. "Yes, I am. You will be too one day, Annie. You're sweet and lovely. You'll see that all men aren't like your father and that hotel owner."

*

The rest of the week went by fast as the women changed Wilbur Fletcher's house into the Cordell home. Jessie also spent time on Tom's neglected lessons, as Matt had purchased new books in town. Annie helped out on occasion, something young Thomas Lane seemed to like. He did his best to impress the girl.

Each evening, Margaret Anne James served their dinner in the dining room, ate in the kitchen, and did the dishes before retiring. Jessie told her she wasn't a servant and it wasn't necessary to wait on them, but Annie seemed to enjoy the task and insisted upon doing it.

*

The professional broncbusters—peelers—arrived on Sunday. Matt introduced them to his wife, then showed the two men where to bunk during their brief stay.

The remuda—cavvy—of half-broken and wild horses was corraled near the barn and ready for busting and training to begin tomorrow. Hands had gathered them over the last few days for the seasonal task of preparing them for roundup and the long drive on the Western Trail to Dodge City, Kansas.

Each man needed three horses for gathering steers and for cowpunching on the trail, a total of one hundred ninety horses. Excluding their regular mounts—which made four apiece—that left the Cordells one hundred and fifty horses to break. Each man was responsible for all the care his four animals would require along the way: thinning and shortening tails, trimming and shodding hooves, treating injuries and sickness, currying sweaty hides, and feeding them.

Geldings were used, as stallions and mares were moody and undependable. The remuda was allowed to roam the range until it was needed in the fall. Most were seven to ten years old; the older were more experienced and easiest to retrain for the next time. Each had its own personality. Some made good cutting horses that were superior at culling market-ready steers from the herds. Night horses were steady of foot in the dark. Rope horses seemed to know when and how to keep lassos tight around stock's necks. Herd mounts were adept at working with steers during drives and skilled at remaining calm and masterful and sure-footed during terrifying stampedes.

The dusty, exhausting, and perilous task of training the horses would begin after breakfast tomorrow. An aura of suspense and excitement already hung over the area as everyone awaited the event.

*

Jessie joined Matt and others at the corral. They talked a while, then parted as he went to handle the chore. She waved to Miguel, Carlos, and Jimmy Joe as they prepared themselves to risk life and limb while challenging half-wild creatures to prove who was master. Hands perched on the fence, ready to lend help if an unseated rider was in danger of being trampled and eager to shout jests and encouragement during the episodes.

Five areas were sectioned off so all the busters could work mounts at the same time. The professional peelers took on six to eight of the wildest beasts a day, while the

Cordell hands rode three to four half-broken creatures into renewed submission. Each man had a helper to rope the right animal and to assist the rider with saddling and mounting a frantic critter.

Jessie stepped onto the bottom rail and looped her arms over the top one to observe the action. This time, she didn't sit atop the fence and risk a fall.

"Tame them good, Miguel," she said to the Mexican who was dressed in his finery to put on a good show.

"Do not fret, *amiga;* I will be resting by high noon," he vowed with a grin.

"On a busted arse!" one of the men joked, then chuckled.

"You wish to make a bet on who gets tamed?" Miguel retorted.

"Yep! Fifty cents for every hoss that throws ye."

"Done" was the confident reply. His dark eyes twinkled with anticipation of earning the wager.

Miguel's assistant pulled a wide-eyed horse to the snubbing post. The animal snorted, backed until a taut noose halted him, then jerked his captive head several times to free it. His mane shook, but the lariat held firm. The critter's ears twitched and he moved his hooves in restless panic.

Miguel tried to calm him with a soft and soothing voice. As he did so, he eased forward and slipped a hackamore onto its head. With caution, he put on the blanket and saddle. While the helper talked to the animal, then twisted an ear to hold its attention, Miguel mounted. The instant the horse felt weight upon its back, he began bucking. His front hooves slammed into the hard ground and his back legs kicked up and out, fast and hard. The beast hunched and reared and bawled in outrage and fear.

Dirty and pebbles were flung in all directions. Dust clouds went into the air. Hands yelled and chuckled. Some waved hats above their heads and rocked their bodies on the fence as if helping the rider who pitched and swayed in a frenzied dance. The area was charged with emotion, and with prayers for safety.

Jessie knew what a jarring strain such a wild ride was on a man. It was as hazardous to his teeth, spine, neck, and innards as a crushing fall could be.

Up and down and around went the pair as the roan and vaquero challenged each other's will and stamina. The Mexican used a quirk and spurs to master the animal, but was careful not to injure the creature. Miguel's hair, bandanna, and batwings flapped about—as did the gelding's tail and mane—as the two whirled and bounced to the music of broncbusting which played inside their heads.

In the end, the beast tired and calmed. Miguel rode him around the area for a time. The procedure would be repeated every day until the buster was certain the animal was tamed. Then its special skills would be cultivated.

Later, Gran and Annie joined the redhead to watch the action and join the fun. Jessie saw how the girl gazed at Miguel. She had seen the two talking several times during the past week, and she suspected a romance was in the making. Jessie witnessed how the Mexican glanced their way and how his admiring gaze lingered on Annie.

Concern nipped at Jessie as she noticed an unnatural cockiness enter the Mexican at the girl's presence. The vaquero grinned and mounted his last horse. It only took the panicked chestnut a few leaps and bucks to send the inattentive rider to the ground. Its back legs kicked ominously near the fallen man's head as it tried to buck off the saddle, too, then, failing, raced around the enclosure while venting its fury. Jessie heard Annie's squeal of fear and the thud as Miguel hit the ground.

"That's three fur you and one fur me!" the wagering hand shouted.

Miguel jumped from the dirt, dusted off himself, and glanced at the group in embarrassment. "Double or nothing I do not eat dirt again, *amigo!*" he shouted.

The gambling hand looked at the frantic horse, then back at Miguel. He saw, as did everyone, that the vaquero limped toward his helper, who had captured the gelding's reins and was having trouble controlling the beast. "That high roller'll toss ye agin. Ye got a bet, *amigo*," he chuckled, then spit tobacco.

Jessie saw the determination and pride in Miguel's expression. "You're wasting good money, Slim; he won't be thrown a second time. I know that look." She was right. When the vaquero had the animal calmed and trotting around the enclosure, she said to the women, "Let's get back to our chores." The others weren't finished yet, and she decided against watching more of the action. She didn't want a distracted rider injured while trying to impress the green-eyed beauty. "See you later, boys," she called out and left with Gran and Annie trailing her.

Over dinner preparations, Annie asked questions about the men and broncbusting. Jessie knew why. She talked about her times with the hands and explained the seasonal chores and schedule of ranch life. She guided the conversation to Annie's obvious object of interest.

"You've met Miguel, the rider we were watching earlier. He's one of our best hands, one of my best friends. He's an expert with guns and horses. He's one of the most skilled ropers and cutters I've known."

"What's a cutter?"

"That's when horse and rider work as one to separate certain steers from the herd. Both must have a natural instinct for that task. I'm sure you realize he's Mexican. He's been with us since he was twenty."

"How old is he now?"

"Twenty-seven."

"Does he . . ."

"What?" Jessie coaxed.

"Does he have a sweetheart?"

"Not that I know about. He is a man to catch women's eyes. You caught his today; that's why he took that spill, showing off for you."

The girl blushed and said, "I'm sorry. I didn't mean to . . . cause an accident. I won't go near the corral again."

Jessie laughed and replied, "No need to stay away, Anie, not if you let him know you're just as charmed by him as he is by you. If he doesn't have to worry about other hands catching your interest and he doesn't have to impress you, he won't get cocky again. I don't want him hurt or killed."

"Killed? It's that dangerous?"

"If a rider's careless or distracted, he can break his neck in a fall. Miguel's good. He doesn't usually act that way. But I can't blame him. You're a beauty."

"Thank you, Jessie. But I know little about romance and men like him."

"Then Gran and I will have to teach you. Of course we won't if you aren't interested in him or ready to learn."

Annie thought a minute, smiled, and admitted, "I'm both." She frowned and asked, "What if *he* isn't interested or ready?"

Jessie and Gran laughed. "I've known him for years," the redhead told her. "He's both, too. Trust me; I'm sure."

*   *   *

By dusk Saturday, the broken cavvy was ready to tackle the tasks ahead of it. The peelers were paid and thanked for a job well done. The three Cordell hands were given bonuses for their additional labors, skills, and dangers. The extra drovers and trail boss were due to arrive tomorrow to begin Monday's roundup.

*

Jessie and Matt took a stroll after dinner. Holding hands and chatting, they paused near the corral to observe the sun's last appearance of the day.

Matt watched the fading rays on his wife's hair. Its golden soul shone through the dark-auburn strands. Her skin glowed in the enhancing light. She seemed tranquil to him tonight. He knew her serene mood came from a successful week, having Annie's help in the house, and the disappearance of her morning sickness a few days ago. "You're beautiful, Jessie," he murmured. "I'm gonna miss you."

Her calm blue gaze met his adoring brown one. She smiled and said, "I'll miss you, too, my comfy old shoe."

They shared laughter at her rhyming reply.

He stroked her hair and cheek. "It's working for us, isn't it, Jessie?"

She nestled against him. "Yes, Matt; it is."

His arms crossed her back and he rested his chin against her sweet-smelling hair. "I'm happier than I ever dreamed I could be, thanks to you, woman."

"Me, too. Everything is going so well for us. We make good partners, Matt."

"Then you aren't sorry I talked you into staying and marrying me?"

"No, I made a good bargain." When his head lifted and he stiffened, she knew she had used the wrong word. She was denied a chance to correct herself.

His voice was strained as he said, "We both got a good deal."

Jessie tried to rectify the mistake, but her meaning went astray. "After the baby's born, it'll be a better one for you."

He sounded sad and serious as he argued, "You don't owe me more than you've given so far, Jessie."

"But you want and need more, don't you, Matt?" she challenged.

He remained quiet for a while, and both knew he was deciding how to respond.

His mood worried her. She tried again to better it. "I know how hard this has been on you, Matt. You're the most unselfish and caring person I've ever met."

"That's more true of you than me, Jessie."

"No, it isn't." She leaned away to look into his eyes. "I've been selfish and unfair just to protect myself, the baby, and the ranch. I've taken advantage of your love and kindness. You've done so much for me, Matt, and I'm truly grateful. How could I help but love you and respect you? And want you? Don't look surprised and doubtful. It's true, Matt. I've always had deep feelings for you, and they've grown since . . . in the last few months. They're getting stronger and clearer. I just need more time to get over the past. After the baby's born, I'll be a real wife to you. I promise."

Matt released her and stepped to the corral. He leaned against it, his back to her. "Don't rush yourself, Jessie. The hurt goes away; I know from experience, but not this fast or this easy. Let it work itself out. I'll be here when the right time comes. When it does, you'll know." He turned to face her. "I don't want Navarro's place, Jessie; I want my own spread in your heart and life. Until you can surrender that terrain for the right reason, let's leave our life as is."

Chapter

20

The drovers and trail boss—Jake Bass—gathered on the ranch Sunday evening. Jake was tough and wise, with quick reflexes and keen instincts. The hands respected and obeyed him without question or hesitation. He kept the men relaxed, but still working hard. He was an expert horseman and gunman. He knew the territory they traveled with the herd: where to find the best grass, ample water, how to avoid the worst perils. He knew cattle, their quirks and needs. Experienced and in great demand, they were lucky to hire him again this year. At one hundred twenty-five dollars a month, he was well worth his high pay.

Matt met with the men and gave the orders. Returning men and Cordell hands separated into groups to talk over old times, tell tall tales, play jokes, and relate their experiences since they'd last worked together. New men joined in to laugh and learn. They would be on the trail for six to eight weeks, so it was important to build good rapport and trust. Matt spent most of the evening with them, enjoying old acquaintances and making new friends.

Jessie watched them for a time from the front porch. She saw Annie and Miguel taking a stroll, and smiled in pleasure. It was obvious to everyone that the couple was smitten with each other. She liked the girl and trusted her. She was in favor of a match between the two, but it was happening awfully fast.

Fast? her mind taunted as she went to her room for privacy. Instant love and attraction were things she knew too well. The moment she had gazed into Navarro's eyes, she had been lost to him. Each hour in his company had entrapped her more, until she hadn't wanted to escape. In all honesty, she had tried to forget Navarro. She had tried to make the hurt and anger go away. Each time he returned to her mind, she had closed the door. Yet cracks around the jamb had allowed parts of him to slip past her barrier. Her mind told her it was wrong and unfair to pine over him and the life they could have shared, but her heart couldn't help but do so at weak moments.

She wanted and needed to get over her lost dream, to embrace her reality, but it was so hard, more than she had realized. Sometimes his memory was so vivid that it seemed as if he would return from a day on the range at any moment, just as on some days she briefly forgot her father was gone forever. Yet Jed's loss was more real than Navarro's was, and she didn't know why. Perhaps because she knew Navarro was still alive somewhere and could reappear before her. She was forced to admit she still loved and desired Navarro Breed, and she still yearned and watched for his return.

Jessie knew that was foolish, and cruel to her husband. It would soon be three months since Navarro had gone. She resented him for not sending word, not letting her know he was safe, that he was suffering as she was—that he still loved her and hadn't changed his mind about returning. She needed a last message from him before she could truly break with the past. The silence was eating at her nerves.

Matt sensed that turmoil, she decided, even though she herself hadn't been aware of it. She had been so caught up in other matters and emotions that she hadn't realized how hard she was struggling to keep Navarro out of her mind; when, all the while, he was lurking in her heart and waiting to spring on her.

That wasn't her fault, she vowed. She wasn't to blame for loving the desperado. Love wasn't something that came and went on schedule like the seasons. It wasn't an emotion that could be controlled. She wasn't guilty of not trying to make a new life and not trying to turn to a new love. But,m did innocence and determination matter? She didn't know, but she wanted it to.

Matt was a good man. He deserved more than half of her, more than a marriage in name only. But Matt was right: she couldn't rush the healing process or make him a substitute for Navarro. Her husband had to win her heart before she could yield her body to him. But was he right about keeping her at a distance?

At times she was tempted to surrender to her husband. She truly desired Matt, and she yearned to free the passions that Navarro had once unleashed. Mathew Cordell stirred them to life some nights with his touch, kisses, and tenderness. He often made her head spin, and her body tremble, but he never tried to make love to her. He seemed content as things were. Perhaps, she worried, he didn't desire her as Navarro had.

She had accused herself of being wanton for thinking of Matt that way so soon after Navarro's departure. But was she so wrong? Wicked? Unnatural? How so, when Matt was her husband? When she had known him forever? When, perhaps, she had always loved and desired him and failed to recognize her feelings? Perhaps it was because the two men and situations were so different.

Navarro had been a wild and urgent temptation. She had been helpless to resist his allure. He had ridden into her heart and life when she was vulnerable and felt so trapped by her role as Jed's "son." He had made her feel strong, alive, and free. He had given her adventure, romance, and her womanhood. He had come along at the right time to become her confidant, partner and solace. Maybe, she mused, those were meant to be his only roles in her life.

Perhaps Mathew Cordell was her real destiny. Matt's love was different. It was calm, tender, safe, and nourishing. It was honest and pure. She knew everything about Matt; no shadows surrounded him. She and Matt were compatible in personality and background, but she hoped not too much alike to prevent sparks of excitement and mystery. Yet, after only a short marriage, they were like a longtime couple. Their marriage was comfortable and tranquil. But what about passion, romance, temptation? Amidst the steady coals, there had to be occasional sparks of fiery sensuality to ignite her soul, to make her burn with desire. Yet she had to think of the fugitive as a turbulent and brief adventure, and Matt as a serene and permanent haven.

She felt her flat stomach. It was hard to believe she was pregnant with another man's child. Often, Navarro seemed only a dream to her. Matt was reality. She had a good life and family. It would be stupid to ruin them. If only she knew how she would feel if she ever saw Navarro again. What if he rode up, took her in his arms, and said, "I love you. I'm free. I can stay forever if you still want me,"?

Jessie knew she could never go on the run with the fugitive. But what if Navarro could return to her side? Could she break her vows to Matt and to God and to herself? And break Matt's heart a second time?

Jessie searched her soul and realized the answer was no. Yet, she comprehended that it would take all her strength to turn Navarro down should he return for her. But Mathew Cordell and their life together was worth that painful sacrifice.

Her conversation with Matt last night returned to haunt her troubled mind. She had accepted his words and had agreed with them, at least verbally. In silence, they had returned to the house. They hadn't touched in bed or kissed good night as usual. All day he had been quiet, serious, and reserved, like the old Matt. She knew he was hurting, and her heart ached for things beyond her control.

Jessie closed her teary eyes and prayed for the next six months to pass swiftly and mercifully. Until Navarro's child was born, her body and life were tied to the past. All she could do was wait, hope, and pray she didn't lose her second love while imprisoned by her first bittersweet experience.

*

The men left for roundup the next morning. While Annie was hanging up wash, Jessie and Gran did the dishes and talked. The distressed redhead told her grandmother of her thoughts.

"What am I going to do, Gran? I feel so helpless. I'm trapped between them. I love them both, but in different ways. I can't have Navarro, but I have Matt. Navarro is a landslide, but Matt is stable ground. I want him and need him, Gran, but he won't reach out to me as long as he thinks I'm bound to Navarro."

Martha sympathized and comforted her troubled granddaughter. "Matt's right, Jessie," she said, "Time is all you need."

"It can work against us as much as for us, Gran. So much happened with Navarro; so many unfamiliar emotions were involved. I was lost in a sandstorm before I knew what was happening to me. I was too susceptible to Navarro's spell, too inexperienced and naive. I was just one of the boys, Jed's 'son' and heir. I'd never had such feelings before. Now, every time I dam them up, something happens to let them break free again. I've honestly tried to forget him, and I usually do a good job at it. But Matt can't forget our past together. It's so hard for him to accept the fact Navarro had me as he hasn't yet."

"He loves you, Jessie. He wants to be the only man in your heart and life."

"It's too late for that, Gran. I wish I could change what happened, but I can't."

"Then you and Matt must learn to accept it."

"I hope we can. I do love him and want him, Gran, but I'm not sure he believes me. I'm so afraid I'll lose him before he realizes the truth. You know how stubborn and destructive pride can be."

"He needs time, love, and patience, too, child."

"Time!" Jessie exploded. "That damned word sounds as dangerous and frightening as our old enemy Fletcher was!"

"Don't work yourself up, Jessie. It isn't good for the baby."

"Good for the baby? Everything I've done lately has been for the baby. Navarro's child is ruining my life with Matt. I wish it were his, Gran; I really do."

"Don't blame an innocent child, Jessie," she scolded in a soft tone.

"I'm sorry, Gran. You're right, as always. I do love it and want it. It's mine. But sometimes it seems so unreal," she said, glancing at her slim waist.

"That's because the daily sickness is gone and you aren't showing yet. Living with Matt while it grows inside you will make it feel like his."

"To me, yes; but to him, no. I'm afraid he'll always see it as Navarro's. Maybe it was a mistake to let us believe it will be ours."

"No, Jessie, it wasn't a mistake. You'll see."

"Will I, Gran? How can Matt bear to watch me bloom from another man's seed? He'll come to hate me. I would rather Navarro feel that way than my Matt. What am I going to do, Gran? How can I hold Matt's love and respect until I become his wife? Losing him would be far worse than losing Navarro." She began to cry.

In a few minutes, Matt called out from the parlor, "Jessie! I'm back! I forgot something! Where are you?"

Jessie panicked. She couldn't let him see her like this. She wiped her eyes on her apron and yelled, "In here, Matt!"

He came to the kitchen, glanced at her, Gran, then back to Jessie again. He came forward and asked, "What's wrong?"

"Something in her eye," Gran said, which wasn't totally untrue: there had been tears.

Matt tilted her head upward and gazed into her eyes. He read anguish and panic in them. "It's gone now. You must have washed it out. I came back for my duster. It gets cool some nights on the range. We'll be back in a few days. If you need anything, send one of the hands. We'll be in the south pasture."

"I'll be fine, Matt. Don't worry about me."

"That's a husband's job. Walk me upstairs?" he asked.

"Of course." With his arm around her waist, Jessie accompanied him.

Jessie leaned against the wall near the bedroom door as Matt fetched his duster from the closet. As he walked toward her, their gazes locked. Matt dropped the boot-length garment of water-resistant canvas to the floor. He stepped in front of her and propped one hand against the wall over her head. The other hand lifted a henna curl and toyed with it. Jessie was baffled and mesmerized.

"I also forgot to tell you I love you," he murmured just before his mouth covered hers. His hand released the curl and shifted behind her head to hold her close.

Matt's kiss was deep and passionate. His other hand left the wall and both cupped her face as his mouth continued to pleasure and stimulate hers.

Jessie was astonished, taken off guard. Going almost limp, she leaned against the wall for support. Matt pressed closer, his full length snug against hers, and his mouth worked hungrier at its tasty feast. Jessie felt dizzy, weak, and breathless. A hot flash spread over her quivering body. She was lost in a golden swirl of emotions. Her hands slipped up his back. She clung to him and returned her husband's tantalizing kiss with an ardor that surprised both of them. A soft moan escaped her throat as Matt spread a fiery trail over it. She trembled with longing for more, much more. She wanted him to carry her to the bed and finish what he had started—a sensual journey to discovery.

Instead, Matt's hands drew her head to his chest and held it there. He kissed her hair, then took several deep breaths. Jessie felt the tension and craving in him. She heard his heavy breathing and thudding heart. She felt the strength of his hard body.

"I love you, Jessie, now and always. Nothing will ever change that. Take care of yourself and our baby. I'll see you in a few days." He scooped up his duster and left in a hurry.

Jessie sank against the wall—enflamed, confused, and shaky. Matt had never kissed her or behaved like this before; and she wondered what it would be like to make unrestrained love to him. Wild, fiery sensations begged her to explore that astonishing mystery. So much, she concluded, for thinking Matt's passions were calm and cozy!

Jessie raced after him. He had secured his duster to his saddle and mounted. She rushed to his horse and looked up at him, flustered and dazed. She just kept staring at him, as if seeing him fully for the first time.

Matt looked down at his wife's rosy cheeks. Her gaze held a mixture of bafflement and desire. "Did I forget something else?" he asked.

His voice returned hers. "You're quite a surprise, Mathew Cordell."

A broad grin revealed his white teeth and played mischievously in his dark eyes. "I figured it was past time I stopped being just a dependable, nice friend and started showing you how I really feel about you, woman. You asked me if I wanted and needed more from you, and I didn't answer. Well, I do, Jessie. I'm not a martyr. My head was clear when I staked my claim on you. I was the one who took advantage during a hard time, not you. But I realized you were believing you owed me something. I must be loco, because I haven't been doing anything to help you get over Navarro and turn to me. If I stand back, it'll take longer to heal and will hurt more. *I'm* the medicine you need, Jessie, not time. From now on, woman, I'm gonna work on proving I can be anything and everything you need in a man, in a husband. Between today and next spring, I'm gonna chase you, romance you, and tempt you until you can't resist me. That's a warning and a promise, Mrs. Cordell."

After the initial shock of his stirring words, Jessie was smiling so much her eyes sparkled. "I'll hold you to both, Mr. Cordell. I love you."

Matt leaned over and Jessie lifted herself on her tiptoes so they could kiss. When they parted, Matt said, "I love you, Jessie."

"Good-bye, Matt. Be careful. You owe me a lot."

"Don't worry; I always pay my debts, and collect what's due me." Matt rode off with love, pride, and hope in his heart. He was glad he had overheard Jessie's enlightening talk with Gran. It warned him that he certainly couldn't win his wife by leaving her alone. He had to show Jessie he was more of a man than she realized. He couldn't do that by behaving like her brother. After that accidental eavesdropping and the passionate scene upstairs, he knew she loved him and wanted him. Whatever it took, he would defeat Navarro's ghost!

*

Matt returned Thursday afternoon. Jessie heard his voice and hurried to greet him. She eyed three days' stubble on his face, grinned, and fingered it. "I let you out of my sight and care for a while and look what happens," she teased.

"You know how we boys are on the trail. I only stopped by to tell you we're on the way to the north pasture. We'll cull the steers there, move the others to the west section, and get ready to pull out next Wednesday."

She toyed with the buttons on his shirt. "I miss you already."

"Good."

"Can't you stay home tonight?"

"Nope, not a good idea. You're too tempting, and my clever plan's working."

"Good . . . I think." They both laughed, and Jessie remarked, "We need to increase our vocabulary, Mr. Cordell; we're overworking *good.*"

"But it's such a . . . good word," Matt chuckled and changed the subject. "Best I can tell, we have between eight and eleven thousand head ready for market. If the price is good"—they both grinned—"we'll have a nice deal."

"I hope so. A weak market could hurt us this year. Our cash will be low soon. If we do, Matt, I want to pay off Mary Louise for the ranch. I don't want to risk problems with her later. You know how she can be. Is that all right with you?"

"It's your cattle and money, Jessie. The decision is yours."

"It's all *ours*, Matt. Tell me what you think. I trust your opinion."

"It's a smart idea. Sorry, Jessie, but I don't trust your sister, either. The sooner our deed is clear, the better. I best ride before the boys get too far ahead."

"You'll be leaving for over two months soon. Will I see you again before you go?"

"Yep. I'll visit before we head out."

"Visit?"

"The less time I spend with you right now, the more you'll miss me, woman."

"Part of that clever plan of yours to drive me loco?"

"Not loco, just into my arms."

"You already have that much."

"Yep, but like I said, I want you craving me something fierce."

"More than I already do?" she challenged.

"Yep, a whole lot more."

"That's cruel, Mathew Cordell."

"Nope, just smart."

"I like you this way," she murmured. "Possessive, masterful, and cocky."

"I've only gained a little confidence about you, Jessie."

"Good. It's about time." They laughed again.

"Yep, it is. See you soon." He brushed her lips with his and mounted.

"See you soon, my love," she murmured, watching his departure.

*

Matt rode in Monday afternoon with Miguel. Jessie excused Annie from her chores so she could visit with the vaquero before he left for the months-long mission. She also wanted privacy with her husband, which Gran and Tom respected.

"By the time you get back, you'll have a beard and long hair, Matt. All you men'l look like drifters before you get home and cleaned up. I wish I could go with you."

"Me, too, but it's too hard and dangerous this time. You need anything?"

She stroked his coarse jawline. "Besides you, my stingy husband?"

He backed away with hands raised and jested, "Behave yourself, Jessica Cordell. We have to get back. We're heading off at dawn Wednesday."

"Why can't you stay home tonight?" she urged.

He waxed serious. "You know why."

"That's no longer a reason, Matt. You can't make it back to camp by dark."

Matt was afraid of hurting Jessie and not giving her pleasure in her condition. He didn't know much about such things. When they came together the first time, he wanted it to be special, passionate, and fulfilling. He wanted only the two of them in bed, not anything of Navarro's sharing it. He dared not tempt them tonight, because he wanted her too badly and she was willing to surrender. "Not yet, Jessie. We need to get closer first. We'll work on it when I return."

By the time he returned, Jessie knew she would be showing. It would then become impossible to forget she was pregnant with Navarro's child. She feared how Matt would react. She wanted him to have her now. She wanted him to know she belonged to *him*. She also felt it would make the baby seem more like his. How could it if they'd never made love? How could he want her so much and hold off taking her?

Matt interrupted her obvious worrying. "We'll ride most of the night. We can catch a nap in camp tomorrow while the boys finish up. Don't work too hard or take any risks while I'm gone," he said as he took her hand and walked to the door. He had to leave before she became even more tempting.

Jessie knew she couldn't stall him. "Be careful, Matt. You know there are all kinds of dangers on the trail: Indians, rustlers, stampedes . . ."

"I'll be home by Thanksgiving." He looked Jessie over and smiled. "The chuckwagons pulled out this morning. They'll load up and join us at Fort Stockton."

"Don't you go visiting those naughty saloons in Dodge, Mr. Cordell. You're a married man now. You need a ring to show my claim on you, like yours on me."

"This lasso around my heart is strong and tight enough to hold me true."

Jessie shook her finger at him and jested, "You try loosening it any to play around and I'll treat you like a male calf at spring branding."

"Ouch!" he yelped and grimaced playfully. "I best shout for Miguel and hightail it before you try something foolish, woman."

"That was sweet of you to bring him along. I think he and Annie have picked up that love chigger you mentioned to Tom."

"I think you're right. I'm glad."

"Me, too. Everybody should be in love."

"Yep." Matt kissed her, took a last look, and left. He and Miguel rode off with Jessie and Annie watching their retreat until they were out of sight.

"Well, Annie," Jessie said with a sigh, "it'll be a long and lonely wait for them."

*

A week later, Jessie was answering Annie's questions about the long drive to Dodge City. "There's about ten thousand steers, two hundred horses, two chuckwagons and cooks, and over sixty men. They spread out for miles across the terrain, Annie; you can't let them bump horns and hooves. It's an awesome sight. But it's loud, dusty, and tiring. At times, the journey seems endless. It's eighteen-hour days and short, chilly night. By the time you make camp, you swallow your grub and hot coffee, then fall onto your bedroll, to start it all again in a few hours. They won't be back for two and a half to three months."

"It takes that long?" Annie murmured.

"I'm afraid so. They have to cross dangerous rivers and harsh country. In the Oklahoma Territory, you have to pay Indians to keep them from scaring off stock just so they can charge you to round them up again. White men try to pull that same trick sometimes. Storms or thirst can spark a herd into stampedes along the way. If you don't stop them fast, the steers can be injured, lose valuable weight, or get killed. A few times, we had trouble with irate farmers and other ranchers not wanting us to cross their land. If you're used to stopping for water and grazing there and have to circle a wide path, it can be bad. Of course, I can't blame them; several large herds during a season can do a lot of eating and trampling. And you always have rustlers trying to pick off a thousand or two. It's exciting, Annie, but exhausting and hazardous." Jessie took a deep breath. "Mercy, it's a slow pace. You almost get rocked to sleep in the saddle, unless you're one of the drag riders responsible for strays and sluggards. Then you eat dust and stay busy."

"You've been with them?"

Jessie grinned. "Many times. Papa was teaching me what I needed to know to take over for him one day."

"But you're such a . . . I was going to say 'delicate woman,' but you aren't."

"I was raised as Jed's son, as one of the boys. Papa and the hands always forgot I was a girl. Sometimes they said and did things they shouldn't because they were so used to having me around," Jessie laughed.

"How could they forget? You're so beautiful and feminine."

"In boy's clothes, a pigtail, and dirty face, I looked the role I had to play."

"*Had* to play?"

Jessie exhaled loudly in the ensuing silence. "I was Papa's heir. I grew up on our ranch doing anything and everything the hands do. Until this year, I almost forgot I was a woman. I opened everyone's eye when I started wearing girl's clothes, leaving my hair down, and acting like a lady."

"Because of Matt—and love?" Annie hinted with a smile.

"Yes, because of love. It's surprising how first love affects a female."

"I'm learning that more and more every day. When you've been independent like me and you, it's scary seeing how much you can lean on another person, how much you want them to share everything with you."

Jessie nodded and agreed. She left the painful area of first love by saying, "We'll be safe while the men are gone. Matt left plenty of hands for chores and protection. And we won't have wasted milk; they took two cows with them. But we'd better get busy with the hands' supper before they're moody with hunger."

*

The following Tuesday, Jessie dropped a bottle of cologne. It struck the shelf in her private water closet and shattered. Fragrant liquid and glass shot in all directions. "Tarnation," she muttered.

With caution, she gathered the broken pieces. She poured water from a pitcher into a basin and set it on the floor. She wiped up the cologne, then removed the items in the cabinet and placed them atop it. With a bathing cloth, she worked to clean up the mess. As she leaned inside to reach the back and corners, she noticed a packet tucked beneath a support board.

Jessie tossed the cloth into the basin. She worked the packet free from its snug and secret hiding place and leaned against the wall and opened it. She withdrew a map, several papers, and a few letters. Unfolding the map first, she gazed at it.

Jessie's eyes widened in confusion, then narrowed in understanding and anger. The map revealed a proposed rail line right through the Lane ranch, past Fort Leaton, and into Mexico. There was a spur to Fort Davis that traveled onward to Fort Quitman and El Paso, and a spur into the Chinati Mountains that were southwest of them. She saw an X marked in the last area. She read the papers. One related the profitability of shipping cattle and supplies to the posts and across the border, and of transporting Mexican precious metals and goods into America. The other exposed that rich silver mines in the Chinati region were owned by the Fletchers! Now she knew why Wilbur Fletcher had craved the Box L Ranch. His motive had been greed, as his railroad and mine could earn him enormous wealth and power. The Lane property was the best route because of easy terrain and ample water and wood for the engines, and proposed stops were marked on the map.

Jessie studied the map and papers. No company names were listed so she assumed it was a private venture by the Fletchers. That was a relief, else any partners might try to finish what Wilbur had failed to accomplish. Worry nipped at her as she realized Fletcher could have accomplices somewhere, waiting until the Lanes were lulled into complacency before starting new attacks. With Matt and most of the hands away for months, she prayed that wasn't true.

Jessie opened the letters to read them, seeking clues as to any future threat. They were from his brothers back East. Dread filled the redhead as she realized they had been in on the plot.

Mary Louise was there now. Jessie had written her late last month to tell her about her marriage to Mathew Cordell, the fire, and their move here. She had mentioned they were in the midst of broncbusting, and that the men were leaving soon for roundup and market. The blonde must have received it about the time Matt left for Dodge. Had her sister shared that news with Fletcher's wicked brothers? If Mary Louise had responded immediately, a letter could arrive with the twice-monthly mail this Saturday.

Jessie wondered how the Fletcher men had taken the news of their brother's marriage, his death, then his widow's arrival to claim her husband's possessions from them. Jessie owned this entire area now, so what destructive action could they take against her? With this evidence in her grasp, they had better not try anything! Yet she had little help and protection available with the others gone, and Mary Louise might have told them she'd be vulnerable now. It would be wise to warn the remaining hands to stay alert, and she would do so today. If nothing more, the villains might want to make certain any evidence against them was destroyed.

Jessie asked herself if she should write Mary Louise again and warn her sister about the Fletchers. No, she decided, as the men might get their hands on the revealing letter and harm Mary Louise. It was best to keep this evidence a secret in case she needed it to stop the Fletchers. She needed to find a good hiding place for it. She also needed to alert Sheriff Toby Cooper of possible danger and a need of assistance. She would send one of the men in the morning. She must do all in her power to prevent another siege.

"I wish you were here, Navarro. I'm scared, and I might need your help again," she murmured to herself.

The moment she spoke these words, Jessie grimaced. She prayed he wouldn't return. She couldn't work with him again; it was too dangerous for him and for them, particularly with her husband away for so long.

*

Jessie met with their new foreman Rusty Jones when he returned from the range. She showed him the papers, map, and letters. "This could be big trouble, Rusty. I want you to take this evidence to the line shack and conceal it under the floor. Then I want you to ride into Davis and explain matters to Sheriff Cooper. Bring him to the old house. I'll meet him there and go over the situation. I don't want Gran, Tom, and Annie to know about this. I don't want them to worry. I trust you, Rusty, so I need you to handle it personally. Put the men on alert, but tell them to keep quiet. At least Matt took all of Fletcher's old hands with him, so we don't have to worry about traitors if his brothers should arrive. I want this information safe. After that trick Fletcher pulled with the bankers, I don't dare risk letting them lock them up for me. Hopefully I'll get a letter from Mary Louise this week."

Jessie told Rusty about the letter she'd sent to her sister. "By now they all know what's happened here. Hopefully they won't take over where Fletcher failed."

"If they do, Jessie, we'll be waiting for 'em. I got a notion they won't try anything soon. They won't know how many men Matt left behind to guard the place. Let's take every precaution we can. We don't want 'em trying to force this proof out of your hands. You women best stay close to the house. Be ready to lock 'er up and have guns nearby. I'll keep one of the men around all day and I'll leave at first light. After I hide this packet on the way, I'll ride into town. Me and Toby should be back Thursday afternoon afore three."

"I'll be waiting over there for you. Be careful, Rusty."

* * *

Jessie was apprehensive for two nights and the next day. She managed to conceal the reason for her strange mood by pretending it was loneliness and worry over Matt. While Gran was napping Thursday after their midday meal, Jessie saddled Ben and rode several hours to the burned-out site of her old home. She had told Annie she was going for a leisurely ride and would return later. She had also sent Tom out with one of the men to keep him in the dark about her actions.

Jessie dismounted, dropped Ben's reins to the ground, and strolled around the blackened ruins. She hadn't been there since the devastating fire almost six weeks ago. Her heart ached at seeing the tormenting reminder of her home.

Her parents had died here, as had two brothers and her grandfather. She had loved and lost Navarro here. She had battled Fletcher here. She had discovered her pregnancy here. She had watched her sister walk out the door.

But there had been happy and special times, too. She had to forget the painful memories and only remember the good ones. She was making a new life in a new place. As with the house and loved ones, the past was dead.

Ben's whinny and movement alerted Jessie to riders approaching. She shielded her eyes from the sun to check their identity. She was holding a rifle, her piebald was alert and protective, and she was a skilled horseman, so she hadn't been afraid to come here alone.

She waved to Rusty and Toby as they joined her. "Good to see you back safe."

Toby Cooper removed his hat and said, "Rusty explained everything, Mrs. Cordell. We'll stay on watch until Matt and the boys return. Then, you should turn that evidence over to the law and let them handle the matter. I always say, head off trouble before it strikes if you can. Once they're unmasked, they won't be a threat to you again. Unless you want to go ahead with it now."

Jessie wanted to wait for her husband's return. She wanted to let Matt take care of the problem. That would increase his pride and confidence. She wanted to use the situation to show she needed him. She was strong, smart, and brave. She could handle the matter, but she wanted Matt to believe she leaned on him for protection and strength and courage. With the sheriff involved, there shouldn't be any danger for a while.

"I'll let my husband settle it, Sheriff, unless there's trouble before his return. I simply wanted you informed in case Fletcher's brothers arrive to cause problems. The Fletchers are rich and powerful. It would be dangerous to challenge them while Matt and the boys are away. We can't even prove they were involved with the fight here; we can only prove they knew what Fletcher was doing to us and why. I'm not sure that makes for a strong case against them. They have plenty of money for smart lawyers and for bribes. I wouldn't want to challenge them alone. It's best to keep quiet for now."

"I agree," Toby said. "If you see anything suspicious, send word. I'll keep my eyes open for strangers in town. I can bring soldiers if you need help."

"Thank you, Sheriff Cooper."

Rusty and Jessie watched the lawman mount and head back toward town.

"I hope we can trust him, Rusty. You know what a rail line could do for Davis and the fort. I only hope none of the men there were involved with Fletcher's plot to bring it in. Big contracts offer big money to businessmen and posts. I didn't want to tell him that I didn't know whom we can trust. I just keep remembering how sluggish he and the Army were about exposing Fletcher."

"Toby's a good man, Jessie. So is Captain Graham. I wouldn't worry about them betraying you and siding with that snake's brothers."

"I'm sure you're right, but I don't want to take any chances. When Matt and the hands get back, we'll have plenty of guns and men. He'll know what to do."

*

Jessie received another shock on Saturday in the mail. There were two letters. One was from Wilbur's brothers. She went to her room, closed the door, and ripped open the envelope. Her eyes widened as she read it. She tore open Mary Louise's, and had the same stunned reaction.

Jessie realized she had to share this news with her grandmother. She called down the steps for the woman to join her for privacy. She and Martha sat on the small couch in the bedroom sitting area. Jessie related how she had found the packet of evidence, what she had done about it, and the gist of today's letters.

"Can they take the house and ranch back?" Before Jessie could respond, Martha asked, "Where will we go till Matt returns? We'll have to separate everything that's been mixed, and put up that boundary fence again."

"Don't be worried, Gran. It's just a bluff. Mary Louise claims her husband's will left everything to his brothers and she had no legal right to sell it to us. She warns us to leave pronto. The Fletchers have threatened to recover this ranch in court if we refuse to get out and turn it over to them. They say they don't want to sell, and we know why, thanks to Wilbur's carelessness. They don't care about this spread; they just want to recover their foothold here. Naturally they offered to buy the Box L again. They're awaiting my answer before starting legal action against us. They're in for a fat surprise."

"What are we going to do, Jessie?" Martha asked in alarm.

Irate, the flushed redhead declared, "Give them an answer, but not one they expect! Will or no will, this land is ours. I don't care if a wife can't inherit without one. That's a stupid law! It isn't right that a man's family can walk in and take over after the husband dies! We aren't in the dark ages any more. Women work as hard on spreads as men do, sometimes harder. If anything happens, she should get the land and home, not his kin. Matt insisted our deed remain in my name, and I see why. He wanted me protected from such injustice. I'll bet my best boots Mary Louise is in the saddle with them!"

"How could she do this to us, Jessie?"

"Because she's just as wicked and greedy as they are! She claims she invested the money I paid her and lost it, so she can't return it. That's a lie! She says she's living off their charity and support, so she has to take their side. More lies, Gran. The deceitful witch even apologized for her *mistake!* She said she didn't get any of Wilbur's holdings and money back there. That could be true or his brothers' trick, but it's the only part of her letter I'm inclined to believe."

"Didn't she tell them about the sale when she got there? Why did they wait so long to threaten us?"

"I'm sure she did. They waited until Matt and the boys were gone. They think I'll panic and run. When they learned we'd moved here, they must have panicked. This means her last letter was nothing but more lies. I should have suspected something was up when she didn't send a boastful one every week!"

"What if we can't fight that will, Jessie? What if the law sides with them?"

"They can't battle us from prison, Gran. I have that evidence, so I'm going to call their bluff. I'll send word we have proof against them and they had better not threaten me or challenge me again! I'll even blackmail them if I have to. We don't know if they're telling the truth about wills and inheritances. I'll let them know I've already seen the Sheriff, and I'll fight them in court. I'll claim I have all of their old letters to Wilbur and have his incriminating journal. That should scare them. I'll threaten them with a scandal and imprisonment."

Martha's blue eyes widened. Her face paled. "That's too dangerous, child. They might come after you. Wait until Matt returns."

Jessie frowned in dismay. "I was going to, Gran, but that's months away. I have to act fast. I don't want them coming here and starting another battle while we're low on men. I have to protect you and Tom and the ranch, not to mention the baby. If I notify the governor, Army, the Rangers, the U.S. marshal, and a lawyer and tell them I've done so, that should at least frighten them into holding off for a while. Hopefully for good."

"Send a letter or telegram to Matt. He'll get it when he reaches Dodge."

"No, Gran; that'll only worry him. Being so far away and hearing we've been in danger for months will frighten him. And there's nothing he can do from there. He'll blame himself for us being in danger. It'll be two months before he's home, and the Fletchers are almost knocking at our door."

"You think we should move into town until he's back?"

"No, Gran; nobody is going to force me off my land or out of my home. If we run scared, they'll smell it and pursue us. We take a stand and don't budge."

Martha clasped the redhead's hands in hers and confessed, "I'm afraid for you and the baby, child, and for Tom. I'm an old woman. I've lived a long and good life. My safety doesn't matter. What if they hurt you? These are violent and desperate men, Jessie."

"I know, Gran. But we took a stand against Wilbur and won, and we'll do the same with his brothers. Lane blood and spirit run in my body; I'm no quitter or coward. After they're exposed, we'll be safe. Don't worry."

*

Jessie met with the foreman and hands. She explained the new predicament. She handed Rusty the letters to the authorities she had mentioned to her grandmother, a terse letter to her treacherous sister, and a bold one to the Fletchers. "These will put our daring plan into motion, Rusty. I pray they work. You men stay on full alert, but don't take any chances."

Jessie returned to the house and related the trouble to Tom and Annie. "I think we'll be safe, but keep your eyes and ears open. Annie, if you want to go into town for a while, I'll pay your expenses there until it's safe to return. You weren't part of this trouble and I can't ask you to risk your life for us."

"I'm staying here, Jessie. All of you are more of a family to me than my parents ever were. If those buzzards come, we'll show them how women clip wings."

"I think you should stay in the house with us. We'll put up a cot in the extra room upstairs. I don't want you out there alone."

*

Over two weeks passed without trouble. Jessie, Gran, and Annie occupied themselves making clothes for the baby and working on Jessie's garments, as she had told the girl about her pregnancy and let Annie think the child was Matt's. She did not give any details about her due date, but she knew Annie would realize how far along she was in a few weeks.

Jessie knew her letters had reached the Fletchers and the authorities by now, and she wondered what was happening.

It was five weeks since Matt left home, and she was anxious for his return. She prayed for his safety on the trail, and she missed him. Some nights she found her hand stroking his side of their bed, and she wished he were lying there in his arms. It was strange, but she thought and dreamed about him more now than Navarro.

Yet a few times she had allowed herself to think and worry about the desperado. She hated to think of him alone, bitter, and in danger. There had been moments when she was tempted to write the Arizona governor to see if she could help exonerate him. Each time she warned herself it was too risky. It could stir up new interest and a search for him. She could be the reason he was captured and hanged. It might bring the authorities to her ranch.

Navarro had told her that day at the windmill she needed a man raised as she was, a rancher. He had pointed out Matt's love for her several times. Had he knowingly pushed for this union? Navarro had said, "Be strong and never look back," so how could he blame her for believing and obeying him? His failure to return or write had proven she had made the right—the only—choice.

*

Tuesday, October seventeenth, a rider approached the house with Rusty. Jessie walked outside to see who it was and what he wanted. Her heart pounded in dread.

Jessica Cordell studied the stranger. It was obvious to her that he was not a horseman from the awkward way he sat the saddle and dismounted. His neat brown suit and white shirt suggested he was a businessman. His looked aggravated and uncomfortable. As he straightened his clothes, dusted himself off, and walked toward her, she read arrogance and purpose in his gaze and stride. The Fletchers' lawyer? she posited.

Rusty accompanied him to Jessie and said, "I found him heading this way, so I rode in with him. Says he's here to fetch Annie."

"That's right. Where is she? I've come a long way and I'm in a hurry."

Jessie took an instant dislike to the impatient and unfriendly man. There was something about him that made her uneasy. "Who are you, sir?"

"I'm Jubal Starns from El Paso. I've come to fetch her home. Call her out."

It was the hotel owner who had given Annie a hard time. "Home, Mr. Starns? annie *is* home; she lives here with us."

"I assume you're Mrs. Cordell?"

"That's right. How can I help you?"

"You can't. I'm here to speak with Annie and take her back to El Paso."

"Annie didn't like El Paso, Mr. Starns; that's why she moved here. I'm sure she has no intention of leaving her new home with us."

"That's not for you to say, Mrs. Cordell. Call her out," he demanded.

"Everyone on this ranch is my responsibility, sir. She doesn't want to see you."

"That's none of your business, woman. I insist you not interfere."

"I'm afraid it *is* my business. I know why Annie left El Paso and your employ. I'm positive she doesn't want to see you or speak with you again, and I agree with her. You should leave. I don't like your manner."

Starns glared at Jessie. "I'll discuss this with your husband."

"He's away on business. However, I am the owner of this ranch, not him, so you'll have to deal with me. Annie isn't leaving here with the likes of you."

He puffed with anger and his eyes narrowed. "You can't keep her prisoner here. I'll fetch the law if necessary. You can't keep me from my fiancée."

"I'm not your fiancée!" Annie shrieked from the doorway and joined them.

The man turned to face her. "You promised to marry me, girl, after my wife died. I buried her two weeks past. You have to keep your word to me. Get your things and let's go. I'll buy a horse for you to use. The folks in town told me I couldn't make this ride in a carriage."

"While your wife was dying, you asked me to marry you, but I didn't accept. I never will. I hate you, Mr. Starns. And you know why."

"Don't be airing our private affairs before strangers, girl," he warned.

"I know all about you, Mr. Starns. Annie told me," Jessie informed him. More anger and now embarrassment colored his expression. "Rusty, show Mr. Starns the way back to town."

"I'm not leaving without her," Jubal announced coldly.

"Yes, you are," Jessie stated.

"If you don't come, Annie, you'll leave me no choice but to put the law on you. I don't want to do that, girl, but I will."

That threat infuriated Jessie. "For what reason?" she asked.

"Annie knows" was his reply as he stared at the wide-eyed girl.

"What is he talking about, Annie? Maybe I can help."

"I borrowed—"

"She ran out on a legal debt," the man interrupted. "It's against the law to flee a creditor. I had a man track her to Davis, then here. As soon as time allowed, I came after her. Since she couldn't repay me, I told her I would forget the loan if she married me. I understood her answer to be yes."

"That's absurd, Mr. Starns!" Jessie declared. "A woman like Annie James doesn't sell herself into marriage. She could have repaid you, if she hadn't quit your employ because you were forcing your unwanted attentions upon her. You also made it impossible for her to get another job in El Paso. She had no choice but to move to another town. You have no legal claim on her."

"I have a contract that says she owes me money. I thought Annie was honest and reliable, so I trusted her. Her father cheated lots of men out of money. Some folks in El Paso still hold a grudge against him. The law wouldn't be lenient with his kin doing the same."

"That wasn't my fault," Annie cried. "When Father died, his creditors took all I had but for my clothes. After what you did to me, I had to move to support myself."

"And flee without telling me? And no word since. Can you pay me off, girl?"

"No, sir, but I'll send you money every month until it's settled."

"The contract says it must be repaid within a year. Your time has lapsed. Cost me more money to track you here. If you don't settle up today, I can have you jailed for escaping your debt. You sneaked off without telling me and making arrangements to honor your liability. That's the same as cheating or stealing. The law is on my side. Think hard, girl. Me or debtor's prison?"

Annie looked terrified of the man and of going to jail. "Please, Mr. Starns, give me more time. I promise to repay you, but I can't marry you."

"A deal is a deal, girl. If I leave without you, I'm going straight to the law."

"How much did you borrow, Annie, and why?" Jessie inquired.

"One hundred dollars. It was to pay off a debt of my father's or go to jail."

"I don't understand. A sixteen-year-old isn't responsible for her parents' debts. Who told you such a lie?"

"Mr. Hobbs. He said he talked to the sheriff and a lawyer. They told him I had to pay the bill or go to jail. I was already working for Mr. Starns, so he agreed to loan me the money. I was to repay him out of my salary. By the time I paid for boarding, meals, and clothes, there was little left. The same was true in Davis. I was going to start sending him money this month to avoid trouble."

"But you went to work for a seamstress after your parents died," Jessie reasoned. "Why did Mr. Hobbs wait so long to approach you?"

"I don't know. He said he was giving me time to heal and work."

"Did you speak to the sheriff and lawyer?"

"No, Jessie; I was afraid to cause trouble."

"I see," the redhead murmured. "Are Mr. Hobbs and Mr. Starns good friends?"

"Yes, they—"

"Hold on a minute! What are you implying, Mrs. Cordell?"

"You know what I'm charging, sir. You had this man frighten and trick Annie into a corner so you could take advantage of her. She can't be held accountable for her father's old debts. She was almost a child."

"I don't know about the law or if Hobbs tricked her, but I made a legal loan."

"Did you, sir? I wonder what the El Paso sheriff, that alleged lawyer, and Mr. Hobbs will say when I contact them. Better still, when the U.S. marshal does."

"How dare you threaten me or insinuate I'm a liar!"

"I think you're despicable, sir. If you press this matter, so will I. However, I am willing to see if Mr. Hobbs lied and Annie's debt to you is real. If it is, I'll gladly send you the money to settle her account. Please give me their names and addresses. I'll have my lawyer check it out and handle it for us."

"You're making a big mistake intruding in my affairs!"

Jessie saw how flustered and outraged he was. "No, sir, you made all the mistakes in this offensive matter. You dared to push yourself onto a helpless girl. Worse, while your wife lay dying! You had a man trick her into an illegal debt. You tried to ruin her life by driving her into poverty anhd desperation. You dared to come here and threaten her. Get off my land. If we ever hear from you again, sir, you'll be the one in court, then in jail."

"Try to do something nice for someone, and this is what happens!"

"You don't have a nice bone in your body, sir."

"If your answer to my proposal is no, Annie, I'll be leaving."

"It is," the girl replied, having gained courage from her boss and friend.

The defeated man slyly eyed Jessie and Rusty, then said to the girl, "I guess I should apologize for being so mean. I love you and want you so much, Annie, that I lost my wits. You're what's important, not the money. If you change your mind, you know where to find me. If you're scared to travel alone, just send for me. You were a good worker, so I'll cancel your debt to me."

"That would be wise," Jessie said, although she didn't trust him.

"Good-bye, Mrs. Cordell. Annie." Jubal Starns went to his mount and struggled onto its back with difficulty. Then he rode away from the watchful group.

"Thank you, Jessie," the tearful girl said, then embraced the redhead.

"You'll never see that vile beast again, so forget him," Jessie advised.

After Annie returned to her chores, Jessie remarked to the foreman, "I thought Sheriff Cooper was going to alert us to strangers in town, especially one who asks for directions to our ranch. I'm surprised that greenhorn made it alone. Of course the sheriff might not have been around to take notice."

"I'm willing to bet Toby never saw Starns in town. He would have come along."

"You're probably right. At least we solved one nasty problem. I'm sure Annie's been afraid something like this might happen. She can relax now."

"That was a low-down man, Jessie. He needs a good lashing with a whip."

"I know. It's a shame there are so many like him around who take advantage of vulnerable females. I'm glad Matt found her and brought her here."

Rusty grinned. "So is Miguel."

"I've noticed. I think they'll be good for each other . . . Any problems on the range?" she asked, leaving the subject of romance behind them.

"None, but the boys are still on alert."

"We should have news by the end of the month. Hopefully we can settle it as quickly and easily as we handled Mr. Jubal Starns."

*

On Monday, October thirtieth, Jessie hurried to meet the mail deliverer, as she had been watching for him all morning. She took the twine-bound letters, thanked him, and returned to the house. She hadn't bothered to put on a wrap, as the days in southwest Texas were still pleasantly warm. She closed the front door and sat in the parlor to learn the news.

Jessie dreaded opening the letters. There were so many of them today. She began with the ones from the authorities she had written for help. She sighed in relief as the Texas Rangers and U.S. marshal offered any assistance needed to avert more trouble with the easterners and revealed that the Fletchers had been notified of such intentions. She smiled as the governor said he would never sign permission for a rail line across her ranch, and particularly if something happened to drive the Cordells off their land. He also related that he had informed the authorities back East of the charges against the Fletchers and that he would press for an investigation of them if Mrs. Mathew Cordell was harmed in any way.

Jessie's smile and satisfaction increased as she read a letter from the lawyer who had handled the sale from Mary Louise Fletcher. He was certain it was legal and would stand up in court. He offered his services to fight the case for her.

Feeling confident, Jessie ripped open the missive from the Fletchers. Her gaze traveled it rapidly, then slowly, to absorb each word. It was apparent the Texans had reached the eastern men with their warnings before this letter was written. It was also obvious that the brothers feared challenging the "alleged evidence" she possessed. They retreated by giving the ranch to Wilbur's widow, to dispose of as she desired. They even apologized for the "shameful trouble" with their "headstrong and misguided" brother! And they swore they were not involved in that attempted landgrab and could prove it. They had assumed Wilbur was obtaining the land needed for the proposed railroad by legal means. To prevent a "scandalous, time-consuming, and costly battle in court," they suggested the matter be dropped.

Jessie whooped with elation and victory. Gran came to see what was wrong. "Nothing, Gran. I'm just excited. We won! They backed down." She read the letters to the older woman, who laughed and cried in joy.

"We beat them this time without a bloody fight. Matt will be so relieved. I can't wait until he gets home, so I can share all this wonderful news with him."

"You've got a long wait, child, at least another month," Gran reminded.

"A busy one, too. My waist and tummy are changing. I'd better work faster on my clothes. I'll be five months on Wednesday and I'll start getting fat."

"It doesn't happen overnight, child. Your waist will thicken slowly and your tummy will begin to round. You won't be very big when Matt returns."

"I hope not. I want him around as it happens; then, it won't be such a shocking change. I should write Mary Louise about the baby, but I hate— I forgot; we haven't read her letter yet. Let's see what little sister has to say about all this trouble. I dread to," she murmured, ripping open the last envelope.

Dear Jessica, You have no idea how much trouble, misery, embarrassment, hard feelings, and money your actions have caused me. The Fletchers have now refused to grant me any support and friendship. They are making my social life and acceptance here impossible. It's all your fault. How could you accuse such fine men of such wickedness? Just because Wilbur made a mitake, that gave you no right or reason to attack them. They will have nothing to do with me now, and are encouraging everyone to ostracize me. I shall have to move to another city to begin a new life for a second time. I will send you my address when I'm settled. I shall expect my yearly payments on schedule or I shall be forced to confiscate the ranch for your debt. If you've read the Fletchers' letter, you know they gave Wilbur's ranch to me. That means, dear sister, you still owe me forty thousand dollars as the balance of our deal. Family or not, it is a legal contract that states I regain possession if you happen to default. Tell Gran and Tom hello.

The letter was signed, Mrs. Mary Louise Fletcher.

"What a little bitch she is," Jessica said in exasperation to her grandmother. "If she ever steps foot here again, I'll take a whip to her buttocks!"

"And I'll hold her for you," Gran replied. "Such an ungrateful and selfish girl. How could she have turned out so badly?"

"That fancy school and those so-called friends filled her head with crazy ideas. I'm glad she's gone. Sometimes I can't believe she's my sister. There isn't any Lane in her. How can she say the Fletchers gave her no widow's support, when they deeded her the ranch. And I paid her forty thousand dollars cash four months ago, and she'll get five more every year for eight years. How much money does that girl need?

"My sister better lasso herself another rich husband before she spends all her money. I won't give her a dollar more than I owe her or another pinch of sympathy. She's trampled our love and loyalty into the ground. She'll never be welcome here again. I'm finished with her. I'll settle my debt with her as soon as Matt returns with the money, all of it. I want the ranch title clear of any threat from her and those devious Fletchers."

"Don't get yourself so worked up over her, Jessie. It isn't good for the baby. Mary Louise made her choice; she deserted and betrayed us. One day she'll be sorry. The Good Lord always punishes such wickedness."

Jessie tried to calm herself. "I used to feel sorry for her, Gran. I tried to believe her problems weren't her fault. But they are. She made herself and us miserable. She wanted to capture a dream that she'll discover in the future is a nightmare. Love and family are the most important things in life. She's turned her back on them for pleasures of the flesh. Heaven only knows what's in store for my little sister."

*

Thursday, against her grandmother's pleas, Jessie rode into Davis with Rusty to get rid of Mary Louise for good . . .

*

In mid-November, the three women and Tom were sitting in the parlor after dinner before a cozy fire. Jessie giggled and caressed her stomach.

"What is it?" Gran asked, looking at her glowing granddaughter.

"The baby—it moved. I thought it was my imagination the last few times. It's like . . . a feather tickling my insides."

"Baby?" Tom echoed, dropping his book and coming to sit beside her.

Jessie smiled at her brother and said, "Yes, Tom; Matt and I are expecting a baby next spring. You'll be an uncle."

"You'll be a mother," he said, amazement shining in his wide gaze.

"That's right." She ruffled his hair and grinned.

"This is exciting!" he shouted. "Annie, my sister's gonna have a baby!"

"I know, Tom. Isn't that wonderful?"

"Am I the last one to learn anything around here?" he asked, feigning anger.

Gran cuffed his chin and said, "It's women's business until it shows, Tom."

"Does it hurt?" he asked, gazing at her stomach.

"Not yet, but I hear birth can give a few pains," she jested.

"Don't be funny. You'll be all right, won't you?"

"Of course. Having babies is woman's work, a natural thing. When he's born, you can play with him. Would you like that, Uncle Tom?"

"Is it a boy?" he questioned, seriousness filling his gaze and voice.

"I don't know. Unborns are usually called *he*, but it might be a girl."

"I bet she'll be as pretty as you and Annie," he remarked.

"It could be a boy. Then he'd be like a little brother to you."

"I'll be fourteen. Big boys don't play with babies."

"Said who, Mr. Thomas Lane?" she teased.

As if enlightened to something wonderful, he replied, "You're right, Jessie. Can I feel him move?"

"Not yet, just me. When he starts kicking hard, I'll let you feel him."

His eyes were full of wonder, then panic. "Will he be all right, Jessie."

"What do you mean?" she inquired.

"Will he be good?"

"Good?"

"Not broken like I am. Or die like my brothers."

Martha gasped Tom's hand and squeezed it. "He'll be a fine baby, Tom."

The boy looked at his silent sister. "I'm sorry, Jess. I didn't mean to scare you. He'll be perfect. Won't he, Annie?"

"I'm sure he will, Tom. Why don't I help you with that arithmetic?" the girl offered.

After the two went to Tom's room, Jessie glanced at her grandmother and asked, "He will be all right, won't he, Gran? God wouldn't punish an innocent child for my wickedness?"

"I'm sure he'll be fine, Jessie. But if he isn't, you won't be to blame."

"Are you certain, Gran? You said God punishes wickedness."

"What you did with Navarro was love, Jessie, not evil. It should come after marriage, but that doesn't make it any less special."

"I did love him, Gran."

"*Did?*" the older woman repeated.

"Do," Jessie admitted. "But it's different now. I still think about him, but most of the pain and bitterness are gone. I just want him to be safe and happy like I am. I accept we can't share a life together. I have Matt now, and I'm happy."

"I'm glad, Jessie. But if you want to keep the baby safe, you should stay home. Riding is hard and dangerous for both of you."

"I had to go into town, Gran. I wanted Mary Louise paid off, so I wouldn't have to worry about her treachery any more. That puts us low on money, but Matt will be home in a few weeks to replace it."

"It was risky, child. What if the market was bad or they get robbed? You should have waited and talked it over with your husband."

"Perhaps, but I'd rather owe the bank than any Fletcher, Gran. If the worst happens, we can get a loan until next season, or sell stock to the Army and miners. I wanted that debt and title cleared."

"You sure you trust that Brazel detective you hired to carry it to her?"

"Yes, Gran. I do. While he's there, he's to check out the Fletcher brothers. I have to make certain they've really backed down. I don't trust men like them. Or that Jubal Starns. I'm having him checked on, too. Before we start a new year, I needed all those problems laid to rest. They will be soon."

*

Jessie heard the commotion of men and horses outside and realized—after over ten weeks—her husband and the hands had returned. Joy was her first reaction and she started to race outdoors to welcome the boys and Matt. Panic halted her. She fretted over how Matt would take her news. Men were considered the heads of homes, the protectors, and the decision-makers. They wanted wives to be dependent upon them, and submissive.

Jessie had known Mathew Cordell for ages, but she wasn't sure of his innermost views on marriage, and a wife's role. What, she asked herself, if he was annoyed and disappointed with her? The forty thousand dollars she had withdrawn and spent was theirs. What if he considered her action impulsive and hasty? What if he had decided not to pay off Mary Louise in a lump sum?

Time passed, and Matt didn't join her. Jessie began to pace the bedroom and wonder what was delaying him. Why hadn't he rushed to her side? She wanted to have their reunion in private. If he didn't come soon, she would go downstairs to greet him.

Jessie went into the water closet and glanced out the window that overlooked the front yard. She saw her husband talking with Rusty Jones. She had asked the new foreman and longtime hand to let her be the one to relate the news to Matt. She wondered if Rusty was obeying. Judging from Matt's face and his rigid stance, he was pretty upset. She saw Matt yank off his hat and run his fingers through tousled, shoulder-length brown hair. He hadn't shaved since the first week of September when roundup began, three months ago. His clothes were dusty and wrinkled. He looked tired and distressed.

When Matt glanced toward the front door, then up at the window, Jessie jerked aside and her heartbeat increased. She admonished herself for her silly reaction. She wasn't actually spying on him. So why did she feel guilty and devious? Why did she wish so hard that she could overhear them? Why did she have this oppressive feeling that something terrible was wrong?

Jessie turned from the window to check her appearance in the mirror. Her freshly washed hair was brushed and hanging free. Her complexion was clear, but her cheeks were a little too rosy. At least the let-out waist and full skirt of her dark-blue dress didn't blatantly show her condition. Yet her bosom was noticeably fuller. She knew the bodice was snug and revealing, as there had been no excess seam to enlarge. This dress would have to be put away soon, if her sensitive breasts grew any more. But it was too late to change clothes.

What are you doing out there, Matt? Hurry, so I can get my confession over with, so we can enjoy your homecoming. The timing is perfect: tomorrow's Thanksgiving. I don't want to spoil your return. What is Rusty telling you?

*　*　*

Matt felt an urgent need to speak with his wife about his visit to the jeweler, and, even more, his strange talk with Rusty Jones echoed through his mind:

"Been any trouble, Rusty?"

"Let Jessie tell you everything. She's anxious to see you, Boss."

"Anything wrong?"

"She'll explain."

"Why don't you tell me, so I won't have to tire Jessie?"

"I promised Jessie she could give the news."

"Any visitors while I've been gone?"

"Not many."

"Who were they? What did they want?"

"Why don't you go on inside, Boss, and let Jessie talk to you? I ain't the one to speak in her place."

Rusty hadn't exposed anything, but Matt had perceived that plenty was afoot. His anxiety mounted when Gran refused to give any clues, and Tom didn't come greet him. Even Annie wasn't in the kitchen, and he suspected she had sneaked out the back door to avoid him. Something was wrong.

Matt trudged upstairs and entered their bedroom. He closed the door and glanced at his wife as she left the water closet. She didn't run into his arms as he'd hoped and dreamed since leaving her side. She, too, looked worried and wary.

"Has Navarro returned, Jessie? Is he here now?"

Stunned at those queries, Jessie stared at him in confusion. "No, why?"

"Are you sure?" he pressed.

"Yes, Matt, I'm positive. Why would you think about him? Or doubt me? I swear I haven't seen him or heard from him since he left over five months ago."

"Did you give him this?" he asked, withdrawing her locket from his vest and dangling it before her pale face.

Jessie's quivering hands took it. She opened the catch, stared inside, then asked, "How did you get it back? Did you see him? Where is my picture?"

It was sold to a jeweler in Dodge, where your father bought his last watch. I went in to buy you a Christmas gift while the papers were being drawn up for the cattle sale. I saw it and realized I hadn't seen you wearing yours since the fire. I figured you'd lost it that night, and it would be nice to have a new one for the baby's picture. The jeweler said he hadn't been able to sell it because it was marked with the last owner's initials: JML. Said he'd make me a good deal on it if we didn't mind. JML, Jessica Marie Lane," Matt ventured. "Right?"

Jessie swallowed hard. She was confused, and frightened for Navarro. She was also hurting for Matt. "Yes, it's mine. And yes, I gave it to Navarro. It was a farewell gift, Matt. I don't understand. Why would he remove the picture and sell it? He must have needed money badly."

"The man who sold it didn't fit Navarro's description. He told the jeweler he won it in a card game in New Mexico in late June. That means Navarro headed that way after leaving here."

"I don't know where he headed or where he is now. I swear it. Maybe the man stole it from him, or maybe it didn't mean anything special to Navarro, or maybe that man took it after he . . ."

"Killed Navarro?" Matt finished for her. "A man like that lives by his guns, Jessie, and usually dies by them."

"Don't say that!" she shrieked.

Matt looked and sounded crushed by her reaction. "I'm sorry this hurts you so deeply, Jessie. I know you still love him and hope he isn't dead. Maybe he isn't. Maybe he's on the way here now, after you."

"Don't say that, either, Matt. It isn't true. Even if it were, it wouldn't change anything between us. I'm your wife; I'll always be your wife. I love you."

"But you loved him first; you love him more," he remarked sadly.

"First, yes; but more, no. You must believe that, Matt. I don't want him killed or hanged, but I wouldn't leave you for him. There had to be a good reason why he gave up the locket. I'm afraid for him, but I'm happy you bought it. Maybe this is fate's way of proving to us that it's over between me and Navarro. Maybe he didn't love me as much as he thought he did. Maybe he's found someone new to love. If he truly cared about me, don't you think he would have at least sent me word that he's safe? I think it's time I told you the whole truth about Navarro Breed, so we can forget about him."

"Breed? I thought his name was Jones."

"No, Matt, it isn't. Navarro Breed is a fugitive from an Arizona prison. He was convicted of a gold robbery. He killed a guard to escape a few months before we met." Jessie related Navarro's life history to her shocked husband. "If he's captured, he'll hang. But he swore he would never let them take him alive. That's why he left and why he can't ever come back. Never, Matt."

Matt paced the room, deep in thought. Everything made sense now. He knew Navarro loved Jessie and had given her up to protect her. The desperado hadn't betrayed and deserted Jessie. Losing and leaving her must have been the hardest thing he'd endured in his grim existence. Matt felt a wave of sympathy for the fugitive. "I'm sorry. I didn't know or understand how hard it had been on both of you."

"Matt, I don't want him to return to me, but I do want him to be safe and happy somewhere far away. He's no threat to you; I promise."

He walked to her and caressed her cheek. "I'm glad you told me the truth, Jessie. I can relax now. I was plenty worried. When Rusty acted so crazy and wouldn't answer my questions, I thought Navarro was back."

"That isn't what I asked Rusty to let me tell you. I'm glad you're home, Matt. So much happened while you were gone. I wanted to wait until you got back so we could handle the situation together, but I couldn't. Please don't be angry with me. I did it all for us. I had to."

"Did what, Jessie?"

She explained about finding Wilbur Fletcher's packet of information in the water closet two weeks after his departure. Matt looked shocked to hear about the railroad line. She told him about her meeting with Sheriff Toby Cooper and about hiding the evidence in the line shack. She explained that she had planned to wait for him before taking action against the villains, but the letters from the Fletcher brothers and Mary Louise had forced her hand. She told him what she'd written to the authorities, Fletcher's brothers, and her sister, and about the answers she'd received. She hurriedly went on to tell how she had withdrawn the forty thousand dollars, sent it to her sister, hired detectives to check on the brothers and on Jubal Starns, and what had happened with the hotel owner.

"I should have Mary Louise's receipt soon; then the ranch title will be clear. Gran was upset with me for paying her off without asking you, but I just wanted it over with, Matt. And I had to be sure the Fletchers and Starns wouldn't try anything else against us, especially before your return."

"Mercy, a lot happened while I was gone. I should have stayed home, Jessie. I should have let Jake Bass handle the drive. He's the best trail boss in the west. You could have been hurt. You shouldn't have had to deal with this by yourself."

"Are you angry because I did all that without you?"

Matt gathered her into his arms. "No, my love. You're strong and smart. I knew you could take care of yourself and the ranch. That's why I didn't worry much leaving you here. But I thought the trouble was over or I wouldn't have gone. You've always run or helped run everything for Jed. Your strength and courage are parts of you that I love and respect. I don't want to change you, Jessie. I don't feel less of a man because you can manage alone. I'm relieved, in case anything ever happened to me."

"Most men don't feel that way about their wives, Matt. Most men would be furious about a woman taking control."

"I'm not most men, Mrs. Cordell," he said, then chuckled as he hugged her.

"I thought I knew you, Matt. But you surprise me more and more."

"I hope in a good way."

"Yes, a very good way." She nestled closer to his broad chest.

"You see, Jessie, I always had to hide my feelings and real self around you. Jed was always ordering me to watch out for men trying to get their hands on what you'd inherit one day. I knew he liked me and trusted me, but I was afraid of how he would react to me pursuing you. He didn't want anybody taking you away from him. After your mother died, he was even more possessive and scared about losing you to a man. He didn't mean to be like that. He loved you and needed you. He felt steady and strong with you at his side. He fired Navarro because he sensed a threat from him, not because he believed your sister."

"I know, but it doesn't matter now. Except . . ."

"Except what, love?" he coaxed her to finish.

"Papa might still be alive if Navarro hadn't been sent away. I think he was at Mama's grave alone because he felt guilty over what he'd done. But we can't change the past. Let's not think or talk about it again. You don't have to worry about Navarro's return or my feelings for him. I'm yours forever, Matt."

His body ached with desire for her, but he was a mess. He didn't want to hold her or kiss her until he'd had a chance to clean himself up. "I'll never doubt that again, Jessie." He released her and said, "It's civilizing time. This beard and hair have to go. I need scrubbing head to foot. I'm about as filthy as a pig wallowing in mud, and stink about as bad. I'll go over the trip with you after I'm clean and fed."

*

Friday, Jessie and her husband sat down to insert the drive expenses and profit into the ranch book. Matt figured and called out amounts for his wife to enter.

"Salaries for the sixty drovers at forty a month, forty-eight hundred. Trail boss at one-twenty a month and bonus, four hundred. Supplies, five thousand. Indian pay, three hundred. No tricks or troubles this time, Jessie. Paying them to cross their lands is a lot better than having them spook the cattle. We lose less time and no beeves this way. Meal and lodging for our boys in Dodge, two hundred," he said. The seasonal hands had left them after receiving their pay to look for their next jobs. "Feed and holding pens, $8,823. He charged twenty-five cents a day each for four days. That's the highest so far. Supplies for the return trip, three hundred. Bonuses, four twenty-seven. Total expenses, $20,250.00."

"That's wonderful, Matt, less than last time."

"Thanks, Jessie. We got thirty dollars a head, and we had 8,823 by the time we reached market. Didn't lose many this trip. Our profit is $244,440. That'll give us plenty to use until next year."

"Sounds as if four is our lucky number this year," Jessie remarked.

"Yep. I'll assign shifts to give the boys a few days off apiece. They deserve it. They worked hard."

"Oh, Matt, I'm so excited and pleased. I have so many dreams about our spread." Her eyes glowed as she spoke. "We'll give the boys those raises we promised. And I want to add a large room onto the bunkhouse with a fireplace, billiard table, comfortable chairs, and a couple of poker tables. A sitting room will be nice for them, especially in the winter. They've been loyal to us for years. I'd like to show our appreciation. I also want to buy more bulls, and some Hereford cows. It's time we start improving our bloodlines like Papa planned. And we can purchase blooded studs. A hearty breed will sell good to the Army. And I want to raise or buy more hay this year; Fletcher grasslands aren't as good as ours for so much extra stock. We'll need more windmills here and on the southern range in case of drought. We can keep them shut down until needed. I want to replace the things we lost in the fire. We'll be so successful. Things are finally brighter than a sunny day for us. And I want to build a new entrance to the ranch, a large arch of stone with a new sign: L/C Ranch; it'll be our new brand," she finished, almost breathless from her rush of words.

Matt chuckled at her exuberance. "Whoa, Jessie," he teased. "Money only goes so far. We can't do everything in one good year. The next one or two could be bad. We'd better hold plenty back for emergencies and hard times."

Jessie gazed at her handsome husband who was smiling ear to ear. His brown eyes shone with love, joy, and pride. He looked rested and at ease today. "That's why I married my expert foreman, to keep me from leaping onto a runaway stallion," she jested.

"We'll do it all, Jessie, just not at once. We have plenty to be thankful for."

"Yes, we do," she agreed, then reflected for a few minutes on their happy Thanksgiving yesterday. Her parents had always made it a special event. She would continue that family tradition.

"What are you thinking about now? More dreams?" he asked.

"Yesterday, and all our years to come. They'll be good ones, Matt."

"I know. I love you, Jessie."

"I love you, too, Matt."

Feeling aroused by her adoring gaze and nearness, Matt suggested, "Let's get finished here, so we can make those dreams come true one day."

*

Christmas was a wonderful time for the Cordells and Lanes. Annie and the hands joined them inside the night before to sing and eat and drink. At seven months, Jessie's pregnancy was showing. The men shared their joy with their bosses at the blessed event. Small gifts were given to the regulars and Annie. In turn, Matt and Jessie were presented with a cradle that Big John had made. The hands had contributed money for the materials and for the covers inside it, which Margaret Anne James Ortega had selected in town.

Miguel and Annie had wed on Saturday, so that added to the party spirit. He had moved into the small foreman's house with her. Everyone was pleased.

There was more for the family to celebrate. Reports had come in from the Brazel detectives that week. They learned that Jubal Starns had died during a stage holdup on his return to El Paso, so he couldn't cause future trouble. They discovered that the

Fletcher brothers had sold their holdings and moved to England, so vengeance from that distance should be impossible. Mary Louise had moved to Philadelphia, and had sent a receipt for the balance that Jessie had owed her for the ranch. Now the title was free of any threat from her sister and Wilbur's kin.

Jessie had given Matt a light wool shirt that she had made, and he wore it Christmas day. He presented her with a lovely wool shawl he had purchased in Dodge, feeling the locket was only a return of her property.

When the special day was over, Jessie and Matt stood gazing down at the cradle in the extra room beside theirs. It and her protruding stomach made the baby's impending arrival more of a reality. The redhead leaned her back against Matt's body and nestled her head to his neck. Matt's arms overlapped hers.

When the baby began to kick, Jessie shifted their arms to let him share the sensation. "Feel it?" she murmured in wonder, her hands covering his.

"Yep. He's getting stronger and busier. Anxious to bust outta his cell, too. I hope it's a girl who looks just like you."

"What if it's a boy who looks just like his father?"

She and Matt both reacted to her slip. She feared from his last two sentences tht he was thinking about Navarro again. She hoped and prayed not. "I'm sorry, Matt, but I think of you as his father."

He smiled, knowing she was being honest. "That's how it should be, Jessie. I love you and I'll love the baby. Let's get you to bed. It's been a busy season."

*

Matt's soft snoring told Jessie he was asleep. She hoped she hadn't hurt him tonight with her accidental remark. He was her husband and was with her all the time, and she had come to think of the baby as theirs. Matt was a good man, a special man. Every day she realized how lucky she was to have him. She only wished her parents were there to share the joy of her success, her child, and her marriage. A new year was approaching, and she must put the past behind her, behind *them*.

But tonight had brought back thoughts of Navarro Breed. She wondered where and how he was. He could be cold, miserable, and alone. She couldn't forget about Fletcher's sketch. She wondered why nothing had come of it. Perhaps it hadn't fallen into the right hands, or more accurately, the *wrong* ones. Perhaps Fletcher had lied about it to scare the skilled gunslinger away. If not for the sketch, perhaps Navarro wouldn't have left her, or he might have returned by now, at least for a brief visit.

What would Navarro have done if he'd learned about their baby? What could he have done with the law on his back and the threat of a noose hanging over his head? It would have hurt him deeply to learn he had put her into such a bind. Had he forgotten her? Had he met someone else to love, someone with no responsibilities who could run off with him? Had he realized he didn't truly love her as much as he had thought?

If only he'd sent a letter by now that he was alive and well. Surely six and a half months were long enough to go without a single word. But maybe he felt writing to her was unfair and cruel. He had told her to forget him, to seek a new start with another man, that he could never return. Had he meant those tormenting words? Or had something terrible happened to him on the trail?

Jessie asked herself for the hundredth time if she should contact the Arizona authorities about him. Her letters to the Texas authorities had helped her out of a dangerous situation with the Fletchers. Perhaps she could help Navarro by sending the truth to the Arizona governor, U.S. marshal, and prison officials. If they learned he had been sentenced and imprisoned unjustly and had been forced to escape, it could save his life and clear his name.

But she was afraid to act on her hopes. If they didn't believe her or if it didn't change things for him, it could stir up a new search for the fugitive. If the prison was as bad as Navarro said, the men there would want to silence him. It could also spur those lawmen to come here to probe about the desperado, to stir up the painful past. To protect all of them, Jessica Cordell asked herself, shouldn't she let the matter go?

Chapter

22

Jessie's back had ached for hours, since early morning. Contractions hardened her stomach every ten to fifteen minutes, like her insides were twisting into painful knots. She was tense and scared. She's told Gran and Annie that she suspected her labor had begun, and everything was prepared on this still chilly day in March. All she could do was wait, and try to ease her fears.

Jessie wished Matt would hurry home. He was due back anytime from the range. It was almost four o'clock. Gran had explained the birthing process. She was ready to get started, to see her first child, to get the pain behind her. Her stomach was so large. She had been miserable and uncomfortable for weeks. Getting up and down was difficult now. Sleeping was almost impossible, so she was tired and edgy.

It had been a long wait. Once the baby was born, she and Matt could settle down to their life together. So many times she had desired him, and she was looking forward to their first night of lovemaking. That would make her truly and finally his, something she needed and wanted.

More time passed, and the pains increased in frequency. Each one hurt more than the last. Jessie paced her bedroom floor to distract herself. But each knifing slice through her body reminded her of what was in store. She dreaded the suffering she must endure to bring a new life into the world. She hoped and prayed she would be brave, that the child would be safe and healthy. She groaned, held her distended belly, and gasped for breath. Tears blurred her vision. Standing was hard on weak legs, but sitting was worse. Besides, Gran told her that moving around would help lessen the agony.

Every few minutes, Gran or Annie checked on her. They kept Tom away so his nervous jabbering wouldn't bother her. Water was kept hot on the stove. Cloths, sheets, cord, scissors, and basin were ready for use nearby.

Jessie glanced out the window and wondered what was keeping Matt. She wanted him there to keep up her strength and courage, to help her keep silent. She wanted to scream with each pain, yet she didn't want Tom and the men outside to hear her yells. Each time, she clamped her hand over her mouth to keep her torment from escaping. Gran said it could take all day, and Nature was trying her best to prove the woman right.

Jessie was in a loose nightgown and was barefoot. Her hair was braided to keep it out of the way. She grabbed a bathing cloth to wipe the beads of moisture from her flushed face. When Gran entered the room, Jessie murmured through clenched teeth, "It hurts so bad, Gran. They just keep coming and coming."

Gran patted her hands and comforted, "It'll be over soon, child."

Jessie moaned and gripped her stomach, bending forward as if that helped, which it didn't. Gran spread old covers on the bed and told her to lie down. Jessie crawled onto the bed and curled to her side.

Martha handed her a knotted rag and said, "Bite on this when it strikes."

Jessie seized it and obeyed; she felt as if she were being ripped apart.

Gran timed the contractions. Five minutes apart. "Let's get you ready. Won't be long." She helped Jessie work up her nightgown to the waist. She covered her bare bottom with a sheet. "I'll tell Annie to be ready when I shout."

"Gran, I'm scared," the suffering redhead confessed.

"I know. Try to think of something pleasant."

"How can I?" she gritted out as she bit into the cloth and groaned.

Matt hurried into the room. He sat down on the bed, gazed at his wife, and captured her hand in his. Although she gripped his tightly, he felt her tremble. He was worried and frightened by her pale, wet face and flushed cheeks. "We had to pull some calves out of the mud. You doing all right?"

Jessie was about to answer when she stuck the rag into her mouth, closed her eyes, stiffened, and groaned. The labor pain was long, deep, and hard.

"Jessie?" he hinted in panic.

"She's fine, Matt. You're just used to seeing and helping deliver animals. We women make a little more noise than they do. Watch her until I get back."

Matt wiped her brow with his hand. "I love you, Jessie. Don't worry."

When Martha came back, he asked, "Have you sent for the doctor yet?"

"No need. The baby'll be here before he could make it from town. I know what to do, son. Relax. It'll be a while. Why don't you get some coffee and food?"

"I can't leave her like this, Gran."

"Go ahead, Matt, I'll be fine," Jessie encouraged.

Matt obeyed, but reluctantly. When he heard Jessie scream, he dropped his fork and took the steps two by two to get to her side. "What is it?"

"Sorry," she murmured, breathing hard and fast. "It caught me by surprise."

"They're close, Matt. You'll have your first child soon."

But hours passed, Jessie's torment mounted, and no baby entered the world. She had been in labor since eight that morning; it was now eleven. Jessie was writhing in agony. Matt was frantic. Gran was worried.

The older woman bathed her granddaughter's brow with a cool cloth. Jessie's hair was soaked, as was her gown and the bedding. She looked pale, weak, and frightened. She had suffered too long without release.

"Matt, I think you should send for the doctor," Gran whispered.

Jessie halted her rolling motions and stared at her grandmother. "Why, Gran?"

"It's taking longer than I expected. We might need help," she admitted.

"Is something wrong with my baby?" Her eyes were large and dark.

"I don't think so, but he's being stubborn," she tried to jest to calm her granddaughter.

Matt kissed her cheek and left to send one of the boys into town.

"Tell me, Gran, what's wrong," Jessie persisted during his absence.

"I think he might be turned wrong. He might need help getting out."

Jessie's water broke and saturated the area beneath her. Blood flowed onto the wet padding. "What was that?"

Grand reminded her of the birth process. "That's a good sign."

The contractions were coming fast and lasting long. Matt lifted Jessie while Gran and Annie pulled the soaked padding from beneath her and placed a new one there. Gently he lowered his wife to the bed. Gran kept the cover aside to watch for the baby's head.

Jessie was too dazed and was hurting too much to think of modesty or to realize this was the first time her husband had seen her nakedness.

More time passed, and still the baby refused to be born. Labor was almost one continuous agony now. Jessie was exhausted and terrified. Her braid had loosened itself during her thrashings, and her hair was damp and tangled. Her body was covered in perspiration. Her breathing was harsh and loud. She no longer tried to silence her screams, and her throat and lips were dry from them. She yanked on the loops Matt had tied to the bed at Gran's instruction.

By noon the next day, the fatigued and alarmed rider returned to the ranch. Matt hurried to meet him. "Where's the doctor?"

"Not there, Matt. He's in El Paso getting some supplies."

While her husband was outside and Annie was downstairs, Jessie asked, "Is my baby going to die for my sins, Gran? Am I going to die, too?"

"No, child. You'll both be fine."

Matt returned and gazed at his weakened wife. He feared he was going to lose her. He came to the bed and told the older woman, "If the baby's breech, what can we do to get it out? We can't let her go on like this. It's dangerous for both of them. I've turned and pulled out plenty of calves and colts."

"It isn't that easy with a woman, Matt."

"I've got to try it, Gran." Matt moved between Jessie's legs. He examined her stomach, then tried to push the baby into another position. Matt slipped his fingers inside his dilated wife. He felt a foot. Trying not to increase Jessie's pain, his fingers gently searched for the other one. Locating it, he shoved it near the first. With care, he tugged on them inside the expanded area. The baby moved downward. Matt prayed he wasn't injuring the child or his wife. "Hold on, Jessie; it's coming now."

Jessie ordered herself to be brave. Those ripping pains grew worse. She felt as if her womanly opening was splitting asunder when the baby's legs and hips were expelled. She took deep breaths and shoved with all her might to assist the action. She felt Matt's fingers helping those tiny shoulders outside, but they felt as wide as her own at that trying moment. Jessie pushed and grunted several more times between prayers . . . and the baby was delivered. With the pain and pressure gone for a time, she gasped for breath and collapsed into the bed. She let go of the grabbing loops and tossed the biting knot aside.

Matt hurried to clear the child's nose and mouth. He popped its bottom to make it inhale its first breath of air. When it did so and began to cry, he laughed and whooped with joy and relief. "A boy, Jessie, a fine son."

She tried to lift herself to see him. "Is he all right?"

"Beautiful and healthy," Matt promised. "Lie still. We aren't done yet."

"I'll finish up," Gran told the smiling man. She tied off the cord in two places an inch apart and close to the baby, then cut the umbilical link to its mother. "You and Annie tend him while I do a woman's work here."

A nervous Matt accepted the tiny boy. It took twenty minutes for the placenta to pass, but luckily with little bleeding. While Matt and Annie cleaned and dried the infant, Gran bathed Jessie and cleared away the cloths and afterbirth. She called Matt to help her get Jessie into a fresh gown and to help put clean covers on the bed.

Jessie ignored her pain and exhaustion. "Let me see him." She struggled to raise herself.

Matt brought the blanket-wrapped infant to his wife and placed him in her arms.

Jessie cuddled the child close and gazed at him in amazement and love. He had lots of hair, black fuzz. What little she could see of his eyes were dark, too. She moved aside the covering to look him over from head to foot. She saw nothing to worry her. He was wrinkled and pale, and crying in a high baby pitch. She smiled and nestled him against her. "He's perfect, Matt. Let's call him Lane, Lane Cordell."

That brought a broad grin to Matt's face. "It's a good, strong name."

"You saved our lives, Matt," she remarked, love and gratitude shining in her eyes. "Our son. Our first child," she added, and smiled at him.

He beamed with pleasure. "Get some rest. You've worked hard, Jessie."

Gran took the baby from her. "We'll tend him while you sleep a while."

"You're all as exhausted as I am." Her weary lids looked heavy.

"We can take turns napping and watching Lane. Get some rest before he's hungry and shouting for his milk."

Matt bent over, kissed her forehead, then her lips. "I love you, Jessie."

"I love you, too," she replied, drifting off to sleep.

*

Jessie finished bathing and dressing Lane, then nursed him and put him down to nap. She gazed at the sleeping infant of two and a half months. He was a healthy baby, and a good baby, a joy to tend. His hair was still dark, and she believed his eyes would be hazel, like his father's.

Jessie and Matt loved him so much that neither minded that resemblance. If anyone else had noticed, nothing had been said to them or within their hearing. Of course, it helped that Matt had dark hair and eyes. The baby had been so small that everyone believed he had arrived early.

Jessie realized that Lane Cordell had been born on the very day she had met his father a year ago. She felt as if it were God's way of replacing Navarro in her heart and life. It had been a difficult birth, but she and the baby were fine now. She had Matt's quick thinking to thank for their survival.

Today was June first of 1877, a year after she became pregnant by Navarro Breed. It was the right day for beginning her life as Matt's wife. She had thought of her husband all morning and afternoon. He had taken such excellent and gentle care of her since Lane's arrival. He had waited upon her, bathed her, washed her hair, and helped tend their son. Nature had healed her body, and time had healed her heart.

It was time to settle her life and love, time to belong fully to Mathew Cordell. She would always love and remember Navarro Breed, but it was totally and finally over between them. She hadn't heard from the desperado in almost a year. If he ever returned, she would remain Matt's wife. Matt was her life and love now.

Or would be tonight, she decided. Jessie bathed and donned a lovely dress. She splashed on fragrant cologne. She brushed her hair and let it tumble down her back. She planned a special meal for dinner, including wine from Wilbur Fletcher's old stock. Everything was prepared for a romantic evening.

When Matt entered the house, his gaze widened. Candles were lit on the dining-room table, which was set for two. He walked into the kitchen to find Jessie humming as she worked on their meal. "What's going on?" he asked.

"I thought we would enjoy a quiet meal alone tonight. Lane doesn't need attention for another few hours. Tom is camping on the range with the boys. Gran wanted to turn in early. I gave Annie the night off with Miguel. It's just you and me, if that's all right," she said with a sly grin and twinkling eyes.

"It's more than all right," he replied in a hoarse voice. He noticed how beautiful she was tonight and sensed her strange and tantalizing mood.

"I heard you arrive, so I got everything ready for your bath in the closet outside," she remarked, motioning to the room for bathing on the back porch near the kitchen door. "I couldn't carry water upstairs, so I prepared your bath down here. Get busy, sir; dinner's almost ready."

"Is there something I should know?" he inquired, his gaze and tone hopeful.

"You said I would know when the time was right for us," she said. "That's tonight, Mathew Cordell, if you're ready and willing to make a fresh start with me."

Matt's mouth fell open and his brown gaze enlarged. "Are you saying . . . "

"Yep, and about time, don't you think?" she teased.

Matt felt a tingle and flush race over his body. His heart pounded in joy and suspense. "Are you sure, Jessie?"

"More than sure, Matt," she replied with confidence. "Get along," she coaxed.

Jessie grinned to herself as the happily confused male left the room. All day she had fantasized about tonight. She had daydreamed of what it would be like to be in Matt's arms, unrestrained and passionate. She was eager to make love with her handsome and virile husband. She had envisioned them in bed with his fingers and lips working magic upon her body. She had made a lovely gown for this special event, and couldn't wait for Matt to see it on her. She wanted to hurry the meal; yet, she wanted to prolong the enticing prelude to the wonderful evening ahead.

Matt returned and glanced at Jessie. She sent him an encouraging smile. He followed her into the dining room, and they took their places with her next to him. Jessie passed him the food, and his hands trembled slightly as he handled the dishes. He watched her pour two glasses of wine.

"To us, Matt, and our bright future," she toasted and tapped their glasses, but only took a small sip or two since she was nursing the baby.

"Delicious," he murmured, but his appetite was whet for a different kind of meal. He tried not to eat too fast, but it was hard. He had been waiting for this night for almost a year. No, he had wanted Jessica Lane for much longer. Joy and anticipation coursed through his body.

Jessie noticed how excited and pleased Matt was. The meal was wonderful, but not nearly as wonderful as what was in store for them later. She watched candlelight dance on his bronzed face and in his deep brown eyes. She realized he was nervous, and that touched her heart. As they finished the dinner, she suggested, "Why don't we have our pie and coffee later—much later—Mr. Cordell?"

He agreed, then said, "I'll help you with the dishes."

"I'll put them in hot soapy water and do them later. Why don't you go up and get ready for bed? I'm sure you're tired," she jested.

The eager Matt followed her request.

When Jessie entered their bedroom, only candles were burning, casting a soft glow that enhanced the romantic mood. She closed and bolted the door. She didn't want anything or anyone to disturb them for hours. The redhead gazed at the man awaiting her. He was propped against the headboard, resting on a pillow. His bare torso was exposed, but a light sheet concealed his lower half.

Jessie started to enter the bathing closet to change into her new gown, but changed her mind. She sat on the small couch instead and removed her shoes. She unbuttoned her dress and peeled it off her shoulders, then worked it over her hips. She placed the garment over the couch back. Jessie was aware that Matt was watching her with speechless surprise. She found that undressing before him aroused her as much as it did him. She unlaced her chemise and slipped it off her arms. Her breasts were full and taut. She eased off her knee-length bloomers and stood naked before him. She had gained little weight during her pregnancy, and her figure was almost back to normal.

"You're beautiful, Jessie," he murmured in pride and desire.

Mathew Cordell stared in wonder as she walked to the bed. Her auburn hair cascaded over her shoulders like a dark-red river over creamy sand. Her enticing eyes looked bluer than usual. Her body was no longer that of a tomboy. She was bewitching and seductive, knowing and innocent. She appeared soft and fragile, but Matt knew she was firm and strong. He ached to get his hands and lips upon that silken skin.

Jessie sat down near him. She trailed her fingers over his hairy chest, making tiny dark curls along her way. She felt his heart beating at a swift pace. As her fingers journeyed upward, they paused a moment on the pulse point at the base of his throat to feel it racing beneath them. She traced over his jawline, avoiding the small nick from his hasty shave. They traveled down his straight nose and teased over his wide mouth. "I was around you for so many years, but failed to realize how handsome you are." When he smiled, she said, "You have the most beautiful smile in the world. It makes your eyes light up."

"Only when I'm looking at you, Jessie." His hand lifted to caress her cheek.

"I wish I had known about your feelings for me sooner. We wasted so many years. Let's not waste any more," she said, then sealed her mouth to his.

Matt grasped her body and rolled her over his to place her at his side. The cover twisted around his hips as he lay half atop her. His mouth and tongue worked with hers to send their senses spinning. His fingers drifted over her silky flesh, trailing down her arm and over her back. They entangled themselves in her lush mane and didn't seek freedom for a time.

Their bare torsos met and Jessie gasped at the sensation. They explored each other's bodies with equal and rising passion.

Matt's mouth left hers to roam the smooth flesh of her neck, then traveled downward to move slowly and purposefully toward one beckoning breast. He brushed his lips over its peak, his hot breathing enflaming the taut bud and causing it to stiffen. His tongue lavished sweet nectar upon it, and he felt Jessie quiver in pleasure. His hand drifted over her hip and lower, to the very center of her passion. With skill and tenderness, he teased and and caressed her moist, satiny flesh.

Jessie closed her eyes and savored the blissful sensations her husband was creating. His hands and lips were skilled and knowing. If ever she had doubted she loved and desired Matt Cordell, those qualms were over. If ever she had doubted she could respond to him in this way, she had been mistaken. Her body was sensitive and receptive to every move he made. She wanted to touch him, to pleasure him, to tantalize him, too. The cover prevented her bold explorations. She yanked at it and Matt caught her intention.

Without taking his lips from her body, he grasped the edge and tossed it aside, leaving nothing between them. He felt Jessie's hands stroke his back, tease over his buttocks, and seek his throbbing hardness. He sucked in air and stiffened a moment when she touched him.

Jessie smiled at his reaction and her hand curled around him. As her desire increased, her fingers roamed up and down his hot, hard length. Her mind was dazed by the wall of fire around her. Her body was engulfed in passion's flames. She wanted to be consumed by them. "I want you so much, Matt."

Jessie didn't have to tell him she was ready to receive him; her actions spoke for her. Matt moved atop her and when she eagerly parted her thighs, he thrust into her with a cry of ecstasy.

Jessie groaned with pleasure as their bodies united and worked as one. Their hands and lips continued to heighten their hunger. Their lovemaking was blissful and stirring. But they had waited a long time and were unable to restrain themselves. They moved with urgency, their hearts and bodies demanding to be sated.

"I love you, Jessie. It's more wonderful than I dreamed."

"Oh, yes, Matt, it feels wonderful." she murmured as the bittersweet sensations charged through her writhing body. "You're driving me crazy."

Unable to hold back any longer, he carried them to the edge of restraint and into paradise itself. Together, they shared a rapturous delight, then lay contented in each other's arms, savoring the glowing aftermath of their first union.

Jessie teased her fingers over her husband's damp chest. "Mathew Cordell, you're one surprise after another. Why did you keep me starving so long?"

He laughed. "Don't you know food tastes better when you're hungriest?"

"Ah, yes, that devious scheme of yours to conquer me," she jested.

"Seems it worked," he retorted, hugging her possessively.

"I must admit it did, and most delightfully."

Matt rolled to his side and propped on his elbow. He gazed down into Jessie's radiant and serene face. "And I'll confess that was worth waiting for."

"You're right. We did need time to get this close. I'm yours now."

As he studied her gaze and mood, he knew that was true in all ways.

Jessie heard the baby cry. She laughed and said, "Now, our son wants his dinner. For a while, we'll have to work our schedule around his. I won't be long. Keep the bed warm, my love." Jessie rose and donned her gown. "On second thought, Mr. Cordell, keep yourself warm until I get back. Seems I haven't had my dessert yet."

Jessie nursed Lane and tended his needs. As she rocked him to sleep, she smiled and hummed. She realized it was possible to love two men. There was still a special place in her heart for Lane's father, but her life was with Matt. Surely Matt was her destiny.

She wouldn't allow the bittersweet past and her lost first love to torment her again. She wouldn't dream of how it could have been with Navarro. She wouldn't fantasize about his eventual return. She would live in the present and for the future. She was lucky to have captured a beautiful second chance.

Jessie tucked in her son and gazed at him for a short time. Lane Cordell had been meant to be born, and she would no longer scold herself for making a sinful mistake. He would be loved and nurtured by two happy parents. That was more than Navarro had had and more than Lane would have had if she'd escaped with the fugitive that day long ago.

Despite sharing love and passion, she and Navarro had been too different to have made a life together. She would have been lost in Navarro—overwhelmed by him. But she and Matt were equal halves that made a healthy whole.

No doubt Navarro had realized such truths, too, and that was why he hadn't visited or written: to let them both heal and forget. With all her heart, she wished Navarro well, but she loved Matt and their happy life. There would always be a small corner in her heart that only Navarro had touched and where he would reside. She would always be grateful to him for what he had done for her and for her family. There was no shame or sin in such pure love and harmless loyalty. Yes, things were as they should be.

Matt was awaiting her return to share more pleasure. Peace ruled their ranch and lives, Miguel and Annie Ortega were expecting their first child next year. Everyone was safe and happy.

Jessie took one more glance at her son, smiled, and left to rejoin Matt. Her life was perfect, and nothing or no one could spoil it . . .

Chapter

23

Matt entered the parlor where Jessie and Gran were sewing and chatting. Tom was in his room doing lessons. The November day was cool, and a cozy fire glowed on the large hearth. Lane sat on a rug near his mother's feet playing with wooden toys that Big John Williams and other hands had carved for him. Annie was in her small home tending to her new infant. The two women halted their hands and looked at Jessie's husband as he approached them.

He scooped up the twenty-month-old boy and said, "How's my fine son tonight? Getting bigger and smarter every day."

Lane laughed and squealed with delight as Matt played with him for a time.

After Matt set him down and kissed Jessie's cheek, he withdrew an envelope from his pocket. He held it out to his wife and said, "A letter from Mary Louise."

The redhead stared at the mail as if it were a viper about to strike her, and that was just how she felt. With reluctance, she took the envelope. She glanced at her grandmother, then at Matt, and murmured, "I wonder what she wants. It's been two and a half years of peace. I hope she isn't going to try to end it for us."

Jessie exhaled in dread. "Might as well get it over with." She ripped open the missive and read it to the others. The redhead blinked and shook her head, doubting what her eyes and wits were gathering. No one had spoken. She realized Matt and Gran were as shocked by the news, too. "I don't believe it."

"She sounds sincere, Jessie," Gran remarked.

"I have to admit, I think she does too," Matt added. "Never thought to see the day when she would change."

"It must be a trick," Jessie said, but somehow didn't believe it was.

"What would she have to gain with this offer?" Matt reasoned.

"Matt, watch Lane for me. He's curious about fire, so don't take your eyes off of him," she advised. "I want to study this closely." Jessie went into the kitchen, sat down at the table, and read her sister's letter once more:

Dear Jessica, Gran, and Tom,
You must be surprised to hear from me again after all these years of silence. I beg your forgiveness for the wicked things I did. I realize I was a terrible person, and I'm sorry. I was selfish, defiant, impulsive, and cruel. If you can't find it in your hearts to forgive me, I shall understand. You're wondering what caused this

drastic change in me. Love, Jessica, something you can understand. But not only love.

I was so confused when I returned home from school and left home years ago. I had convinced myself Father hated me and that I had to escape. I was so mean to myself and all of you. Being on my own and alone was frightening, but I could not admit it, not after the awful way I behaved there. When I reached Boston and related my news, the Fletchers took the money you gave me. Wilbur's will left them everything. He lied to me and used me, as you warned. He sent his money here and made an iron-clad will the day we wed to keep the Lanes from getting his estate! I was forced to survive off their charity and had to aid their cause to get it. I couldn't confess my stupidity and dire straits to you. They composed that wicked letter I wrote to you. When you called their bluff, I told them you couldn't be tricked or scared off your land. When they were forced to yield, they blamed me, and my life worsened.

I used the final payment you sent for survival and a second escape. I fled to Philadelphia and was fine for almost a year. But I had more to learn, all the hard way. I sought another rich man and profitable marriage. Again, I was used and discarded by several targets. Looks and wiles aren't enough without a good heart behind them. I was living high to gain attention and success, so my money was running out fast. Then a terrible thing happened to me. I was robbed and beaten, and worse. I nearly died. I wanted and needed my family, but I had betrayed them. I feared you would think it was only a trick to get more money or sympathy. I was so ashamed and scared. A wonderful and gentle—and handsome, too, Jessica—doctor saved my life and tended me like a child. Under his care, I realized love and family are what's important in life. He's so like Matt, a good and kind man. His name is John Blye. He's thirty-three.

After I'd healed, John dismissed me. He had heard what an awful person I was, and he wanted to escape my greedy clutches. But I had fallen in love with him. I chased him until I convinced him I had changed. We had a glorious courtship, and we married. He has an office in our home. Many times I help him with patients. We love each other so much and we're so happy. Each day I changed even more. I'm so like Jessica now that no one at home would recognize me.

But I'm writing for another reason, too. I told John about Tom's problems. John is certain he can help improve them or find a specialized doctor who can. If you'll send Tom to us, we'll help him. He can live with us during treatments, for as long as it requires. Please allow him to come. His life can be so much better.

Jessie put the letter down and rubbed her eyes, tired from sewing all day. She heard Lane and Matt playing in the parlor and smiled. She wanted to join them, but she had a serious decision to make. She lifted the astonishing letter again and read on about Mary Louise's life and work with Dr. John Blye, about her experiences before and after her marriage, about her many changes, and about her dreams for helping their brother.

Jessie got up to pour herself a cup of coffee, then sat down to think. She yearned to believe she could trust her sister. She prayed it was possible to treat Tom's clubfoot and bad eyes. She hated to think of him going so far away to endure pain and loneliness in his effort to seek a better chance in life. Yet Tom deserved any help he could receive. Jessie knew he would want to take this risk when he learned of this opportunity. He was going on sixteen, but times weren't much different for him today than years ago. He didn't want to be a rancher, and could never manage a spread on his own. Yet, if surgery and treatments couldn't improve his conditions, she didn't want to give him false hopes. But it was Tom's choice to make, not hers.

Jessie took the letter and headed for the parlor stairs. She told Gran and Matt she was going to talk with Tom. Neither tried to discourage her. Jessie knocked on his door, then entered after he responsed. She looked at her brother. He was tall and lanky, and sat erect. His dark-auburn hair was mussed from running his fingers through it countless times while studying. Many of his childhood freckles had vanished, but there was still a charming smattering of them across his nose and cheeks. He had become quieter and more serious over the last year. He spent a great deal of time reading and studying.

"Yes, Jessie?" he asked in a voice that seemed to deepen more each day.

Jessie sat on his bed. He was such a nice and smart young man, with excellent manners. When she remained silent, he squinted to see her better through his thick glasses.

"Is something wrong?" he pressed.

"I have some news to share with you, Tom."

When she hesitated once more, he grinned and asked, "Another baby?"

Jessie laughed and sent him a sly grin. "Yes, but don't tell Matt before I do. Due next fall, you perceptive young man."

"He'll be excited. Why tell me first?"

Jessie noticed how his grammar had improved due to all his hard work and her assistance. "That isn't what I came to say, but you're so clever to have guessed my secret. I was waiting to make certain before I told Matt. But what I wanted you to know is that we received a letter from our sister today."

Tom frowned. "What does she want now?"

"That was my first reaction, but we're wrong this time. I want to read it to you, then discuss her suggestion." Jessie read the letter to a shocked Tom. As she lowered it to her lap, she asked, "Do you want to think about it for a while, or talk about it now?"

Tom glanced at his disabled foot, then removed his glasses to rub his strained eyes. He replaced them and looked at his older sister. "Do you think it's possible?"

"I don't know, Tom. But I doubt a doctor would say he could help if he knows for certain he can't. He will have to examine you first to make sure. I hope he can, but I don't want to raise your hopes."

Tom drifted into deep thought. His eyes darted about as he deliberated this unexpected opportunity. "He can't make things worse, but he might make them better. It's a risk, Jessie, but I want to take it. When did she say to come?"

Jessie was not surprised by his choice. "There's a train from Dallas on December second. Mary Louise will meet it in Philadelphia on the chance you're on it. That'll give us time to get your things ready. I'll send Rusty with you."

"I'm not a baby, Jessie. I can travel by train alone."

"But it's such a long trip, Tom. You've never been away before. You aren't grown yet, little brother."

"I'll behave and study all the way. Will you and Gran and Lane be all right without me? She said it'll probably take a year of surgery and exercises."

"We'll miss you terribly. It's going to be scary, hard, and probably painful, Tom. You'll have to be brave and work hard to get well. You'll also have to be patient and not push too fast to recover. I would go with you to get things started, but you know why I can't. There's Lane and . . ." She patted her stomach.

"Don't worry, big sister. I can take care of myself. I can take the pain and work to be normal. Even if Dr. Blye can't cure me, Jessie, can I stay there to go to college? Could I get in and do the work?"

Jessie's eyes widened. "You want to attend college back East?"

"More than anything," he confessed. "I've dreamed about it. This is my chance to make it come true. Please, Jessie, say yes. I'm not dumb."

"Of course you aren't. I'm sure you can do it, but it would keep you away so much longer. It takes years, Tom."

"Only a few. I don't want to ranch or farm, Jessie. I want to study business and lots of other things. I want to be around other students. I want to learn and do fun stuff. I want to see what it's like over there. Please."

"So many surprises in one day," she murmured. Jessie studied Tom's pleading look and realized how sincere and serious he was. "I'm sure John could help. And I'll give you the funds, if this is really what you want."

"Whoopee! It is, Jessie. I'll make you proud of me; I promise."

Jessie returned his impulsive embrace. "I *am* proud of you, Tom."

"But it'll be better for me after I'm fixed and educated. Even if the doctor can't repair me, who laughs at somebody who's been to college? This will give me the chance to be somebody, to get respect, to stop the jokes. I'll become too smart for them to hurt me or ignore me anymore. I can live at school, Jessie, so I won't be any trouble for Mary Louise and her husband."

"You've learned enough at home to do any of their lessons."

"Then, it's all right?"

"Why not gamble for the whole pot while you're at the table?" she quipped. "I'll bet John tries to talk you into medicine or law. Just don't let that eastern school ruin you like it did Mary Louise."

"Don't worry; I'll only change for the better. I swear."

"If you're sure about this, we'll start preparing for your departure tomorrow."

"I'm sure, Jessie. You and Mary Louise have good lives now. I have to seek mine."

*

"I'll write Mary Louise tomorrow, so she can get things prepared for Tom's arrival. I just hate to see him hurt and disappointed if John can't help him. Science and medicine are so tricky, but they change all the time."

"We'll hope and pray for the best," Matt replied.

"Do you think I'm doing the right thing, Matt? It's so serious. Tom's never been away from home before. Is he too young to face so much alone?"

"I don't think so, Jessie. He's mature for his age, and he's smart. He'll have Mary Louise and John with him. He needs this chance to prove himself. We can afford to send him for treatment and school. That rail strike last year didn't hurt us. And our sale this time was good," he added, referring to the long drive from August to November that he had completed two weeks past.

"I'm glad you started the roundup and drive early this year, so you're home now to advise me on this. We were lucky that cattlemen's war in New Mexico didn't affect us at market. This is the third season I've missed."

"Lane keeps you busy at home, love. Surely you don't miss the hard riding and trail dust," he teased.

"Sometimes I do. I was used to being a ranch hand. It takes a while to adjust to being a mother and wife who stays home. I miss the excitement and good times with the boys. I don't feel much a part of my old life anymore."

"What about missing me?" he jested.

She smiled. "I miss you most of all during market season."

"Two weeks hasn't caught me up for what I missed for three months."

"Me, either," she responded. Jessie slipped off her garments and got into bed fast to avoid a chill. "Let's make up for lost time," she hinted.

Matt grinned. "I'll check the fire in the hall and make sure Lane's asleep."

Jessie snuggled under the covers. She was glad Big John Williams had made a sturdy crib for their son, who loved to climb on things and investigate every curiosity. Jessie had worried over Lane falling down the steps or exploring the fire in the second-floor hearth. John had constructed the bed so the small boy would stay put and not get into dangerous mischief.

Matt closed the door behind him and joined his wife in bed. He nestled her close to his naked body. "Cold?" he whispered.

"Not anymore."

Matt's mouth met hers. He kissed her many times before sending his hands on a skilled search for pleasure. His fingers and lips teased and tantalized his responsive wife until she was riding with him toward bliss.

Jessie's hands roamed Matt's well-muscled body as she trailed kisses over his neck and face. Sometimes their lovemaking was calm and leisurely. Sometimes it was urgent and swift. Sometimes it was a mixture of both. But every time it was fulfilling and pleasurable. She had come to love him more each day since their marriage. Both had mellowed, and she knew it was because they were a good match. They were friends and partners and mates. Lane was like their son. She was eager to share her other news with him later, as he would be ecstatic to learn she was carrying his child this time.

Matt's touch brought her attention back to the spell he was weaving. She soared with him, knowing he gained as much satisfaction as he gave. She stroked his hard back where muscles rippled with his movements. She arched to meet each thrust he made into her welcoming womanhood. She loved being with him in this special way that bound their bodies and hearts as one. He was such a gentle and skilled lover. He knew what to do to drive her mindless with desire. She enjoyed the taste of his mouth on hers and savored each caress.

And Matt could never seem to get enough of Jessie. He wanted to be near her every day, if only to see her smile. He savored the way she clung to him and responded with such eagerness and passion. He had no doubts that she loved him, desired him, and found ecstasy in his arms. To realize he could reach her so deeply thrilled him. At first he had worried he couldn't or might not satisfy her like Navarro had. But those doubts and fears had vanished. He was confident that Jessica Cordell was his forever.

Matt and Jessie rode the waves that crashed over, around, and through them. Their lovemaking became more frenzied as the power of it urged them higher, then carried them to ecstasy. They kissed and embraced until they lay exhausted and breathless but happy.

Matt turned and kissed her ear. "You're the most precious treasure a man could have, Jessie," he whispered.

She stroked his cheek. "Isn't it strange how lovemaking gets better each time. You'd think it would become commonplace after so many times. But the feelings just get stronger. It's almost as if it's new and different each time, but . . . It's strange and wonderful," she finished, unable to describe how marvelous each union was.

"I feel the same way. We're perfect for each other."

"Yes, we are. By the way, you left a gift behind before the drive. Thank you."

"A gift? I don't recall one," he said in confusion.

Jessie grinned, candlelight revealing her expression. "I'm three months' pregnant, Matt. You'll be a father again in early May."

"A baby?" he murmured, gazing into her merry eyes.

"Yep, cowboy, you've saddled me with another child," she teased. "It happens when two people make love as often as we do. In fact, it took longer than I imagined it would. It's been quite a while since you and I started these delightful bouts in bed, and Lane is nearly two. Aren't you pleased?"

A mixture of elation and dread filled Matt. "You had such a hard time with Lane's birth. Will you be all right, Jessie? I'm worried."

She caressed his face and kissed him. "I'm fine now, Matt. First babies can be difficult. Don't be afraid. Your child would never give its mother trouble."

"My child," he murmured. "That's wonderful, Jessie."

"It'll be a busy time with spring roundup and branding."

"Don't worry. I'll stay home. Rusty and the boys can handle the roundup of calves and colts next year. I want to make certain I see our child born."

"Want to play doctor again, huh?" she jested.

He chuckled, then responded, "I'll be satisfied just to be in the house this time. I don't want you to suffer like you did with Lane."

"Gran said it's only hard the first time. The others come fast and easy."

"I hope so. You scared me last time. I can't lose you, Jessie."

"You won't, Matt, not ever."

"I wonder if it'll be a boy or a girl."

"Does it matter?"

"Nope." He ran his fingers through his hair. "This is good news, woman."

Jessie spread kisses over his chest. "We have months to get used to it and make our plans. With Tom leaving for school, we can put Lane in his room. Then the nursery will be ready for use again."

"I want to fill up this house with our children."

"Whoa, boy, one at a time, please. If I get too busy with lots of children, that'll leave less time for you, for us. For this," she added, then moved atop him.

*

March thirteenth of 1881 was a lovely spring day. The last two years and four months had been successful and happy ones for the Lanes and Cordells. Matt was outside with four-year-old Lane, keeping the boy busy while his birthday meal and cake were being cooked. Alice Cordell—named after Jessie's mother—was napping in the nursery. At twenty-two months, she was a beautiful child, with Matt's brown eyes and Jessie's red hair. Gran was tickled to have a little girl to help raise, and Alice's father adored both child and mother.

Gran was stiffer these days from her arthritis, but she still insisted on doing chores. Jessie did as much as possible, but the two children took much of her time and energy. Matt had suggested hiring another girl, as Annie Ortega had two children of her own to tend. With Gran now seventy-five and with Jessie three months pregnant with a third child, the redhead knew she should seek hired help soon.

"Did you write to Tom and Mary Louise about the new baby?" Martha inquired.

"Not yet. Mary Louise is depressed about not getting pregnant so far. She's afraid she can't have children. She thinks she's being punished by God or tested to see if she'll make a good mother. I told her not to worry. It'll happen."

"How much longer does Tom have at school? And is he walking again?" she asked. She was forgetful some days.

Patient and loving, Jessie gave the same answers again. "He'll be home next summer. He's already talking about starting a business in town. Matt and I told him we'll back him. I'm so glad the surgery worked, Gran. Tom says he only has a slight limp now. His foot is almost straight. One of his greatest pleasures in life is wearing shoes, even if they are specially made. I can't wait to see his new glasses; he says he can see so much better. Things are going wonderfully for him. He's happy. Mary Louise and John are happy. All of us are happy and safe."

"We wouldn't be safe if those soldiers and Rangers hadn't whipped those renegades. They sure we won't have no more trouble?"

"We're fine, Gran. It's been two years since Victorio went on the warpath. We were lucky the Apaches liked to cross into Mexico between Fort Davis and El Paso, instead of over here like the Comanches did. I was nervous when Fort Davis was made the headquarters for West Texas. But Captain Baylor and his Rangers did more than the Army to stop the outbreak."

"I remember. They licked the Apaches good at Quitman Canyon in July of last year. Then they got 'em good again at Rattlesnake Spring in August."

Jessie smiled at the woman who sometimes thought clearly and other times was muddled. "That's right, Gran. Then Victorio was beaten in October by the Mexicans. The survivors took a last stand in January at Quitman Canyon, but Baylor and his men defeated them. The papers say Indian wars are over for Texas."

"What about those two chiefs who escaped?"

"Nana and Geronimo are living and raiding farther west, Gran. They won't be any trouble to us. Besides, we still have those Apache symbols painted on our fence posts. If any renegades came our way, they honored them."

"I still think we should keep on extra men to be sure."

"We did, Gran. Matt doesn't want to take any risks until the other chiefs and renegades are stopped or back on the reservations. You can't blame the Indians for wanting to roam free like their ancestors did. I read that some of those reservations are terrible. I think the Apaches prefer the Warm Springs location to San Carlos. It's a shame we can't all live in peace. A lot of people have died from these wars."

"I bet Navarro could lick a whole band by himself."

Jessie stiffened, and her hands stopped spreading icing on her son's cake. It had been five years ago today that she had met the desperado, and four since she'd borne their child. Gran had mentioned his name several times to her lately. She hoped the aging woman didn't do the same with Matt or Lane. She didn't know why Navarro Breed was on her grandmother's mind so much these days, unless it was because Lane was favoring his real father more and more. Jessie always ignored the mentions with hopes they would pass out of the woman's head as fast as so many other things did.

Not today. "He sure beat that Fletcher good," Gran added.

"Yes, he did. Are the biscuits finished?" Jessie asked to distract her.

"Does Matt know he's Lane's father?"

Jessie halted her task and took her grandmother's gnarled hands in hers. "Yes, Gran, but we don't talk about that secret. Someone might overhear." The redhead worried over slips the aging woman might make in front of others. Jessie fretted over the clouding of the woman's memory, and her occasional bouts of stubbornness, which the doctor had said couldn't be helped. This was one of those irrational moments. Gran looked at her and scowled.

"A boy should know who his father is, Jessie."

"Matt is Lane's father, Gran. Matt is rearing him. You must keep this secret." Jessie explained the past and their need to protect Lane Cordell.

The cloud lifted for now. "You're right, Jessie. I'm sorry."

"Let's get finished before Lane's cake is a mess."

*

By Monday, Navarro and Gran were still on Jessie's troubled mind. In her condition, Jessie knew she didn't need this tension plaguing her. It was making her miserable and edgy. Perhaps the only way to get it behind her was to do what she had thought about years ago: send letters to the authorities to help clear Navarro. She had succeeded with those against the Fletcher brothers, whom they hadn't heard from since she had taken that action. Perhaps, if Navarro was still alive and free, she could end his torment.

If she wrote the President, the Arizona governor, the U.S. marshal, and the Arizona law, perhaps things could be changed for the fugitive. It could initiate an investigation into the false charges against him and the brutalities at the prison. If she could get Navarro pardoned, then if she ever heard from him again, she could tell him he was free. That would pay any debt she owed the man for his being denied a life with her and their son and for all his years of suffering.

Too, if Lane ever discovered the truth about his birth, it would be better if his real father wasn't a wanted criminal. If Lane learned his heritage was Breed, it would be better if that name was cleared of its blackness and shame.

Navarro had given her a new life, and she owed him one. He had refused to carry her away and to sweep her into his perilous existence. He had refused to intrude by letter or visit. It was time to pay him back for his generosity.

Matt was confident enough now in their love to endure any questions the authorities might ask. She was carrying his second child, and he trusted her. She had to take this risk for Navarro and their son.

But, she fretted, what if Navarro was pardoned and returned? How would she feel when she saw him again? She honestly didn't know. How would seeing her married with children affect him? She didn't know that, either. But if he was the man she believed him to be, he would thank them and leave to make a fresh start elsewhere. She had been compelled to start over, and it had worked for her. She had found a rich, fulfilling love and a happy life; that would show him that he could, too. A pardon would give Navarro a new beginning.

Yet all he would need was one look at Lane for him to guess the truth. Was it fair for her to protect herself and family at Navarro's expense? Was it just for him to keep suffering while she was free and happy? Especially when she might could change all that for him with a few letters? She could tell the authorities his side and what kind of man he truly was. At least she might get his sentence reduced so he'd only have to serve a few more years.

The more Lane favored his father, the more her secret was in jeopardy. If her son learned the truth, how would he feel about her not helping his father? Faith, hope, love, and charity: she believed in those things, and tried to practice them. Yes, she decided, it was worth the risk to help Navarro, even if the fugitive never discovered she had done so. And, what better day than the momentous March thirteenth to begin her task?

Chapter

❦

24

On an early June day in 1881 Mathew Cordell rode to the old Lane settlement and dismounted. He and Jessie had discussed building a few small houses on this location for the hands who married so they wouldn't have to leave their employ, as several had reached that age and inclination. Last night they had sketched out their plans and figured the construction cost. Reasonable rent would give them enough to pay the bank note each month, and the chosen amount wouldn't be a hardship on the families. Both had decided it would be nice to have neighbors and other families nearby. Workers' children would give the Cordell family playmates. Matt had ridden over to check the location.

As Matt worked and made notes, he knew it was an excellent spot. The site had plenty of water and fertile gardening space. They would start with three houses, and perhaps later increase it to five. If spaced and arranged creatively around the existing structures as Jessie had suggested, each family would have its own yard and privacy. The couple knew the men's wives and children would be safe in this area, as some of the wranglers and a cook still occupied the Lane bunkhouse. Since there was so much work in this area and beyond, it made their schedules easier. Presently those hands were off riding herd and fence. Their cook was at the river fishing, to give the men a change in their diet while he enjoyed himself.

It was a quiet and peaceful setting with no one around an hour past the noon meal. The sky was clear and blue in all directions. A gentle breeze wafted over him and the sun-drenched landscape, stirring grass and bushes as it passed. With sufficient rain so far this year, everything was green and growing. The ranch structures still in use were kept in excellent condition. Flowers that Jessie and Gran had planted long ago and a variety of wild ones bloomed here and there to add color and beauty. Chickens scratched and a milk cow grazed contentedly at a distance, occasionally sending forth a few clucks and moos. Only the stone foundation and chimneys of the original Lane home were standing; the charred debris had been cleared long ago to prevent an eyesore. They could use the stones for future construction, but not build over them, as the old Lane home was larger than the cozy houses they were planning.

Jessie had wanted to come with him; but in the sixth month of her pregnancy, both knew horseback riding was unwise and a leisurely carriage trip would have taken six hours over and back. Matt hurried his task, eager to get back to her.

As he completed it, galloping hooves caught his attention. Matt looked in that direction and saw a man heading toward him. As the rider neared the location, dread filled the rancher. Matt realized his only nightmare was coming true: Navarro Breed was back. He had feared his past rival's return ever since he gave Jessie permission to write the authorities three months ago on Navarro's behalf.

As Matt awaited his approach, he wondered if the fugitive knew about their efforts to help him. He wondered if those letters had worked in Navarro's favor, or if the loner was unaware of them and was stealing a visit. Matt had suspected this event would take place one day, but his tender-hearted wife had convinced him with little effort that it was the right thing to do.

At least, Matt admitted, he was being given the chance to speak with Navarro first. Hopefully he could persuade the man to do the right thing, too: keep riding without seeing and upsetting Jessie in her condition. Not that Matt distrusted his wife's loyalty or doubted her feelings for him, but there was time later for her to learn the truth, after the baby's birth when she was well. *Lord help us both do the right thing for everyone,* he prayed.

Navarro dismounted and joined the unsmiling rancher. Neither spoke for a short time. Sweat beaded on both men's faces and dampened their shirts. Both had dark tans, white teeth, strong features, and matching garments; but they didn't favor each other in the least. Both were strong, proud, and skilled, but the confidence of both men was shaky at that moment. At six foot two, Navarro stood taller than Matt, but they had about the same build.

"Hello, Matt," Navarro finally greeted him, perceiving that the man was anything but happy to see him return. "Where's Jessie? And what happened here?" he asked with a worried look, nodding toward the ruins of the Lane home where he had bid his beloved Jessie good-bye.

"A fire, two months after you left," Matt replied. He prayed again for the power and words to handle this trying situation.

Panic filled Navarro and showed in his expression. "Was Jessie hurt?"

"No, she's fine. Everyone got out safely."

"Where is she? I have to see her."

"She moved to Fletcher's place. She bought it, remember?"

"I'll ride over," he said as he turned to mount.

Matt's hand on Navarro's arm halted his intention. "Don't," he said simply.

Navarro stared at Matt. "Why not?"

"Jessie is married now. The past is over. Leave her be."

Navarro couldn't conceal his shock and dismay. "Married? To whom?"

"To me. For years," Matt added, trying to feed him the truth in small bites.

Navarro couldn't swallow that bitter piece. "I don't believe you."

"It's true. If you love her, stay out of her life."

The loner knew that Matt had loved and wanted Jessica Lane years ago. Could she . . . "How did you manage that? Take advantage of her after this fire and my leaving?"

"We got married before the fire," Matt hinted.

"Before? But you said it was two months after I left. She wouldn't have."

"She did. She needed me."

Navarro was confused and angry. He couldn't accept that Jessie had wed so soon after his departure. "You made her think she did! I'm going to see her, your wife or not!"

"Don't do this, Navarro. We have children. Don't spoil our lives."

"She married you and had your children! How could she? She said she loved me. She said she'd wait for me."

"For how long? It's been five years without word or a visit."

"But she didn't even wait a few months! I thought she was honest and special. How could she have loved me, then turned to you so soon?"

Matt read the man's bitterness and resentment, and knew he would feel the same in Navarro's place. He tried to be kind and gentle, to avoid involving Jessie. "She *is* honest and special. She *did* love you. When you deserted her and never contacted her again, she didn't think you'd ever return."

"She could have waited for a while! Longer than two months! She'll have to tell me herself why she betrayed me. I risked everything for her."

Knowing Navarro's past from Jessie, Matt used the only weapon he could use on the man to defeat him. "If she had waited for you to return, seeing as how it took five years, your son would have been born a bastard like his father."

Navarro's heart pounded. "Son? What are you talking about?"

Matt prayed that Navarro's love was strong and pure, that his rival would make the right sacrifice for his wife and child. It was a risk worth taking, since Navarro would recognize the truth if he saw Lane. Matt tried to work on the loner's conscience. "You deserted Jessie while she was carrying your child. You left her alone and in a mess. You never came back to help her. What did you expect her to do? Live in shame? Run off somewhere to have the child, where nobody knew she wasn't married and where she had no friends around to protect her? If you're the man I think and hope you are, you wouldn't have wanted her life to be that way."

The stunned man asked in a strained voice, "Why didn't she tell me? Was she afraid I'd think she was trying to trick me into staying?" Yet Navarro suspected it was all because of what he'd told her during their last meeting. His confession had silenced hers, as she realized they couldn't wed. She had let him leave without knowing of their child, then married Matt to protect them both. Cruel life had given her no choice, but how he wished he had known about his child.

Matt had waited a few minutes for the news to settle in. "She didn't know she was pregnant until August. You were long gone by then, and she didn't know where to locate you. I know why you left, Navarro; Jessie told me all about your past and troubles. I'm glad you didn't draw her into them. I know how hard it was to give her up, but you did the right thing. She couldn't wait any longer to see if you'd ever be back. Time was against her. Even if she had waited and you'd returned for a visit, what did a fugitive have to offer her and the child? Nothing but trouble and danger. She was frantic and sick. She had everything put on her shoulders: the ranch, her family, the baby, and losing you and Jed. She was going to move somewhere, claim she was a widow, and have the baby. She asked me to take care of the ranch until she could return. I persuaded her not to give up her home, to stay here where me and the boys could protect her and help her, to marry me to give your child a name. Jessie didn't want to take advantage of me, so I had to talk long and hard to convince her it was the best path to take. I loved her and wanted her; I was even glad you'd shoved her into my arms. She agreed to marry me and stay home. As time passed, she came to love me. She was right not to wait; it's been five years!"

Navarro exploded from guilt and bitterness. "I didn't desert her! I couldn't put her in danger by staying or by taking her with me. I told her everything, and she understood. But she vowed to wait anyway, and I believed her. We both hoped something would happen to clear me so I could come back to her. I was captured by the law two days after leaving here. I was on my way back to tell Jessie I loved her when they trapped me and carried me back to that Arizona prison. I realized it wasn't fair to leave her without telling her something that important. I'm sure she knew the truth, but I never said those words aloud. I wanted her to hear from me how I felt. I never wanted her to think I had selfishly taken so much from her without loving her. I said I'd never return, but we both knew I would. It had to hurt her bad to think she was wrong about me."

Navarro grimaced and clenched his teeth. "Fletcher's sketches helped them catch me. Did she tell you about them?" When Matt nodded, he continued. "I couldn't send word about my capture because I didn't want the law to think she'd been hiding me and get her into trouble. I've been in that stinking hole for five years. They made sure I had no chance to escape again. I was released two weeks ago. The governor started an investigation into that place; he cleaned out the vermin and set me free. I came straight here. I have to see her and explain everything, Matt."

Matt was glad to hear the news about the prison reform, and he felt compassion for all Navarro had endured for years—no, since the man's ill-fated birth. Yet protecting Jessie was the most important thing on his mind. "Don't, Navarro. She's accepted your loss. Don't stir up new pain for her. Seeing you can't change anything now. We have a good and happy life. Besides your son, we have a daughter two years old and another child on the way."

"You said you married her to give my child a name. Now you're telling me you're a real husband to her. How could she love me and be a wife to you?"

"*Loved* you, Navarro, long ago. She loves me now. Time heals wounds and changes lives. If you love her, let her be. Think what you'll do to her and Lane if you suddenly appear or try to lay claim to them. That's cruel and selfish."

"Lane?"

"Your son, Lane Cordell. *My* son. I've raised him as my own for four years, Navarro. He's smart and good. He favors you, but that doesn't trouble me. I love him. I'm a good father to him, a good husband to Jessie."

"But he's my son. She's my woman. You stole them while I wasn't around to guard them."

Matt reasoned with the distressed man. "Would you rather I had stood back and let your baby be born a bastard? Let Jessie be shamed? Let her run off and be alone? I've always loved her. If you hadn't come along and stolen her from me, she'd have been mine first. Be satisfied with the time and love you shared with her. You have us to thank for getting you out of prison." Matt related what they had done to help Navarro and why. "Repay us by leaving us in peace."

Learning that his beloved was behind his release made Navarro wonder. "What if Jessie still loves me and wants me? Is it fair not to give her a choice? Is it fair to keep the truth about me from her?"

"She would never leave her family for you, even if she did love and want you more than me. But she doesn't, Navarro; believe me. She's expecting another baby in a few months. Confronting you after all this time could be dangerous for them both. She almost died giving birth to Lane. She suffered bad after you left. Don't make her hurt like that again!"

"I'm a free man now," Navarro broke in. "Let her choose between us. I can settle down with my son and the woman I love. I'd raise your children like you've raised my son."

"If Jessie and I didn't share a real marriage and our children, I would agree. I know how you must be suffering. But others have suffered, too, Navarro. They'll suffer more if you don't back down. Lane thinks I'm his father. If you ride up and spill the truth, he'll be hurt and confused. You'll ruin Jessie's name if people learn our secret. You have a responsibility to protect both of them. Think about them, not yourself," Matt urged.

Navarro had to work through his anguish, guilt, and disappointment. "Like you did years ago when you laid claim to what's mine? You're thinking of yourself now, Matt. You don't want to lose Jessie and all you have with her. You can't know what I've endured. You've never been thrown into prison for something you didn't do. You haven't been beaten and starved. You were never treated like a half-breed bastard. You've never had to give up everything you ever wanted and needed when it was in your grasp because you thought it was too late to keep it. You had a home, a family, a good life. You've had Jessie for years, and my son. I can be blamed for many things in my past, but not for deserting my love and child. How can you ask me to walk away, to never see them, to not explain? How can you expect me to give up this second chance?"

"You're right about some things. You had a bad life, and I'm sorry about that. But I thought Jessie had changed you. I guess prison undid all the good she did you. Call it back to mind, Navarro. Think and feel with your heart. Be unselfish—for her and Lane. Doesn't it matter how much she loved you and suffered?"

"If Jessie had loved me as I love her, she couldn't have turned to you so quickly. I understand why she married you. But how could her love for me die? How could she love you and truly become your wife so soon?"

Matt grasped the crux of his confusion and torment. "It wasn't soon or easy, Navarro. Our love came from sharing years of days and nights together, tending each other when sick, giving help and comfort in times of trouble and hardship, raising our children, planning for our future, and in providing each other with hope and courage and strength. It came from all of those things that draw two people together over a period of time. We didn't sleep together as man and wife until a year after you'd been gone. Before she could turn to me, Jessie had to lay your ghost to rest. That was a hard and painful battle, Navarro, for both of us."

The rancher knew that hearing such facts and details was rough on the troubled man before him, but Navarro didn't interrupt. Matt continued in a soft-spoken and understanding tone. "You know what kind of woman Jessie is; you can grasp why she finally accepted your loss and why she wanted and made a new life with me. She had so much to give, and it was crying for release. I was the one there to receive it."

"Because I wasn't around to defend my claim on her and Lane."

"Partly, but face the whole truth, Navarro. Even if you hadn't been recaptured, you couldn't have built a good life with Jessie, not the kind she deserves. You wouldn't have risked staying and you wouldn't have taken her on the run. You wouldn't have sentenced your love and child to a miserable existence of stolen visits. I think you're more of a man than that and your love is stronger than that, too. Don't punish her for seeking the safe and happy life you wanted for her, the kind you wanted with her but couldn't have. I know it's hard to see another man in her life. I felt that way about you from the moment you arrived here long ago and I saw that gleam in her eyes for you. I held her in my arms and comforted her while she cried over you. I watched her bloom with your seed. I was with her when she almost died bearing your child. I delivered your baby and tended both of them. Yes, I know what it's like for the woman you love to belong to another man. But all those days we spent together and all those things we shared made us cling to each other."

Matt saw his rival was listening closely to him. "We always liked each other and respected each other. I watched Jessie grow from a tomboy into a woman. I saw her open up and come alive because of you. She was hurting, and needed me for comfort and strength. You two met at a time when each needed the other. That time has passed, Navarro. You and Jessie have different destinies. You have to seek yours elsewhere, but hers is with me, here with our children. Your relationship was meant to help you both change and grow, to prepare you both for your real destinies."

"She was my destiny, Matt," Navarro argued. "She *is* my destiny."

The rancher shook his head. "No, each of you was a marker on the other's trail to point the way, but not a final destination. She loved you, but she had to get over you. I helped her do that. I admit I did everything I could to slay your ghost. You'd have done the same in my place. Surely you didn't want her to pine and suffer for years. I swear to you we love each other and have a good life together. I don't think it could be the same for you and her because you can't have a real life based on fiery passion alone. You have to have all of that time and those things that Jessie and I have shared."

"I was denied them because of prison, Matt."

"For whatever reason, Jessie was taken from your arms and put into mine. Be honest with yourself, Navarro—what kind of life could you have given her for the past five years, even if you hadn't been recaptured? What would it have been like if she'd run off with you? Or been like for her as Jessie Breed, wife of a prisoner or widow of a hanged man? You didn't want such an existence for her; that's why you left, left alone. You told her you wouldn't return, to start a new life. Now you act as if her doing so was a sin and betrayal."

Those words stung, because Matt was right. Navarro had told Jessie he was never coming back, not to wait for him. He had pushed her toward another man, toward Matt. Jessie and Gran had said Matt was a lot like him, and Matt had been like part of their family for a long time. He had witnessed their closeness. How could he blame Jessie for turning to Matt for love and comfort?

"I need her, Matt. She is my heart. Dreams of her kept me going in prison."

"That's over and you have to wake up. What you need is what she's already done for you. Don't ask for more; I'm begging you."

Navarro knew he had lost this vital battle, but he made one last thrust at his rival. "If you aren't afraid she'll pick me over you, why can't I see her and let her choose? At least explain the truth and say a final good-bye? If you're so confident and what you've said it true, what difference can our meeting make?"

Matt perceived his victory, but he didn't gloat. "Jessie doesn't deserve to be pulled between us, and I don't want to put her under such tension. I told you she's expecting another child. It could be hard on her to see you and talk to you, knowing she had to hurt you again. There's also the men, our hands; if they see you with Lane, much as you two favor each other, they'll guess the truth. You don't want them to know about the truth of his birth. They'll wonder why you left Jessie in that condition and why you never returned. If you didn't relate the whole truth about your past and prison, they'd think badly of you. They liked you and respected you, Navarro; leave it that way."

"But I want Jessie to know the truth, Matt. I don't want her to hate me for what she thinks I did."

"She doesn't, Navarro. Can't you see that in how she helped with your pardon?

You were Jessie's first love; she'll always have special feelings for you. After she has the baby, I'll tell her everything, I swear it. I'll even walk farther with you: when you get settled somewhere, send me your address and I'll keep you informed about Lane and Jessie. If either of them ever needs you, I'll let you know. But you'll need to pick a name to use until I can tell her everything. And if anything happened to me, I'd make certain Jessie knows how to reach you."

"I was offered a job by the Arizona governor. Seems the remaining Apaches, under Nana and Geronimo, are raiding again. They know I'm part Apache so they think I can help them prevent more bloodshed. I've scouted before."

"Do it, Navarro; make your new chance work. Use all the things Jessie taught you." He told him about the loss of his own first love and his acceptance of it. "I found a second love; Jessie did, too. So can you, Navarro. A life with Jessie isn't possible for you now, so why torment all of us? It's in your power to be kind or cruel. I won't try to stop you from seeing Jessie and Lane, but I'm pleading with you to leave us in peace."

Navarro paced as he considered Matt's words. He comprehended what it took for a strong, proud man like Mathew Cordell to beg, and he grasped the man's true motives. His heart ached over this unexpected dilemma. He had been so happy when he was exonerated and set free. Now he felt as if he were staked to a frozen earth and talons of fire were ripping his body apart. "Before I decide, tell me what's happened during the last five years. How's Tom, Gran, and the boys?"

Matt told him all he could. He finished by telling Navarro about the locket incident.

Navarro explained. "When I was trapped, I knew I'd be searched once they'd captured me . . . or killed me. I removed Jessie's picture and hid it in a small crevice in the rocks. I didn't want the law to learn about her. While I was distracted, one of the lawmen sneaked up and clobbered me senseless. When I reached prison, one of the prison guards took the locket. I guess he was the man who gambled it away. I surely could have used its comfort while I was there." He didn't tell Matt he had recovered the picture, worn and faded.

"Why didn't they hang you? Jessie said you killed a guard to escape."

"I was lucky, for once. Another prisoner escaped that same day and he got blamed for that bastard's death. He was shot, so the law never knew I did it. That's why I was returned to prison, not swung from a rope. If I'd known I wasn't charged with murder, I would have turned myself in and finished my sentence so I could earn freedom to return to Jessie. She'd have waited for me."

"Don't you see that it wasn't meant to be for you two? You were cleared of all charges, Navarro. You have an important job offer, a new chance for a fresh beginning. Go after them without hurting everyone here. We're part of your past, too. Let it die, all of it. Please."

Navarro paced again in deep thought. If he were the same man he had been years ago, he wouldn't hesitate a moment before slaying this obstacle to his dream. But he wasn't the Navarro Breed of five years ago; he had changed because of Jessica Lane. As he lived and breathed, he wanted her with every part of his being!

But, Navarro confessed to himself, Jessie must have changed, too, because their long separation had changed everything. Their destiny was no longer as one. Their trails had parted. It was cruel and wrong to force himself into her new life. He couldn't think about what might have been; he had to accept reality. He must make this choice

—sacrifice—for his love and his child. Jessica Lane . . . Cordell had earned a new life, and he could not destroy it and her.

Navarro halted and faced his love's husband. "You win, Matt. You're right. I love Jessie too much to hurt her again. I love my son, too, even if I've never seen him and didn't know about him until today. Promise me you'll take care of Jessie and Lane. Promise you'll send word if they ever need me. You can reach me through the Arizona governor; I'll accept his job offer. That'll give me a starting point."

The rancher shook Navarro's hand, knowing how hard his decision had been. "You have my word of honor, Navarro. I love them and want what's best for them. If I believed that was you, I'd step aside. When the time's right after the baby's born in September, I'll tell Jessie everything about today. Thanks, Navarro," Matt said with a smile of gratitude and tear-filled eyes.

"No, Matt, you can't tell her about today. That would cause trouble between you two."

Shocked, Matt argued, "But that isn't fair to either of you. I can't lie to my wife."

"Staying quiet to prevent trouble and heartache isn't lying."

"It's cows in the same pasture," Matt refuted. "I'd feel dishonest."

"Listen to me," Navarro persisted. "Jessie is a proud and tender-hearted person. She'll be upset we didn't let her make the choice about seeing me or not. She won't believe she needed this kind of protection from either of us. She'll think we treated her like a child. If she learns I was recaptured while trying to return to her, she'll blame herself for what happened to me after I left here. She'll feel guilty and tormented for all the years I had to suffer in prison; I told her what that place was like. If she learns her letters got me freed, she'll feel worse for not trying to help me sooner. I'm sure that's how she'll react. She can't find out you were involved today. She'll be angry at you for withholding the truth for months and for excluding her from our decision today. I don't want Jessie to suffer again, or to cause trouble between you two."

"But—"

"There's a better way for her to hear only what she needs to learn," Navarro interrupted. "Around Christmas, I'll write her a letter. I'll tell her I've been cleared and have a new life. She doesn't have to learn about my troubles of the past five years. I'll tell her I'm fine and safe. I'll say a friend checked on her for me. I'll tell her I'm glad she's married to you, has children, and is doing so well. I'll thank her for all she did for me, but say it's best if we don't meet again. That'll let her know I'm all right and won't be back, let her know I'm aware things are good for her. Hearing about today and the last five years would do more harm than good for Jessie and for your marriage. For her to learn you convinced me to leave without seeing her will make her think you doubted her loyalty, love, and strength; she may think I love her more than you do." Navarro saw the older man grimace at those words. "You told me not to be cruel and selfish, so you do the same. Every time you're tempted to confess, think of the damage the truth can do to your marriage. We both want her happy and protected; this is the best way, the only way, Matt. A short letter will tell her all she ever needs to know about what happened after we parted."

When Matt looked worried and reluctant, Navarro added, "If I can accept and conceal the truth because it's best for Jessie, Lane, and your marriage, so can you. Be strong and generous, Matt; that's what you're asking of me. It's only fair that we partner up this last time to share the responsibility of Jessie and Lane. How could you feel bad about doing what's right for everyone?" Navarro reasoned.

"But you're asking me to deceive my wife. Jessie and I have always been honest with each other."

"Don't be foolish, Matt; it could cost you the same things my mistakes have cost me. You can't just tell Jessie part of what happened here today; if you tell her all of it, you'll hurt her beyond reason. What happens when she comes to find me to make sure I'm all right? What will happen when we talk and try to comfort each other? I'm afraid I wouldn't be able to resist her. You'd have her all confused about love and loyalty, gratitude and guilt. Let it go, Matt, for all our sakes. All I ask is that you contact me if Jessie or Lane ever need me. Otherwise, forget the past, forget today, and forget about me."

Matt contemplated the man's words. He admitted they made sense, but for another woman, not his Jessie. Navarro didn't grasp how it was with married couples who loved and trusted each other. Matt was certain his wife would understand and concur with his decision to protect her in her condition. Matt realized that Navarro hadn't known Jessica Lane well enough long ago, and she had changed—matured—over the years since then. She would not react as the man believed. But Matt was happy and relieved that Navarro was being so unselfish. To prevent fears and worries or Navarro changing his mind, the rancher pretended to agree. "We'll do it your way, Navarro. Thanks." Yet Mathew Cordell knew he would reveal the truth about the other man and today as soon as possible.

*

It was dark outside the Cordell home, but the children were still up, as Matt's tardy return had made the evening meal late. While Jessie and Gran sewed, the rancher read a bedtime story to Lane and Alice, named after Jessie's beloved mother. Sometimes he did the storytelling; other times it was Jessie or her grandmother. A story always settled down the children after an active day.

Lane sat on one leg and Alice on the other, with Matt's arms around them and his hands holding the book they were using tonight: *Adventures of the Smallest Pony*. It had been read many times before, but they never tired of hearing it again. Matt's delivery was entertaining as he used several voices for the different characters and created sound effects for the creatures and events. The children smiled and laughed, and sometimes halted their father to ask the same questions or to make the same comments as in past readings.

With love and patience, the rancher replied with the same answers. Often he glanced at his wife and grinned or winked. Jessie would return his smile with adoring eyes. Neither scolded the children for interrupting or quelled their enthusiasm.

"Got out," Alice squealed with joy when the pony escaped a brush enclosure. "See, run," she said, giggling and clapping her pudgy hands.

At two, the girl's vocabulary increased every week. Jessie and Matt were proud of both their children.

"I wanna pony, Papa," Lane informed his parents as he had done countless times.

"Get a little bigger first," the soft-spoken Matt told him.

"When I'm five?" the four-year-old asked, eyes wide with hope.

"Six is better, son. These legs have to get longer," Matt explained, releasing one hand from the book to playfully shake the boy's knees, then tickle his tummy.

"Why, Papa?" Lane inquired.

"To reach the stirrups. You have to use them for balance when learning to ride. If you don't, you fall off and get hurt."

"I'm going with you tomorrow," Lane reminded Matt.

"Yep, I haven't forgotten, son. We'll ride over to check on the horses after breakfast."

"Me go," their daughter stated, looking at her father with bright eyes.

Matt kissed her forehead and smiled. "Not tomorrow, Alice. You'll get to go on the picnic Saturday to the new pond the boys dug."

"Let your father finish the story, children," Jessie said. "It's very late."

After Matt did so, Lane coaxed, "Read it again, Papa."

He put the book aside. "Another night, son. It's off to bed with you two."

As the couple and their children talked a few minutes, no one noticed the man hiding outside the nearby window who was observing the poignant scene. Navarro Breed had left his mount at a safe distance, then sneaked to the house to see his son and his lost love before riding out of their lives. His secrecy was aided by the wall around the home and bushes near the structure. The hands were all inside the bunkhouse.

Navarro witnessed the love and closeness of the family he was observing. Bittersweet emotions tugged at him. He wished it were he enjoying this family and this special life. He knew for certain now that Mathew Cordell had not lied to him; that made him feel both good and bad.

He gazed at his son as Matt gathered the boy into his arms to put him to bed. Lane did resemble his real father, and that pleased Navarro. He devoured every word, movement, and expression his son used. It hurt to hear the boy call another man "Papa," but the love and rapport those two shared was undeniable. The little girl favored Jessie; Alice was pretty, bubbly, and delightful. Navarro saw Lane hug and kiss his little sister, and the action made the man smile.

Gran, looking older and weaker, took charge of Alice to put her to bed for Jessie. The white-haired woman and Matt left the room to do their tasks. Gran had bid them good night, as she was turning in, too.

Navarro's hungry eyes consumed every inch of Jessica Lane Cordell as she put toys and sewing away. She was more beautiful than five years ago. She wore a loose dress that did not conceal her pregnancy, and Navarro imagined that was how she had looked carrying his son. Her auburn hair was unbound; it flowed silky and wavy down her back. She still kept it cut shorter on the sides and top as she had done for her disguise so long ago in San Angelo. Her skin was smooth and flawless, and glowed with her happiness. Her expressive eyes seemed bluer and clearer; no doubt from peace and joy, he decided. How lovely she was, and he yearned to kiss her and hold her one last time . . . No, he wanted her forever. But that could not be. Once more, it was too late for them. Years ago, he had lost his love because of his dark past. Now, he would lose her again because of her bright future, into which he could not intrude.

Navarro remembered all Jessie had taught him and all she meant to him. When he had met her, he hadn't loved or needed anybody. That was no longer true. She had inspired love, compassion, unselfishness, and courage. He had learned about what makes a home and a family from this unique woman. She had made him laugh and smile, even learn to dance. She had gotten him a pardon and job, even though the law hadn't revealed her part in it when they set him free. Even after thinking he had deserted her, she didn't hate him.

On her ranch, he had made real friends. He had shared a special bond with her brother, one that had helped both of them. But he was not a part of their lives anymore, and that saddened him.

If he hadn't met Jessica Lane and fallen under her influence, his existence would be bleak today. He wouldn't have cared about life or even a new chance. He would still be on the run or dead. He would have been in and out of trouble for the rest of his miserable life. She had saved him and changed him.

He had a fine son. He had beautiful memories. He had a fresh start. Hard as it was to ride away, this time forever, he must and he would. One day his son would own this splendid ranch. Lane would have a better life with Matt than he himself could have offered; and it wasn't right to confuse and hurt the boy now. Lane had a loving and wonderful mother, a good father, and kin. Lane would be happy, respected, be somebody important: things his natural father had been denied. Matt had promised to contact him if trouble arose in the future, and he trusted the rancher. It was time—

Navarro watched as Matt returned to his wife and embraced her. "All done, love."

They sat on the couch and talked, cuddled together. Matt's arm was around Jessie, and her head rested on his strong shoulder. The couple discussed their construction plans for the hands' homes; they spoke of their future, of the child Jessie was carrying. They talked of how much they looked forward to seeing Tom after college ended. They spoke of Mary Louise Lane Blye, who wanted children and who would be visiting them with her physician husband next summer. Matt joked about Miguel and Annie Ortega trying to catch up with them, as they were expecting their third child, too. Jessie reminded Matt of their intention to replace Annie before their next child was born, as Annie had her hands full with her own family. The couple smiled when Matt related that Biscuit Hank, their chuckhouse cook, had finally proposed to a lovely widow in town.

"It's perfect timing, Matt. Hank and his bride can move into one of the new houses, so he can remain with us. Annie and Miguel have asked for one; they need more room. If we get busy, they can be settled before Christmas."

"It shouldn't take long, Jessie. It was a good idea. You're always thinking about everybody else. That's why I love you so much, woman."

"I just want everyone to be as happy and comfortable as we are. If the . . ." She halted and laughed. "The baby's moving. It tickles. Maybe it's a son. Feel."

"Doesn't matter, love; I have a fine son, the best a man could want."

Jessie nestled closer to him. "You're a good father to Lane, Matt."

"It's easy; I love him. Jessie . . ." he began rather hesitantly. "If the day ever comes when Lane needs to know about his real father, we'll tell him the truth. Navarro would be proud of Lane. He left to protect you, so that proves he's a good man. After the baby's born, do you want me to get you the truth about him?"

Jessie turned her head and gazed into her husband's warm brown eyes. "That isn't necessary, Matt. We've done all we can for him. After he left years ago, I had terrible feelings and nightmares that he was in danger. Maybe there was some kind of mental connection to him because I was carrying his child. But lately, especially today, I have this strong feeling that he's all right. I can't explain it, but I sense he truly is safe and free. It's almost as if he knows the truth about us and accepts it. I hope so. It would be so hard to face him and hurt him again. Navarro doesn't deserve more pain and sacrifice. He was a special part of my life, but that was long ago. I'm glad you don't feel threatened by our past. I love you for being so kind and understanding."

Matt kissed her brow. "Perhaps Navarro knows the truth and that's why he's left us alone. He wouldn't do anything to hurt you and Lane. You gave him the strength and courage to fight for a fresh start. Navarro's a special man; he'll win this time. Wherever he is, he knows he's done what's best for all of us."

"I honestly hope so, Matt; that's what I want to believe. Let's get to sleep. The children will be up at dawn and pulling us from our bed."

Matt stood and helped Jessie to her feet. The rancher doused the lamps. With their arms around each other, they headed for the steps and a cozy bed.

Neither saw the man who eased away from the open window, sneaked over the stucco and stone wall, and slipped from their happy life without turning it inside out. Navarro Breed mounted his horse and rode toward Arizona to capture a new dream.

Upstairs, Mathew and Jessica Cordell peeked in on their children. All was quiet. The couple entered their room. Matt undressed and eased into bed. Jessie donned a pretty cotton gown and joined him. They snuggled and kissed.

"Sweet dreams, Jessie," Matt murmured into her ear.

"You, too, my love," she replied, at last feeling as if that was the only kind she would have forever. *You, too, Navarro,* her peaceful heart added.

Epilogue

———— ⊙✑⊙ ————

Mathew and Jessica Cordell stood before the new entrance to their ranch. A large sign hung from the stone arch over the dirt road to their home, one that said L/C Ranch: their stock brand, ranch name, and the initials of their two sons. Matt was behind Jessie, his arms wrapped around her slender waist. Both gazed at the sign and thought of the bond it represented.

Jessie reflected on all that had brought them to this September day in 1882. She knew her father and mother would be happy, and proud of her. She had never learned who had slain Jedidiah Lane six years ago, but she had to believe his killer had met justice. At least, the man who ordered his murder had been punished.

Jessie didn't want to dwell on sad matters today. She had two fine sons: Lane and Lance Cordell, brothers who would share this magnificent and profitable spread one day. She had a beautiful vivacious daughter who would be given the chance to choose her own path; Alice would never be treated or viewed as a son, as she herself had been for twenty-four years. Yet the redhead was not bitter about the way she'd been raised. Jed had never meant to harm any of his three children. They all loved him. She knew her father must be resting easier now that Mary Louise and Tom were so much happier.

So much had happened this summer. A healthy and happy Thomas Lane had returned from college in June, with only a slight and almost unnoticeable limp. His new glasses provided perfect vision and looked appealing on the handsome auburn-haired nineteen-year-old. Tom had brought home a lovely girl named Sarah Jane Tims, and the engaged couple had wed in late July. With the Cordells' backing, Tom and his bride had opened a mercantile store in Davis that was doing well.

Mary Louise and Dr. John Blye had accompanied Tom home. They had visited with her family until after the wedding. Everyone, but particularly Jessie and Gran, had been astonished and pleased by the good changes in the beautiful blonde who radiated with happiness. Powerful love, Jessie decided, was a great medicine for the sick in heart, spirit, or body. Since returning home to Philadelphia, news had arrived by letter this month revealing Mary Louise's first pregnancy. Both the Blyes and Cordells were thrilled.

Gran, at seventy-six, still insisted on doing chores in the house. She loved her grandchildren and great-grandchildren, and was happy all the family were friends at last. The few bouts of forgetfulness or confusion she had these days were harmless.

Most of the original Lane hands still worked for them. Five couples—including

Annie and Miguel Ortega, Hank Epps and his wife, and Jefferson Clark and his new bride—occupied the cozy houses on the site of the old homestead. It was nice having good neighbors for the adults and playmates for the children. Since both towns—Davis and Stockton—were so far for daily travel and both schools were crowded, Jessie and Matt had decided to construct a small schoolhouse on their property for all the children.

As Jessie had thought over the last six years, she realized how one dream had been exchanged for another, one man for another. She could not help but wonder how Navarro Breed was doing.

Following Lance's birth a year ago, Matt had told her about Navarro's visit and the men's talk last June. Jessie had been relieved and saddened to learn why Navarro had been unable to contact her or return to her. At last she was able to understand and forgive. She was proud of her role, and Matt's, in his new life. She believed the two men had made the right and kindest decision for everyone last year. She understood why Navarro hadn't wanted Matt to tell her about their meeting, but dear Matt knew her so well, as it should be between a husband and wife.

Hopefully Navarro had found real peace and happiness, as his brief letter last December had indicated. Jessie wanted those things for him; she prayed his claims were true, not just meant to protect her from some awful truth. More and more Lane favored his real father; but the dark-haired, hazel-eyed boy had Mathew Cordell's personality. In all but blood, Lane was Matt's son.

In his letter, Navarro had told how he'd been exonerated of all charges, found a good job and a contented life. He had said he stayed away all those years to protect both of them and to give each a chance for a fresh start alone. He had revealed that he'd checked on her to make certain she was all right. Since she was also doing so well, he had felt it was best not to meet again and stir up the past. He had thanked her for her role in changing him. He had intended to let the past stay buried, but her letters to several Arizona authorities—passed on to him because of his job—encouraged him to write so she wouldn't worry about him any longer. He had mentioned prison reforms, and she was delighted about them. He had said he was happy for her, and knew she'd feel the same for him.

Jessie was relieved Navarro had written instead of visiting. Yet she hated that he would never know his son, even though it was important for everyone's happiness. He was living and working in Arizona as a scout, translator, and peacemaker between the whites and Apaches. She was relieved the skilled half-white warrior was there to keep the raiding Apaches from heading this way. But she hadn't tried to contact him, as gently ordered. Jessie was glad Navarro Breed had made a fresh start, and she treasured not only his sacrifices of six years ago but the final one of last year. Knowing he was alive and well gave her peace and joy.

For most of her life, she had lived as Jed's "son," as Jess Lane. Navarro had ended her passionless existence. She had loved him wildly and freely, rashly and blindly. If he had returned in time, she would have lost herself again as Navarro's woman.

With Matt, she had found her real self, the woman she was meant to be. She had grown and matured; she had stayed strong, and had gotten stronger. She loved her husband and needed him, just as he loved and needed her. They were so alike, so special as one. Mathew Cordell was her destiny. A turbulent life was behind her. A good life was with and before her.

Jessie turned to face her husband. She hugged him tightly. When he laughed and questioned the meaning of her emphatic squeeze, she gazed into his eyes and said,

"For so long I was searching for a beautiful dream, and it was right before me when I awoke from my girlish sleep. I love you, Matt; I think I always did. I just had to become a woman before I could understand that. I'm glad you gave me time to grow up and you let me capture you."

The grinning man returned her smile. "I love you, too, Mrs. Cordell." Matt could not help but think about the man—the half-breed drifter—who had helped make this blissful life possible. He knew Navarro would keep his word about staying away. Yet, if trouble came down the road one day, Jessie knew where and how to locate Navarro Breed for help, protection, and comfort.

Jessie cuddled closer to her husband. With Matt at her side and in her arms, the L/C Ranch would become famous far and wide. Jessie lifted her head and kissed him deeply. She had sought to follow the wind with a daring desperado, but now she possessed a beautiful and priceless love.

Kiss of the Night Wind

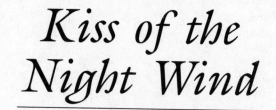

Come with me, my fiery vixen,

"And I would love you all the day,
Every night would kiss and play,
If with me you'd fondly stray
Over the hills and far away,"

JOHN GAY

"And o'er the hills and far away
Beyond their utmost purple rim,
Beyond the night, across the day,
Through all the world she followed him."

ALFRED TENNYSON

Until for Rogue Vixen's heart did burn,
Until for Rogue Vixen's soul did yearn,
Until for Rogue all else did fade,
Until Vixen Rogue had betrayed . . .

Chapter

1

If this doesn't work out and you get caught, Carrie Sue Stover, as surely as the summer's hot, you'll either swing from a rope or waste away in some awful prison! Ever alert and wary, Carrie Sue scanned her surroundings and strained to hear each sound, her senses sharpened from years on the run. Being with strangers always made her nervous, as she constantly feared being recognized and arrested even this far from Texas and her infamous reputation.

The redhead continued dressing in a small room which she had shared last night with another female passenger at the "home station." She had traveled from Fort Worth on this stage line, a coach which halted every night, unlike the Butterfield stage which halted once every twenty-four hours for passengers to get sorely needed sleep. Between these rustic inns which were owned and operated by the Garrett Overland Company, the coach stopped for fresh horses at relay stations where the passengers could eat and freshen up.

Her roommate, a soldier's wife from back East, had completed her grooming quickly and left the cramped room, almost as if she were afraid of Carrie Sue. The redhead frowned, knowing that her thoughts were groundless and it only proved that she was too mistrustful of most people. She had given the timid woman no reason to be afraid of her. The soldier's wife, who had joined them yesterday at Fort Bowie to complete her journey to Fort Verde, had jumped at every twist and turn, at every sudden voice or stranger's glance. Without a doubt, she concluded, the Eastern female was petrified of her own shadow. How, the redhead wondered, would the pitiful creature ever survive the wild west?

Carrie Sue shook her head in sympathy. She vigorously brushed her long hair to remove as much trail dust as possible. Whether it be in a rented tub of hot suds or in a cold stream, she hated not having daily baths. She was eager to reach her destination where a good scrubbing from head to toe would be her first priority.

Carrie Sue glanced at the brush she was holding whose handle was marked with a painted "C.S.S." Suppressing guilt, she repacked the confiscated belongings of Miss Carolyn Sarah Starns. She wanted to believe that fate had decreed that the Butterfield Stage would overturn between St. Louis and Fort Worth during a robbery attempt by her brother's gang. All the passengers had been killed, including a Texas Ranger and the young woman whose identity and possessions she had stolen in a moment of desperation.

If the driver had reined up that day near Sherman, Texas as ordered by Darby

Stover instead of recklessly charging her brother's gang and trying to outrun them, the fatal crash would not have occurred. Carrie Sue wished it could have been avoided, but no one could bring the innocent victims back to life. Upon learning the female passenger was dead, Carrie Sue had been compelled by some inexplicable force to search her belongings to learn something about the unfortunate woman. From the woman's letters and detailed diary, Carrie Sue had made a startling discovery and found the answer to her problems.

Carolyn Starns had been a twenty-one-year-old orphan who was heading to Tucson to become the town's new schoolmarm. The lovely brunette would be a stranger there. By the time the gang had completed their task, Carrie Sue knew what she wanted to do, what she had to do. The chance at a new life had been too tempting to ignore. Carolyn looked enough like Carrie Sue . . . but their initials and sizes were eerily the same. It had to work!

So, after her brother helped her bury the teacher's body miles from the scene of their crime, on April twenty-eighth of '76, Carrie Sue Stover became Miss Carolyn Sarah Starns. Today, May tenth, she was on her way to blissful freedom in a Tucson schoolhouse as long as no one recognized her. That was a strong possibility since her wanted poster was done so poorly, by Quade Harding's nefarious design!

The redhead was tired of running and hiding, tired of being scared, tired of being shot at, and tired of being pursued until she was exhausted or provoked into lethal self-defense. She was tired of innocent people getting hurt, and of being accused of crimes which she and the gang hadn't committed. She'd been forced into a life of crime at the tender age of seventeen—she'd never wanted to live this way! Several times she had tried to "go straight" and once she had risked turning herself in to the law and ending this awful existence. All of those desperate actions had failed. Too, she had heard of how horrible prison was for women, and that three female outlaws had been hanged in the last few years by crazed mobs!

Carrie Sue wanted a normal life. She longed for peace and safety. She wanted to fall in love, to have a husband, a home, a family. She wanted this soul-wrenching loneliness and misery to end. She wanted to ranch again, to work alongside her family. She wanted to be the Carrie Sue Stover she had been at seventeen before her life was torn asunder by a greedy man named Quade Harding.

The lovely outlaw sighed wearily as she braided her hair. She secured the long plait near her nape and fluffed her thick, wavy bangs over her forehead in an attempt to avoid calling attention to the fiery locks that had caused the law to brand her the "Texas Flame." How she yearned to gaze toward a bright future rather than looking over her shoulder for trouble. This opportunity had fallen into her lap like a miracle, and she had taken advantage of it. In a way, she was giving God a helping hand with her survival. If no one recognized her, her dreams could be realized. She had to make this work. She had to!

So far, Quade Harding had still not released an accurate sketch of her that could insure her capture or possibly cause her death. No, Quade Harding wanted her alive, wanted her as his private prisoner. In May of '74, Quade had furnished the law with her name and a poor drawing of Darby Stover's sister, but only to frighten her and to remind her of her precarious existence which he could destroy at any moment.

Unlike posters for the other members of the Stover Gang, her wanted poster demanded that she be turned in *alive* to Quade Harding for a payment of five thousand dollars in gold. The law, on the other hand, was offering two thousand paper dollars for her capture, *preferably* alive. She knew the reason for Quade's stipulation; he wanted to use his power and money to obtain control of her. As long as no one learned she was the "Texas Flame," Carrie Sue was safe; she could make a fresh start in Tucson. But what, she mused frantically, if Quade decided he would see her dead if he couldn't have her alive? All he had to do was release a better description.

"Breakfast!" the station keeper shouted and interrupted her worrying.

With increased haste Carrie Sue finished her task. As she buttoned the front of her dress, she was relieved that Carolyn's clothes, although rather plain and inexpensive, were comfortable and appropriate for her new status. Judging from the way she had packed her belongings, Carolyn had been a precise and careful person.

"It's on the table and going fast!" the second announcement came.

Carrie Sue entered the adjoining room. The mouth-watering smells of cat's-head biscuits, fried bacon, perked coffee, and flour gravy reached her nose. She inhaled, realizing how hungry she was. *No more trail food,* her mind sang happily, and no more choking down food on the run or on the impatient Butterfield stageline which she had used earlier. Thank goodness the frugal Carolyn had wanted to save money by purchasing a ticket between Fort Worth and Tucson from Garrett lines which traveled more cheaply but much more slowly. Knowing the routine by now, she walked toward a wooden table to join the driver, guard, woman, and the men who had caught the stage two days ago.

Instantly she sighted a handsome stranger sitting there and eating calmly. At her approach, he glanced her way for a moment, his rapid and probing gaze sliding over her before it returned to his meal. Everything and everyone in the room except him vanished briefly. Her heart pounded in trepidation. Numerous questions about him filled her mind. She trembled, but struggled to regain her poise.

The only vacant seat was across from the black-haired male whose presence seemed to fill the room, and Carrie Sue took it. She eased her chair to the table and placed the red-checked napkin in her lap as her mother had taught her long ago. *Relax,* she ordered. *He's only a customer. If not, you can bluff your way out with Carolyn's identity.*

When he looked up from his plate, she was astonished to feel weakened and warmed by his smokey gray gaze. Why was she feeling this way? She had lived among men for years!

In what seemed to be only a second, the darkly tanned stranger scrutinized her thoroughly. She could tell his mind was quick and keen, so she tried to keep her expression blank. His stubbled jawline and upper lip said he hadn't shaved in a day or two, but his face and hands were freshly scrubbed and his collar-length hair was combed. He was dressed in a faded gray shirt and jeans, both snug enough to evince a muscular body and worn enough to imply his funds were limited. Sleeves rolled to his elbows revealed a lean hardness in his forearms. He looked up again and nodded a polite greeting which caused a midnight lock to fall across his forehead, and he left it there as he returned to his meal.

A drifter? she wondered. *Can't be,* she reasoned. *His body is too well-honed and his movements are too controlled for an easy-going cowpoke. Who is he and what's he doing here? That sketch hardly favors me, but what if he guesses the truth and challenges me?*

Carrie Sue tried to keep her hands from shaking and rattling the dishes as she served herself. For a reason which she couldn't grasp and a reaction which she couldn't halt, she had difficulty eating, and more difficulty keeping her disobedient eyes off of him. She had been around countless men, but none had affected her this way. She found herself wanting to stare at him, to talk with him, to share passion with him. That was crazy! He was a stranger, perhaps even a threat to her.

Beneath lowered lashes as she nibbled at a large biscuit, she eyed the enticing span of hairy chest which was showing above the three buttons which he had left unfastened. His features were strong and appealing.

She observed the way he sat in his chair, leaving room between his chest and the table and between his back and the chair to allow for rapid movement if it was required. The other men chatted amiably, but the stranger kept quiet. Even so, she realized that he caught every word spoken and each move made, that he was in full control of himself and any situation. The others might think he was totally relaxed or distracted, but she knew better. Yes, he was alert and guarded; those were traits which she recognized too well. She knew he could spring into action swifter than she could blink if danger approached. She wondered on which side of the law this man stood. And was he here to eat or was he biding time for an unknown purpose?

The stranger finished his breakfast and laid his fork on the empty plate. After his coffee cup was refilled, he propped his left elbow on the table and placed his thumb along his sturdy jawline with his first two fingers entrapping a cleft chin between them. As if in deep thought, he absently rubbed his jawbone with his thumb, causing the dark stubble growing there to make a noise which he did not seem to hear. Those smokey gray eyes boldly studied her in a manner which warned her that he knew she had been furtively doing the same with him, studied her as if he were trying to figure out a crucial puzzle. Maybe, as Kale Rushton had told her long ago, fear had an odor, and this man had detected it in the air. Certainly that would cause a gunslinger, if that's what he was, to become intrigued.

Carrie Sue struggled to ignore him, but his pull was too strong. Her gaze fused with his, and she felt as if he was probing the depths of her soul. Her cheeks flushed slightly. The handsome stranger glanced at her dark blue cotton dress with small white cuffs and collar and at her neat hairstyle. She heard a deep inhalation and exhalation of air through his shapely nose as his eyes narrowed, but not in a menacing way. For an instant she read doubt in those smokey depths. His gaze shifted to her left hand. One brow lifted inquisitively. He studied her again and confusion—an obviously unusual emotion for him—briefly filled his eyes.

"Can I give you anything, Miss?" he asked, his voice teasing over Carrie Sue's flesh like blazing sunshine on a frigid day. When her expression said she was astonished at him speaking to her, he half-grinned—only the left corner of his sensual mouth lifting—as if to imply she should have expected his response to her behavior. He lifted his cup and sipped coffee as he brazenly observed her over its rim.

While she collected her wits, Carrie Sue watched the steamy curls from the hot coffee tickle his nose and dampen it. She noticed the enticing humor in his potent gaze which implied that his real query had nothing to do with food. She was baffled, as he did not seem to be the kind of male who flirted with a strange woman, or one who had to make any effort to get a female's undivided attention. There was something about the way he was eyeing her that made her tension increase. This was something more than a man admiring a pretty face; there was an array of emotions battling within him.

What if he's a bounty hunter? What if he's playing games with me? Or trying to decide what to do about me? How she wished she had her Remington revolvers nearby for comfort, but they were concealed in Carolyn Starns's baggage. Besides, she doubted she could defend herself against this particular man. The way he moved, looked, even breathed told her of his enormous prowess. The flaming haired female shifted in her chair, unnerved by his overt attention. Maybe he was only intrigued by her scent of fear, or responsive to her unintentionally enticing behavior. She reminded herself to behave as the respectable and studious schoolmarm. "No, thank you," she replied in a ladylike manner and dismissive tone. She focused her eyes on her food, but was intensely aware of him.

Suddenly he stood, pushing back his chair with his legs, and walked to the front wall. Recovering his gunbelt from a peg, he strapped it around his firm waist, the way he buckled it exposing that he favored his . . . *right* hand. Strange, she would have sworn he was left-handed. The holsters held two Frontier Colts, the '73 model, six-shot, forty-five caliber, single action. As he bent forward to secure the dangling thongs about his thighs, Carrie Sue observed his lithe movements. Before putting a dark hat on his ebony head and settling it into place, he pulled on a brown leather vest which was as worn as his shirt and jeans. He retrieved a Winchester '73 lever-action rifle from where he had leaned it against the door jamb.

"A fine meal, Sam," he told the station keeper and smiled broadly, a smile which captivated Carrie Sue and sent tingles over her body.

The burly man in a stained white apron smiled and responded, "Most folks say I got the best vittles on any line. Stop in again to fill yore belly. I cook a kill-for stew on Tuesdays and Thursdays."

The appealing stranger tossed Sam an extra coin, glanced back at the beautiful redhead, shrugged as if she puzzled him, then departed.

Carrie Sue heard a horse gallop away, but only half-prayed she had seen him for the last time. She waited patiently while the other passengers, the two men and the soldier's wife, completed their meals. The driver and guard loaded their baggage and summoned them.

For a moment, the fleeing desperado wondered if she should buy or steal a horse and escape this area as swiftly as possible, just in case that virile stranger was after her. No, she bravely decided. This chance for a new life was too good to pass up without proof he was on her trail. If he had delayed her capture with the hope of her leading him to Darby and his gang, he would have a long wait!

"All's away!" the driver shouted to let the passengers know he was leaving so they wouldn't be thrown backwards roughly when the horses jerked against the harnesses and the stage's weight.

Tomorrow night, she would be in Tucson. There were only a few more stops for fresh horses, meals, and one night's sleep between her and her destination. Suspense, eagerness, and hope filled Carrie Sue Stover and diverted her from thoughts of the stranger.

The stage had passed the Dragoon Springs station where an Apache massacre had occurred in '58. The road was flanked by impressive mountains. They had made it through the Chiricahua range which had been Cochise's stronghold until four years ago when the infamous Apache chief had agreed to settle on a reservation. Carrie Sue looked out the window, as did the other three passengers. No one chatted, which suited her just fine.

The arid countryside possessed a wild beauty with its abundance of blooming yuccas, entangling catclaw, bean laden mesquite, paloverde, snakeweed, and countless other sturdy plants and small trees which could survive this harsh area and climate. A variety of cacti, some crouching low to the ground and some standing tall and green against the blue skyline, was scattered before her line of vision. The coach had passed through many mountain ranges, but the landscape in this flash flood region was relatively flat.

She watched the scenery alternate between scrub-covered areas with an occasional hill, to sparsely vegetated areas, and sites with countless boulders and brown mountains on all sides. In some places, grass was a yellowy tan, or pale green, or nonexistent. At times thousands of yuccas grew on both sides of the road; at other times, only scrubs and small trees were visible. She noticed that the mountains had an almost purply brown color—unlike the vivid reds, grays, and blacks of Texas mountains or the heavily forested green ones of Georgia.

Carrie Sue's eyes had rested enough to return to her task, which was a difficult one in the jouncing coach. She wanted to read Carolyn Starns's letters and diary as many times as possible before she reached Tucson so she would know the woman's life by heart. She could not afford any slip-ups when she met her contact tomorrow and began her new job. She had practiced signing Carolyn's name until she could do it perfectly. She had learned why Carolyn had purchased a ticket for this cheaper stageline, to save money. The brunette was intent upon saving enough to buy a dress shop with a small home attached.

Carrie Sue hated sewing. But when she claimed the money which Carolyn had transferred to the Tucson bank, she would not squander those hard-earned dollars; she would use them wisely. Carolyn had no need for them and she had no family to claim the shattered-dream fund. Carrie Sue would use the money for a promising future, just as Carolyn had meant to do.

She also studied the school books in Carolyn's baggage to refresh herself on "reading, writing, and arithmetic," along with history and geography. She was glad her mother had insisted on educating her and that she'd always loved learning. She went over sample lesson plans to familiarize herself with presenting information to various ages, as the Tucson school included first through eighth grades. Carrie Sue smiled, for she felt confident she would make a good schoolmarm. If she didn't like teaching, she could change jobs later, after she was certain her new identity cloaked her securely.

Following the midday meal, the other three passengers dozed in the warm stage which was traveling at an almost rocking pace in the heat of the day. Carrie Sue leaned her head against the coach and closed her eyes to think about her brother and their stormy past. While there was not an accurate picture of herself on her wanted poster, Darby and his gang were not as fortunate. She worried about her brother. Darby had been such a cheerful, easy-going, likable person before Quinn Harding and his lecherous son Quade had ruined his life. She fretted over how Darby was changing, especially during the last two years since Quade had released her brother's picture and name and had tagged his band the Stover Gang: a vicious trick to flush her into the open again. The longer Darby was an outlaw and the more he was forced to do to survive, the harder he would become.

She and Darby had been born and raised in Georgia, until a greedy Carpetbagger wanted their farm following the War Between the States. The northern controlled law had refused to protect them when they were forced to sell out for less than half of the land's value or risk imprisonment for allegedly unpaid taxes. After her father secretly took revenge on the villain, they had left Georgia to make a new life elsewhere, finally settling in Texas. Her parents, Martha and John Henry Stover, had come upon another Southerner in dire straits and purchased his ranch near Brownwood. But Quinn Harding and his son had wanted to add it to their large spread, the QH Ranch, a fact the seller—who despised the Hardings—had not told them. Her father had refused to sell out to the Hardings, refused to be forced from his land and home again. Within a year, her parents had been killed and the Hardings had taken control of the small ranch with a coveted water supply and lush grasslands. This time, their unpaid bank loan had been used as the so-called legal means to steal all the Stover's possessions. Lacking evidence against the Hardings, there had been nothing she and Darby could do, or so the Hardings had believed.

In '69, at the age of seventeen, she had gone to work in the Harding home as the housekeeper's helper to spy on them for her brother. The elder Harding, a hateful man, had treated her as a slave—someone to dominate and cruelly tease. She had despised waiting upon Quinn Harding, who had been crippled three months earlier from a fall. It was that accident which had placed Quade in control of the QH Ranch, their evil plans, and all of their hirelings. She had learned about payroll shipments, cattle drives, auctions, and more—information she had passed on to Darby and the gang he had formed to destroy the Hardings. The unknown band of outlaws had cut fences, rustled cattle, burned barns and fields, and stolen payrolls—anything to punish the Hardings.

In the beginning, she and Darby had been concerned only with justice and revenge. But her furtive activities had been discovered by the lustful Quade who had watched her too closely. After seven months on the ever-increasing QH Ranch, she had been compelled to flee Quade's wicked demands and his threats about unmasking her brother.

From his wheelchair, "Old Man Harding" had ordered his devious son to hire gunslingers to guard his spread and bounty hunters to destroy his persistent enemies. Quade had agreed to a certain point but, despite his family's losses, he had not told his father or the law about Carrie's involvement or about the gang's identity. She had been surprised and confused by Quade's silence, until she guessed his motive: he wanted to capture her, not have the law do it.

After several run-ins with detectives Quade had hired, Darby had ceased his harassment of the Hardings, and they had fled into the Oklahoma Territory. They had lain low there all winter, until a lack of supplies had forced them to pull off raids in Oklahoma and Kansas. For a year, dressed as a boy and masked, she had ridden occasionally with Darby's gang as they eluded Quade's relentless detectives and struggled to survive. But unless it was too perilous to leave her behind, she remained in hidden camps because Darby didn't want her—a fiery-haired female—to be sighted and remembered. The same was true when the boys visited towns in small groups, which was possible since their faces and names were unknown. Still, no matter where they journeyed, they had to be on constant guard. And she, at eighteen, could do nothing except tag along for safety.

With no place to live and on the run from Quade's cohorts and the law, Darby's gang had begun to commit other crimes, mainly robberies and rustlings. Carrie Sue had realized her brother's gang was becoming too much like other outlaws or the men she wanted to punish, but she was caught up in the band's crimes and too fearful of capture to leave.

When the men had grown restless in camp and supplies had run out, the gang had made their raids. Yet, Darby Stover was careful not to kill, and he never attacked poor folks. Sometimes, he gave money to people in dire straits whom they met along the way. For those reasons, his reputation became the colorful one of a hero more than that of a ruthless outlaw. Darby's rule had been "Never kill anybody unless you have to save your hide 'cause it only gives lily-livered men the guts to join posses and chase our tails to kingdom's come. Folks will allow robbing but not killing. They know we'll treat them fair, so they yield without trouble. Some of them even enjoy being held up by the Stover Gang."

In late 71, she was desperate to break free from her offensive life and Quade's obsessive pursuit. She tried to make a fresh start by working in a mercantile store in Sante Fe. To go unnoticed, she dressed plainly, kept her eyes lowered timidly to hide their color, and covered her fiery hair with a dark brown net. Her freedom lasted only ten months before one of Quade's detectives tracked her down and delivered his intimidating threat: "Marry me and I'll get the charges against you dropped. If not, I'll see to it you and your brother are imprisoned and hanged."

Carrie Sue had heard tales about the treatment of female captives. The law could kill her as punishment, but never send her to prison! She would do just about anything to avoid that degrading existence. She had used her wits and skills to overcome the clever detective. She had fled to one of Darby's hideouts and nervously waited for three wintry months until her brother arrived to lay low and found her there.

At twenty, she was thrown into the gang again, and rode with them from March of '72 until April of '73. To protect her identity, she continued to dress as a boy, to conceal her hair, and to wear a mask.

Things had changed over the years, mainly because they were charged with crimes which they hadn't committed. Clearly the gang's reputation was suffering from the false accusations and wild newspaper stories, and sometimes from the bitter truth. During her absences, Darby had begun hiring other outlaws to help pull certain jobs. Her brother was a strong leader who tried to choose his men carefully, but a "rotten seed" sometimes slipped past his keen wits. It was those rare mistakes who were hard to control at all times, mistakes who got them into trouble with unwanted violence. Still, Darby Stover was responsible for his gang's actions.

Carrie Sue admitted to herself that she wished she had never gotten involved in such a wicked existence, even to punish the Hardings. Perhaps the grief and anger she'd felt after her parent's deaths had made her too susceptible to Darby's scheme.

In April of '73, Darby and his men had grown tired of roaming and of being chased. They had realized their luck could not last forever. One truth could not be denied or halted: every fast gun and strong body eventually slowed, every keen eye and mind dulled with age.

The men who had ridden with Darby from the start put their money together and purchased a ranch near Laredo from a widow who could no longer manage alone. On April nineteenth, for a pleasant change, she had celebrated her twenty-first birthday in happiness and peace. As they had always been masked during their crimes and Quade had continued to hold silent, their identities had remained unknown. Still, they had taken the precaution of changing their names. For eight wonderful months all went well, even if Darby wouldn't allow her to leave the new seclusion of their new home. Then, Quade's detectives had located them again, forcing them to leave the ranch and new life behind. They had fled to Mexico for the next few months.

That time, Quade became desperate, impatient, and dangerous. He released the descriptions and names of Darby and his men in hopes of flushing the gang—no, her—into the open. He hired an artist to provide the law with accurate sketches of the men. Yet, Carrie Sue's wanted poster still lacked her sketch and identity, containing only a vague description of a fiery-haired female. He had labeled her the "Texas Flame," a nickname which had stuck to her.

She had been lucky to remain a secret over the years. Her family had not lived near Brownwood very long when they were slain, so few people had met her there. She had been over seven years younger and her looks had changed greatly since '69. Her short, dark auburn hair was now—due to hours beneath the sun and years of growing—a long "flaming red mane with a golden soul" as Darby put it. Nor was she a "skinny kid" any longer. Anyone who might have met her as the sixteen or seventeen year old Carrie Sue Stover was either employed by the Hardings or had been run out of Texas by them. No doubt, Quade had ordered everyone on the ranch to keep silent about her looks and, considering her scanty poster, his father must have agreed to let Quade have his way in this matter, if the old man even knew about it.

Maybe Quade's relentless pressure was partly her fault. At times, she had led him on, boldly and vindictively tantalizing him with what he could never have. She had made him crave her to the point of taking any risk or paying any cost to have her. Yet, as an innocent seventeen-year-old, she had not fully understood the hazardous trail she was taking with that unpredictable villain. But marry her? She didn't believe him. Probably Quade wanted to force her to become his defenseless and slavish whore, to punish her for duping and eluding him! Without a doubt, both Harding men were evil and cold-blooded.

For the past two years, she had stayed with the gang, becoming widely known as the mysterious "Texas Flame." She had given up trying to tuck her thick hair beneath a hat and banding her breasts tightly to conceal the shapely feminine figure which her cotton skirts and snug jeans insisted on revealing. But she still wore a mask to hide her identity and made certain to keep her distance from their victims to prevent anyone from noticing her unusual periwinkle eyes.

She knew what most men thought and said about her, "a wildcat to be tamed" or a "sly vixen to be captured and punished." Yet, Carrie Sue only shot in self-defense if she was cornered. Even then, she gave her pursuer many chances to retreat or yield before firing.

But things had worsened over the years. With the men's faces and names known, they could no longer travel at will. And they all feared that Quade would panic and expose her at any time. Carrie Sue was sickened by the accidental deaths like Carolyn's and the Ranger's two weeks ago, and a mother's and her child's in March near San Angelo.

Her worst experience had been in August of '75 when a Texas Ranger snared her. She had the drop on him, but couldn't shoot him, so she surrendered. The vile lawman had physically and mentally abused her, and had tried to ravish her. With skills taught to her by Kale Rushton—a half-Apache member of Darby's gang—she had thwarted the wicked Ranger and escaped. That experience had taught her that the law couldn't be trusted. She also had learned that the authorities were no longer lenient with female criminals, especially those without children.

She had been given no choice except to stay with the gang. Anger and resentment gnawed at her. Being a woman, she couldn't take off to faraway places without plenty of money, a job, or a partner. Often women were trapped in terrible situations because good and safe choices were so few. To have raced off with the blind hope of finding a lucky opportunity would have been reckless. Every time she had been on her own, numerous men had tried to take advantage of her. She was a good shot and fighter, but she could not call attention to herself by going around killing or beating wicked men all the time! And once Quade raised the amounts of his rewards, listing "Dead or Alive" in all cases but hers, bounty hunters and vicious gunslingers became a threat to them. Everyone knew that bounty hunters were like badgers; they never let go of their prey. At least she had her brother and his gang to protect her from beasts like the Hardings, their detectives, bounty hunters, posses, lawmen, and gunslingers.

Off and on for seven years she was a daring desperado in Texas, Oklahoma, New Mexico, and Kansas. But she had faced the truth long ago. Her deeds were no longer a matter of honor and vengeful justice. The harsh demands of a criminal's life—the cold, the rain, the dust, the hunger, the desperation—were wearing. She couldn't pretend to be cold, hard, and tough any longer. She was tired of having no home, no meaning to her life, and no friends except other bandits. And, she admitted, she hated what people thought about her.

Too, real life was passing her by swiftly. She was twenty-four, a spinster by custom. She had never been married, never had a child, never even had a lover! To keep galloping down the wrong road was like recklessly racing toward a box canyon with a crazed posse hot on your tail. Surely Fate had forced this life-saving decision upon her.

After concealing Carolyn's body and fleeing the soldiers who were approaching the overturned stage, Darby and his men had headed for a hideout in the Oklahoma Territory, hoping to stay unnoticed for a few months while "heads cooled a mite in these parts."

The soldiers had taken "Carolyn Starns" to the next Butterfield station to continue her journey following a "lucky rescue just in the nick of time." Since that tragic day, she had switched to this Garrett stage in Fort Worth for the remainder of her trip to Tucson.

The redhead knew her brother was worried about her daring plan, but he had agreed with it because he was more concerned about himself and his gang endangering her on the trail. If anything went wrong, she knew where and how to contact Darby.

Gunshots filled the air and ceased her musings. Carrie Sue glanced out the window and sighted the trouble. As the driver urged the horses to outrun the bandits who were attacking it, the stage lurched wildly, hurling the two passengers on the other seat toward her and the man beside her. Obviously the driver had seen the six masked men galloping from behind a hill toward them and had decided to make a desperate race for the next relay station, which baffled and alarmed her because it was twenty miles down the road. It was a policy of stagelines to yield to robbers to safeguard passengers' lives, but the rash driver must have felt that he and the guard could successfully discourage the bandits, as he surely could not race the horses at breakneck speed for hours.

Carrie Sue and the other man helped the two fallen passengers back into their places. The holdup made no sense to her, as it was common knowledge that the Garrett line carried no mail or strongboxes; the Butterfield line performed those perilous tasks. The Garrett line was known for its passenger comfort because of its slower pace and fewer robberies. Averaging five miles an hour for nine to ten hours a day in comparison to Butterfield's rapid nine miles per hour and fewer stops, this line only covered forty to fifty miles a day and halted every night instead of every twenty-four hours for sleep. They had been on the road for five hours today, and Tucson was about sixty miles ahead of them. So close for trouble to defeat her!

The stage bounced up and down roughly, shaking them about like cotton balls in a flour sack. Many sounds assailed her ears: the driver's whip slapping against horse-flesh; the metal and wood creaking in protest; the pounding of many hooves and the labored breathing of the frantic animals; the exchange of gunfire. The soldier's wife began screaming hysterically and the two men cursed in fear.

Carrie Sue saw the guard's body fall from the stage and tumble several times upon the hard ground. Hills, trees, yuccas, and brown mountains flashed by swiftly. The man on the seat beside her slumped into her lap as a bullet caught him in the head, staining her dress with blood. She did not shove his body aside because it would probably only fall her way again. The other man drew a small pistol and began firing at the outlaws. She shouted a warning but he sneered at her. He, too, was shot and killed.

As Carrie Sue peered out the window to see how close the gang was, the soldier's wife—in a panic over the horrible tales she had been told about the Wild West—screamed, "They'll rape us and murder us!" The woman seized the dead man's gun and shot herself in the head before Carrie Sue could grab the weapon from her. The redhead gasped at the shocking sight. She looked at the three bloody bodies which surrounded her and heard the peril closing in on her. These bandits were merciless, and she did not want to imagine what they would do to her. Now she knew what it was like to be a helpless victim. As Kale vowed, she had actually smelled fear and death in the air, and its odor was foul in her nostrils. Carrie Sue knew she wasn't anything like these heartless outlaws; yet, she wanted to gun them down! Dare she reveal who she was? Would it matter to them that she was Darby Stover's sister, that she was the "Texas Flame?" If she exposed herself, probably they would take her with them and there was no telling what would happen to her in their camp!

Outlaws were galloping on both sides of the coach. The driver reined in and yielded only to be shot by the bandit leader. Carrie Sue wished fervently she had her revolvers or rifle inside the coach. She was an excellent shot and her aid might have swung the odds in their favor. She knew better than to hide her money—no, Carolyn Starns's money—even in her bodice. She knew better than to give the cutthroats any trouble. She knew from experience.

Suddenly she wondered if the handsome stranger at the relay station was in this gang, if he had been scouting the stage while pretending to eat. Would his presence help her?

During her brief distraction, the door was jerked open and Carrie Sue was yanked outside. She lost her balance and fell, skinning her hands and dirtying her already ruined dress. Quickly she flipped to her seat and glared at the despicable ruffian, preparing to defend herself. She watched the man's expression change upon viewing her face.

A lecherous grin revealed his perilous interest in her. "Whatda we have here? Seems this stage was carrying two prizes, boys. Get that strongbox while I have a look-see at this pretty thing."

As the lawless bully bent forward to seize her, he was shot in the throat near his collarbone. His body fell past Carrie Sue, hitting the ground with a thud. The other bandits whirled to check out their danger, but not in time to prevent two more from taking lethal rifle bullets.

The rescuer, who was galloping toward them without fear or hesitation, nearly concealed behind his horse's head, shoved his rifle into its saddle holster and drew two pistols. The remaining two outlaws fired at the lone gunman who rode to the side of his horse Indian-style and fired guns from either side of the animal's neck. One bandit yelled in pain as his chest accepted two deadly shots.

The last man grabbed Carrie Sue's wrist and yanked her to him to use as a shield and hostage. Wanting to protect herself and to aid her defender, she fought the cowardly villain like an unleashed wildcat as he struggled to control her while defending himself. Their actions caused her braid to fall. He cursed her and threatened her, but she did not let up on her attack of nails, fists, and kicks. As his hand tried to band her chest to imprison her, his rough fingers snagged the edge of her bodice and, as she attempted to escape his grasp, popped off several buttons and scratched her tender flesh. Provoked further, she whirled on him and landed a fisted blow to his mouth. "The Devil take you, you bastard!" she screamed.

Carrie Sue broke free and scrambled beneath the stage to give her rescuer a clear shot at him. She knew the bandit didn't have many more bullets in his two revolvers and he was winded from his fight with her. As he damned her to hell and scurried behind the coach for cover, she saw him shove an emptied weapon into one holster.

She kept her gaze on the nearby bandit and shifted her position as he did. Hurriedly her mind plotted how to help defeat this killer. She risked a quick glance at her rescuer, but he had dismounted and rushed behind a tree which was too small to offer much protection. Yet, the faded gray shirt and ebony head were familiar. Excitement traveled through her. She saw him duck a bullet, and knew she could not allow the bandit time to reload his weapons. She looked about for a rock or stick; none were available. If she tried to climb on the driver's box or into the coach to get a weapon, the outlaw would hear and feel her movements. Then, she spotted a dead outlaw's pistol not far away.

Carrie Sue checked the bandit's stance which said he was peering around the back of the stage. Rapidly she scooted toward it. Her rescuer fired several times. Obviously he had seen her action and was giving her time and cover by distracting the ruffian. Seizing the weapon, she turned and fired beneath the coach at the man's legs.

He yelped in pain and staggered into the handsome stranger's view. The raven-haired man jumped into the open. His right hand cocked the hammer and his left hand pulled the trigger in one fluid motion which required no more than a split-second. The last bandit was slain.

The smokey-eyed gunslinger with whom she had eaten breakfast shoved his revolvers into their holsters and stalked forward in a purposeful stride, a black stallion trailing him out of love and protection. He glared at her and shouted, "That was a stupid thing to do! You could have gotten killed! Why didn't you stay under the stage?"

Distressed by the mayhem of the day, and angered by his ridiculous attitude, she shouted back, "If you had gotten yourself shot playing the hero, I would have been in deep trouble by now! I couldn't take a chance on your being killed for helping me! I wasn't about to let that ba . . . beast get his hands on me again!"

The man glared at her as if no female had ever dared to argue with him, and she glared back. His left thumb tipped up his hat and that obstinate ebony lock fell over his forehead once more. He sighed loudly in annoyance and shook his head. "What about the others?" he finally asked.

Carrie Sue knew he meant the people inside the coach. "All dead."

He rubbed his jawline as if saving her life had cost him precious time and energy which he resented spending. This vexed the redhead even more than his previous behavior. She suggested coldly, "If you'll help me load the bodies, I'll drive the stage to the next relay station and you can be on your way."

His eyes widened as he looked her up and down in astonishment. She was the most beautiful and desirable woman he had ever seen, even more so in her highly agitated state. Her tawny red hair seemed aflame beneath the brilliant sun. Strands had pulled themselves free of her plait and now danced about her dirty face like a fiery glow. A defiant expression filled her violet-blue eyes and tightened her enticing lips.

She faced him squarely able to meet his gaze without craning her neck though he was over six feet tall. What an armful she would be!

When she wiped at the perspiration on her face, it mingled with the dust and created playful smudges on her forehead, nose, and above her upper-lip. Her dress was dirty, torn, and blood-stained. He noticed the scratches on her chest where the bodice gaped and revealed a white chemise. Observing his line of vision, her free hand lifted to clutch the severed garment together. The revolver was still dangling from the loosened grip in her right hand. He recalled how she had fought the bandit, even shot him. And hadn't he heard her curse the man? Where had that prim and proper lady from breakfast gone? What a surprising spitfire she was!

All that shyness and gentleness which he had observed this morning was now masked by a strength, confidence, and boldness which he found unexpected, befuddling, and appealing. Yet, he still sensed that same wary nature he had detected earlier. This intriguing vixen could definitely take care of herself, if the odds weren't too uneven.

Long ago he had built a strong wall around himself to prevent ever being hurt again, and had honed his skills to make certain no one ever took advantage of him. In a few minutes this morning, this wild filly had nearly kicked a hole in that sturdy wall, and he had been willing—eager—to let her! That was crazy! He was a loner and she was a stranger, a ravishing and troublesome type. At the station this morning, he had lost his wits for a while. No, this beautiful thief had stolen them! He had tried to dismiss her from mind after leaving, but found that task impossible. He had caught himself riding slower and slower and sticking close to the road just to be near her once more when the stage halted for the night at the last home station. While he halted to get control of himself, the stage had passed his hiding place. Now he was glad he had hung back.

What was so different and alluring about this particular creature? Was it her entrancing eyes which exposed such vulnerable innocence and such defiant fire? Her beautiful face with its rosy gold hue? Her shapely body in that simple cotton dress? Her fiery mane which enticed his fingers to enter it? Or some elusive and irresistible aura which he couldn't name just yet? Whatever her magic, he didn't have time to test it, enjoy it, or become ensnared by it! He had to get to Tucson to kill a man. Afterwards, there were other men to track and slay.

As the man stared at her, Carrie Sue felt that strange heat and tension crawl over her body once more like a dangerous viper seeking a vulnerable spot to strike. She had not expected him or wanted him to be so . . . whatever! Being alone with him was intimidating. Never had she been more aware that she was a woman. "Why do you keep gaping at me so rudely, just like you did at breakfast? Your mother should be whipped for failing to teach you any manners!"

The stranger's eyes chilled and narrowed. He forcefully jabbed his thumbs into his gunbelt as if controlling the urge to strike her. "Why is it people always blame a mother's failure for their bad traits and weaknesses? Obviously your mother failed in the same task or you'd be thanking me for saving your pretty hide instead of being so smartmouthed," he scolded. "When a man sees such a beautiful woman, naturally he's gonna stare a minute or two. At your age, I would think you'd be used to it by now," he added, but made it sound more like an insult than a compliment. He watched her violet-blue eyes blaze with fury. He lowered his head and inhaled deeply several times, chiding himself for his callousness. Obviously she had endured a bad scare and wasn't herself just now. When he looked back at her, he asked, "Have you ever driven a stage or wagon before?"

His mood, expression, and tone had changed. Maybe it was the heat or lethal battle which had put him on edge. They both had to settle down because there was a grim chore to perform. "A wagon, yes; a stage, no," she replied, mastering her own unleashed temper.

He was visibly impressed by her self-control. In a teasing tone, he said, "No insult intended, Ma'am, but you don't look strong enough to handle six half-broken horses and a heavy stage. If you have no objection, I'll drive it to the next station."

"You seemed in such a hurry that I didn't want to put you out any further," she responded in like manner.

"Won't delay me much. I'm heading for Tucson just like you."

"Why?" the question jumped uncontrollably from her lips.

His expression waxed to one of curiosity. "Does it matter?"

Carrie Sue dared her cheeks to turn that unnatural red again. Her body must have feared her threat, because it obeyed. "Not to me. I was just wondering why you didn't travel with us. If you'd been . . ."

Knowing her words, he interrupted, "I travel alone, unless it suits me otherwise. Your stomach strong enough for this task, or you want me to load the bodies alone?" he inquired, his voice softening.

The lovely fugitive liked the change in his tone and expression. "I've seen and touched plenty of dead people before. I'm just angry because this attack was stupid, a waste of lives. The Garrett line never carries anything of value. I'm glad you came along when you did. I've never witnessed more courage or prowess than you displayed," she said without thinking. Unnerved by her slip, she rushed on, "Let's get busy. It's four hours to the next station. What about those bandits?"

His smokey gray eyes glanced over them. "I would leave 'em here for the vultures, but there might be a reward or two on their heads. I see no reason not to collect it for my trouble. I might even be persuaded to split it with you. Let me check your hand," he said and reached for the one which had struck the last bandit.

Carrie Sue jerked it from his light grasp and stepped away from him. She hoped her face didn't pale and her trembling didn't show. "Are you a bounty hunter?" she asked, her tone laced with revulsion.

Chapter

2

He was surprised by her reaction. "A bounty hunter?" he echoed in a matching tone of aversion. "Not me, but it's foolish to pass up a possible reward when you've earned it. Why do you feel so strongly about them?"

She looked relieved by his reply, but ignored his question. "You're awfully good with a gun," she hinted for information.

He responded to her evocative tone and expression, "I manage to stay alive and healthy. What riles you about bounty hunters?" he persisted.

"I've heard many times that they hunt men down like wild animals, that they get their shooting and questioning out of order. They're nothing but glorified killers using the law to carry out the evil within them. What do you do for a living?"

"Rescue beautiful women in trouble," he quipped. The stubble on his face and his dark tan made his teeth appear snowy white when he smiled.

She frowned. "Hold the jests, please. What are you? A gunslinger? A drifter? A lawman?" she inquired.

He chuckled to prevent her from realizing that he was aware of her excessive anxiety. He knew she was afraid of something or someone because her lips remained parted, her respiration was shallow and swift, and she seemed to hang on every word he spoke as if seeking life-sustaining clues in them. In a casual tone and manner he said, "I'm intrigued by your choices. I've had lots of jobs in the past. When I get bored with one or the place I'm in, I move on to the next challenge. I guess that makes me a drifter of sorts, doesn't it?"

"Not necessarily. A real drifter roams aimlessly, but you sound as if you plan your moves before taking them. You left the station before the stage and a horse travels faster, so how did you fall behind?"

He eyed her up and down and grinned. "Very observant and sharp-witted. Was I supposed to be in a hurry to reach Tucson?"

"What's in Tucson to lure you there?" she kept firing questions at him since he seemed willing to answer them, which surprised her.

"Mighty nosey about strangers, aren't we?" he teased.

"Since we're trapped out here alone, I'd like to make certain I can trust you. For all I know, that could be your gang you double-crossed and gunned down so you could steal that alleged strongbox for yourself. You could have been checking us over this morning at the station. Do you mind answering my questions to calm my worries?"

"I certainly don't need or want an hysterical female on my hands. I'm heading for the mines near Tucson. You've heard of the Specie Resumption Act of '75. The government needs lots of gold to trade for those worthless greenbacks. Arizona has plenty of gold and silver."

"You don't look like a miner to me."

He laughed. It sounded rich and mellow, and his smokey gray eyes filled with amusement. "I'm not. Freight lines need drivers and guards, and those jobs pay plenty. Might be interesting for a while."

Carrie Sue tugged on her lower lip with her upper teeth, a habit which revealed her suspicion of him and his words. "You don't look like a wagon driver or guard either."

He was impressed by her cunning, wits, and courage. She was direct without being forward. From now on, he needed to pay close attention to what he said and did around her. "I take it you've seen enough miners, drivers, and guards to recognize them at forty paces."

She frowned again at his new jest. "What I meant was, you don't strike me as a man who takes or follows orders from others. Isn't that right?" she probed.

"Maybe that's why I can't stay put for long in one place. But a man has to eat, so he needs money. If he gets it the wrong way, his lazy days are over. Frankly, Ma'am, I don't hanker to have the law on my tail day and night, so I watch my steps and guns."

Once more Carrie Sue's teeth toyed with her lower lip, exposing her mistrust. This man was not behaving as he should! She knew that loners were not talkers, so why was he doing so much of it?

The gunslinger wondered the same thing. Everywhere he went, people accused him of being silent and moody, of being cold and hard and tough. Yet, this clever female had a strange way of pulling words from his mouth, of warming and disarming him. He was actually enjoying their controlled banter. But he wanted to know a few things about her. He wanted to ask why she hid her exceptional looks beneath plain dresses and simple hairstyles; why she had no ring on her finger; why she was so curious about him; why her hand had gone to her waist at the home station like a reflex of a gunslinger; why her hands were so rough and her nails so jagged; why she was scared of him; and why she had watched his presence and departure so intensely. Those queries would certainly frighten her into silence. Perhaps she was fleeing a brutal father or a cruel marriage and was wary of strangers. All he asked was, "Why are you heading for Tucson, Miss Starns?"

"How do you know my name?" she demanded, looking and sounding angry and distressed.

He wondered if he had read a brief gleam of terror in her lovely eyes. He also noticed how her hand tightened on the gun butt in her hand. "I asked the guard before I rode off this morning."

"Why?" she asked in a strained voice.

He shrugged and replied, "You caught my eye."

Carrie Sue could not suppress a smile. "What's your name?"

"T.J. Rogue."

Her violet-blue gaze widened and she looked him over again. She recognized his name. He was a famous gunslinger. Gossip said he was one of the fastest, if not the fastest gun in the West. Rumor also said he hired out to settle dangerous problems for other people. He was supposed to be tough, cold, hard, and relentless, but she did not find him that way. If anybody knew how gossip could be exaggerated or fabricated, she did! At times she had observed a resentful, almost bitter, air about him and wondered what had birthed those emotions. One thing, he was careful and highly intelligent because he wasn't wanted by the law, as far as she knew.

T.J. realized she had heard his name before, but if he had met her in the past, he would certainly recall it. "You've heard of me," he said, a statement instead of a question. "Where? When? What were you told?"

"Are you really as good as your reputation claims? One of the best guns in Texas? A man who settles problems others can't? Or should I say the fastest gun in the entire West?"

"No man is the fastest and best for very long. Another gunman always comes along who is swifter and better. Does it frighten you to be alone with the notorious T.J. Rogue, Miss Starns?"

"Actually, Mr. Rogue, having heard of your enormous reputation and having witnessed your skills, it makes me feel safer. If rumor can be trusted, you're more legendary than notorious. Tell me, does it make you feel odd to be the subject of countless campfire tales?"

"A man can't help what others say or think about him. Let's get moving. I want to reach the next station before dark." He tugged his hat down on his forehead and wiggled it into place, indicating their conversation was closed for now.

The redhead inquired, "Don't you think you should check those bandits. Someone could be alive."

"Not unless I'm losing my touch, Miss Starns. When I pull my gun, I shoot to kill. That's something you should always remember: never draw a weapon unless you intend to use it or you'll get hurt. You know any of these passengers?"

"No. They've only been on the stage a day or two, and I caught it at Fort Worth. None of us were talkers."

They gathered the outlaw's bodies and loaded them inside the stage with the slain passengers and driver. Carrie Sue glanced at the soldier's wife and unwillingly recalled another woman's murder in March near San Angelo. But that time, a small girl had been slain, too. She had to forget those incidents; she had to look to a bright future.

While her ebon-haired partner retrieved the guard's body down the road and fetched the horses, Carrie Sue recovered her purse and buttons and hurriedly changed clothes, a fact T.J. noticed when he returned. He liked the multi-colored dress she was wearing; its brighter colors suited her better. He secured the horses' reins to the back of the stage, but allowed his black stallion to remain free.

"You forgot your horse," she told him.

"Nighthawk stays with me unless I order him otherwise. He'll run alongside of us." As he replaced her smaller bag atop the coach, he pointed to the large chest hidden beneath the driver's box and commented, "Gold makes men go crazy with greed; it gets 'em into trouble. Obviously those bandits knew this stage was loaded."

"I wonder how," she mused. "I thought Garrett lines didn't haul mail or strongboxes to insure passengers' safety and comfort. That's why I chose them over Butterfield in Fort Worth. They're responsible for this slaughter. I'll register a complaint when I reach the next station."

He concurred, "I would too; it nearly got you killed. Let's tend those scratches and get moving."

The daring desperado allowed T.J. to doctor her scrapes with soothing ointment from his saddlebag. His touch was surprisingly gentle and warm. She wondered if he was tempted by the gold. All he had to do was get rid of her—the solitary witness—and take it. No one would guess the truth and he'd be rich.

When she trembled, his eyes left her injuries to look at her. She hurriedly averted her gaze and stood silently before him. When she began to fidget, he knew he was affecting her in the same way she was affecting him. He released her hand. "What's in Tucson for you?"

Carrie Sue kept her telltale gaze on her hands. "I'm heading there to become the town's new schoolmarm."

His gaze narrowed, but remained pleasant. He inhaled and exhaled deeply through his nose, a clue the redhead already guessed revealed his doubts about something. "A teacher. That explains why you're so inquisitive and ask so many questions."

"It's the best way to learn anything and to stay out of trouble."

"Only if people tell you the truth," he nonchalantly refuted.

"If you're smart enough to know they're lying or being evasive, that tells you a great deal about them and the situation."

He chuckled and his smokey eyes glowed. "You're right on that point, Miss Starns. You're very smart and brave."

"For a woman?" she teased.

"For anybody," he replied, then grinned.

T.J. helped her onto the driver's box and lifted the reins and whip. "Ready?" he asked.

Carrie Sue placed the pistol in her lap and nodded.

The gunslinger glanced at it, then looked into her periwinkle eyes.

"Just in case there's more trouble, I want to be prepared."

"Like I said, smart and brave."

As they traveled along the dusty road, Carrie Sue contemplated the man beside her. He didn't seem tempted by the large amount of gold beneath his feet if it meant killing her and breaking the law to obtain it. Perhaps if they'd all been dead when he attacked the bandits, he might have taken it just as she had stolen Carolyn Starns's identity and possessions. He was basically a decent and honest man, but private. He had not tried to capture her. Surely that also meant he hadn't guessed her dark secret, as that much gold should be more tempting to a gunslinger than the rewards posted on her and her brother's gang. Normally she was not this open and talkative, nor was he. Obviously there was an attraction between them which relaxed them. She wondered how long he would stay in Tucson. Yet, it couldn't matter to her. It was too risky starting a romance with any man, particularly a man like Rogue. It would make her too vulnerable to discovery and defeat. She had to resist him.

T.J. was thinking much the same. She didn't look like a school teacher, and she possessed a trail instinct which most men would envy. Her lips were full, her nose was wide, and her eyes were large. Separately none of those features were beautiful, but put them together beneath a flaming head of hair and the result was exquisite. At this moment, she looked so soft and vulnerable. But he knew better. Lordy, what a fetching and intriguing vixen she was. And frankly, he was aching to make her *his* vixen.

That was impossible. He would never be able to love her as she deserved to be loved. He was always on the move and doubted he could settle down in one place. He had tried, but had failed in every attempt. To date, the women he had known fell into two sacks: spoiled daughters of rich and powerful men, who pretended to be angels outside but were black devils inside, and whores in saloons who were filled with bitterness, most too weak to break away from a life they despised. But this woman was different, and different could mean trouble for him!

For the first time he asked himself if he was as cold and hard as people claimed, or he led them to believe. He had been forced to become that way to survive. His parents had been killed by Apaches when he was seven and he had been raised by the Indians until he was thirteen. After being rescued by the cavalry, he had been placed in Father Rafael Ortega's mission in San Antonio, Texas. He had become a street kid—"a half-savage rogue"—until running off to the war in '62 to see how the white tribes battled. Upon returning to Texas in '65, he had wandered aimlessly, facing new challenges every day, always into trouble, never fitting in anywhere.

Yes, he admitted, he had been tough, unrelenting, embittered. He had been separated from his brother after their capture and had never seen Tim again. Then, last winter he'd learned that his brother was a major at Fort Davis near the Mexican border. But fate had played him cruel again, allowing Tim to be slain by Mexican renegades before they could be reunited.

Then, the beautiful Arabella and precious little Marie had been murdered two months ago during a holdup near San Angelo. He had planned to give up his perilous existence and settle down with them, but that ill-fated dark cloud over his head had prevented it. As soon as he hunted down and killed the piece of scum who had barbwired him to a tree, he would stalk the gang responsible for Arabella's and Marie's deaths. The law wouldn't interfere if he killed them on the spot!

Despite his earlier troubles and "sorry attitude," he had always managed to stay an inch on the right side of the law by finding a way to provoke an enemy into a legal showdown. Hopefully he could do the same with those cold-blooded killers of his loved ones. Nearly everyone and everything he had loved had been taken from him, so it was a big risk to lean toward the woman beside him. Maybe his destiny was to remain a loner who cleared the earth of vermin, so why keep fighting it?

He glanced at the gold chest below his feet. That much treasure would tempt any man, including him. He couldn't steal it. But, Lordy, he could dream about taking it and the fiery treasure beside him! What a fine life that would be. . . .

Carrie Sue furtively observed T.J. She wondered what was more important to this man than easy riches. When he glanced her way, she read such resentment and anguish in his smokey eyes before he swiftly looked ahead again. Her heart twinged in empathy. She wanted to ease his suffering. Terrible things must have compelled him into his miserable existence. She wondered if he even realized how unhappy he was, how much he wanted and needed love. Yes, underneath that hard exterior was a gentle man aching for peace. She was certain of it because she felt the same. Was he the kind of man, the only man, who could understand what she had done and been, could forgive it and forget it?

Back off, Carrie Sue. You're dancing too close to the fire, she warned herself. She didn't know much about love and commitment, but she knew a tormented man like T.J. Rogue could burn her badly.

"Where are you from, Miss Starns?" he interrupted her musings.

Carrie Sue called Carolyn Starns's life to mind. "Originally from back East, but I've been teaching in St. Louis for the past two years. I lost my job to the mayor's daughter. She wanted it, so papa got it for her. I read about the position in Tucson in the paper. Fortunately I was the only teacher to answer their advertisement. I don't know why because the pay is excellent. Lots of successful ranchers and miners in that area. I've been traveling for weeks, so I'm more than ready to get there and take on those little hellions."

"Little hellions?" he echoed.

"If you've been to school, Mr. Rogue, surely you remember how boys behave when cooped up like feisty roosters all day."

They shared laughter before he remarked playfully, "You don't look like a school-marm to me."

"And you would recognize one at forty paces?" she teased.

They laughed again. "Nope, but I've never seen one who looks like you. Those boys will be lucky to face you every day."

"Only if they do their lessons the night before. I can be very tough."

"I know you can, but I wouldn't have believed you if I hadn't seen how skillfully you handled yourself back there. You surely know a lot about a lot of things."

Carrie Sue smiled. "I read and study all the time, an occupational necessity and curse. Too, if I weren't strong and hard, those children would run all over me. Fear, Mr. Rogue, is the only way to control boys twice your size and nearly your age."

He eyed her with a sensual grin. "I'd imagine you have other ways to control rowdy males. Just give 'em a smile and they'll do anything you ask." She smiled radiantly and he laughed. "I didn't mean for you to use that power on me. You forgetting we're out here alone? If you want me to remain a gentleman, better holster that weapon and don't draw it again unless you intend to use it."

As if trying to obey his mischievous warning, Carrie Sue placed her left hand over her mouth as merry laughter spilled forth. "You're quite a charming man, Mr. Rogue."

"That's one word which hasn't been used before to describe me. Why don't you call me T.J.?" he suggested.

"If you'll call me Ca-rolyn and tell me more about you."

"Why not? My folks were killed by Apaches when I was a boy. Then, I was raised in a mission orphanage. I ran away at fifteen to see what all the ruckus was about in the East. I fought a few battles and returned to Texas when the war ended. I've had just about every kind of job there is, but none of them kept my interest, and certainly didn't pay me enough to become my own boss. The last job I had was herding cattle to market. Months on a dusty trail in all kinds of weather. I plan to rest up a spell in Tucson, then hire out as a mine guard. When I get bored, I'll move on. One thing, you learn a lot while drifting around and trying out different jobs. You a widow?" he asked suddenly, returning the conversation to her.

"No, I've never been married. Have you?"

"Was that your choice or was every man you've met dumb and blind?"

He guided the stage off the public road to the Garrett station. Although it couldn't be seen through the dense growth of billowy mesquite, thick paloverde, and numerous branches of cacti, T.J. knew something was wrong: It was too quiet, and he smelled recent smoke. Just as those perceptions settled in, the winding road reached the clearing.

Before she could respond to his question, he shouted, "Hold on tight, Carolyn! Trouble ahead! Whoa, boys!" The moment she braced herself, he stomped on the brake lever and pulled back hard on the reins, halting the stage with skill and strength. He scolded himself for his lack of attention, a result of his intriguing companion.

Carrie Sue's eyes went from his scowling face to the scene before them. The home station had been destroyed by a fire and bodies were sighted here and there, with arrows protruding from them.

"Renegade Apaches," he commented knowingly from their colors and patterns. "Must have broken from the reservation. No buzzards circling yet. Stay here while I take a look around."

He climbed down slowly, adjusting his gunbelt when his boots touched the ground. He retrieved his rifle from Nighthawk's saddle and cocked it. He closed the distance between the stage and the station. He scanned all directions with keen eyes, then dropped to the ground and listened for any sound of hoofbeats as the Apaches had taught him. He examined the bodies, the charred remains of the house and barn, the empty corral, and tracks on the earth. He returned to the coach and said, "Happened late yesterday. She was dry and burned quickly, but the odor's still fresh. They won't be back this way. We'll camp here for the night, then leave at dawn."

Her wide eyes checked their surroundings and her ears strained to pick up any unnatural sound. Mountains were visible in all directions over the tops of the thick growth which encircled the clearing. Her lips were parted and her breathing was shallow and swift. She knew what Indians on the warpath could do, and was wisely afraid. If Indians came galloping down the narrow road, they would be trapped. "I don't like being boxed in like this. You're sure it's safe?" she pressed.

"No reason for them to return. They stole the horses and supplies and destroyed everything else. Besides, our horses have to rest and graze before they can take us on to Tucson. We'll load those bodies in the stage to keep the vultures off them and leave the stage here. We can make better time on horseback. I'll let you ride Nighthawk and I'll use one of these horses. Can you ride?"

"Yes, but what about the gold and my baggage? Other bandits might come along and steal everything before the company can send someone to recover them. Can't we just take the stage on into town?"

T.J. gave her reminder some thought. The gold was too heavy for them to lift out and bury. If anything happened to it, someone might point an accusatory finger at them and mess up his schedule. "You're right, Carolyn. We can't risk losing that gold and falling under suspicion for its theft. We'll take the stage on to Tucson at dawn."

Although he hadn't mentioned her possessions, she thanked him for agreeing with her. She certainly didn't need to fall under suspicion for a robbery! She climbed over the edge of the driver's box and made her way down, with T.J.'s hands securely about her waist. "What's first?" she asked.

"Let's put these bodies inside the coach. Too many to bury, and families might want to claim them for burial at home."

Carrie Sue and T.J. carried two more bodies to the stage and added them to the eleven already there. To foil vultures, they had no choice except to pile them on the seats and floor. She wished there were blankets in which to wrap the bodies, but none were available in the warm month of May. She watched her partner lower the leather window shades and secure them tightly to keep insects away.

Afterwards, he unhitched the team and placed the horses in the corral where unsinged hay and a water trough were located. Nighthawk was placed with them so he could drink and feed. T.J. motioned to a spot on the western side of the clearing where a few trees didn't have limbs teasing the dry ground. "We'll camp there in the shade. Your nose is already pink. You need a hat, Miss Starns."

She touched the sensitive area and said, "I didn't even think about it in all the excitement. I'll unpack one for tomorrow's ride."

Carrie Sue followed T.J. beneath the trees, both having to duck to avoid low branches. He spread out a blanket and told her to have a seat while he gathered firewood and prepared them some "grub."

"I can help, T.J.," she offered. "My rear can use some relief. That shotgun seat is harder than the benches inside the coach."

He chuckled when she rubbed her sore behind. He was accustomed to doing chores alone, but he welcomed her company and assistance.

Being careful around the bristly cacti, sharp-tipped yuccas, and thorny catclaw, they scouted amongst the scrubs for dead branches and dry weeds to use for a fire. When they finished, T.J. raised his left pant leg and withdrew a large knife from a sheath which was strapped to his calf. He dug a shallow pit and built a fire within it.

On the lip of the hole, he placed a circle of rocks to contain the flames and heat. Around it, he jabbed a three-prong metal holder into the ground from which to suspend a small cooking pot. He opened his pouch and dropped strips of dried meat into the pot, then cleaned and used the sharp blade to open a can of beans to add to it. Next, he put some coffee on to perk near one edge of the fire. "It'll take a while. Which one of your bags do you need for the night?"

"Why don't I go with you? There's no need to lift a heavy bag down and up when I can climb up there and pull what I need from it."

"Good idea. Come along, partner."

They went to the coach and mounted the driver's box. T.J. pulled her largest bag forward so she could reach it easily.

Carrie Sue opened Carolyn's bag and withdrew a washcloth, dress, hat, and under-garments for the next morning. She was glad she had hidden her rifle and six-guns on the bottom of the case where he couldn't see them. She closed the bag and fastened the straps, leaving a tiny gap which would tell her if the bag was tampered with during the night. If he was anything more than the gunslinger T.J. Rogue, she would know by morning. And if he was, she would deal with that problem then. She inhaled deeply to distract him and said, "That coffee smells wonderful."

"Let's see if it's ready." He helped her down and they walked back to their small camp. "Not yet," he said while stirring the beans.

Carrie Sue excused herself to use the outhouse, the only unburned structure. Borrowing his canteen upon her return, she washed her dirty face and hands. T.J. handed her the ointment from his saddlebag and suggested she rub more on her scratches, which she did.

"I only have one set of dishes and utensils. You can use the plate and fork, and I'll eat from the pot with a spoon. I'm afraid we'll have to share the cup," he told her. "Sorry, but I don't have any sugar."

"It doesn't matter; I drink mine black," Carrie Sue replied, having been forced by years on the trail to adjust to unsweetened coffee. "You're handy to have around, T.J., and you're most generous. I'm sorry I accused you of not having manners; clearly you have plenty."

He glanced at her and teased, "Don't swell my head, woman. I guess we were both a little edgy back there. Sorry." He pulled two biscuits from a cloth and put them on a hot rock to warm. "Sam gave 'em to me this morning. Been craving 'em all day."

After dining on coffee, beans, biscuits, and dried beef, darkness surrounded their cozy campfire. T.J. suggested, "We'd better turn in so we can get an early start at dawn. We only have one bedroll, so we'll have to share it too. You mind?"

"Not if you remember you're a gentleman," she teased pointedly.

"I promise not to forget that fact, Miss Starns. I wouldn't want the Tucson town council tracking me down for molesting their teacher."

Carrie Sue stayed in her clothes as she settled down to spend the night beside the handsome man. She turned on her side away from him, and he did the same. Yet, as time passed, she remained aware of his close proximity and her body burned to feel his touch again.

T.J. couldn't sleep; the woman near him was too desirable. He wanted to turn to her and pull her into his arms, to smother her lips with kisses, to caress her shapely body, to run his fingers through her fiery mane. He knew that would be a mistake, for both of them.

Carrie Sue struggled to locate dreamland where she could unite her torrid flesh with his, but her search was in vain. He was too real; this moment was too real. She attempted to concentrate on their surroundings. Not far away was a coach filled with bodies. She was heading for a new life, one free of complications. He was T.J. Rogue, a famous—or infamous—gunslinger who could destroy her without meaning to do so. He would call attention to her presence. Their match was perilous; their attraction was dangerous.

"Carolyn?" he whispered, "are you awake?"

"Yes," she replied.

"I'm going to bed down near the corral, else neither of us will get any sleep. Don't be afraid; I'll be nearby."

"T.J. . . ."

"Yes?"

"Thank you."

"I know," he murmured hoarsely.

He left the area and his body was engulfed by darkness. She listened as he crossed the open space and flopped down on hay near the corral. How she yearned to call him back to her side, but she dared not. How long, she wondered, before she would feel safe to yield to her desires? How long before another man like this appeared?

Carrie Sue thought about Quade Harding's lust for her. It had been seven years since they'd met. Why couldn't he forget about her and settle down with another woman? How could he sustain his obsession for so long? He must have spent a fortune on detectives. Anyone would think he'd weary of the chase and setbacks. But time seemed to increase his hunger for her. Merciful heavens, what would he do next to locate her?

The lovely fugitive's mind drifted to her brother. Had Darby and his men made it to their hideout? What if peril forced him northward and she needed him to rescue her? Would he head to El Paso in early July as planned? If she ran into trouble, would that old Mexican deliver her message to Darby as promised? Would Darby keep his gang out of Arizona as promised so her new life wouldn't be threatened? And, how long would Quade hold silent? Or that Ranger she had shot and thwarted last year? If the vile lawman had reported her deed, news of it had not been released. After all, it would be her word against his that she had surrendered, then been forced to shoot and flee.

Carrie Sue recalled the Stover farm in Georgia before the War Between the States had destroyed their lives the first time. Her family had raised cotton and done very well at it. She remembered how to plant it, pick it, and gin it. After the war, greedy northerners had forced them off their prized land and out of business. Finally her father had yielded reluctantly, bitterly, and sold out to a persistent Carpetbagger in

'67. The moment the evil man moved into their home, her father had robbed him and had burned the barns, house, and fields so he couldn't profit from his wickedness. Afterwards, they had made their way to distant Texas and purchased a ranch in early '68 with the villain's stolen money. Perhaps that was where Darby had learned the motives and means of just revenge which he had used against the Hardings in '69.

Men, could any of them be trusted? Carrie Sue wondered sadly. First, the northern soldiers had terrorized her family in Georgia. Next, northern Carpetbaggers had ruined their life and driven them from their home and land. Then, the Hardings had destroyed their new chance for happiness in Texas. Now, countless lawmen, bounty hunters, and others wanted nothing more than to see her and her brother's gang dead.

If only they could be left alone for a while, allowed to cease their criminal life and settle down. Both she and Darby should be wed by now with homes and families. But fate had dealt them heavy blows. Everywhere they went, trouble followed. Everyone they loved, fate destroyed. T.J. Rogue had enough trouble without taking on hers!

Carrie Sue grimaced as if in physical pain. Never had she known a man whom she wanted to know intimately. It was too late. When she reached Tucson and he departed, she must forget him.

T.J. glanced toward the cluster of trees. It was too dark to see the woman camped beneath them; yet, he knew she was still awake, awake and miserable like he was. He felt the heavy tension in the air, sensed the odd mingling of powerful attraction and necessary rejection in both of them. Why had he allowed her to get under his tough hide? How could he simply scratch her out like a troublesome chigger? He had to ignore her, resist her pull, forget her. But could he?

At last, the distraught redhead and agitated smokey-eyed male were fast asleep and the remainder of the night passed swiftly.

Chapter

3

Carrie Sue stirred and awakened on T.J.'s bedroll. She nestled her cheek against the material which held manly scents along with those of leather and horseflesh. Accustomed to such smells, she did not find them offensive. In fact, the gunslinger's scent was quite arousing.

To break its hold over her, she sat up and looked around, but didn't see the charming Rogue anywhere. The sun was just peeking over the distant mountains to the east, so her shade would be stolen soon. Except for the neighing and movements of the corralled horses, few sounds were heard in the "Southwest Corner of Hell," as early travelers had described this dry and sunny area. At first glance one might think this landscape was desolate and dreary, but on closer inspection, it was filled with life and wild beauty.

The creaking of metal and splashing of water caught her attention and she turned to find the black-haired man near a water pump at the corral. She stood, straightened her dress, removed the washcloth from an overhead branch, and headed his way. Used to being around males who were half-dressed, she thought nothing of joining him. "Good morning, Mr. Rogue. We did pass the night safely as you promised."

He met her smiling gaze and grinned. "I was hoping I wouldn't have to awaken you to start breakfast, but I was getting mighty hungry." His mellow gaze roamed her sleepy face and rumpled clothes. "I found a bucket in the yard and filled it with fresh water. I put it behind the coach. Why don't you get washed up and changed behind the stage while I prepare some coffee and vittles?"

"Sounds marvelous to me," she replied, stretching and yawning. She watched T.J. fingercomb his wet hair and use his dirty shirt to dry off his muscled torso and darkly stubbled face. That willful lock fell forward to tease at his temple and she had the urge to twirl it around her finger. She eyed the two rows of curious scars which ran across his furry chest, arms, and over his flat stomach. Then, she noticed matching ones across the backs of his wrists. It appeared as if he had been bound tightly by a metal rope with jagged edges.

T.J.'s smokey gray eyes went from her inquisitive expression to his chest and arms, then returned to her face. He reached for the bib-shirt which he had thrown over the fence and began pulling it on. "Barbwire," he murmured as he fastened the buttons.

"What?" she said in confusion.

He left the top part of his shirt unbuttoned and flapped to one side. As he tied a brown bandanna around his neck, he revealed, "I ran afoul of a man in Texas so he had his hirelings ambush me and tie me to a tree with barbwire."

"Merciful Heavens, T.J.! How did you get loose without tearing yourself to pieces?" she asked, imagining those sharp points biting viciously into his handsome body.

His eyes narrowed and chilled, but he joked lightly, "I stayed real still until somebody came along and cut me free. Didn't take but two days. I was so hungry and thirsty and mad by then, damage or naught, I would have broken myself free in another hour or two. Worst part was all those blood-sucking insects wanting a drink from me."

"How could anyone do such a despicable thing? Did you kill him?"

T.J. withdrew a comb from his saddlebag and ran it through his ebony hair. "I caught two of them later and let them enjoy the same experience for a while. Their friend will cross my path one day and I'll make certain he recalls who I am. As for their boss, I couldn't prove he was involved, as if anyone would believe a notorious gun-slinger over a respectable rancher. He even had a different kind of wire used on me so the evidence wouldn't point a finger at him. But he'll make another mistake some day, and I'll be there to repay him. I know right where to find him and he isn't going anywhere."

"Was he trying to kill you for some reason, or just torture you?"

"Yep, I made a fool of him in front of others. A man doesn't forget or forgive humiliation. He planned for me to rot at that tree, real slow and painful, but I fooled him." T.J. chuckled coldly.

"Why didn't you sneak to his ranch one night and get revenge?"

"I'm letting him simmer and sweat. Fear is a perfect first course to a fine meal of vengeance. About the time he stops looking over his shoulder, I'll be standing there. Guess that sounds pretty cold-blooded to a genteel lady like you, Miss Starns."

"No, it sounds like justice to me. Sometimes men have to take the law into their own hands to obtain it. Evil men don't deserve to live."

"Lordy, woman, you think like me."

"Is that why your reputation says you take on villains the law is afraid to touch or can't touch?"

"It's a job like any other, but one I seem to enjoy a lot," he admitted. His gaze wandered over her lovely face and tousled hair. Her eyes were wide and alert, but enticingly soft. When she looked away, fell silent, and shifted her weight nervously, he knew he was making her uncomfortable with his stare. "We'd better get busy."

T.J. headed for the campsite beneath the fragrant mesquites and squatted by the fire ring. Carrie Sue's gaze followed his retreat and lingered on his back for a time as he pulled items from his saddlebag. She sighed heavily and made a trip to the outhouse before going behind the stage to bathe and change clothes. She wanted to look her best when she entered Tucson later today, as the impression she made on the people there would be vital. With their grim baggage and tale to be exposed, their arrivals certainly wouldn't go unnoticed; that worried her.

At least she would look fairly well-rested. Actually, she was amazed at herself for sleeping so deeply; she hadn't even noticed T.J.'s stirrings at dawn. Obviously she felt at ease with him. But, she wondered, should that please her or make her nervous? Merciful Heavens, it was scary to trust a stranger!

She slipped off the dress, glad Carolyn was accustomed to dressing alone and had all of her garments made with buttons up the front. The only exception was an elegant gown and it wasn't appropriate for her mission today. But at least she had a proper dress if a special occasion arose.

Carrie Sue discarded the cotton petticoat, chemise, and bloomers. Using the bucket of water and washcloth, she bathed as quickly and thoroughly as possible. She dried herself and pulled on the clean undergarments and dark green dress. She wondered if Miss Carolyn Starns favored darker garments because of her position as a schoolmarm. She knew the dress was plain and sturdy, yet it did nothing to flatter her coloring and figure. But she shouldn't want to appear beautiful to T.J., or showy to the town council in Tucson. She must present the image of a virtuous and respectable school teacher.

Delectable odors assailed her nose and her stomach rumbled in hunger. She climbed upon the driver's box to stuff her things inside her baggage. She smiled when she noticed the case had not been tampered with during the night. If the gunslinger mistrusted her or was playing games with her, he would have searched her baggage while she was asleep. Relief and joy swept over her. She placed her hat on the shotgun seat, ready for use later this morning when the sun's heat and glare increased.

Taking her brush, she joined T.J. beneath the trees. He looked her way as she unbraided her hair and brushed it. The fiery mane was long, thick, and wavy, and golden highlights shone in the sunny light. T.J. felt his groin tighten at the ravishing sight before his eyes.

Carrie Sue rebraided her hair neatly and secured the looped plait to the back of her head as she had done yesterday. When she put aside her brush and looked his way, T.J. was still staring at her. "Is something wrong?" she inquired apprehensively.

T.J. shook his head and murmured, "Nope." He returned his attention to his chore. Lordy, she was one tempting female! With that flaming hair unleashed, she looked like an angel imprisoned on earth.

Carrie Sue grinned as she realized what kind of expression had filled his eyes: desire. Her own body was burning with it. She noticed what he was cooking and asked, "Where did you get those?"

Without looking up again, he replied, "One of the chickens must have gotten loose during the Apache attack. She was nesting in a thicket, but a coyote got her. Wasn't a total loss; she left behind three eggs. I fried enough salt pork to stuff inside our last two biscuits so we won't have to halt at midday to make dinner. Sam gave me six, so we can have two this morning. I can't wait to reach Tucson and get some good food," he chatted on nervously.

"What could be better than fried pork, scrambled eggs, coffee, and biscuits? You're an excellent cook, Mr. Rogue. I'm going to miss all this attention when we reach Tucson."

"Attention is what you'll get plenty of, Miss Starns," he muttered, sounding resentful.

"Not like yours, T.J., not without demands attached."

T.J. glanced at her again. "I guess that is a problem for a beautiful lady like you."

"It's nice meeting a real gentleman for a change."

T.J. eyed her up and down and shrugged. It might be nice, but it surely was damned hard where she was concerned! "It's ready." He dished up her portion of the meat and eggs and placed a warmed biscuit on the plate. He set the coffee cup near her and focused on eating his own share of the meal.

Feeling happy and relaxed, Carrie Sue devoured the food and sipped on the coffee, from a metal cup which he occasionally used. When they finished the silent meal, she gathered the dishes and carried them to the pump to wash. After rolling up his sleeping bag and collecting his supplies, he joined her there and put them away.

"I'll hitch up the team and we'll be off."

The redhead observed the smokey-eyed man as he worked efficiently with the horses and harnesses. He saddled Nighthawk but did not secure his reins to the coach. "Let's get moving," he called out.

Carrie Sue mounted the stage and took her seat beside him. She tied the sun bonnet on her head and placed the pistol nearby. When he handed her his folded blanket to sit on to soften the bench, she smiled and thanked him. She held on while he got the stage and team into motion. The black stallion galloped beside them, on his side of the coach.

T.J. was aware of the gun on the bench between them, just as he was aware that she hadn't slept with it. Since she knew who and what he was, why did she trust him so fully? Why was she at ease in his company? Not many women would strip, bathe, and change clothes within a hundred yards of a total stranger, even with a stagecoach between them. Maybe she was one of those women who was attracted to dangerous men, to adventurous rogues. No, he concluded, she wasn't like that. He was pleased that she hadn't complained one time about the heat, dust, dangers, food, or hardships of their journey. He couldn't figure her out, and that astonished him.

The wind tugged at their hats and clothes. Yet, he didn't think there was any danger of a sandstorm. He glanced at the benches on the sides of the slopes where countless cacti grew. Some places were so abundant with it that cross-country travel was impossible for man or beast. Everything around them seemed to warn people to stay out of this harsh countryside or risk a terrible death. It was rugged terrain: hot, dry, and hostile to everyone except the Indians and critters who knew how to survive in it.

They traveled in silence until midday, when they halted to rest the horses and eat the fried salt pork in biscuits, washed down with water from his canteen. For a short time, she vanished behind bushes to the right of the coach while he did the same to the left. When the journey continued, he almost hated to reach their destination, knowing she and their circumstances would alter drastically. Once she was in town, the rough edges which had surfaced briefly with him would be forced to disappear. Again, she would become the sedate lady he had met at breakfast at the way station, and his fantasy would end.

Carrie Sue hated to reach Tucson today, knowing this stimulating adventure with T.J. Rogue would be over and she probably would never see him again. She was tempted to try to prolong his visit in town, but was afraid to do so. What could come of it? Nothing. He was a drifter, and she had to settle down, settle down safely and permanently. But she longed for more time with him.

As she gazed out over the desert terrain, tears stung her eyes. She couldn't help but feel that she would be losing something special when they parted, that she would never forget him or cease wanting him. They were a good match; they could grow, change, and mature together, but she could not afford to entice him. She could cause him grave trouble, and he could do the same for her. Fate, cruel fate, was ruining her life again. Every time a glimmer of hope and beauty entered her life, vindictive fate would appear to show her the bleak reality of her destiny, her destiny to be an outcast, to have nothing and no one for very long. Bitterness chewed at Carrie Sue's soul. It wasn't fair! But she had to accept it.

Maybe, just maybe, one day they would meet again, meet when there were no threats to their relationship. If she prayed real hard and was very good, perhaps God would answer her prayers.

T.J. could almost smell the troubled air which surrounded the woman beside him. She was watching the passing landscape as if she were taking a ride to the gallows. Why were tears glistening in her lovely eyes? Why were her shoulders slumped in dejection? Why was he so afraid to ask those disturbing questions and to offer her help to solve her problems? He wasn't a coward or a weakling, but Lordy she scared him! Who was this contradiction beside him? What was in her past? Could he allow himself to get involved with her and those dark shadows?

The ground became drier, sandier, and rockier. In most spots, vegetation was sparser than it had been along their journey. Mesquite was laden heavily with green and yellow pods like cleverly decorated Christmas trees. Clusters of white flowers topped the uplifted arms of the giant Saguaro cactus. Some were over two hundred years old, over fifty feet high, and weighed more than the stage. Mountains appeared to form a distant ring around them. Dry washes occasionally crossed the road to remind travelers of the flash flood threat.

In some places, the road was narrow and winding, often causing trees and bushes to slap their limbs against the coach. Several times a white sea of blooming yuccas stretched for miles beside and beyond them. On some rolling hills, cacti stood like green soldiers at attention, ready and eager to defend their terrain against invasion. Most of the wildflowers, trees, bushes, and plants were in full bloom; their reds, golds, blues, yellows, pinks, whites, oranges, and purples fused into a blanket of color to make Spring the desert's most beautiful season.

Tucson loomed on the horizon. Along one mountain range west of town, three peaks rose higher than others and reminded T.J. of teepees without poles out the top. It was one of the markers which had guided travelers to this area before the road had been cleared. "We'll be there soon, Carolyn. Do you need anything before we ride into town?"

"No," she replied in a hoarse tone. "I'm fine, thanks, just a little nervous. I've only spoken to these people through the mail. What if they don't like me? And refuse to hire me?"

T.J. sent her a smile of encouragement. "How could anyone not like you and want you?" he chided softly, touched by her vulnerability.

Carrie Sue bravely fused her gaze to his. "I'll miss you," she rashly confessed, then averted her eyes and scolded herself. "You saved my life and took good care of me. Thanks, T.J."

"I'll miss you too," he replied. "I'll . . . be in town for a while, if you get a hankering to spend time with a . . . real gentleman again." Carrie Sue grinned. "That's much better," he murmured, pleased with his affect on her.

It was three o'clock and the town ahead seemed quiet. Later, it would probably get rowdy when the cowboys and miners drifted into town for the evening. From reading Carolyn's notes, Carrie Sue knew that Tucson was situated on the Santa Cruz River, in a wide valley which was rimmed by mountains and surrounded by desert. In the latter seventeen hundreds, Tucson had been a presidio of the Spanish Army. Today, it was the territorial capital, and had existed under four different flags: the Spanish, Mexican, Confederate, and United States.

Carrie Sue called the brunette's diary to mind and tried to remember all Carolyn had written about this town. As a teacher, she should know such things. As a desperate fugitive, they could be vital to her.

The town had sprang up around the presidio of *San Agustin del Tucson* which had been built in 1775 by Hugo O'Connor of the Royal Spanish Army. Since that year, men and women from many countries and all walks of life had added to her history: Indians, soldiers, padres, Mexican colonials, cowboys, miners, gamblers, outlaws, merchantmen, prostitutes, wives, children, and countless others.

As they neared town, the stage passed adobe huts and houses, their sunbaked mud blocks held in place by straw-laced mortar, some with light stucco surfaces. Other homes, probably those of Anglos, were built of wood and most had lengthy porches to keep out as much sun as possible. There were barns, lean-tos, rough corrals, out-houses, and a few small stores. The ground was dry and dusty and little vegetation grew around the homes. She noticed a heavy use of dark stone which T.J. told her came from nearby Sentinel Peak, meaning "dark mountain," which gave Tucson its name.

The town was much larger and more settled than she had imagined. It seemed to spread out over a great distance in the valley. They passed two cheap cantinas which were silent this early in the day. They passed Mission Lane which led across farmlands to the *Convento of San Agustin.* She was amazed by the lovely townhome of rancher Francisco Carrillo, and asked T.J. how he knew who owned it.

"I've been in and out of this area more than a dozen times. I've watched her grow from a hole in the desert to a real town. I probably know as much about this area as I do any other. When you get settled in, you might enjoy me showing you the surrounding area. You certainly don't want to visit such secluded terrain without a gentleman guide."

T.J. described the interior of the Carrillo home with its mesquite and pine beams and its saguaro-ribbed ceilings. "Maybe you can visit it when he comes to town on business. I surely was impressed."

"How did you meet him?" she asked eagerly, not daring to make a quick acceptance of his polite offer to be her guide. She feared she couldn't allow "Miss Carolyn Starns" to be seen in his company.

"Did a little job for him years ago. Look over there." He told her about the *El Ojito,* an artesian spring which had supplied Tucson with water since the Spanish Colonial days. He pointed out *Casa del Gobernador,* a breathtaking home built by Jose Maria Soza over twenty years ago. They passed *Calle de La India Triste,* a street meaning "the sad Indian girl."

"The Garrett office is near *Calle de la Guardia* and *Calle Real.* We'll be there shortly. I guess you've noticed the attention we're getting," he hinted.

Carrie Sue had been too busy staring at the enormous adobe fort which stood before them to take note of the crowd gathering beside and behind the stage. She knew the people's curiosity and attendance had nothing to do with a slightly tardy schedule. She and the man near her were the center of attention. She discarded her study of the Presidio to focus on her task.

T.J. reined in the team before the stage office. Men hurried outside, questions spilling rapidly from their mouths at the ominous sight. The handsome man climbed down from the driver's box and helped Carrie Sue to the ground.

Sheriff Ben Myers, whose office was next door, heard the commotion and joined the crowd. T.J. related their misadventures to the gaping men. Myers introduced himself and said he'd take a look at the bandits inside the coach to see if any of them had prices on their heads. Before doing so, he sent for the undertaker.

The thirteen bodies were unloaded and laid out on the plankway in front of

Garrett's office. Ben Myers checked each man and said, "Far as I know, three of 'em have rewards posted. I'll check on the others."

"No hurry, Sheriff, I'll be in town for a while," T.J. informed him.

"I'll alert the Army about those Apaches. Until March we didn't have much trouble with 'em after Jeffords persuaded Cochise to settle down. Some of 'em riled the Mexicans and did some raiding nearby. Governor Safford got Jeffords fired last month 'cause he couldn't control 'em, and the Army's to move 'em soon to New Mexico. The Apaches are real mad. I got news a band had jumped the reservation with that Geronimo. Maybe they just needed supplies to get 'em across the border."

T.J. knew that Cochise had died two years ago and his body had been buried in a secret place in his beloved Chiricahua Mountains. T.J. remembered Geronimo and doubted that great warrior would flee to Mexico. The Indian agent Tom Jeffords was about the only white man the Apaches trusted, but Tom's hands were tied by government ropes.

A nice looking businessman joined them, and the crowd parted to let him move about as he desired. Even the noise quieted. "I heard the news, Ben. Did they get my gold shipment?"

Carrie Sue eyed the man closely, and took an instant dislike to him. He had brown eyes and brown hair; and his clothes were costly, clean, and neatly ironed though the day was hot and the hour late. She realized he was a man of power, wealth, and status . . . like the northern Carpetbagger who had stolen their Georgia farm and the Hardings who had slain her parents and stolen their Texas ranch. He noticed the bodies, but made no comments or apologies for the destruction he had caused. His only interest was his gold! "Sir, you are to blame for this slaughter of good people." She bravely scolded. "The Garrett line is not supposed to carry such perilous baggage. It was your gold which lured those beasts to attack us. I shall file a complaint with the company."

The middle-aged man looked her over, then smiled. "You must be Miss Carolyn Starns, our new school teacher. We've been expecting you. I'm Martin Ferris. I own a ranch and silver mine nearby, and I'm head of the town council which summoned you."

Carrie Sue's heart lurched in panic. She could not make an enemy of this important man, important to her new beginning here. She searched for her lost poise and a safe way to disentangle herself. "Why would such a responsible man encourage the stage company to break its rules and endanger so many lives?" she inquired, her tone softened.

"My gold shipment was supposed to be a secret and it's gravely needed here for expansion. Since everyone knows Garrett doesn't haul mail or strongboxes, we thought the gold and passengers would be perfectly safe this one time. We have men who won't accept paper dollars for skills or goods, scared the government might back down on its promise to rebuy them with gold. I traded silver from my mine for that chest of gold so I can loan it to our local bank. I'll have the sheriff investigate who revealed its presence to those outlaws. He's the one to blame for this bloody attack. I hope you weren't injured."

Carrie Sue cautioned herself to behave as Miss Carolyn Starns. "I'm fine, thanks to this kind gentleman," she remarked, nodding to T.J.

Martin Ferris glanced at the gunslinger, then told the redhead, "There's no need for a lady to endure a situation like this, so I'll have someone escort you to Mrs. Thayer's boarding house. We can meet and talk in the morning after you've rested and unpacked. If we see eye-to-eye, I'll hire you after our talk." To her ebon-haired companion, he said almost coldly, "I'll have to reward you for saving Miss Starns and my gold. I'm surprised to find you're such an honest man."

"Your gold isn't worth dying for, Ferris, or rotting in jail over," T.J. replied in a casual tone, which concealed his past trouble with this man. He didn't like the way Martin Ferris was observing Carolyn or how the man had spoken to her. Too, there was something strange about the attempted theft of a "secret" shipment.

Two men gathered the bags which Carrie Sue pointed out and she followed them to the boarding house, after thanking T.J. again for saving her life. One of the men spoke privately with Mrs. Thayer—as he had done with Martin Ferris—before she showed Carrie Sue to her new home. It was a lovely set of two rooms which received neither the morning nor afternoon sun, which meant they would be cooler day and night.

The woman said there was a tub and pump in the water closet down the hall and informed Carrie Sue that supper was served promptly at six each evening, with breakfast at seven and dinner at twelve. "I'm sure after days on a hot stage you'll be wanting to get scrubbed first. The food and lodgings are good here, Miss Starns, so I know you'll enjoy living at my place."

"I'm certain I will, Mrs. Thayer. Thank you," she responded. "What do you charge for rent and when is it due?"

"I charge fifteen dollars a month for board and ten for food, due the first day of each month you plan to live here. You'll be wanting to take your meals here because the restaurants are higher and my food is better." She laughed merrily and her pale blue eyes twinkled. "Leave your key with me every Monday for changing bed linens and cleaning up your rooms. The other days are your responsibility. I don't allow no cussing or drinking or misbehaving." The fifty-year-old woman laughed again as if she'd told a joke. "There's a laundress down the street who does a good job of washing and ironing, and her prices are cheap. It might be better to hire her rather than doing your own clothes. But if you like, you can use my washtub and iron. If you have a guest for a meal, it's fifty cents extra. You can have gentlemen callers in the downstairs parlor, but you have to leave your door open for decency if a man visits you up here. Any more questions?"

Carrie Sue returned the woman's warm smile. She liked the grandmotherly landlady. "Today's the eleventh, so how much do I owe you for May?"

"The town council is paying until the fifteenth, then you can pay for half a month's charges. If you need anything, let me know. I have to get back to my supper. We'll talk more over a hot meal."

The moment the owner left, Carrie Sue examined her surroundings. The front room, a small private parlor, was clean and decorated nicely. It contained a short couch against one wall and matching chair in a floral print on one corner. Beside each was a round table with a glass lamp. In the middle of the floor before the couch was a thick rug which looked several years old but was in excellent condition. In another corner was a desk and chair, and Carrie Sue wondered if this set of rooms had been reserved for the new schoolmarm, or had Martin Ferris requested it after meeting her earlier? She wanted to know what he and his man had said, and what the man had told the owner of this fine boarding house.

There was a window on one side of the room which overlooked a side street. The bedroom had two windows for fresh air, one which looked out over that same side street and one which overlooked a quiet back street. Situated away from the main section of Tucson, it should be a serene home. The structure, two stories high, was built of sturdy wood. The walls were covered with a pale floral wallpaper and the woodwork was painted a light yellow, giving the rooms an airy and bright effect which appealed to Carrie Sue. The floors were scrubbed and the furniture was polished. It was clear that Mrs. Thayer took good care of her property and would expect her guests to do the same.

The bedroom was furnished with a double bed, a small side table with an oil lamp, a braided rug, a squatty chest with a second oil lamp, and a washstand with a pitcher and bowl and a mirror mounted over it. Surprisingly the room had a large closet for storage, which meant no hanging of clothes behind a curtain in one corner.

Carrie Sue twirled around, eyeing everything once more. Her daring ruse was working! Everyone believed her! At last, her dreams were coming true. She had a real home.

She lifted a bag to the bed to begin unpacking. A knock on her door halted her. She froze and panicked. Then, she heard Mrs. Thayer call out to her. Carrie Sue took several deep breaths to steady her jittery nerves before she opened the door to find Martin Ferris's two men standing there with the older woman.

"They brought up the trunk which you had sent ahead. Carry it into the bedroom, boys. After you unpack it, if you don't have space for it in your closet or bedroom, you can store it in my shed out back."

"You're most kind, Mrs. Thayer. In all the excitement yesterday and today, I almost forgot about it. Thank you," she told the men as they departed.

Mrs. Thayer remarked, "They told me about the holdup and Indian attack. You've had a rough time getting here, but you're gonna like Tucson. Why don't you relax in a nice bath before supper? You can settle in tomorrow when you're rested."

"That's an excellent suggestion," Carrie Sue responded.

"You'll find towels and soap in the water closet. Don't forget to wash out the tub when you're done. There's a chamber pot under your bed. I have a Mexican girl who empties them every morning and helps me around here. You'll meet her tomorrow."

After Mrs. Thayer's second departure, Carrie Sue fetched her string-purse and retrieved the key to the lock on the trunk. First thing, she needed to make certain there were no clues inside of it to her and Carolyn's identities. If so, they must be destroyed immediately.

To Carrie Sue's surprise, the clothes inside the trunk were prettier and nicer than the ones in Carolyn's travel bags. She examined each one with pleasure and interest. There was even a riding skirt and three lovely nightgowns. Of course, there were more books, and one picture: Carolyn with her family. Carrie Sue studied it and decided it had been made several years ago. She hated to get rid of it, but she looked nothing like the parents or girl there.

Taking her knife from another bag, Carrie Sue entered the closet and knelt. She searched for a loosened board on the floor and found one. As quietly as possible, she worked it free. In the space between her floor and the ceiling of the room below, she concealed the picture and her weapons. She had the most trouble with her rifle, which barely fit because of the support beams. With great caution, she replaced the board and sat the empty bag atop the disturbed area. The clothes from it were placed inside the chest of drawers to be sorted later.

After deciding which dress to wear tonight, she put the other bags near the large trunk at the foot of the bed. Tonight, she would bathe, eat, and get a good night's sleep. Tomorrow she could unpack at her leisure, after her meeting with Martin Ferris.

Chapter

4

Friday morning, Carrie Sue dressed with great care for her meeting. She donned a lovely pale blue day dress from Carolyn's trunk and placed a matching sunbonnet on the bed, which was straightened neatly. As she brushed her hair, her mind drifted back to last night.

Her lengthy bath had been wonderful, but she hadn't washed her hair because there hadn't been enough time for it to dry before supper. She had met the other guests during a splendid meal. Mrs. Thayer had not boasted deceitfully about her cooking, and Carrie Sue had savored each bite of chicken and dumplings.

On the second floor were two more sets of rooms similar to hers and two single rooms for traveling men, who "don't need as much space as a woman or a couple," according to the genial owner. One set was occupied by a young couple who was awaiting the completion of their new home; they were too much in love and excited over their bright future to take much notice of her. Another was occupied by a couple whose home had recently burned; they were too depressed to take much notice of her. One of the single rooms was rented by a man who was having his home repaired and painted for his bride-to-be who was to arrive soon from El Paso, and he couldn't stop talking about her. The other single room was vacant.

Mrs. Thayer's private rooms, into which she invited very few people, were located on one side of the first floor. The other side of the large house contained a kitchen, dining area, large social parlor, and a small sitting room for privacy.

There was a storage shed built against a small barn for the residents' horses, to the rear of which was a small corral. At the back of the house had been attached two more single rooms, both of which were rented by men who were going to be in Tucson long enough to make staying here cheaper than renting hotel rooms. Both men—one married and one single—were taken by Carrie Sue's beauty and presence, and each did his best to obtain her full attention until the evening ended.

Mrs. Thayer had introduced her to everyone at supper and had shown her around afterwards. Carrie Sue had been impressed by the woman's property and success. She had learned of Mr. Thayer's death a few years back and of the woman's determination to keep the boarding house.

The redhead braided her hair again, twisted it into a ball near her nape, and covered it with a thick brown net from Carolyn's trunk so only her fiery bangs were exposed. Carrie Sue checked her image in the mirror and smiled; it was an excellent disguise for her flaming locks. Once her sunbonnet was in place, she concluded happily, no one would be overly aware of her hair. It would be wise to do this every day.

Last night she had gone to sleep thinking about Darby and T.J., wondering what both men were doing. To imagine never seeing either one again pained her deeply. Was freedom worth such a high price? She thought about the horror stories of women in prison and—

Someone knocked at her door and interrupted her mental study. She tensed, but not as much as she had yesterday afternoon. She was far away from Texas and her crimes. She had been accepted here as the new schoolmarm. She had fooled everyone. She had to calm her fears and worries. She was Carolyn Starns now, and forever.

But what would happen if she opened her door one day to find Quade Harding standing there, or one of his hired hunters? The lovely fugitive reprimanded herself for her cowardice. If it happened, it happened, and she must deal with it that day! She couldn't live her new life in constant terror of discovery and capture. Yet, realistically she knew she would be looking over her shoulder for a long time.

The knock came again. Carrie Sue responded to find a dark-haired girl standing there. "Señor Ferris waits downstairs for you."

"You must be Maria Corbeza, Mrs. Thayer's helper," Carrie Sue hinted. The young girl smiled shyly and nodded. "Tell him I will be down shortly. Thank you, Maria."

Carrie Sue checked her appearance once more, gathered her hat and purse, and went to join the man. She assumed he was picking her up to escort her to a council meeting.

Martin Ferris had other plans in mind. Carrie Sue found him awaiting her in the private parlor. "Sit down, Miss Starns, and we'll complete our business quickly. Then, I can show you around."

"What about the rest of the town council? Don't they wish to meet me and question me?" she inquired.

"It isn't necessary. They trust my opinion. Would you care for some coffee or hot tea?" he inquired, as if this were his home.

"No, thank you. What do you need to know about me that wasn't included in our correspondence?" she asked, getting down to business.

"Relax, Miss Starns, there's no rush, or need to be afraid." Carrie Sue didn't like his tone or his lecherous gaze. "I'm certain we'll become very good friends. If you satisfy me, the rest of the town council will go along with my wishes."

Carrie Sue recognized his kind of man. He was a cruel and greedy tyrant who took advantage of weaker people, especially defenseless females. She wanted and needed this job badly, but not badly enough to cow to a man like this! With Carolyn's money and identity and credentials, and with her determination and wits, she could find another job, even another town farther west, if this one didn't work out as expected. She couldn't allow him to get the upper hand this early in their relationship, or she would have trouble with him from now on! She had to be firm, but cautious.

In a pleasant tone and with a calm expression, she asked, "Why should I be frightened, Mr. Ferris? Either you hire me or you don't. If not, I can look elsewhere. From your recent experience, I'm sure you realize that well-trained teachers are in great demand these days and that it's difficult to lure them to a town in the desert. One point confuses me—it was my understanding that I had already been hired through the mail by Mr. Payne. Am I mistaken?"

Martin Ferris studied her intently, especially her eyes and hair. "Not exactly, Miss

Starns. But I do need to interview you further before placing the children of our town in your hands."

"How many children do you have, sir?"

"None," he responded, but not a glimmer of sadness was exposed in his piercing brown eyes.

"You've never been married?"

"My wife met with a fatal accident years ago and I haven't remarried. I'm sorry to say she was unable to give me children."

Carrie Sue mentally scoffed, *Just like you to blame her for having weak seeds!* "Ask your questions because I would like to get our matter settled as quickly as possible. I've had a long journey and I'm still fatigued. Too, I have a great deal of unpacking and planning to do."

"Right to the point—I like that in a person. I've gone over your credentials and correspondence. You didn't say why you left St. Louis."

"Another woman wanted my job, and she had a powerful father who made certain she got it. I can assure you the school there will suffer greatly for hiring her; she isn't as qualified as I am." Carrie Sue wanted to demand, *if you read the correspondence, why don't you know those facts?* Fortunately Carolyn had kept a copy of every letter to and from this town, so the redhead knew Martin was lying.

"Confidence and courage are good traits to have, Miss Starns. I'm certain every word you've spoken and written is the truth." He watched for her reactions as he continued. "The salary is one hundred dollars a month. I know you were quoted sixty in the letter, but I convinced the council that isn't enough for a lady to live on in Tucson. It's a growing town, getting more expensive every week." Naturally Martin didn't tell her he was supplying the additional forty dollars, not yet anyway.

"I'm delighted to learn your town council is so generous and wise, Mr. Ferris. Most teachers are terribly underpaid for the difficult job they perform. The salary is most agreeable. What else?"

"The school is open Monday through Friday from eight until four. Since the children have been without a teacher for some time, we expect you to begin classes on June fifth. You can give them August off, then resume teaching in September. That allows you three weeks to get the schoolhouse in order and get settled here. I'm sure you know from experience that the care and cleaning of the schoolhouse is part of your job, unless you hire a helper from your salary. You will also receive a small budget for supplies. Is that part also agreeable?"

"Certainly."

"There will be a trial period of two months, June and July. If all goes well, your position becomes permanent in September. I have been appointed to drop in occasionally to observe your methods and control of the children. We do expect good results, Miss Starns."

Appointed, my rump! Carrie Sue's mind refuted. She didn't need to spend time and energy on this offensive distraction when she had so much to do! "I assure you that you'll have them, Mr. Ferris. But it's my policy to hold a parent's day once every month so they can see how their children are progressing. At that time, any problem either of us has can be discussed and resolved. I'm afraid your presence in the classroom would be most distracting to the students. Most of them, especially the older ones, are shy about participation in front of strange adults. I'm certain you don't wish to disrupt the class over something you can observe one Saturday a month."

Carrie Sue sensed the man's annoyance at her quick wits and obstinance. She had been playing Carolyn Starns for weeks and her old life seemed far away, so she had the courage to battle him.

The well-dressed man stood and said, "I'll show you the schoolhouse if you'll follow me."

Carrie Sue tied the ribbons of her sunbonnet beneath her chin and trailed Martin Ferris to the door. A carriage was waiting outside with a driver, a black man who was as neatly dressed as his boss. Martin turned to assist her into the carriage. Carrie Sue did not want to sit so close to him, so she suggested, "Is it within walking distance? I can use the exercise."

"It isn't far, but you must learn to be careful in this sun. It can be a killer. Newcomers don't realize the danger because the heat dries up warning perspiration so quickly. Always remember to keep plenty of drinking water available for you and the children. We'll take the carriage today, so we can head on into town afterwards."

"I would ra—"

Martin did not let her finish her refusal. "There are plenty of people eager to meet you, and you need to learn your way around. I promised to bring you by for introductions after our talk."

The desperado did not believe him, but she couldn't call him a liar. She reasoned politely, "Couldn't we make our visits tomorrow or Sunday after I've settled in?"

"Some of the council members and important people live outside of town. It's best to catch them at their stores and offices today."

Carrie Sue felt trapped by the ride and his demands, but she had to yield. "As you wish, Mr. Ferris."

The wealthy man thought it was the bright sun which made the beauty beside him squint her eyes, tighten her lips, and flush her cheeks. He did not know that the exquisite redhead had a temper as fiery as her hair, one which Carrie Sue had learned to leash on most occasions. He felt the heat of her body, touching his from thigh to shoulder, and passion for her blazed into life.

They reached the schoolhouse soon, three blocks away, an easy walk for anyone except a man who didn't like to sweat or work. It was a stark wooden structure. The boards were weathered by harsh nature and its dull facade was unappealing. *If schools were prettier, perhaps children wouldn't be so frightened by them!* she mused as she followed Martin's lead around the outside of the building. There were windows on all sides for fresh air flow, including one near the apex of the front roof and one in the same place on the back to allow the rising hot air to escape.

The earth around it was dry, rocky and nearly barren, except for a tall saguaro cactus near the front door and a few small scrubs here and there. A bell beneath a cover was attached to the roof near the front, and two steps—over which was nailed a sign that read "Tucson School"—led inside to the one large room. Behind the school was an outhouse which looked as if it would collapse if it weren't repaired soon.

As if reading her mind, Martin remarked, "I'll have a carpenter work on it next week. We don't want parents blaming you for an accident." He pointed to a partially fenced area and informed her, "That's where the children play during recess. The boards near the ground keep out snakes and other undesirable creatures. It also keeps the children in an area you can control. Let's go inside."

There was no moisture on Carrie Sue's face, but she felt as if her clothes were getting damp. Obviously the man's warning about the climate here was accurate, something to remember. The shade of the schoolhouse felt good to her flesh and eyes. She let her gaze grow accustomed to the lack of glare before looking around. There were twenty student's desks placed in rows of fives, all facing the lengthy wooden desk upon a raised section of flooring. On the wall behind the teacher's desk was a chalkboard, flanked by shelves on each side. A long pole sat in one corner for pushing up and pulling down the two high window sashes. In the other stood an American flag with its thirty-seven stars. The bell rope was wound about a peg near the door, and she had a mischievous urge to ring it. On one side of the doorway was a bench, and on the other side was a row of pegs for winter garments.

The floors, desks, window sills, and shelves were covered in dirt. The window panes were so clouded that seeing outside was nearly impossible. It appeared as if the school hadn't been cleaned in months, and the windows had been left open during a violent dust storm. This meant she had a lot of sweeping, mopping, scrubbing, and polishing ahead of her. Perhaps she could hire Maria to help with the first cleaning.

Carrie Sue approached the shelves behind her new desk. Small chalkboards, boxes of chalk, pencils, paper, books, and other items were stacked there. "You furnish such supplies rather than the families?"

"The parents pay a small fee which makes up that supply budget I mentioned earlier. It's easier for everyone if the teacher provides them on the first day of school. When it closed, the children were asked to leave them here so they wouldn't get lost while we sought a replacement for Helen Cooper."

"What happened to Miss Cooper? Did she move or retire?"

"I'm afraid Miss Cooper met with a terrible accident."

"What happened?" she pressed.

"Mining's a big part of our territory, so she wanted to teach the children about it. She asked to take them out to the one I own. I agreed to let her visit first to make certain she knew what she was doing. Once we got inside where it was dark and narrow, she panicked and started running for the entrance. She fell into a pit and broke her neck. Since it was my mine and she was in my care, I've taken a responsibility to help replace her. If you get the same idea, I'll have to refuse your request. But I can send one of my men here with samples to give a lesson."

"That's very kind and thoughtful, Mr. Ferris. Shall we begin our tour of your town?"

As they were leaving, he said, "I'll have notices sent out to all parents to let them know we have a new teacher and school will open again on June fifth. That is, if you've found everything agreeable today."

"Everything is fine with me, Mr. Ferris." Actually, she was getting excited about this new challenge.

"Excellent, Miss Starns. I promise you'll love it here."

As they rode past homes and businesses, Martin Ferris told her who lived there or owned them, and sometimes their history. His driver took them to where the streets *Calle de la Guardia* and *Calle Real* met near the entry to the Presidio. He helped her out of his carriage and told the driver, "We'll walk a spell."

As they did so, he pointed out the size of the old Spanish fort. The adobe wall was twelve feet high and ran for about seven hundred and fifty feet on each side. He explained how the soldiers and their families had lived inside the Presidio and how settlers had lived and farmed beyond it. He pointed out where the fiestas were still held on special occasions, and she could almost hear the music and laughter and smell the Mexican foods. She saw the home built by Edward Nye Fish and the one beside it which belonged to Hiram Stevens, his friend.

She was shown *La Casa Cordova,* one of the oldest buildings in Tucson. She saw the unusual outside of Leonardo Romero's home which was built over part of the Presidio wall. He told her that Soledad Jacome's residence had been completed only last year, that it had saguaro rib ceilings, expensive woodwork, and several corner fireplaces.

She noticed people of many races and cultures, living and working as if no one here was aware of any differences between them. Shops with Spanish and American names and goods were located here and there, and she was amazed by what this walled area contained. She studied its columns and arches, its highly decorated facade, the tile roofs, and traditional canales: drain pipes to allow water to flow off the flat roofs. Most of the private homes had been built ten to fifteen years ago, but some were much older. It was a splendid blend of cultures.

"How do you like Tucson so far?" he asked.

"It's breathtaking and amazing," she commented.

"Just as you are, Carolyn," he murmured.

As if she hadn't heard him, she glanced his way with an innocent expression and asked, "What did you say, sir?"

"I said, I promised you would love it here. We'll meet a few people, then have some dinner. It's already three o'clock. You must be famished. I didn't mean to starve you during our tour."

This man could be very charming, she concluded, but deceitfully so. She had been so engrossed by the scenery that she had forgotten about time and business, and his company. "Learning new things is always fascinating to me, so I forget everything else. Lead on, Mr. Ferris," she teased, having decided to spend more time with him to observe him. Too, she might encounter T.J. Rogue along the way. Her handsome rescuer had told her he would be in town for a while, and he did know where she was staying and working. Surely he hadn't already dismissed her from mind.

After meeting the other members of the town council, Carrie Sue sat down in a nice restaurant to eat with Martin. They were served baked chicken, rice with gravy, biscuits, jam, and canned carrots. The delicious meal was finished off with dried apple pie and coffee.

Carrie Sue shifted in her chair and sent him a rueful smile. "I must get home now, Mr. Ferris; it's late and I'm exhausted. I can see that my unpacking will have to wait another day."

"If you'll call me Martin, I'll escort you home this moment."

"As you wish," she responded with a lightness which she didn't feel.

Mrs. Thayer met her in the front parlor and asked, "Are you all right, Miss Starns? I was worried about you when you missed dinner and supper is nearly ready to go on the table."

As she removed her hat, she explained, "I'm sorry, Mrs. Thayer, but Mr. Ferris practically refused to return me home until I knew Tucson by heart and had met everyone he called 'important.' He insisted we stop to eat at four-thirty. He's a most persistent man and I didn't want to offend him so soon after my arrival."

"I thought I saw a twinkle in his eye when he arrived this morning. Be wary of him, Carolyn," she advised, switching to her first name and lowering her voice to prevent being overheard. "He's a rich and powerful man, and he likes to have his way."

"Did Helen Cooper live here, too? Did he pester her like this?"

Mrs. Thayer's smile faded completely. "She moved here about a month before her death. She saw him now and again, but she seemed afraid of him. He always sent his carriage and driver after her, didn't come himself like a real gentleman should."

"He said she had an accident in his mine. Is that true?"

"She left here to visit it with him, but she didn't want to go. She'd been feeling poorly ever since she moved in. She never came back. He told everyone she got scared inside the mine and took a fall while trying to get outside."

"You sound as if you don't believe his tale."

"I've talked too much as it is. Just keep this between us, but watch him with a tight eye. And stay out of that dangerous mine," she warned like a frightened mother. "I have to get back to work."

"Thank you, Mrs. Thayer. I'll be careful."

The older woman smiled at her and tweaked her cheek. "I know you will, girl. You're smart and brave—noticed that right off. Helen weren't nothing like you. She was weak and scared. Can't blame her; she needed this job to keep her out of the whorehouse. There ain't many jobs for a woman alone, 'specially if she ain't got no money. Maybe it's best she went to her final resting place. She couldn't get enough sleep, tired all the time, tired and nervous and sick. Didn't a morning pass that girl didn't empty her stomach into her potty."

Carrie Sue noticed how the woman's speech pattern became rustic as she spoke hurriedly, apprehensively. She wondered if the woman realized what sickness she had just described: pregnancy. Was it, she asked herself, a coincidence that the single and expectant Helen Cooper was seeing a man she disliked and met with death in his mine?

"I suppose you won't be needing supper tonight since you just ate, but I'll save some pie and coffee for you later."

Carrie Sue impulsively hugged the older woman. "You're wonderful, Mrs. Thayer. I'll get my hair washed; it feels awful."

*

Carrie Sue sat on the floor in her bedroom with her long hair hanging out the window so it could dry before bedtime. She had unpacked a few things, taken a bath, scrubbed her head, and consumed the pie and milk which Mrs. Thayer had brought to her room.

Her lids kept closing as her mind drifted lazily. How she wished her brother was here to enjoy the sweet taste of freedom.

Another safe day had passed. Tomorrow, she would visit the school again and the laundress. And she might stroll around to see if she could sight T.J. somewhere. Of course that presented the risk of running into Martin Ferris and being unable to get rid of him.

"Who knows?" she murmured. "Perhaps he would make a powerful ally if trouble struck. If I can use him without being used!"

*

The following morning, Maria delivered a package to her room. When Carrie Sue unwrapped it, she found a lovely parasol and a note from Martin Ferris. She read it:

> Carolyn,
>   To protect that beautiful head from our hot sun. Please join me for supper tonight. I'll send for your answer at noon.
> Martin Ferris.

Carrie Sue hurriedly rewrapped the package and retied the string. She seized her hat, purse, dirty clothes, and the gift and rushed downstairs. She found Mrs. Thayer in the kitchen and explained her dilemma. She entreated, "Please put this somewhere. When Mister Ferris or his man arrives at noon, tell him I was gone when it arrived and you don't know when I'll return today to get his message."

The woman grinned with anticipation of their ruse. "It's done, Carolyn. If you see his carriage waiting outside, slip in the back and up to your room. I'll bring your meal there later. Be careful."

"I will. But don't worry about me. We'll think of some plausible excuse tonight."

Carrie Sue followed Mrs. Thayer's directions to the home of the laundress. The sturdy woman agreed to do the redhead's washing and ironing each week. Carrie Sue was to bring it to her each Monday and pick it up each Thursday, unless she had a special need of a garment.

Carrie Sue walked to the schoolhouse. She did not open the windows or leave the front door ajar, just in case Martin Ferris came by. She examined the room again and mentally made notes about its cleaning and preparation. She sat at the desk; she walked back and forth on the raised flooring; she pretended to write on the chalkboard; she imagined herself teaching a room filled with children.

Anticipation surged through her as she decided this job would be fun and challenging. She would be filling young minds, making friends, and earning respect. She wanted these people—especially the children in her class—to like her, to trust her, to want to learn from her. She recalled her school days and teachers in Georgia. Having loved school, she remembered a great deal about them, memories which would aid her now.

The room was getting hot. Carrie Sue realized she had to open the doors and windows, or she had to leave. The noises of an approaching carriage caught her attention. She grabbed her purse and hid under the lengthy desk, relieved that the front and sides were enclosed so she couldn't be seen from the door. Nor could she be sighted if Martin walked around the building, as the back window was too high.

She heard the carriage halt. She controlled her respiration so it wouldn't expose her presence. The steps creaked as Martin mounted them and opened the door. There was momentary silence as he must have glanced around the large room. She heard him swear irritably. Then, she sighted another peril. . . .

A Bark Scorpion was clinging deftly to the underside of the desk, poised there and ready to strike an unsuspecting leg or hand. She was lucky he hadn't attacked earlier when she was sitting in the chair with her legs near his hiding place. He was about two inches long, rather slender, straw colored, and had two dark bands along his back. His pinchers were moving in a threatening manner, as was his raised tail with its venomous stinger. It was said that more people died from its sting than from the bites of all poisonous snakes combined!

Carrie Sue remained motionless, keeping her full attention on the scorpion, who seemed content to hold his position for the time being. She was crouched on the other end, but her feet and legs were beneath him. If he released his hold on the wood and dropped to them . . . She knew Martin had not closed the door and left. If she scrambled from her position, her ruse would be exposed. She waited; the tiny foe waited; and Martin seemed to stall his departure for some reason.

A horrible thought entered the lovely desperado's mind: what if the scorpion had family or friends nearby, such as behind her? She dared not turn her head and look. She kept her hands in her lap with her purse. There was nothing within reach to use for a weapon. Despite her fear and peril, she knew it was best not to alert Martin to her ruse. She had been in tight spots before, so she could endure this one.

Finally she heard him close the door and descend the steps, but he walked around the schoolhouse, even called her name several times. Perhaps he thought she was in the outhouse. The scorpion took a few menacing steps forward. Carrie Sue held her ground. She kept her respiration slow and shallow to prevent as much motion as possible. She wondered if the deadly creature could sense her fear, perhaps smell it as she had smelled the passengers' terror during the holdup.

Even when she heard the carriage leave, she remained in her hiding place for a time, her gaze glued on the arachnid. Martin Ferris was sneaky, and could be standing outside to see if she suddenly appeared after his departure. The scorpion began to make his way in her direction. She had no choice but to wiggle cautiously from beneath the desk. The moment her dress cleared a spot, the venomous creature dropped to it with stinger and pinchers lifted ominously.

Carrie Sue seized a heavy book and dropped it on the scorpion. She placed her foot on it and shifted her weight. When she heard a "crunch," she leaned against the chalkboard and took a deep breath. Her shaking ceased, and she went from window to window making certain the persistent man was gone. No doubt he would return later to look for her again when she failed to appear at the boarding house.

She left the school and went to visit a seamstress which Mrs. Thayer had recommended. She didn't need any new clothes for a while, but it would take time to meet the woman and to chat for a while. Carrie Sue did not plan to alter Carolyn's image until she was assured of her unquestionable acceptance here. Then, *Carolyn* could buy and wear some prettier and nicer clothes. After subtracting her monthly expenses, she would have thirty-five to forty dollars left over to save or to spend.

One thing she needed to do was conceal money and supplies in her closet, just in case she had to flee in a hurry. And it might be a good idea to do the same outside of town, in case she couldn't get to her room following her unmasking. A horse for a quick getaway was a good idea, and it shouldn't arouse suspicion for Miss Carolyn Starns to own and ride one in this western town.

Carrie Sue made a lengthy visit with the seamstress who was close to her age, the widow of a soldier from Fort Lowell nearby. She revealed that she wanted lovelier and better quality clothes, but she had to wait a while because people had a preset idea of how a teacher should dress. The woman had laughed and understood.

Afterwards, Carrie Sue strolled down backstreets where she assumed she was safe from Martin Ferris's seeking gaze. She realized that Tucson was a rapidly growing town of very wealthy people and very poor people. Some of the poverty she observed tugged at her heart. She saw homes which were little more than adobe or wooden shacks with dirty children playing around them in near rags.

The air was hot and dry, yet she smelled a variety of odors of which Mexican food was most noticeable. The people seemed to move and work slowly in the heat of the day, aware of the demands of their harsh climate. Carrie Sue's body was warm and her clothes were damp. She knew she should get out of the unrelenting sun for a time.

She sighted a Mexican cafe which looked clean and safe for a lady to enter, as she had learned to judge places fairly well during her years on the trail. She entered it to find only a few customers present. She took a seat near a window for fresh air.

A plump Spanish woman took her order with a smile, and returned shortly with her meal: refried beans, browned rice, a floured tortilla rolled with a chicken filling, and coffee. Carrie Sue ate slowly to enjoy the tasty meal and to waste time. She wished she could order a few sips of tequila to calm her nerves, but she dared not.

She watched Martin Ferris's carriage go down the street and wondered how long the man would search for her. Perhaps, she fretted, his patience and persistence would rival Quade's! Unable to hold another drop of coffee or food, she paid the woman and left.

She made a stop at a saddlery shop, concluding that no one would think to look for her in such a place. She told the man she was considering the purchase of a horse and a saddle, so he delighted in showing her the different kinds and making recommendations for a lady. She pretended to know little about western saddles and let him talk for over an hour. She promised, when she bought her horse, she would make her saddle purchase in his shop.

Carrie Sue was hot and tired and tense. She sneaked to the boarding house only to find Martin's carriage sitting out front as suspected. She went into the barn and climbed into the loft. She sat on loose hay which was used to feed the horses in the corral out back. She sank to her back, gazing at the beams overhead as she eased into deep thought.

She had hidden in lofts many times, sometimes while on the run during her outlaw days, and sometimes for hide-and-seek with Darby on their Texas ranch. Her location stirred many memories of those days.

Suddenly the beautiful fugitive bolted upright. She asked herself what she was doing hiding out like a terrified child. She didn't owe Martin Ferris or anyone here an explanation for her choices. This was like being on the run again! She had work to do. She was fatigued. She needed a soothing bath. She needed the tranquility of her new home. All she had to do was refuse his invitation firmly. She couldn't hide from him every day. And she hated this feeling of being watched, followed everywhere. It hadn't left her all day or yesterday!

"What's the matter with you, Carrie Sue Stover? You're too damn edgy and suspicious. No one is trailing you, or you'd have noticed him. Get your butt in the house and get busy with something!"

Carrie Sue left the loft and entered the back door. She heard Martin Ferris's voice in the front parlor. She scowled, then headed up the back steps. She made it to her room without meeting anyone, and locked her door. After removing her hat, she fanned herself with it a few minutes. A bath would have to wait because it would alert the others to someone's presence upstairs. No matter, she had plenty of unpacking and sorting to do until Martin gave up and departed.

*

T.J. Rogue leaned against the building nearby. He was baffled by the redhead's behavior, yesterday and today. Something had her spooked. But what? he wondered. It couldn't be his tail because he was too good at that job to give himself away, especially to a woman. There was something weird going on with that contradictory vixen. He wanted answers to her mystery.

Chapter

5

Sunday morning, Carrie Sue dressed to attend church with Mrs. Thayer. She knew such behavior would be expected of her, as she was an example for the children to follow and it would reveal her morals to the adults of this town. She had not attended church since her parent's deaths, and because of her past sins she found it difficult to enter one. Yet, her ruse demanded it of her, and she was probably in need of God's protection and guidance.

She had completed her unpacking last night and had taken a late bath. When Mrs. Thayer had come to check on her after Martin's departure, she had revealed her actions of the day, and her decision to confront the man when next he appoached—no, pestered—her.

Carrie Sue pinned her hair atop her head and put on a lovely pink and blue floral hat which she had purchased yesterday during her wanderings. It went nicely with the soft blue dress she had found in Carolyn's trunk. She rode with Mrs. Thayer and one of the couples to the other end of town to where a large white church was located. From the number of horses and carriages and wagons, the attendance was good.

They took seats on a pew which was halfway to the front of the church. They had arrived just in time for the service to begin. A woman started playing an old organ which needed tuning; the crowd rose to its feet with hymnals in hand; and the minister took his position behind the pulpit and led the opening song.

Martin Ferris slipped into the row where they were standing. He took a place next to Carrie Sue and boldly shared the songbook which she and Mrs. Thayer were holding. His action caused him to lean close to the redhead, too close for her liking. She kept her gaze either on the page or the minister and sang softly.

After several songs were completed and they were taking their seats, he whispered, "Good morning, Carolyn. I missed you yesterday."

She glanced his way and smiled politely, then shifted toward Mrs. Thayer as she pretended to settle herself. The preacher gave them a heated lesson on the Ten Commandments from Exodus 20: 1–17. He shouted about the "wages of sin" being death. He urged them to repentance and to obedience of "God's Holy Word."

Carrie Sue felt her heart flutter when the minister expounded on God's views on theft and murder. She had not coveted the possessions of others, but she had needed some of them for survival. She had not entered her life of sin because she was evil or weak; she had done so to seek justice against the Hardings. She had not turned "the other cheek" or waited for "God to punish vile sinners." But as the preacher shouted on and on, she had to admit she had taken the law into her own hands and sought vengeance—a sin in itself.

Carrie Sue's mind wandered to the innocent victims of the Stover Gang's deeds. She had condemned herself by being a part of them, however innocent in the beginning. Guilt nibbled at her. She promised, *If you let this new life work out for me, I'll never be bad again.*

Immediately the preacher yelled that you couldn't make deals with God: live morally or pay the consequences. Carrie Sue's mind argued that she had been forced into a life of crime. But the minister yelled as he pounded his fist on the pulpit, "God don't accept no excuses for being wicked! You'll pay for your black sins in the fires of Hell, and He'll make you suffer terribly here on Earth!"

Carrie Sue's mind shouted back at him, *I have suffered terribly! I've paid for my mistakes! I've earned a right to freedom! What about those whom God hasn't punished or destroyed?*

The service finally ended, and she wanted to get away from Martin Ferris. Carrie Sue was forced to chat with him though. When he questioned her whereabouts the day before, she eyed him rather oddly, sending him a look which said he was being too forward and nosey.

Her reaction did not trouble or dissuade him. He alleged, "I was worried about you, Carolyn. You don't know this town yet and you aren't accustomed to our tricky weather. What did you do all day?"

She noticed his use of her first name. She was standing in a church, so she tried to be as honest as possible. "I visited the school to decide how much time and work was involved in getting it clean. Then, I just wandered around familiarizing myself with the town and people. I also did a little shopping," she remarked, touching her new hat.

"It's very pretty. How did you like the parasol?"

"It was kind of you to send it, Mr. Ferris, but a lady shouldn't accept gifts from strangers. I'll return it tomorrow."

He chuckled and shook his head. "It's a welcome gift from the town council, so you can't refuse it and hurt everyone's feelings." In a smug tone, he informed her, "We need to get moving, Carolyn. I planned for you to join me and some friends for Sunday dinner."

Carrie Sue was annoyed. They were standing outside now, so she lied calmly, "Thank you for the invitation, but I always rest and study my Bible on Sundays as the Scriptures insist."

"Surely you don't want to disappoint our Mayor Carlson and his wife. They're expecting us to join them at their home within the hour. I was certain you'd want to go, so I accepted their invitation for the both of us."

Carrie Sue eyed him again, then exhaled loudly to reveal her vexation. "I will dine with them today, Mr. Ferris. But in the future, please ask first before you accept invitations on my behalf."

Carrie Sue was introduced to numerous people, many of them parents of children who would be her students very soon. The adults were delighted to learn that the school would open again on June fifth, but the children seemed none too happy about attending classes in the hot summer. Carrie Sue laughed and joked with the youngsters to relax them.

Before she left the church yard, many of the children were won over by the beautiful and genial schoolmarm.

In his carriage, Martin teased, "Don't you think it's unwise to get so friendly with your students? How will they obey you?"

Carrie Sue did not smile. "It has been my experience, Mr. Ferris, that people—especially children—obey better out of friendship and respect than out of fear and dislike. A friend will go a second mile for you, but an enemy halts your journey or heads the other way."

"You're very wise for such a beautiful young woman. I stand corrected, my fetching schoolmarm."

Carrie Sue did not respond to his overture by word or expression. "Did the other council members agree to our deal, Mr. Ferris?"

"Please, you promised to call me Martin," he scolded mockingly.

"I'm afraid I find it difficult to call a man of your status by his Christian name. I am only the school teacher here, and some people might think that improper." Her remarks did not put him in his place.

"I don't care what people say or think about me," he vowed.

"I can't afford such a luxury, Mr. Ferris."

"If anyone is nasty to you, just report it to me. I'll handle him."

They reached the mayor's home and were greeted by a stocky man with heavy jowls and a prominent belly. Carrie Sue became alert.

Lester Carlson invited them inside. "We're so happy you two could join us for Sunday dinner. The wife is finishing up in the kitchen now."

"It was kind of you to invite me, sir."

"Please, call me Lester, and my wife's name is Mertle."

The man beside her jested, "If you accomplish that feat, Lester, I'll be shocked. Carolyn insists on calling me Mr. Ferris. She's worried about people's opinions of her."

"That isn't necessary, Carolyn. You're amongst friends here."

"See there. What did I tell you?" Martin teased.

"We only met recently, so it will require practice." Carrie Sue felt that Martin was responsible for this invitation and treatment.

Lester Carlson's wife and children joined them, and they took their seats at the table with Martin beside her. The petite woman served a roast of beef, rice, gravy, dried peas, cornbread, and canned peaches. The conversation was light during the early part of the meal. As everyone started on dessert—cake and coffee or milk—the talk increased, except for the three children who were trained to hold silent.

"Martin is one of our best citizens, Carolyn. I own the local bank and we can do a lot with loans on the gold he had shipped in on your stage. I know it caused you a great deal of trouble, but that was an unforeseen accident," the local banker informed her.

Probably at Martin's request, Carrie Sue concluded. She talked with the children for a while, noting how well-mannered they were.

The mayor boasted, "I have good children, Carolyn. They're going to enjoy having you as their new teacher."

"I was told Helen Cooper was a good teacher. It's a shame about her accident." She watched the children's faces and realized they had liked the woman who had preceded her. "I promise you're going to like school and not mind spending the summer there. Learning can be fun. I'm sure I won't teach in the same way she did, but that doesn't matter."

Lester remarked uneasily, "We don't talk about that tragedy, Carolyn; it makes the children sad. I'm sure you won't mind. Martin tells us you're from St. Louis. We have family there. Their children are grown, but perhaps you know them: John and Clindice Carlson."

Carrie Sue had not considered such a problem arising, but she held her poise and wits. She smiled and replied, "Naturally I've heard of them, but we're not well-acquainted."

"Doesn't matter. You can meet them when they come to visit this fall. John wrote us about how well you were liked there."

"That was kind of him," she replied, hoping her voice didn't quaver as she obviously had given the correct response. There was no way of knowing if Carolyn Starns knew the St. Louis Carlsons, as they had not been mentioned in the woman's diary. Carrie Sue was tense. What if they came here and exposed her as a fraud?

As the two women were doing the dishes in the kitchen while the men enjoyed cigars in the parlor, Mertle Carlson asked, "How do you like Tucson, my dear?"

"It's quite lovely, like your home, Mrs. Carlson. I deeply appreciate the invitation to dinner, and I've enjoyed the meal and company."

"Martin says you're living at Mrs. Thayer's boarding house. I hear it's the best one."

Carrie Sue smiled and nodded agreement. "Mrs. Thayer is wonderful. She's like a mother hen. I feel right at home there."

The woman's next words were alarming to the redhead. "Martin is very fond of you, my dear. I haven't seen him this interested in a woman since his wife's death, nor this happy in a long time."

Carrie Sue felt as if she'd walked into a conspiracy. "He seems very nice and respectable. What grades did your children say they were in?" she asked, trying to change the subject.

"We can talk about the children another time. I'm having a party in two weeks. You will come with Martin, won't you? It's the perfect occasion for you to meet everyone."

Carrie Sue realized she had no choice except to reply, "I'll be delighted, Mrs. Carlson. You will let me know if there's anything I can do to help."

"Certainly, my dear."

*

When Carrie Sue was dropped off at the boarding house, she was relieved that the man did not insist on coming inside for a short visit. She found Mrs. Thayer gone to visit friends and the other boarders were occupied. She paced her rooms, and they suddenly felt confining. She was being thrust toward Martin Ferris and she hated that disagreeable problem. Her new life was not developing as she had hoped. She had left one trap only to find herself ensnared by another! She had to face the truth: Martin Ferris was not going to let up on her and, if she made an enemy of him, things would not go well for her here.

"What to do?" she murmured anxiously. Quit this job and move on quickly? Try again to discourage Martin's interest in her? Lead him on for a while until he tired of his amorous pursuit?

"Not in a flea's jump!" she scoffed, recalling that Quade Harding hadn't given up on his chase in over seven years. "The Devil take you, Martin Ferris! Merciful Heavens, what am I going to do now?"

Carrie Sue longed to see T.J. Rogue. She yearned to have soothing and protective arms around her. She wished he would come to visit her, but she doubted he would.

And she certainly couldn't go scouting for him! Besides, what could that handsome Rogue do to help her? Nothing, except perhaps to stain her new image. She was on her own now, and this new problem was hers to solve.

*

At supper, the two men with back rooms were exceedingly quiet, even slightly sullen. Carrie Sue wondered if Martin Ferris had warned them to stay away from her or he would damage their business in town. She knew such a threat was not beyond the offensive man, nor was carrying it out if he was challenged. He was so like the Hardings!

Instead of remaining downstairs in the parlor after supper, Carrie Sue returned to her room. She sat at the desk to go over Carolyn's class plans, and was relieved the woman had made out those for the first month. By that time, she should have learned enough to do them.

She compared the notes to the pages marked in Carolyn's books. The brunette had been very intelligent and the lessons were easy to grasp. Between now and the opening day of school, she needed to study the books daily to refresh herself on all the facts contained there.

When she grew weary of reading, she went to the couch. She leaned her head against its back and closed her eyes to rest them. She could not get over the feeling that she was being watched all the time. Yet, she never saw anyone spying on her. Perhaps she was just nervous and tired. Perhaps it was because of too many years on the run. Or because she was too afraid of letting down her guard too soon. She was worried about Darby, and yearning for T.J. Rogue. She was irritated by Martin Ferris. She was unaccustomed to this dry heat.

And, she was afraid of what Quade Harding had in store for her. How long would his obsession for her continue? Surely there was no way he could track her to Tucson. Was there?

Monday morning, Carrie Sue put on one of Carolyn's oldest dresses for her task today. When she went downstairs, she paid her rent for the remainder of May. She borrowed cleaning rags, a broom, a mop, soap, vinegar, and two pails from Mrs. Thayer. She left her key with the woman, as this was the cleaning day for her rooms. With Maria's help, Carrie Sue carried the supplies and water to the schoolhouse.

After the Mexican girl's departure, Carrie Sue pushed up all the windows and left the door open. She tied a bandanna around her head to protect her hair from dust. To stay as cool as possible, she hadn't worn a petticoat or chemise under the cotton dress which was thick enough to be modest. She removed her shoes, and hoped no one would come by and see her in such a state.

The first thing she did was search beneath the desks, bench, and bookshelves for scorpions and spiders. She removed the webs and killed the spiders so they couldn't rebuild and endanger the children, but she found no more scorpions. She brushed down the walls and swept the floor, twice to make certain all the loose dirt was removed. Next, she washed the desks and mopped the floor.

While they dried, she sat on the front steps to eat a light snack which Mrs. Thayer had sent over with Maria. As Carrie Sue did so, the Mexican girl retrieved more water for her.

The heat absorbed the water quickly, and Carrie Sue was eager to finish as much work as possible before she needed to head home for a bath and supper. Already her arms and back were aching for relief.

She climbed upon a chair to wash the windows, using a mixture of water, soap, and vinegar to remove the grimy dirt. She had completed the door and two of the side windows when she suddenly sensed a powerful presence behind her. Instinctively her right hand dropped the wet cloth and went to her side, but naturally she wasn't armed. She hadn't heard anyone approach, but she knew someone was there. Her flesh tingled and her respiration increased. She half-turned to find T.J. Rogue leaning against the door jamb. Her eyes widened, then she smiled as she stepped off the chair to recover the rag. "Hello, stranger. How long have you been standing there watching me slave?"

He chuckled, the sound of it mellow. "Not long. I didn't want to startle you and make you fall." He straightened and walked forward, teasing, "I see they put you right to work. How are you doing?"

Carrie Sue felt dirty, sweaty, and a mess. But she was too happy to see him to let her condition trouble her too much. She mopped at the smudges and perspiration on her face, and tossed the rag into the water pail. She flexed her sore body as she replied, "Fine I guess. The boarding house and Mrs. Thayer are wonderful. I finally got settled in Saturday night, and I even went to church yesterday."

They exchanged grins. "They treating you all right?"

She inhaled deeply and nodded. "Mr. Ferris interrogated me on Friday before hiring me and showing me around. I've met so many people in the past few days that I can't recall everyone."

"Keeping you busy, huh?"

"They did on Friday, but I sneaked off Saturday to look around and shop. Yesterday I was practically forced to eat Sunday dinner with the mayor and his family." She sighed heavily. "I almost feel like a puppet performing for these people. That Mr. Ferris . . ." She halted and glanced away from his engulfing gaze. "I'm chattering like a raucous bluejay! What have you been doing since Thursday? I haven't seen you around since we got here."

"Not much of anything," he answered nonchalantly. "Playing cards and lazing about. I've had to repeat our tale a hundred times. You'd think these people were dying for news and excitement." His smokey gray eyes slipped over her from covered head to bare feet. She was a hard worker. And, she was a beauty even in her disheveled state.

Carrie Sue warmed at his tone and at his use of "our." He looked so handsome today. His face was freshly shaven; his ebony hair was combed neatly, even if that defiant lock was hanging over his forehead. His clothes, a red shirt and new jeans in a dark blue, were clean. A blue bandanna was tied about his throat, and two Frontier Colts were strapped at his waist. "How long do you plan to stay in Tucson being lazy and entertaining?"

He shrugged his powerful shoulders. "Until Nighthawk's hoof gets well. He caught a stone under it on our way into town. He's got a nasty rock bruise which needs to heal before I ride him again. Besides, I have to wait for those rewards to arrive. With a jingle in my pocket, I can be more choosey about my next job and boss. I have four hundred dollars coming. You earned fifty of it by helping me defeat that last man; that's half of his reward."

"Shooting a man in the leg hardly makes a rewarding experience. You keep the money, T.J.; I have a good salary here. And I have savings from my last job in St. Louis. If I have too loud of a jingle in my own pocket, I'll spend it foolishly. Keep it all, please, for saving my life and getting me here."

He shook his head and grinned. "I've never known any woman to have enough money, and you don't appear a foolish spender. I can't leave Tucson before settling my debt with a partner. Ain't my way."

"Then, you'll be here an awfully long time," she playfully warned.

"Don't tell me you're one of those difficult females who loves to give any man a hard time," he jested.

"I suppose I can be bullheaded on occasion," she admitted. "Haven't you heard that redheads are stubborn, impulsive, and fiery-tempered?"

"And they like to keep you indebted to them until they need to call in a favor?" he accused with a laugh, recalling how she felt about bounty hunters who earned blood money. "Name it, woman."

"I tell you what, Mr. Rogue. Why don't you work off your debt today? And take me to supper Friday night?" she suggested in a brave attempt to keep him in town a while longer. Maybe that would give her time to make a decision about staying here, and about chasing him. The more she saw him and thought of him, the more she wanted him, the more she weakened in her resolve to avoid him.

T.J. observed her intently, surprised by her temerity. "What do you need from a gunslinger like me, Miss Starns? A bodyguard?"

She wanted to say, I want you! And didn't realize her gaze did it for her. "I don't need a bodyguard since I only have one man pursuing me, and I can handle him," she revealed in a tone which exposed her ill feelings about Martin Ferris. "What I need is a ladder from Mrs. Thayer's barn so I can reach those high windows. And I can use a strong back to fetch more water. The school doesn't have a well."

"Anything else, partner?" he inquired mirthfully.

She laughed and replied, "I'll give it some thought while you're gone, partner. I never turn down free help or a willing spirit."

"Free?" he echoed. "It'll cost you fifty dollars, Ma'am. Haven't you heard? T.J. Rogue doesn't work cheap, most of the time. Not unless he's starving and needs a quick dollar, or owes a favor."

She watched T.J. mount a strange horse, probably a rented one to use while his black stallion healed, and ride away from the secluded school. Carrie Sue hurriedly checked her appearance, doing as much as possible to improve it during his absence. She removed the scarf and rebraided her hair. She dusted her dress and put on her shoes.

The handsome Rogue returned, dragging the ladder behind the horse and balancing a water pail in each hand. She took a bucket and set it on the ground, then took the other one. T.J. dismounted and carried them inside the schoolhouse, then returned for the ladder. Together they placed it before the window over the door.

Carrie Sue added soap and vinegar to one bucket. She wet a rag in the mixture and climbed the ladder very slowly and apprehensively.

T.J. noticed her neatened appearance and wondered if she had prettied herself up for him or because she was a proud female. Even if she was mussed, she was still ravishing. He wouldn't mind sticking her in a tub and washing her all over before carrying her to— "Careful, woman," he cautioned as the ladder wiggled under her.

Without looking down, Carrie Sue began scrubbing the highest panes. As she was about to go down the ladder for rinse water and a drying cloth, T.J. mounted it, carrying both.

"I'll hold these close so you can get done quickly. You make me nervous up here. A fall like this could break your neck."

"I'm nervous, too. I'm afraid of heights," she revealed, smiling sheepishly.

"Why didn't you say so?" he softly chided her.

"This is part of my job, so I have to do it. Besides, you should know that the best way to overcome fears is to confront them."

"Even if you break your neck or kill yourself in the process?"

"I'm being careful," she avowed nervously.

"Get down and let me do these high ones."

"That's asking too much of you, partner."

"You didn't ask; I offered. Better accept my help before I get mad and leave you to do it all."

Carrie Sue glanced down at him. He was standing a few rungs below where her feet were positioned, his face near her waist. Their gazes met and searched, as if each was looking for something special to be written in the other's. She trembled. "Just hold the bucket within reach and I'll hurry," she told him, averting her gaze and going silent. His touch made her more jittery than the fearsome height!

Soon, the window over the door was sparkling clean. They shifted the ladder to the back one, and finished it within thirty minutes. When Carrie Sue's feet touched the floor, she realized she was shaking.

So did T.J. Rogue. "You always been afraid of heights?" he asked.

"For as long as I can remember. Every time I go to a loft or up high stairs, I don't look down. It makes me feel so silly. I thought if I kept doing it, the fear would finally go away, but it hasn't."

"Fear is a way of warning us to be extra careful about certain things. We usually mess up by trying too hard to overcome it, by being too reckless so we won't look like fools or cowards."

"You aren't afraid of anything or anyone, are you, T.J.?"

"Only myself," he replied too quickly.

"What do you mean?" she probed.

"A man like me is his own worst enemy, only he can hurt himself."

"How?" she persisted for a clearer answer.

"Drop it, woman, or you'll make me look and feel silly."

The lovely desperado knew it was best to let the matter pass. She smiled and nodded. As she started on the lower windows again, T.J. went to fetch more clean water. Had he meant that he was self-destructive? Weren't all gunslingers that way? Surely a man who lived by his gun expected to die by the gun. She wondered if the ebon-haired man yearned to settle down. If so, where and how and when? If she was not mistaken, she sometimes read deep anguish in him. Somewhere in his past, or more than once, he had been hurt terribly.

Carrie Sue felt sad and hungry, but not for food. She knew that T.J. was not the kind of man who opened up to many people. Yet, he seemed to be reaching out to her, even if he didn't realize that fact. If she turned her back on him, wouldn't he withdraw even more into himself? But what would happen if she didn't . . . ?

While she labored and the smokey-eyed man observed, T.J. asked, "What happened to their last teacher?"

Carrie Sue related part of what she knew about Helen Cooper. She wondered if she should reveal what Mrs. Thayer had said, and decided she shouldn't expose those suspicions at this time.

"You know more than you're saying, Carolyn. What is it?"

She glanced at him, astonished that he had read her so well. "What are you, T.J., a detective hired by Helen Cooper's family to investigate her murder?"

"Nope, but why did you say murder?" he jumped on her slip.

She halted her chore to meet his direct gaze. She cautioned herself to choose her words wisely, as such an accusation could result in an investigation that called light to her. "I don't know any facts about her tragic accident. I just think it sounds like a strange one."

"But you have a suspicion it wasn't an accident. Why?"

"Why are you so interested?"

"Because you've taken her place here and I wouldn't want the same thing to happen to you. I've seen you with Martin Ferris several times. There's something about him I don't like."

The redhead gaped at him, asking herself if his were the eyes she had felt spying on her. "You've seen us together?"

"Couldn't help it, woman; you've been with him nearly every day since our arrival," he remarked, sounding a little jealous.

Carrie Sue smiled in pleasure, assuming interest in her to be his motive for observing her secretly. T.J. had been given plenty of chances to take advantage of her, but he hadn't, so she felt she could trust him. She needed to talk openly and honestly about this problem with someone who wasn't involved. "You're a man of keen instincts, T.J., and you've earned my trust." She told him what had happened between her and Martin Ferris and revealed her ill feelings about the man, with the exception of Mrs. Thayer's revealing words and her dark suspicions. "Do you think I'm being too suspicious of him?"

"Not suspicious enough, if you ask me. I think you've sized him up right, and I think you should steer clear of him. He's dangerous."

Carrie Sue frowned. "How do you propose I do that? He is one of my bosses, probably my only boss considering everyone yields to his wishes."

"Have you ever dealt with a man like him before?"

Her expression said yes, but she replied, "What difference does that make? Aren't all men and situations different in some way?"

"Yep, but we learn from past experiences what works and what doesn't. I'd say you should make him dislike you and avoid you."

"How?" she questioned seriously. "The best way for a woman to frighten off a man is to make it obvious she's seeking marriage. Somehow I don't think that ploy would work with Mr. Ferris."

"You don't want to get married?"

"Not to him! In fact, I haven't met any man I've wanted to marry," she added, then wished she hadn't made such a deceitful reply with the truth staring her in the face.

He ignored her last statement and suggested, "Look for his weaknesses, then work on them. A man can't stand for a woman to belittle him in any way. Annoy the hell out of him and he'll scat."

"That sounds good, but it hasn't worked so far. He hears and sees only what pleases him. I've done everything but slap his face in public."

"It didn't look that way Friday afternoon while you two were looking around. You both seemed to be having a good time."

"Well, I wasn't!" she snapped angrily. Her periwinkle eyes squinted, her full lips tightened, and her cheeks flushed. "I don't like to feel like I have a noose around my neck! He's demanding, and persistent, and overbearing, and pushy! He's lower than a snake's belly! But he's a powerful man here, so I can't afford to offend him."

T.J. laughed heartily. "You do have quite a temper, Miss Starns, but don't get mad at me. I'm not the one chasing you. You think you can handle him after I'm gone?"

"I'll have to, but it'll be tough," she answered, trying to master her wild temper. Her outburst was foolish. She snatched up a wet cloth and returned to her chore. She was being too talkative with this disarming stranger!

"I don't like him or trust him, Carolyn. I'll be worried about you."

She halted and turned to face him again. There was something in his tone and expression which lassoed her heart. "I don't either, T.J., but I'll have to tolerate him. I can't just pick up and leave like you do. A woman makes a bad drifter. You men can get jobs anywhere and any time, but that isn't true for women. At least not the kind of jobs we want." She began washing the window again, working the rag swiftly and roughly over the filthy panes to release her rising tension.

T.J.'s hand covered hers and halted it. He felt her tremors, from anger and resentment and from his contact. "If you need anything, any help at all, you will send for me, won't you?"

Carrie Sue leaned her forehead against the window. She wanted to fling herself into his arms and beg him to carry her away from all her troubles, away from her loneliness and pain, and further away from her dark past. "Where? You move around all the time."

T.J.'s other hand reached out to stroke her hair, but then he stopped himself and let go of her hand. Her pull was nearly overpowering, and it alarmed him to feel such weakness. It was reckless to play with this fiery torch! He could get burned badly. "I'll let you know where I can be reached in case of trouble here."

"T.J. . . . ," she began, but forced herself to cease.

He probed tenderly, "What is it, Carolyn?"

"Have you ever wanted to stay in one place, to get your life settled, to be off the trail for good? No more running just ahead of real life? No more suffering and loneliness? No more killing? Just to find a place where you can be accepted and respected? Where there wouldn't be any more cold, and dust, and rain, and hunger? A place where you can be free and happy?"

Her understanding caused him to respond, "I was going to try it once."

She faced him. "What happened to stop you?"

Lordy, she was beautiful and desirable! She made him feel hot and weak all over. Such empathy blazed within her eyes. She was so special, so precious. He could have this woman if things were different, but they weren't. He couldn't remain here, and he couldn't carry her off. Bitterly he scoffed, "Fate. I've got a bad one, haven't you heard? Men like me can't settle down." When he sighted warning moisture in her eyes, he flinched and said, "I need to go. I have a poker game set up."

Carrie Sue guessed the reason for his turn-around. She, too, was scared of the potent feelings which were passing between them, scared to surrender and scared to flee. From experience she knew it was rash to push a man or to respond to him falsely. There was no future with a gunslinger who drifted. "Thanks for the help, both times."

He inhaled deeply, then slowly released the spent air. He grabbed his hat and holster off the bench. "Anytime, Miss Starns."

As he strapped on his weapons, she teased to lighten his parting mood, "You always so formal with your past partners?"

He grinned and winked. "See you around, Carolyn."

"I hope so. You will let me know before you leave town?"

From the steps, he glanced back at her. "It's a promise."

Chapter

6

Carrie Sue worked until five o'clock. By that time, she was exhausted and soaked with perspiration. She left her supplies, except for the water pails, at the school and returned to the boarding house.

Mrs. Thayer met her at the back door with a genial smile. "I saw you coming, Carolyn, so I sent Maria to fill the tub for you. You can't clean up a mess like that in one day. I bet you're bone tired."

The redhead leaned against the door jamb for a few minutes, hating to challenge those steps with her aching legs. "I am, but I got a lot of work done. I think I can finish most of it tomorrow. That place was covered in dirt."

"Now you are," the woman teased. "Who was that handsome gent helping you today? I don't recall seeing him around town."

Carrie Sue told the woman who T.J. was and how they met.

Excitement and intrigue filled the woman's eyes and voice. "There's a man who knows how to defend himself and protect his woman."

Carrie Sue laughed. "I'm not his woman, Mrs. Thayer. This is the first time I've seen him since our adventures together."

"Do you want to be?" the graying haired woman asked.

Carrie Sue was almost too weary to think straight. "Honestly, I don't know. We're nearly strangers and it's probably best to keep it that way. He's a wild gunslinger and I'm a respectable schoolteacher."

"But you like him, don't you?"

"Yes, but T.J. Rogue has quite a colorful reputation, Mrs. Thayer. He's a most unusual and mysterious man. He could cause trouble for me. If I started seeing him socially, people might think something wicked happened between us on the trail, which it didn't. Besides, he'll be leaving soon and I probably won't ever see him again, so why take a chance of staining my reputation here?"

"Men can be changed, Carolyn."

"Not all of them. Consider Martin Ferris. He's cast in stone."

*

Following a long bath, hair washing, and delicious meal, Carrie Sue returned to her room for rest and quiet. It wasn't long before she was asleep, to dream of T.J. Rogue.

*

Tuesday she returned to the schoolhouse to work again. She polished the desks and dusted the books. She checked their condition and recorded their number, as well as the available supplies. When she heard hammering outside, she went to see what was going on out back.

A carpenter told her that Martin Ferris had paid him to repair the outhouse and the play-yard fence. The redhead thanked him and returned to her chores inside, fearing a visit from the vile man.

Surprisingly, Martin did not appear for a visit, which pleased Carrie Sue immensely. When her chores were completed, she closed the windows and door and walked home, to spend a night similar to the one before.

*

Wednesday, Carrie Sue remained in her rooms, relaxing and studying for her new job. She made notes on school supplies to be purchased tomorrow, and on her own secret supplies for a quick escape in case of trouble. She had concealed Carolyn's letters and diary in her hiding place in the closet. She had decided to buy a horse and keep him in Mrs. Thayer's corral. Perhaps she could look around for one tomorrow while she was shopping.

With the door bolted, she cleaned and oiled her weapons, then replaced them in the secret compartment. Handling the guns brought back an assortment of memories, such as the day Darby had given her the pistols and the rifle, and the days she had target shot for hours with her brother. She was a good shot, nearly perfect.

Her mind drifted to her brother's gang. Off and on for years she had lived with or around the six men: Kadry Sams, Walt Vinson, Tyler Parnell, Dillon Holmes, John Griffin, and Kale Rushton. She knew the men liked her, and would do anything for her because she was Darby's sister. She was fond of them, but they had never seemed like family to her, except for Kale. She was close to the half-Apache bandit, and he viewed her as a sister. She could talk to Kale, be honest with him. He had taught her most of the skills which she possessed and he had honed them. Without a doubt, Kale would die defending her. But, she admitted, so would the others.

She wondered what Dillon—a die-hard Southerner—was doing. He had pursued her for years. She wondered if Griff—a black man—was chewing on a stick this minute as usual, and if Tyler was sipping too much whiskey, and if Walt was collecting his badges and fingering his gunbutts.

She knew Kale was watching over Darby, his best friend, and few men had his prowess. But what about the blue-eyed blond Kadry Sams? Was he pining over her? Was his Scottish burr filling another woman's ear? Would he come after her and beg her to return? Kadry loved her and wanted her fiercely, but that feeling wasn't mutual. She had tried to return his love, especially at the Laredo ranch; it hadn't worked and never would.

Carrie Sue's mind shifted to the local men in her life. She hadn't seen or heard from Martin Ferris since Sunday, and was a bit baffled by his sudden distance for days. No doubt it was some ploy of his to seize her attention. That would never work either!

As for T.J. Rogue, she was disappointed that he hadn't returned to the school Tuesday or come to visit her today. But she had expected his distance; she had seen that flicker of apprehension in his gaze, the one which said a woman was getting too close too fast.

"I bet that's the most talking you've done with a female, Mr. Skittish Rogue. Do I dare try to tame you, to really trust you?"

The flaming haired ex-outlaw called his image to mind. Her body warmed all over and the pit of her stomach tightened. "What's gotten into you, Carrie Sue Stover?

You've never behaved this way before. Merciful Heavens, loving him scares the life out of me!"

Her face paled and she felt her heart drum rapidly. "Love him?" she murmured hoarsely. "You hardly know the man. Maybe it's only because he's a handsome and virile man. Not so, girl, you've seen too many of them and not been affected like this." Most women would kill to win Kale, or Dillon, or Kadry, but none of them affected her like this. "Nope, it's T.J. Rogue who's got you snared."

Carrie Sue squirmed in agitation. Now that she had admitted the truth to herself, what was she going to do about it? Could she risk messing up her new life for him? Could she risk losing this unique man forever just to remain here? "You're a fool, Carrie Sue Stover! What makes you think you can win him even if you tried? He's a loner, a drifter, a famous gunslinger. If he discovered who you are, he'd be waiting around Tucson for your reward to arrive!"

He wouldn't do that, her heart argued.

"I suppose you think he would understand and forgive you?" she scoffed. "He would just let those thousands of dollars slip through his hands so he could caress you with them!"

He likes you, fool, her heart reminded her.

"He likes Miss Carolyn Starns, a pretty schoolmarm, not an outlaw with a high price on her head."

No, he likes you. That's why he's hanging around Tucson. You saw how he looked and behaved with you the other day.

"He was just being nice."

A gunslinger just being nice? Never. Get off that loco horse, girl.

"I can't love him and chase him. It's too dangerous."

For whom, you coward, you liar?

"For both of us, idiot. T.J.'s already a gunslinger tottering on the line between good and bad. Think what loving you would cost him. You're a wanted fugitive. Do you want that bitter life for him too?"

Her heart remained silent, and she knew why. There was no reasonable comeback to her last words.

*

Thursday, Carrie Sue arose late, as she hadn't slept well after her talk with herself. Her final decision had been to leave the matter in T.J.'s hands. If he stayed around Tucson and seemed to feel the same way she did and she felt she could trust him fully, she would tell him the truth. Then, they could decide what to do about a future together. She cautioned herself to be patient with him because she didn't want to scare him off. He had to more than want her as an attractive woman; he had to love her, love her enough to discard her past as he would an unwanted poker card.

She headed for the mercantile store a few blocks away. She spoke with the owner for a time, then began shopping. The man told her to pick out what she needed and he would have it delivered to the school. He said he would charge the items until she decided how to pay for them.

Carrie Sue rounded one tall counter toward the rear of the large store and nearly bumped into the man who now haunted her dreams day and night. "T.J., what are you doing here?"

"I needed some ammo and a new rope. I saw you come in, so I decided to sneak up on you and check your reflexes," he teased, warming her with a blazing smile.

"They're dull today because of fatigue," she said with a laugh. "I could have used your help again Tuesday to finish up the schoolhouse. You sure you worked off your entire debt in one afternoon?"

"Nope, I still have to take you to supper tomorrow night. What time you want me to call on you, Miss Starns?"

"I thought you might have forgotten that part of our bargain."

"Calling on a lady is new for me, but I'll try my best to do it right. Any place special you want me to take you?"

The thought of spending an evening with him thrilled her. How else was she going to test her feelings for him or his for her? How else could she discover if he was a risk worth taking? "I'm sure you know this town better than I do. You choose and surprise me."

"Some place quiet and relaxing, away from your adoring crowd?" he hinted with a twinkle in his smokey gray eyes.

"Perfect."

"What did you do yesterday?" he inquired to continue their talk and his observation of this fascinating woman.

"Worked on lessons and tried to rest up." She gave a mock sigh of distress. "School begins in two weeks, so I have to prepare myself."

"To challenge those little hellions?" he teased near a whisper.

Carrie Sue glanced around before replying softly, "Want to help me tame them, Mr. Rogue?"

"Not on your life, woman. You couldn't pay me enough to go back to school. Always hated 'em. Father Ortega used to stand over me with a switch making me do my lessons. I wasn't lucky enough to have a teacher like you. Mine was real strict and cold."

"You went to school while you were at the mission in San Antonio?"

"Yep. The priest made all the orphans do it. But he was especially hard on me. Said I was too wild and needed settling down."

"Did it work?" she asked, suppressing laughter.

"What do you think, Miss Starns?" he answered, then grinned.

"It must have because you're very smart and well-mannered."

"For a gunslinger," he added teasingly.

Carrie Sue smiled. "For anyone."

They fused their gazes and looked at each other for what seemed a lengthy spell. Suddenly both smiled at the same time.

"I like you, T.J., you're so easy to talk to," she confessed. "It's going to be awfully dull around here after you leave."

"I know what you mean, Carolyn; you're easy to talk with, too." The moment after he made that admission, he cleared his throat and asked, "You need me to help carry your packages home?"

"Thanks, but the owner's going to deliver most of them to the school, and I can manage the rest. I'm not going straight home from here. I have some other stops to make. I'm thinking about buying a horse, so I planned to look around while I'm out today. Some places are too far for walking in the heat, and I hear it gets worse."

"Why don't I look around for you? Men sometimes take advantage of a female customer by selling her a bad horse or charging her too much. I'll pick out a couple and take you to see them in a few days."

"That would be very nice of you, if you don't mind."

Of course he didn't mind, for two reasons. He didn't want her to get cheated, and he couldn't let her visit the stable where Nighthawk was staying and discover he had lied about the stallion's injury. "Be my pleasure, Ma'am," he said in a heavy Southern drawl. "I best get moving along. I'll see you tomorrow night at six."

"Thanks again, T.J. You're always there when I need help."

"What are friends for?" he murmured and left.

Carrie Sue finished her shopping and walked to the laundress's home to pick up her washing. I'll see you Monday," she told the woman.

At the boarding house, she related her encounter with T.J. to Mrs. Thayer, who seemed genuinely pleased with the news.

*

Friday seemed like a particularly long day as Carrie Sue planned her evening over and over while she tried to study, bathe, and dress. She had selected a lovely dress in pale yellow from Carolyn's trunk. The skirt was full and swishy, the waist snug, and the sleeves ending at her elbows. Matching lace trimmed the collar and cuffs, and Carolyn even had slippers to match the pretty dress which didn't look as if it had ever been worn. Sadly, they were too small for Carrie Sue's feet. She put them aside to drop into the school's outhouse to correct an oversight which could be dangerous if noticed by someone.

The soft shade of the dress brought out the golden highlights in her red hair and flattered her skin color. It even made her eyes appear darker and more noticeable. Carrie Sue gazed in the mirror, wondering why she wasn't covered in freckles like most redheads. She also noticed, as if for the first time, that her skin was not exceptionally pale or florid, but was a rosy brown from the sun. Her brows were reddish gold to match her hair, although her long lashes were a dark brown. She knew her features were too large, her nose and lips and eyes. Yet, she decided, they blended together enhancingly.

She had washed her hair early so it could dry before this evening. It hung to her waist, thick and shiny, and curled ever so slightly to spread around her shoulders like a tawny red mane. She recklessly decided to let it hang free tonight. She gathered up the sides and pinned each behind her ears, then fluffed her bangs over her forehead.

Carrie Sue Stover stood and twisted before the mirror. She was amazed by how different she looked in a dress, compared to a cotton shirt and jeans and boots. She actually looked like a real lady, and that delighted her. She hoped T.J. liked her appearance tonight.

She paced the floor as she waited for him. He was fifteen minutes late. She worried that he had changed his mind about coming tonight. Worse, what if something had happened to him? He was a famous gunslinger, and they were often challenged by men who wanted to increase their own reputations by outdrawing legends. Who would care if T.J. Rogue died except her? She trembled. She clenched her teeth and vowed to slay any man who—

Mrs. Thayer's voice called from outside her door, "Carolyn, he's here. Are you ready?"

Carrie Sue rushed to the door and opened it. She beamed as she nodded. "Thank you, Mrs. Thayer. I was getting worried."

"So was I," the woman confessed with a sly grin.

Carrie Sue went to the front door and joined T.J. there. She smiled when he couldn't seem to take his eyes from her or speak. "I'm ready," she said to bring him back to reality before his stimulating loss affected her even more deeply and noticeably.

T.J. said he had rented a carriage. She followed him to it and he helped her inside.

The redhead watched him walk around the horse and take his seat next to her. She noticed his purposeful and confident stride, his alert gaze, his proud and fearless carriage, and his sensual aura. Carrie Sue had to remind herself not to snuggle up to his broad shoulder, as she was tempted to do. Happiness filled her as they rode away and she furtively studied him.

T.J. was wearing a dark gray shirt that fit his muscled chest as if molded for it. His hips were clad in ebony pants and his feet in freshly polished midnight boots. From the rich colors and excellent condition of his garments, she concluded, they were new. She wondered if he had purchased them to make a good impression on her, and she wanted to believe he had done so. A black hat rested comfortably on his dark head of neatly combed hair, and a matching bandanna was tied loosely around his neck, its edges fluttering playfully in the breeze created by the carriage's movement. His ever-present gunbelt hung below his waist, the holsters strapped securely to hard thighs. Her heart beat faster as his overpowering looks and nearness enchanted her. Courting, she decided, was delirious fun, with the right man.

T.J. asked, "You like Mexican food, Miss Starns?"

"Love it, Mr. Rogue."

T.J. wondered where an Eastern girl, even one from St. Louis, had learned to "love" Mexican food. He had seen her stop to eat at a small Mexican cafe the other day and had thought it strange. He headed for the other end of town as he, too, furtively studied the woman beside him. The gunslinger decided she looked vivacious and stunning in the yellow dress that made her appear so much the lady. He was glad she was not attired in one of those depressingly dark gowns which she seemed to favor for some odd reason. This color was sunny and warm, like she was. His hands begged to slip around her waist, which looked so small in its snug confines. His fingers itched to caress the silky skin of her arms that was exposed by her elbow length sleeves. Tonight, she seemed as delicate as the lace on her dress; yet, he knew she was a woman of strength and will, a ravishing woman of compelling traits.

T.J. halted the carriage behind a large building. He helped her down—wisely not allowing his hands to linger too long and inflamingly on her body—and escorted her inside. As he walked behind her, he watched the gentle and enticing sway of her hips beneath the flowing skirt. Although he had never been one to attend many socials, he wondered what it would feel like to have her pressed against his body while dancing dreamily to romantic music. Every time he was with the flaming redhead who got under his skin, he felt hot and itchy all over and he had to be extra careful to keep himself under tight control.

A dark-haired woman greeted them and smiled at T.J. before she led the couple to a back table. T.J. assisted her with her chair and was rewarded with a radiant smile. Lordy, he thought, how those beautiful eyes glow when she smiles. He asked himself if he was crazy to spend time with this unobtainable lady. He yearned to touch her soft hair, and to catch another whiff of her fresh and heady fragrance. He cleared his throat and asked, "How do you like my choice?"

Carrie Sue glanced around. It was decorated with Mexican tapestries, sombreros, a bull's head, colorful ponchos, braided lariats, silver spurs, and other items to give the flavor of Mexico. A mariachi trio was strolling around the front of the room, playing their native music for the customers. The serving girls were dressed in Mexican clothes. Delightful aromas filled her nostrils. She closed her eyes, inhaled, and smiled. She was out for the evening with the most appealing man alive. "It's wonderful, T.J.," she remarked, opening her eyes. It reminded her of times she had spent over the border in hiding with Darby, but those were good memories of lazy and pleasant days.

The woman returned to take their order. Relaxed and happy, without notice, Carrie Sue ordered her favorite dishes in Spanish.

T.J. noticed, but he quickly ordered in English. After all, she was a teacher and they often knew more than one language. He watched her listen to the musicians and sway her head in time to their beat, as if it were a natural thing to do. He realized that she was utterly relaxed with him and that was why her guard was down, because she did have a guard up on most occasions. Certain things she had said and done raced through his keen mind. Who, he mused, was this beautiful woman who had him at a loss of wits? Why did she seem like a born and bred Westerner hiding behind an Eastern face? If that was true, why the act? From whom or what was she hiding? How would it affect him?

"How old are you and how long have you been a teacher?" he asked.

"I'm twenty-one, almost twenty-two. I've been teaching for two years," she replied without looking at him. Lying to T.J. left a bad taste in her mouth, but it couldn't be helped.

"How did you get into teaching?"

"My parents were teachers back East. We lived in Charleston. But there were many problems in South Carolina after the war. Northern Carpetbaggers tried to take over everything. They even wanted to control what the children learned in school, and the new books were very biased against the South. One of the newcomers kept giving my mother a hard time. My father was forced to kill him for trying to attack her. We were lucky there were witnesses in his favor, but the law warned us it would be best for everyone if we left Carolina. We tried a few towns in neighboring states, but they didn't work out. Papa decided to move to St. Louis and open a private school there. Mama and I were going to teach in it. But there was an accident, our buggy overturned while we were looking for a place to build. They were killed and I was knocked unconscious. When I recovered, I took over the job at a local school, until a spoiled brat wanted it."

T.J. wondered why she sounded like she was reciting a lesson rather than relating her history. His intrigue gave him the chance to get other things off his mind, such as where and how this stimulating evening would end. "So you found this job and headed for Tucson."

Their conversation did the same for Carrie Sue, as she focused on her false tale. "It was in the newspaper, and I responded. Many people heading west get stranded in St. Louis, so I guess they thought it was a good place to search for a teacher. I caught the Butterfield stage to Fort Worth, then the Garrett line from there. Garrett was supposed to be cheaper and safer, and I could see more sights at a slower pace."

"What's a teacher's existence like?"

Carrie Sue hoped that her willingness to converse would inspire him to do the same. "I'll have grades one through eight. Classes run Monday through Friday from eight until four. I'm suppose to start school on June fifth and work until August. If I do a good job during that two month period, I'll be hired permanently to begin in September. I'll be paid one hundred dollars a month, which is an excellent salary."

"You don't sound too thrilled about such a good job and pay."

"Can you blame me? Martin Ferris wanted to come observe, but I hope I talked him out of it." She related what she had told the man. "He would make me and the students nervous with his little visits. This was a big move for me, T.J.; I have to do good and make it work. It could be my last ch—," she faltered at his alert gaze. "Chance to prove myself. It's important to me. Tell me more about you," she encouraged when the music halted.

"There isn't anything more to tell you than you already know. I'm a simple man. I live, I breathe, I travel." Mentally he added, *And I want you like crazy, woman!* He lowered his gaze for a time to master his runaway emotions.

"And you're private and shy," she added and laughed. Carrie Sue watched him grin and listened closely to his merry chuckle, a reaction that mellowed his smokey gray gaze and softened his features. She liked the way his dark gray shirt seemed to make his arresting eyes appear the same shade and the way his sun-bronzed skin made his teeth appear white when he smiled broadly. She longed to run her fingers through his midnight mane and over his tanned face. She wanted her hands to roam his chest. He looked so splendid tonight, so clean, so healthy, so vital and alive, so downright irresistible. *Concentrate, girl, or you'll make a fool of yourself in front of everybody, especially him!* "Where are you staying?" she asked nervously.

His gaze shifted to the ceiling as he said, "Up there. That's how I know the food here is good."

"I thought that woman smiled too long at a stranger," she teased.

"Jealous?" he hinted with a mirthful laugh.

"Of course. I don't like women looking at my partner like that."

"I see," he murmured with a lopsided grin. "Possessive, huh?"

"I suppose that bad trait goes along with being stubborn, impulsive, and fiery-tempered: the ill fortunes of being a redhead."

T.J. leaned forward on the table. His left thumb rubbed his jawline as his first two fingers captured his strong chin between them. His gaze slipped over her tawny red hair, and he liked how she was wearing it tonight. The pulled back style revealed more of her lovely face and made her look more genteel and exquisite than when she tried to hide it beneath a hat or secure it in a snug bun. "Do you honestly have any bad traits, Miss Starns?"

Carrie Sue tingled at the way he was watching her. Surely his mood and gaze meant she was having the same effect on him that he was having on her, and that pleased her. She relaxed even more as she replied, "Plenty of them. Haven't you noticed?"

T.J. stared into her merry eyes and said, "Nope."

"Good, then I don't have to worry about trying to conceal them."

"Have you noticed mine?" he asked.

"Do you have any?" she parried, feigning playful innocence.

"Of course not," he answered, then licked his lips. Lordy, he mused, how his mouth hungered to close over her sweet one and to feast there. She was absolutely bewitching, and he didn't mind her magical pull at all. In fact, he found it amazing and intriguing that a near stranger—even a beautiful one—could touch him this way. As a man who liked and needed to grasp all angles of a matter, he knew this curious one would require lots of study, close and pleasant study.

The food came: enchiladas, refried beans, Spanish rice, soft tacos, and tasty burritos. *"Gracias,"* she told the woman. It was spicy, but delicious. Carrie Sue ate with eagerness.

"Well?" he hinted as he watched her with keen interest.

The smiling fugitive noticed that T.J. was using his left hand to hold his fork. Either he used both hands equally, or he wanted challengers to think he was righthanded. If so, it was a clever ruse to entice foes to watch the wrong fingers during a gunfight. She said, "The best I've had, Mr. Rogue. You were right about this place."

He grinned and asked her if she wanted to taste his tequila. She looked around, smiled, and reached for his glass. She took a small sip, rolled it on her tongue, and swallowed. "Strong," she murmured.

As he refilled the glass from the bottle left on their table, he said, "It's made from the agava, that tall yellow plant you mainly see on hillsides. It's potent, so drink it slow. If you drink too much, you get real thirsty and your head kills you the next day."

"Perhaps I shouldn't have any more."

"Perhaps, Miss Starns. I wouldn't want you getting drunk on me," he said, but knew he would love to see her with her guard completely lowered and with all inhibitions gone, but in private.

"The town council would love that news," she teased.

"I bet they would, especially Martin Ferris."

"Let's don't spoil our supper with talk of him," she entreated. All she wanted tonight was to think of T.J., to be with him, to be the only thing on his mind. She wanted and needed to know all about him and all about the wild emotions he stirred within her.

"Fine with me," he concurred, leaving the full glass of tequila near her plate. As he sipped his and ate his meal, he asked, "What do you plan to do when you retire? How long do teachers usually stay on the job and in one place?"

Carrie Sue unthinkingly took sips from the glass. She liked tequila, and it relaxed her tonight. It made her feel happy, weightless, and trouble-free. "I haven't planned that far ahead," she replied, her wits clear enough to realize he wouldn't buy Carolyn's story about a dress shop. "I have lots of good years left. You normally remain in the same place until you retire, unless there's a problem."

"Like the one you had in St. Louis?"

"Yep, or the one I might have here with . . ." She halted and sighed in annoyance. She downed the remaining inch of golden liquid in her glass. "It's your turn to do some talking, mister."

The smokey-eyed gunslinger refilled their glasses. "And say what?"

"When are you going after that man who used barbwire on you? And what mine are you planning to work for? Surely not Ferris's!"

"Nope, not his, but I haven't looked around yet. I'll hold off a while longer on my revenge; he's probably still watching out for me. First, I have to find the best way to ruin him, and catch him by surprise."

"If he's a rancher, snag him where it'll hurt the most. Cut his fences. Burn his barns and fields. Steal his payrolls. Rustle his cattle."

T.J.'s eyes widened. "Where did a gentle schoolmarm like you learn about such stuff? Most of it's illegal."

Carrie Sue pushed aside her drink and reached for her black coffee. "I read those ten-cent novels. They have some good ideas in them. The good man always finds a way to defeat his enemies, even bad lawmen and cattle barons and politicians. You have to take risks with enemies, or they'll get away with their crimes. Have you ever been tempted to become an outlaw? Didn't that gold tempt you to take it?"

"Yep, that gold was tempting, but not enough to challenge the law." He didn't add, *what tempted me most was you, woman, but taking you captive was more dangerous than taking that gold.*

Carrie Sue suddenly remembered something: he had been in this area "a dozen times," and he had worked for Francisco Carrillo once. She wondered if he had known Martin Ferris before she arrived here, but didn't ask. "Do you have family, T.J.?"

"Nope. How about you?"

She looked sad as she shook her head, believing her brother was lost to her if she remained as Carolyn Starns. "What do you plan to do when you retire from being a gunslinger and a drifter?"

"Don't know yet." He asked himself how a St. Louis schoolmarm had heard of him and why she'd said "campfire tales." He had to start paying closer attention to her words! That, he concluded, was nearly impossible with the stunning creature so near and inviting! He tried another subject, "You certainly had a tough time getting to Tucson. I'm surprised you didn't turn back."

Tensed and lightheaded, the redhead remarked before thinking clearly, "That holdup and Indian raid weren't my only misadventures on the way here. The soldier's wife you saw at the station killed herself right in front of me. She was terrified of what those outlaws would do, so she grabbed a gun and shot herself before I could stop her. When I was on the Butterfield stage, it crashed outside Sherman trying to get away from outlaws. A Texas Ranger was killed. I only survived because the cavalry arrived in time to chase them away. It was scary. But I don't want to talk about that. Tell me about your travels," she encouraged.

"I've been lots of places, but none of them were special enough to entice me to settle down there. This hot box certainly doesn't."

"I know what you mean. I'm not sure I'm going to like it here." She dabbed at perspiration from the hot food, strong drink, and heat.

T.J. eyed her intently, thinking how much he would enjoy a bath in a cold stream with her. He watched her dab at the glistening moisture on her face, and had the oddest urge to taste the salty liquid forming there. He shifted in his chair and warned himself to discard such thoughts. "What will you do if your opinion doesn't change?"

"Look for a cooler and prettier place to move. Maybe Colorado, or California, or back East. The South is beautiful and pleasant."

"I noticed that during the war, but I'm pretty much a Texan."

"A Texan?" she echoed, her voice sounding strained. What if he'd heard about that holdup near Sherman? What if he knew it was the Stover Gang? What if he thought it was odd that two redheads were involved? She was wanted in Texas, Oklahoma, New Mexico, and Kansas. But Quade's detective had not exposed her in Sante Fe or Laredo, so no one in those towns could reveal her appearance. She had to chain her tongue and clear her wits!

The ebon-haired man had been furtively watching her strange reaction, and he became alert. "Most of the people I know best live there. Lots of jobs with high pay. She's a big state so it gives me plenty of room to stretch my legs."

"Which area do you like best?"

"The middle."

"Why?" she probed.

He chuckled. "I just told you why. You getting dazed on that tequila? Maybe I should take you home now," he suggested playfully.

Carrie Sue took his last words as a hint the wonderful evening was over. Yet, she teased, "Because you have other plans or because I'm being too nosey?"

He wished he did have other plans for tonight, other than taking this lady home after supper! But, she was a lady, so he could do no less without scaring her off or soiling her reputation, and he didn't want that to happen. He looked her in the eye and answered, "Both."

"Good, an honest man, and a brave one," she said with a smile. "I'm finished, so we can leave now," she said reluctantly. She didn't think he was trying to end the evening abruptly because he wasn't having a good time, but she knew she was making him apprehensive. A man like this one would value his privacy.

T.J. didn't want to take her home, but he was anxious about talking with her. There was little he could tell her tonight, and he didn't want to sit around in strained silence or fire too many curious questions her way. A few minutes at a time with her was what he needed, time enough to see her but not enough to get a probing conversation going about him. Lordy, she made him nervous, like a green soldier on his first Indian raid. Too, he made her awfully nervous, but why? She had him plenty confused!

They traveled to the boarding house without talking. Carrie Sue pretended to observe her surroundings. "It's cooler tonight."

"Yep, it is." As he halted the carriage, he asked, "Is it all right if I come by tomorrow to show you a horse I've found?"

She smiled. "What time?"

"About ten, so you can ride him before it gets hot. I don't want the sun roasting that pretty head of yours."

"Thanks, I'll be waiting," she said as he helped her down. She realized he wouldn't try to kiss her tonight; he was too much of a gentleman, despite his rough existence. This contradiction in character and personality intrigued and delighted her. It also told Carrie Sue that he believed she was a real lady, and he was a hard man to dupe. That conclusion gave her confidence about succeeding in her new life here in Tucson.

T.J. wanted to pull her into his arms and kiss her but it was too soon to expose such hot desires, and someone might see them. He watched the moonlight dance on her tawny highlights and caress her face. He couldn't risk speaking again because his throat felt constricted with yearning. He smiled, tipped his hat, and left in the carriage.

Carrie Sue watched him ride away, thinking how tight-lipped he could get at times. She hadn't learned much more about him. Why was he so secretive? How could he expect to spend time with her without talking? Maybe he just didn't know how to deal with women, or maybe she made him extra nervous. At least he kept coming back to see her. Surely, she reasoned dreamily, that was a good sign.

When she went inside, Mrs. Thayer broke bad news to her: Martin Ferris had dropped by for a visit and one of the male boarders had told him she had left to spend the evening with T.J. Rogue.

"He was red-faced with anger. He's gonna be trouble, Carolyn."

"I was afraid of that."

"He said to tell you he'll call on you again tomorrow after dinner."

"It won't do him any good. I'm going riding with T.J. to try out a horse I'm considering purchasing. I need one to get around in this heat and he was kind enough to scout about for a good buy. He's coming for me at ten before it gets hot. Do you think I could take a picnic basket along so I won't have to return so early and confront Martin Ferris again before Sunday?"

"I'll prepare it myself," the woman answered happily. "You two look good together, Carolyn. I bet you're the first woman to turn his handsome head."

"I know he's the first to turn mine," the redhead confided. "But I'm hesitant about seeing him. My reputation's at stake."

"Don't fret over what people here will say. People gossip no matter how spotless your reputation is. Be happy, girl. They need a teacher badly so they won't fire you without good reason."

"If Martin Ferris has his way, he'll convince them my seeing a gunslinger is a good reason, or he'll make that threat tomorrow. You wait and see, Mrs. Thayer; I'll bet a month's rent on it."

"I ain't into losing a sure bet, girl," the woman concurred.

*

T.J. arrived on schedule the next morning with two horses. She met him at the corral, with a smile and a picnic basket. He told her the pinto was two years old and in excellent condition. "Do you know how to ride, Miss Starns?"

"Yes, Mr. Rogue, even schoolmarms have to get around."

As she stroked the brown and white mare and examined the beast visually, he teased, "I thought ladies always used carriages."

"A mount is cheaper than a buggy horse and a carriage and harnesses, and much easier to take care of. I've had several horses in the past, so I know how to tend them."

"What about riding? You used to side saddle?"

"Side saddles out here are for genteel ladies and sissies."

"What about a gun? Do you know how to shoot?" When she stared at him oddly, he explained, "The West is a dangerous place, Miss Starns. You should know how to defend yourself. I'll give you some lessons today if you like. I even picked up a small pistol for you to try out, but we'll need to get a good ways out of town to practice. Sheriff Myers wouldn't like us shooting up his town and scaring his folks."

Carrie Sue became edgy. He was asking some alarming questions. Had he heard of the hold up by the Stover Gang near Sherman? Had he put two and two together? Or had he been suspicious of her all along? Was he trying to test her skills with a horse and a gun? Should she play dumb? No, that pretense could make it worse.

"You afraid of guns, Miss Starns? They aren't dangerous if you learn how to fire them and take care of them properly. I'd feel better about leaving you here if I knew you could protect yourself in a scrape."

"My father taught me how to protect myself before he was killed. I've even been hunting with him. But as you told me on the trail, if you pull a weapon on a man, you have to be prepared to use it."

"Some men back down when threatened."

"And most men won't, especially the really dangerous ones."

"You're saying you couldn't shoot a man even if your life's in peril?"

"Have you forgotten what happened on the trail? Yes, I could shoot a man, but I'd prefer to wound him. We do have lawmen to protect us and our property."

"Like they did on your way here. Johnny Law isn't always around when you need help, and sometimes he's as bad as the villains."

"That's true," she murmured, recalling the evil Ranger.

"Well, you want the infamous Rogue to teach you to shoot?"

"If the . . . legendary Rogue will join me for a picnic," she coaxed. "My pursuer came by last night and was furious to find me out with you. He's dropping by again at high noon. If you don't mind, I'd rather not return until later today. How's a bribe of fried chicken, biscuits, and canned fruit sound to you?"

"If you throw in riding and shooting lessons, it's a deal."

"You drive a hard bargain, Mr. Rogue. It's a deal."

Carrie Sue mounted agilely, and T.J. nodded approval. He slid sideways on his saddle and scooped up the fragrant basket. "Move 'em out, partner," he announced and led the way out of town.

Martin Ferris watched them ride away, then scowled with suppressed fury. . . .

Chapter

7

They rode out of town to the west. A dirt trail led toward hills not far away which rose up from the harsh flat landscape. The ground was dry, sandy, and rocky, and scattered ravines were cut into its surface. The cacti were thick in this direction, especially the taller variety. Red or white flowers topped many of the towering cactus plants were birds darted amongst the sharp spines to collect bugs or to enter abodes they had made in the green giants. The further they rode, the higher the hills reached skyward. Huge boulders with clusters of small rocks were situated at intervals as if they'd been dropped from heaven by a mischievous spirit. They didn't see any water, but dry washes snaked over the rugged terrain to remind them this area wasn't always dry.

They had left town at a slow pace, then settled into a steady gallop. T.J. was pleased about how well she rode and how she treated the animal. As he slowed his pace, he asked, "How do you like Charlie?"

Carrie Sue laughed. "Who named her Charlie? She's a mare."

"The man at the stable said a rancher nearby left her with him to sell. He's had some hard luck and needs money."

The redhead lovingly stroked the pinto's neck. She gathered part of the white mane into her hand and studied it. She leaned forward and checked the animal's eyes. "How much is he asking?"

"One-twenty-five. She seems well-trained and in good condition."

Happy to find a good getaway mount, the redhead added, "She has strong legs and a sleek hide. Her teeth are good and she has healthy hooves. And her eyes are clear. She's worth it."

T.J. was impressed by her knowledge and skill, but they increased his curiosity. She sat the pinto and handled her as if she'd been born in a saddle. If she'd been a rancher's daughter, he could understand such traits, but how did a schoolmarm know so much about horses?

"I love riding," she murmured dreamily. "I did it all the time back home. The horse I had in St. Louis was too old to make the trip here. I'm glad you found this one for me to buy. She's special."

"I'm glad you like her," T.J. replied, telling himself to relax or he wouldn't get any additional information out of her.

"I love her," the daring desperado corrected. "I'm going to buy her."

"You planning to change her name?" he teased.

"No. Charlie sounds good for a bright-eyed pinto. You ready to eat? I skipped breakfast and I'm starving."

T.J. guided her into a ravine where small bushes and squat trees along its eastern rim provided shade in the narrow, winding gulch. He dismounted and went to help her, but she was off the animal's back with noticeable agility. He put the basket on the ground and spread his blanket against the gully wall. "Let's eat, woman."

Carrie Sue sat on a blanket near T.J. and unwrapped the chicken and biscuits. She handed him a cloth and said, "I didn't want to risk breaking any of Mrs. Thayer's dishes on the trail. She's a wonderful woman. We've become good friends."

As they helped themselves and began to eat, he remarked, "It was smart of you to get up early to fry chicken and bake biscuits."

The redhead grinned and confessed, "I didn't. Mrs. Thayer insisted. She likes you, but she doesn't care for Martin Ferris at all and likes to help me avoid him."

He stopped eating to question, "Why?"

Carrie Sue decided to be completely honest on the matter. "Helen Cooper used to live at her boarding house. Mrs. Thayer didn't like the way Mr. Ferris treated the woman," she disclosed. "She doesn't believe Miss Cooper's death was an accident."

"Why do you think he killed her?"

Carrie Sue eyed him intently. "You sure she wasn't a friend of yours? Did you visit her when you came to town?"

"Nope. I didn't know her." He reached for another chicken thigh.

"Then why are you so interested in how she died?"

He drank from his canteen and offered her some water. "Because of you, Carolyn, your safety. Why do you think he did it?"

She was glad he cared enough to worry about her. "I think she was pregnant and he didn't want to marry her or create a scandal."

Surprise registered on his face. "What makes you think that?"

"Mrs. Thayer told me she was sick every morning just before she died. She also said Martin would summon her every few days and she didn't want to go, but seemed afraid not to mind him. He was probably threatening to fire her and she was terrified of him and losing her job."

"You aren't scared he'll do the same with you?"

"No, because I won't let him get to me," she vowed with confidence. "I would like to avoid any problems with Martin Ferris, but that's up to him. Can you open this can?" she asked, handing it to him.

He drew his concealed knife and complied. "He's gonna be plenty mad when he discovers you gone with me again."

"That's too bad because I can't let him control my new life and I can't hide from him every day. The last time I tried, I nearly got stung by a scorpion." She related the perilous incident at the school.

T.J. was amazed again by her courage and wits. This woman was not an ordinary schoolmarm, or an ordinary female! "You're a mighty brave and clever woman, Carolyn."

She handed him a fork and placed the can between them. "Thanks, but I have to be. My parents taught me to be independent. I've had to learn to take care of myself. I just hope I remember how next week."

After he took a bite of a peach, he asked, "What happens next week?"

She put her chicken biscuit aside. "The Mayor is giving a party for the so-called important people in town. I have to attend."

"Have to?" he stressed evocatively.

"Unless I want to offend everyone. Haven't you ever had to do something you didn't want to do, but felt you must to avoid trouble?"

"I try my damnedest to do as I please." He chuckled. "You know Ferris isn't going to leave you alone. He wants you, Carolyn, and he goes after what he wants. He can be sly and deadly."

Her purply blue eyes widened and her lips parted. She licked her dry lips. "You've met him before during your visits here, haven't you?"

He realized he had to tell her a few things about himself for her to keep opening up to him, and he wanted to know all about her. Besides, she could learn about his connection to Ferris from the man himself. "Yep. The problem I settled for Carrillo was over a land dispute with Martin Ferris, mainly water rights. You must realize how valuable water is out here, and Ferris wanted it all. Carrillo paid me to make sure his cattle got water until the court settled the matter, which went in Carrillo's favor. Riled Ferris pretty badly."

"Merciful Heavens, you two are old enemies! That makes my seeing you worse for him. I bet he's burning like a wildfire about now."

"You care if it riles him to see me?"

She considered the dilemma. "I guess not. I can't live my new life worrying about pleasing a ba . . . beast like that. Either Tucson will work out for me or it won't. I can always move on to another town."

T.J. wondered why she kept saying "new life" and why she almost slipped into rough language ever so often. "Become a drifter like me?"

She stared out over the desert terrain. "No, I want to settle down this time. I'm getting too old to move around so much."

"Too old at twenty-one?" he jested.

"No, I'm . . ." Carrie Sue focused her attention on the food in her lap. "I'm just ready to grow some roots. I haven't had a real home since . . . back East."

"You women want and need homes, don't you?"

"Doesn't everyone, T.J., at some point in their lives? Wouldn't you like to shake the dust from your boots? Wouldn't you like to have a nice place to run to instead of bad ones to run from?"

T.J. forced himself not to look at her. Carolyn affected him in a curious way, a potent one. He was wary, though, because she was the kind of woman who would insist on love, commitment, and marriage from a man: things he had no time for at this point in his life. Lordy, he wanted her badly, but his surrender held a big price. Yet, he absently murmured, "Someday."

"This is my someday, partner. I was hoping it would work out, but I'm afraid Martin Ferris will mess it up for me."

She looked sad and frightened for a moment, which tugged at his embittered heart. He was responsible for the deaths of Arabella and Marie because he had asked them to meet him in Fort Worth where they could become a family and settle down, where he could carry out his responsibilities to the woman and child. Fate hadn't allowed him to become a husband and father, to perform his duty, to find peace and happiness. Now, he wanted Carolyn Starns to settle down with because she made him feel comfortable and enlivened, because she respected him and accepted him as is, because she created a white-heat in him which burned throughout his mind and body. Yet, he was afraid such an entrapping blaze would consume him and destroy her, and he despised fear and weakness. By seeing her, he was endangering her, especially where

Ferris was concerned. The moment he left her side, Ferris would be on her like a starving bee on an exquisite flower! "You want to hire me to make certain he doesn't?"

Carrie Sue fused her gaze to his. He wasn't smiling. "Are you serious? What could you do to get him off my back? Legally."

"Don't want me breaking the law for you, huh?" After she shook her head, he suggested, "We could find a way to pin that woman's murder on him."

"It happened too long ago. We'd never find any evidence or a witness against him. That's one crime he'll get away with."

"What about pinning that attempted holdup on him. It was a secret, so he had to be behind it. Rumor said he wasn't responsible for the gold until the shipment was in his hands. If it never reached him, publicly that is, he has the gold and his silver. Quite a clever scheme. He probably knows I suspect the truth."

"Aren't you afraid he'll come after you?" she questioned anxiously.

"He's too smart to challenge me."

Carrie Sue knew he wasn't boasting, just confident in his skills and wits. "How can we prove he was involved?"

"I'll give it some thought." He wanted to have Martin Ferris out of the way before he left her here alone.

They ate silently for a time, then she asked, "Which side did you fight on in the war?"

"I fought with a man named Grant. He's President now."

She looked shocked. "You sided with the Union?"

"I reckon so. I saved Grant's life once. This man called Sharpe was playing on both sides of the fence and nearly got Grant killed. It happened in August of '64 at City Point, Virginia. Some Confederate spies got into camp and set off explosions. Stuff went flying everywhere, and Grant just sat there calm as could be."

"But I thought you saved his life."

"I did. One of the spies tried to shoot him before escaping, but I shot the careless Reb first. From then on, I was Grant's bodyguard till the war ended and I returned to Texas."

"Why did a Texan fight for the North?"

"I didn't start out on either side, just went there to look around. Since I hated slavery and the South favored it, I put in with the Yanks."

Carrie Sue didn't want to argue the reasons for the war, as she believed both sides had been in error, partially from misunderstandings. She had detected a coldness, a bitterness, in the way he said *slavery*. How curious for a gunslinger to have such strong feelings about it!

"What happened after the war?" she inquired pleasantly.

He shrugged as he put away his fork and napkin. It wouldn't hurt to relate things she already knew or seemed logical. "Nothing much. I was always getting into trouble. I didn't seem to fit anywhere. Maybe that's why people think I'm so tough; I had to be to survive. I lost my entire family at age seven, so I had to learn to be independent while I was still a snot-nosed kid. I guess I grew up too fast and too hard. I had a reputation as a gunslinger before nineteen, so my path was marked."

"Were you ever in trouble with the law?" she inquired. If he had, then perhaps he could understand where and how she had gone wrong.

"Yep. That priest who helped raise me was murdered, but not before he told me who shot him and why. It was a crooked deputy. I went after him and killed him. The law didn't take much to having a starred man shot, so I was put in jail. I can tell you, woman, it ain't a good place to be. You could say that's why I've always stayed just over the line; I don't want that experience again."

Her heart pounded. Her lips were parted and dry. Her respiration was erratic. She hung on every word he spoke. "It must have been terrible."

"Try being a legend without your gun. Every prisoner in there wanted a piece of me, and every guard too. I'm lucky I survived to be released. Make sure you watch your step 'cause it's worse for women, especially one who looks like you. Those guards would devour you like dessert."

If the truth about her came out, at least he could understand why she wanted to avoid prison at any cost. When she had gotten entangled with the law, she had been young, reckless, and bitter. She had been blinded by hatred for the Hardings and misguided by love for her brother. She had thought only of the present, the punishment of her parent's killers, not considered or foreseen her future as an outlaw. Yet, even a man like T.J. Rogue had managed to stay on the right side of the law. Would he blame her for not doing so? "How did you earn a pardon?" she asked eagerly.

"I didn't. I told them everything when I was arrested. There was one lawman who wanted justice done so he tracked down the truth. If not for him, I'd be dead. 'Course, that same lawman will track me down and stick me in prison the moment I walk crooked." He reflected on his friend Hank Peterson, but didn't mention his name.

"You were lucky, but you were innocent."

"Lots of innocent men filling up prisons, Carolyn."

"I suppose that's true. What about men who've made mistakes but want to go straight? How do they earn pardons?"

"Don't ask me. Never heard it done before, not to anybody I know." T.J. watched her eager anticipation alter to sadness and misery. He wondered if she knew someone in that predicament, someone special.

"That's a shame. I'm sure lots of men would do it if given the chance. Life on the run must be awful. Didn't it make you feel wonderful to do something good, like when you saved Grant's life?"

He looked at her oddly. "You know what I mean, T.J.," she explained nervously. "Don't you like doing things which improve your reputation?"

"I don't have a good reputation to worry about."

"You could have if you worked at it. You aren't as cold and hard as people say. Why don't you let people see the side of you I've seen?"

He stared at her. His body temperature was rising by the second, and not from the sun. Those periwinkle eyes were softly caressing him; those full lips were enticing him; and her gentle, hungry spirit was reaching out to him. Lordy, self-control was nearly impossible to maintain! He felt as if he were in a hot oven being baked by that smoldering gaze and fiery aura. "What side is that, Carolyn?"

She noticed how long he had observed her and how his body was responding to her intentional allure. She had to know what it was like to kiss him, to be in his arms. She had to help him learn to relax, to trust, to find peace, to yield to love. How wonderful it would be to learn those things together. If he came to love her and want her, her dark past wouldn't matter to him. "You're kind and gentle and courteous. You have a sensitive, generous nature, Mr. Rogue, but you try to hide it. Why?"

"Traits like those make a man look weak, and weak men get themselves killed out here. I'm not as nice as you think," he remarked, praying she would halt her innocent attack on his warring senses. If she didn't in a few minutes, he would lose his head and be all over her!

Carrie Sue shook her head. "You'll never convince me of that. You're too hard on yourself, T.J."

He looked away and teased, "Then I'll let you remain stubbornly mistaken, woman. The food was good. Thank Mrs. Thayer for me," he said, changing the subject.

She accepted his clue to back off for now before she scared him too much. "Maria helped her, so I'll thank both of them."

"Maria?" he echoed, his gaze narrowing and chilling. The name reminded him of the deaths of Arabella and Marie. He swore once again to track down and kill the gang who attacked their stage and murdered them, just as soon as he killed a man who was to arrive here soon.

"You know Maria Corbeza at the boarding house?"

"No."

"She's the Mexican girl who helps Mrs. Thayer with the cooking and cleaning. She's very nice, but shy and quiet." She had noticed his reaction to the female's name. He was now moody and silent, and rapidly packing up the remains of their picnic so they could leave. She tried to draw him out by asking, "Which mine are you going to try?"

"None soon. I have business to finish here first."

"What about my shooting lessons?"

"Another day."

"Is something wr—" Gunfire cut off her question.

T.J. tossed aside the items in his hands. He grabbed her head and shoved her face down on the blanket, shouting, "Keep down and still!" His gaze followed the line of fire to a large pile of rocks near the curve of the deep gulch. He concluded that the men—just out of pistol range—were either bad shots with rifles and were only trying to scare them, or pin them down beneath the blazing sun which was overhead by this time of day.

"Can you see anyone?" she asked, her voice muffled by her position.

"Looks like three men in the rocks over there. Stay put while I get my rifle," he ordered. But when he tried to move in the direction of the horses, more bullets splattered the dry earth around them like a heavy rainfall. "We can't stay here in the open; they have a clear shot at this ravine. I'm going to push you up the bank on three. Get behind those bushes and lie flat on the ground."

Carrie Sue readied herself to scramble up the steep incline. When he reached "three," she struggled with the sandy bank and finally conquered its rim with T.J. pushing on her rear and feet. She stretched out her hand toward him and shouted, "Hurry!"

He threw her one of his revolvers as he commanded, "Get down, woman! Don't worry about me!" He raced for the horses and yanked his rifle from its saddle holster before vanishing around a bend in the gully. He wanted to use the hill nearby to get a closer view and better advantage. By the way the men opened up rapid fire on him after Carolyn was out of danger, he knew the men were after him and she would be safe for a while.

Carrie Sue realized what T.J. was trying to do, get behind their attackers. But their foes would make the same conclusion and be prepared to thwart him. She aimed T.J.'s pistol and fired toward the men to check its range. Gunfire wasn't returned. The bullet struck short of their foe's hiding place. It was rifle range, and she didn't have one to help her partner. She studied the landscape between her and their peril. Several smaller piles of large rocks were between them. Since the men seemed to have their full attention on T.J., she decided she could move closer and get into pistol range.

The redhead peered around the bushes to plan her path to the rocks, which included dodging cactus, scrubs, and spiny yuccas. She brushed the dirt and grit from her bloody hands and gripped the butt firmly, noticing the "T.J.R." carved into it. She was wearing a split-tail riding skirt which reached the tops of her boots, so she needed to be careful of the bushes and cacti snagging it and delaying her progress. She took a few deep breaths, then raced for the rocks. Three warning shots were sent her way, but no man was that bad of a shot, she reasoned.

Carrie Sue remained low for a short time, then peeked around the edge of the largest rock. Her gaze scanned for T.J. and she saw him sliding forward on his belly just behind a rise of the hard ground. To give him time and cover, she fired two shots at their foes, nicking one in the arm. Suddenly she heard a sound which made her freeze. Without moving, her gaze searched the rocks for the rattler she had disturbed.

If T.J.'s gun had been fully loaded when he gave it to her, she had three bullets left. She dared not lift the pistol to check her ammunition, as movement would antagonize the already annoyed viper. Since he was shading himself during the heat of the day, he didn't want to move, and he was making it loudly known that he wanted her to do so.

The redhead knew she could not shift her legs to rise without being in the rattler's striking range. She hurriedly gave the manner serious thought. If she used her bullets on the snake, if the gun contained more, she would be defenseless against the villains nearby. So far, the men seemed interested only in T.J., but she couldn't be certain.

The ebon-haired man began firing at their attackers from his new position. Carrie Sue had faith in his prowess, so she fired twice at the rattler who was coming her way to make his threatening point. The wounded viper thrashed on the ground, fighting death to the last moment.

Her shots confused T.J. and he shouted, "Carolyn, what's up?"

"A rattler, but I got him! I'm fine!" she yelled back to him.

The three villains rushed to their horses and galloped away, a hill protecting their escape. T.J. ran to where she was sitting, as he knew the men would be out of range before he could pursue them. He glanced at the snake, then at her. "You're a damn good shot, woman."

"We had snakes in . . . Charleston, too. Sorry I wasn't any help."

"That was a stupid thing to do. You challenge danger like you have nine lives. They got away, but two of them are wounded. Not badly enough to suit me. Let's get moving before they come back."

The flaming haired fugitive knew the attackers wouldn't return, and knew T.J. didn't think so. "What about my lessons?"

His smokey gray eyes looked her over, then he replied, "From what I've seen, you don't need any shooting or riding lessons. You hurt?" he asked, noticing bloody spots on her skirt.

"Just scuffed hands. I'll tend them when I get home. What do you think they wanted?"

T.J. stared in the direction of the villains' flight. He was intrigued by the skill and ease with which this schoolmarm handled a gun. But he had other matters to consider at this time. He suspected that Martin Ferris was behind this reckless attack. Obviously the cattle baron hadn't forgotten their run-in years ago and didn't like the relationship with the woman he'd staked out for himself. Ferris probably wanted to show Carolyn that she needed the protection of a wealthy and powerful man once her rescuer was gone. But if Ferris wanted to make him look weak in front of Carolyn, it hadn't worked, as his hirelings would report soon. Or maybe Ferris wanted him dead.

"Well?" she hinted. "What do you think?"

"Probably was Ferris trying to scare me off his woman."

"I'm not his woman," she protested.

"We know that, but he doesn't. I'll check on those men after we reach town."

"Did you get a good look at them?"

"Nope, but two wounded men can't hide easily. Let's go, Red."

"Don't call me that!" she stated harshly.

"Sorry, Miss Starns, no insult intended."

Carrie Sue lied to cover her slip, "When I was a child, that's how I was teased. I hated it, but I didn't mean to snap at you."

"Don't worry about it. I understand."

They gathered the remains from their picnic and mounted their horses. In silence they rode for town.

Carrie Sue reflected on the despicable detective who had tracked her down twice for Quade Harding. He had loved calling her "Red." If given half a chance, he would have discarded Quade's reward and orders to take her for himself! She hated both of those evil men!

T.J. furtively watched the woman nearby. Something was eating at her, something she tried to keep under control. She was such a compelling mystery. The more she related and exposed about herself, the more confused and ensnared he became. She had been so relaxed with him, but her guard was up again and he wondered why.

At the boarding house corral, Carrie Sue asked T.J. if he would tell the man at the stable she was buying Charlie on Monday when the bank opened. "Do you think he'll mind if I keep her until I pay him?"

"I'll pay him today, then you can repay me on Monday when I bring you the sale papers. A rough livery stable is no place for a lady."

Carrie Sue wondered what a gunslinging drifter was doing with so much money and why he was willing to handle the transaction. She smiled and thanked him for his many kindnesses. He didn't mention the gun he had taken along today for her to try out, so she didn't either. She watched him leave, then went inside to see Mrs. Thayer.

The woman listened to the redhead's tale and frowned. "I bet Martin Ferris was sending you a message to keep away from Mr. Rogue or he'd kill him. You two be careful," she urged.

Carrie Sue also frowned, as she hadn't taken the attack in that light. If Martin Ferris was as dangerous and determined as she believed, then he would have T.J. slain without another thought. A famous gunslinger's death would entice a great deal of attention and gossip, but that wasn't why she wanted to protect the ebon-haired man. She cautioned herself to rethink her situation, her desires, her perils.

*

T.J. saw three men go out the back way to Ferris's office. They were wearing different clothes. One man was rubbing the edge of his shoulder like he had a flesh wound there, and another had something thick beneath his right sleeve, the size of a bandage. He trailed them to a saloon and watched them go inside. He carefully approached their horses at the hitching post. Two saddles displayed fresh drops of dried blood. He had an answer to the question of who was involved. He just didn't know the real motive yet. Without evidence the sheriff could use for arrests, all he could do was antagonize them into a showdown to punish them. He warned himself against calling out the men today and exposing his hand. But before he left Tucson, Ferris and his hirelings would pay their debts to him.

*

Carrie Sue went to church again Sunday morning with Mrs. Thayer. They made certain they sat on a pew which didn't allow room for Martin Ferris to squeeze into when he arrived shortly after them.

She paid little attention to the preacher's sermon as she was ensnared by deep concerns. She wondered if she should try to get a message to Darby to let him know she had arrived safely and had been accepted here as the schoolmarm. She didn't want her brother distracted by worry over her. She was also distressed over Martin Ferris's attack on T.J. Rogue. She asked herself if she should not see him again before his departure to protect him from further attempts on his life. She also needed to protect herself against suspicion and dislike once he was gone, and she never doubted he would leave town soon. Even if he was as drawn to her as she was to him, their bond wasn't strong enough to hold him here or to bind him to her yet. When and if he realized and accepted the truth about them, hopefully he would return to her.

After the service ended, Carrie Sue and Mrs. Thayer tried to leave quickly. Her ploy to avoid Martin Ferris didn't work. He hurried after them, calling her name. She had no choice but to halt and speak.

"I need to talk with you privately, Miss Starns," he said sternly.

"We can talk tomorrow at the boarding house if you like."

"This can't wait," he persisted, taking her arm and excusing them to walk a few feet away from the dispersing crowd and Mrs. Thayer.

"What is it, Mr. Ferris?" she inquired innocently.

"I don't think it's wise for you to be seeing that gunslinger socially. Some friends saw you two out to supper the other night and are gossiping about it. You have to be more careful with your behavior. You two were alone on the road after that attempted holdup, and people might think bad things about you if you continue seeing a common drifter. You have to be above reproach as our schoolmarm. I wouldn't want you getting fired over a rash friendship with a gunslinger."

"That gunslinger saved my life, Mr. Ferris, and I like him."

Martin frowned. "I've already rewarded him for saving your life and my gold, and you've thanked him; that's sufficient for a man like him. That little picnic yesterday was most foolish. What do you think people will say about you two taking off into the wilderness alone?"

"I didn't know there were any restrictions on my private life, Mr. Ferris. I'm unaccustomed to being told with whom I can make friends or see socially, as long as I conduct myself like a lady, which I have."

"It isn't ladylike to spend time alone with a man like Rogue."

"Do you know him personally?" she asked.

He shifted and glanced at the ground. "Not well, but I know his type. I know he's handsome and exciting to you women, but he has a bad image. Men like that take advantage of good women and ruin their reputations. I'm giving you a friendly warning, Carolyn; he'll cause you trouble here. Considering your example to our children, especially to the young boys who are duped by colorful legends, I must insist you don't see him again. If you need a horse, I'll gladly furnish one for you. If you're too proud to accept one as a gift, I'll make you a good price and let you pay me off a little each month."

"That's very kind, Mr. Ferris, but unnecessary. I purchased one yesterday, a beautiful pinto from a local rancher. Mr. Rogue found her for me at the livery and I was trying her out today."

"I see. You will consider my warning before the town council hears about this offensive manner and summons you for a serious meeting."

"Of course," she responded in a casual tone. "But I don't like justifying innocent actions to strangers. If they feel they must interfere in my personal life, I may have to reconsider such a demanding job. Good-bye, Mr. Ferris. I'll see you in church next Sunday."

"I'll pick you up Saturday night at six-thirty for the party at Mayor Carlson's. You haven't forgotten about it, have you?"

"Certainly not. I'll be ready. Thanks for the kind escort." Carrie Sue walked off while he was gloating over his minor victory. She would accept a ride with him to the party. Maybe that would keep him sated for a while! One thing, she knew he had lied to her, had exposed himself without realizing it: Mrs. Thayer had not told him about the picnic, she told him Carolyn was out looking at horses with T.J. Rogue. There was only one way he could have known about the picnic.

*

Carrie Sue completed her bath. She had been sweaty and dusty from a windy walk with Mrs. Thayer and other boarders after supper. She had spent a quiet afternoon in her rooms, studying lessons. It was nine o'clock and most of the guests were in their rooms for the night. She left the water closet and returned to her room, bolting the door.

She leaned against the door and sighed heavily with her eyes closed. The sitting room was dim, as only one oil lamp was burning low. She sensed a presence. Her eyes opened quickly. Her hand rushed to her right side as she shifted rapidly to check out the front corner of the room.

Chapter

8

Carrie Sue didn't know what to say to the handsome man who was lazing in the corner as if this was his room, or theirs. One elbow was resting on the chair arm, causing that shoulder to rise slightly. His other arm was laying across his flat stomach. His head was leaning against the back of the chair. His long legs were stretched before him and were crossed at the ankles. Yet, he didn't look totally relaxed as his negligent position implied. He didn't move or speak. Nor did she.

The dim light cast a rosy glow in the room and on T.J.'s face. He kept staring at her. She struggled to break the tight hold of his gaze, and finally succeeded. His gunbelt was draped over the chair at the desk, where his hat was placed. She looked back at him. His shirt was unbuttoned to his heart, exposing a hard and hairy chest. His smokey gray eyes were locked on her face.

She felt tension in the room, within herself, exuding from T.J., but it was a strange suspense and excitement. It was almost as if they were communicating on a mental level. Each seemed to be summoning the courage to say and do something important.

T.J. stood and walked to her. Their gazes fused. He was aware of her state of dress, a nightgown and wrapper. She was barefooted, fresh from a bath. Damp wisps of fiery hair clung to her face, the remaining blaze of glory cascading down her back. Her periwinkle eyes were entreating. She was hesitant, but unafraid of him. This time, she did not avert her gaze when he aroused her.

His fiery gaze traveled down her face to her throat where he watched the pounding of her heart revealed at her pulse point. Lordy, sneaking here to speak with her was a stupid thing to do! If he didn't get out of here pronto, he would complicate her life and his, and the tasks before him. Right now, he had nothing to offer her, at least nothing she needed in her unpredictable existence in this new town. He lowered his gaze to where her chest was rising and falling erratically beneath her cotton garments. *Get out fast, Rogue!*

Carrie Sue knew she wanted and needed this man. He would be leaving soon, and she couldn't bear that, not without having him first. She had to let him know how she felt about him, about them, and hopefully that knowledge would lure him back to her one day. Her hands cupped his jawline and she lifted his head to lock their gazes. "It's all right, T.J.," she murmured, then kissed him.

She was pressed to the door by his strong body and ardent response. His hands went into her hair and pulled her mouth more tightly against his. The kiss exposed their deepest longings, their fiercest desires. His mouth roamed her face, his lips tasting the sweetness of her flesh and savoring its soft texture. Each trembled.

"Lordy, how I want you and need you, woman," he murmured.

Fires licked at Carrie Sue's body. She kissed him greedily, her mouth seeming to ravish his neck and upper chest. "I'm glad you're here," she whispered against his muscled torso.

After several more stimulating kisses, he gathered her into his arms and carried her into the other room to lay her on the bed.

They embraced, caressed, and kissed for a long time, even though their aching bodies were screaming for release. It wasn't necessary to whet their appetites or to enflame their senses; they had wanted this moment since meeting that morning at the home station. It just seemed natural to tantalize each other and themselves. His lips brushed over her features, and her hands caressed his lean back. His fingers trailed down her neck, and hers wandered over his shoulders. His mouth followed the path his fingers had burned down her chest, and her lips pressed against his ebony hair. He unbuttoned her gown, and she let him continue without protest.

Carrie Sue shifted to assist him with the removal of her garments. She finished unbuttoning his shirt and he yanked it off with eagerness to rejoin her, flinging it to the floor. He pulled off his boots and removed his jeans, then snuggled with her again.

He wished he could see her, but the room was too dark. Yet he remembered every line and curve on her face and body. He closed his eyes and thought of the prettiest sunset he had viewed. She was even more beautiful, more tranquil, more colorful, more inspiring. Her hair flamed like the rich reds and golds of a setting sun in the hottest of summers, or like the sleek hide of a wild sorrel racing across a sunny landscape. Sometimes her eyes reminded him of the purplish blue shade of the sky at dusk, or the periwinkle haze over the mountainous horizon. Other times her eyes were like two violet-blue flowers which bloomed in spring and demanded he gaze at them. Her flesh smelled like a morning rain, fresh and clean and scented with wildflowers. Her skin was soft, and golden where the sun had kissed it. Her body was lean, yet supple and stimulating. Pressing their naked bodies together made him shudder with need.

As he caressed her and kissed her, Carrie Sue felt like honey warmed and softened by a brilliant sun, as if she were so limp she would melt into the bed beneath them. His hands were strong, yet fondled her with amazing gentleness. His kisses were urgent, but tenderly stirring. She loved the feel of him, his hard muscles which were honed to perfection, his downy soft skin, his lithe limbs which moved with agility, the rises and falls of his shapely frame where her bold fingers wandered. She loved his smell: masculine, clean, invigorating. There was such a strength about him, such an aura of confidence, such a fiery glow which spread to her. She savored the way he made her feel, the way he worked so lovingly, so leisurely, so skillfully on her body. She had never felt this way before and she wanted to burn every moment into her memory.

"You've been driving me crazy with hunger, woman. I don't think I could have resisted you another day. This is loco, but I can't help myself," he admitted hoarsely as he nibbled at her ear. She was exciting and mysterious. She was intelligent, but never made others feel inferior. She was gentle, sensitive, hard-working. She had a compelling strength and courage about her. Yet, she could be bold and stubborn and impulsive, a feisty spitfire.

Consumed by desire and ravenous for him, she replied, "Neither can I, T.J., neither can I."

His lips and tongue drifted to her breasts and stimulated her to writhing passion.

When his hand roamed lower and touched her where no man ever had, she arched her back and inhaled sharply. With patience and gentleness, he aroused her until she cried out for a blissful end to this madness which had her engulfed.

T.J. entered her womanly domain, knowledgeable enough to know this was her first time. Joy and pride surged through him when he realized she had chosen him for this special moment. He was very careful not to move too swiftly or forcefully. Once she adjusted to his size and presence, he set a steady pace to carry her back to the fiery heights of passion's peak which she had left briefly.

Carrie Sue seemed to know instinctively what to do. She curled her legs over his and responded to his thrusts and withdrawals with a matching pace and pattern. She returned his kisses and spread her own over his face and neck. His back was moist and her fingers ardently slipped along its surface, admiring its feel and labor beneath them.

T.J. couldn't believe this was happening for him. Lady Luck was finally smiling on him. This fiery treasure had been dangled under his nose for twelve days but he never thought he could claim it and enjoy it, or be allowed by cruel fate to do so. Maybe she was his good luck charm, the woman to change his life, his means of escaping his troubled past. She was here with him, joined to him as no other person had ever been, responding to him as no female ever had. It wouldn't have worked out with Arabella; Carolyn was proving that at this moment.

He didn't know much about love, but he had heard enough to know what he was feeling for this woman had to be love, and that she was responding to him because she felt it, too. But how would she feel about him tomorrow? Next week? Next year? He had vengeful promises to keep, promises made before this mute one to her. How would she feel when she discovered he was little more than a hired killer? A man who used his guns and skills to solve other's problems? She would hate him when he walked away from her soon, hate him for misleading her tonight. And he had misled her by allowing her to believe this action would lead to marriage, for she was that kind of woman. He couldn't marry her until he settled some old debts . . . if he survived. By then, since he couldn't explain anything to her, she would be lost forever. Maybe that was why he had needed her so badly tonight, maybe why he had taken this perilous risk. For some reason, he didn't have the strength to leave Tucson without knowing her this way.

Passions built higher between them, taking away his fears and worries. His mouth covered hers, his tongue dancing wildly with hers. He felt her tense and arch, her nails digging into his back but not as painfully as the barbwire had done.

Over rapture's peak they fell together, riding on ecstasy's powerful waves. They came together blissfully, almost savagely, until they were drained of all tension. They lay nestled together on the damp sheet, reluctant to move apart, reluctant to speak and break the magical spell around them.

Carrie Sue's head rested on his chest and she listened to the thundering of his heart which surely beat with the same emotions that filled hers. She loved him and he belonged to her now. She had wanted him; she had staked her claim on him. She had branded him with her love and he could never run free again like the wild mustang he had been. By coming to her tonight, he had surrendered his freedom, he had torn down the wall around him, he had exposed his feelings for her.

T.J. heard her sigh peacefully as she snuggled closer to him. He wished it could be this way forever for them, but it couldn't. Should he tell her the truth about their situation? No, he didn't want to spoil this special night, or hurt her so soon after it. He would tell her tomorrow, tell her as much as he dared.

When he realized that the woman in his arms had fallen asleep, he gingerly shifted her to the other pillow to keep from awakening her. He rose from the bed and dressed. A dim glow entered the door from the lamp in the next room. He looked down at the dark form in the bed and his heart pained him deeply. She had been so honest and giving with him, but he had not done the same with her. She had let down her guard to allow him to enter her life, but he couldn't back away from his destiny. He retrieved his holster and hat. He locked the door from the outside and shoved the key under it into her room. Stealthily he left the boarding house without being seen or heard.

*

Carrie Sue stretched lazily and yawned. She felt wonderful, rested, happy, free. She knew T.J. was gone, else she would have sensed his presence and inhaled his manly odor the moment she awoke. Her hands moved over the bed where she had first experienced blissful love. Yes, love, she vowed peacefully. No matter what happened to her now, she loved T.J. and he loved her. They would have each other.

Carrie Sue bolted upright in bed. No, she warned herself, she couldn't be so dreamy-eyed and naive. Fate always stepped in and ruined things for her! She had to walk slowly and carefully this time. Making love was not the same as being in love. What if T.J. didn't feel the same way? At least not yet? And if he did, what should she tell him about herself? When should she expose the dark truth? Would it change things between them? What if she remained as Carolyn Starns and told him nothing about her criminal past? If she was never unmasked . . . No, she argued with herself, she couldn't continue her lies into their future. If he learned the truth weeks or months or years from now, it could damage their relationship.

"You're riding too fast down an unfamiliar path, Carrie Sue. First, you need to discover his intentions before you mark your trail for him to follow."

The daring desperado remembered something else: she hadn't told T.J. what she had learned yesterday from Martin Ferris. Perhaps she could go to the bank, withdraw the money for Charlie, then head for the stable to see if her love was there checking on his horse. If not, she could . . . wander to the place he was staying and see him under the public pretense of eating there.

Carrie Sue bounded eagerly out of bed. She used the water pitcher and basin to remove the sights and scents of rapturous lovemaking. She quickly checked the sheets, relieved to find no telltale blood there. She donned one of the prettiest dresses in her closet and a matching sunbonnet, bravely allowing her tawny red mane to flow freely down her back. She felt aglow, as if nothing could go wrong today. After speaking briefly with Mrs. Thayer, she was off to the bank and the livery stable.

Sheriff Ben Myers was in the bank. He smiled genially and greeted her. Carrie Sue did the same with him. Recalling that the rewards were one thing keeping her love in Tucson, she inquired innocently, "When do you expect the rewards for those stage bandits to arrive? I'm certain Mr. Rogue wants to get them before he leaves town."

Sheriff Myers's left brow lifted quizzically. "Did he forget to share with you, Miss Starns? I paid him that day you two arrived. The bank always keeps a fund for rewards so bounty hunters and the likes won't have to hang around waiting for them. When they come in, I just replace the money I withdrew. Is he cheating you out of your part?"

"Oh, no, sir," she vowed. "I told him I didn't want any of that blood money. I just wondered why he was hanging around so long. Drifters don't usually do that, do they?" Carrie Sue hoped she didn't sound like a blithering idiot.

"No, ma'am, they don't. I think he just wants to rest up a spell before heading out. He ain't been into no trouble here, so I leave him be. Men like to do heavy drinking and gambling when they get unexpected money in their pockets."

They chatted for a few more minutes before Carrie Sue left with the money to pay for Charlie, from Carolyn Starns's account. She fretted over T.J.'s lie, but did she have any room to fault him when she'd concealed worse things from him? Maybe he had only used that excuse to explain why he was lingering here because he hadn't wanted her to know how he felt about her.

The beautiful redhead reached the livery stable which was within walking distance from the bank. The smithy met her at the door as he was leaving for his midday meal. When she asked if T.J. Rogue had paid him for Charlie, the dirty but amiable man nodded. She thanked him for finding the pinto for her and asked about Nighthawk's injury.

The burly man who had more muscles than wits sent her a cordial grin. "Rogue's black stallion is fine, Miss. He ain't got no injured leg."

"A stone bruise under his front hoof," she clarified.

He scratched his greasy head and replied, "Nope. He was in perfect shape when Rogue got here, and he's still thataway. 'Course he needs a good run. Rogue's been renting a horse from me for some crazy reason. That black stallion is strong; he don't need no rest."

Carrie Sue laughed at what appeared her mistake. "Perhaps I misunderstood. I thought his horse must be injured since he was riding a strange one. Anyway, thanks for helping me find Charlie."

"You want me to give Rogue a message if he comes by?" he offered.

"No thanks. I'll have someone take the money over to his hotel. Since the bank was closed Saturday and I didn't want to risk losing Charlie to another buyer, he loaned me the payment."

"You got a good deal. That's the best horse in the territory. I told bill I wouldn't show him to nobody but a good buyer."

Carrie Sue headed for the boarding house to get her dirty clothes to take to the laundress before she went shopping for a saddle. She was baffled by T.J.'s two lies. If Nighthawk wasn't hurt and he had received his rewards, what was keeping him in Tucson? If he had needed a woman, there were plenty for sale in the saloons, and he had plenty of money in his pockets. Had he stayed because of her? For what reason? Because she was irresistible as he had claimed last night, or because he knew or suspected who she was?

Surely the famous T.J. Rogue, a Texan, had heard of the Stover Gang, and might have met some of its members. But he wasn't an outlaw and he seemed determined not to become one. She knew from gossip that he was a troubleshooting gunslinger who hired out for pay, but he wasn't a cold-blooded killer or a bounty hunter. At least she had never heard of him doing such things. He had to move around a lot because she had never run into him.

Maybe her lover was on a secret job here, but he couldn't or wouldn't tell her about it. Maybe he'd been paid by the Garret line or someone else to protect that gold shipment, which would explain why he hadn't stolen that yellow treasure after the attempted holdup and why he was so resolved to get it to Tucson safely. That would also explain why he'd been close enough to the stage to give assistance. Or perhaps he had gone into the bounty hunting business and had been after those men who tried to rob the stage.

Or perhaps he was after Martin Ferris again. He did ask a lot of questions about the slain schoolmarm. Maybe he was working for her family or a friend of Helen Cooper's. Maybe Martin Ferris had made enemies with someone else or was harassing Carrillo again. Something had happened between the two men long ago and perhaps it hadn't been settled to T.J.'s liking. A horrible thought entered her warring mind, surely Martin Ferris wasn't the one responsible for that barbwire incident! If so, it was a good reason for Martin to fear T.J. and want him dead. Or, want him slain for intruding on his affairs years ago. T.J. was interested in Martin and asked plenty of questions about the offensive man. If he was after Martin again, that told her why he kept warning her away from the vile beast. And if that was the case, she needed to avoid becoming entangled in their private war and drawing attention to herself.

But none of those possibilities revealed why T.J. gave her the impression he was hanging around Tucson for a crucial reason, as if he was waiting for something to happen or someone to arrive. Half the time she felt as if she were being watched, but by whom? By Martin Ferris for personal reasons or because of her tie to that handsome Rogue? By T.J. for personal reasons or because of her association with Martin Ferris? Perhaps she was being used by either or both men to get at an old enemy. Whatever was between the two powerful men, she must not get involved!

In the beginning, she had warned herself that T.J. Rogue could be perilous to her future. He could unmask her by accident, or by intention. She had been rash to get this close to a man like him, especially so soon after meeting him. But she had fallen in love with him and couldn't help herself. Merciful heavens protect her if T.J. was pursuing the Texas Flame! And heaven help him if he had duped her! She would never let him take her in or lead him to the Stover Gang!

Back off from him, Carrie Sue, and see what happens. If he makes no threats or intimidating moves, you'll know he isn't after you for your reward. If he is after you for yourself, he'll fight to keep you. But if he's trying to get to Darby, he'll slip up and expose himself.

"Carolyn," Martin Ferris called out from behind her.

Carrie Sue gritted her teeth before she turned to speak with the man. "Good day, Mr. Ferris."

"You busy?" he asked, looking her over appreciatively.

"I have some chores I'm tending," she replied, not in the mood to banter with him this afternoon.

"What if I tag along and we can chat?" he coaxed.

"Some of them are personal, Mr. Ferris. I have a great deal to do before classes start in two weeks. I hope you don't feel it's necessary to warn me a second time against seeing Mr. Rogue."

"You're a smart woman, so one warning is sufficient. Have you seen him again?" he questioned boldly.

Carrie Sue met his gaze without smiling. He was dressed and groomed immaculately, but he was beginning to sweat and flush. "Do you have the right to ask or to interfere?" she responded coolly.

He sent her a falsely rueful smile. "I'm afraid I do. The town council asked me to handle the problem."

"I wasn't aware there is a problem, sir."

He withdrew a handkerchief from his pocket and mopped at the beads of moisture on his face and the backs of his hands. "If you persist in this repulsive friendship, I assure you there will be."

"Explain why that's true," she coaxed in a demanding tone. "Why is Mr. Rogue so disliked and disrespected here?"

"Because you're a respectable lady and he's a no-count drifter."

"Are you certain of your facts, sir?" she challenged.

Martin Ferris looked shocked by her behavior and words, then annoyed. "Why are you so determined to see a man like that?"

"You misunderstand. That isn't the point. I just don't like being ordered about by anyone. I'm not a slave here, sir. I was hired to teach school, and I'll do it efficiently. As far as I've witnessed, Mr. Rogue is a kind and polite gentleman. I've met many so-called upstanding citizens who aren't as nice or as good as he appears to be."

"That's part of your trouble, Carolyn, you don't know him or his type. Every time he comes to town there's trouble. His business here is finished, so he should move on. He won't as long as you're keeping him company, and the good folks of Tucson don't want his kind around."

Carrie Sue laughed. "Mr. Rogue isn't hanging around because of me. He's his own boss. He comes and goes as he chooses. I'm not enticing or encouraging him to remain here. He's smart, so he knows a prim schoolmarm and a gunslinging drifter can't mix. As far as I know, he's planning to get a job at a mine nearby or further north."

"Rogue ain't no miner," he refuted peevishly.

"A job as a guard or freight-wagon driver. You own a silver mine. Perhaps he'll check with you about a job."

"He'd be wasting his time! I don't want any hired guns around here."

The redhead decided to do a little detective work. "Somebody does because we were attacked by three gunmen while we were out riding Saturday. I was nearly killed."

"Who would shoot at you?" he asked skeptically.

"I don't know but it was a cleverly planned ambush, not a robbery attempt. They made certain not to get too close."

"Maybe they were after Rogue. He attracts trouble."

"Then why were they shooting at me after we got separated?" She noticed the surprise and vexation which flared in his dark eyes, telling her she hadn't been the intended target. "To make it worse, I was nearly bitten by a rattler while hiding in the rocks for Mr. Rogue to flank them. I couldn't move because they were firing at me. So you see, sir, he's saved my life more than once. If Mr. Rogue does have enemies here, they're fools to attack him. He's the best shot and smartest man I've met."

"If someone is after him, that's another good reason to keep your distance. You could get hurt or killed in the crossfire."

Carrie Sue pretended to consider his last words. "You could be right. No matter, I have too much work to do to spend time with him or any man. I'm sure he'll be moving along very soon."

At the same time, the lovely desperado and the man beside her saw T.J. leaving the telegraph office down the street. Without turning her head, she glanced at Martin Ferris who was scowling, his brown eyes cold and his jawline clenched. T.J. saw them and halted on the plankway. He walked toward them.

Carrie Sue didn't want to confront him while standing with Martin Ferris. "If you'll excuse me, I must tend my chores." She turned and headed for the saddlery shop, making it obvious to both men that she was leaving because of Rogue's approach.

Martin Ferris stopped T.J. from walking past him in pursuit of the rapidly departing redhead. "Leave her be, Rogue. She ain't your type."

"How would you know, Ferris?" the ebon-haired man taunted.

"She's too nice to tell you to keep away from her, so I'll do it for her. You're making trouble here again, and I don't like it. The town council wants her to stay clear of the likes of you. If you don't want to cause her problems here, then get out of Tucson today."

T.J. chuckled, vexing his foe. "The town council wants me to keep my distance, or you do?"

"Both," Martin replied coldly. "You could never get a woman like her, so give up before you harm her image."

T.J. scoffed casually, "You people can't boss her around."

"We hired her as a respectable schoolmarm, so we can fire her for unladylike conduct. We both know what people will say and think about her if she keeps seeing you. She needs this job, so don't make her lose it over gratitude to you for saving her life."

"You asking or telling?"

"Both," Martin replied again, his brown eyes narrowed.

"Sometimes I don't hear so well, Ferris," he teased pointedly.

"This time, you better clean out your ears because you won't irritate me again. I'm going to make certain that young lady gets a good start here, even if that means challenging you again."

"Like your hirelings did Saturday?" he hinted.

"Is that what you told Carolyn? It's my bet they were friends of yours trying to fool her into thinking you saved her life again."

"Is that what *you* just told her?"

"I didn't have to. She's beginning to doubt you. Didn't you see how she ran from you just now? She's tried to be nice to you, but she realizes you're taking advantage of her kindness to lost pups."

"Don't tell her any lies about me, Ferris," he warned.

"She's opening her own eyes, boy, but I'll help her any chance I get."

"I just bet you will," T.J. sneered. He had noticed the look Carolyn had given him, and it worried him. From the window in the telegraph office he had seen them standing here, talking like old friends. There was something odd about that woman which he couldn't put his finger on. Surely she wasn't leading him on for Ferris, hadn't lured him on a picnic so his men could kill him. She did probe him a lot about Ferris, but was it to see how much he knew about the man? No way, he decided, could that vixen be working for this man!

Martin gave a final warning before strolling away, "Keep your distance, Rogue, or you'll be sorry."

T.J. glanced in the direction Carolyn had taken, but she wasn't in sight. Should he go after her to see what was wrong with her today? What could he tell her to soothe her worries and fears? Maybe she had guessed the truth about the impossibility of their situation and was angry with him for tempting and seducing her, angry with herself for yielding to him last night. Maybe she was scared she would be exposed and sent packing. Maybe she did need this job, or want it. Once he told her he didn't have marriage in mind and would be moving on soon, things would be worse between them. Maybe it was best to let her cool off, or to let her believe the worst of him to make their parting easier for both.

* * *

Carrie Sue hurried to where T.J. was staying. She left the money and a note with the woman who had waited on them that night. In her message to T.J., she had asked him to leave her alone before she got into trouble here. She wrote that it was impossible and dangerous for them to be friends. To protect herself from gossip and an impulsive relationship with no future, they couldn't see each other again. She entreated him to understand and comply with her request. She did not mention what she had learned from the sheriff and stableman.

Afterwards, she returned to the boarding house and gathered her laundry. She delivered it to the woman for washing and ironing. Then, she went to the saddlery shop and purchased a saddle. The man was delighted to assist her and have her sale, and promised to have it delivered to Mrs. Thayer's barn before the day ended.

Carrie Sue went to a small mercantile store on a back street and purchased supplies for the trail, just in case she had to make a run for it. She returned to her home and concealed the supplies in Carolyn's large trunk which she had placed in the corner of her bedroom.

She hated mistrusting T.J., the man she loved and had given herself to just last night. Yet, she was afraid to trust him fully. He was so mysterious and could be so dangerous, even though he had revealed a few things about himself. Still, she realized he had related nothing which wasn't common knowledge or couldn't be true of any man like him. She had to be wary of everyone until her life was settled.

*

The following day, Carrie Sue remained in her room studying except for taking her meals downstairs. She told Mrs. Thayer she wasn't to be disturbed by anyone, and she explained her misgivings about a friendship with T.J. to the kind woman. Mrs. Thayer had seemed to comprehend her dilemma and agreed with her decision to avoid him.

On Wednesday, Carrie Sue realized she needed ammunition if she were forced into a fast escape. She hadn't seen or heard from T.J. or Martin Ferris. She prayed she wouldn't run into either man when she went out to make her purchase at that same small store. She also prayed that her purchase wouldn't seem strange to the owner. No matter, she had supplies, a horse, a saddle, and weapons ready for quick use, but she needed bullets and a rope and a rifle holster.

Something inexplicable was nagging at her. She felt overly tense today. She felt as if some threat was hanging over her head like a storm cloud. Usually she was right when she got such ominous feelings, and that worried her. Kale Rushton had trained her to trust her instincts, and she did. Yet, it was hard around that disarming Rogue. Her heart kept beating swiftly and her respiration was labored. Her skin tingled and felt flushed. She was edgy and insecure. Her instincts were telling her something, but she didn't know what!

Maybe it was an aching for T.J., or maybe it was the anxiety of wondering why he hadn't tried to reach her, by note or in person. They had slept together, then she had spurned him. Didn't he care? Didn't he want to resolve the trouble between them? Why hadn't he contacted her and asked for an explanation of her crazy note after their passionate night together? How could he take possession of her, then walk away as if she meant nothing to him?

Her heart argued, *Maybe he's scared and uncertain too. Maybe you hurt him with your demand for distance. Maybe he's staying away because you asked him to. Or maybe he's giving you time to change your mind and come to him.*

Her keen mind shouted, *Or maybe he got what he wanted from you and he's left town! Or he doesn't want a green girl again!*

Carrie Sue's heart and mind ceased their argument the moment she saw Curly James walking toward her. Her lips parted and her eyes widened. A feeling of intense apprehension washed over her. The blond gunslinger had ridden with her brother's gang, until he kept getting them into lethal trouble. Curly had always been an uncontrollable, cold-blooded bastard and Darby had told him to pack up and move on one day. Curly was boastful and arrogant, but there was no wanted poster out on him, as far as she knew. Surely there wasn't or he wouldn't be walking calmly down the streets of Tucson.

What, she wondered frantically, was he doing in Tucson? What if people saw them talking, as the man was grinning broadly and heading straight for her? He knew who she was! Merciful heavens, if anyone recognized him and put the clues together, she was in deep trouble!

Chapter
9

The ruggedly handsome gunslinger halted before her and looked her over from head to foot. "How kin you git more beautiful ever' time I see you, Carrie Sue? What are you doin' here? Darby tol' me you'd left the gang. You think it's safe to be out in the open?"

"You've seen Darby?" she asked anxiously.

"Yep, he's in Texas. You remember that hideout in the mountains. He was camped there when I passed through."

"I thought he was heading for Oklahoma to lay low for a while," she said to draw out information. She didn't like this particular man knowing such perilous facts about her and Darby's gang.

"The trail was too hot for 'em. They're holed up in the Guadalupes. I plan to join 'em when I leave here in a few days. Darby said I could."

Carrie Sue recalled the hideout in the mountains which were half in Texas and half in New Mexico. Her brother was now closer to her if she needed help. Yet, she doubted his claim that Darby would hire him again, but Curly didn't appear to be lying; that worried her. "Is Darby all right?" she asked nervously, glancing about to see if anyone was watching them, but sighted no one. She had to hurry.

"Tough as ever. Why'd you run out on him?"

"I was getting too old to gallop all over the countryside a mile ahead of a posse. No one here knows who I am, Curly. I've been hired as a schoolteacher by the name of Carolyn Starns. Please don't give me away. I'm trying to start a new life for myself."

He leaned against a post and rolled a cigarette. "That might be hard since Darby's gang has wanted posters out on 'em, exceptin' yourn don't have no good picture. You're lucky, 'cause I doubt anybody can recognize you from it. If he'd gotten out of Texas like I warned him, they'd all be safe. I tol' him to leave that Hardin' fellow alone. He's one mean bastard. I did some work for him, but he'd a killed me afterwards if given the chance. I got my pay and took off."

"You took a job for Quade Harding?" she asked disdainfully.

"I needed money and I couldn't do nothin' illegal. The law was breathing down my neck as it was and watchin' me like a hawk over a slow rabbit. I can't let my face git on one of them posters. I been hirin' out as a gunslinger and bounty hunter. I got me a good paying job here. Then, I'll be riding with Darby and the boys again."

"You've turned on your old friends?" she asked fearfully.

"Naw, only cheap outlaws we never met. I got to eat."

Carrie Sue wondered if this sly outlaw would turn on her.

Curly James grinned and shook his head, as if she'd asked the question aloud. "I'd never hurt you, Carrie Sue. You was always nice to me. I was hot-headed back in the ol' days, but I ain't no more. That's why Darby's givin' me another chance. I sure am glad. You'll be safe here, if Hardin' don't come after you."

"You wouldn't tell him where to find me, would you, Curly?" she asked, her tone pleading.

"Naw. Fact is, I may have to kill the bastard myself. Those other two who helped me with his job turned up dead. It's my thinkin' Hardin' got rid of 'em and plans to get rid of me if he can. They was to meet me in El Paso and head here. They never showed, and I heard they was killed. Made me too late for one job, but I got another. I figured I might as well earn some dollars while the boys are laying low. From what Darby said, they plan to laze around for a month or so."

Curly's expression and tone seemed odd to her, but she didn't show it. "Stay clear of Quade; he's an evil man." she warned. "If it weren't for him and his father, Darby and I wouldn't be in this mess. I'm trying to break away from my old life. People believe I'm this schoolmarm. If this doesn't work out, I'm either dead or in prison. Help me, Curly."

"Don't worry none about me, Carrie Sue. Honest," he vowed.

"I believe you," she lied with a radiant smile. She knew Curl James couldn't be trusted. Money—especially a reward as large as hers—had a way of blinding a man. But, she mused, what could she do about Curly? He could turn her in to the law or to Quade Harding. When his money ran out, he would, and she knew it.

She knew the word *give* was a mistake with a bastard like this villain, so she said, "If you need any money, Curly, I can loan you some or tell you where a large gold shipment is stashed."

His eyes brightened. "Where?" he asked eagerly.

"In Martin Ferris's safe. It won't be hard to find his office; he's a big man here." She didn't care if he robbed that vile man, and gold would make her reward less appealing. She noticed the instant glimmer of disagreement and disappointment in his gaze. "You know him?"

"I went on his payroll today. That's why I'm here. I did some jobs for him before, and he sent for me again. I guess he likes my work."

Carrie Sue felt weak and shaky. "Why? he's as bad as Harding!"

"To git rid of a snake named Rogue for him."

"Why?" she asked again, her heart drumming in alarm.

"Two reasons." He took a deep drag off his cigarette.

"Like what, Curly?" she pressed in a panic. If she warned T.J., he would wonder how she got her information. If she didn't . . .

"Like I'm gittin' paid good to do him under and it'll be great for my reputation. Rogue's notch on my gun will set me for life."

"Please don't do this, Curly. He's good, damn good." She told him about the attempted stage robbery and how T.J. had saved her life. "You know I've seen the best guns around, Curly, and they're nothing compared to him. He's lightning fast and cold-blooded. Don't challenge him for any amount of money or glory."

"I kin beat him or any man to the draw."

"Did Martin Ferris tell you he'd already sent three men against him at the same time and they failed? I was there, Curly, and I wouldn't lie to a friend. Please, back off this time."

"I can't. I done took the money and gave my word, and Curly James don't run from nothing or nobody."

Carrie Sue realized that the blond didn't want to back down from a gunfight with T.J. Rogue, even if he wasn't being paid highly for it. The handsome fool honestly believed he could beat T.J. to the draw.

"You got problems with Ferris?" the man asked.

She tried to dupe him, win him over to her side. "He took a liking to me the day I arrived and he hasn't left me alone since then. He's been trying to force me to become his sweetheart. When his charm didn't work, he tried blackmailing me with my job. The town council does what he wants, Curly, so he threatened to get me fired if I wasn't nice to him. He thinks I'm friends with Mr. Rogue because the man saved my life and he fears Rogue will protect me against his pursuit."

"Zat true?"

She lied convincingly, "Mr. Rogue likes me and saved my life, but there's nothing more between us; I swear it. The real war is an old one between them and they're putting me in the middle of it. If you get rid of Rogue, I'll be at Martin Ferris's mercy. If I fight Mr. Ferris, he might learn who I am and use it against me. Please, Curly, let this one pass; I beg you. You can get Rogue another day in another town when I'm not involved. He'll be leaving here soon."

She dropped the disturbing subject for a time to ease her worries on another subject. "Is Darby laying low or working?" she asked. If the gang didn't stay on the opposite side of the neighboring territory, their presence could endanger her. Darby had promised not to come near Arizona Territory. She hoped he kept his word.

The blond eyed her intently. "Mostly layin' low. You want me to take him a message when I leave here?" he offered.

"Just remind him to stay out of Arizona or I'm done for. I'd better get along before someone sees us together. I'll contact you later."

Curly caught her elbow to halt her and suggested, "If you help me git that gold and stay with me a few nights, I'll drop off Ferris's payroll and forgit about Rogue."

Carrie Sue knew she couldn't do as he demanded, sleep with him, not after Rogue, not for any reason. She mused, what to do? If she coldly spurned him, all was lost. If she sought T.J.'s help and confessed the truth, all was lost. If she duped Curly, he would expose Darby's location and get her captured. Desperately she replied, "Give me a day or two to work out the details. Make sure we aren't seen together again or someone might get curious about both of us."

Curly James grinned at the prospect of laying his hands on a golden treasure and a fiery one. He had wanted this woman for ages, but Darby always kept the men away from his sister, even his friend Kadry Sams. Now she was in a bind as snug as wet rawhide and had no choice but to lean his way. If she liked him in bed, maybe she would take off with him after he finished his business for Ferris, which he had no intention of dropping, especially with Rogue sweet on her. He didn't want that gunslinger tailing them because of her. Of course taking Carrie Sue would rile his boss Harding something terrible, but he would betray any man for lots of gold and the Texas Flame, even dangerous men like Harding and Ferris. He had planned to do Ferris's job while waiting for Darby to surface again to join him. After finding where the gang was holed up and learning their plans, he knew he had time to complete it before going back to work for Harding again. Now, he wouldn't need Harding's job. "It's a deal, Carrie Sue."

She cautioned, "Don't call me that again or someone might hear you. I'm Miss Carolyn Starns, schoolmarm, here. I'll contact you soon. Where are you staying?"

"The Morris Hotel, room ten. Let me hear from you by Friday."

"You will. It's a promise, Curly. Thanks." She smiled and left.

*

T.J. witnessed the curious interaction between the beautiful woman he loved and the violent outlaw he was waiting here to kill. He had seen Curly James in town this morning and had been dogging him for a chance to cause a *legal* showdown. He wondered what they were talking about and how they knew each other, as their conversation seemed too friendly to suit him. Had they met while she was passing through Texas, where Curly was from? Didn't she know who and what that blond was? Something wasn't right here. . . .

T.J. intentionally bumped into Curly James. The sunny-haired man gaped at him, recalling where and how they had met. T.J. was aware that Curly's fingers were stroking his gunbutt and the man was tense.

Martin Ferris walked up and commented, "I see you found him, Mr. James. This man has been looking for you, Rogue."

T.J. noticed the look of astonishment which filled Curly's eyes.

The outlaw swallowed hard and tried to master his infuriating rush of fear. "You're T.J. Rogue?" he finally asked, wondering why Quade hadn't told him that fact before he barbwired this man to a tree. If he had known, he could have killed Rogue that day.

"Yep. We have some old business to settle, don't we?" he said with a cold smile.

"You two know each other?" Martin inquired, baffled.

"We've met before, but we weren't properly introduced. Were we, Curly?" There was a steely edge to T.J.'s voice and gaze.

"Why don't we step into the street and git it done?" Curly sneered, his false courage having returned. He mentally cursed Quade for getting him into this bind. He had heard that Rogue was good, but hatred made an opponent even more dangerous. Curly thought of his Brownwood boss and chuckled. Quade would be the one in a tight bind when Curly didn't carry out his part of their bargain!

"You calling me out?" T.J. asked loudly for the witnesses who had gathered around them.

"If you ain't no coward, Rogue, you'll give me satisfaction."

"I guess I'll be obliged to send you back to your maker below. You'll count for us, won't you, Ferris?"

"I'll be more than happy to," Martin answered with a grin. Curly had been too late to do that stage job which had caused him problems, but not too late to rid him of this intimidating foe.

The two gunslingers stepped into the street. Martin counted off the paces and the men halted. Slowly they turned. "On three!" Martin shouted, rubbing his hands together in eagerness.

T.J.'s left hand was hanging loose at his side. His right one was poised near his waist as if he were planning to use it, and he knew Curly James would watch the wrong hand. He waited.

Carrie Sue had seen the action beginning from the store window. She had hurried to the doorway and listened to the men's conversation. How, she mused worriedly, did T.J. and Curly know each other? Yet, Curly had looked shocked to learn the black-haired man was Rogue! Who had Curly believed he was? The hatred between them was thick and black like mud in the bottomlands. What was the "old business" to be settled between them? It looked as if Curly was going to try to do his job for Martin Ferris, which she hadn't doubted for a moment, but not this soon. Was the Rogue as good as legend claimed? She dearly hoped so.

Martin counted to three and a flurry of action took place. T.J. drew his left revolver, fired twice, and replaced it before Curly's gun cleared its holster. Suddenly Curly lay in a heap on the dusty street. Never had she seen a man pull a gun, fan the hammer, and shoot as swiftly and accurately as T.J. Rogue had done. If she had blinked, she would have missed everything! She asked herself if Curly James was the reason for T.J. coming to Tucson. Had he been waiting for this "old business" and showdown before leaving? Did he know Martin Ferris had hired Curly to slay him? It was terrible, but she was relieved by the outcome of the gunfight, because now Curly couldn't betray or blackmail her, and T.J. was uninjured. Her peril was over for now. Yet, she wished she had asked Curly if Darby had told him she was here. And, she wondered if the other job he had mentioned was the foiled holdup. That would have given her evidence against Martin. Then, she realized she couldn't have used it.

The sheriff came running down the street. Ben Myers went to where T.J. was standing beneath the sun, calm as a windless day. The two men chatted for a few minutes, then shook hands! Wariness filled her. Why was T.J. always gunning down outlaws? Had he lied to her about being a bounty hunter? Or was he something else? Carrie Sue wondered what was going on. . . .

Carrie Sue walked rapidly toward the boarding house to do some serious thinking, but T.J. caught up with her.

"Wait just a minute, woman," he ordered sternly. When she turned to face him, he read doubt and fear in her gaze. "I saw you back there."

Carrie Sue misunderstood his hint. She alleged, "He wanted directions and information, but I told him I couldn't help him because I was new here. He started flirting with me, but I set him straight. I told him I didn't like gunslingers. You surely do a lot of killing," she murmured in an attempt to focus the attention away from her.

T.J. knew she was lying and he needed to learn why, but later. "I meant, I saw you during and after the showdown. I'm sorry you had to see something like that. What else could I do, Carolyn? He called me out in front of witnesses. If I'd backed down, he'd have kept pushing until I got riled and fought him, or I'd have gotten a reputation as a coward. Besides, he's one of the men who barbwired me to that tree in Texas. We had an old score to settle. Myers said there's a reward out on him now, so he wasn't as smart as he believed he was. He was thanking me for taking him on 'cause the sheriff's old and slow with a gun. Curly James would have killed him in a showdown."

"Was Curly James the reason you were lingering in Tucson?"

Rogue knew she had learned the truth about the rewards and his horse, and he guessed those were the real reasons behind the note she'd sent him. He had left her alone since Monday afternoon, but had planned to see her tonight to straighten out the misunderstanding which he had created to explain his continued presence. She did not want him to leave her alone, he had reasoned, and she was not that afraid of Ferris, the town council, or of losing her job here! She had been angered, hurt, and alarmed by his lies. She had to wonder why he had duped her and others, and she had to question his honesty about his feelings for her. But, why hadn't she confronted him about those deceits? She was a brave and forthright woman, but a proud and cautious one. No matter her reasons for spurning him and for writing the seemingly desperate note, he had to earn her trust and respect again.

He replied carefully, "Yep, but I couldn't tell you I was lying in wait to kill a man. I caught up with his friends and they told me they were to meet him in El Paso to head here for a job. Their tongues got real loose after I barbwired them back-to-back. I was afraid Curly wouldn't show up when they failed to meet him as planned. It's my guess Ferris hired them for that holdup, but Curly got waylaid somewhere. You can bet he's worked for Ferris before, because men like Ferris don't use their own men for dirty work and risk exposure. I'm sure he hired Curly to kill me for thwarting his plans for that gold and you." He breathed deeply before saying, "You already know I didn't tell you the truth about those rewards and Nighthawk. Is that why you're mad at me?"

"After what Curly and those men did to you, I don't blame you for making them pay. I suppose you'll be moving on now."

She didn't answer his last question, and he didn't press her. That telegram had told him Curly was on the way, and Darby was on the move again. He had to get to Texas. "I'll be pulling out at dawn, but I'll send word where you can locate me in case you have trouble with Ferris and need my help. I hate for that bastard to outdo me, but you know we can't prove he was behind that robbery attempt or that he hired Curly to gun me down. Seems he made a mistake there, one he won't take lightly. I best move on to prevent trouble for both of us."

Carrie Sue realized she had to let their relationship end here in the open, not in her room tonight. She wanted him badly, but it would only make losing him more painful. His business was done and he wasn't hanging around because of her, so she needed to keep her pride and wits intact. "You've been a good friend, T.J., and I wish you luck wherever you go. Good-bye," she said and shook his hand.

T.J. clasped it snugly between his and met her gaze. "I wish it could be different for us, Carolyn, but it can't. You understand?"

Carrie Sue forced herself not to break their visual contact and expose the pain which was tearing through her soul. "Yes, I understand."

"You sure you'll be all right here?" he asked, his gaze tender.

She smiled and jested. "Of course I will be, Mr. Rogue. After seeing you in action today, Martin Ferris will be too scared to harm me."

T.J. mentally added, *Especially after I get rid of his three hirelings tonight.* "Would you like to have a farewell supper tonight?"

She shook her head. "That wouldn't be wise for either of us."

"You aren't sorry, are you?" he asked, needing to know.

"No, only sorry we are too different to make it work."

T.J. breathed a deep sigh of relief. "If either of us ever changes—"

Carrie Sue squeezed his hand and interrupted, "Don't say it because we won't change, T.J. We can't change and survive. Go celebrate your victory—the men in the saloon will be drinking to you all night."

"You're one unique woman, Carolyn Starns," he murmured.

"Be careful, T.J.; Martin Ferris hates you." She told him about the man's slip about the picnic. "Watch your back, Rogue. An enemy like that doesn't give up easily."

"I'll be careful, woman, and you do the same."

She smiled radiantly and left him standing there. She was glad he had come after her to explain, to apologize, and to say good-bye. That told her he did care about her.

T.J. exhaled forcefully. Lordy, he hated to leave her behind, but he couldn't ask her to go with him. And it wasn't fair to her to try to see her tonight. By the time he finished his next task, maybe he would be ready to give up this wild life and settle down. And maybe she would still be willing to give him a chance. But that was months away.

*

T.J. was sprawled on his bed, trying to get some sleep before dawn. He wanted to sneak over to see his woman, but he didn't want to make his leaving any harder than it was on her. He had read the pain and disappointment in her gaze, and he was feeling the same way.

A knock sounded softly at his door. He came to alert. Surely it wasn't Carolyn taking such a risk to see him one last time! He opened the door. A man hurried inside and bolted it. T.J. eyed him inquisitively. "What are you doing in Tucson?"

"Trying to protect your cover, Thad. Captain McNelly got your telegram and sent me to see you about it. I was in Tombstone tracking down the Kelly boys, so I rode here as soon as I got his message. None too soon from what I heard tonight about your run-in with Curly James today. Now that's over, you can move on to the Stover case. I've been ordered to partner up with you."

T.J. stared at Texas Ranger Joe Collins, an old and close friend. Joe was one of the few men who knew his real identity, and they had worked together many times in the past. "Captain McNelly has agreed to let me take it on? He's been fighting me on it. I told him if he didn't relent I was going to resign and take it anyway."

Joe Collins replied, "He thought you were too personally involved to keep a clear head. He didn't want you getting yourself killed. He thinks you've probably settled down by now. If anyone can get to that gang, it's Thaddeus Jamison. Curly was one of those men who did that barbwire number on you, wasn't he?"

T.J. glanced down at his scars and said, "Yep, the last one except for Quade Harding. Are Will Clarke and Captain McNelly still having Harding watched?" T.J. asked, referring to a Texas sheriff, and to Capt. L.H. McNelly of the Texas Ranger Special Force—one of his bosses. When he was in that trouble over killing a deputy, President Grant had come to his rescue with the offer of exoneration if he'd go to work as an undercover Special Agent and U.S. Marshal. Thaddeus Jerome Jamison had accepted the entwined jobs and been at them for years. As a cover, he had used the reputation of a famed gunslinger and the name Rogue, which he'd chosen because he'd often been called a savage rogue during his orphanage days. Two years ago he had added Texas Ranger to his jobs, a position that gave him all the authority he needed anywhere and any time to accomplish the most difficult and dangerous assignments, if he couldn't carry them out as Rogue and remain undercover.

Joe replied, "They know the Hardings are gobbling up land illegally. All they have to do is get evidence against them. You can't work on them again because they know your face. Besides, you can do more as T.J. Rogue than as Thad Jamison, Ranger," he remarked.

Half the time all he felt like was a hired killer who was paid and ordered to clean up the dirty West. "Yep, I can kill off lots of scum as Rogue. Just make sure they get Harding for me, or I'll have to give it another go," he warned. "Before you join me, Joe, contact Charlie Shibell. Have him check out a man named Martin Ferris. He owns a big ranch and silver mine." T.J. related the facts and his suspicions about the attempted holdup of the gold shipment and the probable murder of Helen Cooper which he wanted the Pima County Sheriff to investigate. "I thought it would look odd if Rogue contacted an Arizona lawman. Since I couldn't use a coded telegram, I was afraid Ferris might get hold of my message to him. I planned to wire Charlie after I left town."

"You had trouble with Ferris years ago when you worked on the Carillo case. He still after you?" Joe inquired.

"Yep. But he's after a friend of mine more, Carolyn Starns. She's the woman I rescued on the stage and we've gotten pretty close. Ferris has his mind set on getting her, like he did on Helen Cooper. I want Charlie to make certain he doesn't harm her. Handle it for me while I get a lead on the Stover Gang. Headquarters is keeping a file on their attacks, watching for a pattern. I need to learn what they've done since that Fort Worth job Monday. I haven't been asking about them 'cause I figured it might entice me to head after them before I finished this task. After you see Charlie, join me in El Paso at Mitch's."

"That's why I'm here. That holdup Miss Starns survived near Sherman was pulled by the Stover Gang. She might be able to give us some information about them. Your friend Jacob was killed on that stage, so McNelly wants that gang as badly as you."

"They murdered Arabella and Marie in March. Now they got Jacob. If they give me any trouble, I won't bring them in alive."

"I know, Thad. I'm sorry about your family and friend."

"Me, too. I hadn't seen Tim since I was seven. When I heard the name Major Timothy David Jamison, I couldn't believe he was still alive. Those Mexican bandits got him before we could be reunited." He gritted his teeth.

Joe Collins thought about T.J.'s three badges: U.S. Marshall, Department of Justice for President Grant, and Texas Ranger for L.H. McNelly of the Special Force. Few people knew about Thad Jamison, but plenty were aware of the legendary gunslinger named T.J. Rogue. Thad took on secret missions, reaching far and wide, ignoring perils and hardship to solve crimes and stop criminals. Thad did those jobs other men couldn't handle and didn't want. Joe didn't like, respect, or trust any man more than this one.

"Old man Harding is the one who's offered the biggest rewards for the Stover Gang's capture. They used to harass him all the time. Quade's the one who furnished the names and descriptions for their new posters, claimed he got them from a detective he hired to track them down. He wants them real bad, even Darby Stover's sister. But there's something strange going on there—her poster says "Alive Or No Reward." He's raised it to ten thousand each for the sister and brother, and he's even offering five each on the others. That Texas Flame is a real beauty, Thad. Flaming red hair to her waist and strange blue eyes. I brought along one of her new posters; it has a different sketch. Take a look," he said, withdrawing the paper from his pocket and unfolding it. "Did you ever see prettier eyes or hair? She looks as innocent as an angel. 'Course we know she isn't. A real shame she went bad."

Before he even glanced at it, T.J. had a terrible feeling in his gut. Carolyn had been on a stage robbed by the Stover Gang, a sole survivor, a flaming redhead with violet-blue eyes. She had appeared the same time the gang had dropped from sight. Everything about her flashed through his mind at lightning speed. He stared at the beautiful face of Carrie Sue Stover, and grimaced. It all made sense now.

T.J. reflected on what he knew about the mysterious outlaw. The early reports had listed a flaming haired female who rode with the gang but rarely participated in their crimes. Many had assumed she was one of the bandit's sweethearts or a female who lived with and worked for all of them. Later, she had ridden with them all the time, but always hung back, probably to avoid being recognized. She was an expert shot and rider—he knew from witnessing her skills. Yet, she seemed so gentle, such a lady, when she wasn't a little spitfire! She had almost fooled him. Yet, there was something about her which didn't add up, but she was one of them. She was one of Arabella's, Marie's, and Jacob's killers. He was heading after that notorious gang. The time had come and Carrie Sue, guilty or not, was in his path.

T.J. kept staring into those exquisite eyes as he reminded himself of who and what she was, allowing his anger to mount so he could carry out his unpleasant task. "I'll get on their trail first thing in the morning, Joe. Tell McNelly this case is mine, all mine."

The Ranger looked at the sullen man and said, "They're laying low right now. Until they surface again, we can't get a lead on them."

"Yes, I can, through her," T.J. replied moodily.

"But how can we locate her?"

T.J. flung the poster on the bed. "I know just where to find her. She's pretending to be Miss Carolyn Starns, the new schoolmarm here. T.J. Rogue will help her escape to her brother, then I'll get them all. I have to do this alone, Joe. Do me a favor and see if you can get her posters destroyed. I'd like to carry out this mission without looking over my shoulder for bounty hunters and wild posses."

"She's the woman you telegraphed Captain McNelly about? This Carolyn Starns is actually Carrie Sue Stover?" he asked incredulously, and T.J. nodded. "She's a reckless one to live in the open like this."

"It wasn't reckless until this sketch was released. It's my guess they killed Miss Starns, and Darby's sister took her place. I'm going to dupe her into leading me to his gang. She could be here to wait for her brother and his men to arrive, could be staking out the town. She knows about Ferris's gold shipment and she's gotten familiar with Tucson. This could be their next target and she's the scout."

"It's a clever plan using her like that," Joe murmured.

"That Darby's a real snake. I should have known she wasn't what she claimed to be; she acted too wary and strange. Lordy, she can be mighty convincing. I'll have to keep a sharp eye on her."

"Can you trust her, Thad? She could lead you into a trap."

"Once she sees that poster, she'll have to trust me and that's all that counts. I want the Stover Gang dead."

"I'll have to get permission to recall her posters. I can say they were a mistake. I'll handle it tomorrow. Keep in touch if you can."

After the men made further plans, Ranger Collins sneaked from T.J.'s room. The ebon-haired man threw himself on the bed. Fury surged through him. He berated himself for getting involved with Carrie Sue Stover. He felt as if she had betrayed him. He loved her and wanted her, but that was impossible now. "Lord help you for doing this to me, woman."

The heartsick lawman seized the wanted poster and stared at the lovely image printed there. Was it possible she had left the gang and was trying to begin a new life? Was that why she had said they were too different to make a go of a future together? She had let down her guard for him, but why? He remembered how hard she had worked at the school and how she had tried to avoid Martin Ferris. If she was scouting Ferris out, she wouldn't be spurning him. She had been studying books and planning lessons as if she honestly intended to teach there. Maybe something in the past had compelled her into a life of crime which she didn't want. Maybe she had gotten entrapped by her brother's deeds. Maybe she really was trying to escape her old life.

"If you're for real, Carrie Sue Stover, I'm sorry because I need you to lead me to the others. This time, I'll be the one betraying you."

T.J. realized the danger he would be placing her in on the trail, but she wouldn't be any safer here with those posters around. He was thrice a lawman. Could he let her slip through his fingers after he had the gang in sight? Could he capture her and send her to prison, knowing what it would be like for her or any woman? Could he watch her hang? What else could he do? His hands were tied and her fate was marked because she was an outlaw, a member of the gang he had sworn to destroy. This wasn't a mistake and she wasn't working undercover. She was just as guilty and wanted as they were, and he had to do his job.

Carrie Sue returned to her room after breakfast to find T.J. waiting for her. "I thought you would be gone by now," she said, her gaze softening as it roamed his features. She walked toward him and halted. She knew something was wrong because he was oddly quiet and seemed to be in deep thought. Maybe he wanted and needed to leave town, but couldn't because of her. An air of uncertainty exuded from him. Her fingers touched his taut lips as she asked, "Are you sure you can't stay in Tucson a while longer? I'm not afraid of what Martin Ferris will do to me after you leave. I want you, T.J., at least a' while longer. I'm not pressing for a commitment. I'm just afraid we'll never see each other again after you leave. There's so much I wish I could share with you, but I can't. If only we were other people," she murmured sadly.

T.J. clasped her hand in his and lowered it. This choice was hellish for him, especially after her stirring words. He inhaled deeply as if making a difficult decision, then said, "Get some things packed, Carrie. You're leaving here with me."

She paled and trembled. Her misty gaze locked on his piercing stare. He was armed, and she wasn't. He had the advantage, as she hadn't suspected treachery from him. Her energy and joy drained away swiftly. "So," she murmured, "you are a bounty hunter and you know who I am. I should have known better than to trust you or any man. Every time I do, I get into more trouble. Damn you."

Her gaze and expression sent pangs of guilt and anguish through him. "No, Carrie, I'm not a bounty hunter. But they'll be on your trail soon if you don't get out of here with me." He unfolded the poster and held it before her face. He watched her face pale even more and her eyes enlarge with panic. "Quade Harding released your real description. It says so at the bottom. When the mail came in, I was at the sheriff's office to sign papers to collect the reward on Curly James. Myers had to fetch my payment from the bank. While he was gone, I got nosey and opened an envelope from Texas because I always like to know what's going on there. The Sheriff's supposed to print up lots of these and post them. I stole it, so he doesn't know about you yet. He will soon, so you won't be safe here anymore."

"If those posters are out everywhere, I won't ever be safe again. Dammit!" she scoffed bitterly. "I thought it was over this time. Everything was working out fine for a change, except for Martin Ferris. Why can't they just let me disappear and start over? If they'd leave me alone, I wouldn't cause them any more trouble! I should have known Quade would pull this trick when he got impatient. I was stupid to think this ruse would work. I just wanted out so badly. Heavens, ten thousand dollars in gold. That'll be the end of me."

"I don't want to see you hurt, Carrie. I don't know what happened back in Texas to create your troubles, but they can get you shot or hanged before you can straighten them out. You have to get out of here and lay low for a while. And you need someone you can trust to guard your pretty backside. I'm more than willing," he offered.

"You can't help me, T.J.—no one can. I'm in too deep. Merciful Heavens, if I could go back to '69 and take a different trail, I would. I guess you realize this is what I couldn't share with you, T.J. This is why I was so edgy half the time. I have to get moving, fast."

"You don't stand a chance traveling alone, woman. I'm going with you and I won't take any lip from a cornered wildcat. I mean it."

"You don't understand what you'd be getting yourself into! I'm an outlaw. I'm wanted in four states. I have more charges against me than a dog has ticks! That bastard Quade Harding is responsible for everything that's happened to me. I should have killed him long ago, and his cold-blooded father. He'll never leave me alone."

T.J. had to know why his foes were so hot on this girl's trail. "Why do the Hardings want you so badly? Alive?" he asked. "That's a pretty big reward and a crazy demand. Where did he get your sketch?"

Carrie Sue met his gaze and told him the truth. "Why are you willing to help me escape? You don't want to become a wanted man."

"You know why I have to help you, Carrie," he replied tenderly, his hand lifting to caress her anger-flushed cheek.

She was scared; she was wary; she was emotionally torn between a loving faith and an instinctive mistrust. "What about my big reward?"

He captured her forearms and shook her lightly. "Listen to me good, woman! If I wanted money that badly, I would have stolen Ferris's gold. I took the rewards for those varmints I killed because it would have been silly not to, but I could never sell you to the law like a piece of prized meat. Surely you've been around me long enough to know you can trust me. I've been more open and honest with you than anyone else in my life. And it scared the hell out of me! Lordy, Carrie, I know what jails and prisons are like; I can't let you get caught."

His sincere words and gaze worked; they duped her. "Don't you understand, T.J.? If you're caught with me, you'll be in as much trouble as I am. I can't let you mess up your life for me."

He assumed his next cunning question was a safe one to ask. "All I have to know is how did you get Carolyn Starns's identity? I have to hear you say you didn't kill an innocent woman for a new life."

Carrie Sue inhaled deeply, fighting back unusual tears. She explained about the coach accident and her impulsive action. "I could have been a good teacher, honestly. It was like I was being given a chance to break free from the gang, and I took it. But Quade has tired of his cruel games and released my sketch. What now?" she murmured to herself. "They'll be looking for me everywhere."

T.J. knew she might get suspicious of him if he suggested taking her to Darby for protection. "We'll figure something out later. Right now, we need to get out of Tucson, fast. Get packed, woman. We're wasting valuable time arguing. You're stuck with me."

"I can't let you ruin your life," she protested weakly, needing him.

"It's my life, what there is of it. If anything happened to you, it would be my fault. Like it or not, I'm going to help you get through this. Now, get in there and get ready to leave. Move it, woman!" Carrie Sue rushed into the bedroom to follow his order. She changed into a riding skirt, boots, and a cotton shirt. T.J. joined her. She retrieved her weapons from the hiding place in her closet and her supplies from the trunk, on which T.J. was now sitting and watching her.

She stuffed clothes into a small satchel. Suddenly a voice spoke to her from outside the bedroom door, inside the front room.

"I'm Charlie Shibell, Sheriff of Pima County. I'm here to arrest you, Miss Stover.

Stay clear of those guns," Joe Collins warned. "I saw you in town the other day. When I got this poster, I remembered you. I want to get you out of Tucson and into my jail before bounty hunters see those new posters and try to take you away from me."

T.J. motioned to her to keep silent about his presence in the corner. When the Ranger entered the room, T.J. hit him over the head with his gunbutt, as planned. Joe had glanced his way, as planned. "He saw me. Let's get out of here. We're in this together now."

"He isn't dead, is he?" she asked frantically. "I don't want you to kill anyone because of me, T.J., please. I'd rather be jailed or hanged than make you an outlaw."

T.J. checked his friend, and wished some of her words and looks weren't affecting him so strongly. "Nope, just out cold and will be for some time. Let's ride, woman. I'll get the horses saddled."

"No," she protested. "You sneak out of here and meet me at the southeast edge of town. I'll take the backstreets from here and you leave from the livery stable. I don't want us seen riding out together. If that sheriff dies, I don't want anyone else knowing about your help. If he doesn't, it's your word against his, later. Don't act rashly. I don't want you on the run. It's a terrible existence."

He reasoned, "What if you run into Martin Ferris? He'll get suspicious and try to stop you."

"I'll handle him. I'll meet you on the road we came in on by stage, five miles beyond the last house."

He realized he couldn't argue with her. "I have supplies at the livery stable with Nighthawk. Be quick and be careful. If you try to protect me by not showing up, I'll track you down. Until you're safe, you need me to guard your back and I fully intend to do a good job."

"I'll be there soon. Now get out of here, Mr. Rogue."

After T.J. left, Carrie Sue checked the sheriff to make sure he was alive. She took the poster from Joe's pocket and stuffed it inside her satchel. She wrote Mrs. Thayer a quick note telling the woman how much she appreciated everything she'd done for her and how much she would miss her new friend. She said she was in trouble and had to leave town in a hurry, and that the woman would understand why very soon. She revealed that she had been trying to start a new life here in Tucson, but her wicked past was preventing it. She left the note on the desk, gathered her things, and sneaked out the back door. After saddling the pinto, she rode northward out of Tucson along the backstreets, even though the stage had entered town from the southeast.

Chapter

10

Carrie Sue hadn't ridden far before she realized she was being followed. The redhead pulled out her fieldglasses and stared at the rider trailing her. It was T.J., and she sighed in relief. She waved to him to let him know she had sighted him, and she waited for him to join her.

She laughed and accused, "You don't trust me, Mr. Rogue? You're supposed to be on the other side of town waiting for me. You've ruined my brilliant strategy. I wanted to be seen leaving town northward, alone. If anyone saw you, they'll know you're with me."

He frowned at his bad decision, then grinned. "Don't worry; they'll think I was on to your ruse and was dogging you for capture. I was worried about you. I was scared you'd skip out on me to protect me."

Now that they were out of Tucson and could easily make a run for it, her tension had lessened. She felt safer in a saddle, out in the open, away from strangers, and heavily armed. She was with her love and he was determined to protect her and help her, to be with her. If his feelings were as strong for her as hers were for him, perhaps they could escape and make a future together. She would give him a few days to prove his love and commitment, then she would suggest her stirring plan. She merrily admitted, "The thought crossed my mind, partner, but I remembered your threat to hunt me down. I certainly don't want to get on T.J. Rogue's bad side. I have enough troubles as it is."

He liked seeing her relaxed and confident. He teased, "I'm glad you decided not to dupe me, woman. I would hate to think I clobbered that sheriff and got into real trouble for no good reason."

"You still have time to back out. Maybe he didn't recognize you."

"He knows me all right. We had a foul disagreement one night in a saloon. If I recall him accurately, he won't tell anybody about us too soon. He'll want to track us down so he can say he captured the Texas Flame and the notorious Rogue. And he won't want anybody to know we skunked him."

She sent him a playful grin. "At least we have male pride working on our side. Let's go before he comes to. I was going to tie him up, but I might need my rope for something else."

T.J. was glad she hadn't bound and gagged Joe Collins because that would be hard for the Ranger to explain. "Where to, Carrie?"

"I'm called Carrie Sue, but it doesn't matter. Let's ride for New Mexico. It's fairly secluded and I know some places there we can hide."

"As long as we're partners, it sounds fine to me."

They exchanged smiles and headed across country to avoid the public road south of their location. They traveled for hours through wild fields of saguaro cactus and into the Rincon Mountain range. They steadily pushed onward until the sun seemingly burned into their skulls and dampened their clothes. When they found a couple of taller trees, they dismounted and relaxed in the shade. While Carrie Sue strolled around loosening up her stiff muscles, T.J. poured water from one canteen into his hat and let the thirsty horses drink.

"I can tell I've been out of the saddle for weeks," she remarked, rubbing her lower back and flexing her shoulders. Her hair was twisted and tucked beneath her hat to keep her cooler. She sipped water from a second canteen and handed it to her handsome partner.

He took several deep swallows, then pushed up his hat with his thumb. "I wonder what Ferris will say and do when he finds you gone."

Carrie Sue laughed and retorted, "You mean when he discovers who I really am. Can't you imagine his face when he sees my wanted poster? He'll probably be relieved he didn't try to attack me."

He replaced the top on the canteen and hung it over the saddle horn. "I know what I thought and felt when I saw it."

Carrie Sue met his engulfing gaze and asked, "What was that?"

His smokey gray eyes enlivened as he grinned and eyed her head to foot. "How it didn't do you justice. You're one beautiful woman. I haven't been able to get you off my mind since we met."

She smiled and asked, "Was that all that came to mind?"

"Nope. I realized you were in deep trouble and would need my help to survive, if I could convince you to accept it. We've spent a lot of time together, Carrie Sue, and I think I know you by now. You may have done some things you're wanted for, but not all of them, and not because you wanted to do any of them. Isn't that right?"

"I guess a man like you would know that half the stuff said and written about people like us isn't true, or it's greatly enlarged. It all started out so innocently, T.J. All I wanted was justice and revenge. The Hardings killed my parents and took our land, but the law didn't do anything to them. I was bitter, and too young to know any better. So was Darby. Somewhere along the way, everything got out of control and there was no turning back. Twice before I tried to start fresh, but Quade's detective always found me and sent me on the run again. Sometimes I wished it were over any way possible." She leaned her head against the tree and closed her eyes to relax.

T.J. observed her profile and mood. He hated tricking her like this, but it was necessary. He had sworn personal revenge on the Stover Gang, and it was his lawful mission to defeat them. To get to Darby and his men, he had to strengthen the bond between Carrie Sue and himself so she would trust him completely and lead him to those murderous bastards. If this beauty was telling the truth about her entanglement with her brother, he would try to find a way to help her when this matter was settled, though it wouldn't be easy. After all, she was guilty, was an outlaw. If the crimes against the Hardings were the only ones involved, he wouldn't have a problem getting her a pardon. There were countless other charges, including three murders he needed to avenge. He knew she hadn't killed anyone, but she was an accomplice. She knew what those bastards were like, but she had stayed with them.

T.J.'s keen gaze scanned the horizon in all directions. If anyone remembered this redhead on the stage, and who could forget a beauty like her, other men were probably on her trail right now. He had to be careful until those posters for her were withdrawn, if Joe could get them pulled out of circulation so he could do his job. But something else troubled him—her acting skills. He had fallen for her ruse just like everyone else, and she hadn't confessed anything even after their passionate night, until today when she was forced to do so to escape. Even now, she was on guard, and that worried him. Had she tried to sneak out of town and lose him? To spare him from a criminal life because she loved him? Or to flee to her brother alone?

He glanced in her direction and she appeared to be dozing. Lordy, she looked so innocent and vulnerable. But he had witnessed the spitfire in her and he was aware of her reputation. He had observed her skills and he knew a desperate person was the deadliest of all enemies. What if she was fooling him more than he was fooling her? What if she was suspicious of him and was pretending she wasn't? What if she was letting him tag along only until she could elude him? Worse, maybe he was duping himself, being dreamy-eyed, because he wanted to believe her story, wanted to trust her, wanted to help her survive so he could have her later. But could he, after betraying her and using her? Would she be able to understand and forgive him?

Carrie Sue sensed powerful emotions in the air. Now that she was on the trail again, her instincts were alive. Merciful Heavens, how she wanted and needed to believe T.J., but could she afford to do so? She felt guilty about making him prove himself, but her life depended on it. She sighed heavily and stretched.

T.J. revealed, "I may as well confess something right now. Quade Harding is the man who had me barbwired to that tree. When he hears you're with me, he'll be furious. One day, I'm going to kill him. He'll pay for what he did to both of us." He smiled when she moved closer to him. "You know something strange? We have the same enemy and our lives have been similar. We both lost our parents and we both got into trouble, and we both wound up in the same place at the same time. It's almost like some force has been pushing us toward each other."

"Maybe that's why we find each other irresistible," she jested.

"Could be, woman. Let's get moving before Shibell tracks us here."

They journeyed until it was nearly dark and made camp in a treed area near the bank of the San Pedro River, about six to ten miles north of the road between Dragoon Springs and Tucson. Fortunately, the river—which could often nearly dry up—was flowing tranquilly at this time of year. T.J. tended the horses while Carrie Sue built a small fire to prepare a meal of canned beans and coffee. The moment they were ready, Carrie Sue doused the fire.

Along with the biscuits which Carrie Sue had sneaked from Mrs. Thayer's kitchen on her way out, she and T.J. ate the simple beans and drank black coffee. For the first time, trail food didn't seem so bad or—each decided—maybe it was the company they were with tonight. He washed the dishes in the river while she refilled their canteens. In case a swift start was needed, everything was repacked. The horses were nearby, watering and grazing contentedly, and the serene mood encompassed T.J. and Carrie Sue.

"You want to take a swim and cool off before we turn in?"

She smiled at him and answered, "I always say take advantage of water when you're near it. We'll probably sleep better afterwards."

T.J. grinned at her, a grin which said he had more in mind than a late night swim. "I'll meet you in the water."

Carrie Sue knew what she wanted tonight, him, and she was quivering with anticipation. Maybe this situation was crazy and dangerous, but she had to have him! In view of her stormy existence, they could be parted or slain at any time. For now, for a while, she couldn't leave him or resist him. Yes, that made her vulnerable, but she had to take this risk. She headed for the river's edge and undressed near a tree. She knew, and so did he, that no one should ride by this spot this late at night. She stepped into the cool water and submerged her body to her neck. She liked the feel of the sand under her feet and the sensuous splashing of water against her bare flesh.

T.J. surfaced before her, within inches of her body. She gasped in surprise and bolted upwards, the water striking her above her waist. Her eyes were transfixed on his handsome face where moonlight was playing over his solid features and enhancing his good looks. Just a glance from him seemed to awaken every sleeping emotion within her and whetted her appetite for the loving only he could give. His eyes seemed to burn into her very soul, into the core of her being, to ignite her senses into flaming desire. "I couldn't tell you were there."

"Old Apache trick," he jested with a devilish grin, his gaze caressing her as his hands yearned to do. She had really gotten to him and he ached to possess her. No blaze of passion could burn brighter or fiercer than his for her. She had kindled a flame within him the first moment he sighted her, and he doubted that the ensuing wildfire could ever be doused. But that was a problem he would deal with later. "You're even more beautiful than I imagined you were beneath that simple dress at the home station." His arms encircled her waist and he sank slightly in the water to nestle his right cheek against hers, crushing her supple curves against his broad chest. He closed his eyes and inhaled the sultry scent of her salty body. Except for her infamous reputation, he knew little, if anything, about this mysterious and irresistible vixen. He wanted and needed to know everything about her, but he had to move cautiously.

Carrie Sue's fingers came up to rest lightly on his shoulders. Her naked breasts pressed against his collarbone, her stomach snuggled to his taut abdomen. Despite the cooling water around them, she felt aflame with blazing desire. She trembled as his lips nibbled at her ear and trailed slowly across her jawline to her chin, before they sealed over her mouth. She had promised herself never to trust another man, not after her grim experiences with them. But how could she not trust this man she loved and craved? Merciful Heavens, could she even trust herself?

They touched lightly, questioningly, leisurely. Their bodies ached to be joined, but neither wanted to rush this moment. His mouth was soft and smooth and stimulating as it claimed hers. They shared numerous kisses which increased their hunger. Their lips parted and they gazed at each other: hesitating, longing, burning.

Her fingers slipped through his dripping hair, brushing it away from his face. His hair was full and thick, nape length, as black as a moonless midnight. Her eyes slid over his features, and her fingers followed the trail of her gaze, encouraging her lips to join the stirring journey. She felt him stiffen a moment, then relax as a moan escaped his throat. The midnight sun glowed on his torso and was reflected in his smokey gray eyes. He was like a wild stallion, an unbroken mustang, who allowed her to approach him and ride him. His frame was sleek and hard, yet supple. No ounce of extra fat detracted from his magnificent form. She traced the hairy path over his hard chest.

T.J. pulled her toward him. He had to feel her, taste her, inhale her. She couldn't be a vicious outlaw, not this proud and gentle creature. His mouth found her cheek first, then her lips, nibbling at them and mutely inviting her to do the same with his. His kisses were deep, greedy, pervading, and she responded in the same manner. His tongue enticed hers to mischievous play. His hands left her waist and drifted up her bare arms, delighting in the wet slipperiness which enlivened his senses. He sent them roaming over her shoulders and down her chest. Her wet skin was silky to his touch, responsive to him. His hand cupped her breasts and gently kneaded her taut nipples as his mouth labored tenderly down the silky column of her neck.

A tingling chill raced up Carrie Sue's back, which arched toward him when he lowered himself into the water so his mouth could taste the sweet rosy brown buds that were blooming beneath his toiling lips. His mouth seared over her tingling flesh with a white-hot heat which threatened to drive her mad. He was so warm and so tempting, so pervasive. His touch was tantalizing on her sensitive skin and it aroused every inch of her being. His tongue skillfully fluttered over her breasts like a delicate butterfly's wings. His hands shifted to her buttocks and pulled her tightly against him. Her head was spinning with pleasure and happiness. Countless sensations washed over her. She felt hot as a boiling pot, taut as a calf-rope during branding, and as giddy as a child at Christmas.

T.J. stood before her, eight inches taller than she was. His quivering hands untied the bandanna around her head and loosened her fiery mane. He spread the blazing glory around her shoulders and admired it as his fingers savored the texture. The flaming locks seemed to hint at Carrie Sue's leashed sensuality, her fiery nature, her imprisoned soul, her secret self which had been jailed with all men except him. Only from love could she have given herself to him. Without a word, he lifted her in his strong arms and carried her to the blanket which he had spread for them before entering the water. He lay her on it and gazed down at her, his hungry eyes traveling her full length. She didn't appear the least bit shy or inhibited with him. She reached for him and drew him down to her, boldly, possessively, enticingly. His heart pounded, sending fiery blood racing through his veins.

T.J.'s mouth fastened to hers and his hips pressed against hers. Carrie Sue felt his manly hardness and it heightened her desire to feel him within her. His ebony hair fell forward and grazed her face. Beads of water dripped from him and trickled down her face into her hair. His caresses were amazingly soft, yet urgent. His respiration was erratic, and it excited her to know how aroused he was. She thrilled to his masterful touch, his titillating kisses, his caring mood. He gently stroked her breasts, then suckled them without mercy.

Carrie Sue was breathing fast and shallow; her heart was thundering. His mouth and hands seemed to be everywhere at once and she was awash with searing passion. Stirring moans kept reaching her ears, some of them hers and some of them his. She pressed against his body; she clung to him; she ached for him to be inside of her. She shuddered, and so did he.

The Texas Rogue entered her slowly and sensuously, and the blissful sensation tore away her light restraint as she gasped for undizzying air. She clutched at him savagely as he gently set his pattern and pace. It was as if they were melting into each other like slabs of butter beneath a hot sun. They were one, joined in spirit and need. Her head tossed and her body writhed as if she would perish if he didn't feed her ravenous hunger soon. He moved deeper within her, his movements strong and skilled. The daring desperado caught his rhythm and responded feverishly.

T.J. wanted to surrender himself to Carrie Sue's spell, but he would lose all control if he didn't concentrate. He pushed himself deep within her as the beautiful redhead wrapped her legs around him, pleading for a race to passion's summit. Their bodies were locked together and moving rapturously as if one. He needed to withdraw a few minutes to cool his torrid flesh, but she wouldn't release him even for a moment.

Carrie Sue squirmed beneath her handsome Rogue as his lips brushed her breasts. She knew his restraint was stretched tightly, but she couldn't control herself as he filled her with wonderful strokes. She clasped his head between her hands and lifted it, wanting to stare into those smokey depths when that special moment of ecstasy arrived. She fused her gaze to his, as snugly as her body was sealed to his. She smiled when he kissed the tip of her damp nose. Then, the explosion came, long, deep, achingly sweet, powerful.

As she cried her victory aloud and meshed her mouth to his, his strokes became swifter and more forceful. His mouth feasted ravenously on hers as his body shuddered with his own release. His face moved to her neck as he gasped for air and continued his movements until he was fully sated. Her fingers stroked his dark, wet head and she smiled as she felt the throbbing pulsations cease within her.

T.J. rolled to his back and carried her along with him. His breathing was labored and his body was drenched with sweat. He was totally exhausted, a wonderful and thrilling fatigue.

Neither spoke nor moved as they shared the closeness of this serene aftermath. They listened to the songs of nocturnal insects and birds and the rush of the nearby river. They inhaled the sweet fragrances of the flowers that bloomed around them. The trees overhead were still, as no breeze stirred them at this peaceful moment. The night was cooling steadily, as was their flesh as it dried. Their respirations slowed to normal and their bodies relaxed fully.

T.J. knew this proud woman couldn't demand, and probably wouldn't request, a commitment from him. Her hazardous existence didn't lend itself to one. But she was the kind of strong woman who would not compromise over love, over trust. She would settle for nothing less than the one man who unleashed her inner soul and bound his heart to hers. When he stroked her silken body and experienced the overpowering force of their raging desire, he knew he was the one man who could earn her love and share it forever, even without marriage. He was the one man who could fulfill her, and she could do the same for him. But he was also the one man who could hurt her the worst, who could selfishly use and then cruelly destroy her.

He couldn't run away with her, no matter how badly he wanted her or how much he loved her. He couldn't become a hunted man, always looking over his shoulder. He couldn't let the Stover Gang continue their crimes, or get away with the murders of Arabella and Marie, or of Carolyn Starns and that Texas Ranger, a man he had known and worked with in the past. He had to stop them; he had to punish them. And this woman was the only path to victory.

Carrie Sue sighed peacefully and sat up. She gazed down at T.J. who was resting with one hand behind his head. She smiled and said, "I'm going to take a bath and get dressed. It's getting cool and we might have to take off in a hurry. I'll be back shortly."

He caught her hand and kissed her palm before letting her rise to leave his side. He watched her naked body as she headed for the river. A curious loneliness chewed at him. He closed his eyes and imagined his life without her, then dreamed of what it could be with her at his side forever. He had experienced so many bitter times. He had endured such misery and loneliness. He had been so empty, so hard, almost unfeeling in many ways. He had found his brother, only to lose him again before their reunion. He had lost Arabella and little Marie to brutal deaths. Now, he had found the one woman who could change his life, but he was going to lose her; it was inevitable. Bitterness attacked his gut. Why did that flaming redhead have to be Carrie Sue Stover? Why couldn't she have been born Carolyn Starns? Why had taunting fate thrown them together after her life was ruined, when she had little hope for survival and freedom? Why couldn't they have met years ago when her only criminal deeds were against Quade Harding?

He wanted to help her, but how could he? She had dug a pit and cast herself inside, and he didn't have a rope to haul her up with and couldn't think of how or where to obtain one. What a stupid thing for a lawman to do, to fall in love with a fugitive!

Catching the Stover Gang had seemed hopeless until he had met Darby's sister. If he could spare Carrie Sue somehow, he wouldn't use her to get at them. But he couldn't pardon her or get her a pardon, not after the things she'd done; so he might as well let her unknowingly help him get his task done quickly. Maybe, in the eyes of the law, that would make up for some of the wicked things she'd done.

He had come a long way from that quiet and terrified kid who had been kidnapped and half-raised by Apaches. He had come a long way from the white Apache warrior he had become before age thirteen. A boy grew up fast and hard under such harsh and demanding conditions, or he didn't survive them. He had come a long way from that "half wild rogue" at an orphanage in a San Antonio mission. He had traveled even further than the tough and embittered youth who went off to war, where he met the man who had become President of the United States. His journey had carried him through days of trouble and into the jail from which he was rescued by President Grant and befriended by several unique lawmen. Their trust in him had changed him forever. He couldn't look the other way when such malicious crimes had happened. He couldn't betray Grant, McNelly, Collins, Peterson, Clarke, and others close to him. He couldn't betray himself and what he knew was right and just, not for a woman he couldn't have.

Most people didn't know it and few would probably believe it, but he did have a code of honor, one instilled by his parents and the Apaches, and fortified by the good men he knew. He could hold his own against any man, match his skills and prowess against the best, and that wasn't boasting. He had traveled far and wide during his missions, and had left behind him a reputation as a legendary gunslinger. He sometimes wished people knew the truth about him so he would have their respect and acceptance. But he couldn't get his vital tasks done if people knew him as Thaddeus Jerome Jamison, Special Agent to the President, or U.S. Marshal, or Texas Ranger.

He was obligated to defeat criminals, especially the Stover Gang. But he hadn't bargained on this beautiful complication. This was a desperate situation which would force him to battle everything he was and all he believed in; yet, he couldn't hold back or retreat. He was honor-bound to seize victory any way necessary.

Lordy, last night seemed ages away from this one. After his shocking talk with Joe Collins, he had hunted down Martin Ferris's three henchmen and slain them. He hoped Charlie Shibell, the Pima County Sheriff and his good friend, would be able to get evidence against Ferris so the man couldn't give them trouble on the trail. He wanted Ferris to pay for his many crimes. T.J. realized that Martin would send men after them the moment they were discovered missing, even if he did or didn't know the truth. But once he saw Carrie Sue's poster, the Tucson mineowner would be determined to possess the fiery-haired vixen who had duped him and enflamed his desire.

Strange, but reality seemed distant and unimportant at this moment. All he wanted at this maddening time was the redheaded vixen at the river. He would have to keep reminding himself of who and what she was.

*

Carrie Sue completed her bath and dried off with her dirty shirt. She washed it and tossed it over a branch to dry by morning, along with the cotton riding skirt and undergarments. She needed to keep her clothes and body washed whenever possible, as she couldn't always count on having water for such chores. She donned a deep blue shirt and snug jeans, and braided her golden red hair. She had been so calm and limp when she began her bath, but it had stimulated her. Now, she was strangely tense and alert. Perhaps it was her garments, braided hair, and being on the trail again which altered her from the lovestruck woman to the wary desperado.

As she gathered her things to rejoin her lover, Carrie Sue's mind was in turmoil. She had been given time to think, time for her fear to be leashed, time for her wits to come to full strength. T.J. had her confused and agitated. He was the only man besides her brother and Kale that she had trusted, to whom she had gotten this close. But she had lied to him, and he knew it. She was a valuable prize, and he knew it. She was a notorious outlaw, and he wasn't. She admitted she needed his help in escaping, as she couldn't imagine how many men were chasing her at this moment. Prison or a hanging was staring her in the face and, yes, she was scared. Only a fool wouldn't be!

But was it fair to involve her love in such perils? There was no future for them, and she didn't even know if T.J. Rogue wanted anything permanent with her. Wherever she went, someone would know about her, would have seen her poster, would endanger any new life she tried to begin. She couldn't get him killed. Bounty hunters would be eager to track her down for ten thousand dollars, and lawmen would be anxious to arrest the Texas Flame just for glory.

But something else was nagging at her. T.J. hadn't questioned her about her brother, his gang, and their past actions. Wouldn't any man, particularly a lover, want to know what she had done and why? He had stolen her wits and heart as easily as drawing his revolver. He had sneaked to see her Sunday night to unleash her passion for him, conveniently in time to seal their bond before this trouble began. Too, she had seen him leaving the telegraph office in Tucson. Why?

But there was more to worry her. That sheriff had sneaked into her room just as they were escaping, to compel T.J. more tightly into her hazardous life. The handsome Rogue had been at the home station for an *accidental* meeting and had *accidentally* been around when the stage was attacked so he could rescue her. Then, shortly after her talk with past gang member Curly James, T.J. had gunned him down.

What if it all was a clever ruse to get at her? What if T.J. wasn't who or what he claimed to be? What if that poster he had shown to her was false? What if he had printed it and shown it to her to send her on the trail toward Darby and his gang? What if he had been using his cunning to get close to her before tricking her? What if he was using her to get to Darby? And what would her brother say if and when she turned up with T.J. Rogue?

It was terrible not trusting a man under such conditions; yet, she had trained herself to be wary. Before she made her final conclusions, she had to discover the truth about her love. If he was after Darby and the Stover Gang, once she told him where they were or led him there, their love affair would be over and she would lose him. Perhaps she would have to kill him for betraying her. Carrie Sue returned to camp to find two bedrolls stretched out.

T.J. grinned and said, "If we're going to get any sleep tonight, it has to be separately. I won't be able to leave you alone if I'm touching you. We have a long, hard ride tomorrow."

"Yes," she concurred, "we do, Mr. Rogue."

*

They rose at dawn, ate quickly and quietly, and were on the trail shortly after sunup, T.J. and Carrie Sue rode as swiftly as the rugged terrain and heat would allow, not wanting to overtire or overheat the animals and themselves. She watched the landscape become hilly and rolling. The flatlands were lost for a time, as were the numberless yuccas and variety of cacti—except for occasional prickly pears which fanned out on the dry earth, often to cover spaces of three to five feet. Trees were taller and mesquites were rarer. Loose boulders formed piles of rocks which seemingly spread out for miles on both sides of them. It made her nervous because there were so many places where they could be attacked and entrapped; yet, they continued.

The beautiful fugitive and the handsome gunslinger covered less distance that day than on Thursday. They camped in the Little Dragoon Mountains in a small valley between towering rock formations where lush grass was growing and a shallow seep was located, making the fatigued redhead glad her lover was familiar with this territory.

They had talked little during their arduous journey that day and in camp that night. They both knew their silence was not totally due to their exhaustion. Yet, they watched each other furtively and smiled when their gazes met, and they shared the few chores genially. Even though the rock-enclosed valley was off the nearby road, they were careful to watch and listen for stages and riders as they took turns sleeping.

*

Again, they arose early. As they headed out Carrie Sue couldn't help but wonder why T.J. did not bring up the questions she thought should be asked. At least he should try to discuss why they were riding toward the very states in which she was wanted! He should want to know if she knew where to find her brother and if she was heading to rejoin the Stover Gang! As the day progressed, her worries, fears, and doubts increased.

T.J. guided them safely past Dragoon Springs and the Butterfield Stage station. He told her they needed to travel swiftly through this area which was so close to her last known location. He promised they could halt for rest for a few days in the Chiricahua Mountains: a day to a day and a half beyond them.

The air was hot and dry, too arid for cooling perspiration to form on her body. The blazing sun seemed to penetrate her shirt and jeans and sear her flesh, and she knew from experience that even clothed flesh could burn badly. She felt as if her hat was doing little good, as if her brains were being cooked slowly. She stayed thirsty, but knew the danger of drinking too much water too quickly; it was safer to sip frequently than to guzzle large amounts. She also didn't want to use up their water supply before reaching the next source. She concluded that the desert was wildly beautiful, but deadly. As the landscape of boulders and deep ravines continued on both sides of them, the daring desperado's apprehension mounted and she struggled to remain alert in the dazing heat.

Just after their midday break, they rode into the midst of concealed Indians who rapidly surrounded them. Carrie Sue paled with fear. T.J. held himself erect and proud.

"Don't touch your weapons; they're Apaches." he warned. "That's the infamous Geronimo coming toward us. Keep silent and let me get us out of this. If you speak, woman, they'll be insulted and very angry."

Chapter

11

T.J. lifted his hand and greeted the renegades with the correct Apache words and signal. He touched his chest and revealed, *"Biishe, nagushnlti-ye Cochise, shitaa' daalk'ida."* The ebon-haired man told them he was "Nighthawk, adopted son of Cochise, his father long ago."

Carrie Sue did as her lover ordered; she kept still and silent. Yet, she was amazed by T.J.'s knowledge of the Apache language and signals, and she was baffled by how calm he seemed around warriors who had slain his parents years ago. There was something he hadn't told her. . . .

A stocky warrior approached them. Slowly the Apache circled the white couple and looked them over thoroughly. He said, *"Benasi'nldal,"* which meant Nighthawk had forgotten about him.

"Duuda," T.J. refuted. He explained that he had needed to return to *keeya',* his homeland to search for his family. In Apache, he continued, "I needed to learn of the white man and my history. I have never forgotten my Apache brothers and history. I have never turned against them or battled them."

"Andi," a second warrior replied as he left his hiding place and joined them, saying T.J.'s words were true. "Nighthawk told me of his hungers before he left our camp and my father's side."

T.J. smiled and nodded at Naiche, the second son of Cochise who had become chief after his father's death, a blood chief who was being compelled to share his power with the notorious Geronimo. For the benefit of Geronimo and others, T.J. said, "I heard of our father's death and it saddened my heart. He was a great leader."

Geronimo scoffed. "The white man forced him to a reservation, and it killed his spirit first and then his body. It is evil!" *"Ntu',"* he stressed coldly and bitterly.

"But he wished peace and survival for his people. It was wise."

"Naagundzu!" Geronimo shouted, meaning they were at war again.

T.J. kept his attention on his blood brother. "It is bad to begin the raids and warfare again, Naiche. You must find a way to make peace so your people can survive, as our father wished. The whites are many and powerful. They will hunt down your people."

Geronimo stated belligerently, "The bluecoats try to corral and tame us like wild horses. They track us as animals!"

"Because you prey on them as wolves after helpless sheep," T.J. reasoned softly. "The white man is here to stay, so you must make peace or your tribe will perish under his advance and guns. He does not understand the Apache way; he must be taught to do so."

Carrie Sue intently observed the two Apaches closest to them. The younger one was nice-looking. His dark eyes were shiny and alert, filled with intelligence and courage, and noticeably lacked any glint of hatred and danger to her and her lover. The only thing which detracted from his looks was his slightly drooping right jawline which caused the left corner of his mouth to lift slightly as if he were always half-smiling. He was clad in a striped cotton shirt, tan breeches, a knee-length loin drape, and the distinctive leather boots which could be drawn over the knees to protect them against cactus and other prickly plants. A red cloth was rolled and tied around his black hair, making a sharp contrast in colors. It reminded her of Kale Rushton who was half-Apache and wore his black hair long and wore a red sash around his forehead. The other man was much different.

He looked to be middle-aged, but it was hard to tell because his skin was so darkened by the Arizona sun. His features were nearly harsh, as was his piercing gaze. His hair, which was parted down the center of his head, only fell to his shoulders, unlike the long hair of the other Indians. His nose was large, very full at the bottom. His mouth appeared a mere slit across his face, a line which turned downward at both ends as if set in a permanent frown. Furrows cut into his forehead and between his brows, but she didn't know if they were due to the sun's glare or his ill-feelings toward them.

Carrie Sue's attention was drawn to the older man's deep-set eyes beneath overhanging brows. They were small, and glittered with powerful emotions. His gaze and expression hinted at a man who was short-tempered, suspicious, tough, a man with an unyielding spirit and fierce courage. She didn't need to be told this stocky man was Geronimo. She wished she could understand what the men were saying, but she didn't know a word of Apache; Kale had never tried to teach her.

Cochise's second son and chief of this band of renegades said, "You know why we have taken to the warpath again, Nighthawk. They invaded our land and made us prisoners. They force those on the reservations to work for them as slaves. Women and children are given a metal penny to gather hay for their horses, but this white money buys little. We were told to gather piles of cottonwood and mesquite, but were allowed only small shares for our campfires. We were forced to make a line to claim rations of flour and beef as the treaty promised if we halted our raids. Seven days' supply the Army said, but it was gone in four. Yet we were forbidden to hunt game on lands which have belonged to us since Grandfather made them. Men must dig holes in the body of Mother Earth to do what is called irrigation so we can grow evil things within her belly for the whiteman to eat. Apaches are not farmers and we do not care for such foods. If we refuse to cut into the earth, we have nothing to do but drink, gamble, and repeat tales of past glories. Many warriors have become scouts for the bluecoats so they can ride free. We grew restless and escaped."

T.J. inquired patiently, "What of Tom Jeffords, Naiche? Can you not trust him as our father did? Can you not make a new treaty with him for the sake of your people?"

"The whites sent him away because he sided with us. Jeffords forced the whites to give us our sacred mountains as part of our reservation, but they have taken back their words and our lands. He was with my father before he left Mother Earth. They were friends. He is gone now and can no longer help us battle the evil whites."

T.J. knew that Cochise had died on the day and the hour he had told Indian agent Tom Jeffords he would. His people had painted his body yellow, black, and vermilion, had shrouded him in a red blanket, and had taken the chief's body into the sacred mountains and buried it in a secret place where it would never be found.

For the last two years, Jeffords had maintained peace, but Cochise's death had made it difficult. When Geronimo and other leaders began raiding across the Mexican border, trouble had begun.

T.J. hadn't been in this area in some time, but he always found ways to keep up with the local events and the tribe which had raised him. He hated the thought of the Apaches being wiped out, but there was little he could do to help prevent what seemed to be their grim fate. For the past few months, things had gotten worse.

The Mexican government had insisted that Jeffords and the American authorities halt the Apache raids in their country. One bitter incident in March had brought the conflict to a head. It had been rumored that the marauding Indians had stolen gold and silver along with horses and cattle. Two white men had sold the Indians whiskey and gotten them drunk so they would reveal where the treasure was hidden. When the Indians refused to comply and the treacherous whites wouldn't give them more whiskey, the inebriated Indians had killed them. The taste of blood had brought back memories of olden times and sent the Apaches to raiding locally. Jeffords and the Army had tried vainly to capture the renegades and halt their attacks, and all Apaches had been blamed.

In April the *Arizona Citizen* of Tucson had declared, "The kind of war needed for the Chiricahua Apaches is steady, unrelenting, hopeless, and undiscriminating war, slaying men, women, and children, until every valley and crest and crag and fastness shall send to high heaven the grateful incense of festering and rotting Chiricahuas." The outcry of the Arizonians and Governor Anson Safford had been heard in Washington, and Tom Jeffords had been fired. The decision had been made to dissolve the Chiricahua reservation and to transfer its people to the San Carlos Reservation which was shared by over four thousand Apaches of all tribes. Geronimo had gotten wind of the offensive plan and fled, enticing four hundred followers to do the same.

T.J. had learned of Jeffords's firing and the intent to move the reservation; he had protested both actions to the President, knowing how the Apaches would react. But Grant had many problems and pressures at the time and couldn't relent to T.J.'s request, suggestions the special agent had known would prevent plenty of bloodshed on both sides. Now, it was too late to influence the President; war was on.

"There is nothing more I can say to you, my brother. You must ride the path you know is best for Naiche. Will you allow us safe passage through your territory?"

"Who is the woman?" Geronimo asked, staring up at her.

"Kada'ultan," T.J. replied, telling him Carrie Sue was a teacher. *"Shiisdzaa,"* he added, claiming she was "my woman."

Both Apache leaders looked her over again, making her nervous.

"She must be brave and smart to be the woman of Nighthawk," Naiche remarked. "We need more women. Is she for trade or sell?"

T.J. grinned and shook his head. *"Duuda."*

"Lltse 'i'nagu 'akahugal," Naiche told him, inviting them to return to their camp to talk and eat before they left this area.

Geronimo shouted, *"Duuda!"*

The two leaders argued for a time, alarming Carrie Sue who couldn't understand what the heated debate was about, except for the constant motioning to her and her lover. Finally, Geronimo relented, if they were blindfolded on both trips, to and from their hidden camp.

T.J. nodded acceptance of the requirement. He told Carrie Sue, "They want us to go to their camp to eat and spend the night to prove we offer them no harm. They'll release us in the morning. If we don't agree, they'll be insulted by our mistrust and scorn."

The redhead eyed the two chiefs. "Will we be safe?"

The smokey-eyed man replied, "Yes, I know this leader. His word is his honor. We'll have to be blindfolded first. Don't be afraid."

Carrie Sue glanced at Naiche again. "I'm not. His eyes say he speaks the truth. Besides, they could have captured us or slain us here if they wanted to. I sense no danger from him. Who is he?"

"The second son of Cochise and my blood brother. I lived with the Apaches from seven to thirteen. My Indian name is Nighthawk."

Carrie Sue stared at him. Was he telling the truth? She gazed into his blackish gray eyes and glanced at his midnight hair and dark tan. Had he been raised as an Indian captive? Was that why he had reacted so strongly to slavery and why he had sided with the Union? Or was he half-blooded and didn't want to tell her? Could he be Cochise's son with a white woman? Was the leader before them his half-brother? Was that why it would be safe for them to enter the Apache stronghold? "I see."

"Does that bother you, woman?" he asked after her intense study.

"No, I have nothing against Indians. In fact, I can't blame them for what they're doing. If we'd treat them fairly, we could co-exist peacefully. You have good and bad Indians, just like you have good and bad whites. I won't have a problem with them unless they declare themselves my enemy just because I'm white. I don't even care if you're half-Indian, which you could be with those eyes and hair. I'd still feel the same way about you."

Naiche wanted to grin, but that would tell the white girl he understood her words. For a while, it would be nice if she didn't know.

But T.J. knew and he was glad she answered as she had.

Carrie Sue and T.J. were blindfolded and led away. The group rode across open land which soon became scattered with mesquites and scrubs. The land was relatively flat and grassy so the riding—despite the blindfold—was easy. They entered a protective rampart of granite domes and sheer cliffs. They headed for the natural fortress where Cochise had made his home and from which he had carried out his stunning raids. Years ago, Cochise's lookouts had stood on towering pinnacles of rock to sight their enemies or targets in the valley below, a stronghold from which the Apaches could swoop down without warning to attack wagon trains and stages and other travelers.

Carrie Sue missed seeing the awesome rock formations of the Dragoon Mountains and the concealed entryway to a narrow, six-mile long canyon which suddenly opened up into a forty-acre valley where water, grass, and security were seemingly provided for the Apaches by some Higher Being who desired their survival.

The blindfolds were removed so the redhead and ex-captive could dismount. There were numerous wickiups and rope corrals located in the valley. She was amazed by how many Indians had escaped the reservation. They were escorted to one of those dome-like abodes made from canvas which had been stolen from wagon trains and the Army.

T.J. told her they had been ordered to remain there while the men had a meeting. "About us?" she probed.

"Nope, survival strategy. Relax, woman, they won't harm you."

Carrie Sue needed some answers. "I take it you were more than their prisoner long ago after your parents were killed. Why do they treat you so well? Why weren't we disarmed?"

"Because Cochise took a liking to me and adopted me. I earned their respect and was allowed to join them, until I left at thirteen."

"You weren't rescued by soldiers?"

"In a way."

"What does that mean?" she asked, confused.

He revealed, "I was out with a small band when soldiers sighted us and attacked. I had one hand tied behind me to prove my skills at hunting, so the soldiers thought I was a captive who'd gotten one hand free trying to escape. I let them believe it so they'd send me back to Texas. That's what the Army did with white boys they rescued so they wouldn't be tempted to return to the Apaches and the only life they knew."

She removed her hat and fanned herself with it. "Did you want to come back to them? Did you ever try?"

"Nope. I wanted to search for my older brother. He'd been taken by Mescaleros right after our captures. Since their territory was New Mexico and eastern Texas, I figured if my brother got free or was rescued, he'd be sent to one of those Texas missions."

She noted the haunted look which filled his eyes and darkened them, and she felt empathy toward him. She knew what it was to lose family, to lose an only brother. "Did you ever find him?"

"I checked all the missions when I got older, but no one had heard of him. I got news of him last winter by accident, but he was killed by Mexican bandits before we could catch up with each other again."

Such bitterness filled his gaze and tone that she questioned him no further on that subject. "I'm sorry, T.J.; that must have been hard for you to accept."

"Yep, fate was determined to defeat me, but I wouldn't let her."

"The Indians don't seem mad at you for escaping and never returning. What did you tell them back there?"

"Naiche and Cochise knew I would leave one day. The braves who escaped told them I was taken by the soldiers. They knew I would seek my own path and they accepted my hunger for the truth."

Still something didn't add up right. She inquired, "How could you accept the tribe who'd killed your parents?"

T.J. glanced at her, comprehending her confusion. "They were soldiers at war, and innocent people get in the way sometimes. They aren't the only ones who kill women and children during battles." He told her about the newspaper article and the events which had spurred this outbreak from the reservation.

That wasn't what baffled her. "But you're a Texan. How did you get to Arizona to be captured? If you were thirteen when you left, how could they remember you after so many years. I'm confused."

"It's been sixteen; I'm twenty-nine. Are you forgetting I've been in and out of this area lots of times? I've seen them plenty since my departure. I left as a friend, and I always return as one."

She noted that he said "departure" not *escape*. She waited for him to continue.

"The Chiricahuas were helping the Mescaleros battle the whites. They knew if the whites got past their brothers' territory, they would advance here next. We were heading for El Paso to sell cattle, and the stock was needed by the Indians. It was the first time papa had taken all of us along on a cattle drive. If he'd let the Apaches have the cattle without a fight, they'd be alive."

To get off the painful past, T.J. started another subject to distract her. He explained how boys were trained for cunning and toughness, the two most important traits for survival in a harsh landscape. He told her how they were taught trickery as a better strategy than raw courage. A leader and his band were more highly praised for stealing a few horses or goods with no losses of life rather than stealing an abundance of them and incurring many deaths and injuries.

T.J. stood and looked toward the mountains to his left. He related how boys were forced to stay awake for long periods to learn how to thwart fatigue. They were compelled to run through miles of harsh terrain, carrying a mouthful of water all the way. If the boy spit it out or swallowed it, he must do the four-mile run again and again until he succeeded. A grown warrior could run seventy miles a day over any landscape. "We trained with arrows and bows and slings and rocks. We acted out battles and raids. We were shown how to use the land to conceal ourselves. We had to learn to survive using only our shields, wits, strength, and prowess."

He took a deep breath and continued, "By the time a boy was twelve, either he was ready to become a warrior-in-training or he had to go through pre-training again from the start. To prove yourself, you were taken miles from camp and told to find your way back within a few hours, without being captured by braves in hiding."

"You made it, didn't you?" she asked, but knew the answer.

He nodded. "Yep, I had to. I was white so I had to prove myself more than worthy of being Cochise's adopted son."

"They're finding lasting peace hard to achieve, aren't they?"

"Yep. After the war, countless soldiers were assigned out here to string telegraph lines, build roads, protect settlers and miners, and control the so-called hostiles. The whites didn't realize how tough it would be to battle the Apaches. They're experts at striking from ambush; they can hide right before your eyes and you wouldn't see them. They know this terrain; they know how to live off of it and how to fight on it. The whites were at a big disadvantage out here. Until they got more fighters and better weapons than the Apaches."

A beautiful Indian girl called T.J. out to speak with her. They laughed and talked for nearly an hour. Carrie Sue felt her temper rising as she watched how the darkhaired beauty looked at and touched her lover, and how T.J. was behaving in return. Surely thirteen year old warriors didn't take girls to marry or to bed! Or did they?

When T.J. rejoined her, she asked, "Who was that?"

"Windsong, an old friend. She's grown into an eyecatching filly."

"Is she married?" Carrie Sue inquired, trying to sound calm.

"Not anymore. Her husband was killed a few months ago, from whiskey and a whiteman's disease."

She watched the woman vanish inside a nearby wickiup. "What was she doing, trying to entice you to rejoin them and take his place?"

T.J. eyed her with a mischievous grin. "Yep, but I told her I already had more woman than I could handle."

That jest did not soothe her ire. "I see."

He chuckled. "What do you see, my fiery vixen?"

"A roguish man playing tricks with me," she accused.

"Can I help it if a woman flirts with me? Made me feel good. I don't get much of that in the white world. Women are scared of me."

She frowned at him. "I could tell you were enjoying yourself."

T.J. sat on the blanket with her and tugged the red braid. "I'll remind you of your behavior when I act the same over another man."

"If we live that long," she murmured, feeling foolish.

"I told you they won't harm us," he comforted her.

"I'm not worried about the Apaches," she replied pointedly.

T.J. took her hand in his and vowed, "I won't let the whites harm you either, *Tsine*."

"You shouldn't make promises you can't keep, Mr. Rogue. We both know my situation is impossible, just like the one with the Apaches."

"We'll figure something out. Trust me," he urged.

Naiche returned from the meeting, and he and T.J. talked in Apache for a time. Then, another warrior approached them. He spoke with T.J., pointing at her and making unknown remarks. She caught two of the words, but couldn't translate them: *"Naaki." "Tai."*

Coyote held up four fingers and said, *"Dii lii."* T.J. shook his head and smiled amiably. Coyote held up eight fingers and said, *"Tsaabi lii,"* and motioned eagerly at her.

"Duuda, Naaldluushi," T.J. responded genially.

The warrior eyed Carrie Sue and frowned at T.J. before leaving.

"What did he want?" she asked, knowing she had just been discussed.

T.J. laughed. "He wanted to buy you for his wife."

"Buy me!" she shrieked. When T.J. chuckled merrily, she added, "I hope you told him you can't sell what doesn't belong to you!"

"He went from two horses, to three, to four, then eight. That's a big price; you really captured his eye. I told Coyote he wouldn't want a sharp-tongued spitfire like you."

"And I wouldn't want a sa—"

T.J. hurriedly cut her off, "Calm down, *Tsine*. Women aren't allowed to be nasty to men in public. You don't want your hot temper and impulsiveness to cause trouble for us. If you behave like a rotten child, I'll be forced to spank you to save face and protect us."

"You try anything, Rogue, and I'll slit both your throats!"

Naiche remarked in English, "Her temper flames as brightly as her hair of fire, my brother. Why do you travel with such a defiant woman? Do you wish to borrow my lash to punish her?"

"Sometimes her mouth runs faster than her wits, Naiche, and she forgets how valuable she could be to someone who needs money for survival. She isn't usually so rude and forward. She's just tired and hungry. She'll tame down or else I'll punish her."

Carrie Sue caught the warning in his first sentence and fell silent. She must not offend these Indians, or enlighten them to her value. She hadn't realized Naiche could speak her language, but she should have been more careful. "I'll behave, partner."

Naiche and T.J. exchanged pleased smiles. They sat on blankets before his abode and consumed *ch'ilae'bitsi, 'iigaa'i, 'itsa'ich'i'i,* and *lees'an:* roasted antelope meat, Apache cabbage, dried cactus fruits, and bread cooked in the ashes. The men drank *inaada*—mescal—while she had *tl'uk'axee'*—wild tea.

Afterwards, she thanked Naiche and smiled at him. The chief called Windsong over to take Carrie Sue to the river for privacy and a bath. She gathered her belongings and followed the Indian woman.

"She is very brave, my brother," Cochise's son remarked. "It was wise to use the blindfold to fool her. No outsider can see the hidden passage into our secret valley, not even your woman. But you have not forgotten it as Geronimo believes. It has been a long time since your last visit. Why have you returned?"

"I'm taking her back to her land. The dangers here are too many for her. Her brother is an evil man who causes the whites much trouble. People fear her and chase her to get at him."

"But you will protect her from them, as you tried to protect us from the evil whites. You lived amongst us when our father allowed the building of the Butterfield station near our mountains. He let the whites use our water and lands, but their greed increased. You were gone when the white man named Bascom destroyed the peace between us."

"I learned it was the Pinal tribe who caused the treaty to be broken, my brother. When they attacked white ranchers and stole a child, the soldiers had to ride against them. But they did not understand, all Apaches are not the same, of the same tribe. Bascom was eager for glory and he did not know the truth. I revealed it to them, but it was too late. No man can undo a past deed."

"Bascom insulted our father when he accused him of theft and lying. He shamed Cochise before the Indian and white man. He tried to hold my father and others captive for the black deeds of the Pinals."

"If Jeffords had been here in those days, the mistake would have been corrected before it led to war."

"Bascom hanged my uncle and his two sons. We were challenged."

"Was the new war worth the price, my brother? During the white man's big war against himself, he sent soldiers here with powerful weapons called howitzers. Do you wish them to return with such guns?"

"Have you forgotten what our father told you during one visit? He said, 'We kill ten; a hundred come in their place.' We destroy little weapons and they return with bigger ones with more power than our bows and lances. After you left, whites of all kinds poured into our lands like the summer rains. They do not wish to share; they wish to take. It cannot be."

T.J. knew the white population had grown to thirty-seven thousand by 1870, ten times larger than the Indian population. He recalled that Cochise had told him that he was intrigued by the white man's courage. That had been the great chief's reason for meeting with Tom Jeffords, a courageous man who became his friend for life.

"Four summers past, you talked the Great White Father into making peace with us again. Our father hunted and talked with General Howard for eleven days. Our father said, 'The white man and the Indian are to drink of the same water, eat of the same bread and be at peace.' He agreed to the treaty and reservation life until the Great Spirit called him two winters past. We tried to keep the peace, my brother; you know this. It cannot be. We will never go to the San Carlos prison."

As Naiche had said, there had been many times T.J. had tried to help make peace between the whites and the Apaches, especially after making contact with and going to work for President Grant in '70. But he could not change history or control an inevitable future. At times, he experienced bitterness over what both peoples had done to his life. But he had come to understand the Apaches who had raised him. They had taught him many things which had saved his life when threatened by man or nature.

He had grasped their desperation to survive, to challenge the people they viewed as invaders of their lands and destroyers of their people. The Indians had disciplined him, but never abused him; they had adopted him. They were simply different from the whites, a difference which prevented lasting peace.

Thad Jamison had been forced to accept the truth long ago about his past. He remembered the day his parents had died, his father while shooting at the Apaches and his mother from a stray bullet. He knew he and Tim had been separated only because white brothers would adapt better to new lives if they didn't have each other to whom to cling. Yet, he still sometimes felt resentment burning in his heart against the Apaches, and he knew that was only normal.

"When you leave this time, my brother, we will never see each other again," Naiche concluded.

"Your words are true, and it saddens me."

The chief offered, "If you wish to remain here with your woman for safety, no Apache will take your lives."

T.J. sighed heavily. "I cannot, my brother. There is something I must do. I will tell no one how to reach this stronghold. Your war is with the whites, not with me."

Naiche saw how troubled his blood brother was and knew the man needed to speak openly and honestly to someone he could trust. "Your word is your honor, Nighthawk. What bitterness eats at you?"

T.J. looked at his friend and replied, "What I must do is hard, Naiche; I must capture and slay the brother of my woman."

"She does not know this," the chief concluded aloud.

"No, and it will cause her much pain. My task will endanger her life. The whites wish her dead. By taking her back to lead me to her brother, she could be captured and slain by the white law."

"Can you do this thing, Nighthawk?"

"I must, for her brother killed my loved ones and friend. They ride as outlaws, murdering and robbing the innocent. I have promised the Great White Father to defeat them. She must be my path."

Naiche knew the truth about Thad Jamison. "You are a powerful man with the white law. Is there no way to save her?"

"Long ago, she rode with her brother's gang. She is guilty by white law and must be punished. My powers cannot save her."

"Can you not let her escape after you capture her brother?"

"My word is my honor, Naiche. To do so I must turn my back on it. I swore justice and vengeance before I knew her. It is hard to deceive her and betray her, but it is too late to retreat."

"You must not leave the path marked for you, Nighthawk. You cannot show weakness and lose face for any reason."

"I know," T.J. murmured. "It is a dark and dangerous path I travel this time, my brother; it will demand much from me."

"If there is a way to bring light and safety to it, you will find it and use it. But do not weaken and betray yourself."

"Her pull is powerful, Naiche," he confessed.

"But you are stronger and more cunning. Have you forgotten how to make an enemy a friend? Have you forgotten how you hated the Apaches and swore vengeance on us? It was that strength and courage which caused my father to adopt you. Nighthawk found understanding. He became a son, a brother, a man. Use what you learned amongst us. If you could run seventy miles across the desert in the heat, surely you can travel this path. You found the way to become one of us. When you left, you found the way to become a white man again. Can you not find a way to save this woman who causes your heart to burn?"

"It's different this time, Naiche. She has made many enemies."

"More than the Apaches have made?" he reasoned cunningly. "Yet we find ways to survive, to challenge our foes."

"Yes, Naiche, she has more foes than the Apache. They seek her everywhere. She has no stronghold such as this one. She cannot remain in hiding forever, for someone will find her. When she travels the land, she is in more peril than when you leave this place. You are a warrior, but she is a woman. How can she defeat such forces? How can she change what has been done in the past? She is like you, my brother; she is in a white man's trap."

"From your words, there is no way to save her. You must do what your honor demands. As with us, find happiness until death takes her. As with us, if you side with her, you will also die. You were sent from us to find the path you were meant to walk. Travel with her for a time, then ride on without her when she is lost to you."

"I have lost many things, my brother." T.J. told him. "I want this woman."

"As Apaches want survival and peace. Sometimes it cannot be."

*

Carrie Sue completed her bath under the curious gaze of Windsong who either couldn't or wouldn't speak to her in English. She sensed the Indian woman's irritation and intrigue, and she wondered what T.J. would do if she weren't with him on this visit. She had learned something new about her lover, his rearing and training by these Apaches and his adoption by the famed Apache chief who was now dead. Surely he felt a sense of loyalty to him, but how much? Which pull was strongest in a bind, the Indian or the white? And why, with his previous training and keen instincts, hadn't he detected their presence? Or had he? No doubt he had allowed their "capture."

She pondered the experiences and losses he had endured, at least those she knew about, and realized what had made him as he was. And, there was no telling what else had happened to him over the years to create the legendary gunslinger T.J. Rogue. He had been forced to become a strong, self-reliant male, a loner, a man feared by people on both sides of the law. He was a man driven by ghosts, scarred and molded by events out of his control, urged onward in search of peace and respect: a story similar to hers. Perhaps that was why he had taken her side and was helping her.

But what had happened, she wondered, to him during the war between the North and South? Where had he gone? What had he done? How had he prevented becoming an outlaw, which usually happened to a man with his skills and nature?

If T.J. didn't seem to fit anywhere, what did he have to make his existence worthwhile? What did he want in life? Why couldn't he, if he loved her and wanted her, escape far away with her? What could possibly hold him to this area? And, why did she perceive that expectant air about him again, one similar to the one in Tucson?

There was, she decided, even more to this man than she had learned. But what were those secrets and how would they affect her?

Carrie Sue knew that T.J. loved her hair unbound, so she brushed it and let it flow down her back like a wild river of tawny red. She donned the one dress she had brought along, as she would have time to change clothes before they left this Indian hideout. She wanted to look as lovely as possible, to tempt him, she admitted.

Carrie Sue followed Windsong back to camp. It was nearly dark. T.J. told her to take a seat on a blanket near a campfire and to remain silent and respectful. She observed the ceremony of music and dances with awe. She watched the men drink mescal and talk, and she sipped the fiery liquid which her lover passed to her. She watched the women observe her, taking special note of her fiery mane.

The hour grew late, and she was exhausted. The drum of the music seemed to fill her head and chest; yet, she began to doze, to feel utterly relaxed, limp and warm.

"Why don't you turn in, Carrie Sue?" T.J.'s voice asked.

"Where?" she replied, too weary to argue or to be aroused.

"In Naiche's wickiup. We're his guests."

"Good-night," she murmured and headed that way. T.J. didn't follow. She fell on the bedroll and was asleep quickly.

*

T.J. finally joined Carrie Sue on the bedroll. She snuggled against him but did not awaken. He lay beside her in deep thought, musing over how their lives were so entangled.

Last summer Quade Harding had learned he was Thad Jamison, undercover Texas Ranger, from a careless officer who unwittingly had exposed his name and task during what the man thought was a private conversation in a Brownwood livery stable. T.J. had been investigating rumors about the Hardings and their illegal actions, but he had been compelled for the first time to leave a mission unfinished because of the man's rash slip, and that didn't sit well with him. Luckily the villainous bastard hadn't told his hirelings—Curly James and two friends—that secret when he had ordered T.J. Rogue's murder at the end of September. T.J. hadn't told Curly and his boys the truth either, as it wouldn't have changed what they did to him, unless entice them to murder him quickly and with certainty instead of leaving him to die a horrible death!

The Ranger who had been on the stage with Carolyn Starns had found him in time to save his life; now, his friend was dead at the hands of the Stover Gang. After healing, a vital mission had intruded on his search for Curly and his boys.

T.J. knew that Quade Harding assumed he was dead and there was no way the evil rancher would reveal his involvement with a Texas Ranger's death, so his secret identity was safe. If possible, he'd like to stay out of Quade's sight and hearing a while longer. Later, he would kill the snake for himself and his woman!

Bitterness chewed at the handsome lawman. It had been those cases which had prevented him from seeing his brother again. Actually Tim had been the one to hear of Thaddeus Jerome Jamison, a lawman who was heading soon to Fort Davis to work secretly on a case. Major Timothy Jamison had contacted Ira Aten of the Rangers and asked questions. T.J. had gotten the shocking news of his brother's survival and location in January, shortly before completing his mission in the Oklahoma Territory. Then, he had gotten wind of Quade Harding's cohorts, who were reported to be in Sante Fe. In February, Tim and his troop had been ambushed and killed by Mexican bandits who kept raiding over the border. T.J. had gotten the infuriating news a few days later, just as he was about to set aside his pursuit in order to visit his brother. The reports on Curly had proven to be wrong.

For a while he had been enraged and resentful. He had planned to quit his overlapping jobs for state, country, and President. He had intended to settle down with a lovely woman and her beautiful little girl, but the Stover Gang had murdered them in March. He hadn't quit his jobs; he had sworn revenge on the Stover Gang and Quade Harding. He had sworn revenge on the Mexican raiders, but the Army had done that task for him in late March. In April he had picked up clues on Curly's boys and tracked them down, to learn they were to meet their boss in El Paso on May first. Again fate had stalled him until May second. Assuming Curly had left El Paso, T.J. had gone to Tucson to await the bastard's arrival.

Along the way, he had met Miss Carolyn Starns, alias Carrie Sue Stover. If his life hadn't been complicated already, it was now, for the woman who had stolen his heart and wits was connected to both enemies! And, she had known Curly James, a curious fact considering the blond gunslinger had worked for the Stover's enemy. His love certainly had traveled with some vile types. Yet, he knew for a fact she hadn't gotten cozy with any of those criminals. Didn't that say something important and good about the woman he loved and desired?

There was something else Thad Jamison wanted, his Texas Ranger badge with his name engraved on the back. He knew from reports that Darby Stover or one of the gang members was a collector of badges off the chests of slain officers of any kind of law enforcement, and his badge was among them. The Ranger who had been slain with Carolyn Starns during the holdup near Sherman had been keeping it for him until he completed a tricky case. That badge represented a lot to him, and he wanted it back! Soon, he promised himself.

When it was safe and the opportunity presented itself, he needed to telegraph his superiors on several matters . . .

He looked over at the sleeping vixen in his arms. *What the hell am I going to do with you, woman?*

His warring mind shouted back, *You mean, what the hell are you going to do about her, Thad?*

Chapter

12

TJ. awakened Carrie Sue so they could head out soon. With the flap down, she washed her face and hands and donned her riding clothes. After packing her possessions, she lifted the entry covering and joined the two men outside.

T.J. and Carrie Sue were served *itl'anaasdidze* and *banxei,* Apache mush and fry bread. They were given a supply of *tsguust'ei* and *bii bitsi,* Apache tortillas and dried venison, for the trail. When they finished eating, her lover went to bid old friends good-bye.

Carrie Sue asked Naiche, "What does *Tsine* mean?"

The Indian chief sent her a lopsided grin and responded, "It is what a man calls the woman he loves. You whites have many words for it, so it is difficult to translate. Do not tell my brother we have spoken of this word or he will be angry with me," he teased, hoping his revelation might help Nighthawk get closer to the woman and carry out his mission as quickly and painlessly as possible.

As T.J. and Naiche said their farewells, Carrie Sue wondered if the endearment had been used to fool the Indians into believing she was his woman to prevent problems, or if T.J. had meant it. Right now, her head ached from too much mescal to think clearly! She shouldn't have consumed any of the potent drink, but she had been so nervous last night not knowing how to act with T.J. here. She still wasn't certain of the Apache woman's role, and she didn't want to offend or insult any of them. Soon, she could relax.

Relax? her throbbing head scoffed. *When? Where? How? You're on the run again!*

In Apache, T.J. told Naiche, "I will send the Great White Father another message about Jeffords and the San Carlos movement. If I can change his mind about them, my brother, I will do so. It will take time for my words to reach his hands and ears. If he takes them to heart, it will take more time for him to respond and take action. Until that day, try to work with the new Indian agent for peace and a compromise."

Naiche replied, "I will give your words to the council, but I can make you no promises, my brother. While your words travel to the white leader and his words travel back to my lands, the whites and soldiers will not be at truce with the Apache. If they strike at us, we must defend our lives and lands."

T.J. coaxed, "Try to encourage your tribe not to raid on the whites from this full moon to the next. That will give time to make a new treaty to halt more bloodshed on both sides."

Naiche inhaled deeply, expanding his broad chest. "I will try."

"I can ask nothing more of you, my wise brother."

After a few more minutes of conversation in Apache, Naiche blindfolded them and led them out of the valley via the secret canyon. Miles away, the eye coverings were removed and they parted.

T.J. and Carrie Sue headed across a terrain of mostly yuccas, scattered bushes, and desert grassland. There were mountains in all directions, some distant and some close. It was fairly easy riding, except for her headache and excessively dry mouth.

They had traveled about twenty miles when he halted them for rest and water. T.J. knew she was in discomfort, but they needed to push on toward Apache Pass where he could conceal her in the Chiricahua Mountains while he rode to Fort Bowie to send critical telegrams. He had to complete his obligations to Naiche and his tribe before continuing his mission with Carrie Sue. He had to inform the President of what could happen out here if quick and fair decisions weren't made.

The lawman also needed to make certain the wanted posters on this beautiful fugitive had been withdrawn and that his superior knew all was going well on the Stover case. Too, he wanted to have an agent assigned to investigate her charges against Quade Harding. Since those events took place in June of '69, evidence would be hard—if not impossible—to find. But proving what had turned her bad was the only chance he had!

To give Carrie Sue more time to rest, T.J. said he was going to scout ahead for a short while. He told her to remain in the shade and to sip water slowly. He smiled when she simply nodded in her misery.

Carrie Sue watched the handsome Rogue leave, and frowned. She knew what he was doing, and it vexed her that it was necessary. She scolded herself for being so foolish last night. She knew that by nightfall the scorching sun would have sweated out most of the devilish liquid and she would feel like herself again.

She leaned her head against the tree and closed her eyes to shut out the sun's tormenting glare. She liked having T.J. be so caring and sensitive; she liked him calling her a romantic name, even if he didn't know she understood it. Before she reached El Paso and then headed for the Guadalupes where Darby was hiding—if Curly had spoken the truth—the matter of T.J. Rogue would be solved one way or—

Galloping hooves interrupted her musings. She jumped up, drew her revolver, and positioned herself for defense. T.J. came into sight, dismounted, and rushed toward her. She holstered the weapon.

"Trouble ahead, woman! I need you to hide here while I ride back to Naiche's camp and warn him. From those rocks, you can see miles beyond, even without fieldglasses. Several regiments of soldiers are coming this way with Apache scouts and Gatling guns. You know what that means. They'll be led straight to Naiche's camp and those Apaches won't stand a chance against those guns."

T.J.'s heart had pounded in dread when he had sighted those multibarreled weapons on their field carriages. He knew they could fire hundreds of rounds a minute. If the soldiers got into the secret valley or simply waited for the Apaches to ride out, it would be a slaughter. He had to do something to prevent such bloodshed, but he couldn't go reason with the Army. Without authorization, they wouldn't listen or change their minds, and his cover and mission would be destroyed for nothing. Besides, he had no proof he was Thad Jamison and he couldn't reveal that he worked for the President, who had given the order to move the Apaches to the San Carlos Reservation. Even if he told the Army he was trying to reach Grant to change his mind, they wouldn't back off on such weak words. "I have to persuade Naiche and his people to flee into Mexico until this current trouble settles down."

"How can you find their camp again?" she asked.

"They have guards posted who can see everything nearby. I know which direction to take. Remember, the sun was to our left, then at our backs. I can guess how many miles we rode and which way. All I need to do is be seen by them. They'll know something's wrong."

Carrie Sue didn't quite believe he didn't know the camp's location, but she didn't challenge his code of honor. "Does this mean your loyalty lies more with the Indians than the whites?"

"Nope, they're usually divided in matters like this because I know both sides. But I can't let a slaughter take place when I can stop it. There are women, children, and old ones in that camp, but those Gatling guns won't know the difference between them and warriors. If they'll just cross the border and lay low for a while, maybe things will cool down here with the new Indian agent in charge. At least I will have done the only thing I could."

Carrie Sue wondered why she wasn't surprised by his behavior. "Why would those Apache scouts help the Army track down their own people?"

"They're caught in the middle too. And it's the only way they can ride and live free of reservations. Besides, they're probably from other tribes and don't feel they owe this band any loyalty."

She wondered if, because of his troubled background, he had a penchant for helping the downtrodden or vulnerable. "Do you always help bad people like us when we're in trouble?"

"What makes you think that either side is totally wrong or bad?" T.J. asked. "You both got bad breaks in life and you have to accept them and deal with them. You can't believe that you or the Apaches are totally to blame for what's happened in your lives. Everybody makes mistakes and has flaws. Yours just multiplied before you could correct them. I think you and the Apaches are caught in other people's traps, but there's little I can do for either of you, except help you both survive until things change, if they ever do."

The redhead eyed him strangely. "What's in it for you, T.J.?"

He shrugged, then grinned. "With you, I'll get paid for my trouble and danger by getting to spend time with a beautiful and enjoyable woman. As for the Apaches, I owe them for what they've done for me."

She argued, "But you're breaking the law in both cases. I thought you always liked to steer clear of such perils."

"I have to do what I think is right and fair, so any more talk will have to wait until later. The Apaches only have a few hours to get packed and get away before those soldiers reach attack position. Right now the Army's camped during the heat of the day and, when they get going again, they'll have to move slowly with those heavy guns. Will you stay here until I return? I can move faster alone."

Carrie Sue realized he didn't want to leave her alone, but he wanted to warn his friends. She jested to cease his worry, "Without my protective partner, I have no choice but to await his return." Her expression and tone became serious when she added, "I'll keep hidden. You be careful, T.J., and please convince them to leave quickly."

"Be here when I return, woman, or I'll tie you naked to the first cactus I find after I recover you." The ebon-haired man pulled her tightly against him and kissed her with a feverish force that revealed his hunger for her, and his fear she wouldn't keep her word.

Carrie Sue caressed his cheek and jested, "Do you want to take my weapons along to prove I'll have to wait for you?"

"Nope, 'cause you might need them if another rattlesnake shows up, with no legs or with two of them. I'll get back as soon as I can."

Carrie Sue watched him ride off and she sighed wearily. At least this would give her time to relax and recover from her reckless drinking. She left her pinto concealed in the deep arroyo nearby, and she stretched out on her blanket beneath the low limbs of a shady mesquite.

Time passed as the day's heat, the lack of any breeze, the near silence of the terrain, and the soothing buzz of insects on the fragrantly flowering tree lulled her into a peaceful doze.

*

Suddenly Carrie Sue sensed danger and bolted upright, entangling her braided hair on a mesquite branch. Rapidly her hand had gone to her holster, to find it empty. As she freed her hair, she angrily watched the man who was squatting before her with a broad grin on his face. She realized what had aroused her from her too deep slumber—he had taken her gun. "What is the meaning of this, Martin?"

The cattle baron and silver mine owner chuckled. "So, I was courting a legend and didn't even know it," he murmured. "I should have known you were too tough and sassy to be a schoolmarm." His brown eyes lazily walked over the beautiful redhead and he laughed again.

"I suppose you're here to arrest me so you can collect my reward," she said with a contemptible sneer. "How did you find me?"

"Arrest you, my famous Texas Flame?" he leaned back his brown head and laughed almost wildly. "No, Miss Stover, I'm here to capture you for myself. As for finding you so quickly and easily, I have my Apache scout to thank; he's the best around," he boasted, nodding toward one of two men nearby. "As soon as Ben Myers showed me your poster Thursday afternoon, I came after you. Naturally our old sheriff didn't want to call out such a famed gunslinger, even if she is a woman." He pushed out his lips in a silly pout and said, "But you had taken off with that Rogue. Were you two friends before that bungled holdup?" he asked, his tone now demanding and cold.

"We'd never met before, but I figured I could use his help in case trouble came along before I could convince everyone I was Miss Starns. Men are easy targets when they think they'll get something from you out of gratitude," she remarked, trying to sound poised and cold like he was. If she was going to control this situation, especially get out of it, she had to fool Martin Ferris, to pretend she was like him.

"What was that little schoolmarm act about?" he questioned.

Carrie Sue watched the sweat roll down his face, too much for even the dry heat to consume. His cheeks were flushed as red as blood, and his lips were trying to parch. He definitely was not an outdoor man! He looked miserable in his soaked and rumpled clothes. He acted as if he were surrounded by hell's flames instead of desert heat. And the holster around his waist looked totally out of place on him. She almost laughed at the comical sight, but knew that would be unwise, as he was a dangerous foe. She didn't think he would believe her story about starting a new life and it wouldn't matter to a villainous beast like him if he did, so she related what would seem obvious and credible. "I was staking out the town for Darby's gang. I was supposed to decide if there were any easy, profitable targets there. If Tucson looked good to me, I was to send him a telegram on June first. Seems I messed up this time." She laughed softly and curled her arms around her upraised knees, wanting to appear relaxed and confident.

"It was working perfectly until those wanted posters arrived, and I'm not fooled easily. How did you find out about the wanted posters before they reached town? You took off like you had been warned."

She sent him a sly smile before answering, "I was, by Curly James, before Mr. Rogue inconveniently shot him. He used to ride with my brother's gang. We were old friends. We bumped into each other only minutes before his death and he told me my description and sketch had been released and I best get moving. I took off at dawn the next morning, but Rogue saw me leaving and followed. I persuaded him that Darby would ransom me for more than my ten thousand dollar reward, so he agreed to escort me to my brother. Of course, I planned to elude him along the way, after he and his guns had served me well as guards on the trail."

Carrie Sue lowered her legs and curled them to the left of her buttocks so she could lean forward, closer to the man's face. After sending him an enticing smile and seductive gaze, she asked, "Well, Martin, what are you planning to do with your helpless captive?"

"I have a big ranch and it's mighty private. No one will find you there unless I want them to. If you do as you're told, you'll be safe with me. I don't care about your measly reward."

Carrie Sue watched his tongue lick his lips in anticipation of having her at his mercy. She saw the lust glowing in his eyes, causing his face to redden even more. She heard his breathing alter as he became aroused just by looking at her, being near her, and having control over her. Those were weaknesses of which she could take advantage if she were clever and careful. The intelligent woman knew what this lecherous and wicked man wanted from her, and she had to pretend she was agreeable. "Since I have either a rope or a cell staring me in the face, your offer sounds most appealing, Martin. In fact, very appealing," she added, moving closer to him. When T.J. sneaked up, which she hoped was soon, she needed to be close enough to grab the vain man's weapon. The only problem was, she didn't know how long her lover had been gone or when he would return!

Martin extended his hand and helped her from beneath the tree. "You made the right decision, Carrie. You will understand if I take precautions with you until we're home and I'm certain I can trust you?"

"Of course. What would a woman want with a stupid or reckless man?" she teased. "Where is your ranch? What's it like?" she inquired to stall for time for her partner to rescue her.

"You'll see," he murmured, eyeing the area between her throat and cleavage where her shirt was opened for air. "Where is Rogue now?"

Beyond where they were standing, she saw the Apache scout studying the signs on the ground. "He went scouting. There's a detachment of soldiers miles up that way. He was looking for the safest path around them. I was asleep, so I don't know how long he's been away," she informed him, trying to sound as if she were being totally honest with him. Besides, if these men had been tracking them or observing them, Martin Ferris knew the truth.

"Does she speak the truth?" Martin asked the Indian.

The dark-skinned man who was dressed half in white man's clothes and half in

Apache garments replied, "The white man rode in the direction she said. He returned and talked. He left again and rode toward the Dragoons. He left two hours past."

Martin Ferris already knew before reaching this makeshift camp which direction T.J. had taken and when he had left because he had been watching the scene with his fieldglasses from a rocky peak in the distance. He also knew from their tracking that the couple had been captured and released by the renegade Apaches, which he found odd. He just wanted to see what the redhead would say before and after the Indian's words. "Why would Rogue be heading for the Apache stronghold after he sighted those soldiers?"

Carrie Sue had sensed trickery in the man, so she was prepared not to look surprised or unmasked. "I wouldn't know, unless he wanted to warn them of danger. He didn't tell me he was heading back to their camp, and I'll be surprised if he can locate it again. I wasn't feeling well, so he told me to wait for him here. I assumed he was doing what he said, looking for the best way out of this area. He gave me a kiss and galloped off, then I took a nap."

"What do you mean he was 'heading back'?" Martin asked, though his tone and expression made it all too clear he already knew the answer.

Nonchalantly, Carrie Sue sighed. "The Apaches captured us on the trail, blind-folded us, and took us to their camp for questioning. They seemed to know who Mr. Rogue was and admired his courage, so they released us this morning. For all I know, they could be old friends. I was kept in a separate tepee, so I didn't hear or see anything to tell me otherwise. He could have made some trade with them for our freedom."

"I'm glad you're being truthful with me, Carrie," he remarked in a pleased tone. "Let's get moving out of this heat." He ordered the Apache scout to stay behind and ambush T.J. to prevent him from following them. "After you're done here, catch up with us on the road or meet me back at my ranch for payment. I want his guns for souvenirs," he added, but they all knew he meant he wanted them as proof.

Carrie Sue had no choice but to do as Martin Ferris ordered, and to pray that her lover wouldn't ride into the trap set for him. She had faith in T.J.'s keen wits and skills, so he should be fine. She thought she had this lecherous villain at least partially duped, and the odds would be only two-to-one on the road, which might aid her escape. She gathered her things and mounted the pinto.

"Sorry about this, Carrie," he said with a falsely rueful grin as he bound her hands before her and took control of her reins. "What the hell are you looking at, Jess," he scowled at the other man, whose eyes had been glued to her curvaceous form. Jess quickly looked away.

Her quivering hands clung tightly to the horn, relieved she was such a good rider, skills she tried not to reveal to the two men who rode on either side of her. That idea didn't work too well since the pace and terrain forced her to use them to remain in the saddle. If she were thrown off at this speed, she could be severely hurt. She wondered if Martin was testing her in some cruel way, or merely assumed she was an expert horsewoman.

They traveled fast for the perilous terrain and heat, but Carrie Sue didn't say anything to slow them. When the horses got winded and Martin became overheated, he would be forced to take it easier. She hated to push her animal this hard, but if she suggested a lesser pace, Martin might take it the wrong way and watch her too closely. She had to let him get over-confident where she was concerned!

They reached the road to Tucson and continued to gallop swiftly. She finally decided that Martin was afraid his Indian hireling might not kill T.J. and the handsome gunslinger would be dogging them any time now. They only halted twice for short breaks before reaching the San Pedro River at dark where they made camp in a sparsely treed area.

Carrie Sue was aware of how close they were to Tucson, one day's ride. By using the cleared road and swift pace, they had covered a great distance today. She wondered why they hadn't met anyone along the public road. Where were all the soldiers, renegades, stages, and solitary travelers? Was T.J., she worried, alive and chasing them?

She was annoyed when Martin Ferris refused to untie her hands so she could relieve herself more easily behind thick bushes not far away. Nor did he unbind her hands while she ate her helping of canned beans and stale tortillas, a sparse and untasty meal prepared by Jess. Her headache had eased up, but was not totally gone. She blamed the lingering discomfort on the hot sun and swift pace, but tried to ignore it to keep her wits clear. At least their fast ride had prevented any talking on the trail which would have kept her on alert for many strenuous hours. She teased him flirtatiously, "Is this necessary, Martin? You have my weapons, horses, and supplies. Surely you know I'm not going to escape into the desert without them. Besides," she hinted seductively, "we both know I'll be safer at your ranch than anywhere else."

"Apaches can use this land with ease, and a smart woman like you might have those same skills. I would hate for you to trick me, Carrie, and force me to hurt you. This way, you won't be tempted to act rashly during the night. Relax, we'll be home before sundown tomorrow."

It was apparent that Martin was exhausted from his uncommon exertions, too fatigued to even make any sexual overtures. No doubt he assumed he had plenty of time to tame her and use her.

After she was secured to a tree for the night, Martin and his man took turns guarding the camp, with Jess taking the first watch and keeping his lustful eyes on her. She assumed their caution had as much to do with marauding Apaches as with T.J. Rogue. She fretted over what Sheriff Ben Myers was doing and thinking. Had the Tucson lawman sent out telegrams about her presence in and escape from his town? Did the lawman know about Martin Ferris's pursuit?

Carrie Sue's turbulent mind would not allow her to stop thinking so she could get some sleep. She asked herself if T.J. didn't catch up with them on the trail, would he come to Martin's ranch to rescue her? Wouldn't her lover guess that was where she would be taken? Wouldn't he guess that Martin Ferris would have his men watching for his stealthy approach?

And what of dear Mrs. Thayer? What had the woman been told? How had she accepted the shocking news about Carrie Sue Stover? One day, she hoped to get word to the woman and explain everything. But right now, she had to worry about escape from this beast.

The night was strangely still and quiet, and a full moon eerily brightened the landscape which was wild and rugged. It was too quiet, she fretted, because she didn't hear any bird, animal, or insect stirring about or making noises in the bushes or in the distance! It was as if some evil force had every living creature imprisoned, as if some oppressive and eerie heaviness was covering the landscape. In every direction, tall cactus looked like large fingers or hands pointing heavenward. She glanced skyward and saw clouds increasing on the midnight blue horizon. Maybe, she mused, a storm was brewing. That suited her fine, as it would cool the air and her body and it would release her tension. It might offer a chance for escape and wash away her tracks from even that Apache's keen eyes.

The redhead tested the strength of the ropes again. Too tight, she decided helplessly. She wanted water, but she refused to ask Jess to come near her to bring the canteen. She was exhausted, achy, and hot. The way she was bound to the tree, she couldn't shift to get comfortable. All she could do was spend a tormenting night on a complaining rump.

As Carrie Sue reflected on her dire situation, she was amazed by Martin's pursuit without a large band of men behind him. No doubt the conceited rancher believed no harm could come to him, and he didn't want anyone to know she was in his possession. Else, the law would take her away from him. Mercy, he was so like Quade Harding!

She knew it was long past Martin's watch time when Jess awakened him. She feigned sleep to prevent any conversation between them. While pretending, she dozed lightly.

*

After allowing her to excuse herself in the near darkness, Carrie Sue's hands were untied for a short time so she could eat another sparse meal and rub her wrists. Neither man was close enough to permit her the opportunity to seize a weapon from his holster. She had to figure out a plan to get away and return to Darby. But first, she had to earn Martin's trust. Maybe she would be forced to remain at his ranch until an opening presented itself, if she could control his sexual demands! As she drank her coffee, she asked her cocky captor, "What did Sheriff Myers say when you told him you were going after me?"

The brown-eyed man chuckled. "I didn't tell him anything about my plans. Except I did warn him to telegraph the Texas authorities that you'd left our area long ago so those bloodthirsty bounty hunters wouldn't pour into Tucson. I believe he was going to tell them you were seen heading northward toward Colorado. Doesn't matter; we'll be at my ranch before news gets out and you're in danger."

"What about Mrs. Thayer? What did she say when you went to check on me? She was nice and I liked her. Does she know the truth?"

"She knows you were using her place to hide, and she was mighty surprised. You had her fooled. People don't like being fooled, Carrie."

The redhead doubted Mrs. Thayer was really angry with her. Now, her new friend understood the meaning of her letter. With luck, Mrs. Thayer would give her the benefit of explaining before she judged her too harshly.

"Mount up so we can get out of here," Martin ordered.

While they were talking, Jess had doused the fire, packed the supplies, and saddled the horses. Her hands were bound again, and off they rode at breakneck speed just as the sun was rising.

It was clear and hot, so Carrie Sue realized it wasn't going to rain. She noticed the air was very still again today, and she could use a nice breeze. She realized that T.J. would guess their pace from the condition of their tracks, and hopefully he would race to catch up with them. Yet, he had used a great deal of time riding back to Naiche's camp, so she couldn't surmise how long that trip would take. Then, he had to battle that Apache scout and track her. With this pace and so few stops, could her love overtake them? He and his horse would already be tired from their long ride, and he would probably doubt that Martin would keep such a fast pace on this terrain.

A terrible thought came to mind: what if Martin had ordered the scout to conceal their departure trail? What if T.J. didn't guess who the scout worked for, or withdraw clues from the Indian before slaying him? How would he know where to search for her?

Following that alarming talk with herself, the day went by sluggishly despite their rush.

*

A shot rang out from behind them, and Jess fell to the road. Carrie Sue twisted in her saddle to see who was coming. Her heart fluttered with excitement.

Martin guided his horse in front of hers, his hand extended backwards to hold her reins as he positioned her between himself and T.J.'s gunfire. She realized the Tucson rancher was making a desperate race for town while using her as a shield. They were near the Old Spanish Trail, making Tucson about twenty miles up the road.

Carrie Sue could not allow them to reach town. She took hold of Charlie's mane and leaned forward. When she had herself steadied there, she released her grip and struggled to loosen the animal's bridle. She forced it over the mare's ears and shoved it down Charlie's forehead. The animal instinctively opened its mouth and the bridle was yanked free. Instantly the redhead caught Charlie's mane and tried to halt her swift gallop so she could turn around and ride toward her lover.

The moment her reins went loose in his grip, Martin pulled back on his own. Before Carrie Sue could gain full control over her startled mare, Martin was beside her, a revolver aimed at her chest. He shouted, "Stay back, Rogue, or she's dead!"

She and Martin were sitting sideways in the road. She saw T.J. stop. Nighthawk paced apprehensively, and her lover did not pull out his rifle. She knew Martin could not shoot T.J. with a revolver at that range, nor could her lover shoot her captor without his rifle. She wondered what was going through T.J.'s mind, as he was not a man to surrender or retreat. Her heart pounded with fear.

Martin backed his mount until she was between the two men again. He handed her the bridle and ordered, "Put this on!"

It was obvious to everyone that T.J. didn't have a clear shot at Martin. "I have to dismount first," she told the villain.

"Do it, and no tricks!" the annoyed and scared man shouted. "Go for that rifle, Rogue, and I'll fill her with bullets!" he warned.

Since Martin had his attention on her lover, Carrie Sue decided to use a clever dismount to get the upperhand. As she was moving her right leg over the saddle horn, she was muttering, "Jess should have put it on correctly, and he should have been guarding our—" Carrie Sue forcefully kicked Martin in the stomach and knocked him to the ground. She hurriedly put her boot back into the stirrup and galloped toward safety with her love, who was racing toward her.

"Get down!" T.J. shouted as he took the right side of the road.

Carrie Sue urged Charlie to the left and bent over the animal's neck. The moment she had attacked Martin, T.J. had drawn his rifle and galloped toward them. She heard shots behind her, but didn't know if Martin was shooting at her or her rescuer. T.J. returned Martin's fire.

Carrie Sue gently tugged on Charlie's mane. When she turned, she saw Martin Ferris lying on the ground and T.J. approaching him. She guided Charlie back to the scene to find her captor dead.

She dismounted and stared at the man's bloody chest. Weariness and dejection filled her. "What now, Rogue? They'll surely hunt us down for this so-called murder of an upstanding citizen. No one will believe he wasn't taking me in for that reward.

Merciful Heavens, another false charge against me!" she scoffed bitterly. "Now you're involved. I'm sorry."

This was one time the law knew she wasn't to blame for a foul deed, and T.J. couldn't help but wonder how many other charges against her were either false or exaggerated or self-defense. Her mood tugged powerfully at him. He reasoned to comfort her, "He was trying to shoot you in the back, not kill me, woman. I had no choice but to get him first. You had nothing to do with this shooting," he vowed as he drew his knife and cut her hands free.

Carrie Sue rubbed her chaffed wrists as she explained, "You don't understand, T.J.; it's another charge against me. They just keep piling up no matter what I do or where I go. I'll never get out of this mess alive; it'll never be over, for either of us." she glared at Martin's body and wanted to kick it in frustration. "I have only myself to blame. If I weren't an outlaw, things like this wouldn't happen to me. I wouldn't be forced to do the things I do and keep breaking more and more laws."

He argued, "He was trying to kill you; it was self-defense."

She sighed deeply. "In my position, nothing is viewed as self-defense. The law will say I murdered him while trying to escape capture."

"But I know better, woman."

"What difference does that make? They'll only charge you for siding with me. They'll say you're just as guilty and you'll be in as much trouble and danger as I am. This isn't fair to you, T.J. I shouldn't have dragged you into this mess."

"I'm in it, so it's too late. Forget it for now."

She asked, "How did you overtake us so quickly?"

"I met Naiche halfway back to his camp, so I wasn't away that long. He agreed to take his tribe across the border for a while. When things quiet down, he's going to try for another truce."

She smiled in relief and said, "That's good. How did you elude that Apache scout Martin left behind to ambush you?"

"I didn't. He's dead. When something's wrong, I get this crazy itch. I sneaked back through the rocks to take a look around before I whistled for Nighthawk. I got the drop on him first."

"And he told you who captured me?"

"Nope, and he'd brushed away most of your trail for a ways."

She looked baffled. "Then, how did you know where to find me?"

"An Apache can hide a trail real good, but not from another Apache, and I was trained by them. I turned his horse loose; he can graze until he's found by someone or he'll join up with a herd of wild horses. I hid his body, so no one will be suspicious of us." He chuckled. "I guess Martin forgot I'd seen his scout in town, so I knew who had you. I took a shortcut by Dragoon Springs and found where you'd camped for the night. Not a comfortable one I could tell. Besides, Nighthawk is one of the fastest horses alive."

"What are we going to do now, partner?" she asked again. She told him about Ben Myers getting the wanted poster and telegraphing she was gone. She also revealed what had been said and done between her and Martin.

"That's perfect, Carrie Sue. It'll give us time to rest before we get out of this area. I know a place we can use, a large cave off the Old Spanish Trail, not far from here. We'll hide the bodies and horses there. You'll feel better after you're rested."

She smiled at him and said, "This is the fifth time you've saved my life. Won't that become a tiring job?"

"Fifth time?" he said, surprised.

"During that holdup, during our picnic, with that sheriff in my room, with those Indians, because there's no telling what they would have done to me if you hadn't been along, and today. That's five."

He didn't expound on her remarks because those incidents had sapped some of her confidence. Yet, he had to point out how much she needed him to strengthen their bond. "You're a skilled, smart, and brave woman, but you can't take on every lawman and bounty hunter alone. I told you I was needed to guard this pretty backside."

She admitted he was right and she couldn't do it alone. "You've convinced me I need your help and protection, T.J."

To lighten her somber mood, he tugged on her braid and teased, "No matter what happens, I'll stick with you. I'm surprised you weren't worried about me."

"Why should I have been? You're the best."

He grinned in pleasure and gratitude. "I'm glad you have so much confidence in me, but you're drowning yourself too much. You're just as good as I am in most areas. Are you forgetting you saved my life at that picnic? If you hadn't been there to shoot at them, it would have been three-to-one odds, and I might have been killed."

"You're only trying to swell my head, Mr. Rogue. I recall how you took on more bandits than that during the stage holdup. Besides, there wouldn't have been any danger to you if not for my presence."

He shook his ebony head and refuted, "You're wrong, woman. Martin did it because we're old enemies. If his men hadn't attacked me out there, they would have ambushed me another time."

"What's to stop those three men from coming after us now? They know who I am and probably know Martin came after me."

"They can't; I got rid of them before we left town."

Sadness troubled her mind and heart. "You've had to kill too many times to save my miserable life, T.J. It has to stop."

"I didn't kill anybody who didn't need killing or who didn't provoke it. You're not to blame, Carrie Sue," he murmured and caressed her flushed cheek. He wanted to yank her into his arms and kiss her soundly. Lordy, she was getting a powerful grip on him! "We can't stand here jawing. Somebody might come along and there's a storm brewing. Let's get these bodies loaded and get to the cave."

T.J. retrieved Jess's body and horse, then loaded Martin Ferris on his. He guided her to the Old Spanish Trail cut-off and headed toward the Rincon Mountains which were twenty-two miles from Tucson.

They rode for a few miles, then left the trail to head into the hills. It was an area of small trees and bushy scrubs, mostly mesquite and catclaw. Large clusters of prickly pear, yuccas with tall shoots, towering agave plants, and numerous saguaro cactus were scattered around them. The land was rolling in places, and many dry washes ominously cut across the terrain. They journeyed uphill where rocks ribbed the landscape. Finally, they reached the cave's yawning mouth which was almost concealed by rocks and brush until one was right on it.

They dismounted near sunset. T.J. pointed out the Sonora Desert, the highest crag of the Santa Rita Mountains, and peaks which were in Old Mexico. It was a lofty spot, a perfect hideout with a view of the surrounding area. They entered the hollow mountain, and she was surprised by how cool and refreshing the interior was with a temperature in the low seventies.

"Wait here at the entrance while I fetch some brush for a fire. We'll need light and something to cook over. I'm starved. I haven't eaten since I took off after you," he confessed before leaving to gather wood. When he returned and unloaded it, he guided her to a large cavern not far into the hillside. He built a fire for light, then took the bodies into a side tunnel to keep her from having to look at them. After unsaddling the horses and hobbling them, he smiled and said, "I'll be back soon. I want to cover our trail and see if I can get some fresh meat to roast. Don't leave here. Understand?"

"I promise. Please, be careful," she urged.

Carrie Sue sat on a low ledge in the dancing shadows of the campfire, anxiously waiting for her love's return. She wasn't afraid of the darkness which engulfed the rocky tunnels in all but the area where she was standing. She was aware of every minute that passed. She recalled what he had said about a storm brewing and the area outside this protective cave was a flash flood location. She knew how treacherous dry washes were when they gushed with violent water.

Carrie Sue jumped when it thundered loudly. She grabbed a torch and rushed to the entrance. The storm broke overhead. The lightning and thundering seemed continuous, powerful, endless. The rain poured so heavily that she couldn't see outside to watch for T.J.'s approach. With visibility near nothing, how could he find his way back? What if he got injured in the obscuring storm?

Suddenly she realized he had known the storm was close! He knew the signs and dangers of this territory. Why hadn't he let the rain conceal their tracks? Why couldn't they eat the food from Naiche, or eat from their supplies, or from Martin's? She panicked again. . . .

Chapter

13

Carrie Sue paced the entry tunnel from the opening to the first cavern. She knew T.J. was planning to return because he had left his supplies with her. But, she fretted, where had he gone and why? Had he ridden into Tucson to send a telegram to someone, perhaps the same person he had telegraphed last Monday? Who? For what reason? To let someone know he had been delayed by this grim set-back? Could he possibly be a bounty hunter who was after bigger game than her? Was he hoping to romance her into leading him to Darby and his gang? T.J. Rogue was a loner and a talented gunslinger, but a man who stayed just within the boundaries of the law, a man who made his own decisions and went his own way, not a man to become just another gang member, even to be with her.

The daring desperado admitted that ten thousand dollars was a lot of money, and the capture of the Texas Flame would bring any man a lot of glory. Why would a legendary gunman ignore both to help her? If he loved her, he hadn't said so. He seemed to be enjoying their wild and wonderful romance, but did he consider it a permanent one, a special one? Or something to pass the time? Although he was passionate and protective with her, he was also mysterious and guarded. Maybe what had her so anxious was that he was a little too glued to her for a loner like he was and a fugitive like she was! If he was so crazy about her that he was willing to put his life and reputation on the mark, why didn't he tell her? Why couldn't she trust him fully?

Carrie Sue had never surrendered her heart and body to a man before, and she prayed she wasn't wrong about him. Because of her lifestyle, she had been given very few opportunities to be romanced by any man except outlaws like Kadry Sams and Dillon Holmes. She trusted few people, and she feared she couldn't trust her lover or herself. Maybe that was the problem, the source of her apprehensions. Maybe she was trying to convince herself she didn't and couldn't trust him because she was afraid of what it would mean to believe and accept him.

She was so confused. By pushing him away, was she only trying to spare herself from a hard and painful choice? Was she only trying to prevent his possible betrayal? Or was she trying to keep him safe from the dangers that haunted her? She was scared to trust him and to yield fully, scared he wasn't for real, scared he wasn't as serious about her as she was about him; and she was scared he was for real and she would lose him or destroy him.

Her head was spinning from dismay. Even if she was mistaken about his good feelings and motives, would he soon tire of her and this unlawful adventure and betray her? She had to clear her wits because he was too disarming. He could be so gentle and persuasive, but he was also tough and hard, and something was eating at him. Yes, she was leery of this enchanting rogue and distressed by her own warring emotions. She hated these fears and doubts, but she couldn't seem to master them. Her next actions depended on what he said and how he acted when he returned to the cave. . . .

Carrie Sue walked to the ledge and took a seat again. She scanned her surroundings. The ceiling in this area was soot-blackened, no doubt from fires used by ancient people, Indians, outlaws, and others. She—

"Carrie Sue," her lover's voice broke into her musings.

She hurried to the entrance to find a drenched T.J. and Nighthawk coming in out of the violent storm. He handed her a pail and asked her to fetch rain water for the horses while he unsaddled his stallion and fed the horses the bound hay he was carrying. She noticed a lantern tied to his saddle horn. She questioned, "Where have you been, Rogue? You could have let the rain wash away our tracks."

"I know," he agreed, then chuckled. "But we needed something for the horses to eat because I can't let them roam outside and be seen. We needed light, and a pail to give them water. This cave is dry."

She followed him inside to get her answers. "A campfire would give light," she hinted.

"And use up too much wood. If it went out while we're sleeping, this cave gets mighty dark. We're camping way back in there," he told her, motioning to the tunnel to their right.

"Go back in there?" she murmured almost inaudibly, her eyes widening in astonishment as she glanced in that dark direction. "What if we get lost?"

T.J. set the lantern aside and removed his soaked saddle. He tossed it on the ledge where she had been sitting so it could drip. There was no need to hobble Nighthawk, so he guided the animal to where the others were standing. He cut the cord around the bundle of hay and spread it on the rock floor so they could eat.

"Did you hear me, Mr. Rogue? What if we get lost in there?"

"Sorry, woman, my head is getting dizzy from hunger and fatigue. We won't get lost. I've been here plenty of times. This was one of the Apache tests for entering manhood. You were taken way back into the tunnels, given a small torch, and told to use your wits and courage to find your way back before the torch burned up. The area we'll camp in is where boys were taken to spend the night waiting for visions. It's flat and sandy, and we'll be safe there if anybody shows up. Don't worry; I've camped, explored, and played here many times."

His confidence dispelled her worries. "Where did you get this stuff? Did you go into Tucson?"

He lit the lantern and began unpacking supplies. "Nope, too dangerous. I stole it from a rancher not far away. I also shot us a rabbit. Roasted meat," he murmured and licked his lips. He was honest on those replies. He hadn't dared enter Tucson to look for Joe Collins or to send telegrams to his superiors from Ben Myers's town. "I knew if I told you my plans when I left here, you would argue and worry."

"You're right," she concurred. "That was quite a risk."

He shrugged wearily. "The horses have to eat and drink, and we have to see. Why don't you fetch that rain water for them while I take some of this stuff to our camping area? I'll build a fire and be back shortly for you." He didn't want her to see the wood and supplies he had brought here early Thursday morning after his Wednesday night talk with Collins. Just in case they had needed to escape quickly and conceal themselves for a while, he had prepared things to camp here. If she noticed his preparations, she would wonder about them. "I'm sure there's plenty of brush back there from old camping trips, but I'll check while I'm gone." He loaded up and lifted the lantern to illuminate his path. Within minutes, he and the lamp's glow vanished.

Carrie Sue held the bucket outside and let the pouring rain fill it. She carried the pail to the horses and let each one drink. Afterwards, she refilled it again and placed it nearby. While she waited T.J.'s return, she stroked the pinto. As always, she mused, T.J. had logical reasons and credible explanations for everything. Either he was the cleverest man alive or he was being honest with her!

The redhead's partner rejoined her, without his shirt and boots. His wet hair curled in mischievous black waves, as did the hair on his hard chest. His saturated jeans clung enticingly to his hips and thighs, hinting at their strength and sleek shape. He was carrying two blankets over his left arm and a hunk of soap in his hand, and two lanterns.

T.J. nodded at the items and suggested, "Why don't we take turns getting a bath in nature's shower right outside the entrance? It'll be easier than poking holes in a pail and hanging it from a rope. After what we've been through during the past two days, I know it'll make me feel better. You wanna be first or last?"

"Last," she responded. "Where did you get the other lantern?"

"It was in the back. Somebody left it there, thank goodness."

She waited in the large cavern for T.J. to walk to the entrance, strip off his jeans, wet himself, lather up, rinse off, and return to her location. While he was busy, she stripped and wrapped the blanket around her to be ready to do the same task after he finished.

Before leaving him there, she admired his magnificent body clad only in a blanket around the hips. She smiled when he warned her to walk carefully, as the rock flooring was slippery when wet.

Carrie Sue dropped the blanket just inside the cave. She stepped outside and drenched her hair and body, aware that no one could sight her in the blinding downpour. She gingerly stepped beneath the protective ceiling of stone and lathered herself from head to foot. It felt exhilarating to scrub the dirt and sweat from her hair and flesh, and she savored the refreshing chore as long as possible. She let the water rinse away the suds before standing just inside the cave to dry off with the blanket. She shivered from a chill as a blast of wind blew rain against her.

Carrie Sue stepped further into the passageway and dried off again. She wrapped the damp blanket around her and tucked it snugly above her breasts. Carefully she made her way back to T.J. "It's getting dark and cool outside," she remarked as she squeezed more water from her long hair. She shuddered again.

T.J. had placed one lantern on the rock shelf near his saddle, out of reach of horses' hooves. He doused the campfire and said, "That'll give them plenty of light and I won't have to keep checking on the fire. Let's get you to that warm blaze in back. Dry your feet good or you could slip on these rocks. Some of the pathway is steep."

As she obeyed, Carrie Sue didn't mention the two bodies in the side tunnel, but she remembered they were there in the darkness. Even though they were enemies, now that their peril was over, she hated to just discard them like unwanted trash. Yet, they couldn't turn the bodies in and there was no way to bury the two men. She gathered her clothes and boots and followed her love into the shadows.

They headed into the right tunnel, then rounded a sharp bend whose passageway led into a nice sized chamber. They zig-zagged left into an even larger chamber where draperies of stone looked like a frozen waterfall. T.J. paused for a while and moved the lantern back and forth so she could view the awesome sight.

In all areas the walls were mostly shades of brown—ranging from tan to chocolate hues—with a few shades of gray and white intermingled. Most of the side walls and flooring were smooth, almost slick, even when dry. It appeared as if a massive underground river had created this series of chambers and passageways and had rubbed them smooth over a long period of time. She was amazed by the wildly beautiful formations from the floor and the ceiling, which were sometimes unending like columns holding up a structure.

Here and there, they had to walk on sideways slants or down almost too steep paths of solid stone. On occasion, they had to duck low ledges with sharp and jagged tips. She noticed how some formations looked like the saguaro cactus set in stone. They passed areas where the flooring seemed to have ripples like stone waves on a strange sea. Many of the chambers were enormous, others small and cramped. The tunnels ranged from narrow and low to wide and tall. They followed the often snaking path through the darkness lighted by one lantern, which she prayed wouldn't go out. Merciful Heavens, she decided, it would be black as soot and scary as hell in there.

T.J. told her these passageways ran for miles in numerous directions. In one side tunnel there was a sink hole which had no doubt ensnared some unlucky explorers. They walked deeper into the crystal caverns until the path opened up into an oblong chamber where a cheery fire chased away more darkness. Even though a river had once eaten away at this underground area, it was totally dry now. A sandy bed had been left behind upon which T.J. had made their camp.

She glanced around, relieved this area was flat and large. She saw brush and wood piled in several places, and she saw evidence of old campfires. She looked at her lover when he put aside their things and told her to follow him again before she got comfortable.

They retraced their steps for a few feet. "This isn't far, Carrie Sue. When you reach this fork, go left and round this corner. This is the outhouse when you need it."

Without further delay or embarrassing words, he guided her back to their campground. "I'll start the rabbit roasting while you get that head dry and get on something warm."

Carrie Sue pulled a nightgown from her pouch, glad she had brought it along impulsively. Since no one could find them, she could be comfortable. As T.J. was facing away from her, she didn't turn her back to drop the blanket and pull the gown over her head. Then, she bent forward to dry her hair with the blanket. When she went to sit near the fire, she brushed and braided her flaming mane while T.J. prepared coffee and readied the Johnnycake mix of plain flour and water with a pinch of salt. She watched him cut strips of salted pork for obtaining grease in which to cook the flatbread, and he placed them in a small frying pan.

"You're handy to have around, Mr. Rogue. I could get mighty spoiled with all this attention."

"I thought all women were spoiled," he teased, grinning at her.

"Most men think we are." She retorted and laughed. A contradictory sensation filled her; it seemed strange being here with him, yet perfectly normal. It was as if they were the only two people in existence, or as if they had escaped far from grim reality. Primitive feelings were aroused by their simple and cozy setting and his state of dress.

Dreamily she remarked, "With that blanket wrapped around you, if your hair was long, you'd look like an Indian."

"I'm glad you didn't say half-breed. That's a nasty name, and I sure was called it a lot after my so-called rescue by the cavalry. That and a savage rogue," he added unthinkingly. He caught himself before telling her that was how and where he had gotten his undercover name. He rubbed his smokey gray eyes and said, "Lordy, I'm tired."

Carrie Sue gazed at him and agreed, "You look it, partner. Did I thank you for losing all that sleep to catch up with us and rescue me?"

"Yep." His gaze met hers, and they stared at each other. He noticed the azure gown which flowed over her soft curves like sensuous waves, and his body warmed. He drowned himself for a time in the bluish depths of her engulfing gaze. He wanted to loosen her hair and let the red mane flow around her face and shoulders like a tranquil and inviting waterfall. He longed to caress that silky flesh of rosy gold. He wanted to run his forefinger over brows which matched her tawny red hair. He yearned to kiss her nose and full lips, her shapely cheekbones. He craved to trail his hot tongue along her collarbone, to tease it over the throbbing pulse in her neck, to dip it into the hollow at her throat, to send it between her breasts and down her stomach and . . . "You have the prettiest hair and eyes I've seen on any woman," he complimented her unexpectedly, uncontrollably. He shook his head to clear it and his hand stroked his whiskered jawline. "I need a shave," he murmured as if suddenly feeling awkward.

Carrie Sue realized this secluded and intimate situation made the carefree loner a little nervous. She was certain he had had plenty of sex, but love and closeness were new for him, and no doubt intimidating. Tonight they were totally alone, so either they talked casually or they would create an uneasy silence. She was touched by his near loss of poise, and it enflamed her passions to witness it. Surely that told her how deeply and strongly he was affected by her. "Thanks, partner; I like your looks too. What do you want me to do to help?" she inquired, aware of the heavy sensual aura around them.

"Just sit there and let me admire you," he replied huskily, then cautioned himself to stop acting like . . . Like what, a lovesick boy? He had to get control of himself and the situation or he'd foul up!

His words, expression, and mood aroused her. "That's too easy. Give me something harder," she almost whispered in a strained voice.

He rubbed his jawline again and looked hesitant. His keen mind shouted, *Get on with your work and stop acting like an ass! She's opened the door, so jump in fast before she slams it again!* "Would you get mad or upset if I asked you about Curly James? I saw you two talking that day and couldn't figure it out. It didn't look like strangers meeting. How did you know a bastard like him?"

The ex-outlaw drew up her knees and banded her legs with her arms, interlocking her fingers. She wet her lips and answered, "I'll admit I lied to you that day, but you now realize I had no choice. I was pretending to be a schoolmarm, and I hadn't known you very long. Curly James rode with my brother a long time ago in Texas. He recognized me and wanted to know what I was doing in Tucson. I told him the truth and he agreed to keep my secret. To answer your next question, no, I didn't believe him and I was wondering if I should leave town before he could trick me. You saved me from that choice and problem when you gunned him down. Curly never was one to be trusted. He was wild, reckless, and mean. He was always disobeying Darby's orders and getting the gang into trouble, so Darby asked him to leave."

He hinted, "I don't imagine Curly took that news well."

"No, but the other men agreed with Darby's decision." She told him what Curly had said about Quade and Ferris, and of her suspicions about both men. He agreed with her. Yet, she didn't tell him about Curly claiming to have seen Darby and his plans to rejoin the gang.

T.J. shifted his position on the ground. He cleared his throat and asked bravely, "Speaking of your brother, don't you think it's about time you tell me about him and your life with his gang? I've been biting my tongue to keep silent. I was afraid of making you nervous if I pressed for more information, but I need to know more about you, woman. I figured you'd speak up when you were ready, but you've stayed tight-lipped. I kept thinking you'd open up when you realized you could trust me. Why haven't you, Carrie Sue?"

She fused her violet-blue gaze to his entreating one and responded, "I was wondering why you haven't asked me those questions. Frankly, it had me worried. You're right; you deserve to know more. My brother didn't like killing unless it couldn't be helped. But Curly did a lot of shooting; then, he'd tell Darby he was forced into it. Darby knows that robberies and rustlings don't create posses the way killings do. Despite what people think and say about my brother, he isn't cold-blooded. Like me, he was forced into this miserable life and he can't get out of it. Mostly he uses the same six men, but some jobs called for extra guns. He was always careful about the men he let join his gang for a while, but sometimes he got fooled and let a bad one in. As soon as he realized his mistake, he corrected it."

T.J. wanted to ask if one of those *mistakes* was responsible for the deaths of Arabella and Marie and Jacob, but he couldn't, not yet. "You love him a lot, don't you?"

Carrie Sue's eyes softened and glowed. "Yes, I do. We've always been close." She told him about their Georgia farm and its loss to a wicked Carpetbagger, and how her father had obtained vengeful justice. She related facts about the Texas ranch and how the Hardings had taken it from them, killing her parents during the process, and how she and Darby had gone after revenge. She explained about her years with the gang and her attempts at new beginnings, chances always spoiled by Quade Harding, the man who had barbwired her love to a tree to die. She explained how her identity had been kept secret until Quade unmasked her with that new poster.

She went on, "In '73, Darby and a few of his closest friends tried to go straight. They bought a ranch near Laredo. We stayed there for eight months and everything was wonderful. I even had my twenty-first birthday there in April. Then, Quade Harding had us tracked down. We had to leave everything behind but the clothes on our backs and our horses. We hid out in Mexico for months. That's when Quade released the men's descriptions—I suppose to get a line on me. May of '74 was when he put out that bad sketch just to scare me. We've been on the move ever since, surviving the only way left open to us."

She talked about how people used to love Darby's legend—until false charges, mistakes, and sensational newspaper accounts had darkened his image. She admitted they had shot several of Quade's men during raids and pursuits, and shot other men in self-defense. She told him they had been accused of Quinn's accident, which was a lie. She claimed that their "groundless harassment" of the Hardings and responsibility for Quinn's crippling were the devious lies which Quade used to explain his large rewards.

Her story moved him deeply, but he had to ignore such feelings to do what had to be done. Maybe she was telling the truth about Darby Stover, or perhaps she was blinded by her love for her brother. Either way, he had to capture the Stover Gang. He quelled his guilt to continue. "Your dealings with Quade Harding explain why he's so determined to capture you and get rid of Darby. Until now, he's held silent to get you back alive and safe. I guess he finally realized you're too smart to get snared. Maybe he's hoping you'll rush back to him for help and protection.

"Never!" she vowed coldly. "I'd hang first!"

T.J. understood Quade's obsession with this ravishing vixen. But he would go down shooting before he let Harding get his vile hands on her! As he turned the rabbit to roast the other side, he asked, "Have you ever been captured or tried to clear yourself?"

She sighed heavily, bitterly. "Yes, I was captured once. Darby busted me out of jail just before two deputies raped me. Another time, I turned myself in to a Texas Ranger. I had the drop on him, but I couldn't gun him down to escape. Besides, I figured if anybody could help me get a fair shake, it was a Ranger. He cursed me and beat me and nearly broke my arm before I wounded him and escaped. I wore a sling for two months. Then, Quade's detective caught up with me several times with his threats and abuse, but I always managed to get away. I guess that explains why I have trouble trusting men."

T.J. was shocked by those confessions, and he didn't doubt them. But he'd never heard of a Ranger capturing the Texas Flame. Considering her treatment by the tainted lawman, no wonder he'd kept silent! Later, he would get the man's name from her and take care of him! "Yep, I understand. I wish I could think of someone to help you, but I can't." Even if he did know some powerful men, he couldn't tell her at this time and he didn't believe there was anything his friends could do for her.

Carrie Sue smiled sadly, but gratefully. "There is nothing and no one to help me, T.J. Darby and I got in too deeply and there is no escape for us. We'll have to keep running and hiding until we're jailed or hanged or we get far enough away to be left alone. When I locate him, I'm going to try to persuade him to head for Montana or California or the Dakotas. He thinks fleeing is useless because somebody finds us wherever we go, if we don't stay in hiding. We can't do that forever. We have to eat." She gazed at him tenderly. "I wish you could have met Darby before all this mess changed him. I'm worried about him. He's been forced to stay in a life of crime too long. I'm afraid it's going to make him hard and cold, and make him do things he doesn't want to do. If you want to know the truth, partner, I'm not as afraid of hanging as I am of prison. And that's probably what the law would do with a young woman. If only I could rub out my past as easily as you get rid of your trail or enemies, but I can't. Quade has forced me out of hiding again. After trying so many times to start over, I'm beginning to doubt it's possible. I suppose the only thing I can do is rejoin Darby."

"Do you know where to find your brother?" he asked.

Carrie Sue wished he had replied in another way, had offered a safe and happy life with him far away. Perhaps he didn't want that solution with her; or perhaps he hadn't thought of it yet. She responded carefully, "When we split up near Sherman, he was heading for Oklahoma to lay low for a while. I figured I'd head toward Brownwood and leave messages at our old hideouts along the way. It'll be hard chasing him with my poster nailed up everywhere. Maybe when he sees it or hears about it, he'll come looking for me. I know he won't come to Tucson because he promised to stay clear of this area to give me a chance to start over, and he knows I would take off the moment I sensed danger. While Quade was holding silent, Darby wouldn't attack him, to protect me and the boys. Once he learns what Quade has done to me, he'll go after him again."

T.J. noticed the way she'd hesitated before answering him. Fatigue and depression, he wondered, or planning a devious reply? Lordy, he had to convince her to be totally honest with him, for both their sakes! "That's why you want to head for Brownwood?" When she nodded, he asked, "That's too risky with Quade Harding searching for you. Don't you realize he'll be on the lookout for Darby's revenge?"

Carrie Sue lifted the frying pan and started cooking the Johnnycakes. "I guess you're right, but what else can I do?" She glanced at him and said, "I didn't want to drag you into this mess, and I'm sorry you're involved. It will be too late to change things if you don't back away from me and leave now."

When she reached for a fork to turn the pork strips, he captured her hand, compelling her gaze back to his. "It's already too late to back away, woman. I can't leave you until this matter is settled."

Settled how? she helplessly wondered. "If you have as much brain in that handsome head as I think you do, you'll get out while you can. If you don't, you'll get in as deeply as me and Darby. Once you're entangled with the law, T.J., there's no going back to your old life. This isn't the existence either of us wants for you. Nobody knows about you except that sheriff. It'll be your word against his, unless you can provoke him into a gunfight and get rid of the one witness against you."

"It's already too late to turn back. He's probably reported my actions by now."

"It'll be worth the risk to make certain you aren't on the wanted list. If I were you, T.J. Rogue, I would call his bluff. I'll be fine alone, so stop worrying about me and get on with your life."

Defiance clouded his smokey gray gaze. "I can't. You mean too much for me to desert you. I can't imagine you being an outlaw on the run forever, much less being the notorious Texas Flame. You're nothing like your reputation, Carrie Sue. If you give me some time, maybe I can think of a better way to help you."

"People do a lot of things when they have to. Don't waste your time and strength fighting my battle, T.J.; I lost it long ago."

As if angered and challenged by her loss of spirit, he argued almost harshly, "No battle is lost until you're dead, woman, and you have plenty of life and prowess left. If you want something badly enough, you'll find a way to get it, and you can with my help."

What she wanted most of all was the man sitting near her, that and a bright future with him, and her brother's survival. If only the three of them could leave the West and start a ranch somewhere together. But where would they get enough money? And where could they go where the law couldn't reach them? It was hopeless. "I'm starving, and I can't think straight anymore. Can we finish this talk later?"

T.J. saw how agitated she was becoming. "You've told me enough to know I made the right decision joining up with you. Lordy, I wish I knew of some way to get you out of this mess. About the only thing I can do right now is get you back to your brother for protection. Much as I hate to think it, Carrie Sue, that's the safest place for you because we can't hide out here forever, or hide anywhere long. If I don't find work by the time that reward money runs out, we'll be forced to commit crimes for it and dig ourselves in deeper."

"That's my point, T.J.; one bad thing leads to another. I was going to withdraw some of Carolyn's money and hide it for an emergency, but I forgot. I was too busy with the school and you and Martin. At least I did get a horse and supplies. Mercy, this will be dangerous."

T.J. guided them back to his mission. "I like your idea of getting Darby to go straight in some town far away; that's the only way you two can survive. When we find your brother, if I can help you convince him to take off for distant places, I will."

Carrie Sue realized he did not say he would go with her or with them. She decided this was not the time to ask him if he was in love with her and if he'd seek a future together. She wanted him to recognize those facts and make those decisions for himself without any pressure from her; that was the only way it would work between them. Maybe he hadn't confessed love and a hope for a life together because he was too honest or too proud to lie about his feelings for her, which could be nothing more than the passionate desire and kindness he had exposed to date.

She smiled and said, "Thanks, T.J.; I'll probably need your help."

Together they completed the meal and devoured every bit and drop. She helped him clean up the area, then he went to the entrance to wash the dishes and to check on the horses one final time. While he was gone, she spread out their bedrolls, on opposite sides of the cozy fire to prevent looking overly eager to spend the night in his arms. Since she didn't know for certain what he wanted from her, she didn't know how to act tonight.

T.J. returned and put away his belongings. He watched Carrie Sue take the lantern and vanish from the chamber for a while. When she came back, she sat on her bedroll. He had noticed instantly where she had placed them and took her unintended hint. Considering her emotional state tonight, he didn't want to press her romantically. He wanted her to realize he was with her for more than sex, and he didn't mean his case or his revenge. He wanted her to see that he could be unselfish and understanding. He wanted her to realize that he could be a friend as well as a lover.

Thad Jamison admitted to himself that he loved and wanted this woman in bed and out! All he had to do was figure out how to pull off the impossible feat of winning her and being able to keep her. He wasn't the kind of man who ran away from trouble like a coward, but he would leave his present life behind after this mission if he could save her and take her along with or without the law's permission. Much as he hated the reality of using and betraying his love, he couldn't turn his back on who and what he was. He couldn't become a weakling just to win her. He couldn't let that murderous gang go free any longer, and he was the only lawman with a path to them. With Carrie Sue involved, he couldn't turn the case over to another Ranger or marshal. Yet, once she realized what he was doing or had done . . .

T.J. dropped those troubling thoughts. He withdrew a bottle of whiskey from his saddlebag and offered her a few sips to relax her and help her sleep.

As she smiled and accepted the bottle, Carrie Sue wanted to shout at him that all she needed tonight was him, but she didn't. He looked exhausted, and he was jittery. Perhaps making love after their serious talk would intimidate him further. She needed for him to hold her, but she would settle for having him nearby and pledged to aiding her survival. Besides, she was tense too, tense over her tormenting confessions, tense over her doubts, and tense over the two bodies somewhere in this cave. Considering the twists and turns they had made between here and the entrance, Martin and Jess could be lying around that far corner! She almost felt as if Martin Ferris's eyes were on her this very moment and his evil mind was plotting revenge. She knew that was ridiculous and only proved how fatigued and clouded her mind was. She returned the bottle to her lover and thanked him.

"Get a good night's sleep, woman; we have a lot of lost ground to make up tomorrow. I don't want anybody figuring out to look in the last place you should be, still near Tucson. That poster's been out for a week or more, so there's no telling who's on your trial by now. I want us out of Arizona pronto."

"Are there any bats or slithery critters in here?" she asked to change the subject. She didn't like those flying and crawling creatures, but she wasn't afraid of them.

He caught her ruse and grinned. "Nope. Besides no food supply, this cave system is too dry and rocky, and too dark back in here for anything without a lantern. If you get scared, you can join me over here. I promise I won't let the fire and lantern go out."

All she could hear was their breathing and movements and words and the crackling of the fire. There was a curious aura in this secret place, a spiritual one, an eerie one. Maybe there were Indian spirits here, or ghosts of unlucky men or ancient people who had died in this place. She wasn't afraid, just uneasy.

"Did you hear me, Carrie Sue?" he asked, lifting his head and looking in her direction. "I won't let the light go out."

Without moving from her back, she replied softly, "Thanks, but I'm not scared. I was just wondering because I hadn't seen anything or heard any noises. It's so quiet, not even any echoes. I can't even hear the storm or horses."

"The storm's over. Most of the water should be gone by sunup. Those dry washes take it away quickly, what the ground doesn't suck up fast. You'll be surprised when you go out in the morning; you won't even be able to tell it rained, much less stormed like crazy."

"If the light did go out, would you be lost in here?" she asked.

"Nope. I could find my way out by feeling along the walls. I know which tunnels to take even in pitch black, and I know where the pitfalls are located, and believe me there are plenty of them. Don't you get up during the night and go roaming. There are sinkholes, bottomless pits, narrow ledges, and worse. You'd be lost in less than five minutes." He lowered his voice to a whisper as if relating a secret. "All through these caverns are trail markings, if you know where and how to look for them. With or without light, we're safe."

"So if we got trapped in here, you could douse the lantern and guide us to safety or into hiding?"

"Yep, so relax and get to sleep before I have to pour more whiskey into you to settle down that pretty head and silence that tasty mouth."

Carrie Sue laughed before responding, "That's all I needed to know, partner. Good-night, T.J."

*

The redhead tossed aside her light blanket. She stretched and yawned contentedly. She rubbed her grainy eyes and sat up. Smiling, Carrie Sue turned to awaken her love.

Her smile faded rapidly and she paled. There was no bedroll across the small fire. There were no saddlebags or supplies in sight. There was no T.J. Rogue!

Carrie Sue jumped up and looked around in panic. Nothing except her, her bedroll, a campfire, and some brush was left behind!

The anxious woman frantically realized—except for her gown and bedroll—she had no clothes, no weapons, no boots, no supplies, no food, no water! Worse, she realized she was imprisoned in this hazardous labyrinth which would be Satan black when that pile of brush was used up within a few hours.

How clever, she ranted to herself, for him to leave her in the one place from which she couldn't escape! How had she slept so deeply as to not hear his treacherous movements? It couldn't have been anything in the whiskey because he had drank from the same bottle. She realized his wits and skills were far superior to what she had imagined, and she had imagined them to be the best. Where had he gone? Why had he left her here without even food and water? Was he fetching a posse? A partner? Was this a terrorizing tactic? A test?

"**D**amn you, you bastard!" she screamed as loudly as she could. "I hate you! I'll kill you when I get my hands on you!"

Her previous thoughts echoed through her mind, *In the one place from which she couldn't escape* . . . "Think, Carrie Sue. No man can outwit you or capture you if you keep your wits clear."

The angry fugitive realized she couldn't remain there and wait for the fire to burn up all the brush. She comprehended the perils involved in her decision, but she had to risk finding her way to the entrance. She closed her eyes, envisioned the cave opening, and mentally retraced their steps; first right, around a left bend, bear right after the first large cavern, pass a tunnel on her right, through that large chamber with the frozen waterfall, use last tunnel to left, horseshoe into this oblong chamber. All she had to do was reverse those directions and backtrack to safety; no, only to light.

Carrie Sue didn't know what she would do when she reached her entrance in only her gown, but she would be in the light there to make her next decision. She left her sleeping roll where it was. She tied the tail of her gown in a secure knot above her knees to prevent tripping over it. She grabbed the largest piece of wood for a torch and held it in the fire until it flamed on the end. She headed toward freedom.

Just as she reached the end of the sleeping chamber, she nearly crashed into T.J. Rogue who eyed her strangely, then set down his lantern. She glared at him and accused, "You bastard! You're lower than a sidewinder's belly. I should have known not to trust you. Who did you fetch to turn me over to? Will I be allowed to dress first?" she inquired sarcastically. She accepted the fact she couldn't pass the strong man who was blocking the tunnel, for now. She wanted to rave at him and tear into his handsome face with her nails, but she needed to conserve her strength for a better opportunity.

T.J. stared at her in confusion. "I heard you screaming while I was on my way back to awaken you for breakfast. What has you so riled? Did you sleep with burrs in your blanket? You cuss worse than I do when that temper flares. I'll have to change that bad habit."

Her violet-blue eyes narrowed and chilled. She balled her fist with the urge to strike him. "You filthy vermin! How dare you betray me, and leave me trapped here! Give me a gun and I'll kill you!"

The ebon-haired man was still baffled. "What are you talking about, woman? I was up front cooking breakfast, right where I said I would be. I haven't been anywhere, and you were never in any danger. I sneaked out to let you sleep as long as possible."

"Sneaked out with everything and left me here defenseless!" she scoffed. "That fire will be out soon, and I want my clothes!"

Was that, he wondered, the problem? She had panicked when she found him and everything gone? But why? Didn't she believe his note? "How else could I prepare our meal? I woke up early so I decided to save time by carrying our things up front and having our food ready. I figured you were exhausted because you didn't even stir."

Carrie Sue brought up the blazing torch in her hand to strike him forcefully across the head so she could escape this cunning rogue and cease his tormenting lies.

T.J. seized her wrist and wrestled the torch from her grip, casting it aside. He grabbed her and pinned her against his bare chest, which was difficult with her fighting him like wild. "Settle down, you little spitfire. I left a note by your bedroll so you wouldn't panic before I returned for you."

"Liar! There was no note!" she shouted again, struggling to free herself from his powerful grasp. She couldn't, so she glared at him.

T.J. was mad, but he pretended to be angrier than he was. "I'm going to release you, you little wildcat, and you go look beside your bedroll. Go on," he ordered sternly, freeing her and pushing her in that direction. "Damnation, woman, I'm telling the truth and I can prove it!"

Carrie Sue calmed slightly. He was blocking the escape tunnel, so she decided to put some distance between them. Since he knew these passageways and she didn't, it was rash to flee in the other direction into the perilous darkness. She stalked to the bedroll and looked at the sandy floor around it. "Nothing here, Rogue."

"Look again!" he shouted back at her.

Carrie Sue picked up the blanket which she had tossed aside upon awakening. A note was lying there. She glanced at T.J. before scooping it up to read. Just as he claimed, the message said he was up front packing and cooking and would return for her soon. Had she accidentally concealed it? Or had he hidden it long enough for her to panic? She scolded herself for behaving like a fool and for instantly doubting him again. The vexed redhead crumpled the slip of paper and tossed it into the fire. She watched it burn before turning to face her sullen lover.

"Get your bedroll and follow me," he commanded without a smile.

Carrie Sue was still edgy, but she rolled it and secured it with the leather ties. "What about the fire?" she asked contritely.

"It'll go out soon. There's no danger of it spreading anywhere." He lifted the lantern and ordered gruffly, "Let's go."

Carrie Sue followed close behind the moody man who wasted no time guiding them back to the entrance where a campfire was going and their meal was ready to be completed. It was easy to see he had spoken the truth, and remorse consumed her. The smell of freshly perked coffee filled her nostrils, as did the odor of horse droppings. She glanced that way and frowned, not at the odor common to her, but at herself for her impulsive behavior. The horses were saddled, and her clothes were lying on the nearby ledge.

As if reading her mind, he said in an unapologetic tone, "Sorry about that oversight. We can stand outside and eat where there's fresh air. What's gotten into you, woman? I was just trying to give you as much sleep as possible. Get dressed while I finish here."

Carrie Sue watched him kneel at the fire and begin working on their meal. She felt terrible about her behavior and words. "I'm sorry for what I said and did, T.J.; that wasn't fair of me."

Without turning, he replied in a cool tone, "No, it wasn't fair, woman. After our serious talk last night, I thought you were beginning to trust me, but obviously I was wrong and that worries me."

"Surely you can understand why I panicked when I found you and everything gone and didn't see that note," she entreated.

He halted his chore to look at her. "I know all your secrets and I trust you, so why do you find it so difficult to trust me? Have I said or done anything to make you doubtful?" His gaze returned to the fire.

She joined him on her knees, his profile to her. Her gaze slipped over his bronzed face, chest, and shoulders. She wanted to fling herself into his arms and beg his forgiveness. She released a deep breath whose intake she hadn't noticed. She said in a rueful tone, "No, but I find it difficult to trust anybody, especially a man, except Darby and Kale. After all I told you last night, can you blame me?"

He didn't appear to soften and he didn't meet her troubled gaze. "Nope, but Darby's the one who got you into all this trouble, so why is he the only one you trust? Brother or not, he was wrong." He didn't mention the other man, but committed this information to memory.

She was miffed. "You can't blame him, T.J.; he didn't twist my arm. I agreed to help him battle the Hardings. You know why."

He briefly glanced at her to check her expression. "Yep, you agreed to help him get justice and revenge on the Hardings, but you didn't agree to become an outlaw, to do all those other crimes."

She reasoned, "Once Quade found out about us, which was my fault, we didn't have any choice in our actions. We had to survive."

He poured her a cup of coffee and sat it nearby. He refuted, "Yes, you did have a choice, Carrie Sue, just like I do every time I'm tempted to break the law or I run into trouble. If you'd gone to the authorities, perhaps you could have gotten it straightened out before your landslide came."

She looked stunned, hurt. "Who would have believed us over the Hardings? They wouldn't even investigate Darby's charges after our parent's deaths and the seizure of our ranch. Darby went to every law office he could think of, but no one would help us. We were young and scared and foolish. We didn't think about going straight because of Quade's pursuit and the crimes we'd committed. I'll even admit that the boys found their new lives exciting. They were reckless and daring, and having fun together. It was like being caught in a flood; things kept pushing us onward to a waterfall. Once we were carried over it, we couldn't fight our way upstream again."

T.J. realized he had to back down. "I guess you're right, but it riles me how you were ensnared in this trap by Harding and your brother and you can't get free. You shouldn't have to live like this."

Carrie Sue misread his meaning. She thought he was angered because she was unavailable because of her past, a past for which Quade Harding was responsible. He even blamed Darby for her predicament. She asked, "Why did Quade have you barbwired to that tree?"

He looked at her as if surprised by the change of subject. He shrugged. "We were in a poker game and I accused him of cheating. I caught him red-handed and he was humiliated. The bastard didn't admit he was guilty. He tossed his winnings to the table, got up, and said the money wasn't worth dying over and he wasn't about to call me out over a silly misunderstanding. He just strolled out of there, red-faced. I couldn't shoot him in the back, so I let him play the coward," he related deviously. "Nothing makes a foe quicker than humiliation, and nothing settles that offense except death."

"Then what happened?" she pressed when he fell silent.

As he worked on his task, he went on in a casual tone, "He didn't want to use any of his men and he didn't even use his brand of barbwire so it couldn't be traced to his ranch. Since you've ranched, you know how many kinds of barbwire there are and most cattlemen prefer a certain brand. Curly James and two of his friends were in town, probably smarting from being tossed out of Darby's gang. Quade hired them to do his dirty work."

"How did you know Quade was responsible? Is he your only enemy? And how did they get the drop on you? I wouldn't think that possible."

"Curly boasted about how much Harding was paying him to get rid of me, in a very slow and painful way, one to give me plenty of time to suffer and to pray for death." He paused a moment before saying, "I hate to confess it, but they took me by surprise while I was bathing. A woman helped them, so I have little reason to trust sly vixens," he teased pointedly. "While I was in the tub without my weapons, the girl who was supposedly helping me scrub and fetch stuff, unlocked the door and made lots of noise while they slipped in."

"You let a woman bathe you?" she asked, astonished and jealous.

He chuckled and seemed totally relaxed by now. "I heard it was a real nice pleasure, so I tried it, and I'm sorry I did. They caught me with my pants down and guns missing. I was knocked unconscious, taken out the back way, and pinned to that tree with wire stickers."

"Does Quade know you're still alive?" she asked worriedly.

"I don't think so. No, I'm certain of it." He related what the Ranger had done, but as if he had taken that precaution. "I stole a drunk's body and dressed him in my clothes and put him in my place. I figured by the time Harding checked on me, if he ever did, wouldn't be anything left but bones and clothes."

"What if Quade went back too soon and realized it wasn't you?"

"If that problem exists, I'll deal with it later. We both have a debt against Quade, and one day I'll settle it for us when he least suspects it." He poured himself another cup of coffee and sipped it.

"Something I don't quite understand, T.J.: with your reputation, how would Quade not know that you're still alive?"

"Because I left the area right after I got loose and replaced myself on that tree. I've been tracking Curly and his two friends since I healed. I got them all, one by one, just like they deserved. I doubt Harding knows I'm still around and plotting revenge."

"If he does, he'll be sending someone after you. Quade doesn't give up on something he wants. Those detectives will track you down just like they tracked me down several times. As with me, Quade knows what you look like and can provide your description."

"Then maybe I'll have to take care of him sooner than I planned. In fact, I'll probably do him under when we reach Brownwood. I'll turn you over to your brother and I'll go after Harding. That way, he'll be off both our backs for good. It's a shame I didn't take care of him before he released your description. I was heading back to Brownwood after I finished off Curly James, but I met a distraction."

She smiled warmly. "I wish you had. Then, I'd still be a schoolmarm in Tucson. I'd have been free forever."

"I guess that's something else for you to hold against me."

She asked, "What do you mean by something else?"

His gaze locked with hers. "Evidently you've got something against me because you can't seem to trust me."

She caressed his smoothly shaven cheek and vowed, "I promise I won't ever mistrust you again."

"We'll see," he hinted, then returned her smile. "We have a long way to ride together, woman. I'm afraid the next time something strange comes up, you'll forget this promise."

She stroked his jawline with the back of her hand. "I swear I won't."

"I'll be counting on you, Carrie Sue, because there will be times when you'll have to get me out of trouble. I have to know I can depend on you like you can depend on me."

"You can, T.J. honestly." She leaned forward to kiss him.

He imprisoned her face between his hands and kissed her with a hunger greater than the one in his belly. Suddenly smoke and a sizzling noise caught their attention. They jerked apart to find their meal about to be ruined. They laughed and hurried to save it.

When they finished eating and cleaning up, T.J. repacked their supplies while she dressed nearby with her back to him. She pulled on jeans, boots, and a long-sleeved faded blue shirt. She strapped on her holster, checked her weapons as usual, and told him she was ready.

"We'll leave the bodies where they are. No better place for an evil man to be buried forever than in total darkness. We'll take the horses along for a while. If we release them here, they might find their way home or back to town. I don't want anyone in Tucson to be alerted to a problem and begin a search. By the time Martin Ferris and his sidekick are missed, we'll be long gone."

Carrie Sue agreed. She twirled her long braid and tucked it beneath her hat. Taking Charlie's reins, she led the brown and white pinto outside. T.J. joined her with Nighthawk and the other two horses. She noticed only bridles on them as she mounted.

"Let's try to put this area behind us again," he murmured.

They headed down the Old Spanish Trail. When they reached the road into Tucson, he didn't have to slow down because they could see for miles in both directions.

T.J. halted. He pointed southeastward and said, "You ride toward those mountains while I hang back to cover our tracks. Use the terrain to set your pace, and I'll catch up soon." He passed the two horses reins to her. "Keep your canteen handy. This ride will be slow and hot, and we don't want to halt until necessary."

Carrie Sue left the road and headed across country at a sluggish pace, weaving her way around mesquites and scrubs and cactus. It didn't take long for the morning sun to get high enough to cause sweat to ease down her face and slide down her stomach from beneath her breasts. Riding toward the sun created a glare in her eyes which was too low for her hat to prevent. Her eyes soon grew weary and red from the dryness and squinting. The terrain jostled her in the saddle, almost as badly as the stage ride had done weeks ago. Time passed, but she couldn't sight her lover when she halted a moment and twisted in her saddle to look behind her. She scanned the area in all directions and saw nothing moving. She continued, trying to ignore the heat.

She traveled alone for two hours before T.J. joined her. She smiled and said, "Everything all right back there?"

"Stop a minute while I take these coverings off Nighthawk's hooves. The Apaches taught me this trick to conceal tracks."

She watched him dismount, untie the leather squares, and pack them. He glanced up at her and grinned. "That should protect us for a time, unless somebody hires another Apache scout. Won't fool him."

T.J. took the reins of Martin's and Jess's horses. They headed off again, with her lover in the lead. They passed north of the Santa Rita Mountains and rode for the Whetstones. They halted there to rest and eat strips of jerky, which wasn't her favorite meal.

As if establishing a new rapport after the incident this morning, they talked little as they moved along beneath the blazing sun and through the difficult terrain. It was dark when they reached the San Pedro River and stopped to camp.

"When we head out at dawn, we'll leave Ferris's horses here near water and grass. Why don't you freshen up after that hot ride while I tend ours? It's cold beans tonight, woman, because I don't want anyone seeing a fire and coming to investigate."

"That's fine. Think a bath is too risky?" she inquired.

"Yep. It'll have to wait until we're camped in the Chiricahuas. Lots of water there, cool and pretty area. We'll stay there a few days to rest," he murmured as if visualizing a dreamy setting. "Stay dressed and ready to take off like a hare before a coyote. I'm going to take off the saddles, rub 'em down a bit, and resaddle them for a fast getaway. We can't take any chances tonight, woman."

Carrie Sue caught the underlying meaning of his words, no lovemaking. She followed his suggestions, knowing he was right.

The redhead removed her shirt at the riverbank, rinsed off, dried with it, then donned a clean one. The nights were cooler, sometimes chilly, so a clean, dry shirt would feel better tonight. She removed her boots, rolled up her pant legs, and dangled her feet in the water. Afterwards, she dried them and replaced her boots on soothed feet.

Carrie Sue returned to where T.J. had lain out their bedrolls, side-by-side. She sat on hers and ate the beans, warmed only by the sun, and washed them down with water and one sip of whiskey to put a more pleasant taste in her mouth for the night. She tried to wash the dishes, but T.J. insisted on that task.

"I'm used to taking care of chores around camp, so I don't mind. Besides, I want to freshen up, too," he remarked, then peeled off his damp shirt and tossed it on his saddlebag. He headed for the riverbank.

Carrie Sue reclined. She commanded her heart to stop racing madly and her mind to stop thinking up reckless ways to seduce him tonight. She craved him fiercely, but lovemaking here was too dangerous. She eagerly looked forward to those cool and secluded mountains ahead.

She closed her eyes and fantasized about her irresistible partner. She reflected on their sensual nights together, and longed to repeat those blissful sensations. Maybe she could slow this trip to Darby and spend as much time with her love as possible before something parted them. The desperado could not imagine what her brother was going to say when she suddenly appeared in his camp, without or with her lover. T.J. was doing exactly what he had promised, defending and helping her, but she wanted more from him, so much more. Slowly she drifted off to sleep with images of them dancing peacefully in her head.

T.J. found her asleep when he reached his bedroll. He gazed down at her and intense longings surged through him. She was right about him tricking her with that note. He knew how brave and strong and smart she was, so he had to prove to her how alone and vulnerable she was without him. He had used that situation to scare her, to panic her, to push her closer to him. He had noticed how, even though she was righthanded, she always grasped her blanket and threw it aside with her left hand. And, even though the fire had been to her left, it was too far away to entice her to change her habit, as neither slept close enough to the fire for a spark to jump on their bedrolls.

Before they reached Darby's camp, he had to find other ways to eat up her remaining mistrust, which he was certain still existed. He had to make their bond so powerful that, if trouble arose for him in that outlaw's haven, she would side with him against those murdering bandits, even against her brother. He felt that she was falling in love with him and he needed to strengthen that bond. He planned to do just that while they were camped in the Chiricahua Mountains for days.

There were baffling parts of this mission which he needed to know, but it would create more suspicions if he probed them even casually. No matter what she said or thought about her brother's character and intentions, Darby Stover was a cunning outlaw who had to be stopped any way possible.

T.J. stretched out on his bedroll and tried to relax. He wished he could tell her the truth and obtain her help, but he doubted she would ever betray her only brother. Even if he could dangle a pardon beneath her beautiful nose, she probably wouldn't aid him.

A pardon for her aid, his keen mind stressed. He knew that wasn't possible, but should he pretend it was? If offered her freedom and a life with him, would she take his side and help defeat her own brother and his gang? T.J. asked himself if he could accept such rewards if it meant betraying and killing his brother Tim. He tried to put himself in her place, and Tim in Darby's. In all honesty, what would he do if his trickery meant earning a pardon and winning her? Could he live with himself afterwards? Would he come to despise himself, and her for tempting him to such treachery? Would it make a difference to him if Tim had killed her family? He couldn't answer.

Lordy, what was he doing in love with a woman like Carrie Sue Stover? How could she seem so innocent, so gentle, so kind and caring when she had been an outlaw for years? How could she not have been touched, tainted, by such a lengthy existence? Those big periwinkle eyes and rosy gold face appeared to glow with purity and warmth, but what if she had learned to use her special traits to her advantage? What if he was totally wrong about her? What if she was the one using and duping him? She had been ready and willing to kill him this morning! She had played Carolyn Starns with a skill to be envied by the best actress! Lordy, what if she was just like her brother?

You're grabbing for a dust devil, Thad, and it can't be captured. All it will do is dirty your hands and choke you. Forget this nonsense until your mission's over and you discover the truth. If she isn't guilty, you'll find a way to save her from prison and the rope, even if she refuses to forgive you and stay with you. But what in blue blazes will you do if she is guilty? Or if you get her killed by accident? He couldn't answer those questions, either. . . .

*

The following day, they traveled between the Dragoon Mountains where Naiche's camp had been and Tombstone, a town known for its savageness. Since that wild town was Ike Canton's domain, they didn't linger there. The ride was long and hard because T.J. was determined not to halt before reaching their enticing campsite.

After telling her it was sixty miles, he reminded her that an Apache warrior could run on foot under these same conditions to cover seventy miles in one day, so covering less by horse would be easier.

Many times they were allowed by the terrain to ride side-by-side at a leisurely gallop; other times, they were compelled to ride single file through scrubs and desert vegetation at a snail's pace. Often T.J. scanned all directions with his fieldglasses, as one could see for miles in this area. Even though they were far from the road, he didn't want to take any chances of their dust attracting unwelcome visitors.

The sun was behind them now. It beat down unmercifully on their bodies, urging them to continually sip water to prevent dehydration. They steadily journeyed, eating away the miles to their destination. Yet, they were careful not to overtire or overheat the horses.

Carrie Sue sensed her flesh burning beneath the garments. She couldn't remove her hat to cool her head or roll her sleeves to cool her arms as the sun would attack her fiercely. She rubbed her salty brows with the backs of her forefingers, and winced when the tiny balls of fire drifted into her eyes. When they teared, she blinked to help wash away the stinging sensation. She felt sticky all over, and a salty residue was left behind by her perspiration—moisture which dried almost instantly everywhere except on her clothes. She wondered if steam could rise from her head which seemed saturated by boiling liquid, as was her hatband. She wished she could pull off her boots if only for a few minutes and pour water over her scorching feet. She was miserable, but she never complained to her partner or slowed their progress.

At last, the baking sun lowered itself toward the earth, and the heat lessened. Soon, the Chiricahuas rose like magic from the Sonoran Desert. The lowlands drifted upwards into a cool forest of spruce, fir, oak, juniper, pinyon, aspen, pine, and cypress. The heavily forested mountains offered shady glens which were breathtakingly sheltered by massive and unusual rock formations. She noticed a variety of shrubs, mosses, flowers, and ferns set amongst the trees and rocks. They journeyed through the foothills, beside creeks, and through canyons. T.J. guided her toward a camping area which he remembered. When they arrived, she beamed with pleasure and relief. It was cool and lovely, and plenty of water was nearby in a stream-fed pond.

T.J. told her, "You rest while I scout the area. I want to make certain no one is around in any direction. We'll eat when I get back."

She watched him vanish from sight. She unsaddled her pinto and led the mare to water. Carrie Sue encouraged the animal to step into a shallow area where she could splash water on her sweat-drenched hide. She rubbed the pinto and talked softly to her. When the animal was cooled and relaxed, the pinto began grazing peacefully near the water's edge.

The redhead discarded her hat and weapons. She knelt and washed the salty surface from her face. The water was wonderful, inviting. Unable to resist the impulse, she stripped and went swimming. When her fiery body was refreshed, she fetched her soap and blanket to bathe leisurely. Her arms and thighs were pinkened by the searing sun and she rubbed them gently. She could tell the same was true of her back. She loosened her braid and washed her hair, ducking over and over to rinse it. Finally she left the stream-fed pond, dried off, and put on her gown. Carrie Sue sat on a rock and brushed her wet hair.

Dusk was nearly gone beneath the rising three-quarters moon when T.J. returned and wearily dismounted. He looked at the gown clad beauty on the rock who was nonchalantly brushing her fiery mane, and scowled. He gently caught a handful of drying hair and demanded, "What is this, woman?"

She laughed and teased, "My clean head, Mr. Rogue."

He chided, "Don't jest with me, woman. It looks more like a matador's red cape and this area could be filled with raging bulls. You were supposed to stay on guard until I returned. Taking a bath was a damn stupid thing to do while I was gone! I told you that's how I got snared by Quade's men. When I'm not around, keep a gun in your hand."

"I was miserable, T.J.," she explained. "I knew you'd—"

He irritably cut her off, "Miserable is better than killed, raped, or captured! Do you even realize how tempting you are?"

"I hope I am, but only to you," she replied boldly.

T.J. glared at the beauty. "Sometimes you're too damn tempting and I can't keep my head clear for wanting you!"

She smiled. "Good, that makes two of us in that uncomfortable predicament. Besides, I like having you rescue me all the time."

He warned angrily, "One of these times, I might not get back in time to rescue you from one of these stupid stunts."

"But you always arrive in the nick of time, my handsome gunslinger. I've come to depend on you for everything. You've had very little sleep in the last few days; you're just tired and edgy. Why don't you get cooled off and relaxed while I prepare supper?" she suggested, calm as the wind in the secluded valley.

"That sounds like a perfect idea," he agreed. He unsaddled his horse and set aside their supplies. Nighthawk followed him to the water and was rubbed down before he joined the mare to graze. T.J. stripped and entered the soothing water.

Carrie Sue noticed his absence of modesty and grinned. She liked him not feeling inhibited or embarrassed around her, and that mood spread to her. She walked to the bank, lifted his holster, and called out, "I guess this means it's safe here?"

He glanced at her and replied, "From everyone but me, woman. I still might punish you for being so reckless."

Carrie Sue laughed softly and teased, "Be careful of the Texas Flame, Mr. Rogue; she may singe your hands when you spank her. What would you like me to prepare for supper, partner?"

"You," he answered without jest.

Carrie Sue stared at him in astonishment, then her face softened into a radiant smile. "Consider your supper ready and waiting, partner." She replaced his weapons, returned to their gear and laid out one bedroll.

In seconds, T.J.'s wet hands gripped her shoulders and turned her to face him. His smokey gray gaze locked with hers as he asked, "Did I hear right?"

In answer, Carrie Sue eased her arms around his neck and pulled his head downward to kiss her. Her breath was taken away as he possessively yanked her against his nude body, its moisture dampening her nightgown. There was a desperation in his kisses to which she readily responded. He was no longer elusive; at this feverish moment, he seemed so vulnerable, so susceptible to her allure. It had been a week since they had made love and she craved him wildly.

Overcome with a passion which had been restrained since last Thursday night, his fingers roamed into her wet hair and pulled her head more snugly against his mouth. He shifted them to capture her jawline so he could spread kisses over her face. He hugged her tightly, resting her head against his drumming heart with a quivering hand. "Lordy, you make me go crazy when I'm near you."

"But you're with me all the time," she whispered in a voice hoarsened by powerful emotions.

"I know," he murmured with his lips pressed to her head. "What am I going to do about you, woman?" he unintentionally asked aloud.

Carrie Sue mistook his meaning, but it thrilled her to learn what an overwhelming affect she had on him. Evidently, she concluded, he was panicked over his urgent feelings for her, especially in light of her situation. To relax him, she murmured, "You'll have plenty of time to decide, T.J.; there's no rush. We'll take it slow and easy until we figure out this crazy predicament. For now, just love me."

T.J. leaned back his head and looked into her arresting eyes. Nothing could be easier than to love her, emotionally and physically; and nothing could be more demanding. He was relieved by her lack of pressure and was enflamed by her unleashed desire for him. "You're the only woman who's wanted to understand me and accept me as I am. I don't have any experience in matters like this, so be patient."

She nestled against him and heard what she wanted to hear in his words. "I know what you mean, T.J.; it's scary as hell, isn't it?"

"Worse," he admitted. "I want you so badly I feel like an overfilled feed sack about to burst and scatter my existence in all directions. Lordy, these feelings make me nervous. I've never let anybody get this close to me and, when I do, it's . . ."

Carrie Sue trailed her fingertips over his parted lips when he halted. "It's an outlaw," she calmly finished for him. "Can't we forget about that problem tonight and just be together? Talking about it isn't going to change anything, only make us feel worse. While we're together, can't we just enjoy each other until we have to separate?"

He stared into her glowing gaze and asked seriously, "Can you accept that, Carrie Sue? It isn't much to offer."

She entwined her fingers in his hair and smiled encouragingly. "You're wrong, T.J.; it's the most I've ever gotten from anyone."

Guilt charged through him like a cattle stampede. Yet, he wasn't being totally dishonest with her. He wasn't lying about his feelings and desires for her, and he wasn't leading her to believe there was a future for them. "But we only have until—"

She silenced his weak protest with, "That's better than no time at all," and a passionate kiss. When her lips left his, her fingers replaced them as she coaxed, "Don't say anything else. I accept things the way they are between us, they way they have to be. For tonight and for as long as we have together, just need me and love me."

T.J.'s mouth slanted across hers in a tender kiss which answered her urging truthfully. As one kiss dissolved into another, the pressure of his lips varied from firm and demanding to tender and soft. His capable hands wandered up and down her back as if they were explorers trying to map every inch. His mouth journeyed down her neck and over her ears, driving her mad with uncontrollable cravings.

Carrie Sue wondered if her kindled body would burst into a roaring blaze and consume her if the rising heat within her was not doused soon. She yearned to feel her bare flesh against his. She wiggled her hands between their close bodies and unbuttoned her cotton nightgown to the waist. She pushed it over her shoulders and let it slide down her lowered arms and off her fingertips. She knew that T.J.'s eager hands had helped peel it over her shoulders and send it along its snaking way to curl around her feet. She pressed her naked frame against his, and both moaned at the tantalizing contact.

Her senses were alive and responsive to any and all stimulation. When Carrie Sue leaned her head backwards as T.J.'s lips roved down her silky throat, her long hair tickled the tops of her buttocks and caused her to arch toward her lover. As she moved her head back and forth, and she pressed her hips against his, he shuddered and returned his lips to hers to ravish her mouth with undeniable urgency.

T.J.'s body itched and tingled all over, and it begged for appeasement. His tension was mounting fast as he tried to move slowly and skillfully with her and he wondered if he could explode just from touching and being touched by her. Lordy, no woman had ever aroused him to such heights of hunger and to such a perilous strain on his control!

T.J. shifted his hands to her breasts and kneaded them with a gentle strength, feeling the buds grow hard beneath his fingers. His knees were weak and shaky, so he guided them to the bedroll. His mouth left hers to trail down her neck to the valley between her breasts before allowing his hot tongue to circle each peak and pleasure both. His left hand was sent down her ribcage, moving over each bone slowly and sensuously as if his fingers were counting them. His palm flattened against her stomach and shifted back and forth between the ridges of her hips, each passing taking him lower and lower.

Carrie Sue quivered in anticipation. When his fingers deftly caressed her, she squirmed in delight. She trailed her right hand over his shoulder and stroked his extended arm. She wanted him to continue this thrilling play of hands and lips, but her body yearned to have him within her. "Please, T.J., I can't take any more teasing. Love me now before I go mad. It's been so long."

T.J.'s mouth went to her lips and he moved his body over hers. He entered her slowly, delighting in her welcoming warmth. As passion threatened to overwhelm him, he moved with powerful thrusts, then paused a moment and lifted his head to take in several deep and steadying breaths. When she moaned in protest and her hands and hips urged his firm buttocks to continue their tantalizing movement, he revealed huskily, "Go easy, woman; I'm on the edge. Hellfire, I've been on the edge since I touched you. My control is about gone. Lordy, I want you so bad."

Carrie Sue pulled his mouth back to hers after telling him, "There's no need to control yourself, my love." She was already experiencing tiny waves of ecstasy. She wrapped her legs over his and arched toward him as he rocked his body against hers, causing those waves to build in force until they crashed over her and swept her away in their wild current. He stiffened and paused briefly, then pushed himself deep within her womanhood. She felt him throbbing within her and knew he was obtaining the same potent victory which she was enjoying.

He buried his face in her flowing hair and drove into her over and over until every drop of love's liquid had been drained from him. He held her tightly as he caught his breath and rolled to his back, carrying her along with him.

They lay there in each other's arms, sharing and savoring their closeness. A little less than a full moon glowed down on them and bathed their moist bodies in her romantic light. A mild breeze waved over their naked flesh and dried it. She sighed peacefully and snuggled closer as the fingers of his right hand drifted up and down her arm. His left arm rounded her back with a loving embrace and held her close to his side.

Dreamily her fingertips grazed through the field of black hair on his chest. They roamed a supple terrain of lean and hard flesh. They wandered over boney ridges and firm valleys. One took a mischievous dip in his navel pool of moisture. Suddenly her left arm banded his firm waist and she hugged him tightly. As she relaxed again, her fingers went back to their appreciative play.

A joyful smile slipped over T.J.'s face, for he grasped her serene mood and knew he'd given her great pleasure. At this time, not an ounce of tension troubled him. The most ravishing and unique woman in the entire world was lying in his arms and belonged to him. Whatever problems existed beyond this tranquil haven could be handled and considered later. He didn't want any troubling thought or mood to spoil this wonderful moment. He closed his eyes.

Twenty minutes passed and Carrie Sue believed her lover had fallen asleep from exhaustion. She was tired and sore and sensuously sated, but she was too hungry to drop off to sleep. She eased from his arms and bedroll to see what she could find to eat in his supply pouch. She moved quietly and carefully so as not to awaken him.

Just as she reached for the pouch, T.J. asked in an odd tone, "What are you doing?" He bounded forward and halted her action.

She looked up, his face shadowed by its lowered position and that of the moon's behind him, and replied, "I'm starved. I was looking for something to eat. I thought you were asleep. Did I disturb you?"

"I was just resting and giving you time to rest. I'm too hungry to sleep, too. I'll find us something quick and easy. Why don't you wash off and put on your gown?" he suggested, tugging playfully at her hair.

Carrie Sue did as he asked to prevent him from witnessing her reaction to his curious behavior. It was almost as if he was hiding something in that pouch. Of course, some people just didn't like others going through their belongings. Yet, he always was the one to unload and load the supplies, and usually the one to prepare them. Was there something concealed in his possessions that he didn't want her to see?

She stepped into the water and rinsed swiftly because its temperature and the air's had dropped since sundown. She dried off, donned her nightgown, and loosely braided her hair to prevent its tangling. She sat on the bedroll and waited for him to join her.

T.J. didn't build a fire. When he sat down beside her, he teased, "You almost spoiled my surprise. I've been saving these treats until we got here to enjoy them." He handed her a metal plate with several items on it. "Naiche gave these to me. This is saguaro fruit. It's sweet and delicious. The Apaches gather it in early summer. You can eat the fruits raw, or make thick cakes with them and store them for a long time. They also make a tasty juice."

"Saguaro? Isn't saguaro that huge cactus that only grows in certain parts of Arizona and New Mexico?" she inquired, eyeing one.

"Yep, try it," he coaxed.

She did, and smiled, "It's good. I wouldn't have thought about eating part of a cactus. I guess that's why the Apaches can survive in this desert; they know what to eat and how to get water."

"Try this," he urged, pointing to another item on her plate.

Carrie Sue lifted the vegetable which resembled an artichoke heart. It was warm from being in his pouch beneath the sun. She tasted it, and was reminded of a sweet potato. "I like it. What is it?"

"Parry Agave. You remember, those tall tree-looking plants with clusters of yellow flowers."

"The ones tequila is made from?" she asked and grinned. "Is this going to get me drunk?"

"Nope. The Apaches used to spend four months a year gathering, roasting, and drying agave. Once its prepared, it lasts up to a year."

"How do they prepare it?" she asked, then continued eating.

"They gather the shoots and roast them over hot coals. Then, you peel 'em and eat 'em until your belly wants to burst. Tequila is made from the stalks, not these roots," he stated merrily and licked his lips. "Naiche's people dig up the roots, bake them for two nights and one day in stone-lined pits with the agave covered by hot rocks."

He chuckled and leaned closer to whisper in a roguish tone, "But he did give me a skin of tequila if you want some tonight."

"After the last time, I think I'll stick to whiskey when I have need of a sip of lively spirits." They both laughed in recall of that night in the Mexican cafe and in Naiche's camp, and her sufferings afterwards.

T.J. ate and drank from his plate and cup because Carrie Sue had her own now. He was impressed by the preparations she had made in case a swift flight from Tucson was needed, and it had been. He offered her jerky and almost stale Jonnycakes.

She rejected the dried beef strips, but ate two cakes. When he asked if she wanted him to warm some beans, she shook her head. "This is plenty for tonight, thanks. You're a good cook even when you don't cook, partner. I can learn a lot from you."

"How about starting your lessons another time? I'm ready to fall out on my feet." Carrie Sue handed him her empty plate and cup, and he put everything away. He spread her sleeping roll beside his.

They took their places, both choosing their backs. Just as she closed her eyes, his hand found hers and squeezed it. She returned his gesture, and they drifted off with fingers entwined.

*

Breakfast—fried salt pork, flour gravy, Jonnycakes, and black coffee—had been cooked and eaten. The dishes were washed and stored. Both were dressed, and the horses were tending themselves.

T.J. told her to relax with that book he had seen her place in her saddlebag in Tucson, while he went to cover their trail from yesterday. He explained, "It was too late last night to conceal our tracks and set a false trail. I also want to do some hunting for fresh meat. You stay here and rest, but stay on alert, woman. Keep your pistol close and your ears open. I'll be back in a few hours. No bathing or swimming alone," he added as he mounted Nighthawk. He needed to do and learn a few vital things today, and she would be safe. A telegraph line was situated not too far away . . .

Carrie Sue waved and watched him leave. She glanced at the possessions T.J. had left behind. She wanted to go through them just as soon as she was certain he wasn't hiding nearby and spying on her to see if she could be trusted not to pry into his belongings or to desert him during his absence. She fetched her book and sat down to read, placing her revolver beside her. Soon, she would discover why he didn't want her looking inside his pouches. . . .

Chapter

15

Carrie Sue pretended to read for thirty minutes while she reflected on T.J. Rogue and her situation with him. Sometimes he gave off an arrogant air, but—she concluded—it was only enormous self-confidence and his custom of being self-reliant. Sometimes he found it hard to be open with her, but that was due to his being a loner for so many years. He was a man resolved to fight all obstacles in his path, a man who could endure anything he encountered and survive. His experiences had toughened him and honed him into an undefeatable force, except for that one incident with Quade. There was a powerful strength about him: physical, mental, and emotional. She felt that until meeting her, he had been satisfied with his carefree existence; now, he wanted and needed more, and often didn't realize that fact or want to accept it.

Yet, T.J. Rogue could be vulnerable, susceptible to her pull, worried over the danger she presented to and for him, distracted and disarmed by her. Too, he was a man with a haunted past which still troubled and plagued him. He could be easygoing one minute and guarded the next. What, she wondered, drove him the hardest?

The redhead didn't sense any eyes watching her and decided T.J. wasn't spying on her from the rocks which surrounded this small valley. She lay the book aside and went to search his pouches. She didn't find anything unusual inside them. Then, she remembered he had taken his saddlebags with him. She frowned, then decided that might be only from force of habit.

Why, she asked herself, couldn't she trust him completely? Why did she sense there was something crucial going on inside his head, something which involved her? As far as she knew, they only had one connection, Quade Harding, and one bond—their mutual attraction. So, why did she feel as if there was more between them, something mysterious and dangerous? On the other hand, why should he trust her? That wasn't a common trait of a gunslinger or an outlaw. Yet, both wanted to believe the other; she was positive of that.

Tensed by her thoughts and actions, Carrie Sue strapped on her holster and went to gather wood. She jumped when she spooked a slumbering Whitetail deer and the animal fled swiftly. She remembered T.J. cautioning her about snakes in this region, particularly in July and August. "Stay alert," she warned herself.

The flaming haired woman used an extra knife to dig a fire pit and gathered rocks to encircle it. Afterwards, she took a walk to admire the scenery and to dispel her anxieties.

T.J. had described the northwestern section of these mountains and she longed to ride there to observe those magnificent scenes. He had drawn verbal pictures of the "Land of the Standing-Up Rocks" as the Apaches called that area. Maybe she could persuade him to take her there tomorrow.

She wondered what was taking her lover so long to conceal their trail and to shoot fresh meat. He had left early, and it was past midday. She was bored and restless. She didn't want to read, although she loved reading. Today, her concentration was missing.

She recalled the fishing hooks and string in T.J.'s pouch. She fetched them and secured them to the sturdy limb she located. Taking his extra knife, she dug in the clumps of grass near the stream for several worms. While her pinto aimlessly grazed, she fished.

She laughed aloud when she snagged the first one, a little over a pound. Quickly she imprisoned the squirming creature on a thin rope by running it through his mouth and out his gill and looping the end. She tied the rope to a bush and dangled the fish in water so it would stay alive and fresh until she finished her task. She attached another worm to the hook and tossed it beneath the surface. It took her longer this time, but she caught another one about the same size. Excitement and satisfaction filled her. If her luck held out, she could surprise her lover with a tasty meal tonight.

Carrie Sue caught one fish bigger and one smaller than the other two. She put away the fishing supplies and found a distant spot to clean her nice catch. Expertly she scaled and gutted the fish, then washed them in the lake.

From the sun's position, it was around three o'clock. She built a fire and let it burn down to smouldering coals. While doing so, she scouted for more rocks and placed a stack on either side to form two support ledges. She located four sturdy sticks and sharpened one end on each. Carefully she shoved a stick through each fish. Afterwards, she suspended the largest one horizontally between the rock ledges.

Considering the hour and the length of cooking time at that height over the coals, T.J. should return by the time the last one—the smallest—was ready to be placed over the pit. When the largest was done enough to meet her schedule, she positioned the two medium fish on either side of it.

She mixed flour and water and salt for fresh Jonnycakes. Added to the remaining agava roots, which she would warm soon on the hot rocks, T.J. was in for a special treat tonight. At last, she placed the last fish over the fire and turned the others once more.

She was getting annoyed with her tardy lover when he rode up and dismounted. "No luck?" she hinted, noticing his empty hands and saddle.

He grinned as he eyed the beautiful vixen and feast before him. He replied, "Looks like I have plenty right here. How did you manage this?" he asked, surprised and pleased. He hunkered down opposite her.

"My father and brother taught me to fish and camp cook. It passed the time today," she remarked, sounding and looking as vexed as she felt. "I borrowed your supplies. I hope you don't mind."

"Of course not, woman. Feel free to use any of those supplies. You did better than me. Thank goodness or it'd be beans again tonight." He frowned playfully. "I'm afraid I didn't see anything small enough to shoot, and I don't like killing more meat than I can use."

"I'm glad. Senseless killing distresses me," she remarked as she began cooking the circles of bread in the edge of the fire. She placed the agavas on the other side to absorb heat. "You want to get the dishes and pour us some whiskey?" Carrie Sue stood and unbuckled her holster. She laid it aside.

T.J. eyed her intently and pondered her request for liquor instead of water or coffee. He asked, "You mad at me again?"

Her periwinkle eyes were cool when they met his smokey gray ones. "You've been gone since early morning. I was worried."

He knew she meant suspicious, not worried. He knew he had to dispel her mood quickly. "I backtracked a good ways and covered our trail. Then, I made several new ones in various directions to confuse anyone who comes along. Afterwards, I did some hunting, but we wouldn't want to eat the only small game I spotted: Apaches fox squirrels, lizards, coatimundis. That takes time, woman, lots of it."

The redhead realized she was acting oddly. She sighed and smiled. "I know, but it's sundown. What if something had happened to you? I wouldn't know how or where to find you so I could help."

He relaxed. "You're right. Just in case we get separated, we need a plan for joining up again. What do you suggest?"

"Since we're heading for Commanche, why don't I give you a map of where we're going and mark a few spots between New Mexico and there?"

"Commanche? Is that where you're to meet Darby?" he asked.

She shrugged as she continued her chore. "I'm not certain. After we parted near Sherman, he was heading for Oklahoma to lay low a while. If he knows about my trouble, he'll either head for a spot on the Pecos River or the cabin and hope to join up with me there. Since the river comes first on the trail, we'll check there before heading for Commanche. I'll draw you a map later."

T.J. wondered if she was telling the truth, or if she was testing him. If she suspected that he was after Darby and his gang, maybe she figured he would take the map and be done with her, one way or another. "I'll take the map, Carrie Sue, but we'll make sure we don't get separated. It's too dangerous out there for you alone, and you aren't familiar with this territory. If you want to call off your search for your brother, I'll guide you anywhere you want to go. What about it? You want to give a new life another chance? In your place, I would."

The desperate fugitive considered his answer, and what action he would take if she accepted his offer of escort. If he was after her and/or Darby, once she gave him a map and if he believed it was real, he wouldn't have any further use for her. If that was his motive, he certainly wasn't going about obtaining victory in a logical manner!

Carrie Sue didn't know what to think. If he loved her enough to go to such perilous lengths to help her, why didn't he want to remain with her, to run away with her? Perhaps he knew she wouldn't take his advice about escaping, so he was unafraid to use his offer as a clever ruse. And, perhaps he thought he had her in his control and could entrap all of them. "I have to see Darby first. If I can't persuade him to go straight some place far away, then I'm going to give it one last try. If your offer's still open after you get rid of Quade Harding, you can guide me some place wonderful and safe."

T.J. sent her a broad smile, one which brightened his eyes and softened his features, one which looked totally honest and sincere. "That's a wise choice, woman. I'm proud of you. I give you my word of honor to become your future escort. Just as soon as we finish with Darby and Harding, it's Montana or wherever you want to go. Who knows, maybe I'll stick around a while and get you started on this new life, make sure no Ferrises are around. Would that be all right?"

"More than all right, partner. Thanks. Our wonderful meal isn't going to be so wonderful if we don't pay attention to it," she jested.

"I'll fetch the dishes and drinks, Ma'am," he said, then bowed comically before doing so.

As she served their plates, he said, "I need to draw you a map of this area and all the way through New Mexico, just in case of trouble. I'll mark some places and give you some names of friends who might help if anything happens to me. I said, might help, Carrie Sue. I can't promise anything because of who you are. You understand?"

She looked at him, her gaze wide and her lips parted in surprise. "I understand, and thanks."

T.J. cunningly added, "Just so you'll know you can trust me, don't give me a map so I won't know where we're heading. When we get near Darby's hideout, you can take my weapons and bind my hands."

This time, total astonishment was exposed in her expression and voice. "That would look as if I don't trust you at all."

He shook his head. "Nope, it'll be the smart and careful thing to do. In your place, I'd do the same. I don't mind. Just promise me I'll be safe when we reach him. I wouldn't want your brother acting like an irate father when he learns about us."

Carrie Sue laughed. "He won't. Darby trusts me to make my own decisions. He knows I wouldn't do anything foolish, and he knows I would die before endangering him. If I take you into his camp, he'll know you can be trusted."

T.J. smiled. "Let's eat before all your work is wasted."

After they devoured the fish, agava, and Jonnycakes and washed them down with sips of whiskey, they shared the cleanup chores.

T.J. suggested they take a swim before turning in for the night. When she agreed, he walked to the bank, stripped, and dove in. Carrie Sue did the same. They laughed and relaxed as they played chase-and-tag in the cooling water, and shared provocative kisses each time they touched. Their game lasted for over an hour until they were winded, and highly aroused.

T.J. left the water, dried off, and wrapped a blanket around his hips. He sat on a bedroll and leaned his back against a large rock. He watched Carrie Sue leave the water and dry off, delighting in the way the moonlight shimmered over her wet body. After she secured a blanket around her, he enticed, "Come over here and sit with me."

The redhead eagerly did as he said and sat on the bedroll between his legs. She snuggled against him and sighed peacefully. Her body was turned slightly to the left, one hip resting on the bedroll. Her legs were curved backward to the right and her ankles were crossed. T.J.'s left arm crossed her breasts and lightly captured her right arm near the elbow. Her left shoulder was under his with her fingers curled over his arm. Her weight was partially on his extended left leg, but his right one was raised and lying against her buttocks. His right fingers began to draw little designs on her right shoulder, and he bent his head forward to nuzzle her ear on that side. The position was so comfortable, so intoxicating, so perfectly meshed.

She dreamily entreated, "Tell me more about you, T.J."

He ceased nibbling on her ear and replied, "Like what? You know about all there is to learn about me."

She nestled closer to him and stroked the outside of his left thigh with her fingertips. "Like what you've been doing since the orphanage and war. Why haven't you found a place to settle down by now?"

His fingers began to trail up and down her bare arm. "A man like me hasn't needed a home and, when you travel around all the time, you make few friends. I've been a cowhand, a guide, a shotgun messenger, a guard for gold or silver wagons, a trail boss, and lots of other things. I guess I've had about every kind of job there is to make a few dollars. Between jobs, I rest and look around, and try to stay out of trouble, which isn't easy sometimes."

She laughed. She wondered if there was a special meaning to his words that he hadn't needed a home, as he hadn't said doesn't need. "I'm surprised that a man with your skills and prowess hasn't become a lawman of some kind. Have they ever approached you about one of their jobs?" She felt him tense, then relax.

He chuckled heartily, his chest movements shaking her lightly. "T.J. Rogue, a lawman? Lordy, woman, what office would trust me that much? Besides, I hear the pay is small and the perils large."

Although it wasn't a firm denial, she let it pass. "What about a bounty hunter? You could easily track down the worse criminals and earn big money."

Scorn filled his tone when he responded, "I feel the same way about bounty hunters as you do. My reputation isn't the best, woman, but I don't want it becoming any worse. Bounty hunters can't be trusted; they're cold-blooded and greedy. They shoot too many innocent men, or shoot men they could bring in alive. I've seen boys who couldn't be more than fifteen or sixteen strapped over their saddles, or men old enough to be grandfathers many times over with bullets through their heads. Nobody can tell me that's necessary, just easier for those snakes."

"What hunger drives you onward the most, T.J.?"

"What do you mean?" he asked, baffled by the deep question.

"Why do you stay in this unrooted and dangerous existence?"

"I don't know, Carrie Sue, but I will when I find it. I guess I just have a restless nature and I don't mix too well with regular people." As she fell silent, T.J. thought about the wires he had sent today. He hoped the President would heed his warnings and requests on the Apaches. He knew he couldn't risk using his operator key to tap into the telegraph lines again until they reached Deming, and that was a long time to wait to learn if her posters had been recalled by the Texas Rangers. At the same time, he would discover if the Stover Gang was on the trail again and where they were attacking. At least his office knew he was on the case and all was going as planned with Collins. Joe was to tell the Pima County sheriff of his lethal run-in with Martin Ferris. All of those messages had been sent in code.

T.J. stiffened. His hand covered her mouth and he strained to pick out a certain noise in the rocks to their left. "Stay here behind cover while I check on something," he whispered. After handing her a revolver, he vanished into the darkness.

He was back soon, grinning and chuckling. "Just a gray fox on the prowl. I scared him off. You ready to turn in?"

Without hesitation, she answered. "Yes."

"Would you like to sleep with me tonight?" he invited huskily.

"I'd like to sleep with you every night," came her bold response.

Looking into her moon-lightened face, he said, "Suits me, woman." T.J. put the two bedrolls together and Carrie Sue lay down. He joined her, and placed a revolver nearby.

Their mouths met in a tender kiss which soon became a series of passionate ones. T.J. deftly loosened the blankets around their bodies, bringing their heated flesh into contact. She closed her eyes as his lips started a fiery trail down her throat, one which eventually covered her entire body. Soon, she irresistibly joined his bold adventures along new paths of lovemaking and she followed his hoarsely spoken instructions with eagerness and ecstatic delight. For hours they made love leisurely, uninhibitedly, blissfully, until they fell asleep cuddled together.

*

Carrie Sue jerked upwards when a rifle shot abruptly awakened her. She had slept late, as the sun was peeking over the tall peaks to the east. She looked around, but didn't see her lover. Quickly she wrapped the discarded blanket around her and grabbed her weapons. Then, she saw T.J. weaving through rocks and heading her way, carrying something. "What is it?" she shouted to him.

When he reached her, he held up the small animal and replied. "A javelina, small enough to be real tender and delicious after roasted. He must have gotten separated from his band. Usually they travel in herds of five to nearly thirty. Ever seen one? Or eaten one?"

Carrie Sue shook her head as she eyed the creature with small ears, a protruding snout, and almost no tail. He looked to weigh about fifteen to twenty pounds and was dark gray. "He looks like a pig with hair," she remarked, mischievously wrinkling her nose.

T.J. put down his burden and rifle. "You're right. The Apaches hunted them for their hides and meat, so I've eaten plenty, and killed plenty with a bow and arrows or a lance. These little boys usually nose around at night or real early in the morning, and get real mean if cornered or chased. When they send out an alarm to the herd, it's almost like a bark. They scare your pants off if you spook 'em. They chatter their teeth like the rattling of a sidewinder. I think you know what that is since you called me one in the cave," he jested.

Carrie Sue stuck out her tongue at him. She asserted, "You deserved it, partner, for scaring me witless."

T.J. chuckled merrily and teased, "Better watch it, Red, or I'll clip off that tasty tongue and cook it for my breakfast."

When he roguishly yanked her against him and brushed his lips over hers, she murmured, "Is that what you like best about it?" She flicked her tongue over his lips as her subtle words reminded him of how rapturously it had worked on his body last night.

"You're a woman of many surprises, Carrie Sue Stover."

As if it had been weeks since they had been together, they hurriedly undressed and fell upon the rumpled bedrolls, making love in an urgent and stimulating rush. Both were panting breathlessly when they finished and rolled to their backs to rest.

"Lordy, you keep me boiling all the time! But I surely do like how you cool me off. Shame that lack of heat doesn't last long."

Carrie Sue wiggled half atop him and teased, "I'm glad it doesn't. If you didn't crave me as much as I do you, I'd have to get the drop on you and force you to do my bidding at gunpoint."

He locked their gazes and said, "Yep, it's good we're matched."

She nibbled at his sensual lips as her naked body rubbed against his. "I like all the things you're teaching me, partner. I'm glad I brought you along. Just look what I'd be missing."

"There's plenty more to learn and experience, Red. Just make certain you don't use these facts and skills on anybody but me."

Carrie Sue gazed lovingly into his smokey gray eyes. She didn't care if she was naked in daylight with this man. She also didn't care that he was calling her "Red," because he did it in such a provocative and seductive tone. "As long as you're satisfied to remain my private teacher, I'll stay your devoted student."

"That's a bargain, my ex-schoolmarm. Right now," he said, capturing her in his arms and coming to a standing position with ease and strength, "let's get washed up and cook some breakfast."

T.J. carried her to the water and waded into it. They were waist deep before he placed her feet against the bottom. After kissing her soundly, he coaxed, "Get busy, woman. I'm starved."

Following their baths, they dressed and began their chores. While Carrie Sue gathered more wood, T.J. skinned and carved the peccary. She built a fire in the pit and made coffee as he took the unusable parts of the animal away from camp. She mixed Jonnycakes and started them while he cooked small strips of meat, the larger hunks to be roasted slowly to eat later. As he watched the cakes, she fetched their dishes and poured them coffee. They talked and ate.

Carrie Sue smiled after the first few bites and said, "It's good."

T.J. seemed utterly at ease this morning, smiling and chatting freely. He related some of his experiences during the war between the Northern and Southern states. He talked about some of the famous gunslingers and lawmen he had met over the years, and about a few run-ins with each. He told her about some of his adventures on the trail. Yet, everything he revealed, which could be checked out or might have been heard by her, was true about T.J. Rogue.

Carrie Sue enjoyed their conversation and rapport, which continued while they cleared the dishes and he put the rest of the meat on to roast slowly over the next few hours. They strolled around as she related more about her farming days in Georgia and her ranching days in Texas. She revealed more about her experiences with Quade Harding on the QH Ranch near Brownwood, below Commanche on a map.

When their talk came around to her brother, she spoke of their days growing up, not of their years on the trail as outlaws.

But T.J. did. "Money, cattle, and goods can be replaced, but a life can't. If you get caught, killings will be the hardest crimes to justify. I hope you don't get involved again." T.J. asked her about the killings they had been forced to commit.

Her bright smile faded and her sunny mood darkened. The lovely fugitive looked dismayed by the direction of their conversation. She admitted that killing was repulsive to her and to Darby and that they always tried to avoid it, unless it was necessary.

T.J. had to ask, "I know what makes killing necessary in my existence, Carrie Sue, but what makes it necessary in yours?"

She began to fidget as she explained, "Stages are always ordered to halt when bandits approach, but some drivers are reckless or cocky. Unless they tried to escape us, there never was any shooting. Or unless we were being shot at and our lives were at stake. You already know why we had to defend ourselves against Quade and his men."

Despite her unease, he continued, "What about the innocent victims of your attacks, the old men, women, and children?"

A haunted expression clouded her violet-blue eyes. "Can we skip over such a painful part of my life?" she entreated sadly.

He nodded and asked, "Who was the Texas Ranger who abused you?"

The flaming haired woman looked surprised by his unexpected question. Yet, she answered, "Virgil Ames. Why?"

"Well, I won't be able to teach him a lesson about how to treat women, even women in your predicament. He was shot by Bill Longley. Ever heard of him or met him?"

"Heard of him, yes. Met him, luckily no. They don't come any lower or viler than Longley. He hates Negroes and kills one every chance he gets. I hear he wears a goatee which gives him a devilish look. Doesn't he do a lot of bounty hunting?"

"Yep, every time he's low on money. He's only about twenty-five, but he has at least thirty killings to his name. He's a wild and savage man. He's just lucky the law hasn't gotten something on him yet. If he comes after the Texas Flame, the law won't have to worry about him anymore; I'll take him coffin deep."

T.J. returned to the fire pit to check on the meat. He poured more coffee and leaned against a rock while he sipped the hot liquid gingerly. He smiled when she joined him. He resumed their conversation. "If Longley hadn't gotten Virgil Ames, the Rangers would have soon. I hear they don't like anybody, especially their own men, giving them a bad name. Ames gave me a hard time back in Texas, but I didn't let him provoke me into being reckless. I suppose he tried the same thing with Bill Longley and it didn't work. I don't exactly know what happened but the law didn't arrest Longley. That's one less revenge we have to worry about."

"That's a relief. I've always been nervous about running into him again. I knew that if that day ever came, I'd have to kill him and be in more trouble. You can't go around shooting Rangers, even with good reason. I have to admit, Virgil Ames was the only bad one I've met."

He concurred, "Yep, you don't run across many bad Rangers. Usually they're straight talking and fair. If Ames had been a good one, things might be different for you today."

"And we wouldn't have met," she added meaningfully. "I wonder which episode will prove best for me," she murmured evocatively.

He grinned and asserted confidently, "I will, naturally."

Carrie Sue smiled and relaxed again. "We'll see, Mr. Rogue."

"Yep, Red, we will," he replied, licking his lips.

Time seemed to move by swiftly today, too swiftly to suit either of them. Both were acutely aware of their plans to leave this tranquil haven at dawn the next morning.

Carrie Sue asked, "Will you take me to see that area northward?"

"Yep, let's saddle up. Grab your canteen and fill it."

Slowly they rode through the mountains located between the Sonoran and Chihuahuan Deserts. She saw and heard many bird species: busy flycatchers, Mexican chickadees, rufous-sided towhees who were scratching in the leaves, wrens with their laughing echoes in the canyons, raucous gray-breasted jays, and exotic-looking coppery tailed trogons.

There was a variety of plant life which seemed unlikely to grow in the same or nearby location, but it did. There were cactus in the lowlands; stunted oaks and pines, twisted alligator junipers, and cypress in the dense forests in the canyons; and scrubby manzanita, buckthorn, and skunkbush on the ridges. Forests of ponderosa pines, Douglas firs, and aspens filled the higher slopes. There were dry, sandy spots; there were lush grassy ones.

They reached their first destination, "the wonderful land of cliff formations." She saw hedgehog cacti with their red blossoms sprouting between rocks. There was an abundance of creeks, supplying plenty of water for the animals of this wondrous world. T.J. lead her from place to place, sometimes on horseback and sometimes on foot.

Extraordinary rock sculptures greeted her ever widening eyes. There were acres of pinnacles, organ pipe rocks, towering spires, massive stone columns, and enormous boulders delicately balanced on small pedestals. The incredible formations were a spectacular sight. The couple traveled the riparian trails through floral meadows, and cool woodlands, and along paths made by thousands of moccasined feet over the years.

T.J. escorted her to the area called "Heart of Rocks." There he showed her an echo canyon where she bounced words off the mocking stones, and a rock grotto which they could walk over, under, around, or through. She could see from the well-worn trail that it had been used many times in the past. They halted at Turkey Creek to rest and refresh themselves before heading back to their camp in the southern region of this splendid location.

When they reached their campsite, T.J. checked on the meat which was cooking in the fire pit. He asked later, "Do you have any kin back in Georgia? Some relative who'll take you in if you can get back there safely?"

Her gaze was locked to his. "No, I don't."

He clarified, "Once I get you back to your brother, if anything happens to Darby, you'll be all alone?"

"Yes," she responded, if she didn't have her lover at her side.

T.J. exhaled loudly. "That's something you have to think about, Carrie Sue. Considering the kind of life you two lead, he could get killed at any time. I'm sorry, but that's a reality you have to face. What would you do?"

She had faced that grim reality long ago, even if she hated to think about it. "If you mean what I think, T.J., I'm confused. I'd never stay with the boys if anything happened to Darby. I've already told you I'm leaving the gang after I see Darby once more."

"That isn't what I was asking. What would happen with Darby's gang if anything happened to him after I left you there to go after Harding? I mean, what would they do with you? How would they treat you? You're a beautiful woman, and they're violent outlaws. Would you be safe with them until you escaped or I returned?"

When she hesitated, he said, "I can see from your reaction that you aren't certain you can trust them."

Carrie Sue was thinking more of his words "violent" and "escape" than she was about his disturbing questions. She hated to spoil their lovely day with such dismaying conversation. She told him, "They've been with Darby since the beginning and are friends of his."

He pressed, "But that doesn't mean they're friends of yours, right?"

She frowned and answered, "I've been around them off and on for seven years, but they're not family to me. What's your point?"

T.J. was relieved to learn her only affection and loyalty lay with her brother, but he replied, "That worries me, woman."

Carrie Sue had never thought of being alone with the gang. Frankly, she didn't know how the outlaws would behave without her brother's guidance and influence, especially Kadry and Dillon. As for Kale, she would be safe with him. Yet, T.J. seemed to be probing her loyalties and affections for the men. Surely he didn't think she'd change her mind after seeing them again. Maybe he was only worried about one of them being too special to her, or worried that she would take their side if trouble struck. The gang members were all right, but she had avoided getting close to men who could die at any moment, except for Kale. She thought it best not to go into detail with her lover over that amiable relationship. She stated confidently, "Don't let it. If there's a problem, I can take care of myself."

"Against how many men, Carrie Sue?" he asked skeptically, slyly.

"The last time I was with Darby, he had six men, seven including himself. Sometimes for bigger jobs like robbing trains or rustling cattle or holding up a well-guarded Wells Fargo freight, he hires additional men for a week or two. I can trust Darby's friends, but I don't know about any others who might be in camp. Rest easy, love; the boys wouldn't harm me or allow anyone else to do so." Carrie Sue knew there were posters out on the Stover Gang, so she wouldn't be giving away any secrets by speaking the men's names. To let him believe she trusted him fully, she listed the gang members, "He normally rides with Kadry Sams, Walt Vinson, Tyler Parnell, John Griffin, Dillon Holmes, and Kale Rushton."

"A man would have to be deaf and blind not to have heard and read about them. Six expert gunmen are a lot for one woman to handle, especially one as desirable as you are, Carrie Sue. Any of them ever try anything with you in the past? You know what I mean."

"Why? You planning to challenge them to a showdown for my honor?"

"Nope, for your protection, if necessary."

"It won't be, partner. My brother takes care of me in camp."

"What if he isn't around or gets wounded or killed? Who would give you trouble? I'd like to look 'em over before I leave you there."

She wanted to drop the subject, but knew her lover wouldn't let her until he had the answers he was seeking. To appease him—but to lighten his grave mood—she continued in a playfully mischievous vein. "You promise no trouble, you possessive male?"

"Not if they leave you alone and give you time to leave safely."

"The worst is Kadry Sams. He's Darby's best friend, so don't start anything with him or Darby won't take kindly to my bringing you along. Kadry never harmed me, but he was always after me in public and in private. His chase was worse when Darby wasn't looking or nearby, but he never succeeded. The other one is Dillon Holmes. He's the one I'll have to watch the most. He's sneaky around the others and bold around me, if I got alone with him, which I avoided like a chigger patch. Kadry is part of the reason I left so many times. He wanted to marry me and didn't want to be put off much longer. If I hadn't left near Sherman, it would have come to trouble between us."

"I'm surprised he let you go without a fuss. Why did he?"

She laughed. "He had no choice; Darby agreed with my decision. Kadry said he knew I'd be back soon, and it appears he was right."

T.J. cleverly hinted, "What if Kadry is the one who released your description to force you back into the gang, not the Hardings?"

"Friend or not, Darby would kill him," she vowed.

"If his deed ever came to light," her lover added. "I'm serious."

Carrie Sue contemplated his words, then shook her head. "No, Kadry would never endanger me; he wants me too badly. I could get killed and he'd never get his hands on me again. Too big of a risk."

"Isn't that also true of Quade Harding? Somebody betrayed you to the law, and it surely wasn't me. I didn't even guess your secret. If that poster hadn't come out, I doubt anyone else would have either."

"You worry too much," she teased, and he frowned. "I tell you what, partner; when we reach Darby's camp, you study Kadry and Dillon before you leave and tell me your opinion of them. If you're still available after handling Quade, you can take me far away."

"You have another bargain, woman. But what do you mean by if I'm still available?" he queried with intrigue.

"You said Darby could get killed at any time. The same is true of you, T.J. Rogue, my famous gunslinger with a highly coveted reputation. Even if you defeat Quade, he's not the only man after your handsome hide. You're more enticing to other gunslingers than nearly naked women hanging over saloon bannisters are to sex-starved cowpokes when they ride into town. Who'll be my escort then?"

"Don't worry about me or your escape, Red. I won't die before getting you far away from your threat. If Darby is near Brownwood, after I leave you in his camp, you'll have one week to say good-bye while I finish off Harding. Then, I'll drag you away even if I have to face down Kadry, Dillon, your brother, and the entire gang." T.J. knew where he would go after dropping her off, to alert the Rangers and plan their captures, not to Brownwood after Harding.

"I guess that means you aren't planning to join the gang?"

"I doubt it. If I do, it won't be for long. 'Course, that all depends on if I'm a wanted man now. We'll decide later. It's time to eat supper. Coffee or whiskey? What do you want tonight?"

She was glad the subject was back to pleasant ones, and she intended to keep it that way for the rest of the evening! "Coffee with supper, and you later, if you don't mind my working you so hard. You're like water in this desert area, my handsome and creative teacher; I have to take every advantage of it when it's available, 'cause you can't ever tell when it won't be."

Chapter

∽⦿∽

16

A s they were packing the next morning to leave, Carrie Sue tested a suspicion of hers. She picked up T.J.'s saddlebag and remarked, "I'll fetch some paper so you can draw me that map before we ride out."

The raven-haired man nearly yanked the bags from her and said, "I'll get it. You finish your chores. I have an Apache charm in here and it's bad luck for a woman to touch it. Besides, a lady shouldn't handle men's underwear." He chuckled to pass off his odd reaction.

"I've handled my father's and brother's many times."

"That's different. We're strangers," he reasoned playfully.

"Considering our relationship, Mr. Rogue, we're hardly strangers anymore. I know what you're hiding in there," she teased.

His head jerked in her direction and his expression was strange. To hide her suspicion, she jested, "You have keepsakes from your old conquests and you're afraid I'll get wildly jealous if I see them."

He laughed and retorted, "How did you know?"

With a seductive grin, she ventured, "Don't all men keep souvenirs of such victories? I'll have to think of something special to give you when we separate so you'll always remember this one as your best. Do the map, partner, while I finish with Charlie. I promise not to peek at your feminine treasures or order you to throw them away."

He chuckled and said, "Thanks, you're a wise woman, generous, too." When the map was done, he handed it to her and cautioned, "Don't lose it. It might save your life if anything happens to me."

"I'll keep it close to my heart," she replied and shoved it into her shirt pocket, more intrigued than ever about his saddlebag contents. How, she plotted, could she get a peek at them?

*

On the way to Deming, New Mexico, they passed more brown mountains on both sides, mountains which looked purple in the distant haze. Hills varied in size and height, many with rocky ridges and craggy protrusions which formed unusual shapes and gave the scenery a wild and rugged appearance. Some rocks were side by side like towering stone cactus which grew from the earth to the peak like sturdy walls holding back the tall mounds behind them. The terrain was covered by scattered scrubs and thick grassland. There was a large dry wash to their left, as they traveled near—but not on—the public road. The area had flattened out; the tall cactus and yuccas were gone for a while. It was almost like traversing a vast prairie.

They by-passed the rough settlement of Shakespeare, which was a mining town and a brief stop on the Butterfield and Garret stage lines. The quiet couple weaved through the Pyramid Mountains. They came to areas where no trees or bushes grew, where the mountains and hills were a great distance away, where the ground was sandy and dry. They crossed several playas where the desert terrain sent forth the mirage of water, of beautiful lakes and rivers which weren't really there, unmerciful illusions which played havoc with heat dazed senses. Occasionally clumps of grass were seen, but nothing more. It was a barren location, one which put them in the open for a long stretch.

Carrie Sue wondered if this area wasn't hotter and dryer than Arizona had been. She didn't like this valley, this lack of cover from the heat and from human perils. There was no place to hide, no cover for shade. T.J. told her they were about seventy miles west of Deming, and she eagerly looked forward to reaching that area.

They did very little talking because they needed to stay alert in the almost mesmerizing heat and glare of the blazing sun, and talking also dried their throats even more than the arid climate. Overhead were wispy clouds on a pale blue sky which offered no shade beneath their skimpy sizes, a trick often used by travelers in the open. Neither cared for this hazardous stretch of their journey which made them easy targets for attackers and the weather. Yet, it had to be covered.

Suddenly, a tree-lined dry wash seemed to spring miraculously from the barren earth to entice them toward it. Nearby was an abandoned shack and well. They halted to water the horses, refill their canteens, and refresh themselves. They only rested there for a short while because T.J. warned that other travelers could come along at any time.

Soon, they continued their ride, but the demands eased up for a while as small trees and bushy scrubs again dotted seemingly endless grasslands. Yet, the ground was still very dry, and Carrie Sue realized how hardy the plants must be to survive under such harsh conditions. She was amazed by the way the bushes and clumps of grass made the deserty region look cool and green, almost inviting!

At last they halted, forty miles from their secluded haven in the cool Chiricahua Mountains of Arizona. The heat and terrain had been responsible for their slow progress today. The sun was setting and the western horizon was ablaze with shades of rich colors: reds, pinks, oranges, golds, and violets on an ever darkening blue backdrop.

T.J. chose a scrub-lined arroyo which put them out of sight of any late passerby. They unsaddled and tended the loyal horses first, then made camp. He warned against a fire, as smoke would give away their location and presence. He handed her weather-heated strips of peccary meat and a plate of beans, to be washed down with water as whiskey only made one more thirsty and sweaty in such heat.

The couple was tired from their demanding ride, so they claimed their bedrolls quickly, side by side. Neither mentioned lovemaking, as both knew it was impossible at this spot. It was even too hot to cuddle during sleep, but they did kiss good-night several times.

*

The ride was much the same the following day with landscape varying back and forth as with yesterday. It was hot on this fourth day of June in the year of eighteen-seventy-six. They were forty-five miles from Deming, where T.J. planned to make a stop for supplies.

Carrie Sue realized that the Tucson school was to have reopened for classes tomorrow. She wondered what Mrs. Thayer and Maria were doing and thinking. She wondered what the town residents, especially those who had met her on the streets and in church, thought about Miss Carolyn Starns turning out to be the notorious Texas Flame, a thought she did not find the least bit humorous. She wondered if Martin Ferris's body had been found, or if friends were searching for the mysteriously missing rancher at this moment.

The fiery redhead tried not to think about eager posses and greedy bounty hunters tracking her. She tried not to think about Darby's perils. She hoped he was resting in the Guadalupe Mountains which straddled the New Mexico-Texas border. She also tried not to let tormenting doubts about her lover gallop into her sluggish mind, but she couldn't master that runaway topic.

As she traveled near T.J. Rogue, she was plagued by doubts, fears, and worries. She wished she could halt such feelings, but she had learned to survive by her instincts, instincts which warned that he was trouble. She had just spent days making love to him and talking with him; yet, she distrusted the legendary Rogue! Loving T.J. was easy, irresistible, but believing him was difficult. Maybe that was the core of her problem; she was too emotionally involved with this peak of prowess to judge him accurately.

The desperado reflected on the *evidence* against him. Why had a loner taken to a proper lady, a staid schoolmarm, a passing stranger in a relay station? Even if he was attracted to her, men like him would have avoided her or believed her out of his reach. Yet, he had continued coming around her even before she appeared receptive to his pull. Perhaps it had been her connection to Martin Ferris which had enticed him to keep company with her; perhaps he had wanted to aggravate his past foe and provoke Martin into a battle. Later, he had been waiting for Curly James to arrive, and had seen them talking. Somehow, T.J. had always been around—as with the stage holdup and the attack during their picnic—always been there when she needed help, as if he had advance notice of trouble in the wind. Had those numerous incidents been coincidental or created by his design?

Then, he had just happened to be in Sheriff Ben Myers's office when her first poster arrived! He had just happened to be in her room to rescue her from that other sheriff. His questions in camp and on the trail could be normal or sly ones. Yet, he was asking plenty about Darby and his men, particularly about their skills and weapons. He had said it was information needed in case he had to defend and rescue her from that gang. Yes, he always had logical explanations!

Lately he had pressed her about her actions with the gang, wanting to know exactly where she had gone and what she had done over the years. He had wanted to know if she had spent most of her time in the gang's camp and if she had taken care of the men by cooking and cleaning and washing for them. He had seemed pleased when she had told him she had rarely been involved in the heart of crimes, and she didn't tend to the men's chores, only to Darby's.

The inquisitive male had wanted to know why no one had realized the Texas Flame was Darby Stover's fiery-haired sister and gotten her description out sooner. She knew she had explained that before, but she did so again. She also told him that the few men who had seen and met her face-to-face were outlaws who wouldn't or couldn't release information on her without incriminating themselves.

Since that night in the colossal cave and later in their romantic hideaway, T.J. had gone from refusing to ask any personal and probing questions to pouring them from his loosened lips! What worried her now was his main topic always seemed to be Darby Stover and his gang! And, there was the curious matter of what was inside his saddle-bags.

On the other hand, she knew Martin Ferris had been behind that picnic attack. She knew from Martin that her poster had arrived in Tucson on Thursday, but after her morning departure. Had there been another one in the early mail as T.J. claimed, the one he had seen and stolen? Did he make it a practice of opening others' mail? Could it be true, as he claimed, that fate had guided his hand to that letter? Why two posters to Ben Myers, if that was where T.J. had gotten his copy? Who had released her new description: Quade or his father? Or T.J. to force her onto the trail with him? Had it been in his possession all along, with him waiting for the perfect moment to use it? Had someone tipped him off by telegraph, ordering him to speed up his ruse? Had he left during the night while they were at the cave? Where had he gone that day in the Chiricahua Mountains?

There were too many unanswered questions about her lover, too many *coincidences* and pat explanations. If only she dared to demand answers, but that would alert him to her lingering mistrust. If T.J. Rogue was a threat to her and Darby, she was no match for his prowess at this moment. It was a quandary which only time and events could settle for her. Was it, she asked herself, wise to let T.J. keep forging a stronger bond between them, uncontrollably or intentionally on his part? She would make her final decision about her lover at El Paso. Merciful Heavens, she wished she could trust him completely, but she was afraid she couldn't. Until she was certain of him, she couldn't lead him to her brother. . . .

*

They neared Deming at dusk. T.J. showed her an excellent place to hide while he went into town for supplies.

"It's too risky," she protested his decision.

"I know a man here that I can trust. I'll get supplies from him. We have to eat, woman. And I'd like to get some news. We've been out of contact for days. I want to see if your posters are everywhere and if I'm a wanted man. I have a gut feeling that Shibell didn't let it be known you slipped through his hands and I got the drop on him. He's a proud and stubborn lawman. He'll want to correct his mistake without anybody learning about it. Trust me; I know what I'm doing."

"I'll go with you," she announced.

"You can't; that's definitely too risky. If I get chased, I can flee better alone. I'll work my way back to you after I lose them."

"If you aren't back by morning, I'm coming after you, Rogue."

He grinned at her defiant expression and warning. "I will be."

Carrie Sue and her pinto stayed hidden in the trees while she watched her lover ride off again. She was tempted to follow him, but knew he would catch her and it would cause trouble between them. She glanced at the possessions left behind. No saddlebag was among them. If they were careful, they had enough supplies to get them to Mesilla where he had another friend who had a place they could use. Without a doubt, he had another reason for going into town!

She withdrew the map from her pocket and studied it. She read the names and locations of T.J.'s friends, and wondered who—no what—they were. The one in Mesilla was Hank Peterson, but she'd never heard of him. Nor had she heard the name Mitchell Sterling who was in El Paso. One owned a cantina and the other owned a mercantile store. The map ended there because T.J. knew she was familiar with Texas. Whatever happened, she'd never look up strangers for help.

The flaming haired fugitive remained there, fretting, until T.J. returned. He grinned lightheartedly as he served her fried chicken, biscuits, and steamed vegetables which were rolled inside a clean cloth.

"Good news for me, woman," he said, "but I'm afraid you aren't as lucky. Your poster's up all right, but they don't know about me. Shibell kept his mouth shut just like I presumed."

She tried to pass him some food, but he shook his head and said he'd already eaten with his friend. She wished she could see one of those wanted posters and compare it to the one in his possession. If they weren't alike, that would answer one question for her! Somewhere and somehow, she had to get a look at one of those *real* posters. As she ate, she listened intently to his words.

T.J. sipped tart tequila as he reluctantly related his devious tale to cover his trip into town to use the telegraph. He hoped she would credit the unusual tone of his voice to the strong liquor, not as the effect of his guilt and deceit. Many times he had fooled people easily, but he found it hard to look at her while lying. "Matthew Grimes, that's my friend, saw a marshal today and he learned a lot which he passed along to me. You were reported last seen in Tucson, but nothing was mentioned about me escaping with you. The law assumes you left town Wednesday night before your posters reached Ben Myers on Thursday. They figure by now you're either heading north to safety or you're back in Texas with your brother. His last strike was two weeks ago near Fort Worth, and Monday after our picnic. That means he isn't laying low in Oklahoma. Either he has to be near Brownwood or the Pecos River, like you predicted. You must know Darby well."

Rapidly she figured the distance and time involved in Curly leaving her brother at the Guadalupe hideout on May eighteenth and Curly's arrival in Tucson on the twenty-third against Darby's being able to reach Fort Worth to commit a robbery by May twenty-second. Darby would have to have left the hideout immediately—after telling Curly he was staying there for a while—ridden hard and fast, known his target ahead of time, and carried off the deed in less than five days. She knew from experience that schedule was impossible, and Darby never struck a target without careful preparation and observation!

Who, she mused worriedly, was lying? T.J. to trick her, or the law? If it was the law, was the reported charge a mistake or a sly trick to lure her there for capture? If it was T.J., did her lover expect her to panic and refute the information, then rashly disclose the whereabouts of Darby's location? It could be that another gang was impersonating them; that happened sometimes with them and with other well-known bands!

"What's wrong, Carrie Sue?" he questioned her moody silence. Excluding his remorse over his ruse, he felt wonderful; the Rangers had withdrawn her posters as requested, claiming it was a sketch of the wrong woman. That compliance should reduce her peril during his case. He yearned to tell her she was safe for a while, but he couldn't without exposing himself and his mission.

The keen-witted outlaw realized her lover wasn't fusing his gaze to hers as he spoke, and his voice was strange despite the scratchy tequila. He seemed an odd mixture of joy and tension. He seemed alert and wary, a little too edgy for an unwanted man. "What did Darby hit?" she asked, trying to look and sound sad at his so-called news.

He answered honestly, "A Union Express office. Got away with a big haul of greenbacks. Maybe he's planning on trading them for gold like the President promised. Paper is easier to carry off than heavy gold."

She frowned, not at his unamusing assumption, but at his or someone's chosen target. Unless Darby had changed his mind since they parted, her brother never struck at Union Express, which was too heavily guarded. Darby Stover wasn't one to get desperate enough to be reckless! She noticed how many times her lover unconsciously wet his lips and dried his sweaty palms on the knees of his jeans, and she observed how the pulse point in his throat exposed his rapid heartbeat. These, combined with his odd anxiety, unnatural tone of voice, and curious expression, were signs of dishonesty that any astute and intelligent person could read, as Kale had taught her. Anguish seized her, but she concealed the reason. "I wonder if he knows about my trouble. If he's working near a big town, then I would imagine so. That also puts him nearer Brownwood than West Texas. Still, we should check there first as we pass by."

He sensed that something was wrong, but he couldn't surmise what. To draw her out, he said, "Once we reach Texas, we'll have to be more careful than ever. It's about seven to ten days from the border to Commanche. You still determined to see your brother?"

Carrie Sue realized another peril. What if they—the law or her beguiling lover—used her reported capture to lure Darby into a trap? If her brother didn't know where she was, he might fall for such a clever ruse. She nodded and replied, "I have to. There's no way I can reach him to let him know I'm all right and what my plans are. I want to convince him to join me; that has to be done in person."

"You think he'll listen?" T.J. probed.

She sighed heavily and shrugged. "He'll listen, but I can't decide what he'll do afterwards. Darby thinks he's trapped in this miserable life; Quade saw to that with his action near Laredo. And he knows how many times I've tried to go straight and my description wasn't even out. I'm not sure I can persuade him we'll be safe anywhere. But I'm going to try my hardest. I don't want my brother killed or hanged or jailed, T.J.; he made a mistake which carried him away like a flood. He kept getting pulled down by currents he couldn't fight. It isn't fair! It's all Quade's fault. If you don't kill him, I will. That bastard! He's going free while his victims are on the run!"

"Don't worry this pretty head about Harding; I'll take care of him. All you have to think about is getting to Darby, talking to him, and escaping before the law closes in on you two. I'll help, Carrie Sue."

She looked at him and smiled faintly. If he loved her, why wasn't he insisting she leave the hazardous West immediately? He was tough and strong, so why wasn't he binding her and dragging her far away? He was smart and careful, so why wasn't he trying to convince her that searching for Darby Stover was too perilous? He wasn't a wanted man and didn't plan to become one, so why wasn't he more worried about the enormous price on her head and the countless men who were pursuing her at this very time? His words and actions didn't make sense!

Yes, her warring mind argued, it did make sense if he was after Darby Stover! In light of his many contradictions and curious behavior, it certainly seemed that way to her, much as she hated to accept that grim fact. The questions were: who did he keep contacting, and why did he want her brother so badly, and when would he betray her?

Not wanting her to watch him defeat her brother, T.J. suggested desperately, "Since I'm safe for now, Carrie Sue, why don't you conceal yourself and let me take a message to Darby? You can use one of your old hideouts and tell me how to locate him. If you put something in your letter that only you and Darby know, that'll convince him I came from you. I can tell him it was too dangerous for you to travel and I can bring him back to where you're camped. You know, with him in the open again, the law and bounty hunters are going to be everywhere. Please let me go after him alone while you stay safe," he urged.

"Even with a lock of my hair and all our family secrets written in a note, Darby Stover wouldn't believe you. He'd think those things were tortured out of me. He knows I would never, under any circumstances, reveal his location. He'd probably kill you!"

"It was worth a try, Red; I don't want to see you harmed."

She smiled, wanting to believe that last statement. Maybe it was true; maybe he had fallen enough in love with her to forget about capturing her; maybe all he wanted now was the Stover Gang. But didn't he realize she could not betray her brother, even for him? And if he loved her and wanted her afterwards, didn't he realize that could never happen if he was responsible for Darby's capture and death? How could she ever surrender her heart and body to the man with her brother's blood on his hands? She couldn't.

Carrie Sue comprehended his worry over her, and that teased warmly at her heart. She would let T.J. Rogue use his prowess and wits to get her to El Paso safely, then she would take off on her own. She could easily find Darby's hideout from there. If her lover tried to stop her from leaving him . . .

"Quit frowning, love; everything will be fine soon," he murmured tenderly and stroked her lined forehead.

She focused misty eyes on him. "I'm not sure, T.J.; I have this terrible feeling something is going wrong somewhere."

"What, love?" he asked. "I'll protect you with my own life. No one is going to harm you again. Once this is over," he paused a moment before continuing, "you'll be safe and happy forever. I swear."

Tears, which were unlike her, gathered in her eyes as she thanked him. He had called her "love" twice. Why? And why did it seem as if he was being totally honest at this moment? If he knew how much his betrayal would hurt her, and the sharp-witted male had to know, why would he continue his ruse? Why was he so resolved to capture her brother? And, surely he was. For a man to have such consuming bitterness and determination and to be willing to sacrifice anything for a particular victory, there had to be a good reason. What was T.J.'s?

Merciful Heavens, if only she could demand the truth! If she did, he would either lie or he would end his cruel ruse or he would jail her and continue his trek after Darby Stover. No, she couldn't let him know she was on to him! She had to reach her brother first and get him far away from peril. Then, she would seek the truth about her devilish Rogue . . .

Chapter

17

Early the next morning, almost before dawn, they broke camp and headed for Mesilla and another of T.J. Rogue's friends.

Before pulling out, T.J. had questioned her silence. She had told him she was worried about Darby being on the move again. If he was captured or slain before she could reach him, her brother wouldn't stand a chance of having a new beginning, and he deserved one. She told T.J. she had a horrible feeling that she had seen her brother alive for the last time, that some unknown threat was stalking him.

T.J. had replied, "A man who lives by his guns expects to die by them. You aren't responsible for his fate, Carrie Sue, and you can't halt it. Whatever happens, I'll take care of you."

As they traveled, she considered her dilemma for the seemingly hundredth time. How could she love a man she distrusted? Yet, she knew it was far more than physical attraction for him, and she suspected it was the same for T.J. Rogue. The only thing she didn't doubt was the fact they were in love and wanted to be together for keeps!

T.J.'s grudge against Darby had to be vitally important to him. What, she pondered, could it be? Had one of their victims been his father or brother? No, one was killed long ago by Apaches and the other had died at the hands of Mexican bandits. Or so her lover had claimed. What if the Stover Gang had killed his brother? What if they had killed his best friend? For a man with so few friends, each one would be precious to him, worth dying for while seeking revenge.

Yes, she concluded, T.J.'s motive had to be personal revenge. That would be the only thing important enough to sacrifice their new and unexpected love and to risk his life and hers. Who was the victim?

Maybe T.J. had had other family, members he hadn't mentioned to her, members left behind on that ill-fated journey into the Apaches' hands. Perhaps a baby brother or sister, she mused. The possibilities were endless and frustrating. For all she knew, one of the men riding with Darby could be T.J.'s long-lost brother who'd gone bad. The ages of most would figure out correctly, and her lover was mighty interested in each one. No, she protested, that was too far-fetched.

But something else wasn't. If another gang was impersonating them, why couldn't another gang have killed this person whom her lover wanted to avenge? What if Darby and the others were innocent of T.J.'s mental charges? What if her love was after the wrong killer?

Darby Stover and T.J. Rogue were the only people in the world that she loved with all her heart and soul. If it came to a choice between the two men, and Darby's life was at stake, she would have to take her brother's side. Merciful Heavens, what would she do if it came to a shoot-out between them? If Darby had to die because of his wicked deeds, she prayed that it wouldn't be at her love's hands.

Those agonizing thoughts finished making her decision. Trust him or not, there was no way she could lead T.J. to Darby's hideout. The two special men in her life must never meet and battle. Besides, she couldn't endanger T.J.'s life by delivering him into the hands of his unsuspecting enemies, skilled gunmen who made the odds seven-to-one against him! And, since he wasn't a wanted man, she couldn't be the one to ensnare her love in a life of crime. Guilty or not of her mental accusations, she had to part ways with T.J. Rogue in El Paso.

After leaving the Deming area, the landscape was back to dry and sandy terrain which was pancake flat. On occasion it drifted into scrubby spots that abounded in snakeweed, a bushy plant which appeared globular in shape and gave off stinky black smoke when burned. The "matchweed" was known to be poisonous to some stock, but fortunately its foul taste kept them away from it. Most were densely crowded into scattered patches and were covered in clusters of yellow flowers, adding green and yellow coloring to the pale brown earth.

Suddenly an exquisite section filled their vision, and she was amazed anew at how rapidly and unexpectedly the landscape could alter. All around them thousands of yuccas in full bloom were sighted and enjoyed. The patches were thick and beautiful, appearing like countless white torches held skyward by skinny green hands. Carrie Sue twisted in her saddle to take in the view from all directions.

Amongst the cloud white abundance were mesquites and cacti. Along the dry washes they passed, blue paloverde edged the rims. She wondered why the tree-like bush was called blue, when it was covered in masses of yellow blossoms! In locations where there were plenty of them, it looked as if the desert washes were lined with a golden trail. She knew that paloverde was Spanish for "green stick" and referred to the bark color. This display of life and beauty distracted her for a time from her troubles. She cleared her mind and let Mother Nature entertain and relax her.

They were less than forty miles from Las Cruces, a large town adjoining the smaller one of Mesilla. Northward, she could make out the Robledo Mountain in a whitish blue haze which made it appear a ghostly outline against the distant horizon. Southward were the Potrillo Mountains. Eastward—their direction—were the Organ Mountains, before which was spread Las Cruces in a tranquil valley.

T.J. remained on alert, knowing there would be bounty hunters and lawmen who hadn't gotten the word about withdrawing her posters from circulation. And, there would be some men who wouldn't believe the posters had been a mistake. He had to be careful. Wanting to reach Mesilla with its protective cover by nightfall, he urged them onward at an increased pace which wasn't too demanding on the horses.

At their mid-way break, they finished off the chicken and biscuits which had been left over from last night. They rested quietly for thirty minutes, then hit the trail once more.

*

Carrie Sue didn't realize the land wasn't flat ahead until they reached the edge of a downward slope which entered the valley where their destination was located. She reined up and looked at the sight of Las Cruces snuggled at the base of the large mountains. "This is a perfect place to build a house," she remarked to her companion.

T.J. lifted himself in his stirrups and looked around, smiling and agreeing, "Yep, this is some pretty view, woman." He glanced at her and asked, "How does a bed sound for tonight? We're almost there."

"Sounds wonderful, partner. That and hot food and a cool bath. Lead on, my faithful Apache scout," she jested.

They crossed a narrow section of the Rio Grande, which miles ahead formed the boundary between Texas and Mexico, and bore south. The area was shrouded in shadows by the time they reached the outskirts of Mesilla. Beneath a half moon, T.J. guided her to his friend's house.

For a brief moment as they dismounted, Carrie Sue was consumed with panic and wondered if his betrayal would come here, tonight. No, he needed her to lead him to Darby.

The trees were larger in this area of adobe homes and Spanish structures. As he put their horses into a small corral, fed and watered them, T.J. related how La Mesilla had started as a Mexican civil colony in eighteen-fifty with around eight hundred Hispanos. He told her that one of the buildings had housed the territorial capitol of the Confederacy. Not too far from his friend's house was a plaza, to its right was his friend's saloon, near the La Posta.

He led her inside the Mexican-style house and put her things down. "You rest while I go tell Hank we're here. I'll bring some food back and help you prepare a bath. Stay inside and out of sight, woman; we don't know what's waiting out there," he cautioned.

Carrie Sue nodded wearily, took a seat, and removed her boots. She flung her hat into another chair and leaned back on the comfortable couch. "Take too long, partner, and I'll be asleep," she murmured. She watched T.J. flash her a breathtaking smile, toss his saddlebags over his shoulder, and depart. Without delay or hesitation, she grabbed a colorful poncho from a chair and wiggled it over her head, settling the blanketlike cloak over her feminine body to conceal it and her weapons. She seized a sombrero from a wall hook and stuffed her braid beneath its tall crown. She slipped out the back way to follow him. She peered around the house and edged toward the front.

Carrie Sue looked in both directions and located her lover's retreating back as he headed down a narrow street. She waited until he rounded the corner and, sighting no one, she hurried that way. She was careful not to make any noise, and her bare feet aided her.

She saw him enter a fancy cantina on the next street near a long, cream-colored building which was marked "La Posta." So far, he had told the truth. She heard the music and laughter and voices from her concealed position, but she couldn't see inside the swinging doors. She had to get closer! Cautiously she crept toward her destination.

When two men came outside, she flattened herself against the wall behind her, and her heart pounded in alarm. Fortunately they headed in the other direction and vanished soon. She made it to the side of Hank's place and peered through a window which looked dirty enough to prevent anyone from sighting her face. It was a large room with wooden tables and chairs, much like most saloons. There was a lengthy bar at the other side, and a hazy glow filled the room from lantern and cigar smoke. Men were drinking, playing cards, and chatting. Mexican girls waited upon the customers, smiling and teasing them. Then, she spotted her lover; he was speaking with a man shorter than he was, an American in a Mexican settlement. . . .

The redhead studied the stranger. He was dressed in a white shirt, a black and gray striped vest, and dark trousers. She supposed he looked authentic for a gambler and saloon owner. He wasn't wearing a visible weapon, but most men like him carried smaller ones concealed. His graying hair had once been blond and his face was tanned from hours beneath the sun. Odd, she mused, for a business man who kept late hours and spent so much time inside during the day? Nothing really to go on, she concluded.

She watched them head into a back room and close the door. She worked her way around the building, but the only window was too high for observation or eavesdropping. She frowned, wondering what was being said inside the room she was leaning against.

A door opened nearby and a woman walked outside. She glanced in Carrie Sue's direction and asked in Spanish, "What do you want there?"

The daring fugitive ignored her and quickly left the scene before the woman summoned her boss and she was caught red-handed. She hurried back to Hank's house and replaced the borrowed items. Removing her gunbelt and laying it aside, she half-reclined on the couch.

In twenty minutes, T.J. was back, carrying a meal of floured tortillas, enchiladas oozing with sauce, and other Mexican dishes. He smiled as he placed the food on the table. "Ready?" he hinted.

Carrie Sue pretended to drag herself wearily from the couch. "Did you find him?" she asked as she sat down at the table.

"Yep, he'll be working a few more hours. You'll have to meet him in the morning, my exhausted vixen. After we eat, you're getting a bath and turning in." He dropped his fork and leaned to recover it, taking a look at her feet. As suspected, they were dirty. He grinned, aware she was the one sighted by one of Hank's woman. He also realized that either his guard was down too low or she possessed more skills than previously believed, as he hadn't seen or heard her!

As if reading his thoughts, she remarked, "I checked on Charlie and Nighthawk. We pushed them hard these past few days. I think I got a stone bruise; I should have put on my boots."

"It'll feel better after you soak it a while. Be glad it isn't a cactus spine; they're hell to remove. How's the food?"

"Delicious, Mr. Rogue, even better than what we had in Tucson. Or I'm twice as hungry." She laughed and took a few bites before asking, "What did your friend say about you bringing me here?"

"I trust Hank Peterson. He understands your problem. I told him you're going straight, so he's willing to help by hiding us tonight."

"Why?" she probed, observing him more closely than he realized.

"Why what?" he asked, looking baffled.

She clarified, "Why is he willing to aid a criminal and endanger himself? And why do you two trust each other so much? I'm valuable property, remember?"

Enlightenment brightened his smokey gray eyes. "We've worked together several times in the past. He's one of my best friends, and he feels the same about me. We've saved each other's lives a few times, so we're close and tight. He knows I wouldn't be taking this risk unless I trusted you and believed you, and had good reason."

"Which is?" she prompted before sliding a forkful of enchilada into her mouth and licking the mischievous sauce from her lips.

He stopped eating to gaze at her across the table. "Don't you know the reason by now, Carrie Sue?" he asked in a quiet tone. "Isn't it the same reason you let me tag along and have allowed me to stay?"

"If that's a sly way of asking me how I feel about you, Mr. Rogue, I think I've pretty well exposed myself in that area. Like it is with you and Hank, I think we're tight and close. You did say your friend has to work late, didn't you?" she hinted audaciously.

Passion darkened his eyes and his respiration altered as his heart speeded up with anticipation. "Yep, lucky for us," he murmured.

They finished their meal quickly, each continually glancing at the other and smiling in suspense and eagerness. T.J. fetched a metal tub and filled it with tepid well water while she cleared the table. As she bathed inside, T.J. stood at the well in the moonlight to scrub and rinse himself. When he went inside, she was waiting for him in the bed which he had pointed out to her. He approached it, and she lifted her arms in summons.

T.J. released his blanket and it dropped to the floor. He joined her on the bed and gathered her into his arms. "Lordy, this feels good."

"The comfortable bed or me?" she teased.

"Both, but you best of all," he murmured, closing his mouth over hers. His hands wandered over her body, caressing here and fondling there. He was glad he had asked Hank to give them some time alone tonight, and that his friend had understood their need for privacy. Yet, Hank Peterson was worried about the relationship between them and how it might affect T.J.'s judgment and mission. T.J. was too, but it couldn't be helped. He loved this woman and needed her. He thought she had come to trust him almost fully, but evidently he was wrong. Her following him tonight proved she possessed lingering doubts, and it had been her in Hank's poncho and sombrero.

T.J. couldn't blame her for being cautious, even suspicious of him. After all she was a famous outlaw with a large price on her head and she was guiding him to one of the most notorious bands in the West, which was led by her brother. Yet, she needed him for protection and aid, so she wouldn't pull any tricks any time soon. Perhaps tonight was one last test to make certain of his loyalty, and he had passed.

Carrie Sue's fingers drifted over her lover's back and shoulders. She liked the smooth texture of his flesh and the hardness of the muscles beneath the bronzed covering. She was stimulated by the contact of their bodies and their mouths. She was painfully aware this could be the last time she ever made love to T.J. Rogue, as El Paso was their next stop. She clung to him and kissed him urgently, feverishly.

T.J. trailed his lips over her face, returning time and time again to her insistent mouth. He tried not to nuzzle her face and throat too roughly as he hadn't shaven in his rush to fuse their bodies into one wild and blissful union. His mouth roamed down her chest and his hand traveled down her sleek side. Gently he teethed the rosy brown buds on her breasts, and deftly his fingers tantalized her to squirming desire.

Carrie Sue closed her eyes as she absorbed these rapturous memories which might have to last a lifetime. Her fingertips traced little patterns on his shoulders as she mentally marked the splendid territory as her own private possession. She felt as if she were drifting on a cloud and being pleasured to the fullest degree by the only man she had ever and would ever love.

T.J. adored this woman, this gentle creature who filled his life with joy, this wild vixen who challenged him to risk all to have her, this prized lover who made his body ache with hunger and his heart sing with happiness. Carrie Sue Stover was one helluva woman! She was his woman, and he would do whatever necessary to keep her safe and with him.

As they rested in the golden afterglow of lovemaking, Carrie Sue suspected that her lover knew about her mischief, so she slyly murmured, "I didn't tell you the truth earlier. I followed you to the saloon. I wanted to see who you were meeting. I'm sorry."

T.J. hugged her tightly as he revealed, "I know what you did, and I understand. You can't be too careful, love, even with me. Luz, that's Hank's woman, told us she saw someone outside wearing Hank's poncho and sombrero. You see, my sneaky redhead, that poncho is a special design, a one-of-a-kind, which Luz had made for him."

Carrie Sue giggled when T.J.'s fingers played over her ribcage. "I never thought of that angle. Snared by a lover's gift."

"That was a stupid thing to do, woman," he chided softly. "You could have been seen and captured."

"I'll be more careful in the future, and more trusting."

"Good. Now, we need to get cleaned up and turn in. Hank insists you use his bedroom. He and I will bunk down in the other room."

Carrie Sue protested that hospitality, but T.J. held firm. They rinsed off, emptied the tub water, cleared away their things, and she went to bed in the back room with the door closed.

*

Hank and T.J. stood near the corral the next morning and talked. The graying blond asked, "How are you planning to handle this case once you locate them? You can't take on seven men alone, and you know she's going to kick up a ruckus when she realizes she's been duped."

T.J. glanced at the ex-Ranger with whom he had worked many times, a good friend whom he trusted fully, a man who still served as a contact for Rangers on the trail. "I just want to discover their hideout. Then, I'll alert the Rangers and let them take care of the problem. I'm going to try my damnedest to keep from being the one to take out her brother. She'd never forgive me if I killed Darby."

"What about her, Thad? You know you can't get a pardon for her. I gave you the answer to that question last night. The President understands your feelings, but she's an outlaw, has been for seven years. Even if she helped you capture her brother's gang, that wouldn't make up for all she's done. The law says she has to pay."

T.J. began to fidget; that wasn't the answer he had wanted and prayed for from his superiors. "I'll think of something, Hank. I can't let her go to prison or die. Lordy, man, I love her."

Hank Peterson's faded blue eyes settled on Thad Jamison's pained expression. "I never thought I'd hear such words from those lips. You've really settled down over the past two years and I'm proud of you. I just hate it that she's on the most wanted list, and that she's as guilty of breaking the law as a rustler caught with a hot branding iron in his hand. If you don't cool your head and heart, my friend, you're in for one tough time when you have to arrest her."

"I can't do that, Hank," T.J. revealed sadly, stubbornly.

"You'll have to, Thad; this is your case, by your choice and insistence. You can't back away now; it's too late. You're too close to her and she's the only one who can end this madness by that gang. Like I told you last night, their last few crimes have been vicious."

"From the reports I've been getting along the trail, it doesn't sound like the same man she describes as Darby Stover. I wonder . . ."

Hank reasoned with a clear head and keen wit, "What do you expect from her? She's his devoted sister. Rest assured, it is the real Stover Gang on the rampage again.

They're smart and fast and real mean, Thad. The only way we're going to stop them any time soon is through her. You have to do this, for justice and yourself."

T.J. caught the implied hint. "I haven't forgotten what they did to Arabella and Marie, nor to our friend on that stage. I'll stop them, but I won't let her get harmed."

"There's no way you can prevent that from happening, Thad."

"There has to be a way, some legal crack she can wiggle through."

Hank shook his head. "I've asked a lawyer friend of mine to look for it, but he doesn't think one exists either, not for the Texas Flame. I'll let you know what he uncovers. Keep me alerted by telegraph."

"Don't forget to send those coded messages this morning after we leave. I'll pick up the answers in El Paso. That'll probably be my last contact for a while. I don't want her getting suspicious of me again. I just earned her trust, though Lord knows I don't deserve it."

"Don't be hard on yourself, Thad; you didn't expect to fall in love with her. By the time you were on to her, it was too late. It took some doing and lots of telegrams to get those posters on her recalled. You can bet your boots there are still some around or people who haven't gotten the news, so be careful." Hank passed along other facts, "Quade Harding and his father were furious about it. We've tried to quiet them down, but they suspected something is up. We told Quade that poster he released wasn't the Texas Flame and he could get an innocent woman killed. He was ordered to stop interfering in our affairs. Harding claimed he put out that recent sketch to protect Carrie Sue Stover, to get her taken alive and delivered to him so he can help clear her of the mixup. He says he knows she isn't the Flame, but others believe she is so she's in great peril. Of course, we don't buy that story; he's up to mischief. We told him his poster on Carrie Sue was illegal, so he agreed to pull it and cancel his reward on her. That'll help maintain our secrecy. The newspapers were forced to print retractions. I doubt you've seen the stories about her; the papers gobbled up news on that sketch and big reward. They're using that old picture again, which doesn't pose a threat to her or you. Dave's still working on the Harding case."

T.J.'s smokey gray eyes darkened with anger. "You know Harding's the one who forced her into a life of crime. Dave better get him."

Hank Peterson conceded, "What she and her brother did against the Hardings was justified, but their crimes since then aren't. Don't deny that truth to yourself."

"I don't, but it riles me how she got entrapped."

"I know, but they've become hardened criminals over the years."

"Not Carrie Sue. You'll see when you meet her."

"A person can't live that kind of life without being affected by it."

"She was affected, but not in a bad way. That's why she kept trying to escape that existence, but Harding wouldn't let her."

"We'll get Harding: don't worry."

"If you don't, I will, one way or another," he vowed coldly. "You did send that messenger to Mitch last night?"

"Yep. He'll be ready to play along with your deceit. We'd better get inside and get breakfast going. She should be awake by now. I'm eager to meet this woman who stole your heart."

*

Carrie Sue finished dressing in a clean blue shirt and jeans. She brushed her hair and let it hang free, knowing that style made her look innocent. She wanted to meet and impress Hank Peterson. She packed her things, made the bed, and left the room.

The two men were in the kitchen. She joined them, timidly smiling first at her lover, then at his friend. "Good morning, gentlemen. That was the best night's sleep I've had in days. Thanks for the loan of your bed, Mr. Peterson. I know that we're putting you in danger by accepting your many kindnesses; you're a good friend to T.J."

He looked her over and entreated, "Please, call me Hank. You ready for some coffee, bacon, eggs, and biscuits?"

"Sounds marvelous. Thank you," she replied, licking her lips.

Hank studied the ravishing beauty whose shapely figure was displayed by her snug garments. Those large periwinkle eyes stunned him with their color and expression. She looked as pure as a newborn babe. Her hair was like a golden red halo about a glowing face which could halt a runaway train on its tracks. Her skin was downy soft and unmarred. Her voice was cultured and musically appealing. She had real breeding and good manners. She was exquisite and delightful, not what he had imagined.

Carrie Sue realized the man was impressed with her, and surprised to see she wasn't some terrible monster. She wanted those thoughts and feelings to continue. She was extra careful with her words, looks, and behavior. She offered politely, "I can prepare breakfast while you two have your coffee and talk over old times."

T.J. said, "We've already talked for an hour and had two cups of coffee while you were snoozing, woman. The biscuits and bacon's about done. Scrambled eggs all right with you?"

"If you cook them good and done," she replied with a bright smile.

"Good and done it is. The dishes are there," he remarked when she looked around for them to set the table.

"Sometimes I think you read my mind, T.J. Hank, you should tell him how dangerous it is to do that with a woman," she teased.

Hank laughed and agreed, "She's right; it gets you into trouble."

As they ate, Carrie Sue remarked, "T.J. told me you two have worked and traveled together many times."

"Yep," he responded like her lover would. "We've pushed cattle, ridden a dusty trail, guarded strongboxes, branded stock, got stages in on time, hauled freight, and done a passel of odd jobs together over the years. I got too old and retired here with my cantina. Ever so often, . . . T.J. stops by to see me. I miss those old days, but I like being settled down when winter and bad weather comes around."

Carrie Sue caught his hesitation over her lover's name and wondered what it meant, if anything. She smiled warmly and said, "I know what you mean. Trail life can be rough, unbearable at times. Is there anything you want to ask me while I'm here?"

"Nope. The less I know about you, the better for all of us."

"Thank you, Hank. I just didn't want you thinking so badly of me, or of T.J. for helping me. Sometimes people aren't as bad as their reputations make out."

"Now that I've met the beautiful woman he described last night, I believe it." He saw her blush. He was astonished, moved. "Of course, from knowing T.J. Rogue, I realize reputations get colored."

The redhead didn't know why or how she had blushed, but she was glad, as it had a nice affect on Hank Peterson. "I'm lucky T.J. came along when he did. He's saved my hide several times. He's a very special man, Hank, not many would do what he's doing for me."

T.J. teased, "Don't go telling my secrets to Hank. He thinks I'm a tough and cold son-of-a-bitch. You'll spoil my image, woman."

She laughed merrily and added, "You're special too, Hank, but you'd have to be to be his friend. I know how tempting it must be to have a ten thousand dollar prize sitting across the table from you and you can't collect on it."

"It isn't tempting at all, Carrie Sue. A man would have to be a fool to sell out a woman like you. I think T.J.'s right to help you; I just hope he doesn't get into any trouble being so kind and reckless."

"I promise to do my best to protect him," she vowed.

They finished off the food and cleared the table.

T.J. looked at Hank. "I hate to say it, old friend, but we have to get moving. I'd like to make El Paso by nightfall."

Hank shook Carrie Sue's hand and said, "It was good meeting you. I hope everything works out just fine. T.J., you let me hear from you."

"I will, Hank," the ebon-haired man replied, affectionately slapping his friend on the back and giving him a bearhug.

The lovely fugitive observed the scene with interest. It was clear their friendship was not a pretense, and that warmed and relaxed her.

As they mounted, Hank said, "You two be careful."

T.J. and Carrie Sue replied simultaneously, "We will."

Hank scratched his head as the couple waved and rode off, skirting the town. Nope, he concluded, the girl was nothing like her reputation. In fact, he couldn't believe she was an outlaw, and he'd met plenty. Now he understood how and why Thad Jamison was in love with her.

*

Shortly after dusk, Carrie Sue and T.J. entered El Paso at the base of the Franklin Mountains and situated on the Rio Grande River. Here, she realized, she could escape across the Mexican border if there was trouble. They worked their way to another friend's home: Mitchell Sterling, who owned a large mercantile store in town.

The man greeted them at the back door. T.J. grasped his hand and said, "Good to see you, Mitch. Thanks for the help. Hank said he'd send you a telegram to expect me and a guest."

The brown-haired man of about forty replied, "I got it this morning. I sent my wife and children to visit kin in the next town so we'd have privacy. If there's one thing I owe you, friend, it's plenty of favors. All you have to do is ask for one. I take it this is the lady who needs protection and privacy?" When Carrie Sue stepped forward, his eyes widened in exaggerated surprise. Then, he looked at his friend oddly.

T.J. smiled at him. "Yep, she's the one in the papers and on those wanted posters, but it's a mistake, Mitch. She isn't the Texas Flame. I got to know her in Tucson; we're good friends. When those posters came out, I helped her escape. I'm getting her to Ranger Headquarters in Waco so we can straighten out this crazy error. I knew I could trust you to help us and keep quiet. We have to be real careful until we clear up this mess. Her name's Carolyn Starns; she's a schoolmarm. Somebody mixed her up with Carrie Sue Stover after that holdup near Sherman. Probably because there aren't many flaming redheads around these parts and some people are eager to get their hands on that big reward. We'll talk more later. We're starved."

Mitchell Sterling shook hands with her and said, "Pleased to meet you, Miss Starns. You two come in. I held supper for you."

Carrie Sue loved the big house, but wished she didn't have to put this family man on the spot. She wondered what her lover had done for Mitchell Sterling to earn such respect and loyalty, and why her love would take unfair advantage of the man's generosity. Over dinner of a beef roast with fresh vegetables, she received her answer.

"I don't suppose T.J.'s told you what all he's done for me." When the redhead shook her head, Mitch filled her in after a genial smile. "About a year ago, I had some bullies giving me trouble at the store. The law couldn't catch 'em and stop 'em, but T.J. did. Those ruffians had me and my family terrorized until he came to town and took over. They cost me plenty of money, but T.J. here refused to take payment. Said he didn't like their kind and enjoyed sending 'em on their way."

After a few bites, Mitchell added, "But that wasn't the first time he saved my life. We met during the war and served together for a year. I'll admit I was pretty scared, but T.J. always looked out after me. He's a man who takes care of his friends."

"I'm glad to hear that, Mitch, since I'm a new one. I hope he can help me solve my problem as well as he solved yours," Carrie Sue said.

"If anybody can help you, it's T.J. Rogue," Mitchell asserted.

T.J. chuckled and pleaded, "Come on you two, stop praising me or my head will swell and my hat won't fit anymore."

They chatted lightly for a while longer, then cleared the table. They retired to the parlor and sat down. Mitchell served them an after dinner wine and they all relaxed as they sipped it.

"From experience, I know you like to keep your business private, T.J., so I won't ask anymore questions about her troubles. I'm sure you'll find a way to solve them." He turned to the topic to politics. "I've been hearing some interesting things about our commander during the war. I'm sure you remember President Grant since you saved his life once. Word is, he's eager to run for a third term, but his Republican friends can't get the nomination for him. The majority's afraid of this upsurge of Democratic strength and the third term issue."

"You can't blame them, Mitch. Grant's been surrounded by scandals for eight years. Guilty or not, soot around him has to blacken him. But he'd get my vote if he's listed again. He seems to be running the country as well as anyone else before him. I haven't forgotten him. He taught me plenty during the war. He was a damn good commander."

"Word is, if they get another candidate, they might lure those Liberals back into the Republican Party. Looks like it'll be that Hayes fellow from Ohio. He was a Union officer with a spotless record. He's been a congressman and the Governor of Ohio three times, so he knows plenty about politics and government. It doesn't hurt any that he's a champion of civil service reforms. I surely hope they choose him over that Senator Blaine who's been linked to one of those railroad scandals."

"Who do you think the Democrats will push?" T.J. asked, worried about his friend Grant's loss of power and distraction when he needed the President's help in the Stover matter.

After taking another sip of his wine, Mitchell surmised, "I think it'll be Samuel Tilden of New York. He's the Governor and doing a good job at it. Made lots of powerful friends with plenty of money."

"Never heard of him, but I miss lots of papers and news on the trail."

"You been near Pine Springs lately?" Mitch asked. T.J. shook his head.

Carrie Sue had sat quietly listening to the two men and observing them. Her ears perked up when Mitchell Sterling mentioned the area near the Guadalupe Mountains, her destination! Coincidence? she mused, then told herself that was possible. Curly James hadn't told T.J. anything before dying, and no one else knew where to look.

"That damn Salt War is boiling like a wild kettle again. We had trouble there in '63, then again in '67 and '68. Charles Howard and that fiery-tempered Italian Don Louis Cardis are at each other's throats again. And that Mexican Padre Borajo in San Elizarie isn't helping matters. It could get real dangerous at Salt Flats and here. Borajo is siding with Cardis and trying to stir up his people against Howard and the Americans. The Padre was ordered by the church back to the Mexican interior, but he refuses to go. I don't like the smell of the air, T.J. Both sides have been taking salt from those flats for years. I don't see why anybody has to go and claim them and try to charge everyone else for what's lying free on God's earth. Governor Hubbard is keeping a keen eye on the situation, but I think he's holding back too long. He needs to get soldiers or Rangers in here immediately to handle matters before there's killing. If you asked me, I think it's coming to a silly war over that white powder. You stay in touch with me, after you finish with the little lady here, in case I need your help protecting my property. Borajo is inciting his people against all Americans in this area; that worries me."

T.J. leaned forward and propped his elbows on his knees, clutching the glass between his hands. "Don't worry, Mitch; I'll let you know where I can be reached when I complete her job. What do you read on King Fisher? Is he still operating near Castroville and Eagle Pass?"

"He surely is, and I hope he stay there. Papers say a Ranger called Captain McNelly is pursuing him. If I were him, I'd be mighty careful. Reports say Fisher has one hundred outlaws terrorizing the countryside down there. Fisher boasts publicly he's seizing control of the entire area. I surely do hope he never takes a liking to El Paso."

T.J. had one answer he needed, where Captain McNelly was and how he was doing with his case. He knew from Hank Peterson that Rangers Jones and Steele were entangled by the range wars caused by the introduction of barbed wire in '74. With the inventions of barbwire, the well drill, and the windmill, ranchers were spreading across the previously unusable grasslands and fencing off rangelands and waterholes, which created a whole series of problems for the law. He needed to learn who was available to assist him when the time came for action against the Stover Gang. Later, he told himself. He teased ex-Ranger Sterling, "I believe the King loves Mexico and the border area too much to take on your town. I met him once. He's a real mean cuss who's provoked easily. I surely would like to avoid another run-in with him, especially with all his boys around. A gun can only hold so many bullets at a time."

Mitchell Sterling, who still lent the Rangers—especially his close friends like Thad —a hand when needed, poured himself and T.J. more wine. Carrie Sue politely refused another glass. "You heard any interesting news recently during your travels?" he questioned T.J.

The ebon-haired male leaned back in his chair and stretched out his legs. "I hear tell the train is extending its tracks this way soon. That should help your business. Makes goods easier and cheaper to get."

The man scowled. "Yes, but it lures train robbers into the area. If there's anything we don't need, it's more trouble over this way."

"What do you mean?" her dark-haired companion inquired.

Mitch began their ruse. "That Wes Harding's kicking up his heels all over, and the Stover Gang's raiding again." He glanced at the redhead and asked, "You mind if we talk about them, Miss Starns?"

Without flinching, she replied, "Certainly not. Since it involves me now, T.J. and I need to learn all we can about that gang."

"Maybe they'll catch the Texas Flame before you two reach Waco. That'll make it easier for you to clear yourself. They hit the Union Express Office in Fort Worth a few weeks back, a bank in Hillsboro on the twenty-fifth, and did some rustling near Eastland on the thirtieth. Then, last Saturday, they struck a stage near Big Spring. Since you weren't around and T.J. can vouch for your whereabouts, that should prove your innocence. Everybody knows he tells the truth, so they'll accept his word. We've been warned to keep our eyes and ears open because the law thinks they're heading toward El Paso. They're probably on their way to New Mexico or Arizona where there's plenty of gold and silver, if they don't ride for San Angelo and circle back toward Waco. The soldiers from Fort Davis are on the prowl after 'em. They're real mean cusses, T.J. I hope they get caught real soon. Been lots of killing on this spree, and lots of boasting like they want everybody to know they're the best outlaws in the state. Nearly every day the paper reports some new crime."

Mitch retrieved a small bundle of newspapers and handed them to T.J. "I kept them; so if you'd like to take them along and read them on the trail, you're welcome to them. You can't ever tell who you'll cross in the road, so you'd better keep up with where the trouble is. That story about you is in there, Miss Starns. It says you were hiding out in Tucson as a teacher. The law thinks a Martin Ferris helped you escape because he vanished at the same time. They think you two headed further west or northward; that's where they're searching." The ex-Ranger knew that story had been retracted or corrected, but that was one paper he hadn't included in the bundle to keep her in the dark. He also knew his friend would prevent her from seeing it anywhere. By the time they hooked up with the Stover Gang, if Darby knew about the weird incident, the bandit leader would hold Harding responsible.

T.J. sent her a keep-quiet look. "Good. That'll give us time to clear you and get the truth out." He rose and said, "I think my partner's exhausted, Mitch. Why don't you show her where to bed down for the night. I'll bring her things along."

Mitchell Sterling glanced at the beautiful redhead and said, "I hope we haven't talked your ears off, Miss Starns. Kind of rude of us to leave you out of the conversation."

Carrie Sue smiled genially and said, "I enjoyed listening to such intriguing subjects, Mitch. If you don't mind, I'd like to read those papers tomorrow and catch up on the news."

"Sure thing. I'll leave them in the parlor." He led her to a small room near the back of the house. "Will my daughter's room be all right?"

"Yes, thank you, Mitch. I'll see you in the morning." She smiled again and shook his extended hand.

After Mitchell returned to the parlor, T.J. sent her a rueful smile and said, "I'm sorry about what he said, but he believed our story."

"We're placing him in deep peril. That isn't fair or right, T.J., not even from a friend who owes you a mountainous favor."

"I know, woman, but we needed a safe place tonight and a chance to get supplies. Even if Mitch knew the truth, he would help. I just think it's best not to let too many people in on our secret. It makes things awkward for them."

"When the truth comes out, he'll know we deceived him, used him. Nothing is worse than to betray a loved one or a friend."

"If I ever see him again, I'll say you gave me the slip along the way. He believes you're Carolyn Starns and a terrible mistake's been made, so he'll think I believed you, too. Your life's at stake, woman; we have to fool Mitch and others. I don't like it, but it can't be helped."

She replied wearily, "I understand, T.J., but I hate doing this. Our being in his home can get him arrested as an accomplice. You'll have to tell him those other lies so he won't get into trouble later or feel betrayed by you."

T.J. said, "I will, honest, as soon as we reach a safe place where I can send him a telegram. Get some sleep. We'll rest here tomorrow and take off before dawn on Thursday. From here on, it'll be more dangerous for you than before."

He caressed her cheek. "We'll talk more in the morning. Afterwards, I want to do some scouting around, see what I can pick up about your brother. He may be nearer than we know. Try to think of any places around here where he might hide. We'll check them out when we leave day after tomorrow."

As T.J. walked down the hall, he was worried about this new outbreak of crimes by Darby Stover and his gang. The message last night had told Mitch to reveal anything he had heard recently in front of Carrie Sue, but he hadn't expected that enlightenment to include so many crimes! He wondered if the gang was indeed heading this way, or if they would turn south toward the Davis Mountains or Mexico to hide. Considering the number of targets they had taken in the last few weeks—which wasn't like Darby Stover—surely they wouldn't strike at the other towns near Brownwood. Maybe, he surmised, Darby had a new style, or a sly plan to work around Brownwood and Commanche while awaiting news of his sister, or her arrival. His flurry of criminal activity could be to let her know where to look for him. He wondered if Darby knew about the posters, stories, and retractions, and what the outlaw thought about the crazy incidents.

From the window, Carrie Sue watched T.J. Rogue and his friend walk down the street together, talking seriously. She shook her head in mounting sadness, for Mitchell Sterling was a terrible liar. She hadn't fallen for their clever pretense tonight, not even surrounded by all that genial and masculine talk. Mitch had been prepared to deceive her; no doubt Hank had sent him a detailed message last night while she was sleeping in his bed. Mitch had known who she was before her arrival, and not from posters or newspaper stories. Mitch's conversation about her brother had been carefully planned. Mitch couldn't be trusted, nor could those false newspaper accounts.

Far worse, T.J. Rogue could not be trusted at all. A man like him would never bring her here and dupe his good friend, and they could have gotten plenty of supplies in Mesilla from Hank. There was a crafty motive and keen mind at work. If T.J. was bringing others into his duplicity and they were obliging, something terrible was at work around her. Obviously Hank and Mitch were two of the men he had been contacting in Tucson and along the way. And, for all she knew, that man in Tucson wasn't a lawman, just another one of her lover's accomplices. But what did these men want from her? Merciful Heavens, could it be the sixty-six thousand dollars in gold and paper money? Maybe it was more now if the gang's big targets had contributed to their reward offers. Would her lover do this to her?

Chapter

18

After breakfast, Mitchell Sterling headed for his mercantile store, leaving T.J. alone with Carrie Sue. He told them he would pick up food for dinner from a local restaurant and be home about six-thirty.

Carrie Sue had observed Mitch closely this morning. It might be crazy, but he didn't seem like a treacherous man, nor had Hank. Maybe T.J. had duped them into willingly helping their friend. Maybe her lover was the only one of them who was being deceitful. She didn't doubt that Mitch knew who she was, but he was following T.J.'s request to pretend he didn't. Perhaps her love was afraid she'd skip out on him, so he had asked Mitch to scare her with those false reports.

T.J. said, "I'm going to do some scouting around town today and see what I can learn. I'll get a newspaper and see if there's any current news on your brother; you can read those other ones while I'm gone and maybe draw a clue from the reports. I can always pick up information in saloons from drifters, gamblers, and cowpunchers passing through town. Men get real talkative over a drink and card game."

She clasped his hand and stroked its back with her cheek. "I'll make sure no one sees me here at Mitch's. I hate putting you in this awkward position, T.J., and I appreciate all you're doing to help me. When we leave town tomorrow, we'll head for a spot where the gang's camped lots of times when we needed rest and distance. It's where the Toyah Creek joins with the Pecos River, about three days from here. If they didn't head there after that holdup at Big Spring, then we'll ride for Commanche. There's a cabin north of town which can't be found easily."

"It should take us about eight or nine days to reach the first town between here and there, so we'll need a pack horse and additional supplies to get us to San Angelo. I'll buy one while I'm out today. Do you mind if I trade Charlie? That pinto could be recognized and give us away," he suggested with reluctance, knowing she liked the animal.

Her eyes and voice were sad. "I think that's wise, but I hate to lose her. In eleven days, we should be near Brownwood and hopefully so will Darby so we can settle this matter. I wonder if people, especially lawmen, think it's strange the Hardings want us so badly. I mean, it's been years since we harassed them. In fact, I think it's odd that Quade Harding put his name at the bottom of my poster."

"Not really," T.J. asserted. "That's to let everyone know who's offering the highest reward. It's much more than the government's two thousand each. He also wants to make certain you're captured alive and delivered to him. Who would claim two thousand when he can get ten by taking you to Brownwood and the QH Ranch?"

"Is that legal?" she inquired.

"Yep, he can have you taken to him for payment, then he can turn you over to the law for their reward. Lawmen don't like it, but there isn't anything they can do about it. I would imagine the law's keeping an eye on the Hardings over this suspicious affair. I would be."

"But if it isn't illegal, what good would spying on them do?"

"A man who bends or breaks one law, usually does it with others. If I were a lawman, I'd think he was up to no good, and I'd watch him. If we're both lucky, Quade will do something wrong and get caught. Then, we won't have to worry about endangering ourselves for revenge."

"Don't count on it, partner. He's been evil for years and never been caught. I'll admit, Quade's as clever as he is mean and wicked."

"Very few men get away with their crimes forever, love."

Carrie Sue stretched and yawned. "Merciful Heavens, I'm tired. I didn't sleep well last night. I think I'll read those papers and get plenty of rest before we hit the trail again. You be careful today."

"You need anything before I leave?" he asked.

"You can hold me and kiss me," she answered, knowing where their contact would lead, but she needed him one last time.

T.J. pulled her into his arms and covered her parted lips with his. His heart ached for this secret breach between them to be destroyed. His body yearned to fuse with hers. His mind pleaded for peace.

Carrie Sue feverishly kissed and caressed T.J. as she peeled off his shirt, and he did the same for her. Their chests touched, then they swiftly pressed together to remove any space between them. He scooped her up in his arms and carried her back to her borrowed bed. They both hurriedly removed their boots and jeans. She flung aside the covers and they fell entwined upon the bed.

They made love with a tender and tantalizing urgency which neither understood in the other. Their lips and tongues meshed in a wild and stirring dance. Their arms and hands embraced and caressed. Their bodies united as one. And afterward, they remained locked together, kissing, touching, holding, savoring, until a tranquil glow relaxed them.

T.J. arose and rinsed off in the basin nearby. He said, "I'll wait to trade Charlie as we're leaving, just in case her description is out. You take it easy today, and I'll see you about six. Don't unlock the doors for anybody, or stick this beautiful head outside."

She stretched and yawned again. After a radiant smile, she said, "I plan to be wickedly lazy today, partner, while you get our chores done. After my bath, I might not leave this bed until dinner time."

T.J. bent forward and kissed her on the nose. "I wish I could join you all day, but one of us has work to do."

"We'll have plenty of time on the trail for other . . . business," she teased guilefully in a seductive tone.

As her love reached the bedroom door, she called out, "T.J., please be careful out there. I don't want you forgetting about that sheriff we clobbered in Tucson. And don't get into any trouble in those saloons. You stay away from those fancy dressed gals there!"

"You don't have to be jealous or worried, love; I have all I need right here. Relax today; I'll be safe and careful."

"If you're not, partner, I'll thrash you good after I rescue you."

T.J.'s gaze fused with hers for a moment, and both smiled as each felt as if they had the other exactly where wanted. . . .

*

Carrie Sue noticed that T.J. didn't take his saddlebags with him, but she couldn't locate them during a brief search. She did find a Mexican blouse, skirt, and sandals in Mrs. Sterling's closet. She took them to use as a disguise to get her out of town. She packed enough supplies for a two day trip, careful to use two canteens to give her and her horse plenty of water between creeks. She clipped out the newspaper articles on Darby's false raids and packed them.

She knew her brother hadn't committed those robberies and rustlings, but she couldn't decide if another gang posing as them had. That was something she needed to discuss with Darby. Either it was a ruse to draw them into the open, a trick to lure her into the area, or they had a serious problem of impersonation.

She wrote T.J. a carefully worded note. In case their paths crossed again, she didn't want him to know she was suspicious of him.

She clipped a lock of her hair and bound the end with a blue ribbon. She placed both on her pillow. Using extra blankets, she formed a body roll and covered it, making it appear she was asleep if her lover returned earlier than planned and looked in on her. She drew the heavy curtains over the lace ones to darken the room and aid her ruse.

Carrie Sue donned the Mexican garments and covered her head with a colorful shawl, normally used to ward off the sun's heat, but one which would conceal her fiery hair. She carried her things to the barn behind Mitchell Sterling's home. From recall on their arrival, she knew the merchantman had around ten fine horses in his corral.

"Sorry, Charlie, but you have to stay behind this time," she murmured as she stroked the pinto's neck. "That hide of yours is too easily recognized." She chose a sturdy sorrel and saddled him. Taking one of Mitchell's saddles, she placed it where hers had been and hoped it wouldn't be noticed as the wrong one until she was long gone.

She secured her saddlebags, bedroll, and supplies behind her cantle and looped the canteens over her pommel. She mounted, tossed the shawl over her head, and left the barn. The daring desperado left the area by the back way, hardly enticing any notice in her disguise, which made her grateful this town was populated so heavily with Mexicans. Once El Paso was behind her, she kneed the reddish-brown stallion into a gallop toward the Guadalupe Mountains, northeast of town.

Carrie Sue knew the Hueco Mountains would come first, then the Cornudas, Salt Flats, and Guadalupes. She wasn't worried about the Salt War which Mitchell had mentioned last night, but she would be on alert for any threat in that region.

Outside of town, she encountered scattered scrubs and grass clumps on dry and sandy ground. Sometimes the land was flat; other times it was covered with rolling hills, deep ravines, and shallow dry washes. She could make out the Huecos in the distant haze. Above her the sky was a rich blue shade, unlike the pale blue of Arizona. The clouds were large and billowy. A rider could take refuge under them from the blazing sun. She loved Texas and found its climate and landscape less demanding than Arizona's and New Mexico's desert terrain and soaring heat.

She journeyed steadily, aware that T.J. would head southeast to search for her when her disappearance was discovered this evening. She took the time to cover her tracks for a while. Yet, if his Apache training was still in full force and his investigation into her escape paid off, it wouldn't do any good to conceal her trail from his keen wits.

After a few hours, she located a safe place to change her clothes and don her boots, packing the stolen ones in case they were needed another time. She took breaks only when her mount needed them. She wanted to put as much distance as possible between her and El Paso as quickly as possible. Too, she wanted to reach Darby soon. Besides, her appetite was missing as she reflected on T.J. and Darby.

The riding was easy in this less rugged region. The grassland and scrubs were green this time of year and following a recent rain. She always saw mountains, or hills, or mesas, or buttes in the distance on all sides. Often the hills appeared to be covered by green fuzz which she knew was shortgrass. She was familiar with this area, so she didn't worry over getting lost.

Her Remington revolvers were strapped around her waist and to her thighs, the forty-fours giving her confidence and a sense of security, as did her enormous skills with them. Her Henry rifle, a fifteen-shot repeater with lever-action, was close at hand if needed. She missed her lover something terrible, but she could take care of herself. Still, she hoped and prayed she wouldn't run into anyone who'd seen her poster. She hated the thought of killing someone to defend herself, but ten thousand dollars would make a life-and-death struggle for anyone.

Despite what she had told T.J. about a lack of sleep last night, she had slumbered fairly well under the circumstances. She watched the sunset's reflections on the clouds before her. They were shades of pink against a backdrop of intermingled blues, grays, and lavenders. It was a serene sight, but it didn't relax her. She remained on guard as she continued her slowed pace after dark, as she intended to go on for a few more hours before napping.

*

When T.J. returned, he stabled the pack horse before he fed Nighthawk and Charlie, then put their supplies in the barn, which he packed and readied to move out early in the morning. He checked to make certain his saddlebags were still where he had concealed them, and noticed they hadn't been disturbed. He smiled in pleasure, not wanting her to find the telegraph key, picture of Annabelle and Marie, and his badges. He walked to the house and found it quiet.

T.J. went to the back room and eased open the door. He saw the shapely form lying in the darkened room. He smiled again, and decided to let her rest a while longer. Mitchell had gotten a late supply of goods and wouldn't get home until seven.

T.J. returned to the parlor and fetched himself a drink from the sideboard. He relaxed in a chair and called to mind the telegram he had received two hours ago, telling him of Darby Stover's raid on a Wells Fargo office in Brady, a good day's ride from Brownwood, eleven days from El Paso. That told him where the Stover Gang was operating and where he and Carrie Sue needed to head in the morning.

He hadn't learned much at the two saloons, only heard more about President Grant's problems with the election later this year and more about the Stover Gang's movements. T.J. wondered if his position would be affected by the election of a new president. Currently he could come and go anywhere as he pleased with his three badges. They came in handy if a certain mission took him out of Texas into other states. They always gave him more jurisdiction, authority, and power than local or state lawmen, if the undercover T.J. Rogue was forced to become Thaddeus Jamison. He used whichever badge was needed for that time, place, and task. Sometimes he ran into bad or stubborn lawmen and had to pull rank on them with one or more of his badges. Yet, he always tried to work as Rogue so few knew him as Lawman Thaddeus Jerome Jamison, especially in Texas.

Actually, he liked being a Special Agent for the President, a United States Marshal, and a Texas Ranger. If he ever had to chose one job and rank over the other two, he didn't know which one it would be. He only wished the possession of so much power could help his love, but it didn't. He sipped his drink and sighed deeply.

When he realized it was nearly dark outside, he decided to awaken Carrie Sue. He lit a lamp and carried it down the hallway. He opened the door and approached the bed. His hands reached out and pulled back the covers.

T.J.'s eyes widened, then narrowed as he angrily scooped up the lock of golden red hair and the folded note. He sat down the lamp and read it:

Dear T.J.,

Please forgive me for deserting you like this. Since you aren't a wanted man and we keep endangering your friends, it's best if I continue alone to Commanche. I know bounty hunters and lawmen will be searching for me, but I have to take those risks without involving you further. I can't keep using and duping your friends. And I can't allow you to be killed because of me.

The newspapers are wrong about Darby. He never strikes Union Express and he never gives his name boastfully. He never makes that many hits so close together. Another gang must be using his reputation and name or it's a trick by the law to lure us out and capture us. If he doesn't know what's happening, I have to warn him. I have to let him see for himself that I'm fine, in case the papers tell more lies and claim I've been captured to entrap him.

Thanks for everything. When I'm settled somewhere far away, I'll contact you through Hank Peterson because you trust him. I took his address, so I'll write or telegraph you as Sue Starns. I love you and will miss you dreadfully. Please be careful and don't come after me. I would die if you were slain trying to help me. And I couldn't bear it if you were sent to prison because of me.

I know where Darby is hiding. Curly told me that day in Tucson, but I had to keep it from you. I am certain Darby is lying low for a month or two like he told Curly, so he can't be guilty of all these suspicious attacks.

I swear to write you later and hope you'll want to hear from me and come to see me. I've left you a souvenir on my pillow from the Texas Flame. I hope it's the only one in your collection with real meaning. I can't wait until we're together again. I'll try to make it happen very soon. Forgive my new ruse. I love you, T.J. Rogue.
C.S.S.

T.J. sank to the bed, staring at the shocking note and worrying over her reckless action. He had to find her, and fast! But how had she gotten away? Charlie was still in the barn. He realized she must have stolen one of Mitchell's horses.

The distressed lawman hurried to the corral. He had studied his friend's horses earlier and decided which one to trade for Charlie. He had to smile when he saw that the chosen sorrel was missing. It was obvious she had good taste in horseflesh. He checked the saddle near his, and grasped that clever precaution. He hadn't noticed it wasn't hers when he was in the barn earlier. He checked their old supplies, to find some missing and two canteens gone. At least she would have plenty of water and food. And, she was well-armed and skilled.

He returned to the house, impressed with her preparations, wits and courage. He couldn't track her at night beneath such a scanty moon, and it was too late to question possible witnesses. He went to her room and admired her handiwork there before making the bed. In the parlor, T.J. took a seat to think.

Mitchell came home with their dinner. He smiled and greeted his dark-haired friend. He sensed T.J.'s sullen mood and questioned it.

T.J. informed him, "I've got bad trouble, Mitch. Carrie Sue took off right after my departure this morning, so she has a good headstart on me." The intelligent lawman related what the redhaired fugitive had said to him last night and this morning and most of what her note had revealed. "Lordy, Mitch, where is she heading?" He paced anxiously as he made his plans. "I'll head for Brownwood to see what's happening there. Maybe Dave has some news by now. If she's right about her brother's innocence in these crimes, where is Darby Stover and who's to blame? If Carrie Sue honestly believes her brother headed for Oklahoma to lay low, could she be riding in that direction?"

T.J. sighed. "I just can't decide what's she's thinking and doing. Telegraph Dave in the morning, then send word to me in San Angelo. I should get there in a few days. Maybe we can meet in Commanche. I'd like to know what I'm riding into before I reach Brownwood."

The ex-Ranger asked gravely, "Do you think he's being framed?"

"Lordy, I don't know. From what she's told me about Darby, it doesn't sound like him, and he's surely changed his pattern. If anyone should know how he thinks and operates, it's his sister. But if she's mistaken or Darby's changed and she's heading for Brownwood, she'll be riding into danger with all that's going on in that area. Even with her poster recalled, she could get snared by accident."

Mitchell remarked, "At least we know why she wants to see him in person. I can't blame her. She's a real prize, T.J., and I don't mean reward-wise. Frankly, I like her and believe her."

T.J. jumped up to pace nervously, which was not like him. His smokey gray gaze was somber and his body was taut with unnatural fear. "I wish you were still working with me. We've solved some tough cases together and I can use your help and wits on this one. Lordy, I'm too closely involved with her to think straight."

"Sorry, old friend, but I'm enjoying my retirement and family. But I'll do whatever I can to assist you from here. You think she would listen if you confessed the truth? Would help you with your mission? If she truly loves you, it's got to be real tough on her being in this mess."

T.J. halted and looked at his friend. "She would never betray her brother for any reason or any person, including me and a pardon, which I can't arrange. Even Grant refuses a presidential pardon for her."

"That shouldn't surprise you. She's an outlaw. And he's trying to secure a third term. He won't do anything to cause more doubts about himself. He's already been accused of doing illegal things for his friends."

"I understand, but it riles me to be so damn helpless!" T.J. revealed, "She took those newspaper clippings to show Darby. Lordy, Mitch, much as I hate the man and want to see him punished, I hope she doesn't find out those reports are accurate. It'll crush her." T.J. inhaled deeply and let the spent air out loudly. "Maybe Darby Stover wants to go straight and he's desperate to get enough money to take off to parts unknown. Or maybe he wants enough money to send his sister far away to safety. I just can't figure it out yet. I need to locate her and meet this clever brother of hers."

Mitchell questioned, "What if Curly James lied to her about seeing Darby on his way to Tucson? What if she's riding into a trap? Didn't you say he worked for Harding in the past? I think I'll check to see if he telegraphed anyone from Tucson and betrayed her."

T.J. whirled and gaped at Mitchell Sterling. "Lordy, I overlooked that angle! What if that bastard was still on Harding's payroll? Curly knew exactly where Carrie Sue was at and maybe where Darby was camped. He used to ride with the Stover Gang, so Darby wouldn't be suspicious of him. Curly could have alerted his old boss to their locations for those rewards. You're right; we need to learn if any messages were passed between them. Check the office here, too. If Curly saw Darby before he reached the Texas border, he might have contacted Quade from here. This is where he was to meet his boys before I got to them."

"I'll handle it first thing in the morning and wire you in San Angelo," Mitchell promised. "I'll also wire Dave in Brownwood and let him know you're on the way and what's going on. Check with him when you arrive."

"Damn!" T.J. swore irritably. "If only I'd arrested Curly, then I could question him or have him questioned. Revenge stinks this time!"

"That would have broken your cover, Ranger Jamison. At least he's out of the way and can't do more harm to her. You want me to wire Hank to tell him to be on the alert for news from her?"

"Yep. Thanks. I'll keep in touch with you and him. At first light, I'll do some scouting and questioning. Surely someone saw a beautiful redhead leaving town. I need to know which direction she took. Damn that Curly! There's no telling where he sent her! Or to whom. . . ."

"Just hope it's toward her brother so she'll have some protection."

T.J.'s eyes brightened and enlarged. "You know something, Mitch? If Darby's gang is being framed, Curly was the perfect one to let that other gang leader know Darby was out of reach for weeks so they could impersonate him and his men. With Darby laying low and out of touch, the law would put the blame on the Stover Gang. I wonder . . ." He paused to contemplate the matter. "What if there's more to this alleged frame than money? What if someone wants Darby in deeper trouble? Make it so he can't go anywhere without being hunted? Maybe even force Darby to seek revenge to halt his imperiling intrusion? Make it too dangerous for Carrie Sue to approach and rejoin her brother?"

"Quade Harding?" the astute Mitchell hinted.

"Damn right!" T.J. shouted angrily. "If there is a frame and has been for years, that means Carrie Sue and her brother might not be responsible for all the charges against them. And if Quade Harding is in the middle of this mischief, we'll get him for sure this time."

"You're overlooking another point, my friend; they are still outlaws and they're guilty of plenty of crimes. Taking a few away won't help her much, if any," Mitchell warned.

"I know," T.J. murmured and clenched his teeth. He withdrew the fiery lock from his pocket and passed it beneath his nose. The hair was soft and fragrant and brought her image to mind. The words in her note raced through his head. Was love, he pondered, her real reason for deserting him? What did she think he would feel and do after discovering her escape? Had he done anything to arouse her suspicions against him? Anything besides his crazy behavior over his saddlebags? He had to admit every-thing about their meeting and relationship was curiously coincidental. As smart and instinctive as she was, Carrie Sue had to realize most of those incidents were strange. No wonder she couldn't dismiss her lingering doubts!

T.J. thought about their lovemaking this morning. She had known she was run-ning out on him soon. *Lordy, her emotions must be in turmoil.* She had exposed love and urgency, a desperation he now understood.

Mitchell queried him on his plans, and they discussed them in detail. Except for his Ranger badge, T.J. left the others and his papers with Mitch for safekeeping and secrecy.

T.J. told his friend about the stolen horse, which had been traded last night for the pinto. "I'm glad she was smart enough to change mounts; that mare is probably associated with her by now. You best keep it in the barn and sell it across the border real quick."

"Don't worry; I'll take care of it tomorrow."

T.J. fumed as he tried to eat the chilled dinner in his highly agitated state. He didn't like not knowing what and whom he was up against. He was worried about his love's safety. How could he calmly eat dinner when she was out there somewhere alone, facing no telling what? He had to find her quickly. Yet, all he could do was head for the area in which Darby Stover was supposedly working and hope to get a line on her. If it was another gang as she believed, he'd be no closer to her there than he was here tonight. *Damnation, you frustrating vixen! If this case gets any more dangerous or complicated, I might have to expose my identity and rank to solve it without you getting harmed.*

*

It was nearing dusk Thursday afternoon when Carrie Sue reached the salt basin. It had been a grueling two day journey. She had eaten, slept, and rested very little along the way. Rocky ramparts seemed to leap skyward in the distance to present a harsh, but majestic, view. The Guadalupe Mountains were starkly barren when approached, but they concealed many hidden meadows, forests, canyons, and streams. A variety of life filled the interior, ranging from desert to canyon woodland to highland forest varieties: yuccas, cacti, rattlesnakes, scorpions, the poisonous desert scorpion, agaves, walking-stick chollas, sotol, coyotes, mule deer, mountain lions, pines, firs, maple, ash, walnut, aspen, chokecherry, elk, racoons, wild turkeys, and sometimes black bears. It was a primitive area whose trails into the highcountry were rough and steep, whose inner canyons rimmed shady glens and cool creeks. The precipitous cliffs and surrounding desert belied the beauty and tranquility of the inland, except when late summer thun-derstorms violently attacked here.

El Capitan peak loomed before her and over the sparse settlement of Pine Springs. She skirted the tiny settlement of Salt Flats, knowing that a lone rider at that distance wouldn't attract much attention or interest, and her sex couldn't be detected that far away.

The sun-bleached salt flats looked pearly gray this late in the afternoon. They seemed to stretch for miles on either side and before her. It was a dry terrain, one of value to many people. Yet, she found no trouble crossing that trouble-torn region. She weaved through the Patterson Hills and passed the sentinel peak. She slipped by the Pine Springs area and The Pinery, where a Butterfield stop had been situated since '58. The exhausted redhead halted at Manzanita Springs for her horse to rest and drink.

She had ridden a little over a hundred miles and had about ten to fifteen to go, if

Darby was camped in McKittrick Canyon as Curly James had told her. The freshwater springs were cool and inviting. She removed her boots and dangled her feet beneath the surface. She splashed her face and arms and took long drinks.

The sun's heat was gone. The temperature was in the comfortable seventies. She was glad it wasn't spring, as high winds with forceful gusts often lashed unmercifully at this area.

She knew this area was frequently the base for the Mescalero Apaches, but she wasn't afraid. Those Indians knew who she was. They liked and respected Darby Stover and allowed him to camp here whenever he desired, as her brother was truthful with the Apaches and always brought them many gifts of friendship and gratitude. It helped that one of Darby's men—Kale Rushton—was part Apache and was admired by the Mescalero tribe for his harassment of the whites.

The Apaches made their camps to the far western side of the mountains, so they rarely saw the Indians when camped here. Usually Darby and Kale Rushton went to visit them when they reached this area to let the Apaches know they were at their campsite in the canyon. Since most whites feared the Apaches, Darby's gang didn't have to worry about being located in this secluded and peaceful region.

Knowing now that T.J. Rogue had been raised by Apaches, she wished she had met them and learned their language. She wondered if the Mescalero tribe in these mountains was the one who had captured and raised his brother. She hadn't been able to speak that question in fear of giving away a vital clue about her destination.

Carrie Sue reached the eastern entrance to McKittrick Canyon and headed along the winding trail. She followed the perennial spring-fed stream whose banks were edged by grey oak, velvet ash, bigtooth maple, willows, and lacy ferns. In the rapidly fading light, she admired the beauty of prickly pear cacti, alligator junipers, and the sparkling water. She inhaled the mingled scents which surrounded her, noticing the pines and madrones most of all. She saw a mule deer browsing at the edge of the woods, and other creatures scampering home for the coming night. She noted the rapid and stealthful movement of a coyote, a misunderstood animal who was no threat to man. She experienced the solitude of this vast wonderland, but wished it weren't getting dark so quickly.

She knew her way blindfolded, but accidents did occur on shadowy paths, and the moon was nearing its crescent stage of little light. She made certain her rifle was cocked for use, just in case a mountain lion challenged her or a spooked elk charged. She knew that Darby always posted a guard at the entrance to the canyon, but no one had called out to her or presented himself. The weary redhead hoped that wasn't a bad sign. She had about two to three miles to ride to reach the rough cabin, located at a spot on the stream where the canyon split north and south, making two escape routes over the ridges if ever needed. Yes, Darby Stover was too clever to box himself into a trap!

Carrie Sue tossed back her hat and loosened her hair to let the fiery mane glow in the receding light to reveal her identity. Still, no one joined her. Darby had trained and ordered his men to be careful, but only a stranger wouldn't recognize her as the Texas Flame, his sister. Even so, her hair should alert an unknown guard to her identity.

She halted and listened as she looked around, but heard and saw nothing but movements of nocturnal animals, insects, birds, and other creatures. She sensed no piercing eyes or threatening presence. She wondered if Curly had lied or if her brother had left this area and was—

Carrie Sue mentally scolded herself for thinking such ridiculous thoughts for even a moment. Darby Stover was a natural-born leader of men, too bad they were outlaws.

She knew why the regular gang followed him, trusted him, would die for him. Darby had the kind of personality which made people like him and want to be around him. He was clever, fearlessly brave, coolheaded, and highly skilled with physical and mental prowess. He always had a crafty backup plan. He never got caught. He was never reckless and impulsive. He was a smart planner. He wasn't arrogant or cocky. And he had a smile which could melt the coldest woman's heart, a smile which made his eyes glow on a tanned face with white teeth and handsome features, a dazzling and boyish smile which relaxed, charmed, and disarmed even men. He always robbed companies, not people. He always tried never to harm innocent bystanders. For those two reasons, he hadn't been feared like a common criminal, and many had considered him an admirable rebel, until the last few years.

At least Darby Stover had been that way. Over the past months before their separation, she had watched him changing, watched him accepting his life and reputation as an outlaw, watched him decide to become the best and most well-known bandit leader in history. Life had made it too hard for him to stay on the right side of the law, so he'd quit trying. What happened to him at the Laredo ranch had changed him, made him believe he could never escape his trap, so why delude and punish himself? The posses never gave him time to halt long enough to go straight, unless he vanished from sight as when he came here. But the moment he was seen anywhere, the maddening and exhausting chase was on again. It was like a grim challenge he had to meet.

When her brother and his men were younger, their bloods had been boiling for excitement and adventures, for conquests and riches. After a taste of money and suspense, none of them had wanted to work hard for a meager salary from sunup to sunset and be too fatigued to care if life was passing them by. Those early days of battling Quade Harding had been fun and profitable for them, but their first killing had turned the tide, had provoked more than the Hardings after them.

Carrie Sue sighed heavily. Maybe T.J. was partially right. Maybe she did have a rosy, inaccurate view of her brother. Maybe he had become hardened and chilled by his lifestyle. Maybe it was too late for him to change again, to change back to that happy-go-lucky boy who had taken on a powerful enemy with the hope of obtaining justice. Those admissions hurt. Yet, at last, she had to face the truth.

She had given Darby the benefit of the doubt. She had loved him and followed him into great perils. She had ruined her life doing so. Maybe she had refused to look at him and their lives with an unbiased mind. Maybe she hadn't wanted to believe what they both had become. Maybe she inwardly resented the gang because Darby wouldn't be in this mess without them, still in this existence without them. She would give anything if the only charges against them had to do with the Hardings, charges a good lawyer might be able to argue successfully.

Following the deaths of innocent victims in March and April, she had suspected the truth and desperately fled it. Now, she was riding back into the hopeless situation she had escaped. The redhead was too tired to deceive herself. She loved Darby and wanted to see him. She prayed she could talk some sense into him, but she doubted it. No matter what happened, she had to get far away as soon as possible. She should have done so long ago, after leaving the Harding Ranch.

She would reach the campsite soon, but she realized Darby wasn't here because no guard had been posted at the entrance. She hoped no one else was using the crude cabin tonight. She would rest, then decide how to locate him safely. How she wished T.J. was here to help, comfort, and understand—

Someone leaped on her horse behind her and banded her chest tightly with his arms, preventing her from drawing her weapons or battling him. In his right hand he held a shiny blade near her face. Her heart pounded in alarm as she suddenly wondered if Curly had someone waiting for her, and she berated herself for being so careless.

He said in Spanish, *"Hola, chica. Que me cuenta?"*

The man reined in her horse, dismounted agilely, and assisted her to the ground. She angrily pounded his hard, bare chest and scolded, "Damn you, Kale Rushton! You scared ten years off my life!" She wasn't amused by his joke and, even though she was not a young girl anymore, he continued to call her *chica* as he had since seventeen.

Kale chuckled and looked her over in the waning light. "What's wrong with you tonight, *chica*? I've been trailing you since you entered the canyon. You're guard's much too low, *mi belleza*. I might have been a hungry *leon* and gobbled you up in two bites."

Carrie Sue relaxed and grinned. "I'm exhausted, that's what's wrong," she replied, softening her tone. "I've been on the trail for two days with hardly any rest. I'd about decided you all weren't here."

"How did you know?" the half-Apache asked, his black eyes alert.

"Curly James told me. He came to Tucson and got himself killed there in a showdown. We've got trouble, Kale, but we can discuss it in the morning. I need some sleep badly before I collapse."

The twenty-seven-year-old man with flowing black hair past his shoulders smiled and nodded. Kale Rushton was half Spanish and half Apache, and was an appealing male of good looks and a virile body. His hips were clad in snug jeans and his ever present red sash was secured around his head. Kale was only four inches taller than her five-seven height, but he was solidly built. He had been with Darby since the Quade Harding affair. She liked Kale because she always felt she could trust him. "It's good to see you, *amigo.*"

"*Lo mismo digo,*" he murmured, saying "the same to you."

"Is Darby all right?" she asked worriedly.

"*Si,* only restless to be on the trail again. Why are you here, *chica*? What happened to drive you from Tucson?" he asked, perceptive.

"I was exposed and had to flee for my life."

"You came all this way alone?" he queried, his gaze widening.

"Let's talk about it later," she coaxed, yawning and flexing.

Kale suggested, "Why don't you bed down where I stand guard? If you enter camp this late, it will disturb everyone and you won't get any rest for hours. I'll be on guard until dawn."

"That's a good idea, *amigo*. Let's go before I hit the ground."

They mounted double-back and returned to a grassy area near the entrance. Kale unpacked her bedroll and spread it out for her. As he unsaddled her horse and tended the sorrel, Carrie Sue drank cool water from the stream. She stretched out on the bedroll and closed her eyes.

When Kale took his place nearby, she lifted her head and looked at him, asking, "How long have you been camped here?"

"For weeks, why?" he questioned, sensing there was an important meaning to her query.

"I thought so. See you at dawn, Kale," she said and went to sleep.

Kale Rushton withdrew his knife and stone. He began sharpening the already incisive blade, a habit when he was in deep thought. The half-Apache observed the redhaired beauty for a long time, deciding something terrible had driven her from her new life, something which would affect all of them. Patience was one of his best traits, so he could wait until morning to discover that reason. If danger was close, she would have aroused the others.

Kale removed the fiery red sash from across his forehead. He grasped his long black hair and bound the flowing mane at the nape with it. His Apache hairstyle was his badge of honor, his pride in and acknowledgement of that part of his heritage, a sign of his rebel spirit.

He had met Darby Stover during a saloon brawl in Brownwood, shortly after Darby's parent's deaths and a week before his new friend went on the vengeance trail against his enemies the Hardings. Kale remembered those days clearly. The twenty-one-year-old Darby had been suffering badly over his parent's deaths and the loss of his property, and the law's refusal to punish those responsible. Darby had needed a friend, a helper, a confidant, a comforter. As for Carrie Sue, the young beauty had no place to live and no money for support, and jobs were few for seventeen year olds with her looks. Besides, Darby hadn't wanted his sister to slave for strangers, and Kale had agreed.

Even at twenty, Kale had done plenty of gunslinging, horse thieving, and cattle rustling. Because of his looks and mixed blood, he had endured lots of trouble, hatred, taunting, and challenges—incidents which had made him into a tough and self-reliant gunman who enjoyed getting the best of his physical and mental attackers. Men who gave him trouble or ridicule found their properties burned or stolen, but no one had ever been able to pin one of those deeds on him.

Kale had been the one to suggest revenge on the Hardings, telling Darby he should do similar things to Harding as punishment. He was the one who had taught Darby many Apache tricks, trained the youth in how to pull off crimes and get away with them. He owed Darby Stover his life and loyalty, as Darby had saved his life during that saloon brawl when a man was going to shoot him in the back. He and Darby had taken an instant liking to each other and become fast friends.

Kale had worked with Walt Vinson, Tyler Parnell, and John "Griff" Griffin many times in the past. He was the one who had introduced Darby to them and suggested they form a gang to harass Quade Harding. Knowing they needed another couple of men, they had observed prospects in saloons, gunslingers and drifters passing through town. They had met Kadry Sams in a saloon following a showdown with a famed gunslinger. They had picked up Dillon Holmes while visiting Miss Sally's brothel in San Angelo, after witnessing a fight between Dillon and another customer who favored the same "soiled dove."

Kale knew he preferred following Darby, helping with the plans and suggestions, and teaching his friend all he knew, but he didn't care about being the leader. Too, the half-Apache realized that Darby Stover was a natural-born leader. He liked and respected his friend, and nothing Darby did turned Kale against him. He also liked being a member of the famous Stover Gang.

Kale knew he was the most loyal outlaw in the band. Except for Kadry and Dillon, the other men weren't as smart and skilled as Darby and Kale and they just naturally followed along behind a superior leader and expert warrior. Kale knew that Kadry Sams would like to be a leader, but he would never go against Darby Stover, nor would the rest of the gang back him. But if anything happened to Darby, Kadry would be the one to take control of the gang.

Kale Rushton liked Kadry, but he realized the light-haired bandit with impenetrable sky blue eyes was more conniving, cold-blooded, and harder than any of the others. Kadry was also more daring than Kale and Darby, almost to the point of being recklessly brave.

Over the years, Darby had let other outlaws or gunmen join their gang for certain jobs, but never for any length of time. It was obvious to the seven men who composed the Stover Gang that they had a special rapport, trusted each other, and liked each other.

Kale loved this life. It was exciting, stimulating, challenging. They were always seeking a bigger haul, taking on a more dangerous target, getting away quicker and cleaner, outsmarting the law and their targets, and moving from place to place. Kale knew he was part of the reason why Darby and the gang had done so well and why Darby had remained in the outlaw business so long. He was aware that Kadry was a little jealous of his tight bond with Darby, but not to the point of leaving the gang or going against Darby. Sure they had had occasional squabbles, but nothing serious. Disagreements sometimes arose under the conditions in which they were forced to survive and work. Sometimes they got edgy and nervous during lengthy pursuits or during long periods of laying low. But mostly they lived in close and tight rapport like a family of brothers with Darby as the father.

The only thing Kale Rushton didn't like was Darby bringing his younger sister into this dangerous and difficult existence. Kale trusted Carrie Sue, and had confidence in her skills, but he didn't believe a woman like her should endure this kind of life. He also didn't like Kadry Sams pursuing her hotly. His only quarrel with Darby was that his friend didn't see that such a relationship couldn't work; yet Darby wouldn't discourage it.

Years ago when Carrie Sue learned of their plans to destroy the Hardings, she had demanded to help seek justice and vengeance. Kale had warned both they must be careful and that they needed to know more about Harding's business and schedule. Since the villainous bastard had offered her a job several times, she had taken it to be the spy whom they needed. When Harding figured out their plot and gave her false information to entrap them, their task had fallen apart, but the gang had gotten away without deaths or injuries. After Harding confronted her, she had managed to use her wits and skills to flee the beast. Ever since that day, she had ridden with them off and on.

Darby hadn't been too worried about Quade's threats because Quade wanted her too badly to endanger her; his refusal to give out her description over the years had proven it. Yet, the harassment of Quade had been halted to protect her, something which still riled Darby.

Kale Rushton knew Quade Harding would never give up trying to possess Carrie Sue Stover. Quade was like a ferocious badger with his teeth locked into a delicious piece of meat; he would hang on until he wore her down and devoured her, unless he was killed.

Kale was worried about her return to them tonight. Things had gotten hot for them all over the territory. That was the reason why they had been unable to make it into Oklahoma and why Darby had suggested this distant place for resting and keeping out of sight for a while. Nowadays, they were chased everywhere they went by wild posses and bounty hunters and eager lawmen. Yet, this far from central Texas where they usually operated, they were safe in this Apache place.

The ruggedly handsome bandit glanced at the sleeping woman. Evidently something had gone wrong in Tucson because she had been determined never to ride with the gang again. Kale decided to persuade Darby to get her plenty of money so she could get further away from the hazardous West. Maybe next time she could find success.

As dawn approached, Kale nudged Carrie Sue's shoulder and awakened her. Softly he murmured, *"Chica,* it's time to stir your blood and clear your head before Griff comes to take over."

The drowsy redhead sat up and flexed her sore body. She smiled and said, "I'm getting too old and stiff for this kind of life, *amigo.* I'm going around the bend to take a quick bath and change clothes." She gathered her things and left him sitting there.

When she returned, she was clad in the Mexican skirt, white blouse over a camisole, and sandals. Her tawny red hair was flowing about her shoulders. She greeted Kale with a bright smile. She looked rested, fresh as the pleasant summer morning which surrounded them.

"I'm starved, but food needs to wait. I trust you most of all, Kale, so please convince Darby to do what's best for all of us when you hear my news later. First, I need to speak with him privately. Can you fetch him for me and keep the others in camp?"

Kale nodded. "The boys will be stirring soon. I see smoke which means coffee. I'll send some to you with Darby. Watch the entrance for me." Kale headed toward camp at a steady run which would take him ten minutes in his well-honed condition.

She guessed accurately, for Darby came into sight within fifteen minutes, riding bareback. In his excitement, he hadn't even buttoned his shirt or donned his boots. He leapt off the horse and embraced her.

He held her away from him and studied her with affection and intrigue. His eyes were soft like warmed chocolate and sparkled like the sun-lit stream nearby. A broad smile revealed white teeth and deep grooves at the sides of his mouth. His face was perfectly shaped, as were his features. Yes, she concluded in love and pride, he could stop a woman's heart or cause her to stare and stumble.

"What are you doing here, Sis?" he asked, eagerness brightening his dark eyes even more than before. "I thought Kale was teasing me."

Carrie Sue's fingers combed through his mussed dark auburn hair which was shaggy on the sides, but didn't conceal his ears. Sideburns crept to his lobes and brought attention to his strong jawline. The nape curled boyishly at his collar and she playfully fluffed that area. "You need a haircut, Darby Stover, and a shave," she added merrily as her hand teased over two day's growth of dark whiskers.

"Surely you didn't come here to make sure I'm taking care of myself. How did you find us? Why are you here?"

"Did Curly James pass through here recently?" she asked.

Darby sent her an odd look. "Yep, why?"

"On the eighteenth?" she probed.

"Yep, he had business in Tucson. He was coming back to join up with us again for the next few jobs. I'll need some extra men 'cause I'm planning to hit some big targets. I know he was hard to control, but he promised no trouble or killing," Darby asserted when she frowned.

"Did you tell him I was in Tucson?"

"No way, Sis. I was hoping he'd miss you. What's going on?"

What business did he have in Tucson?"

"Don't know. Give, Sis," he demanded, getting impatient. "All Kale told me was you arrived late and slept here."

Carrie Sue sat down on her bedroll and patted the area next to her to indicate he was to sit there. "We need to have a serious talk, big brother. We've got lots of trouble." She told Darby about running into Curly James on the street and what passed between them, letting him know that's how she located him. When she related news of the showdown with T.J. Rogue, her brother's eyes widened in astonishment.

"Curly challenged Rogue? Is he crazy?" Darby scoffed.

"Not anymore. Rogue had him on the ground before his pistol cleared his holster. Ever met him?" she inquired.

"Met him, no, but heard plenty about him. He's taken down more gunslingers than I've met, killed more men than a dog has fleas. So, what are you doing here? Did Curly cause trouble for you?"

"Not really, but I didn't trust him to keep his promise to me. Not with my new poster out. It has an accurate picture of me, Darby. I found out just in time to get out of town before I was arrested. The Hardings have upped our rewards to ten thousand each, and five each on the boys. Add that to the law's offer of sixteen, and the gang is worth sixty-six thousand. That makes us real tempting to everyone, big brother. I've no doubt Curly would have collected on mine if Rogue hadn't kill him."

"Damn that Quade Harding! I didn't think he'd ever do this to you! Wasn't killing Papa and Mama and stealing our ranch enough for the bastard? I know he wants you badly, Sis, but this can get you killed."

Hurriedly, Carrie Sue went over her experiences in Tucson and her problem with Martin Ferris. Then, she related her many rescues and adventures with T.J. Rogue, omitting their love affair. She told him why T.J. killed Curly and about T.J.'s helping her flee Tucson. She went over her plights on the trail and admitted, "I deserted him in El Paso, but I feel awful about deceiving him after all he's done for me. I didn't want to get him into trouble by tying in with us." She did not tell her brother about her suspicions of T.J., in case the two men ever met. She didn't want Darby gunning down her lover if he wasn't guilty, and there was a slight chance he wasn't.

Darby eyed her intently. "You're in love with him, aren't you?"

Carrie Sue licked her lips and nodded. "Crazy, isn't it?" she jested.

Darby scowled, but replied, "Not after what he's done for you. He's got quite a reputation, but he isn't an outlaw."

"I know, but he was willing to do anything to help me."

"That means he probably loves you, too. What about Kadry? He loves you and wants to marry you. This'll bust him up badly."

"You know I don't love Kadry. I've tried to tell both of you that many times. Love isn't something you force, big brother; it either happens between two people or it doesn't. It just isn't there for Kadry. Besides, I'm leaving again to give it another try farther away. I can't see Kadry as a husband, father, and rancher."

"What about Rogue? Do you see him that way?" Darby asked.

"I don't know, but I'll let him know where I am once I get settled."

"You trust him that much?"

"Yes. And it won't endanger you if I'm far away when I contact him. I had to see you in person, Darby. I had to let you know I'm all right in case the law tries to trick you by saying I've been captured. Once I leave, don't believe any stories in the newspapers." She reached for her saddlebag and withdrew the articles. "Read these and the dates."

"What the hell?" Darby exploded in disbelief as he scanned the report of *his* crimes on May twenty-second, twenty-fifth, thirtieth and June third. "I wasn't anywhere near those places! This isn't the first time we've been accused of the wrong crimes!"

Carrie Sue urged, "You have to give it up, big brother. It's too dangerous out there. Either the law is boxing you in with lies, or trying to lure me into a trap, or some gang is playing yours. If you're being framed, it has to be Quade Harding, with Curly's help."

"Curly's help?" he echoed, baffled.

She reasoned, "How else did this other gang know you were out of touch so they could operate freely as the Stover Gang? I knew you weren't responsible, so I had to warn you. I know your style and I know you, Darby Stover. You don't go around killing people on every job or telling your victims they've been taken by the Stover Gang. Besides, Curly worked for Quade in the past. He and two men barbwired T.J. to a tree to die slowly for Quade; that's why T.J. killed Curly and wants to go after Quade. We have a mutual enemy."

"You believed that tale? Rogue getting ambushed by Curly and his boys? From what I hear, he's the best gunman around; you don't snare a man like Rogue easily."

"I saw the scars, and he told me that story before he knew who I was. I'm certain it's true, Darby."

"Or you want to believe it is 'cause of how you feel about him."

Carrie Sue related the incident as T.J. had told her. "When Curly saw T.J., he went white. He did that because he recognized him as the man he'd hired out to kill for Quade." She moved closer to her brother and clasped his hand in hers. She entreated, "Please, let's ride for Montana while it's safe. We can buy a ranch there and be happy and free. This other gang has stirred up everyone against you, and your large reward is tempting even for friends. Ten thousand dollar in gold, Darby, that's more than most of our takes. Give it up, please."

Darby jumped up to pace, agitated by this unexpected turn in events. He argued sullenly, "We don't have enough money for a ranch or anything else, Sis. Give it up to do what? Live how? Like dirt farmers or poor cowpunchers? We'd never make enough to have any kind of decent life. Always looking over our shoulders? Never able to relax or feel safe? I don't hanker to be strung up to a cottonwood and have my innards dumpthemselves down my legs while I dangle on that tree and people gape and joke and have a good time like they was at a Sunday picnic."

He continued at her silence, "They'd never put me in jail and, if they did, I couldn't stand being locked up forever. Our faces are known everywhere, and Harding won't quit hiring detectives and bounty hunters until he has our bodies! It's too late to turn back, Sis. But I want you out of this mess for keeps. I'm going to get you plenty of money so you can get away. Alone, you stand a chance of making it. I don't want you getting killed and I don't want you around when that last bullet strikes me down."

"Don't say that, Darby!" she shrieked at him.

"It's coming one day, Sis; it can't be stopped. Accept it and get out while you still have a chance to survive and start over. You deserve a home and a family. You ought to have them by now. If Rogue is the man you want, find him and convince him to join you. I'll stake you two," he vowed.

Carrie Sue tried another angle. "What if Curly told Quade where you're hiding? If Quade's your framer, he won't come here or send anyone after you while he's blackening your name. But if he isn't, he could be on his way here now, with a large posse. Curly didn't have time to betray me, so Quade can't know where I was."

Refreshing that treachery in his mind, Darby cursed, "Damn that bastard Curly! If Rogue hadn't killed him, I would! He's fooled me twice, and I don't fool easy! Looks like Harding's given up on catching you first and wants you dead if he can't have you."

She ventured, "Or he hopes I'll figure out his ruse and rush into his arms and save you and myself."

"You think that's his motive?" Darby asked.

"I don't know, big brother. Too much has happened lately and my wits aren't clear. What else could he want from this ruse? If he's the one behind it," she added, but somehow knew he was.

"Let's get back to camp and talk with the boys. We'll need to pull out in the morning. Just so there won't be any trouble with Kadry, let's keep quiet about this romance with Rogue."

"How did you guess the truth?" she teased.

"I've alwasy been able to read you, Sis, so don't start keeping secrets from me. How far has this romance gone?" he asked gravely.

Carrie Sue lowered her lashes a moment. "I'm a grown woman, big brother; I'm twenty-four and that's private."

"That far, huh? Oh, well, I can't say much. I've had me plenty of women and I didn't love any of them. At least you love this man."

"No more than I love you, Darby Stover."

The outlaw leader helped her to her feet and hugged her tightly. "I got you into this mess, Sis, and I'll get you out. Soon, I promise." He eyed the poster and clipping about her. "With these around, you're in big danger, Sis. You'll have to stick with us until I get you away."

They gathered her things and rode to the cabin. It was a crude structure made of oak logs from the area. There was no stove, so all cooking was done outside, near the stream. The cabin backed up to steep rocks, and trails led off to its right and left and traveled into the interior of the mountains. From there other trails snaked into New Mexico and into western Texas, providing many escape routes.

Carrie Sue saw the boys sitting around the campfire drinking coffee. As they approached, all except Kale came to greet her.

Tyler Parnell, a simple man of thirty with light brown hair and hazel eyes, helped her down and said in a thick Arkansas accent, "Shore good ta have ya back, Miss Carrie Sue. We done missed ya."

She smelled the ever present hint of whiskey on Tyler, who towered over her at six-feet-two inches. When he hugged her, his short beard and wiry mustache scratched her cheek. She glanced at his first cousin Walt Vinson who was a man of thirty with medium brown hair, hazel eyes, a shorter beard but softer mustache, and about Tyler's height. She smiled and nodded hello. As always, those two men reminded her of brothers because they looked and talked so much alike with their rough country tongues. Walt fingered his gunbutts and nodded in return. Neither had changed their habits she realized.

John "Griff" Griffin shook her hand energetically and said, "Yes'm, good ta have you back, Missy Stover. It dun been quiet without you."

"Thank you, Griff," she remarked to the black man with a cleanly shaven jawline and a long black mustache. Griff was thirty-one, the oldest of the group. His obsidian eyes sparkled when he grinned. He jammed a stick in his mouth and began chewing on it, as always.

Dillon Holmes grabbed her and hugged her and kissed her on the cheek, but only because she turned her head when he boldly went for her mouth. As usual, he smelled of aromatic cigarillos from Mexico. At six feet, the twenty-nine-year-old man had dark brown hair and intensely green eyes. His hair was straight and, for a side part, fell across his forehead in a haphazard manner. "Hello, Dillon."

"You're one sight for sore eyes, Carrie Sue," he murmured in his heavy southern drawl from Mississippi. "Glad you're home again."

Kadry Sams parted the group with his six-one frame. His sky blue eyes trailed over her leisurely. He habitually finger-combed his wavy hair which was a mixture of dark and sunny blond. At twenty-eight, Kadry Sams was a handsome man with a splendid physique. She dreaded the confrontation, but smiled genially and said, "Hello, Kadry."

"Ye been gone tae long, me beautiful lass," he murmured with a Scottish burr. He captured a lock of her hair and teased it under his nose. "I been awaitin' ye return. Canna git ye anything?"

"Coffee, please," she replied.

"Ye wish is filled, me bonny lass. Gie me ae moment. 'Tis ae fine day fer ye tae return home. I've missed ye." He went for her coffee.

Walt asked, "Whatcha doin' back, Miss Carrie Sue?"

"Did dat Tucson turn out a bad place?" Griff added.

"Let her catch her breath, boys," Dillon drawled.

While Carrie Sue sipped the hot liquid, Darby related the news to his gang, who were just as shocked and vexed as her brother was, except for Kadry Sams whose blue eyes burned with jealousy.

Kadry hinted, "Sae, ye met tha famous Rogue, did ye?"

"I wouldn't be here now if he hadn't saved my life a few times," she replied, bravely looking at the blond while speaking.

"Why dinna ye bring him along?" Kadry asked, fingering his hair.

"Why should I?" she asked in aflippant tone.

Kadry eyed her suspiciously and shrugged. "Nae reason."

"What'll we do, boss?" Tyler asked.

"I don't lack nobody playin' usins," Griff said.

"Naw, me neither," Walt added.

Dillon's mysterious green eyes remained locked on Carrie Sue as if he weren't listening to the important conversation. Kadry nudged him, and glared when Dillon glanced his way. Dillon grinned and shrugged. Carrie Sue realized with annoyance that a new challenge for her had been given and accepted. Nothing and no one had changed. She frowned at both men, then returned her attention to her brother.

Darby caught the interaction. He warned sternly, "Settle down, boys. We gotta think this through." He showed them the clippings.

Kale Rushton remained quiet and alert, sharpening his knife.

While the men were passing around the newspaper articles with the false stories, Kadry whispered to her, "Ye best stay with us frae nigh on, lass. We should hae seen ye poster comin'. Old Quade willna e'er gie up on ye."

Carrie Sue recalled what T.J. had suggested about this man possibly being the one who had released her description to force her back into his reach. No, she concluded, there was no way he could have done it. Not that it wasn't a clever and daring idea, but Kadry hadn't been given the opportunity to pull off such a dangerous ruse.

She divulged, "I'm not staying long, Kadry. I only came to warn Darby and to let him know I'm safe."

"Wha' mean ye, lass?" he asked, staring at her.

"I'll tell you what she means," Darby answered for her. "I'm getting her plenty of money, then she's hightailing it far from here. I'm sending her to Montana to buy a ranch, or a hotel, or store, or something. If all goes well, we might even join her in a few months."

Carrie Sue's head jerked in her brother's direction. She returned his broad smile which made him look so boyish. "You will?"

Darby caught her free hand in his. "I ain't making no promises, Sis, but I'll think about it. For sure, you're getting your butt out of this area. We'll pull out at dawn tomorrow. We need to make a big hit to let folks knew we didn't pull those other ones. We'll head for San Angelo, supply up there, and make a strike a few days later. We can head for Miss Sally's Parlor House and get some news from her. She always protects us and she knows everything."

The men agreed, as always. As breakfast was being cooked by Walt and Tyler, Kadry and Dillon surrounded Carrie Sue.

"Dinna worry, lass; I'll take care o' ye."

Dillon's heavy southern voice refuted, "I do it best. I'm the one who took a bullet in the shoulder to save you."

Carrie Sue didn't want any trouble, so she said, "You're both good friends and I'm grateful, but I can take care of myself."

Kadry's blue eyes darkened. "I'll kill him with me bare hands!"

"If I don't get the sorry bastard first," Dillon remarked.

Trying to make light conversation, Carrie Sue said, "I think he's the one framing us, but how can we prove it? Even if we catch him red-handed, who'd believe us?"

"Just kill the sorry trash and be done with him and his troubles."

"Ye make that sound easy, Dillon. How canna we do it?"

"Yeah," Tyler agreed. "He's been a pain in our arses fur years!"

"We can't risk going after Harding," Darby told them. He'll be on the lookout for us. It's too dangerous for Carrie Sue. Us, too, if we want to live much longer. Nope, we can't be reckless or stupid."

"I lack Montanee. Sounds good ta me," Walt murmured.

Tyler teased, "Ya ain't never been there, Cuz, so how'd ya know?"

"Well, I heared it was great," Walt retorted with a grin.

Griff hinted, "Yes'm, a man could git lost up thar."

Dillon murmured dreamily, "I like the idea of settling down. We been at this for years. I'm tired of running and hiding and having nothing. I may get me a wife, and home, and children up there."

"Dinna go ae lookin' at her, Dillon. She be mine."

Dillon chuckled and replied, "That's up to Carrie Sue, isn't it?"

Darby wasn't one to deceive his friends and he saw trouble was brewing over his sister, so he revealed merrily, "Stop it, boys. Carrie Sue has her sights set on T.J. Rogue, so you're wasting your breath."

Carrie Sue wasn't totally surprised by her brother's disclosure as he lived with these men like brothers, and it would halt their sieges.

Kadry's blue eyes narrowed. "Wha' be this, lass?' he demanded.

"My private business," she responded in a cool tone, glaring back.

Tyler asked, "Will Rogue be joinin' us, boss?"

"I wouldn't mind having him, if we run across him."

"Rogue ain't no outlaw. We couldn't trust him," Dillon argued.

The leader explained, "He's an expert, boys, and he saved her life."

"Dinna matter tae me who or wha' he is. He canna steal her."

"Shut up, both of you," she commanded. "I'll choose whom I'll see and not see. I like you both as friends, but nothing more. Get it?"

Kale spoke up for the first time since returning to camp to announce her arrival, "When we leave, we'll have plenty to do, so let's stay limber and alert. We have that other gang to worry about."

Walt suggested, "If'n Miss Carrie Sue rides with us, they'll know we're th' real Stover Gang. The other un don't have no Texas Flame."

Kale instantly said, "No. It's too dangerous."

Dillon concurred, "I agree. She stays in camp."

Walt said, "I didn't mean no harm. I just want 'em unmasked. Them stories in th' papers are gittin' us in trouble lack she says."

Carrie Sue grinned. "I have a better idea on how to unmask those pretenders. It's dangerous and we might get caught, but it could work."

Chapter 20

"What do you mean?" Darby asked as the men gathered around to hear her suggestion.

She reasoned, "Since they're using the newspapers against us, why can't we use the papers in our favor? When we reach San Angelo, you can kidnap a reporter, bring him to our hideout, and we'll give him the facts. Any newspaper man would die for exclusive interviews with the Stover Gang, and every paper in Texas and probably in other states will carry his story on us. We'll tell him our backgrounds and how we got ensnared in this business. That should put Quade Harding and his father in the boiling pot. Maybe other victims of theirs will step forward to give evidence against him. Or get the law to looking in his direction. Quade will be too busy defending himself to give us much trouble. Maybe our story will flush that other gang into the open or make them stop framing us. And . . ."

She paused for affect before adding, "It should make the law get suspicious of who and why we're being framed and start them to investigating the situation. If Quade's involved, it could get him caught and punished. It's worth a try since we can't get near him to avenge Mama and Papa. After reading the truth, most everyone will have sympathy for us and it'll brighten our reputations. People used to like us, but bad stories and lies have hurt our image. We need to win over the people again. If we get caught, a friendly jury would be a big help. Besides exposing Quade, it may get his huge rewards withdrawn. If so, those two thousand dollar government ones won't look as good to our pursuers."

"You think it'll work?" Darby murmured, eagerness filling his eyes.

Carrie Sue smiled at her brother. "We'll tell the reporter they can be certain of any jobs we pull because we'll give our target a lock of the Texas Flame's hair. Before I leave, I'll cut off a few inches and make ribbon-bound curls. Very few people have hair my color, so this false leader won't be able to hand out convincing locks. It's simple: no golden red curl, no Stover Gang responsible. Without locks of my hair, that other gang can't pretend to be us anymore. This way, the Stover Gang will get blame or credit only for the jobs you pull."

Kale grinned. "You are one clever woman, *chica*. It's good."

"Does this mean we won't haveta shave, boss?" Tyler asked.

When Carrie Sue glanced inquisitively at Darby, he explained, "We got new horses and planned to disguise ourselves so we could move about safer. Tyler, Griff, and Walt were going to shave off their beards and mustaches. Me, Dillon, and Kadry were going to grow some here before leaving. Kale's got too much Indian blood to grow more than a faint shadow," he jested. "We planned to do our hair different, too. Except Kale; he refuses to cut his, but he said he'd tuck it under his hat and stop wearing that red sash."

Carrie Sue didn't ask why the three men involved hadn't begun their facial hair yet, probably the habit of shaving wasn't noticed or they had planned to stay here a long time. "That won't benecessary now. You want people to recognize the gang. Don't wear masks anymore so they can see that your faces match those on the posters. Your crimes aren't doing the gang as much damage as those pretenders' are. They're killing people and hitting reckless targets. Those big companies will fight back harder and meaner than our usual targets. They have the money and power to hire large bands to hunt us down."

"Damn those Hardings!" Dillon shouted and lit a cigarillo.

"Are ye sure 'tis him?" Kadry asked.

The redhead replied, "At first, I thought the law might be tricking me or endangering the gang with false reports by turning everyone against us. They know we have people who give us aid sometimes. Then, I decided those stories are true, just not about us. Who, but Quade Harding, has the motive, money, and guts to pull this off?"

Kale concurred, "She's right. Good thinking, *chica*."

Walt queried with a frown, "Won't it be dangerous ta steal a reporter an' show 'im our hideout?"

"Darby can learn from Sally who's the best one, where he works, and where he lives. He can take one of you to help him abduct the man from his home or office. You can blindfold him and lead him around in circles to disorient him. He'll be too excited to be scared or reluctant. This will be the biggest story of his lifetime. He'll be plenty willing to oblige us with printing the truth. I'll give him a lock of my hair to use for comparison in future jobs. Think what a famous man we'll make of him. He won't turn us down."

"You're right about that, Sis. It's a damn good idea. It'll work. We been laying low for weeks. We're getting restless. This is the perfect first job to pull. Before a week's out, we'll have that other gang in a stew. This is gonna be fun. We head for San Angelo at first light. You boys get plenty of rest today, and get everything packed."

Carrie Sue added, "If Curly was the one tipping off Quade, his boss will be in a terrible fix when he isn't warned we're on the move again and he pulls a job at the same time we do."

*

Late that afternoon, Carrie Sue took a walk with Kale Rushton after his lengthy nap. Kadry was on guard duty, and Dillon wouldn't approach her while she was in the half-Apache's company. Walt, Griff, and Tyler were playing poker with Darby. She had talked over old and future times with her brother, a conversation which made her restless.

"Kale, how is Darby these days? He seems different since I last saw him. He's quieter and moodier. What's wrong?"

"Seven years is a long time to be chased around the countryside, *chica*. I think he misses what he lost, a home and a family, and he's missed you like crazy. A long time ago, we could ride into towns for fun and rest. Nowadays, we can't. What good is money if you can't spend it somewhere and enjoy it?"

"Then, why is he so reluctant to go straight some place?"

"He doesn't want to admit it, but he's getting worried about how long he can survive and when he'll make his first mistake and get us all killed or captured. This kind of life gets tiresome, *chica,* for men like them. Me, it's all I've ever known. 'Course, I'm not stuck like they are. I can return to the Apaches or to Mexico and live fine."

Carrie Sue spoke softly, "T.J. Rogue was raised by the Chiricahua Apaches in Arizona." She told Kale about the experiences T.J. had while growing up in the Indian camp. She related her visit to Naiche's camp and her meeting on the trail with Geronimo. She revealed how T.J. had gone back to warn them of the Army's approach with Gatling guns, and how Naiche's tribe had fled into Mexico until it was safe to return. "You two are much alike, Kale; I think you'd make good friends."

"Now I see why Rogue is so powerful with his guns and wits—Apache training. You love this gunslinger, *chica?*"

Carrie Sue glanced at him and admitted, "Yes."

Kale probed, "You trust him?"

Carrie Sue hesitated before replying, "Because of my existence, Kale, it's hard for me to trust anybody fully except you and Darby. He had plenty of chances to betray me for money or glory, but he didn't. He took a lot of risks to help me. I think he loves me, too."

"Will he go to Montana with you?"

"I don't know. I did run out on him in El Paso. Several times he tried to persuade me to stop searching for Darby and get away. But I had to warn Darby about that other gang and let him see I was all right."

"Why did you leave Rogue behind?"

"Two reasons. I didn't want him joining us and getting into trouble, and I didn't want to endanger all of you if I'd misjudged him."

Kale liked the honesty of her answer, but wished she weren't so miserable over her decision. "If he crosses our trail and joins us, I will study him for you. Eyes and voices cannot lie to Apache wits."

"If he does lie, Kale, please don't kill him. He did save my life many times and he helped me get here. Just send him away."

"You love him too much, *chica,* if you do not wish his death even if he is an enemy. That is unlike the woman I helped raise and train. Love must be a powerful emotion, and a dangeorus one." Kale eyed her closely. If Rogue made trouble for Darby, he would have to kill him. No threat to his friend could be allowed to live.

"When we reach San Angelo, let Kadry and Dillon go with Darby, and you stay in camp with me. After we finish with the reporter and I get some money, I'm gone, Kale. I have to. Understand?"

"*Si, chica,* I understand." He withdrew his knife and whetstone and began passing the blade back and forth along its surface.

"One day, *amigo,* you're going to cut off your fingers," she teased.

He chuckled. "A good knife can be your best friend if you take good care of it. I can peel off a man's hide in ten minutes or less."

She grimaced and asked, "Whyever would you want to do a gory thing like that, Kale?"

"A foe deserves no less than to lose his mask, *chica.*"

She swallowed hard. "I wouldn't want you as a foe, Kale Rushton."

"Nor would I, *chica,* nor would I," he concurred honestly. "If anyone ever harmed you or Darby or one of the boys, you'd see what me and this shiny blade could do."

* * *

After a supper of venison stew and Johnny cakes, the camp quieted down. The boys began playing cards, making new plans, and sipping whiskey—especially Tyler Parnell. Kadry went to where Carrie Sue was standing near their brush corral with her new horse and asked her to take a walk with him.

When she refused as politely as possible, he asked, "Ye willna e'en gie me a chance tae fight fer ye?"

She focused her violet-blue eyes on him. "It won't do any good, Kadry. I don't love you. When are you going to accept that?"

He ran his spread fingers through his mixed blond hair. His sky blue eyes darkened. "Because o' this Rogue fellow?"

"Not really. I've known you for years, Kadry, and I haven't fallen in love with you. I tried it once to make you and Darby happy, but it didn't work, remember? Even if T.J. didn't exist, I still wouldn't love you and marry you. You're only making yourself miserable and me uncomfortable with this useless pursuit when you can't win."

"If that's a challenge, me darlin', I accept it."

She frowned to show her annoyance and to discourage him. "It wasn't a challenge, Kadry Sams, it's a fact."

He stroked her cheek and vowed, "One day, ye might find ye love me an' need me when this Rogue betrays ye or turns ye down."

"Whatever happens or doesn't happen between me and T.J. Rogue, it doesn't affect how I feel about you. I don't love you," she stressed. "You can't make somebody love you just because you want them to."

He argued, "I kin love enough fer both o' us, lass. Gie me a chance. Let me come ta Montana with ye. We kin start a new life. We kin buy a ranch, hae a home an' family. I kin make ye happy."

She shook her head. "No, Kadry, it wouldn't work. Please stop this. It isn't doing either of us any good to keep talking about it."

"I love ye an' want ye, Carrie Sue. I canna gie up on ye."

"I wish that weren't true. What can I say or do to make you stop pressing me? You're only punishing yourself. I don't want to hurt you, Kadry. Why do you force me to keep rejecting you?"

He captured her hand and carried it to his lips. "Tha only thin' I'ma forcing ye tae do, me luv, is face tha truth. Ye canna e'er hae a man like Rogue. He'd ne'er settle down. Men wad always be after him, challenging him. Ye'd ne'er be safe with him."

She pulled her hand away and placed it behind her. "The same can be said of you, my infamous friend."

"Nae in Montana, me luv, I promise ye, nae trouble."

Dillon Holmes joined them and halted Kadry's earnest pleas for love and marriage. The green-eyed southerner asked, "Why don't you let it go, Kadry? She's not going to choose you over me."

Carrie Sue groaned loudly. "I'm not going to choose either one of you, so please stop this bickering and pestering. You two are part of the reason I had to get away so many times. You drive me loco."

Dillon said, "I can give you anything you want or need, Carrie Sue."

She responded, "No, you can't, Dillon, nobody can. Please, both of you leave me alone, I'm tired. I'm going to bed. We have a long ride ahead of us." She walked away, leaving the two outlaws bickering.

In her bedroll, Carrie Sue wondered if there was any way T.J. could track her here.

If so, what would she do and say? She hoped he didn't. Much as she wanted to see his handsome face, she didn't want to cause trouble with any of the men or for her lover.

Carrie Sue pondered T.J.'s reaction to her escape. How had he felt? Where would he head to search for her, for surely he would? To Brownwood, she concluded, because that was where the gang was allegedly operating. She doubted that T.J. believed her note's claim that her brother wasn't to blame for those recent crimes. Even if he did believe her, he would still head for that area, either to take care of Quade Harding or hopefully to join up with her again. What would happen when Darby and T.J. met, if they did?

"Darby?" she whispered, her bedroll beside his.

"Yeah, Sis?" he responded, turning toward her in the dim light of a crescent moon. He was unable to make out much in the darkness.

She kept her voice low so the others couldn't overhear them. "Did you mean what you said earlier about going to Montana with me?"

Darby stayed silent.

Carrie Sue quivered in alarm and asked, "Did you hear me?"

"Yeah, I heard you. Once we get this mess cleared up about that false gang with that reporter, things should cool down for us. Me and the boys will probably head for Arizona after you leave. I hear there's lot of gold and silver to be had out there. You have a better chance of survival and making a new life if me and the boys aren't around to mess it up for you. If I leave them here, they'll only get into trouble and get themselves killed. I can't run out on them and I couldn't take them along to Montana 'cause we'd draw too much attention to you. I owe them, Sis; they've been with me from the start. They're my friends, like family to me."

"You don't owe them your life, big brother."

"Yeah, maybe I do. They've risked theirs lots of times for me."

"You can't keep on with this, Darby. One day, one of those lawmen is going to outsmart you or one of those bounty hunters is going to catch up with you. They're going to kill you, Darby, all of you."

"I know, but we don't have any choice. It's too late for us."

"Yes, you do. You can pull out now. Let's forget about the reporter and money. Let's just leave from here and head north."

"I can't, Sis."

"You mean, you won't," she corrected, anger chewing at her.

After a pause, he replied, "Yeah, I guess you're right about that."

With teary eyes, she urged, "Darby, please."

Darby ignored her tone and words. "Why don't you leave from here, Sis? You can take some supplies and all the money we have left. The boys won't mind; we'll get more soon."

"No, I want to go to San Angelo with you and work with that reporter. I want the truth out before I take off." Carrie Sue didn't tell him she thought the reporter would trust her and believe her more than the men and she could make the newspaper man grasp the truth. She had to remove that threat to her brother before she deserted him for the last time. She owed Darby that much. Besides, she needed better supplies and more money if she was going to make it to Montana and have a real chance at a new beginning. If only she could get to Carolyn Starns's money in the Tucson bank, but that wasn't possible.

Carrie Sue also wanted to send T.J. a message through Hank Peterson to let her love know she was all right and was heading for safety far away. She realized there was no need to keep reasoning or arguing with her brother; she couldn't change his mind. She hated the fact he was choosing his friends over her, but Darby thought and felt like a man. Sometimes misguided loyalty was more important to men than family bonds. His male pride and his fealty to his gang would never let him desert them. He had pulled them together, led them, made all the decisions for them, and taken care of them. He felt responsible for the gang as a good father would for his family. They were six, and she was only one, so the odds were against her.

"Good-night, Darby," she murmured, her heart heavy with sadness.

" 'Night Sis," he replied in a matching tone.

*

Carrie Sue spent a restless night with bad dreams about her brother's capture and death. Each time she awakened, she tried to return to sleep to dream about a bright future with T.J. Rogue, but her mind refused to cooperate. Whenever she saw her lover in her dreams, he was dogging her persistently and trying to destroy Darby and his gang. Two hours before dawn, she finally fell into a deep slumber.

*

Saturday morning, June tenth, the Stover Gang left the cool and secluded canyon in the Guadalupe Mountains, heading for San Angelo. It was a journey which would require five days.

*

To the east in Brownwood, Ranger Dave Clemmens rode into a lethal trap by the gang impersonating Darby and his men. Pinned to the lawman's chest by his silver star was a note saying, "Stop chasing the Stover Gang or you'll all end up like this. You'll never catch us, so give it up and survive." It was signed "Darby Stover."

Tuesday night, a weary and moody T.J. Rogue arrived in San Angelo. He had tried to make town before the telegraph office closed for the day so he could pick up his messages. A storm had slowed him yesterday by forcing him to take cover for hours. He had no choice but to wait for morning to see what had taken place while he'd been out of touch. He also needed a newspaper to learn whatever he could.

He stabled Nighthawk, took his gear, and checked into a small hotel near the edge of town. Two buildings away was Miss Sally's Parlor House, a luxurious brothel famous for its food, music, drinks, gambling, and well-trained prostitutes. Tonight, he needed nothing more than a bath, hot meal, cool drink, and comfortable bed.

No, he corrected himself, what he needed and wanted most was Carrie Sue Stover in his arms. It had been seven days since he'd made love to her, then lost her to her recklessness. If, his mind scoffed, he could call her fleeing from his threat being rash. Lordy, he wished he knew where she was and how she was. Even if her posters were down, she was with the gang again, and in great peril. For all he knew, she could be captured or killed by now.

When morning came, after a long and troublesome night, T.J. arose early, had a quick breakfast, and headed for the telegraph office. There were two messages awaiting him. He read Hank Peterson's to discover his friend in Mesilla hadn't heard from Carrie Sue and didn't have any further news on the gang. Mitchell Sterling's message said that Ranger Dave Clemmens had been killed outside Brownwood last Saturday, allegedly by "Darby Stover."

T.J. knew from study that Carrie Sue's brother was not known to ambush and murder any man in cold blood, and Darby certainly never incriminated himself with reckless boasting! He wondered if Dave had stumbled onto something important about Quade Harding. The skilled Ranger had been working the Harding case for some time and had made a mistake somewhere along the trail. That meant T.J. needed to investigate Dave's death when he reached Brownwood. If Quade was in on more than a land grab and local crimes, his two cases would overlap. He hoped Harding was involved in the frame of the Stover Gang. If one existed, and he believed it did, that would give him another reason and way to entrap his foe.

Mitchell also said he had nothing new to report on the gang's movements and deeds since T.J. left El Paso. If Darby and his men had committed those recent crimes and Carrie Sue was back with them, they were laying low again and she would be safe, hopefully.

T.J. faced another reality. When he rode into Brownwood and confronted Quade Harding again, what would happen? The man knew he was Ranger Thad Jamison, and he would know his murder attempt had failed. Harding would be forced to try again to cover his guilt. T.J. asked himself if he should skip Brownwood for now, which could lead to him exposing his identity on this case. He couldn't arrest Quade without evidence and he couldn't get near the man to obtain it! If he revealed himself there, his undercover days were over. And, Carrie Sue would learn the wrong way who he was. Besides, Harding was probably on alert after that curious poster business.

The best thing to do was wait to learn if Dave Clemmens had reported anything before his death. T.J. sent a coded wire to the head of the Texas Ranger unit for which he worked. He told his superior about his suspicions of a frame and Quade Harding's possible involvement in that and Dave's murder. He asked the officer to reconsider a pardon for Carrie Sue, if she helped with the Stover and Harding cases. He vowed to marry her and keep her out of future trouble. He said he would take full responsibility for her, that he would do *anything* to get her pardoned.

T.J. sent a similar coded message to President Grant and prayed his old friend wouldn't let him down. If Grant didn't have a chance at a third term, then, this being an election year shouldn't control his decision on a pardon. If fact, the man whose life he had saved and whom he had served faithfully owed him this chance at happiness.

T.J. sent answers to Mitchell and Hank, then went to the newspaper office. He met William Ferguson, owner and reporter. He asked for the last seven day's papers to check out the news. While Ferguson gathered them, T.J. asked, "Hear much about the Stover Gang?"

"There was plenty of news for weeks, but nothing since that Wells Fargo office in Brady. Why are you so interested, son?"

T.J. used one of his genial and disarming smiles. "There's a ten thousand dollar reward out on Darby Stover and his sister and five each on his men. That's a lot of money. I travel around all the time, so if I run into them, I wouldn't mind collecting it. I hear she's a real beauty."

"Are you a bounty hunter?" William Ferguson asked.

T.J. sent him a scowl to reveal his feelings. "Nope. I'm what you might call a drifter or gunslinger. Name's T.J. Rogue."

William Ferguson looked the young man over and smiled. "In this business, I've heard of you many times, son. I must say it's a pleasure to meet such a famous man. I've printed stories about your . . . shall we say, colorful adventures? I also enjoy meeting the people I write about in my paper. I bet you could fill an entire edition with tall tales. You want to set the record straight? I always print the truth."

T.J. chuckled and shook his head, the man's words and mood telling him which approach to take to extract the most information. T.J. knew men like this had facts they often didn't or couldn't print. "Nope. If men learned I was tame as a kitten, they'd be stomping on my tail all the time. Sometimes a bad reputation serves you well, sir, so I'd better keep mine a while. A fierce lone wolf gets challenged less than a pussycat, and I try to do as little killing as I can. It isn't like people think it is. It's a bad and hard way to survive."

Ferguson laughed heartily. He liked this direct young man and concluded he couldn't be evil. "You staying in town long?"

"I think I'll be leaving for Commanche in a few hours. That's one place the gang hasn't struck lately. Maybe I'll get lucky. I get tired of searching for odd jobs or taking offensive ones. It'll be nice to have enough money to maybe settle down some place peaceful. If you add up the Hardings' rewards and the law's, that comes to sixty-six thousand. A man can get out of the gunslinging business with that much."

"That's a wise and brave decision, son. I hope you succeed. But I wouldn't count on the Stover Gang being in central Texas. If they were, they'd be after whoever's impersonating them. I've studied and followed the Stover Gang for years and I can tell you, those last five crimes weren't committed by Darby's boys. Not his style, and a man doesn't change a perfect one and start acting crazy and reckless."

Tipping up the brim of his hat so the man could see his clear eyes better, T.J. chuckled and alleged, "That was my thinking too, sir. That's why I wanted your papers; I hear you're the best in Texas. From those I've been reading, something didn't sound right to me. I wonder if the law has noticed anything strange."

"I doubt it. They're too busy trying to capture and hang them to realize they're innocent of those charges. It's a real shame to see Darby's reputation sullied like this. He's been mighty careful over the years to shoot only when necessary. I think that's why people always yielded to him without a fight; they trusted him to ride off afterwards and leave them safe. These recent jobs all had vicious killings."

T.J. realized that Carrie Sue knew her brother well and she was right about suspecting impersonation. "You think somebody could be doing this on purpose, Mr. Ferguson? Say, framing Darby?"

"What makes you think that, son?" he asked, intrigued.

T.J. propped his elbows on the counter. He tucked his thumb under his chin and curled his index finger over it. "I'd say there has to be a traitor or spy somewhere, somebody who knows when his boss can play Darby. There hasn't been a robbery by both at the same time; that's why he looks guilty. Suppose one of his men is in cahoots with another gang and tipping them off on where and when to attack. Or," he began and paused dramatically, "what if some enemy is framing him to get him killed? Say, that Harding fellow in Brownwood who's so eager to get the Stovers. I hear he wants the sister alive or no payment. Isn't that a mite strange? I wonder what he's up to?" T.J. murmured, uncurling his fingers to stroke his jawline as if in deep study.

Ferguson was stimulated by the conversation. "I hadn't considered that angle, son. You could have something there. I thought it was strange that the Hardings took over the Stover ranch just before Darby became an outlaw. At first, he was Darby's only target, and the boy had done some shouting to the law about murder and theft. Could be a revenge motive in there some place. I'd give a box of gold pieces to question that boy and his sister about those early days."

"What would you say was their last strike, Mr. Ferguson?"

"That stage holdup near Sherman the end of April."

"That's over six weeks past. Isn't that a long time to lay low?"

The older man chuckled. "Not for Darby Stover. He doesn't need much money. Where can he go to spend it? He's wanted everywhere. He doesn't care about making a reputation for himself. I think he's stayed an outlaw because he had no choice in the matter. I think that boy would have gone straight long ago if the law had punished the Hardings. A real shame, but I believe he got himself into a trap trying to destroy the men who killed his parents and took his ranch."

"That's some theory, Mr. Ferguson. How could you prove it?"

"I can't, neither can he; that's why he's still on the run. I've worked on this story for years, son. It fascinates me how and why good men go bad. I've talked to folks who won't even talk to the law, scared to talk to them. I know things I can't even print because I can't back them up with proof or witnesses. Those Hardings have power and wealth, and they're real mean. It wouldn't surprise me any if there is a frame and they're behind it. I really hate seeing that boy and his sister get maligned and killed. You know something strange?" he said, then looked behind him to make certain no one was around.

"They put out a wanted poster on Carrie Sue Stover, then withdrew it, said it was a mistake, the wrong woman. Harding claims Carrie Sue Stover isn't the Texas Flame. He says he was with her when the Flame was seen with the Stover Gang. I can tell you, son, it wasn't the wrong woman. I don't know what's going on, but I'm trying to find out. The law isn't talking."

"How do you know it was her? And why would the law call it back?"

The older man moved closer and talked in a lowered tone. "I paid one of Quade Harding's ex-detectives for some information. He was fired from the agency for drinking too much, and he must have realized Quade wouldn't give him the chance to loosen his tongue while drunk. He identified the poster I showed him as Carrie Sue Stover. He swore she's the Flame, and he vowed that Quade Harding knows the truth. While he was considering my lucrative offer about coming forward with evidence, he was killed by a gambler for cheating. Blasted bad luck!" He glanced around again, then said, "Harding's son wants her badly, and it isn't for revenge. What I can't figure is why the law called in her posters and how they persuaded Harding to cooperate. They must have threatened him with legal action for withholding evidence all those years. I think the Rangers did it because they have one of their men with her and he's trying to get her to lead him to the gang. Sometimes she vanishes for months. It could be she's linked up with an undercover lawman and doesn't know it. They could be doing this to protect him and to give her time to lead him to her brother's gang."

"That means I don't stand a chance of locating them and bringing them in alive. I surely do hate to see bounty hunters get them."

"So do I, young man, so do I," the older man murmured sadly.

T.J. studied the gray-haired man for a time and made a quick decision. "Mr. Ferguson, I think you can be a big help to the law and possibly save their lives. What I'm about to tell you is in strictest confidence, but I need your help. You have a lot of knowledge we'll need if we're going to stop the Stover Gang and arrest the Hardings. I'm Thad Jamison, Texas Ranger, U.S. Marshal, and Special Agent to President Grant; I have official papers and badges to prove my claims if you need to see them. I've been on this case for weeks. Our man in Brownwood, Dave Clemmens, was killed recently, and I don't believe it was Darby's doing like that note on his chest claimed. Obviously he uncovered something about Quade Harding or this false gang and had to be silenced. I always work in secret, so I'll have to trust you not to tell anyone who or what I am." He divulged, "I was the one traveling with Carrie Sue Stover, but she gave me the slip in El Paso. From the message she left me, she was afraid she'd get T.J. Rogue into trouble for helping her. She said her brother was being framed, but how do we prove it? If we can, this will be the biggest story of your life." T.J. related most of the facts to the astonished man and entreated his help with this vital case.

After some thought, William Ferguson said, "If she's back with her brother by now, he knows about this frame job. If I know Darby Stover, he'll find a clever way to let people know the truth. Believe me, he'll make a strike this week and leave positive proof it was him."

"If Darby doesn't know her poster's down and he lets Carrie Sue ride with him again, our ruse won't be worth a damn, and there's no way I can save her. Lordy, I can't even help her if she doesn't!" he stated angrily. "If she had only stuck with me a while longer."

Ferguson eyed him, then said, "You're in love with her, son."

"That's one story you can't ever print: Lawman Thad Jamison in love with the notorious Texas Flame. Can you help me save her?"

The newspaper owner and reporter smiled and said, "I'll try, son."

The two men discussed the case in length, comparing and sharing information. It was decided that T.J. would head on to Commanche while Ferguson tried to gather more facts through the sources. If anything was discovered, Ferguson was to wire T.J. in Commanche. If T.J. moved on, he was to let Ferguson know where to locate him. The two men shook hands and T.J. left the San Angelo newspaper.

He returned to the telegraph office and sent another coded message to McNelly, revealing these new facts and plans. By noon, T.J. was on his way to check the hideout which Carrie Sue had mentioned.

*

There was two hours of daylight left on Wednesday when the Stover Gang and Carrie Sue reached their old hideout west of San Angelo. It was little more than an old lean-to beside the Middle Concho River. Built in a heavily treed and bushy area, only a person riding in the water could see the cleverly concealed structure.

They had traveled for days across undulating fields of shortgrass with trees which often looked like balls of greenery. They had journeyed over lush, rolling hills and passed picturesque mesas and buttes. It had been easy riding, but everyone was tired.

Carrie Sue had not had a bath since the Pecos River, three days ago. She was eager for the men to head into town to Miss Sally's so she could strip and dive into the river. Along the way, she had been lucky and careful to stay clear of Kadry and Dillon. She hoped she could continue avoiding them until she was gone.

Miss Sally's, Carrie Sue thought with a grin, was a delightful place for ranchers, soldiers from Fort Concho, cowboys, and other males to visit. The bawdyhouse had plenty to offer with its entertainment downstairs and upstairs. She had been there several times in the past and had gotten quite an eye, ear, and head full of enlightenment. Miss Sally more than liked Darby Stover and his boys. Often she had concealed them while they rested, and enjoyed her establishment.

Carrie Sue was not worried about her brother and his friends going there tonight. Miss Sally had a sly system of corded bells which warned men in certain rooms to flee out secret doors. Miss Sally's Parlor House was near the edge of town, and it would soon be dark. The men would be able to slip into and out of town without a problem, especially if Darby spent time with Miss Sally as usual.

After camp was set up, Carrie Sue encouraged all the men to go into town for diversion, but Kale Rushton refused. The half-Apache insisted on remaining with her for protection. She and Kale were relieved when Kadry and Dillon decided not to cause trouble tonight by trying to remain there to court her.

When the gang rode off, Carrie Sue glanced at Kale and said, "You stand guard, *amigo,* while I take a much needed bath. I want to look my best when they bring back that reporter. I hope the boys don't get too liquored up and make bad impressions on him. We need to clean up our image, not make it worse. I'm sure the man will start out prejudiced toward us, so we'll have to win him over with charm."

Kale told her, "Darby warned them to behave tonight because this task is important. The only one he'll need to watch is Tyler. He still drinks too much whiskey. I worry about him getting us caught. You know Darby and the boys wouldn't leave him behind if he got snared. Darby wouldn't leave any of us behind to face a rope."

"I know, Kale. He would die for any or all of you."

"You get cleaned up, *chica,* while I cook us some grub. I'm as hungry as a longhorn after a prairie fire burned all the grass."

*

It was long after midnight when Darby and his gang returned to camp. Kale Rushton and the redhead ceased their talk and set down their coffee cups. The half-Apache pocketed his whetstone and sheathed his knife before rising to go meet the boys. Two strangers were riding with them, and only one was blindfolded.

Darby dismounted and handed his reins to Kale. He grasped Carrie Sue's hand and said, "Come with me, Sis; we have to talk, now."

Carrie Sue realized something was wrong. She glanced at the man between Kadry and Dillon who was staring at her, then took a walk with her brother.

"What is it, Darby? Did anything happen in town tonight?"

"Plenty. Sis, there are a few things you and me need to discuss," he hinted, locking his eyes with hers.

Chapter

21

"What is it, Darby?" she asked when he continued to stare at her.

"We got that newspaper man and he was plenty willing to come along for the story. Sally said he's the best in Texas and a fair man. Name's William Ferguson. We'll give him our side tomorrow."

She smiled and hugged him. "That's wonderful, so why the sullen face? And who's the stranger with you?" she queried.

He replied to her last question, "Cliff Thomas. He was at Sally's tonight. I can use another man on the next few jobs. He rode with us when you were in Sante Fe all those months."

"That was years ago, Darby. You sure you can still trust him?"

"Yep, and it hasn't been years since our last job together. He rode with us after that ranch mess in Laredo and other times while you were holed up in camp."

"Why haven't I met him before?" she asked.

"He didn't come to camp between jobs. You know I never let many extras visit our hideout and see you; they met us other places. Now that your poster's out, it isn't necessary to protect your identity. That time we were on the trail for weeks, Cliff was with us. He's always been careful, so his face isn't known. He'll make a perfect scout for us like before. Don't worry about him; he's a good man."

"I'm confused," she murmured. "If everything went so well in town, why are you acting so strangely? Was Sally mad at you?"

"Nope. Sally was better than ever tonight," he responded with a devilish grin. "She'd never betray me and the boys. What has me spooked is that friend of yours, T.J. Rogue, and your wanted posters."

Carrie Sue became alert. "Was he in town? Did you meet him?"

The auburn-haired man leaned against a tree. "He left yesterday morning, I'm sorry to say, 'cause I'd like a few words with your sweetheart about his feelings for you. If he loves you, maybe he'll help you escape when I get you some money. Least he can do is protect you in camp while me and the boys are raiding. He must be trying to locate you or he wouldn't be in this area. Too bad he's gone."

Carrie Sue wondered if T.J. was heading for Brownwood to battle Quade Harding like he said not long ago. If so, he was in danger. Quade had tried to kill him once and probably would try again. Or, he could be riding for Commanche just to see if she was there. Should she try to reach him, or was that a crazy idea?

"Cliff told me something real strange, Sis. Your posters were recalled by the Texas

Rangers right after they were released. Most of them didn't even get put up anywhere. Cliff only saw two or three, 'cause they were yanked down quick as a wink. He said they weren't up any other place he's been lately. And that story about you in the papers was called a mistake. Now, the Rangers are claiming that new poster is Carrie Sue Stover, but you aren't the Texas Flame. They're saying that old poster is her and it ain't you."

"I don't understand," she murmured in total confusion.

"Quade told the law he was using your poster and reward to save your life until the real Texas Flame was captured. He said he was afraid you'd be killed by mistake before he could clear you. The law told Quade he couldn't put one out on someone who isn't a criminal, so they called them in. How do you make that out, Sis?"

She appeared baffled. "What could Quade be up to? It's crazy. T.J. showed me a poster, and Martin Ferris had one, and that sheriff who came to my room had one. For them to be called in so swiftly, a lot of them got loose! Are you sure Cliff's telling you the truth? I've never heard of wanted posters being withdrawn."

Her brother added, "I asked that newspaper man, and he said the same thing: no posters are out on Carrie Sue Stover with your picture, only one about a redhead called the Texas Flame. Mr. Ferguson said Quade Harding told the law they had the wrong woman. Said you'd worked for him for a long time and couldn't be involved. Quade vowed you two were together when the Flame was spotted riding with us. He's withdrawn his reward offer for Carrie Sue Stover."

She was shocked and alarmed. "Quade is crazy, but he's smart, too smart to pull this ridiculous stunt. How can he lie to the law? Doesn't he realize they'll discover the truth and arrest him?"

"Harding's never been worried about lying to the law. He's done it plenty of times. I think Curly wired him from Tucson and told him you weren't with us anymore, that you were starting a new life there. Harding was probably afraid you'd get killed before he could reach you, so he pulled that trick about the poster to get it called in. Don't you see, Sis? You aren't wanted now. Your names been cleared. When I get you some money, you can get away clean." He tugged on a golden red curl and advised, "You need to cut this long hair and use some berries to darken it 'cause some folks have seen it. Thank goodness you were always masked. We'll make up a name for our famous sidekick and your past will be destroyed."

Carrie Sue paced in deep thought. Something wasn't right. Curly was killed right after seeing her, so he couldn't have wired Quade. Unless he wired Quade from El Paso after visiting Darby and told his boss she had quit the gang. It was like that sneaky Quade to disclaim her poster and guilt to give him time to locate her. Once she was cleared, he would assume he could force her to marry him! She related her conclusions to her brother, who agreed with them.

"You can always say you escaped Tucson because you were innocent but you knew no one would believe you. Good thing you didn't harm that sheriff and make yourself look guilty. This'll clear Rogue too."

She scoffed, "Until Quade admits he lied just to entrap me, or one of his hirelings does. It'll never work, Darby. There's something weird going on, and the law won't be fooled very long, if they're fooled at all. This could be a trick to ensnare Quade. They have to think it's odd that he's reversing his story. They'll figure out he lied and be on my trail again. I still have to vanish to be safe."

"You're right, Sis. I was too excited to think straight. Here in Texas, you'll always be Darby Stover's little sister. We'll let Harding help us clear you before I silence him forever. Once you're gone and Quade's dead, the law can't get to you or the truth. Let's get back to camp. We'll go over this again later."

He straightened up to leave. "I plan to hit the San Angelo bank tomorrow while you hold Ferguson captive here, talking his ears off. Then, we'll strike a gold coin shipment at Big Spring. Sally read a customer's telegram about it, a marshal who's to be there Monday to escort it to El Paso with his deputies. Me and the boys will take it on Sunday before they arrive. Gold coins can't be traced and they're worth plenty. Your freedom's in sight, Sis. You be sure to convince that newspaper man you've never ridden with us."

"That won't work, Darby. The minute Quade is dead, one of his men or hired detectives will come forward with the truth and I'll be on the wanted list again. He must be paying them plenty to keep them silent." Her violet-blue eyes enlarged and she frowned. "We know where he's getting the money for hush payments and our reward offers, from those frame jobs he's pulling. I have to tell Mr. Ferguson the truth so he can help us. Besides, people saw me in Tucson living as a woman killed during one of our robberies; that's too coincidental. It will make things worse for us, for me, if I mislead that reporter and the facts come out soon. People, especially the law, will assume that if we've lied about one thing, we've lied about others and we're no better off than before. He can get the truth out and lessen our perils."

Darby sighed heavily. "I guess I'm too tired to think straight. You're right, Sis. We need to unmask Harding and get you out of here."

*

William Ferguson spent hours questioning the men and taking notes. He couldn't believe his good fortune. He didn't mind that his legs and chest were secured to a chair when the gang got ready to leave camp to rob the bank in San Angelo. His hands were left free for writing and he promised not to pull any tricks with Carrie Sue, his guard.

Carrie Sue watched the eight men gallop away before taking a seat before the newspaper man with a pistol in her lap. She urged, "Please don't try anything, Mr. Ferguson, because I don't want you making me into a killer. Things have gotten desperate for us with that other gang on the loose, so I can't take any chances with my brother's life. It's time everyone learned the truth about us. I'm glad you came so willingly to hear it and report it."

They talked until two o'clock with the man taking down every word. Carrie Sue told him she was the Texas Flame and that Quade Harding had lied about knowing that fact. "Hopefully that will get him into deep trouble with the law. If they'll start investigating him, maybe they'll uncover other crimes. He's up to something, and I don't want to get entangled by his deceit."

William Ferguson knew Quade was not responsible for the poster ruse, but he could not tell her. "When I print this story, new posters will go out on you. This is a big risk, Carrie Sue."

"I know, but it'll unmask Quade Harding. I hate him."

"Why didn't you stick to Harding's lies and go free?"

She sighed wearily. "The law is too smart to be fooled very long, Bill. The truth would eventually come out and it would start over again. This is my one chance to tell our side. Your story can't clear us, but it can reveal the truth and help people understand."

Ferguson knew he couldn't print this story and endanger Thad Jamison's mission or risk having Quade expose the Ranger's demands. When it was over, he would print everything. He needed to get these facts to the lawman who might link up with her again soon.

*

In Commanche, T.J. was resentful over the two telegrams he picked up and read. His Ranger superior and the president still refused to consider a pardon for his love, and he was ordered to stay undercover as T.J. Rogue. That meant, no Brownwood and Harding yet. After he checked out the hiding place Carrie Sue had mentioned, he would decide what action to take next. It was frustrating. How, he worried, could he help her and protect her if he couldn't locate her? If anything happened to her, he'd never forgive himself. How could he live without his heart and soul, for she had stolen them. If he could just see her and reason with her, tell her the truth and convince her to comply with his plans.

*

In Stephenville, between Fort Worth and Brownwood, a train robbery was carried off by the alleged Stover Gang. One of the men was wounded while getting away. The masked Quade Harding reined in his horse, pulled his rifle, and shot his hireling to make certain he was dead and couldn't expose him. Before passing out, the outlaw saw Quade pull the trigger.

In San Angelo, the unmasked gang of Darby Stover was also having bad luck. After robbing the bank and handing the clerk a golden red lock from the Texas Flame, the frightened man pulled a small pistol from beneath the counter and shot the last man out the door: Cliff Thomas, who had turned to warn the people to stay quiet and motionless.

Walt Vinson checked Cliff quickly and said he was dead. Darby ordered the men to flee, and the gang got away with success.

*

In the Stover camp, Carrie Sue and William Ferguson were still talking, but she was calling him Bill now, as requested. She had given him their history and he had told her his impressions before and after meeting them, which pleased her. He believed the account of their frame and who was behind it. He told her about the witness he had found, the man who had been killed before speaking with the law.

"I can't print anything as fact without proof, Carrie Sue, but I can quote your statements. I think every newspaper in the country will print this. Everyone will be excited by it and wonder about your guilt. All you need to do is alert the authorities to Harding's mischief. They'll start an investigation which should help you. It won't clear any of you, but it will get many of those charges dropped. The shorter and weaker the list, the better your chances for a good defense when you're all captured. You have to face facts, Carrie Sue, criminals don't get away with their illegal deeds forever. What will happen to you?"

"As soon as the story's printed, I'm leaving. I may go to California, or Mexico, or Canada, or back East. I might even take a ship and get further away, maybe to England or one of those beautiful islands. I have to find a safe place to start over, Bill. You understand why I can't be clearer on that fact."

"Of course I do, young lady." He sent her an encouraging smile. "People want to know what makes honest folks go bad; this story will teach them something, maybe prevent other youngsters from taking the law into their own hands. It should also put a halt to the Hardings' crimes. After all these years, his treachery might get you justice in that matter. Is there anybody who can help you?"

Carrie Sue looked up from her evening meal preparations and gazed at him sadly for a moment as she thought about her lover. Where was T.J.? What was he doing and feeling? Would he trust her and want her back after her desertion and lies? Would any proud man? "No one. I told you what happened every time I tried to go straight or seek help."

"Those are some strong points in your favor that I believe the law will find of great interest, if you get a judge and jury who're fair. It's a shame you got in so deeply before this trouble could be cleared up with the Hardings. Those boys, too. They don't seem like bad fellows to me, not even that Kale Rushton. I could tell he didn't want to reveal anything about his experiences, but he did that just to help the rest of you. I don't often come across loyalty and love like that."

"The boys are real close, Bill. Any of them would die for the other."

"I'm sure of that, Carrie Sue. What else do you want me to print?"

The gang returned and halted their conversation. She was distressed to learn Cliff Thomas had been left behind. "Are you sure he was dead?"

"Yes, Walt checked him. Took a bullet in the heart. We left that lock of hair like you suggested, Sis. Make sure you put that in the story, Mr. Ferguson. That'll stop whoever's framing us."

"That was a clever idea, Carrie Sue, but a dangerous one. Those curls will tie you to the gang more tightly," Ferguson warned.

"It couldn't be helped. It was the only way to prove which gang was attacking where. I'll be gone soon and out of danger."

*

The men eagerly devoured the beef stew and biscuits. Afterwards, they planned their departure in the morning for Big Spring. . . .

Darby asked Walt Vinson to show him his badge collection so he could find one or more to use during their next job, as Darby didn't want any trouble getting into the building where the gold was being held in secrecy. The men went to where Walt's possessions were outside near his bedroll, leaving Carrie Sue and William Ferguson in the shack.

When Darby saw the Texas Ranger badge with "Thad Jamison" on the back, he asked, "Where did you get this one, Walt?"

Walt looked at it and replied, "From that stage near Sherman. I took it offin that dead Ranger."

"What it is?" Kale questioned his friend's reaction.

"Read it, Kale. It says Thad Jamison. If we killed him, those Rangers will hunt us down forever. He's a legend."

"Legend," Dillon scoffed, "More like a mystery. You think he's for real?"

Kale Rushton responded, "He's for real, all right. He moves like a morning mist; you never see him, but you see where he's been. He hits an area, does his job secretly, then vanishes. Few people know him in person. You don't want to tangle with him; he's deadly, an expert in every area: guns, knives, bows, bare hands.

"We didn't kill Jamison, I met him at an Apache camp years ago. You remember that time I left you boys in camp and went to visit my mother's tribe. He was there, trying to work out some trouble between the whites and Indians. It wasn't him on the stage. Maybe that Ranger was carrying him a new badge."

Darby licked his lips nervously, then dropped the matter from mind. "We have one U.S. Marshal badge and three deputy badges. I'll take this one. Kadry, Dillon, and Tyler will take the other three. With them, we'll get those guards to open the doors to that hotel room. After we get the drop on them, we'll let the rest of you inside. With these new beards and mustaches on me, Kadry, and Dillon, and with Tyler clean shaven, they won't recognize us 'til it's too late. I don't want any shooting, boys. We're trying to wash up our dirty reputations, not splatter 'em with fresh blood. If we make our next few hits without shedding blood, it'll go in our favor with that story."

*

At dawn on Friday, Darby Stover and his men rode off again, to return Monday night, leaving Carrie Sue to guard Ferguson once more.

Over coffee, she told him, "I'm sorry, Bill, but we can't release you until they return from Big Spring. I promise you will leave safely."

"Don't worry, Carrie Sue. We can talk easily for four more days. What was that talk about using badges last night?" he asked.

Carrie Sue explained how Darby intended to use badges which Walt Vinson collected to prevent any unnecessary killing during their holdup. "As I told you, my brother doesn't shoot unless his life's threatened, and he doesn't allow his men to do so either. Nearly every killing against us was committed by a man who was a temporary gangmember. Darby's always careful about who he lets join, but sometimes a bad seed gets past him. He gets rid of them the moment they disobey."

*

In San Angelo, the sheriff was questioning Cliff Thomas who had just aroused from his bullet wound. "You're damn lucky that slug was so small, Thomas. You can live through this and get pardoned if you help us catch the Stover Gang. They can't have gotten too far. Which way were they heading? Speak up, man, or you'll hang tomorrow."

Cliff was in pain and was scared. "They didn't go nowhere, Sheriff. You put that promise in writing and I'll draw you a map to their camp."

The sheriff complied, but he knew he wouldn't keep his promise to this outlaw or to any criminal whom he tricked into capture. Cliff Thomas was propped up to draw a map to Darby's hideout on the Middle Concho River, west of town. "That ain't all, Sheriff," he hinted, but began to cough strenuously. He grabbed his chest as the bullet shifted in his heart and blocked a main artery, killing him before he could expose the Big Spring threat.

The doctor checked the outlaw and said, "Gone for sure this time."

"Don't matter; he would have hanged when he got well." He ordered his deputy to gather a posse, "a large one with plenty of guns."

*

Carrie Sue was glancing out the paneless window when she spotted movement around the trees and bushes. She hurried from side to side where wooden flaps were lifted for air flow and assessed the situation.

"What's wrong, Carrie Sue?" the gray-haired man asked.

"We've got a posse closing in on the shack. We're surrounded."

"Why don't you use me as a shield and hostage to bluff your way out?" he suggested, not wanting her captured.

"It's too dangerous, Bill. You could get shot by accident; posses are nervous men. I have to surrender peaceably to protect you." She went to William Ferguson and cut him free. Yanking off her bandanna, she ordered, "Tie my hands, Bill, quickly. Take my pistol and pretend you've overpowered me and captured me. There's no chance of escape for me, so it's rash to challenge them. I want you to get my reward, if there's one left. Just think what a wonderful story this will make: Newspaperman Captures Texas Flame!"

"Oh, my heavens," he murmured worriedly. He tied her wrists together, collected his valuable notes, and stuffed them inside his shirt. He led her outside at gunpoint with her bound hands lifted skyward. "Don't shoot!" he yelled when men showed their faces from behind trees. "It's me, William Ferguson, from the newspaper."

"Where are the others, Bill?" the sheriff shouted from cover.

"Gone. They left early this morning. I was kidnapped, but I got free and captured Darby's sister. She's harmless."

The sheriff and his posse came forward, eyeing the beautiful fugitive with great interest. "What in blazes are you doing here, Bill?"

The crafty newspaperman explained, "The Stovers say they're being framed. They vow they didn't commit any of those recent crimes. They abducted me to tell me their story so I could print it and inform the authorities. They claim Quade Harding, that fellow in Brownwood who offered those big rewards, is responsible. The gang's gone there to face him down and pull a job. She was guarding me, but I got the drop on her." He glanced at the silent beauty. "She's too nice and trusting," he added. "I believe their story."

The San Angelo sheriff studied Carrie Sue for a time. "It don't matter none. They're still outlaws. We'll catch 'em and they'll all hang."

No murmurs of approval were heard as the local men continued to stare at the ravishing creature beside William Ferguson, a woman whose expression was one of vulnerable innocence. They were awed by those large periwinkle eyes, her flowing tawny red mane, her soft rosy gold skin, and her gentle and delicate air.

"You say they left for Brownwood early this morning?" After Ferguson nodded, the sheriff said, "That should take them about three or four days round-trip. We'll have a posse waiting for them when they return. By Monday, we'll have them all in jail."

Carrie Sue recalled telling Ferguson that her brother always set out markers in all directions when leaving camp; that way Darby knew if it was safe to return there following a job. The gray-haired man also knew that the Stover Gang was heading northwest to Big Spring, not easterly. What she couldn't figure out was why this newspaper man lied to protect all of them because he knew Darby and his men, no matter which direction they had taken, would not ride back into a trap.

The offensive sheriff appeared to gloat when he said, "The Rangers called in your posters, but I guess this proves they were mistaken for a change. I'm sure the Flame's hair matches yours perfectly,. I'll wire them we caught you dead-to-rights. You got anything to say, Miss Stover?" he asked tersely. "Where's the bank money?"

The redhead gazed at the belligerent lawman and, despite knowing it was a waste of breath, said, "I don't know. We're being framed, and the truth will come ot soon. That's all."

"I suppose you've been framed all these years?" he scoffed.

Carrie Sue glared at him. "Of course not, but I've nothing more to say. Mr. Peterson has all the facts. He'll print the truth."

"If the law lets him print such crap."

"Freedom of the press, Sheriff. I can print what they told me."

"Why would you want to do such a stupid thing, Bill?"

Calmly the man replied, "Two reasons, Sheriff. First, it's big news. No other paper has ever gotten an interview with the Stover Gang or any other gang. Second, I believe their account. I've studied this gang for years, and those recent crimes don't match their set style."

"Gangs don't have a style, Bill; they just rob and murder."

Ferguson smiled and shook his head. "I think the Rangers will disagree with you there. I'm ready to get back to town and get moving on this news. For my story, how did you find this place?"

"That bastard they left behind recovered long enough to spill his guts about this place. Then, he keeled over before he could tell me about Brownwood. He's dead, not that it matters any."

Ferguson asked, "Can I come to the jail later and talk to her again?"

"Sure, but she'll be guarded heavily. I don't want that brother of hers busting her out. 'Course, he won't be back for a few days, and me and my men will be waiting right here to welcome him."

Ferguson didn't protest the grounds for her arrest. He figured jail was the safest place for her until he could reach Thad Jamison.

Carrie Sue's things were gathered and her horse was saddled. She was taken into town at the front of the posse and locked in the jail.

Time passed as the daring desperado contemplated her perilous predicament. She didn't think she needed to worry about her brother because he shouldn't fall for a trap. Yet, he might figure out what had happened to her and try to get her out of jail. Carrie Sue couldn't send word to Sally to warn him because that would expose the woman who loved and aided her brother. She couldn't get William Ferguson more involved than he already was. She dared not wire Hank Ferguson or Mitchell Sterling and call attention to them. If only T.J. were here, but she didn't know how or where to locate him. She was trapped, and all she could do was wait for the firm hand of justice to punish her.

*

William Ferguson sent a wire to Commanche, but T.J. Rogue didn't respond to it. He visited Carrie Sue briefly in her cell and was tempted to reveal news about Thad Jamison's help, but decided against exposing the lawman who had trusted him. He went back to his office and continued to work on the legendary story. He wished Jamison would answer his telegram and wondered why the man hadn't done so.

An hour later, the *San Angelo Tribune* owner and writer received news of a Stover Gang robbery in Stephenville which had occurred almost simultaneously with Darby's hit in San Angelo. A reporter there telegraphed that a wounded outlaw had been captured and jailed, and asked Ferguson to come interview the man and split the story. Ferguson chuckled—the Stephenville reporter said that Bill could get information out of a silence-vowed monk.

Ferguson went to see Carrie Sue again and told her about the other crime and his trip to Stephenville tomorrow. "I need to get there before he dies or decides not to talk, or gives somebody else his story. If he incriminates Quade Harding, this could be the break you need, Carrie Sue. But whatever happens with him, the law will realize Darby Stover couldn't be in two towns on the same day. They'll have to begin an investigation. I'm glad your brother hit the bank here yesterday to back up my story and your claims, but I surely did hate to lose my money in that holdup." He chuckled.

She promised in a serious tone, "Darby hid it, but I'll make certain he gets it back to you. And don't forget about collecting the reward for my capture. Good luck, Bill, and thanks . . . for everything."

Ferguson grasped the meaning of her last two words. He smiled and nodded. "I'll get you the best lawyer in the state, and I'll keep after the authorities until they listen to our side."

The sheriff unlocked the cell and ordered Bill to end his task.

Before leaving, Ferguson said, "I'm going to Stephenville for a story tomorrow. You take good care of Miss Stover. Make sure she isn't harmed or harassed, or you'll see yourself in bad print."

"Come on, Bill, don't threaten me," he said with a vexed laugh.

"No threat, Sheriff, a promise."

*

T.J. showed up at William Ferguson's home at nine o'clock. The newspaper owner was delighted and surprised to see the lawman. He told T.J. what had happened and of his impending plans.

The stunned T.J. said, "I heard about both robberies Thursday when I was in the telegraph office in Commanche, so I hightailed it back here when this one mentioned a fiery lock of hair as proof it was the Stover Gang's. Leaving such evidence against her was a stupid thing for her brother to do!" he stated with rising fury. He ordered himself to calm down and handle this matter with clear wits. "I didn't get your wire about her capture, but I wanted to see you before I met with three Rangers at the hotel. I wired them to meet me here tonight so we can make a plan to end this matter before she gets hurt. You head on to Stephenville and get that man to talk. Offer him anything, just open his mouth. I'll arrange a jailbreak for Carrie Sue tonight and get her to lead us to her brother's gang. I have to end this quickly."

Ferguson brushed over the highlights of his visit and interview with the gang. He cautioned, "Don't trust the sheriff here, Thad; he's set on taking them any way necessary. I said they were heading for Brownwood, but it's Big Spring like I told you. I knew it was better to give you that information rather than to tell him. You and those Rangers should head that way or they'll be gunned down if they return to his camp on the Concho River. You going to warn Big Spring?"

T.J. pondered his movements carefully. "Nope. If they plan an ambush for Darby and his boys on Sunday, it'll be a slaughter. Let them carry out the robbery and we'll capture them on their way back. With Rangers heading up the posse, everything should go smoothly."

"What will Carrie Sue say when she discovers the truth?"

"You didn't tell her anything about me, did you?"

"Certainly not, my friend, but I was sorely tempted."

"I'll have a talk with her before we reach her brother. I'll make her understand this is the only way to save his life. You get that evidence against Quade Harding because we'll need it at Darby's trial. I have another plan I'll need help with, Bill, so hurry back to town."

"What is it?" the newspaper owner inquired, intrigued.

When Lawman Thaddeus Jerome Jamison explained, William Ferguson's eyes widened in disbelief. Then, he smiled and nodded . . .

*

T.J. met with the three Texas Rangers who agreed with his bold plan to cature the Stover Gang in a location which wouldn't endanger town citizens. The San Angelo sheriff was summoned and persuaded to go along with her jailbreak. After the sheriff left to dismiss his deputies, T.J. told the Rangers how he would mark the trail for them to follow.

"Hang back at night, 'cause she's alert and wary. I'll need time to convince her I'm on her side. Monday morning, move in closer. That's when we should meet up with her brother on the trail back to San Angelo. We'll need a posse to prevent any gaps they can slip through. I want this case over with as quickly and cleanly as possible. Warn the men, no shooting unless fired upon and you give the signal. I want this gang taken alive. Understand?"

*

In Brownwood, Quade Harding left his ranch with his gang. The San Angelo sheriff had telegraphed him, in case the man was still interested in Carrie Sue Stover and her reward was still available. But Quade hadn't heard about the curious happening in Stephenville . . .

Carrie Sue realized she could not wait for Darby or T.J. to hear about her capture and risk freeing her. she had to escape, tonight! The sheriff seemed to cooperate unknowingly when he returned to the jail and dismissed his two deputies, telling them he was going to sleep there and to replace him at seven in the morning.

When the jail was quiet, she walked to the bars and called out, "Sheriff, can I see you a minute? I have something to say." As he got off the bunk, she pretended to trip and fall. She slammed her hand against the bars so it sounded as if her head had struck them. She groaned and lay still.

"Damn!" the man swore, worried about her being injured while in his care. How would he explain this to those Rangers? He hurriedly fetched the key and unlocked the door.

As he knelt beside the redhead and tried to help the dazed woman to her feet, Carrie Sue yanked the pistol from his holster. "Don't move or shout, Sheriff, or you're dead before help arrives. Just back away, real slow and careful."

While keeping her eyes on him, she left the cell and got his handcuffs. She returned to fasten them on his wrists. Afterwards, she gagged him, then secured him to the bars using his belt. The redhead locked the cell door and tossed the keys on the man's desk.

Ignoring her aching wrist, Carrie Sue strapped on her gunbelt and checked her revolvers. She gathered her belongings from a pile in the front corner. She would have to steal a horse, any one she could find close by. She stiffened in alarm when someone knocked on the door and called out in a muffled voice, "It's me, Sheriff, open up."

Carrie Sue knew she had to let the man inside or he would know something was wrong and sound a warning. She stood behind the door as she unlocked it and opened it, her pistol in her hand. She closed it quickly and said, "Don't move or you'll catch my bullet in your gut."

The masked man turned to face her, his twinkling eyes revealing his identity. He glanced toward the imprisoned sheriff, then back at her. He laughed and said, "I see you didn't need my help after all, Sis."

She smiled and said, "Darby! I knew you'd come, but this is reckless. Let's get moving before somebody sees us."

They gathered her things and sneaked out the door, locking it behind them. He had horses waiting around back. They mounted and left San Angelo quietly. Outside town, they changed to a swift gallop.

They rode for over an hour before halting to speak briefly without dismounting. It was Saturday, June seventeenth, in the wee hours of the morning. They edged their mounts close together and caused their legs to make contact. Beneath the half-moon, they gazed at each other.

"You all right, love?" he asked, unable to pull his eyes from hers.

"Wonderful, partner. That was a good trick we pulled back there. I'm glad I told you Darby calls me Sis. That sheriff will be utterly confused and annoyed. At least I was quick-witted enough not to expose you. How did you find me, T.J., and why take such a big risk?"

He leaned forward and pulled her head toward him to kiss her before saying, "I should yank you off that horse, woman, and spank you good. Running out on me in El Paso was a dumb thing to do. See where it got you. From now on, you stick with me. Understand?"

Carrie Sue grinned as she caressed his stubbled jaw. "Yes sir, partner. Merciful Heavens, it's good to see your handsome face." She leaned toward him to kiss him again, savoring his lips and touch.

Both trembled and warmed. When they parted, he said, "We don't have time to fool around, you hotblooded vixen, so we'd better stop tempting each other before we lose our heads and lives. We need to put plenty of miles between us and San Angelo. We'll talk later, woman; you just behave for now."

"You didn't say how you found me," she pressed.

"I was in the Commanche telegraph office when word came in about the bank job here and your capture. I was sending Hank a message to see if he'd heard from you. I've been half-crazy with worry. Lordy, I'm glad you're safe and sound." He looked her over as if making certain she was unharmed. "You sent me on quite a wild chase, you sly woman. I checked out that place you mentioned near Commanche, but clearly you weren't heading there. I understand why you gave me the slip, Carrie Sue, but I don't agree with you being so impulsive just to protect me and Darby. I actually panicked when you were captured. I rushed here pronto to get you out of trouble. When that story comes out, the law won't know what to think or do."

"What story?" she inquired, new suspicions flooding her.

His eyes glowed. "Haven't you heard? That other band robbed a train in Stephenville and called themselves the Stover Gang. It happened on the same day Darby hit the bank here. The law has to realize somebody's framing them, just like your note said. Why did you think I wouldn't believe you? If anybody knows your brother, it's you."

"I was too scared and dull-witted. Quade Harding's to blame; I'm certain of it. You'll never guess what's been going on here," she hinted, then explained quickly what had taken place since they parted.

T.J. grinned as if her revelations were news to him. "That's a clever trick, woman, using the papers to clear yourselves. After those two holdups at the same time, the law will have to listen to your brother's side. I just wish all of his crimes were frame jobs." His tender gaze locked with hers. "You want to warn him before I take you far away? 'Cause that's exactly what I'm going to do, pronto."

She appeared surprised. "What about your revenge on Quade?"

"If the law doesn't get him this time, one day I'll come back for him. Right now, you're my main concern. I love you, Carrie Sue Stover, and I want you to marry me when this mess is cleared up. I have to make certain you get out of this perilous existence."

Her mouth parted and her eyes enlarged with astonishment. "You what?" she asked, hoping she had heard him correctly.

He responded, "I love you and want to marry you. We'll go to Wyoming, or Montana, or some place and start a new life together. You did say you love me in that note. It wasn't a lie, was it?"

Happiness surged through her at his unexpected proposal, and at the engulfing look in his smokey gray eyes. "No, it wasn't a lie. I love you, T.J. Rogue, and I want to marry you. If we can just get far enough away from my past, it'll work."

He lifted her from her saddle and placed her on his thighs. He kissed her deeply and longingly. "I love you, woman, and I would do just about anything for you. I'll make certain you stay safe and happy from now on. I promise I won't ever let you change your mind about us."

"I could never stop loving you and wanting you," she murmured.

"I hope not, Carrie Sue, because you're mine forever."

They kissed and embraced again, then parted.

T.J. helped her back into her saddle. "We have to make tracks, love. There's only one question left: do we head for parts unknown this minute or do we locate your brother to warn him and say good-bye?"

Her heart bubbling with love and joy, she disclosed, "Darby's in Big Spring, waiting to pull off a robbery on Sunday. If we head that way, we'll meet him on the trail. I'd like to warn him and tell him good-bye, and I'd like him to meet my future husband. He heard you were in San Angelo before our arrival. He said he wished you'd hung around so he could question your intentions toward his little sister and entice you to take on my permanent protection."

A broad smile lifted the corners of T.J.'s mouth because she had told him the truth. At last, she trusted him completely. Lordy, how he hated to tell her his truth tomorrow night, at least part of it. Hopefully she wouldn't lose faith in him or change her feelings toward him before he could confide the rest of it. "That's the best job offer I've ever received, woman. Consider me hired."

Carrie Sue asked, "You think we should swing by the camp and make sure those warning markers are down in case we miss Darby and the boys on the road? Thoughts of a trap make me cringe."

"I think it's too dangerous. If that sheriff gets free before morning, he'll have a posse on our tail. He'll probably look in the last place he thinks we would think he wouldn't look." He chuckled.

Carrie Sue laughed too. "You're right, my love. Let's put some miles between us and talk later. Which way, partner?"

T.J. had taken off from town in an eastward direction to prevent suspicion. He took the lead and off they galloped northwesterly, to travel for many hours before taking a break, then journeying until dark.

*

William Ferguson left on the nine o'clock stage for Stephenville to question the bandit in jail there. He wanted to hurry this interview and return to San Angelo before the final story came to light. . . .

*

Quade Harding and his boys were heading toward San Angelo, but would arrive long after the posse—led by three Texas Rangers—left town to trail undercover Ranger Thad Jamison and his unsuspecting sweetheart Carrie Sue Stover . . .

*

Near Big Spring, Darby Stover and his gang camped outside town to await their action the next morning. The settlement had grown up around a natural spring on Sulphur Draw, a past and present watering hole for buffalo, antelope, wild mustangs, Indians, stage passengers, soldiers, and drifters. At ten o'clock in the morning, when most folks were in church, they would sneak into town, use their stolen badges, take the gold, and ride back for camp. It was a simple and crafty plan, and the boys were eager to get money for Carrie Sue's future.

*

As the last light of day was vanishing, T.J. and Carrie Sue halted to make camp. She asked, "You think it's safe to stop for the night?"

He gave a sly response, "You told me that sheriff thinks the gang was heading for Brownwood, and we did set a trail in that direction."

"But I called you Darby, so he'll think my brother rescued me. There's no telling which area he'll search, maybe all of them."

"You don't imagine he'll think Darby had a lookout posted who warned him about your capture so he could return and rescue you? Or maybe he'll think the guard rescued you," he hinted to mislead her.

Suddenly she laughed and said, "I bet he thinks I called the lookout Darby just to fool him into believing my brother wasn't heading for Brownwood. That sheriff was hateful. When he gets loose, after what that newspaper man told him, I'm sure he'll head straight for the Harding Ranch to look for the Stover Gang. Besides, we've ridden hard and fast for hours, so we have to be way ahead of any posse. They'll have to stop for rest, too, and they can't track in the dark."

T.J. noticed how she was flexing and rubbing her right wrist. "What's wrong, love. That wrist giving you trouble? Let me take a look."

He examined it and heard how she had injured it in the cell. "It's swollen and discolored, probably sprained." His fingers checked the area as gently as possible. "I don't feel any break. I'll wrap it tightly to take off the pressure. You should have told me sooner."

"We didn't have time to fiddle with a complaining wrist. It'll be fine in a day or two. Just sore and tingly. Ouch," she muttered when she flexed it too roughly to prove her point.

"You can't fool me, woman; I know it hurts. I've had sprains before. Holding that heavy pistol had to annoy it. You even burst a vein or two and it's bled under the skin." T.J. wrapped one of his bandannas securely around her wrist to remove the strain on it. "Try not to use it more than necessary. I'll do the chores. You rest."

He chuckled and teased, "I know how you love cold biscuits, beans from the can, and no coffee, so that's what I'll serve tonight. We shouldn't have a fire, just in case that sheriff is smarter than you think."

Carrie Sue observed her lover at work while she leaned against a tree and sipped water. She jested, "Maybe we should ride south to the Mexican border and ask King Fisher to hide us a while. From what Mitch was saying, the law's scared of him and can't snare him. I've met the King, twice."

"You have? When? How?"

"After that trouble in Laredo, we rode to Eagle Pass to cross the Rio Grande into Piedras Negras to lay low a while. He halted us and questioned us, then let us pass through his territory, after spending the night in his hidden camp, just like with Naiche. Then, he insisted we stop by again on our way back into Texas."

"You know where King Fisher's camp is located?"

"Sure, it's easy to find if you know where to look." She told the lawman how to reach the hideout of the bandit leader whom the Rangers were eager to apprehend, along with his band of around a hundred men.

T.J. sent her a pleased smile which she didn't grasp the meaning of, which was one of relief. Surely this piece of valuable information would be worth something to the Texas authorities. If Carrie Sue could help him get the Stover Gang, Quade Harding, and King Fisher, surely that would earn her a pardon! What difference did it make to T.J. that she wasn't helping him willingly or knowingly? After the fact, he would claim she had assisted him in all three cases and make her agree! But if the authorities and his friends in high positions still didn't help him save his love, he would take that matter into his own hands!

Carrie Sue broke into his line of thought with, "We should link up with Darby by tomorrow afternoon, if nothing went wrong in Big Spring. He always travels one mile right of the road so me or the boys can catch up if any of us gets separated during a job. We'll ride in that area and eventually meet up with him. I can't wait to see his face when we turn up together. He'll be glad you're with me."

"I hope so; Darby sounds mighty protective to me. Where'd you get those clothes?" he asked, eyeing the Mexican garments which she had donned to look more feminine to William Ferguson.

"I stole them from Mitch's wife," she admitted. Carrie Sue related how she had disguised herself to get out of El Paso. "Was your friend upset with me for stealing his sorrel? How did you get him back?"

T.J. chuckled. "Seems our tastes run the same in horseflesh, love. That's the horse I traded for Charlie. Mitch was going to take your pinto across the border to sell so he wouldn't get caught with it."

"You mean I stole my own horse?" she ventured merrily.

"Yep. But those clothes were definitely a theft. I'll send Mitch the money to pay for them. You do look good like that." He licked his lips and let his gaze roam her silky flesh before answering her other query. "I figured the sheriff had stabled Charo at the livery. I sneaked him and your saddle out before I came to rescue you."

"Charo, that's a good name. I'm glad you got him back for me."

After they ate and T.J. cleared the dishes, he asked, "Want to take a cool swim before we turn in? That was a hot and dusty ride."

Carrie Sue glanced at the inviting North Concho River nearby with moonlight dancing on its surface. "Yep, partner, sounds wonderful."

They walked to the bank and removed their clothes, after T.J. asked huskily if she needed any assistance with hers. He swam for a time, and the happy redhead was content to bathe and to watch her lover's sleek body.

T.J. knew they wouldn't be disturbed tonight because he had dropped a marker where he wanted the Rangers and posse to camp for the night, miles behind them. He had also warned them to hang back at night so as not to spook her. He needed to tell her part of the truth tonight, but he dreaded it because he couldn't decide how she would react.

The ebon-haired man joined her in the shallow water, resting on his knees before her. His smokey gray eyes studied her compelling beauty in the moonlight. "Lordy, you get me hotter than a horseshoe in the flames. I can't imagine what it's going to be like to have you as my wife forever, to be with you day and night, but I've surely dreamed about it countless times. How will I ever get any work done on our new ranch knowing you're in the house and I can go see you any time?"

Her wet hand drifted through his mussed hair. "The best way to solve that problem is to have me work at your side during the day and sleep there at night. I've worked a ranch twice, so I'll be helpful. We'll be good together, T.J., perfect."

T.J. captured her hand and pressed kisses to it. "I'm sure there's plenty I don't know about ranching, but you can teach me or we can learn together. Just like I'll help you in the house after we finish our chores outside. I've taken care of myself for years, so I know how to cook, sew on buttons and stitch up tears, wash dishes, and do other stuff. I've been in homes where an exhausted wife had to share the husband's chores during the day, then get no help with hers at night. I don't think that's fair, Carrie Sue, and it won't happen with us."

"You're one special man, T.J. Rogue. I love you." She pulled his mouth to hers and kissed him with a rising fever of desire.

Their lips fused into passionate kiss after tender kiss. Their hands caressed bare, wet flesh and caused each other to tingle and glow. Their bodies blazed with love's consuming flames. T.J. lifted her and placed her on the soft grass, and they embraced with eagerness.

T.J.'s lips seared over her face and his hands roved her body. He murmured hoarsely, "I love you, Carrie Sue. I've never told another woman that, and didn't know what love was until I met you. This has to be love because I feel all kinds of things for you. Not just physically," he confessed, "but everything. I want to be with you all the time. Just to talk or have fun. You make me feel good all over, taut as a bow and loose as a broken string at the same time. I get pleasure just from looking at you or hearing your voice. Sometimes I can't even control myself around you, and Lord knows that's never happened with a female before. I want to protect you and make you happy. Lordy, I'd die if I lost you."

"You won't ever lose me, my love. We're a perfect match in spirit, body, and lives. We'll be so happy together; I'm certain of it." Her fingers wandered over his firm shoulders and into the crevice of his spine. She loved the feel of his cool skin beneath her warm hands. She loved the possessive—but gentle—way he held her, touched her, responded to her, made love to her. Their relationship was nothing like the unions she had heard about at Sally's; her man didn't just take satisfaction from her. T.J. gave to her, shared with her, made sure she enjoyed their union as much as he did.

Carrie Sue sighed with contentment, knowing that soon she could have him any time she desired him and as many times as her body burned for his. Soon, they would have a home, a family, freedom. It was going to be sheer ecstasy to be his wife.

"The first time I saw you, T.J. Rogue, you scattered my wits and sent my mind to day-dreaming about you. That night at the burned station, I knew something was going to happen between us. I'd never been pulled toward a man like that before, and I didn't want to resist you. I was just too scared to chase you because of my past. After you visited my room that night, I was afraid not to tell you who and what I am, but I was more afraid you'd discover the truth one day and hate me, Merciful Heavens, I wanted and needed you so badly, but it was such a terrible risk to take. I love you so much."

Their loving words ceased as they kissed. Their bodies joined, fusing their spirits and souls. The blissful tensions mounted within them until they could no longer hold back the flood of desire which coursed through them. Their dams of restraint shattered and they were washed away by stormy passion.

Carrie Sue and T.J. were swept passed beautiful islands of sensation which tossed blossoms of delight into their paths. They were carried onward by powerful waves, caressed and stimulated by love's waters, and sent gasping for breath as they were pulled beneath the rapturous surface time and time again. The stormy tide seemed endless; yet, eventually they arrived on a peaceful shore. There, they lay exhausted from their stirring efforts, savoring their wondrous triumph.

They were tired, but it was a serene fatigue. They knew they needed sleep, so they didn't tarry long at their location. They rinsed in the river, dried off, and donned their riding clothes. They would sleep dressed, in case they had to make a fast getaway.

As T.J. put a dry wrap on Carrie Sue's sprained wrist, she laughed and said, "I don't even know your name. What does T.J. stand for?"

He completed his task and sat beside her on the bedroll. "It's time for you to learn more about me since we're going to be married soon. Just hold your temper, Red, until I explain everything. I took the name Rogue because I was angry with my father for getting himself and my family killed. I was pretty bitter and was striking out at anything. When I was at the orphanage, the people in town called me a half-savage rogue, and the name stuck to me.,"

"You mean it isn't your name?" she inquired, all ears.

"Nope. My real name is Thaddeus Jerome Jamison, but I've gone by T.J. since I was born. Sometimes close friends call me Thad."

"Thad Jamison? *The* Thad Jamison, the mysterious legend?" she said, panic striking her when he nodded. "You're a . . . a *Texas Ranger,* aren't you?" When he kept his tender gaze locked to hers and nodded, her mouth went dry and her lips remained parted. Her heart pounded. Her chest rose and fell rapidly. She felt cold, weak, nauseous. She felt as if he had just stabbed her in the heart with a knife. she stared at him.

T.J. vowed in a serious tone, "I meant everything I said tonight, Carrie Sue. I love you and want to marry you. I want us to go to Montana where you'll be safe. If we stay here, I can't have you."

"But you're a lawman, a famous lawman. Why would you help me escape? Are you hoping I'll be tricked into leading you to Darby? That's what I suspected all along, but I let you get to me with your lies!"

He demanded, "Hear me out, Carrie Sue. Dammit, I love you and want to marry you. I swear I'm taking you to safety. I could never let you be captured, or jailed, or hanged. The only way to save you and have you is to leave Texas and the Rangers; that's what I'll do. Give me a chance to explain everything, please."

"What have I got to lose? I'm your prisoner already. Talk, Mr. Ranger, and I'll listen, but don't expect me to be duped again."

"Just keep an open mind until you hear what I have to say. When I met you, I was on Curly James's trail, for the reason I told you. He did barbwire me to that tree and leave me to die, on Quade Harding's orders. Harding discovered who I was and that I was investigating him. The Rangers had received tips on his underhanded dealings and I was sent to check them out. He overheard me talking with another Ranger. That's why I've had to stay clear of him; he knows I'm Thad Jamison. We figured if he believed I was dead, he would relax and make a slip. We assigned another undercover Ranger to him, Dave Clemmens, but he was killed recently. When they found his body, there was a note pinned to his chest." He told her what the note said and how it was signed. When she gasped in shock and her eyes widened, he added, "You don't have to convince me your brother didn't do it. I know Darby Stover wasn't involved in any way."

Carrie Sue remained quiet and alert.

"If you're wondering if I was spying on you in Tucson, yes, I was. You can hardly blame me for being suspicious of a woman who acted so strangely and had such skills. But I had no idea who you were; I swear. I lied about Nighthawk's injury and collecting those rewards because I needed a logical reason to hang around town waiting for Curly."

"How did you know he was heading for Tucson?" she probed.

"The other two men told me before I killed them. They were to link up in El Paso, then head for Tucson to work for Ferris. I got them first, then beat Curly there. Mitch sent me a telegram about that Union Express job. That's the day you saw me coming out of the telegraph office when you were with Ferris. The Stover Gang was my next assignment, but I didn't connect you with the Texas Flame. I suppose because I was too involved with you to think clearly. You had my head clouded. But what could I do? I couldn't tell you who and what I am: I'm sworn to secrecy by the Rangers and the President. And I couldn't offer you anything without being honest with you. I figured, whatever would a proper schoolmarm see or want with a common gunslinger like T.J. Rogue? But Lordy you twisted up my guts with crazy feelings."

"Which is more important, your job or me?" she challenged.

He urged, "Let me finish first, then you'll know the answer. When Joe Collins came to my room the night before we escaped, he showed me the new poster for Carrie Sue Stover. I was stunned. I couldn't believe you were the Texas Flame, but it all made sense."

"Joe Collins? He's that lawman who came to my room?"

"Yep, but that was a ruse to force you to take me along when you fled. He wasn't hurt, and he was never on our trail. That's why I could come and go as usual; he wasn't after me. I'm sorry, love, but it was the only way I could get you out of town safely and quietly. I realized why you were in Tucson and I was sorry it wasn't going to work out for you, thanks to that damn Quade Harding!"

He mastered his anger so he could continue. "I wanted to save you and help you, Carrie Sue. I couldn't let you face posses and bounty hunters alone. And I wasn't about to put the woman I love in prison or at the end of a noose. At first, I was going to offer you a pardon if you'd help me capture your brother's gang. But I knew you'd never betray or endanger him for any reason. Yet, I hoped you'd want to stop his life of crime on innocent victims. If I could help you get a pardon, then you could lead a normal life somewhere, hopefully with me. I knew you must be tired of running and hiding and being an outlaw. I recalled little clues you dropped about your old life, about prison and such. I believed you wanted out, and I was determined to help you go straight. But first, I had to defeat your brother. Nobody's ever been able to get near Darby Stover, so I used you. I'm sorry and I feel guilty as hell, but I felt I had to get him any way necessary."

T.J. propped his elbows on his raised legs and rested his chin on interlocked hands. "But something happened along the way. I had rescued and was protecting a beautiful desperado with hopes of her assisting my case, but there was no one to protect me from you. I discovered I loved you and wanted you desperately. I had to find a way to clear you. The problem is, you're guilty; you're an outlaw. No frame or misunderstanding to clear up for exoneration. What could I do? Lordy, I was as ensnared by your past as you were. I didn't want to ask myself what you would do and say when you learned the truth about me. I didn't want to think about how my capturing your brother would affect our relationship. I kept telling myself I should be thinking only of my mission, but how could I with you nearby? Lordy, I've never been in such a predicament, such a scary trap."

"So what happens to me? To us?" she inquired sadly.

He didn't reply. "That day I vanished in the Chiricahuas, I went to tap into the telegraph line. I sent messages asking for the government to help the Apaches, as I promised Naiche when I saw him. I wired Collins about Martin Ferris. And I wired the Rangers and President about granting you a pardon. I told them you were aiding my case."

"But that was lie!" she shrieked.

"I know, but I was desperate, Carrie Sue. I had to remove the threats to you. How could we have a life together if you were killed or imprisoned? I told you, I was going loco over our situation. When we reached Deming, I sent more telegrams and picked up some waiting for me. I learned about those jobs in Hillsboro, Eastland, and Big Spring which your brother supposedly committed. I know he's innocent of those charges, Carrie Sue, and I'm certain Harding's to blame. I also let Hank Peterson know we were on the way to his place."

She asked, "Who is Hank Peterson? And Mitchell Sterling?"

"Retired Rangers who still give help when we need it. They're deeply respected and the authorities listen to them. They're both good friends of mine. I've worked with them many times in the past and they agreed to help me in this matter. They know I love you and I'm trying to carry out this mission without damaging our relationship."

She murmured, "That can't be done, T.J. How can I marry you if you destroy my brother? How can you marry me if I'm captured?"

· "That's why I found myself in such a tight bind, woman. To get the Stover Gang, I had to risk losing you. Unless I could get you pardoned. They've refused to cooperate on one, but I kept hoping they would reconsider because of all I've done for them," he revealed.

"And?" she hinted.

"No luck," he admitted. "One reason is the law thinks the gang's behind those recent crimes, and they're bad ones. When we were at Mitch's, I wired Dave Clemmens to speed up the Harding case, but he was killed a few days later. Maybe because I provoked him into doing something rash just to help us. After you ran out on me, I was afraid you'd messed up any chance I had of getting you exonerated. Then, I got word on the Brady holdup. I'd studied your brother's gang, so something didn't seem right. I came to the same conclusion you did, a frame job by Harding. I had to find you before you fell into his hands again, or got into more trouble with Darby."

Carrie Sue made no attempt to battle him or escape. "Quade is up to something more than framing us. He had my posters yanked until he could get to me. The law will know soon, because I told that newspaper man the truth to entrap Quade. I'm certain Curly was working for him, but you killed the snake before he could betray me."

T.J. gave her a stunning response. "It wasn't Quade, Carrie Sue. I convinced the Rangers to withdraw those posters so you would be safe on the trail. I told them I couldn't get near the gang with you if we were being chased. They were pulled down right after we left Tucson."

She stared at him. "I don't understand. William Ferguson told me Quade did it. It was in all the papers."

"That's the story we put out to explain yanking them. We told Harding we had proof Carrie Sue Stover wasn't the Texas Flame, and we were pulling her posters. He was madder than a hornet with his nest shot down, but he was worried about how much we knew. He guessed we were up to something; either we were using you, or you were helping us to earn a pardon. He figured he'd better comply or risk exposure and charges for suppressing evidence for years. He agreed to tell the papers his poster and reward were put out to protect you until he could prove your innocence, which was what the lying bastard claims is true. In return, the Rangers said he didn't know what he did was illegal and no charges would be filed against him. Your posters were yanked and those old ones were put out again as the Flame."

"If I was cleared publicly, why was I arrested?"

"Because you were caught in Darby's camp, holding a prisoner. And that business with the Flame's lock proved you were guilty. The sheriff wired the Rangers and told them he had captured you red-handed." T.J. shifted his position. "I rode to Comanche with hopes you'd told the truth about going there, but you hadn't. While I was wiring Hank about news from you, I heard about the simultaneous San Angelo and Stephenville crimes. I knew Darby was on the move again and you'd be with him. Then, word came of your capture. Lordy, I was afraid Harding would bust you out of jail before I could."

Both were silent for a while. Then, the flaming haired fugitive asked, "Why do you hate my brother, T.J.? There had to be more than your job driving you after him. If you truly love me and want me, then you'd have given up this mission for our future. There has to be a personal motive in here somewhere. What is it?"

"As I always said, woman, you're too smart to be fooled very long. You're right; I did have revenge in mind. I insisted on having this assignment, before I met you and discovered who you are. Ever since March, all I could think about was killing the entire gang."

"Why?" she demanded when he fell silent again.

T.J. needed strength on his side to win her over to his until everything was resolved, and he hoped the truth would do that vital job for him. "There was a stage holdup near San Angelo on March twenty-second. A woman and child were murdered. Do you recall that incident, Carrie Sue? Were you along that day?"

At his tone and expression, a cold chill swept over her. "Yes I was there. I can't forget what happened."

"Do you also remember the robbery on April twenty-eighth when you became Carolyn Starns? A Ranger was killed when the stage was pursued and crashed. He was a good friend of mine. He saved my life when I was barbwired to that tree. I owed him justice, vengeance."

Her frantic mind was still lingering on his earlier hint, so she asked, "Who were the woman and child? Did you know them?"

"Arabella and Marie Jamison."

"Jamison?" she echoed in dread, wondering if his next words would be *my wife and child,* and she prayed they wouldn't be.

In a strained tone, he disclosed, "My brother's wife and daughter. Tim and I hadn't seen each other since our captures by the Apaches. We got news of each other's survival and location around Christmas time. We were planning to be reunited soon, but Tim was killed by Mexican bandits in February. When I received the news of his murder, I sent for his widow and child. I had intended to marry Arabella and raise Marie as my own daughter, but they didn't reach Fort Worth because of the Stover Gang."

Carrie Sue gaped at him as those staggering words sank in. Her heart was tormented by anguish and was filled with sympathy. "I'm sorry, T.J.; I didn't know. . . ." She lapsed into remorseful silence.

"Those three deaths in March came right atop my brother's in February. I was furious. Within two months, I'd gone from finding my family to not having one again. I wanted to kill every member of that gang, including Darby's sister. I was on Curly's trail, and the Stover Gang was laying low, so I decided to finish with him before taking off after your brother and his boys, which I figured would take a long time. Headquarters was keeping a file on Darby's movements, but I didn't know that the Sherman job was pulled by Darby until Joe Collins came to fill me in. You were acting strange, so I thought you were in trouble. I asked a Ranger friend to check you out so I could help you. Joe told me the Stover Gang pulled that holdup and he showed me your poster. That's the first time I knew about you; I swear it."

T.J. couldn't let her believe she was his second choice or that he fell in love with her because he was agonizing over a lost family. "There's something else I have to explain, Carrie Sue. I wasn't in love with Arabella—I didn't even know her—but I would have married her if she'd reached Fort Worth alive. You know from experience what happens to a woman alone, especially one with a child. I couldn't let anything happen to my brother's family. Maybe I was weakened by Tim's recent death, but I honestly was going to do my best to make a home for them. Then, a crazy thing happened to me: I met you while I was chasing Curly. I fell in love with you before I learned who you were. You're the only woman I've ever loved, and I could never have married Arabella after meeting you. When I discovered the truth about your identity, it was too late to back away from you and these feelings."

Tears were rolling down Carrie Sue's cheeks. T.J. turned to her and wiped them away, saying, "I don't hold you to blame, love."

"But we are to blame, T.J. That's why I was so desperate to get away; I couldn't stand the accidental deaths. If that driver hadn't tried to outrun us, that stage wouldn't have crashed and killed your friend and Carolyn. And if we hadn't attacked that other stage, that passenger wouldn't have panicked and shot your brother's wife and child. We didn't kill them, T.J., honestly. This man was babbling about them being captured and abused, so he shot them. Darby winged him, but it was too late. I swear we'd never kill women and children. If you can locate that coward, you can force the truth from him." As with T.J., she didn't know the irrational man had committed suicide following that grim incident.

"After all you've told me about Darby, I realized something didn't ring true. Your brother isn't what I imagined him to be. You said he ordered no killings, and I believe you. I understand that you two got shoved into this miserable life and were forced to stay there. But the accidents have to stop, Carrie Sue. I know you two don't deserve what happened to you, but neither do the innocent people the gang attacked. If Darby doesn't get out soon, he'll be dead, and we both know it, woman. You have to convince him to do the right thing, to turn himself in and face his punishment."

"He won't listen to me, T.J.; he thinks he's in too deep."

"When a man's in the right, sometimes he has to kill another man who wrongs him or challenges him. But when he's in the wrong, there's no justification for murder. That's why I never became an outlaw and why gunslinging never agreed with me, even as a cover for my job. I knew if I told you the truth about me, you'd offer me anything to give up this mission. But what kind of man shows such weakness and lack of character? I did change my mind about killing Darby and his boys, but I still felt I had to arrest the Stover Gang, for the law and for my friends and family. I was hoping after it was over, you'd love me enough to understand my predicament. I figured, if your love was strong and real, you'd keep on loving me even after I got justice."

"He's my brother, T.J.; I can't help you. I can't. Has it all been a lie? You've stayed with me and . . . just to get to Darby?"

"No, you frustrating vixen. I've pulled all kinds of tricks with you and my superiors so I could stay with you for protection. I love you, Carrie Sue Stover, and want to marry you. You have to believe that much. I've done everything I could to secure you a pardon: bargained, begged, threatened, reasoned, misled. Nothing worked. I can't lose you, woman, so I have to quit the Rangers and leave Texas with you."

Carrie Sue looked deeply into his smokey gray eyes. "You really mean that don't you? You would give it all up to get me away safely."

"Yep. I can live without the Rangers and Texas, but I can't live without you, woman. If I led the law to your brother or told them where to locate his hideout, you'd be captured, too. I can't have that. To be honest, woman, if I could have gotten you a pardon, I'd have finished this mission to stop your brother's crimes. You love him, Carrie Sue, but what he's doing is wrong. Someone has to stop him."

Carrie Sue jumped up to pace. T.J. told her, "If you don't trust me near Darby, then we'll leave from here. Several times before I've given you the chance to test my word. I won't let anything happen to you. The only imprisonment you're facing is marriage to me."

"You'll forget your revenge?" she asked.

"You said Darby didn't kill Arabella and Marie; I believe you."

"What's in your saddlebags? You guard them like gold."

T.J. tossed them to her feet. "Look for yourself. You know the truth now. A telegraph key to tap into lines, a picture of Arabella and Marie, and a Ranger badge. That's what I couldn't let you see."

Carrie Sue unbuckled the straps and looked inside. Amidst clothing and ammunition were the items he stated. She didn't do more than glance at the picture because she would never forget those faces. She held his badge in the palm of her hand and wondered how much it meant to him. She was filled with mixed emotions: love, hope, joy, suspicion, and anger at his deceit. She studied the telegraph key and asked, "You won't use this to betray Darby after we see him and escape?"

"You can keep it or throw it away right now. I don't need it anymore. Maybe we can persuade Darby to turn himself in and serve his time. I can ask the Governor to intercede for him, and I can, too. Maybe he can get off with fifteen to twenty years with a chance of early parole for good behavior. After all, he didn't commit all the charges listed against him. He'll still be young when he gets out with a clean slate. That's better than being chased, hanged, or killed. He's welcome to join us in Montana."

Carrie Sue smiled at him, then flung the telegraph key into the river. She replaced the Ranger badge and picture of his brother's family in his saddlebag. "He'd never turn himself in," she said.

Her lover encouraged, "Still work on him because that may be the only way to save him. Surely you'd rather see him in jail for a few years than see hm hanged or gunned down."

The redhead knelt before T.J. and cupped his knees with her palms. "Swear to me I'm not making a mistake to trust you."

T.J. gently captured her lovely face between his hands and pulled her closer to him. He worded his response carefully, trying to deceive her no more than necessary tonight. He had to stop the Stover Gang before he ran away with her, and he was being forced to flee afterwards. Once this matter was settled, he would expose everything to her and make her forgive him. "I love you and want to help you, woman. I swear to take you far away and marry you. I won't let you get harmed."

Carrie Sue knew those words were true, his clear gaze and calm voice told her they were. Besides, she mused, if they were being trailed by this lawman's order, T.J. wouldn't stop to make love! And if he was tricking her, he wouldn't tell her such things tonight. He had had her fooled into leading him to Darby, so he wouldn't take this risk. He wanted to prove he trusted her, and she must prove she trusted him. "We'll see Darby tomorrow, then head north, my love."

*

It was seven o'clock, not yet dusk, when Carrie Sue and T.J. found Darby Stover's camp on Sunday night. She hurriedly dismounted and raced toward her brother. She hugged and kissed him. Rapidly she related her capture, jailbreak, and flight with T.J. Rogue. "We're leaving at first light to head for Montana to get married, big brother. Are you sure you won't go with us?" she entreated.

Kale Rushton sneaked up behind the distracted lawman and put a gun to T.J.'s back and said, "This liar ain't going nowhere, *chica*. He may call himself Rogue to you and others, but he's Texas Ranger Thad Jamison, and your jailbreak was nothing but a sly trick."

Kadry and Walt grabbed T.J.'s arms and Dillon took his weapons.

Carrie Sue shouted, "Stop it! I know who he is. He's told me everythig about him. He's giving up his badge and job to help me escape so we can start a new life together. Let him go!"

Darby faced T.J. and studied him. His brown eyes roved the lawman from head to foot, then settled on T.J.'s smokey gaze. Darby sensed power and peril, integrity and prowess. He perceived an undeniable strength of mind, body, and spirit. "You're wrong, Sis. He's used you to get to us. Tie him up, boys. We'll kill him later."

Carrie Sue yanked on her brother's arm. "You're mistaken, Darby! He loves me and is helping me escape. Don't you dare harm him!"

The auburn-haired man turned and glared at Carrie Sue to silence her. He was angry with his sister for being duped into a lethal trap by a crafty lawman, because he knew the treacherous Ranger had taken everything—everything—from her. "There are things you don't know and understand, Sis. Jamison has to die. Tonight."

Chapter

23

"What don't I understand?" she shouted at her icy-eyed brother. "Lawmen like Thad Jamison wouldn't give up a mission or toss away their job for a woman. He's charmed you into bringing him here. There's probably a posse tight on your tails. Tie him up snug, boys."

As T.J. was being bound, she refuted, "That isn't true, Darby. I watched him set a false trail out of town, and he's covered our tracks for miles. We weren't even heading in this direction. I was the one who insisted we find you and warn you before we headed north."

He scoffed in a sarcastic tone, "I bet. Don't you see, Sis? He let you think it was your idea. He knew you would be fooled after he busted you outta jail and filled your ears with pretty lies."

"From what I hear, Thaddeus Jamison can wipe out a whole gang by himself. Let's see how tough he is," Dillon suggested, then punched T.J. forcefully in the stomach.

Both rejected suitors vengefully attacked the helpless lawman who had stolen their love's heart and had betrayed her affections and trust. Kadry slammed his fist into T.J.'s gut. Dillon struck him across the jaw, making the lawman stagger backwards. When T.J. failed to go down, Kadry landed another, much harder, blow to his chin. That time, T.J. was sent to the dirt.

"Stop them, Darby, Or I will," she threatened seriously, fingering her gunbutts as she was tempted to draw against Darby and his men.

"Just because you're sweet on him, Sis, don't mean we have to get killed over it," her brother reasoned impatiently.

"My feelings for him have nothing to do with you allowing your men to murder him. If I loved him more than I love you, Darby, I wouldn't have come to warn you. I've proven myself to you plenty of times. You owe me this favor. Let us leave peacefully. He loves me."

"Sorry, Sis, but I have me and the boys to think about. Even if we let Jamison go or left you two behind, he'd be dogging us again the minute he's loose, or he'd alert his friends. It's him or us, Sis."

"No, it isn't. He's taking me to Montana; I swear it. He's even given up his revenge on us. That was his brother's wife and child that crazed man killed in March. T.J. thought we did it; that's why he was after us. I explained to him what happened that awful day. He knows the truth now, and he's giving up everything so I can go free and marry him. He even knows Quade Harding is framing us. He told me everything last night. If he was trying to trick me into leading him to you and the boys, he would have held silent. I trust him, Darby; that's why I brought him here to meet you."

Darby glared at her lover. "He's lying to you, Sis! He's been lying all along, and he'll keep on lying until we're all dead! I've met plenty of men like him, so I know his kind and feelings. He can't love you or want you. Don't be blind and stupid. We're riding out of here and you best come along. He probably has the law on to you."

T.J. was helpless, and decided against doing anything rash, but he couldn't let Darby's inflammatory words go unchallenged. "Don't listen to him, Carrie Sue. I love you, and I'll get you out of this mess if you'll trust me and convince them to let us go. That's no trick or lie."

"He lied tae ye, me darlin'. We hae tae kill him as punishment."

The redhead looked at the blond outlaw with her eyes chilled. "No, Kadry. There'll be no killing over me or I'll never forgive you."

"Whatcha gonna do, boss?" Walt asked.

"Give 'im time ta think, Cuz," Tyler suggested, his hazel eyes reddened by the whiskey everyone could smell on his breath.

"I say kill tha bastard now. Nae need tae wait until morn."

"Yeah," Dillon agreed with Kadry. "Kill him now. Let me do it." He lit a cigarillo as he eagerly awaited his leader's decision.

The black man pulled the ever-present chewing stick from between his snowy white teeth. "Missy Stover loves 'im, boss. Ya thinks ya ought to kill 'im a'fore 'er?"

Darby answered, "I have to, Griff. He's a threat to all of us."

"Yeah, he lied ta Miss Carrie Sue," Walt added, fingering his gun butts. As he looked at the lawman, fear permeated him.

Dillon tossed his cigarillo to the ground and crushed it forcefully. "I say get it over with, then pull out. If he's got a posse back there—"

Carrie Sue injected, "I told you he doesn't. Kale taught me plenty about tracking and covering trails. T.J. did a good job concealing it."

Kale Rushton reminded her, "He's Apache trained, *chica;* he could leave a trail you'd never notice. Maybe he is sweet on you, but I still think he was looking for our camp and planned to warn the others tomorrow before he left Texas with you. That's what I'd do in his place. A man like this doesn't give up once he has victory in sight. Now that he's found us, he can't just walk away and forget about us. That's not to his thinking and training."

She reasoned desperately, "How? He had a telegraph key, but he threw it into the river to prove he had no way to expose you."

The man with the red sash around his head asserted, "That was just another sly trick to keep you fooled."

"No, it wasn't," she protested. "I'm certain of it."

"Are you really certain, *chica,* certain enough to risk all our lives?"

She eyed Kale intently. "Don't put a burden like that on me. You're my friend. Make them listen. If anybody can read T.J., it's you."

"I know, *chica,* that's why I vote to kill him."

Panic flooded her. No one would take her side.

Darby said, "We're responsible for that Ranger's death on the stage. They'll never stop chasing us. They'll hound us into hell to capture us and kill us. Rangers don't forget or forgive."

Her voice was strained as she argued, "T.J. understands it was an accident. He holds the driver to blame for not yielding to us."

Darby tried to make her see his point of view. "I bet he recognized you from the start, Sis. He's been playing games with you. It's us he's after, not you."

"He didn't know who I was until he saw my poster the night before we escaped from Tucson. He's been protecting me and helping me."

T.J. spoke up and said, "That's true, Darby. I didn't know who she was until I was already in love with her. I'm telling you the truth; I'm going to take her far away to safety and marry her. If you kill me, she'll never forgive you."

"I wish I could believe you, Jamison, but I don't and can't. If she wasn't in love with you, she wouldn't trust you, either."

"She loves us both, man. She doesn't want to see us kill each other. The least you can do for her is leave us here and take off."

"Not after what you've done to my sister, you lying bastard."

Tyler said, "Let's kill 'im an' git outta 'ere before that posse comes."

Kale told them, "They can't track at night. They're probably camped by now. We should get some sleep and head out before daybreak."

Carrie Sue warned, "If you slay him, Darby, the Rangers will surely hunt you down and kill you. They don't know he's siding with me. They won't give up until you're dead, until you're all dead."

"Not if we head for Wyoming and lay low for months. We've got enough money. That'll be far enough away to fool them."

"He knew about the Big Spring job Friday night after he broke me out of jail. If he wasn't on my side, he would have wired them to set a trap for you. He could have captured me and had all of you ambushed."

"He just wanted tae catch us himself, lass, but we got him first."

"Capture seven men alone? Don't be ridiculous. No lawman is that good. He's had no chance to send for help, Darby; I swear it. You know I would never endanger you."

"There's a posse out there, *chica;* I can smell them miles away."

T.J. stated angrily, "Dammit, man, at least let her go. Stop dragging her into your crimes or you're going to get her killed."

"Dinna worry, Lawman. I'll take care o' her. I'll make her forget ye, ye cauld bastard. Ye took her frae me, but she'll be mine ag'in."

Carrie Sue eyed her brother and his men, then looked at the bound T.J. Rogue— no, she corrected herself, Thad Jamison, Ranger. T.J., R., the initials on his gun. Merciful Heavens, how she loved him and wanted to believe him. He had lied to her, but she knew he loved her and wanted to rescue her. Whatever was awaiting her out there, she couldn't let him die. It was useless to argue with the outlaws, so she made her decision. "Just wait until morning, Darby, and give yourself time to think this over. Don't kill him in haste. If you feel the same way at first light, then I'll leave and you can handle the matter. I'm going far away to where nobody has ever heard of the Stover Gang. I can't live this way. Whatever you do and wherever you go after tomorrow, just make certain you don't come near Montana and ruin things for me. The same goes for you two," she told Kadry and Dillon. "Don't ever try to find me."

"Ye canna mean that, me darlin' Carrie Sue."

"I've never meant anything more, Kadry Sams." She glanced from man to man. "If you kill him, I never want to see any of you again. You'll all be cold-blooded murderers, including you, big brother."

Darby said, "Let her be, boys; she's upset. Tie him to that tree and put a guard on him. We'll take care of him before we leave in the morning. Carrie Sue, you stay clear of him tonight, understand? I don't want to get tough with you, Sis, so let me handle this matter. When you've had time to cool down, you'll see I'm doing the right thing. Dammit, girl, he betrayed you in the worst way! How can you forgive him and take his side against me and the boys?"

"That isn't what I'm doing, Darby Stover! I just don't want you committing a rash murder. I know he lied to me and might have used me, but he had his reasons, just like we had good reasons for going on this outlaw trail years ago. No matter what he's done, murdering him is wrong. You never used to kill without good cause, Darby, and I'm sorry I've witnessed this wicked change in you."

Darby watched his sister walk away, and sighed deeply. He looked at T.J. and said, "This is your fault, Ranger. She doesn't understand I'm avenging her honor. You know you're guilty and deserve to die."

Thad Jamison said, "No matter what I've done to apprehend a notorious gang like yours or what you think about me, Darby, I do love her." He ordered through clenched teeth, "Leave her alone tomorrow. Give Carrie Sue the chance to be free and happy. If you really love her, you'll keep your men away from her or they'll lead the law to her new location. Carrie Sue deserves better than what you've given her over the years."

*

To avoid suspicion, Carrie Sue ate her supper and didn't go near her lover, even to give him food and water. She had tended their horses, and prayed T.J. could ride bareback as skillfully as she could. The redhead knew she would be watched tonight, just like T.J. would. But the only man she had to worry about was Kale Rushton.

Carrie Sue lay on her bedroll until three o'clock. The longer she hesitated, the fewer doubts the men would feel about her. Darby had taken her weapons until morning, and she was furious with him for making her helpless. At least her brother hadn't order her bound!

She slipped from her bedroll and walked to the river which ran from San Angelo nearly to Big Spring. She sat on the bank, after placing a heavy rock beneath her full Mexican skirt. She knew the sharp-witted half-Apache would follow her and she would be forced to render him unconscious so she could do the same with Dillon and help her love escape. With luck, the boys wouldn't chase them. If they believed there was a posse nearby, they should take off swiftly in the other direciton. *Please don't let anyone get hurt*, she prayed.

As expected and hoped, Kale Rushton joined her. "What's wrong, *chica*, can't sleep?"

Carrie Sue looked up at the man who was standing to her left. "You're my friend, Kale, so how can you do this to me?"

His dark eyes settled on her pale face. "To save our lives and to punish his tricks on you," came the easy answer.

"Have you never lied to someone you love to get what you wanted or to keep from hurting that person? Nearly all men deceive women for their own pleasures or reasons. T.J. is no different," she alleged.

"I've never told a woman I loved her just to use her."

"To let her believe you do is the same thing. Don't kill him."

"We have to, *chica*, or he'll dog us forever. Jamison is good, the best. If we get caught, he's the one who can do it."

"He'll leave with me today, honestly, Kale. He's not after you all anymore. He loves me and wants to get me away from this peril."

"Even if that's true, he'd expose us somewhere along the way or convince you to betray us."

She vowed heatedly, "I'd never do that; you know I wouldn't."

"He'll work on you until you weaken and see things his way. He's a lawman, *chica*, and he'll always be a lawman first. Jamison isn't the changing kind, or the relenting kind. He'll insist on finishing this last mission before running off with you, if that's the truth. He has a personal stake in this matter; have you forgotten about his brother's wife and child, and that Ranger friend of his? His honor will force him to destroy us. We're both Apache raised, so I know what he's like inside."

Carrie Sue stood up, holding the rock securely behind her in her left hand because her sprained right one was still weak. "You see that campfire in the distance," she remarked, pointing southward with her right hand. When he glanced that way, she lifted the rock and struck his head with it. He collapsed to the ground. She yanked the red sash for his bleeding head and bound his hands tightly behind his back. She knew his head would pain him but he wasn't badly injured. Taking Kale's bandanna, she gagged him for silence. She took his knife and gun and concealed them beneath her untucked blouse.

The redhead made her way to where Dillon was guarding the bound T.J. She whispered, "Can I see you privately for a minute, Dillon?"

Dillon knew the lawman couldn't escape as he was secured to a tree. He saw she was unarmed so he followed Carrie Sue into the bushes.

She turned to him and asked, "What do I have to do for you to let him escape before the others get up? I don't want him murdered."

Dillon studied her for a minute. "Anything for his freedom?"

"Yes," she replied guilefully. "What will it take to cut him loose?"

Dillon Holmes responded confidently, "Promise you'll marry me as soon as we reach Wyoming, 'cause you'll keep your word."

"What's that over there?" she asked, leaning forward and pretending to strain to see into the shadows. When Dillon turned, she rendered him unconscious with Kale's gun. She used his belt to bind his hands behind him and gagged him with his bandanna.

The desperate woman took Dillon's weapons and sneaked to her lover. Using Kale's sharp blade, she cut T.J. free and handed him Dillon's holster. "Let's get out of here," she whispered.

T.J. made no attempt to get the drop on the sleeping men because he knew Carrie Sue wouldn't stand for it, and wild shooting from the slumber-dazed outlaws could imperil her. He led her to their horses and they mounted bareback to prevent extra noise. They walked the horses from camp, then galloped southward.

At nearly four-thirty, they rode into the midst of the posse's camp before Carrie Sue realized what was taking place. Several men surrounded them and startled her.

One asked, "What's up, Thad? We trailing you too close?"

Carrie Sue stared at the Ranger badge on the man's chest and grasped his words. Kale had been right! It was a trap! She tried to bolt, but T.J. grabbed her from the sorrel's back. "Let me go, you lying bastard!" she shouted and struggled for freedom.

"Calm down, woman, this is for the best. I have to stop your brother's gang before he gets himself or more people killed. I'll explain everything when I get back.

Saddle up, men. We can take them while they're asleep. No shooting except in self-defense."

"No, T.J., he'll be gunned down. Please. You owe me!"

T.J. handed her to two men who held her captive between them. He pulled his silver star from his jeans pocket and pinned it on his shirt. "Sorry, Carrie Sue, but I have to do this. Darby's crimes have to stop and I'm the only one willing to take him alive. You'll be safe. Bob, you stay here and protect her," he commanded one of the men.

The posse mounted up and rode off with Rangers in the lead.

*

Carrie Sue paced frantically. Even if the posse sneaked up on Darby's camp, there would be shooting and killing. Darby would never surrender, nor would Kale or Kadry or Dillon, if Kale and Dillon weren't still disabled by her impulsive actions. This trap was her fault. She had trusted the wrong man, and he had used her vilely and betrayed her. He had sworn love, marriage, and freedom: all cruel lies! He had promised she would be safe, but she was a prisoner who would soon be facing either her Maker or a lengthy incarceration! He had alleged he couldn't pursue and capture the gang because she had no pardon and would be endangered, but he was doing it anyway! Her jailbreak had been a clever ruse to ensnare them, including her, because there was no way he could save her now that she was in custody. He had lied to her ever since their first meeting. Surely he had duped her in all areas, including lovemaking, which hurt the most. She had to escape. She had to ride like a blizzard wind and warn Darby to flee; she had to make up for her foolish mistakes.

She was standing near low hanging limbs. She pretended to toy with one while she asked, "Who planned this trap, Bob? How long has the posse been—" She yanked back the limb and released it, forcing the branch to slap the Ranger in the face and knock him backwards. She was on him in a flash, taking his weapon and getting the drop on him, a trick taught to her by Kale Rushton. Her friend had said that men could be duped easily by a female because they never expected or believed a mere woman could overpower and defeat them.

"Toss me your cuffs!" she demanded, then changed her mind. "No, snap one on your right wrist. Do it or I'll shoot you where a man doesn't want to be injured," she threatened, pointing the pistol at his groin. "I'm not a killer, Bob, but I can make you suffer badly if you don't do as I say. I'm not going to let them ambush my brother!"

After Bob obeyed, she gingerly stepped forward and locked the other cuff around his left wrist. She mounted Charo and, taking his horse along to prevent his pursuit, she galloped toward Darby's camp.

*

Before the posse reached their destination, T.J. halted them to give his final orders. "They're camped in those trees about a mile ahead on the river. I want the camp encircled. I don't want any of them to get away and risk a jailbreak later. I want them taken alive, all of them. They're outnumbered, so they should give up without a fight. Give 'em that chance." He told which men to take each position. "The Rangers will close in and order them to yield."

The groups quietly took their positions. T.J. sneaked to the spots where Kale and Dillon were still bound and only half-conscious. He led them back to the Rangers. "Hold these two, Harry. That leaves only five in camp. Let's go," he told the third Ranger.

They moved in closer and took cover behind two trees.

The lawman was distracted by worry over his love. Without thinking clearly, T.J. called out in a loud voice, "Darby Stover! This is Captain Thad Jamison and the Rangers. We have your camp surrounded. Give up peaceably and there won't be any killing. We've captured Carrie Sue, Kale, and Dillon. There's only five of you and plenty of us."

Darby Stover was awakened by the commotion. He roused the other men fully. He warned, "Hold your fire until we see where the boys and Carrie Sue are. We don't want to hit them by mistake." T.J. yelled out, "Give it up, Darby, and you'll get a fair trial. You don't stand a chance of escape. Don't force us to kill you."

Tyler Parnell panicked at the thought of being surrounded by Rangers and going to prison. He shouted, "Ya ain't gonna send me ta no jail." He ran for his horse, shooting wildly in all directions.

Several shots answered his challenge and he dropped to the ground.

Walt Vinson heard his first cousin moan and saw Tyler attempt to get up. He raced from cover, yelling, "I'll git ya, Cuz." He dodged back and forth, firing into the trees, as he ran to Tyler's aid.

More shots rang out and Walt went down near Tyler, both dead.

Seeing there were only three of them left, John Griffin threw down his pistols and stepped into the open with his hands raised. "Don't shoot. I'm comin' out," the black bandit shouted nervously.

"Hold your fire, men!" T.J. called out to the posse. To Griff he said, "Come this way and no tricks. You'll get a fair deal from us."

Griff followed the voice into the shadows and was taken prisoner by the Ranger with Thad Jamison.

Behind a tree, Kadry Sams turned to Darby. "I'm nae fool, man. I dinna want' tae die." He looked ruefully at his guns as he laid them down.

"I'm comin', tae, Rogue," he called out, then walked into the clearing with his hands above his head.

T.J. called to the gang leader, "It's just you left, Darby. Let me come in and talk to you. I don't want Carrie Sue seeing you gunned down, so don't be foolish. I'll get you a good lawyer. Harding will be captured soon and those fake charges against you will be dropped. Serve your time, man, and go free afterwards. You can't keep up this killing and robbing. Give it up, for your sister's sake."

There was no answer from the auburn-haired bandit. T.J. said, "I'm holstering my weapon and coming over there. Let's talk." T.J. told the Ranger, "I'll handle him." He left his cover and walked toward camp. "I'll help you, Darby, if you'll let me."

Darby allowed T.J. to get to within five feet of him. His revolvers were aimed at the lawman's chest. He yelled, "Any of you get itchy fingers out there and Jamison will be dead before I hit the ground!"

T.J. knew their words couldn't be overheard by the posse at that distance. He said, "I ordered them not to fire, Darby. Drop your guns and give yourself up. I promise you a fair trial. I'll do all I can to get you the shortest sentence possible, then you can join me and Carrie Sue in Montana. I'm serious about loving her and saving her."

"Where is my sister?" Darby demanded.

"She's safe with the Rangers, so are Kale and Dillon. This isn't for revenge, Darby, but I had to stop you. Can't you see this isn't any kind of life for you? You got into this mess by accident. I think the judge and jury will understand and be lenient. I have evidence to clear you of many false charges. One of Harding's men was wounded in that Stephenville train robbery. He talked plenty," T.J. alleged, hoping the witness had lived and chatted plenty to William Ferguson.

"You're a fool to walk into my gun sights," Darby told him.

"You aren't a cold-blooded killer, Darby Stover, and we both know that. When Harding's convicted, you'll probably get your ranch back. It's a prize piece of land, worth plenty. If you sell it and pay back those people you've robbed, the law will probably look on you with favor. You can serve your time and have a good life when you get out. Plenty of men go straight in prison and get paroled early. Hell, they'll probably hire a man like you as a lawman when you get out."

"You expect me to believe such crap?" Darby scoffed, but was intrigued by the man's words and expression.

T.J. saw the wavering in his love's brother. "I can help you, man, but only if you lay down those guns and come with me. I—"

T.J.'s words were cut off when Carrie Sue galloped into camp and dismounted near the two men. With a pistol in her hand, she ran toward them. "Darby!"

A shot rang out and Carrie Sue was thrown backwards by the force of the blast into her chest. T.J. and Darby raced toward her.

Thad Jamison shouted, "Hold your fire, damn you!"

Darby gathered the wounded Carrie Sue into his arms. "I didn't want it to go this way, Sis. Why did you do it? You can't help me."

"I know, Darby. I . . . love . . . you. Don't fight . . . them . . . or you'll . . . get killed," she murmured through a blackening haze. "It's over, Darby . . . finally over." Searing pain racked her shoulder and blood poured from the bullet wound.

T.J. knelt beside her and said, "You'll be all right, love. I'll get you to a doctor. Hold on, woman, or I'll beat you." Sheer terror flooded his body. Would he be the cause of her death? He couldn't lose her; he loved her and needed her.

With the last of her strength and awareness, Carrie Sue looked at her traitorous lover and murmured, "I . . . hate you. . . . Let me die . . . get . . . it over . . . with."

Before others reached them, T.J. told Darby, "I love her. I'll protect her. Don't worry or do anything foolish. They'll kill you."

Darby Stover met T.J.'s frantic gaze and knew the man was telling him the truth. He realized he should have let them go last night. "Get her away from this mess or I'll hunt you down when I get out and kill you."

When the posse closed in on them, T.J. ordered, "Bring Kale Rushton over here. He's probably got some Indian medicine in his saddlebag. Get me something to use for bandages. I have to halt this bleeding. Harry, send one of the men to fetch the doctor in Big Spring."

Harry informed his panicked friend, "Doc Pritchard died last month. They don't have a doctor in Big Spring anymore. You'll have to get her back to San Angelo."

"That's too far and too rough a ride in her condition!"

"There's no choice, Thad," the Ranger reasoned.

T.J. thought swiftly. "There's a ranch a few miles away. Borrow a wagon from it while we tend her."

Harry sent two men to fetch the wagon. After cuffing Darby's hands, he searched the saddlebags for something to use as bandages. He handed them and a canteen of water to Thad Jamison.

The man who had done the impulsive shooting babbled anxiously, "She hada gun

in 'er hand. I thought she was going to shoot Cap'ain Jamison. I didn't mean to ki
'er, just wound 'er."

Kale was unbound and brought forward to help Carrie Sue. T.J. ordered the posse
to move away with the prisoners to give them working room and privacy. Harry urged
the man backwards to the river.

After everyone cleared the area, Kale pushed the red splotched blouse to her waist
and unlaced her camisole. He and T.J. studied the wound and glanced at each other.

"It's bad. Deep. Lots of bleeding," Kale remarked. He opened his Apache medicine pouch and withdrew a smaller pouch of powder. He shook some onto the wound,
then bound it. "Bullet's in too far. If I dig around in there, I'll kill her. She needs a
good doctor, fast."

T.J.'s voice was choked and his eyes were glittery with moisture as he asked, "You
sure that's all you can do, Kale? She can't die on me. Dammit, I should have kept
riding like I promised her."

Kale looked at the famous lawman. "She was right; you do love her."

"Yep, but I might have just killed her with my stubbornness. Not even the capture
of the Stover Gang is worth her life. This was crazy."

"*Si, amigo,* but something a *verdadero hombre* had to do," Rushton remarked.

T.J. scoffed, "This is anything but honorable. No *real man* would do what I've
done, but thanks, *-ch'uune'.*"

The outlaw was impressed when the Indian-raised lawman called him a friend and
helper. "I wish I could do more. I can't."

"When that wagon arrives, I'll get her back to San Angelo and the doctor. I won't
let her die on me," he vowed with determination.

*

While T.J. was busy with Carrie Sue, the other Rangers assigned men to return the
gold to Big Spring. Harry took control of Walt Vinson's badge collection, pulling out
Thad Jamison's to return it to him. The bodies of Walt and Tyler were secured to their
horses for burial in San Angelo. The prisoners—Kadry Sams, Dillon Holmes, John
Griffin, Kale Rushton, and Darby Stover—were ordered to mount up to be taken to
the jail in San Angelo. From there, they would be escorted to Waco for trial and
sentencing.

The wagon arrived. Darby entreated, "Please, let me ride with my sister. She could
die along the way and I should be with her."

T.J. ordered, "Harry, you come along with me to guard Stover. I'm going to let
him stay with his sister. I'll drive the wagon. The rest of you men take those prisoners
back to town. Watch them closely, and no trouble. I promised them a fair trial, so get
them to town alive and well or you'll answer to me personally."

T.J. and Darby loaded Carrie Sue with gentleness and worry. Her blouse had been
replaced but the camisole was being used to help stop the continuing blood flow.
Charo, Nighthawk, and Darby's mount were tied to the wagon gate. T.J. put their
supplies in the wagon and told Darby to watch her carefully, to call out if he needed to
halt and give her relief. Both men were scared because she hadn't regained consciousness. They pulled out with Harry riding beside them and guarding the notorious
bandit leader whose lap cradled his sister's head.

*

It was a long and difficult trip back to San Angelo with T.J. and Darby trading places as
the driver while the other man tended Carrie Sue. They halted only for the horses to

est and water. The men ate cold beans and chewed on dried strips of beef. They forced water into Carrie Sue, but she remained in her world of silent blackness.

They traveled all of Monday, most of Monday night, and part of Tuesday. The wagon had to move slowly to keep from jarring her too much and causing more bleeding. They reached town about five o'clock and took Carrie Sue to the doctor's office.

The physician checked the wound and shook his head. Carrie Sue moaned and moved slightly. The doctor said he had to use ether to make sure she held still while he removed the bullet. It was lodged near her lung and he didn't want to puncture it. He poured ether onto a clean rag and laid it over her nose and mouth. Soon, she quieted and lay motionless.

The skilled man took a long instrument with a slightly curved tip called a sound and probed the hole until he heard it make contact with metal. He eyed the spot and assessed the location. With slender gouging forceps, he wiggled them into the wound and grasped for the bullet. The bleeding was profuse now, but he couldn't stop groping. Finally he captured the lead between the forcep tips and carefully withdrew it. He tossed the bullet into a pan of water with his bloody instrument.

The doctor dabbed sweat from his brow and above his upper lip. He pressed a cloth to the fiery location to halt some of the bleeding so he could see to make stitches. He poured antiseptic—a wonder product by Robert Johnson—on the area, then sutured the wound with silk thread. After bandaging her, he said, "That's all I can do for her, Ranger Jamison. Keep her quiet and still. Try to force water and soup into her. If the bleeding stops soon and no infection sets in, she could survive. I would recommend holding her prisoner at the hotel. That jail isn't any place for her in this condition. As for me, I'd like to speak with that Indian fellow. Whatever he poured on the wound kept her alive until I could treat her. If he hadn't, she'd either have bled to death or been too enfevered to save. I've heard those Indians have magical cures we whites know nothing about. If he would work with me, we could advance medicine ten years."

"His name is Kale Rushton. He's half-Apache and half-Spanish. Talk to the Governor; maybe he'll work something out for you two."

The doctor smiled and said, "It's worth a try."

T.J. suggested, "You should check her right wrist; she sprained it badly a few days back."

After the doctor looked at it, then bandaged it snugly.

*

Carrie Sue was taken to the hotel and placed in bed. T.J. sat down to watch over her. To him, she looked so pale and weak lying there, and it ripped at his heart to know he was responsible.

"Don't leave me, love, and I promise you won't ever be harmed again," he murmured, placing kisses over her face and parted lips. He tasted and inhaled the bitter remains of the ether. He took a cloth and washed her face. "You're so beautiful, Carrie Sue Stover," he said as he gazed into her serene face. He wanted to see her lovely eyes open again. He stroked her tawny red hair and lifted her left hand to kiss each fingertip.

"I need you with me, woman. Hang on to life, love, please," he beseeched the unconscious redhead.

A knock summoned T.J. to the door. Two of the Rangers came inside and questioned her condition.

T.J. glanced toward the bed and informed them. "I don't think she's going to make it. Why don't you head on to Waco in the morning? If she gets well, I'll escort her there. If not, I'll join you soon."

"That's what we came to see you about, Thad. We need to keep the prisoners here a few days. Quade Harding and his boys left town late this morning. I've called the posse back together to ride after them at first light. You want to come along? I know you have a score to settle with him, and you are the superior officer here."

"I'm putting you in charge, Harry. Just get the bastard and his gang for me. I want to stay here with Carrie Sue. It's my fault she got shot helping me. With her brother in jail, she has no one to take care of her. We got close on the trail, so I'd prefer to tend her."

One of the Texas Rangers asked, "What will happen to her, Thad, if she survives?"

"I've requested a pardon for her from the President and Governor. I expect it to come through any day now. She did help us capture the Stover Gang and she's given evidence against Quade Harding. She also told me where and how to locate King Fisher's hideout." He drew a map and handed it to one man. "Wire this information to the Rangers near Eagle Pass. That should help Major Jones put a stop to his raids."

T.J. hated to lie to the Rangers—his friends—but if Carrie Sue was taken to Waco to stand trial with the Stover Gang, she would probably be convicted. He couldn't allow that to happen to his love. Since they had refused her a pardon, he had no choice but to get her away from there as soon as she was able to travel. He prayed that day would come. He had hoped the Rangers would depart for Waco in the morning with the prisoners and leave him here with Carrie Sue. Then, as soon as she was able to travel, instead of heading for Waco as he promised, he would sneak her to safety in Montana.

"She's a special woman, Thad, and I hope she makes it," Bob told him. "She's mighty clever, too. Got the drop on me in a flash."

The three men discussed their plans and case. Afterwrds, the Rangers left him alone with his love.

William Ferguson arrived for a visit. "How is she, Thad?"

"Not doing good, Bill. I'm worried."

The newspaper man glanced in her direction and said, "I hope she pulls through; I really like her." Ferguson eyed Carrie Sue again before saying, "I told the other Rangers Harding just left town and, if they hurried, they could overtake him and capture him." He told T.J. about his interview with the wounded bandit in Stephenville and how he turned the evidence over to the Rangers today. "That outlaw talked his head off. It seems that Harding shot him and left him for dead so he couldn't expose him. The man was furious, but he was scared. He was afraid no one would believe his account against such a powerful and wealthy rancher. When I told him the law was investigating Harding and he would be arrested soon he opened up and told me everything."

"That's good, Bill. Thanks for the help; I surely need it."

Ferguson took a seat and continued, "Curly James was feeding Quade Harding information, just like you suspected. From what that bandit said, Curly was suppose to join the Stover Gang after he left Tucson. Before he did, he was to wire Harding and warn him to cease those fake raids. That's how Harding messed up; he didn't know Curly was dead and Darby was on the move again, so he never got his warning against that Stephenville holdup. You'll be surprised how many raids they've pulled over the years and blamed the Stover Gang; that should help Darby's defense."

"I hope so. He's not a bad man by choice," T.J. murmured.

"I agree," the gray-haired man concurred. "I hired a good lawyer, one of the best available. He's to meet Darby in Waco. I'm going there myself to cover the end of this story. I've written up all the evidence I've gathered and I've recorded my conclusions for the lawyer and the authorities. I think those notes will aid Darby's defense."

"If we're lucky, but I haven't seen much luck lately."

"Don't get dispirited, Thad. I also sent a telegram to the President and Governor, asking them to pardon her."

T.J. muttered with resentment, "It won't do any good, Bill. I've begged them for a pardon, offered to do anything for one. They've refused. They've made up their minds the answer is no. I was going to sneak her away, but this shooting messes up things for us. When the posse gets back with Harding and his gang, if they don't leave with all the prisoners before she's well enough to travel, we're done for." He glanced at his injured love and murmured, "If she doesn't survive, it won't matter what I do."

The two men—new, but good, friends—talked and planned a while longer. . . .

*

T.J. watched and tended his love all night, forcing cool water between her dry lips. Not once did she arouse, and his fears increased. For a time, while the ether and her weakness held Carrie Sue entrapped in a dark world, he sneaked away to handle a pressing matter. . . .

*

Early the next morning, one of the Rangers stopped by to say they were pulling out to pursue the Harding gang. Harry remarked with concern, "You look terrible, Thad. Did you get any sleep?"

"Very little. There's no change. I doubt she'll survive to stand trial."

*

As he was flexing his stiff body, T.J. looked out the front window. He saw the doctor heading for the hotel. He went o Carrie Sue's bed and prepared her for this crucial examination.

When the doctor arrived, he checked the still unconscious woman. He tended her wound with antiseptic and placed new bandages on it. "No change, son. I'm sorry. It's real bad when they don't wake up soon. It could be that ether's fault; it can be unpredictable at times. I might have used too much," he said, detecting a faint odor of it on her.

"You think she'll pull through, Doc?" he queried, looking very worried.

"I'm afraid I don't, son," he revealed. "I have to go out of town to deliver a stubborn baby. I'll be back tonight. I'll check on her then."

*

The doctor reported to the local sheriff as ordered by the man. "She hasn't regained consciousness; that's a bad sign. I don't think she's going to make it, Sheriff, but that Ranger's trying his best to save her. If you asked me, I think he has strong feelings for her. He hasn't left her side for a minute, for the little good it's doing."

The sheriff said, "Maybe it'll be best if the Texas Flame doesn't recover to stand trial. Prison's a bad place for a woman like that." The lecherous man imagined the beauty as his helpless captive for years.

"Why didn't you ride out with the posse?" the doctor inquired.

"Those Rangers don't need any help," the offensive lawman scoffed.

Darby overheard those tormenting words about his sister's condition and begged the lawman to let him go see her. The auburn-haired man was furious and distressed when the sheriff laughed and refused. "If she dies and I get loose, I'll kill you for this," he theatened.

*

T.J. forced water and soup into Carrie Sue again today as he had last night. He wanted her to have the strength to battle for her life.

William Ferguson came to visit again. He stayed with Carie Sue while T.J. went to see Darby Stover. The Ranger and the outlaw talked privately for a time, then Thad Jamison returned to the hotel.

T.J. checked his love and said, "It's too late to change things, Bill. I'll handle the arrangements as we agreed. You sure about helping me with this?" When the man nodded, T.J. said, "You stay here until I return, then fetch your things. It'll be a long, hard day."

T.J. went to see the undertaker and ordered a coffin sent to his hotel room in an hour. As he was passing the dressmaker's store, he halted and went inside. He purchased the beautiful white gown in the window. With a heavy heart, he returned to the hotel room. Lordy, how he hated to do this, but he had no choice.

Ferguson left to fetch his camera. While he was gone, T.J. put the white dress on Carrie Sue and brushed her tawny gold mane. The coffin was delivered. When William returned, he and T.J. placed a lovely quilt in the bottom and a pillow. They put Carrie Sue inside. Ferguson placed flowers from his yard beneath her overlapping hands. T.J. straightened her white lace dress and flaming hair.

"All right, Bill, do what you must."

Ferguson set up his camera and took pictures of the grim sight. Tomorrow, his stories and pictures of the ill-fated Stover Gang would fill the *San Angelo Tribune*. "I have most of the articles written, Thad, and I'm going to re-run a few that I've already printed. I'll prepare the one on her death today. I'm also getting pictures of the gang in jail and taking their statements this afternoon. I'll go fetch the sheriff so he can bear witness to her demise. I'll see you at my house tonight. Make yourself at home there until the Rangers and posse return."

After the newspaper man departed, T.J. stood over the coffin and stared at the lovely face of the Texas Flame. "I'm sorry it had to be this way, love," he murmured, then bent forward to kiss her.

The sheriff arrived and looked into the coffin. "A real shame, she was a beauty. You burying her here?"

"Nope, in Waco where I live. I'm having her delivered to William Ferguson's home until we pull out of town. I don't want curious folks gaping at her on display. If they want to see her, they can buy one of Bill's papers tomorrow. He took pictures earlier to print. I want you to cuff Darby Stover and send him over with two deputies. Any man deserves to tell his sister good-bye, even an outlaw."

The sheriff argued, but had to obey the Ranger. Two deputies arrived shortly with a handcuffed Darby.

The bandit leader gazed at his sister a long time and kissed her cheek before murmuring, "Good-bye, Sis, I'll never forget you. This is all my fault and I'm sorry. I love you, Carrie Sue."

*

At the jail, one of the boys asked, "Is she really dead, boss?"

Darby leaned his head against the stone wall and said, "Yes."

The coldhearted sheriff remarked, "Don't worry, boys; you'll all be joining her soon when you swing from ropes in Waco."

Chapter

24

Thursday morning, the doctor came to Ferguson's home. "I got back to town too late last night to check on her. I saw the paper this morning. You sure she was dead, not just in deep unconsciousness?"

"I've seen plenty of people die, Doc. She had no heartbeat, no pulse in her throat. I put a mirror to her nose and mouth to check for breathing, and nothing happened."

"I didn't expect her to make it, not after staying unconscious so long." The doctor glanced at the sealed coffin, then at the disheveled lawman. "She was real special to you, so I'm mighty sorry she's gone."

*

Friday afternoon, the Rangers and posse returned to San Angelo with a few prisoners, but Quade Harding and others had been slain during a violent shoot-out on the trail. After filing their reports, the three Rangers went to William Ferguson's home to see Thad Jamison.

Harry related the news about Quade Harding and his gang. "We'll take the others back to Waco with us on Monday. We plan to rest here a couple of days." He shifted uneasily. "We heard about her passing on, Thad, and we're real sorry. What are your plans?"

T.J. took a hammer and loosened the coffin lid. He let the lawmen glance at Carrie Sue Stover before he nailed it shut again. He dropped into a chair as if soul-tired. His hair was mussed and he hadn't shaven for days. From the look of his wrinkled garments, he hadn't bothered to bathe or change them lately. "I'll head out with you on Monday morning. I'm taking her back to Waco to bury it so she'll be near me. That's the only place I spend much time." He sighed deeply before adding, "I'm thinking of quitting the Rangers. Playing T.J. Rogue gets as many innocent people killed as her brother's gang did. Besides, after she was shot, we blew my cover, so I won't be any more use to the Rangers or the President as T.J. Rogue."

"The Rangers still need Thad Jamison," Harry told him.

T.J. ran his fingers threw his ebony hair, then stroked his stubble. "I doubt they'll be too happy that I exposed myself on this case. I was ordered to remain undercover. After the trials, I think I'll find me a quiet town somewhere and settle down as a town marshal."

"Why don't you get cleaned up and join us for supper and a few drinks?" another of the Rangers asked. "You can use both, friend."

T.J. stood. He walked to the coffin and placed his hands on it. "Thanks, Bob, but

I prefer to stay here and guard her until we leave town. I need to keep the curiosity seekers away. I won't let anyone gape at her or steal souvenirs. You know how folks behave when a famous person gets killed."

"Yep, I'm afraid I do. Will you be all right, Thad?"

He nodded. "I was going to marry this girl when her pardon came through. I just need some time alone to adjust."

"We understand," said Harry.

As they were leaving, William Ferguson returned home. Harry said, "You did a fine job on the Stovers' lives and on the Harding case. You want to report on King Fisher for your paper?"

"You have news on him already?" William inquired.

"Yep. The Rangers and Army joined forces and attacked that hideout she told us about. They didn't get King Fisher, but they sent him on the run. Good thing is, his gang is scattered, what's left. Fisher won't be terrorizing that area any longer, thanks to Miss Stover."

"Why don't we have supper and you can give me all the facts on Harding and Fisher?" Ferguson suggested. "The restaurant at the hotel has a fine cook. When we're done, I'll bring Thad something to eat."

The four men left and T.J. bolted the door. Again, he checked all the windows and doors to make certain they were locked. He went to the coffin and unsealed it. He lifted Carrie Sue and carried her back to the bed. After removing the white dress, he checked her healing wound and put on her nightgown. He hoped the ether would wear off soon and he wouldn't have to use it again on her. Yet, he was glad it put her under deep enough to fool everyone into believing she was dead.

He murmured to the soundly sleeping woman, "I know you're getting tired of that foul ether, love, but I have to convince everyone you're dead. I just hope Doc won't miss what little I stole from his office the other night or figure out my ruse. 'Course, he's got no reason to mistrust a Texas Ranger." He stroked her hair and kissed the tip of her nose. "We'll be leaving Monday, love. Hank will have everything ready for us in Waco. Just as soon as the trials are over, we can sneak away without suspicion. But if I don't gothere and retire, someone might realize what I've done and come after us. We'll be far away and safe soon, love. We'll get married and be happy forever."

As he tucked her in, he continued chatting to himself, "You don't have to worry about Darby suffering over your death; I told him my wild plan before I pulled it off. He played his part good and he's glad you'll be safe." He checked her wrist and saw it was doing fine now.

T.J. washed Carrie Sue's face and hands. He put the flowers in water and sat them near the bed. She had aroused only a few times since being shot—slipping in and out of consciousness—but not enough to comprehend what was happening. Her wound was looking better and no fever or infection had attacked her body, thanks to Kale's prompt treatment. She had swallowed the soup and water each time he had forced it into her mouth, and she was getting stronger.

T.J. felt bad about lying to his Ranger friends, but he had to think only of Carrie Sue now. His duty had been met, and he had done far more than should be expected of any man. He had used and betrayed his love and almost gotten her killed. They deserved freedom and happiness, and it was up to him to obtain them.

T.J. left her sleeping peacefully while he took a bath, shaved, and changed clothes. Until they left town, he would remain at her side. Once they were on the trail, the

Rangers and prisoners would go on ahead while he drove slowly in a wagon with the coffin. When he and Carrie Sue were alone, he could unseal the wooden box. At the outskirts of Waco she would be compelled to hide again until he reached the house which Hank had rented for him. While he was filing his reports, attending the trials, and retiring from the Rangers, Hank Peterson would take care of her. Afterwards, it was off to Montana and a new life together.

As T.J. looked down at his love, he murmured, "From the moment I first laid eyes on you, I knew I couldn't rest until you were mine. I'll make you understand and forgive me, Carrie Sue. We're meant to be together."

T.J. stretched out beside her and closed his eyes. He was exhausted from nightly vigils and daily worry. He could relax and rest now because he knew she was going to get well and his ruse had worked perfectly.

*

Carrie Sue awakened off and on Saturday. T.J. was always at her side. While her head was clear, she was worried about her brother, but T.J. kept telling her that Darby was fine.

The last time she awakened that day, after feeding her nourishing soup, T.J. told her of his impending plans.

In a weak voice, she asked, "You really are taking me away?"

"I never lied about that, Carrie Sue. I love you and want to marry you, but this is the only way. You have to trust me and cooperate."

Carrie Sue's eyes were heavy. She closed them and went to sleep, his last words running through her mind each time she stirred.

*

Sunday morning, Carrie Sue was more lucid and for a longer period of time. She asked for coffee, bringing a smile to T.J.'s lips.

"I hope this means you're feeling better," he hinted.

She was propped against pillows. "My shoulder hurts like heck. I feel as if I've honestly died and been dragged back to life."

T.J. stroked her silky hair—which he kept brushed—and said, "I was determined not to let you go, woman. You owe me."

Her violet-blue eyes gaped at him. "I owe you? How did you come to that crazy conclusion, you conniving lawman?"

"You're the one who tempted and teased me until I lost my head and heart over you. You're to blame for making me pull those stunts so I could have you. At least we got Harding, so you have your revenge and justice." He told her about Quade Harding's deeds and death.

"I feel too bad for that news to enliven me. What about Darby?"

T.J. explained what he had told Darby before and after her shooting. He related what he believed would happen to the bandit leader. "That's the best I can do for him, love." He sat beside her. "Aren't you relieved his outlaw days are over? Now, he can work on getting his head and life straight. I told him that when he gets out of prison, he can come live with us. He knows where to look, and he's plenty welcome. None of the other boys know the truth. Darby and I figured it was too dangerous to tell them you aren't dead. This way, none of them will come looking for you after they get out of prison."

"You mean Kadry Sams and Dillon Holmes."

He grinned and chuckled. "That's right, my clever vixen. I'm a possessive and jealous man. I don't want either of those lovesick cowboys chasing my wife. I'd like a peaceful existence for a change."

She tried to move away from him, but she couldn't. She was too weak and it hurt her shoulder. Touching him caused a mixture of feelings: anger, irritation, confusion, love, and desire. "What if I refuse to marry you, Mr. Traitorous Rogue? Am I supposed to forget and forgive just because you had a mission to carry out? How do I know this isn't another one of your crafty tricks?"

He captured her hand and kissed it. "For what reason, woman? The Stover Gang is in jail. And you're in no condition to rescue them. Even if you were, I think you're smart enough to realize this is for the best. You don't want Darby killed or continuing as an outlaw. I saved his life, Carrie Sue, and he has a chance for a fresh start after he's served his time. There was no way you would help me stop him, so what did I do so wrong by tricking you for a while? I never lied about the important things like love and marriage."

She wanted to discuss this further, but she was drowsy. "The problem is . . . Rogue, I don't know . . . if I can ever trust you again."

"Let's get you tucked in and comfortable. You need sleep, love. You'll have lots of time to punish me with this sharp tongue later. Right now, you have to get plenty of rest. We leave in the morning. It'll be tough going for you until I get rid of them and unseal that coffin."

"I don't . . . want to . . . ride . . . in a coffin," she argued.

"Would you prefer to travel with the prisoners, stay in jail with them, stand trial with them, go to prison with them? Are you that angry with me, Carrie Sue? Do you hate me that much?"

"Behave, Rogue, I'm . . . too tired to quarrel. Good-night." She closed her eyes and went to sleep.

T.J. settled her in bed and kissed her forehead. "You might be furious with me, woman, but you love me. It'll work out for us."

When she awakened again later, T.J. showed her the newspaper with her coffin picture and read the stories to her. He told her about the sheriff checking her at the hotel and what he told the doctor.

Carrie Sue was amazed, and impressed. "You're one clever and daring man, Rogue. Or should I call you Thad now?"

He grinned and shrugged. "Whichever name you prefer, love. I mostly go by T.J., but a few friends and Rangers call me Thad. You'll be Mrs. Thaddeus Jerome Jamison, Carrie Sue Jamison."

"If I marry you," she scoffed, jerking her hand from his.

He glued his gaze to hers. "You have no choice, woman. I saved your life and I'm keeping you out of prison. You belong to me."

"I see, swap one prison for another kind? Is that my choice?"

He sighed loudly in frustration. "Come on, Carrie Sue, give me another chance," he entreated.

"Another chance to use me and betray me?"

"Lordy, you stubborn vixen! You really want to punish me, don't you? What can I say or do to convince you I love you?"

She replied, "I don't doubt you love me, Ranger Jamison, but trust is a big part of love and marriage. You lied to me."

He countered, "And you didn't lie to me plenty of times?"

Carrie Sue felt a rush of guilt. "I suppose I did," she admitted. "But I had to," she claimed.

His voice tender, he responded, "Just like I had to deceive you, just for different reasons. Even so, I still trust you and love you."

Carrie Sue frowned in consternation. He was right, but . . .

"I know this is all hard on you, love, but I'll prove myself. Just give me time and patience and understanding. I promise you it's been just as hard on me. Imagine Thad Jamison, lawman, falling in love with an outlaw, the notorious fugitive he's sworn to arrest. Now, I'm turning my back on everything I know and have just to win you."

T.J. told her of his three badges and jobs. He went on to explain, "I was a Presidential agent and U.S. Marshal before I became a Texas Ranger in '74. That was when they were reorganized. Maybe you didn't know they were disbanded after the war by military authorities and corrupt politicians; I guess it was punishment for seceding from the Union in '61. The Texas Legislature passed a bill in '74 starting them up again with six companies. Major John Jones was assigned the Frontier Battalion to combat the Indian and border problems. I work under Captain L. H. McNelly of the Special Force. We're suppose to rid Texas of cattle thieves and outlaws, reestablish law and order. The President, Marshal's office, and Rangers sort of share me for various missions, but I've almost always used the gunslinger Rogue as a cover. My missions took me all over Texas and the surrounding territories. That's how I met Hank, Mitch, and Joe Collins." He related the full story of Arabella and Marie. Then, he filled in any gaps which she questioned.

With a sad tone, he said, "I tried to get you a pardon, Carrie Sue, but they won't grant one. And, if I hadn't brought your brother in alive, someone would have killed him. I've tried to do what's right for everyone. Can't you understand my side?"

Finally she said, "I need time, patience, and understanding, too. Maybe I'm just too weak and weary to think and feel right now."

"Just answer one question for me; do you love me and want me?"

She stared into his smokey gray eyes and said, "Yes, I do."

He smiled broadly. "That's plenty for now. Take a nap, love. Bill wants to visit later if that's all right with you."

"Why are we at his home? Why is he helping you? Don't tell me he's an ex-Ranger too," she jested, feeling as if an oppressing weight had been lifted from her body.

T.J. explained when and how he met the newspaper man. He told her what they had done together and separately. He explained why Bill hadn't betrayed the Stover Gang to the local sheriff. "By the way, the sheriff was killed last night trying to capture some rustlers. I doubt he'll be missed very much. He wasn't a good man."

"William Ferguson is," she remarked. "I'd like to see him later. I want to thank him for all he's done for me and Darby. See you next time, partner," she murmured and snuggled into bed.

*

Monday morning, June twenty-sixth, it had been a week since Carrie Sue was shot. She was recovering slowly and steadily. She asked, "What if they want to view my body again?"

"They won't, love. You've been dead too long. But just in case, I'll help you into that white dress again and you can hold these," he said, yanking the dead flowers from the vase. "We're damn lucky they didn't send for a prison wagon to haul those men to Waco. That would have caught us in a bind, made us travel at the same pace."

Carrie Sue was helped into the dress, and she admired it. "Where did you get this, Rogue? It's beautiful."

"At a local dress shop. I saw it in the window. Luckily it fit. You sure do look great in it. Why don't you wear it when we marry?"

She glanced at him, but didn't respond. She was trying to remain calm; she was trying to be understanding. She knew T.J. wouldn't allow her to recuperate here where he couldn't watch her. For now, the best thing was to cooperate. Also, she wanted to be near Darby's trial. T.J. had promised to find a way for them to visit one last time before he was sent to prison. Too, she wanted to see if T.J. truly meant what he had said about retiring and escaping with her.

Carrie Sue Stover loved Thad Jamison with all her heart and soul, but she was afraid to let down her guard this soon after his deceit. Time and his imminent actions would tell her what to do.

She was helped into the quilt-lined coffin. "I don't like this," she muttered as she lay down, wincing when her shoulder protested.

"You all right, love?" T.J. asked.

"Yep," she muttered unconvincingly.

He placed a canteen and some food in the wooden box within her reach. He laid a gun near her hand. "Just in case something happens to me and you need to protect yourself," he informed her when she glanced at him oddly. "Just stay quiet and still. I'll try to get rid of them as soon as possible. I love you, woman," he vowed, then bent forward to kiss her.

Carrie Sue looked at him when he straightened. She parted her lips to speak, but didn't. It was dark when he sealed the lid. She settled herself for the grueling experience ahead.

"It might get warm in here, love, but be patient." He cautioned, "They're here, so no more talking or moving."

T.J. and another man loaded the coffin onto a wagon. William tossed her saddlebags beside it. T.J. added his belongings and supplies. The lawman tied the reins of Nighthawk and Charo to the tail gate. He shook hands with William Ferguson and said, "I'll see you in Waco on Saturday. Thanks for everything, Bill."

"Take care of yourself, Thad. I'll be seeing you soon."

T.J. mounted the wagon seat, clicked the reins, and the team pulled out to join the group of men nearby. He glanced at Darby Stover, but their looks revealed nothing suspicious to the others. "Let's go."

Ten miles outside of San Angelo on the road which passed through Brownwood and Hamilton on the way to Waco, T.J. halted the men. "This is slow moving, Harry. Why don't you ride on and I'll catch up in Waco. If I go any faster, I'll bounce her coffin out of the wagon. I didn't think about it, but I could have headed out Saturday or Sunday. I guess my mind was elsewhere." He tried to look and sound sad, but it was hard with his love and happiness so close at hand.

Harry smiled sympathetically and said, "If you don't mind traveling alone, Thad, I would like to make better time."

T.J. despised lying to his friends and hated being compelled to take illegal actions, but he couldn't avoid this path and save his love too. "I wouldn't want to walk my horse that far. I'll be fine. I can use the peace and quiet, if you understand my meaning."

Harry thought he did, so he nodded. "All right, boys, let's pick up the pace and let the wind cool us."

Kadry Sams shouted, "I need tae see her an' sae good-bye. Just gie me one look at her."

Harry shook his head and replied, "She's been dead for nigh unto a week, boy; you don't want to look at her now. Remember her like she was."

When Bob offered to hang back with T.J., Harry said, "Let him be alone; he needs it before he puts her away for keeps."

The Rangers, appointed deputies, and prisoners galloped off and left the wagon there.

T.J. said, "Just a while longer, love. I want to make sure they're gone. You all right in there?"

When the wounded woman didn't respond, T.J. panicked. He knocked on the coffin and asked, "You all right, Carrie Sue?"

A muffled voice answered, "Just hot and sore, but fine."

They traveled for another half-hour, then halted. T.J. removed the lid and lifted her out of the wooden confinement. Carrie Sue's cheeks were flushed and her skin glistened with moisture. T.J. poured water on a bandanna and washed the sweat from her face. He waved it before her, trying to cool her faster.

"How's the shoulder?" he inquired. "We'll get you out of this hot dress and into something cooler. I washed those Mexican garments; they should do the trick. I want to check for bleeding."

She noticed he had stopped near the eastern flow of the Concho River. She was glad. The grove he had selected was cool and shady. She let him remove the lovely white dress, check her wound, and rebind it with antiseptic bandages which he had stolen from the doctor. She helped him as much as possible as he pulled on her blouse and skirt.

"That better?" he asked.

"Much. Thanks." She sipped water slowly because she felt weak.

When he tossed the white lace dress into the wagon, she summoned the strength to scold, "Don't do that, T.J. Rogue! You fold that dress and put it away before you ruin it. Are your hands clean? I don't want you to stain it. It took all I had to keep from bleeding on it."

T.J. chuckled and said, "Yes, ma'am. Don't worry. I'm glad to see your spirit returning. You must feel better if that fiery temper is aglow today."

"I want to walk a minute. Can you help me? My legs feel like a mellow pear, so I can't do it alone. I need to get some blood flowing in this aching body. I'm not used to lying around for days. Makes me tense and moody."

T.J. smiled in pleasure. He put his right arm around her waist and held her left elbow with his free hand. He guided her around for a short time with her leaning against him for support. He felt her telltale tremors and the amount of pressure she was putting on his body. "I hope that ride wasn't too rough on you."

"I've had worse, and plenty better. Damn," she swore underbreath. "I hate feeling this way, helpless as a baby."

T.J. coaxed, "Just take it easy, love; you nearly died. You're strong and healthy; you'll be well soon. Until then, just lean on me. Whatever you want or need, I'll get it or do it for you."

For some inexplicable reason, Carrie Sue began to cry. "Damn," she swore again, feeling stupid, "First I'm feeling like a baby, now I'm bawling like one. I hate acting like this!"

T.J. knew what it was like to feel utterly helpless. He had experienced similar bouts of that offensive condition when he had been barbwired to that tree, when he hadn't been able to secure her a life-saving pardon, when she had been shot and nearly died, and when the Stover Gang had captured him. He knew how nerve-racking it was!

He swept her into his arms and walked to the riverbank with her. He sat her down and placed her feet in the refreshing water. "You're just hot and tired, love. You've been very sick. It's nothing but your body fussing at you and trying to heal. I was like this while recovering from Quade's little attack. I nearly died. I was weak and fussy and miserable, too. It'll pass, honest."

"I bet you didn't cry," she murmured, wiping at the tears.

He answered truthfully, "Nope, but I sure did want to lots of times. It was frustrating, maddening, irritating. My nerves stayed on edge. I was moody and bitter, downright foul-tempered all the time. I hurt like hell. I couldn't even take care of myself or defend myself. I had to be fed and tended for days. Really stung my pride." He didn't mention the Ranger who had saved his life and taken care of him; he didn't want to remind her of one of the Stover Gang's victims.

Carrie Sue looked at him. Maybe that was it: singed pride and damaged modesty. She hadn't even been able to tend to her private business alone! At least it was T.J. helping her and not a stranger. She dangled her feet in the soothing water and rested against his chest. "I feel nasty. What I need is a bath, a good bath, not just a light rinsing off. That would make me feel better; I know it would."

T.J. gently refused, "When we get to the house in Waco, I'll wash you from head to toe, woman, but it's too dangerous on the trail. I want you to take a nap and gather some energy before we pull out. Mind me, and I'll prop you up in the wagon for our afternoon ride."

She was exhausted, so she didn't battle him with foolish words. She stretched out on the bedroll he spread for her and closed her eyes.

*

T.J. saw the dust cloud down the road and knew someone was coming. He glanced at the sleeping Carrie Sue and didn't want to disturb her yet. He slipped to his horse, untied Nighthawk's reins, and headed in that direction to ward off any visitor to the wagon.

It was William Ferguson. "What is it, Bill? You were to catch the stage Thursday."

"How is Carrie Sue?" the newspaper man asked.

"She's doing fine, just tired and sleeping. What's up?" he pressed.

The excited man revealed, "Good news, Thad. Her pardons came through today. When the telegrams arrived for you, the man brought them to me because he knew you had been staying at my house and I was seeing you soon. It has to be a stroke of good fortune for them to arrive on the same morning, and before you're out of this area."

"From whom?" the shocked lawman asked.

"The President and Governor Hubbard. It seems our reports and pleas had a profound effect on them. What will you tell the Rangers about this death ruse?" Ferguson inquired.

T.J. shoved his hat to his shoulders and ran his fingers through his damp hair. "I don't have any idea, Bill. I didn't give it any thought when I believed they weren't going to pardon her. To be honest, it didn't bother me as much when I thought they'd never learn I'd lied to them, but now they'll know the truth. Either I have to keep pretending she's dead, or I have to confess what I've done. You know what that means.

I broke the law by faking the death of a fugitive so she could escape justice, so they could bring charges against me."

Ferguson reminded him, "But if you clear up this mess, then neither of you will have to go into hiding. Her name will be cleared. You won't have to run away."

"I still plan to head for Montana. We're both too well known here to have a real chance at a fresh start. Lordy, man, why couldn't this pardon have come through last week, or before she was shot?"

"Maybe you should read those telegrams," Ferguson hinted. "I hope you don't mind my opening them, but I figured if they were important, you needed to know immediately."

T.J. smiled and said, "You did the right thing, Bill." He read them and scowled. The wire from the Governor of Texas said reports on the evidence had been sent to him and he was requesting that the court go light on Darby Stover and his men, since all the charges against them weren't true, especially those violent killings and raids which the Harding gang had pulled off as a frame. Too, there were mitigating circumstances for Darby and his men becoming and remaining outlaws. With King Fisher, the Stover Gang, and Harding and his men halted, people would feel more comfortable about the law going lenient on the Stovers. Both telegrams said that official papers were enroute by mail, but wires had been sent to the Ranger Headquarters in Waco. Both men were particularly impressed with Carrie Sue Stover and affected by T.J.'s love for her.

Ferguson agreed, "People will be glad to have all of those villains taken off the roads. They'll be delighted to learn that Darby Stover wasn't responsible for those terrible crimes. Folks have always liked him; he's a colorful legend in this area."

T.J. concurred, "Yeah, but that doesn't help me with my situation."

Ferguson suggested, "Why don't you get the President to say the death ruse was his idea until he could decide on her pardon? Who would say anything bad against him? Or hold you to blame? He's going out of office soon and has nothing more to lose, but you do."

T.J. argued, "But that means I'll have to tell him I lied. He'll lose all respect for me. One thing he knew was that he could trust me."

Ferguson reasoned, "Which is more important, Thad, his respect or you two going free?"

T.J. considered his words. He realized that was the only path to take. "It's best if I 'fess up and take any punishment coming my way."

Ferguson said, "Carrie Sue is going to be surprised and pleased when she hears this news."

T.J. informed him, "I can't tell her any time soon because she hasn't made up her mind about me yet. If she learns she's free to come and go as she chooses, there's no telling what that woman will do. She's still upset with me, so I don't want her taking off and doing something foolish or dangerous. I need for her to think she has to stay in hiding. Otherwise, she'll be at the court every day. I don't want her witnessing what happens to her brother, in case things don't go well with him."

Ferguson looked worried. "You've been honest with her lately, son. If I were you, I wouldn't risk deceiving her again."

"Lordy, man, do you know how headstrong that vixen is? I can't imagine what she'll do when she finds out she's been pardoned."

"I know, Thad. But you know what she'll do later when she discovers you've tricked her again."

Reluctantly T.J. admitted the older man was right. "Lordy, this thing called love is complicated. I guess I'm learning about it the wrong way because I keep making stupid mistakes with her. As soon as I find the best time, I'll tell her about the pardon."

Ferguson said he had to get back to San Angelo to complete his paper and business before packing and heading for Waco to cover the end of this fascinating story.

"You know where we'll be. Look us up when you arrive." T.J. gave the man a message to wire to President Grant, and T.J. prayed that the country's leader would understand his motive and forgive him.

Ferguson mounted and departed. T.J. returned to camp. While his love finished her nap, the lawman contemplated the requirements which Grant had placed on her pardon. . . .

When the redhead awakened, T.J. made her comfortable in the wagon and they continued their journey.

*

On Tuesday while they were camped, to distract her from her tension and discomfort, T.J. told Carrie Sue about Waco in the midst of the fertile and lovely Brazos River Valley. It was a town known for its cattle, cotton, corn, and culture: the four "C's." He explained how the town's cold springs had been popular with the Waco Indians and how the Ranger fort had been constructed there in '37. He spoke of the beautiful and prosperous plantations which had lined the river before the war, estates which had fallen greatly when the plantation economy had collapsed and the population had scattered. But, he said, renewed western movement following the war and the Chisholm Trail had brought new life into Waco, referred to as "Six-shooter Junction." He talked of Fort Fisher, Texas Ranger headquarters in this area, the place to where he reported after each mission. He mentioned the nation's largest suspension bridge across the Brazos River, built in '70 and rivaled by none in America.

When Carrie Sue's eyes glowed and she said she wanted to see all those wondrous sights, T.J. told her that maybe she could when this predicament was settled. He intended to wait until reaching Waco and getting the official papers and word before telling her about the pardon, which proved a wise decision.

*

On Wednesday night after they camped, they talked about their pasts, separately and together. Carrie Sue realized what good and gentle care he was taking of her. He had not pressed her romantically, nor had he argued with her or tried to browbeat her into thinking his way. He appeared to be giving her the time she had requested. Often along the way, he had halted at farms, ranches, or small towns to purchase hot meals for them, while she remained hidden in the coffin until they were out of sight and camped. He made certain she had nourishing food and plenty of rest, and that the journey wasn't too demanding on her condition. The longer she was with him, the harder it was to fault him for the necessary deceit.

She said, "You've been good to me, T.J., and I'm grateful. I'm feeling better every day, and it's because of your generous care."

He smiled at her relaxed air tonight. Her color and mood were improved. "I owed you, woman. I love you and you saved my life."

She placed her coffee cup aside and said, "Not really. Darby wouldn't have killed you or let his men murder you."

T.J. refuted in a tender tone, "Don't stay blinded by love and loyalty to him, Carrie Sue. We both know Darby would have killed me because he thought he had to.

That's why I had to end this matter; I had to stop him from doing things he didn't want to do but felt he had to in order to survive. I think he's glad I stopped him."

Carrie Sue tried not to be miffed with him because his answer was an honest one, even though it pained her deeply to admit the truth. "How was my brother when you last saw him?"

T.J. leaned against the wagon spokes. "Actually he was very calm, relieved, I must say. I think he's resigned himself to serving his time and starting over one day with a clean slate. At least he isn't furious with me anymore. He knows why I completed my mission before taking off with you to parts unknown. I believe your brother likes me and trusts me, even if you don't, my fickle vixen."

"I am not fickle," she retorted.

"What do you call it when a woman loves you in sunny weather but not during a storm?" he jested.

"This was more than a simple storm, T.J. Rogue. I mean, Thad."

"Exactly what was it, Carrie Sue?" he asked seriously.

She scoffed, "It was your damned deceit, Mr. Ranger!"

His gaze fused with hers. "Yep, one I was sworn to carry out long before I met a distracting spitfire who turned my life and guts inside out and seared them good. Tell me something, you feisty little wildcat, what would you think of me if I had turned my back on my duty and become an outlaw just for you?"

"I didn't want you to become an outlaw. I didn't want my brother to be an outlaw. I didn't want to be an outlaw. What's your point?"

"Then, what was an honest lawman supposed to do, woman? Let you go your merry way and get killed because you loved your brother too much to betray him? Let the Stover Gang continue their raids when I knew I could get to them and stop them? Was I supposed to look the other way to keep from hurting you? Was I supposed to forget I knew you, which was damned impossible? Should I have forgotten the law and my duty, the promises to my friends and superiors? Could I allow more innocent people to suffer or die like my brother's family, Miss Starns, and that Ranger when I had a way to halt any future deaths? Surely you of all people can understand loyalty, desperation, and love. Look what you've done because of them."

T.J. seized her hand and compelled her gaze to his while he asked, "Tell me, Carrie Sue, if you had been in my place, what would you have done differently to solve this case without damaging our relationship? I did everything within my power to protect you and to save your life and Darby's. He's alive today because I used you to capture him. He has one of the best lawyers in Texas defending him. I gathered evidence to go in his favor and yours. I offered the President, the Governor, and the Rangers *anything* in exchange for your pardon. If you had been in my position, if you had met me and fallen in love with me after you were on this same trail to justice and revenge, what would you have done to end this matter while retaining your self-respect and mine? If you can honestly say you would have done anything differently, then I'll set you free as soon as you're fully recovered and I'll never trouble you again. Don't answer me now, just think about it."

Chapter

25

Carrie Sue had not answered T.J.'s question the night before, but she had given the matter serious consideration all morning as they traveled. She had to admit he was right. If he had done any less, she would not have respected him, nor would he have respected himself. He was a man of considerable honor and conscience, a good man, a strong and dependable one. She had spent more than a week nearly alone with him. They had talked many times on various subjects. No one could have done more for her than T.J. had.

It was evident to the redhead that Thad Jamison loved her and wanted her understanding. It was clear that he had done all in his power to help her and Darby. It was also undeniable that he could not have carried out his actions any differently for all concerned. He had taken big risks to protect her. She knew his mind must be in turmoil over betraying his friends, superiors, and his duty, all to save her. He was turning his back on all of them so she could be happy and free, and become his wife. Yes, she admitted, he had done his duty many times over to everyone, including her.

Both had been quiet all morning during their ride, and she knew why. Both were entrapped by deep thought and warring emotions. They had fallen in love, but were confronting serious problems. Both wanted a future together, a bright and happy fresh start. But if she couldn't forgive him, he—as vowed—would release her soon. She knew that that was not what she wanted and needed; Thad Jamison was.

At William's and along the way, they had been uneasy around each other, fearing to reach out, fearing to trust each other and themselves, but fearing not to do so. The strain had been tough on them, something they needed to end before they could make a new beginning. Each knew what a refusal of understanding and forgiveness would cost them. False pride and stubbornness had to be cast aside. They needed to relax, to reform their bond.

They reached the outskirts of Waco late that afternoon. Carrie Sue was concealed in the coffin one last time. T.J. drove the wagon to the house which Hank Peterson had rented for them. When they arrived, the ex-Ranger was waiting there and helped T.J. unload.

Inside the small house, T.J. removed the lid and assisted Carrie Sue out of the wooden box. He sat her in a chair and smiled, a loving and tender smile which warmed her from head to foot.

Hank said, "I think I have everything here you need, Thad. But if I overlooked something, I'm staying at the Merry Hotel." The man grinned as he thought of the happy news in his possession, but he would let his friend reveal it to Carrie Sue. When he had agreed to this daring ruse, somehow he had known the pardon would come through and dismiss them of guilt. He hadn't been able to allow this woman to go to prison or be hanged for mistakes in her past, mostly in her misguided and embittered youth. She hadn't wanted that vile existence and had tried to escape it many times. Carrie Sue Stover was worth saving and helping. Yet, if he had still been a Ranger, he couldn't have aided Thad with this illegal deception. Currently, he was only a private citizen, a good friend, and a romantic at heart.

Just as those last words traveled through Hank's mind, Carrie Sue asked, "Why are you doing this, Hank? It's against the law, I'm sure."

Hank sent her a genial smile. "Because I'm a darn fool, Carrie Sue, and Thad's my best friend. He wouldn't ask me to help him pull this off if it wasn't vital to his survival. I know you two love each other, and I know this is the right thing for me to do. I guess you could say the law sometimes needs a helping hand to make the right decision. For certain, I couldn't let you hang or go to prison, and I couldn't let Thad's life be ruined because of mistakes you were forced to commit long ago. You deserve another chance, Carrie Sue, and Thad deserves happiness. This was the only way to make both happen."

A radiant smile crossed her face and settled in her periwinkle eyes, eyes brightened by unshed tears of joy and gratitude. Those emotions were revealed in her voice when she replied, "Thank you; this is one of the nicest things anybody's ever done for me. I'll make certain you're never exposed because I wouldn't want you getting into trouble over me. I hope you don't mind if I consider you my friend, too."

The man responded with ease and verity, "I'd see it as an honor, Carrie Sue. I'm glad to see you survived your accident. Thad's telegram sounded a bit panicky when I got the news."

Carrie Sue glanced at T.J. and smiled. To show her lover she was relaxing and relenting, the redhead jested, "That's because my sneaky partner went to such trouble and pains to capture me."

T.J.'s heart fluttered wildly at her softened gaze and tone. He playfully retorted, "Only because my impulsive vixen went to such trouble and pains to thwart me. But I was determined not to give up hope. I needed a wife real bad to straighten me out and you're the only woman who's been able and willing to tolerate me and my craziness."

They all laughed. Then, Carrie Sue replied mirthfully, "Only because I had no choice, my sly and domineering partner."

"Right now, woman, I'm issuing another order. You need to hop into bed and take a nap. If you want to collect on that favor I promised you, you'll need lots of strength."

Carrie Sue blushed as she wondered how the word "favor" struck Hank Peterson. "If you renege on my bath, I'll pitch a tantrum."

Hank laughed and said, "I need to get moving so you can rest. I'll see you tomorrow, Carrie Sue. You want me to stable that team and her horse at the livery?" he asked his friend.

"That would be a big help, Hank. I'll keep Nighthawk here. Just let me fetch the rest of our things from the wagon." He looked at Carrie Sue and said, "Stay in that chair, woman. I'll be right back and help you into bed. I don't want you falling and hurting yourself."

Outside, Hank passed the official pardon papers to Thad Jamison. "I'll sit with her tomorrow afternoon while you go to headquarters and straighten out this situation. I kept my mouth shut because I figured you'd want to tell her the good news. There's a telegram in there from President Grant; you might want to read it before you decide what to do. Oh, yes, there's food in the warming oven over the stove."

Hank tied his reins to the wagon with Carrie Sue's sorrel. He mounted the driver's seat and headed for the livery stable. T.J. secured Nighthawk's reins to the short hitching post out front, placed his saddle inside the door, and rejoined Carrie Sue.

"I want you to get a nap, love. Then, we'll have a long talk after supper." He lifted her and carried her to bed with her mildly protesting she could walk with his help. As he placed her on the bed, he chuckled and said, "But I love carrying you around, woman."

T.J. leaned over and kissed her, then gazed at her. "I love you, Carrie Sue, and everything's going to work out for us. You'll see."

"What if your friends come to visit? How will you explain me?"

"No one will find us here, love. They don't know we've reached town yet and they don't know about this house." He kissed her again and stroked her hair. "Sleep, woman," he ordered with a grin and left the lovely bedroom.

When she awakened nearly two hours later, T.J. washed her face and hands amidst shared laughter and playful jests. He helped her to the kitchen and into a chair. They devoured a hearty meal of fried chicken, brown gravy, biscuits, coffee, and green beans with small potatoes which he had warmed.

"Delicious," she murmured, licking her lips. "You're spoiling me."

"I wish I could say I cook this good, but Hank got it at the hotel. I only heated and served it, ma'am. And I'll clean it up while you rest."

"You've been doing all the work lately; let me help."

"No way, woman. Don't you realize how weak you are? That was a bad wound; you're still recovering."

"For once, partner, I won't be stubborn. You're right. My body still feels like flowing water, and this shoulder pains me to annoyance."

"How's the sprained wrist?" he queried.

"It's fine now. The pain and swelling are gone thanks to you, doc."

"Good. I'll take you in the parlor while I finish here."

"No, I'll drink coffee and watch you. I want to see how good you are in the kitchen, see if your skills here match those on the trail."

They exchanged smiles and laughter.

She observed and sipped coffee while he cleared the table and washed the dishes. "Who's home is this?" she inquired. "You said it was rented, but it's furnished. It's charming and lovely."

"It belonged to a widow who died recently. She had no family to claim her possessions. The bank has it for sale. The money's going to an orphanage like the woman requested. Hank lucked up on it."

"I'm glad he did; it's wonderful. When I worked at the Harding ranch, I had a small room in the back of the house. I had to stay there unless I was doing chores in the other rooms. Then, while I was in Sante Fe working, I had a tiny room, which was all I could afford on that meager salary. Some businessmen really take advantage of women on their own by treating us like slaves and paying us hardly enough for survival, unless you're willing to do special chores after work," she hinted meaningfully. "The boarding house in Tucson was nice." She brightened, then looked sad.

"What's wrong?" he asked, noting her change in mood.

"I was thinking about Mrs. Thayer in Tucson. I wish I could write to her and explain things. She was so good and kind to me. But I'm suppose to be dead. I wonder if she's heard the news."

T.J. said, "You can still write her a letter. You can date it before June twenty-first. I'll mail it for you." After she learned of her pardon, she could write the woman with the whole truth.

"Thanks. I like this place," she murmured. "Except for that ranch in Laredo, this is the first home I've lived in since my parents—"

T.J. glanced up from his task when she fell silent. "I know how you feel, Carrie Sue; I haven't had a home since my parents died. It's either been strange hotel rooms or rowdy bunkhouses, crumbling shacks, or sleeping on the trail. I enjoyed our visits with Hank and Mitch, and I surely do like this place. Real homey and pretty."

"I liked visiting with them, too. We didn't have time in Laredo to fix up that place into a real home, but it was nice until Quade's detective made us flee. Being on the trail is a lousy existence, isn't it?"

"I didn't think much about it until I met you. Lordy, woman, you showed me how miserable my life was. Yep, this is real nice."

T.J. completed his chore and suggested, "Let's sit in the parlor, ma'am. We can behave like real folk here. No dessert or wine though."

Carrie Sue laughed and took his extended arm. With his assistance, she walked into the cozy room and sat on the floral couch, leaving room for him. T.J. sat beside her. He leaned his head against the back and closed his eyes, sighing deeply in contentment.

"These next few days will be busy ones," he remarked without opening his smokey gray eyes. He dreaded what was ahead tonight.

She looked at him. "You're tired, aren't you?"

"Yep. Driving a slow wagon for days beats on your neck and back when you're used to a fast horse and a comfortable saddle."

"So does tending and hauling around a helpless invalid."

He turned his head and met her gaze. "You aren't heavy or any trouble, woman."

"I'm both, and you know it, Mr. Rogue." She laughed again. "It's going to be hard to get used to your real name. It's going to take a lot of attention and practice. Are your superiors mad at you for breaking your cover to help me?"

"I haven't given them the chance to fire me or scold me." He stood up and fetched an envelope. He returned to the couch and handed it to her. "Hank gave me this. You need to read it."

"What is it?" she questioned as she accepted the envelope.

"Good news for you. Maybe a bit of trouble for me."

She read the official notices of a full pardon for Carrie Sue Stover, then stared at the page with the President's seal and signature, and those of the Texas Governor on the other paper. Her astonished gaze shifted to T.J.'s face.

"Yep, those are for real, woman, just a little late."

"I'm free? I can come and go as I please?" she queried.

"Yep, but that would be dangerous until everyone learns the truth. Until it's written up in the newspapers and gets widely known, you'll still be in peril if anyone sees you. And, there's another problem. I have to figure out a way to explain your so-called death to everyone before they see you walking around, alive and well. I faked your death before this pardon was granted, so I have to clear up that deception before you come out. Else, Bill, Hank and me are in big trouble for breaking the law. You were a wanted criminal and we were helping you escape justice. I'll take those two pardons and go to Ranger headquarters tomorrow and try to straighten out this mess I've created."

As the reality of the joint pardons sank in, she said with excitement, "This means I can attend Darby's trial next week."

T.J. shook his head and dashed her joy and eagerness. "That's not a wise idea, Carrie Sue. Your presence would be much too distracting in the courtroom. People, including the judge and jury, will be gaping at you instead of paying attention to the evidence Bill and I gathered. They'll also realize I lied about your death, so they might assume I lied about the evidence to favor your brother. If I could fake your death, then I could fake evidence for him, which might cause Darby big trouble with his defense. That isn't all, woman. There'll be a large crowd observing and you're still weak and injured. I don't want you bumped around while people are trying to get a closer look at the Texas Flame. They'll be pushing and shoving just to touch you. They might even be yanking at your clothes to snatch souvenirs. You aren't well enough to face a mob scene like that. You need to stay here, resting and healing. I'll give you a full report every day."

Carrie Sue realized he hadn't given orders or threats. "But I could testify for him, T.J.; I know the truth. I might do him some good."

"I doubt it. Once everyone sees how beautiful you are and they discover the truth about our love and ruse, they won't believe a thing either of us says. Some of those envious women might convince their husbands you used your beauty to trick me into helping you and Darby. The President and Governor have requested the court to go lenient on Darby and the boys. If you show up and flaunt our deceit in their faces, it could be damaging for his case."

Carrie Sue realized he was right. She had to do what was best for Darby and everyone else involved—T.J., William, and Hank. They had taken great risks to help her and she owed them her loyalty.

T.J. added, "There are some stipulations on your pardon, love. Grant's message was in code, but I've translated it for you. Read it."

Carrie Sue discovered that her freedom was based on Thad Jamison marrying her and keeping her out of trouble and on his resigning from the Rangers and as a Special Agent for the President who would be leaving office after this term. He was required to continue as a U.S. Marshal, but in Colorado. The decoded message also said that Grant was taking full responsibility for the death ruse, ordering T.J. to say it was his idea and command. The man claimed it was his hesitation which forced T.J. to become so desperate. Grant said he understood T.J.'s love for her and didn't fault his action. Clearly the President was giving her love a way out of his predicament. "If I don't marry you and go to Colorado as a marshal's wife, this pardon isn't effective?"

"Those are the conditions, what I promised in exchange. I told him I would do anything to get you pardoned, and he finally accepted my offer." When she became silent and thoughtful, T.J. walked to the window and gazed outside, worried about her reaction and response. He knew she loved him, but he had betrayed her. She was upset with him and was afraid to trust him again. He couldn't blame her.

Carrie Sue broke her silence by saying, "I'll do whatever you order here in Waco, T.J., because I'm certain you know what's best for everybody concerned. I would like to see Darby. Is that possible?"

T.J. didn't know how to take her oblique answer. "When his trial's over, I'll find some way to sneak Darby here or to slip you into the jail for a last visit. But right now, it's too dangerous. Too many curious people are hanging around the jail day and night. Once the trials ends, things will settle down and it'll be safe."

They both fell silent. T.J. felt dejected. Why was she so quiet? What in blazes was going on inside her head?

"That's fine," she remarked. She said suddenly, "I'm going to marry you, T.J., not because of this pardon, but because I love you. I accept what you had to do in the line of duty."

T.J. turned and looked at her. He walked to the couch and sat down, pulling her into his embrace. He kissed her with a fiery passion which ignited his entire body, a passion which had been denied a long time. He cautioned himself not to let his hungers run wild; she was in no condition for urgent lovemaking tonight. When she cuddled against him, he vowed, "You won't be sorry, Carrie Sue. We'll be happy."

She hugged him and replied, "I know we will."

As her fingers absently teased over his chest and her body nestled to his, T.J. felt his control lessening by the instant. "You've been up long enough, woman. It's time for you to get back into bed. That journey here was hard on this healing body. I have to take care of you. I want you up and around soon so we can get married and head for our new home." When her head shifted and she gazed up at him, he added, "I know I promised you a bath, but it'll have to be in the morning after you're rested. I'll scrub this hair and body good; that'll give you some energy. I'm afraid it's too late to dry and you need to recover from that rough wagon ride. Is that all right with you?"

Carrie Sue felt her body aching for sweet release, but she knew he was exhausted and she hadn't had a bath in days. If she yielded to the temptation to cover his face with eager kisses, she would be unable to control her urgent desires. They hadn't been together as one since her jailbreak, nearly two weeks ago. She was starving for him. Yet, she wanted their reunion to be something special. Tomorrow night was the perfect occasion.

"You're the boss, my husband-to-be," she teased.

T.J. chuckled merrily as he carried her to the bed. Flames licked greedily at his body as she spread kisses on his neck. After she was tucked in, he only brushed her lips lightly with his, not daring to really kiss her. "See you in the morning, love."

She halted him at the door by saying, "Where are you sleeping?"

"I'll bed down in the parlor."

"A hard floor over a comfortable bed?" she hinted mirthfully.

"That's best, woman. You need a full night's sleep to get well. It would be much too dangerous for me to sleep in here tonight."

Carrie Sue gazed into his smokey gray eyes. She smiled knowingly. "It won't be hazardous tomorrow night," she hinted with a seductive smile.

His eyes glowed with happiness and desire. "The things you women will exchange for a bath," he teased.

Soft laughter left her throat. She mischievously retorted, "No more than a famous lawman would exchange to get himself a wife."

"Good-night, you lusty vixen," he murmured. "I love you."

"Good-night, my handsome Rogue. I love you, too."

*

After a delicious breakfast of bacon, scrambled eggs, biscuits, and coffee, T.J. heated plenty of water and filled the widow's tub in the kitchen. He helped Carrie Sue get undressed. Then, he scrubbed her hair and waited while she bathed.

Afterwards, he dried her quickly to prevent his kindled body from bursting into flames, and put on a fresh bandage on her shoulder. As he did so, he told her how he had stolen the ether and bandages from the doctor's office in San Angelo. Being careful with her wounded shoulder, he pulled on the cotton gown which she had brought along from Tucson. She sat in a kitchen chair while he brushed her hair, a task they both enjoyed.

"You're definitely spoiling me, my love. This is wonderful."

"Maybe you can repay my services when you get stronger."

"I'd love to, my virile Rogue." She tilted her head backwards and enticed her to kiss him.

"Behave, woman. I have work to do and it's back to bed with you."

"Sounds perfect to me," she could not help but say.

"I meant, I have to go to Ranger headquarters and settle our problem. Hank will be here soon to stay with you while I'm gone."

"You still don't trust me?" she jested.

"Of course I do. I just want him here for your protection. You're too weak to defend yourself if trouble struck. I'll stop by to see Darby and fill him in on the news. Up, vixen, it's nap time."

*

Since she didn't have a robe, Carrie Sue wrapped a lacy coverlet around her shoulders so she could visit with Hank Peterson in the parlor.

As they chatted, Hank told her how much T.J. loved her, how he had panicked after her escape in El Paso, and how frightened he had been after she was wounded. "You've made a big difference in his life, Carrie Sue, and he's done the same in yours. Thad and I have worked together and guarded each other's backs many times." To pass the time, Hank related some of their adventures.

*

Hank left when T.J. returned to the cozy house. Her love related his meeting with the Rangers, saying he had let the President take the blame since his authority outweighed the Texas law. "They don't like what I did, but they accepted it. I was a Special Agent before I was a Texas Ranger and that position carries more power. They realize I didn't have any choice but to obey President Grant's orders."

"Did you tell them about the President's requirements?"

T.J. shook his head. "That's a secret bargain between us, but I told them I was resigning to become a marshal in Colorado. Considering how well-known we both are, it sounded like a good idea to them." He grinned and quipped, "At least they were reluctant to lose me even after learning I had deceived them. I told them you agreed to stay in hiding until the trials were over, so they agreed to let you see Darby one night when it's safe. There's too much commotion in town for the next few days, so you'll have to wait a while. See where cooperation gets you, woman; right where you should be."

He chuckled, then revealed, "The story's being released today of your survival and pardon. It'll claim you've been sent back East to relatives. Nothing's going to be said about our love and marriage. That'll protect our privacy. The report will read that your death was faked until your pardon could arrive and you could be sent away secretly."

She sighed in relief. "I'm glad that worked out all right."

"Me too. Darby was in good spirits when I saw him. Even better after he heard you're doing fine and you've been pardoned. He's accepted his fate, Carrie Sue, and I'm glad. I told him you'd be seeing him before he left for prison. He's happy about that."

"How do you think the trial will go?" she queried with anxiety.

"His lawyer had just left. He thinks Darby has a strong defense. It helps that there wasn't a shoot-out when he was captured. And no one was hurt in either San Angelo or Big Spring, and all money was returned. That lawyer's as smart as Bill said he was; he's gotten those false charges of Quade's dropped. The newspapers have been filled with good reports on Darby and that frame's been exposed in colorful detail. The papers here picked up Bill's stories and interviews, so Darby's going to trial almost a hero, a real Western legend."

"Like I said, let the papers help you after they've hurt you."

T.J. went on, "I picked up some mighty interesting information today. Quinn Harding had a heart attack when he heard about his son; he's dead. The law has taken control of his ranch. They plan to return the stolen parcels to their rightful owners, including the Stover Ranch to Darby. His lawyer is handling a sale so the money can be used to pay back Darby's targets and get those charges reduced. The judge says it'll go in his favor. I hope you don't mind."

The redhead beamed with joy. "Certainly not. Besides, I have a new home to make in Colorado with my handsome husband. I don't have any money, so it's a good thing you'll have a job awaiting you."

T.J. smiled and informed her, "I have plenty of money saved, so we'll do just fine, Miss Stover. A man doesn't spend much money when he's on the trail alone most of the time."

Carrie Sue ventured, "Right now, partner, I'm not so fine. I have this ache all over that Dr. Jamison needs to tend."

"That's good, woman, because I'm suffering from that same condition. Let me lock up so we won't be disturbed for a long time."

After he did so, he carried the laughing Carrie Sue to bed. With gentle hands, quivering from anticipation, he undressed her. After she lay down, he removed his garments and boots and joined her.

He lay to her good side and gazed into her violet-blue eyes. His fingers carefully touched her bandaged shoulder as he murmured, "Lordy, I was afraid I had lost you forever when this happened. Then, I was afraid you'd never be able to forgive me and take me back. You don't know what it means to me for us to be together like this again. I love you, woman, and I need you. I'm glad you came to your senses," he teased, assailing her face and neck with kisses.

"I'm glad you came to your senses, too, Mr. Ranger Man," she murmured, embracing him. Overwhelming love and desire coursed through her body. She had never imagined she could be this content, this much in love. T.J. had entered her life and changed it, changed her.

A feeling of intermingled tranquility and tension consumed her. At last, she felt totally safe and deliriously happy. It had been a long and hard road to this safe and loving location, but she was glad she had found it, discovered it with T.J.'s help and persistence. Her spirit was relaxed with T.J., and her body was highly susceptible to his actions. Her heart belonged to him.

It seemed as if this was the man she had awaited all her life, as if he was the only one who could unleash her passions, the only one who could tame her wild spirit, the only one who could fulfill her. Carrie Sue's fingers lightly skimmed his supple flesh—his powerful shoulders, his brawny arms, his hard chest—relishing the way it felt beneath them and responded to her touch. She hugged him tightly against her naked body and trembled at that stirring contact.

T.J.'s lips roamed her rosy gold face, placing kisses in each area. He loved the way her skin felt beneath his mouth and hands. He wanted to kiss and caress every inch of her. He wanted to give her enormous pleasure; yet, self-control to carry out that enticing task was difficult. He fingered her flaming hair and kissed the throbbing pulse at her throat. She seemed eager to join their bodies, and that thrilled him.

Carrie Sue realized how gentle and hesitant he was with her; she knew he was trying not to hurt her. She knew his body was aflame for hers, just as hers were burning wildly for his. No matter how many times they made love, each time was better, if that was possible.

T.J.'s skilled hands searched out those hidden places that made her squirm with rapture. His tongue worked in the hollows of her neck and between her breasts, then traveled to her snowy mounds and titillated the rosy brown peaks upon them. He loved the way she moaned in rising need, the way she reacted to his trek, the way she entreated him to continue his journey toward a mutual discovery of passion's haven. He explored her like a virginal area, slowly, thoroughly, excitedly. He yearned for their new life to begin, and knew it would soon.

Carrie Sue's tongue darted about T.J.'s sensual mouth, craving his taste. Her hands were bold and confident today, wandering over his virile frame at will and causing him to tremble with mounting intensity. She wanted to tantalize him beyond reality and endurance, and was doing a wonderful job of it. She wanted him to experience the most blissful union of his life, today, in her arms, within her.

They played their enticing games until both were breathless and consumed by a ravenous hunger. They joined their bodies to feed those fierce appetites which both had whet. They teased and tempted each other. They took and gave and shared. They were as one.

He looked down at her, enjoying the way her hair flamed a vivid golden red against the stark white pillow. He noted the flush on her face, but knew it was from a different kind of fever than he had feared last week. He listened to her moans, this time from passion, not physical pain. He watched her violet-blue eyes close, grateful it was from dreamy pleasure and not unconsciousness. He kissed the area around her bandage, and mutely thanked God for saving her life.

Carrie Sue was enraptured by his skilled lovemaking and gentleness. Her body felt aglow and her mind adrift. The sea of passion within her coursed back and forth between peaceful waves to stormy ones. She was swept along helplessly by the awesome force. She felt that blissful tension building higher and higher within her until she felt dizzy from its height and power.

T.J. trembled in restraint, fearing it was about to be lost uncontrollably. His body was searing from the heat of their union, burning from her touch, blazing from her brave actions. His manhood quivered in warning. It had been so long since they had made love, and he craved her urgently. His fingers roved her body, stimulating her. When he felt her clutch his shoulders and kiss him feverishly as she arched her back toward him, he knew the moment of victory had arrived. He cast aside his guard and raced swiftly to join her.

Surges of ecstasy shot through them like tiny bolts of lightning. Blood pounded in their ears like roaring thunder. They clung together to ride out passion's downpour of fiery sparks, their bodies glistening from its blissful rain. Their mouths meshed and their tongues danced wildly in their own mating ritual. The wondrous experience, the culmination of lovemaking, washed over them and carried them away to a serene shore where they lay panting for breath and savoring this special fusion of bodies, hearts, souls, and spirits.

They continued to kiss and caress, to lie enjoined in the paradise of contentment which they had built. As they cuddled, the strength of their love filled their minds and consumed them. Each knew their love had been predestined, their first encounter by fate guided.

T.J. looked into Carrie Sue's eyes and asked happily, "So you won't mind becoming a lawman's wife, my beautiful Texas Flame?"

Carrie Sue's hands lifted to caress his face. She stared into his smokey gray gaze and replied with a straight face. "Not at all, Marshal Thaddeus Jerome Jamison, but I still prefer being your vixen." Her face and eyes glowed as her naked body shook with merry laughter.

"You'll always hold that intoxicating position, my love," T.J. murmured, then closed his mouth over hers.

When their lips parted, she whispered mischievously, "I suppose you can teach this daring desperado to become a lawful citizen. After all, my handsome Rogue, you've taught me everything else."

"Not everything," he hinted with a devilish grin. "But give me time and I will." He knew that if anyone came to visit today, no one would answer the door, not with his tantalizing vixen beside him, not when love's urgent summons were being heard again. . . .

Epilogue

William Ferguson arrived Saturday afternoon to cover the upcoming trials of Darby Stover and his gang. He enjoyed a long visit with Carrie Sue and T.J. before he began his prizewinning work.

Carrie Sue and T.J. spent Sunday alone, making love and making plans for their bright future in Colorado.

Monday, July third, the trial of Darby Stover began. Excited crowds filled the courtroom and others packed around the building to listen through the open windows. Often they cheered the boyishly handsome man whom they considered a Wild West legend.

Tuesday was a big holiday, the country's centennial. Carrie Sue and T.J. celebrated in the cozy house with Hank Peterson and William Ferguson. A congratulatory telegram from Mitchell Sterling had arrived yesterday. He said he wished he could join them.

Wednesday, the trial resumed. It ended Thursday morning with an expected verdict of guilty and a sentence of fifteen years in prison. The crowd screamed for a pardon, but the judge finally quieted them down and told them it was impossible because Stover had broken the law. The crowds then shouted for an early parole for their hero, and the judge smiled.

Thursday night, Carrie Sue's and T.J.'s weapons were taken by the Rangers who stood guard around the outside of the house while Darby Stover was allowed to have supper and a visit with his sister before leaving on Friday for a prison in eastern Texas. Following a delicious meal and a pleasant visit, Darby Stover and Thad Jamison shook hands and parted as friends.

T.J. had told her, "With good behavior, he'll be out sooner."

Darby had given T.J. a letter to Sally in San Angelo, thanking her for her help and love in the past, telling her not to wait for him. But Darby—and Sally—knew she would because she loved him. He had finally admitted to himself that he loved her.

On Friday, the trials of Kale Rushton, Kadry Sams, Dillon Holmes and John Griffin began, to end much the same way as Darby Stover's. The doctor from San Angelo attended Kale's trial and requested to be allowed to visit and work with the half-Apache while he was serving his prison term, hopefully to learn from the man and teach him as well. In fact, he hoped to persuade Kale to study in prison so he could become a doctor one day, combining the skills and knowledge of the Indian and white worlds. To everyone's surprise, Kale was open to the suggestion.

On that same day, Carrie Sue Stover wrote a letter to Mrs. Thayer in Tucson, explaining everything to the kind woman who had befriended her.

After church on Sunday, July nineth, Carrie Sue Stover, wearing the white lace dress, married Thad Jamison in a secret ceremony attended by their closest friends. A small party followed, and a passionate night.

On Monday, July twenty-fourth, Carrie Sue and Thad Jamison left the cozy house in Waco to head for their new life in Colorado. By then, they knew there would soon be three people riding in their wagon. . . .

Author's Note

———— ⚬⚬⚬ ————

I would like to thank the staffs of the Texas Ranger Museum in Waco (with its marvelous examples of barbwire and guns, and displays of Ranger exploits) and the Texas Tourist Bureaus for their extremely generous help. One Texan in particular, Richard Roberts, supplied me with loads of informative material, especially on early Texas.

I would also like to thank the people at the U.S. Department of Interior (National Park Service) for the many maps and brochures which provided information and guidance on the Guadalupe and Chiricahua Mountains.

One note to prevent confusion: In *The Great Chiefs* (Time/Life Books) it says "After both Cochise and his oldest son died, Naiche, the second son, succeeded to the position of chief of the Chiricahuas in 1876." But, *The Indian Wars* (Utley and Washburn) said, "In 1874 the legendary Cochise died. Neither of his sons, Taza or Nachez, proved equal to the test of chieftainship." You know which source I used.

Finally, I would like to thank each of you for your letters and encouragement over the years, and I look forward to writing many more enjoyable books for you. If you would like to receive a Janelle Taylor Newsletter, send a legal-sized Self-Addressed Stamped Envelope (or a stamp and a mailing label) to:

Janelle Taylor Newsletter
P.O. Box 211646
Martinez, Georgia 30917-1646

UNTIL NEXT TIME, GOOD READING . . .

ABOUT THE AUTHOR

JANELLE TAYLOR has won many awards for her writing, and has had seven *New York Times* bestsellers: *First Love, Wild Love; Savage Conquest; Stolen Ecstasy; Moondust and Madness; Kiss of the Night Wind; Whispered Kisses;* and *Follow the Wind.*

The University of Georgia's library houses a collection of her books, manuscripts, and papers. She is the author of twenty-seven novels, with more than twenty-three million copies in print.